McDougal Littell
CLASSZONE

Visit **classzone.com** and get connected.

ClassZone resources provide instruction, practice and learning support for students and parents.

Animated History & Geography

- Brings history to life with interactive activities and visuals
- Provides interactive maps, charts, and graphs

Current Events

- Takes you beyond the text and keeps you up-to-date on world events
- Reflects the most recent political, economic, and social issues
- Provides weekly current events quizzes to help check comprehension

Interactive Review

- Provides a unique way to review key concepts and events
- Includes geography games, crossword puzzles, and matching games
- Helps ensure lesson comprehension through graphic organizers, animated flipcards, and review/study notes

Research and Writing

- Includes links to primary sources, chapter resources, biographies, and state-specific resources
- Provides support for your writing assignments through complete writing models, rubrics, and research guides

Access the online version of your textbook at **classzone.com**

Your complete text, along with animated maps, charts and infographics, is available for immediate use!

McDougal Littell
Where Great Lessons Begin

ILLINOIS EDITION

McDougal Littell

American HISTORY

Robert Dallek

Jesus Garcia

Donna M. Ogle

C. Frederick Risinger

Senior Consultants

Dr. Robert Dallek is an acclaimed historian of the American presidency and an authority on leadership and crises. His biography of President John F. Kennedy, *An Unfinished Life*, spent eight weeks on *The New York Times* bestseller list. A former professor of History at Boston University, Dr. Dallek also spent three decades as a professor at UCLA, and a year as a visiting professor at Oxford. In recent years he has also been a visiting professor at Dartmouth College. In addition to his books, he is the author of more than 100 publications and the recipient of numerous honors and awards. He is a frequent commentator on radio and television networks, including NPR, CNN, and NBC, on subjects concerning the presidency, current events, and foreign policy.

Dr. Jesus Garcia is professor of Curriculum and Instruction at the University of Nevada, Las Vegas, and past president of the National Council for the Social Studies. A former social studies teacher, Dr. Garcia has co-authored many books and articles on subjects that range from teaching social studies in elementary and middle schools to seeking diversity in education. Dr. Garcia has also worked for both the Chicago and Washington, D.C., public schools and the Arkansas Department of Education as a consultant on social studies standards.

Dr. Donna Ogle is professor of Reading and Language at National-Louis University in Chicago, Illinois, and is a specialist in reading in the content areas, with an interest in social studies. She is past president of the International Reading Association and a former social studies teacher. Dr. Ogle is currently directing two content literacy projects in Chicago schools and is Senior Consultant to the Striving Readers Research Project. She continues to explore applications of the K-W-L strategy she developed and is adding a Partner Reading component—PRC2 (Partner Reading and Content 2).

C. Frederick Risinger is the former Director of Professional Development and coordinator for Social Studies Education at Indiana University. He is past president of the National Council for the Social Studies as well as past president of the National Social Studies Supervisors Association. Mr. Risinger also served on the coordinating committee for the National History Standards Project. He writes a monthly column on technology in the social studies classroom for *Social Education* and is the current president of the Social Science Education Consortium.

ISBN-10: 0-618-92143-5
ISBN-13: 978-0-618-92143-0

03 04 05 06 07 08 09 DWO 12 11 10 09 08

Internet Web Site: http://www.mcdougallittell.com

Consultants and Reviewers

 ILLINOIS REVIEWERS

Helene Blangin
Clarence E. Culver School
Niles, IL

Christine Bojanowski
St. Dennis School
Lockport, IL

David S. Brothman
District Social Studies Specialist
North Chicago School District 187
North Chicago, IL

Student Panel

The following Middle School Student Panel reviewed textbook
materials and technology products for this program.

Jessica Baker
Nelly Benitez
Ameer Cannon
Katie Conley
Murad Dajani
Will DiFrancesca
Tom Foydel
Philippa Gillette
Jenny Gorelick
Michael Grassle
Danielle Jackson
DeJauna Jackson
Mark Johnson
David Lenz
Andrew Mack

Madelaine Martin
Jabari McIntyre
Victoria Meliska
Sarah Peters
Brianna Ransom
Andrés Rivera-Thompson
Simone Samuels
Ben Shoaf
Gabriel Siegal
Kyle Siegal
Brock Snider
Hank Strickler
Jasmine Wright
Hannah Wyler

Teacher Consultants

The following educators provided ongoing review of key components or contributed teaching ideas and activities for this program.

Venise N. Battle
Shady Hill School
Cambridge, Massachusetts

Paul C. Beavers
J.T. Moore Middle School
Nashville, Tennessee

Cristy Berger
Wilkinson Middle School
Madison Heights, Michigan

Holly West Brewer
Buena Vista Paideia Magnet
Nashville, Tennessee

David Brothman
North Chicago School District
North Chicago, Illinois

Ron Campana
United Federation of Teachers
New York, New York

Patricia B. Carlson
Swanson Middle School
Arlington, Virginia

Regina L. Colquitt
Chute Middle School
Evanston, Illinois

Meg DeWeese
Thoreau Academy
Tulsa, Oklahoma

Kelly Ellis
Hamilton Middle School
Cypress, Texas

James Grimes
Middlesex County Vocational
Woodbridge, New Jersey

Julie Guild
Carl Albert Junior High
Oklahoma City, Oklahoma

Brent Heath
De Anza Middle School
Ontario, California

Suzanne Hidalgo
Serrano Middle School
Highland, California

Cathryn Mahan Hinesley
Seneca Ridge Middle School
Sterling, Virginia

Alan Hornbecker
Walt Whitman Middle School
Alexandria, Virginia

Barbara Kennedy
Sylvan Middle School
Citrus Heights, California

Pamela Knifflin
Navasota Junior High
Navasota, Texas

Tammy Leiber
Navasota Junior High
Navasota, Texas

Lori Lesslie
Cedar Bluff Middle School
Knoxville, Tennessee

Christine Loop
Glasgow Middle School
Alexandria, Virginia

David Mack
Sarah Banks Middle School
Wixom, Michigan

Brian McKenzie
Buffalo Public School #81
Buffalo, New York

Kayne Miller
Longfellow Middle School
Falls Church, Virginia

Ronnie Moppin
Sunny Vale Middle School
Blue Springs, Missouri

Caroline Ona
Washington Irving Middle School
Springfield, Virginia

Jean Price
St. John's School
Houston, Texas

Meg Robbins
Wilbraham Middle School
Northampton, Massachusetts

Philip Rodriguez
McNair Middle School
San Antonio, Texas

Matthew Scheidler
Wayzata East Middle School
Plymouth, Minnesota

Leslie Schubert
Parkland School
McHenry, Illinois

Robert Sisko
Carteret Middle School
Carteret, New Jersey

Jim Sorenson
Chippewa Middle School
Des Plaines, Illinois

Amy Smith
Lanier Middle School
Fairfax, Virginia

Marci Smith
Hurst-Euless-Bedford ISD
Bedford, Texas

Nicholas Sysock
Carteret Middle School
Carteret, New Jersey

Susan Weber
Maple Point Middle School
Langhorne, Pennsylvania

Becky Wedeking
Eisenhower Middle School
Topeka, Kansas

Lisa Williams
Lamberton Middle School
Carlisle, Pennsylvania

ILLINOIS

OVERVIEW
Illinois Student Edition

Cambridge Lakes Charter School

Lessons with Embedded Illinois Benchmarks

 Look for the Illinois symbol throughout this book. It highlights targeted benchmarks to help you succeed on your test.

ILLINOIS CONTENTS

Buckingham Fountain, Chicago, Illinois © Mark Segal/Getty Images

UNIT 1 ILLINOIS

Three Worlds Meet

Online Activities
at CLASSZONE.COM

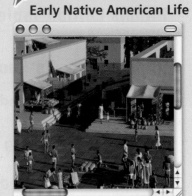

Animated HISTORY
Early Native American Life

Experience the activity and commerce of a Native American market, p. 10.

Interactive Review

Play the GeoGame to test your knowledge of the European explorations of North America, p. 21.

Online Test Practice
Review test-taking strategies and practice your test, pages 23, 55.

UNIT 2 ILLINOIS

The English Colonies

Online Activities at CLASSZONE.COM

Animated HISTORY
A New England Seaport

Visit a busy New England seaport in the 1700s, p. 108.

Interactive Review

American writer, publisher, scientist, inventor, and diplomat

Use Interactive Flipcards to review key people, places, and events in the American colonies, p. 149.

Online Test Practice

Review test-taking strategies and practice your test, pages 91, 123, 151.

Creating A New Nation

IL8

Online Activities
at CLASSZONE.COM

Animated HISTORY
Battle Tactics

See a Revolutionary War battle come alive, p. 202.

Interactive Review

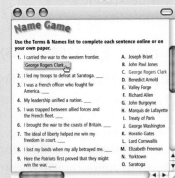

Play the Name Game to test your knowledge of the Revolutionary War, p. 229.

Online Test Practice

Review test-taking strategies and practice your test, pages 191, 231, 259, 299.

UNIT 4 ILLINOIS

The Early Republic

Online Activities
at CLASSZONE.COM

Animated HISTORY
An American Textile Mill

Experience what life was like in an 1800s mill town, p. 370.

Interactive Review

Play the GeoGame to test your knowledge of the new republic, p. 333.

Online Test Practice

Review test-taking strategies and practice your test, pages 335, 361, 389.

UNIT 5 ILLINOIS

A Changing Nation

Online Activities
at CLASSZONE.COM

Animated HISTORY
The Journey West

Endure the hardships and dangers of the westward journey across America's wilderness, p. 424.

Interactive Review

I fought with the *Tejanos* at the Battle of the Alamo.

Use Interactive Flipcards to review key people, places, and events of the mid-1800s, p. 445.

Online Test Practice
Review test-taking strategies and practice your test, pages 415, 447, 475.

Online Activities
at CLASSZONE.COM

 HISTORY
Naval Action at Vicksburg

See Union naval power in action at Vicksburg, p. 556.

Interactive Review

Play the GeoGame to test your knowledge of the history and geography of the Civil War, p. 505.

Online Test Practice
Review test-taking strategies and practice your test, pages 507, 533, 567, 591.

UNIT 7 ILLINOIS

America Transformed

Online Activities
at CLASSZONE.COM

Animated HISTORY
Ellis Island

Visit historic Ellis Island to experience the immigration process in turn-of-the-century America, p. 648.

Interactive Review

CROSSWORD PUZZLE
ACROSS
1. I started the Standard Oil Trust. ____

Solve a crossword of key terms and names for the era of Industrialization and Immigration, p. 667.

Online Test Practice
Review test-taking strategies and practice your test, pages 627, 669, 691, 715.

UNIT 8 ILLINOIS

War and the Jazz Age

Online Activities
at CLASSZONE.COM

Animated HISTORY
Trench Warfare

Get a bird's-eye view of the action on a World War I battlefield, p. 726.

Interactive Review

Serbia

Play the GeoGame to test your knowledge of the history and geography of World War I, p. 747.

Online Test Practice

Review test-taking strategies and practice your test, pages 749, 771.

Depression, War, and Recovery

Online Activities
at CLASSZONE.COM

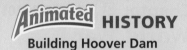
Animated HISTORY
Building Hoover Dam

Tour the Boulder Dam for a first-hand look at one of America's engineering marvels, p. 782.

Interactive Review

CROSSWORD PUZZLE

ACROSS
1. General ____ was the Supreme Allied Commander in Europe.

Use your knowledge of history to solve the crossword of key terms and names from World War II, p. 839.

Online Test Practice

Review test-taking strategies and practice your test, pages 803, 841, 867.

UNIT 10 ILLINOIS

Tensions at Home and Abroad

Online Activities
at CLASSZONE.COM

Animated HISTORY
The Space Program

Explore America's 1960s space program and walk the moon with United States astronauts, p. 944.

Interactive Review

Play the GeoGame to test your knowledge of the history and geography of the Civil Rights Movement, p. 903.

Online Test Practice

Review test-taking strategies and practice your test, pages 905, 933, 965.

FEATURES

CONNECTING ▸ History

CONNECT ▸ To Today

CONNECT ▸ Economics and History

CONNECT ▸ Citizenship and History

Reading Primary Sources

Daily Life

FEATURES

PRIMARY SOURCE

❝ Government is instituted for the protection, safety and happiness of the people. . . The origin of all power is in the people, and . . . they have an [incontestable] right to check the creatures of their own creation, vested with certain powers to guard the life, liberty and property of the community. ❞

—Mercy Otis Warren

PRIMARY SOURCES

PRIMARY SOURCE

❝ That we here highly resolve that these dead shall not have died in vain—that this nation, under God, shall have a new birth of freedom—and that government of the people, by the people, and for the people, shall not perish from this earth. ❞

—Abraham Lincoln

PRIMARY SOURCES

PRIMARY SOURCE

❝ I have a dream that one day this nation will rise up and live out the true meaning of its creed—we hold these truths to be self-evident . . . that all men are created equal. ❞

—Martin Luther King, Jr.

Underground Railroad

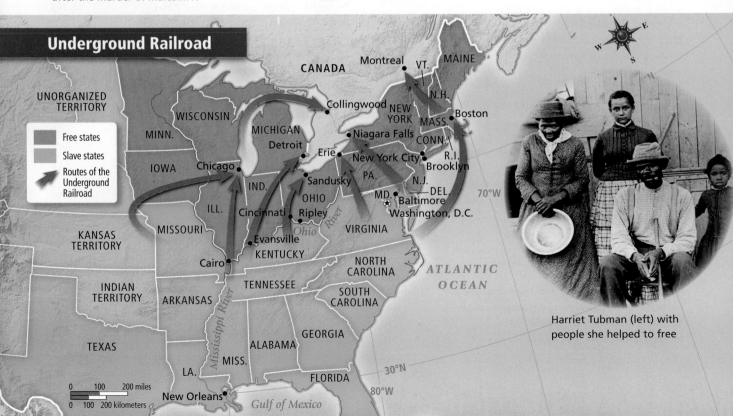

UNORGANIZED TERRITORY

Free states

Slave states

Routes of the Underground Railroad

CANADA

Montreal VT. MAINE

N.H.

Collingwood NEW YORK MASS. Boston

WISCONSIN

MINN.

MICHIGAN

Detroit

Niagara Falls CONN.

Erie R.I.

New York City

Brooklyn

IOWA

Chicago

IND.

Sandusky PA.

N.J.

OHIO DEL.

Cincinnati Ripley MD. Baltimore

Washington, D.C. 70°W

ILL.

MISSOURI

Ohio River

VIRGINIA

Evansville

KANSAS TERRITORY

KENTUCKY

Cairo

NORTH CAROLINA

ATLANTIC OCEAN

INDIAN TERRITORY

ARKANSAS

TENNESSEE

SOUTH CAROLINA

Mississippi River

GEORGIA

TEXAS

ALABAMA

MISS.

30°N

LA.

FLORIDA

80°W

0 100 200 miles

0 100 200 kilometers

New Orleans

Gulf of Mexico

Harriet Tubman (left) with people she helped to free

TABLES AND CHARTS

African American Voter Registration in the South, 1960–1971

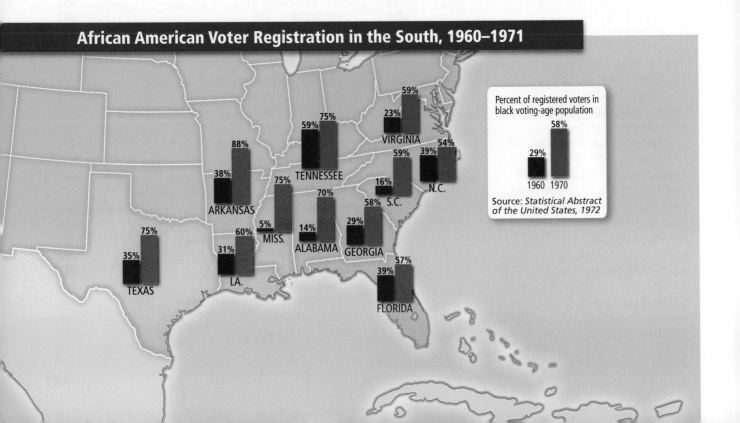

Percent of registered voters in black voting-age population

1960: 29% 1970: 58%

Source: *Statistical Abstract of the United States, 1972*

TEXAS 35% / 75%
ARKANSAS 38% / 88%
LA. 31% / 60%
MISS. 5% / 75%
TENNESSEE 59% / 75%
ALABAMA 14% / 70%
GEORGIA 29% / 58%
FLORIDA 39% / 57%
S.C. 16% / 59%
N.C. 39% / 54%
VIRGINIA 23% / 59%

Graphs

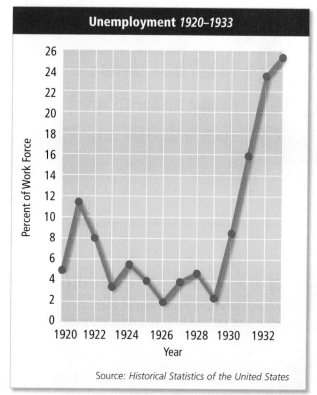

Unemployment *1920–1933*

Source: *Historical Statistics of the United States*

Time Lines

Infographics

Four Steps to Being a Strategic Reader

These pages explain how the *American History* chapters are organized. By using the four key strategies below, you'll become a more successful reader of history, and more knowledgeable about your state's standards.

1 Set a Purpose for Reading

2 Build Your Social Studies Vocabulary

3 Use Active Reading Strategies

4 Check Your Understanding

Can you find it?

Find the following items on this and the next three pages.

- **one** chapter Essential Question and **one** chart that helps answer it
- **two** places where important words are defined
- **three** online games
- **four** key strategies for reading

1 Set a Purpose for Reading

Key features at the beginning of each chapter and section help you set a purpose for reading.

A **Essential Question** This key question sets the main purpose for reading.

B **Connect Geography & History** This feature helps you to consider geography's impact on history.

C **Animated Geography & History** sets the stage for where the history you'll study takes place.

D **Before, You Learned** and **Now You Will Learn** This information helps you to connect what you've studied before to what you'll study next.

E **Key Question** Each topic covered in the chapter is followed by a Key Question that sets your purpose for reading about that topic.

2 Build Your Social Studies Vocabulary

The Reading for Understanding pages provide three important ways to build your vocabulary.

A **Terms & Names** cover the most important events, people, places, and social studies concepts in the section.

B **Background Vocabulary** lists words you need to know in order to understand the basic concepts and ideas discussed in the section.

C **Visual Vocabulary** features provide visual support for some definitions.

D **Terms & Names** and **Background Vocabulary** are highlighted and defined in the main text so that you'll understand them as you read and study.

CHAPTER 7

1. The Early Years of the War
2. The War Expands
3. The Path to Victory
4. The Legacy of the War

The American Revolution
1775–1783

A ESSENTIAL QUESTION

How was it possible that American Patriots gained their independence from the powerful British Empire?

B CONNECT Geography & History

How might the geography of the United States have affected the course of the war?

Think about:

1. how **Saratoga** lies in the Hudson River valley, a major g the Appalachian Mountains

C Animated GEOGRAPHY & HISTORY
Revolutionary America

Click here to preview the Revolutionary War @ ClassZone.com

---

② Reading for Understanding

D Key Ideas

BEFORE, YOU LEARNED

Despite the Continental Army's difficulties, the Patriots triumphed at Saratoga.

NOW YOU WILL LEARN

The expansion of the war weakened the British by forcing them to spread their military resources around the world.

A Vocabulary

TERMS & NAMES

Marquis de Lafayette (mahr•KEE•deh laf•eye•EHT) French aristocrat who volunteered to serve in Washington's army

Valley Forge site in southeast Pennsylvania where Washington and his army camped in the winter of 1777–1778

George Rogers Clark frontiersman who helped defend the Western frontier

John Paul Jones sea commander who attacked British ships near the British coast

Wilderness Road a trail into Kentucky

B BACKGROUND VOCABULARY

ally (AL•eye) a country that agrees to help another country achieve a common goal

desert (duh•ZERT) to leave military duty without permission

privateer (pry•vuh•TEER) a privately owned ship that has been granted permission by a wartime government to attack an enemy's merchant ships

C Visual Vocabulary
privateer

photograph courtesy of Peabody Essex Museum

Reading Strategy

Recreate the diagram shown at right. As you read and respond to the **KEY QUESTIONS**, use the center box to record the main idea; use the outer ovals to note important details. Add ovals or start a new diagram as needed.

See Skillbuilder Handbook, page R2.

MAIN IDEAS AND DETAILS

Other nations join the war.

The War Expands

GRAPHIC ORGANIZERS
Go to Interactive Review @ ClassZone.com

Connecting History

Expansion

Europeans would continue to settle and claim lands in the West until they reached the Pacific Ocean. You will see this theme emerge when you study westward expansion in later chapters.

Americans Seize the Frontier Determined to retake Fort and his men set out for Vincennes from Kaskaskia in Febru ilton wasn't expecting an attack because the rivers were floo But Clark's men slogged through miles of icy swamps and chest-deep water. They caught the British at Vincennes by su

When Hamilton and his troops tried to remain in pretended to have a larger force than he really had. Clark also Native American allies of the British in plain view of the fort to do the same to the British unless they surrendered. Frighte gave up.

Clark's victory gave the Americans a hold on the vast r the Great Lakes and the Ohio River (even though Fort Detro remained in the hands of the British). This area was more tha size of the original 13 states. The expansion of the war into t had another consequence: it forced the British again to sprea over a larger area and further weakened the British war effort

▲ **CAUSES AND EFFECTS** Explain why the war spread to the fronti

War on the Waves

E KEY QUESTION How did Americans expand the naval war?

The war expanded not only west into the frontier but also e high seas. By 1777, Britain had over 200 warships off the Ameri allowed Britain to control the Atlantic trade routes to Europea

British Trade Disrupted Because the American navy was sm Congress encouraged American **privateers** to attack British m A privateer is a privately owned ship that has permission by a wartime government to atta merchant ships. After capturing a ship a privateer sold its cargo and shared America commissioned more than 1, to prey on the British. They captured ships, causing British merchants to government to end the war.

Though outnumbered, the Con scored several victories. A daring c **John Paul Jones** inspired America across the Atlantic to attack British the coast of Britain itself.

"I Have Not Yet Begun to Figh Jones became the commander of a *Bonhomme Richard*. With four oth patrolled the English coast. In Septem vessels approached a convoy in which warships were guarding a number of suppl

James Forten, who later became famous for his efforts to end slavery, joined a privateer at the age of 14.

READING FOR UNDERSTANDING

③ Use Active Reading Strategies

Active reading strategies help you note the most important information in each section.

Ⓐ Reading Strategy Each Reading for Understanding page contains a Reading Strategy diagram to help you track and organize the information you read.

Ⓑ Skillbuilder Handbook Every Reading Strategy is supported by a corresponding lesson in the Skillbuilder Handbook at the back of this book.

Ⓒ Active Reading Strategies in the Skillbuilder Handbook will help you to read and study *American History*.

BACKGROUND VOCABULARY
redoubt (re•DOWT) a small fort

Battle of Charles Town British siege of Charles Town (Charleston), South Carolina, in May 1780, in which the Americans suffered their worst defeat of the war

Lord Cornwallis (korn•WAHL•ihs) British general whose campaigns in the South led to his defeat at Yorktown

Battle of Yorktown final battle of the war, in which French and American forces led by George Washington defeated British General Cornwallis

Visual Vocabulary
redoubt at Yorktown

▶ Reading Strategy

Re-create the diagram shown at right. As you read and respond to the **KEY QUESTIONS**, use the diagram to record important events in the order in which they occurred.

Ⓐ

📖 See Skillbuilder Handbook, page R5.

SEQUENCE EVENTS

British capture Savannah, 1778.	British capture Charles Town, 1780.	
	British capture Georgia.	

GRAPHIC ORGANIZERS
Go to **Interactive Review** @ ClassZone.com

212 Chapter 7

Skillbuilder Handbook

Ⓑ Table of Contents

Ⓒ 1.3 Finding Main Ideas

Defining the Skill

The **main idea** is a statement that summarizes the main point of a speech, an article, a section of a book, or a paragraph. Main ideas can be stated or unstated. The main idea of a paragraph is often stated in the first or last sentence. If it is the first sentence, it is followed by sentences that support that main idea. If it is the last sentence, the details build up to the main idea. To find an unstated idea, you must use the details of the paragraph as clues.

Applying the Skill

The following paragraph describes the role of women in the American Revolution. Use the strategies listed below to help you identify the main idea.

How to Find the Main Idea

Strategy ❶ Identify what you think may be the stated main idea. Check the first and last sentences of the paragraph to see if either could be the stated main idea.

Strategy ❷ Identify details that support that idea. Some details explain the main idea. Others give examples of what is stated in the main idea.

> #### WOMEN IN THE REVOLUTION
>
> ❶ Many women tried to help the army. Martha Washington and other wives followed their husbands to army camps. ❷ The wives cooked, did laundry, and nursed sick or wounded soldiers. ❷ A few women even helped to fight. ❷ Mary Hays earned the nickname "Molly Pitcher" by carrying water to tired soldiers during a battle. ❷ Deborah Sampson dressed as a man, enlisted, and fought in several engagements.

Make a Chart

Making a chart can help you identify the main idea and details in a passage or paragraph. The chart below identifies the main idea and details in the paragraph you just read.

> *Main Idea:* Women helped the army during the Revolution.
>
> *Detail:* They cooked and did laundry
> *Detail:* They nursed the wounded and sick soldiers
> *Detail:* They helped to fight.
> *Detail:* One woman, Molly Pitcher, carried water to soldiers during battles.

Practicing the Skill

Turn to Chapter 5, Section 2, "Roots of American Democracy." Read "Parliament and Colonial Government" on page 137, and create a chart that identifies the main idea and the supporting details.

④ Check Your Understanding

One of the most important things you'll do as you study *American History* is to check your understanding of events, people, places, and issues as you read.

Ⓐ Connect to the Essential Question

This chart summarizes the information that will help you understand the most important ideas in the chapter.

Ⓑ Interactive Review includes a Name Game

and provides two online activities to test your knowledge of the history you just studied.

Ⓒ Section Assessment reviews the section

Terms & Names, revisits your Reading Strategy notes, and provides key questions about the section.

---

large segments of the population were actively involved in a poli Even if the British had succeeded in defeating an American army, would never have been able to conquer the American people.

Ⓐ CONNECT ▶ to the Essential Question

How was it possible that American Patriots gained their independence from the powerful British Empire?

AMERICAN STRENGTHS		BRITISH WEAKNESSES
Patriots fought for their lives, their property, and their political ideals.	**Motivation**	The British and their Hessian mercenaries fought merely for pa
Many civilians actively supported the Revolutio technique Rebellion	**Popular support**	The British were unprepared for a popular uprising. There was no wic
Amerie mistakes patriotisr		
France su and Spair expandir French m		
America		

Ⓑ CHAPTER 7 Interactive Review

Chapter Summary

① Key Idea
Although the Continental Army had difficulty fighting in a divided America, the Patriots triumphed at Saratoga.

② Key Idea
The expansion of the war weakened the British by forcing them to spread their military resources around the world.

③ Key Idea
The Continental Army, their allies, and the American people brought about an American victory.

④ Key Idea
Americans emerged from the Revolution as citizens of a unified nation that valued the ideal of liberty.

To create **Review and Study Notes** go to **Interactive Review** @ ClassZone.com

Name Game

Use the Terms & Names list to complete your own paper.

1. I carried the war to the western frontier. George Rogers Clark ___
2. I led my troops to defeat at Saratoga. ___
3. I was a French officer who fought for America. ___
4. My leadership unified a nation. ___
5. I was trapped between allied forces and the French fleet. ___
6. I brought the war to the coasts of Britain. ___
7. The ideal of liberty helped me win my freedom in court. ___
8. I lost my lands when my ally betrayed me. ___
9. Here the Patriots first proved that they might win the war. ___
10. Here the Continental Army endured a difficult winter. ___

Defining Religious Freedom For many Americans, central to the liberty was the idea that religion is a private matter and that people have the right to choose and practice their personal religious belief such as James Madison and Thomas Jefferson called for a "separ church and state," meaning that the state should not be involved in affairs.

In 1777 Thomas Jefferson proposed his **Virginia Statute for Religiou** In it, he claimed that people have a "natural right" to freedom of including religious opinion. Jefferson opposed state laws that p Jews or Catholics from holding public office. He also opposed the using tax money to support churches, because, he wrote, "to com to furnish contributions of money for the propagation of opini he disbelieves, is sinful and tyrannical."

Jefferson's statute was eventually adopted as law in Virgin became the basis of the religious rights guaranteed by the Bill the U.S. Constitution.

Uniting the States For almost two centuries each colony ha erned independently of its neighbors. The colonies had been and often uncooperative. However, as the war turned colonie Americans saw how important it was for these states to work nation. The great challenge that lay ahead was how to remai nation of independent states, despite regional and religious d

▲ **SUMMARIZE** Describe the ideals that emerged from the Revolutic

Activities

CROSSWORD PUZZLE

Complete the online crossword puzzle to show what you know about the American Revolution.

ACROSS
1. ___ captured the British warship *Serapis*.

GEOGAME

Use this online map to reinforce your understanding of including the locations of important battles and geogra drop each place name in the list at its location on the m you keep track of your progress online.

Trenton
Saratoga
Lake Ontario
Valley Forge
Hudson River

More place names online

Lake Ontario

Ⓒ

ONLINE Q
For test practic
Interactive

TERMS & NAMES
1. Explain the importance of
   • Treaty of Paris
   • Elizabeth Freeman
   • Richard Allen
   • Virginia Statute for Religious Freedom

USING YOUR READING NOTES
2. **Categorize** List and categorize the major results of the Revolutionary War.

Boundary disputes — Deaths and casualties
Results of

KEY IDEAS
3. What groups gained least from
4. How did the goals of the Revolu toward a more just society afte

CRITICAL THINKING
5. **Connect Economics & History** Treaty of Paris protect America's economic interests?
6. **Causes and Effects** How did the Patriot victory affect Native Americans?
7. **Historical Perspective** What might have happened if, during the peace negotiations, each state had tried to negotiate independently?
8. **Writing** **Citizenship Report** Use the Internet

Themes of American History

Themes are ideas and issues that arise and reappear through American history. Understanding these themes will help you to connect the past and the present and to make sense of U.S. history. *American History* focuses on nine of these themes.

Democratic Ideals

Americans have built their society around the principles of democracy. In a democracy, power lies with the people, and every individual enjoys basic rights that cannot be taken away. Throughout the nation's history, however, some Americans— mainly women and minorities—have had to struggle to gain their full rights. Still, the ideals of democracy remain the guiding principles of this land.

Citizenship

The citizens of the United States enjoy rights and freedoms found in very few other places in the world. Yet Americans know that with such freedoms come responsibilities and duties. Whether they stand in line to vote or spend a weekend to clean up a local river, Americans recognize that citizen participation is what keeps a democracy strong.

Diversity and Unity

The United States has been a land of many peoples, cultures, and faiths. Throughout the nation's history, this blend of ethnic, racial, and religious groups has helped to create a rich and uniquely American culture. The nation's many different peoples are united in their belief in American values and ideals.

Impact of the Individual

The history of the United States is the story not only of governments and laws but of individuals. Indeed, individuals have made the United States what it is today through their extraordinary and ordinary achievements. American history provides a variety of examples of the impact of the individual on society in both the United States and the world.

Immigration and Migration

This country was settled by and has remained a magnet for immigrants. Also, within the United States, large numbers of people have migrated to different regions of the country. However, movements to and within the United States have not always been voluntary. Africans were brought against their will to this country. Native Americans were forced from their homelands in order to make room for European settlers.

Martin Luther King, Jr.

Economics in History

Economics has had a powerful impact on the course of U.S. history. For example, the desire for wealth led thousands to join the California Gold Rush in 1849. The nation as a whole has grown wealthy, thanks to its abundant resources and the hard work of its citizens. An important economic issue, however, has been how to make sure that all people have opportunities to share fully in the nation's wealth. This issue will continue to be important in the 21st century.

Mid-1800s telegraph

Science and Technology

Americans have always been quick to embrace inventions and new ways of doing things. After all, this country was settled by people who turned away from old ways and tried new ones. In the past two centuries, new inventions, new technologies, and scientific breakthroughs have transformed the United States—and will continue to do so in our lifetimes and beyond.

America and the World

As the power and influence of the United States have grown, the nation has played a much more active role in world affairs. Indeed, throughout the 20th century, the United States focused much of its energy on events beyond its borders. The nation fought in two world wars and tried to promote democracy, peace, and economic growth around the globe. As one of the world's political and economic leaders, the United States continues to be a key player in world affairs.

Expansion

When the United States declared its independence from Great Britain, it was only a collection of states along the Atlantic Ocean. But the new country would not remain that way for long. Many Americans shared a sense of curiosity, adventure, and a strong belief that their destiny was to expand all the way to the Pacific Ocean. Driven by this belief, they pushed westward. Americans' efforts to increase the size of their nation is a recurring theme in early U.S. history.

Exploring History Online

American History provides a variety of tools to help you explore history online. See history come to life in the Animation Center. Find help for your research projects in the Research and Writing Center. Review for tests with the Interactive Review, or create your own activities in the Activity Center. Go to ClassZone.com to make *American History* interactive!

ClassZone.com

is your gateway to exploring history. Explore the different **ClassZone Centers** to help you study and have fun with history.

(A) Interactive Review
provides you with flip cards, a crossword puzzle, section quizzes, drag-and-drop map activities, and more.

(B) Activity Center
You'll find a variety of interactive tools that will help you engage with history *your* way.

(C) Activity Maker
lets you create your own activities so that you can focus on what *you* need to review.

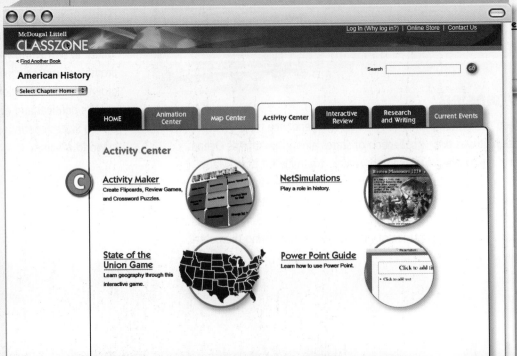

Animation Center

A rich collection of interactive features and maps on a wide variety of historical eras and topics

(A) Roll-overs
Explore the illustration by clicking on areas you'd like to know more about. This Battle Tactics animation links to features about tactics, cannon loading, a soldier's gear, and more.

(B) 3D models
Study this soldier's gear by rotating the 3D model.

(C) In-depth Views and Information
Click each box to find out what a soldier carried during the war.

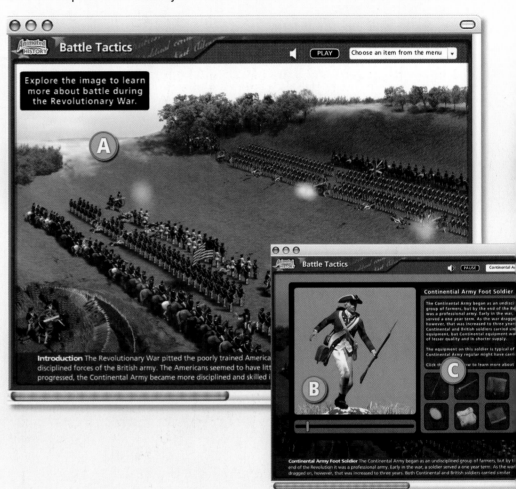

Review Game

- Create your own review game to study history *your* way.

- Select your own topics from any chapter to help you focus on specific people, places, or events to review.

- Help your friends to explore history online. Challenge them to play a review game that you create and modify!

STEPS TO SUCCESS

Guide to Understanding
Illinois's Learning Standards for
Social Science   IL37

- The Illinois Learning Standards for Social Science are organized into five goals. Each goal is divided into standards and benchmarks.

Guide to
Test-Taking Strategies and Practice   S1

- These test-taking strategies and practice are designed to help you tackle many of the items you will find on a standardized test.

 For a complete list of the Illinois Learning Standards for Social Science, see page R100.

Buckingham Fountain, Chicago, Illinois © Mark Segal/Getty Images

ILLINOIS LEARNING STANDARDS

TEST-TAKING STRATEGIES AND PRACTICE

Why Study History?

When you study U.S. history, you will see how the past informs your everyday life. Many things, such as the clothes you wear and the music you listen to, have been influenced by America's past.

Learn how to think like a historian! Dive into the dramatic events of America's past and uncover the lives of the people who shaped our nation's history.

▶ *Be An Informed Citizen* Your textbook will show you how the United States were founded, and how our current government came into existence.

Your textbook will also encourage you to be a more active participant in your community and to make a difference in our nation's future.

▶ *Become a Better Critical Thinker* Many questions throughout this book will encourage you to form your own opinion.

For example, what would *you* have done during the Civil War if fighting for what you believed in meant fighting against your own family?

▶ *Know Your Heritage* By learning about the diverse cultures that make up the United States, you will gain a better understanding of your own heritage.

What Will I Learn?

Guide to Understanding

Illinois's Learning Standards for Social Science

Illinois's Learning Standards for Social Science are organized into five goals. All of the goals are covered in this book.

State Goal 14 **Political Systems**

State Goal 15 **Economics**

State Goal 16 **History**

State Goal 17 **Geography**

State Goal 18 **Social Systems**

Each goal is divided into standards and benchmarks.

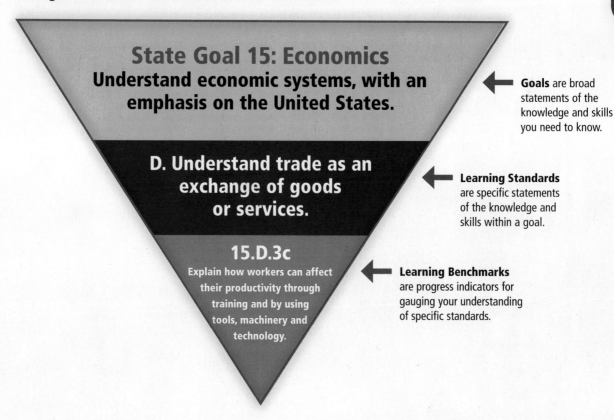

State Goal 15: Economics
Understand economic systems, with an emphasis on the United States.

← **Goals** are broad statements of the knowledge and skills you need to know.

D. Understand trade as an exchange of goods or services.

← **Learning Standards** are specific statements of the knowledge and skills within a goal.

15.D.3c
Explain how workers can affect their productivity through training and by using tools, machinery and technology.

← **Learning Benchmarks** are progress indicators for gauging your understanding of specific standards.

Overview
Illinois Learning Standards for Social Science

The charts that follow provide a brief overview of each goal and its learning standards and benchmarks. The benchmarks are the progress indicators addressed by each standard. Look for them at the beginning of each section.

 For a full list of the Illinois Learning Standards for Social Science, see page R100.

Goal 14 F. Understand the development of United States political ideas and traditions.

Learning Benchmarks	What It Means to *You*
14.F.3a Analyze historical influences on the development of political ideas and practices as enumerated in the Declaration of Independence, the United States Constitution, the Bill of Rights and the Illinois Constitution.	Preparing informed, capable, and responsible citizens is an important goal of civic education. Understanding the historical foundations, values, and principles of the U.S. system of government prepares you to make effective choices as a voter, worker, consumer, and member of your local, state, and national communities.

Goal 15 D. Understand trade as an exchange of goods or services.

Learning Benchmarks	What It Means to *You*
15.D.3a Explain the effects of increasing and declining imports and exports to an individual and to the nation's economy as a whole. **15.D.3b** Explain how comparative advantage forms the basis for specialization and trade among nations. **15.D.3c** Explain how workers can affect their productivity through training and by using tools, machinery and technology.	You are called on to make economic decisions every day as a consumer, producer, saver, and investor. Your decision making is improved if you understand how our economy works and how it is affected by political actions and natural events. Today, for example, U.S. businesses face both opportunities and challenges as they compete in world markets and deal with new technologies and areas of specialization.

Goal 16   C. Understand the development of economic systems.

Learning Benchmarks	What It Means to *You*
16.C.3a (US) Describe economic motivations that attracted Europeans and others to the Americas, 1500–1750. **16.C.3b (US)** Explain relationships among the American economy and slavery, immigration, industrialization, labor and urbanization, 1700-present. **16.C.3c (US)** Describe how economic developments and government policies after 1865 affected the country's economic institutions including corporations, banks and organized labor.	Economics has always had a strong influence on this nation. The Age of Exploration that led to the founding of the United States began with the desire for global trade. Economics also brought waves of people to our shores. Some came involuntarily as slaves. Many others ventured across the oceans in search of economic gain. This desire for economic gain spurred industrialization and urbanization, creating the country we have today.

Goal 17   D. Understand the historical significance of geography.

Learning Benchmarks	What It Means to *You*
17.D.3a Explain how and why spatial patterns of settlement change over time. **17.D.3b** Explain how interactions of geographic factors have shaped present conditions.	The movement of people from the cities to the suburbs, increased immigration, and the shift to a service economy are important geographic factors that shaped U.S. society. Since the 1970s, the nation's population center has moved westward and southward. Today, three of the four most populous states are in the West and the South— California, Texas, and Florida. This shift has changed the balance of political and economic power in the nation.

C. Understand how social systems form and develop over time.

Learning Benchmarks	What It Means to *You*
18.C.3a Describe ways in which a diverse U.S. population has developed and maintained common beliefs (e.g., life, liberty and the pursuit of happiness; the Constitution and the Bill of Rights). **18.C.3b** Explain how diverse groups have contributed to U.S. social systems over time.	United States citizens share many beliefs. As a country, we strongly believe in the democratic principles outlined in the Constitution and the Bill of Rights. We are also a nation of many different cultures. Appreciating this diversity and understanding how U.S. culture has developed and changed will help you better contribute to your community and society.

Guide to
TEST-TAKING STRATEGIES AND PRACTICE

This section of your book helps you develop and practice the skills you need to study history and to take standardized tests.

The **Test-Taking Strategies and Practice** offer specific strategies for tackling many of the items you will find on a standardized test. It gives tips for answering multiple-choice, constructed-response, extended-response, and document-based questions. In addition, it offers guidelines for analyzing primary and secondary sources, maps, political cartoons, charts, graphs, and timelines. Each strategy is followed by a set of questions you can use for practice.

CONTENTS for Test-Taking Strategies and Practice

The chart below provides a guide to the test-taking strategies and practice that will help prepare you for standards-based assessments.

Find online test practice @ ClassZone.com

- **Learn** each strategy by reviewing the numbered steps on the page listed in the column.

- **Practice** the strategy on the following page.

- **Apply** the strategies you learned in the **Illinois Standards-Based Assessment** at the end of each chapter.

Strategy	Learn	Practice	Apply
Multiple Choice	p. S2	p. S3	p. 191, Chapter 6
Primary Sources	p. S4	p. S5	p. 55, Chapter 2 p. 231, Chapter 7 p. 335, Chapter 9
Secondary Sources	p. S6	p. S7	p. 867, Chapter 27 p. 965, Chapter 30
Political Cartoons	p. S8	p. S9	p. 361, Chapter 10 p. 415, Chapter 12 p. 669, Chapter 20
Charts	p. S10	p. S11	p. 22, Chapter 1 p. 334, Chapter 9
Line and Bar Graphs	p. S12	p. S13	p. 335, Chapter 9 p. 361, Chapter 10
Pie Graphs	p. S14	p. S15	p. 690, Chapter 21 p. 770, Chapter 24
Maps	p. S16 p. S18	p. S17 p. S19	p. 447, Chapter 13 p. 507, Chapter 15 p. 533, Chapter 16 p. 591, Chapter 18
Timelines	p. S20	p. S21	p. 360, Chapter 10
Constructed Response	p. S22	p. S23	p. 23, Chapter 1 p. 55, Chapter 2
Extended Response	p. S24	p. S25	p. 91, Chapter 3
Document-Based Questions	pp. S26–27	pp. S28–29	p. 231, Chapter 7 p. 361, Chapter 10

Multiple Choice

A multiple-choice question consists of a stem and a set of choices. The stem is usually in the form of a question or an incomplete sentence. One of the choices correctly answers the question or completes the sentence.

1 Read the stem carefully and try to answer the question or complete the sentence without looking at the choices.

2 Pay close attention to key words in the stem. They may direct you toward the correct answer.

3 Read each choice with the stem. Don't jump to conclusions about the correct answer until you've read all of the choices.

4 Think carefully about questions that include *all of the above* among the choices.

5 After reading all of the choices, eliminate any that you know are incorrect.

6 Use modifiers to help narrow your choice.

7 Look for the best answer among the remaining choices.

---

stem

1 **1.** At the beginning of the Revolution, (most) Americans were

2 *Most* is a key word here. Replacing it with *all* or *some* changes the sentence and calls for a different answer.

3 choices

  A. united in support of the war.

  B. Patriots who wanted independence from Great Britain.

  C. against a war with Great Britain.

  D. Loyalists who supported the British point of view.

2. Which of the following weapons were first used effectively during World War I?

  A. airplanes

  B. machine guns

  C. tanks

  D. all of the above

4 If you select this answer, be sure that all of the choices are correct.

3. In June 1945, Germany was divided into four zones controlled by

  A. Great Britain, France, the United States, and Japan.

  B. Great Britain, France, the United States, and the Soviet Union.

  C. the Allied Powers.

  D. (all) of the countries of Europe.

5 You can eliminate **A** if you remember that the Allies were still at war with Japan in 1945.

6 Absolute words, such as *all, never, always, every,* and *only,* often signal an incorrect choice.

7 Either **B** or **C** could be correct. The Allied Powers did control Germany after World War II. However, Great Britain, France, the United States, and the Soviet Union controlled the four zones. Therefore, **B** is the correct answer.

answers: 1 (C), 2 (D), 3 (B)

Directions: Read the following questions and choose the *best* answer from the four choices.

1. New inventions that helped open the Great Plains to farming included

   A. the steel windmill.

   B. barbed wire.

   C. the spring-tooth harrow.

   D. all of the above

2. Which of the following statements *best* explains why, by the year 1500, there were hundreds of Native American groups with diverse religious beliefs, economies, and languages?

   A. The local environment influenced each group in different ways.

   B. Spiritual beliefs dictated many groups' distinct cultural growth.

   C. Contagious disease caused the people to form smaller groups.

   D. Trading practices led to the establishment of specialized cultures.

3. During the presidency of Thomas Jefferson, the United States was able to foster westward expansion when it acquired territory in what is known as

   A. Seward's Folly.

   B. the Missouri Compromise.

   C. the Kansas-Nebraska Act.

   D. the Louisiana Purchase.

4. In 1950, the United Nations Security Council voted to intervene after an act of aggression by which one of the following countries?

   A. Libya

   B. Great Britain

   C. the Democratic People's Republic of Korea

   D. the People's Republic of China

Primary Sources

Primary sources are materials written or made by people who took part in or witnessed historical events. Letters, diaries, speeches, newspaper articles, and autobiographies are all primary sources. So, too, are legal documents, such as wills, deeds, and financial records.

1 Look at the source line and identify the author. Consider what qualifies the author to write about the events discussed in the passage.

2 Skim the document to form an idea of what it is about.

3 Note special punctuation. Ellipses indicate that words or sentences have been removed from the original passage. Brackets indicate words that were not in the original. Bracketed words often are replacements for difficult or unfamiliar terms.

4 Carefully read the passage and distinguish between facts and the author's opinions. (That the groups of soldiers were wandering in all directions is a fact. The reasons for their wandering offered by Madison are her opinions.)

5 Consider for whom the author was writing. The intended audience may influence what and how an author writes.

6 Before rereading the passage, skim the questions to identify the information you need to find.

answers: 1 (D), 2 (B)

The Flight from the White House

Wednesday Morning, twelve o'clock. Since sunrise I have been turning my spy-glass in every direction, . . . but alas! I can [see] only groups of military, wandering in all directions, as if there was a lack of arms, or of spirit to fight for their own fireside.

Three o'clock. Will you believe it, my sister? We have had a battle, or skirmish, near Bladensburg, and here I am still, within sound of the cannon! . . . Two messengers covered with dust come to bid me fly. . . . At this late hour a wagon has been [found], and I have had it filled with plate and the most valuable portable articles belonging to the house. Whether it will reach its destination . . . or fall into the hands of British soldiery, events must determine. Our kind friend, Mr. Carroll, has come to hasten my departure, and is in a very bad humor with me, because I insist on waiting until the large picture of General Washington is secured. . . . It is done! and the precious portrait placed in the hands of two gentlemen of New York, for safe keeping. And now, dear sister, I must leave this house. . . . When I shall again write to you, or where I shall be tomorrow, I cannot tell!

The author is Dolley Madison, the wife of President James Madison. She personally oversaw the evacuation of the White House in 1814.

—Dolley Madison, in a letter to her sister describing her flight from the White House in August 1814

This is a letter. If it were an official report to Congress, the style and content would be much different.

1. Dolley Madison's letter describes her preparations to flee the White House in advance of a British attack. In which war did this attack take place?

A. War of Jenkins' Ear

B. French and Indian War

C. Revolutionary War

D. War of 1812

2. Why might Dolley Madison be considered a good source of information on the British attack on Washington, D.C.?

A. She was the wife of President James Madison.

B. She was an eyewitness to the attack.

C. She helped her husband develop military policy.

D. She had intercepted British war plans.

Directions: Use this passage from a letter on conservation, written by President Theodore Roosevelt, and your knowledge of U.S. history to answer questions 1 through 3.

In the East, the states are now painfully, and at great expense, endeavoring to undo the effects of their former short-sighted policy in throwing away their forest lands. Congress has before it bills to establish by purchase great forest reserves in the White mountains and the southern Appalachians, and the only argument against the bills is that of their great expense. New York and Pennsylvania are now, late in the day, endeavoring themselves to protect the forests which guard the headwaters of their streams. Michigan and Wisconsin have already had their good timber stripped from their forests by the great lumber companies. But the western states, far more fortunate than their eastern sisters in this regard, can now reserve their forests for the good of all their citizens, without expense, if they choose to show the requisite foresight.

—President Theodore Roosevelt, in a private letter in 1907

1. According to President Roosevelt, forests not yet damaged by timber companies could be set aside at no expense in the

   A. Midwest.

   B. East.

   C. South.

   D. West.

2. You can tell from this letter that President Roosevelt

   A. favored changing forests to farmland.

   B. was a good president.

   C. supported environmental protection.

   D. was an owner of a large lumber company.

3. Which one of the following statements from the letter is most strictly a fact?

   A. "Congress has before it bills to establish by purchase great forest reserves in the White mountains. . . ."

   B. "New York and Pennsylvania are now, late in the day, endeavoring themselves to protect the forests. . . ."

   C. ". . . States are now painfully, and at great expense, endeavoring to undo the effects of . . . throwing away their forest lands."

   D. "But the western states, far more fortunate than their eastern sisters . . . can now reserve their forests. . . ."

Secondary Sources

Secondary sources are descriptions or interpretations of historical events made by people who were not at those events. The most common types of written secondary sources are history books, encyclopedias, and biographies. A secondary source often combines information from several primary sources.

1 Read titles to preview what the passage is about.

2 Look for topic sentences. These, too, will help you preview the content of the passage.

3 As you read, use context clues to help you understand difficult or unfamiliar words. (You can tell from the description of the battle in the previous sentences that the word *fiasco* must mean something like "disaster," "failure," or "blunder.")

4 As you read, ask and answer questions that come to mind. You might ask: Why did Dolly Madison take a bed with her? Why would the British burn public buildings?

5 Before rereading the passage, skim the questions to identify the information you need to find.

1 The British Offensive

2 Ironically, Britain achieved a far more spectacular success in an operation originally designed as a diversion from their main thrust down Lake Champlain. In 1814 a British army sailed from Bermuda for Chesapeake Bay, landed near Washington, and met a larger American force . . . at Bladensburg, Maryland, on August 24. The Battle of Bladensburg quickly became the "Bladensburg races" as the American militia fled, almost without firing a shot. The British then descended on Washington. Madison, who had **3** witnessed the Bladensburg fiasco, escaped into the Virginia hills. His wife, Dolley, pausing only long enough to load her silver, a bed, and a portrait of George Washington onto her carriage, hastened to join her husband, while British troops **4** ate the supper prepared for the Madisons at the presidential mansion. Then they burned the mansion and other public buildings in Washington. A few weeks later, the British attacked Baltimore, but after failing to crack its defenses, they broke off the operation.

—Paul S. Boyer, et al., *The Enduring Vision* (4th ed.)

5 1. Why do you think the authors refer to the Battle of Bladensburg as a "fiasco"?

A. because the American forces fled almost without a fight

B. because President Madison had to flee the White House

C. because it allowed the British to attack Washington, D.C.

D. because it was a famous victory for the British forces

2. What, according to the authors, did the British raid on Washington, D.C., accomplish?

A. It paved the way for the British capture of Baltimore.

B. It drove all the American militia out of the city.

C. It helped the British offensive on Lake Champlain.

D. It burned down the presidential mansion and other public buildings.

> Remember to be wary of choices that contain absolutes, such as *all*, *every*, or *only*.

answers: 1 (A), 2 (D)

PRACTICE

Directions: Use this passage and your knowledge of U.S. history to answer questions 1 through 3.

African-American Sailors

African Americans contributed greatly to the growth of maritime commerce in the United States. Beginning in colonial times, slaves, with their masters' permission, hired themselves out as sailors. Some served as translators on slave ships. Merchant ships also offered a means of escape for runaway slaves. A few escapees even took to the sea as pirates.

Seafaring was one of the few occupations open to free African Americans. They served on clippers, naval vessels, and whaling ships from the 1700s into the late 1800s. Federal crew lists from Atlantic seaports show that during this time, African Americans made up 10 percent or more of sailors on American ships. Seafaring was an especially dangerous line of work for free blacks. They risked capture in southern ports, where they were often thrown in jail or sold into slavery.

1. What records show that African Americans made up 10 percent or more of sailors on American ships?

   A. shipyard records

   B. family bibles

   C. federal crew lists

   D. ships' logs

2. The passage implies that free and enslaved African Americans went to sea for all of the following reasons *except* to

   A. escape slavery.

   B. live as pirates.

   C. earn wages as sailors.

   D. discover new lands.

3. The author states that life was especially dangerous for free African-American sailors because

   A. American prosperity depended on their work alone.

   B. the worst jobs on board ship were always assigned to them.

   C. they ran the risk of capture and enslavement in southern ports.

   D. they were more likely than white sailors to contract scurvy.

Political Cartoons

Political cartoons are drawings that express views on political issues of the day. Cartoonists use symbols and such artistic styles as caricature—exaggerating a person's physical features—to get their message across.

① Identify the subject of the cartoon. Titles and captions often indicate the subject matter.

② Identify the main characters in the cartoon. Here, the main character is Horace Greeley, a candidate in the 1872 presidential election.

③ Note the symbols—ideas or images that stand for something else—used in the cartoon.

④ Study labels and other written information in the cartoon.

⑤ Analyze the point of view. How cartoonists use caricature often indicates how they feel. The exaggeration of Greeley's physical appearance— short and overweight— makes him appear comical.

⑥ Interpret the cartoonist's message.

The cartoonist shows Tammany Hall, New York's Democratic political machine, as a tiger. Uncle Sam, a symbol for the United States, is shown looking on.

The writing on the wall suggests that Tammany Hall wants reform. The "Whitewash" label on the bucket suggests that the tiger's true, corrupt, stripes are just being covered up.

Thomas Nast, *Harper's Weekly*, August 31, 1872

"WHAT ARE YOU GOING TO DO ABOUT IT," IF "OLD HONESTY" LETS HIM LOOSE AGAIN?

① "What are you going to do about it, if 'Old Honesty' lets him loose again?"

1. Based on the cartoon, what do you think was Horace Greeley's major issue in the 1872 presidential campaign?

A. political reform

B. states' rights

C. abolition

D. temperance

2. Which one of the following statements do you think *best* represents the cartoonist's point of view?

A. Horace Greeley is an honest man.

B. Tammany Hall supports political reform.

C. Tammany Hall, regardless of Greeley's view, is still corrupt.

D. Horace Greeley, like most Tammany politicians, is corrupt.

answers: 1 (A), 2 (C)

Directions: Use the cartoon and your knowledge of U.S. history to answer questions 1 through 3.

Rollin Kirby, *New York World*, 1917

"That's my fight, too!"

1. The cartoon character is a symbol of

    A. Americans opposed to war.

    B. the president of the United States.

    C. old soldiers retired from the United States Army.

    D. the United States as a whole.

2. The "fight" in the cartoon caption refers to

    A. the War of 1812.

    B. World War II in Europe.

    C. World War II in the Pacific.

    D. World War I in Europe.

3. The cartoonist's point of view is *best* described by which of the following statements?

    A. The United States believes it has an obligation to join in this foreign war.

    B. Uncle Sam is too old and too late for every battle.

    C. The United States should stay out of other countries' wars.

    D. A country should equip its soldiers with the best weapons and other supplies.

Charts

Charts present information in a visual form. History textbooks use several types of charts, including tables, flow charts, Venn diagrams, and concept webs. The type of chart most commonly found in standardized tests is the table. It organizes information in columns and rows for easy viewing.

1 Read the title and identify the broad subject of the chart.

2 Read the column and row headings and any other labels. This will provide more details about the subject of the chart.

3 Compare and contrast the information from column to column and row to row.

4 Try to draw conclusions from the information in the chart. Ask yourself: What trends does the chart show?

5 Read the questions, and then study the chart again.

> Review difficult or unfamiliar words. Here, the term *nativity* means "place of birth."

1 **United States Population by Region and Nativity** *1890–1920*

2	**1890**	**1900**	**1910**	**1920**
Northeast				
Total Population	17,407,000	21,047,000	25,869,000	29,662,000
% Native Born	78	77	74	77
% Foreign Born	22	23	26	23
North Central				
Total Population	22,410,000	26,333,000	29,889,000	34,020,000
% Native Born	82	84	84	86
% Foreign Born	18	16	16	14
South				
Total Population	20,028,000	24,524,000	29,389,000	33,126,000
% Native Born	97	98	97	97
% Foreign Born	3	2	3	3
West				
Total Population	3,134,000	4,309,000	7,082,000	9,214,000
% Native Born	78	75	76	79
% Foreign Born	22	25	24	21

4

Source: *Historical Statistics of the United States*

> Compare changes in population over time and contrast statistics among regions.
>
> **3**

5 1. The two regions with the highest percentage of foreign-born inhabitants are the

   A. Northeast and the West.

   B. West and the South.

   C. South and the North Central.

   D. North Central and the Northeast.

2. When did immigration to the Northeast peak?

   A. between 1910 and 1920

   B. before 1900

   C. between 1900 and 1910

   D. after 1920

answers: 1 (A), 2 (C)

PRACTICE

Directions: Use the chart and your knowledge of U.S. history to answer questions 1 through 4.

Percentage of Population Free and Enslaved, by States and Territories *1790*						
North				**South**		
States/Territories	**Free**	**Enslaved**		**States/Territories**	**Free**	**Enslaved**
Connecticut	98.9	1.1		Georgia	64.5	35.5
Delaware	85.0	15.0		Kentucky	83.1	16.9
Maine	100.0	0.0		Maryland	67.8	32.2
Massachusetts	100.0	0.0		North Carolina	74.5	25.5
New Hampshire	99.9	0.1		South Carolina	57.0	43.0
New Jersey	93.8	6.2		Virginia	60.9	39.1
New York	93.8	6.2				
Pennsylvania	99.1	0.9				
Rhode Island	98.6	1.4				
Vermont	100.0	0.0				

Source: Inter-University Consortium for Political and Social Research

1. The state with the highest percentage of enslaved people was

   A. New Hampshire.

   B. North Carolina.

   C. Rhode Island.

   D. South Carolina.

2. Which of the following *best* describes most states in the North?

   A. The population was more than 98 percent free.

   B. More than 10 percent of the population was enslaved.

   C. Less than 60 percent of the population was free.

   D. The population was more than 20 percent enslaved.

3. Which statement about the percentage of enslaved people is true?

   A. It is much lower in the South.

   B. It is much higher in the South.

   C. There is no difference between the regions.

   D. There is a slight difference between the regions.

4. What economic factor *best* explains the population differences between the regions?

   A. The North focused on manufacturing.

   B. The North was wealthy enough to free enslaved people.

   C. The South focused on plantation agriculture.

   D. The South needed enslaved people for factory work.

Line and Bar Graphs

Graphs show statistics in a visual form. Line graphs are particularly useful for showing changes over time. Bar graphs make it easy to compare numbers or sets of numbers.

1 Read the title and identify the broad subject of the graph.

2 Study the labels on the vertical and horizontal axes to see the kinds of information presented in the graph. Note the intervals between amounts and between dates. This will help you read the graph more efficiently.

3 Look at the source line and evaluate the reliability of the information in the graph. Government statistics on education tend to be reliable.

4 Study the information in the graph and note any trends.

5 Draw conclusions and make generalizations based on these trends.

6 Read the questions carefully, and then study the graph again.

1 **High School Graduates** *1880–1920*

2 Graduates (*in thousands*)

2 Dates

Grid lines make the information on the graph easier to read.

5 A generalization you might make here is that the number of students enrolled in school increased markedly in the first 20 years of the 1900s.

3 Source: *Historical Statistics of the United States*

6 **1.** How many students graduated from high school in 1905?

   A. exactly 100,000   **C.** about 150,000

   B. about 125,000   **D.** exactly 175,000

1 **Public Secondary School Enrollment** *1880–1920*

2 Thousands of Students

2 Dates

3 Source: *Historical Statistics of the United States*

2. Which one of the following sentences do you think *best* describes the trend shown in the bar graph?

6

   A. The number of students enrolled steadily increased.

   B. The number of students enrolled showed little change.

   C. The number of students enrolled rose and fell.

   D. The number of students enrolled steadily decreased.

answers: 1 (B), 2 (A)

PRACTICE

Directions: Use the graphs and your knowledge of U.S. history to answer questions 1 through 4.

Motor Vehicle Registrations *1930–1960*

Source: *Historical Statistics of the United States*

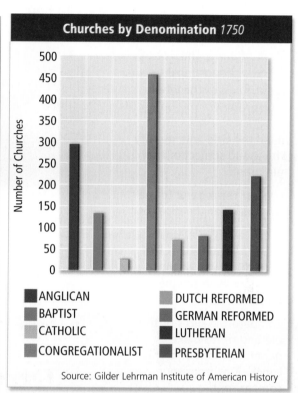

Churches by Denomination *1750*

- ANGLICAN
- BAPTIST
- CATHOLIC
- CONGREGATIONALIST
- DUTCH REFORMED
- GERMAN REFORMED
- LUTHERAN
- PRESBYTERIAN

Source: Gilder Lehrman Institute of American History

1. In which time periods did motor-vehicle registrations decline?

   A. 1930 to 1935 and 1935 to 1940

   B. 1930 to 1935 and 1940 to 1945

   C. 1935 to 1940 and 1940 to 1945

   D. 1935 to 1940 and 1945 to 1950

2. Which one of the following would be another good title for this graph?

   A. The American Love Affair with the Automobile

   B. Industrial Decline After World War II

   C. The Automobile Industry During the Great Depression

   D. Automobiles Through the Ages

3. Which one of the following statements accurately reflects information in the graph?

   A. There were more Congregationalist churches than all other denominations combined.

   B. There were more Presbyterian churches than Anglican churches.

   C. The Baptists had the fewest churches.

   D. The Congregationalists had the most churches.

4. Which denomination had the fewest churches?

   A. Anglican
   B. Catholic
   C. German Reformed
   D. Lutheran

Pie Graphs

A pie, or circle, graph shows relationships among the parts of a whole. These parts look like slices of a pie. The size of each slice is proportional to the percentage of the whole that it represents.

1 Read the title and identify the broad subject of the pie graph.

2 Look at the legend to see what each of the slices of the pie represents.

3 Read the source line and note the origin of the data shown in the pie graph.

4 Compare the slices of the pie and try to make generalizations and draw conclusions from your comparisons.

5 Read the questions carefully and review difficult or unfamiliar terms.

6 Eliminate choices that you know are wrong.

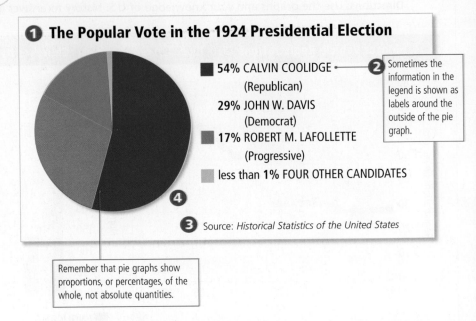

1 **The Popular Vote in the 1924 Presidential Election**

- 54% CALVIN COOLIDGE (Republican)
- 29% JOHN W. DAVIS (Democrat)
- 17% ROBERT M. LAFOLLETTE (Progressive)
- less than 1% FOUR OTHER CANDIDATES

2 Sometimes the information in the legend is shown as labels around the outside of the pie graph.

3 Source: *Historical Statistics of the United States*

Remember that pie graphs show proportions, or percentages, of the whole, not absolute quantities.

1. In the 1924 presidential election, Calvin Coolidge won

   A. by a landslide.

   B. a plurality of the votes cast.

   C. a majority of the votes cast.

   D. by a narrow margin.

   5 In electoral terms, the word *landslide* refers to an overwhelming victory, *majority* means "more than 50 percent," and *plurality* means "the most but less than 50 percent."

2. Which party's candidate won the second largest share of the popular vote?

   A. the Democratic Party

   B. the Other Party

   C. the Progressive Party

   D. the Republican Party

   6 You can eliminate **B** because there is no political party named "Other."

answers: 1 (C), 2 (A)

PRACTICE

Directions: Use the pie graphs and your knowledge of U.S. history to answer questions 1 through 4.

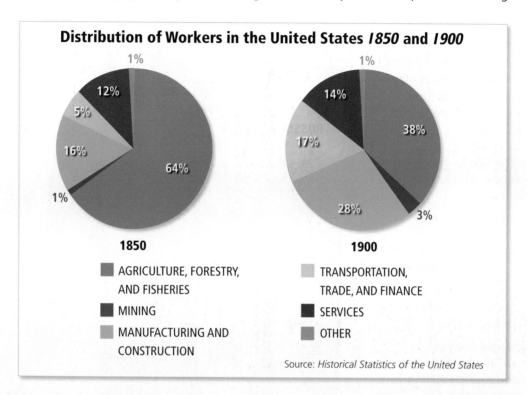

Distribution of Workers in the United States *1850* and *1900*

1850

1900

■ AGRICULTURE, FORESTRY, AND FISHERIES

■ MINING

■ MANUFACTURING AND CONSTRUCTION

■ TRANSPORTATION, TRADE, AND FINANCE

■ SERVICES

■ OTHER

Source: *Historical Statistics of the United States*

1. In 1850, most people worked in

   A. agriculture, forestry, and fisheries.

   B. mining.

   C. services.

   D. transportation, trade, and finance.

2. In 1900, more people worked in manufacturing and construction than in

   A. agriculture, forestry, and fisheries.

   B. mining and agriculture, forestry, and fisheries combined.

   C. services and transportation, trade, and finance combined.

   D. transportation, trade, and finance.

3. Which occupation category showed an increase between 1850 and 1900?

   A. manufacturing and construction

   B. services

   C. transportation, trade, and finance

   D. all of the above

4. What helped to bring about the changes reflected in the two pie graphs?

   A. the passage of new immigration laws

   B. the growth of industry

   C. the decline of world agricultural markets

   D. all of the above

Political Maps

Political maps show countries and the political divisions within countries, such as states. They also show the location of major cities. In addition, political maps often show physical features, such as rivers, seas, oceans, and mountain ranges.

1 Read the title to determine the subject and purpose of the map.

2 Read the labels on the map. This will reveal information about the map's subject and purpose.

3 Study the legend to find the meaning of symbols used on the map.

4 Look at the lines of latitude and longitude. This grid makes locating places much easier.

5 Use the compass rose or the North arrow to determine directions on the map.

6 Use the scale to estimate the distances between places shown on the map.

7 Read the questions, and then carefully study the map to determine the answers.

1 Alaska: Political

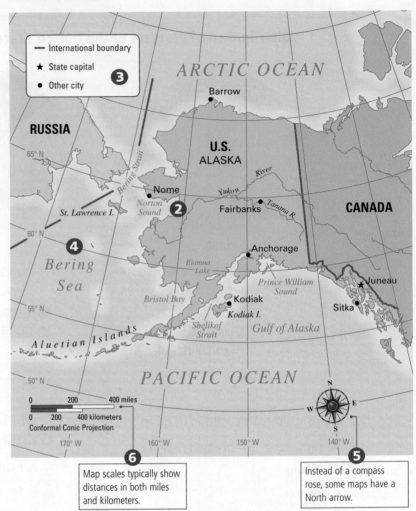

Map scales typically show distances in both miles and kilometers.

Instead of a compass rose, some maps have a North arrow.

7 **1.** Which one of the following cities is located closest to 65° N 150° W?

   A. Anchorage

   B. Barrow

   C. Fairbanks

   D. Nome

2. If you took an airplane trip from Juneau to Anchorage, in which general direction would you be traveling?

   A. north

   B. south

   C. east

   D. west

answers: 1 (C), 2 (D)

Directions: Use the map and your knowledge of U.S. history to answer questions 1 through 4.

San Francisco Bay Area

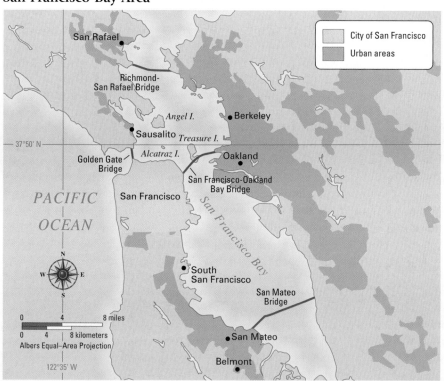

1. Which one of the following describes the location of Sausalito?

   A. north of 37° 50′ N latitude

   B. east of 122° 35′ W longitude

   C. west of Berkeley

   D. all of the above

2. About how far is San Rafael from San Mateo?

   A. 15 miles

   B. 30 miles

   C. 60 miles

   D. 120 miles

3. Which location would figure prominently in a history of immigration to the United States?

   A. Angel Island

   B. Golden Gate Bridge

   C. Treasure Island

   D. Belmont

4. Which one of the following place names does *not* reflect California's Spanish heritage?

   A. San Rafael

   B. Sausalito

   C. Alcatraz

   D. Oakland

Thematic Maps

A thematic map, or special-purpose map, focuses on a particular topic. The location of baseball parks, a country's natural resources, election results, and major battles in a war are all topics you might see illustrated on a thematic map.

① Read the title to determine the subject and purpose of the map.

② Examine the labels on the map to find more information about the map's subject and purpose.

③ Study the legend to find the meaning of the symbols and colors used on the map.

④ Look at the colors and symbols on the map and try to identify patterns.

⑤ Read the questions and then carefully study the map to determine the answers.

① Americans on the Move, 1970s

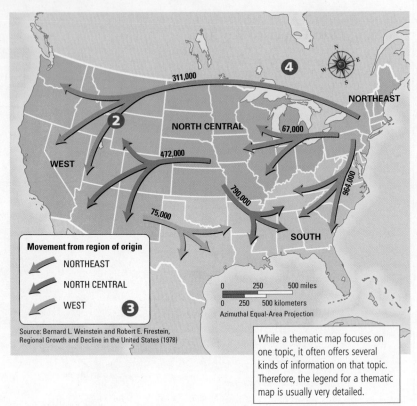

Source: Bernard L. Weinstein and Robert E. Firestein, Regional Growth and Decline in the United States (1978)

While a thematic map focuses on one topic, it often offers several kinds of information on that topic. Therefore, the legend for a thematic map is usually very detailed.

⑤ 1. Which region made the greatest gain in population because of people moving from one part of the country to another?

A. the South

B. the West

C. the North Central

D. the Northeast

2. The region that lost the most population from migration was the

A. North Central.

B. South.

C. Northeast.

D. West.

answers: 1 (A), 2 (C)

PRACTICE

Directions: Use the map and your knowledge of U.S. history to answer questions 1 through 4.

U.S. School Segregation, *1952*

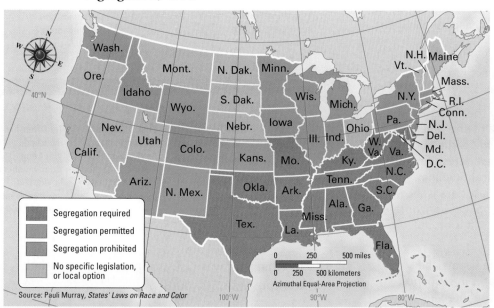

Source: Pauli Murray, *States' Laws on Race and Color*

Legend:
- Segregation required
- Segregation permitted
- Segregation prohibited
- No specific legislation, or local option

1. In what region of the United States was segregation in schools most widespread?

   A. the Northeast

   B. the Midwest

   C. the South

   D. the West

2. In which of the following western states was segregation in schools prohibited?

   A. Arizona

   B. California

   C. Oregon

   D. Washington

3. What was the name given to laws passed by various states to separate the races?

   A. apartheid

   B. Jim Crow

   C. affirmative action

   D. emancipation

4. Which U.S. Supreme Court case struck down segregation in schools as unconstitutional?

   A. *Brown* v. *Board of Education*

   B. *Plessy* v. *Ferguson*

   C. *Hazelwood School District* v. *Kuhlmeier*

   D. *Williams* v. *Mississippi*

Timelines

A timeline is a type of chart that lists events in the order in which they occurred. In other words, timelines are a visual method of showing what happened when.

1 Read the title to discover the subject of the timeline.

2 Identify the time period covered by the timeline by noting the earliest and latest dates shown. On vertical timelines, the earliest date is shown at the top. On horizontal timelines, it is on the far left.

3 Read the events and their dates in sequence. Notice the intervals between events.

4 Use your knowledge of history to develop a fuller picture of the events listed in the timeline. For example, place the events in a broader context by considering what was happening elsewhere in the world.

5 Note how events are related to one another. Look particularly for cause-effect relationships.

6 Use the information you have gathered from the above strategies to answer the questions.

1 The Vietnam War, 1960–1969

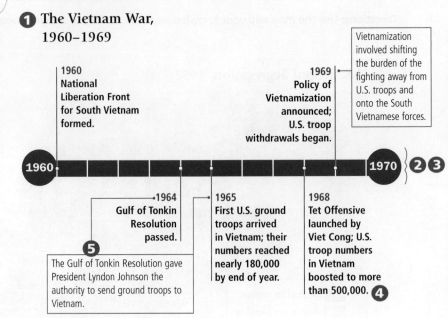

Vietnamization involved shifting the burden of the fighting away from U.S. troops and onto the South Vietnamese forces.

1960
National Liberation Front for South Vietnam formed.

1969
Policy of Vietnamization announced; U.S. troop withdrawals began.

1964
Gulf of Tonkin Resolution passed.

1965
First U.S. ground troops arrived in Vietnam; their numbers reached nearly 180,000 by end of year.

1968
Tet Offensive launched by Viet Cong; U.S. troop numbers in Vietnam boosted to more than 500,000.

5 The Gulf of Tonkin Resolution gave President Lyndon Johnson the authority to send ground troops to Vietnam.

6 **1.** In what year was U.S. troop strength boosted to more than 500,000?

A. 1964

B. 1965

C. 1968

D. 1969

2. What event led to a reduction of U.S. troop strength in Vietnam?

A. passage of the Gulf of Tonkin Resolution

B. announcement of the policy of Vietnamization

C. launch of the Tet Offensive

D. formation of the Viet Cong

answers: 1 (C), 2 (B)

S20

PRACTICE

Directions: Use the timeline and your knowledge of U.S. history to answer questions 1 through 3.

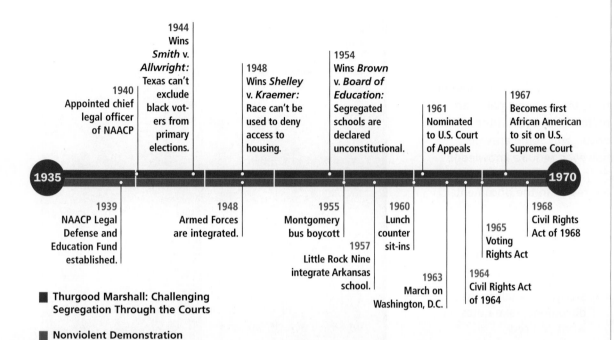

1940 Appointed chief legal officer of NAACP

1944 Wins *Smith* v. *Allwright:* Texas can't exclude black voters from primary elections.

1948 Wins *Shelley* v. *Kraemer:* Race can't be used to deny access to housing.

1954 Wins *Brown* v. *Board of Education:* Segregated schools are declared unconstitutional.

1961 Nominated to U.S. Court of Appeals

1967 Becomes first African American to sit on U.S. Supreme Court

1935 — **1970**

1939 NAACP Legal Defense and Education Fund established.

1948 Armed Forces are integrated.

1955 Montgomery bus boycott

1957 Little Rock Nine integrate Arkansas school.

1960 Lunch counter sit-ins

1963 March on Washington, D.C.

1964 Civil Rights Act of 1964

1965 Voting Rights Act

1968 Civil Rights Act of 1968

■ **Thurgood Marshall: Challenging Segregation Through the Courts**

■ **Nonviolent Demonstration and Legislative Action**

---

1. In what year did the NAACP achieve a major victory in its goal to desegregate schools throughout the United States?

A. 1939

B. 1944

C. 1954

D. 1964

2. How many years after *Brown* v. *Board of Education* did Arkansas integrate a public school?

A. three years

B. five years

C. seven years

D. ten years

3. Thurgood Marshall was known as "Mr. Civil Rights" because he was

A. a lawyer who successfully argued to end legal segregation in voting, housing, and education.

B. the chief legal officer of the NAACP beginning in the late 1930s.

C. the first African American appointed to the Supreme Court.

D. an African-American lawyer and judge before the civil rights acts were passed.

Constructed Response

Constructed-response questions focus on various kinds of documents. Each document usually is accompanied by a series of questions. These questions call for short answers that, for the most part, can be found directly in the document. Some answers, however, require knowledge of the subject or time period addressed in the document.

1 Read the title of the document to discover the subject addressed in the questions.

2 Study and analyze the document. Take notes on what you see.

3 Read the questions and then study the document again to locate the answers.

4 Carefully write your answers. Unless the directions say otherwise, your answers need not be complete sentences.

1 Joseph Glidden's Patent

2 Constructed-response questions use a wide range of documents, including short passages, cartoons, charts, graphs, maps, timelines, posters, and other visual materials. This is a copy of a legal document called a patent.

J. F. GLIDDEN.
Wire-Fences.
No. 157,124.   Patented Nov. 24, 1874.

FIG. I.
FIG. II.
FIG. III.

Witnesses:

Inventor:
Joseph F. Glidden
By Cyd. Chapin
atty.

Source: National Archives and Records Administration

3 **1.** What invention is illustrated on this patent?

4 *barbed wire fence*

2. What suggests that this is a legal document?

It is signed by witnesses and an attorney.

3. What other developments had a major impact on farming on the plains in the 1800s?

steel plows, reapers, threshers, dry farming

Directions: Use the photograph below and your knowledge of U.S. history to answer questions 1 through 3. Your answers need not be complete sentences.

Exercise Desert Rock: Six Miles from Ground Zero

Troops of the Battalion Combat Team, U.S. Army 11th Airborne Division: Yucca Flats, Nevada, November 1, 1951

Source: National Archives and Records Administration

1. What are the soldiers in the photograph looking at?

2. What major nonmilitary global conflict caused the United States to conduct tests like "Exercise Desert Rock"?

3. Name the 1963 agreement that ended above-ground tests like the one pictured here, and identify the two nations that signed it.

Extended Response

Extended-response questions, like constructed-response questions, usually focus on one kind of document. However, they are more complex and require more time to complete than typical short-answer constructed-response questions. Some extended-response questions ask you to present information from the document in a different form. Others require you to apply your knowledge of history to information contained in the document.

1 Read the title of the document to get an idea of the subject.

2 Study and analyze the document. Take notes on your ideas.

3 Carefully read the extended-response questions.

4 If the question calls for a graph or some other kind of diagram, make a rough sketch on scrap paper first. Then make a final copy of your drawing on the answer sheet.

5 If the question requires a written response, jot down ideas in outline form. Use this outline to write your answer.

1

Carbon Dioxide Output of Average U.S. Single-Family Home	
Sources	**Pounds of Carbon Dioxide per Year**
Space Heating	10,132
Air Conditioning	2,609
Water Heating	3,618
Refrigerator, Freezer	3,429
Cooking	935
Other Appliances	6,337
Lighting	2,460
Automobile	20,960

Source: Rocky Mountain Institute, 1999

2

3 1. Use the information in the chart to create a bar graph showing the annual carbon dioxide output of the average American single-family home.

Annual Carbon Dioxide Output of the Average American Single-Family Home

4 For graphs and other diagrams, remember to include a title and all appropriate labels.

3 2. Write a short essay discussing the steps that the typical American family could take to reduce its carbon dioxide output.

5 **Essay Rubric** The best essays will point out that families could reduce their carbon dioxide output by reducing their use of appliances and vehicles. Walking, carpooling, and taking public transportation would greatly reduce carbon dioxide output. So, too, would setting thermostats at a reasonable level to cut the use of heaters and air conditioners. Finally, replacing old appliances with newer, more efficient ones also would cut carbon dioxide emissions.

PRACTICE

Directions: Use the passage and your knowledge of U.S. history to make a chart like the one below. Complete the chart by providing the information requested at the end of the paragraph.

A Country Dividing

As the United States grew during the 1800s, Congress and the people argued about what form of government each new territory and state would have. The differences of opinion centered on one issue more than any other: slavery. Eventually, those sectional arguments led to the Civil War. The left side of the chart below lists three acts of Congress that addressed the issue of slavery in the West. Describe at least three provisions of each of these acts. (Note that the first provision of each act has been written for you.)

Act	Provisions
Missouri Compromise, 1820–1821	1. Slavery was to be prohibited in the Louisiana territory north of the 36° 30′ parallel. 2. 3.
Compromise of 1850	1. The territories of New Mexico and Utah were created without restrictions on slavery. 2. 3.
Kansas-Nebraska Act, 1854	1. Two new territories, Kansas and Nebraska, were created. 2. 3.

Document-Based Questions

A document-based question focuses on several documents—both visual and written. These documents often are accompanied by short-answer questions. You then use the answers to these questions and information from the documents to write an essay on a specified subject.

1 Carefully read the "Historical Context" to get an indication of the issue addressed in the question.

2 Note the action words used in the "Task" section. These words tell you exactly what the essay question requires.

3 Study and analyze each document. Think about how the documents are connected to the essay question. Take notes on your ideas.

4 Read and answer each of the document-specific questions.

Introduction

1 **Historical Context:** After the United States entered World War II, many men left their jobs to join the military. Millions of women stepped in to take their place in factories and offices.

2 **Task:** Discuss how life for women in the U.S. changed during World War II and note the gains that women made in the field of employment.

Part 1: Short Answer

Study each document carefully and answer the questions that follow.

3 Document 1: Working Women During World War II

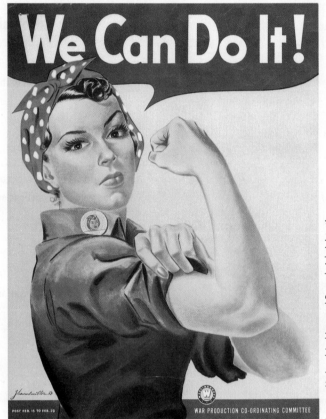

Source: National Archives and Records Administration

4 How does this image of women workers differ from the traditionally accepted image of the time?

This image shows a woman in the nontraditional role of a factory worker. It also shows the woman as self confident and physically strong.

Document 2:

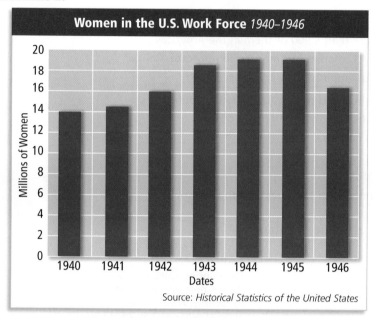

Women in the U.S. Work Force *1940–1946*

Millions of Women (y-axis: 0 to 20)

Dates (x-axis): 1940, 1941, 1942, 1943, 1944, 1945, 1946

Source: *Historical Statistics of the United States*

What trends in women's employment does this graph show?

The graph shows a marked increase during the war years with a decrease after the war's end.

Document 3: The Future of Women's Work

Despite the surge of women into heavy industry, markedly larger numbers of new women entrants into the wartime work force took up clerical and service jobs, . . . and there women's gains proved far more durable. The number of women factory operatives plummeted at war's end. . . . By 1947 the proportion of working women in blue-collar occupations was actually smaller than it had been at the war's outset. . . . The future of women's work lay not in the wartime heavy industries, . . . but in the [growing] service occupations, which within a decade of the war's conclusion eclipsed factory work as the nation's principal source of employment.

— David M. Kennedy, *Freedom from Fear*

In what jobs did women make the most long-lasting gains?

clerical and service jobs

❺ Part 2: Essay

Using information from the documents, your answers to the questions in Part 1, and your knowledge of U.S. history, write an essay that discusses how life for women changed during World War II and notes the gains that women made in employment. ❻

❺ Carefully read the essay question. Then write an outline for your essay.

❻ Write your essay. Be sure that it has an introductory paragraph that introduces your argument, main body paragraphs that explain it, and a concluding paragraph that restates your position. In your essay, include extracts or details from specific documents to support your ideas. Add other supporting facts or details that you know from your study of American history.

Sample Response The best essays will point out that the greatest change for American women during World War II was that many entered the work force for the first time (Documents 2 and 3) and that many took jobs that were not traditionally held by women (Document 1). Essays also should note that while many women took jobs traditionally held by men, more entered clerical and service jobs (Document 3). And while the number of women in industrial jobs declined after the war, the number in service jobs grew (Document 3).

Introduction

Historical Context: In 1775, Great Britain had an army of 48,647 men located throughout the world, more than 8,500 of them in the Americas. A rebellion by the small group of 13 colonies in America did not scare the keepers of such a large colonial empire.

Task: Discuss how the colonists' beliefs and military actions contributed to their victory in the Revolution. Include the significance of the American alliances with European nations.

Part 1: Short Answer

Study each document carefully and answer the questions that follow.

Document 1: First Georgia Regiment of Infantry Continental Line, 1777

The hunting shirt, or rifle dress, shown here was recommended by George Washington in his general order of July 24, 1776. Declaring it a practical item to be given to the troops, he also claimed that ". . . it is a dress justly supposed to carry no small terror to the enemy, who think every such person a complete marksman."

Source: New York Historical Society

What unusual military tactics did patriots like the man in the picture use to surprise and outsmart the British during the Revolution?

Document 1: *Uniforms of the American Revolution: 1st Georgia Regiment Continental Infantry, 1777, Private Field Dress,* Charles Lefferts. Watercolor, gouache on paper. Copyright © Collection of the New York Historical Society.

Document 2: Philadelphia, September 12, 1777

> I close this paper with a short address to General Howe. . . . We know the cause which we are engaged in, and though a passionate fondness for it may make us grieve at every injury. . . . We are not moved by the gloomy smile of a worthless king, but by the ardent glow of generous patriotism. We fight not to enslave, but to set a country free, and to make room upon the earth for honest men to live in. In such a case we are sure that we are right; and we leave to you the despairing reflection of being the tool of a miserable tyrant.
>
> —Thomas Paine, *The American Crisis No. IV*

Although this excerpt is addressed to the British General Howe, how might it also have encouraged the colonists to continue their fight against the British?

Document 3: The Battle of Yorktown, 1781: Winning the American Revolution

Estimated American, French, and British Forces and Casualties

Generals and Their Divisions	Forces	Casualties
General Washington (American colonies)	15,000	76
General Rochambeau (France)	7,800	186
General Cornwallis (Britain)	8,000	482

Source: U.S. Army Center of Military History

Estimated French and British Naval Strength*

French and British Fleets	Ships	Guns on Board Ship
Admiral Graves (Britain)	19	1,450
Admiral DeGrasse (France)	24	2,610

*Does not include small craft or transport ships

What support was provided by the French in the Battle of Yorktown?

Part 2: Essay

Using information from the documents, your answers to the questions in Part 1, and your knowledge of U.S. history, write an essay that discusses how the colonists' beliefs and military actions contributed to their victory in the Revolution. Include in your essay the significance of American alliances with European nations.

Geography Handbook

The Landscape of America

The best place to begin your study of American history is with the geography of America. Geography is more than the study of the land and people. It also involves the relationship between people and their environment.

The United States is part of the North American continent. The United States ranks third in both total area and population in the world. It is filled with an incredible variety of physical features, natural resources, climactic conditions, and people. This handbook will help you to learn about these factors and to understand how they affected the development of the United States.

Chicago's waterways—its river system, canals, and location on Lake Michigan—have made it the commercial hub of the Midwest.

Turbines in a California "wind farm" use coastal winds to generate electricity. California is the birthplace of both windsurfing and America's first wind farms.

ROCKY MOUNTAINS

WEST

NORTHEAST

MIDWEST

A P P A L A C H I A N   M O U N T A I N S

SOUTH

Rhode Island is world-renowned for its commercial fishing.

The climate and soil of Alabama are well-suited for growing cotton. The United States grows over 4 million tons of cotton annually.

The Landscape of America **A1**

Themes of Geography

One useful way to think about geography is in terms of major themes or ideas. These pages examine the five major themes of geography and show how they apply to Boston, Massachusetts.

Location

"Where am I?" Your answer is your location. One way to answer is to use absolute location. That means using the coordinates of longitude and latitude (see page A6). For example, if you're in Boston, your absolute location is approximately 42° north latitude and 71° west longitude.

More likely, however, you'll use relative location to answer the question. Relative location describes where an area is in relation to another area. For example, Boston lies in the northeast corner of the United States, next to the Atlantic Ocean.

THINKING ABOUT GEOGRAPHY What is the relative location of your school?

One of the world's best natural ports, Boston has been a center of international shipping for more than 300 years.

Region

Geographers can't easily study the whole world at one time. So they break the world into regions. A region can be as large as a continent or as small as a neighborhood. A region has certain shared characteristics that set it apart. These characteristics might include political division, climate, language, or religion. Boston is part of the northeast region. It shares a climate—humid continental—with the cities of New York and Philadelphia.

THINKING ABOUT GEOGRAPHY What characteristics does your city or town share with nearby cities or towns?

Place

"What is Boston like?" Place can help you answer this question. Place refers to the physical and human factors that make one area different from another. Physical characteristics are natural features, such as physical setting, plants, animals, and weather.

Human characteristics include cultural diversity and the things people have made—including language, the arts, and architecture. For instance, Boston includes African Americans, as well as people of Irish, Italian, Chinese, and Hispanic ancestry.

THINKING ABOUT GEOGRAPHY What physical and human characteristics make where you live unique?

The dragon dance is a holiday tradition in Boston's vibrant Chinatown neighborhood.

Movement

Movement refers to the shifting of people, goods, and ideas from one place to another. People constantly move in search of better places to live, and they trade goods with one another over great distances. Movement also causes ideas to travel from place to place. In recent years, technology has quickened the movement of ideas and goods.

Boston became known as the Cradle of Liberty because of the movement of ideas. The concepts of freedom and self-government that developed in Boston spread to the other colonies and helped to start the American Revolution.

THINKING ABOUT GEOGRAPHY What are some of the different ways you spread information and ideas?

Human-Environment Interaction

Human-environment interaction refers to ways people interact with their environment, such as building a dam, cutting down a tree, or even sitting in the sun.

In Boston, human-environment interaction occurred when officials filled in swampy areas to make the city larger. In other ways, the environment has forced people to act. For example, people have had to invent ways to protect themselves from extreme weather and natural disasters.

THINKING ABOUT GEOGRAPHY What are ways that people in your city or town have changed their environment?

Boston's subway system, which runs both above and below ground, is the oldest in the nation.

Themes of Geography **Assessment**

MAIN IDEAS

1. What is the relative location of your home?
2. What are three characteristics of the region in which you live?
3. What are at least three ways in which you have recently interacted with the environment?

CRITICAL THINKING

4. **Forming and Supporting Opinions** Which aspect of geography described in these themes do you think has most affected your life? Explain.

Think about
• ways that you interact with your environment
• how you travel from place to place

Map Basics

Geographers use many different types of maps, and these maps all have a variety of features. The map on the next page gives you information on a historical event—the final two years of the Civil War. But you can use it to learn about different parts of a map, too.

Types of Maps

Physical maps Physical maps show mountains, hills, plains, rivers, lakes, oceans, and other physical features of an area. (See Atlas p. A29.)

Political maps Political maps show political units, such as countries, states, provinces, counties, districts, and towns. Each unit is normally shaded a different color, represented by a symbol, or shown with a different typeface. (See Atlas p. A28.)

Historical maps Historical maps illustrate such things as economic activity, migrations, battles, and changing national boundaries.

TECHNOLOGY *of the* TIME

GIS—Geographic Information Systems

A GIS is a collection of digitized geographic datasets.

Before computers, some geographers created maps on transparent paper or plastic sheets. Overlaying these maps on each other enabled the geographer to discover patterns and relationships.

Today, a computer-based GIS does the same thing with digital map layers. (See diagram at right.) It allows a geographer to select relevant information and combine many datasets in a single, composite map.

The user selects layers of information that answer the question "What characteristics make for a good airport site?"

GPS—Global Positioning System

GPS uses an array of 24 satellites, called Navstars, in synchronized orbit around Earth. A hand-held GPS device communicates with the satellites. The device determines the exact distance from the nearest Navstars and calculates its exact position on Earth's surface.

A A terrain map (top) shows areas that are flat enough for landing airplanes.

B A land use map shows areas that have few homes.

C The base map shows where roads are located.

D The layers are combined to create a composite map showing possible sites for the airport.

Reading a Map

A **Lines** Lines indicate political boundaries, roads and highways, human movement, and rivers and other waterways.

B **Symbols** Symbols represent such items as capital cities, battle sites, or economic activities.

C **Labels** Labels are words or phrases that explain various items or activities on a map.

D **Compass Rose** A compass rose shows which way the directions north (N), south (S), east (E), and west (W) point on the map.

E **Scale** A scale shows the ratio between a unit of length on the map and a unit of distance on the earth. A typical one-inch scale indicates the number of miles and kilometers that length represents on the map.

F **Colors** Colors show a variety of information on a map, such as population density or the physical growth of a country.

G **Legend or Key** A legend or key lists and explains the symbols, lines, and colors on a map.

H **Lines of Longitude** These are imaginary, north-south lines that run around the globe.

I **Lines of Latitude** These are imaginary, east-west lines that run around the globe. Together, latitude and longitude lines form a grid on a map or globe to indicate an area's absolute location.

Vicksburg and Sherman's March 1863–1864

Legend
- Controlled by Union
- Won by Union, 1863–1864
- Controlled by Confederacy
- → Union forces
- ✦ Union victory
- ✦ Confederate victory

Longitude lines

- are imaginary lines that run north to south around the globe and are known as meridians
- show the distance in degrees east or west of the prime meridian

The prime meridian is a longitude line that runs from the North Pole to the South Pole. It passes through Greenwich, England, and measures 0° longitude.

Longitude Lines (Meridians)

Latitude lines

- are imaginary lines that run east to west around the globe and are known as parallels
- show distance in degrees north or south of the equator

The equator is a latitude line that circles the earth halfway between the North and South poles. It measures 0° latitude.

The tropics of Cancer and Capricorn are parallels that form the boundaries of the Tropics, a region that stays warm all year.

Latitude and longitude lines appear together on a map and allow you to pinpoint the absolute location of cities and other geographic features. You express this location through coordinates of intersecting lines. These are measured in degrees.

Latitude Lines (Parallels)

Hemispheres

Hemisphere is a term for half the globe. The globe can be divided into Northern and Southern hemispheres (separated by the equator) or into Eastern and Western hemispheres. The United States is located in the Northern and Western hemispheres.

Northern Hemisphere

Southern Hemisphere

Projections

A projection is a way of showing the curved surface of the earth on a flat map. Flat maps cannot show sizes, shapes, and directions on a globe all at once with total accuracy. As a result, all projections distort some aspect of the earth's surface. Some maps distort distances, while other maps distort angles. On the next page are four projections.

Mercator Projection

The Mercator projection shows most of the continents as they look on a globe. However, the projection stretches out the lands near the North and South poles. The Mercator is used for all kinds of navigation.

Azimuthal Projection

An azimuthal projection shows the earth so that a straight line from the central point to any other point on the map gives the shortest distance between the two points. Size and shape of the continents are also distorted.

Homolosine Projection

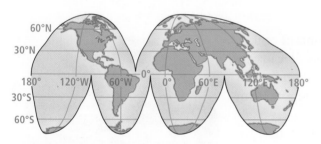

This projection shows the accurate shapes and sizes of the landmasses, but distances on the map are not correct.

Robinson Projection

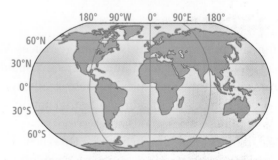

Textbook maps commonly use the Robinson projection. It shows the entire earth with nearly the true sizes and shapes of the continents and oceans. However, the shapes of the landforms near the poles appear flat.

Map Basics Assessment

MAIN IDEAS

1. What is the longitude and latitude of your city or town?

2. What information is provided by the legend on the map on page A5?

3. What is a projection? Compare and contrast Antarctica on the Mercator and the Robinson projections.

CRITICAL THINKING

4. **Making Inferences** Why do you think latitude and longitude are so important to sailors?

Think about
• the landmarks you use to find your way around
• the landmarks available to sailors on the ocean

Physical Geography of the United States

Physical geography involves all the natural features on the earth. This includes the land, resources, climate, and vegetation.

Land

Separated from much of the world by two oceans, the United States covers 3,717,796 square miles and spans the entire width of North America. To the west, Hawaii stretches the United States into the Pacific Ocean. To the north, Alaska extends the United States to the Arctic Circle. On the U.S. mainland, a huge central plain separates large mountains in the West and low mountains in the East. Plains make up almost half of the country, while mountains and plateaus make up a quarter each.

An abundance of lakes—Alaska alone has three million—and rivers also dot the landscape. Twenty percent of the United States is farmed. Urban areas cover only about two percent of the nation.

These sandstone buttes in Monument Valley Navajo Tribal Park (Utah) are nicknamed "the Mittens."

THINKING ABOUT GEOGRAPHY What is the land like around your city or state?

Resources

The United States has a variety of natural resources. Vast amounts of coal, oil, and natural gas lie underneath American soil. Valuable deposits of lead, zinc, uranium, gold, and silver also exist. These resources have helped the United States become the world's leading industrial nation—producing more than 20 percent of the world's goods and services.

These resources have also helped the United States become both the world's largest producer of energy (natural gas, oil, coal, nuclear power, and electricity) and the world's largest consumer of it. Other natural resources include the Great Lakes, which are shared with Canada. They contain about 20 percent of the world's total supply of fresh surface water. Refer to the map on the next page to examine the nation's natural resources.

THINKING ABOUT GEOGRAPHY What are the different natural resources that you and your family use in your daily lives?

Coal mining is an important industry in parts of the Northwest, the Southwest, and the East.

Melting glaciers thousands of years ago left deposits of sand and gravel in ridges, called eskers, like this one in North Dakota.

Land and Resources

ALASKA

70°N

60°N

Zn

160°W   150°W   140°W

PACIFIC
OCEAN

0   300 mi
0   300 km

Some timber harvested in Washington
is transported by tugboat.

UNITED STATES

40°N

PACIFIC
OCEAN

ATLANTIC
OCEAN

30°N

Zn

Zn

Zn

Zn

Zn

Elevation

13,100 ft.   (4,000 m)
6,600 ft.   (2,000 m)
3,280 ft.   (1,000 m)
650 ft.   (200 m)
0 ft.   (0 m)
Below sea level

Texas is the nation's leading producer of oil.

HAWAII

22°N

20°N

PACIFIC OCEAN

160°W   158°W   156°W

0   100 mi
0   100 km

0   250   500 miles
0   250   500 kilometers

Major resources

Aluminum		Natural gas	
Coal		Oil	
Copper		Silver	
Gold		Timber	
Iron ore		Uranium	
Lead		Zinc	
Hydroelectric power			

110°W   100°W   90°W   80°W

Physical Geography of the United States **A9**

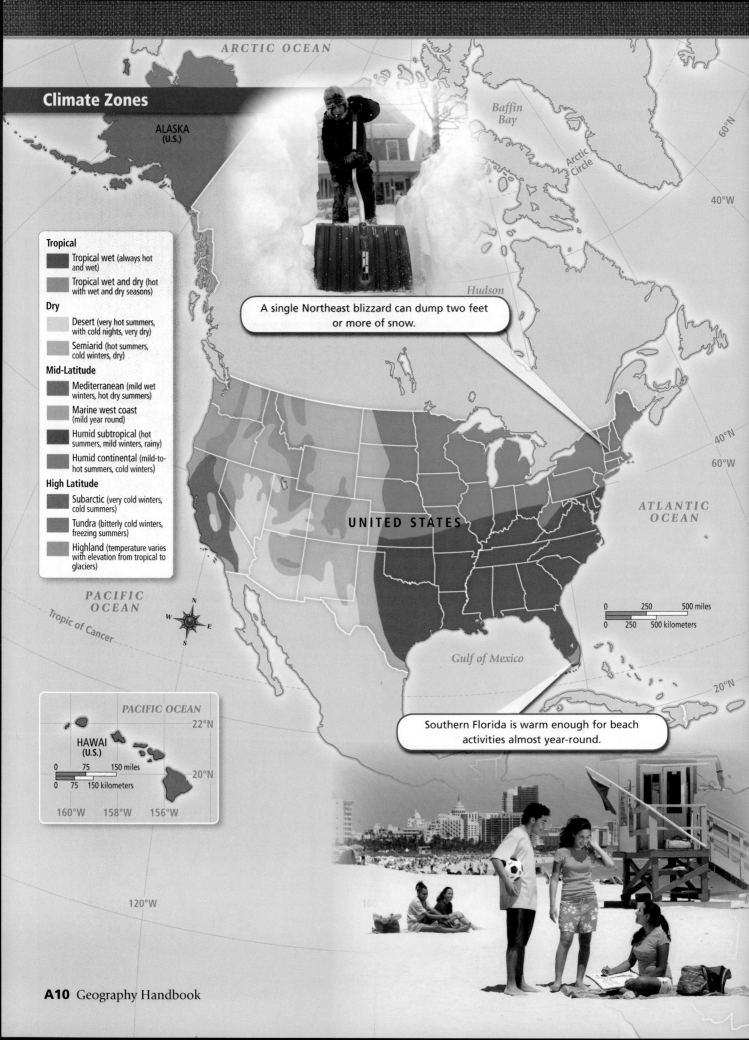

Climate Zones

Tropical

- Tropical wet (always hot and wet)
- Tropical wet and dry (hot with wet and dry seasons)

Dry

- Desert (very hot summers, with cold nights, very dry)
- Semiarid (hot summers, cold winters, dry)

Mid-Latitude

- Mediterranean (mild wet winters, hot dry summers)
- Marine west coast (mild year round)
- Humid subtropical (hot summers, mild winters, rainy)
- Humid continental (mild-to-hot summers, cold winters)

High Latitude

- Subarctic (very cold winters, cold summers)
- Tundra (bitterly cold winters, freezing summers)
- Highland (temperature varies with elevation from tropical to glaciers)

A single Northeast blizzard can dump two feet or more of snow.

Southern Florida is warm enough for beach activities almost year-round.

ALASKA (U.S.)

ARCTIC OCEAN

Baffin Bay

Arctic Circle

Hudson

UNITED STATES

PACIFIC OCEAN

Tropic of Cancer

ATLANTIC OCEAN

Gulf of Mexico

0 250 500 miles
0 250 500 kilometers

PACIFIC OCEAN

HAWAI (U.S.)

0 75 150 miles
0 75 150 kilometers

22°N
20°N
160°W 158°W 156°W

60°N
40°W
40°N
60°W
20°N

120°W

100

Climate

The United States contains a variety of climates. For example, the mean temperature in January in Miami, Florida, is 67°F, while it is 11°F in Minneapolis, Minnesota. Most of the United States experiences a continental climate, or distinct change of seasons. Some regional climatic differences include hot and humid summers in the Southeast versus hot and dry summers in the Southwest. Harsh winters and heavy snow can blanket parts of the Midwest, the Northeast, and the higher elevations of the West and Northwest. Refer to the map on the previous page to see the nation's climatic regions.

Human activities have affected the climate, too. For example, pollution from cars and factories can affect local weather conditions and are contributing to a dangerous rise in the earth's temperature.

THINKING ABOUT GEOGRAPHY How would you describe the climate where you live?

Vegetation

Between 20,000 and 25,000 species and subspecies of plants and vegetation grow in the United States—including over 1,000 different kinds of trees. Climate often dictates the type of vegetation found in a region. For instance, cold autumns in the Northeast contribute to the brilliantly colored autumn leaves. Rain nourishes the forests in the Northwest and Southeast. The central plains, where rainfall is less heavy, are covered by grass. Cactus plants thrive in the dry southwestern deserts.

Along with natural vegetation, climate dictates the nation's variety of planted crops. For example, temperate weather in the Midwest helps wheat to grow, while warm weather nourishes citrus fruit in Florida and California.

THINKING ABOUT GEOGRAPHY What kinds of trees or plants grow in your region?

Spanish moss grows in coastal areas from Virginia south to Venezuela. This scene is of Cumberland Island, Georgia.

Physical Geography Assessment

MAIN IDEAS

1. What are the different aspects of physical geography?
2. Which state contains the largest variety of climates?
3. What two states contain most of the country's oil resources?

CRITICAL THINKING

5. **Drawing Conclusions** What do you think are the advantages of living in a country with diverse physical geography?

Think about
- the different resources available in your region
- the variety of recreational activities in your region

Geography Dictionary

cape
a pointed piece of land extending into an ocean or lake

volcano
an opening in the earth, usually raised, through which gasses and lava escape from the earth's interior

sea level
level of the ocean's surface, used as a reference point when measuring the height or depth of the earth's surface

strait
a narrow strip of water connecting two large bodies of water

bay
part of an ocean or lake partially enclosed by land

harbor
a sheltered area of water, deep enough for docking ships

(river) mouth
the place where a river flows into a lake or ocean

marsh
soft, wet, low-lying, grassy land that serves as a transition between water and land

island
a body of land surrounded by water

delta
a triangular area of land formed from deposits at the mouth of a river

flood plain
flat land near the edges of rivers formed by mud and silt deposited by floods

desert
a dry area where few plants grow

swamp
an area of land that is saturated by water

oasis
a spot of fertile land in a desert, fed by water from wells or underground

butte
a raised, flat area of land with steep cliffs, smaller than a mesa

prairie
a large, level area of grassland with few or no trees

steppe
a wide, treeless plain

mountain
natural elevation of the earth's surface with steep sides and greater height than a hill

valley
low land between hills or mountains

glacier
a large ice mass that moves slowly down a mountain or over land

mesa
a wide, flat-topped mountain with steep sides, larger than a butte

cataract
a large, powerful waterfall

canyon
a narrow, deep valley with steep sides

cliff
the steep, almost vertical edge of a hill, mountain, or plain

plateau
a broad, flat area of land higher than the surrounding land

Human Geography of the United States

Human geography focuses on people's relationships with each other and the surrounding environment. It includes two main themes of geography: human-environment interaction and movement. The following pages will help you to better understand the link between people and geography.

Humans Adapt to Their Surroundings

Humans have always adapted to their environment. For example, in North America, many Native American tribes burned forest patches to create grazing area to attract animals and to clear area for farmland. In addition, Americans have adapted to their environment by building numerous dams, bridges, and tunnels. More recently, scientists and engineers have been developing building materials that will better withstand the earthquakes that occasionally strike California.

THINKING ABOUT GEOGRAPHY What are some of the ways in which you interact with your environment on a daily basis?

The Fred Hartman Bridge, completed in 1995, crosses the Houston Ship Channel, connecting two suburbs of Houston, Texas.

The multi-level cliff dwellings of Mesa Verde, Colorado, were built by Ancestral Pueblo people between 700 and 900 years ago.

Humans Affect the Environment

When humans interact with the environment, sometimes nature suffers. In the United States, for example, major oil leaks or spills occur each year—fouling shorelines and harming wildlife. Building suburbs and strip malls has also destroyed forests, farmland, and valuable wetlands.

THINKING ABOUT GEOGRAPHY What are some of the environmental problems in your city or town?

Workers use heavy equipment to attack a Gulf of Mexico oil spill.

Preserving and Restoring

In 2003, Americans recycled more than 30% of their garbage—about 72 million tons. In 2005, the Kyoto Protocol began to take effect, requiring the signing countries to limit or reduce greenhouse gas emissions. As of 2006, 165 nations had ratified Kyoto.

THINKING ABOUT GEOGRAPHY
What are some of the ways in which you help the environment?

Destruction of Original Forests

1620

1850

1926

This maps show that, over the years, human beings have nearly cut down all the original forests in the United States. Each dot represents 25,000 acres.

More than 3,000 volunteers each year participate in Hands on Miami Day by planting trees and cleaning up neighborhoods.

Human Geography of the United States A13

Human Movement

In prehistoric times, people roamed the earth in search of food. Today, people move from place to place for many different reasons. Among them are cost of living, job availability, and climate. Since the 1950s, many Americans—as well as many new immigrants—moved to the Sunbelt. This region runs through the southern United States from Virginia to California. Since 1990 the nation has seen a population shift from the North and East to the South and West.

- The fastest growing county in the United States—Riverside—and three of the country's ten fastest growing cities are in Southern California. Yet the state has seen a steady outmigration.

- Cities such as Dallas-Forth Worth, Atlanta, and Minneapolis-St. Paul show net outmigration while their surrounding suburbs have net immigration.

THINKING ABOUT GEOGRAPHY
Has your family ever moved? If so, what were some of the reasons?

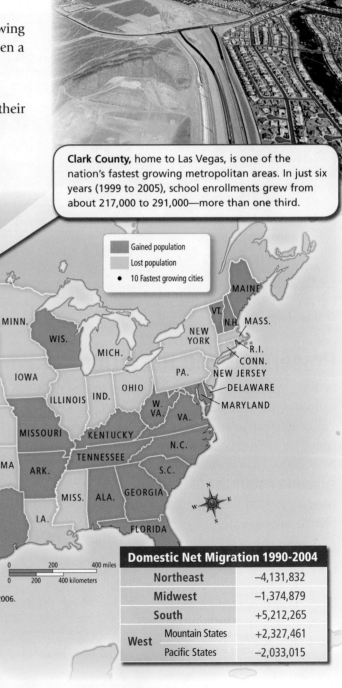

Clark County, home to Las Vegas, is one of the nation's fastest growing metropolitan areas. In just six years (1999 to 2005), school enrollments grew from about 217,000 to 291,000—more than one third.

Domestic Migration *2000–2004*

Legend:
- Gained population
- Lost population
- ● 10 Fastest growing cities

Cities labeled: Elk Grove, North Las Vegas, Rancho Cucamonga, Moreno Valley, Irvine, Chandler, Gilbert

Source: *"Domestic Net Migration in the U.S.: 2000 to 2004"*, U.S. Census, April, 2006.

Domestic Net Migration 1990-2004		
Northeast		−4,131,832
Midwest		−1,374,879
South		+5,212,265
West	Mountain States	+2,327,461
	Pacific States	−2,033,015

Humans Spread Ideas and Information

Throughout U.S. history, people from all over the world have come to the United States. They have brought with them food, music, language, technology, and other aspects of their culture. As a result, the United States is one of the most culturally rich and diverse nations in the world. Look around your town or city. You'll probably notice different people, languages, and foods.

Today, the spreading of ideas and customs does not rely solely on human movement. Technology—from the Internet to television to satellites—spreads ideas and information throughout the world faster than ever. This has created an ever-growing, interconnected world. As the 21st century continues, human geography will continue to play a key role in shaping the United States and the world.

THINKING ABOUT GEOGRAPHY How have computers and the Internet affected your life?

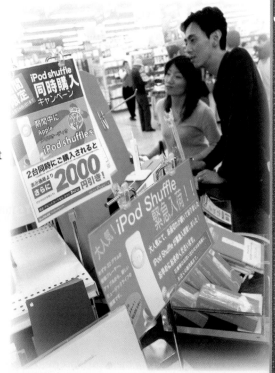

American consumer products are for sale around the globe.

Puertorriqueños celebrate the National Puerto Rican Day Parade in New York City.

Human Geography Assessment

MAIN IDEAS

1. What are some of the ways that people have helped to restore the environment?

2. What are some of the ways that residents of your region have successfully modified their landscape?

3. What are some of the reasons that people move from place to place?

CRITICAL THINKING

4. **Recognizing Effects** In what ways has technology helped bring people in the world together?

Think about

- the different ways in which people communicate today

- the speed in which people today can communicate over long distances

Geography Handbook Assessment

TERMS

Briefly explain the significance of each of the following.

1. physical map
2. political map
3. longitude
4. latitude
5. hemisphere
6. projection
7. flood plain
8. sea level
9. human geography
10. human movement

Compare and contrast each pair of terms.

11. place; location
12. parallel; meridian
13. climate; temperature

REVIEW

Themes of Geography (pages A2–A3)

14. What is the difference between absolute location and relative location?

15. What is meant by the theme of place?

16. What are the themes of movement and human-environment interaction?

Map Basics (pages A4–A7)

17. What do you think are some of the benefits of using technology to study geography?

18. What are the three major kinds of maps?

19. What are latitude and longitude lines?

Physical Geography (pages A8–A11)

20. How have the natural resources in the United States helped its economic development?

21. What are the different climates within the United States?

Human Geography (pages A14–A16)

22. How is human geography different from physical geography?

23. What aspects of human geography might cause people to move?

CRITICAL THINKING

24. **Forming and Supporting Opinions** Which of the five themes of geography do you think has had the most impact on history? Why?

25. **Causes and Effects** How do the climate and natural resources of an area affect its economy?

26. **Categorizing** Create a diagram to organize information from this Handbook about the regions of the United States.

	West	South	Midwest	Northeast
Landforms	Rocky Mountains	Mississippi Delta		
Resources				

27. **Drawing Conclusions** How have computers helped geographers make more accurate maps?

28. **Making Inferences** Why do you think the Mercator projection is used for all types of navigation?

Use the photograph below to answer 29–31.

29. What region of the United States is pictured here?

30. What are some of the physical features of this area?

31. What is the climate of the area pictured?

MULTIPLE CHOICE

✓ **TEST PRACTICE**

• **Online Test Practice** @ ClassZone.com

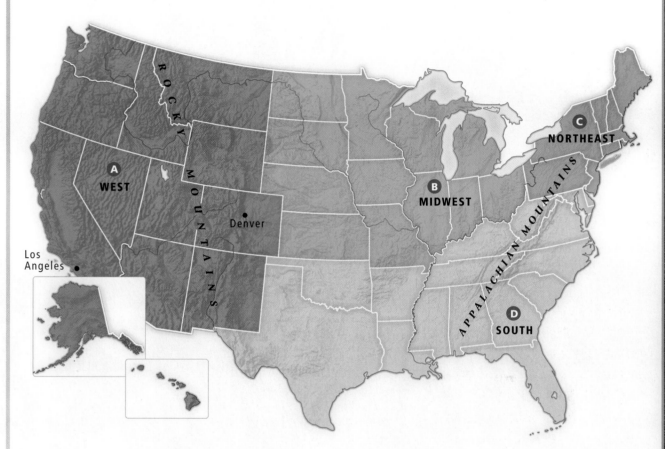

Use the map and your knowledge of geography to answer questions 1–3.

1. **Which describes the absolute location of Denver?**

   A. approximately 39°N 105°W, elev. 5,280 feet
   B. 844 miles ENE of Los Angeles
   C. mountainous; highland climate
   D. state capital of Colorado

2. **Which region is a source for uranium ore?**

   A. Ⓐ   B. Ⓑ   C. Ⓒ   D. Ⓓ

3. **Which region has a primarily humid subtropical climate?**

   A. Ⓐ   B. Ⓑ   C. Ⓒ   D. Ⓓ

Read each question and choose the best answer.

4. **The United States is located in which hemispheres?**

   A. Northern and Western
   B. Southern and Western
   C. Northern and Eastern
   D. Southern and Eastern

5. **Constructing a breakwater in Boston harbor is an example of how humans—**

   A. adapt to their environment.
   B. affect their environment.
   C. spread ideas and information.
   D. restore their environment.

RAND M^cNALLY
World Atlas

CONTENTS

Legend for Physical and Political Maps

Water Features

ATLANTIC OCEAN	Ocean or sea
	Lake (physical map)
	Lake (political map)
	Salt lake (physical map)
	Salt lake (political map)
	Seasonal lake
Mississippi	River
Niagara Falls	Waterfall

Land Features

Mt. Mitchell 6,684 ft. 2,037 m. △	Mountain peak
Mt. McKinley 20,320 ft. 6,194 m. ▲	Highest mountain peak
Great Basin	Physical feature (mountain range, desert, plateau, etc.)
Nantucket Island	Island

Cultural Features

———	International boundary
———	State boundary
CANADA	Country
KANSAS	State

Population Centers

National capital	State capital	Town	Population
⊙	✪	■	Over 1,000,000
⊙	✪	▣	250,000 – 1,000,000
⊙	✪	·	Under 250,000

Land Elevations and Ocean Depths

Land elevation

3,000 meters	9,840 feet
2,000 meters	6,560 feet
1,000 meters	3,280 feet
500 meters	1,640 feet
200 meters	656 feet
0 Sea level	0 Sea level

Water depth

0 Sea level	0 Sea level
200 meters	656 feet
2,000 meters	6,560 feet

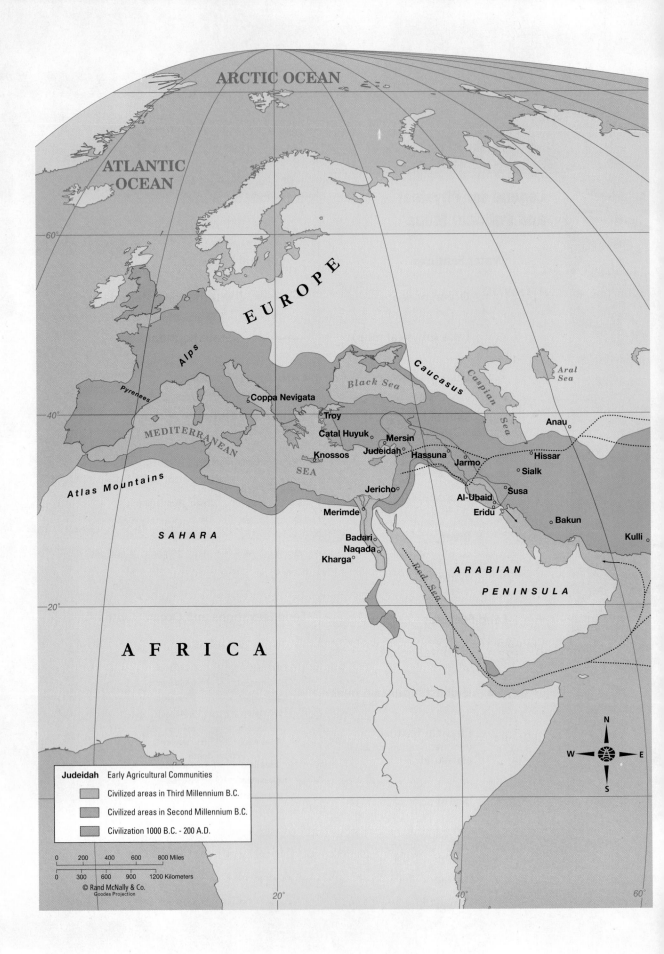

ARCTIC OCEAN

ATLANTIC
OCEAN

EUROPE

Alps

Pyrenees

Black Sea

Caucasus

Caspian Sea

Aral Sea

Anau

Coppa Nevigata

Troy

MEDITERRANEAN

Catal Huyuk

Mersin

Judeidah

Hissar

Knossos

Hassuna

Jarmo

Sialk

SEA

Al-Ubaid

Susa

Jericho

Eridu

Atlas Mountains

Merimde

Bakun

Kulli

SAHARA

Badari

Naqada

Kharga

ARABIAN

PENINSULA

Red Sea

—20°

AFRICA

N
W   E
S

Judeidah Early Agricultural Communities

Civilized areas in Third Millennium B.C.

Civilized areas in Second Millennium B.C.

Civilization 1000 B.C. - 200 A.D.

0   200   400   600   800 Miles

0   300   600   900   1200 Kilometers

© Rand McNally & Co.
Goodes Projection

SIBERIA

ASIA

Tien Shan Altai Mts.
Silk Route First Millennium B.C.

GOBI DESERT

40°

TAKLIMAKAN
DESERT

Qijia Cishan Lungshan
Banpo Anyang
Yangshao
Peiligang

Quetta Harappa

Amri THAR
DESERT Himalayas

Hemudu

PACIFIC
OCEAN

Hoa-Binh

20°

Sea Routes
First Millennium B.C.

CEYLON
(SRI LANKA)

INDIAN
OCEAN

0°

80° 80° 100° 120°

RAND M^cNALLY

A23

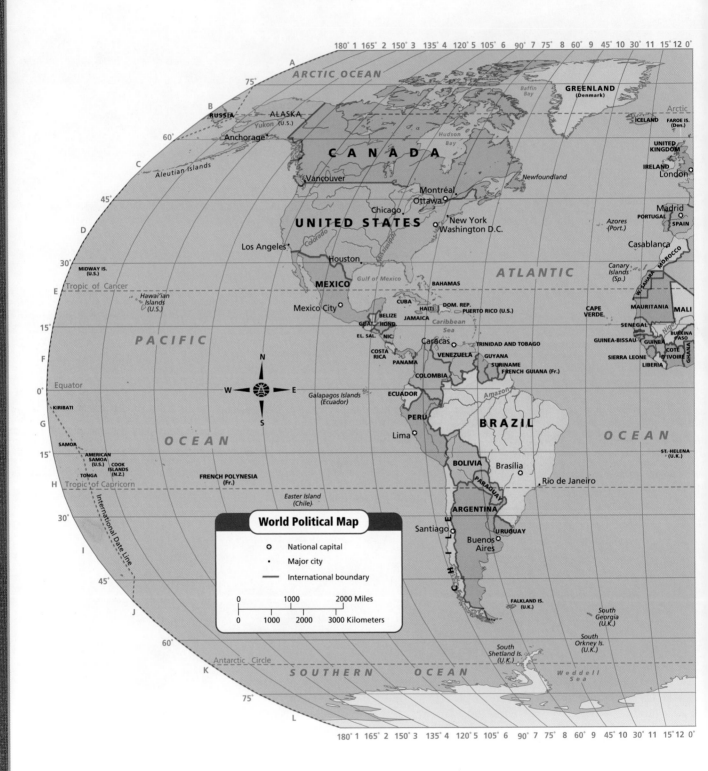

ARCTIC OCEAN

GREENLAND
(Denmark)

Baffin
Bay

Arctic

ICELAND   FAROE IS.
(Den.)

RUSSIA   ALASKA
Yukon (U.S.)

UNITED
KINGDOM

Anchorage

Aleutian Islands

IRELAND
London

C A N A D A

Vancouver

Newfoundland

Hudson
Bay

Montréal
Ottawa

Madrid

Azores
(Port.)

PORTUGAL
SPAIN

Chicago

UNITED STATES

New York
Washington D.C.

Casablanca

MOROCCO

Los Angeles

Colorado

Houston

Canary
Islands
(Sp.)

W. SAHARA

MIDWAY IS.
(U.S.)

Tropic of Cancer

MEXICO

Gulf of Mexico

BAHAMAS

ATLANTIC

CAPE
VERDE

MAURITANIA   MALI

Hawai'ian
Islands
(U.S.)

CUBA

DOM. REP.

Mexico City

HAITI
PUERTO RICO (U.S.)

BELIZE
JAMAICA
GUAT. HOND.

SENEGAL

GUINEA-BISSAU GUINEA

BURKINA
FASO

PACIFIC

EL. SAL.
NIC.

Caribbean
Sea

CÔTE
D'IVOIRE

SIERRA LEONE

COSTA
RICA

Caracas

PANAMA

VENEZUELA

TRINIDAD AND TOBAGO

GUYANA
SURINAME

LIBERIA

GHANA

Niger

COLOMBIA

FRENCH GUIANA (Fr.)

N

Equator

W   E

ECUADOR

Galapagos Islands
(Ecuador)

Amazon

KIRIBATI

S

PERU

BRAZIL

OCEAN

Lima

OCEAN

SAMOA

BOLIVIA

ST. HELENA
(U.K.)

AMERICAN
SAMOA
(U.S.)

COOK
ISLANDS
(N.Z.)

Brasília

TONGA

FRENCH POLYNESIA
(Fr.)

PARAGUAY

Rio de Janeiro

Tropic of Capricorn

Easter Island
(Chile)

ARGENTINA

URUGUAY

International Date Line

Santiago

CHILE

Buenos
Aires

World Political Map

⊙ National capital

· Major city

—— International boundary

0   1000   2000 Miles

0   1000   2000   3000 Kilometers

FALKLAND IS.
(U.K.)

South
Georgia
(U.K.)

South
Orkney Is.
(U.K.)

Antarctic Circle

SOUTHERN   OCEAN

South
Shetland Is.
(U.K.)

Weddell
Sea

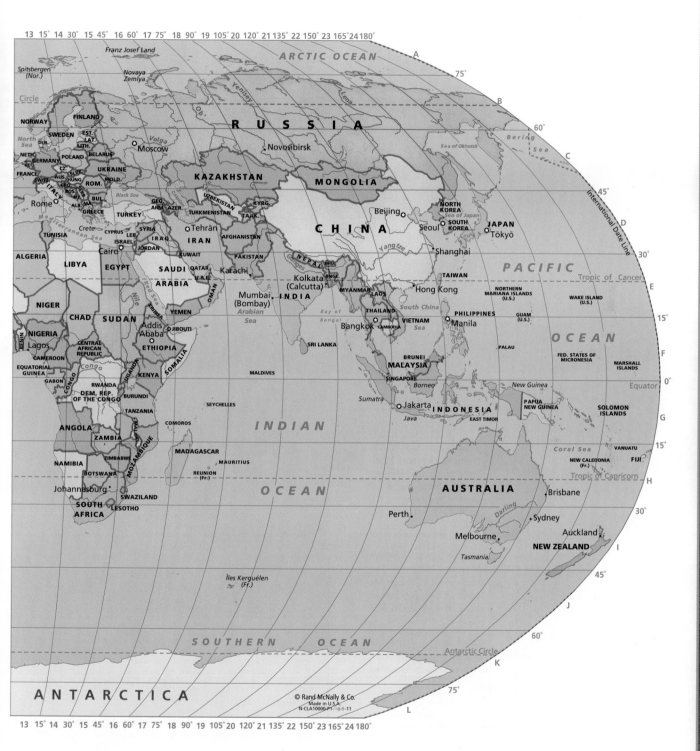

13° 15° 14° 30° 15° 45° 16° 60° 17° 75° 18° 90° 19° 105° 20° 120° 21° 135° 22° 150° 23° 165° 24°180°

ARCTIC OCEAN

Franz Josef Land

Spitsbergen (Nor.)

Novaya Zemlya

75°

Circle

RUSSIA

60°

NORWAY

FINLAND

SWEDEN

EST.

LAT.
LITH.

Moscow

Novosibirsk

Bering

Sea of Okhotsk

Sea

60°

NETH.

North
Sea

DEN.

POLAND

BELARUS

Volga

KAZAKHSTAN

MONGOLIA

International Date Line

45°

GERMANY

FRANCE

BEL.

UKRAINE

MOLD.

SWITZ.
AUS. HUNG.
ITALY CRO. ROM.
BOS. SERB.

Yenisey

Lena

NORTH
KOREA

Sea of Japan

JAPAN

ALB. MAC. BUL.

Black Sea

UZBEKISTAN

KYRG.

Beijing

SOUTH
KOREA

Tōkyō

D

30°

Rome

SLVK.

GREECE

GEO.
ARM. AZER.

TURKMENISTAN

TAJIK.

Seoul

CHINA

TUNISIA

TURKEY

SYRIA

CYPRUS LEB.

Crete

Mediterranean Sea

ISRAEL

IRAQ

JORDAN

IRAN

AFGHANISTAN

Yangtze

Shanghai

PACIFIC

ALGERIA

LIBYA

EGYPT

KUWAIT

SAUDI

QATAR

PAKISTAN

NEPAL

BHU.

Ganges

BNGL.

Kolkata
(Calcutta)

TAIWAN

Hong Kong

Tropic of Cancer

30°

Cairo

Nile

ARABIA

U.A.E.

Karachi

INDIA

MYANMAR

LAOS

NORTHERN
MARIANA ISLANDS
(U.S.)

WAKE ISLAND
(U.S.)

E

NIGER

CHAD

SUDAN

OMAN

YEMEN

Red Sea

Mumbai
(Bombay)

Arabian
Sea

Bay of
Bengal

THAILAND

Bangkok

CAMBODIA

VIETNAM

South China
Sea

PHILIPPINES

Manila

GUAM
(U.S.)

15°

NIGERIA

Lagos

BENIN

CENTRAL
AFRICAN
REPUBLIC

Addis
Ababa

DJIBOUTI

SRI LANKA

BRUNEI

PALAU

FED. STATES OF
MICRONESIA

MARSHALL
ISLANDS

OCEAN

F

CAMEROON

Congo

ETHIOPIA

SOMALIA

MALAYSIA

EQUATORIAL
GUINEA

GABON

UGANDA

KENYA

MALDIVES

SINGAPORE

Borneo

New Guinea

0°

Equator

CONGO

DEM. REP.
OF THE CONGO

RWANDA

BURUNDI

Sumatra

Jakarta

Java

INDONESIA

EAST TIMOR

PAPUA
NEW GUINEA

SOLOMON
ISLANDS

G

ANGOLA

TANZANIA

SEYCHELLES

INDIAN

15°

ZAMBIA

MALAWI

COMOROS

Coral Sea

VANUATU

NAMIBIA

ZIMBABWE

MOZAMBIQUE

MADAGASCAR

MAURITIUS

NEW CALEDONIA
(Fr.)

FIJI

BOTSWANA

REUNION
(Fr.)

OCEAN

Tropic of Capricorn

H

Johannesburg

SWAZILAND

SOUTH
AFRICA

LESOTHO

AUSTRALIA

Brisbane

Perth

Darling

Sydney

Auckland

30°

Melbourne

NEW ZEALAND

I

Tasmania

Îles Kerguélen
(Fr.)

45°

J

SOUTHERN

OCEAN

60°

Antarctic Circle

K

ANTARCTICA

© Rand McNally & Co.
Made in U.S.A.
N-CLA10000-PT-9-9-11

75°

L

13° 15° 14° 30° 15° 45° 16° 60° 17° 75° 18° 90° 19° 105° 20° 120° 21° 135° 22° 150° 23° 165° 24°180°

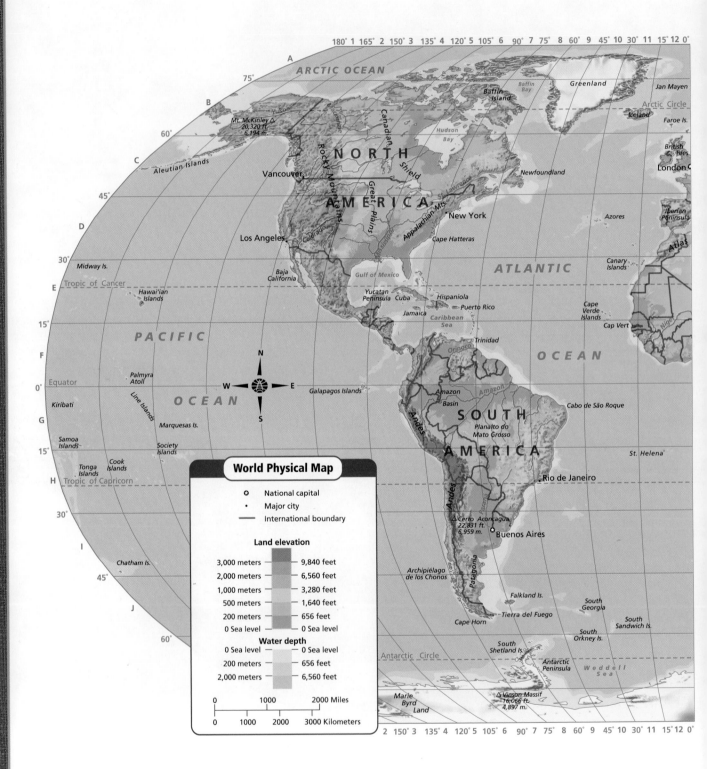

World Physical Map

⊕ National capital
• Major city
— International boundary

Land elevation

3,000 meters	9,840 feet
2,000 meters	6,560 feet
1,000 meters	3,280 feet
500 meters	1,640 feet
200 meters	656 feet
0 Sea level	0 Sea level

Water depth

0 Sea level	0 Sea level
200 meters	656 feet
2,000 meters	6,560 feet

0   1000   2000 Miles

0   1000   2000   3000 Kilometers

RAND McNALLY

RAND McNALLY

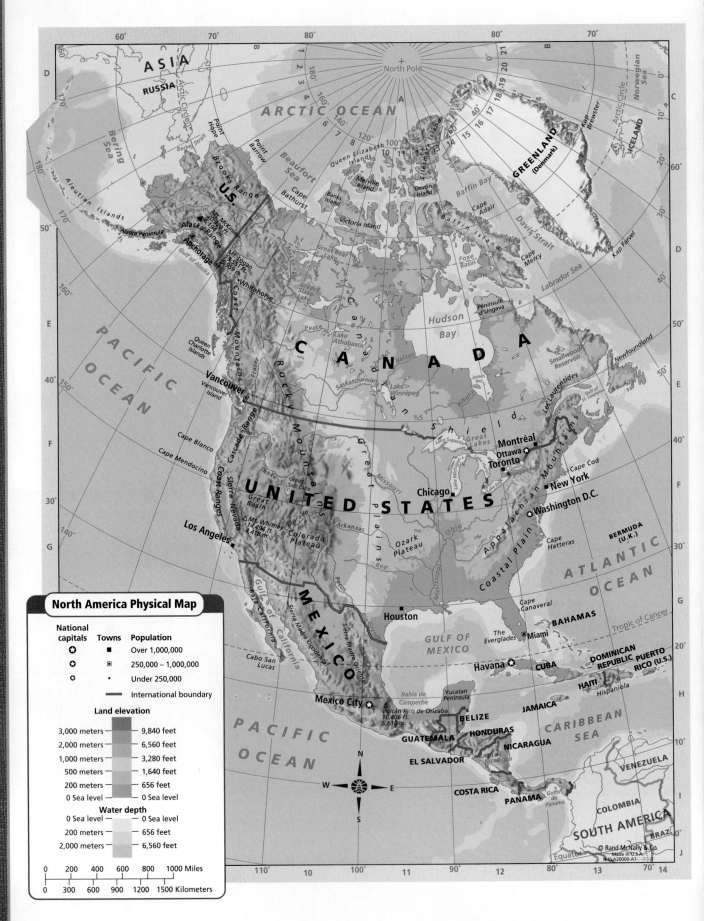

North America Physical Map

National capitals
⊕ Over 1,000,000
⊕ 250,000 – 1,000,000
⊕ Under 250,000

Towns **Population**
■ Over 1,000,000
▣ 250,000 – 1,000,000
• Under 250,000
— International boundary

Land elevation
3,000 meters — 9,840 feet
2,000 meters — 6,560 feet
1,000 meters — 3,280 feet
500 meters — 1,640 feet
200 meters — 656 feet
0 Sea level — 0 Sea level

Water depth
0 Sea level — 0 Sea level
200 meters — 656 feet
2,000 meters — 6,560 feet

0 200 400 600 800 1000 Miles
0 300 600 900 1200 1500 Kilometers

RAND M?NALLY

South America Physical Map

National capitals | **Towns** | **Population**
- ⊙ | ■ | Over 1,000,000
- ⊙ | ▣ | 250,000 – 1,000,000
- ⊙ | • | Under 250,000

— International boundary

Land elevation

3,000 meters	9,840 feet
2,000 meters	6,560 feet
1,000 meters	3,280 feet
500 meters	1,640 feet
200 meters	656 feet
0 Sea level	0 Sea level

Water depth

0 Sea level	0 Sea level
200 meters	656 feet
2,000 meters	6,560 feet

0 200 400 600 800 1000 Miles
0 300 600 900 1200 1500 Kilometers

NORTH AMERICA

GULF OF MEXICO

MEXICO
BELIZE
GUATEMALA
HONDURAS
EL SALVADOR
NICARAGUA
COSTA RICA
PANAMA

CUBA
JAMAICA
HAITI
DOMINICAN REPUBLIC
PUERTO RICO (U.S.)

Yucatán Channel
Greater Antilles
Lesser Antilles

CARIBBEAN SEA

Tropic of Cancer

ATLANTIC OCEAN

TRINIDAD AND TOBAGO
Boca Grande

Punta Gallinas
Pico Cristóbal Colón △ 18,947 ft. 5,775 m.
Lago de Maracaibo

✪ Caracas
Orinoco
Llanos
VENEZUELA
Angel Falls
Pakaraima Mts.
GUYANA
SURINAME
FRENCH GUIANA (FR.)
Cabo Orange

Golfo de Panamá
Magdalena

✪ Bogotá
COLOMBIA
Nev. del Huila △ 18,865 ft. 5,750 m.

Punta Galera

ECUADOR
△ Chimborazo 20,702 ft. 6,310 m.
Galapagos Islands (Ec.)
Equator

Punta Pariñas

Putumayo
Japurá
Negro
Amazon
Manaus ■
Amazon Basin
Selvas
Juruá
Madeira
Tapajós
Xingu
Tocantins

BRAZIL

Ilha de Marajó

Cabo de São Roque

PERU
Andes
Nev. Huascarán 22,133 ft. 6,746 m.
Ucayali

✪ Lima
Punta Carreta

Lago Titicaca
Nev. Illampu △ 21,066 ft. 6,421 m.
La Paz ✪
Cordillera Real
BOLIVIA
Nev. Sajama △ 21,463 ft. 6,542 m.

Planalto do Mato Grosso

Represa de Sobradinho

São Francisco
Serra do Espinhaço

Brasília ✪

Recife ■

Atacama Desert
Isla San Ambrosio (Chile)
Isla San Félix (Chile)

Nev. Ojos del Salado △ 22,615 ft 6,893 m.

Gran Chaco

Pilcomayo
Paraná
Paraguay

PARAGUAY

Iguassu Falls
São Paulo ■
Cabo de São Tomé

Rio de Janeiro ■

Tropic of Capricorn

URUGUAY
Uruguay
Lagoa dos Patos
Lagoa Mirim

PACIFIC OCEAN

Archipiélago Juan Fernández (Chile)

Cerro Aconcagua △ 22,831 ft. 6,959 m.

Santiago ✪

CHILE
ARGENTINA
Andes

Buenos Aires ✪
Río de la Plata

Punta Lavapié
Pampas

Isla Grande de Chiloé

Archipiélago de los Chonos

Golfo San Matías
Península Valdés

Cabo Dos Bahías
Golfo San Jorge
Cabo Tres Puntas

Patagonia

Isla Wellington

Bahía Grande
FALKLAND ISLANDS (U.K.)
West Falkland
East Falkland

Strait of Magellan
Isla Santa Inés
Tierra del Fuego

Cape Horn

South Georgia (U.K.)

Drake Passage

South Shetland Islands (U.K.)
South Orkney Islands (U.K.)
South Sandwich Islands (U.K.)

ATLANTIC OCEAN

N W E S

© Rand McNally & Co.
Made in U.S.A.
N-CLA40000-A1-4-4-4

RAND McNALLY

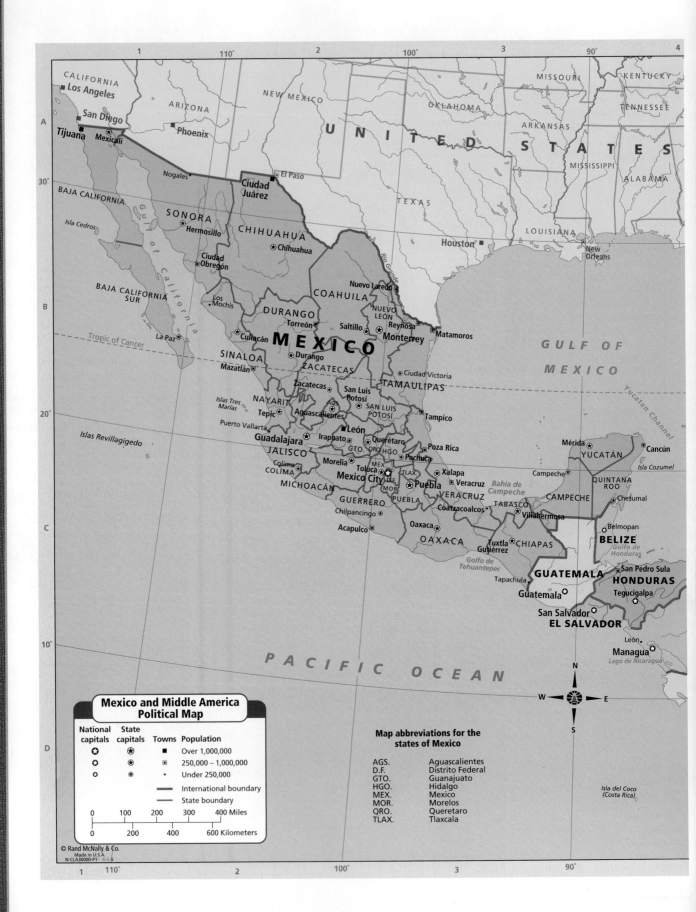

1   110°   2   100°   3   90°   4

CALIFORNIA
■ Los Angeles
■ San Diego
Tijuana
Mexicali
ARIZONA
■ Phoenix
NEW MEXICO
OKLAHOMA
MISSOURI
KENTUCKY
TENNESSEE
A

30°
Nogales
El Paso
Ciudad Juárez
BAJA CALIFORNIA
SONORA
CHIHUAHUA
TEXAS
U N I T E D   S T A T E S
ARKANSAS
MISSISSIPPI
ALABAMA

Isla Cedros
● Hermosillo
● Chihuahua
LOUISIANA
Houston ■
New Orleans

Ciudad Obregón
BAJA CALIFORNIA SUR
Los Mochis
Nuevo Laredo
COAHUILA
Rio Grande
B

DURANGO
Torreón
Saltillo
NUEVO LEÓN
Reynosa
Matamoros
GULF OF MEXICO
Yucatan Channel

La Paz
Tropic of Cancer
Culiacán
M E X I C O
Monterrey
SINALOA
Durango
ZACATECAS
Ciudad Victoria

Mazatlán
TAMAULIPAS

Islas Tres Marías
Zacatecas
San Luis Potosí
SAN LUIS POTOSÍ
Tampico

20°
Tepic
AGS
Aguascalientes
Bahía de Campeche
Mérida
Cancún
YUCATÁN

Islas Revillagigedo
NAYARIT
Puerto Vallarta
Irapuato
León
GTO.
Querétaro
QRO HGO
Poza Rica
Pachuca
Campeche
Isla Cozumel
QUINTANA ROO

Guadalajara
JALISCO
Morelia
MEX
Toluca
TLAX
Xalapa
Veracruz
CAMPECHE
Chetumal

Colima
COLIMA
Mexico City
D.F.
MOR
Puebla
VERACRUZ
Bahía de Campeche

MICHOACÁN
PUEBLA
Coatzacoalcos
TABASCO
Villahermosa
BELIZE
Belmopan

GUERRERO
Chilpancingo
Oaxaca
Golfo de Honduras

Acapulco
OAXACA
Tuxtla Gutiérrez
CHIAPAS
BELIZE
C

Golfo de Tehuantepec
Tapachula
GUATEMALA
San Pedro Sula
HONDURAS

Guatemala
Tegucigalpa

San Salvador
EL SALVADOR

León
Managua
Lago de Nicaragua

P A C I F I C   O C E A N
N
W   E
S

Mexico and Middle America Political Map

National capitals	State capitals	Towns	Population
⊙	✪	■	Over 1,000,000
⊙	✪	⊡	250,000 – 1,000,000
○	✪	·	Under 250,000

―――― International boundary
――― State boundary

0   100   200   300   400 Miles
0   200   400   600 Kilometers

© Rand McNally & Co.
Made in U.S.A.
N-CLA30000-P1- -5-5-5

Map abbreviations for the states of Mexico

AGS.	Aguascalientes
D.F.	Distrito Federal
GTO.	Guanajuato
HGO.	Hidalgo
MEX.	Mexico
MOR.	Morelos
QRO.	Queretaro
TLAX.	Tlaxcala

Isla del Coco
(Costa Rica)
D

1   110°   2   100°   3   90°

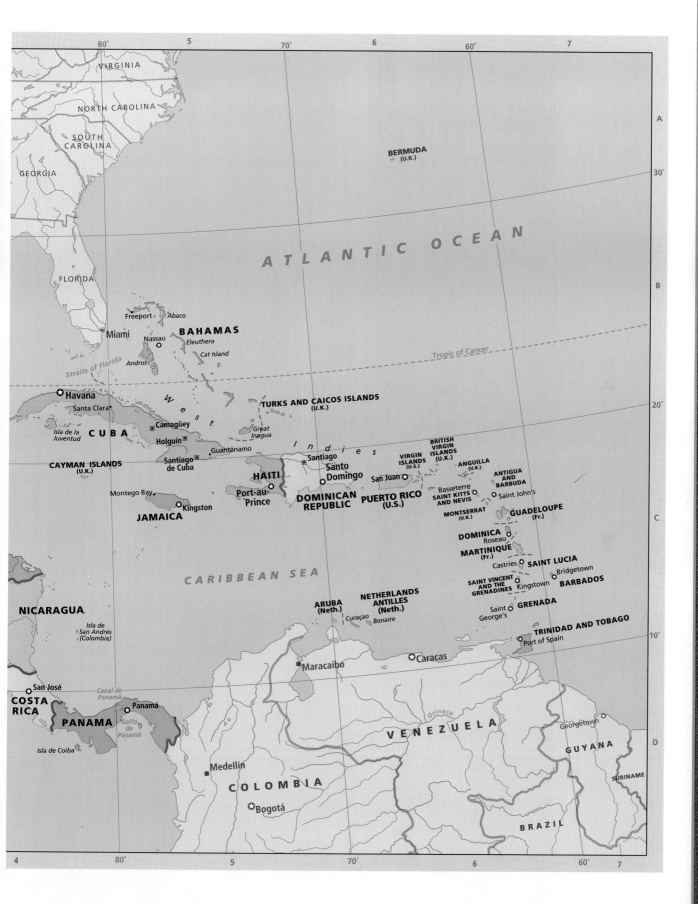

RAND M^cNALLY

ATLANTIC OCEAN

VIRGINIA

NORTH CAROLINA

SOUTH CAROLINA

GEORGIA

FLORIDA

BERMUDA
(U.K.)

30°

Tropic of Cancer

Straits of Florida

Freeport · Abaco

Miami

Nassau · Eleuthera

Andros · Cat Island

BAHAMAS

West

Indies

20°

Havana

Santa Clara

Isla de la Juventud

CUBA

Camagüey

Holguín

Guantánamo

Santiago
de Cuba

CAYMAN ISLANDS
(U.K.)

Montego Bay

Kingston

JAMAICA

HAITI

Port-au-
Prince

Santiago

Santo
Domingo

DOMINICAN
REPUBLIC

San Juan

PUERTO RICO
(U.S.)

Great
Inagua

TURKS AND CAICOS ISLANDS
(U.K.)

VIRGIN
ISLANDS
(U.S.)

BRITISH
VIRGIN
ISLANDS
(U.K.)

ANGUILLA
(U.K.)

ANTIGUA
AND
BARBUDA

Saint John's

Basseterre

SAINT KITTS
AND NEVIS

MONTSERRAT
(U.K.)

GUADELOUPE
(Fr.)

DOMINICA

Roseau

MARTINIQUE
(Fr.)

Castries

SAINT LUCIA

Bridgetown

BARBADOS

SAINT VINCENT
AND THE
GRENADINES

Kingstown

CARIBBEAN SEA

ARUBA
(Neth.)

Curaçao

NETHERLANDS
ANTILLES
(Neth.)

Bonaire

Saint
George's

GRENADA

TRINIDAD AND TOBAGO

Port of Spain

10°

NICARAGUA

Isla de
San Andrés
(Colombia)

Maracaibo

Caracas

Orinoco

San José

COSTA
RICA

Canal de
Panamá

Panamá

PANAMA

Golfo de
Panamá

Isla de Coiba

VENEZUELA

Georgetown

GUYANA

SURINAME

Medellín

COLOMBIA

Bogotá

BRAZIL

80°

70°

60°

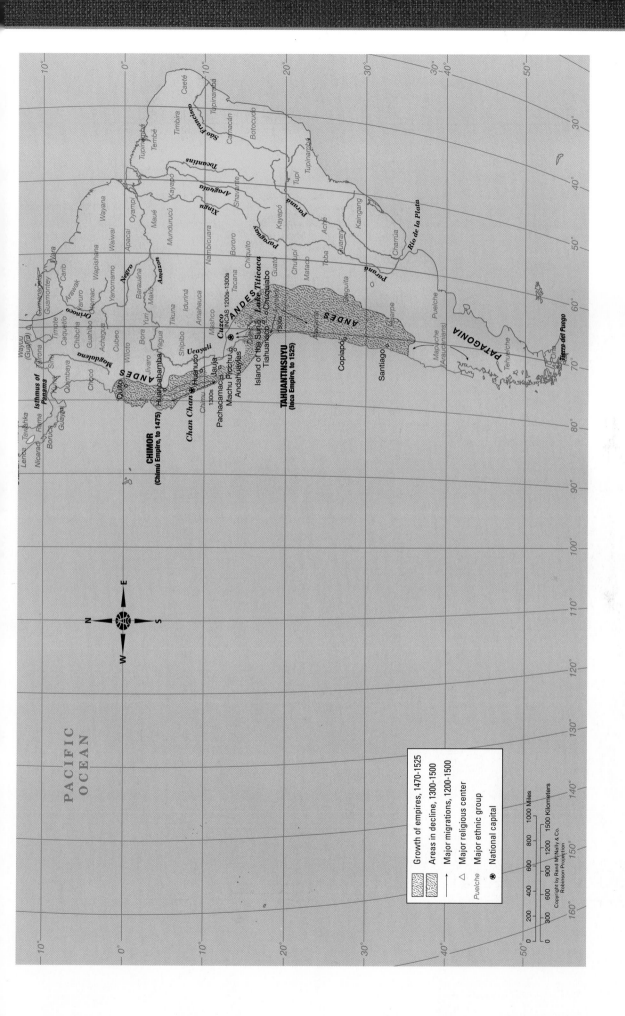

PACIFIC
OCEAN

N
W E
S

Growth of empires, 1470-1525
Areas in decline, 1300-1500
— Major migrations, 1200-1500
△ Major religious center
Puelche Major ethnic group
✷ National capital

Copyright by Rand McNally & Co.
Robinson Projection

0   200   400   600   800   1000 Miles
0 300 600 900 1200 1500 Kilometers

Wayuu
(Guajiro)
Tairona
Carib
Guamontey
Wara
Arawak
Negro
Cumanagoto
Orinoco
Guahibo
Chibcha
Achagua
Cubeo
Barauana
Makú
Yanomamo
Wapishana
Waiwai
Wayana
Apacai
Oyampi
Caqueta
Wioto
Jivaro
Bora
Yuri
Tikuna
Idurina
Amanauca
Masho
Tacana
Chiquito
Mundurucú
Kayapó
Nambicuara
Bororo
Xingú
Arawata
Tocantins
Tupinambá
Timbira
Caeté
Tembé
São Francisco
Camacán
Botocudo
Tupinambá
Tupi
Kayapó
Aché
Guaraní
Kaingang
Charrúa
Río de la Plata
Paraná
Toba
Mataco
Chulpi
Guató
Beguita
Sharpe
Puelche
Mapuche
(Araucanians)
Tehuelche
PATAGONIA
Tierra del Fuego

ANDES
ANDES
ANDES

Lenca
Nicarao
Rama
Boruca
Guatuso
Chiriqui
Chocó
Quimbaya
Quito
Huánuco
Jauja
1300s
Machu Picchu
Andahuaylas
Pachacamac
Chan Chan
Chimú

CHIMOR
(Chimú Empire, to 1475)

Isthmus of
Panama

Magdalena

Cuzco
INCAS 1200s-1300s
Island of the Sun
Tiahuanaco
Chucuito
Chucuabo
Lake Titicaca

TAHUANTINSUYU
(Inca Empire, to 1525)

Copiapó
Santiago

Ucayali
Shipibo
Amazon

Tawahka

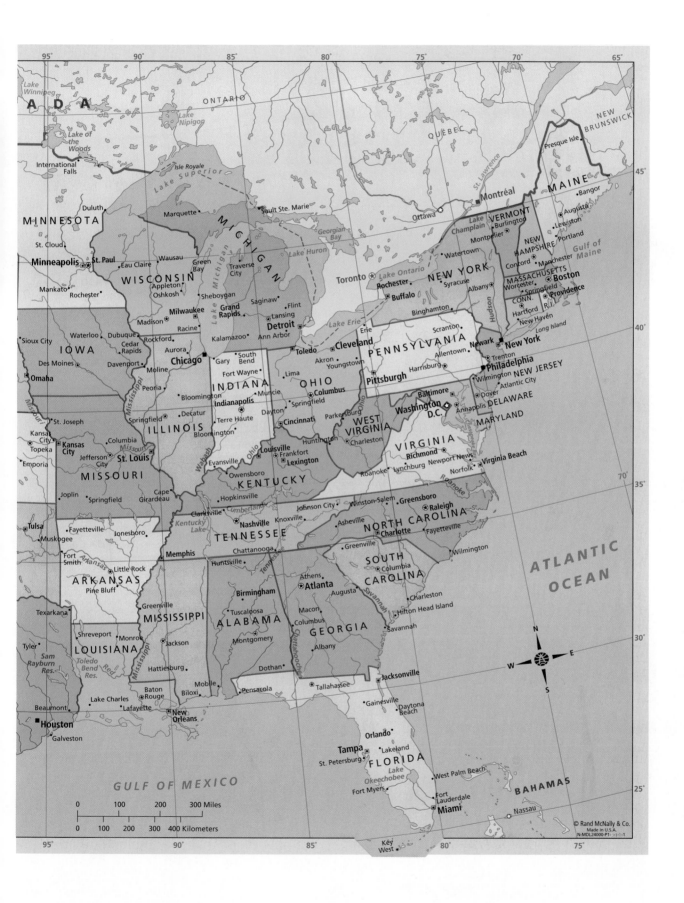

95° 90° 85° 80° 75° 70° 65°

ONTARIO

QUÉBEC

NEW BRUNSWICK

Lake Winnipeg

A D A

Lake of the Woods

Lake Nipigon

Isle Royale

Lake Superior

Sault Ste. Marie

MICHIGAN

Georgian Bay

Lake Huron

Ottawa

Montréal

St. Lawrence

45°

MAINE

Bangor

Augusta

Lewiston

Presque Isle

International Falls

Duluth

MINNESOTA

St. Cloud

Marquette

Georgian Bay

Lake Champlain

VERMONT

Burlington

Montpelier

NEW HAMPSHIRE

Portland

Gulf of Maine

Watertown

Concord

Manchester

Minneapolis

St. Paul

Eau Claire

Wausau

WISCONSIN

Green Bay

Traverse City

Lake Michigan

Lake Ontario

Toronto

Rochester

NEW YORK

Syracuse

Albany

MASSACHUSETTS

Worcester

Boston

Springfield

Providence

Mankato

Rochester

Appleton

Oshkosh

Sheboygan

Saginaw

Flint

Lansing

Buffalo

Binghamton

CONN.

Hartford

R.I.

New Haven

Milwaukee

Grand Rapids

Madison

Racine

Kalamazoo

Ann Arbor

Detroit

Lake Erie

Erie

Cleveland

Akron

Youngstown

Scranton

PENNSYLVANIA

Allentown

Newark

New York

Long Island

Sioux City

IOWA

Waterloo

Dubuque

Cedar Rapids

Rockford

Aurora

Chicago

Gary

South Bend

Toledo

Lima

OHIO

Columbus

Springfield

Harrisburg

Pittsburgh

Trenton

Philadelphia

Wilmington

NEW JERSEY

Atlantic City

Des Moines

Omaha

Davenport

Moline

Peoria

Fort Wayne

INDIANA

Muncie

Dayton

Cincinnati

Parkersburg

Baltimore

Dover

DELAWARE

Washington D.C.

Annapolis

MARYLAND

St. Joseph

Springfield

Decatur

Bloomington

ILLINOIS

Terre Haute

Bloomington

Indianapolis

Ohio

Louisville

Frankfort

Lexington

Huntington

Charleston

WEST VIRGINIA

VIRGINIA

Richmond

Newport News

Kansas City

Topeka

Kansas City

Jefferson City

Columbia

St. Louis

Missouri

Evansville

Owensboro

KENTUCKY

Wabash

Cumberland

Roanoke

Lynchburg

Norfolk

Virginia Beach

70°

Emporia

MISSOURI

Joplin

Springfield

Cape Girardeau

Hopkinsville

Kentucky Lake

Clarksville

Nashville

Knoxville

Johnson City

Winston-Salem

Greensboro

Raleigh

35°

Tulsa

Muskogee

Fayetteville

Jonesboro

Memphis

Chattanooga

TENNESSEE

Tennessee

Asheville

NORTH CAROLINA

Charlotte

Fayetteville

Fort Smith

ARKANSAS

Little Rock

Pine Bluff

Arkansas

Huntsville

Greenville

SOUTH CAROLINA

Columbia

Wilmington

Texarkana

Greenville

MISSISSIPPI

ALABAMA

Birmingham

Tuscaloosa

Macon

Columbus

Atlanta

Athens

Augusta

Savannah

Charleston

Hilton Head Island

ATLANTIC OCEAN

Tyler

Shreveport

Monroe

LOUISIANA

Jackson

Montgomery

GEORGIA

Albany

Savannah

N

30°

Sam Rayburn Res.

Toledo Bend Res.

Red

Hattiesburg

Dothan

Chattahoochee

W E

Beaumont

Lake Charles

Baton Rouge

Mississippi

Mobile

Biloxi

Pensacola

Tallahassee

Jacksonville

S

Houston

Galveston

New Orleans

Lafayette

Gainesville

Daytona Beach

Orlando

Lakeland

Tampa

St. Petersburg

FLORIDA

Lake Okeechobee

West Palm Beach

BAHAMAS

25°

GULF OF MEXICO

Fort Myers

Fort Lauderdale

Miami

Nassau

0 100 200 300 Miles

0 100 200 300 400 Kilometers

Key West

© Rand McNally & Co.
Made in U.S.A.
N-MDL24000-P1- -1-7-1

95° 90° 85° 80° 75°

RAND McNALLY

A35

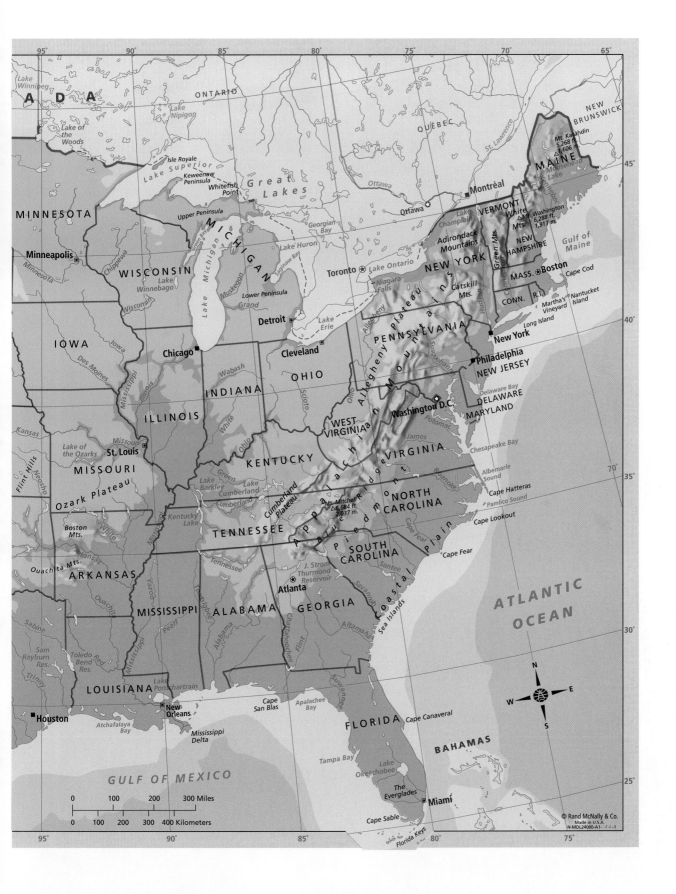

A D A

ONTARIO

Lake Winnipeg
Lake of the Woods
Lake Nipigon

MINNESOTA

Minneapolis

Minnesota

Lake Superior
Isle Royale
Keweenaw Peninsula
Whitefish Point

Great Lakes

QUÉBEC

Ottawa

NEW BRUNSWICK

MAINE
Mt. Katahdin 5,268 ft. 1,606 m.
Moosehead Lake

St. Lawrence

Ottawa

Montréal

Lake Champlain
VERMONT
White Mts.
Mt. Washington 6,288 ft. 1,917 m.
NEW HAMPSHIRE

Gulf of Maine

WISCONSIN

Chippewa

Lake Winnebago

Wisconsin

MICHIGAN

Upper Peninsula

Georgian Bay

Lake Huron
Saginaw Bay

Lower Peninsula
Grand
Muskegon

Lake Michigan

Toronto
Lake Ontario
Niagara Falls

Adirondack Mountains

Green Mts.

MASS. Boston
Cape Cod

NEW YORK

Catskill Mts.

CONN. R.I.
Martha's Vineyard
Nantucket Island

Long Island

IOWA

Des Moines

Iowa

Detroit

Lake Erie

Cleveland

Allegheny Plateau

Hudson

New York

Chicago

Wabash

OHIO

Scioto

PENNSYLVANIA

Philadelphia
NEW JERSEY

ILLINOIS

Illinois

White

Ohio

Allegheny Mountains

Delaware Bay

DELAWARE

MARYLAND

Kansas

Missouri

St. Louis

MISSOURI

Lake of the Ozarks

INDIANA

KENTUCKY

Green

Lake Barkley

Lake Cumberland

Cumberland

Ohio

WEST VIRGINIA

Washington D.C.

Potomac

VIRGINIA

James

Appalachian

Chesapeake Bay

Roanoke

Albemarle Sound

Cape Hatteras

Pamlico Sound

70°

35°

Flint Hills

Neosho

Ozark Plateau

Boston Mts.

Kentucky Lake

White

TENNESSEE

Cumberland Plateau

Mt. Mitchell 6,684 ft. 2,037 m.

Blue Ridge

Piedmont

NORTH CAROLINA

Cape Fear

Cape Lookout

ARKANSAS

Ouachita Mts.

Ouachita

Arkansas

Tennessee

J. Strom Thurmond Reservoir

SOUTH CAROLINA

Santee

Cape Fear

Coastal Plain

Sabine

MISSISSIPPI

Yazoo

ALABAMA

Alabama

Atlanta

GEORGIA

Chattahoochee

Flint

Savannah

Sea Islands

ATLANTIC OCEAN

30°

Sam Rayburn Res.

Toledo Bend Res.

Red

Pearl

Altamaha

Trinity

LOUISIANA

Lake Pontchartrain

Mississippi

Cape San Blas

Apalachee Bay

Suwannee

Houston

New Orleans

Atchafalaya Bay

Mississippi Delta

FLORIDA

Cape Canaveral

BAHAMAS

25°

GULF OF MEXICO

Tampa Bay

Lake Okeechobee

The Everglades

Miami

Cape Sable

Florida Keys

N
W E
S

© Rand McNally & Co.
Made in U.S.A.
N-MDL24000-A1- -J -J -1

0   100   200   300 Miles
0 100 200 300 400 Kilometers

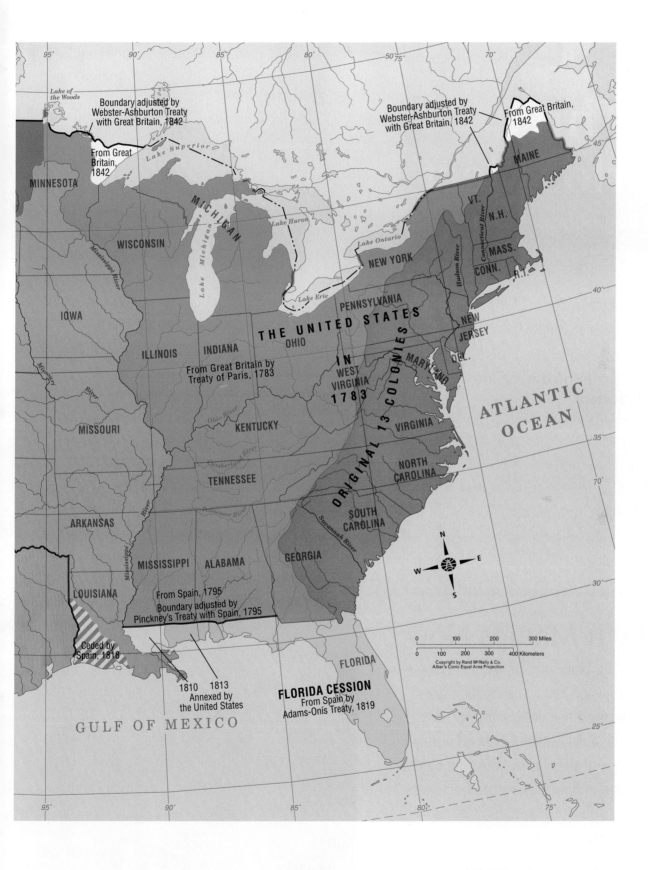

Boundary adjusted by Webster-Ashburton Treaty with Great Britain, 1842

Boundary adjusted by Webster-Ashburton Treaty with Great Britain, 1842

From Great Britain, 1842

Lake of the Woods

From Great Britain, 1842

MINNESOTA

MAINE

Lake Superior

MICHIGAN

Lake Huron

WISCONSIN

VT.

N.H.

Lake Michigan

Connecticut River

MASS.

Hudson River

IOWA

Lake Ontario

CONN.

R.I.

Mississippi River

NEW YORK

Lake Erie

PENNSYLVANIA

THE UNITED STATES

ILLINOIS

INDIANA

OHIO

NEW JERSEY

From Great Britain by Treaty of Paris, 1783

IN

DEL.

Missouri River

MARYLAND

WEST VIRGINIA

Ohio River

1783

ORIGINAL 13 COLONIES

ATLANTIC OCEAN

MISSOURI

KENTUCKY

VIRGINIA

Cumberland River

TENNESSEE

NORTH CAROLINA

Tennessee River

ARKANSAS

SOUTH CAROLINA

Savannah River

GEORGIA

MISSISSIPPI

ALABAMA

Mississippi River

LOUISIANA

From Spain, 1795

Boundary adjusted by Pinckney's Treaty with Spain, 1795

N

W   E

S

Ceded by Spain, 1818

1810   1813
Annexed by the United States

FLORIDA

FLORIDA CESSION
From Spain by Adams-Onís Treaty, 1819

GULF OF MEXICO

0	100	200	300 Miles
0	100	200	300	400 Kilometers

Copyright by Rand McNally & Co.
Alber's Conic Equal Area Projection

Three Worlds Meet

Beginnings–1650

Why It Matters Now

In the 1400s, brave men from Europe crossed uncharted waters to find new trade routes and to discover their destiny. Their actions would write a new chapter in world history. Their story—of their interactions with other peoples and of how they learned from those peoples—is our story, and has made us who we are today.

Until lions have their historians,
tales of the hunt shall always
glorify the hunters.
—African Proverb

The World Before 1500

Beginnings–1500

 ESSENTIAL QUESTION

How did American, African, and European societies differ from one another before 1500?

CONNECT Geography & History

How did world geography both divide and connect the different cultures of the Americas, Africa, and Europe?

Think about:

1 how the Atlantic Ocean's currents affected early navigation, exploration, and trade

2 how people might have first arrived in the Americas

3 ways in which Africans and Europeans might have come into contact

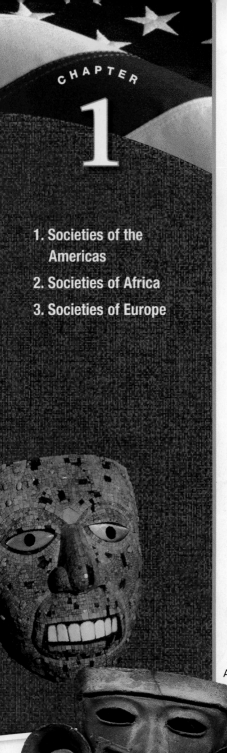

Aztec masks

A.D. 1200s Kingdom of Mali takes over Ghana.

▼

Effect Islam spreads through West Africa.

Victims of the Black Death that killed millions in the 1300s

35,000 B.C.

The "first Americans" migrate from Asia.

▼

Effect Native peoples spread throughout the Americas, forming numerous societies.

Inca figure

1300s The Inca and Aztec Empires expand in the Americas.

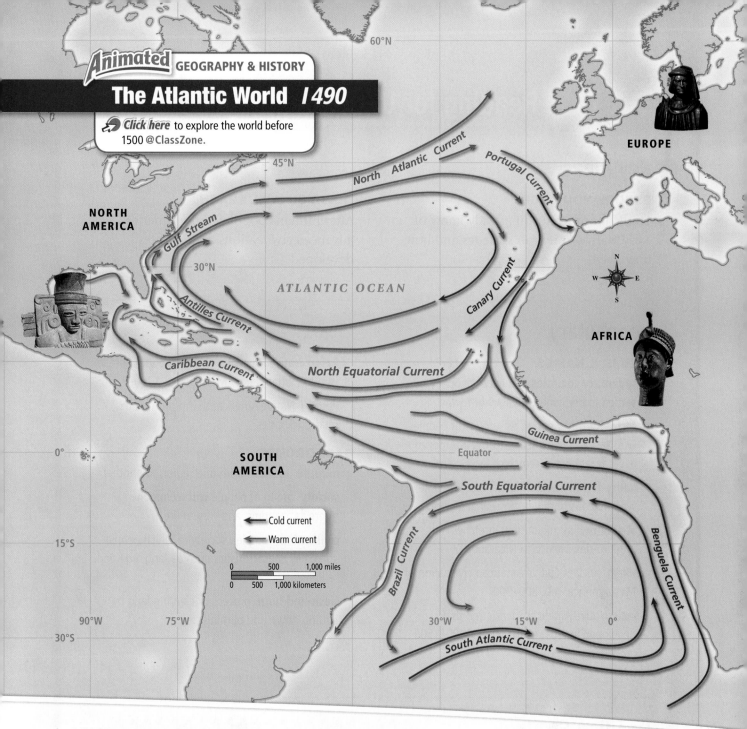

The Atlantic World *1490*

Click here to explore the world before 1500 @ClassZone.

EUROPE

NORTH
AMERICA

60°N

45°N

North Atlantic Current

Portugal Current

Gulf Stream

30°N

ATLANTIC OCEAN

Canary Current

Antilles Current

AFRICA

Caribbean Current

North Equatorial Current

Guinea Current

0°

SOUTH
AMERICA

Equator

South Equatorial Current

15°S

Brazil Current

Benguela Current

← Cold current

← Warm current

0   500   1,000 miles
0   500   1,000 kilometers

90°W   75°W   30°W   15°W   0°

30°S

South Atlantic Current

1350 The Renaissance begins in Italy.

▼

Effect New ideas about the world, science, and human nature spread throughout Europe.

late **1400s**

1400s European sailors begin to understand the Atlantic Ocean's currents.

▼

Effect Routes to Africa and the Americas open for exploration.

Kongo and Ndongo rule Central Africa.

▶ Key Ideas

BEFORE YOU BEGIN

Think about what you already know of early Native American societies and how they lived.

NOW YOU WILL LEARN

After humans populated the Americas, advanced civilizations and cultures developed.

▶ Vocabulary

TERMS & NAMES

sedentary societies groups of people who settled in permanent villages or towns

semisedentary societies groups of people who settled in villages or towns but moved every few years in search of food

nonsedentary societies groups of people who moved continually in search of food

Mesoamerica region that stretches from modern-day Mexico to Nicaragua

Maya ancient Native American civilization of Mesoamerica, A.D. 200–900

Inca Native American civilization that developed in what is now Peru, 1400–1500

Aztec Native American civilization that spread through what is now Mexico, A.D. 1300–1520

Pueblo Native Americans who built great mud-brick cities

BACKGROUND

migrate to move from one region to another

society group of people with common interests, customs, and way of life

civilization complex society in which people share key characteristics such as language and religion

slash-and-burn process of clearing land by cutting down and burning trees

▶ Reading Strategy

Re-create the spider diagram shown at right. As you read and respond to the **KEY QUESTIONS**, use the main branches to note categories of facts about each of the early cultures of the Americas. Add stems to record important details in each category.

 Skillbuilder Handbook, page R6.

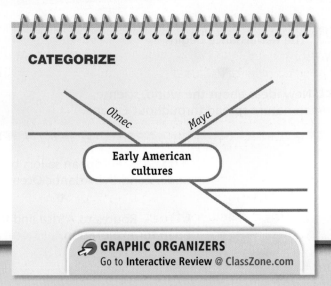

CATEGORIZE

Olmec

Maya

Early American cultures

⌁ **GRAPHIC ORGANIZERS**
Go to **Interactive Review @ ClassZone.com**

Societies of the Americas

17.C.3c Analyze how human process influence settlement patterns including migration and population growth.
17.D.3a Explain how and why spatial patterns of settlement change over time.

One American's Story

Many Native Americans tell stories that describe the origins of their people. Some are very detailed and explain how the gods created their ancestors. Others describe ancient events and early travels from distant lands. Montezuma, who ruled the Aztecs between 1502 and 1520, shared one such story with the Spanish explorer Hernando Cortés.

PRIMARY SOURCE

❝ We have known for a long time, from the chronicles of our forefathers, that neither I, nor those who inhabit this country, are descendants from [its original people], but from strangers who came to it from very distant parts. ❞

—-Montezuma

Aztec emperor Montezuma

While some historians debate the accuracy of this account, most agree that it provides useful insight into the background of the early Americans.

The First People in America

▼ **KEY QUESTION** What kinds of societies emerged in the Americas?

Who were the "first Americans"? Where did they come from? How did they live? These are questions historians have been struggling with for decades.

The Mystery of Migration Although there remains some disagreement among experts, most historians believe that the "first Americans" were men and women from Asia. They **migrated**, or moved, eastward between 15,000 and 35,000 years ago by crossing a land bridge between Siberia and Alaska. It is likely that they made this journey in search of food and shelter.

As the first Americans spread throughout the continent, groups of people often split off from one another. This process created many different **societies**, or groups of people with common interests, customs, and ways of life. Over time, three basic types of societies developed throughout North, Central, and South America. (See chart on next page.)

- **sedentary societies** created permanent towns or villages. These towns were densely populated and included wide streets, large farms, markets, and hundreds of dwellings.
- **semisedentary societies** built towns or villages, but moved them every few years in search of migrating animals and new land for farming.
- **nonsedentary societies** did not construct permanent villages or towns but created small, temporary camps that could be easily moved in a continual search for large game, fish, and edible plants.

🔺 **CATEGORIZE** Describe the early societies of the Americas.

The Rise of Civilizations

🔻 **KEY QUESTION** What led people to form complex civilizations?

Around 1200 B.C. the first Americans began to form larger communities. This occurred when several small societies joined one another through political alliance or military takeover. Over time, some of these communities grew into vast **civilizations**—complex societies in which people share important characteristics such as language, religion, art, dress, and political structure.

The Growth of Complex Societies The first great American civilization emerged in **Mesoamerica**, a region that stretches from modern-day Mexico to Nicaragua. Between 1200 B.C. and 400 B.C., the Olmec people dominated the region by creating large farms on the region's rich soil. There they grew enough maize, or corn, to feed thousands of people.

After the Olmec, Mesoamerica was ruled by the **Maya** peoples. During the period from A.D. 250 to 900, the Maya made many advances in art and architecture that endured through the centuries. They constructed large cities that included giant temples, numerous shrines, vast marketplaces, and even ball courts for games and contests.

Early Civilizations Fall Living in a complex civilization had many advantages. With more workers available, it became possible to build bigger cities, cultivate larger farms, store extra food, and form immense armies for protection. But despite these advantages, each of these early civilizations declined before Europeans reached the Americas in 1492.

No one knows why the early civilizations fell. Some historians blame major environmental changes such as rivers drying up or volcanic eruptions. Others suggest that catastrophic weather, disease, warfare, widespread famine, or internal political revolt are more likely causes.

🔺 **SUMMARIZE** Identify the advantages and disadvantages of living in complex civilizations.

Connect *to the* **World**

Social Organization
As you will see in the next section, similar patterns of social development occurred in Africa.

Perhaps the most recognizable pieces of Olmec art are the colossal heads carved of stone. Some are over ten feet tall and weigh thousands of pounds.

COMPARING *Societies*

EARLY SOCIETIES OF THE AMERICAS

By 1500, Native American societies displayed a variety of customs, languages, cultures, and ways of life. These societies can be categorized into three major groups.

The Americas before *1500*

Source: Adapted from Lockhart and Schwartz, *Early Latin America: A History of Colonial Spanish America and Brazil*

NONSEDENTARY
Chichimecs, Caribs

- Hunter-gatherers wandered from place to place.
- no permanent settlements or farms
- populations smaller than one hundred
- no political leader, laws, or taxes

SEMISEDENTARY
Tupians, Iroquois

- combination of farming and hunting
- small villages; people moved frequently to follow food supply
- Populations number in hundreds and thousands.
- some political leadership to enforce laws and taxes

SEDENTARY
Aztecs, Inca, Maya

- Large-scale farming was basis of life.
- permanent cities with roads, markets, and many dwellings
- Populations number in the millions.
- Political leaders create laws and enforce taxes.

CRITICAL THINKING **Compare and Contrast**

What characteristics distinguish sedentary societies from nonsedentary societies?

A product of the Chaco culture (A.D. 850–1250) that developed in what is now New Mexico

Pre-Contact Societies

▼ **KEY QUESTION** How did the environment affect the way native peoples lived?

When the great civilizations declined, native peoples broke apart into small, self-governing societies. But these groups faced difficult times. Often they had to fight one another for land, crops, and valuable trade goods. Once again, people sought the advantages of living in larger communities.

Aztec and Inca Empires Between 1300 and 1500, two great empires dominated Mesoamerica. In what is now Peru, the **Inca** people created a vast civilization that included as many as ten million inhabitants. Originally these people were part of smaller, independent groups. Over the years, the Inca united the population under a single government and a new set of laws.

In addition to creating a new political system, the Inca created many important cultural and scientific advances. Inca achievements include an accurate calendar, an early clock, and a system of paved roads that ran most of the length of South America's Pacific coast.

To the north, in what is now Mexico, the **Aztec** people also created a major civilization. The capital, Tenochtitlán, was an island in Lake Texcoco. The city was built upon logs and mud and served as a natural fortress for a population of more than 140,000 people.

Like the Inca, the Aztecs united many small communities under a single government. They did this by using military alliances and warfare to control their weaker neighbors. Upon defeating their enemies, the Aztecs enforced new laws, collected taxes, and demanded a share of crops and labor.

Native North Americans Societies to the north were not as complex as those in Mexico and Peru, but their populations were larger. Some historians believe that by 1400, as many as seven million Native Americans lived in what is now the United States.

Throughout North America, a diverse range of native societies developed as various groups adapted to unique environments—whether arctic ice fields, scorching deserts, muddy swamps, or dense forests. In each case, the land, plants, and local animals influenced how native peoples lived.

In the far north, near present-day Alaska, the Inuit (IHN•yoo•iht) peoples lived on frozen tundra by building homes made of ice. They hunted whales, seals, and walrus and used these animals for food, fuel, and clothing.

(top) Inca earrings, A.D. 200 *(bottom)* Macchu Picchu ruins can be visited today, high in the Andes. *(inset)* close up of typical Inca stonework

Toward the southwest—in modern-day Arizona and New Mexico—the **Pueblo** people made their homes. Pueblo people used irrigation to build large farms in the valley regions near the desert. In addition, they constructed multi-storied mud-brick houses under steep mountain cliffs. This design provided both shade from the sun and protection from enemies.

In the Northeast, between the Great Lakes and the Atlantic Ocean, lived the Iroquois and Algonquin peoples. In this region, Native Americans built large villages and farms using **slash-and-burn** agriculture, a process of chopping down trees and burning the land to clear it. Often, this method was repeated annually—clearing large tracts of land for only one season of farming.

Native American religions were also influenced by the environment. Native Americans worshipped many gods whom they believed controlled the sun, moon, sky, crops, rivers, and animals.

Built by the Pueblo people, Mesa Verde stands in present-day Colorado.

An Isolated World Although Native Americans interacted extensively with their neighbors, and sometimes traveled great distances, they remained isolated from the rest of the world. As a result, before the 1400s, people throughout the Americas had no experience of European technology, warfare, culture, or disease.

 SYNTHESIZE Explain why the natural environment was so important to early societies.

Illinois Learning Standards *Review*

 ONLINE QUIZ
For test practice, go to
Interactive Review @ ClassZone.com

TERMS & NAMES

1. Explain the significance of
   - sedentary societies
   - semisedentary societies
   - nonsedentary societies
   - Mesoamerica
   - Maya
   - Inca
   - Aztec
   - Pueblo

USING YOUR READING NOTES

2. **Categorize** Complete the diagram you began at the beginning of this section.

Olmec   Maya

Early American cultures

KEY IDEAS

3. How did ancient people migrate to the Americas?

4. How did the natural environment affect the development of early societies?

CRITICAL THINKING

5. **Analyze** How did sedentary societies differ from semisedentary societies and nonsedentary societies?

6. **Causes and Effects** How did warfare and military alliances affect early societies?

7. **Connect** *to* **Today** What are the advantages of living in a modern civilization?

8. **Art** Research the civilizations that developed in the Americas. Then draw a picture representing some aspect of an early Native American civilization.

Click here for more information on the Aztec market
@ ClassZone.com

Aztec Market

As the sun rises over the Aztec capital at Tenochtitlán, merchants and customers begin arriving at the city's largest market. The market, in an area called Tlatelolco, attracted around 25,000 people each day to buy and sell gold, silver, flowers, cloth, food, and slaves.

Click here Modern Mexico City, which stands on the site of the Aztec capital.

Click here A woman at a Mexico City market prepares *nopales*, or cactus pads, a traditional food.

Click here Diagram of the city of Tenochtitlán.

Activity

Build a Model of Tenochtitlán

1 In groups of 2 or 3 students, use the internet to research the layout and buildings of Tenochtitlán.

2 With your group, build a model of an important building in the city.

3 Present the model to the class, explaining its place and importance in the city.

▶ Key Ideas

BEFORE, YOU LEARNED

After humans migrated to the Americas, a variety of civilizations developed.

NOW YOU WILL LEARN

In Africa, complex and simple societies competed for resources and trade in three geographical zones.

▶ Vocabulary

TERMS & NAMES

Sahara a large desert in Northern Africa

Islam religion that teaches there is one God, named Allah, and Muhammad is his prophet

Muslim follower of the religion of Islam

Ghana West African kingdom that prospered between A.D. 700 and 1000

Mali West African kingdom that ruled from about 1200 to 1400

Kongo Central African kingdom in the 1400s that engaged in warfare and slavery

Ndongo Central African kingdom that ruled during the 1400s

BACKGROUND VOCABULARY

savanna flat grassland with abundant wildlife, thorny bushes, and scattered trees

slave someone who is captured for use in forced, unpaid labor

Visual Vocabulary Sahara

▶ Reading Strategy

Re-create the cluster diagram shown at right. As you read and respond to the **KEY QUESTIONS**, use the outer circles to record important information about how each cultural group adapted to its environment.

 Skillbuilder Handbook, page R4.

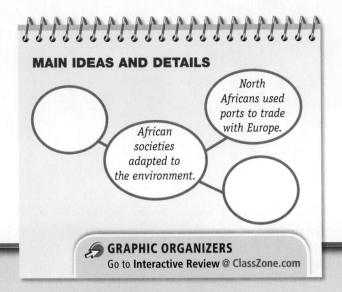

MAIN IDEAS AND DETAILS

North Africans used ports to trade with Europe.

African societies adapted to the environment.

GRAPHIC ORGANIZERS
Go to **Interactive Review** @ ClassZone.com

Societies of Africa

 15.D.3b Explain how comparative advantage forms the basis for specialization and trade among nations.
17.C.3a Explain how human activity is affected by geographic factors.

One African's Story

As early as the 1300s, Africans were exploring the Atlantic Ocean, traveling north to Europe and west into the uncharted sea. In 1324, emperor Mansa Musa of Mali told the historian Al-Umari of the previous emperor's attempt to discover the edge of the Atlantic Ocean.

PRIMARY SOURCE

“ The ruler who preceded me would not believe that it was impossible to discover the limits of the neighboring sea. . . he had 200 ships equipped and filled them with men. . . water and supplies in sufficient quantity to last for years. . . . They went away; their absence was long before any of them returned. ”

—Mansa Musa, as told by historian Al-Umari

Mansa Musa

As the story goes, only one ship returned to Mali. No one knows what happened to the others. But Musa's account shows that Africans looked westward into the Atlantic Ocean in hopes of finding new lands to conquer and goods to trade.

African Kingdoms Before 1200

🔻 **KEY QUESTION** How did Africa's three geographic zones influence the development of early societies?

Although geographically isolated from Europe and Asia, early African societies were connected to the world through extensive trade and commerce.

Geography and Culture The African continent consists of three large geographic zones. In the north is the **Sahara**, a huge, hot desert area with little or no vegetation. In the south is a vast **savanna**, a long and flat grassland with abundant wildlife, thorny bushes, and scattered trees. And in the middle, in Central and Western Africa, is a great transitional, or midway, zone where dense rain forests and broad rivers meet the Atlantic Ocean.

S A H A R A

Algiers
Tunis
Tripoli
Marrakech
In Salah
Sabha
Cairo
Taghaza
Ghat
Walata
Timbuktu
GHANA
Gao
MALI
Djenne
Kano

ATLANTIC
OCEAN
Mbanza
Kongo
KONGO
Luanda
NDONGO

0°
10°S

— Major trade route

0   500   1,000 miles
0   500 1,000 kilometers
10°W   0°   10°E   40°E

Connect Geography & History

1. **Place** What geographic feature separates North Africa from West Africa?

2. **Make Inferences** Why were so many West African towns located on rivers?

In each region of Africa, the natural environment greatly influenced how societies lived. In Northern Africa, people created extensive trade routes through a series of ports on the Mediterranean Sea. This allowed Northern Africans to exchange a wide variety of goods, including grain, cloth, and wine, with their European neighbors.

In the west, life and trade centered around the Niger, Volta, and Senegal rivers. Here people farmed the rich soil and used the rivers to transport their crops to ports and cities on the Atlantic Ocean. From there, goods traveled north by sea to Europe.

At the same time, the vast and barren Sahara limited trade and travel to Central and Southern Africa. There, people lived in relative isolation from the rest of the world and their African neighbors. Despite these harsh conditions, however, the religion of **Islam** was carried throughout the region by traders, travelers, and merchants. The Koran, the book of Islam, teaches that there is one God, Allah, and that Muhammad is his prophet. Those who follow Islam are called **Muslims**.

West African Kingdoms Like the great American civilizations, some of the early African kingdoms were large and complex societies that included thousands—perhaps millions—of people. **Ghana**, located in Western Africa along the Niger River, prospered between A.D. 700 and 1100 by controlling valuable trade routes for gold and salt. By the 1200s, the Kingdom of **Mali** had taken over Ghana and become West Africa's most powerful state. Mali's ruler, Mansa Musa, was a devoted Muslim. Musa promoted Islam throughout Western Africa and even funded a university to teach the religion.

🔺 **MAIN IDEAS & DETAILS** Describe Africa's three geographical zones.

Later African Kingdoms

🔻 **KEY QUESTION** Why was warfare an important aspect of early African society?

(right) Statue from West Africa

Not all African kingdoms were large empires. More often, kingdoms were small territories—sometimes only a few miles wide—and included hundreds rather than thousands of citizens. But each had its own ruler, laws, and an army for protection.

War and Slavery in African Kingdoms By the mid-1400s, more than one hundred small independent kingdoms dotted the landscape of Western and Central Africa. As in the Americas, neighboring African kingdoms often fought one another for rights to land, crops, and valuable trade goods. During these wars, African kings preferred to capture rather than kill their enemies so they could be used as **slaves**, or people who are captured for use in forced, unpaid labor.

Often, kingdoms went to war just to enslave their enemy's population. By enslaving their enemies, African kings achieved three important goals. First, they gained a large population—mostly young and strong men—that could be put to hard work. Second, they depleted, or wore out, their rival's military strength. And third, slaves could be traded to distant kingdoms for crops, weapons, gold, and other valuable resources.

By the late 1400s, two kingdoms dominated Central Africa. **Kongo,** located on the Zaire River, and its southern neighbor **Ndongo** waged numerous battles to capture their enemies and sell them into slavery. By the 1480s, when Europeans arrived in Central Africa, the slave trade was a well-established and profitable business.

 SUMMARIZE Describe the role of warfare and slavery in early African kingdoms.

Illinois Learning Standards *Review*

 ONLINE QUIZ
For test practice, go to
Interactive Review @ ClassZone.com

TERMS & NAMES

1. Explain the importance of
- Sahara
- Islam
- Muslim
- Ghana
- Mali
- Kongo
- Ndongo

USING YOUR READING NOTES

2. Main Ideas and Details Complete the diagram you started at the beginning of this section. Then write a summary of how each group adapted to its environment.

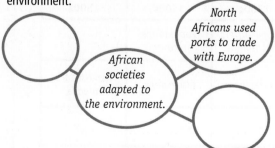

African societies adapted to the environment.

North Africans used ports to trade with Europe.

KEY IDEAS

3. Describe the three geographical zones of Africa.

4. How did the Sahara affect trade and travel to southern and central Africa?

5. How did Islam spread throughout Africa?

CRITICAL THINKING

6. Drawing Conclusions How did African kings benefit from warfare?

7. **Connect** *to* **Today** Use library and Internet resources to research one African group mentioned in this section. Write a paragraph describing the culture today, including its current population and location.

8. **Writing** **Travel Description** Imagine you are a traveler in Central Africa. Write a short description of your travels including the natural terrain and the people you encounter.

▶ Key Ideas

BEFORE, YOU LEARNED

In Africa, large and small societies competed for resources and trade.

NOW YOU WILL LEARN

Between 1300 and 1500, Europe experienced major changes in social, political, and economic life.

▶ Vocabulary

TERMS & NAMES

great famine widespread food shortage that killed thousands of Europeans

Black Death deadly disease that spread through Europe in the 14th century

Renaissance time of increased interest in art and learning in Europe

Reformation movement that divided the church between Catholics and Protestants

Catholics Christian followers of the Roman Catholic Church

Protestants Christian group that broke away from the Catholic Church

North Atlantic Current clockwise ocean current that flows between Northern Europe and the Caribbean Sea

South Atlantic Current counterclockwise ocean current that flows between Africa and South America

BACKGROUND VOCABULARY

printing press device that mechanically printed pages by pressing inked forms onto paper, invented around 1440

Visual Vocabulary printing press

▶ Reading Strategy

Re-create the diagram shown here. As you read and respond to the **KEY QUESTIONS**, use the chart to record the major changes that occurred in Europe between 1300 and 1500.

 Skillbuilder Handbook, page R8.

COMPARE AND CONTRAST

1300s	1400s	1500s
Europe suffers great famine.	*Populations recover.*	
	Cities grow.	*Renaissance spreads.*

 GRAPHIC ORGANIZERS
Go to **Interactive Review** @ ClassZone.com

Societies of Europe

18.A.3 Explain how language, literature, the arts, architecture and traditions contribute to the development and transmission of culture.
18.B.3a Analyze how individuals and groups interact with and within institutions (e.g., *educational, military*).

One European's Story

During the 15th century, many European monarchs encouraged exploration of new lands and distant oceans. One such ruler was Queen Isabella I of Spain. During her reign, Isabella sent several expeditions to seek new territories, spread Christianity, and capture valuable resources. Like other European monarchs, Isabella believed she had a royal right to profit from the conquest of foreign lands.

PRIMARY SOURCE

❝ The kings of glorious memory . . . always had [the right to] the conquest of part of Africa and of Guinea, and they received a fifth of the merchandise that was recovered from those places. ❞

—Queen Isabella, as quoted in *Isabel the Queen*

Queen Isabella I

During Isabella's time on the throne, Spanish explorers traveled to Africa, the Canary Islands, and throughout the Mediterranean. Eventually, her royal adventurers would venture further west to the Americas.

A Modern Europe Emerges

🔻 **KEY QUESTION** What key changes occurred in Europe between 1300 and 1500?

As in Africa and the Americas, Europe experienced major changes in social, political, and economic life between 1300 and 1500. During the 1300s, disease and warfare ravaged the continent. But populations recovered in the following century. Towns and cities grew in size and wealth. Trade increased. And a cultural revolution began spreading new ideas across the continent.

Social and Economic Change In the early 1300s, Europe experienced several major catastrophes. Both the **great famine**, a widespread food shortage, and the **Black Death**, a deadly disease, killed millions of people. At the same time, a conflict between France and England known as the Hundred

WARFARE AND EXPLORATION

During the 1300s changes in European warfare forced monarchs to search for new ways of raising money. In the following centuries, this economic need encouraged world exploration.

1200s Warfare in Europe was dominated by feudal knights. For their service in battle, knights were granted land or noble titles.

1300s Monarchs replaced feudal knights with standing armies. These soldiers demanded gold or silver as payment for fighting.

1400s To pay their armies, monarchs encouraged adventurers to explore new lands, in search of taxable goods to trade.

CRITICAL THINKING Make Inferences How did monarchs' increasing need for gold encourage exploration?

Years War took thousands more lives. Yet despite these disasters, prosperity returned to Europe toward the end of the 14th century.

During the 1400s, stability returned to Europe. Populations rose and cities grew larger. Trade also increased as urban merchants began dealing in silk, porcelain, tea, and rugs from Asia. As a result, monarchs began exerting more control over their land by collecting new taxes and strengthening their central governments.

The Renaissance and Reformation In addition to social and economic change, two cultural movements swept Europe during the 15th and 16th centuries. First was the **Renaissance**, a widespread cultural revival of classical art, architecture, learning, and literature. Begun by artists and scholars in Italy around 1350, the Renaissance promoted the achievements of ancient Greece and Rome as models of progress. The Renaissance—meaning "rebirth"—encouraged a new respect for these ancient values, including education, mathematics, and scientific exploration of the physical world.

In the 1500s, people throughout Europe began questioning the role of the Church in society. Many people were upset over corrupt practices among the clergy, including the sale of favors by the priesthood. This discontent led to a movement to reform the Church, known as the **Reformation**. Eventually, the church divided into two groups—the **Catholics**, or followers of the Pope in Rome, and the **Protestants**, or those who broke away from the church in protest.

During the Renaissance and Reformation, one new invention more than any other helped spread new ideas. Around 1440, a German named Johannes Gutenberg invented the **printing press**, a machine that created printed pages. Before this invention, all books had to be written by hand. Because of this, books were too expensive for ordinary people to buy. The printing press allowed hundreds of books to be published and sold throughout the population. As a result many Europeans learned to read and developed a greater curiosity about the world. In this way, the Renaissance and Reformation helped prepare and motivate Europeans for world exploration.

▲ **COMPARE AND CONTRAST** Describe key changes that affected Europe in the 1300s and 1400s.

CONNECT to the Essential Question

How did American, African, and European societies differ from one another before 1500?

	AMERICAS	AFRICA	EUROPE
Important Groups and Kingdoms	• Olmec, Maya, Inca, Aztecs, Iroquois	• Mali, Kongo, Ndongo	• English, French, Italians, Spanish, Norwegians
Social Organization	• sedentary, semisedentary, nonsedentary	• mostly semisedentary and sedentary	• mostly sedentary
Way of Life	• mix of farming, hunting	• mix of farming, hunting	• mainly farming
Religion	• spiritual belief linked to nature	• Islam, Christianity, native African religions	• Christianity
Achievements	• cities, temples, irrigation canals, calendar	• art, Islamic universities, extensive trade and travel	• Renaissance, Reformation, printing press

CRITICAL THINKING **Summarize** What features were common to societies in the Americas, Africa, and Europe?

European Expansion

Pocket compass and sundial of the 1400s

▼ **KEY QUESTION** How did the ocean's currents affect early navigation?

During the 1400s, European explorers sought new trade routes in order to obtain goods from Africa and Asia. Europeans turned their attention to ocean travel. But despite advances in shipbuilding and navigation, ocean travel in the 1400s was controlled by two natural forces: wind and currents.

Navigation and Currents Two strong currents directed ship travel in the Atlantic Ocean. One was the **North Atlantic Current**, a circular current that runs clockwise between Northern Europe and the Caribbean Sea. A similar flow, the **South Atlantic Current,** runs counterclockwise between Africa and South America. Both currents are very strong and extremely dangerous. Until sailors understood these currents, even the largest and most advanced ships were often swept out to sea and never returned.

Early European Exploration Over the centuries, European sailors slowly solved the mystery of the Atlantic Ocean's currents. This led to the opening of two new routes for sea exploration. First, in the 1450s, sailors discovered how to travel south along Africa's coast and return home safely. Then, in the 1490s, explorers uncovered how to travel west into the Atlantic and return again to Europe. These discoveries would play a major role in American, African, and European history for centuries to come.

▲ **MAIN IDEAS & DETAILS** Identify the major currents that direct ocean travel.

 Illinois Learning Standards *Review*

 ONLINE QUIZ
For test practice, go to
Interactive Review @ ClassZone.com

TERMS & NAMES

1. Explore the importance of

- great famine
- Black Death
- Renaissance
- Reformation
- Catholics
- Protestants
- South Atlantic Current
- North Atlantic Current

USING YOUR READING NOTES

2. Compare and Contrast Complete the diagram you started at the beginning of this section.

1300s	1400s	1500s
Europe suffers great famine.	*Populations recover.*	
	Cities grow.	*Renaissance spreads.*

KEY IDEAS

3. What catastrophes affected Europe in the 1300s?

4. What values did Renaissance writers, artists, and scholars find important?

CRITICAL THINKING

5. Causes and Effects What factors caused the Reformation?

6. Evaluate Why was ocean travel so dangerous between 1300 and 1500?

7. Connect *to* Today The printing press changed the way ideas were spread in Europe. What new technology had a similar effect in recent years?

8. Writing Letter Imagine you are a European sailor during the 1450s. Write a letter to a friend, describing the currents around Europe.

Chapter Summary

1 **Key Idea**
After humans populated the Americas, advanced civilizations and cultures developed.

2 **Key Idea**
In Africa, complex and simple societies competed for resources and trade in three geographical zones.

3 **Key Idea**
Between 1300 and 1500, Europe experienced major changes in social, political, and economic life.

For detailed Review and Study Notes go to **Interactive Review** @ ClassZone.com

Name Game

Use the terms & names list to complete each sentence online or on your own paper.

1. The Church in Europe divided during the ____.
   Reformation 👆

2. A ____ has permanent villages or towns.

3. The invention of the ____ helped spread new ideas throughout Europe.

4. The ____ saw renewed interest in classical thought.

5. The ____ ruled Mesoamerica from 1300 to 1520.

6. The current that flows between Africa and South America is called the ____.

7. A follower of Islam is called a ____.

8. ____ was a process of clearing land for farming.

9. The central African nation of ____ ruled during the 1400s.

10. The ____ is a barren region in Northern Africa.

A. slash-and-burn
B. Renaissance
C. Aztec
D. Ndongo
E. Muslim
F. sedentary society
G. Reformation
H. Sahara
I. South Atlantic Current
J. printing press
K. Black Death
J. Protestant

Activities

FLIPCARD

Use the online flipcards to quiz yourself on the terms and names introduced in this chapter.

A disease that killed millions in 14th c. Europe

ANSWER
Black Death

GEOGAME

Use this online map to reinforce your understanding of the Atlantic world before 1500. Drag and drop each label in the list at its location on the map. A scorecard helps you keep track of your progress online.

Andes Mountains

Hispaniola

Portugal

Gulf Stream

Mali

More items online

VOCABULARY

Explain the significance of each of the following.

1. semisedentary society
2. nonsedentary society
3. Maya
4. slash-and-burn
5. Islam
6. Mali
7. Ndongo
8. slave
9. great famine
10. Renaissance
11. Reformation
12. North Atlantic Current

Explain how the terms and names in each group are related.

13. sedentary society, Inca, Aztec
14. Islam, Mali, Muslim
15. great famine, Black Death
16. Renaissance, Reformation, printing press
17. Mesoamerica, Aztec, Maya

KEY IDEAS

1 Societies of the Americas (pages 4–9)

18. Where did the "first Americans" come from?
19. What were some characteristics of civilization in the Americas?
20. What factors led to the decline of some early civilizations?

2 Societies of Africa (pages 12–15)

21. How did the African landscape influence early societies?
22. Why was warfare important to African kingdoms?
23. How were slaves used in African kingdoms?

3 Societies of Europe (pages 16–20)

24. What catastrophes did Europe suffer in the 1300s?
25. What events led to the Reformation?
26. How did the printing press help spread new ideas in Europe?

CRITICAL THINKING

27. **Make Inferences** Why did some societies conquer their smaller neighbors?

28. **Form and Support Opinions** How might trade between Africa and Europe have affected the spread of Islam and Christianity?

29. **Categorize** Fill in the chart below to show the major characteristics of sedentary, semisedentary and nonsedentary societies.

	Sedentary	Semisedentary	Nonsedentary
Settlement type			*No permanent settlements*
Primary food source	*large-scale farming*		
Population Size		*thousands*	
Political Structure			*No organized structure*

30. **Connect to Today** Slash-and-burn agriculture is still practiced today in some parts of the world. Do you think this method of clearing should still be used. Why or why not?

31. **Summarize** How did ocean currents affect navigation before 1500?

32. **Causes and Effects** Why did Europeans seek new trade routes?

33. **Connect Geography and History** Tenochtitlán, the Aztec capital, was built on a small island in Lake Texcoco. What would be some advantages and disadvantages of this location?

DOCUMENT-BASED QUESTIONS

PART 1: Short Answer

Study each document carefully and answer the questions that follow.

DOCUMENT 1

The Venetian Ambassador's Interview in an Oriental City;
artist unknown, Louvre, Paris

1. Examine this painting, which shows European ambassadors from Venice in the North African city of Cairo. What do you think might have been the purpose of this visit, given that Venice was the leading commercial center of Europe?

DOCUMENT 2

PRIMARY SOURCE

❝ If there chanced to be in those lands . . . some havens, into which it would be possible to sail without peril, many kinds of merchandise might be brought to this realm . . . and also the products of this realm might be taken there, which traffic would bring great profit to our countrymen. ❞

—Azurara, *Discovery and Conquest of Guinea*

2. What does this European writer reveal about the fears and hopes of traders in the 1400s?

PART 2: Essay

3. Using information from the documents, your answer to the question in Part 1, and your knowledge of history, write an essay about the importance of trade in encouraging contact between Europe and other lands.

YOU BE THE HISTORIAN

34. Causes and Effects How did constant warfare affect African populations? Think about who fights in battle and who was most often enslaved.

35. Problems and Solutions How did European society recover after the plague?

36. Form and Support Opinions Was any society in the Americas, Africa, or Europe more advanced than the others? Explain your opinion.

37. WHAT IF? Suppose Europeans had never experienced the Renaissance. How might the world be different today?

38. Draw Conclusions What factors might lead to the decline of a civilization today? Think about the reasons why civilizations declined before 1500.

39. Summarize What new ideas about science and art surfaced in Europe between 1300 and 1500?

40. Make Inferences How did advances in navigation open up new trade routes between Europe, Africa, and the Americas?

 Answer the
ESSENTIAL QUESTION

How did American, African, and European societies differ from one another before 1500?

Written Response Write a four-paragraph response to the Essential Question. Be sure to consider the key ideas of each section, as well as the most significant similarities and differences between the three worlds. Use the Response Rubric below to guide your thinking and writing.

Response Rubric

A strong response will

• discuss the major cultures of each world

• describe major cultural aspects of each world, such as religion and trade

• explain the similarities and differences of each world

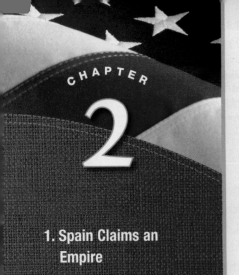

2

1. Spain Claims an Empire

2. European Competition in North America

3. The Spanish and Native Americans

4. Beginnings of Slavery in the Americas

European Exploration of the Americas

1492–1650

 ESSENTIAL QUESTION

How did Europeans transform life in the Americas?

CONNECT Geography & History

How might the physical geography of the Americas have affected European exploration?

Think about:

1 the major landforms and rivers

2 the distances covered. For example, the distance between Spain and the east coast of North America is almost 4,000 miles

3 the harsh conditions under which people traveled

This map of the Americas was drawn about 200 years after European settlement began.

Christopher Columbus

1521 Cortés conquers the Aztec Empire for Spain.

1534 Cartier explores the St. Lawrence in search of the Northwest Passage.

1492

Columbus lands in the Americas.

1494 Treaty of Tordesillas signed.

Effect Set boundary for Spanish and Portuguese exploration.

1531 Pizarro conquers the Inca Empire for Spain.

16th-century Inca goblet

A New
and accurate MAP of
NORTH
AMERICA,
Laid down according to the
latest, and most approved
OBSERVATIONS,
and
DISCOVERIES.
Univ. Mag. J.Hinton,
Newgate Street

1588 English navy
defeats Spanish Armada.

▼

Effect Spain loses its
reputation of invincibility.

Gold
doubloons

1650

1626 Dutch purchase
Manhattan Island from
Native Americans.

The Dutch town of New Amsterdam is
where New York City is now located.

t' Fort nieuw Amsterdam op de Manhatans

▶ Key Ideas

BEFORE, YOU LEARNED
Trade and social changes spurred Europeans to explore the world.

NOW YOU WILL LEARN
After Columbus' voyages, the Spanish quickly conquered the Native American empires of the Aztecs and the Inca.

▶ Vocabulary

TERMS & NAMES

conquistador (kahn•KEES•tuh•dawr) Spanish soldier that explored the Americas and claimed land for Spain

Hernando Cortés *conquistador* who brought the Aztecs to ruin

Christopher Columbus Italian navigator who looked for a faster water route to Asia

Treaty of Tordesillas (tawr•day•SEEL•yahs) 1494 treaty in which Spain and Portugal agreed to divide lands of the Western hemisphere between them and moved the Line of Demarcation to the west

mercantilism economic system that increased money in a country's treasury by creating a favorable balance of trade

Amerigo Vespucci Italian sailor who explored what is now the Americas

Francisco Pizarro *conquistador* who defeated the Inca

BACKGROUND VOCABULARY

missionary person sent by the Church to convert Native Americans to Christianity

alliance people or nations involved in a pact or treaty

Visual Vocabulary
Amerigo Vespucci

▶ Reading Strategy

Re-create the diagram shown at right. As you read and respond to the **KEY QUESTIONS**, use the diagram to record important events in sequence.

 See Skillbuilder Handbook, page R5.

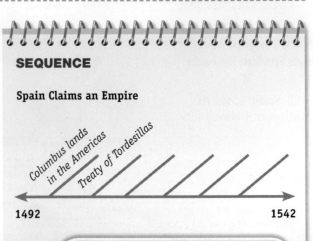

SEQUENCE

Spain Claims an Empire

Columbus lands in the Americas

Treaty of Tordesillas

1492   1542

GRAPHIC ORGANIZERS
Go to **Interactive Review** @ ClassZone.com

Spain Claims an Empire

16.C.3a Describe economic motivations that attracted Europeans and others to the Americas, 1500–1750.
17.C.3c Analyze how human process influence settlement patterns including migration and population growth.

One European's Story

In 1519, soldiers known as **conquistadors** (kahn•KEES•tuh•dawrz), or conquerors, explored the Americas and claimed them for Spain. **Hernando Cortés** was a leading *conquistador*. He led a Spanish army into Tabasco, an Aztec province in southeastern Mexico.

Cortés took advantage of the weaknesses of the Aztec Empire. He relied on a young Aztec woman, named Doña Marina, or Malinche (mah•LEEN•kay), to help him. One of the Spanish foot soldiers wrote about Malinche.

Malinche acted as translator and guide to Cortés for the Spanish conquest of the Aztecs.

PRIMARY SOURCE

❝ Doña Marina . . . although she had . . . seen us surrounded in the late battles, and knew that all of us were wounded and sick, yet never allowed us to see any sign of fear in her, only . . . courage. ❞

—Bernal Díaz del Castillo, quoted in *Notable Latin American Women*

Malinche played a key role in the Spanish conquest of the Aztecs. Spanish colonists followed to create a rich new empire in the Americas.

Exploring the Americas

▼ **KEY QUESTION** Why did the Europeans want to explore the Americas?

In the 1400s, Italian and Arab merchants ran the trade with Asia. Other Europeans, envious of Italian wealth, began to look for different routes to Asia.

Shortcuts to Asia Sailors seeking a route to Asia depended on the skill of their navigator. A navigator plans the course of a ship by using maps and nautical instruments to find its position. In the 1400s, a Portuguese prince,

Henry the Navigator, began a school of navigation. He paid for sailing expeditions to explore the Atlantic and the west coast of Africa. His ships traveled further down the African coast than Europeans had ever gone. Those voyages began Europe's age of discovery. This age of discovery eventually led Europeans to the Americas.

History Makers

Christopher Columbus   1451–1506

Genoese sailor Christopher Columbus thought he had found a faster way to reach Asia by sailing west across the Atlantic. But he underestimated the distance around the globe. In 1484, Columbus asked the king of Portugal to finance his voyage. The king refused, citing Columbus' miscalculations and the promising progress of his own explorers. Columbus then asked the Spanish court. In January 1492, his plan was accepted, and on August 3, 1492, Columbus set out on a voyage that changed history.

With one voyage to present-day Hispaniola, Columbus changed European views of the world. People soon realized that he had reached continents that had been unknown to them. Thanks to Columbus, the Atlantic Ocean became a bridge that connected Europe, Africa, and the Americas. Columbus completed a total of four voyages.

CRITICAL THINKING **Evaluate** What qualities and character traits, shown in Columbus' actions, may have made him a good leader?

 ONLINE BIOGRAPHY   For more on Christopher Columbus, go to the **Research & Writing** Center @ ClassZone.com

Under the sponsorship of Henry the Navigator, the Portuguese developed an improved ship called the caravel. The caravel had triangular sails as well as square sails. Square sails carried the ship forward when the wind was at its back. Triangular sails allowed the caravel to sail into the wind. The caravel was better than other European ships of the time at sailing into the wind.

In January 1488, Bartolomeu Días (DEE-uhs), a Portuguese explorer, reached the southern tip of Africa. After sailing around it, he returned to Portugal at the urging of his crew. Días is said to have named the tip the Cape of Good Hope because he hoped they had found a route to Asia.

A Water Route to Asia Ten years later, another Portuguese explorer, Vasco da Gama, followed Días's route around the Cape. He continued north along the eastern coast of Africa. Then he sailed east across the Indian Ocean to India. At last, someone had found an all-water route to Asia.

This route meant that the Portuguese could now trade with Asia without dealing with Muslim or Italian traders. Portugal took control of the valuable spice trade. Portuguese merchants grew wealthy. Spain and other European rivals wanted to take part in this rich trade. They began to look for their own water routes to Asia.

Christopher Columbus Before da Gama's voyage, an Italian sailor and navigator named **Christopher Columbus** thought he knew a faster way to reach Asia by sailing west across the Atlantic, which he calculated to be a shorter journey.

Spain's rulers, King Ferdinand and Queen Isabella, liked Columbus' plan because they wanted a share of the rich Asian trade. The Queen also welcomed a chance to spread Christianity. After years of waiting, Columbus assembled his ships —the *Niña*, the *Pinta*, and the *Santa María*—at the port of Palos de la Frontera in southern Spain. His fleet left the harbor on August 3, 1492.

Columbus' Explorations 1492–1504

Click here to see the interactive map
@ ClassZone.com

20°W

40°N

60°W

EUROPE

SPAIN

PORTUGAL

NORTH AMERICA

ATLANTIC OCEAN

1492–1493

Tropic of Cancer

20°N

AFRICA

1493–1496

1502–1504

1498–1500

PACIFIC OCEAN

SOUTH AMERICA

0°

Equator

N
W E
S

Connect Geography & History

1. **Movement** In what direction did Columbus sail on his voyages from Europe?

2. **Make Inferences** Why was a shorter route west important to European explorers?

The astrolabe was invented by the ancient Greeks. Sailors used it to help find their latitude.

Reaching the Americas The ships sailed southwest toward the Canary Islands, off the northwest coast of Africa. From there, Columbus was relying on trade winds that blew toward the west to speed his ships across the ocean. (See map on page 1.) But by October 10, he had been at sea for about four weeks and had not sighted land during that time. The crew were close to mutiny, or open rebellion, when they finally saw land.

The ships landed on an island in the Caribbean Sea. Columbus believed he had reached somewhere in India, or Asia, where spices grew. Columbus named the island San Salvador and claimed it for Spain. Eager to reach the rich country of Japan, which he believed to be nearby, he left San Salvador with a group of islanders. For the next three months he visited several of the Caribbean islands.

Finally he reached an island he named La Española, which today is called Hispaniola. There, Columbus and his men found gold and pearls. This convinced Columbus that he had reached Asia. He decided to return home. In 1493 he sailed back to Spain. Believing that he had found a water route to Asia, he wrote to Ferdinand and Isabella. No one suspected that Columbus had landed near continents entirely unknown to Europeans.

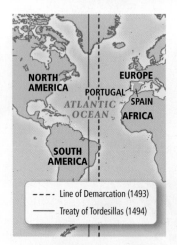

The Line of Demarcation between Spain and Portugal was adjusted by the Treaty of Tordesillas.

Dividing Up the World Due to the surge in explorations, in 1493, Pope Alexander VI drew an imaginary line around the world to decide who would control the lands that sailors were exploring. It was called the Line of Demarcation. Portugal could claim all non-Christian lands to the east of the line. Spain could claim the non-Christian lands to the west.

Portugal's King John II was unhappy—he believed the line favored Spain. He demanded that the Spanish rulers meet with him to change the pope's decision. In June 1494, the two countries agreed to the **Treaty of Tordesillas** (tawr•day•SEEL•yahs). This treaty moved the Line of Demarcation more than 800 miles farther west. The change later allowed Portugal to claim much of eastern South America, which later became the Portuguese colony of Brazil. This agreement led to an increase in Spanish and Portuguese voyages of exploration.

Europeans had three main goals during this age of exploration: first, they wanted to spread Christianity beyond Europe. Many expeditions included **missionaries**, or people sent to covert the native people to Christianity. Second, they wanted to expand their empires. Third, they wanted riches.

By increasing their wealth, European countries could gain power and security. An economic system called **mercantilism** was the way Europeans enriched their treasuries. For example, colonies provided mines that produced gold and silver. They also produced goods, such as crops, that could be traded for gold and silver. Finally, they served as a market for the home country.

European Exploration of the Americas *1500–1550*

Connect Geography & History

1. **Region** Which areas did the northern European countries explore?

2. **Make Inferences** Why did so many explorers stay close to the coastline?

Europeans Explore New Lands After Columbus' first voyage, many explorers went to sea. **Amerigo Vespucci** (vehs•POO•chee) was one of the first. He was an Italian sailor who set out in 1501 to find a sea route to Asia. Vespucci realized, however, that the land he saw on this voyage was not Asia. A German mapmaker, impressed by Vespucci's account of the lands, named the continent "America" after him.

This is a 1596 engraving of the historic voyage of Amerigo Vespucci.

Another famous explorer was the Spaniard Vasco Núñez de Balboa. Balboa heard Native American reports of another sea and a province rich in gold. In 1513, he led an expedition through the jungles of Panama and reached the Pacific Ocean. Balboa claimed the ocean and all the lands around it for Spain.

But perhaps no explorer was more capable than the Portuguese sailor Ferdinand Magellan. He proposed to reach Asia by sailing west around South America. The Spanish king agreed to fund Magellan's voyage. In 1519, Magellan set out from Spain with five ships and about 270 men. After a stormy passage around South America, Magellan entered the Pacific Ocean. For several months his crew crossed the Pacific, suffering great hardship.

Eventually, Magellan reached the Philippines, where he became involved in a local battle and was killed. But his crew traveled on. In 1522, the one remaining ship arrived back in Spain. The sailors in Magellan's crew were the first people to sail around the world.

▲ **ANALYZE MOTIVES** Explain why Europeans wanted to explore the Americas.

Conquering the Americas

▼ **KEY QUESTION** Why did Native American civilizations fall so quickly?

When Columbus arrived in the Caribbean, Native Americans had been living in the Americas for tens of thousands of years. In what is now Mexico and Peru, complex civilizations had developed. But these civilizations were unprepared for the Spanish attacks that began in the early 16th century.

The Invasion of Mexico While Magellan's crew was sailing around the world, the Spanish began their conquest of the Americas. Hernando Cortés landed on the Mexican coast with 508 *conquistadors* in 1519. He already knew that the Aztec Empire was not a single unified nation. Rather it was made up of several hundred mini-states who fought one another and hated their conquerors—the Aztecs.

The Spanish arrival shook the Aztec Empire, which ruled most of Mexico. The Aztec emperor Montezuma II feared that Cortés was an Aztec god sent to reclaim the throne. Montezuma sent Cortés precious gifts to get him to leave. But the gifts only excited Spanish dreams of riches.

The Spaniards marched inland and formed pacts or treaties, called **alliances**, with the native peoples who hated Aztec rule. After a few months,

Cortés reached the Aztec capital, Tenochtitlán (teh•nawch•tee•TLAHN). Montezuma welcomed Cortés with great ceremony. However, Cortés took Montezuma captive and tried to rule the Aztec by giving commands through the Aztec emperor.

But the Aztecs rebelled and trapped the Spanish in Tenochtitlán. On June 30, 1520, the Aztecs caught the Spaniards trying to escape, and fighting broke out. About 1,800 Spaniards and their allies were killed. The Spaniards called the event *La Noche Triste* (lah NAW•cheh TREES•teh)—the Sad Night.

Despite this defeat, Cortés led his forces back to Tenochtitlán in May 1521. At this point, the Spaniards got help from an unusual source—disease. Many Aztecs fell victim to an outbreak of smallpox, which severely weakened their ranks. The germs that caused this disease had been brought to America by the Europeans.

On his return, Cortés placed Tenochtitlán under siege for several months. When Tenochtitlán finally fell in August 1521, the empire lay in ruins. On the rubble of the Aztec capital, the Spanish built Mexico City. Over time, the populations and cultures of Spain and Mexico merged and produced a new society, that of the present-day nation of Mexico.

Aztec calendar

COMPARING *Aztec & Inca Civilizations*

In 1521, Cortés conquered the Aztecs. Pizzarro had subdued the Inca by the mid-1530s. Both were powerful empires for about 400 years and left a rich cultural heritage to their regions.

	Beliefs	Social structure	Economy	Writing	Agriculture
Aztec (Present-day Northern Mexico; capital: Tenochtitlán)	Supreme sun god; total loyalty to the king	1. king 2. nobles (military and priests) 3. commoners 4. slaves	State-controlled: provinces pay tribute in gold, food, and other products	Pictographic (picture) writing on paper made of deerskin or fiber	Terraced farming; floating gardens, causeways, aqueducts
Inca (Parts of present-day Argentina, Bolivia, Chile, Ecuador, and Peru; capital: Cuzco)	Supreme sun god; total loyalty to the emperor	1. emperor 2. royal families 3. small units of commoners	State-controlled: provinces pay tribute in labor	No known writing system; kept records on knotted cords, or *quipus.*	Terraced farming; steep mountainous region

CRITICAL THINKING

1. **Compare and Contrast** What were the biggest differences between the Aztec and Inca societies?

2. **Make Inferences** Why did the Aztecs demand tribute in goods rather than labor?

Silver llama figurine from Peru, after 1438

The Inca Empire Falls Despite the fall of the Aztec, the Inca still had a powerful empire in the Cuzco Valley in what is now Peru. By 1525, the Inca ruled a 2,000-mile-long territory in the Andes Mountains along the western coast of South America. The Inca also possessed much gold and silver. Stories of Incan wealth reached the Spanish. In 1531, a *conquistador* named **Francisco Pizarro** led 180 men into Peru.

Incan emperor Atahualpa (ah•tuh•WAHL•puh) went to greet the Spaniards, but the Spanish killed thousands of Inca and took him captive. To free himself, Atahualpa gave the Spanish a treasure of gold, but the Spaniards killed him anyway. With the Incan emperor dead, the Inca Empire collapsed. Then Pizarro took control of this area for Spain, which he had already called Peru.

How did the great Aztec and Inca empires fall to such small groups of *conquistadors*? Spanish success can be explained by three major reasons.

- The Spanish weakened the Aztec and Inca empires by making alliances with their enemies
- The spread of European diseases killed millions of Native Americans
- Over time, the Spanish acted brutally toward the Native Americans under their control.

Spain conquered the major Native American empires in Central and South America. Then the Spaniards began to look at other parts of the Americas.

 CAUSES AND EFFECTS Describe the impact Europeans had on native societies.

Illinois Learning Standards *Review*

 ONLINE QUIZ
For test practice, go to
Interactive Review @ ClassZone.com

TERMS & NAMES

1. Explain the importance of

- *conquistador*
- mercantilism
- Hernando Cortés
- Amerigo Vespucci
- Christopher Columbus
- Francisco Pizarro
- Treaty of Tordesillas

USING YOUR READING NOTES

2. Sequence Complete the diagram you started at the beginning of this section.

Spain Claims an Empire

1492   1542

KEY IDEAS

3. Why did Europeans set their sights on reaching Asia?

4. Why did Spain succeed in conquering so much of the Americas?

CRITICAL THINKING

5. Evaluate How effective was the Treaty of Tordesillas?

6. Summarize What factors enabled the Spanish to conquer the Aztecs?

7. Connect *to* Today How are Spanish and Native American traditions present in North American culture today?

8. Writing Journal Imagine you are a sailor on Columbus' first voyage. Write a journal entry about reaching Hispaniola.

▶ Key Ideas

BEFORE, YOU LEARNED

Following Columbus' voyages, the Spanish conquered the Native American empires of the Aztecs and the Inca.

NOW YOU WILL LEARN

Competition for the riches of the Americas led to tension and conflict among European powers.

▶ Vocabulary

TERMS & NAMES

Henry Hudson English explorer who sailed for the Dutch and landed at the coast of present-day New York

John Cabot Italian sailor who sailed for the English and is believed to have landed in Newfoundland, Canada

Giovanni da Verrazzano Italian sailor who sailed for the French with hopes of finding an all-water route to Asia

Jacques Cartier French sailor who sailed up the St. Lawrence River to present-day Montreal

Spanish Armada large fleet of ships sent to invade England and restore Catholicism

Samuel de Champlain founder of fur-trading post at Quebec

New France first permanent French colony in North America

New Netherland first permanent Dutch colony in North America

BACKGROUND VOCABULARY

galleon sailing ship

Visual Vocabulary Spanish Armada

▶ Reading Strategy

Re-create the diagram shown at right. As you read and respond to the **KEY QUESTIONS**, use the diagram to record important events in this section.

 See Skillbuilder Handbook, page R6.

CATEGORIES

England	Sent Cabot to find a western route across the Atlantic (1497)
France	Founded Fort Caroline (1564)
Netherlands	
Spain	

 GRAPHIC ORGANIZERS
Go to **Interactive Review** @ ClassZone.com

SECTION 2

European Competition in North America

16.C.3a Describe economic motivations that attracted Europeans and others to the Americas, 1500–1750.
17.D.3a Explain how and why spatial patterns of settlement change over time.

One European's Story

In 1609, the Englishman **Henry Hudson** set sail from Europe. He sailed under the Dutch flag and hoped to find a route to China. Arriving at the coast of present-day New York, he sailed up the river that now bears his name. In his journal, Hudson described what he saw.

PRIMARY SOURCE

❝ The land is the finest for cultivation that I ever in my life set foot upon, and it also abounds in trees . . . . These natives are a very good people; for when they saw that I would not remain, they supposed that I was afraid of their bows, taking their arrows, they broke them in pieces and threw them into the fire. ❞

—**Henry Hudson, quoted in *Discoverers of America***

Henry Hudson sailed into Hudson Bay, Canada, in 1610. The bay became the center of a thriving fur-trading region.

Hudson did not find a route to Asia, but continued to try. In 1610, while sailing for the English, his crew rebelled and set Hudson adrift in a small boat. Hudson, his son, and seven others were never heard from again.

The Race to Explore North America

▼ **KEY QUESTION** What drew European explorers to North America?

Dazzled by Spain's success, other European nations hoped to enjoy the riches of the Americas. As England and France searched for a Northwest passage, Spanish explorers sought a Native American civilization in North America as rich as the ones they had discovered in South and Central America.

Hudson's Explorations

Hudson Bay · NORTH AMERICA · EUROPE · 1610 · 1609 · ATLANTIC OCEAN

Seeking a Quick Route to Wealth Hudson's voyages showed that some European countries hoped to find a westward route to Asia as late as the 1600s. While Spain was taking control of the Americas, other Europeans were sending out expeditions to find a hoped-for Northwest Passage, or a water route through North America to Asia.

One of the first explorers to chart a northern route across the Atlantic in search of Asia was the Italian sailor **John Cabot**. In 1497, Cabot crossed the Atlantic Ocean to explore for the English. He landed in the area of Newfoundland, Canada. He was certain that he had reached Asia and claimed the land for England. The next year he set sail once more, hoping to reach Japan. He was never seen again. Even so, his voyages were the basis for future English colonies along North America's Atlantic shore.

In 1524, another Italian, **Giovanni da Verrazzano**, set out under the French flag to find an all-water route to Asia. He explored the Atlantic coastline of North America, but there was no such passage to be found.

France tried again between 1534 and 1536 with the voyages of explorer **Jacques Cartier** (ZHAHK•kahr•TYAY). Cartier traveled up the St. Lawrence River to the site of present-day Montreal, but rapids blocked the way and ended his search. Cartier returned to North America in 1541. But French settlements were not seriously attempted again until 1603.

Spain Responds to Competition French and English claims to North America angered Spain, which had claimed the land under the Treaty of Tordesillas. Other tensions between Spain, England, and France came from religious conflicts in Europe. These conflicts led to fighting in the Americas.

The Spaniards hoped to collect treasures from North America as they had from Mexico and Peru. Spanish explorers began to survey the North American mainland. They heard Native American stories about cities of gold.

In 1528, *conquistador* Cabeza de Vaca was shipwrecked off the west coast of Florida. He was the first European to explore the continent from Florida to Arizona. Between 1539 and 1540, many other Spaniards set out to find gold. Vázquez de Coronado, for example, explored the southwest, and Hernando de Soto traveled throughout the southeast. In addition, Rodríguez Cabrillo sailed up the California coast. All failed to find cities of gold.

Florida became one of the battlegrounds between the Spanish and the French. In 1564, a group of French Protestants founded a colony called Fort Caroline. Before long, Spanish troops arrived in the area. The Spaniards built a fort, St. Augustine, nearby. Then they massacred the French settlers.

Spain and England Clash Religious differences and English piracies against Spanish trade also led to conflict. In 1558, Queen Elizabeth I, a Protestant, came to the English throne. Elizabeth fought to defend England and to challenge Catholic Spain's power at sea. Daring English sailors, known as sea dogs, used small ships to attack the bulky Spanish sailing ships—called **galleons**—that brought gold and silver from the Americas.

This colorful portrait is believed to be the work of artist George Gower. Completed around 1588, the painting is of Queen Elizabeth I of England and is commonly known as the *"Armada Portrait."*

The portrait pays tribute to the power and wealth of the popular queen. She is shown basking in the glory of England's naval victory over Spain. The English navy is framed on the left and the Spanish Armada, battling high seas in the English Channel, is on the right.

CRITICAL VIEWING Why do you think the queen's right hand rests upon a globe?

In 1577, Sir Francis Drake, a famous sea dog, began a three-year voyage around the world. Drake and his men were the first Englishmen to sail around the world. They raided Spanish ports in South America. In the summer of 1588, the Spanish king sent a large fleet of 130 sailing ships—called the **Spanish Armada**—to conquer England and restore Catholicism.

England Defeats Spain The English and Spanish navies met in the English Channel, which separates England from the European continent. In their smaller but faster craft, the English darted among the Spanish warships, firing deadly rounds with their cannons. The Spanish were forced to retreat. But Spain remained strong. It quickly rebuilt its navy and kept its large colonial empire. But Spain would never again be as powerful as it was in 1588.

The English victory over Spain had two important effects. First, England remained Protestant and proved it could defend itself. Second, the world saw that Spain could be beaten.

English settlers were already coming to America. In addition, by 1600, England and France were chief rivals among many claims for Newfoundland. Even so, England took a cautious approach to overseas expansion. The government did not provide money to start colonies, leaving funding for colonies to private citizens. As a result, England did not establish a successful colony in America until after 1600.

▲ **SUMMARIZE** Explain what drew European explorers to North America.

Quebec
1608

St. Lawrence R.

NEW FRANCE

Montreal
1642

Port Royal
1605

Boston 1630

NEW NETHERLANDS

New Amsterdam 1625

NEW SWEDEN

Great Lakes

Missouri

Mississippi

R.

Ohio R.

R.

ROCKY MOUNTAINS

APPALACHIAN MOUNTAINS

Santa Fe
1609

Rio Grande

St. Augustine
1565

**ATLANTIC
OCEAN**

40°N

30°N

60°W

20°N

**VICEROYALTY OF
NEW SPAIN**

Gulf of Mexico

Havana
1515

Cuba

Hispaniola

*Puerto
Rico*

Dominica

80°W

70°W

90°W

British
Dutch
French
Spanish
Swedish

0   250   500 miles
0   250   500 kilometers

Connect Geography & History

1. **Region** Which nation settled the largest geographic region?

2. **Draw Conclusions** Compare this map to the map on page 30. Where did the European nations tend to start settlements?

The French and Dutch Establish Colonies

▼ **KEY QUESTION** How did the French and Dutch profit from the Americas?

France and the Netherlands were also looking for ways to gain wealth through exploration and colonization. At first, their goal in the Americas was to find the Northwest Passage to Asia. When that search failed, they began to focus on the resources of North America itself as a possible source of new wealth and territory.

New France is Founded The French explorer **Samuel de Champlain** (sham•PLAYN) explored the St. Lawrence River. In 1608, he founded a fur-trading post at Quebec, now a major eastern Canadian city. This post became the first permanent French settlement in Canada. Champlain's activities opened a rich fur trade with local Native Americans.

After about 50 years, **New France**, as the colony was called, began to thrive. From the start, New France differed from the British colonies. Typical French colonists included fur traders and Catholic priests who wanted to convert Native Americans.

The French colonists also developed friendlier relations with Native Americans than did the British. They relied on Native Americans to do most of the animal trapping and then traded with them for the furs, which were in great demand in Europe. This trade relationship led to several military alliances. As early as 1609, for example, the Algonquin and other Native American groups used Champlain's help to defeat their traditional enemies, the Mohawk Iroquois.

The Dutch Establish New Netherland Sometime later, the Dutch built a colony called **New Netherland.** It was located along the Hudson River in present-day New York. It was a welcoming place for people of all religions, which helped attract a diverse, or varied, population. After Hudson's voyage up the river in 1609, the Dutch built Fort Nassau in 1614, near the site of the modern city of Albany, New York.

The Dutch also founded the town of New Amsterdam on Manhattan Island. Soon after, in 1626, they purchased Manhattan Island from Native Americans. New Netherland was soon thriving from the fur trade with Native Americans. (Present-day New York City is located where the Dutch settlement of New Amsterdam was founded.) These early French and Dutch colonies, however, were small compared to the large empire Spain was building in the Americas.

Connecting History

Diversity & Community
To attract settlers, the Dutch of New Netherland opened their colony to people of all backgrounds, including free Africans. From these actions resulted communities of extraordinary diversity and vitality.

RECOGNIZE EFFECTS Explain how the French and Dutch were able to profit from their settlements in North America.

Illinois Learning Standards *Review*

ONLINE QUIZ
For test practice, go to
Interactive Review @ ClassZone.com

TERMS & NAMES
1. Explain the importance of
   - Henry Hudson
   - John Cabot
   - Giovanni da Verrazzano
   - Jacques Cartier
   - Spanish Armada
   - Samuel de Champlain
   - New France
   - New Netherland

USING YOUR READING NOTES
2. **Categories** Complete the diagram to show the most important events of this section.

England	Sent Cabot to find a western route across the Atlantic (1497)
France	Founded Fort Caroline (1564)
Netherlands	
Spain	

KEY IDEAS
3. What were the English, French, and Dutch searching for in their early voyages of exploration?
4. Where did the French and Dutch set up their first American colonies?

CRITICAL THINKING
5. **Cause and Effect** What impact did the English defeat of the Spanish Armada have on England's overseas goals?
6. **Compare and Contrast** How did the French and British colonies in North America differ?
7. **Compare and Contrast** How did the Dutch colony of New Netherland differ from colonies established by Spain?
8. **Connect** *to* **Today** Spanish and Portuguese colonists did not practice freedom of religion. Why is this freedom protected by American law?
9. **Technology** Web Page Research the life of one of the explorers discussed in this section. Sketch a Web page about that person.

▶ Key Ideas

BEFORE, YOU LEARNED
European powers faced conflict and tension as they competed for riches in North America.

NOW YOU WILL LEARN
Native Americans' lives were transformed as Spain grew rich from its new empire.

▶ Vocabulary

TERMS & NAMES

encomienda (en•koh•mee•YEN•duh) grant of Native American slave labor

hacienda (HAH•see•YEN•duh) large farm or estate

mission settlement created by the Spanish church in order to convert Native Americans to Christianity

Bartolomé de Las Casas Spaniard who fought for Native American rights

Columbian Exchange transfer of plants, animals and diseases between the Western and Eastern hemispheres

BACKGROUND VOCABULARY

plantation large farm that raises cash crops

export to send abroad for trade or sale

Visual Vocabulary Mission

▶ Reading Strategy

Re-create the diagram shown at right. As you read and respond to the **KEY QUESTIONS**, use the diagram to note important details that support the main idea of this section. Add ovals as needed.

 See Skillbuilder Handbook, page R4.

MAIN IDEAS AND DETAILS

Spanish Colonies

Locations

Governance

GRAPHIC ORGANIZERS
Go to **Interactive Review** @ ClassZone.com

The Spanish and Native Americans

17.C.3b Explain how patterns of resources are used throughout the world.
17.C.3c Analyze how human process influence settlement patterns including migration and population growth.

One American's Story

Guamán Poma de Ayala, a Peruvian Native American, wrote to King Philip III of Spain in the early 1600s. He described the treatment of Native Americans at the hands of the Spanish.

PRIMARY SOURCE

❝ It is their [the Spanish] practice to collect Indians into groups and send them to forced labor without wages, while they themselves receive the payment. ❞

— **Guamán Poma, Letter to a King**

In his letter, Poma de Ayala asked the king to help the Native Americans and uphold the rule of law in Peru. If the king actually read the letter, it made no difference. Spanish colonists continued to mistreat Native Americans as the Spanish Empire expanded in the Americas.

A Spanish missionary forces a Native American woman to work at a loom.

Spanish Colonies in the Americas

🔻 **KEY QUESTION** How did Spain draw wealth from its new lands?

The Spanish Empire grew rapidly, despite competition from other European countries. Eventually, Spain controlled much of the Americas. Spain took several steps to establish an effective colonial government. It also transformed the landscape and reorganized societies throughout the Americas.

Organizing the Empire First, Spain divided its American empire into two provinces called New Spain and Peru. Each province was called a viceroyalty. The top official of each viceroyalty, called the viceroy, ruled in the king's name.

The Spanish also built new roads to transport people and goods across the empire. These roads stretched outward from the capitals at Mexico City and Lima. The roads helped Spain control the colonies by allowing soldiers to

European Exploration of the Americas **41**

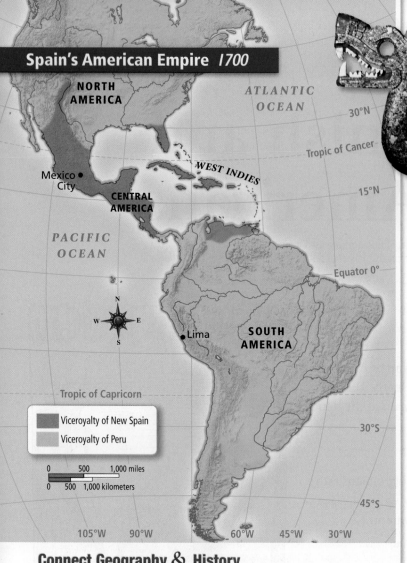

Spain's American Empire *1700*

NORTH AMERICA

ATLANTIC OCEAN

30°N

Tropic of Cancer

Mexico City •

WEST INDIES

15°N

CENTRAL AMERICA

PACIFIC OCEAN

Equator 0°

Lima •

SOUTH AMERICA

Tropic of Capricorn

Viceroyalty of New Spain

Viceroyalty of Peru

0   500   1,000 miles
0   500   1,000 kilometers

30°S

45°S

105°W   90°W   60°W   45°W   30°W

Aztec two-headed snake

Connect Geography & History

1. **Location** Which viceroyalty included the West Indies?
2. **Draw Conclusions** What advantage did Spain have by dividing its empire into two provinces?

move quickly from place to place. Roads also improved the Spanish economy because materials, such as gold and silver, could be transported efficiently to the coast and then to Spain.

The Spaniards made sure that people with Spanish backgrounds held power in the colonies. Spanish-born colonists such as Cortés made up the top layer of colonial society. Just below the Spanish were the Creoles—people of Spanish descent who were born in the colonies. The next step down the social order were the *mestizos*. *Mestizos* are people of mixed Spanish and Native American ancestry. The people with the least power and fewest rights were Native Americans and enslaved Africans.

Making the Colonies Productive Spanish colonists received ***encomiendas*** as a way of collecting tribute from the conquered peoples. An *encomienda* was a grant of forced Native American labor. The *encomienda* system helped the Spanish colonies become more productive.

The Spanish rulers also created large estates, called ***haciendas***, to provide food for the colony. *Haciendas* usually became large farms where Native Americans worked to grow cash crops, such as coffee and cotton. The *encomienda* and *hacienda* systems put much of the power and land in the hands of a few people. The Spanish also forced Native Americans to work on **plantations**, large farms that raised cash crops. These crops were usually **exported**, or sent to Europe. The most important crop was sugar.

Although sugar was in great demand in Europe, there was not much land there to grow it. The demand led to the development of sugar plantations in the Americas. On his second voyage to the Americas, in 1493, Columbus brought sugar cane to Hispaniola, one of the Caribbean islands he had landed on in 1492. He found ideal conditions for sugar production. Spanish planters expanded operations to the nearby islands that Spain colonized.

Sugar plantations required many workers, so the Spanish planters turned to native peoples, such as the Taino. Through *encomiendas*, the Spaniards forced thousands of Taino to work in the fields. The plantations thrived, but many of the Taino suffered and died.

▲ **SUMMARIZE** Explain how the Spanish got wealthy from their new lands.

The Church in the Spanish Colonies

▼ **KEY QUESTION** How did the Church contribute to colonization?

The Spanish monarchs did not intend for the *conquistadores* to destroy the native populations of the Americas. In fact, the Spanish crown wanted Native Americans to become tax-paying subjects and adopt Spanish culture. The Catholic Church played an important role in this process.

The Church Sets Up Missions The Spanish church leaders were key players in Spanish colonial society. In places like New Mexico and California, the Church built **missions**, settlements that included a church, a town, and farmlands. The goal of the missions was to convert Native Americans to Christianity. The missions also increased Spanish control over the land.

Missions helped the Native Americans to create a better supply of food. They also offered Native Americans protection against enemies. Many Native Americans learned how to read and write in the missions. Others developed skills such as carpentry and metalworking.

Over time, however, many Native Americans grew increasingly unhappy. The missionaries often worked them as if they were slaves. The missionaries also tried to replace Native American religions and traditions. As a result, some Native Americans ran away, while others rebelled. Some destroyed churches and killed missionaries.

Las Casas Condemns Abuse Most Spaniards treated the Native Americans as little more than beasts of burden. Fray Toribio de Benavente, a Catholic missionary, wrote that the Spanish "do nothing but command. They are the drones who suck the honey which is made by the poor bees, the Indians."

Not all Spaniards approved of this treatment. One man in particular fought for better treatment of Native Americans. His name was **Bartolomé de Las Casas**. Las Casas had come to Hispaniola in 1502 and taken part in the conquest of Cuba a decade later. For his part in the conquest, he received an *encomienda*. Las Casas was also a Catholic priest, however, and he soon faced a moral dilemma: How can a person serve God and enslave Native Americans at the same time?

In 1514, Las Casas gave up his claim to the Native Americans who worked for him. For the next 50 years, he fought for Native Americans, earning the title "Protector of the Indians."

Because of his efforts, the Spanish king issued the New Laws in 1542. These laws ordered the gradual freeing of all enslaved Native Americans.

Conquistador armor

Holders of *encomiendas* who were found guilty of mistreating Native Americans had their *encomiendas* taken away from them. However, Spanish colonists strongly protested against the New Laws, and the king eventually gave in and reversed many of them.

▲ **DRAW CONCLUSIONS** Explain how the church played a part in Spanish colonization.

The Columbian Exchange

▼ **KEY QUESTION** What were the effects of the Columbian Exchange?

The arrival of the Spanish in the Americas brought more than a clash of peoples and cultures. It also brought a movement of plants, animals, and diseases between the Eastern and Western hemispheres. This movement of living things between hemispheres is called the **Columbian Exchange**.

Trade Brings Disease One result of the Columbian Exchange was the transfer of germs from Europe to the Americas. Before the Europeans arrived, Native American farmland stretched all along the eastern seaboard of what is now the United States. Many of the communities that farmed these lands were wiped out by European diseases before the settlers began arriving in large numbers. The Native Americans had no immunity to the germs that caused such diseases as smallpox, measles, and influenza.

Exact numbers are unknown, but historians estimate that diseases brought by Europeans killed more than 20 million Native Americans in Mexico in the first century after conquest. The population of Native Americans in Central

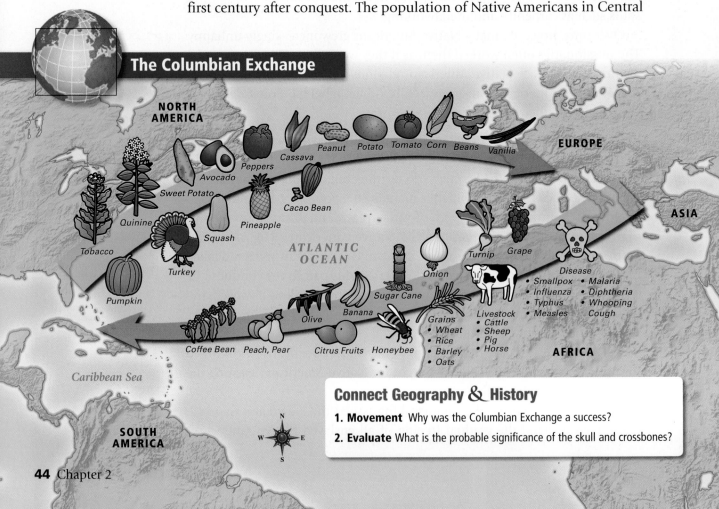

The Columbian Exchange

NORTH AMERICA
EUROPE
ASIA
AFRICA
SOUTH AMERICA

Peanut · Potato · Tomato · Corn · Beans · Vanilla
Cassava
Peppers
Avocado
Sweet Potato
Cacao Bean
Quinine
Pineapple
Squash
Tobacco
Turkey
Pumpkin
ATLANTIC OCEAN
Coffee Bean · Peach, Pear · Citrus Fruits · Honeybee · Olive · Banana · Sugar Cane · Onion · Turnip · Grape
Caribbean Sea

Disease
· Smallpox · Malaria
· Influenza · Diphtheria
· Typhus · Whooping
· Measles   Cough

Livestock
· Cattle
· Sheep
· Pig
· Horse

Grains
· Wheat
· Rice
· Barley
· Oats

Connect Geography & History

1. Movement Why was the Columbian Exchange a success?

2. Evaluate What is the probable significance of the skull and crossbones?

America may have decreased by 90 to 95 percent between the years 1519 and 1619. The result was similar in Peru and other parts of the Americas. Bernardino de Sahagún, a Spanish missionary in Mexico, described the effects of smallpox on the Aztecs: "Very many died of it. . . . They could not move: they could not stir. . . . And if they stirred, much did they cry out. Great was its destruction."

Positive Effects of the Exchange Other effects of the Columbian Exchange were more positive. The Spanish brought many plants and animals to the Americas. European livestock—cattle, pigs, and horses—all thrived in the Americas. Crops from the Eastern Hemisphere, such as grapes, onions, and wheat, also thrived in the Western Hemisphere.

The Columbian Exchange benefited Europe, too. Many American crops became part of the European diet. Two that had a huge impact were potatoes and corn. Potatoes, for example, became an important food in Ireland, Russia, and other parts of Europe. Without potatoes, Europe's population might not have grown as rapidly as it did.

By mixing the products of two hemispheres, the Columbian Exchange brought the world closer together. Of course, people were also moving from one hemisphere to the other, blending their cultures in the process.

 RECOGNIZE EFFECTS Explain the effect of the Columbian Exchange on the Eastern and Western hemispheres.

Illinois Learning Standards *Review*

ONLINE QUIZ
For test practice, go to
Interactive Review @ ClassZone.com

TERMS & NAMES

1. Explain the importance of

- *encomienda*
- *hacienda*
- mission
- Bartolomé de Las Casas
- Columbian Exchange

USING YOUR READING NOTES

2. Main Ideas and Details Complete the diagram you started at the beginning of this section.

KEY IDEAS

3. How did Spain establish a new colonial government in the Americas?

4. How did the Columbian Exchange connect the Eastern and Western hemispheres?

CRITICAL THINKING

5. Analyze Motives Why do you think the Spaniards chose to utilize Native Americans in the new colonies?

6. Draw Conclusions Over time, do you think the Catholic Church's missions were more helpful or harmful to the Native Americans? Explain.

7. Evaluate How did the missions transform the Native American way of life?

8. **Connect** *to* **Today** How is the Columbian Exchange put into effect today?

9. **Art** **Collage** Make a collage that illustrates the plants and animals involved in the Columbian Exchange.

The Iroquois Great Law of Peace

SETTING THE STAGE In the late 1500s the five nations of the Iroquois League created a constitution, called the Great Law of Peace, that had 117 laws and customs. These laws governed all aspects of life and war. In this excerpt, Deganawida, who persuaded the warriors to make peace, introduces the Great Law by describing a tree that symbolizes the permanence and stability of the league. The league brought a long period of peace to the Iroquois.

I am Deganawida and with the Five Nations' Confederate **Lords**[1] I plant the Tree of Great Peace. I plant it in your territory, **Adodarhoh**,[2] and the Onondaga Nation, in the territory of you who are Firekeepers.

I name the tree the Tree of the Great Long Leaves. Under the shade of this Tree of the Great Peace we spread the soft white feathery down of the globe thistle as seats for you, Adodarhoh, and your cousin Lords.

We place you upon those seats, spread soft with the feathery down of the globe thistle, there beneath the shade of the spreading branches of the Tree of Peace. There shall you sit and watch the Council Fire of the **Confederacy of the Five Nations**,[3] and all the affairs of the Five Nations shall be transacted at this place before you, Adodarhoh, and your cousin Lords, by the Confederate Lords of the Five Nations.

Roots have spread out from the Tree of the Great Peace, one to the north, one to the east, one to the south, and one to the west. The name of these roots is The Great White Roots and their nature is Peace and Strength.

If any man or any nation outside the Five Nations shall obey the laws of the Great Peace and make known their disposition to the Lords of the Confederacy, they may trace the Roots to the Tree and if their minds are clean and they are obedient and promise to obey the wishes of the Confederate Council, they shall be welcomed to take shelter beneath the Tree of the Long Leaves.

----

1. **Lords:** chiefs.
2. **Adodarhoh:** the name of the office of the Onondaga chief.
3. **Confederacy of the Five Nations:** the Iroquois League.

The Council Fire

The council fire of the Iroquois League was kept burning for about 200 years.

1. What do you think it would mean if the council fire were allowed to die?

The Great White Roots

The roots of a tree help to anchor it in the ground, and they draw water and food from the soil.

2. Why might Deganawida say the nature of the roots is "Peace and Strength"?

A Relation of Maryland

SETTING THE STAGE A skirmish between the Susquehannock and Wiccomiss tribes of Maryland in 1633 resulted in the death of three Englishmen. Leonard Calvert, the governor of Maryland, ordered that any Indian who killed an Englishman should turn himself in for punishment under English law. The Wiccomiss sent a representative to the governor with an apology.

The Susquehannock

The Susquehannock fought for territory against small tribes like the Wiccomiss, the Patuxent, and the Conoy but had good relations with the English until 1642.

3. How might England's relationship with the Susquehannock have influenced the governor's decision about the Wiccomiss?

"I am a native of Patuxent . . . I married a wife amongst the Wiccomisses, where I have lived ever since, and they have sent me to tell you, that they are sorry for the harm, which was lately done by some of their people, to the English at Monaponson; and hope you will not make the rash act of a few young men (which was done **in heat**[1]) a quarrel to their nation, who desire to live in peace and love with you, and are ready to make satisfaction for the injury . . . But withall, they desire you not to think that they do this for fear, for they have wars with the Susquehannocks, who have by a surprise, lately killed many of their men, . . . yet their desire was to have peace with the English."

The governor returned answer to the Wiccomiss; "Since you acknowledge the injury, and are sorry for it, and only desire to know what I expect for satisfaction; I tell you I expect that those men, who have done this outrage, should be delivered unto me, to do with them as I shall think fit . . .

The Wiccomiss after a little pause, replied; "It is the manner amongst us Indians, that if any such like accident happen, we do redeem the life of a man that is so slain, with a 100–arm's length of roanoke . . . and since that you are here strangers, and come into our country, you should rather conform yourselves to the customs of our country, than impose yours upon us."

Roanoke

Roanoke was a kind of bead that the Wiccomiss used as money.

4. Do you think the payment of money was a fair price for the accidental death of the Englishmen?

----

1. in heat: from anger, without thought

DOCUMENT-BASED QUESTIONS

Short-Answer

1. In what territory was the Tree of the Great Peace planted?

2. How much would the Wiccomiss pay the governor for the death of the Englishmen?

Extended-Answer

3. How do these readings reveal that government was important to both the Iroquois League and the Wiccomiss? What values do the two groups share?

▶ Key Ideas

BEFORE, YOU LEARNED

As the Spanish Empire expanded in the Americas, Native Americans' lives were transformed.

NOW YOU WILL LEARN

Slavery was introduced on a large scale to provide cheap labor for the colonies.

▶ Vocabulary

TERMS & NAMES

slavery practice of one person being owned by another

middle passage middle leg of the triangular trade route that brought captured Africans to the Americas to serve as slaves

slave codes law passed to regulate the treatment of slaves

racism belief that some people are inferior because of their race

BACKGROUND VOCABULARY

maroon runaway or fugitive slave

Visual Vocabulary Middle Passage

▶ Reading Strategy

Re-create the diagram shown at right. As you read and respond to the **KEY QUESTIONS**, use the diagram to compare the experiences of Native Americans and Africans under slavery.

 See Skillbuilder Handbook, page R8.

COMPARE AND CONTRAST

Native Americans — Both — Africans

GRAPHIC ORGANIZERS
Go to **Interactive Review** @ ClassZone.com

Beginnings of Slavery in the Americas

16.C.3a Describe economic motivations that attracted Europeans and others to the Americas, 1500–1750.
17.C.3c Analyze how human process influence settlement patterns including migration and population growth.

One American's Story

In 1546, Diego de Campo was the leader of 7,000 **maroons**, or runaway slaves, on the island of Hispaniola. There were only about 1,000 European men on the island. The Spanish planters greatly feared de Campo. When the Spanish attacked the maroons, de Campo and his followers defeated the Spanish.

Eventually the Spaniards captured de Campo. He offered to lead the fight against the maroons. The Spanish accepted the offer. With de Campo's help, the Spanish defeated the maroons, and slavery in Hispaniola grew. In this section you will read how slave labor expanded in the Americas.

Slavery Takes Hold in the Colonies

▼ **KEY QUESTION** How did slavery bring wealth to Europeans but suffering to millions of Africans and Native Americans?

By the 1600s, **slavery**, the practice of one person being owned by another, was firmly established in the Americas. But slavery was not new. It was a very ancient institution.

Maroons often joined Native American groups.

Origins of American Slavery In some societies, slaves were mainly domestic servants in wealthy households. Some labored in mines and fields. People were enslaved when they were captured in battle or sold to pay off debts. Some slaves were treated with some respect. Some were allowed to marry and own property. The children of some slaves were allowed to go free.

Slavery began to change with the rise of sugar plantations. To work these plantations, Europeans had used slaves in southern Europe since the 1100s. Then, in the 1400s and 1500s, Portugal and Spain set up sugar plantations on islands in the eastern Atlantic. To work these plantations, they used African slaves bought from traders in Africa.

When the Spanish and Portuguese founded their colonies in the Americas, they brought the plantation system with them. At first they tried to enslave Native Americans to work in the fields and mines. But the Native Americans quickly died from overwork and disease. In some cases, they rebelled with the help of local allies.

The Spaniards then looked to other sources of slave labor, including Spanish slaves, black Christian slaves, and Asian slaves. But there was not enough of any of these groups to meet demand.

The Slave Trade The Spanish and Portuguese enslaved Africans to provide plantation labor. Africans proved to be their best resource. They enslaved Africans for four basic reasons.

- Africans were immune to most European diseases.
- Africans had no friends or family in the Americas to help them resist or escape enslavement.
- Enslaved Africans provided a permanent source of cheap labor. Even their children could be held in bondage.
- Many Africans had worked on farms in their native lands.

Over time, the colonies came to depend on slave labor. European slave traders ran the shipment of Africans to the Americas. On the coast of West Africa, local kings captured inland Africans. The kings then traded these captives for European goods, such as textiles, ironware, wine, and guns. This trade made the coastal kingdoms rich while weakening inland African societies. Before the slave trade ended in the late 1800s, between 12 and 15 million Africans had been enslaved and shipped to the Western Hemisphere. Of these, perhaps two million died during the voyage.

The Middle Passage The voyage from Africa to the Americas was called the **middle passage** because it was the middle leg of the triangular trade. The triangular trade refers to the movement of trade ships between Europe, Africa, and the Americas.

Olaudah Equiano (oh•LOW•duh•ehk•wee•AHN•oh) was one of those captured Africans. He made the journey in the 1700s. He was about 11 years old when he was taken from his home and sold into slavery. Later, after he bought his freedom, he wrote about the beginning of the middle passage.

PRIMARY SOURCE

❝ The first object which saluted my eyes when I arrived on the coast, was the sea, and a slave ship . . . waiting for its cargo. These filled me with astonishment, which was soon converted into terror, when I was carried on board. ❞

—Olaudah Equiano, quoted in *Great Slave Narratives*

Olaudah Equiano was brought to the West Indies from West Africa in the 1700s.

Equiano saw a row of men shackled in chains. He also saw a large boiling kettle. He feared that he was going to be cooked and eaten "by those white men with horrible looks, red faces, and long hair."

The scene on the slave deck below was even worse. Several hundred slaves were crammed into a space so small that there was not even enough room to stand up. Foul smells and disease, along with the shrieks and groans of the dying, made the middle passage a terrifying experience.

Many enslaved Africans died from disease or from cruel treatment at the hands of slave traders. Many others committed suicide by plunging into the ocean. It is believed that between 15 and 20 percent of the Africans aboard each slave ship perished during the brutal trip. The captives who did not die faced new horrors in the Americas.

▲ **CAUSES AND EFFECTS** Discuss the results of the African slave trade.

Slavery in the Americas

▼ **KEY QUESTION** What were the long-term effects of slavery in the Americas?

Once the enslaved Africans arrived in the colonies, they were sold at auction. Some worked as house servants. Most were forced to do hard labor in *haciendas* or mines. They were fed and housed poorly.

CONNECT ➤ *to the Essential Question*

How did Europeans transform life in the Americas?

CAUSES	EFFECTS
Europeans explore	Expansion of colonial empires, destruction of Aztec and Inca Empires; growth of wealth and power
establish colonies	Spread of disease; spread of Christianity; brutal oppression of conquered peoples; establishment of *encomiendas, haciendas,* and missions
compete for colonies	Treaty of Tordesillas (1494); establishment of New France and New Netherland; defeat of Spanish Armada; growth of English colonies
introduced the Columbian Exchange	**Brought**—to Americas: disease; livestock, grains, onions, citrus fruits, olives, grapes, bananas, sugar cane **Taken**—to Eastern Hemisphere: tobacco, squash, turkey, peppers, cocoa, peanuts, potatoes, corn
introduced slavery	Provides labor in mines and plantations; slave trade expands quickly between Africa and the Americas; millions of captives die; racism grows

CRITICAL THINKING Make Inferences What were the effects of European colonization on the daily lives of native peoples?

One American's Story

In 1546, Diego de Campo was the leader of 7,000 **maroons**, or runaway slaves, on the island of Hispaniola. There were only about 1,000 European men on the island. The Spanish planters greatly feared de Campo. When the Spanish attacked the maroons, de Campo and his followers defeated the Spanish.

Eventually the Spaniards captured de Campo. He offered to lead the fight against the maroons. The Spanish accepted the offer. With de Campo's help, the Spanish defeated the maroons, and slavery in Hispaniola grew. In this section you will read how slave labor expanded in the Americas.

Slavery Takes Hold in the Colonies

 KEY QUESTION How did slavery bring wealth to Europeans but suffering to millions of Africans and Native Americans?

By the 1600s, **slavery**, the practice of one person being owned by another, was firmly established in the Americas. But slavery was not new. It was a very ancient institution.

Origins of American Slavery In some societies, slaves were mainly domestic servants in wealthy households. Some labored in mines and fields. People were enslaved when they were captured in battle or sold to pay off debts. Some slaves were treated with some respect. Some were allowed to marry and own property. The children of some slaves were allowed to go free.

Slavery began to change with the rise of sugar plantations. To work these plantations, Europeans had used slaves in southern Europe since the 1100s.

 Illinois Learning Standards *Review*

ONLINE QUIZ
For test practice, go to
Interactive Review @ ClassZone.com

TERMS & NAMES

1. Explain the significance of
   - slavery
   - middle passage
   - slave codes
   - racism

USING YOUR READING NOTES

2. **Compare and Contrast** Complete the diagram you started at the beginning of this section.

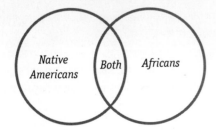

KEY IDEAS

3. Why did Europeans bring Africans to the Americas?

4. What are three examples of bad conditions faced by enslaved Africans?

CRITICAL THINKING

5. **Point of View** Why do you think the slave traders were so cruel to the slaves they transported across the ocean?

6. **Connect Economics & History** How did the enslaved Africans contribute to the Columbian Exchange?

7. **Connect** *to* **Today** What are some of the long-term effects of slavery in the Americas today?

8. **Writing** **Report** Research the contributions of Olaudah Equiano to our knowledge of slavery.

Chapter Summary

1 Key Idea
After Columbus' voyages, the Spanish quickly conquered the Native American empires of the Aztecs and the Inca.

2 Key Idea
Competition for the riches of the Americas led to tension and conflict among European powers.

3 Key Idea
Native Americans' lives were transformed as Spain grew rich from its new empire.

4 Key Idea
Slavery was introduced on a large scale to provide cheap labor for the colonies.

For detailed Review and Study Notes go to **Interactive Review** @ ClassZone.com

Name Game

Use the Terms & Names list to complete each sentence online or on your own paper.

1. _____ led an army to conquer the Aztec empire.
   Hernando Cortés

2. _____ moved the Line of Demarcation to the west.

3. America is named after _____.

4. The large fleet of ships sent to restore Catholicism to England is called the _____.

5. _____ founded a fur trading post in Quebec.

6. _____ was a grant of Native American labor.

7. A large farm or estate is called a _____.

8. _____ earned the title of "Protector of the Indians."

9. For enslaved Africans, the voyage from Africa to the Americas is the _____.

10. _____ is a belief that some people are inferior because of their race.

A. Samuel de Champlain
B. Columbian Exchange
C. Treaty of Tordesillas
D. Bartolomé de Las Casas
E. plantations
F. *encomienda*
G. Jacques Cartier
H. Hernando Cortés
I. Amerigo Vespucci
J. racism
K. slavery
L. Francisco Pizarro
M. *hacienda*
N. middle passage
O. Spanish Armada

Activities

CROSSWORD PUZZLE

Complete the online crossword to show you know about European exploration of the Americas.

ACROSS
1. An instrument used to find latitude.

FLIPCARD

Use the online flipcards to quiz yourself on the terms and names introduced in this chapter

I landed in the Americas in 1492.

ANSWER:
Christopher Columbus

VOCABULARY

Explain the significance of each of the following.

1. Christopher Columbus
2. Columbian Exchange
3. Bartolomé de Las Casas
4. Henry Hudson
5. John Cabot
6. Spanish Armada
7. mercantilism
8. Treaty of Tordesillas
9. Amerigo Vespucci
10. Hernando Cortés
11. Francisco Pizarro
12. Jacques Cartier
13. Samuel de Champlain
14. Giovanni da Verrazzano

Explain how the terms and names in each group are related.

15. *encomienda, hacienda*
16. plantation, mission
17. middle passage, slavery
18. *conquistador*, missionary

KEY IDEAS

1 Spain Claims an Empire (pages 26–33)

19. Why did Europeans seek new trade routes to Asia?
20. Who conquered the Aztecs and Incas?
21. What are three reasons that explain Spain's success in building an empire in the Americas?

2 European Competition in North America (pages 34–39)

22. What was the Northwest Passage?
23. Why did the Spanish Armada attack England?
24. What did the French and Dutch colonists trade?

3 The Spanish and Native Americans (pages 40–45)

25. How did Spanish rule affect Native Americans?
26. How did the Columbian Exchange affect Europe?

4 Beginnings of Slavery in the Americas (pages 48–52)

27. Why did the Spanish and Portuguese use slave labor in their colonies?
28. How did the slave trade work?

CRITICAL THINKING

29. **Analyze Leadership** What leadership qualities helped the *conquistadors* and early explorers succeed in their efforts?

30. **Synthesize** Despite the competition from other nations, how did the Spanish Empire in the Americas grow so quickly?

31. **Causes & Effects** Create a chart to show the causes and effects of European exploration of the Americas.

Causes	Effects
national competition	*European colonies*
spread of Christianity	

32. **Compare and Contrast** How did France and the Netherlands differ in the way they set up colonies in North America?

33. **Recognize Bias and Propaganda** How did slavery influence racial attitudes among Europeans?

34. **Interpret Charts** Read the chart below. About how many slaves were imported to the Americas between 1493 and 1810?

Slaves Imported to the Americas *1451–1810*

Number of Slaves *(in millions)*

7
6
5
4
3
2
1
0

1451–1600   1601–1700   1701–1810
Years

Source: Philip D. Curtin, *The Atlantic Slave Trade*

DOCUMENT-BASED QUESTIONS

Part 1: Short Answer
Study each document carefully and answer the questions that follow.

DOCUMENT 1

1. This image illustrates the meeting of Montezuma and Cortés. What does the picture tell you about the meeting between the Spaniards and the Aztecs?

DOCUMENT 2

PRIMARY SOURCE

❝ On our arrival . . . Montezuma was awaiting our Captain [Cortés]. Taking him by the hand, the prince led him to . . . the hall where he was to lodge. . . . Montezuma had ready for him a very rich necklace, made of golden crabs, a marvellous piece of work, which he hung round Cortés' neck. His captains were greatly astonished at this sign of honour. ❞

—Bernal Díaz del Castillo,
from *The Conquest of New Spain*

2. What can you tell about Montezuma and the Spaniards from this passage?

Part 2: Essay

3. Using information from the documents, your answers to the questions in Part 1, and your knowledge of U.S. history, write an essay that discusses how the Spanish invaders betrayed the trust of the Aztecs and the Inca.

YOU BE THE HISTORIAN

35. **Evaluate** How did advances in shipbuilding and seamanship affect European exploration?

36. **Make Inferences** Why do you think it took France and the Netherlands so long to set up colonies in the Americas?

37. **Economics & History** What were some of the positive and negative effects of the Columbian Exchange?

38. **WHAT IF?** Suppose Spain did not choose to support Columbus in his expedition. How do you think this would have affected colonization?

39. **Citizenship** What kind of values did Las Casas demonstrate in his actions? How effective was he in improving his society?

40. **Connect to Today** How have advances in technology changed exploration?

Answer the

ESSENTIAL QUESTION

How did Europeans transform life in the Americas?

Written Response Write a two- to three-paragraph response to the Essential Question. Be sure to consider the key ideas of each section as well as the most significant factors that led to the European exploration of the Americas.

Response Rubric

A strong response will

• demonstrate an understanding of life in the Americas prior to European exploration
• provide analysis of European motives
• compare European and Native American values
• discuss economic, religious, and social changes brought out by European settlement

The English Colonies

1585–1763

Why It Matters Now

The American identity was initially shaped by the English, both as colonies developed and as tensions arose with British powers. Why England, and not other nations that sought wealth and influence in the new land? The answer lies in the traditions, values, and character of early English settlers, and in their determination to forge a new life in the colonies. Yet just as England established firm roots in early America, it also set the colonies on the path to the freedom and independence that we cherish today.

The history of every country begins
in the heart of a man or a woman.
—Willa Cather

The English Establish 13 Colonies

1585–1732

 ESSENTIAL QUESTION

How did the experience of the early colonists shape America's political and social ideals?

CONNECT ↻ Geography & History

What were the advantages and disadvantages of the location of the first English colonies?

Think about:

1 why these early settlements were not established directly on the coast

2 the poor, sandy soil of Roanoke Island

3 the sand bars and shallow waters that made it difficult for Spanish ships to attack the colonists

A replica of the *Mayflower*

1607 Jamestown founded.

1620 *Mayflower* arrives in **Plymouth**.

1630 Puritan settlers found the **Massachusetts** Bay Colony.

1585

The unsuccessful colony of **Roanoke** is founded in Virginia.

tobacco plant

1614 Virginia sends the first shipment of tobacco to England.

▼

Effect To meet consumer demand, tobacco plantations spread throughout the Chesapeake Bay.

L a n d s   o f   P o w h a t a n   p e o p l e

VIRGINIA

Jamestown

James River

York River

Werowocomoco

Chesapeake Bay

Albemarle Sound

76°W

Roanoke

ATLANTIC OCEAN

36°N

37°N

English settlement

Native American village

Scale varies across perspective view.

ATLANTIC OCEAN

SPANISH

William Penn meets with Native Americans.

1681 Pennsylvania is founded.

1732

British royal seal

1664 The English seize the Dutch colony of New Netherland and rename it New York.

▼

Effect English colonies now stretch from New England through the South.

James Oglethorpe founds Georgia.

Reading for Understanding

▶ Key Ideas

BEFORE, YOU LEARNED

European nations competed to explore the Americas, where they conquered native peoples and introduced slavery.

NOW YOU WILL LEARN

Of the three earliest English colonies in North America, only Jamestown managed to survive.

▶ Vocabulary

TERMS & NAMES

Sir Walter Raleigh (RAW•lee) founder of England's first American colony

mercantilism (MUR•kuhn•tee•LIHZ•uhm) economic system that European nations used to enrich their treasuries

Jamestown first permanent English settlement in North America

John Smith leader of the Jamestown colony

headright land grant given to one who could pay his or her way to the colonies

indentured servant one who worked for a set time without pay in exchange for a free passage to America

House of Burgesses the Virginia assembly, which was the first representative assembly in the American colonies

BACKGROUND VOCABULARY

joint-stock company company funded by a group of investors

investor person who puts money into a project to earn a profit

charter written contract giving the right to establish a colony

royal colony colony ruled by the king's appointed officials

▶ Reading Strategy

Re-create the diagram shown at right. As you read and respond to the **KEY QUESTIONS**, use the boxes to compare and contrast the benefits and risks of colonization.

 See Skillbuilder Handbook, page R8.

COMPARE AND CONTRAST

COLONIZATION

Benefits	Risks
wealth created for mother country	

 GRAPHIC ORGANIZERS
Go to **Interactive Review** @ ClassZone.com

Early Colonies Have Mixed Success

17.C.3a Explain how human activity is affected by geographic factors.
18.B.3a Analyze how individuals and groups interact with and within institutions (e.g., *educational, military*).

One American Story

In 1587 John White was the governor of the English colony at Roanoke, an island off North Carolina. It was here that White's daughter Eleanor gave birth to Virginia Dare—the first English child born in North America.

White went back to England and did not see Roanoke again until 1590. He was shocked by what he found on his return.

PRIMARY SOURCE

❝ We found the houses taken down, and the place very strongly enclosed with a high [fence] of great trees, and one of the chief trees. . . had bark taken off, and five foot from the ground in fair capital letters was [carved] CROATOAN, without any cross or sign of distress. ❞

—from John White's *Journals* (1590)

One of John White's drawings of Native Americans

Croatoan was the name of a local tribe and a nearby island. However, White never discovered the fate of the colonists or his family. Although Roanoke failed, later English settlements in America were successful.

The First English Colonies

▼ **KEY QUESTION** What were the benefits and risks of colonizing America?

In the late 1500s, the English government was envious of the wealth that Spain had taken from its American colonies. The English people, faced with few job opportunities at home, hoped to find riches in America. Most were unaware of the dangers waiting for them on America's eastern shores.

Early Colonies Fail Queen Elizabeth I gave **Sir Walter Raleigh** (RAW•lee) permission to sponsor England's first American colony. Raleigh, a soldier and adventurer, established the colony in 1585 on Roanoke Island. He named the colony Virginia after the unmarried, or virgin, queen. But troubles with local tribes and lack of food forced the colonists to return to England. Raleigh tried to establish Roanoke again in 1587, with the results described in One American Story (previous page). No one knows what happened to this "lost colony." Some historians think that the starving colonists joined a local tribe of Native Americans. Others believe that they were killed.

In 1607, the English tried to found the Sagadahoc colony on the Kennebec River in Maine. Again, hunger forced most colonists to return to England.

Financing a Colony Raleigh lost his investment when his colony failed. Later, other merchants tried financing a colony through a **joint-stock company**. Joint-stock companies were funded by **investors**, people who put money into a project to earn profits. Each investor owned a portion of the company, called shares of stock. Investors shared profits and risk.

Merchants formed two joint-stock companies to colonize America: the Virginia Company of London and the Virginia Company of Plymouth. These companies sought permission to colonize from James I, who had become king after Queen Elizabeth's death. Colonies were important in **mercantilism** (MUR•kuhn•tee•LIHZ•uhm)—an economic system that European nations used to enrich their treasuries.

CONNECT ➤ Economics and History

MERCANTILISM

In mercantilism, a nation would increase its wealth through selling more products to foreign nations than it bought from them.

Colonies helped a nation achieve a favorable balance of trade between exports and imports.

Colonists created a demand, or market, for the mother country's goods and supplied the mother country with cheap raw materials. In this way, the mother country would not have to buy expensive raw materials from rival nations.

RAW MATERIALS

FINISHED GOODS

COLONIES
- provide raw materials to England
- buy finished goods from England
- could trade only with England

ENGLAND
- imports cheap raw materials from the colonies
- exports finished goods to colonies and other nations

CRITICAL THINKING

1. **Make Inferences** How did colonies enrich a nation?

2. **Connect to Today** What do you think would happen if, for several years, your family collected less money than it paid for goods? How might such a situation affect a nation?

King James granted charters to both companies in 1606. A **charter** was a written contract, issued by a government, giving the company the right to establish a colony. Because a charter also gave the company the right to govern the colony, each charter was like a primitive constitution.

🔺 **COMPARE AND CONTRAST** Compare the benefits and risks of colonization.

Jamestown Is Founded in 1607

🔻 **KEY QUESTION** What democratic tradition was planted in Jamestown?

In 1607 100 colonists, sent by the Virginia Company of London, sailed into the Chesapeake Bay. They traveled up the James River until they found a spot that seemed safe from a Spanish attack. The settlement was named **Jamestown** in honor of King James I. This became the first permanent English settlement in North America.

Jamestown Struggles to Survive The colony's early years were troubled. Colonists became ill from diseases carried by water or insects. To make matters worse, the London Company had promised that the colony would be rich with gold, like the Spanish colonies. Settlers searched for treasure instead of building houses and planting crops.

The climate was also a hardship. The English were not prepared for Virginia's hot, humid summers and bitterly cold winters. As one colonist recalled, "There were never Englishmen left in a foreign country in such misery as we were in this newly discovered Virginia."

By January 1608, only 38 of the colonists remained alive. Later that year, **John Smith**, a soldier and adventurer, took control. Smith brought order to the colony. But when Smith returned to England, the colony fell back into confusion. During this "starving time" the colonists ate rodents and snakes. Fortunately, the colony was saved when relief ships arrived in 1610. Lord De La Warr, the new governor, imposed discipline. More attention was paid to farming, and the colony survived.

Although the local Powhatan tribe had traded corn to the colonists, relations between the two groups were tense and sometimes violent. The situation did not improve until 1614, when Chief Powhatan's daughter, Pocahontas, married a colonist named John Rolfe. The Virginia Company brought the couple to England to advertise the colony. Sadly, Pocahontas died there, when she was about twenty-one.

Tobacco Transforms the Colony Unable to find gold, the colonists discovered another product that could bring them wealth—tobacco. In 1614 John Rolfe sent the first shipment of tobacco to England. It became popular in Europe and ensured the colony's survival.

The success of tobacco growing changed the colony. When the colonists demanded a share of the profits, the company responded by allowing them to own land. Settlers worked harder once the land became their own.

Connect *to the* **World**

Colonization
In 1608, a year after the first permanent English colony was established at Jamestown, the French founded their first permanent colony at Quebec.
Chapter 2, p. 38.

Pocahontas in English dress

Tobacco farms began spreading along the James River. This established the pattern for the entire Chesapeake Bay—the region's many rivers allowed planters to ship their crops directly to England.

To attract settlers, the Virginia Company offered a **headright**, a 50-acre land grant for anyone who could pay his or her way to the colony. Those who could not afford passage to America often became **indentured servants**. These men and women agreed to work without pay for a landlord if the landlord paid for their passage to America. After they had served for the time specified in the contract—usually about 4 to 6 years—the landlord restored their freedom.

In 1619 the first Africans arrived in Jamestown. It is not known whether they arrived as indentured servants or as enslaved workers. In the colony's first decades, planters relied more on European indentured servants. Slavery did not become widespread until the late 1600s.

The House of Burgesses Is Formed Settlers soon became frustrated at the lack of self government. So the Virginia Company decided that burgesses, or elected representatives, would meet once a year. The **House of Burgesses**, created in 1619, was the first representative assembly in the colonies.

The House of Burgesses had the authority to pass local laws and to raise taxes. Throughout the colonial period, the power of a local government to raise taxes remained a closely guarded right.

CONNECT ↻ Citizenship and History

VOTING RIGHTS

The creation of the Virginia House of Burgesses did not establish democracy in the modern sense—only male landowners had the right to vote. But it was a step in a long process that gradually extended voting rights to larger and larger sections of the population.

Today, all citizens aged 18 and over have the right to vote. But in order to vote, citizens must first register. This can be done by mail, in person, or in some states, at the Department of Motor Vehicles. Information about voter registration can also be found on the "Rock the Vote" website. Rock the Vote aims to boost voter turnout. Kids who are too young to vote can still participate in America's democracy by educating others.

Activity

Contribute to Voter Education!

1 Let your parents and older relatives know how they can register to vote.

2 As local elections are due, work with your classmates to make signs informing people how to register to vote. Display these signs in public places.

3 With a parent or older relative, speak to people in your neighborhood about the importance of registering to vote

4 Go to the "Rock the Vote" website and send the link via email to people you know.

See Citizenship Handbook, page 303.

Representative Government The colony's government and its very existence were threatened by a Native American uprising in 1622. The local Native American tribe, the Powhatan, were alarmed by the expanding tobacco plantations and the growing English population. On March 22, the Powhatan launched an attack on settlements all along the James River. A quarter of the English population was killed.

A member of the Powhatan watches an English ship; from the film *The New World*.

Jamestown survived, but the Virginia Company did not. After the uprising, King James I took back the company's charter and turned Virginia into a **royal colony**. A royal colony is ruled by the king's appointed officials.

James I, who opposed the idea of elected governments, also got rid of the assembly. This act outraged the colonists. They protested fiercely, sending requests and petitions for the assembly to be restored. After King James's death, his son, Charles I granted the colonists' wishes, and by 1629 the House of Burgesses was meeting once again. In 1639, the King commanded that the governor call an assembly every year.

Thus, the Virginia colonists won for themselves the right to participate in government. As more English colonies were planted on America's eastern seaboard, the political traditions of liberty and representative government took root in America's fertile ground.

▲ **SUMMARIZE** Identify the democratic tradition planted at Jamestown.

Connect *to the* **World**

Representative Government
In the colonies of other European nations, elected assemblies were not allowed.

Illinois Learning Standards *Review*

🖱 **ONLINE QUIZ**
For test practice, go to
Interactive Review @ ClassZone.com

TERMS & NAMES

1. Explain the importance of
   - Sir Walter Raleigh
   - mercantilism
   - Jamestown
   - John Smith
   - House of Burgesses

USING YOUR READING NOTES

2. **Compare and Contrast** Complete the diagram that you started at the beginning of this section.

COLONIZATION

Benefits	Risks
wealth created for mother country	

KEY IDEAS

3. Why did the English want to colonize America?

4. What events saved Jamestown from destruction?

5. What powers belonged to the House of Burgesses?

CRITICAL THINKING

6. **Connect Economics & History** How did the success of tobacco growing change Virginia?

7. **Problems and Solutions** Why were the settlers unprepared for colonizing Virginia?

8. **Connect** *to* **Today** What modern democratic traditions can be traced back to the Jamestown colony?

9. **Art** You want indentured servants to work on your plantation. Design an advertisement that will attract people to the colony of Virginia.

▶ Key Ideas

BEFORE, YOU LEARNED

In Jamestown, Virginia, the first permanent English colony in North America, settlers established representative government.

NOW YOU WILL LEARN

English colonists settled New England, where they planted many political and religious traditions.

▶ Vocabulary

TERMS & NAMES

John Winthrop Puritan leader who became the first governor of the Massachusetts Bay Colony

Pilgrims Separatist group that traveled to America to gain religious freedom

Mayflower Compact document that helped establish the practice of self-government

Puritans English dissenters who wanted to reform the Church of England

Great Migration the movement of tens of thousands of English settlers to New England during the 1630s

Roger Williams Puritan dissenter who established Rhode Island

Anne Hutchinson Puritan dissenter who was banished from Massachusetts

Fundamental Orders of Connecticut document that has been called the first written constitution in America

Quakers group of Protestant dissenters

BACKGROUND VOCABULARY

dissenter (dih•SEHN•tuhr) person who disagrees with an official church

persecute (PUR•sih•KYOOT) to mistreat

tolerance acceptance of different opinions

congregation group of people who belong to the same church

banish to force someone to leave a place

▶ Reading Strategy

Re-create the diagram shown at right. As you read and respond to the **KEY QUESTIONS**, use the boxes to show why the Pilgrims settled in America.

 See Skillbuilder Handbook, page R3.

CAUSES AND EFFECTS

Cause	Effect
	Pilgrims settled in America.

 GRAPHIC ORGANIZERS
Go to **Interactive Review** @ ClassZone.com

New England Colonies

14.F.3a Analyze historical influences on the development of political ideas and practices as enumerated in the Declaration of Independence, the United States Constitution, the Bill of Rights and the Illinois Constitution.

18.B.3a Analyze how individuals and groups interact with and within institutions (e.g., *educational, military*).

One American's Story

One Sunday morning in 1630, **John Winthrop**, a Puritan leader, gave a sermon to a congregation gathered on a ship's deck. The ship was called the *Arbella*, and it was one of four carrying hundreds of English colonists across the Atlantic Ocean to Massachusetts Bay. In his sermon Winthrop stated that success would come only if the settlers worked together as a community to achieve their common goals.

PRIMARY SOURCE

❝ We must be knit together in this work. . . . We must delight in each other, make others' conditions our own and rejoice together, mourn together, labor and suffer together. . . . For we must consider that we shall be as a City upon a Hill; the eyes of all people are on us. ❞

—John Winthrop, "Model of Christian Charity"

John Winthrop, by Charles Osgood

Tens of thousands of English settlers soon followed Winthrop and tried to create a religious society dedicated to the common good.

The Voyage of the Mayflower

🔻 **KEY QUESTION** Why did the Pilgrims want to settle in America?

In the early 1500s, King Henry VIII of England broke his country's ties with the Catholic Church and established the Church of England. Although English Protestants approved of separation from the Catholic Church, many disagreed with certain aspects of the English church. Those who disagreed with England's official church were called **dissenters** (dih•SEHN•tuhrz).

Religious Freedom and Self-Government In the early 1600s, another dissenting group called the Separatists wanted to separate from the Church of England. They thought it was still too much like the Catholic Church. King James **persecuted** (PUR•sih•KYOOT•ted), or mistreated, the Separatists for rejecting England's official church. To escape this persecution, they fled to Holland, a country known for its **tolerance**, or acceptance of different

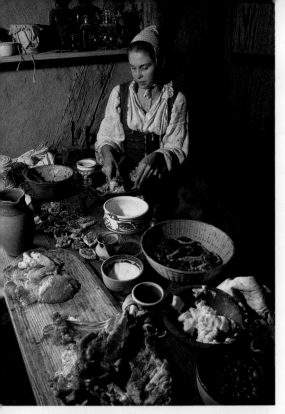

A reenactment of preparation for a Thanksgiving feast. **Why would the Pilgrims need Native Americans' help in order to survive?**

opinions. Eventually the Separatists approached the Virginia Company and gained permission to settle in America. Because this group of Separatists traveled far to gain religious freedom, they later became known as the **Pilgrims**. A pilgrim is a person who goes on a religious journey.

The Pilgrims Found Plymouth On a cold November day in 1620, the Pilgrims, traveling on a ship called the *Mayflower*, arrived off Cape Cod on the Massachusetts coast. Blown north off its course, the *Mayflower* landed in an area that John Smith had mapped and called New England. The Pilgrims settled on the site of an abandoned Native American village. They called their settlement Plymouth.

Because the Pilgrims landed beyond the limits of the Virginia Company, their charter did not apply. They were far from government authority and the laws of England. So most of the men aboard the *Mayflower* signed an agreement called the **Mayflower Compact**. The Mayflower Compact helped establish the practice of self-government and majority rule. (See Reading Primary Sources, page 74.)

Like the settlers at Jamestown, the Pilgrims at Plymouth endured a "starving time." Half the group died during the first winter. However, they were saved by Native Americans who had learned to speak English. Squanto, a Native American, taught the Pilgrims how to plant native crops.

Sometime in the fall of 1621 the Plymouth settlement celebrated a good harvest by holding a three-day feast. It was the first Thanksgiving in New England. This Thanksgiving came to represent the peace that existed at that time between the Native Americans and Pilgrims.

🔺 **CAUSES AND EFFECTS** Explain why the Pilgrims settled in America.

The Puritans Come to Massachusetts Bay

🔻 **KEY QUESTION** What kind of society did the Puritans hope to create?

By the late 1620s, England was troubled by religious and political conflict. Many groups of dissenters were speaking out against the king and the Church of England. The **Puritans** were one such group. Unlike the Separatists, who wanted to break away from the English church, the Puritans wanted to reform, or "purify" its practices. The Puritans faced increasing persecution in England. Many decided to leave and set up a Puritan society in America.

The Great Migration In 1629, the Massachusetts Bay Company, a joint-stock company owned by Puritan merchants, received a royal charter to settle New England. The charter also gave the colony freedom to govern itself. In 1630, 11 ships carried about 1,000 passengers to the Massachusetts Bay Colony. There the Puritans founded Boston, which became the most important town in New England. Between 1630 and 1640 about 20,000 more settlers crossed the Atlantic Ocean in what is known as the **Great Migration**.

The New England Way The Puritans set up their ideal society—a religious "commonwealth" of tightly-knit communities. Instead of a church governed by bishops and king, they created self-governing **congregations**. A congregation is a group of people who belong to the same church. Because Puritan congregations were self-governing, their churches came to be called "Congregationalist." This Congregationalist way of organizing churches became known as "the New England Way."

Each congregation chose its minister and set up its own town. The town's most important building was the meetinghouse, where religious services were held. Everyone had to attend these services. The meetinghouse was also used for town meetings, a form of self-government.

Puritan values helped the colonists organize their society and overcome the hardships of colonial life. Puritan colonists valued:

- **hard work** as a way of honoring God. The Puritan work ethic contributed to the colony's rapid growth and success.
- **education.** Because the Puritans wanted everyone to be able to read the Bible, laws required that all children learn to read.
- **representative government.** Puritans brought their traditions of town meetings and local self-government with them to America.

Democratic rights were quickly expanded. The colony's charter allowed only "freemen" or investors to vote. But when the colonists arrived in America, Winthrop, the colony's first governor, changed the definition of "freeman" to mean any male church member. Although this covered only a limited number of people, it was a major step in expanding voting rights.

▲ **SUMMARIZE** Describe the kind of society the Puritans hoped to create.

New England Colonies 1630

The first colonists built houses with roofs of thatch, or straw, like this one.

Connect Geography & History

1. **Place** How far is Plymouth from Boston?
2. **Make Inferences** Why do you think that Boston became the most important port in New England?

Massachusetts Bay "Seeds" New England

▼ **KEY QUESTION** Why did some colonists leave Massachusetts?

The Puritans worked hard to create an orderly society and felt threatened by those who questioned their ways. But dissenters within their ranks soon began challenging Puritan leaders. Disagreements within Massachusetts forced many to leave and found other colonies. In this way, Massachusetts became a "seed colony" out of which other New England colonies grew.

Rhode Island Welcomes Dissenters In Salem, Massachusetts, the minister **Roger Williams** shocked Puritan authorities by insisting that

- the colonists had no right to take Native American lands by force;
- no one should be forced to attend church;
- the Puritans should not impose their religious beliefs on others; and
- church and state should be kept separate.

Because of his beliefs, the Puritans had Williams **banished**, or forced to leave the colony. In 1636 he fled south and founded Rhode Island, a colony that guaranteed religious tolerance and separation of church and state. Williams also established the first Baptist Church in America.

Anne Hutchinson was another dissenter. She believed that many of the clergy were not among the "elect"—those chosen by God for salvation. She held discussions that challenged church authority. Hutchinson was also tried and banished from Massachusetts. In 1638 she fled to Rhode Island. That same year, John Wheelwright, Anne Hutchinson's brother-in-law and supporter, also fled. He established the town of Exeter, in what is now New Hampshire. The town's founders wrote the Exeter Compact, which was based on the Mayflower Compact. New Hampshire became a separate colony in 1679.

ONLINE PRIMARY SOURCE

Hear the debate at the **Research & Writing Center** @ ClassZone.com

COMPARING *Perspectives*

RELIGIOUS TOLERANCE VS. INTOLERANCE

Puritans began arguing over religious matters almost as soon as they had set up the Massachusetts Bay Colony. Those who disagreed with Puritan leaders were sometimes brought to trial and punished. Issues of religious freedom were widely debated as some colonists argued for and others argued against tolerance.

FOR TOLERANCE

" It doth not a little grieve my spirit to hear what sad things are reported daily of your tyranny and persecutions in New England, as that you fine, whip, and imprison men for their consciences.
—*Richard Saltonstall*

Forced worship stinks in God's nostrils. "
—*Roger Williams, minister*

AGAINST TOLERANCE

" He that is willing to tolerate any religion. . . either doubts of his own [religion] or is not sincere in it.
—*Nathaniel Ward, minister*

We have here Presbyterian churches as well as Congregational. . . .Only we are [reluctant] to be blown up and down. . . by every wind of new notions. "
—*John Cotton, minister*

CRITICAL THINKING

Connect to Today Which group might feel more at ease in modern American society and why?

Connecticut Extends Voting Rights Conservative Puritans also set up new colonies. In 1636, Thomas Hooker moved his congregation to the Connecticut Valley. There settlers wrote the **Fundamental Orders of Connecticut** in 1639. (See pages 74–75.) The Orders extended voting rights to non-church members. This expanded representative government.

▲ **SUMMARIZE** Explain why some colonists left Massachusetts.

The Fight for Tolerance

▼ **KEY QUESTION** Why did the Quakers protest against the Puritans?

Although Puritans had come to America to find religious freedom for themselves, they would not allow all faiths to worship freely. They were particularly intolerant of the **Quakers**, another group of Protestant dissenters.

Puritans Persecute Quakers The name "Quakers" came from a leader's statement that they should "tremble [quake] at the word of the Lord." Quaker beliefs angered the Puritans. The Quakers believed God could be known directly through an "inner light," and that Puritan sermons and ministers were obstacles to the direct experience of God. Because Quakers believed that women were spiritually equal to men, Quaker women served as preachers and as missionaries. These beliefs and practices threatened the very foundations of the New England Way. For this, Quakers were jailed, whipped, or banished from Puritan colonies.

Although often banished, Quaker missionaries defied the authorities, returning repeatedly to Puritan colonies to speak openly about their faith. In frustration, Puritan leaders passed laws with increasingly brutal punishments. Finally Puritans began executing Quakers who returned after being banished.

In response, Quakers became martyrs, people who choose to die for a religious principle. One of the most famous Quaker martyrs was a woman named Mary Dyer. Despite her banishment from the colony, Dyer returned to Massachusetts, determined to "look the bloody laws in the face." Although she was executed, her death led to greater religious tolerance.

▲ **CAUSES AND EFFECTS** Explain why the Quakers protested against the Puritans.

History Makers

Mary Dyer   ?–1660

Mary Dyer, the religious martyr, came to Massachusetts with her husband, William Dyer, in 1635. She supported her friend Anne Hutchinson during Hutchinson's trial. When Hutchinson was banished from Massachusetts, Dyer followed her to Rhode Island. Returning to England, Dyer met George Fox, the founder of the Quakers. In 1657 she was back in New England as a Quaker missionary. For speaking openly about her faith, Dyer was banished once from New Haven before being imprisoned and banished three times from Massachusetts.

Determined to protest against religious intolerance, Dyer again returned, this time to face the sentence of death. She was hanged on June 1, 1660. As she had hoped, her execution helped end the Puritan persecution of the Quakers.

CRITICAL THINKING **Make Inferences** Why do you think the Puritans felt threatened by the Quakers?

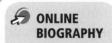 **ONLINE BIOGRAPHY**   For more on the life of Mary Dyer, go to the **Research & Writing Center** @ ClassZone.com

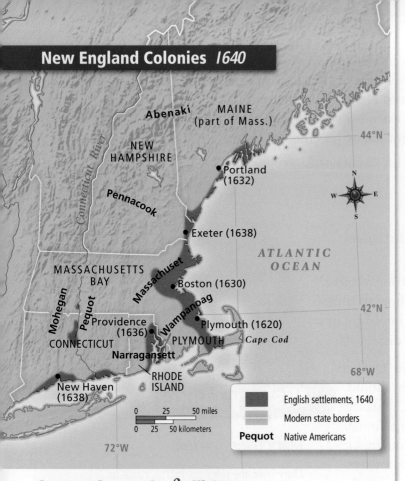

New England Colonies *1640*

Abenaki
MAINE
(part of Mass.)
Connecticut River
NEW HAMPSHIRE
Pennacook
●Portland (1632)

44°N

●Exeter (1638)

ATLANTIC OCEAN

MASSACHUSETTS BAY
Massachuset
●Boston (1630)

Mohegan
Pequot
Wampanoag
Providence (1636)
●Plymouth (1620)
CONNECTICUT
PLYMOUTH
Cape Cod
Narragansett

42°N

68°W

RHODE ISLAND
New Haven (1638)

0   25   50 miles
0 25 50 kilometers

72°W

	English settlements, 1640
	Modern state borders
Pequot	Native Americans

Connect Geography & History

1. **Place** Why did the colonies grow mainly north-south?
2. **Make Inferences** Why did most early settlements develop along rivers and the coast?

Creating a New England

▼ **KEY QUESTION** What did the New England colonies have in common?

By the 1650s, settlers had fanned out across New England, bringing their beliefs, religious disagreements, and political traditions with them. Although a number of colonies were established throughout the region, the New England colonies had much in common.

New England Foundations Many New England settlers came from the densely-populated eastern counties of England. They were used to living in towns and established similar settlements in America. Most New England settlers were also religious dissenters who disagreed with the practices of both the Catholic and the Anglican churches. The New England population was mainly Puritan, but had large numbers of other Protestant groups such as Quakers, Separatists, Baptists, and other dissenters in Rhode Island.

Most New England settlers came from the middle ranks of English society. Many were highly skilled and educated. As they were wealthier than most of the early settlers in the South, they were able to pay their own way across the Atlantic. Few were forced to become indentured servants, who sold their freedom in exchange for passage to America. Unlike the first Jamestown colonists, who were mostly young men, the Puritans traveled in "companies" with their families, friends, and neighbors.

Questions About an Established Church In all the New England colonies, settlers were aware that they were creating new societies in what was, for them, a new world. It is not surprising that they often argued about what direction these new societies should take.

A major argument revolved around a single question: should each colony have one, dominant, "established" church, funded by the taxpayer? In Europe, each national government supported only one established religious group. Other groups might face persecution from the religious group in power.

When the Puritans set up their society in Massachusetts, their church became the only established church in the colony. Other New England colonies were also dominated by Puritans, who tolerated some Christian groups but persecuted others. Only Rhode Island tolerated all Christian denominations, as well as Judaism.

Democratic Traditions Throughout the New England colonies, settlers established democratic practices and self-government. Colonists wove democratic practices into both their local government and their church life.

A modern town meeting

- The Congregational churches of the Puritans were self-governing.
- In Massachusetts, Puritan men elected the governor and the legislature.
- Voting rights were expanded in Massachusetts and Connecticut.
- In the New England countryside, towns controlled their own affairs.

Because of this democratic tradition in the region, the New England town meeting became a symbol of local self-government. At a time when very few Europeans had the right to vote, New England became famous for its democratic practices.

During these early decades of settlement, Massachusetts had the largest population and the greatest influence in the region. Its democratic political trends, its religious beliefs, and the conflicts of its early years influenced the course of American history.

▲ **COMPARE AND CONTRAST** Describe the features that the New England colonies had in common.

Illinois Learning Standards *Review*

ONLINE QUIZ
For test practice, go to
Interactive Review @ ClassZone.com

TERMS & NAMES

1. Explain the importance of
   - John Winthrop
   - Pilgrims
   - Mayflower Compact
   - Puritans
   - Great Migration
   - Roger Williams
   - Anne Hutchinson
   - Fundamental Orders of Connecticut
   - Quakers

USING YOUR READING NOTES

2. **Causes and Effects** Complete the diagram that you started at the beginning of this section.

Cause	Effect
	Pilgrims settled in America.

KEY IDEAS

3. Why did the Puritans leave England?
4. Why was Rhode Island founded?
5. In what ways were New England settlers different from the settlers of Jamestown?

CRITICAL THINKING

6. **Analyze Point of View** Why was religious tolerance an important issue for the early settlers?
7. **Make Generalizations** How did the Puritans weave democracy into their political and religious life?
8. **Connect** *to* **Today** What modern American values might be familiar to a 17th-century Puritan?
9. **Writing** **Research Report** Mary Dyer broke Puritan laws by returning to Massachusetts. This was an act of civil disobedience. Write a paper about other historical figures who used this form of protest.

The Mayflower Compact

SETTING THE STAGE In 1620, 41 colonists aboard the *Mayflower* drew up the Mayflower Compact. This document refers to the area where they landed as "Virginia" because the land grants of the Virginia Company extended into New England. The colonists provided for self-government under majority rule of the male voters.

Reasons for Voyage

The three reasons the colonists give for their voyage to the eastern seaboard of North America are the glory of God, the advancement of Christianity, and the honor of the king.

1. Might there have been more practical reasons for the voyage? Explain.

Guiding Purpose

In signing the compact, the colonists' guiding purpose is the general good of the colony.

2. What does this suggest about the relationship between the individual and the community?

We, whose names are underwritten, . . . having undertaken for the glory of God, and advancement of the Christian faith, and the honor of our King and country, a voyage to plant the first colony in the northern parts of Virginia, do by these presents, solemnly and mutually in the presence of God and one another **covenant**[1] and combine ourselves together into a civil **body politic**,[2] for our better ordering and preservation; and furtherance of the ends aforesaid . . . do enact, constitute, and frame such just and equal laws, ordinances, acts, constitutions, and offices from time to time as shall be thought most [proper] and convenient for the general good of the colony unto which we promise all due submission and obedience. In witness whereof we have hereunto subscribed our names at Cape Cod the eleventh of November, in the year of our **sovereign**[3] lord King James of England . . . Anno Domini 1620.

From B. P. Poore, ed., *The Federal and State Constitutions,* Part I, p. 931.

----

1. **covenant:** promise in a binding agreement
2. **body politic:** the people of a politically organized group
3. **sovereign:** supreme

The Fundamental Orders of Connecticut

SETTING THE STAGE In January 1639, male citizens of three townships in Connecticut (Hartford, Windsor, and Wethersfield) assembled and drew up the Fundamental Orders of Connecticut. This document is often called the first written constitution in America. It contains a preamble, or introduction, and a set of laws.

Preamble

Forasmuch as it has pleased the Almighty God by the wise disposition of His Divine Providence so to order and dispose of things that we, the inhabitants and residents of Windsor, Hartford, and Wethersfield are now cohabiting and dwelling in and upon the river of Conectecotte [Connecticut] and the lands thereunto adjoining; and well knowing where a people are gathered together the Word of God requires that, to maintain the peace and union of such a people, there should be an orderly and decent government established according to God, to order and dispose of the affairs of the people at all seasons as occasion shall require; do therefore associate and **conjoin**[1] ourselves to be as one public state or commonwealth. . . . As also in our civil affairs to be guided and goverened according to such laws, rules, orders, and decrees as shall be made, ordered, and decreed as follows:

Laws, Rules, and Orders

1. It is ordered, sentenced, and decreed that there shall be yearly two general assemblies or courts. . . . The first shall be called the Court of Election, wherein shall be yearly chosen . . . so many magistrates and other public officers as shall be found **requisite**[2]. . . .

4. It is ordered . . . that no person be chosen governor above once in two years, and that the governor shall be always a member of some approved congregation. . . .

5. It is ordered . . . that to the aforesaid Court of Election the several towns shall send their deputies. . . . Also, the other General Court in September shall be for making of laws, and any other public occasion which concerns the good of the Commonwealth. . . .

----

1. conjoin: unite   **2. requisite:** required

Good Government

In the eyes of the colonists, good government is pleasing to God. An orderly and decent government helps to maintain peace and order within a community and between people.

3. How would you define good government today?

The Governor's Role

The person serving as governor can serve only once every two years and must be a member of an approved church or congregation.

4. Why might the colonists have wished to limit the power of the chief executive?

The Courts

The Court of Election chooses officials to serve; the General Court makes laws.

5. Why might it be a good idea to separate these two functions?

DOCUMENT-BASED QUESTIONS

Short Answer

1. Whose rights did the Mayflower Compact protect?

2. In what ways were the Fundamental Orders based on religion?

Extended Answer

3. How do you think these documents reveal the English foundation of American democracy?

▶ Key Ideas

BEFORE, YOU LEARNED
The first permanent English colony in North America was founded in Virginia.

NOW YOU WILL LEARN
New Southern colonies were settled by fortune-seekers, religious refugees, enslaved Africans, and the poor.

▶ Vocabulary

TERMS & NAMES

Lord Baltimore Catholic owner of the colony of Maryland

Margaret Brent attorney of the governor of Maryland

Act of Toleration Maryland law that forbade religious persecution

Huguenots French Protestants

James Oglethorpe the founder of Georgia

BACKGROUND VOCABULARY

proprietary colony colony governed by a single owner, or proprietor

elite highest-ranking social group

Visual Vocabulary
statue of James Oglethorpe

diversity variety

region distinct area of land

Tidewater flat land along the coast

▶ Reading Strategy

Re-create the diagram shown at right. As you read and respond to the **KEY QUESTIONS**, use the boxes to show how each colony was founded because of social or political problems in England.

 See Skillbuilder Handbook, page R9.

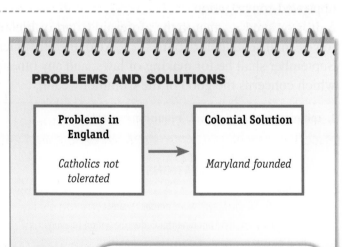

PROBLEMS AND SOLUTIONS

Problems in England	→	Colonial Solution
Catholics not tolerated		*Maryland founded*

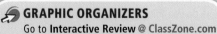
GRAPHIC ORGANIZERS
Go to **Interactive Review** @ ClassZone.com

The Southern Colonies

16.C.3b Explain relationships among the American economy and slavery, immigration, industrialization, labor and urbanization, 1700–present.
18.B.3a Analyze how individuals and groups interact with and within institutions (e.g., *educational, military*).

One American's Story

Margaret Brent demands the right to vote.

In the 1640s fear and confusion spread through Maryland. A Puritan rebellion had been followed by the governor's death. Soldiers demanded their pay, but there was no money to pay them. No one had time to wait for instructions from the colony's owner, **Lord Baltimore**, who lived in England. So **Margaret Brent**, the governor's attorney, took action. First she rose before the Assembly to demand the right to vote. Because she was a woman, her request was denied. However, as the governor's attorney, she still had power. So to raise money to pay the troops, she sold Lord Baltimore's cattle. When Baltimore heard of this sale he was furious. The Assembly defended Brent's actions:

PRIMARY SOURCE

❝ It was better for [the] colony's safety at that time in her hands than in any man's else in the province. She rather deserved favor and thanks from your Honor. **❞**

—letter to Lord Baltimore from the Maryland Assembly

Margaret Brent acted decisively at a time when few women had political power or many legal rights. But the colonies were a new world, where unusual circumstances often led colonists to play unfamiliar roles.

Lord Baltimore Founds Maryland

🔻 **KEY QUESTION** What kind of society was planned for Maryland?

In 1634, the second Southern colony, Maryland, was settled on the Chesapeake Bay. Maryland was also intended to be a new kind of society, free from the religious conflicts of Europe.

The Act of Toleration When Maryland was founded, Catholics and Protestants in Europe had been fighting each other for a century. In England many Anglicans, including King Charles I, sympathized with the Catholics. Charles supported the Catholic Lord Baltimore's plan for a colony where

Catholics would not be persecuted. He gave Maryland to Lord Baltimore as a **proprietary colony**, a colony governed by a single owner, or proprietor.

The first settlement, St. Mary's City, located on the Chesapeake Bay, became the capital. Colonists were allowed to elect an assembly, and in 1649 the **Act of Toleration** forbade religious persecution.

Maryland based its economy on growing tobacco, which required back-breaking work. The tobacco crop quickly used up nutrients in the soil, and workers had to clear more land. Planters were always searching for laborers. Most tobacco workers were either indentured servants or slaves.

Religious Conflict In Maryland The colony did not develop as planned. Some Catholics, such as Margaret Brent, did settle in Maryland. But they were outnumbered by Protestants. In 1645 Puritans tried to seize power in Maryland. Although order was restored, in 1654 Puritans dismissed Maryland's governor. They got rid of the Act of Toleration and replaced it with an anti-Catholic law. Eventually the act was restored. However, it was clear that achieving religious tolerance would be a difficult struggle.

▲ **PROBLEMS AND SOLUTIONS** Describe the kind of society planned for Maryland.

COMPARING ▸ *Religious Groups*

RELIGION IN THE EARLY COLONIES

In the 17th century, conflict between Catholics and Protestants divided Europeans. In England and its colonies, there were also disagreements among Protestants. These disagreements created a variety of religious groups.

Protestants (do not recognize Pope's authority)				Catholic (Pope leads church.)
Quakers	**Baptists**	**Puritans**	**Anglicans**	
Kings and bishops have no authority.	Church & state should be separate.	No bishops; congregations make decisions.	King heads church. Bishops rule.	Bishops help govern.
silent prayer important	sermon important	sermon important	sermon & Catholic-style ritual	ritual important

CRITICAL THINKING Compare and Contrast Which Protestant denomination was most similar to Catholicism?

The Carolinas

▼ **KEY QUESTION** What attracted settlers to the Carolinas?

During the 1640s England was torn by civil war and colonization stopped. In 1649, a Puritan republic was set up in England. Then, in 1660, the monarchy was restored, and Charles II became king. He rewarded eight supporters by giving them land for a new colony named Carolina.

Proprietors Plan Their Colony The proprietors, or owners, hoped to attract settlers by offering religious toleration, large land grants, and political representation. The northern part of Carolina was already populated by colonists from Virginia. The southern area was settled by English colonists who had been living in the West Indies. It was in this region that English settlers from Barbados built Charles Town (later called Charleston) in 1670.

The proprietors offered religious toleration to all Christians and Jews. After 1685, Charleston became a refuge for **Huguenots**, or French Protestants. Many Huguenots fled France to seek religious freedom in America.

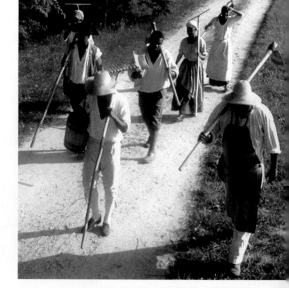

Reenactors portray slave life in the South.

Rice and Slavery In the 1690s, Carolina's colonists started exporting rice. They learned how to cultivate this crop from enslaved Africans, who had grown it in West Africa. Growing rice required a large labor force. So planters imported more enslaved Africans to do the work.

PRIMARY SOURCE

❝ Our Staple Commodity for some years has been Rice, and Tilling, planting, Hoeing, Reaping, Threshing, Pounding have all been done merely by the poor Slaves here. ❞

—letter from a South Carolina doctor, quoted in *American Colonies*

Slave labor helped make Carolina planters the richest **elite**, or high-ranking group, on the eastern seaboard. However, because they were so outnumbered by their slaves, this elite lived in constant fear of revolt.

Colonists also captured and enslaved Native Americans. As a result of this, and the taking of tribal lands, wars broke out between the settlers and Native American tribes, including the Tuscarora and Yamasee. The wars killed so many Native Americans that more lands were opened for the settlers.

The Colonists Rebel In 1691 a group of settlers forced the proprietors to establish a separate government and assembly in "North Carolina." Colonists were unhappy that the proprietors did not provide enough military protection from the Spanish and Native Americans. To gain more military support from the king, in 1719 the colonists overthrew the colony's proprietary rule. In 1729, both North Carolina and South Carolina became royal colonies, ruled by governors appointed by the king.

▲ **CAUSES AND EFFECTS** Explain what attracted settlers to the Carolinas.

Georgia

▼ **KEY QUESTION** Why was Georgia founded?

In 1732, **James Oglethorpe** received a charter for Georgia, named after King George II. A year later Oglethorpe built the first settlement at Savannah.

Ethnic and Religious Diversity The colony was meant as a place where debtors and the poor could make a fresh start. It was hoped that such settlers would protect the English colonies against Spanish Florida to the south and French Louisiana to the west.

A population of great **diversity**, or variety, settled in Georgia. English, German, Swiss, and Scottish colonists arrived. All Protestant groups, as well as Jews, were welcome. However, Catholics were banned in case they might sympathize with Spanish Catholics in Florida.

Oglethorpe's Policies Oglethorpe set strict rules. He opposed large plantations and slavery because he wanted to help poor settlers establish small farms. He believed that a free population could better defend the colony against attack. He also feared that slave revolts might weaken the colony.

The colonists were unhappy with Oglethorpe's policies. They were envious of South Carolina's prosperity, which came from slave labor. In response, the trustees legalized slavery, and Georgia became a royal colony. Georgia turned into a plantation society like that of South Carolina.

▲ **SUMMARIZE** Explain why Georgia was founded.

Southern Colonies *1740*

Legend:
- English settlements, 1660
- English settlements, 1740
- **Powhatan** Native Americans

0 100 200 miles
0 100 200 kilometers

FRENCH

APPALACHIAN MOUNTAINS

Potomac River

MD. • Baltimore (1729)

Nanticoke
St. Mary's City • (1634)

VIRGINIA

James River

Powhatan • — Williamsburg (1699)

Monacan — Jamestown (1607)

Roanoke River

Tuscarora

Cherokee

Yuchi

Catawba — **Lumbee**

Pee Dee River

NORTH CAROLINA

35°N

SOUTH CAROLINA

Savannah River

Creek

GEORGIA

Yamasee

Altamaha R.

• Charles Town (1670)

• Savannah (1733)

ATLANTIC OCEAN

80°W

70°W

SPANISH FLORIDA

• St. Augustine (1565)

Connect Geography & History

1. **Place** Around what geographical feature were the earliest settlements located?

2. **Draw Conclusions** What geographical features allowed some settlements to push farther west than others?

Savannah, Georgia, being built in the 1730s

The Region of the South

 KEY QUESTION What features did the Southern Colonies have in common?

With the addition of Georgia, the Southern Colonies now formed a **region**, or distinct area of land. This Southern region stretched from the borders of the Spanish colony of Florida north through the Carolinas, Virginia, and Maryland. The Southern Colonies shared a common climate and culture.

Southern Culture Develops The Appalachian Mountains bordered these colonies in the west. In the east, the flat land along the coast was known as the **Tidewater**. The soil and climate of the Tidewater encouraged the planting of warm-weather crops such as tobacco, rice, and indigo. These crops required a large labor force, so the region became home to the largest population of enslaved Africans in the colonies.

As large plantations formed along the rivers in coastal areas, landowners became rich from exporting cash crops. A wealthy elite soon developed, especially in Virginia and South Carolina. Meanwhile, poorer settlers were forced west onto the frontier.

Although the Anglican church was the established religion throughout the South, religious diversity increased. Many of the Southern Colonies promised religious toleration in order to attract settlers.

Colonists throughout the South demanded greater say in how they were governed. Eventually, every Southern colony was allowed an elected representative assembly.

 COMPARE AND CONTRAST Describe the features that the Southern Colonies had in common.

Connecting History

Social Conflict
Disagreements between the rich planters of the coast and poorer settlers of the frontier would lead to Bacon's Rebellion in 1676. *Chapter 4, p. 104.*

Illinois Learning Standards *Review*

 ONLINE QUIZ
For test practice, go to
Interactive Review @ ClassZone.com

TERMS & NAMES

1. Explain the importance of
- Lord Baltimore
- Margaret Brent
- Act of Toleration
- Huguenots
- James Oglethorpe

USING YOUR READING NOTES

2. Problems and Solutions Complete the diagram you began at the beginning of this section.

Problems in England	Colonial Solution
Catholics not tolerated	*Maryland founded*

KEY IDEAS

3. Why did Lord Baltimore found the colony of Maryland?

4. What drew settlers to the Carolinas?

5. What kind of society did Oglethorpe want for Georgia?

CRITICAL THINKING

6. Analyze Causes and Effects Why did slavery expand in the Southern Colonies?

7. Connect Economics & History Why did South Carolina planters become such a wealthy elite?

8. Writing Letter Write a persuasive letter to a London newspaper, describing opportunities in the Carolinas and urging other settlers to join you there.

Reading for Understanding

▶ Key Ideas

BEFORE, YOU LEARNED

English colonies in New England and the South struggled with issues of religious tolerance.

NOW YOU WILL LEARN

Religious tolerance and ethnic diversity characterized the Middle Colonies.

▶ Vocabulary

TERMS & NAMES

New Netherland Dutch colony that later became New York

Peter Stuyvesant (STY•vuh•suhnt) governor of the Dutch colony of New Netherland

William Penn Quaker founder of Pennsylvania

BACKGROUND VOCABULARY

patroon person rewarded with a large land grant for bringing 50 settlers to New Netherland

Visual Vocabulary
antique map showing New Netherland

▶ Reading Strategy

Re-create the diagram shown at right. As you read and respond to the **KEY QUESTIONS**, use the boxes to show what attracted settlers to the Middle Colonies.

See Skillbuilder Handbook, page R7.

CAUSES AND EFFECTS

Cause		Effect
		Settlers were drawn to the Middle Colonies.
Cause		

GRAPHIC ORGANIZERS
Go to **Interactive Review** @ ClassZone.com

The Middle Colonies

16.D.3a Describe characteristics of different kinds of communities in various sections of America during the colonial/frontier periods and the 19th century.
18.B.3b Explain how social institutions contribute to the development and transmission of culture.

One American's Story

The Dutch had founded the colony of **New Netherland** (later New York) on the eastern coast of North America in 1624. **Peter Stuyvesant** (STY•vuh•suhnt), the new governor, arrived in the city of New Amsterdam in May 1647. His firm leadership restored order to the wild colonial outpost. But there was one thing about the city of New Amsterdam that Stuyvesant could not control. He complained about this problem in a letter to the directors of the Dutch West India Company, who owned the colony.

PRIMARY SOURCE

❝ The English and French colonies are continued and populated by their own nation and countrymen and consequently bound together more firmly and united, while your Honors' colonies in New-Netherland are . . . peopled by . . . all sorts of nationalities. ❞

—Peter Stuyvesant, from a letter of 1661

Peter Stuyvesant

Stuyvesant was a powerful governor who usually got his way. But he was powerless to stop the growing diversity of the city that would one day be called New York. That diversity became a feature of all the Middle Colonies and one of the region's greatest strengths.

Settling the Middle Colonies

🔻 **KEY QUESTION** What drew settlers to the Middle Colonies?

The Middle Colonies—New York, New Jersey, Pennsylvania, and Delaware—formed a distinct region, located between New England and the Southern Colonies. (See map on page 86.) The Hudson and Delaware rivers, which ran through the region, encouraged shipping and commerce. The Middle Colonies' rich soil and mild winters were good for farming.

Unlike New England, with its large population of English Puritans, the Middle Colonies attracted a population of great ethnic and religious diversity. This diversity began developing very early in the colony's history.

New Netherland As you read in Chapter 2, in the early 1600s the Dutch built the colony of New Netherland along the Hudson River in what is now New York State. The colony's largest town, New Amsterdam, was founded on Manhattan Island in 1625. New Amsterdam was built to defend the Dutch West India Company's fur trading settlements along the Hudson River.

Peter Stuyvesant, the colony's governor, expanded New Netherland by taking over the nearby colony of New Sweden in 1655. The Swedes had settled the land along the Delaware River in 1638.

The Dutch West India Company set up the patroon system to attract more settlers. A **patroon** was a person who brought 50 settlers to New Netherland. As a reward, a patroon received a large land grant. He also received hunting, fishing, and fur trading privileges. The patroon system brought great wealth to the colony's elite.

The social system also included many slaves. Although their lives were harsh, they enjoyed some rights of movement and property ownership.

A Tolerant Society In the 17th century the Netherlands had one of the most tolerant societies in Europe. Dutch settlers brought this religious toleration to their colony. New Netherland welcomed dissenters who had been banished from Puritan New England. Quakers, German Lutherans, and French Protestants all settled in the colony. Twenty-three Jewish settlers arrived in 1654, and others soon followed. New Netherland soon became known as the most tolerant and diverse colony in North America.

🔺 **CAUSES AND EFFECTS** Explain what drew settlers to the Middle Colonies.

The English Take Control

🔻 **KEY QUESTION** How did religious toleration grow in the Middle Colonies?

The English saw the Dutch as a threat. New Netherland lay like a wedge between New England and English colonies in the South. So, King Charles II decided that his brother, the Duke of York, should drive the Dutch out of New Netherland. When the duke's ships appeared off New Amsterdam in August 1664, the colony surrendered. New Netherland was renamed New York after the Duke of York, who became the proprietor of the colony.

New Jersey, Pennsylvania and Delaware The Duke of York was now the largest single landowner in America. He gave part of his claim, the province of New Jersey, to his friends Sir George Carteret and Lord John Berkeley in 1664. They tried to attract settlers by promising freedom of religion. They also promised large land grants and a representative assembly.

William Penn was another landowner. Penn was born into a rich family that had loaned money to Charles II. To pay off this debt, in 1681 the king gave Penn land that came to be called Pennsylvania. The name means "Penn's woods." In 1701, Penn granted the three lower counties their own assembly. The counties became the colony of Delaware.

In his youth, Penn had joined the Quakers, much to his father's disapproval. As you have read, 17th-century Quakers suffered persecution in both

Daily Life *in the Colonies*

CLOTHING, RANK, AND RELIGION

Throughout the colonies, clothing expressed both social rank and religious beliefs. Some colonial governments passed laws controlling what colonists could wear. Puritan laws in Massachusetts required modest clothing to express Christian humility. But in Virginia only the poor were prohibited from wearing extravagant clothes.

Quakers wore the most modest clothing of all religious groups. Quakers thought rich clothes encouraged envy and pride. Their plain clothes were intended to show that they were more concerned with the spirit than with social rank.

STRANGE BUT TRUE

In the 1630s there was a fashion for sleeves slashed to reveal expensive undergarments. While Virginia colonists displayed their wealth through multiple slashes, Massachusetts Puritans passed a law allowing only one slash.

PENNSYLVANIA QUAKERS
1680s

VIRGINIA ANGLICANS
1680s

Artifact File

Imported fabrics and clothing allowed the rich to show off their wealth.

Men wore elegant caps when they removed their long wigs.

Women's shoes were richly adorned.

Women attached fancy "stomachers" to the front of their gowns so that their waists would appear longer.

Connect *to* **Today** **Make Inferences** How do modern clothes express the attitudes, beliefs, or political opinions of the wearer?

England and the colonies. Penn founded Pennsylvania to provide a place where Quakers could practice their beliefs, free of persecution. It was also meant to be a colony where the world could see Quaker ideals at work. Penn declared that Pennsylvania would be a "holy experiment" in Quaker religious tolerance and an "example to the Nations." But unlike the Puritan colonies in New England, Pennsylvania would have no tax-supported church.

The Quakers welcomed those of different religions and ethnic groups. This Quaker ideal of tolerance was written into the Frame of Government of Pennsylvania, which declared

American Colonies 1740

Settled area, 1740

0   100   200 miles
0 100   200 kilometers

MAINE
(part of Mass.)

N.H.

NEW YORK

Connecticut R.

Hudson R.

Delaware R.

MASS.
Boston
Newport
R.I.
CONN.

New York
40°N

PENN.

FRENCH
APPALACHIAN MOUNTAINS

Philadelphia
NEW JERSEY

Potomac R.

DELAWARE
MARYLAND

VIRGINIA

Chesapeake Bay

35°N

NORTH CAROLINA

ATLANTIC
OCEAN

SOUTH
CAROLINA

Savannah R.

75°W

FRENCH

NEW
ENGLAND

MIDDLE
COLONIES

GEORGIA
Charles Town

BRITISH

SOUTHERN

FRENCH

ATLANTIC OCEAN

SPANISH

30°N

SPANISH

N W E S

80°W

Connect Geography & History

1. **Place** What geographical feature acted as a barrier to settlers traveling west?

2. **Make Generalizations** Which settlements were in more frequent contact with the outside world?

PRIMARY SOURCE

❝ [All persons] shall, in no ways, be molested or prejudiced for their religious persuasion, or practice, in matters of faith and worship, nor shall they be compelled at any time, to frequent or maintain any religious worship. ❞

—from The Frame of the Government of Pennsylvania, 1682

In Pennsylvania, Penn extended religious freedom and equality to all. Because of this, settlers from many European countries came to Pennsylvania seeking religious freedom and a better life. Penn himself designed the colony's capital. It was named Philadelphia, meaning "city of brotherly love."

Like the Puritans of New England, the Quakers valued hard work and thrift, or the careful management of money. These Quaker values, combined with Penn's policies, helped poor immigrants become rich. With its long growing season and fertile soil, Pennsylvania became one of the wealthiest American colonies.

Thirteen Colonies By the 1730s, 13 English colonies were thriving along the eastern seaboard of North America. The colonial economies were growing and the population was increasing dramatically. In fact, the American population was doubling every twenty-five years.

In many ways, the earliest English colonies in Virginia and Massachusetts set the pattern of development for the later Northern and Southern Colonies. Virginia, in the South, saw the development of a plantation economy. Massachusetts, in the North, created towns that relied on shipping to produce wealth.

Separated by great distances, distinct colonial cultures developed. But despite differences in climate, religion, and social organization, the colonies had much in common.

Many colonies were born of political events in England. The chart below shows how conditions in England affected the settlement of America.

Animated HISTORY

Founding the Colonies

Click here to explore the founding of the colonies @ ClassZone.com

CONDITIONS/EVENTS IN ENGLAND		COLONIAL RESULT
1600s	Merchants desire wealth-creating colonies; English people seek prosperity.	Effect ▶	**Jamestown, Virginia,** founded 1607.
1620s	James I threatens Separatists. 1625 James dies. Charles I becomes king.	Effect ▶	Separatists flee England. **Plymouth** founded 1620 (later joins Massachusetts).
1630s	Puritans persecuted. Catholics not tolerated.		Puritans flee England in "The Great Migration" 1630 **Massachusetts** Bay Colony 1633–1636 **Connecticut** settled. 1636 **Rhode Island** settled. 1638 Puritans from Massachusetts move into **New Hampshire** and **Maine.** 1634 **Maryland** settled.
1640s	1642 English Civil War begins. 1649 Charles I beheaded.	Effect ▶	Immigration stops. Some Puritans return to England to fight the king and Royalists.
1650s	Puritans control England.	Effect ▶	Royalists flee England and settle in Southern and Middle Colonies.
1660s	Puritan rule ends. Charles II becomes king and rewards supporters.		1664 New Netherland seized and renamed **New York.** **New Jersey** founded.
1670s			1670 Settlers from Barbados arrive in what would become **South Carolina.**
1680s	Charles II grants land to William Penn. 1685 James II becomes king.	Effect ▶	Quakers' migration 1681 **Pennsylvania** founded.
1690s			1691 **North Carolina** established.
1700s			1701 **Delaware** granted its own assembly.
1730s	In England, concern grows over the fate of the poor.	Effect ▶	1733 **Georgia** settled.

CRITICAL THINKING Causes and Effects Which colonies were settled as a result of religious conflict in England?

The colonies were not only connected through their relationship with England. The early colonists shared the same experiences and concerns.

CONNECT to the Essential Question

How did the experience of the early colonists shape America's political and social ideals?

Colonists Left Their Homelands

in order to create a new kind of society.

to escape being persecuted by a more powerful religious group.

in order to improve their lives or to make a fresh start.

In America, Colonists

struggled with issues of religious tolerance.

established representative government and respect for English law.

encountered people from different ethnic backgrounds and faiths.

CRITICAL THINKING

Make Inferences Which experiences helped the colonists value tolerance?

As more immigrants arrived, religious and ethnic diversity increased. Meanwhile, representative assemblies grew stronger and more confident. By the early 18th century, these trends were creating societies that valued religious liberty, freedom of conscience, and representative government.

 DRAW CONCLUSIONS Explain why toleration grew in the Middle Colonies.

Illinois Learning Standards *Review*

 ONLINE QUIZ
For test practice, go to
Interactive Review @ ClassZone.com

TERMS & NAMES

1. Explain the importance of
- New Netherland
- Peter Stuyvesant
- William Penn

USING YOUR READING NOTES

2. Analyze Causes and Effects Complete the chart you started at the beginning of this section.

KEY IDEAS

3. Why did colonists settle in the Middle Colonies?

4. What were the goals of the patroon system?

CRITICAL THINKING

5. Causes and Effects Why did the English seize the Dutch colony of New Netherland?

6. Connect to Today Many modern nations are torn by religious and ethnic strife. What values and ideals helped America move beyond such conflicts?

7. Math Research the population of New England, the Southern Colonies and the Middle Colonies in 1700. Then create a graph to compare the population of the three regions.

Chapter Summary

1 **Key Idea**
Of the three earliest English colonies, only Jamestown managed to survive.

2 **Key Idea**
English colonists settled New England, where they planted many political and religious traditions.

3 **Key Idea**
New Southern colonies were settled by fortune-seekers, religious refugees, enslaved Africans, and the poor.

4 **Key Idea**
Religious tolerance and ethnic diversity characterized the Middle Colonies.

For detailed Review and Study Notes go to **Interactive Review** @ ClassZone.com

Name Game

Use the Terms & Names list to complete each sentence online or on your own paper.

1. I became leader of the Jamestown colony.
   John Smith

2. I founded a colony to protect the other English colonies from attack. _____

3. I founded England's first American colony. _____

4. I wanted to create a colony where Catholics would not be persecuted. _____

5. I was a minister who was banished from the Massachusetts Bay Colony. _____

6. I helped set the Middle Colonies on the road to tolerance and diversity. _____

7. I was a woman who questioned the authority of the clergy. _____

8. This document helped establish the practice of self-government. _____

9. I governed the city that would become New York. _____

10. I acted as attorney for the governor of Maryland. _____

A. James Oglethorpe
B. Mayflower Compact
C. Roger Williams
D. William Penn
E. Jamestown
F. Sir Walter Raleigh
G. House of Burgesses
H. Margaret Brent
I. Peter Stuyvesant
J. New Netherland
K. John Smith
L. mercantilism
M. Anne Hutchinson
N. Puritans
O. Lord Baltimore
P. William Penn

Activities

FLIP CARD

Use the online flip cards to quiz yourself on the terms and names introduced in this chapter.

The first governor of Massachusetts Bay colony.

ANSWER
John Winthrop

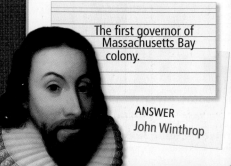

GEOGAME

Use this online map to reinforce your understanding of the early English colonies. Drag and drop each label in the list at its location on the map. A scorecard helps you keep track of your progress online.

Chesapeake Bay
York River
James River
Roanoke
Jamestown

More items online

James River

VOCABULARY

Explain the significance of each of the following.

1. James Oglethorpe
2. Peter Stuyvesant
3. Roger Williams
4. Jamestown
5. Margaret Brent
6. William Penn
7. John Winthrop
8. Lord Baltimore

Explain how the terms and names in each group are related.

9. headright, patroon

10. Anne Hutchinson, Roger Williams

11. Mayflower Compact, Fundamental Orders of Connecticut

12. Puritans, Quakers

13. joint-stock company, mercantilism

KEY IDEAS

1 Early Colonies Have Mixed Success (pages 60–65)

14. What rights did the Virginia Company grant the Jamestown colonists?

15. What was the purpose of the House of Burgesses?

2 New England Colonies (pages 66–73)

16. What was the Great Migration?

17. What religious issues were important to the early colonists of New England?

3 The Southern Colonies (pages 76–81)

18. Why did the Maryland Assembly pass the Act of Toleration?

19. Why did a wealthy elite develop in the Carolinas?

4 The Middle Colonies (pages 82–88)

20. What social values were important to the settlers of the Middle Colonies?

21. What is the difference between a proprietary colony and a royal colony?

CRITICAL THINKING

22. **Synthesize** What similar political traditions did both the Virginia and Massachusetts settlers establish in the colonies?

23. **Analyze Causes and Effects** Why did slavery expand more in the South than in the North?

24. **Summarize** In what ways did issues of religious tolerance emerge throughout the colonies?

25. **Compare and Contrast** Create a table to compare and contrast the people who colonized Virginia and Massachusetts.

Virginia Colonists	Massachusetts Colonists
mostly young men	*families*

26. **Compare and Contrast** In what ways did the difference in climate between northern and southern regions affect the history of the colonies?

27. **Summarize** What democratic customs were practiced by New England congregations?

28. **Interpret Graphs** Use the graph and your knowledge of American history to answer the question: In which decades did the largest population increase occur?

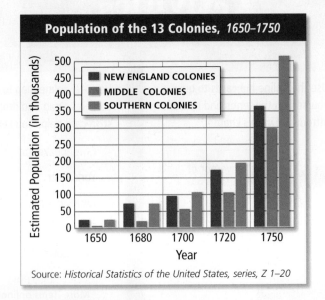

Population of the 13 Colonies, *1650–1750*

- NEW ENGLAND COLONIES
- MIDDLE COLONIES
- SOUTHERN COLONIES

Estimated Population (in thousands)

Year

Source: *Historical Statistics of the United States, series, Z 1–20*

DOCUMENT-BASED QUESTIONS

PART 1: Short Answer

Study each document carefully and answer the questions that follow.

DOCUMENT 1

1. Examine this label that was used to sell American tobacco in late 17th-century England. What does this illustration reveal about the climate and labor force of Virginia in the late 1600s?

DOCUMENT 2

PRIMARY SOURCE

❝ The Planters neglect all other [routes] to wealth and happiness, and fix their hopes only on this vicious weed of Tobacco, which has brought them to that extremity that they can neither [exist] with it, nor without it. ❞

—from Governor William Berkeley's *Discourse and View of Virginia*

2. What is Governor Berkeley's attitude to the planters' dependence on tobacco?

Part 2: Essay

3. Using information from the documents, your answers to the questions in Part 1, and your knowledge of U.S. history, write an essay about the economy of colonial Virginia.

YOU BE THE HISTORIAN

29. **Make Generalizations** William Penn called Pennsylvania a "holy experiment." What other colonies were experiments in creating new societies?

30. **Evaluate** Do you think that John Winthrop achieved his vision for the colony described in One American's Story? Why or why not?

31. **WHAT IF?** Suppose the Great Migration had brought settlers to Virginia instead of to the Massachusetts Bay. How might this have changed the history of the Virginia colony?

32. **Make Inferences** How did the English fear of the Spanish Empire affect the history of the South?

33. **Draw Conclusions** Why would Puritans have felt threatened by the beliefs and practices of the Quakers?

34. **Connect** *to* **Today** **Citizenship** What ideals link the Mayflower Compact, the House of Burgesses, and New England town meetings to modern American democracy?

Answer the

ESSENTIAL QUESTION

How did the experience of the early colonists shape America's political and social ideals?

Written Response Write a two- to three-paragraph response to the Essential Question. Be sure to consider the key ideas of each section as well as the ideals that Americans value today. Use the Response Rubric below to guide your thinking and writing.

Response Rubric

A strong response will

• discuss the values and ideals of modern America
• analyze the colonial events and conflicts out of which these ideals emerged
• explain the unique nature of the American colonies

The Colonies Develop

1651–1753

 ESSENTIAL QUESTION

What factors allowed each colonial region to grow and prosper?

CONNECT ⟲ **Geography & History**

How did the Atlantic Ocean help bring prosperity to American colonists?

Think about:

1 the importance of trans-Atlantic trade

2 how the slave trade fit into the Atlantic trade network

3 the way communities in different regions used natural resources to create wealth

---

detail from *Jamestown: N. Bacon, 1676* by Howard Pyle

1676 Nathaniel Bacon leads a rebellion in Virginia.

▼

Effect After the rebellion ends, the House of Burgesses limits the governor's power.

1651

Parliament passes the first of the Navigation Acts.

seal of Parliament

1675 King Philip's War begins in New England.

1692 The Salem witchcraft trials begin in Massachusetts.

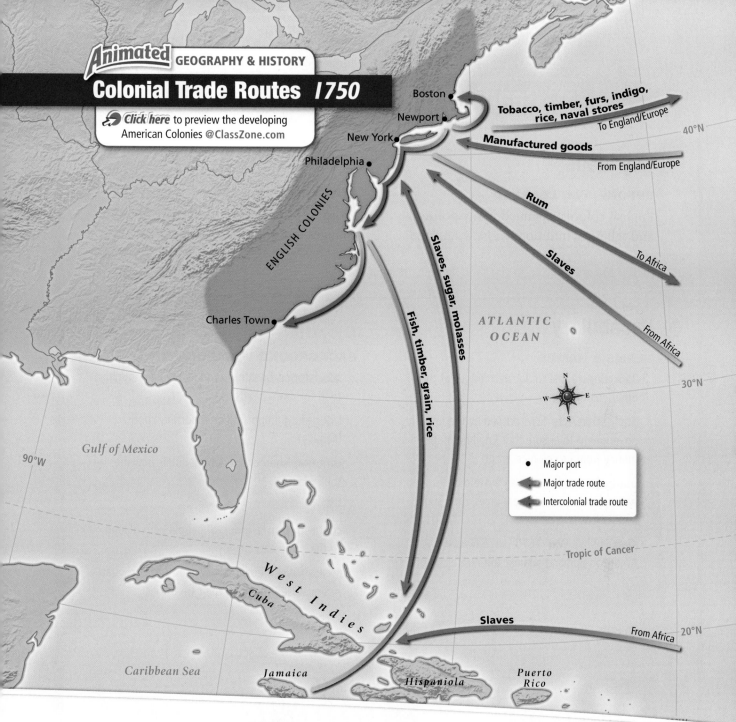

Colonial Trade Routes *1750*

Click here to preview the developing
American Colonies @ClassZone.com

Tobacco, timber, furs, indigo, rice, naval stores

To England/Europe

40°N

Manufactured goods

From England/Europe

Rum

To Africa

Slaves

From Africa

30°N

ENGLISH COLONIES

Slaves, sugar, molasses

Fish, timber, grain, rice

Boston

Newport

New York

Philadelphia

Charles Town

ATLANTIC OCEAN

Gulf of Mexico

90°W

• Major port

⬅ Major trade route

⬅ Intercolonial trade route

Tropic of Cancer

West Indies

Cuba

Caribbean Sea

Jamaica

Hispaniola

Puerto Rico

Slaves

From Africa   20°N

1712 Enslaved Africans rebel in New York City.

1739 The Stono Rebellion, a slave uprising, takes place in South Carolina.

▼

Effect Southern Colonies make slave codes even stricter.

1753

A young officer named George Washington is sent to warn the French to leave the Ohio territory.

slave market on Wall Street, New York in the early 18th century

The Colonies Develop **93**

Reading for Understanding

Key Ideas

BEFORE, YOU LEARNED

English colonists planted many political and religious traditions in New England.

NOW YOU WILL LEARN

Prosperity and religious diversity brought changes to Puritan New England.

▶ Vocabulary

TERMS & NAMES

Backcountry the far western edges of the other colonies

Navigation Acts laws passed by the English government to ensure that England made money from its colonies' trade

triangular trade complex system of transatlantic exchange of slaves, rum, sugar, and molasses

King Philip's War 1675–1676 Native American uprising against the Puritan colonies

BACKGROUND VOCABULARY

subsistence farming producing just enough food for one's needs

smuggling importing or exporting goods illegally

common shared land where public activities took place

REVIEW

congregation a group of people who belong to the same church

mercantilism economic system that European nations used to enrich their treasuries

▶ Reading Strategy

Re-create the diagram shown at right. As you read and respond to the **KEY QUESTIONS**, use the diagram to record the causes and effects of the Navigation Acts.

 See Skillbuilder Handbook, page R7.

ANALYZE CAUSES AND EFFECTS

Cause
England wanted to profit from colonial trade.

Navigation Acts

Effect

Cause

Effect

⚡ GRAPHIC ORGANIZERS
Go to **Interactive Review** @ ClassZone.com

New England:
Commerce and Religion

 15.E.3a Identify the types of taxes levied by differing levels of governments (e.g., *income tax, sales tax, property tax*).
16.C.3b Explain relationships among the American economy and slavery, immigration, industrialization, labor and urbanization, 1700–present.

One American's Story

Like many other New England Puritans, Captain Thomas Smith had grown rich through commerce. In this self-portrait from 1680, he displays his wealthy clothes and surroundings. He was proud of his achievements: the painting includes a scene of a naval battle in which he may have fought. Smith enjoyed his worldly success. But as a Puritan, he was also torn between the joys of this world and the need to prepare for the next. So under the skull appears a religious poem that begins

PRIMARY SOURCE

❝ Why why should I the World be minding
  Therein a World of Evils finding.
  Then Farewell World: Farewell thy Jarres [conflicts]
  Thy Joies thy Toies thy Wiles thy Warrs ❞

—poem in Captain Thomas Smith's self-portrait

Captain Thomas Smith
Self–Portrait, Worcester
Art Museum

The poem reveals a man who was aware of both the "evils" and the "joys" and "toys" of this world. Like other New Englanders, Captain Smith struggled to balance his religious life with his commercial success.

The Resources of New England

▼ **KEY QUESTION** Why did England pass the Navigation Acts?

By the 1700s, the colonies formed several distinct regions: New England, the Middle Colonies, the Southern Colonies and the **Backcountry**, which ran through the far western edges of the colonies. Of all the colonial regions, New England was the most populated. Its people grew rich by cleverly exploiting the region's resources.

Farms and Towns Farming in New England was not easy. The growing season was short, and the soil in many places was rocky. Most farmers practiced **subsistence farming**. That is, they produced just enough food for themselves and sometimes a little extra to trade in town.

Most New England farmers lived near a town. Colonial officials sold large plots of land to groups of people—often to a Puritan **congregation**. The congregation settled the town and divided the land among its members.

This pattern of settlement led New England towns to develop in a unique way. Usually, a cluster of farmhouses and a meetinghouse were built around a **common**—shared land where public activities took place. Because people lived together in small towns, a diverse economy developed. Farmers sold produce to shopkeepers; shopkeepers had enough customers to make a living. Along the coast, seaport towns shipped farm products and provided a marketplace for goods coming into New England.

Harvesting the Sea The Atlantic Ocean offered many economic opportunities. Near New England's coast were some of the world's best whaling and fishing grounds for mackerel, halibut, cod, herring, and other fish.

New England's forests provided everything needed to harvest these "pastures" of fish. Wood from oak trees made excellent ship hulls. Hundred-foot-tall white pines were ideal for masts. Shipbuilders used about 2,500 trees to produce just one ship!

The forests were a valuable resource. Soon New England was exporting timber, as well as fish, to the world. As merchants grew rich from exporting these goods, their ships began carrying goods produced in other places as well. New England's ships became an important part of international trade.

Throughout New England, the population benefitted from the wealth being created in the seaports. The colonists were soon competing with England's fishermen, shipbuilders, and merchants. As coastal towns like Boston, Salem, and Newport grew rich, the English government began to take notice.

The Navigation Acts According to the economic theory of **mercantilism**, the mother country was supposed to profit from its colonies. As the American colonists prospered, England wanted to make sure that it profited

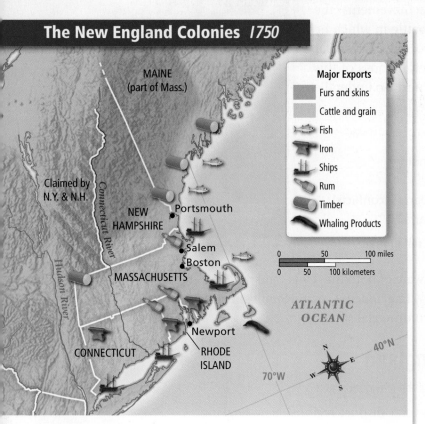

The New England Colonies *1750*

MAINE
(part of Mass.)

Claimed by
N.Y. & N.H.

NEW
HAMPSHIRE   Portsmouth

Salem
Boston
MASSACHUSETTS

CONNECTICUT

Newport
RHODE
ISLAND

Connecticut River

Hudson River

ATLANTIC
OCEAN

Major Exports
- Furs and skins
- Cattle and grain
- Fish
- Iron
- Ships
- Rum
- Timber
- Whaling Products

0   50   100 miles
0 50 100 kilometers

70°W   40°N

Connect Geography & History

1. **Location** All of the New England colonies are located to the east of what major river?

2. **Make Inferences** Why do you think New Englanders exported so many ocean-related products?

from colonial prosperity. So the English government began passing the **Navigation Acts** in 1651. The Navigation Acts had four major provisions designed to ensure that England made money from its colonies' trade.

1. All goods had to be carried on English ships or on ships made in the English colonies.
2. Products such as tobacco, wood, and sugar could be sold only to England or its colonies.
3. European imports to the colonies had to pass through English ports.
4. Officials were to tax any colonial goods not shipped to England.

The colonists resented these laws. Merchants ignored the acts whenever possible. England had trouble controlling colonial shipping and patrolling the long coastline of the colonies. **Smuggling**—importing or exporting goods illegally—was common. England also had great difficulty preventing pirates, like the legendary Blackbeard, from interfering with colonial shipping.

▲ **CAUSES AND EFFECTS** Explain why England passed the Navigation Acts.

CONNECT ⤸ *To Today*

PIRACY

In the late 1600s, England faced a problem that it had helped create—Atlantic piracy. For decades, England had encouraged pirates to attack Spanish shipping. But as England itself grew rich from commerce, pirates began attacking English ships. They also smuggled goods into and out of colonial ports.

Rich cargoes have always attracted pirates. Today, piracy flourishes in southeast Asia, especially in the busy Malacca Strait between Indonesia and Malaysia.

Each year 50,000 ships, carrying half the world's oil shipments, pass through the strait. Hundreds of ships are attacked annually. Vessels are often hijacked and the crew held to ransom. In 2004, Indonesia, Singapore, and Malaysia agreed to fight piracy in their waters.

Modern coastguard on the lookout for piracy near Guam

Pirates in colonial times

CRITICAL THINKING

1. **Make Inferences** Why was piracy a threat to the mercantilist system?
2. **Draw Conclusions** Why are modern pirates attracted to the Malacca Strait?

Atlantic Trade

▼ **KEY QUESTION** How did New Englanders profit from the triangular trade?

New England settlers engaged in three types of trade. First was the trade with other colonies. Second was the exchange of goods with Europe. But the third type, known as the **triangular trade**, had a sinister, or evil, aspect—because it involved trade in human beings.

Human Cargo Triangular trade describes a complex system of trans-Atlantic trade used to exchange slaves, rum, sugar, and molasses. For example, a ship might leave New England with a cargo of rum and iron. In Africa, the captain would trade his cargo for slaves. Slaves then endured the cruel voyage to the West Indies, where they were exchanged for sugar and molasses. Traders then took the sugar and molasses back to New England. There, colonists used the molasses to make rum, and the sequence began again.

New Englanders not only brought slaves to the West Indies but also sent fish to feed the huge slave population there. In this way, the economies of New England and the West Indies were closely tied. This trading system brought prosperity to both New England and the West Indies.

CONNECTING ⟳ *Economics and History*

TRIANGULAR TRADE

America's natural resources brought great wealth to the colonists, who shipped these resources around the world. New England merchants developed a complicated system of trade routes between the Americas, Europe, and Africa. The triangular trade was only one part of this international trade system.

NEW ENGLAND

ATLANTIC OCEAN

EUROPE

MOLASSES, SLAVES

FISH, TIMBER

RUM, IRON

Fortress where slaves were held, West Africa

SLAVES

AFRICA

WEST INDIES
West Indies sugar plantation

CRITICAL THINKING
1. **Make Inferences** How did New England merchants help spread slavery?
2. **Connect** *to* **Today** What countries produce the clothes you wear and the food you eat?

Africans in New England Despite New Englanders' involvement in the slave trade, there were few slaves in New England. In 1700 slaves made up only 2 percent of New England's population. New England had no large plantations, so there was no need for a large labor force on each farm. This is why a large slave population never developed in New England.

Some New Englanders who lived in larger towns and cities did own slaves. Enslaved people worked as house servants, cooks, gardeners, and stable-hands. In the 1700s, New England slave owners seldom had enough room to house more than one or two slaves. Instead, more and more slave owners hired out their slaves to work on the docks or in shops or warehouses. Slave owners sometimes allowed their slaves to keep a portion of their wages.

Occasionally, the enslaved were able to save enough to buy their freedom. In fact, New England had more free blacks than any other region. A free African American man might become a merchant, sailor, printer, carpenter, or landowner. Even so, white colonists did not treat free African Americans as equals.

▲ **SUMMARIZE** Explain how New Englanders profited from the triangular trade.

King Philip's War

▼ **KEY QUESTION** How did Native Americans react to colonial growth?

Europeans and Native Americans had different attitudes about land ownership. Europeans believed that land could be owned. Native Americans had a more communal attitude to land use. Conflict over land resulted in warfare.

Fighting for Survival Native American tribes in New England were alarmed by the increasing numbers of settlers on their hunting grounds and near their crops. They were also troubled by the growing influence of European culture on their people. In 1675–1676, they carried out an uprising against the Puritan colonies. This was known as **King Philip's War**. "King Philip" was the English name of Metacom, leader of the Wampanoag tribe, who led the first attacks against the colonists.

The Wampanoag were soon joined by other tribes. For both sides, the war was a fight for survival. Twelve Puritan towns were destroyed. Forty other towns, including Plymouth and Providence, were attacked. For a while, it seemed as if the New England colonies might be destroyed.

In desperation, the English colonists turned to other Native American peoples for help. Southern New England tribes such as the Pequot and the Mohegan showed the New Englanders how to track down and ambush the rebel tribes. In the summer of 1676 the uprising collapsed. Many Native Americans were killed, while others were sold into slavery in the West Indies. English settlers expanded even farther into Native American land.

▲ **MAKE INFERENCES** Explain how Native Americans reacted to colonial growth.

Why might King Philip (shown above) have been outraged by European attitudes about land use?

Changes in Puritan Society

▼ **KEY QUESTION** What factors helped weaken Puritan religious control?

New England society was changing rapidly by the late 1600s. One of the most noticeable changes was the decline of Puritan power.

Economic Success and Religious Diversity The Puritan values of hard work made many New Englanders rich. But some colonists now seemed to care more about business and material possessions than about religion. Puritan ministers noticed the change and used their sermons to condemn the new interest in worldly success.

History *through* Art

Portraits of Elizabeth, Mary, and John Freake by an unidentified artist, from the collection of the Worcester Art Museum.

A Changing Puritan World

These portraits, painted a few years before King Philip's War, are windows onto a changing Puritan world. Elizabeth, (shown with her daughter Mary) and John Freake were in their 30s when these portraits were painted in the 1670s. Elizabeth was one of the children of the first generation of Puritans, who arrived during the Great Migration. Elizabeth and John enjoyed the fruits of the prosperous society that their parents had created. Their clothes are richly decorated and expensive. For example, John's elaborate lace collar, gloves, and ruffled sleeves display his wealth.

CRITICAL VIEWING How do Elizabeth's clothes and surroundings reveal the wealth of Puritan society in the late 1600s?

❝We have changed our Interest. The Interest of New England was religion, which did distinguish us from other English [colonies]. . . . Now we begin to espouse a Worldly Interest and so choose a new God.❞

—Increase Mather, from the sermon "The Day of Trouble is Near," 1674

The arrival of non-Puritan immigrants also threatened Puritan control. The success of the colony began attracting different kinds of immigrants. Baptists and Anglicans established churches in Massachusetts and Connecticut, where Puritans had once been the most powerful group.

Political changes further weakened Puritan domination. In 1691, a new royal charter for Massachusetts guaranteed religious freedom for all Protestants, not just Puritans. The charter broke Puritan power by ending the churches' control of elections. The loss of power created great uncertainty for many Puritans, which may have contributed to one of the strangest episodes in American history—the Salem witchcraft trials.

The Salem Witchcraft Trials In 1692, a year after the new charter broke Puritan power, a terrifying series of events occurred in Salem Village, Massachusetts. Several girls, pretending to be bewitched, began accusing others of witchcraft.

Hysteria spread through the community. Those accused were forced to name others as witches. More than 100 people were arrested and dozens were tried. Of those, 19 were found guilty and put to death by hanging, including a popular minister. In addition, two dogs were hanged, and a man was pressed to death when he refused to cooperate with the court.

Eventually, important ministers intervened, and the governor stopped the executions. Within a few years, several of the accusers admitted that they had made false accusations. In 1697 one of the judges begged public forgiveness for his part in the trials.

Puritan Legacy Although Puritan power declined, Puritan values survived. These values have influenced American culture. Americans have inherited:

- the Puritan work ethic
- a high regard for education
- opposition to royal power and support for representative government
- the practice of voting on decisions affecting the community

Many of these Puritan values helped put America on the road to independence.

An elderly women being arrested for witchcraft in Salem
Why do you think the girls accused so many people of witchcraft?

 CAUSES AND EFFECTS Describe how Puritan religious control was weakened in the later 1600s.

 ONLINE QUIZ
For test practice, go to
Interactive Review @ ClassZone.com

Illinois Learning Standards *Review*

TERMS & NAMES

1. Explain the importance of
   - Backcountry
   - Navigation Acts
   - triangular trade
   - King Philip's War

USING YOUR READING NOTES

2. **Causes and Effects** Complete the diagram you started at the beginning of this section to show the causes and effects of the Navigation Acts.

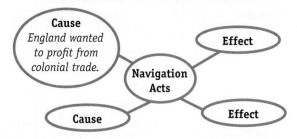

Cause
England wanted to profit from colonial trade.

Navigation Acts

Effect

Cause

Effect

KEY IDEAS

3. How did England profit from colonial shipping?

4. What changes did prosperity bring to New England?

CRITICAL THINKING

5. **Make Inferences** How do you think the enslaved were able to save money if they were not paid for their labor?

6. **Connect Economics & History** Why did New England come to depend on fishing and shipbuilding?

7. **Connect to Today** New Englanders took economic advantage of their environment. Describe modern examples of people using natural resources to gain wealth.

8. **Writing** Letter Write a letter from Metacom to the English colonists. Explain the reasons for the war that is about to be launched against them.

Reading for Understanding

▶ Key Ideas

BEFORE, YOU LEARNED

Southern planters grew rich from exporting tobacco and rice.

NOW YOU WILL LEARN

In the Southern Colonies, the need for cheap labor led to a dependence on slavery.

▶ Vocabulary

TERMS AND NAMES

Bacon's Rebellion 1676 rebellion in Virginia

Eliza Lucas introduced indigo as a successful plantation crop

Stono Rebellion 1739 slave rebellion in South Carolina

BACKGROUND VOCABULARY

cash crops crops raised to be sold for money

overseers people who watch over and direct the work of slaves

indigo plant that produces a deep blue dye

REVIEW

Tidewater the flat land along the coast

elite the highest ranking social group

Visual Vocabulary
indigo plant and dyed yarn

▶ Reading Strategy

Re-create the diagram shown at right. As you read and respond to the **KEY QUESTIONS**, use the chart to show the difference between the Tidewater and the western frontier.

 See Skillbuilder Handbook, page R8.

COMPARE AND CONTRAST

Tidewater *wealthy planters*	Western Frontier

 GRAPHIC ORGANIZERS
Go to **Interactive Review** @ ClassZone.com

The Southern Colonies:
Plantations and Slavery

16.C.3b Explain relationships among the American economy and slavery, immigration, industrialization, labor and urbanization, 1700–present.
17.C.3b Explain how patterns of resources are used throughout the world.

One American's Story

George Mason was born to a wealthy Virginia family in 1725. Mason—who later called the slave trade "disgraceful to mankind"—described the skills of the enslaved people who worked on his family's plantation.

George Mason

PRIMARY SOURCE

❝ My father had among his slaves carpenters, coopers [barrel makers], sawyers, blacksmiths, tanners, curriers, shoemakers, spinners, weavers and knitters, and even a distiller. ❞

—George Mason, quoted in *Common Landscape of America*

The Masons and other wealthy landowners set up self-sufficient plantations and had little need for the kind of densely settled towns that developed in New England. These scattered plantations, and the system of slavery needed to run them, shaped life in the Southern Colonies: Virginia, Maryland, the Carolinas, and Georgia.

The Plantation Economy

🔻 **KEY QUESTION** What tensions developed between Tidewater and Backcountry?

In contrast to the small farms and numerous towns of New England, in the South large plantations developed. The earliest were built on the shores of the **Tidewater**—the flat land along the coast.

Geography and Climate The South's soil and almost year-round growing season were ideal for plantation crops like rice and tobacco. These valuable plants required much labor to produce, but with enough workers they could be grown as **cash crops** and shipped to foreign markets for great profits. The Tidewater's many waterways allowed oceangoing ships to load cargo at the plantation docks. This allowed the plantations to carry on a lively trade with other colonies and with England.

Because most plantations were largely self-sufficient, large urban centers were unnecessary in the South. The port city of Charles Town (later called Charleston) in South Carolina was an early exception.

The Planter Class The owners of the plantations were considered the **elite** of this society. In the early colonies, this class was drawn from the noble families of the south and west of England.

The planter class was relatively small compared to the rest of the population. However, they soon gained control of political and economic power in the South. A foreign traveler in the South commented that the planters "think and act precisely as do the nobility in other countries."

The planters formed the highest level of a class system that included large numbers of poor freemen, indentured servants, and slaves. The social system in the South was dramatically different from New England, where numerous middle-class families had settled. In the South, tension between social groups led to a major conflict in the late 17th century.

Bacon's Rebellion in 1676 The desire for land and wealth had drawn settlers to America, so it is not surprising that many of the early conflicts in the South were over land. By the 1670s many indentured servants had completed their service and demanded land. Because the wealthy planters controlled the Tidewater region, these poorer freemen were forced into the western frontier, where they battled Native Americans for land.

Jamestown: N. Bacon, 1676 by Howard Pyle

Nathaniel Bacon and a group of landless frontier settlers were already angry with Virginia Governor William Berkeley. They complained about high taxes and Governor Berkeley's favoritism toward large plantation owners. Bacon demanded that Berkeley help defend frontier settlements against Native Americans. Berkeley's refusal of Bacon's demand sparked **Bacon's Rebellion** in 1676.

Bacon entered Jamestown, took control of the House of Burgesses, and burned Jamestown to the ground. However, Bacon's sudden illness and death ended the rebellion. Berkeley hanged 23 of Bacon's followers. Angered by Berkeley's actions, King Charles II recalled the governor to England. Afterwards, the House of Burgesses passed laws to prevent a royal governor from assuming such power again. The burgesses had taken an important step against tyranny.

▲ **COMPARE AND CONTRAST** Explain what tensions developed between Tidewater and frontier settlers.

The Search for Cheap Labor

▼ **KEY QUESTION** Why did planters turn to slavery?

In the early Southern Colonies, there were few Africans, either enslaved or free. In 1665, fewer than 500 Africans had been brought into Virginia. At that time, African and European indentured servants worked in the fields together.

In the 1660s, the labor system began to change as indentured white servants left the plantations. Their terms of service were finished, and many moved west in order to buy their own farms. At the same time, fewer European laborers were emigrating to the Southern Colonies. Landowners had to find another source of labor.

Planters Turn to Slavery At first planters tried to enslave Native Americans. But many Native Americans either died of diseases brought by Europeans or were able to escape into the forests that they knew so well.

To meet their labor needs, the planters turned to enslaved Africans. As a result, the enslaved population grew rapidly. By 1750, there were over 235,000 enslaved Africans in America. About 68 percent lived in the Southern Colonies. By 1750 enslaved Africans made up about 40 percent of the South's population.

As the slave population increased, laws were passed to define slavery and to control the growing numbers of people being held against their will. Local militia patrolled the countryside to check that any traveling Africans were carrying passes. Slave quarters were checked regularly for weapons.

Living in Slavery On large Southern plantations, slaves usually toiled in groups of about 20 to 25 under the supervision of **overseers**. Overseers were people who watched over and directed the work of others. Enslaved people performed strenuous and exhausting work, often for 15 hours a day at the peak of the harvest season. If slaves did not appear to be doing their full share of work, they were often whipped by the overseer. If they defied their masters, they could be tortured or mutilated.

Enslaved people usually lived in small one-room cabins with straw for bedding. For a week's food, a slave might receive only around a quarter bushel of cornmeal and around 3 pounds of pork. Some planters allowed their slaves to raise their own food.

In spite of the brutal living conditions, Africans preserved many customs and beliefs from their homelands. These included music, dances, stories, and, for a time, African religions—including Islam. African kinship customs became the basis of African-American family culture.

▲ **CAUSES AND EFFECTS** Explain why planters turned to slavery.

COMPARING *Slave Populations*

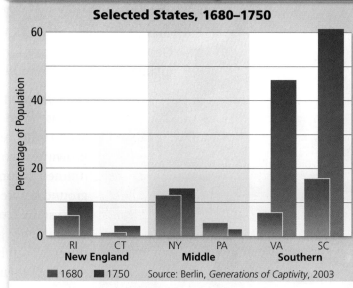

Selected States, 1680–1750

CRITICAL VIEWING Analyze Charts What percentage of the population was enslaved in the South in 1750?

Expansion of Plantations Brings Resistance

🔻 **KEY QUESTION** How did African Americans resist their enslavement?

Slavery allowed plantation farming to expand in South Carolina and Georgia. Without slave labor, there probably would have been no rice plantations in the lowcountry—the region's swampy lowlands.

Backbreaking Labor Rice cultivation required great skill. Because West Africans had these skills, planters sought out slaves who came from Africa's rice-growing regions. Rice growing involved backbreaking labor. Enslaved workers drained swamps, raked fields, burned stubble, and broke ground before planting. They also had to tend the fields and harvest the crop.

On higher ground, planters grew **indigo**, a plant that produces a deep blue dye used to dye clothes. A young woman named **Eliza Lucas** had introduced indigo as a successful plantation crop after her father left her to supervise his South Carolina plantations when she was 17.

The Enslaved Fight Back Although they were kept in bondage, people of African origin found ways to resist their enslavement. They sometimes worked slowly, damaged goods, or deliberately carried out orders the wrong way. A British traveler in 1746 noted that many slaves pretended not to understand tasks they often had performed in West Africa.

Reenactors portray slave labor.

PRIMARY SOURCE

❝ You would really be surpriz'd at their Perseverance; let an hundred Men shew him how to hoe, or drive a wheelbarrow, he'll still take the one by the Bottom, and the other by the Wheel; and they often die before they can be conquer'd. ❞

—Edward Kimber, quoted in *White over Black*

Connecting History

Slavery
In the next century, South Carolina's continuing dependence on slavery would lead the state to secede from the Union in 1860—the event that led to the Civil War.
See Chapter 15, p. 502.

In South Carolina, the enslaved vastly outnumbered whites, who lived in fear of slave rebellions. Their fears came true in the late 1730s when a revolt occurred in South Carolina.

The Stono Rebellion In September 1739, an uprising known as the **Stono Rebellion** took place. The revolt began when about 20 slaves gathered at the Stono River just southwest of Charles Town. Wielding weapons, they killed planters and marched south, beating drums and chanting "Liberty!" They called out for other slaves to join them in their plan to seek freedom in Spanish-held Florida. Many joined them, and their numbers grew until there were perhaps one hundred in open rebellion. Seven plantations were burned along their route and twenty whites were killed. By late that afternoon, however, a white militia had surrounded the escaping slaves. The two sides clashed, and many slaves died in the fighting. Those captured were executed.

Stono and similar revolts led planters to make slave codes even stricter. Slaves were now forbidden from leaving plantations without written permission. The laws also made it illegal for slaves to meet with free blacks. Such laws made the conditions of slavery even more inhumane.

Economy of the South The Southern Colonies' plantation economy and large slave population helped create a unique Southern identity. In northern colonies, with their diverse economies, wealth was more evenly distributed. Southern economies were less diverse, based on crops such as tobacco, rice, and indigo. The wealth from these crops was concentrated in the hands of an elite.

The different economic systems of Northern and Southern Colonies were reflected in the landscape: the north had smaller farms and larger, more numerous towns. The South had scattered settlements, few towns, and self-sufficient plantations. The contrast between northern and southern landscapes, settlement patterns, and economic systems emerged very early in American history. Distinct regionalisms were developing that continue to influence American culture and politics.

▲ **SUMMARIZE** Describe how African Americans resisted their enslavement.

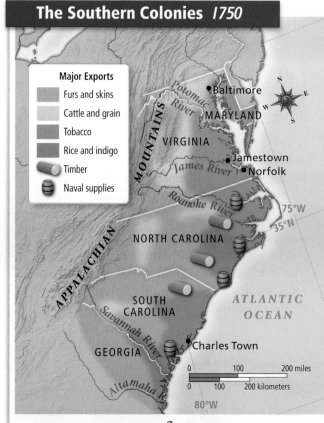

The Southern Colonies 1750

Major Exports
- Furs and skins
- Cattle and grain
- Tobacco
- Rice and indigo
- Timber
- Naval supplies

Connect Geography & History

1. **Place** Which Southern Colonies grew both rice and indigo?
2. **Draw Conclusions** Where would planters have built their plantations if they wanted to keep transportation costs low?

Illinois Learning Standards *Review*

 ONLINE QUIZ
For test practice, go to
Interactive Review @ ClassZone.com

TERMS & NAMES

1. Explain the importance of
   - Bacon's Rebellion
   - Stono Rebellion
   - Eliza Lucas

USING YOUR READING NOTES

2. **Compare and Contrast** Complete the diagram you started at the beginning of this section.

Tidewater *wealthy planters*	Western Frontier

KEY IDEAS

3. Where were most of the early plantations located?
4. How did planters meet their labor needs?

CRITICAL THINKING

5. **Make Inferences** Why did South Carolina's colonists live in fear of a slave revolt?
6. **Summarize** How did the House of Burgesses strengthen colonists' rights after Bacon's Rebellion?
7. **Writing** **Research Report** Use the internet to research the Virginia House of Burgesses. Write a paragraph on the importance of the House of Burgesses in the history of American democracy.

Animated HISTORY
A NEW ENGLAND SEAPORT

 Click here to learn more about how New Englanders created wealth through trade @ ClassZone.com

In New England, densely settled towns developed on the coast. These towns became centers of a worldwide commerce, exporting many different products, such as fish, lumber, and foodstuffs.

This commerce brought wealth to an elite of merchants, bankers, and insurers. However, trade also benefitted the population of New England's smaller towns, rural villages, and farms. For several centuries, New England's sea trade was the basis for the region's prosperity.

COMPARING Economies

By 1700 two economic systems had developed in the colonies—one in the North and one in the South. Both systems created wealth, but in very different ways.

Drayton Hall, near Charleston, South Carolina

Northern Seaport and Southern Plantation

- New England towns had many free workers who bought and sold products among themselves and shipped goods to other places.

- In contrast, the South had few towns. Economic life centered on the plantations. Each plantation exported a limited number of crops.

  A Southern plantation was so self-sufficient that it was like a small town in itself. Plantation slaves produced food and made products in the workshops.

Activity

Seaport and Plantation

1. Divide the class into two groups. Have one group research the layout of an 18th-century plantation. Have the other reseach the types of buildings and businesses found in a New England seaport.

2. Let the plantation group draw a plan of a typical plantation, identifying the various service buildings. Have the seaport group draw the plan of a coastal town.

3. Present the research to the class.

▶ Key Ideas

BEFORE, YOU LEARNED

The Middle Colonies attracted a diverse population who favored religious tolerance.

NOW YOU WILL LEARN

Rich farmland and a climate of tolerance helped the Middle Colonies prosper.

▶ Vocabulary

TERMS & NAMES

Philadelphia settlement on the Delaware River that became the fastest growing city in the colonies

Conestoga wagons covered wagons introduced by German immigrants

BACKGROUND VOCABULARY

artisans skilled craftspeople, such as blacksmiths and cabinet makers

denomination distinct religious group

REVIEW

Quakers group of Protestant dissenters

tolerance acceptance of different opinions

Visual Vocabulary
blacksmith

▶ Reading Strategy

Re-create the diagram shown at right. As you read and respond to the **KEY QUESTIONS**, use the diagram to note important details that support the Main Idea of this section.

 See Skillbuilder Handbook, page R4.

MAIN IDEAS AND DETAILS

Detail	Main Idea	Detail
	Religious tolerance, ethnic diversity, and fertile lands helped the Middle Colonies prosper.	

Detail

GRAPHIC ORGANIZERS
Go to **Interactive Review** @ ClassZone.com

The Middle Colonies:
Farms and Cities

16.C.3b Explain relationships among the American economy and slavery, immigration, industrialization, labor and urbanization, 1700–present.
17.C.3c Analyze how human process influence settlement patterns including migration and population growth.

One American's Story

William Penn, who established Pennsylvania, was aware that earlier English colonists had not treated Native Americans with respect. Writing from England, Penn promised Native Americans that the people of his colony would behave differently.

PRIMARY SOURCE

❝I am very sensible to the unkindness and injustice which have been too much exercised toward you by the people of these parts of the world. . . . I have a great love and regard toward you, and desire to win and gain your love and friendship by a kind, just and peaceable life; and the people I send are of the same mind.❞

—**Letter from William Penn to the Native Americans, 1681**

Penn's Treaty with the Indians by Edward Hicks

The **Quakers**, a group of Protestant dissenters, did develop a good relationship with tribes in Pennsylvania. The Quakers also accepted people who had different religious beliefs. This helped to create a climate of **tolerance**, or acceptance of different opinions, in the prosperous Middle Colonies of New York, New Jersey, Pennsylvania, and Delaware.

A Prosperous Region

🔻 **KEY QUESTION** Why did the cities of the Middle Colonies grow so rapidly?

The Middle Colonies had much to offer in addition to a climate of tolerance. Immigrants were drawn to the region's productive land.

Among the immigrants who came to the Middle Colonies were Dutch and German farmers. Their skills, knowledge, and hard work produced an abundance of foods.

Productive Farms The Middle Colonies enjoyed a longer growing season than New England and a soil rich enough to grow cash crops. These were crops raised to be sold for money. Common cash crops included fruits, vegetables, and, above all, grain. In fact, the Middle Colonies produced so much grain that people began calling them the "breadbasket" colonies.

Growing Cities The excellent harbors of the Middle Colonies were ideal sites for cities. New York City grew at the mouth of the Hudson River, and **Philadelphia** was founded on the Delaware River. The merchants who lived in these growing port cities exported grain and other cash crops from local farms and imported manufactured goods from England.

Because of its enormous trade, Philadelphia became the fastest growing city in the colonies. By the 1750s, it was home to a dozen large shipyards—places where ships are built or repaired.

The city's wealth also brought many public improvements. Large and beautiful buildings, such as Philadelphia's statehouse—which was later renamed Independence Hall—graced the city's streets. In 1748, a Swedish visitor was impressed by the city's beauty and wealth.

PRIMARY SOURCE

❝ And yet . . . its natural advantages, trade, riches, and power are by no means inferior to . . . any, even of the most ancient, towns in Europe. ❞

—Peter Kalm, quoted in *America at 1750*

New York could also thank trade for its rapid growth. This bustling port handled flour, bread, furs, and whale oil. At midcentury, an English naval officer admired the city's elegant buildings and paved streets. "Such is this city," he said, "that very few in England can rival it in its show."

▲ **MAIN IDEAS & DETAILS** Explain why the cities of the Middle Colonies grew.

(*below*) A late 18th-century view of Philadelphia.
In what other respects did Philadelphia grow in the 1700s?

Claimed by
N.Y. & N.H.

Lake Ontario

NEW YORK

Hudson River

ATLANTIC
OCEAN

70°W

40°N

APPALACHIAN MOUNTAINS

Delaware River

PENNSYLVANIA

New York

NEW JERSEY

Susquehanna River

Philadelphia

Major Exports

Furs and skins
Cattle and grain
Tobacco
Iron
Ships
Timber

DELAWARE

75°W

0   50   100 miles
0   50   100 kilometers

Connect Geography & History

1. Place What are the three major rivers in the Middle Colonies?

2. Make Inferences Why might the Middle Colonies' rivers be important for farmers?

Independence Hall,
Philadelphia

African Americans in the Cities

▼ **KEY QUESTION** How did African Americans help build the cities?

Unlike the economy that developed in the South, the economy of the Middle Colonies did not depend on a large slave population. In 1750, only about 7 percent of the Middle Colonies' population was enslaved. Most of these enslaved people lived in the cities.

Racial Tension in New York City New York City had a larger number of people of African descent than any other Northern city. Its African American population was divided between the enslaved and the free.

The slave trade was an important part of the city's economy. Many Africans were brought to New York City in order to serve wealthy families. Enslaved people worked as manual laborers, servants, drivers, and as assistants to **artisans**, or craftspeople. Before New York came under English control, enslaved Africans had built roads, houses, and public buildings—the very foundations of the colony.

A free black community developed in New York City as early as 1644. Free African-American men and women worked as laborers, servants, and sailors. For a time free blacks had the right to own property.

Although both free and enslaved African Americans enjoyed some rights in the Middle Colonies, their lives were harsh. As in the South, fears of a slave revolt grew as the slave population increased. Those fears were realized in 1712 when a group of African-born slaves rebelled. After setting fire to several buildings, the rebels suffered defeat, torture, and death. However, their cruel punishments did not prevent other slave rebellions.

Quakers Condemn Slavery Some white colonists began speaking out against slavery. The Quakers were the first group to condemn it. To many Quakers, slavery was immoral and against Christian principles. In 1688 Quakers in Germantown, Pennsylvania, issued a statement against the practice. In 1712 the Pennsylvania government attempted to discourage the importation of slaves. Throughout the 1700s, Quakers published antislavery petitions and statements. The antislavery efforts of the Quakers were supported by other religious groups in the Delaware Valley, such as the German Pietists. These antislavery ideals influenced immigrants in the Middle Colonies—and eventually the entire nation.

▲ **SUMMARIZE** Explain how African Americans helped build the cities.

Diversity and Tolerance

▼ **KEY QUESTION** How did ethnic diversity encourage tolerance?

Many different immigrant groups arrived in the port cities of the Middle Colonies. Soon the region's population became remarkably diverse.

A Diverse Population The Germans formed one of the largest immigrant groups in the region. Many Germans arrived between 1710 and 1740. Most came as indentured servants fleeing religious intolerance. They were particularly attracted to Pennsylvania because the colony did not tax its people in order to support a particular **denomination**, or distinct religious group. Like the Puritans before them, German immigrants arrived in family groups and tended to settle together in distinct communities. Many moved to the western frontier of Pennsylvania, where land was cheaper.

Famous for their farming skills, these immigrants soon influenced the culture of the Middle Colonies. Germans also brought a strong tradition of skilled crafts to the Middle Colonies. For example, it was German gunsmiths who first developed the long rifle. Other German artisans, or craftspeople, became ironworkers and makers of glass, furniture, and kitchenware.

Reenactors in Pennsylvania portray life on a colonial German farm.

Germans built **Conestoga wagons** to carry their produce to town. These wagons used wide wheels suitable for dirt roads, and the wagons' curved beds prevented spilling when climbing hills. Another important feature of this type of wagon was the canvas covering that offered protection from rain.

Diversity Leads to Tolerance The Dutch in New York and the Quakers in Pennsylvania were two groups that practiced religious tolerance. That is, they honored the right to worship without interference. This laid the foundation for the well-known religious tolerance of the Middle Colonies.

In contrast to New England, where the English Puritans dominated religious life, many different religious groups settled in the Middle Colonies. Because of this diversity, the various religious groups had to learn to accept, or at least tolerate, one another. The tolerance that developed in the Middle Colonies would one day serve as a model for the nation.

Like the other colonial regions, the Middle Colonies have left a lasting legacy. New York City is still a center of commerce and of ethnic and religious diversity. Colonial Pennsylvania produced the model of a society based on tolerance. Although slavery existed in the Middle Colonies, as it did in other colonial regions, some were beginning to raise their voices against it. In fact, throughout the colonial period the Middle Colonies were moving closer to modern America's civil ideals—of a society based on diversity, tolerance, and religious freedom.

 CAUSES AND EFFECTS Explain how ethnic diversity encouraged tolerance.

Connect *to the* **World**

Tolerance
Attitudes in parts of the Middle Colonies may have been influenced by the earliest Dutch settlers. These settlers came from the Dutch Republic, a country famous for its religious tolerance.

 Illinois Learning Standards *Review*

🔁 **ONLINE QUIZ**
For test practice, go to
Interactive Review @ ClassZone.com

TERMS & NAMES

1. Explain the importance of
- Philadelphia
- Conestoga wagons

USING YOUR READING NOTES

2. Main Ideas and Details Complete the diagram you started at the beginning of this section.

| Detail |
| Main Idea |
Religious tolerance, ethnic diversity, and fertile lands helped the Middle Colonies prosper.
| Detail |
| Detail |

KEY IDEAS

3. What factors allowed large coastal cities to develop in the Middle Colonies?

4. How did religious tolerance develop in the Middle Colonies?

CRITICAL THINKING

5. Analyze Graphs Study the graph below of ethnic groups in the Middle Colonies. What two languages might you have heard most frequently?

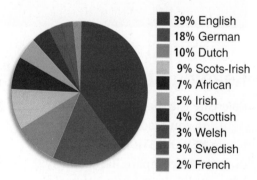

- 39% English
- 18% German
- 10% Dutch
- 9% Scots-Irish
- 7% African
- 5% Irish
- 4% Scottish
- 3% Welsh
- 3% Swedish
- 2% French

Source: *Population of the British Colonies in America Before 1776, 1975*

6. **Math** Use the graph shown above to calculate the number of people speaking each language, given that the Middle Colonies had a population of roughly 297,000. Then create a table to show the results.

Key Ideas

BEFORE, YOU LEARNED

Poorer settlers moved into the far western parts of Virginia and other colonies.

NOW YOU WILL LEARN

Settlers in the Backcountry developed their own regional traditions and culture.

Vocabulary

TERMS & NAMES

Appalachian Mountains mountain range stretching from eastern Canada south to Alabama

Scots-Irish the name given to people from the borderlands of Scotland and England and from the region of northern Ireland

BACKGROUND VOCABULARY

fall line the point at which waterfalls prevent large boats from moving farther upriver

Piedmont the broad plateau that lies at the foot of the Blue Ridge Mountains of the Appalachian range

clans large groups of families that claim a common ancestor

Visual Vocabulary
Appalachian Mountains

Reading Strategy

Re-create the diagram shown at right. As you read and respond to the **KEY QUESTIONS**, use the diagram to compare Backcountry life with life in the other colonies.

 See Skillbuilder Handbook, page R8.

COMPARE AND CONTRAST

Backcountry Life

Life in Other Colonies

Common Features

many resources

GRAPHIC ORGANIZERS
Go to **Interactive Review** @ ClassZone.com

The Backcountry

16.D.3b Describe characteristics of different kinds of families in America during the colonial/frontier periods and the 19th century.
18.B.3b Explain how social institutions contribute to the development and transmission of culture.

One American's Story

In Pennsylvania, the provincial secretary, James Logan, had received instructions from William Penn, the proprietor of the colony. Penn wanted Logan to welcome all religious groups who had suffered persecution in Europe. When Presbyterians from the troubled region of northern Ireland started arriving in the colony, Logan took advantage of their fighting skills. He placed them on the western frontier where they could defend the colony from attack. Years later, Logan recalled his decision.

Scots-Irish arrive in Pennsylvania

PRIMARY SOURCE

❝ About that time [1720] considerable numbers of good, sober people came in from Ireland, who wanted to be settled. . . . I therefore thought it might be prudent to plant a settlement of such men . . . as a frontier, in case of any disturbance. ❞

—James Logan, letter of Nov. 18, 1729

The frontier land where the Presbyterians of Northern Ireland were settled was known as the Backcountry. The Backcountry was one of the four major regions of the English colonies.

Settling the Backcountry

🔻 **KEY QUESTION** What made Backcountry life unique?

The Backcountry extended through the western parts of many colonies. The geography of the Backcountry gave the region its unique appearance and influenced the culture of the people who settled there.

Geography of the Region The Backcountry was a region of dense forest and rushing streams in or near the **Appalachian Mountains**. The Appalachians stretch from eastern Canada south to Alabama.

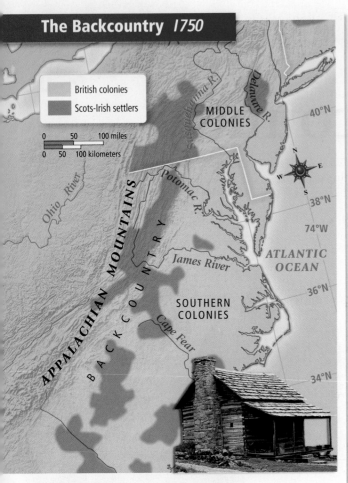

British colonies

Scots-Irish settlers

0   50   100 miles
0   50   100 kilometers

OHIO River

APPALACHIAN MOUNTAINS

B A C K C O U N T R Y

Susquehanna R.

Delaware R.

MIDDLE COLONIES

40°N

Potomac R.

James River

SOUTHERN COLONIES

Cape Fear

74°W

38°N

ATLANTIC OCEAN

36°N

34°N

Connect Geography & History

1. **Region** What geographical feature did the northern and southern areas of the Backcountry have in common?

2. **Make Inferences** Why would geography have helped create an independent spirit in the Backcountry?

In the South, the Backcountry began at the **fall line**, where waterfalls prevent large boats from moving upriver. West of the fall line is the broad plateau known as the **Piedmont**. The Piedmont lies at the foot of the Appalachians.

Early Settlers The first Europeans in the Backcountry arrived to trade with the Native Americans. Farmers soon followed but clashed with Native Americans over land. The Backcountry gained a reputation as a wild place, where independent settlers fought with Native Americans and resented government control.

▲ **COMPARE AND CONTRAST** Explain what made Backcountry life unique.

The Scots-Irish Arrive

▼ **KEY QUESTION** Why did the Scots-Irish emigrate to the colonies?

Most of the Backcountry settlers were forced west because planters had claimed most of the good farmland in the Tidewater, or coastal area. Then, in the 1700s, the **Scots-Irish** arrived.

A Mass Migration "Scots-Irish" was the name given to people who came from the borderlands of Scotland and England. Many were Presbyterian Scots who had lived for a time in northern Ireland. Both Northern Ireland and the Scottish borders were troubled regions, torn by warfare. This hostile environment gave the Scots-Irish survival skills that were useful in the American Backcountry.

In the early 1700s, the Scots-Irish suffered drought, rent increases, and persecution by the Anglican church. As a result, the Scots-Irish sailed to America by the thousands.

Like the English Puritans and the German settlers in Pennsylvania, the Scots-Irish traveled in family groups. But Scots-Irish families formed much larger **clans**. Clans are large groups of families that claim a common ancestor. Clan members were fiercely loyal to one another and banded together when danger threatened. The clan system helped families deal with the perils of the Backcountry.

The Scots-Irish came to Pennsylvania because of its religious tolerance. They were settled on the colony's frontier. From there they spread through the frontiers of other colonies until they occupied the entire Backcountry.

Heritage of the Scots-Irish In the Backcountry the Scots-Irish developed a unique culture. It was here that the music of Scotland and Ireland slowly changed into Bluegrass and American Country Music. Many sports that are now part of track and field competitions also came from the Scots-Irish.

The Scots-Irish reinforced the desire for democracy and freedom that had already been established in earlier colonies. Their loyalty and warrior ethic also had a long-lasting influence on the American military. Their constant migrations may have helped create that unique sense of restless energy in American life.

Regionalisms Develop Between 1700 and 1750, the population of England's colonies in North America doubled and then doubled again. At the start of the century, the colonial population stood at about 251,000. By 1750, they were more than 1,170,000 settlers in North America. These settlers lived in four major regions that were already developing unique characteristics. The chart below describes these different colonial regions and shows how they were able to grow and prosper.

▲ **SUMMARIZE** Explain why the Scots-Irish emigrated to the colonies.

CONNECT ↘ *to the Essential Question*

What factors allowed each colonial region to grow and prosper?

	Climate	Resources	Economy	Ethnic Background	Social Class	Predominant Religion
NEW ENGLAND COLONIES	long winters; short growing season	rocky soil; good fishing grounds	diverse economy small farms, fishing and trade	English, mainly from the eastern counties; few enslaved Africans	middle class	Puritans
MIDDLE COLONIES	short winters	fertile soil	larger farms and cash crops of grain	Europeans; some Africans in the cities	the poor; the middle class	Quakers (Pennsylvania)
SOUTHERN COLONIES	warm; nearly year-round growing season	fertile soil	plantation economy; limited number of cash crops	English and other Europeans; many enslaved Africans	rich, noble families; the poor; indentured servants; slaves	Anglicans
THE BACKCOUNTRY	varied	woods and streams	small farms	Scots-Irish and Native Americans	poor, independent farmers	Presbyterians

CRITICAL THINKING **Compare and Contrast** Which region was least prosperous?

Connecting History

Westward Expansion
The Backcountry settlers started the pioneering movement west that would play an important role in American history.

Beyond the Frontier

 KEY QUESTION How did English colonial growth affect other groups?

As Backcountry settlers pushed west they came into contact with various Native American peoples, as well as French and Spanish colonists. As contact increased, so did conflict over land and resources.

Contact Brings Conflict Native Americans found themselves caught in between advancing French and English colonists. The French had colonized eastern Canada and the territory along the Mississippi River. French fur traders did not want English settlers interfering with their trade. One Native American told an Englishman, "You and the French are like the two edges of a pair of shears, and we are the cloth that is cut to pieces between them." Tensions over land claims often led to war. In 1753 a young officer named George Washington was sent to ask the French to leave the Ohio River Valley, an act which led to the French and Indian War.

Spain also controlled large western areas of North America. Spanish settlers were farmers, ranchers and priests. Priests, who established missions to convert Native Americans, built forts near the missions. In 1718, Spaniards built Fort San Antonio de Bexar to guard the mission of San Antonio de Valero, later renamed the Alamo.

England's colonies often had to unite against these other groups. As a result, an American identity began to form.

▲ **CAUSES AND EFFECTS** Explain how English colonial growth affected other groups in North America.

Illinois Learning Standards *Review*

ONLINE QUIZ
For test practice, go to
Interactive Review @ ClassZone.com

TERMS & NAMES

1. Explain the importance of
   • Appalachian Mountains   • Scots-Irish

USING YOUR READING NOTES

2. **Compare and Contrast** Use the diagram below to contrast Backcountry life with life in the other colonies.

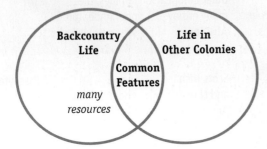

KEY IDEAS

3. What were some cultural characteristics of Backcountry settlers?

4. Why did conflict sometimes develop between English colonists and the other peoples of North America?

CRITICAL THINKING

5. **Make Inferences** How did the clan system help the Scots-Irish survive?

6. **Analyze Point of View** How might the Native Americans have felt as increasing numbers of colonists and trappers invaded their lands?

7. **Summarize** In what ways did the experiences of the Scots-Irish in the British Isles help prepare them for life on the American frontier?

8. **Art** Research the geography of the Backcountry. Draw a map of the routes that colonists might have taken to settle this region.

Chapter Summary

① **Key Idea**
Prosperity and religious diversity brought changes to Puritan New England.

② **Key Idea**
In the Southern Colonies, the need for cheap labor led to a dependence on slavery.

③ **Key Idea**
Rich farmland and a climate of tolerance helped the Middle Colonies prosper.

④ **Key Idea**
Settlers in the Backcountry developed their own regional traditions and culture.

For detailed Review and Study Notes go to **Interactive Review** @ **ClassZone.com**

Name Game

Complete each sentence online or on your own paper.

1. I introduced indigo as a successful plantation crop. Eliza Lucas

2. This city on the Delaware River became the fastest growing city in the colonies. _____

3. These mountains stretch from Canada south to Alabama. _____

4. This region was far to the west. _____

5. This 1739 slave rebellion took place in South Carolina. _____

6. These covered wagons were introduced by German immigrants. _____

7. This was a complex system of transatlantic exchange of slaves and goods. _____

8. This was a 1676 rebellion in Virginia. _____

9. This was a Native American uprising against the Puritan colonies. _____

10. The English government passed these acts to profit from colonial trade. _____

A. Backcountry
B. triangular trade
C. Conestoga wagons
D. Eliza Lucas
E. King Philip's War
F. Stono Rebellion
G. Navigation Acts
H. Philadelphia
I. Bacon's Rebellion
J. Appalachian Mountains
K. Scots-Irish
L. mercantilism

Activities

CROSSWORD PUZZLE

Complete the online crossword puzzle to show what you know about colonial growth.

ACROSS
1. _____ produces a blue dye.

GEOGAME

Use this online map to reinforce your understanding of the growth and development of the colonies, including economic development of the several colonial regions. Drag and drop the groups and products in the list at the location on the map where they were most common. A scorecard helps you keep track of your progress online.

timber

indigo

rice

rum

fur

More items online

VOCABULARY

Explain the significance of each of the following.

1. The Stono Rebellion
2. Conestoga wagons
3. Navigation Acts
4. Scots-Irish
5. Backcountry
6. Appalachian Mountains
7. Bacon's Rebellion
8. triangular trade
9. King Philip's War
10. Philadelphia
11. Eliza Lucas
12. Piedmont

Identify the word that does not fit in each group and explain why it is out of place.

13. Appalachian Mountains, Piedmont, Eliza Lucas
14. Backcountry, Scots-Irish, Navigation Acts
15. King Philip's War, Stono Rebellion, indigo
16. cash crops, indigo, Conestoga wagons
17. triangular trade, overseers, fall line

KEY IDEAS

1 New England: Commerce and Religion (pages 94–101)

18. What were the Navigation Acts meant to do?
19. How did the resources of New England affect its economy?

2 The Southern Colonies: Plantations and Slavery (pages 102–107)

20. Why did slavery spread in the South?
21. Which crops were important to the Southern economy?

3 The Middle Colonies: Farms and Cities (pages 110–115)

22. What attracted settlers to the Middle Colonies?
23. What effect did religious diversity have on the culture of the Middle Colonies?

4 The Backcountry (pages 116–120)

24. How did the geography of the Backcountry foster an independent spirit in the region's settlers?
25. What other groups came into conflict with Backcountry settlers?

CRITICAL THINKING

26. **Make Inferences** Why did the New England colonists' prosperity threaten England's mercantilist goals?

27. **Summarize** In what ways did settlers in New England take advantage of the Atlantic Ocean?

28. **Compare and Contrast** Create a chart to compare and contrast the Middle Colonies with New England.

	New England	Middle Colonies
Religious Groups		
Soil and Climate		
Economy		

29. **Causes and Effects** Why did Southern planters pass such harsh slave codes?

30. **Make Inferences** What made Southern plantations self-sufficient?

31. **Causes and Effects** Why did the tolerant culture of the Middle Colonies encourage even greater diversity in the region?

32. **Make Generalizations** Why were Backcountry settlers often in political conflict with the planters and the elite living along the coast?

33. **Interpret Graphs** Which decade saw the largest increase in the number of slaves imported to the colonies?

Slave Importation Estimates, *1701–1750*	
Years	**Number of Persons** ○ = 5000
1701–1710	⦾⦾ 9,000
1711–1720	⦾⦾⦾ 10,800
1721–1730	⦾⦾ 9,900
1731–1740	⦾⦾⦾⦾⦾⦾⦾⦾ 40,500
1741–1750	⦾⦾⦾⦾⦾⦾⦾⦾⦾⦾⦾⦾ 58,500

DOCUMENT-BASED QUESTIONS

PART 1: Short Answer

Analyze each document and answer the questions that follow.

DOCUMENT 1:

New England Exports 1768–1772

■ 44% DRIED FISH AND WHALE OIL

□ 13% WOOD PRODUCTS

■ 17% LIVESTOCK

■ 25% OTHER

Source: Shepherd and Walton, 1972

1. What industry was the most important for New England exports?

DOCUMENT 2

PRIMARY SOURCE

❝ Of all the American [colonies] his Majesty has, none are so apt for the building of Shipping as New-England. . . and in my poor opinion, there is nothing more. . .dangerous to any Mother-Kingdom, than the increase of Shipping in her Colonies, Plantations, or Provinces. ❞

—Sir Josiah Child, quoted in *American Colonies*

2. What is Sir Josiah Child's attitude to the shipping industry of New England?

Part 2: Essay

3. Using information from the documents, your answers to the questions in Part 1, and your knowledge of U.S. history, write two or three paragraphs to describe the economy of colonial New England.

YOU BE THE HISTORIAN

34. **Compare and Contrast** Why would different cultural attitudes to land ownership have caused conflict between the Native Americans and the colonists?

35. **Synthesize** Why did more large urban centers develop in the North than in the South?

36. **Make Generalizations** How did the South's plantation economy determine who became leaders in the region?

37. **Summarize** Why did changes take place in the population and treatment of African Americans between 1650 and 1750?

38. **Draw Conclusions** Why did regionalisms develop in the colonies?

39. **Connect** *to* **Today** **Citizenship** What modern American values and attitudes can be traced back to the culture of the Middle Colonies?

Answer the
ESSENTIAL QUESTION

What factors allowed each colonial region to grow and prosper?

Written Response Write a four-paragraph response to the Essential Question. Be sure to consider the key ideas of each section. Use the Response Rubric below to guide your thinking and writing.

Response Rubric

A strong response will

• describe the distinct climate and geography of each region

• analyze how climate and geography affected the economy of each region

• compare and contrast the four colonial regions

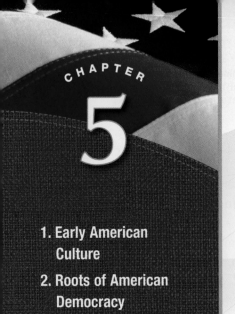

1. Early American Culture

2. Roots of American Democracy

3. The French and Indian War

Beginnings of an American Identity

1689–1763

 ESSENTIAL QUESTION

What traditions, events, and forces helped form an American identity?

Quebec

CONNECT Geography & History

What geographic features helped define colonial borders?

Think about:

1 the difficulty of travel in the days of few roads and thick forests

2 how colonial trade tied the colonies to Britain and foreign ports

3 the Native American nations that occupied the continent's interior

---

The people of Boston announcing the arrest of Governor Andros

1735 The Zenger trial

Effect Jury's decision helps establish freedom of the press.

1689

Massachusetts colonists overthrow royal governor Andros.

1704 *Boston News Letter* is founded.

Ben Franklin's printing press

British territory
French territory
French fort
Miami Native Americans

ATLANTIC OCEAN

70°W
75°W
80°W
85°W
90°W
30°N
35°N
40°N
45°N

R.I.
Boston
CONN.
N.H. MASS.
New York
NEW JERSEY
DEL.
MARYLAND
VIRGINIA
NORTH CAROLINA
Charles Town
NEW YORK
PENNSYLVANIA
Philadelphia
SOUTH CAROLINA
GEORGIA

A P P A L A C H I A N   M O U N T A I N S

Fort Montreal
Iroquois
Fort Duquesne
Fort Niagara
Delaware
Catawba
Lake Ontario
NEW FRANCE
Ohio River
Shawnee
Claimed by British and French
Lake Erie
Cherokee
Wyandot
Fort Detroit
Miami
Potawatomi
Lake Huron
Ottawa
Fort St. Joseph
Chippewa
Lake Michigan
Ojibwa
Fort Vincennes

Joseph Brant (Thayendanegea), Mohawk ally of the British

The Palace of Versailles, where the Treaty of Paris was signed

1763

1754 French and Indian War begins.

1759 Quebec falls to the British.

Effect War turns in favor of the British.

Treaty of Paris ends the French and Indian War.

Reading for Understanding

▶ Key Ideas

BEFORE, YOU LEARNED

Colonial settlers came from different backgrounds and established varied and prosperous economies.

NOW YOU WILL LEARN

The British colonies developed a unique culture shaped by prosperity, literacy, and new movements in religion and thought.

▶ Vocabulary

TERMS & NAMES

Benjamin Franklin American writer, publisher, scientist, inventor, and diplomat

Great Awakening Christian religious movement

Enlightenment philosophical movement stressing human reason

Jonathan Edwards preacher who delivered fiery sermons during the Great Awakening

George Whitefield preacher who drew large crowds during the Great Awakening

John Locke English philosopher who argued that people have natural rights

BACKGROUND VOCABULARY

apprentice (a•PREN•tis) one who is learning a trade from an experienced craftsperson

literacy the ability to read and write

REVIEW

diversity variety

Visual Vocabulary
apprentice

▶ Reading Strategy

Re-create the diagram shown at right. As you read and respond to the **KEY QUESTIONS**, use the diagram to note important details that support the Main Idea of this section.

 See Skillbuilder Handbook, page R4.

MAIN IDEAS AND DETAILS

Detail

Detail

Main Idea
The colonies differed from older, European societies.

Detail

Detail

GRAPHIC ORGANIZERS
Go to **Interactive Review** @ ClassZone.com

SECTION 1

Early American Culture

16.D.3a Describe characteristics of different kinds of communities in various sections of America during the colonial/frontier periods and the 19th century.
18.B.3b Explain how social institutions contribute to the development and transmission of culture.

One American's Story

Colonist Eliza Lucas Pinckney was born in the West Indies. In 1738, she moved to one of her family's South Carolina plantations. Soon after her arrival, her father, a British army officer, was posted to Antigua. When her mother died, Eliza Pinckney was left to manage her family's plantations alone, at the age of 16.

Pinckney enjoyed studying plants. She became interested in one plant in particular.

PRIMARY SOURCE

❝ Much of my time is spent on my experiments with indigo—the plant which produces such a beautiful blue dye. . . . I have also taken pains to bring the ginger [and] cotton . . . to perfection [but] have greater hopes from indigo. ❞

—Eliza Lucas Pinckney, quoted in *Colonies and Revolution*

Pinckney's experiments were so successful that indigo became South Carolina's second largest export. Pinckney's willingness to experiment was a quality well suited to colonial life. By the early 1700s, the colonists' adventurous energies were helping to create a new kind of society in the Americas.

A New Kind of Society

🔻 **KEY QUESTION** How did the American colonies differ from older societies?

British culture remained the foundation of all the colonial societies. But life in the "New World" was unlike life in the old. Settlers faced new climates and new living conditions. As colonists adapted their old ways to a new world, an American identity was born.

(*top*) indigo being processed in South Carolina;
(*below*) indigo-dyed dress

Beginnings of an American Identity **127**

Land, Wealth, and Rights Cheap farmland and abundant natural resources gave colonists a chance to prosper. There was less opportunity in Europe. In England, less than 5 percent of the population owned land. In fact, land rarely went up for sale. By contrast, in the early colonies, land was plentiful—once Native Americans were forced to give up their claims.

Land ownership gave colonists political rights as well as prosperity. In rural areas, only white male property owners could vote. City dwellers could vote by paying a fee. However, because so many colonists owned land, more Americans had the right to vote than did their British counterparts. In its wider democracy, colonial America was becoming a new kind of society.

Social Mobility More widespread land ownership also gave a different shape to the American class system. As in Europe, people were divided into high, middle, and low ranks. Large landholders and their families were high in rank. Owners of small farms were of middle rank. Landless servants or hired workers were low in rank. But America was unique because it had

- no titled aristocracy
- a large middle class
- a huge underclass of slaves

COMPARING *Class Systems*

BRITAIN AND THE AMERICAN COLONIES

Conditions in America created a class system very different from the ancient and rigid class system of Britain. In the diagram below, compare the size of the British and the colonial middle class.

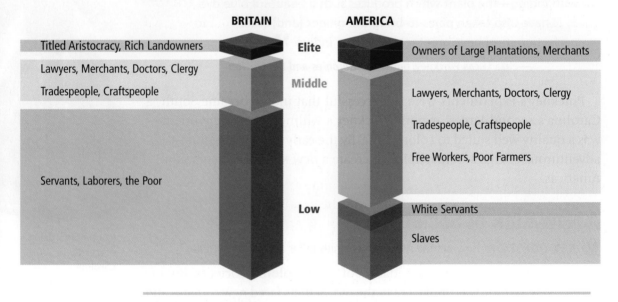

CRITICAL THINKING

1. **Compare and Contrast** What differences do you notice between the two diagrams?
2. **Make Inferences** What do the diagrams reveal about social mobility in the colonies?

America had no class of nobles whose titles passed from parent to child. Not even the aristocracy of the South had the right to titles such as "Lord" or "Lady." Another unique feature was America's huge middle class. The greater opportunities in America allowed poor colonists to rise into the middle ranks.

▲ **MAIN IDEAS & DETAILS** Explain how the American colonies differed from older, European societies.

Colonial Life

▼ **KEY QUESTION** What was life like in the colonies?

Most Americans lived on farms. In this working world, tasks were divided between men and women.

The Working World Farming women cooked; churned butter; made soap, candles, and clothes, and did many other chores. They tended the garden and looked after farm animals.

Reenactor churns butter.

Women who lived in towns and cities had similar chores. However, some urban women ran inns or other businesses. A few women, usually the wives or widows of tradespeople, practiced trades themselves.

Although women contributed to the colonial economy, they did not have many rights. Women could not vote. In most churches, with the exception of Quaker meetings, they could not preach. A married woman could not own property without her husband's permission. By law, even the money a woman earned belonged to her husband.

Farming men were expected to work outdoors. They planted, raised, and harvested the crops and took the surplus to market. They cared for the livestock and butchered the meat. In addition to their other chores, they cut trees and chopped wood for the fireplace.

Life of the Young American families were large. New England families, for example, had about six to eight children. More children on the farm meant more workers. Even toddlers were expected to help with the chores.

Around age six, boys were "breeched." This meant that they no longer wore the skirts or smocks of all young children, but were given a pair of pants. They then began to help their fathers at work. Sons of craftspeople tended their fathers' shops and learned their fathers' trades.

Around age 13, many boys left their fathers to become **apprentices**. An apprentice learned a trade from an experienced craftsman. The apprentice also received food, clothing, lodging, and a general education. He worked for free, usually for four to seven years, until his contract was fulfilled. Then he could work for wages or start his own business.

Girls rarely were apprenticed. They learned sewing and other household skills from their mothers. In New England, girls of 13 or 14 often were sent away to other households to learn specialized skills such as weaving

Colonial schoolroom

or cheese making. Orphaned girls and boys worked as apprentices for families who housed and fed them until adulthood.

Education and Literacy The colonies differed from European societies in level of education. Colonial America had a high rate of **literacy**, or the ability to read and write. In New England, 85 percent of white men were literate, compared with 60 percent of men in England. In the Middle Colonies, 65 percent of white men were literate, and in the South, about 50 percent were.

Most colonists thought that it was more important for males to be educated. In each region, roughly half as many white women as men were literate. Educated African Americans were rare. If they were enslaved, teaching them to read was illegal. If they were free, they were often kept out of schools. Some colonists defied these rules. Eliza Lucas Pinckney educated enslaved children on her plantation.

Children were taught to read so that they could understand the Bible. Education varied according to region. New England had free public schools and a high level of education among the population. Urban areas also provided more free education for the young.

Colonial Literature Literacy also helped unite the colonies. In the early 1700s, the colonies had only one local newspaper, the *Boston News Letter*. But over the next 70 years, dozens more newspapers appeared.

Gradually colonists began to publish their own books. Almanacs were very popular. A typical almanac included a calendar, weather predictions, star charts, farming advice, home remedies, recipes, jokes, and proverbs. In 1732, **Benjamin Franklin** began to publish *Poor Richard's Almanac*. It contained sayings that are still repeated today, such as "Haste makes waste."

Colonists also published poetry, regional histories, and autobiographies. A form of literature unique to the Americas was the captivity narrative. In it, a colonist captured by Native Americans described living among them. Mary Rowlandson's 1682 captivity narrative, *The Sovereignty and Goodness of God*, was one of the first colonial bestsellers. It described how Native Americans held Rowlandson hostage for 11 weeks during King Philip's War in 1676.

A Growing Diversity The American colonies were notable for the **diversity** of their population. Immigrants came into contact with people of different ethnic groups, races, and nationalities. In some colonies, there was religious diversity as well. Settlers had to learn how to adapt to this new situation. In the Middle Colonies, for example, many settlers adopted Quaker principles of equality, cooperation, and religious tolerance.

▲ **SUMMARIZE** Describe daily life in the colonies.

Hornbooks such as these were used to teach children to count and read.

Religious Revival

▼ **KEY QUESTION** How did the Great Awakening change American society?

As colonists developed a new society in America, they drew inspiration from two cultural movements:

- the **Great Awakening**, a Christian religious revival
- the **Enlightenment**, a movement stressing human reason

While the Great Awakening appealed to faith and emotions, the Enlightenment was based on reason and scientific observation. However, both movements offered people ways of changing themselves and their world—which is exactly what the colonists needed as they created a new society.

The Great Awakening In the 1730s and 1740s, a religious movement called the Great Awakening swept through the colonies. Traveling ministers preached that inner religious emotion was more important than outward religious behavior. Huge crowds gathered outdoors to hear famous preachers like **Jonathan Edwards** promise that all could be saved.

PRIMARY SOURCE

❝ And now you have an extraordinary opportunity, a day wherein Christ has thrown the door of mercy wide open, and stands in calling and crying with a loud voice to poor sinners. . . . How awful is it to be left behind at such a day! ❞

—Jonathan Edwards, "Sinners in the Hands of an Angry God"

The Great Awakening offered hope that each person could break from the past and begin a spiritual relationship with God. This would happen during a sudden conversion, or rebirth. This is the doctrine, or belief, of Evangelicalism. The evangelical idea of spiritual renewal or rebirth would be very influential in American culture.

The movement led congregations to argue over religious practices. Some left their churches and joined other Protestant groups such as Baptists. As religious diversity increased, it became more difficult for one "established" church to control a colony's religious life. In colonies like Virginia, the established Anglican church was weakened.

Religion and Social Change In the South, the Great Awakening's focus on spiritual equality threatened the social system. Against the wishes of many plantation owners, the Presbyterian minister Samuel Davies baptized African Americans. Meanwhile Baptist congregations welcomed African Americans and Native Americans. They allowed slaves to preach and women to speak in church.

Reenactors portray African-American worship in the South.

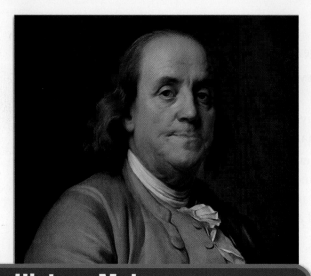

History Makers

Ben Franklin   1706–1790

As an Enlightenment thinker, Benjamin Franklin used reason and scientific methods to improve society. At 42, he retired from business to devote his life to science and public service. He proved that lightning was a form of electricity. Then he invented the lightning rod to protect buildings. The Franklin stove and bifocal eyeglasses were also his inventions. He organized a fire department, a lending library, and a society to discuss philosophy. Later he helped draft the Declaration of Independence.

CRITICAL THINKING

Connect _to_ Today   Consider how Franklin's abilities could be useful today. For example, how might Franklin solve environmental problems?

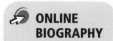 **ONLINE BIOGRAPHY**   For more on Ben Franklin, go to the **Research & Writing Center** @ ClassZone.com

The Great Awakening inspired colonists to help others. **George Whitefield** (HWIT•feeld) drew thousands of people with his sermons and raised funds to start a home for orphans. Other ministers taught Christianity and reading to Native Americans and African Americans.

The Great Awakening helped develop American identity by encouraging a belief in spiritual equality. It also inspired religious debate, which increased religious diversity.

The movement encouraged colonists to challenge authority and question traditional religious practices. Once this had happened, it was easier to challenge other social and political traditions. In this way, the movement laid the groundwork for revolt against British authority.

▲ **EVALUATE** Describe how religion changed society.

The Enlightenment

▼ **KEY QUESTION** How did the Enlightenment influence the colonists?

Unlike the Great Awakening, which explored religious emotion, the Enlightenment emphasized human reason and science as the paths to knowledge. It encouraged the belief that human beings could use rational thought to improve themselves and their society. Benjamin Franklin was a famous American Enlightenment figure. He conducted scientific experiments to discover the laws of nature.

Belief in Progress Writers of the Enlightenment condemned tyranny and superstition and challenged traditional social practices. They valued justice and equality and called for social and political change. Like the Great Awakening, the Enlightenment had far-reaching effects on the colonies.

The Enlightenment began in Europe, as scientists discovered natural laws governing the universe. In the colonies, at first only educated, wealthy people who could afford new books were familiar with Enlightenment ideas. But soon the values of the Enlightenment influenced the wider population.

Other Enlightenment thinkers applied the idea of natural law to human societies. The English philosopher **John Locke** challenged the belief that kings had a God-given right to rule. For many centuries, European kings had claimed that they were divinely appointed by God to rule their kingdoms. Locke challenged this idea. He also claimed that because governments were created by consent of human beings, then human beings had a right to change them. Locke argued that people have natural rights. These are the rights to life, liberty, and property. He insisted that people have the right to change a government that does not protect their natural rights. Locke's ideas would become very influential among American colonists who were dissatisfied with the political relationship with Britain.

Enlightenment writers such as John Locke encouraged a belief in progress—the idea that human beings can improve society and the world. The Enlightenment idea of progress would become one of the fundamental beliefs of American culture. In the following centuries, this optimistic hope for a better future would help Americans through many periods of uncertainty and change.

Ben Franklin experiments with electricity.

Enlightenment ideas of progress, natural rights, and government by agreement had a strong impact on colonial leaders. Such ideas encouraged colonists to reexamine their political ties to Britain. They also sparked political debate throughout the colonies. The colonists were beginning to see the British government as a threat to their rights and freedoms.

 SUMMARIZE Explain how the ideas and values of the Enlightenment influenced the colonists.

Illinois Learning Standards *Review*

 ONLINE QUIZ
For test practice, go to
Interactive Review @ ClassZone.com

TERMS & NAMES
1. Explain the importance of
- Great Awakening
- George Whitefield
- Enlightenment
- Benjamin Franklin
- Jonathan Edwards
- John Locke

USING YOUR READING NOTES
2. Main Ideas and Details Complete the diagram you started at the beginning of this section.

Detail

Detail

Main Idea
The colonies differed from older, European societies.

Detail

Detail

KEY IDEAS
3. How did the abundance of land in America shape colonial society?

4. How did the Great Awakening and the Enlightenment affect the colonies?

CRITICAL THINKING
5. Compare and Contrast How did the colonial class system differ from the class system in Europe?

6. Make Inferences Why was the literacy level so high in New England?

7. **Connect** *to* **Today** What modern American values can be traced back to the Great Awakening and the Enlightenment?

8. **Writing** **Report** Research and write a short report on Benjamin Franklin's contribution to the understanding of electricity.

Climate and Building Traditions

Regional building styles developed quickly in the colonies. In both the North and the South, the local climate changed the way English settlers built their houses.

Annual Mean Daily
Min. Temp. (°F)

20–32
32–40
40–45
45–50
50–55

See Geography Handbook, pages A10–A11.

NORTHERN HOME Several layers of wood protected the house from harsh northern winters. First, planks were fixed to the wood frame. Then a windproof "skin" of clapboards was wrapped tightly over the planks.

clapboards

planks

The rooms, each with its own fireplace, were grouped around a massive central chimney. The chimney absorbed heat from the fires during the day. At night, when the fires had died, the chimney radiated heat back into the house.

To help hold in the heat from the fires, rooms were small and snug with low ceilings.

Through the long winters, the family stored vegetables in the cellar.

SOUTHERN HOME In the milder climate of the South, there was no need for the radiant heat of a central chimney. Fireplaces were placed at the end walls, allowing much of the heat to escape into the outside air.

In wealthier homes, kitchens were placed in a separate building. This helped keep heat away from living areas.

Long central halls allowed summer breezes from open doors to cool the house.

In the South, with its shorter, milder winters and good clay for brickmaking, colonists built houses of brick when they could afford it.

STRANGE BUT TRUE

By the early 18th century, colonists were using American-made materials to build their houses. However, the first English settlers brought materials such as hinges, nails, and tools with them from England.

CRITICAL THINKING

1. Study the temperature chart. How much did the Northern and Southern colonies differ in terms of mean daily minimum temperature?

2. What other features do you think builders might have used to cool a Southern house?

▶ Key Ideas

BEFORE, YOU LEARNED

The British colonies shared a unique culture shaped by prosperity, literacy, and new movements in religion and thought.

NOW YOU WILL LEARN

American democracy has its roots in the English tradition of representative government.

▶ Vocabulary

TERMS & NAMES

Magna Carta charter of English political and civil liberties

Parliament England's chief lawmaking body

Edmund Andros English governor appointed to rule the reorganized northern colonies

Glorious Revolution events of 1688–1689, during which the English Parliament invited William and Mary to replace James II as monarchs

English Bill of Rights 1689 laws protecting the rights of English subjects and Parliament

John Peter Zenger New York publisher who was taken to court for criticizing the governor of New York

BACKGROUND VOCABULARY

prominent important and well-known

heritage tradition

Visual Vocabulary
Magna Carta

▶ Reading Strategy

Create a diagram like the one shown at right. As you read and respond to the **KEY QUESTIONS**, use the diagram to describe how each document or event strengthened English rights over the centuries.

 See Skillbuilder Handbook, page R5.

SEQUENCE EVENTS

1215 Magna Carta → 1688 Glorious Revolution → 1735 Zenger trial *establishes freedom of the press*

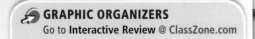
GRAPHIC ORGANIZERS
Go to **Interactive Review** @ ClassZone.com

Roots of American Democracy

 14.F.3a Analyze historical influences on the development of political ideas and practices as enumerated in the Declaration of Independence, the United States Constitution, the Bill of Rights and the Illinois Constitution.
16.B.3a Describe how different groups competed for power within the colonies and how that competition led to the development of political institutions during the early national period.

One American's Story

In 1688, the minister Increase Mather sailed from Massachusetts to England with a complaint. The colonists believed that the new royal governor had trampled their rights as English subjects.

Eventually, Mather came home with a new charter that restored colonists' rights.

PRIMARY SOURCE

❝ For all *English* liberties are restored to them: No Persons shall have a Penny of their Estates taken from them; nor any Laws imposed on them, without their own Consent by Representatives chosen by themselves. ❞

—Increase Mather, quoted in *The Last American Puritan*

Increase Mather

The English rights guaranteed by the Magna Carta and later documents are the basis for the rights that we enjoy today.

The Rights of Englishmen

🔻 **KEY QUESTION** How were English rights strengthened over the centuries?

Throughout the colonies, free Americans enjoyed the rights and liberties of English subjects. England had one of the most advanced political democracies in Europe, and English freedoms were envied throughout the world. The American colonists were fiercely protective of these freedoms, which they called the "rights of Englishmen." The shared belief in certain legal and political principles helped tie the colonies together.

Justice and Self-Government English rights had been developing for centuries. The first step toward guaranteeing these rights came in 1215. That year, English nobles forced King John to sign the **Magna Carta** (Great Charter). By signing this document, the king agreed that he was not above the law. Like everyone else, the king had to obey the laws of the land.

The Magna Carta was the document that guaranteed English political and civil liberties. It limited the king's power by guaranteeing rights to nobles and "freemen," or those not bound to a master. Their property could not be seized by the king or his officials. They could not be taxed, unless a council of **prominent**, or important and well-known, men agreed. They could not be put on trial based only on an official's word, without witnesses. They could be punished only by a jury of their peers, people of the same social rank.

PRIMARY SOURCE

❝ No free man shall be seized or imprisoned, or stripped of his rights or possessions, or exiled . . . nor will we proceed . . . against him . . . except by the lawful judgement of his equals or by the law of the land. ❞

—Magna Carta, translated in *A Documentary History of England*

Over time, the rights promised by the Magna Carta were gradually expanded. One important right was the right to elect representatives to government. The Magna Carta protected the rights of the people and remains the foundation of modern American democracy.

CONNECT Citizenship and History

See Citizenship Handbook, page 300.

TRIAL BY JURY

The Magna Carta promised that no free man would be punished for a crime without being judged by "his equals". By the 1700s, this phrase had helped create a tradition of trial by jury in which jurors listen to the evidence presented in a court and then debate before coming to an agreement.

Jurors are selected from various sources such as voting lists and tax rolls. The Constitution states that jurors in a criminal trial (one that determines the guilt or innocence of a person accused of a crime) must be neutral regarding the case. In addition, a juror must be selected from the community where the crime is supposed to have happened. Every juror is questioned by both defense and prosecuting lawyers, and either lawyer may reject a juror if he/she feels the juror would not serve fairly.

Activity

Set Up a Mock Jury Trial

1 Have one student accuse another of a crime and bring him or her to "trial."

2 Let each student in your class write his or her name on a piece of paper and put the names in a hat.

3 Select twelve jurors.

4 Have the jurors listen to the evidence during the trial.

5 Let the jury discuss the evidence and then vote to determine if the defendant is guilty or innocent.

Parliament and Colonial Government **Parliament**, England's lawmaking body, was the colonists' model for representative government. Parliament had two houses. Members of the House of Commons were elected. Members of the House of Lords were nonelected nobles, judges, and clergy.

English colonists in America did not want to give up the right to representative government. Because the king and Parliament were too far away to manage every detail of the colonies, some self-government was allowed. In all the colonies, the colonists formed their own elected assemblies—smaller-scale versions of the House of Commons. Virginia's House of Burgesses was the first of these. The assemblies imposed taxes and managed the colonies.

The relationship between the assemblies and Parliament was awkward. Although Parliament granted the colonists some self-government, it retained ultimate authority. The colonists disliked many of the laws that Parliament passed without their consent. Conflicts also arose when the king appointed royal governors to rule some colonies on his behalf. These conflicts became more intense in the late 1600s.

▲ **SEQUENCE EVENTS** Describe how English rights were strengthened.

English Rights Threatened

▼ **KEY QUESTION** How were colonial rights affected by political changes?

The political relationship between the assemblies and the English government caused tension on both sides of the Atlantic. In addition, the policies of some kings of England threatened the rights of Englishmen everywhere.

Kings Limit Self-Government In the mid-1600s, Massachusetts and other colonies were smuggling goods and ignoring the Navigation Acts. (See Chapter 4.) When challenged, the people of Massachusetts claimed that England had no right to make laws for them. In response, King Charles II canceled their charter. The charter had given the colony the right of self-government.

When Charles's brother James became king in 1685, he wanted to strengthen royal power. He also changed the way the northern colonies were governed. James combined Massachusetts and the other Northern colonies into one Dominion of New England, ruled by governor **Edmund Andros**. Andros angered the colonists by ending representative assemblies and limiting town meetings.

With their assemblies outlawed, some colonists refused to pay taxes. Andros jailed the loudest protestors. At their trial, they were told, "You have no more privileges left you than not to be Sould [sold] for Slaves."

The colonists sent Increase Mather to England to plead with King James. (See One American's Story on page 137.) However, a revolution in England was underway that changed the situation completely.

Connecting History

Expanding Liberty
Settlers in all the early colonies had quickly established representative government. See *Chapter 3, pp. 65–73.*

Why do you think the colonists resented Governor Andros (*shown below*)?

Colonial Governments

BRITISH CROWN
King or Queen

ROYAL GOVERNOR

- appointed by the crown
- oversaw colonial trade
- had final approval on laws
- could dismiss colonial assembly

COUNCIL

- appointed by governor
- advisory board to governor
- acted as highest court in each colony

COLONIAL ASSEMBLY

- elected by eligible colonists
- made laws
- had authority to tax
- paid governor's salary

CRITICAL THINKING How were lawmaking powers shared?

William and Mary Restore English Rights James II restricted English rights not only in the colonies but in England itself. He severely punished a Protestant rebellion and dismissed Parliament in 1687. Enraged by James's actions, Parliament secretly offered the throne to James's daughter, Mary, and her husband, William of Orange. William was the governor of the Netherlands. With little support in England, James fled the country at the end of 1688. Parliament named William and Mary the new monarchs of England. This change in leadership is called England's **Glorious Revolution**.

William and Mary agreed in 1689 to uphold the **English Bill of Rights**. This was a list of specific rights of English people and of Parliament. The monarch could not cancel laws or impose taxes unless Parliament agreed. Free elections and frequent meetings of Parliament were to be held. Excessive fines and cruel punishments were forbidden. People had the right to complain to the king or queen in Parliament without being arrested.

The English Bill of Rights established an important principle: the government was to be based on laws made by Parliament, not on the desires of a ruler. The rights of English people were strengthened.

Colonists Claim English Rights The colonists were quick to claim these rights. When the people of Boston heard of King James's fall, they jailed Governor Andros and asked Parliament to restore their rights. The Massachusetts colonists regained the right to elect representatives to an assembly. However, they had to accept a governor appointed by the crown. This kind of compromise between royal power and colonial self-government took place in other colonies as well.

The diagram on the upper left shows how most colonial governments were organized by 1700. The royal governor, his council, and the assembly shared power. The governor could strike down laws passed by the assembly, but the assembly was responsible for the governor's salary. If he blocked the assembly, the assembly might refuse to pay him.

After the disagreements between the colonists and the king during the late 1600s, the tension between America and the English government eased. During the early 1700s, England interfered very little in colonial affairs. This hands-off policy was called salutary neglect (*salutary* means "helpful" or "beneficial"). Parliament passed many laws regulating trade, the use of money, and even apprenticeships, but governors rarely enforced these laws. The colonists got used to acting independently.

Zenger and Freedom of the Press Colonists moved toward gaining a new right, freedom of the press, in 1735. That year, **John Peter Zenger**, publisher of the *New York Weekly Journal*, stood trial for printing criticism of New York's governor. Zenger's paper claimed that the governor accepted bribes. It also said that the governor had removed a judge and tried to fix an election.

PRIMARY SOURCE

❝ A Governor turns rogue [criminal], does a thousand things for which a small rogue would have deserved a halter [hanging], and because it is difficult . . . to obtain relief against him, . . . it is prudent [wise] to . . . join in the roguery. ❞

—*New York Weekly Journal*, quoted in *Colonial America, 1607–1763*

At that time, it was illegal to criticize the king in print. Because the governor represented the king, some claimed that no one should criticize the governor. Andrew Hamilton defended Zenger at his trial, claiming that people had the right to speak the truth. The jury agreed, and Zenger was released. Freedom of the press became an important new right in America.

English rights were part of the colonial **heritage**, or tradition. Respect for these principles of law continues to unite the American people.

▼ **CAUSES AND EFFECTS** Explain how colonial rights were affected by political events in England.

Illinois Learning Standards *Review*

⟳ **ONLINE QUIZ**
For test practice, go to
Interactive Review @ ClassZone.com

TERMS & NAMES

1. Explain the importance of
   - Magna Carta
   - Parliament
   - Edmund Andros
   - Glorious Revolution
   - English Bill of Rights
   - John Peter Zenger

USING YOUR READING NOTES

2. **Sequence Events** Complete the diagram you started at the beginning of this section.

1215 Magna Carta → 1688 Glorious Revolution → 1735 Zenger trial *establishes freedom of the press*

KEY IDEAS

3. What English political traditions did colonists bring with them to America?

4. How did King James II restrict the colonists' rights?

5. How did the Zenger trial help expand the colonists' rights?

CRITICAL THINKING

6. **Make Generalizations** How did England's policies toward the colonies change after the Glorious Revolution?

7. **Connect** *to* **Today** What rights enjoyed by modern Americans can be traced back to the Magna Carta of 1215?

8. **Writing** **Speech** Write a speech that Increase Mather might have delivered to the English Parliament, asking for a new charter that would protect the colonists' rights.

▶ Key Ideas

BEFORE, YOU LEARNED

The French had set up colonies and established a trading relationship with the native peoples of North America.

NOW YOU WILL LEARN

Land claims and rivalry among European powers, settlers, and Native Americans led to a war that united the colonies against a common enemy.

▶ Vocabulary

TERMS & NAMES

Pontiac's Rebellion Native American revolt against the British colonies

French and Indian War war of 1754–1763 between Britain, France, and their allies for control of North America

Albany Plan of Union first formal proposal to unite the colonies

Battle of Quebec battle that led to the British victory in the French and Indian War

Treaty of Paris (1763) treaty that ended the war between France and Britain

Proclamation of 1763 British declaration that forbade colonists from settling west of the Appalachians

BACKGROUND VOCABULARY

pact formal agreement; a bargain

smallpox highly infectious and often fatal disease

Visual Vocabulary
Battle of Quebec

▶ Reading Strategy

Re-create the table shown at right. As you read and respond to the **KEY QUESTIONS**, use the table to show why Native Americans became involved in European conflicts.

 See Skillbuilder Handbook, page R7.

CAUSES & EFFECTS

CAUSE	EFFECT
	Native Americans became involved in conflicts between Europeans.

 GRAPHIC ORGANIZERS
Go to **Interactive Review** @ ClassZone.com

The French and Indian War

16.C.3a Describe economic motivations that attracted Europeans and others to the Americas, 1500–1750.

18.C.3a Describe ways in which a diverse U.S. population has developed and maintained common beliefs (e.g., life, liberty and the pursuit of happiness; the Constitution and the Bill of Rights).

One American's Story

Chief Pontiac was a leader of the Ottawa, a Native American group. When the British took over French forts in the Great Lakes area, Pontiac led his people in raids against them. This conflict is known as **Pontiac's Rebellion** (1763–1764). Addressing his followers, Pontiac said

PRIMARY SOURCE

❝ It is important for us, my brothers, that we exterminate from our lands this nation which seeks only to destroy us. . . . Therefore, my brothers, we must all swear their destruction and wait no longer. ❞

—Pontiac, quoted in *Pontiac and the Indian Uprising*

Pontiac

Pontiac's rebellion followed the **French and Indian War**, in which French forces fought British forces in North America. Each side had Native American allies.

Europeans in Native American Lands

🔻 **KEY QUESTION** Why were Native Americans involved in conflicts between Europeans?

The English and the French created rival empires in North America. The competition between these two European powers often led to war.

France Claims Western Lands The French claimed the Ohio River valley, the Mississippi River valley, and the Great Lakes region. The French territory of Louisiana, claimed by La Salle in 1682, stretched from the Ohio River valley to the Rocky Mountains. They called these lands "New France." Some Europeans in New France were fur traders. Others were Jesuit (JEHZH•oo•iht) priests working to convert Native Americans to Christianity.

Native American Alliances The English competed with the French for furs. Different Native American groups also competed to supply furs to the Europeans. The fur trade created economic and military alliances between the Europeans and their Native American trading partners.

These alliances dragged the trading partners into each other's wars. In the 1600s and 1700s, European wars between France and England fueled wars in their colonies. Neither side won a clear victory in these conflicts.

▲ **CAUSES AND EFFECTS** Explain why Native Americans were involved in conflicts between Europeans.

War Begins and Spreads

▼ **KEY QUESTION** What alliances fought in the French and Indian War?

Just beyond the Appalachian Mountains, the Ohio River valley began attracting Pennsylvania fur traders and Virginia land companies. As more British colonists arrived in the area, the French feared losing control of the rivers that linked their Canadian and Louisiana settlements. With tensions mounting, the stage was set for the nine-year-long French and Indian War.

War in the Ohio River Valley The French sent troops to expel the British traders and to build forts to protect the region. This upset the Virginia colony, which claimed the land. In 1753, the governor of Virginia sent a force led by a 21-year-old major named George Washington to tell the French to leave.

Washington neared Fort Duquesne (du•KAYN), a French fort at the forks of the Ohio River, where Pittsburgh now stands. He built a small fort, Fort Necessity. Following Washington's surprise attack on a French force, the French and their allies attacked Fort Necessity on July 3, 1754. Washington retreated to Virginia. The French and Indian War had begun.

The Huron, who lived around the Great Lakes, sided with the French. Meanwhile, the colonists were trying to form alliances of their own. Representatives from the British colonies and the Iroquois nations met at Albany, New York. The colonists wanted the Iroquois to join them against the French.

Benjamin Franklin suggested that the colonies band together for defense. His **Albany Plan of Union** was the first formal proposal to unite the colonies. It called for each colony to send representatives to a Grand Council. This council would collect taxes, raise armies, and make treaties. However, the colonial legislatures rejected the plan because they did not want to give up control of their own affairs.

Braddock's Defeat The British sent General Edward Braddock and two regiments to Virginia. In 1755, Braddock marched toward the French at Fort Duquesne. Washington was at his side. Their red-coated army of 2,100 moved slowly over the mountains, dragging a huge cannon.

On July 9, eight miles from Fort Duquesne, French and Native American troops surprised Braddock's forces. General Braddock was defeated and killed. Americans were stunned by Braddock's defeat and by other British losses over the next two years.

Wolfe 1759

Louisbourg, 1758

ACADIA

Ft. Beausejour, 1755

Quebec, 1759

Halifax

NOVA SCOTIA

45°N

Algonquin

Abenaki

Montreal

NEW FRANCE

1760

St. Lawrence R.

MAINE (part of Mass.)

Monckton 1755

Amherst 1758

Ft. Frontenac, 1758

1756

Ft. Ticonderoga, 1758, 1759

1757

N.H.

Ft. Oswego, 1756

Lake Ontario

Ft. William Henry, 1757

Boston

Ft. Niagara, 1759

Iroquois

NEW YORK

Albany

MASS.

Huron

Lake Erie

Hudson R.

CONN.

R.I.

40°N

Allegheny R.

APPALACHIAN MOUNTAINS

PENNSYLVANIA

New York

Forbes 1758

Ft. Duquesne, 1755

NEW JERSEY

Ft. Necessity, 1754

Shawnee

MARYLAND

DEL.

Ohio R.

VIRGINIA

Cherokee

75°W

70°W

65°W

▨	British territory
▨	French territory
▨	Disputed territory
✸	British victory
✸	French victory
←	British forces
←	French forces
Huron	Native Americans

0   100   200 miles
0   100   200 kilometers

Native American Allies of the French and British

ALLIED WITH BRITISH	ALLIED WITH FRENCH
Iroquois Confederation:	• Abenaki
• Cayuga	• Lenni Lenape
• Mohawk	• Shawnee
• Oneida	• Huron
• Onondaga	• Algonquin
• Seneca	

CRITICAL VIEWING

1. **Place** In what part of North America did the French and Indian War take place?

2. **Make Inferences** What role did the British navy play in winning the war?

Detail of *Braddock's Defeat* by Edward Deming

Quebec Falls In 1757, Britain had a new secretary of state, William Pitt, who was determined to win the war in the colonies. Pitt sent the best generals to America and borrowed money to pay colonial troops. The British controlled six French forts by August 1759, including Fort Duquesne (rebuilt as Fort Pitt). In late summer, the British moved to attack New France at its capital, Quebec.

The British lay siege to Quebec, which sits on cliffs 300 feet above the St. Lawrence River. In September, a scout found a steep path up the cliffs to the plains near Quebec. Under cover of darkness, British general James Wolfe and 4,000 of his men secretly climbed the cliffs.

When the French awoke, the British were lined up on the plains, ready to attack. In the short, fierce battle that followed, Wolfe was killed. The French commander, Montcalm, died of his wounds the next day. Quebec surrendered to the British. The **Battle of Quebec** was the turning point of the war. When Montreal fell the next year, all of Canada was in British hands.

Britain and France battled in other parts of the world for almost three more years. Spain made a **pact** in 1761 to aid France, but this help came too late. When the Seven Years' War ended in 1763, the **Treaty of Paris** was signed. The treaty ended nearly all French control in North America and dramatically expanded Britain's colonial empire.

▲ **SUMMARIZE** Describe the alliances of the French and Indian War.

Connect *to the* **World**

The Seven Years' War
The French and Indian War was part of the Seven Years' War (1756–1763), a worldwide struggle between France and Great Britain.

COMPARING *Prewar and Postwar Boundaries*

Prewar Boundaries *1754*

- British territory
- French territory
- Spanish territory
- Disputed between Great Britain and France

CANADA · Quebec · St. Lawrence R. · 40°N · BRITISH AMERICAN COLONIES · Philadelphia · Ohio R. · Mississippi R. · LOUISIANA · FLORIDA · TEXAS · New Orleans · ATLANTIC OCEAN · 80°W · Tropic of Cancer · 0 250 500 miles · 0 250 500 kilometers

Postwar Boundaries *1763*

HUDSON'S BAY COMPANY · Quebec · St. Lawrence R. · CANADA · 40°N · BRITISH AMERICAN COLONIES · Philadelphia · Ohio R. · Proclamation Line of 1763 · Mississippi R. · LOUISIANA ceded by France to Spain, 1763 · TEXAS · New Orleans · FLORIDA · ATLANTIC OCEAN · 80°W · Tropic of Cancer · 0 250 500 miles · 0 250 500 kilometers

Connect Geography & History

1. **Place** What was the southern limit of British territory in 1754?

2. **Evaluate** Which nation benefited most from the treaty?

What traditions, events, and forces helped form an American identity?

Education
High levels of literacy and education in some regions; children educated to read Bible.

Publishing
Colonists share information in the form of newspapers and books.

Politics and Law
Colonists share legal and political traditions that come from England; expect to enjoy the "rights of Englishmen"; Enlightenment writers help spread idea that people can improve or change their government.

An American Identity Forms

War
French and Indian War unites colonists against common enemy.

Religion and Ideas
Great Awakening unifies colonies and challenges tradition; Enlightenment influences colonial ideas.

Economy
better economic opportunities in the colonies; more chance of owning land

CRITICAL THINKING **Evaluate** Which factor do you think was the most important in creating an American identity?

The New Colonial World

▼ **KEY QUESTION** How did the French and Indian War change the colonial world?

The French and Indian War not only enlarged British territory, it also changed the way that colonial Americans and Native Americans viewed themselves and their relationship with the British empire.

Pontiac's Rebellion After French forces withdrew, the British took over their forts. They refused to give gifts to the Native Americans, as the French had. British settlers also moved across the mountains onto Native American land. In the spring and summer of 1763, Native American groups responded by attacking settlers and destroying almost every British fort west of the Appalachians. They then surrounded the three remaining forts. This revolt was called Pontiac's Rebellion, although the Ottawa war leader Pontiac was only one of many organizers.

British settlers reacted with equal viciousness, killing even those Native Americans who had not attacked them. British officers came up with a brutal plan to end the siege by the Lenni Lenape of Fort Pitt.

❝Could it not be contrived to send the Small Pox among those disaffected [angry] tribes of Indians? We must on this occasion use every stratagem in our power to reduce them.❞

—Major General Jeffrey Amherst, quoted in *The Conspiracy of Pontiac*

The officers invited Lenni Lenape war leaders to talk and then gave them **smallpox**-infected blankets as gifts. This started a deadly outbreak of the disease among the Native Americans.

By the fall, the Native Americans had retreated, and three years later a peace treaty was signed. Pontiac's Rebellion showed the British how difficult it was going to be to govern their vast new empire. To avoid further conflicts with Native Americans, the British issued the **Proclamation of 1763**. This forbade colonists from settling west of the Appalachian Mountains.

A New Colonial Identity The colonists were angry. They thought they had won the right to settle in the Ohio River valley. In turn, the British government was angry with the colonists, who insisted on settling on Native American lands.

The French and Indian War gave the 13 colonies their first taste of unity as they fought a common enemy. This feeling of unity grew as colonists found themselves in another dispute with Britain. With France no longer a threat, colonial leaders grew more confident in their complaints. The stage was set for the final conflict between the colonies and Britain.

 MAKE INFERENCES Explain how the French and Indian War changed the colonial world.

Illinois Learning Standards *Review*

🖰 **ONLINE QUIZ**
For test practice, go to
Interactive Review @ ClassZone.com

TERMS & NAMES
1. Explain the importance of
- Pontiac's Rebellion
- Battle of Quebec
- French and Indian War
- Treaty of Paris (1763)
- Albany Plan of Union
- Proclamation of 1763

USING YOUR READING NOTES
2. Causes and Effects Complete the diagram you started at the beginning of this section.

CAUSE	EFFECT
	Native Americans became involved in conflicts between Europeans.

KEY IDEAS
3. Why did Native American tribes form alliances with European powers?

4. What factors caused the French and Indian War?

5. Why were American colonists angry about the Proclamation of 1763?

CRITICAL THINKING
6. Causes and Effects What were some effects of Pontiac's Rebellion?

7. **Connect** *to* **Today** Many Native American groups were pulled into war because they were trading with the French or British. How do economic alliances continue to pull nations into war?

8. **Art** Imagine you are at the meeting in Albany. Create a poster urging colonial unity.

Chapter Summary

1 Key Idea

The British colonies developed a unique culture shaped by prosperity, literacy, and new movements in religion and thought.

2 Key Idea

American democracy has its roots in the English tradition of representative government.

3 Key Idea

Land claims and rivalry among European powers, settlers, and Native Americans led to a war that united the colonies against a common enemy.

For detailed Review and Study Notes go to **Interactive Review** @ **ClassZone.com**

Name Game

Use the Terms & Names list to identify each sentence online or on your own paper.

1. I was a governor who ended representative assemblies. Edmund Andros

2. I was a popular minister who started a home for orphans. ____

3. This was a battle for a French city. ____

4. I experimented with electricity. ____

5. This was a proclamation that restricted westward movement. ____

6. I argued that people have natural rights. ____

7. My sermons promised that all could be saved. ____

8. This was a war fought for North America. ____

9. My court case won freedom of the press. ____

10. This was a Native American revolt. ____

A. John Locke

B. Battle of Quebec

C. French and Indian War

D. George Whitefield

E. John Peter Zenger

F. Jonathan Edwards

G. English Bill of Rights

H. Benjamin Franklin

I. Albany Plan of Union

J. Pontiac's Rebellion

K. Edmund Andros

L. Proclamation of 1763

Activities

FLIPCARD

Use the online flipcards to quiz yourself on the terms and names introduced in this chapter.

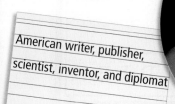

American writer, publisher, scientist, inventor, and diplomat

ANSWER Ben Franklin

GEOGAME

Use this online map to reinforce your understanding of Eastern North America in 1750, including the location of important forts, Native American groups, and geographic features. Drag and drop each name in the list at its location on the map. A scorecard helps you keep track of your progress online.

Iroquois

Fort Duquesne

Ohio River

Fort Montreal

Lake Erie

Ohio River

VOCABULARY

Explain the significance of each of the following.

1. Benjamin Franklin
2. Pontiac's Rebellion
3. Proclamation of 1763
4. English Bill of Rights
5. Enlightenment
6. John Locke
7. French and Indian War
8. Great Awakening
9. Treaty of Paris (1763)
10. Jonathan Edwards
11. Battle of Quebec
12. George Whitefield
13. Albany Plan of Union
14. Magna Carta
15. John Peter Zenger
16. Edmund Andros

Explain how the terms and names in each group are related.

17. Great Awakening, Jonathan Edwards, George Whitefield
18. French and Indian War, Battle of Quebec
19. John Locke, Enlightenment, Benjamin Franklin
20. Parliament, Glorious Revolution

KEY IDEAS

1 **Early American Culture (pages 126–133)**

21. What made American colonial societies different from European societies?
22. How did the Great Awakening challenge social and political traditions?
23. How did the Enlightenment influence Americans?

2 **Roots of American Democracy (pages 134–139)**

24. Why did the colonists value their rights so highly?
25. How did political changes in England affect colonial rights?

3 **The French and Indian War (page 142–148)**

26. Why did the French and Indian War help unite the colonists?
27. Why did the French and Indian War change the relationship between the colonists and Britain?

CRITICAL THINKING

28. **Causes and Effects** Why did a new kind of society develop in the colonies?
29. **Make Generalizations** What political values did English colonists share?
30. **Draw Conclusions** How did colonial publishing help shape an American identity?
31. **Compare and Contrast** Create a diagram to compare and contrast the Great Awakening and the Enlightenment. In the space where the circles intersect, record the common features of the two movements.

32. **Problems and Solutions** Why did the relationship between colonial governments and Parliament cause tension?
33. **Causes and Effects** What do you think was the major cause of the French and Indian War?
34. **Draw Conclusions** What role did the Ohio River valley play in the French and Indian War?
35. **Analyze Primary Sources** Benjamin Franklin published this image during the French and Indian War. Each section of the snake represents a colony. What effect was it meant to have on the colonists?

DOCUMENT-BASED QUESTIONS

PART 1: Short Answer

Study each document carefully and answer the questions that follow.

DOCUMENT 1

1. Examine this painting of the Death of Wolfe by Benjamin West. Why does the painter show a Native American at the scene of Wolfe's death?

DOCUMENT 2

PRIMARY SOURCE

❝ When I go to see the English commander and say to him that some of our comrades are dead, instead of bewailing their death, as our French brothers do, he laughs at me and at you. If I ask anything for our sick, he refuses with the reply that he has no use for us. From all this you can well see that they are seeking our ruin. Therefore, my brothers, we must all swear their destruction and wait no longer. ❞

—Pontiac, 1763

2. What does this quote reveal about Pontiac's Rebellion?

PART 2: Essay

3. Using information from the documents, your answers to the question in part 1, and your knowledge of U.S. history, write an essay that discusses the relationship between Native Americans and the colonial powers.

YOU BE THE HISTORIAN

36. Problems and Solutions Did the French and Indian War settle one dispute or create another set of problems?

37. Evaluate Give an example of bad military or political leadership during the period studied in the chapter. What mistakes were made?

38. WHAT IF? Suppose the British had not taken Quebec in 1759. How might this have changed American history?

39. Make Generalizations What aspects of modern American culture might be familiar to an 18th-century colonist?

40. Analyze Point of View Consider each group's reasons for fighting the French and Indian War. Which group had the most to lose: the British, the French, the Native Americans, or the colonists?

41. Citizenship Why is jury duty a requirement of citizenship?

Answer the
ESSENTIAL QUESTION
What traditions, events, and forces helped form an American identity?

Written Response Write a four-paragraph response to the Essential Question. Be sure to consider the key ideas of each section as well as the most significant factors that led to the development of an American identity. Use the Response Rubric below to guide your thinking and writing.

Response Rubric
A strong response will

• discuss the unique conditions governing colonial life

• explain how deeply colonists valued English political traditions

• describe the cultural and political forces that united the colonists

Creating a New Nation

1763–1791

Why It Matters Now

America at the beginning of its history was an experiment
—a trial to see if democratic and representative government
could work. Patriot colonists imperiled "their lives, their
fortunes, their sacred honor" for the sake of principle. The
values they fought for, and the decisions they wrote into
the Constitution, echo through our history and shape our
government and our lives to this day.

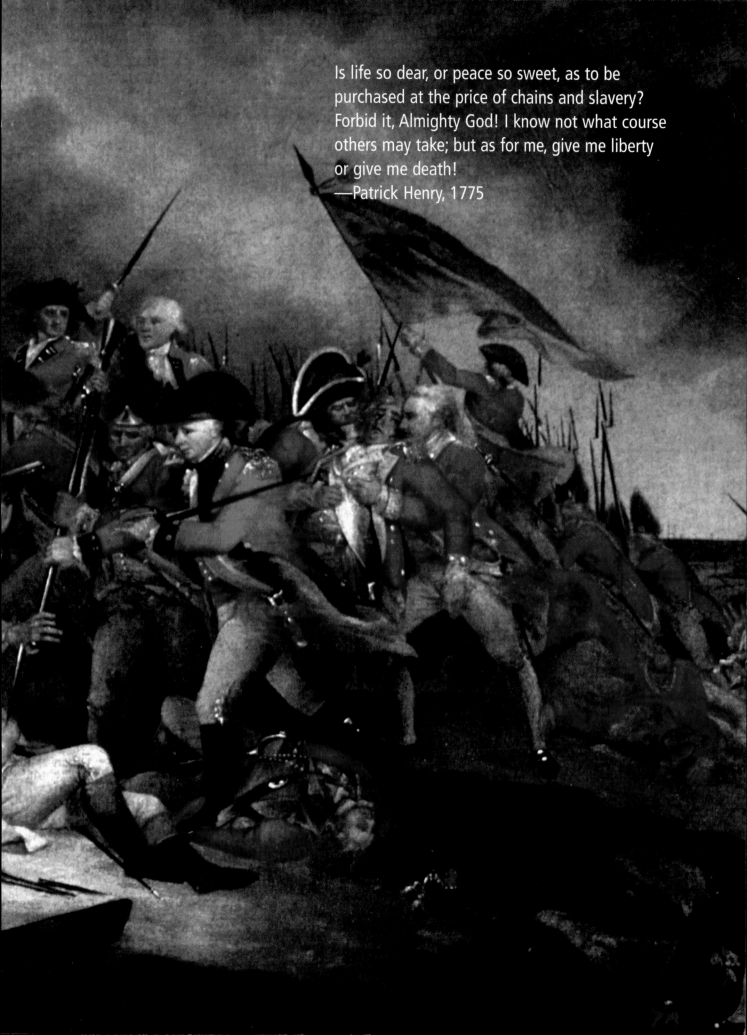

Is life so dear, or peace so sweet, as to be purchased at the price of chains and slavery? Forbid it, Almighty God! I know not what course others may take; but as for me, give me liberty or give me death!
—Patrick Henry, 1775

The Road to Revolution

1763–1776

ESSENTIAL QUESTION

What drove the colonists to declare independence from Great Britain?

2️⃣ To Lexington and Concord

CONNECT ⟳ Geography & History

What role did the geography of 18th-century Boston play in the early days of the Revolution?

Think about:

1 why it was so difficult to invade the town

2 the routes from Boston to Lexington and Concord

3 the strategic importance of the surrounding hills

1️⃣ The only road connecting Boston to the mainland

King George III

Teapot decorated to protest Stamp Act, 1766

1763

Proclamation of 1763 restricts westward expansion.

1765 Parliament passes Stamp Act.

▼

Effect Colonists organize boycott of British goods.

1767 Parliament passes Townshend Acts.

▼

Effect Boycott is resumed; political activism spreads.

Animated GEOGRAPHY & HISTORY
Battle of Bunker Hill *1775*

Click here to preview the events that led to the American Revolution @ClassZone.com

3 Bunker Hill and Breed's Hill overlook the town.

Charlestown burns during the battle.

BOSTON

harbor

British patrols

Massachusetts Minuteman

1774 Intolerable Acts are passed.

▼

Effect Colonists organize First Continental Congress.

1775 Fighting begins at Lexington and Concord.

1773 Parliament passes Tea Act.

▼

Effect Colonists destroy tea in Boston Tea Party.

Bedford, MA militia flag, 1775

1776

Declaration of Independence announces American separation from Britain.

▶ Key Ideas

BEFORE, YOU LEARNED

The British tried to stop colonists from settling on the western frontier.

NOW YOU WILL LEARN

Colonists saw British efforts to increase control over the colonies as violations of their rights.

▶ Vocabulary

TERMS & NAMES

King George III British monarch who reigned during the American Revolution

Quartering Act act requiring the colonists to quarter, or house, British soldiers and provide them with supplies

Sugar Act law placing a tax on sugar, molasses, and other products shipped to the colonies

Stamp Act law requiring all legal and commercial documents to carry an official stamp showing that a tax had been paid

Patrick Henry member of Virginia's House of Burgesses

Sons of Liberty secret society formed to oppose British policies

BACKGROUND VOCABULARY

speculate to buy as an investment

boycott refusal to buy

REVIEW

Proclamation of 1763 British proclamation that forbade the colonists from settling west of the Appalachian Mountains

Visual Vocabulary
King George III

▶ Reading Strategy

Re-create the diagram shown at right. As you read and respond to the **KEY QUESTIONS**, use the boxes to record the opposing points of view of Parliament and the American colonists.

 See Skillbuilder Handbook, page R8.

COMPARE AND CONTRAST

Parliament	Colonists
Colonies should help pay for their own defense.	

 GRAPHIC ORGANIZERS
Go to **Interactive Review** @ ClassZone.com

SECTION 1

Tighter British Control

15.E.3a Identify the types of taxes levied by differing levels of governments (e.g., income tax, sales tax, property tax).
16.B.3b Explain how and why the colonies fought for their independence and how the colonists' ideas are reflected in the Declaration of Independence and the United States Constitution.

One American's Story

In 1765 Sally Franklin's father—the famous American diplomat Benjamin Franklin—was in London to protest the Stamp Act. During his stay, Sally Franklin wrote her father long and detailed letters that were filled with news from the colonies. Often she wrote about family and friends, but Sally also had a keen interest in political affairs. In one letter, she vividly described the colonial reaction to the repeal of the Stamp Act:

PRIMARY SOURCE

❝ We have heard by a round-about way that the Stamp Act is repealed. . . . The bells rung, we had bonfires and one house was illuminated. Indeed I never heard so much noise in my life; the very children seem distracted. **❞**

—Sally Franklin, quoted in *Founding Mothers*

Sally Franklin (Bache)

Similar celebrations occurred throughout the colonies. Many thought the difficulties between Britain and America had finally come to an end.

The Colonies and Britain Grow Apart

▼ **KEY QUESTION** Why were the colonists threatened by Parliament's new laws?

During the French and Indian War, American colonists helped the British defeat the French. The colonists took pride in the British victory, but soon found that their relationship with Britain had soured. In earlier days, the colonies had been allowed, for the most part, to manage their own affairs. In the 1760s, however, Parliament's new laws and restrictions threatened the colonists' freedom.

Westward Expansion Restricted After the French and Indian War, **King George III**, the British monarch, issued many reforms to tighten his control of the American colonies. First, he issued the **Proclamation of 1763**, which forbade the colonists from settling beyond the Appalachian Mountains. Although designed to maintain peace between the colonists and Native Americans, this law angered settlers who hoped to **speculate**, or buy as an investment, in western lands. In addition, King George decided to keep 10,000 soldiers in the colonies to enforce the proclamation. But housing the troops proved very expensive. Therefore, Parliament passed the **Quartering Act**, a law that required colonists to house all British soldiers.

These new laws created great anxiety in the colonies. The colonists feared that Parliament intended to use the troops to control their movements and restrict their freedom.

Parliament Taxes the Colonists In addition to the cost of keeping troops in the colonies, Britain owed massive debts from the French and Indian War. To pay off these debts, Britain needed more revenue, or income. As a result, Parliament looked to the colonies to pay part of the costs for frontier defense and colonial government.

In 1765, Parliament passed the **Sugar Act**. This law placed a tax on sugar, molasses, and other products shipped to the colonies. Making matters worse, in the following year Parliament passed the **Stamp Act**, a law that required all legal and commercial documents to carry an official stamp showing that a tax had been paid. In addition to wills and contracts, all newspapers and diplomas also had to carry a stamp.

From Parliament's perspective, the Sugar and Stamp Acts were reasonable ways to raise money in the colonies to pay off Britain's debt. From the colonist's perspective, however, these acts were seen as serious threats to their political rights. Their anger focused on two complaints: First, that Parliament had no right to tax the colonies—that was a job for the colonial assembly. And second, that no tax should be created without their consent.

▲ **COMPARE AND CONTRAST** Explain why the colonists disagreed with Parliament.

Colonists Defy Parliament

▼ **KEY QUESTION** How did the colonists react when Parliament took over the assemblies' power to tax?

The Stamp Act enraged the colonists. Everywhere people took up the cry "No taxation without representation!" to protest the attack on their rights. **Patrick Henry**, a member of Virginia's House of Burgesses, demanded resistance. When another member shouted that resistance was treason, Henry is said to have replied, "If *this* be treason, make the most of it!"

The Colonists Organize In 1765, delegates from nine colonies formed the Stamp Act Congress in New York. During this meeting, delegates drafted a petition to the king protesting the Stamp Act and declared that the right to tax the colonists belonged to the colonial assemblies, not to Parliament. This was the first time the colonies had united in opposition to British policy.

Meanwhile, some colonists formed secret societies, such as the **Sons of Liberty**, to oppose British policies. Occasionally they encouraged

Under the Stamp Act of 1765, royal stamps such as these were required on legal documents.

people to attack customs officials and burn the stamps. As a result, many customs officials quit their jobs and returned to England.

Colonists Threaten British Profits The colonists' complaints against Parliament were bitter, loud, and sometimes violent. But the most effective protest took the form of a **boycott**, a widespread refusal to buy British goods. By refusing to buy goods from England, the colonists targeted British merchants. The colonists hoped that these merchants, faced with declining sales, would influence Parliament to repeal the Stamp Act. Some British politicians sided with the colonists. Parliamentary leader William Pitt spoke out against the Stamp Act:

(*above*) During the crisis with Great Britian, colonists often met under the Liberty Tree, a symbol of liberty, individuality, and freedom.

PRIMARY SOURCE

❝ The Americans have not acted in all things with prudence and [good] temper. They have been driven to madness by injustice. Will you punish them for the madness you have [caused]? . . . . My opinion . . . . is that the Stamp Act be repealed absolutely, totally, and immediately. ❞

—**William Pitt, quoted in** *Patriots*

The colonists' tactic worked, and Parliament finally repealed the Stamp Act in 1766. But at the same time, Parliament passed the Declaratory Act, which stated that Parliament had supreme authority to govern the colonies. Although the colonists celebrated the repeal of the Stamp Act, the great argument between Parliament and the colonies had just begun.

 CAUSES AND EFFECTS Explain how the colonists reacted when Parliament took over the assemblies' power to tax.

Illinois Learning Standards *Review*

ONLINE QUIZ
For test practice, go to
Interactive Review @ ClassZone.com

TERMS & NAMES

1. Explain the importance of
- King George III
- Quartering Act
- Sugar Act
- Stamp Act
- Patrick Henry
- Sons of Liberty

USING YOUR READING NOTES

2. Compare and Contrast Complete the diagram that you started at the beginning of this section.

Parliament	Colonists
Colonies should help pay for their own defense.	

KEY IDEAS

3. Why did Parliament pass new laws governing the colonies?

4. How did the colonists oppose the new acts?

CRITICAL THINKING

5. Analyze Point of View Why would Britain's new laws have convinced Americans that their freedom was under threat?

6. Connect Economics & History Why was boycotting British goods an effective way to protest the Stamp Act?

7. Writing Protest Song Imagine that you are one of the Sons of Liberty. Write a song protesting Parliament's new laws.

▶ Key Ideas

BEFORE, YOU LEARNED

Colonists saw British efforts to increase control over the colonies as violations of their rights.

NOW YOU WILL LEARN

Many colonists organized to oppose British policies.

▶ Vocabulary

TERMS & NAMES

Crispus Attucks sailor of African-American and Native American ancestry who died at the Boston Massacre

Boston Massacre incident in 1770 in which British troops fired on and killed American colonists

Townshend Acts acts passed by Parliament in 1767 to tax imports in the colonies

writs of assistance search warrants used to enter homes or businesses to search for smuggled goods

Daughters of Liberty organization of colonial women formed to protest British policies

Samuel Adams leader of the Boston Sons of Liberty

committee of correspondence organization formed to exchange information about British policies and American resistance

Boston Tea Party incident in 1773, when colonists protested British policies by boarding British ships and throwing their cargoes of tea overboard

BACKGROUND VOCABULARY

duties taxes placed on imported goods

REVIEW

John Adams lawyer who defended British soldiers accused of murder in the Boston Massacre

▶ Reading Strategy

Re-create the diagram shown at right. As you read and respond to the **KEY QUESTIONS**, use the boxes to record how each aspect of the Townshend Acts angered the colonists.

 See Skillbuilder Handbook, page R7.

CAUSES AND EFFECTS

Townshend Acts...	anger colonists because...
writs of assistance	*customs officials invaded their homes and businesses*
duties on imports	

 GRAPHIC ORGANIZERS
Go to **Interactive Review** @ ClassZone.com

Colonial Resistance Grows

15.E.3a Identify the types of taxes levied by differing levels of governments (e.g., *income tax, sales tax, property tax*).

16.A.3b Make inferences about historical events and eras using historical maps and other historical sources.

One American's Story

Crispus Attucks was born into slavery in Framingham, Massachusetts, around 1723. It is believed that Attucks was the son of an African-American father and a Native American mother. As a young man, Attucks escaped slavery by running away to sea.

In March 1770, Attucks was in Boston, where feelings against British rule were reaching a fever pitch. He joined a crowd who were protesting British troops. A witness described what happened next.

PRIMARY SOURCE

❝ [The British officer] is said to have ordered [the troops] to fire, and to have repeated that order. One gun was fired first; then others in succession and with deliberation, till ten or a dozen guns were fired. ❞

—anonymous account of the Boston Massacre

Crispus Attucks

When the smoke cleared Attucks was dead, one of the victims of the **Boston Massacre**. Throughout America, tension between Britain and its colonies was exploding into violence.

Tightening British Control

🔻 **KEY QUESTION** Why did the Townshend Acts anger the colonists?

After the uproar over the Sugar and Stamp Acts, Britain hoped to avoid further conflict with the colonies. Yet Parliament faced a serious dilemma: how to control the unruly colonists without angering the people with a new set of taxes. The answer, Parliament decided, was the Declaratory Act.

Passed in 1766, the Declaratory Act affirmed Parliament's right to legislate for the colonies "in all cases whatsoever." Importantly, however, no new tax accompanied the act. The purpose of the Declaratory Act was simply to reassert Parliament's control over all colonial affairs.

Most colonists did not feel threatened by the Declaratory Act. Although some politicans did protest the new law in colonial assemblies, most people were not bothered by Parliament's bold political statement. Instead, colonists simply ignored the act and went on with their lives as best they could.

The Townshend Acts Are Passed Parliament's new strategy, however, had one major flaw: with the Stamp Act repealed, Britain still needed to raise money in the colonies to pay for troops and other expenses. So Britain's finance minister, Charles Townshend, proposed a new series of **duties**, or taxes on imports, to raise revenue in America.

Approved by Parliament in 1767, the **Townshend Acts** placed duties on numerous imports to the colonies such as glass, paper, paint, lead, and tea. In addition, the acts allowed British officers to issue **writs of assistance**, or search warrants, to enter homes and businesses to search for smuggled or illegal goods.

Daily Life   *The Colonial Marketplace*

By the 1760s, English merchants were sending hundreds of ships to America with goods for sale to the colonists. Beyond the daily necessities of life—tools, knives, nails, and axes—colonists were eager to buy the latest luxuries and fashions from England, including (**A**) clothing, (**B**) glass and building materials, (**C**) glassware, (**D**) scientific and medical instruments, (**E**) books and periodicals, (**F**) furniture, and (**G**) fine silks.

BOYCOTT PRESSURES MERCHANTS

When the colonists boycotted British goods, many English merchants, shippers, and manufacturers lost business as their products went unsold. As a result, in 1765 many merchants pressured Parliament to repeal the acts so their businesses could recover.

CRITICAL THINKING Make Generalizations
How did the colonial boycotts affect British merchants?

Anger Over the Townshend Acts News of the Townshend Acts sparked immediate protest throughout the colonies. People were furious that Parliament had once again passed a tax without their consent. Colonists felt that only locally elected officials—rather than Parliament—should have the right to create laws and taxes in the colonies. Many people, such as Pennsylvania lawyer John Dickinson, thought the acts were illegal. Dickinson explained his beliefs in a famous pamphlet:

PRIMARY SOURCE

❝ We cannot be happy without being free . . . we cannot be free without being secure in our property . . . we cannot be secure in our property, if [taxed] without our consent. ❞

—John Dickinson, *Letters from a Farmer in Pennsylvania*

The colonists were also angry about the writs of assistance. Many believed that the writs went against their natural rights, as defined by English philosopher John Locke. The law of nature, wrote Locke, teaches that "no one ought to harm another in his life, health, liberty, or possessions."

🔺 **CAUSES AND EFFECTS** Explain why the Townshend Acts angered the colonists.

Colonists Protest

🔻 **KEY QUESTION** In what ways did colonists protest British laws?

In response to the Townshend Acts, merchants in Boston organized another boycott of British goods. By October 1767, other colonies had joined the Massachusetts protests. The colonists were uniting for a common cause.

Political Activism Spreads As the boycott spread throughout the colonies, more people became politically active. Many colonists who had not previously participated in politics now had a way of making their voices heard. For example, some women formed their own protest organization called the **Daughters of Liberty**. They urged colonists to weave their own cloth and to use American products instead of British goods.

Meanwhile, colonial leaders urged the people to remain calm and not to protest violently. "No mobs," the *Boston Gazette* suggested, "Constitutional methods are best." Regardless, some colonists continued to protest with anger and threatened to form a mob.

Fearing disorder in the colonies, British officials called for more troops. This angered the colonists—even those who wanted peace. **Samuel Adams**, a leader of the Boston Sons of Liberty, stated, "We will destroy every soldier that dare put his foot on shore. . . . I look upon them as foreign enemies!"

The Boston Massacre In the fall of 1768, more than 1,000 additional British soldiers (known as redcoats for their bright red jackets) arrived in Boston under the command of General Thomas Gage. With their arrival, tensions erupted into violence.

Connecting History

Representative Government
Ever since the House of Burgesses was established in Jamestown in 1619, colonists had the right to raise their own taxes. See *Chapter 3, page 64.*

Paul Revere's etching of the Boston Massacre fueled anger in the colonies.

Are the soldiers represented fairly in Revere's etching?

On March 5, 1770, a group of colonists—mostly youths and dockworkers—surrounded some soldiers in front of the State House. Soon, the two groups began trading insults, shouting at each other and even throwing snowballs. As the crowd grew larger, the soldiers began to fear for their safety. Thinking they were about to be attacked, the soldiers fired into the crowd. Five people, including Crispus Attucks, were killed.

The people of Boston were outraged at what came to be known as the Boston Massacre. In the weeks that followed, the colonies were flooded with anti-British propaganda in newspapers, pamphlets, and political posters. Attucks and the four victims were depicted as heroes who had given their lives for the cause of freedom. The British soldiers, on the other hand, were portrayed as evil and menacing villains.

At the same time, the soldiers who had fired the shots were arrested and charged with murder. **John Adams**, a lawyer and cousin of Samuel Adams, agreed to defend the soldiers in court. Many people criticized Adams and some even threatened to harm the lawyer. But Adams believed that everyone—including the British soldiers—was entitled to a fair trial. Although Adams supported the colonists' cause, he wanted to demonstrate that everyone was subject to the rule of law.

Adams argued that the soldiers had acted in self-defense. The jury agreed and acquitted the soldiers. To many colonists, however, the Boston Massacre would stand as a symbol of British tyranny in the colonies.

▲ **SUMMARIZE** Describe how colonists protested British laws.

Economic Interference

▼ **KEY QUESTION** How did colonists in the port cities react to the Tea Act?

In April 1770, Parliament repealed the Townshend Acts. Once again, the colonial boycott had worked—British trade had been hurt and Parliament had backed down. But Parliament kept the tea tax to show that it still had the right to tax the colonists.

The Tea Act Increases Anger To demonstrate their displeasure with the remaining tax on tea, many colonists chose not to purchase luxuries from British merchants. Instead, they drank tea that was smuggled from Holland. As a result, many British tea companies lost money in America as their tea went unsold and rotted in ports.

Attempting to save British tea merchants, Parliament passed the Tea Act in 1773. This law gave one company, the East India Company, the exclusive right to sell tea in the colonies. Although the act lowered the price of tea for colonists, it also restricted colonists from acting as shippers and merchants of the valuable product.

Many colonists—particularly those who had traded in smuggled tea—were enraged by the new tax. Colonists saw the tea act as another attempt by Parliament to interfere in the economic life of the colonies.

Colonial Unity Expands By this time, colonial leaders understood the importance of unity among the colonies. Therefore, Samuel Adams urged many towns in Massachusetts to establish **committees of correspondence** to communicate with their neighboring towns and colonial leaders.

In the months that followed, these groups exchanged numerous secret letters on colonial affairs and resistance to British policy. Before long, many other colonies—such as New York, South Carolina, and Rhode Island—had created similar committees of correspondence.

History Makers *Revolutionary Leaders*

Samuel Adams   1722–1803

When Parliament levied taxes upon the colonies, no one responded with greater passion and fury than Boston merchant Samuel Adams. A skillful writer, orator, and popular leader of the Sons of Liberty and the Boston Committee of Correspondence, Samuel Adams persuaded many colonists to unite against British policy and taxation. "It does not require a majority to prevail," Samuel Adams wrote, "but rather an irate, tireless minority keen to set brush fires in people's minds."

ONLINE BIOGRAPHY For more information about Samuel and John Adams, go to the **Research & Writing Center** @ ClassZone.com

John Adams   1735–1826

While his cousin Samuel planned fiery public protests, John Adams used a quieter tactic—the law—to counter British policy. "Facts are stubborn things," Adams wrote, "and whatever may be our wishes, our inclinations, or the dictates of our passions, they cannot alter the state of facts and evidence." Putting this theory into practice, Adams helped draft a legal petition to the king suggesting that Parliament had no right to tax the colonies.

COMPARING *Leaders*

How did Samuel and John Adams differ in the way they protested British actions?

The Boston Tea Party Protests against the Tea Act took place throughout the colonies. In Charlestown, South Carolina, colonists unloaded tea and let it rot on the docks. In New York City and Philadelphia, colonists blocked tea ships from landing. In Boston, the Sons of Liberty organized what came to be known as the **Boston Tea Party**.

On the evening of December 16, 1773, a group of men disguised as Native Americans boarded three tea ships docked in Boston harbor. One of the men, George Hewes, a Boston shoemaker, later recalled the events.

PRIMARY SOURCE

❝ We then were ordered by our commander to open the hatches and take out all the chests of tea and throw them overboard. . . . In about three hours from the time we went on board, we had thus broken and thrown overboard every tea chest to be found in the ship; while those in the other ships were disposing of the tea in the same way, at the same time. ❞

—George Hewes, quoted in *A Retrospect of the Boston Tea-Party*

That night, Hewes and the others destroyed 342 chests of tea to protest the Tea Act. Many colonists rejoiced at the news. British officials, however, were angered by the destructive protest and wanted to punish the culprits.

In the days that followed, some colonial leaders offered to pay for the tea if Parliament agreed to repeal the hated Tea Act. But Britain ruled out any compromise. This decision pushed many Americans into open rebellion.

▲ **CAUSES AND EFFECTS** Describe how colonists reacted to the Tea Act.

 Illinois Learning Standards *Review*

 ONLINE QUIZ
For test practice, go to
Interactive Review @ ClassZone.com

TERMS & NAMES

1. Explain the importance of
- Crispus Attucks
- Boston Massacre
- Townshend Acts
- writs of assistance
- Daughters of Liberty
- Samuel Adams
- John Adams
- Boston Tea Party

USING YOUR READING NOTES

2. Causes and Effects Complete the diagram that you started at the beginning of this section.

Townshend Acts...	anger colonists because...
writs of assistance	*customs officials invaded their homes and businesses*
duties on imports	

KEY IDEAS

3. Why did colonists oppose the Townshend Acts?

4. How did the colonists express their discontent?

5. What prompted the Boston Tea Party?

CRITICAL THINKING

6. Draw Conclusions Why did Parliament keep trying different ways of raising revenue?

7. Problems and Solutions Why did the colonists react so violently to the Tea Act?

8. Summarize Explain the impact of Paul Revere's etching of the Boston Massacre.

9. **Writing** **Letter** Write a letter to Parliament, urging the British government not to interfere in colonial trade.

POPULAR RESISTANCE

The colonists found many ways to resist the new laws passed by Parliament.
Americans from all walks of life joined in the popular protests.

PROTESTS IN THE STREETS

Popular protests echoed through the streets
of colonial towns. In this illustration, an angry
crowd of colonists burns the hated stamps.

WOMEN BECOME ACTIVISTS

For the first time in American history, large numbers
of women became involved in a political cause.
Women played a leading role in the boycotts of
British goods. They also organized and signed
petitions. This British cartoon shows the women of
Edenton, North Carolina signing a promise not to
buy British products.

POLITICS IN DAILY LIFE

Protests against the
Stamp Act appeared
everywhere, from
newspapers and
periodicals to
ordinary household
items.

A mock stamp printed by a Pennsylvania
journal to protest the Stamp Act

Join the Boycott

Imagine you have joined the boycott
of imported goods. Create a political
pamphlet that expresses your opinion
about British products.

▶ Key Ideas

BEFORE, YOU LEARNED
Many Americans organized to oppose British policies.

NOW YOU WILL LEARN
The tensions between Britain and the colonies led to the outbreak of the Revolutionary War.

▶ Vocabulary

TERMS & NAMES

Minutemen group of armed civilians, trained to be ready to fight "at a minute's warning"

Intolerable Acts series of laws, known in Britain as the Coercive Acts, meant to punish Massachusetts and clamp down on resistance in other colonies

First Continental Congress meeting of delegates from most of the colonies, called in reaction to the Intolerable Acts

Paul Revere Boston silversmith who rode into the countryside to spread news of British troop movement

Lexington and Concord first battles of the Revolutionary War

Loyalists Americans who supported the British

Patriots Americans who sided with the rebels

BACKGROUND VOCABULARY

militia a force of armed civilians pledged to defend their community

Visual Vocabulary Paul Revere

▶ Reading Strategy

Re-create the diagram shown at right. As you read and respond to the **KEY QUESTIONS**, record information to support the generalization.

 See Skillbuilder Handbook, page R11.

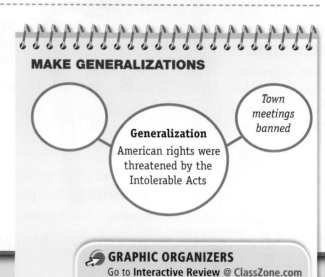

MAKE GENERALIZATIONS

Town meetings banned

Generalization
American rights were threatened by the Intolerable Acts

🖱 **GRAPHIC ORGANIZERS**
Go to **Interactive Review** @ ClassZone.com

The Road to Lexington and Concord

16.B.3a Describe how different groups competed for power within the colonies and how that competition led to the development of political institutions during the early national period.
16.B.3b Explain how and why the colonies fought for their independence and how the colonists' ideas are reflected in the Declaration of Independence and the United States Constitution.

One American's Story

At dawn on April 19, 1775, Captain John Parker and 70 of his men stood on the grassy common at the center of Lexington, a village near Boston. The men under Parker's command belonged to the local **militia**—a force of armed civilians pledged to defend their community. About one-third of the Lexington militia were **Minutemen**, colonists trained to be "ready to act at a minute's warning." A soldier described what happened next:

PRIMARY SOURCE

❝ There suddenly appeared a Number of King's troops . . . They were . . . on a quick pace Towards us with Three officers in there front on horse back and on full gallop Towards us the foremost of which cryed through down your arms you villains you Rebels." ❞

—**John Robbins, quoted in *Redcoats and Rebels***

Colonists battle Redcoats at Lexington, 1775.

Captain Parker was wounded and eight of his men were killed in the first fighting of the War of Independence. Colonial protests had turned into violent revolution.

The Intolerable Acts

🔻 **KEY QUESTION** What rights were threatened by the Intolerable Acts?

The Boston Tea Party infuriated Parliament. One British official said the people of Boston "ought to be knocked about their ears." King George III declared, "We must master them or totally leave them to themselves and treat them as aliens." Britain chose to "master" the colonies.

Attacks on Rights and Liberties In 1774, Parliament passed a series of laws to punish the Massachusetts colony and to clamp down on resistance in other colonies. The British called these laws the Coercive Acts, but they were so harsh that the colonists called them the **Intolerable Acts**. These acts were a direct attack on colonists' traditional rights and liberties, because they

- closed the port of Boston until colonists paid for the destroyed tea
- altered the Massachusetts charter to ban town meetings
- replaced the elected council with an appointed one
- increased the governor's power over the colonists
- protected British officials accused of crimes in the colonies from being tried by colonists
- allowed British officers to house troops in private dwellings

To enforce the acts, Parliament appointed General Thomas Gage governor of Massachusetts.

ANALYZING *Political Cartoons*

HISTORICAL CARTOONS

Historical cartoons show how people viewed the important events of their time. Each cartoon on these pages expresses the point of view of the cartoonist. Notice how the cartoonists use symbols, exaggeration, and humor to get their points across.

The Bostonians in Distress

This cartoon uses symbols to show the situation in Boston after the Intolerable Acts stopped all ships from entering the town's harbors.

Bostonians are trapped in a cage symbolizing the restrictions of the Intolerable Acts.

Other colonists are shown helping the Bostonians by feeding them fish.

The First Continental Congress Meets In 1772, Sam Adams had written, "I wish we could arouse the continent." The Intolerable Acts answered his wish. Other colonies immediately offered Massachusetts their support. They sent food and money to Boston. The committees of correspondence also called for a meeting of colonial delegates to discuss what to do next.

In September 1774, delegates from all the colonies except Georgia met in Philadelphia. At this meeting, called the **First Continental Congress**, delegates voted to ban all trade with Britain until the Intolerable Acts were repealed. They also called on each colony to begin training troops. Georgia agreed to be a part of the actions of the Congress even though it had voted not to send delegates.

The First Continental Congress marked a key step in American history. Although most delegates were not ready to call for independence, they were determined to uphold colonial rights. This meeting planted the seeds of a future independent government. John Adams called it "a nursery of American statesmen." The delegates agreed to meet again in seven months.

The Bostonians Paying the Excise-Man

This cartoon was published in London in 1774. It shows how Tories (those supporting the King) viewed colonial protests.

A customs informer, who has been tarred and feathered, is being tormented.

The protesters are shown as violent thugs.

CRITICAL THINKING

1. **Make Inferences** Which cartoon is sympathetic to the colonists?

2. **Synthesize** How would these images have helped unite the colonists against British policies?

 See Skillbuilder Handbook, page R24.

Abigail Adams 1744–1818

Abigail Smith was born on November 11, 1744, in Weymouth, Massachusetts. She married John Adams in 1764, the same year that Britain enacted the Sugar Act. She was often left alone to manage the family farm and raise their children.

During their long separations, Abigail wrote her husband many letters about government and politics. Often she expressed her opinions to her husband and even gave him advice when creating new laws. In one letter, Abigail asked John to give women more rights. "Remember the ladies," she wrote him, "and be more generous and favorable to them than your ancestors." Abigail's views were well ahead of her time, although it was years before women achieved equal rights.

CRITICAL THINKING Draw Conclusions What might Abigail Adams think about women's rights today?

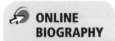 **ONLINE BIOGRAPHY** For more on on Abigail Adams, go to the **Research & Writing Center** @ ClassZone.com

British Control Begins to Slip The colonists hoped that another trade boycott would force a repeal of the Intolerable Acts. After all, past boycotts had led to the repeal of the Stamp Act and the Townshend Acts. This time, however, Parliament stood firm. It even increased restrictions on colonial trade and sent more troops in the colonies. However, in the countryside, British authorities were already losing control of government. Throughout the colonies, Americans acted forcefully to reestablish the rights that Parliament was taking away. In the summer of 1774 in towns throughout Massachusetts, large crowds gathered to prevent British-appointed judges from holding court. They also forced many unelected officials to resign. In defiance of the royal governor, the people of Massachusetts elected a provincial congress with the power to collect its own taxes and raise its own army.

By the end of 1774, some colonists were preparing to fight. In Massachusetts, John Hancock headed the Committee of Safety, which had the power to call out the militia. In Virginia, House of Burgess member Patrick Henry delivered his most famous speech, calling for war:

PRIMARY SOURCE

❝ Gentlemen may cry peace, peace—but there is no peace. The war is actually begun! The next gale that sweeps from the north will bring to our ears the clash of resounding arms! Our brethren are already in the field! Why stand we here idle? . . . I know not what course others may take; but as for me, give me liberty or give me death. ❞

—Patrick Henry, quoted in *Patriots*

But most colonial leaders believed that any fight with Britain would be short. They thought that a public show of force would make the British Parliament change its policies.

▲ **SUMMARIZE** Explain what rights were threatened by the Intolerable Acts.

The Revolution Begins

▼ **KEY QUESTION** Why did the fighting begin at Lexington?

Since 1770, Sam Adams had been building a network of informants to keep watch over British activities. The British had their spies too. It was from these spies that General Gage learned that the Massachusetts militia was storing arms and ammunition in Concord, about 20 miles northwest of Boston. He also heard that Sam Adams and John Hancock were nearby in Lexington. On the night of April 18, 1775, Gage ordered his troops to arrest Adams and Hancock in Lexington and to destroy the supplies in Concord.

The Midnight Ride The Sons of Liberty had prepared for this moment. **Paul Revere**, a Boston silversmith, and a second messenger, William Dawes, were sent to spread the news about British troop movements. Revere would cross the harbor from Boston to Charlestown. From there he would ride to Lexington and Concord. Dawes would take the land route.

Revere had arranged a system of signals to alert colonists across the harbor in Charlestown. One lantern burning in the Old North Church steeple signaled that the British troops were taking the land route out of Boston; two lamps meant that the troops were leaving Boston by water.

CONNECTING ⟲ History

NEW ENGLANDERS OPPOSE THE KING

New Englanders had a long history of fierce opposition to royal authority. During the English Civil War of the 1640s, many New England Puritans returned to England to fight the king. They rejoiced when a republic was set up in England following the king's execution.

Over a century later, in the 1760s and 1770s, descendants of the Puritans were still angered by the same issues that had upset their ancestors:

- the levying of taxes without the people's consent
- the extent of the king's power
- the creation of a standing army that might threaten their freedom

Puritans execute King Charles I in London in 1649.

CRITICAL THINKING **Make Generalizations** Why was New England a hotbed of political protest?

When the British moved, so did Revere and Dawes. They galloped over the countryside on their "midnight ride," spreading the news. In Lexington, they were joined by Dr. Samuel Prescott. When Revere and Dawes were stopped by a British patrol, Prescott broke away and carried the message to Concord.

Lexington and Concord At dawn on April 19, 1775, more than 700 British troops reached Lexington. There they found Captain John Parker and about 70 colonial militiamen waiting. The British commander ordered the Americans to drop their muskets. The colonists refused. No one knows who fired first, but within a few minutes eight militiamen lay dead. The British then marched to Concord, where they destroyed military supplies. A battle broke out at a bridge north of town, forcing the British to retreat.

Nearly 4,000 Minutemen and militiamen arrived in the area. They lined the road from Concord to Lexington and peppered the retreating redcoats with musket fire. "It seemed as if men came down from the clouds," one British soldier later recalled. Only the arrival of 1,000 more troops saved the British from total destruction as they scrambled back to Boston.

Lexington and Concord were the first battles of the Revolutionary War. As Ralph Waldo Emerson later wrote, colonial troops had fired the "shot heard 'round the world." Americans would now have to choose sides and back up their political beliefs by force of arms. Those who supported the British were called **Loyalists**. Those who sided with the rebels were known as **Patriots**. The Revolution had begun.

 CAUSES AND EFFECTS Explain why fighting began at Lexington.

Illinois Learning Standards *Review*

ONLINE QUIZ
For test practice, go to
Interactive Review @ ClassZone.com

TERMS & NAMES

1. Explain the importance of

- Minutemen
- Intolerable Acts
- First Continental Congress
- Paul Revere
- Lexington and Concord
- Loyalists
- Patriots

USING YOUR READING NOTES

2. Make Generalizations Complete the diagram that you started at the beginning of this section.

Generalization
American rights were threatened by the Intolerable Acts

Town meetings banned

KEY IDEAS

3. Why did Britain pass the Intolerable Acts?

4. Why were British troops sent to Concord?

CRITICAL THINKING

5. Draw Conclusions Why did the colonists fear the Intolerable Acts?

6. Analyze Causes What democratic traditions were threatened by Parliament's policies?

7. Make Inferences Why were the British worried about the weapons being stored in Lexington?

8. Geography In the 18th century the landscape of Boston was very different than it is today. Research and write a short paper on how much the landscape around Boston has changed, or build a model of Boston in the 18th century.

Johnny Tremain
by Esther Forbes

In 1775, 16-year-old Johnny Tremain lives in Boston and works as a delivery boy for a newspaper. Because he travels so much around the city, he is able to help the Patriots gather information about what the British are doing.

On the night of April 18, Johnny learns that British troops will be leaving on an expedition to seize the gunpowder at Lexington and Concord. He rushes to tell this news to Dr. Joseph Warren, who is a Patriot. Then Johnny goes to bed, wondering if the war has begun.

So Johnny slept. It was daylight when he woke with Warren's hand upon his shoulder. Outside on Tremont Street he could hear the clumping of army boots. A sergeant was swearing at his men. The soldiers were paraded so close to the house, which stood **flush**[1] with the sidewalkless street, that Johnny at first thought they must be in the room.

Doctor Warren dared speak no louder than a whisper.

"I'm going now."

"Something's happened?"

"Yes." He motioned Johnny to follow him into the kitchen. This room was on the back of the house. They could talk without danger of being overheard by the troops in the street.

Doctor Warren had on the same clothes as the day before. He had not been to bed. But now his hat was on his head. His black bag of instruments and medicines was packed and on the table. Silently he put milk, bread, herrings beside it, and gestured to Johnny to join him.

"Where did it begin?" asked Johnny.

"Lexington."

"Who won?"

"They did. Seven hundred against seventy. It wasn't a battle. It was . . . just target practice . . . for them. Some of our men were killed and the British **huzzaed**[2] and took the road to Concord."

"And did they get our supplies there?"

"I don't know. Paul Revere sent for me just after the firing on Lexington Green."

The young man's usually fresh-colored face was **haggard**.[3] He knew the seriousness of this day for himself and for his country.

"But everywhere the alarm is spreading. Men are grabbing their guns—marching for Concord. Paul Revere did get through in time last night. Billy Dawes a little later. Hundreds—maybe thousands—of Minute Men are on the march. Before the day's over, there'll be real fighting—not target practice. But Gage doesn't know that it's begun. You see, long before Colonel Smith got to Lexington—just as soon as he heard that Revere had warned the country—he sent back for reinforcements. For Earl Percy. You and I, Johnny, are just about the only people in Boston who know that blood has already been shed."

ADDITIONAL READING

Give Me Liberty! by Russell Freedman An exciting and well illustrated account of the events leading up to the Declaration of Independence.

Concise History of the American Revolution, by David C. G. Dutcher This publication from the National Park Service provides a good narrative of the American Revolution.

1. **flush:** in a line with
2. **huzzaed:** cheered
3. **haggard:** tired

▶ Key Ideas

BEFORE, YOU LEARNED

Rising tensions between Britain and the colonies led to the outbreak of the Revolutionary War.

NOW YOU WILL LEARN

As fighting continued, Americans decided to declare their independence from Britain.

▶ Vocabulary

TERMS & NAMES

Ethan Allen leader of a Patriot group of fighters known as the Green Mountain Boys

Second Continental Congress America's government during the Revolutionary War

Continental Army America's Patriot army during the Revolutionary War

Thomas Paine political radical and the author of *Common Sense*

Declaration of Independence document that declared American independence from Britain

Thomas Jefferson delegate from Virginia who wrote the Declaration of Independence

BACKGROUND VOCABULARY

siege when enemy forces surround a town or city in order to force it to surrender

artillery cannon and large guns

Visual Vocabulary Thomas Jefferson

▶ Reading Strategy

Re-create the diagram shown at right. As you read and respond to the **KEY QUESTIONS**, use the boxes to sequence events.

 See Skillbuilder Handbook, page R5.

SEQUENCE EVENTS

Lexington and Concord → ☐ → ☐ → Battle of Bunker Hill

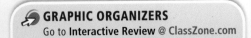

GRAPHIC ORGANIZERS
Go to **Interactive Review** @ ClassZone.com

Declaring Independence

 14.F.3a Analyze historical influences on the development of political ideas and practices as enumerated in the Declaration of Independence, the United States Constitution, the Bill of Rights and the Illinois Constitution.
16.B.3b Explain how and why the colonies fought for their independence and how the colonists' ideas are reflected in the Declaration of Independence and the United States Constitution.

One American's Story

No one knows who warned the colonists about the British plan to march on Concord. But suspicion has always fallen on Margaret Kemble Gage, the American-born wife of British General Thomas Gage. Despite her husband's lofty position as commander-in-chief of the British army in America, Margaret's loyalty remained torn between England and America. Explaining her mixed feelings about the war, Margaret Gage quoted Blanche from Shakespeare's play *King John*:

PRIMARY SOURCE

❝ The Sun's o'ercast with blood: fair day, adieu!
Which is the side that I must go withal?
I am with both: each army hath a hand;
And in their rage, I having hold of both,
They whirl asunder and dismember me . . .
Whoever wins, on that side shall I lose.
Assured loss, before the match be played. ❞

— Margaret Kemble Gage, quoted in *Paul Revere's Ride*

Margaret Kemble Gage
by John Singleton Copley

After the British retreat at Lexington and Concord, even Margaret's husband suspected his wife had revealed the secret plans. Fearing she might do the same again, Gage sent his wife back to England. Like many others, Margaret Gage was forced to make difficult choices as the conflict began to spread.

The Siege of Boston

🔻 **KEY QUESTION** What events led to the Battle of Bunker Hill?

After the fighting at Lexington and Concord, British troops retreated to safety in Boston. As General Gage considered his next move, over 15,000 militiamen from all over New England surrounded the town. Boston was now

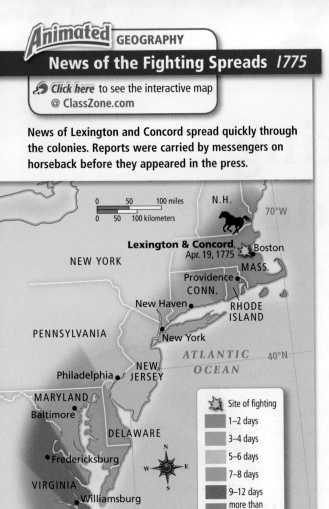

Click here to see the interactive map @ ClassZone.com

News of Lexington and Concord spread quickly through the colonies. Reports were carried by messengers on horseback before they appeared in the press.

Source: Adapted from *Paul Revere's Ride*, D. Fischer

Connect Geography & History

Draw Conclusions How many miles could news spread in a two-day period?

---

under **siege**—encircled by military forces determined to force the British to surrender.

The Continental Army Is Formed In 1775, Boston stood at the tip of a long peninsula that connected the town to the mainland. Because the town was almost completely surrounded by water, it could not be attacked easily by land. However, if the Americans succeeded in placing cannon on the hills overlooking the bays that surrounded the town, the British would be forced to surrender.

The Americans came up with a daring plan. They would capture a British fort, far to the north, and drag the fort's cannon back to Boston. On May 10, 1775, Americans attacked Britain's Fort Ticonderoga on Lake Champlain. **Ethan Allen** led this band of backwoods fighters known as the Green Mountain Boys. They captured the fort and its large supply of **artillery**, or cannon and large guns.

On the same day as the attack on Fort Ticonderoga, the **Second Continental Congress** began meeting in Philadelphia. This would be America's government during the war. Delegates included John and Samuel Adams, John Hancock, Benjamin Franklin, George Washington, and Patrick Henry. They agreed to create a **Continental Army**. George Washington, who was from Virginia, was chosen as its commanding general.

Battle of Bunker Hill Meanwhile, tensions were building in Boston in June 1775. Across the harbor from Boston stood the town of Charlestown. Militiamen were positioned on Bunker Hill and Breeds Hill, which rose above the town. They built fortifications on Breeds Hill. Alarmed, the British decided to attack.

General William Howe crossed the bay with 2,200 British soldiers. Bostonians watched in horror as the British set fire to Charlestown. Then, marching in ranks, the British climbed Breeds Hill toward the American militia. On the hilltop, the militia waited. According to legend, Colonel William Prescott ordered, "Don't fire until you see the whites of their eyes!" When the British got close, the militia unleashed a barrage of fire. The British fell back and then charged again. Eventually, they forced the militia off the hill.

The redcoats had won the Battle of Bunker Hill, but at tremendous cost. More than 1,000 were killed or wounded, compared with some 400 militia casualties. "The loss we have sustained is greater than we can bear," wrote General Gage. The inexperienced colonial militia had held its own against the world's most powerful army.

▲ **SEQUENCE EVENTS** Describe the events that led to the Battle of Bunker Hill.

The Conflict Spreads

▼ **KEY QUESTION** Why were the British forced to leave Boston?

In their coffee houses, inns, and taverns, colonists discussed the deepening crisis. Most colonists still hoped for peace. Even some Patriot leaders still considered themselves loyal subjects of the king. They blamed Parliament for the terrible events taking place.

The Olive Branch Petition In July 1775, moderates in Congress drafted the Olive Branch Petition and sent it to London. This document asked the king to restore harmony between Britain and the colonies. Some members opposed the petition but signed it anyway as a last hope.

The king rejected the petition, however, and announced new measures to punish the colonies. He would use the British navy to block American ships from leaving their ports. He would send thousands of hired German soldiers to fight in America. "When once these rebels have felt a smart blow, they will submit," he declared.

The colonial forces were not going to back down, though. They thought they were equal to the British troops. George Washington knew otherwise. The British soldiers were professionals, while the colonial troops had little training and were poorly equipped. The Massachusetts militia barely had enough gunpowder to fight one battle.

Washington Arrives During the summer of 1775, Washington arrived at the militia camp near Boston. He immediately began to gather supplies and train the army. In the fall, Washington approved a bold plan. Continental Army troops would invade Quebec, in eastern Canada. They hoped to defeat British forces there and draw Canadians into the Patriot cause. One of the leaders of this expedition was Benedict Arnold. He was an officer who had played a role in the victory at Fort Ticonderoga.

After a grueling march across Maine, Arnold arrived at Quebec in November 1775. Under harsh winter conditions, the Americans launched their attack but failed. After several months, they limped home in defeat.

The British Retreat from Boston In Massachusetts, the Continental Army continued its siege of Boston. The British lay trapped in the town, which stood like an island protected by the surrounding waters of the bays. They gazed nervously across the bays to the opposite shores, where thousands of American forces waited on the hills.

Neither side was able or willing to break the standoff. However, help for Washington was on the way. Cannon were being hauled from Fort Ticonderoga. This was a difficult job, since there were no roads across the snow-covered mountains. It took soldiers, under the leadership of American General Henry Knox, two months to drag the 59 heavy weapons to Boston, where they arrived in January 1776.

Washington positioned these cannon on Dorchester Heights, overlooking Boston. The Americans, now in a position of power, threatened to bombard the city. General Howe, who was in charge of

(*below*) This statue, which stands in the Boston Public Garden, commemorates the day General Washington drove the British from the city.

the British forces, decided to withdraw his troops. On March 17, over 7,000 British soldiers departed Boston in more than 100 ships. Boston Patriots joyfully reclaimed their city. Although the British had damaged homes and destroyed possessions, Boston was still standing. The British would never return.

▲ **CAUSES AND EFFECTS** Explain how the British were forced to leave Boston.

Rebellion Becomes Revolution

▼ **KEY QUESTION** What ideas can be found in the Declaration of Independence?

As the British evacuated Boston, Americans debated the crisis. Most Americans hoped to avoid a final break with Britain. However, the publication of a pamphlet titled *Common Sense* helped convince many Americans that it was time to fight for independence.

***Common Sense* Changes Minds** *Common Sense* had been written by **Thomas Paine**, a recent immigrant from England. Paine was considered a political radical. He believed that all men, not just landowners, should have the right to vote. He also ridiculed the idea that kings ruled by the will of God. Calling George III "the Royal Brute," Paine argued that all monarchies were corrupt. He also disagreed with the economic arguments for remaining with Britain. "Our corn," he said, "will fetch its price in any market in Europe." He believed that America should follow its own destiny.

(*above*) political writer Thomas Paine (*below*) the pamphlet, *Common Sense*, that moved many colonists toward revolution

PRIMARY SOURCE

❝ Everything that is right or natural pleads for separation. The blood of the slain, the weeping voice of nature cries, " 'Tis time to part." Even the distance at which the Almighty had placed England and America is a strong and natural proof that the authority of the one over the other was never the design of heaven. ❞

—Thomas Paine, *Common Sense*

Common Sense was an instant success. Published in January, it sold more than 100,000 copies in three months. Americans were beginning to understand that it was time to fight for independence.

A Time for Decision The Continental Congress remained undecided. A majority of the delegates did not support independence. Even so, in May 1776, Congress adopted a resolution authorizing each of the 13 colonies to establish its own government.

On June 7, Richard Henry Lee of Virginia introduced a key resolution. It called the colonies "free and independent states" and declared that "all political connection between them and the state of Great Britain is . . . totally dissolved." Congress debated the resolution, but not all the delegates were ready to vote on it.

In the meantime, however, Congress appointed a committee to draft a

Declaration of Independence. The committee included Benjamin Franklin, John Adams, Roger Sherman, Robert Livingston, and **Thomas Jefferson**.

The group chose Jefferson to compose the Declaration. Two reasons for selecting Jefferson were that he was an excellent writer and that he came from Virginia. The members knew that no independence movement could succeed without Virginia's support.

Jefferson immediately went to work. In two weeks, he had prepared most of the Declaration. (See pages 184–188.) On July 2, 1776, Congress considered Lee's resolution again. Despite some opposition, the measure passed. The colonies now considered themselves independent from Great Britain.

COMPARING *Symbols of Freedom*

REVOLUTIONARY FLAGS

During the Revolution, Patriot militiamen created elaborate flags to represent their colony and military traditions. Often these flags were carried into battle.

This flag was carried to the Battle of Bunker Hill by Massachusetts militiamen in 1775. The Liberty Tree represented freedom in the colonies.

Regiments from South Carolina adorned their flag with a crescent. Another version had the word "Liberty" stitched in the crescent.

This flag was carried to Boston by Rhode Island militiamen in 1775.

This flag, created in 1775, was adorned with the British Union, as well as 13 red and white stripes.

The North Hampton County Militia adorned its flag with 13 white stars, a blue field, and 13 red and white stripes.

This was the flag of Gadsden, South Carolina's Continental Navy. The snake was a warning to those who would tread on liberty.

CRITICAL THINKING Make Inferences Why did some Patriot flags include British symbols? What does that tell you about some colonists' desire for independence?

Activity

Create a Revolutionary Flag

Create a flag that might have been carried in the Revolution. Use symbols to represent your state or hometown.

The Declaration is Adopted Two days later, on July 4, 1776, Congress adopted the document that proclaimed independence—the Declaration of Independence. John Hancock, the president of the Congress, was the first to sign the Declaration. According to tradition, he wrote in large letters and commented, "There, I guess King George will be able to read that." The core idea of the Declaration is based on the philosophy of John Locke. This idea is that people have natural and unalienable rights, or rights that government cannot take away. Jefferson stated this belief in what was to become the Declaration's best-known passage.

CONNECT to the Essential Question

What drove the colonists to declare independence from Great Britain?

All regions and groups	Southern Colonies	New England and Middle Colonies	Backcountry
• feared that British troops might be used against colonists • suffered from tax increases (Stamp Act 1765) • were angered that the right to tax had been taken away from colonial assemblies (Stamp Act 1765) • suffered from duty on imports (Sugar Act 1764; Townshend Acts 1767)	• Planters were angry that the Proclamation of 1763 restricted them from speculating in land beyond the Appalachian Mountains.	• Merchants suffered from interference in colonial trade (Tea Act 1773). • New England merchants suffered from the Sugar Act of 1764, which raised duty on sugar • New Yorkers were angry they had to pay to house troops in New York (Quartering Act 1765)	• angered by Proclamation of 1763, which restricted movement west • Some Scots-Irish had never felt loyalty to Britain.

CRITICAL THINKING **Draw Conclusions** What issues united the colonists against Great Britian?

❝ We hold these truths to be self-evident, that all men are created equal, that they are endowed by their Creator with certain unalienable Rights, that among these are Life, Liberty, and the pursuit of Happiness. ❞

—Thomas Jefferson, The Declaration of Independence

If a government disregards these rights, Jefferson explained, it loses its right to govern. The people then have the right to abolish that government, by force if necessary. They can form a new government that will protect their rights. When Jefferson spoke of "the people," however, he meant only free, white, landowning men. Women, the enslaved, and those without property were left out of the Declaration.

The Declaration also explained the reasons for breaking with Britain. It declared the colonies to be free and independent states. This was a very serious action—treason from the British point of view—and the delegates knew it. John Hancock urged the delegates to stand together in mutual defense. He realized that if the war were lost, they might all be hanged.

The Declaration closed with this pledge: "And for the support of this Declaration, with a firm reliance on the protection of divine Providence, we mutually pledge to each other our Lives, our Fortunes, and our sacred Honor."

Americans had declared independence. Now they had to win their freedom on the battlefield.

▲ **MAIN IDEAS & DETAILS** Explain what ideas can be found in the Declaration of Independence.

 Illinois Learning Standards *Review*

 ONLINE QUIZ
For test practice, go to
Interactive Review @ ClassZone.com

TERMS & NAMES

1. Explain the importance of
- Ethan Allen
- Thomas Jefferson
- Continental Army
- Thomas Paine
- Second Continental Congress
- Declaration of Independence

USING YOUR READING NOTES

2. Sequence Events Complete the diagram that you started at the beginning of this section.

Lexington and Concord → ☐ → ☐ → Battle of Bunker Hill

KEY IDEAS

3. Make Inferences What forced the British to leave Boston?

4. Analyze Primary Sources What does the Declaration of Independence say about government and the rights of the people?

CRITICAL THINKING

5. Draw Conclusions Why did it take the colonists so long to declare independence?

6. Make Inferences Why do you think *Common Sense* was so popular?

7. Sequence Events Why do you think militiamen surrounded the British in Boston?

8. Math Graph Research the population statistics of colonial Boston. Make a graph to show how the population of Boston changed during the Revolution.

The Declaration of Independence

Setting the Stage On July 4, 1776, the Second Continental Congress adopted what became one of America's most cherished documents. Written by Thomas Jefferson, the Declaration of Independence voiced the reasons for separating from Britain and provided the principles of government upon which the United States would be built.

Preamble

When in the Course of human events, it becomes necessary for one people to dissolve the political bands which have connected them with another, and to assume among the powers of the earth, the separate and equal station to which the Laws of Nature and of Nature's God entitle them, a decent respect to the opinions of mankind requires that they should declare the causes which impel them to the separation.

Rights of the People

The ideas in this passage reflect the views of John Locke. Locke was an English philosopher who believed that the natural rights of individuals came from God, but that a government's power comes from the consent of the governed. This belief is the foundation of modern democracy.

1. In what way can American voters bring about changes in their government?

The Right of the People to Control Their Government

We hold these truths to be self-evident, that all men are created equal, that they are **endowed**[1] by their Creator with certain **unalienable**[2] Rights, that among these are Life, Liberty and the pursuit of Happiness; that, to secure these rights, Governments are instituted among Men, deriving their just powers from the consent of the governed; that whenever any Form of Government becomes destructive of these ends, it is the Right of the People to alter or to abolish it, and to institute new Government, laying its foundation on such principles and organizing its powers in such form, as to them shall seem most likely to effect their Safety and Happiness. Prudence, indeed, will dictate that Governments long established should not

----

1. endowed: provided. **2. unalienable:** unable to be taken away.

be changed for light and transient causes; and accordingly all experience hath shewn that mankind are more disposed to suffer, while evils are sufferable, than to right themselves by abolishing the forms to which they are accustomed. But when a long train of abuses and <u>usurpations</u>,[3] pursuing invariably the same Object, evinces a design to reduce them under absolute <u>Despotism</u>,[4] it is their right, it is their duty, to throw off such Government, and to provide new Guards for their future security.

Such has been the patient sufferance of these Colonies; and such is now the necessity which constrains them to alter their former Systems of Government. The history of the present King of Great Britain is a history of repeated injuries and usurpations, all having in direct object the establishment of an absolute Tyranny over these States. To prove this, let facts be submitted to a <u>candid</u>[5] world.

Tyrannical Acts of the British King

He has refused his Assent to Laws, the most wholesome and necessary for the public good.

He has forbidden his Governors to pass Laws of immediate and pressing importance, unless suspended in their operation till his assent should be obtained; and, when so suspended, he has utterly neglected to attend to them.

He has refused to pass other Laws for the accommodation of large districts of people, unless those people would <u>relinquish</u>[6] the right of Representation in the Legislature, a right inestimable to them, and formidable to tyrants only.

He has called together legislative bodies at places unusual, uncomfortable, and distant from the depository of their public Records, for the sole purpose of fatiguing them into compliance with his measures.

He has dissolved Representative Houses repeatedly, for opposing with manly firmness his invasions on the rights of the people.

He has refused for a long time, after such dissolutions, to cause others to be elected; whereby the Legislative powers, incapable of Annihilation, have returned to the people at large for their exercise; the State remaining in the mean time exposed to all the dangers of invasions from without, and <u>convulsions</u>[7] within.

He has endeavoured to prevent the population of these States; for that purpose obstructing the Laws for <u>Naturalization</u>[8] of Foreigners;

----

3. **usurpations:** unjust seizures of power.

4. **Despotism:** rule by a tyrant with absolute power.

5. **candid:** fair, impartial.

6. **relinquish:** give up.

7. **convulsions:** violent disturbances.

8. **Naturalization:** process of becoming a citizen.

refusing to pass others to encourage their migration hither, and raising the conditions of new Appropriations of Lands.

He has obstructed the Administration of Justice, by refusing his Assent to Laws for establishing Judiciary powers.

He has made Judges dependent on his Will alone, for the **tenure**[9] of their offices, and the amount and payment of their salaries.

He has erected a multitude of New Offices, and sent hither swarms of Officers to harass our people and eat out their **substance**.[10]

He has kept among us, in times of peace, Standing Armies, without the Consent of our legislatures.

He has affected to render the Military independent of and superior to the Civil power. He has combined with others to subject us to a jurisdiction foreign to our constitution and unacknowledged by our laws; giving his Assent to their Acts of pretended Legislation:

For **quartering**[11] large bodies of armed troops among us;

For protecting them, by a mock Trial, from punishment for any Murders which they should commit on the Inhabitants of these States;

For cutting off our Trade with all parts of the world;

For imposing Taxes on us without our Consent;

For depriving us, in many cases, of the benefits of Trial by Jury;

For transporting us beyond Seas to be tried for pretended offenses;

For abolishing the free System of English Laws in a neighboring Province, establishing therein an **Arbitrary**[12] government, and enlarging its Boundaries so as to render it at once an example and fit instrument for introducing the same absolute rule into these Colonies;

For taking away our Charters, abolishing our most valuable laws, and altering fundamentally the Forms of our Governments;

For suspending our own Legislatures, and declaring themselves invested with power to legislate for us in all cases whatsoever.

He has **abdicated**[13] Government here, by declaring us out of his Protection and waging War against us.

He has plundered our seas, ravaged our Coasts, burnt our towns, and destroyed the lives of our people.

He is at this time transporting large Armies of **foreign Mercenaries**[14] to compleat the works of death, desolation, and tyranny, already begun

---

Quartering Troops without Consent

The Quartering Act of 1765 required colonists to provide housing and supplies for British troops in America.

4. Why did colonists object to this act?

Taxation without Representation

The colonists believed in the long-standing British tradition that Parliament could tax only those citizens it represented—and the colonists claimed to have no representation in Parliament.

5. How do persons today give consent to taxation?

---

9. **tenure:** term.
10. **eat out their substance:** drain their resources.
11. **quartering:** housing or giving lodging to.
12. **Arbitrary:** not limited by law.
13. **abdicated:** given up.
14. **foreign Mercenaries:** professional soldiers hired to serve in a foreign army.

with circumstances of Cruelty & **perfidy**[15] scarcely paralleled in the most barbarous ages, and totally unworthy the Head of a civilized nation.

He has constrained our fellow Citizens, taken Captive on the high Seas, to bear Arms against their Country, to become the executioners of their friends and Brethren, or to fall themselves by their Hands.

He has excited domestic **insurrections**[16] amongst us, and has endeavoured to bring on the inhabitants of our frontiers the merciless Indian Savages, whose known rule of warfare is an undistinguished destruction of all ages, sexes and conditions.

Efforts of the Colonies to Avoid Separation

In every stage of these Oppressions We have **Petitioned for Redress**[17] in the most humble terms; Our repeated Petitions have been answered only by repeated injury. A Prince, whose character is thus marked by every act which may define a Tyrant, is unfit to be the ruler of a free people.

Nor have We been wanting in attentions to our British brethren. We have warned them from time to time of attempts by their legislature to extend an unwarrantable jurisdiction over us. We have reminded them of the circumstances of our emigration and settlement here. We have appealed to their native justice and **magnanimity,**[18] and we have conjured them by the ties of our common kindred, to disavow these usurpations, which would inevitably interrupt our connections and correspondence. They too have been deaf to the voice of justice and of **consanguinity.**[19] We must, therefore, **acquiesce**[20] in the necessity, which denounces our Separation, and hold them, as we hold the rest of mankind, Enemies in War, in Peace Friends.

The Colonies Are Declared Free and Independent

We, therefore, the Representatives of the United States of America, in General Congress, Assembled, appealing to the Supreme Judge of the world for the **rectitude**[21] of our intentions, do, in the name, and by the Authority of the good People of these Colonies solemnly publish and declare, That these United Colonies are, and of Right ought to be, Free and Independent States; that they are Absolved from all Allegiance to the British Crown, and that all political connection between them and

---

15. **perfidy:** dishonesty, disloyalty.

16. **domestic insurrections:** rebellions at home.

17. **Petitioned for Redress:** asked for the correction of wrongs.

18. **magnanimity:** generosity, forgiveness.

19. **consanguinity:** relationship by a common ancestor; close connection.

20. **acquiesce:** accept without protest.

21. **rectitude:** moral uprightness.

the State of Great Britain is, and ought to be, totally dissolved; and that as Free and Independent States, they have full Power to levy War, conclude Peace, contract Alliances, establish Commerce, and do all other Acts and Things which Independent States may of right do.

And for the support of this Declaration, with a firm reliance on the protection of divine Providence, we mutually pledge to each other our Lives, our Fortunes, and our sacred Honor. [Signed by]

John Hancock *President, from Massachusetts*

[Georgia] Button Gwinnett; Lyman Hall; George Walton

[Rhode Island] Stephen Hopkins; William Ellery

[Connecticut] Roger Sherman; Samuel Huntington; William Williams; Oliver Wolcott

[North Carolina] William Hooper; Joseph Hewes; John Penn

[South Carolina] Edward Rutledge; Thomas Heyward, Jr.; Thomas Lynch, Jr.; Arthur Middleton

[Maryland] Samuel Chase; William Paca; Thomas Stone; Charles Carroll

[Virginia] George Wythe; Richard Henry Lee; Thomas Jefferson; Benjamin Harrison; Thomas Nelson, Jr.; Francis Lightfoot Lee; Carter Braxton

[Pennsylvania] Robert Morris; Benjamin Rush; Benjamin Franklin; John Morton; George Clymer; James Smith; George Taylor; James Wilson; George Ross

[Delaware] Caesar Rodney; George Read; Thomas McKean

[New York] William Floyd; Philip Livingston;Francis Lewis; Lewis Morris

[New Jersey] Richard Stockton; John Witherspoon; Francis Hopkinson; John Hart; Abraham Clark

[New Hampshire] Josiah Bartlett; William Whipple; Matthew Thornton

[Massachusetts] Samuel Adams; John Adams; Robert Treat Paine; Elbridge Gerry

Declaration Signers

The Declaration was signed by 56 representatives from the 13 original states.

8. Which signers do you recognize? Write one line about each of those signers.

DOCUMENT–BASED QUESTIONS

Short Answer

1. What is the purpose of the Declaration of Independence as stated in the Preamble?

2. What are the five main parts of the Declaration?

3. What are three rights that all people have?

Extended Answer

4. Why did the colonies feel that they had to declare their independence?

Chapter Summary

1 Key Idea
Colonists saw British efforts to increase control over the colonies as violations of their rights.

2 Key Idea
Many colonists organized to oppose British policies.

3 Key Idea
The tensions between Britain and the colonies led to the outbreak of the Revolutionary War.

4 Key Idea
As fighting continued, Americans decided to declare their independence from Britain.

For detailed Review and Study Notes go to **Interactive Review** @ ClassZone.com

Name Game

Use the Terms & Names list to complete each sentence online or on your own paper.

1. _____ wrote the Declaration of Independence.
   Thomas Jefferson

2. The _____ was a secret society established to oppose British policy.

3. _____ rode into the countryside to warn of British troop movement.

4. The British used _____ to enter and search the colonists' homes.

5. The African-American sailor who died at the Boston Massacre was _____.

6. During the Revolutionary War, George Washington commanded the _____.

7. The _____ placed a tax on molasses.

8. Parliament passed the _____ in 1767 to tighten control on the colonies.

9. At the _____ in Philadelphia, delegates voted to ban all trade with Britain.

10. The _____ required colonists to house and feed British soldiers.

A. Quartering Act
B. Continental Army
C. First Continental Congress
D. Sons of Liberty
E. Townshend Acts
F. Paul Revere
G. Sugar Act
H. Thomas Jefferson
I. Crispus Attucks
J. Philadelphia
K. Boston Tea Party
L. Writs of Assistance

Activities

FLIPCARD

Use the online flipcards to quiz yourself on the terms and names introduced in this chapter.

He was a political radical and author of *Common Sense*

ANSWER:
Thomas Paine

CROSSWORD PUZZLE

Complete the online crossword puzzle to show what you know about the American Revolution.

ACROSS

1. _____ could fight at a minute's warning.

VOCABULARY

Explain the significance of each of the following

1. King George III
2. Sugar Act
3. Boston Tea Party
4. Townshend Acts
5. Boston Massacre
6. First Continental Congress
7. Minutemen
8. Intolerable Acts
9. Stamp Act
10. Lexington and Concord
11. Thomas Jefferson
12. Declaration of Independence

Explain how the terms and names in each group are related.

13. Sons of Liberty, King George III, Daughters of Liberty
14. First Continental Congress, committees of correspondence, Boston Massacre
15. Sugar Act, Boston Tea Party, Stamp Act
16. Thomas Paine, Patrick Henry, Samuel Adams

KEY IDEAS

1 Tighter British Control (pages 156–159)

17. How did Parliament's new laws reflect a change in British treatment of the colonies?

18. How did the colonists get the Stamp Act repealed?

2 Colonial Resistance Grows (pages 160–166)

19. In what ways did the Townshend Acts attack colonists' rights and freedoms?

20. How did Americans protest the Townshend Acts?

21. Why did protests against the Tea Act take place in the port cities?

3 The Road to Lexington and Concord (pages 168–174)

22. In what ways were the Intolerable Acts harsher than Parliament's previous laws?

23. What did the British troops hope to achieve in Lexington and Concord?

4 Declaring Independence (pages 176–183)

24. How did the Americans force the British to leave Boston?

25. What does the Declaration of Independence say about the relationship between government and the people?

CRITICAL THINKING

26. **Make Inferences** Why were the boycotts of British products so effective?

27. **Summarize** How did protests against British policies encourage women to become politically active?

28. **Make Generalizations** How did the committees of correspondence help unite the colonies?

29. **Make Inferences** Why were the colonists storing weapons in Concord?

30. **Categorize** Fill in the chart below to show how Parliament's new laws threatened the colonists economically and politically.

Economic Threat	Threat to Political Traditions

31. **Causes and Effects** How did ordinary people help change British government policies?

32. **Connect Geography and History** Study this map of Boston during the Battle of Bunker Hill. Why were the British so alarmed when the Americans occupied the hills above Charlestown?

The Battle of Bunker Hill, *June 17, 1775*

✓ TEST PRACTICE

• **Online Test Practice** @ ClassZone.com
• **Test-Taking Strategies & Practice** at the front of this book

MULTIPLE CHOICE

Use the artifact below and your knowledge of U.S. history to answer question 1.

ARTIFACT

1. Examine this teapot that was created to protest the Stamp Act. Why did colonists use this ordinary household item to carry a political message?

   A. to openly demonstrate their support of the cause

   B. to remind themselves which items were taxed

   C. to offend British soldiers and government officials

   D. to declare independence

Use the quotation and your knowledge of U.S. history to answer question 2.

PRIMARY SOURCE

❝ It is inseparably essential to the freedom of a people, and the undoubted rights of Englishmen, that no taxes should be imposed on them, but with their own consent, given personally, or by their representatives. ❞

—from The Declaration of Rights of the Stamp Act Congress

2. According to this declaration, what is essential to freedom?

   A. No taxes should be imposed.

   B. Taxes need the consent of the governed.

   C. America should be independent.

   D. Englishmen should have rights.

YOU BE THE HISTORIAN

33. **Causes and Effects** What were the unexpected consequences of Britain's victory in the French and Indian War?

34. **Problems and Solutions** Was the American Revolution a conflict that could have been avoided? Explain your answer.

35. **Make Inferences** What was so unusual about women becoming politically involved in the 1760s and 1770s?

36. **Make Generalizations** How did British policies plant the seeds of a future American national government?

37. **Draw Conclusions** How did the political protests of the 1760s and 1770s help prepare the American people for the Revolution?

38. **Analyze Point of View** Do you think that any of Parliament's new laws were justified? Explain your answer.

 Answer the

ESSENTIAL QUESTION

What drove the colonists to declare independence from Great Britain?

Written Response Write a four-paragraph response to the Essential Question. Be sure to consider the key ideas of each section as well as the most significant facts that helped determine your answer. Use the Response Rubric below to guide your thinking and writing.

Response Rubric

A strong response will

• discuss why Parliament increased its control and taxation of the colonists

• explain how Parliament's actions threatened the economy and democratic political traditions of the colonies

• describe how the colonists reacted to Parliament's increased control.

The American Revolution

1775–1783

 ESSENTIAL QUESTION

How was it possible that American Patriots gained their independence from the powerful British Empire?

CONNECT ↻ **Geography & History**

How might the geography of the United States have affected the course of the war?

Think about:

1 how **Saratoga** lies in the Hudson River valley, a major gap through the Appalachian Mountains

2 how **Yorktown** stands on the Chesapeake Bay, a wide body of water that allowed ships access to ports and plantations

3 the distance between Britain and America, roughly 3,400 miles

Travel time:
4 weeks to 4 months

Battle of Lexington

1777 The American victory at **Saratoga** convinces foreign powers that America can win.

▼

Effect France enters the war on the American side.

1775

Revolution begins at **Lexington** and **Concord.**

1776 Declaration of Independence

After their victory at the **Battle of Long Island**, the British make New York their base of operations.

1778 The British capture **Savannah**, Georgia—their first major victory in their new Southern campaign.

Lake Superior

Lake Michigan

Lake Huron

Lake Erie

Lake Ontario

1 Saratoga, 1777

NEW HAMPSHIRE

MASSACHUSETTS

Lexington, 1775

Concord 1775

RHODE ISLAND

NEW YORK

Hudson R.

Delaware R.

CONNECTICUT

Long Island, 1776

PENNSYLVANIA

Valley Forge •

NEW JERSEY

MARYLAND

DELAWARE

Chesapeake Bay

VIRGINIA

2 Yorktown, 1781

Wabash River

Ohio River

Mississippi River

Vincennes, 1779

APPALACHIAN MOUNTAINS

NORTH CAROLINA

King's Mountain, 178

SOUTH CAROLINA

Savannah River

GEORGIA

Savannah, 1778

ATLANTIC OCEAN

65°W

35°N

30°N

75°W

✸	American victory
✸	British victory
▮	New England colonies
▮	Middle colonies
▮	Southern colonies

0   100   200 miles
0   100   200 kilometers

1780 The Americans defeat the
British at **King's Mountain**, South Carolina.

▼

Effect This complicates British plans in
the South.

Revolutionary-era Drum
Drums were used to give
instructions to the troops.

Continental Soldier
Most soldiers in the
Continental Army supplied
their own weapons.

1783

1781 After the American victory
at **Yorktown**, British lose their will to
continue the war.

The Treaty of
Paris ends the
war.

▼

Effect British negotiate for peace.

Reading for Understanding

▶ Key Ideas

BEFORE, YOU LEARNED

After the Revolutionary War broke out at Lexington and Concord, the United States declared independence from British rule.

NOW YOU WILL LEARN

Although the Continental Army had difficulty fighting in a divided America, the Patriots triumphed at Saratoga.

▶ Vocabulary

TERMS & NAMES

George Washington commander of the Continental Army

John Burgoyne (buhr•GOIN) British army general in the Revolutionary War

Joseph Brant Mohawk chief allied with the British

Benedict Arnold U.S. army general in the Revolutionary War who later turned traitor

Horatio Gates U.S. army general in the Revolutionary War

Battles of Saratoga (sair•uh•TOH•guh) a series of conflicts in 1777 near Albany, New York

BACKGROUND VOCABULARY

neutral (NEW•truhl) not favoring any one side

pacifist (PAS•uh•fist) someone who is opposed to all war

mercenary (MUR•suh•NAIR•ee) a professional soldier hired to fight for a foreign country

strategy (STRA•tuh•jee) an overall plan of action

rendezvous (RAHN•day•voo) a meeting

REVIEW

guerrillas (guh•RIL•uhz) small bands of fighters who weaken the enemy with surprise raids and hit-and-run attacks

▶ Reading Strategy

Re-create the diagram shown at right. As you read and respond to the **KEY QUESTIONS**, use the diagram to note important events and their effects. Add boxes or start a new diagram as needed.

 See Skillbuilder Handbook, page R7.

CAUSES AND EFFECTS

CAUSE

The Revolution divides Americans.

EFFECT

EFFECT

Some Native Americans join the British. Others support the Patriots.

GRAPHIC ORGANIZERS
Go to **Interactive Review** @ ClassZone.com

The Early Years of the War

16.A.3c Identify the differences between historical fact and interpretation.
16.B.3b Explain how and why the colonies fought for their independence and how the colonists' ideas are reflected in the Declaration of Independence and the United States Constitution.

One American's Story

When John Singleton Copley painted this portrait of his own Loyalist family, the Copleys had only recently escaped the violence of the Revolution. Copley's father-in-law (shown seated) lost his investments during the Boston Tea Party. Copley's wife (in the blue dress) lost her infant son during the siege of Boston. In the background stands Copley himself—an American who became one of the greatest painters in the British Empire.

Copley was born and raised in Boston. Before the war, he left Boston to study overseas. When he received news of the fighting in America, he wrote to his half-brother.

The Copley Family, by
John Singleton Copley

PRIMARY SOURCE

❝ Could anything be more fortunate than the time of my leaving Boston? Poor America. I hope for the best, but I fear the worst. Yet certain I am she will finally emerge from her present calamity and become a mighty empire. ❞

—John Singleton Copley, letter to Henry Pelham

Copley worried about his family as he traveled through Europe. Eventually, he found them safe in London. They had arrived with the first wave of Loyalist refugees. Copley painted this portrait after their reunion.

Americans Divided

🔻 **KEY QUESTION** In what ways was the Revolution like a civil war?

The issue of separating from Britain divided American society. Historians estimate that 20 to 30 percent of Americans were Loyalists, 40 to 45 percent were Patriots, and the rest were **neutral**, or not favoring any one side.

Americans Choose Sides The conflict divided Americans along social, religious, and ethnic lines. New England and Virginia had many Patriots. Loyalists were numerous in cities, New York State, and the South. Judges, councilors, and governors tended to be Loyalists. Many Loyalists were clergy or members of the Church of England. Some Quakers were active Loyalists, although many were **pacifists**—people opposed to all war. The Patriots drew support from Congregationalists, Presbyterians, and Baptists.

Most Southern states did not allow African Americans to enlist. They feared that armed African Americans might lead slave revolts. In contrast, the British offered enslaved persons their freedom if they joined British forces. Many slaves ran away to fight for the British. In the North, however, about 5,000 African Americans served in the Continental Army.

The American Revolution was the largest Indian war in American history. All Native American nations east of the Mississippi were caught up in the fighting. Some Native Americans, like the Mohawks, joined the British because they feared Americans would take Native American land. Others, who lived within areas settled by the colonists, sided with the Americans.

▲ **CAUSES AND EFFECTS** Explain how the Revolution caused divisions among the population.

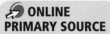

Connecting History

Dissent and Rebellion
The oldest English settlements were in New England and Virginia. They both had a tradition of dissent and rebellion. *See Chapter 3, p. 72, Chapter 4, p. 104.*

ONLINE PRIMARY SOURCE

Hear the debate at the **Research & Writing Center**
@ ClassZone.com

COMPARING Perspectives

Patriots and Loyalists (or "Tories") viewed the political situation from radically different perspectives. These were some of the arguments heard as debate gave way to bloodshed.

◀) Patriots Speak

66 [Shall] a body of men in Great Britain, who . . . know nothing of us . . . invest themselves with a power to command our lives and properties . . . ?
—*a lady from Philadelphia*

If our Trade be taxed, why not our Lands, or Produce . . . in short, everything we possess? They tax us without having legal representation. 99
—*Samuel Adams*

◀) Loyalists Speak

66 They call me a brainless Tory; but tell me, which is better—to be ruled by one tyrant three thousand miles away, or by three thousand tyrants not one mile away?
—*Mather Byles*

Whenever a . . . people . . . prevent the execution of laws, or destroy the property of individuals . . . there is an end of all order and government. . . 99
—*Massachusetts Gazette, and Boston News-Letter*

CRITICAL THINKING

1. **Analyze Primary Sources** What were the Loyalists' greatest fears? What angered the Patriots most?

2. **Analyze Point of View** What would you have said to oppose each argument listed above?

Preparing for War

▼ **KEY QUESTION** Why did both America and Britain have trouble raising an army?

In June 1775, Congress named **George Washington** commander of the Continental Army. This army faced many problems.

Problems of the Army At first, this new national army was formed from state militias, made up of untrained and undisciplined volunteers. The militia were part-time, emergency fighters who were not prepared for the hardship of a long war.

Washington's main goal was to keep the Revolution alive. To do so, he needed to keep an army in the field, win some battles—no matter how small—and avoid a crushing defeat. He knew he could not win a major battle until he had a large, well-trained army.

At the start of the war, Congress asked men to enlist only for one year. When the soldiers' time was up, they went home. As a result, Washington's army never numbered more than 17,000 men. In the early years of the war, Washington always worried about losing men whose enlistments had expired.

Congress's inability to supply the army also frustrated Washington. The soldiers lacked blankets, shoes, food, and even guns and ammunition.

Fortunately, many women helped the army. George Washington's wife Martha and other wives followed their husbands to camp. The women cooked, did laundry, and nursed sick or wounded soldiers. Some women even disguised themselves to help fight. Twenty-two-year-old Deborah Sampson dressed as a man, enlisted, and fought in several battles. But many women who never ventured near a battlefield also helped the nation by managing farms and businesses while their husbands were away fighting. In the days when women had few civil rights and freedoms, the war brought them greater responsibilities.

History Makers

George Washington   1732–1799

When Washington saw the army he was asked to lead, he was shocked by its disunity. Soldiers shared a common enemy but had no sense of national unity. Officers from different regions refused to co-operate with each other. Troops would only obey officers from their own province. Angrily, Washington wrote, "Could I have foreseen what I have experienced, and am likely to experience, no consideration upon earth would have induced me to accept this command." But Washington was determined to hold the army together. His efforts helped create a model of unity for the nation.

COMPARING *Leaders*

As you read through the chapter, look for other examples of Washington's leadership. Compare his leadership qualities to those of British generals described in this chapter.

🔁 **ONLINE BIOGRAPHY** For more on the life of George Washington, go to the **Research & Writing Center** @ ClassZone.com

Britain Prepares Many British viewed the Americans as disorganized, inexperienced rebels who would be easily defeated. In contrast to Washington's troops, the British army was experienced and professional. But the British military faced problems of its own. For personal and political reasons, many British officers refused to fight the Americans. Many British people were not enthusiastic about the war, so the king had trouble recruiting soldiers in

Britain. In addition, British soldiers signed up for life—which discouraged enlistment. Because of these problems, Britain had to hire mercenaries. A **mercenary** is a professional soldier hired to fight for a foreign country. The British mercenaries were called "Hessians" (HEH•shunz) because many came from the German region of Hesse.

🔺 **CAUSES AND EFFECTS** Describe why each side had trouble raising an army.

War in the Middle States

🔻 **KEY QUESTION** How did Washington reverse a series of American defeats?

As Chapter 6 explains, Washington had forced the British to retreat from Boston in March 1776. He then hurried his army to New York City, where he expected the British to go next. One British goal was to occupy coastal cities so that their navy could land troops and supplies. From these bases on the coast, they could then launch their military campaigns.

Patriot Retreat Washington's hunch was correct. In July 1776, Britain's General William Howe arrived in New York with a large army. Then in August, more soldiers arrived, including about 9,000 Hessian mercenaries. At the Battle of Long Island the Americans were defeated.

For several months, the British and American armies fought to control New York. Finally, the British forced Washington to retreat through New Jersey. (See map below.) By December, when the American army crossed the Delaware River into Pennsylvania, it was in terrible condition.

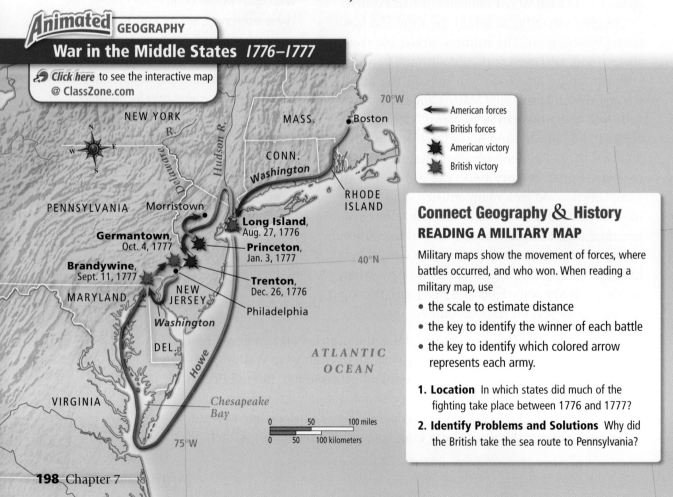

Animated GEOGRAPHY

War in the Middle States *1776–1777*

🐭 **Click here** to see the interactive map @ ClassZone.com

American forces
British forces
American victory
British victory

Connect Geography & History
READING A MILITARY MAP

Military maps show the movement of forces, where battles occurred, and who won. When reading a military map, use

- the scale to estimate distance
- the key to identify the winner of each battle
- the key to identify which colored arrow represents each army.

1. **Location** In which states did much of the fighting take place between 1776 and 1777?

2. **Identify Problems and Solutions** Why did the British take the sea route to Pennsylvania?

Political writer Thomas Paine witnessed the low spirits of the soldiers during the retreat. To urge Americans to keep fighting, Paine published the first in a series of pamphlets he called *The American Crisis*.

PRIMARY SOURCE

❝ These are the times that try men's souls. The summer soldier and the sunshine patriot will, in this crisis, shrink from the service of their country; but he that stands it now, deserves the love and thanks of man and woman. ❞

—Thomas Paine, *The American Crisis*

Washington needed something to encourage his weary men. He also knew that he must attack the British quickly because most of his soldiers would leave once their enlistments ended on December 31.

Victory at Trenton Late on December 25, 1776, Washington's troops rowed across the icy Delaware River to New Jersey. From there, they marched in bitter, early-morning cold to Trenton (see map on page 198) to surprise the Hessians, some of whom were sleeping after their Christmas celebration. The Americans captured or killed more than 900 Hessians and gained needed supplies. Washington's army won another victory at Princeton eight days later before setting up winter camp at Morristown, New Jersey. These victories proved that the American general was better than many had thought. The American army began to attract new recruits.

A Hessian mercenary

▲ **SUMMARIZE** Explain how Washington reversed a series of defeats.

Britain's Northern Strategy

▼ **KEY QUESTION** What was Britain's northern strategy?

Meanwhile, the British were pursuing a **strategy**—an overall plan of action—to seize the Hudson River valley. They believed that New England was the source of the rebellion. If they controlled the Hudson River valley, they could cut off New England from the other states. The strategy called for three armies to meet at Albany, New York.

- General **John Burgoyne** would lead a force south from Canada.
- Lt Colonel Barry St. Leger would come down the Mohawk valley.
- General Howe would follow the Hudson north from New York City.

Burgoyne left Canada in June 1777 with an army of British, Hessians, and Iroquois. In July, they captured Fort Ticonderoga and continued south. (See map on page 200.)

Burgoyne's Slow March Called "Gentleman Johnny" by his soldiers, Burgoyne threw elaborate parties to celebrate victories. But his mood changed as he marched deeper into hostile territory. Not only was the countryside filled with rebel sympathizers, but the forests were swarming with militia from New York and New England. The militia cut down trees to slow Burgoyne's progress. They burned crops and drove off cattle, leaving no food

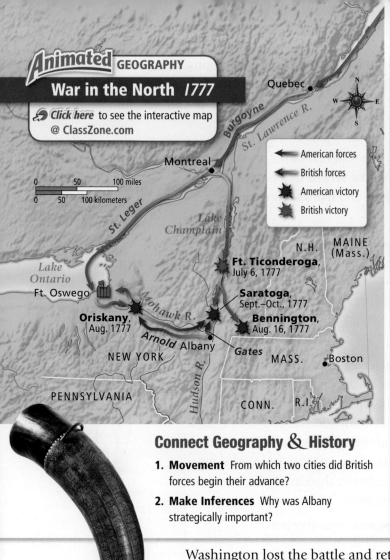

Animated GEOGRAPHY

War in the North 1777

🖱 **Click here** to see the interactive map
@ ClassZone.com

Quebec

Burgoyne

St. Lawrence R.

Montreal

←	American forces
←	British forces
✸	American victory
✸	British victory

0   50   100 miles
0   50   100 kilometers

St. Leger

Lake Champlain

Lake Ontario

Ft. Oswego

N.H.

MAINE (Mass.)

Ft. Ticonderoga, July 6, 1777

Saratoga, Sept.–Oct., 1777

Mohawk R.

Oriskany, Aug. 1777

Bennington, Aug. 16, 1777

Arnold   Albany

Gates

NEW YORK

Hudson R.

MASS.

Boston

PENNSYLVANIA

CONN.   R.I.

Connect Geography & History

1. **Movement** From which two cities did British forces begin their advance?

2. **Make Inferences** Why was Albany strategically important?

Powder Horn
Revolutionary-era soldiers used horns like this to carry gunpowder. **Why was horn a good material in which to store gunpowder?**

for the British. Burgoyne realized that the countryside was rising up against him. It was a lesson that other British generals would soon learn: they were not simply fighting an enemy army, they were fighting an entire people.

Britain's Strategy Unravels Burgoyne still looked forward to the **rendezvous**, or meeting, with St. Leger and Howe in Albany. But on August 4, Burgoyne received a message that Howe would not be coming north; instead, he had decided to try to capture Philadelphia—where the Continental Congress met. "Success be ever with you," wrote Howe. Yet Burgoyne needed Howe's soldiers, not his good wishes.

When Washington heard that Howe was heading south, he rushed to protect Philadelphia. However, in September 1777, Howe defeated Washington at Brandywine. (See map on page 198.) Howe then occupied Philadelphia. In October, Washington attacked Howe at Germantown. Again, Washington lost the battle and retreated to winter camp.

As Burgoyne received Howe's message, St. Leger faced his own obstacle in reaching Albany. In the summer of 1777, he was trying to defeat a small American force at Fort Stanwix, near Oriskany in the Mohawk River valley of New York. St. Leger's forces included Iroquois led by Mohawk chief **Joseph Brant**, also called Thayendanegea (thi•ehn•DAH•nah•gee•ah). Brant had been promised that the British would protect Iroquois land.

During August 1777, American general **Benedict Arnold** led an army up the Mohawk River. He wanted to chase the British away from Fort Stanwix. Arnold sent a captured Loyalist and some Iroquois to spread the rumor that he had a large army. The trick worked, and the British retreated to Fort Oswego. Now no one was left to rendezvous with Burgoyne.

🔺 **MAIN IDEAS & DETAILS** Explain Britain's northern strategy—and why it failed.

Saratoga: A Turning Point

🔻 **KEY QUESTION** Why has Saratoga been called a "turning point"?

Burgoyne's army was running out of supplies. A raiding party was sent into Vermont where it was defeated by New England militia at the Battle of Bennington on August 16, 1777.

British Advance on Albany Despite these setbacks, Burgoyne's army continued south. But an American force led by General **Horatio Gates** blocked their way on a ridge called Bemis Heights, near Saratoga, New York. There the Polish engineer Tadeusz Kosciuszko (TAH•deh•oosh KAWSH•choosh•kaw) had helped the Americans create fortifications, or built-up earthen walls.

Starting on September 19, Burgoyne attacked the fortifications. While Gates commanded the Americans on the ridge, Benedict Arnold led an attack on nearby Freeman's Farm. His men repeatedly charged the British, with Arnold galloping through the battlefield "like a madman." Despite heavy casualties, the British held their position, but on October 7, Burgoyne was forced to retreat.

Burgoyne Surrenders Burgoyne's army moved slowly through heavy rain to a former army camp at Saratoga. By the time they arrived, the men were exhausted. The Continental Army then surrounded Burgoyne's army and fired on it day and night until Burgoyne surrendered. The series of conflicts that led to this surrender is known as the **Battles of Saratoga**.

The victory at Saratoga was a turning point. It prevented the British from dividing the States and isolating New England. It also showed Europeans that the Americans might win their war for independence. Because of this, some European nations hostile to Great Britain decided to help.

 CAUSES AND EFFECTS Explain why Saratoga has been called "a turning point."

Connect *to the* **World**

In London, after hearing the news of Burgoyne's surrender, William Pitt (Lord Chatham) warns Parliament: "You cannot conquer America."

Illinois Learning Standards *Review*

ONLINE QUIZ
For test practice, go to
Interactive Review @ ClassZone.com

TERMS & NAMES

1. Explain the importance of
- George Washington
- John Burgoyne
- Joseph Brant
- Benedict Arnold
- Horatio Gates
- Battles of Saratoga

USING YOUR READING NOTES

2. Analyze Causes and Effects Complete the diagram you started at the beginning of this section. Then create a diagram for each of the other main events in this section.

CAUSE

The Revolution divides Americans.

EFFECT

EFFECT

Some Native Americans join the British. Others support the Patriots.

KEY IDEAS

3. Why did the British want to control the Hudson River valley?

4. Why were the Battles of Saratoga important?

CRITICAL THINKING

5. Analyze Graphs The graph shows how colonists were divided in 1776. Why is it surprising that the Patriots won?

- Patriots
- Loyalists
- Neutral

20% 40%
40%

Source: *Blackwell Encyclopedia of the American Revolution*

6. **Connect** *to* **Today** Use of mercenaries was banned by a United Nations agreement in 1989. Why do you think this was?

7. **Writing** **Letter** Write a one-page letter from Burgoyne to General Howe. Respond to Howe's letter in which he says he will head to Pennsylvania. Describe how this news affects your strategy.

Click here to enter a Revolutionary War battlefield @ ClassZone.com

Formal Battle

The majority of Revolutionary War battles followed a standard sequence. A battle would begin after the armies formed rows, or lines, facing each other. Americans used lines of both "regulars" (members of the Continental Army) and militia.

Click here **First,** field artillery (cannon) blast the enemy's lines.

Click here **Next,** front line soldiers advance to 50–100 yards of the enemy and fire muskets.

Click here **Finally,** soldiers attack with bayonets (knives attached to the end of a gun), while cavalry (soldiers on horseback) charge.

Formal Battle and Guerrilla War

The militia's expert marksmanship played an important role in formal battles. However, the militia often practiced more informal guerrilla fighting. As part-time soldiers, they operated locally to disrupt supplies and communication and ambush enemy units. The militia ensured that the British could not depend on the countryside for supplies or support.

Activity

Take to the Battlefield!

1 Divide into two armies, one on each side of the room.

2 Each group then selects a "general," who divides them into these groups:
   • artillery   • infantry (front & second lines)   • cavalry

3 The two "generals" command their "troops" to move forward as they would in a formal battle.

Reading for Understanding

▶ Key Ideas

BEFORE, YOU LEARNED

Despite the Continental Army's difficulties, the Patriots triumphed at Saratoga.

NOW YOU WILL LEARN

The expansion of the war weakened the British by forcing them to spread their military resources around the world.

▶ Vocabulary

TERMS & NAMES

Marquis de Lafayette (mahr•KEE•deh laf•eye•EHT) French aristocrat who volunteered to serve in Washington's army

Valley Forge site in southeast Pennsylvania where Washington and his army camped in the winter of 1777–1778

George Rogers Clark frontiersman who helped defend the Western frontier

John Paul Jones sea commander who attacked British ships near the British coast

Wilderness Road a trail into Kentucky

BACKGROUND VOCABULARY

ally (AL•eye) a country that agrees to help another country achieve a common goal

desert (duh•ZERT) to leave military duty without permission

privateer (pry•vuh•TEER) a privately owned ship that has been granted permission by a wartime government to attack an enemy's merchant ships

Visual Vocabulary
privateer

photograph courtesy of Peabody Essex Museum

▶ Reading Strategy

Recreate the diagram shown at right. As you read and respond to the **KEY QUESTIONS**, use the center box to record the main idea; use the outer ovals to note important details. Add ovals or start a new diagram as needed.

 See Skillbuilder Handbook, page R2.

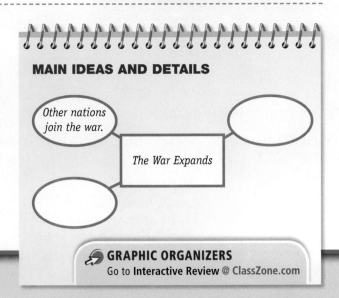

MAIN IDEAS AND DETAILS

Other nations join the war.

The War Expands

GRAPHIC ORGANIZERS
Go to **Interactive Review** @ ClassZone.com

The War Expands

16.A.3c Identify the differences between historical fact and interpretation.
16.B.3b Explain how and why the colonies fought for their independence and how the colonists' ideas are reflected in the Declaration of Independence and the United States Constitution.

One American's Story

In 1778, General Washington hoped to take Newport, Rhode Island, from the British. The French had just entered the war, and their fleet had arrived to help the Americans. But a storm damaged the ships, and the Americans retreated, pursued by the British. A regiment of African Americans saved the day by holding the enemy at bay. An eyewitness described the bravery of the all-black First Rhode Island Regiment.

The First Rhode Island Regiment, by David R. Wagner

© David Wagner
http://davidrwagner.com

PRIMARY SOURCE

❝There was a black regiment in the same situation. Yes, a regiment of negroes, fighting for our liberty and independence,—not a white man among them but the officers. . . . Had they been unfaithful, or given way before the enemy, all would have been lost. Three times in succession were they attacked . . . and three times did they successfully repel the assault, and thus preserve our army from capture. ❞

—Dr. Harris, a veteran of the Battle of Rhode Island

In 1778 the war was expanding on many fronts. Not only were some states allowing African Americans to enlist, but foreign soldiers began arriving to help the American cause.

Help from Abroad

▼ **KEY QUESTION** Why did France and Spain enter the war?

The French were still bitter over their defeat by Britain in the French and Indian War, in which France lost its North American colonies. The French hoped to weaken the British by helping Britain's American colonies break free. In 1776, France began to give secret aid to the Americans. However, the French didn't become an overt American **ally** until the Americans had proved they could win a conventional battle against British forces. An ally is a country that helps another country achieve a common goal.

France and Spain Enter the War After hearing of the American victory at Saratoga, King Louis XVI of France publicly recognized U.S. independence. In 1778, France signed two treaties of alliance with the United States. By doing so, France went to war with Britain. As part of its new alliance, France promised to send badly needed funds, supplies, and troops to America.

In 1779, France persuaded its ally Spain to help the Americans, too. Spain was also Britain's rival. The Spanish governor of Louisiana, General Bernardo de Gálvez, acted quickly. He captured the British strongholds of Natchez and Baton Rouge in the lower Mississippi Valley. From there, his small army went on to take Mobile and, in 1781, Pensacola, in West Florida. These victories prevented the British from attacking the United States from the southwest. However, like France, Spain wanted more than just to help the United States. Gálvez's victories helped extend Spain's empire.

By entering the war against Britain, France and Spain forced the British to fight a number of enemies on land and sea. For instance, the British expected to have to fight the French in the West Indies, so they sent troops there. And thousands of British troops were busy fighting Gálvez in the west. The British now had to spread their military resources over many fronts.

ANALYZE *Political Cartoons*

This cartoon was published in London in 1779, a year after France had formed an alliance with the United States. In political cartoons, sometimes a nation is represented by a figure wearing clothes associated with that nation. For example, in 18th-century cartoons, a Native American symbolized America. Here, figures representing different nations surround a sleeping figure representing Great Britain.

France is on the attack.

Scotland defends Britain.

Britain sleeps through the war.

America steals the cap of liberty.

Holland (whose merchants were trading with the Americans) picks Britain's pocket.

THE PRESENT STATE OF GREAT BRITAIN.

Skillbuilder Handbook, page R18.

CRITICAL THINKING

1. **Analyze Point of View** Why would the cartoonist have shown Britain as sleeping?

2. **Make Inferences** Why is Holland shown picking Britain's pocket?

3. **Synthesize** What is the basic meaning of the cartoon?

Foreign Officers Arrive European military officers from France, Poland, and the German states came to Washington's aid. One of these was the **Marquis de Lafayette** (laf•eye•EHT), a 19-year-old French aristocrat who volunteered to serve in Washington's army. He wanted a military career, and he believed in the American cause. Soon after Lafayette arrived in June 1777, he was given the command of an army division and quickly gained Washington's confidence. Lafayette won his men's respect and love by sharing their hardships. Called "the soldier's friend," he used his own money to buy warm clothing for his ragged troops. Washington regarded him as a son.

Lafayette fought in many battles and also persuaded the French king to send a 6,000-man army to America. He became a hero in both France and the United States. Later he took part in France's own revolution.

Along with Lafayette came the Baron de Kalb, a German officer who had served in the French army. He became one of Washington's generals with a reputation for bravery.

🔺 **MAIN IDEAS & DETAILS** Tell why France and Spain entered the war.

Winter at Valley Forge

🔻 **KEY QUESTION** How did Valley Forge transform the American army?

Help from France and Spain came when the Americans desperately needed it. As you have read, in late 1777 Britain's General Howe had forced Washington to retreat from Philadelphia. In the winter of 1777–1778, Washington and his army camped at **Valley Forge** in southeast Pennsylvania.

Marquis de Lafayette

Hardship at Valley Forge On the march to Valley Forge, Washington's army lacked supplies. Many soldiers had only blankets to cover themselves. They also lacked shoes. The barefoot men left tracks of blood on the frozen ground as they marched.

The soldiers' condition did not improve at camp. Over the winter, the soldiers at Valley Forge grew weak from not having enough food or warm clothing. Roughly a quarter of them died from malnutrition, exposure, or diseases such as smallpox and typhoid fever. Because of this suffering, the name Valley Forge came to stand for the great hardships that Americans endured in the Revolutionary War.

Washington appealed to Congress for supplies, but it was slow in responding. Luckily, private citizens sometimes helped the soldiers. On New Year's Day 1778, a group of Philadelphia women drove ten teams of oxen into camp. The oxen were pulling wagons full of supplies and 2,000 shirts. The women had the oxen killed to provide food for the troops.

Patriotism Unites the Army Despite the hardships, American soldiers showed amazing endurance. Under such circumstances, soldiers often **desert**, or leave military duty without permission. Soldiers did desert, but Lieutenant

A Deadly Winter

Due to poor planning, thievery, and muddy roads, supplies were lacking during the army's winter camp at Valley Forge. An estimated 2,500 to 3,000 men died from exposure, disease, or malnutrition. According to the Marquis de Lafayette,

> " The unfortunate soldiers were in want of everything; they had neither coats nor hats, nor shirts, nor shoes. Their feet and their legs froze until they were black, and it was often necessary to amputate them. "

◀ The **amputation saw** was an important piece of the surgeon's kit.

Data File

WHO	approx. 12,000 regulars, officers, and advisers
WHAT	14′ x 16′ log huts housed 12 privates each; officers had more space, depending on rank
WHERE	25 miles NW of Philadelphia
WHEN	Dec. 19, 1777, to June 19, 1778
WHY	near major crossroads, with plenty of wood and water

HARDSHIPS AT VALLEY FORGE

- In February, almost 5,000 soldiers were too sick to fight; another 3,700 lacked either shoes or clothes.

- Shipments intended for troops were often stolen by government employees.

- Many local farmers were Loyalist and refused to sell food to the army. Others would not sell food because American currency was worthless.

- Common ailments included typhus and dysentery.

- Desertions exceeded 2,000. By February, 8–10 men were deserting each day.

- When frostbitten flesh dies, it turns black. The condition, called gangrene, can spread through the body and can be fatal. Amputations were performed without anesthetics or antiseptics, so amputees often died from infections anyway.

Colonel John Brooks wrote that the army stayed together because of the "Love of our Country." Once again, Washington's determination and patriotic vision inspired the troops to keep fighting.

The Army Grows Stronger Thanks to a German officer, the Baron von Steuben, the inexperienced American army was transformed into a skilled fighting force. Von Steuben began by forming a model company of 100 men. He taught them how to handle weapons properly. He also showed them how to fight the kind of formal battles favored by the British. (See Battle Tactics on page 202.) Within a month, the troops were executing drills with speed and precision. Because of this, the American army emerged from Valley Forge as a more efficient and stronger fighting machine.

▲ **SUMMARIZE** Describe how Valley Forge transformed the American army.

Frontier Fighting

▼ **KEY QUESTION** Why did the war spread to the frontier?

In the late 18th century, the region between the Appalachian Mountains and the Mississippi River was known as the frontier; colonists had only just begun to settle there. In 1763, the British had tried to restrict settlement in this area and had built forts in the region. But some believed that the frontier should be open to settlement. In 1775 Daniel Boone helped build the **Wilderness Road**, a trail into Kentucky. Because Kentucky was claimed by Virginia in 1777, 24-year-old Kentuckian **George Rogers Clark** persuaded Virginia's governor, Patrick Henry, to allow him to raise an army to capture British outposts on the Western frontier. Clark wanted to expand the war into the frontier by attacking the British and their Native American allies in what is now Indiana and Illinois.

Clark's Army In May 1778, Clark led a group of frontiersmen to Kaskaskia, a British fort guarding the Mississippi River. They captured Kaskaskia without a fight.

Then they moved east to take Fort Sackville at Vincennes, in present-day Indiana. Earlier, a small force sent by Clark had taken Vincennes, but British forces under Henry Hamilton had recaptured it. Settlers called Hamilton the "Hair Buyer" because he supposedly paid rewards for American scalps.

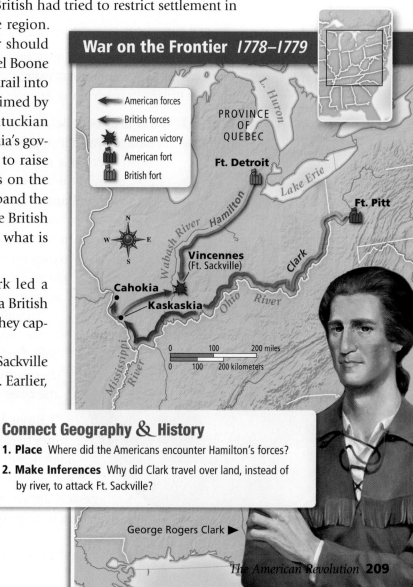

War on the Frontier *1778–1779*

← American forces
← British forces
✸ American victory
🏰 American fort
🏰 British fort

PROVINCE OF QUEBEC

L. Huron
Lake Erie

Ft. Detroit
Ft. Pitt

Wabash River
Hamilton
Clark

Vincennes
(Ft. Sackville)

Cahokia
Kaskaskia

Ohio River
Mississippi River

0   100   200 miles
0   100   200 kilometers

Connect Geography & History

1. **Place** Where did the Americans encounter Hamilton's forces?

2. **Make Inferences** Why did Clark travel over land, instead of by river, to attack Ft. Sackville?

George Rogers Clark ▶

Americans Seize the Frontier Determined to retake Fort Sackville, Clark and his men set out for Vincennes from Kaskaskia in February 1779. Hamilton wasn't expecting an attack because the rivers were flooding the woods. But Clark's men slogged through miles of icy swamps and waded through chest-deep water. They caught the British at Vincennes by surprise.

When Hamilton and his troops tried to remain in the fort, Clark pretended to have a larger force than he really had. Clark also executed some Native American allies of the British in plain view of the fort. He threatened to do the same to the British unless they surrendered. Frightened, the British gave up.

Clark's victory gave the Americans a hold on the vast region between the Great Lakes and the Ohio River (even though Fort Detroit on Lake Erie remained in the hands of the British). This area was more than half the total size of the original 13 states. The expansion of the war into the frontier also had another consequence: it forced the British again to spread their troops over a larger area and further weakened the British war effort.

▲ **CAUSES AND EFFECTS** Explain why the war spread to the frontier.

War on the Waves

▼ **KEY QUESTION** How did Americans expand the naval war?

The war expanded not only west into the frontier but also eastward to the high seas. By 1777, Britain had over 200 warships off the American coast. This allowed Britain to control the Atlantic trade routes to European markets.

James Forten, who later became famous for his efforts to end slavery, joined a privateer at the age of 14.

British Trade Disrupted Because the American navy was small and weak, Congress encouraged American **privateers** to attack British merchant ships. A privateer is a privately owned ship that has been granted permission by a wartime government to attack an enemy's merchant ships. After capturing a ship, the crew of a privateer sold its cargo and shared the money. America commissioned more than 1,000 privateers to prey on the British. They captured hundreds of ships, causing British merchants to call on their government to end the war.

Though outnumbered, the Continental Navy scored several victories. A daring officer named **John Paul Jones** inspired Americans by sailing across the Atlantic to attack British ships along the coast of Britain itself.

"I Have Not Yet Begun to Fight" In 1779, Jones became the commander of a ship named *Bonhomme Richard*. With four other ships, he patrolled the English coast. In September, Jones's vessels approached a convoy in which two British warships were guarding a number of supply ships.

Jones closed in on the *Serapis*, the larger of the two warships. At one point, the *Bonhomme Richard* rammed the better-armed British vessel. As the two ships locked together, the confident British captain demanded that Jones surrender. In words that have become a famous U.S. Navy slogan, Jones is said to have replied, "I have not yet begun to fight!"

The two warships were virtually locked together; the muzzles of their guns almost touched. They blasted away, each seriously damaging the other. On the shore, crowds of Britons gathered under a full moon to watch the fighting. After a fierce three-and-a-half-hour battle, the main mast of the *Serapis* cracked and fell. The ship's captain then surrendered. The *Bonhomme Richard* was so full of holes that it eventually sank, so Jones and his crew had to sail away in the *Serapis*!

Jones's success angered the British and inspired the Americans. Even so, the Americans knew that the war had to be won on land. The next section discusses the major land battles in the closing years of the war.

 SUMMARIZE Explain how Americans expanded the naval war.

John Paul Jones, by N. C. Wyeth

 Illinois Learning Standards *Review*

ONLINE QUIZ
For test practice, go to
Interactive Review @ ClassZone.com

TERMS & NAMES

1. Explain the importance of
- Marquis de Lafayette
- John Paul Jones
- Valley Forge
- Wilderness Road
- George Rogers Clark

USING YOUR READING NOTES

2. Main Ideas & Details List the ways in which the war expanded from 1776–1779. For each, identify one key event and explain its importance.

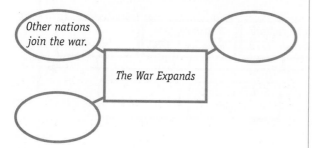

Other nations join the war.

The War Expands

KEY IDEAS

3. List reasons why France decided to help America. Were Spain's reasons the same or different? Explain.

4. How did foreign officers help General Washington?

CRITICAL THINKING

5. Connect Economics & History How did the alliance with France alter America's financial situation?

6. Analyze Point of View Why do you think so many Native Americans on the frontier supported the British?

7. **Connect** *to* **Today** Why has Valley Forge remained an important symbol of America's heritage?

8. **Math** Research to find out how many soldiers fought in Washington's army during each year of the Revolution. Then calculate the average size of the army throughout the war.

▶ Key Ideas

BEFORE, YOU LEARNED

The expansion of the war forced the British to spread their military resources over a wide area.

NOW YOU WILL LEARN

The Continental Army, their allies, and the American people brought about an American victory.

▶ Vocabulary

TERMS & NAMES

Battle of Charles Town British siege of Charles Town (Charleston), South Carolina, in May 1780, in which the Americans suffered their worst defeat of the war

Lord Cornwallis (korn•WAHL•ihs) British general whose campaigns in the South led to his defeat at Yorktown

Battle of Yorktown final battle of the war, in which French and American forces led by George Washington defeated British General Cornwallis

BACKGROUND VOCABULARY

redoubt (re•DOWT) a small fort

Visual Vocabulary
redoubt at Yorktown

▶ Reading Strategy

Re-create the diagram shown at right. As you read and respond to the **KEY QUESTIONS**, use the diagram to record important events in the order in which they occurred.

 See Skillbuilder Handbook, page R5.

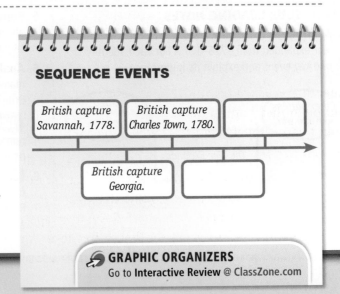

SEQUENCE EVENTS

| British capture Savannah, 1778. | British capture Charles Town, 1780. | |

| | British capture Georgia. | |

GRAPHIC ORGANIZERS
Go to **Interactive Review** @ ClassZone.com

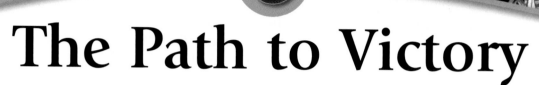

The Path to Victory

16.B.3b Explain how and why the colonies fought for their independence and how the colonists' ideas are reflected in the Declaration of Independence and the United States Constitution.

18.C.3b Explain how diverse groups have contributed to U.S. social systems over time.

One American's Story

James P. Collins, a 16-year-old American, found himself in the midst of a civil war as the Revolution raged in the South. He watched as both sides committed war crimes. At the Battle of King's Mountain, fought on the border of North and South Carolina in October 1780, he saw American Patriots surround and slaughter about 1,000 American Loyalist militia, led by Major General Patrick Ferguson. Collins described the scene.

PRIMARY SOURCE

❝ The dead lay in heaps on all sides, while the groans of the wounded were heard in every direction. I could not help turning away from the scene before me with horror and, though exulting in victory, could not refrain from shedding tears. ❞

—James P. Collins, quoted in *The Spirit of Seventy-Six*

The Battle of King's Mountain

As James Collins's story demonstrates, fighting in the South was vicious.

The War Moves South

▼ **KEY QUESTION** What happened when the British shifted the war to the South?

After three years of fighting in the North, the British were no closer to victory. Although they had captured many important Northern coastal cities, they didn't have enough troops to control the countryside.

The British Change Their Strategy In 1778 the British decided to move the war to the South. They believed that most Southerners were Loyalists, who would support an invading British army.

The British also expected Southern slaves to escape and join them because they had promised to grant the slaves freedom. Although thousands of African Americans did join the British, not all were set free.

The American Revolution **213**

Savannah and Charles Town Fall In December 1778, the British captured the port of Savannah, Georgia. (See Map **Ⓐ** on p. 215.) They then conquered most of Georgia. In 1780, a British army led by General Henry Clinton landed in South Carolina. They trapped American forces in Charles Town (now Charleston), the largest Southern city. **The Battle of Charles Town** ended when the city surrendered. The Americans lost almost their entire Southern army. It was the worst American defeat of the war.

After that loss, Congress assigned General Horatio Gates—the victor at Saratoga—to form a new Southern army. Continental soldiers led by Baron de Kalb formed the army's core. Gates added about 2,000 new and untrained militia. He then headed for Camden, South Carolina, to challenge the army led by the British general **Lord Cornwallis**. (Cornwallis had assumed control of British forces after Clinton returned to New York.)

In August 1780, Gates's army ran into British troops outside Camden. (See Map **Ⓐ** on p. 215.) The Americans were in no condition to fight. They were out of supplies and half-starved. Even worse, Gates put the inexperienced militia along part of the frontline instead of behind the veterans. When the British attacked, the militia panicked and ran. Gates also fled,

CONNECT ↻ *To Today*

MILITARY COMMUNICATION

In the 18th century, military communications were painfully slow. Ships from London might take up to four months to bring orders to British generals.

Mail did not travel much faster within America itself. British General Cornwallis was frustrated by the "delay and difficulty of conveying letters" and "the impossibility of waiting for answers." Not only were journeys long, but bands of Patriots made sure that British lines of communication were constantly disrupted.

Today, wars are fought with the help of technology that provides instant communication. Computers and satellites relay information quickly between sea, air, and ground forces. For example, a video of an attack on enemy forces in Afghanistan can be sent via satellite to the Florida command center and then relayed live to the White House.

A woman gives a message to an officer of the Continental Army.

A modern soldier relays battlefield information.

CRITICAL THINKING

1. **Draw Conclusions** Which side in the Revolutionary War would have suffered most from slow communications? Why?

2. **Evaluate** What are the advantages of today's faster communications?

Map Ⓐ *Dec. 1778–Oct. 1780*

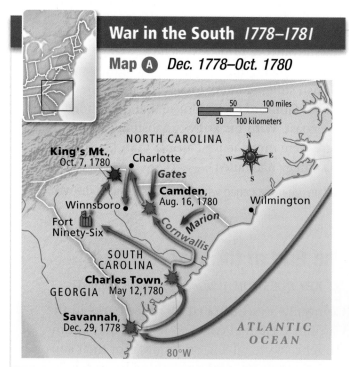

Map Ⓑ *Jan. 1781–April 1781*

Connect Geography & History

1. **Place** Where did the British begin their attacks in the South?
2. **Identify Problems and Solutions** Why do you think Cornwallis headed for the coast after the Battle of Guilford?

but de Kalb remained with his soldiers and received fatal wounds. This second defeat in the South ended Gates's term as head of an army. American spirits fell to a new low.

Guerrilla War Although the Americans had been defeated at Camden, the British were having difficulty controlling the South. The countryside was hostile and filled with more rebel sympathizers than Loyalists. Rebel guerrillas repeatedly attacked British messengers. This made it difficult for British forces moving inland to keep in touch with their bases on the coast. British commanders in the South were discovering what General Burgoyne had realized in the North: the countryside was a dangerous place for the British army.

One of the most famous rebel guerrilla leaders was Francis Marion, called the "Swamp Fox" because he led cunning attacks from his base in the swamps. An American officer described Marion's guerrilla band: "Their number did not exceed 20 men and boys, some white, some black, and all mounted, but most of them miserably equipped." Despite their poor equipment, Marion's men were able to cut the British supply line that led inland from Charles Town.

General Greene Takes Charge After Gates's defeat at Camden, Washington put Nathanael Greene in charge of the Southern army. Greene was one of Washington's best generals. In January 1781, he sent part of his army south to confront Cornwallis. In a formal, linear battle, the Americans won a spectacular victory at Cowpens. (See Map Ⓑ above.) The victory proved that Americans had mastered the formal battle tactics of the British.

Cornwallis's main army now pursued Greene up into North Carolina. The British still had the advantage in a full-scale battle due to their greater firepower. However, the Americans used their knowledge of the landscape to keep one step ahead of the advancing British. Greene's strategy was to let the British wear themselves out. When the Americans did fight, they did their best to make sure the British suffered heavy losses. In fact, Cornwallis lost so many men at the Battle of Guilford Court House that he decided to retreat to Wilmington, on the coast. With his army exhausted, Cornwallis had to face a bitter truth: there were more active Patriots than Loyalists in the South. Britain's southern strategy had failed.

▲ **CAUSES AND EFFECTS** Explain what happened when the British shifted the war to the South.

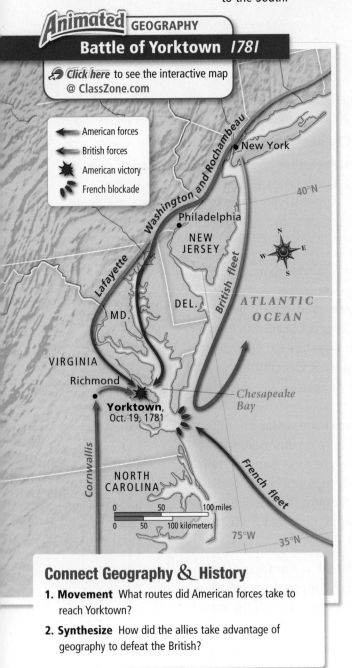

Animated GEOGRAPHY

Battle of Yorktown 1781

Click here to see the interactive map @ ClassZone.com

← American forces
← British forces
✸ American victory
French blockade

New York
40°N
Philadelphia
NEW JERSEY
Washington and Rochambeau
British fleet
Lafayette
DEL.
MD.
ATLANTIC OCEAN
VIRGINIA
Richmond
Yorktown, Oct. 19, 1781
Chesapeake Bay
Cornwallis
NORTH CAROLINA
French fleet
0   50   100 miles
0   50   100 kilometers
75°W
35°N

Connect Geography & History

1. **Movement** What routes did American forces take to reach Yorktown?

2. **Synthesize** How did the allies take advantage of geography to defeat the British?

The End of the War

▼ **KEY QUESTION** How was Cornwallis trapped?

Cornwallis was frustrated by his setbacks in the Carolinas. He had come to believe that Southern rebels were relying on Virginia for their supplies. So, in 1781, without waiting for orders, he marched north into Virginia. In August Cornwallis set up his base at Yorktown, located on a peninsula in Chesapeake Bay. From there, his army could receive supplies by ship from New York. It was a fatal mistake.

Setting the Trap Cornwallis's decision gave Washington a golden opportunity to trap the British on the peninsula. Washington first joined forces with General Jean Rochambeau's French army in New York and headed south. In August 1781, as these armies came south, a large French fleet arrived from the West Indies and blocked Chesapeake Bay. (See map at left.) The French fleet prevented the British ships from reaching Yorktown and delivering supplies—and prevented the British in Yorktown from escaping.

Meanwhile, the **Battle of Yorktown** had begun. The British tried to protect themselves by encircling the town with numerous **redoubts**, or small forts. These forts were meant to keep the allies' artillery at a distance from the town. But as the allies captured British redoubts, they brought their artillery closer to the town's defenses. The American and French cannon bombarded Yorktown, turning its buildings to rubble. Cornwallis had no way out. On October 19, 1781, he surrendered his force of about 8,000.

History *through* Art

Although fighting continued in the South and on the frontier, Yorktown was the last major battle of the war. When the British prime minister, Lord North, heard the news, he gasped, "It is all over!" Indeed, he and other British leaders were soon forced to resign. Britain's new leaders began to negotiate a peace treaty, which is discussed in the next section.

▲ **SUMMARIZE** Describe how Cornwallis was trapped.

Why the Americans Won

▼ **KEY QUESTION** How were the Americans able to defeat the British?

The Surrender of Lord Cornwallis by John Trumbull shows a British officer surrendering to a mounted American officer, with French troops on the left and Americans on the right. Unwilling to face public humiliation, Cornwallis pretended to be ill, sending General Charles O'Hara to offer his sword to the French. The French sent O'Hara to General Washington, who allowed General Benjamin Lincoln to accept the sword of surrender.

CRITICAL VIEWING How does the positioning of the troops symbolize the British defeat?

By their persistence, the Americans won independence even though they faced many obstacles. As you have read, the American army lacked training and experience. American soldiers served only for short periods of time. They often lacked proper supplies and weapons. In contrast, the British forces ranked among the best trained in the world. Yet the Americans had advantages that had not been obvious at first; only as the war progressed did American strengths become apparent. The chart on the next page sets these American strengths against the weaknesses of the British.

The British were defeated not only by the American army, but by civilians who kept the resistance alive. The British were not prepared for a popular uprising. In Europe, only armies fought the wars, and civilians either fled or hid before advancing forces. In America, however, the British discovered that large segments of the population were actively involved in a political cause. Even if the British had succeeded in defeating an American army, they likely would never have been able to conquer the American people.

CONNECT to the Essential Question

How was it possible that American Patriots gained their independence from the powerful British Empire?

AMERICAN STRENGTHS		BRITISH WEAKNESSES
Patriots fought for their lives, their property, and their political ideals.	**Motivation**	The British and their Hessian mercenaries fought merely for pay.
Many civilians actively supported the Revolution. Patriots used many techniques to rally popular support. Rebellion broke out across the continent.	**Popular support**	The British were unprepared for a popular uprising. There was no widespread support for the war in Britain.
American generals learned from their mistakes. Washington inspired loyalty and patriotism in his troops.	**Leadership**	British generals were overconfident and disunited, their efforts often uncoordinated.
France supplied money and troops. France and Spain weakened British forces by expanding the war. The Dutch helped carry French military supplies to the Americans.	**Foreign allies**	No allies. As more European countries turned against Britain, the British were forced to fight many enemies.
Americans fought close to home; the militia made sure that the British could not live off the land.	**Communication and supplies**	Orders from London might take months to reach America. The British were also forced to transport food and supplies over 3,000 miles of ocean.
Although Americans had fewer troops, local militia helped swell American forces. Altogether, 250,000 may have fought for the Patriot cause.	**Troop strength**	By 1781 the British army had around 54,000 troops fighting rebel forces.

CRITICAL THINKING **Compare and Contrast** Which strength do you think was most important to the American victory?

Fond Farewells In late 1783, the last British ships and troops left New York City. As the American army disbanded, soldiers such as Joseph Plumb Martin of Connecticut had mixed emotions. Martin had enlisted in 1776, at the age of 15. He experienced the terrible winter at Valley Forge and the winning battle at Yorktown. Many years later, he wrote about his last day as a regular.

PRIMARY SOURCE

❝ There was as much sorrow as joy. . . . We had lived together as a family of brothers for several years, . . . had shared with each other the hardships, dangers, and sufferings incident to a soldier's life; had sympathized with each other in trouble and sickness; . . . And now we were to be . . . parted forever. ❞

—Joseph Plumb Martin, quoted in *The Revolutionaries*

In his farewell letter to his armies, George Washington wrote that the army's endurance "through almost every possible suffering and discouragement for the space of eight long years, was little short of a standing miracle." Like Washington—and the British—American Patriots were astonished at their achievement.

▲ **SUMMARIZE** Explain how the Americans were able to defeat the British.

 Illinois Learning Standards *Review*

 ONLINE QUIZ
For test practice, go to
Interactive Review @ ClassZone.com

TERMS & NAMES
1. Explain the importance of
- Battle of Charles Town
- Lord Cornwallis
- Battle of Yorktown

USING YOUR READING NOTES
2. Sequence Complete the diagram to show the most importance events of this section.

KEY IDEAS
3. Why didn't the British control of coastal cities bring them victory in the South?

4. When and why did Congress form a new Southern army?

5. How did the allies force the British to surrender?

CRITICAL THINKING
6. Make Generalizations Does military superiority always guarantee victory? Why or why not?

7. WHAT IF? What might have happened at Yorktown without the aid of the French fleet?

8. Connect *to* Today What can the history of the Revolution teach us about modern conflicts?

9. Writing Letter Use books or the Internet to find out about the actions of Lord North after the British defeat at Yorktown. As North, write a letter to your king explaining the defeat.

American Spirit

RALLYING TO THE CAUSE

During the Revolution, American Patriots supported the war effort in a variety of ways. Why was popular support so important for the American victory?

Teens in History

RAISING THE LIBERTY POLE

Americans imagined liberty as a tree grown from a seed planted by the early colonists. Many American communities had a liberty tree (or pole) in the center of town that served as a meeting spot where Patriots rallied supporters and exchanged news.

THE YOUNG ENLIST

Although the Continental Army was not supposed to enlist boys younger than sixteen, recruiters did not usually ask for proof of age. In fact, teenage boys made up a large proportion of the army. Posters like this one were designed to persuade young men to enlist.

> "To the enemies of our country! May they have cobweb breeches, a *porcupine saddle*, a hard-trotting horse, and an eternal journey!"

> "May the enemies of America be destitute of (lacking in) beef and claret (wine)"

PATRIOTIC CURSES

Patriots raised their spirits by laughing at the enemy.

PATRIOT POET

Phillis Wheatley, the first African-American writer to achieve fame, was a poet who supported the Patriot cause. During the war, Washington invited her to his headquarters after she sent him a poem that ended with this verse:

"Proceed, great chief,
with virtue on thy side,
Thy ev'ry action
let the goddess guide.
A crown, a mansion,
and a throne that shine,
With gold unfading,
Washington be thine."

SPYING FOR THE CAUSE

Many women spied for the Patriots. The American-born Patience Wright worked in London as a sculptor. Some historians believe that she coaxed military information out of her subjects as she sculpted their likenesses. Then she apparently passed on the information to Patriot agents in London.

SECRET CODES

Information was often coded, in case letters fell into enemy hands. One kind of secret message did not look like a code at all, but lay hidden in an innocent-looking letter like the one shown here. By cutting the right shape out of another piece of paper and laying it on top of the letter, the secret message would be revealed.

Activity

Decode a secret message!

1 In the middle of a sheet of paper, cut out a triangle with these dimensions:
Base: 6 cm; Height: 4 cm; Sides: 5 cm.

2 Place the sheet over the message below. Align the base of the triangle with the blue line below the message. Then slide the sheet slowly from left to right until you find the secret message.

M. may have told you the secret news by this time. But, if you have not heard, the message is that the city of New York will be attacked by some Americans and French, who are growing bolder day by day and are at this moment moving their armies there. They will not take their armies to the south to attack British forces there because my Lord Cornwallis, who is at Yorktown, is not a threat.

▶ Key Ideas

BEFORE, YOU LEARNED

A combination of factors brought about an American victory.

NOW YOU WILL LEARN

Americans emerged from the Revolution as citizens of a unified nation that valued the ideal of liberty.

▶ Vocabulary

TERMS & NAMES

Treaty of Paris the 1783 treaty that ended the Revolutionary War

Elizabeth Freeman enslaved African American who won her freedom in court

Richard Allen African-American preacher who helped start the Free African Society

Virginia Statute for Religious Freedom statement of religious liberty, written by Thomas Jefferson

BACKGROUND VOCABULARY

disputes (dis•PYOOTS) disagreements

outposts (OWT•posts) military bases, usually located on the frontier

nondenominational not favoring any particular religion

Visual Vocabulary
outpost

▶ Reading Strategy

Re-create the spider diagram shown at right. As you read and respond to the **KEY QUESTIONS**, use the main branches to note categories of facts about results of the war. Add stems to record important details in each category.

 See Skillbuilder Handbook, page R6.

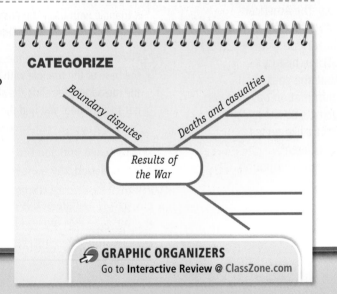

CATEGORIZE

Boundary disputes

Deaths and casualties

Results of the War

GRAPHIC ORGANIZERS
Go to **Interactive Review** @ ClassZone.com

The Legacy of the War

16.B.3b Explain how and why the colonies fought for their independence and how the colonists' ideas are reflected in the Declaration of Independence and the United States Constitution.
16.D.3a Describe characteristics of different kinds of communities in various sections of America during the colonial/frontier periods and the 19th century.

One American's Story

Haym Salomon, a Jew living in Poland, moved to New York before the Revolution in search of liberty. He soon became a successful merchant and banker. During the war, Salomon supported the Patriot cause.

When the British captured New York in 1776, Salomon was arrested. Because he spoke many languages, the British thought he could help them deal with foreign merchants, so they let him out of prison. Unfortunately, prison had permanently damaged his health.

In 1778, Salomon fled to Philadelphia. He loaned the new government more than $600,000, which was never repaid. Like many other Americans, Salomon had sacrificed his health and fortune to help his country survive.

A 1975 U.S. postage stamp honors Haym Salomon.

Costs of the War

▼ **KEY QUESTION** What were the costs of the war?

No one knows exactly how many people died in the war, but eight years of fighting took a terrible toll. An estimated 25,700 Americans died in the war, and 1,400 remained missing. Over 8,200 Americans were wounded. Some were left with permanent disabilities, such as amputated limbs. The British military suffered about 10,000 deaths.

Debts and Losses Many soldiers who survived the war left the army with no money. They had received little or no pay. Instead of back pay, the government gave some soldiers certificates for land in the West. Many men sold that land to get money for food and other basic needs.

Both the Congress and the states had borrowed money to finance the conflict. The war left the nation with a debt of about $27 million—a debt that would prove difficult to pay off.

Those who supported the losing side in the war also suffered. Thousands of Loyalists lost their property. Between 60,000 and 100,000 Loyalists

PAYING FOR THE WAR

The Continental Congress—our first national government—did not have the power to tax; it asked for funds and then hoped that the states would pay. It did have the power to borrow, however. Fighting the Revolutionary War cost America around $100 million, and by 1782, the new U.S. government was approximately $30 million in debt. To fund the Continental Army, the United States borrowed money in several ways.

TREASURY NOTES	CERTIFICATES	PERSONAL NOTES
A treasury note states the government's promise to repay a specified amount at a specified date. Notes were sold to **patriotic investors** and to **foreign countries** such as France.	Printed money, known as "certificates," could be exchanged for an amount of silver—*if* the government had enough. This is how many **"regulars"** (soldiers), **farmers**, and **tradespeople** were paid.	**Wealthy individuals**, such as Haym Salomon and Robert Morris—the country's first superintendent of finance—issued personal notes (or loans) to pay government expenses.

Connect *to* **Today** Do you think it's a good idea for a modern government to borrow money? Why or why not?

---

left the United States during and after the war. Among them were several thousand African Americans and Native Americans, including Mohawk chief Joseph Brant. Most of the Loyalists went to Canada. There they settled new towns and provinces. They also brought English traditions to areas that the French had settled. To this day, Canada has both French and English as official languages.

The Revolution had been a civil war that left both Patriots and Loyalists with bitter memories. Patriots found it especially difficult to forgive the former American general Benedict Arnold. In 1780 Arnold had betrayed his country by trying to turn over an American fort to the British. Throughout American history, the name Benedict Arnold is used to mean traitor.

▲ **SUMMARIZE** List some of the costs of the war.

The Treaty of Paris

▼ **KEY QUESTION** What did America gain most from the Treaty of Paris?

Benjamin Franklin, John Adams, and John Jay began formal peace negotiations with the British on September 27, 1782. The final **Treaty of Paris**, which ended the Revolutionary War, was signed on September 3, 1783.

Favorable Terms The Americans won favorable terms in the peace treaty:

- The United States was independent.
- Its boundaries would be the Mississippi River on the west, Canada on the north, and Spanish Florida on the south.
- The United States would receive the right to fish off Canada's Atlantic Coast, near Newfoundland and Nova Scotia.
- Each side would repay debts it owed the other.
- The British would return any enslaved persons they had captured.
- Congress would recommend that the states return any property they had seized from Loyalists.

Neither Britain nor the United States fully lived up to the treaty's terms. Americans did not repay the prewar debts they owed British merchants or return Loyalist property. The British did not return runaway slaves.

Boundary Disputes The Treaty of Paris led to boundary **disputes**, or disagreements, with Spain, who could now claim control of both banks of the Mississippi river for over 100 miles north of the Gulf of Mexico. This Spanish control threatened American shipping. In the northwest, the British refused to give up military **outposts**, or bases, in the Great Lakes area, such as Fort Detroit.

COMPARING ◄ *Prewar and Postwar Boundaries*

Prewar Boundaries *1775*

Postwar Boundaries *1783*

British
French
Russian
Spanish
United States
Disputed Territory

Connect Geography & History

1. **Place** What was the southern limit of British territory in 1775?

2. **Evaluate** Which foreign nation benefited most from the Treaty of Paris?

Joseph Brant, or Thayendanegea, was not born to be a chief but earned the esteem of his people by his leadership. The giant shell he wears is a symbol of wealth and status.

The Threat to Native American Lands The Treaty of Paris redrew the national boundaries with little concern for Native American interests. In Chapter 5, you learned that the British had attempted to keep white settlers away from Native American territory by establishing the Proclamation Line of 1763. Because of this, many tribes had supported the British in the war. But in the treaty, the British handed over Native American lands without even consulting their former allies. When Mohawk chief Joseph Brant heard the news, he was horrified by the betrayal.

PRIMARY SOURCE

❝ When I joined the English in the beginning of the War, it was purely on account of my forefathers' engagements with the King. I always looked upon these engagements, or covenants between the King and the Indian nation, as a sacred thing. ❞

—Joseph Brant, 1783

Native Americans who lived east of the Mississippi found themselves living within the boundaries of a new nation that was intent on westward expansion. Their lands were now at risk.

🔺 **MAIN IDEAS & DETAILS** Identify what America gained from the Treaty of Paris.

Creating a New Nation

🔻 **KEY QUESTION** What ideals emerged from the Revolution?

"Liberty" had been the rallying cry of the Revolution as Americans freed themselves from British rule. Now, the success of the Revolution challenged the existing world order. For the first time in the Americas, a colonial rebellion against an imperial power had succeeded. By destroying British authority, the Revolution offered political reformers a chance to prove that republicanism, the idea that a country can be governed by the people, and without a king, could work. Imperial powers around the world began to fear this new threat.

At the same time, the war created a new nation—one that valued the ideal of liberty. As Americans built their new society, the ideal of liberty became one of the most important legacies of the Revolution.

New State and National Governments As early as 1775 British rule had become ineffective in many areas of the colonies. Eventually, in May of 1776, the Continental Congress advised the colonies to establish new governments. By 1777 nearly all the former colonies had adopted written constitutions. Two colonies—Connecticut and Rhode Island—retained the governments established by their royal charters.

All the new state constitutions contained some enumeration of individual rights and liberties. For instance, Virginia's new Constitution of 1776 was based on the Virginia Declaration of Rights. It protected many rights and guaranteed freedom of the press and freedom of religion. Some states, including Delaware, prohibited slavery and a state-supported religion. Georgia's constitution established public schools.

The states also realized early on that they needed a national government, if only to conduct the war. By 1777, the Continental Congress had drafted a plan: the Articles of Confederation. (The new government finally took charge in 1781.) The Articles gave very limited powers to the central government—little more than waging war and signing treaties. (See Chapter 8.)

Freedom and Slavery During the Revolution, some people began to see a conflict between slavery and the ideal of liberty. In response, Vermont outlawed slavery, and Pennsylvania passed a law to free slaves gradually. Individual African Americans also fought to end slavery, sometimes suing for freedom in the courts. For example, **Elizabeth Freeman** sued for her freedom in a Massachusetts court and won. Her victory in 1781 and other similar cases ended slavery in that state.

Freed African Americans formed their own institutions. For example, in Philadelphia **Richard Allen** helped start the Free African Society, a **nondenominational** group that encouraged people to help each other. (*Nondenominational* means not favoring any particular religion.) Richard Allen had earned the money to buy his freedom by working for the Revolutionary forces. As a preacher, Allen's leadership was shaped by his belief that he had a special duty to teach and help people, of all backgrounds, who had suffered from discrimination. Allen also founded the African Methodist Episcopal Church, the first African-American church in the United States.

Despite the efforts to end slavery in the North, in the South slavery continued. However, many people, including Southern plantation owners, were troubled by the new nation's dependence on slavery. In 1784, Thomas Jefferson, a slave owner himself, wrote of his fears for America if slavery were allowed to continue: "I tremble for my country when I reflect that God is just; that his justice cannot sleep forever."

Connecting History

Regionalism
The South's dependence on slavery would lead to a terrible civil war that threatened to tear apart the United States itself. You will see this theme emerge as you study events leading to the Civil War.

Richard Allen

Defining Religious Freedom For many Americans, central to the ideal of liberty was the idea that religion is a private matter and that people should have the right to choose and practice their personal religious beliefs. People such as James Madison and Thomas Jefferson called for a "separation of church and state," meaning that the state should not be involved in religious affairs.

In 1777 Thomas Jefferson proposed his **Virginia Statute for Religious Freedom**. In it, he claimed that people have a "natural right" to freedom of opinion, including religious opinion. Jefferson opposed state laws that prohibited Jews or Catholics from holding public office. He also opposed the practice of using tax money to support churches, because, he wrote, "to compel a man to furnish contributions of money for the propagation of opinions which he disbelieves, is sinful and tyrannical."

Jefferson's statute was eventually adopted as law in Virginia. Later, it became the basis of the religious rights guaranteed by the Bill of Rights in the U.S. Constitution.

Uniting the States For almost two centuries each colony had been governed independently of its neighbors. The colonies had been quarrelsome and often uncooperative. However, as the war turned colonies into states, Americans saw how important it was for these states to work together as a nation. The great challenge that lay ahead was how to remain united as a nation of independent states, despite regional and religious differences.

▲ **SUMMARIZE** Describe the ideals that emerged from the Revolution.

Illinois Learning Standards *Review*

🔁 **ONLINE QUIZ**
For test practice, go to
Interactive Review @ ClassZone.com

TERMS & NAMES

1. Explain the importance of

- Treaty of Paris
- Elizabeth Freeman
- Richard Allen
- Virginia Statute for Religious Freedom

USING YOUR READING NOTES

2. Categorize List and categorize the major results of the Revolutionary War.

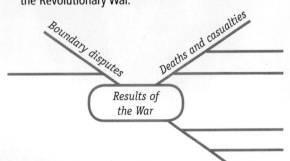

KEY IDEAS

3. What groups gained least from the Treaty of Paris?

4. How did the goals of the Revolution guide Americans toward a more just society after the war?

CRITICAL THINKING

5. Connect Economics & History How did the Treaty of Paris protect America's economic interests?

6. Causes and Effects How did the Patriot victory affect Native Americans?

7. Historical Perspective What might have happened if, during the peace negotiations, each state had tried to negotiate independently?

8. **Writing** **Citizenship Report** Use the Internet to research Elizabeth Freeman and Richard Allen. Write a brief report explaining how their efforts helped improve their communities.

Chapter Summary

1 **Key Idea**
Although the Continental Army had difficulty fighting in a divided America, the Patriots triumphed at Saratoga.

2 **Key Idea**
The expansion of the war weakened the British by forcing them to spread their military resources around the world.

3 **Key Idea**
The Continental Army, their allies, and the American people brought about an American victory.

4 **Key Idea**
Americans emerged from the Revolution as citizens of a unified nation that valued the ideal of liberty.

 To create **Review and Study Notes** go to **Interactive Review** @ **ClassZone.com**

Name Game

Use the Terms & Names list to complete each sentence online or on your own paper.

1. I carried the war to the western frontier.
   George Rogers Clark

2. I led my troops to defeat at Saratoga. ____

3. I was a French officer who fought for America. ____

4. My leadership unified a nation. ____

5. I was trapped between allied forces and the French fleet. ____

6. I brought the war to the coasts of Britain. ____

7. The ideal of liberty helped me win my freedom in court. ____

8. I lost my lands when my ally betrayed me. ____

9. Here the Patriots first proved that they might win the war. ____

10. Here the Continental Army endured a difficult winter. ____

A. Joseph Brant
B. John Paul Jones
C. George Rogers Clark
D. Benedict Arnold
E. Valley Forge
F. Richard Allen
G. John Burgoyne
H. Marquis de Lafayette
I. Treaty of Paris
J. George Washington
K. Horatio Gates
L. Lord Cornwallis
M. Elizabeth Freeman
N. Yorktown
O. Saratoga

Activities

CROSSWORD PUZZLE

Complete the online crossword puzzle to show what you know about the American Revolution.

ACROSS

1. ____ captured the British warship *Serapis*.

GEOGAME

Use this online map to reinforce your understanding of the Revolutionary War, including the locations of important battles and geographic features. Drag and drop each place name in the list at its location on the map. A scorecard helps you keep track of your progress online.

Trenton

Saratoga

Lake Ontario

Valley Forge

Hudson River

Lake Ontario

More place names online

VOCABULARY

Explain the significance of each of the following:

1. Joseph Brant
2. Treaty of Paris
3. Battles of Saratoga
4. privateer
5. Battle of Yorktown
6. neutral
7. Richard Allen
8. Valley Forge
9. guerrilla
10. George Washington

Explain how the terms and names in each group are related.

Marquis de Lafayette

11. George Washington, Marquis de Lafayette, Valley Forge, mercenary

12. John Burgoyne, Horatio Gates, Benedict Arnold

13. Lord Cornwallis, Battle of Yorktown, redoubt

KEY IDEAS

① The Early Years of the War (pages 194–201)

14. What difficulties did the Americans have in readying a military force to fight the Revolutionary War?

15. What events led to British defeat at Saratoga?

② The War Expands (pages 204–211)

16. Explain the importance of George Rogers Clark and John Paul Jones in expanding the war.

17. Explain three effects of America's alliances with France and Spain.

③ The Path to Victory (pages 212–219)

18. Why did the British decide to attack the South?

19. Describe the tactics and technologies used during the fighting in the Southern colonies.

④ The Legacy of the War (pages 222–228)

20. In what ways did the Treaty of Paris of 1783 favor America?

21. Describe three challenges America faced after defeating Britain.

CRITICAL THINKING

22. **Causes and Effects** How did shortages of soldiers and supplies affect Washington's plans at the start of the war?

23. **Summarize** Summarize the role of Britain's navy in the war.

24. **Compare** Create a table to compare and contrast the battles of Saratoga and Yorktown. After you complete your table, explain the significance of each battle.

Battles of Saratoga	Battle of Yorktown
mountainous	*town*
wooded terrain	*flat land*

25. **Synthesize** Why did the war last such a long time?

26. **Evaluate** Refer to the "American Strengths/British Weaknesses" chart on page 218. Which British weakness do you think proved most important in the Patriot victory? Explain your choice.

27. **Draw Conclusions** How was America able to overcome its lack of resources and soldiers?

28. **Interpret Graphs** Study the graph below. How do you explain the change in data from 1779 to 1780?

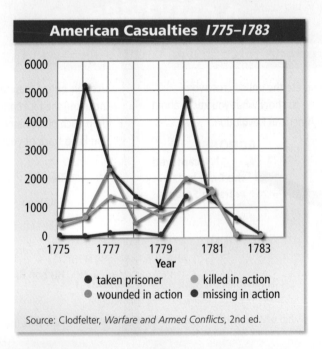

American Casualties *1775–1783*

● taken prisoner ● killed in action
● wounded in action ● missing in action

Source: Clodfelter, *Warfare and Armed Conflicts*, 2nd ed.

DOCUMENT-BASED QUESTIONS

PART 1: Short Answer

Analyze each document, and answer the questions that follow.

DOCUMENT 1

1. This artwork shows Catherine Van Rensselaer Schuyler, the wife of American general Philip Schuyler, setting fire to her own family's fields near Saratoga, New York, in 1777. Why is Mrs. Schuyler burning her fields?

DOCUMENT 2

PRIMARY SOURCE

❝ When . . . it [became] impossible for any but the wealthiest to import anything to eat or wear, and all had to be raised and manufactured at home, from bread stuffs, sugar, and rum to the linen and woollen for our clothes and bedding, you may well imagine that my duties were not light. ❞

—Temperance Smith

2. Temperance Smith wrote this while her husband was serving at Fort Ticonderoga during the American Revolution. How did Temperance Smith's life change during the war?

Part 2: Essay

3. In two or three short paragraphs, explain how civilians contributed to the Patriot victory in the Revolutionary War. Use information from your answers to Part 1 and your knowledge of U.S. history.

YOU BE THE HISTORIAN

29. Make Judgments Do you think America was stronger before or after the war? Explain and justify your opinion.

30. Causes and Effects How did the war change the daily life of an average merchant or farm family?

31. WHAT IF? Suppose France had not come to America's aid. In what ways would this have affected Washington's ability to defeat the British?

32. Analyze Motives Why do you think most Patriots who fought the Revolutionary War to protect liberty did not try to banish slavery?

33. Citizenship How did independence change Americans' responsibilities as citizens?

 Connect *to* **Today** Give some examples of how people in your community fulfill these responsibilities today.

Answer the
ESSENTIAL QUESTION
How was it possible that American Patriots gained their independence from the powerful British Empire?

Written Response Write a four-paragraph response to the Essential Question. Be sure to consider the key ideas of each section as well as the most significant factors that led to the American victory. Use the Response Rubric below to guide your thinking and writing.

Response Rubric
A strong response will

• discuss major events that led to the American victory
• analyze American strengths and British weaknesses
• explain the importance of strong leadership
• describe the role of allies in the war.

Confederation to Constitution

1776–1791

ESSENTIAL QUESTION

How did Americans create a national government that respected both the independence of states and the rights of individuals?

CONNECT Geography & History

How might the geography of the United States have affected the policies of the new national government?

Think about:

1 the newly acquired territory between the Appalachian Mountains and the Mississippi River

2 the regions with the densest population concentration

3 the distance between Maine and Georgia, about 1,300 miles

Independence Hall as it appeared in 1776.

1781 Articles of Confederation passed.

▼

Effect The United States has its first national government.

1776

American independence

1777 Continental Congress passes the Articles of Confederation.

This early flag has 13 stars representing the original 13 colonies.

Claimed by both
U.S. and Britain

MAINE
(MASS.)

Claimed by
N.Y. & N.H.

Lake
Superior

NEW HAMPSHIRE
Boston
MASSACHUSETTS

Lake Ontario

RHODE
ISLAND

NEW YORK

CONNECTICUT

New York

PENNSYLVANIA

NEW JERSEY

Philadelphia

Baltimore — DELAWARE

MARYLAND

Lake Michigan

Lake Huron

Lake Erie

River

A P P A L A C H I A N   M O U N T A I N S

Ohio

VIRGINIA

One dot equals 5,000 persons*

National capital

* 1st U.S. Census, 1790

0   100   200 miles
0   100   200 kilometers

NORTH
CAROLINA

SOUTH CAROLINA

Charleston

ATLANTIC
OCEAN

GEORGIA

Mississippi River

40°N

65°W

35°N

30°N

70°W

Iroquois warrior

Writers of the Constitution used a quill pen dipped in an inkwell.

1791

1785 Land Ordinance of 1785 stakes out Northwest Territory for U.S. settlers.

1788 U.S. Constitution is ratified.

Bill of Rights is ratified.
▼
Effect Preserves and protects individual liberties.

▶ Key Ideas

BEFORE, YOU LEARNED
Americans emerged from the Revolution as citizens of a unified nation that valued the ideal of liberty.

NOW YOU WILL LEARN
The Articles of Confederation created a weak national government.

▶ Vocabulary

TERMS & NAMES

Shays's Rebellion uprising of Massachusetts farmers who demanded debt relief

Northwest Territory lands northwest of the Appalachians, covered by the Land Ordinance of 1785

Articles of Confederation plan for national government ratified in 1781

Confederation Congress national legislative body formed by the Articles of Confederation

Land Ordinance of 1785 law that established a plan for dividing the federally owned lands west of the Appalachian Mountains

Northwest Ordinance law that described how the Northwest Territory was to be governed

BACKGROUND VOCABULARY

republic state, country or nation in which people elect representatives to govern.

ratification act of official confirmation

levy impose or raise a tax

arsenal place where weapons are stored

REVIEW

neutral not siding with one country or another

▶ Reading Strategy

Create an outline like the one shown at right. As you read and respond to the **KEY QUESTIONS**, note the main ideas and supporting details about the Articles of Confederation.

 See Skillbuilder Handbook, page R9.

MAIN IDEAS & DETAILS

The Articles of Confederation

I. Features of the A. of C.
 —
 —

II. Needs addressed by the A. of C.
 —
 —

 GRAPHIC ORGANIZERS
Go to **Interactive Review** @ ClassZone.com

The Confederation Era

14.F.3a Analyze historical influences on the development of political ideas and practices as enumerated in the Declaration of Independence, the United States Constitution, the Bill of Rights and the Illinois Constitution.

17.A.3b Explain how to make and use geographic representations to provide and enhance spatial information including maps, graphs, charts, models, aerial photographs, satellite images.

One American's Story

After the Revolutionary War, the nation faced hard economic times. People had little money, but the states continued to levy high taxes. In Massachusetts, many farmers fell deeply into debt.

PRIMARY SOURCE

> ❝ I have been obliged to pay and nobody will pay me. I have lost a great deal by this man and that man . . . and the great men are going to get all we have, and I think it is time for us to rise and put a stop to it. . . . ❞
>
> —Plough Jogger, quoted in *The People Speak: American Voices, Some Famous, Some Little Known*

Shays's rebels take over a Massachusetts courthouse. Today a stone marker rests on the spot of the rebellion.

From August 1786 to February 1787, Daniel Shays, a Revolutionary War veteran, led Jogger and other farmers in an armed uprising. To protest what the farmers viewed as unfair taxation, they attacked county courts in Massachusetts. At first, using force, they succeeded in stopping the courts from selling farmers' possessions and jailing people who couldn't pay their debts.

The state militia put down **Shays's Rebellion**, as the uprising came to be known. But many people sided with the farmers. America's leaders realized that a popular armed uprising spelled danger to the new nation. It was clearly time to talk about a stronger national government.

Forming a New Government

🔻 **KEY QUESTION** What did the states want from a national government?

Ten years before Shays's Rebellion, the colonists had resisted the harsh rule of a distant government. As Americans planned their first national government, in 1776-1777, their main goal was to prevent governmental tyranny from reappearing in the new nation.

Republicanism and Citizenship American leaders felt strongly that the people needed to exercise control over their government. It was decided that the new nation would be a **republic**, a country in which the people choose representatives to govern them. But not everyone in the United States would be allowed to help select these representatives. Most states had fairly high property qualifications, and only property owners, who were considered citizens, would be allowed to vote. African Americans were generally not allowed to vote. Some states granted voting rights to all white males. All states, except Pennsylvania and Georgia, made property ownership a requirement for voting. Women were also denied the right to vote in most states.

State Constitutions Lead the Way Once the American colonies declared independence in 1776, each of the states set out to create its own government. The framers, or creators, of the state constitutions did not want to destroy the political systems that they had had as colonies. They simply wanted to make those systems more representative.

Some states experimented with giving different powers to different parts of government. By creating separate branches of government, Americans hoped to prevent any one part of the government from becoming too powerful. All state governments limited the powers of their governors because of the colonists' unpleasant experience with the British king.

Some states included a Bill of Rights in their constitutions. Based on the English Bill of Rights of 1689, these bills were lists of freedoms that Americans were most eager to protect. The first constitutional document in the United States was Virginia's constitution of 1776. It protected freedom of the press and freedom of religion.

As citizens set up their state governments, they discussed how to form a national government. During the Revolutionary War, Americans realized that they had to unite to win the war against Britain. Forming a national government was key to national unity. And diplomat John Dickinson's words, "By uniting we stand, by dividing we fall," became a popular slogan.

The Articles of Confederation In 1776, the Continental Congress began to plan for a national government. Congress agreed that the government should be a republic. But the delegates disagreed about whether each state should have one vote or voting should be based on population.

They also disagreed about who should control the **Northwest Territory**, or the lands west of the Appalachians. The Continental Congress eventually arrived at a plan called the **Articles of Confederation**. In the Articles, the national government would be run by a legislative body to be called the **Confederation Congress**. Congress had the power to wage war, make peace, sign treaties, run Indian affairs, and issue money. Each state had only one vote in the Congress.

Connecting History

Growth of Government
The English Bill of Rights limited the power of the English monarch. Among other things, it prevented the monarch from levying taxes, and maintaining an army in peacetime without the consent of Parliament.

Powers Granted and Denied Congress

GRANTED CONGRESS	DENIED CONGRESS
• Conduct foreign affairs	• Establish executive branch
• Declare war and make peace	• Enforce national laws
• Issue or borrow money	• Enact and collect taxes
• Control Western territories	• Regulate interstate or foreign trade
• Control Indian affairs	• Establish federal courts
• Run postal service	• Amend the Articles

CRITICAL THINKING Evaluate Why did the powers denied Congress lead to a weak government?

But the Articles left most important powers to the states. These powers included the authority to set taxes and enforce national laws. The proposed Articles left the individual states in control of the lands west of the Appalachian Mountains.

The Articles Are Ratified The Continental Congress passed the Articles of Confederation in November 1777. It then sent the Articles to the states for **ratification,** or approval. By July 1778, eight states had ratified the Articles. But some of the small states that did not have Western land claims refused to sign. These states worried that they would be at a disadvantage unless the Western lands were placed under the control of the national government. The states with Western lands could sell them to pay off debts left from the Revolution and possibly become overwhelmingly powerful. But states without lands would have difficulty paying off the high war debts.

Gradually, all the states gave up their claims to Western lands. This led the small states to ratify the Articles. In 1781, Maryland became the 13th state to accept the Articles. As a result, the United States finally had an official government.

▲ **SUMMARIZE** Discuss the powers of the states under the Articles of Confederation.

Western Land Claims 1789

Connect Geography & History

1. **Location** How far west did the Western land claims extend?

2. **Draw Conclusions** The western lands were vast. What might be some of the challenges of governing such a large territory?

Strengths and Weaknesses of the Articles

▼ **KEY QUESTION** What were the weaknesses of the national government?

The Confederation Congress had run the country during the Revolutionary War and had some success in handling land issues. But Americans began to realize the Confederation Congress was too weak to deal with most other national issues.

The Land Ordinance of 1785 One issue the Confederation Congress successfully handled was what to do with the Western lands that it now controlled. Starting in 1785, the Congress passed important laws on how to divide and govern these lands.

The **Land Ordinance of 1785** called for surveyors to stake out six-mile-square plots, called townships, in the Western lands. These lands later became known as the Northwest Territory. The Northwest Territory included land that formed the states of Ohio, Indiana, Michigan, Illinois, Wisconsin, and part of Minnesota.

Governing the Northwest Territory The **Northwest Ordinance** of 1787 outlined how the Northwest Territory was to be governed. The bill had many democratic features. As the territory grew in population, it would gain rights to self-government. When there were 5,000 free adult males in an area, men who owned at least 50 acres of land could elect an assembly. When there were 60,000 people, they could apply to become a new state. Slavery was outlawed. Rivers were to be open to navigation for all. Freedom of religion and trial by jury were guaranteed.

The Northwest Ordinance was a big success for the Confederation Congress. The bill created a model for the orderly growth of the United States well into the 19th century. But the Northwest Ordinance was bad for the lands' original inhabitants. The Ordinance promised Native Americans fair treatment, and Native American lands were not to be taken from them. However, the increased contact between settlers and natives led to territorial conflicts that were not easily resolved.

Problems with Britain and Spain To fight the Revolutionary War, Congress had borrowed large sums of money. With the war over, it was now time to pay back the loans. Yet the Confederation Congress did not have the money to do so. Congress also found that it did not have the power to deal on an equal basis with other nations. Some of the challenges Congress faced with other nations were:

- Britain competed against the American fur trade by refusing to evacuate its military forts south of the Great Lakes.
- Britain barred American-owned ships from British waters in the Caribbean.
- Spain also put up barriers to American shipping in the Caribbean.
- Spain refused to allow Americans to use the Mississippi River or to deposit goods in New Orleans.
- Spain and Congress argued over the boundary of Florida.

In the late 1700s, Spain held the crucial port of New Orleans. **Why did this have an impact on American traders?**

The problems the Confederation faced in foreign relations revealed the basic weaknesses of the national government. The United States did not have the strength to face up to the superior forces of the British or the Spanish.

Economic Problems and Shays's Rebellion With American trade weakened, the nation was facing a serious economic crisis. Much of the Confederation's debt was owed to soldiers of the Revolutionary army. Upset at not being paid, approximately 300 soldiers demonstrated before the Pennsylvania State House where Congress was meeting in June 1783. The delegates were forced to flee the city. The event was another clear sign of Congress's weakness.

One reason Congress was unable to raise money to pay the soldiers was that it did not have the power to **levy**, or collect, taxes. The national government depended on the states to send money. The states, who also owed money because of the war, tried to raise money through taxes. However, few ordinary Americans could afford to pay them. Taxes on imported goods raised the cost of everyday necessities, further hurting average Americans.

Taxes in Massachusetts were some of the highest in the nation. The government's refusal to grant debt relief led to an uprising known as Shays's Rebellion. In January 1787, Shays led a march on a federal **arsenal**, a place where weapons are stored. Around one thousand soldiers from the state militia quickly defeated Shays's men.

America's leaders realized that an armed uprising of common farmers spelled danger for the nation. Some leaders hoped that the nation's ills could be solved by giving more power to the national government.

 PROBLEMS AND SOLUTIONS Identify the reasons why the national government was not strong enough.

 Illinois Learning Standards *Review*

ONLINE QUIZ
For test practice, go to
Interactive Review @ ClassZone.com

TERMS & NAMES

1. Explain the importance of
   - Shays's Rebellion
   - Northwest Territory
   - Articles of Confederation
   - Confederation Congress
   - Land Ordinance of 1785
   - Northwest Ordinance

USING YOUR READING NOTES

2. **Problems and Solutions** Complete the outline you started at the beginning of this section.

   The Articles of Confederation

   I. *Features of the A. of C.*
      —
      —
   II. *Needs addressed by the A. of C.*
      —
      —

KEY IDEAS

3. How did the Articles of Confederation prevent the national government from becoming too powerful?

4. Why was the Confederation Congress unable to resolve problems with Britain and Spain?

CRITICAL THINKING

5. **Connect Economics and History** Which side would you have supported in Shays's Rebellion—the farmers or the officials who called out the militia? Why?

6. **Analyze** Why were the states afraid of centralized authority and a strong national government?

7. **Writing** **Letter** Write a one-page letter from Daniel Shays to the governor of Massachusetts. In your letter, ask the governor to pardon, or forgive, your rebellion against the government.

The Northwest Territory

In the mid-1780s, Congress decided to sell the land known as "the Territory Northwest of the river Ohio" to settlers—although this policy was often fiercely resisted by the Native Americans living in the region. The sale of land solved two problems. First, it provided cash for the government. Second, it increased American control over the land. The first organized American settlement in the Northwest Territory was Marietta, Ohio, founded in 1788.

The Land Ordinance of 1785 outlined how the land in the Northwest Territory would be divided. Congress created townships that could be divided into sections, as shown on the map below. Each township was six miles by six miles. This was an improvement over earlier methods of setting boundaries. Previously people had used rocks, trees, or other landmarks to set boundaries.

Township 1785					
36	30	24	18	12	6
35	29	23	17	11	5
34	28	22	16	10	4
33	27	21	15	9	3
32	26	20	14	8	2
31	25	19	13	7	1

Each township contained 36 sections. Each section was one square mile.

NATIVE AMERICANS

This area that became the Northwest Territory was the homeland of many Native American tribes — such as the Miami and Shawnee. The tribes grew crops and supplemented their diet with hunting and fishing. Some built bark houses. Besides trading with European fur traders, Native Americans traded with other tribes. Miami corn, for example, was valued for its high quality and the ease with which it could be turned into fine flour.

Shawnee fishing

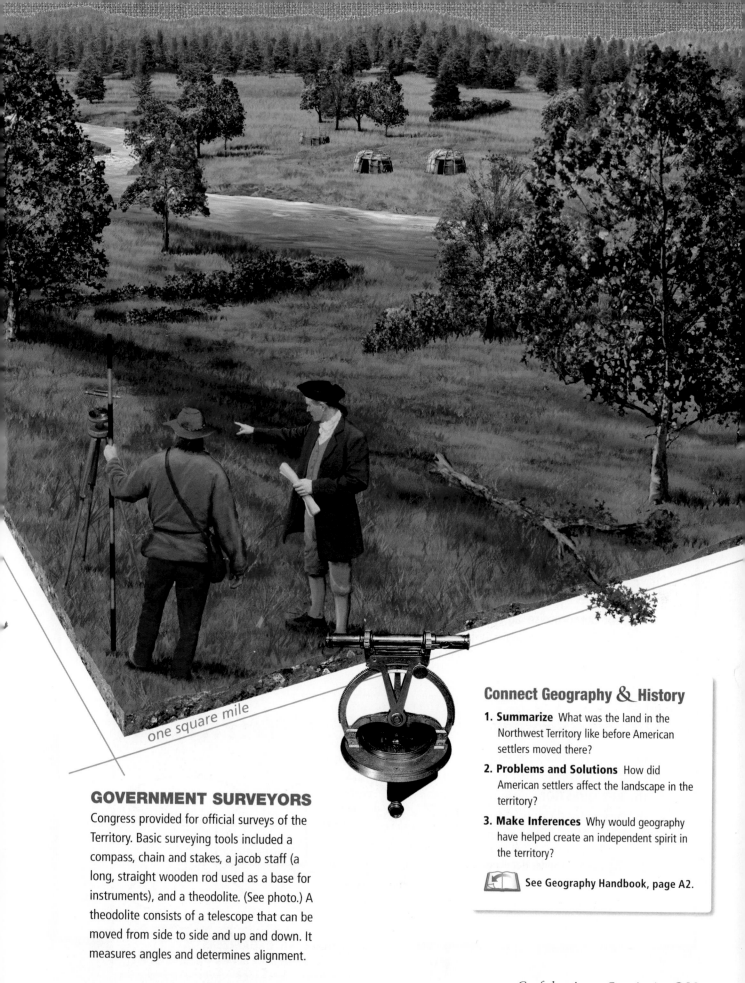

one square mile

GOVERNMENT SURVEYORS

Congress provided for official surveys of the Territory. Basic surveying tools included a compass, chain and stakes, a jacob staff (a long, straight wooden rod used as a base for instruments), and a theodolite. (See photo.) A theodolite consists of a telescope that can be moved from side to side and up and down. It measures angles and determines alignment.

Connect Geography & History

1. **Summarize** What was the land in the Northwest Territory like before American settlers moved there?

2. **Problems and Solutions** How did American settlers affect the landscape in the territory?

3. **Make Inferences** Why would geography have helped create an independent spirit in the territory?

See Geography Handbook, page A2.

▶ Key Ideas

BEFORE, YOU LEARNED
The Articles of Confederation created a weak national government.

NOW YOU WILL LEARN
The Constitution created a new, stronger government that replaced the Confederation.

▶ Vocabulary

TERMS & NAMES

Constitutional Convention 1787 meeting at which the U.S. Constitution was created

Founders people who helped create the U.S. Constitution

James Madison prominent adviser to the Constitutional Convention

Virginia Plan proposal for a two-house legislature with representation according to each state's population or wealth

New Jersey Plan proposal for a legislature in which each state would have one vote

Great Compromise agreement to establish a two-house national legislature, with all states having equal representation in one

house and each state having representation based on its population in the other house.

Three-Fifths Compromise agreement that three-fifths of a state's slave population would be counted for representation and taxation

executive branch government department that enforces laws

judicial branch government department that interprets laws

legislative branch government department that makes laws

checks and balances the ability of each branch of government to exercise checks, or controls, over the other branches

▶ Reading Strategy

Re-create the diagram shown at right. As you read and respond to the **KEY QUESTIONS**, use the ovals to show why there was a need for a Constitutional Convention.

 See Skillbuilder Handbook, page R3.

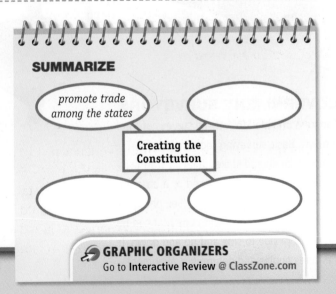

SUMMARIZE

promote trade among the states

Creating the Constitution

GRAPHIC ORGANIZERS
Go to **Interactive Review** @ ClassZone.com

Creating the Constitution

14.C.3 Compare historical issues involving rights, roles and status of individuals in relation to municipalities, states and the nation.
14.F.3b Describe how United States political ideas and traditions were instituted in the Constitution and the Bill of Rights.

One American's Story

On May 15, 1787, Virginia Governor Edmund Randolph arrived in Philadelphia. The young nation faced conflict, as Shays's Rebellion had shown. Now delegates from throughout the states were coming to Philadelphia to discuss reforming the government.

Early in the convention Randolph spoke.

PRIMARY SOURCE

❝ Let us not be afraid to view with a steady eye the [dangers] with which we are surrounded. . . . Are we not on the eve of [a civil] war, which is only to be prevented by the hopes from this convention? **❞**

—Edmund Randolph, quoted in *Edmund Randolph: A Biography*

The Pennsylvania State House is where (*inset*) Edmund Randolph attended the Constitutional Convention.

At first, many Americans doubted that the national government needed strengthening. But fear of rebellion and lawlessness had changed people's minds. For over four months, Congress debated how best to keep the United States from falling apart.

The Call for a Constitutional Convention

🔻 **KEY QUESTION** Why was there a call for a Constitutional Convention?

In September 1786, delegates from five states met in Annapolis, Maryland, to discuss ways to promote trade among the states. At the time, most states charged high taxes on goods imported from other states. The Annapolis delegates believed that creating national trade laws would help the economies of all the states. However, making such changes required amending the Articles of Confederation, because the national government had been granted no

History Makers

James Madison 1751–1836

James Madison was a soft-spoken, scholarly man. In the months before the convention, Madison studied the history of other confederacies that had failed. He saw that without a strong central government, states tended to concentrate too much on their individual interests and not enough on the common good. He came to believe that simply revising the Articles of Confederation would not be enough. Out of this research emerged the Virginia Plan, which provided the basic structure of the new government.

Madison may have made the greatest contribution of any of the Founders at the Constitutional Convention. His contributions were so important that he earned the title "Father of the Constitution."

COMPARING *Leaders*

As you read through the chapter, look for other examples of Madison's leadership. Compare his leadership qualities to those of American statesmen described in previous chapters.

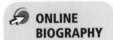 **ONLINE BIOGRAPHY** For more on James Madison, go to the **Research & Writing Center** @ ClassZone.com

power to regulate trade among the states. Some delegates, led by Alexander Hamilton, called for a convention in Philadelphia the following May. Twelve states sent delegates to the Convention. Only Rhode Island declined.

Constitutional Convention The convention opened on May 25, 1787. The first order of business was to nominate a president for the convention. Every delegate voted for the hero of the Revolution, George Washington. Washington's quiet and dignified leadership set the tone for the convention.

The delegates did not want to be pressured by the politics of the day. For this reason, they decided their discussions would remain secret. Much of what we know today about the debates and drama of the Constitutional Convention is thanks to Virginia delegate **James Madison**. In addition to contributing many ideas that shaped the Constitution, Madison took detailed notes on the proceedings.

Who Was There? The 55 delegates to the **Constitutional Convention**, as the Philadelphia meeting became known, were a very impressive group. Many had been members of their state legislatures and had helped write their state constitutions. Along with other leaders of the time, these delegates are called the **Founders**, or Founding Fathers, of the United States. Many of the delegates who helped draft the proposals presented at the Convention were already well known. Roger Sherman, a Connecticut delegate, was a signer of The Declaration of Independence and the Articles of Confederation. Pennsylvania's Gouverneur Morris had also signed the Articles of Confederation. Morris and Washington were friends.

Another prominent Pennsylvania delegate, Scots-born James Wilson, was known for his brilliant legal mind. Wilson worked with James Madison in pushing for a system of **popular sovereignty**, which is a government system in which the people rule. He backed the election of a national legislature by the people to be "not only the cornerstone, but the foundation of the fabric."

Who Was Missing? A number of key people were unable to attend. Thomas Jefferson and John Adams were overseas at their diplomatic posts. But they wrote home to encourage the delegates. Others had a less positive outlook. For example, Patrick Henry, who had been elected as a delegate from Virginia, refused to go. He said he "smelled a rat . . . tending toward monarchy."

Also, the convention did not reflect the diverse U.S. population of the 1780s. There were no Native Americans, African Americans, or women among the delegates. These groups of people were not recognized as citizens and were not invited to attend. However, the framework of government the Founders established at the Constitutional Convention is the very one that would eventually provide full rights and responsibilities to all Americans.

▲ **SUMMARIZE** Explain why the United States needed a constitutional convention.

Some Challenges of the Convention

▼ **KEY QUESTION** What were some of the major challenges facing the Convention?

By 1787, many Americans realized that people and states often came into conflict and needed a government that could keep order. They wanted a government that was strong enough to protect people's rights but not so strong that it would oppress them.

Disagreements over Representation As the Convention began, the delegates disagreed about what form the new government would take. Two plans emerged. James Madison and the other Virginia delegates had drawn up their plan while they waited for the convention to open. Edmund Randolph presented the plan. The **Virginia Plan** proposed a government with three branches. The **executive branch** would enforce the laws. The **judicial branch** would interpret the laws. The third branch, the **legislative branch,** would create the laws.

The Virginia Plan wanted the legislature to have two sections: an Upper House and a Lower House. In both houses, the number of representatives

COMPARING *Plans for Government*

	VIRGINIA PLAN	NEW JERSEY PLAN
Legislative branch	Two (branches) houses: representation determined by state population or wealth	One house: one vote for each state, regardless of size
	Lower House: elected by the people Upper House: elected by lower house	Elected by state legislatures
Executive branch	Appointed by Legislature	Appointed by Legislature
Judicial branch	Appointed by Legislature	Appointed by Executive

CRITICAL THINKING Analyze Which plan appealed more to the smaller states?

from each state would be based on the state's population or its wealth. The legislature would have the power to make laws "in all cases to which the separate states are incompetent [unable]."

As well as having its own distinct powers, each branch could check the powers of the other branches in certain circumstances. This system of "**checks and balances**" is a way of controlling the power of government. As James Madison said, "All power in human hands is liable to be abused." The Founders designed the new government to limit that abuse.

Delegates from the small states strongly objected to the Virginia Plan because it gave more power to states with larger populations. In response to the Virginia Plan, New Jersey delegate William Paterson presented an alternative. Like the Articles, the **New Jersey Plan** called for a single-house congress in which each state had an equal vote. Small states supported the New Jersey Plan.

The Great Compromise Emotions ran high as the delegates struggled to solve the problem of representation in the legislature. In early July, a committee led by Roger Sherman and other delegates from Connecticut offered a deal known as the **Great Compromise**. Sherman proposed:

PRIMARY SOURCE

❝ That the proportion of suffrage in the first branch should be according to the respective numbers of free inhabitants, and that in the second branch or Senate, each State should have one vote and no more. ❞

—Roger Sherman, June 11, 1787

In other words, to satisfy the smaller states, each state would have an equal number of votes in the Senate. To satisfy the larger states, representation in the House of Representatives was set according to state populations. On July 16, 1787, the convention passed the plan.

🔺 **PROBLEMS AND SOLUTIONS** Describe the major challenges of the Convention in creating a stronger national government.

Challenges Over Slavery

🔻 **KEY QUESTION** How did the Constitutional Convention compromise over slavery?

Because representation in the House of Representatives would be based on the population of each state, the delegates had to decide who would be counted in that population. For example, were slaves to be counted as part of the population?

Slave Population 1790

Number of Slaves
300,000
100,000
25,000
10,000
1,000
100

Connect Geography & History

1. **Place** Which state would have the greatest interest in having slaves counted as part of their population for purposes of representation?
2. **Clarify** Why did the North and the South have differing opinions on whether or not slaves should be counted as part of a state's population?

The Three-Fifths Compromise Representation based on population raised the question of whether slaves should be counted as people. The Southern states had many more slaves than the Northern states. Southerners wanted the slaves to be counted as part of the population for representation but not for taxation. Northerners, whose states had few slaves, argued that slaves were not citizens and should not be counted for representation but should be counted for taxation.

The delegates reached an agreement, known as the **Three-Fifths Compromise**. Three-fifths of the slave population would be counted for both purposes: representation in the legislature and taxation.

The delegates had another point of disagreement. Slavery had already been outlawed in several Northern states. Many Northerners wanted to see this ban extended to the rest of the nation. But Southern slaveholders disagreed. The delegates from South Carolina and Georgia stated that they would never accept any plan "unless their right to import slaves be untouched." Again, the delegates settled on a compromise. On August 29, they agreed that Congress could not ban the slave trade until 1808.

On September 17, 1787, the delegates passed the Constitution. All but three of the 42 delegates present signed the Constitution. It was then sent to each state for approval.

 ANALYZE POINT OF VIEW Explain how the Constitutional Convention compromised on the issue of slavery.

Connecting History

Individual Rights vs. Majority Rule
Congress decided to end the importation of Africans after 1808. However, the slave trade continued in the slave states.

 Illinois Learning Standards *Review*

ONLINE QUIZ
For test practice, go to
Interactive Review @ ClassZone.com

TERMS & NAMES

1. Explain the importance of

- Constitutional Convention
- Founders
- James Madison
- legislative branch
- Virginia Plan
- checks and balances
- New Jersey Plan
- Great Compromise
- executive branch
- judicial branch
- Three-Fifths Compromise

USING YOUR READING NOTES

2. Summarize Summarize the important achievements of the Constitution.

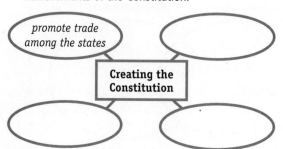

promote trade among the states

Creating the Constitution

KEY IDEAS

3. What was the relationship between the Annapolis Convention and the Constitutional Convention?

4. Why did the Virginia delegates insist that the new government have three branches?

5. Under the Three-Fifths Compromise, how would each state's population be decided?

CRITICAL THINKING

6. Analyze Point of View Why did supporters of the Virginia Plan believe their plan was the best way to create a new government?

7. **Connect** *to* **Today** What American political traditions can be traced back to the Constitutional Convention?

8. **Art** Think about the Three-Fifths Compromise. Draw a political cartoon that expresses your views on the issue.

▶ Key Ideas

BEFORE, YOU LEARNED
The Constitution created a new, stronger government that replaced the Confederation.

NOW YOU WILL LEARN
American liberties are protected by the U.S. Constitution and a Bill of Rights.

▶ Vocabulary

TERMS & NAMES

Antifederalists people who opposed ratification of the Constitution

federalism system of government in which power is shared between the national (or federal) government and the states

Federalists people who supported ratification of the Constitution

The Federalist **papers** ratification essays published in New York newspapers

Bill of Rights first ten amendments to the U.S. Constitution

BACKGROUND VOCABULARY

majority rule a system in which more than one half of a group holds the power to make decisions binding the entire group

amendment addition to a document

REVIEW

Parliament Britain's chief lawmaking body

Enlightenment 18th-century movement that emphasized the use of reason and the scientific method to obtain knowledge

▶ Reading Strategy

Re-create the diagram shown at right. As you read and respond to the **KEY QUESTIONS,** use the circles to compare the positions of Federalists and Antifederalists.

 See Skillbuilder Handbook, page R8.

COMPARE AND CONTRAST

Federalists   Antifederalists

both

🔗 **GRAPHIC ORGANIZERS**
Go to **Interactive Review** @ ClassZone.com

Ratification and the Bill of Rights

14.F.3a Analyze historical influences on the development of political ideas and practices as enumerated in the Declaration of Independence, the United States Constitution, the Bill of Rights and the Illinois Constitution.
14.F.3b Describe how United States political ideas and traditions were instituted in the Constitution and the Bill of Rights.

One American's Story

In February of 1788, **Antifederalists**, people who opposed the Constitution, sent out a pamphlet voicing their concerns over the form of the new government. The title of the essay was "Observations on the New Constitution, and on the Federal and State Conventions." To the surprise of many people, a woman, Mercy Otis Warren, was responsible for the pamphlet. The pamphlet stressed the importance of a democratic nation ruled by the people.

PRIMARY SOURCE

❝ Government is instituted for the protection, safety and happiness of the people. . . . That the origin of all power is in the people, and that they have an [incontestable] right to check the creatures of their own creation, vested with certain powers to guard the life, liberty and property of the community. ❞

—Mercy Otis Warren, quoted in *Mercy Otis Warren*

Mercy Otis Warren was an Antifederalist and a respected historian of the American Revolution.

Warren's essay became an important part of the debate between supporters and opposers of the Constitution.

Federalists and Antifederalists

▼ **KEY QUESTION** What key issues divided Federalists and Antifederalists?

By the time Warren's essay was published, Americans had already been debating the new Constitution for months. The document had been widely distributed in newspapers and pamphlets across the country. The framers of the Constitution knew that the document would cause controversy. At once they began to campaign for ratification, or approval, of the Constitution.

Concerns of the Federalists The framers suspected that people might be afraid the Constitution would take too much power away from the states. To address this fear, the framers explained that the Constitution was based on federalism. **Federalism** is a system of government in which power is shared between the central (or federal) government and the states. Linking themselves to the idea of federalism, the people who supported the Constitution took the name **Federalists**.

The Federalists promoted their views and answered their critics in a series of essays, known as *The Federalist* **papers**. Three well-known politicians wrote *The Federalist* papers—James Madison, Alexander Hamilton, and John Jay. These essays first appeared as letters in New York newspapers. Calling for ratification of the Constitution, *The Federalist* papers appealed both to reason and emotion. In *The Federalist* papers, Hamilton described why people should support ratification.

PRIMARY SOURCE

❝ Yes, my countrymen, . . . I am clearly of opinion it is your interest to adopt it [the Constitution]. I am convinced that this is the safest course for your liberty, your dignity, and your happiness. ❞

—Alexander Hamilton, *The Federalist* "Number 1"

ONLINE PRIMARY SOURCE

Hear the debate at the **Research & Writing Center** @ ClassZone.com

COMPARING *Perspectives*

Federalists and Antifederalists had very different ideas about how the United States should be governed. These were some of the arguments made as Americans passionately debated ratification of the Constitution.

◀ Antifederalists

❝ Your president may easily become king: Your Senate is so imperfectly constructed that your dearest rights may be sacrificed by what may be a small minority; and a very small minority may continue for ever unchangeably this government, although horridly defective. Where are your checks in this government?

—*Patrick Henry*

The mode of levying taxes is of the utmost consequence; and yet here it is to be determined by those who have neither knowledge of our situation, nor a common interest with us. ❞

—*George Mason*

◀ Federalists

❝ I am persuaded that a firm union is as necessary to perpetuate our liberties as it is to make us respectable; and experience will probably prove that the national government will be as natural a guardian of our freedom as the state legislature[s] themselves.

—*Alexander Hamilton*

As all the States are equally represented in the Senate, and by men the most able and the most willing to promote the interests of their constituents, they will all have an equal degree of influence in that body. ❞

—*John Jay*

Patrick Henry

John Jay

CRITICAL THINKING Analyze What was it about a strong federal government that frightened the Antifederalists?

Concerns of the Antifederalists The Antifederalists thought the Constitution took too much power away from the states and did not guarantee rights for the people. Some feared that a strong president might be declared king. Others feared the Senate might become a powerful ruling class. In either case, they thought, the liberties fiercely won during the Revolution might be lost.

Antifederalists received support from rural areas, where people feared a strong government that might add to their tax burden. Large states and those with strong economies, such as New York, which had greater freedom under the Articles of Confederation, also were unsupportive of the Constitution at first.

New Yorkers cheer a "Ship of State" float in honor of the new Constitution of 1798. **Why did Alexander Hamilton deserve a float in his honor?**

▲ **COMPARE AND CONTRAST** Describe the disagreements between Federalists and Antifederalists.

The Battle for Ratification

▼ **KEY QUESTION** How did the lack of a bill of rights endanger the Constitution?

The proposed U.S. Constitution contained no guarantee that the government would protect the rights of the people, or of the states. Some supporters of the Constitution, including Thomas Jefferson, wanted to add a bill of rights—a formal summary of citizens' rights and freedoms, as a set of amendments to the Constitution.

The Call for a Bill of Rights Virginia's convention opened in June of 1788. Antifederalist Patrick Henry fought against ratification, or approval, of the Constitution. George Mason, who had been a delegate to the Constitutional Convention in Philadelphia, also was opposed to it.

Antifederalists wanted written guarantees that the people would have freedom of speech, of the press, and of religion. They demanded assurance of the right to trial by jury and the right to bear arms.

Federalists insisted that the Constitution granted only limited powers to the national government so that it could not violate the rights of the states or of the people. They also pointed out that the Constitution gave the people the power to protect their rights through the election of trustworthy leaders. In the end, Federalists yielded to the people's demands and promised to add a bill of rights if the states ratified the Constitution.

Final Ratification In December 1787, Delaware, New Jersey, and Pennsylvania voted for ratification. In January 1788, Georgia and Connecticut ratified the Constitution, followed by Massachusetts in early February. By late June, nine states had ratified. The Constitution was officially ratified with nine votes. It was vital, however, to get the support of Virginia, the largest state, and New York. Without New York, the nation would be split geographically into two parts. James Madison recommended that Virginia ratify the Constitution, with the addition of a bill of rights.

As other states ratified, however, the Virginia Antifederalists played on Southern fear of Northern domination. Under the Articles of Confederation, each state had one vote, and major decisions required the approval of nine of the 13 states. The Constitution, however, provided for **majority rule**, which means that more than one half of a group holds the power to make decisions binding on the entire group. The North, Virginia Antifederalists warned, would then dictate policy in trade, slavery, and other important issues bearing on the southern economy.

After bitter debate, at the end of June, Virginia narrowly ratified the Constitution with 89 in favor and 79 opposed. The news of Virginia's vote arrived while the New York convention was in debate. Until then, the Antifederalists had outnumbered the Federalists. But with Virginia's ratification, New Yorkers decided to join the Union. New York also called for a bill of rights.

It would be another year before North Carolina ratified the Constitution, followed by Rhode Island in 1790. By then, the new Congress had already written a bill of rights and submitted it to the states for approval.

EVALUATE Explain how the lack of a bill of rights made ratification of the Constitution more difficult.

CONNECT ⟳ *Citizenship and History*

DEBATE AND FREE SPEECH

To debate is to engage in argument by discussing opposing points of view. Debate has long been an important method of exploring public issues. The Founding Fathers engaged in intense debate before the ratification of the U.S. Constitution.

Today, many students learn about the ideas of democracy through programs like the YMCA Youth in Government program. Most of these programs consist of a model legislature composed of high school students writing legislation. Participants then meet to debate their proposed laws in their actual state capitol building.

Activity

Organize a Debate!

1. Choose a debate opponent and an issue to debate. Research the topic you chose.
2. Agree on a format for your debate—presentation, rebuttal, and closing.
3. Debate your opponent in front of the class. Ask the audience to cast their votes; then report the result to the class.

See Citizenship Handbook, page 300.

How did Americans create a national government that respected both the independence of states and the rights of individuals?

	CONFEDERATION WEAKNESSES	NEW GOVERNMENT STRENGTHS
Taxes	Congress could not levy or collect taxes.	Congress empowered to levy and collect taxes
Trade	Congress could not regulate trade carried on between states or with foreign nations.	Congress empowered to regulate interstate and foreign commerce
Courts	No regular Confederation courts; Congress depended on state courts to settle legal disputes arising from its laws.	A national system of courts set up with district and circuit courts and a supreme court
Executive	No national executive branch; enforcement of acts of Congress left to the states.	National government had the power to enforce federal laws.
States' Rights	Equality of states in voting, regardless of size or population	Proportional representation in the House; equality of states in the Senate.
Amendments	Unanimous vote required to amend Articles	Two-thirds vote in each House of Congress
Laws	Nine states had to approve an ordinary bill.	A majority required to pass a bill

CRITICAL THINKING Evaluate How were states' rights protected under the new government?

The Bill of Rights and the Constitution

▼ **KEY QUESTION** How does the Bill of Rights protect people's rights?

Madison, who took office in the first Congress in the winter of 1789, took up the cause of the bill of rights. Madison submitted ten **amendments**, or additions to a document, to the Constitution. Congress proposed that they be placed at the end of the Constitution in a separate section. These ten amendments to the U.S. Constitution became known as the **Bill of Rights.**

The Bill of Rights Of these amendments to the Constitution, the first nine guarantee basic individual freedoms. Jefferson and Madison believed that government enforcement of religious laws was the source of much social conflict. They supported freedom of religion as a way to prevent such conflict. Even before Madison wrote the Bill of Rights, he worked to ensure religious liberty in Virginia. (In 1786, Madison had helped pass the Virginia Statute for Religious Freedom, originally written by Jefferson in 1779.)

Freedom of religion is an important part of the First Amendment, which states: "Congress shall make no law respecting an establishment of religion, or prohibiting the free exercise thereof . . ." This means that the government may never support one particular religion, favor one faith above another, or interfere with anyone's religious freedom.

In this way, the Constitution put an end to the kind of religious conflict that had divided the early colonies. In the words of Thomas Jefferson, the first amendment built "a wall of separation between Church and State." Taken as a whole, the Bill of Rights creates an invisible but powerful shield that protects people from government abuse.

Amending the Constitution But the Bill of Rights was more than that. It was the first step in making the Constitution a living document, one that can be amended to reflect the changes in society. The Constitutional Convention provided for such changes. Two-thirds of each house of Congress or two-thirds of the state legislatures can propose an amendment. To become law, an amendment then needs the approval of three-fourths of the states. By this process, the Bill of Rights became the first ten amendments. Since then seventeen more amendments have been added to the Constitution.

 SUMMARIZE Explain how the Bill of Rights ensures American freedoms.

TERMS & NAMES

1. Explain the importance of
   - Antifederalists
   - *The Federalist* papers
   - federalism
   - Bill of Rights
   - Federalists

USING YOUR READING NOTES

2. **Compare & Contrast** Complete the diagram you started at the beginning of this section.

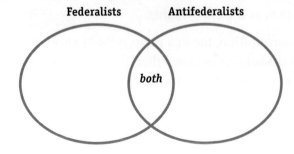

Federalists   Antifederalists

both

KEY IDEAS

3. What arguments did the Federalists use to convince people to support the Constitution? What arguments did the Antifederalists use against them?

4. Why was ratification of the Constitution in Virginia and New York especially important?

5. What did the framers of the Constitution do to prevent religious conflict?

CRITICAL THINKING

6. **Compare & Contrast** How was the battle over ratification similar to the conflicts among the states over the writing of the Constitution?

7. **Analyze Point of View** Why did the Antifederalists demand the Bill of Rights?

8. **Language Arts** Review the major arguments for and against ratification of the Constitution. Hold a press conference or write a news report on the ratification debate.

The Federalist "Number 51"

SETTING THE STAGE James Madison wrote 29 essays in *The Federalist* papers to argue in favor of ratifying the Constitution. In *The Federalist* "Number 51," Madison explains how the government set up by the Constitution will protect the rights of the people by weakening the power of any interest, or group, to dominate the government.

It is of great importance in a republic not only to guard the society against the oppression of its rulers, but to guard one part of the society against the injustice of the other part. Different interests necessarily exist in different classes of citizens. If a majority be united by a common interest, the rights of the minority will be insecure. There are but two methods of providing against this evil: the one by creating a will in the community independent of the majority—that is, of the society itself; the other, by **comprehending**[1] in the society so many separate descriptions of citizens as will render an unjust combination of a majority of the whole very improbable, if not **impracticable.**[2] . . .

Whilst[3] all authority in it will be derived from and dependent on the society, the society itself will be broken into so many parts, interests and classes of citizens, that the rights of individuals, or of the minority, will be in little danger from interested combinations of the majority. In a free government the security for civil rights must be the same as that for religious rights. It consists in the one case in the multiplicity of interests, and in the other in the multiplicity of **sects.**[4] . . .

In the extended republic of the United States, and among the great variety of interests, parties, and sects which it embraces, a **coalition**[5] of a majority of the whole society could seldom take place on any other principles than those of justice and the general good. . . .

It is no less certain than it is important . . . that the larger the society, provided it lie within a practicable sphere, the more duly capable it will be of self-government. And happily for the republican cause, the practicable sphere may be carried to a very great extent by a judicious **modification**[6] and mixture of the *federal principle*.

----

1. **comprehending:** understanding.
2. **impracticable:** not practical or realistic.
3. **whilst:** while.
4. **multiplicity of sects:** large number of groups.
5. **coalition:** alliance of groups.
6. **judicious modification:** careful change.

Minority Rights

In the 1700s, people feared that democratic majorities could turn into mobs that would violate other people's rights. Madison had to explain how the Constitution would prevent this.

1. What two methods does Madison suggest a society can use to protect minority rights?

Large Republics

For centuries, people believed that only small societies could be republics. But Madison argues that large societies are more likely to remain republics.

2. Why does Madison believe that a large republic is likely to protect justice?

Objections to the Constitution

SETTING THE STAGE George Mason was one of the leading Antifederalists. In "Objections to the Constitution of Government Formed by the Convention," he listed his reasons for opposing ratification. Above all, he feared that the Constitution created a government that would destroy democracy in the young nation.

Declaration Of Rights

At the time of the ratification debate, Americans across the nation complained that the Constitution did not include a bill of rights.

3. What arguments does Mason make about the lack of a Declaration of Rights?

Abuse Of Power

Mason believed that presidents might abuse the power to grant pardons for treason in order to protect the guilty.

4. What reasons might favor a presidential power to pardon?

There is no Declaration of Rights; and the Laws of the general Government being **paramount**[1] to the Laws and Constitutions of the several States, the Declaration of Rights in the separate states are no Security. Nor are the people secured even in the Enjoyment of the Benefits of the common-Law. . . .

In the House of Representatives, there is not the Substance, but the Shadow only of Representation; which can never produce proper Information in the Legislature, or inspire Confidence in the People; the Laws will therefore be generally made by Men little concern'd in, and **unacquainted**[2] with their Effects and Consequences.

The Senate have the Power of altering all Money-Bills and of originating Appropriations of Money and the **Sallerys**'[3] of the Officers of their own Appointment in **Conjunction**[4] with the President of the United States; altho' they are not the Representatives of the People, or **amenable**[5] to them. . . .

The President of the United States has the unrestrained Power of granting Pardon for Treason; which may be sometimes exercised to screen from Punishment those whom he had secretly **instigated**[6] to commit the Crime, and thereby prevent a Discovery of his own Guilt.

This government will **commence**[7] in a moderate **Aristocracy**;[8] it is at present impossible to foresee whether it will, in (its) Operation, produce a **Monarchy**[9] or a corrupt oppressive Aristocracy; it will most probably vibrate some Years between the two, and then terminate in the one or the other.

—George Mason

- -

1. **paramount:** most important.
2. **unacquainted:** unfamiliar.
3. **sallerys:** salaries.
4. **conjunction:** joining.
5. **amenable:** agreeable.
6. **instigated:** caused.
7. **commence:** begin.
8. **aristocracy:** rule by a few, usually nobles.
9. **monarchy:** rule by one, usually a king.

DOCUMENT-BASED QUESTIONS

Short Answer

1. Why does Madison believe that a fragmented society will not endanger minority rights?

2. What does Mason argue might happen if the president had the power to pardon people?

Extended Answer

3. Compare how each writer supports his opinions with facts.

Chapter Summary

1 Key Idea
The Articles of Confederation created a weak national government.

2 Key Idea
The Constitution created a new, stronger government that replaced the Confederation.

3 Key Idea
American liberties are protected by the U.S. Constitution and a Bill of Rights.

For detailed Review and Study Notes go to **Interactive Review** @ ClassZone.com

Name Game

Use the Terms & Names list to complete each sentence online or on your own paper.

1. The first government of the United States was established by the ⌐Articles of Confederation⌐

2. A group known as _____ opposed ratification of the Constitution.

3. Angered by new taxes, farmers attacked the courts in Massachusetts during _____

4. In a _____, the people elect representatives to govern them.

5. State representation in the House and Congress was determined by the _____

6. The _____ established law in the Northwest Territory.

7. _____ was the primary author of the Virginia Plan.

8. The Constitution was created at the _____ in 1787.

9. The _____ interprets the law.

10. The first ten amendments of the Constitution are known as the _____

A. New Jersey Plan
B. Constitutional Convention
C. Republic
D. Articles of Confederation
E. Legislative Branch
F. Shays's Rebellion
G. Antifederalists
H. James Madison
I. Northwest Ordinance
J. Judicial Branch
L. Land Ordinance of 1785
M. Founders
N. Bill of Rights
O. Great Compromise
P. Federalist Papers

Activities

CROSSWORD PUZZLE

Complete the online crossword puzzle to show what you know about the Constitution.

ACROSS
1. _____ is known as "Father of the Constitution."

GEOGAME

Use this online map to reinforce your knowledge of the Confederation Era, including the locations of important cities and events. Drag and drop each name in the list at its location on the map. A scorecard helps you keep track online.

Constitutional Convention

Shays's Rebellion

Northwest Territory

Confederation Congress

The Federalist papers published here

More items online

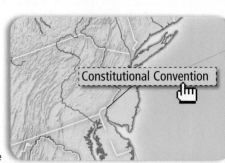

Constitutional Convention

VOCABULARY

Explain the significance of each of the following.

1. Shays's Rebellion
2. Great Compromise
3. Constitutional Convention
4. Bill of Rights
5. James Madison
6. Northwest Ordinance
7. Founders
8. Three-Fifths Compromise
9. Articles of Confederation
10. Confederation Congress

Explain how the terms and names in each group are related.

11. ratification, amendment
12. Virginia Plan, New Jersey Plan
13. Confederation Congress, Land Ordinance of 1785
14. Federalists, Antifederalists

KEY IDEAS

1 The Confederation Era (pages 234–239)

15. What problems did the Continental Congress successfully address?

16. How did Shays's Rebellion affect people's views on the Articles of Confederation?

2 Creating the Constitution (pages 242–247)

17. What groups of people were not represented at the Constitutional Convention?

18. What compromises did the delegates make during the convention?

3 Ratifying the Constitution (pages 248–254)

19. Why were Virginia and New York important in the battle for ratification of the Constitution?

20. Why did some states think that it was necessary to add a bill of rights to the Constitution?

CRITICAL THINKING

21. **Causes and Effects** How did America's history as a British colony cause the Confederation to fail?

22. **Evaluate** Why is the Northwest Ordinance sometimes called the Confederation Congress's only success?

23. **Problems & Solutions** Create a chart to identify the specific problems faced by the new nation, and the solutions it tried.

Problem	Solution
Western lands	Northwest Ordinance, 1787
Postwar depression	
Representation in the new government	

24. **Compare and Contrast** How do the Articles of Confederation and the Constitution each carry out democratic ideals?

25. **Evaluate** How did the Antifederalists have an impact on the Constitution?

26. **Interpret Maps** In which states did the Federalists have statewide majorities?

Ratification in Middle States *1790*

- Federalist majority
- Anti-federalist majority
- Evenly divided
- Sparsely populated

NEW YORK

PENNSYLVANIA

NEW JERSEY

DELAWARE

DOCUMENT-BASED QUESTIONS

PART 1: Short Answer

Study each document carefully and answer the questions that follow.

DOCUMENT 1

THE CONSTITUTIONAL CONVENTION · 1787

1. Examine the mural that shows (left to right) Hamilton, James Wilson, Madison, and Franklin at the Constitutional Convention. What does the art tell you about the type of delegates who attended?

DOCUMENT 2

PRIMARY SOURCE

❝ I like much the general idea of framing a government which should go on of itself . . . [but] I do not like. . . . First, the omission of a bill of rights. . . . Let me add that a bill of rights is what the people are entitled to against every government on earth, general or particular; and what no just government should refuse. . . ❞

—Thomas Jefferson, December 20, 1787

2. Is Jefferson stating the Federalist or Antifederalist point of view?

PART 2: Essay

3. Using information from the documents, your answers to the questions in Part 1, and your knowledge of U.S. history, write an essay that explains the events leading to the ratification of the Bill of Rights.

YOU BE THE HISTORIAN

27. **Make Decisions** How might the United States have developed if the Articles of Confederation had continued to provide the basis for government?

28. **Draw Conclusions** In what ways was the land of the Northwest Territory distributed democratically?

29. **Connect Economics & History** How did the Three-Fifths Compromise satisfy both North and South?

30. **Compare & Contrast** Consider the two groups that rebelled against the government: farmers and Revolutionary War veterans. Compare what life was probably like for these people as opposed to what life might have been like for the Founders.

31. **Connect _to_ Today** How does the Constitution give Americans a voice in their national government?

 Answer the
ESSENTIAL QUESTION

How did Americans create a strong national government that respected both the rights of states and the rights of individuals?

Written Response Write a two-to-three-paragraph response to the Essential Question. Be sure to consider the key ideas of each section as well as the ideals that Americans value today. Use the Response rubric to guide your thinking and writing.

Response Rubric
A strong response will
• discuss the values and ideals of modern America
• analyze the post-revolutionary events and conflicts out of which these ideals emerged
• explain the unique nature of the American constitution

The Living Constitution

The Framers of the Constitution created a flexible plan for governing the United States far into the future. They also described ways to allow changes in the Constitution. For over 200 years, the Constitution has guided the American people. It remains a "living document." The Constitution still thrives, in part, because it echoes the principles the delegates valued. Each generation of Americans renews the meaning of the Constitution's timeless ideas. These two pages show you some ways in which the Constitution has shaped events in American history.

> ❝ In framing a system which we wish to last for ages, we should not lose sight of the changes which ages will produce. ❞
>
> —James Madison, Constitutional Convention

1787
Delegates in Philadelphia
sign the Constitution.

1963
Reverend Dr. Martin Luther King, Jr. addresses demonstrators at the civil rights march on Washington in August 1963.

1971

The 26th Amendment to the Constitution gives young people "18 years of age or older" the right to vote. Here, the Voters Project encourages young people to register and vote.

1981

A Supreme Court decision rules that Congress can exclude women from the draft. In the early 2000s, there were 215,243 women in the U.S. military.

MR. ASHCROFT, IT'S THE NATIONAL ARCHIVES HERE ··· PLEASE RETURN THE CONSTITUTION AND BILL OF RIGHTS YOU CHECKED OUT ···

~ RIGHT···
WAY
PAST
DUE···

2002

Attorney General John Ashcroft's positions on privacy and civil liberties issues made him a controversial figure in the George W. Bush cabinet. Ashcroft was a key supporter of the passage of the USA Patriot act. The act, which was dubbed the "anti-terrorism" act, drew fire from both liberals and conservatives. Critics of the act said it endangered the basic freedoms guaranteed under the U.S. Constitution.

Seven Principles of the Constitution

The Framers of the Constitution constructed a new system of government. Seven principles supported their efforts. To picture how these principles work, imagine seven building blocks. Together they form the foundation of the United States Constitution. In the pages that follow, you will find the definitions and main ideas of the principles shown in the graphic below.

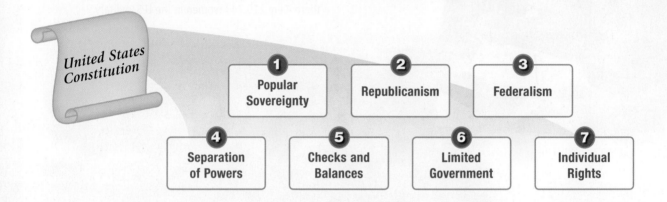

United States Constitution

1 **Popular Sovereignty**

2 **Republicanism**

3 **Federalism**

4 **Separation of Powers**

5 **Checks and Balances**

6 **Limited Government**

7 **Individual Rights**

1 Popular Sovereignty
Who Gives the Government Its Power?

"We the people of the United States . . . establish this Constitution for the United States of America." These words from the Preamble, or introduction, to the Constitution clearly spell out the source of the government's power. The Constitution rests on the idea of **popular sovereignty**—a government in which the people rule. As the nation changed and grew, popular sovereignty took on new meaning. A broader range of Americans shared in the power to govern themselves.

In 1987, Americans gathered in Washington, D.C. to celebrate the 200th anniversary of the Constitution.

② Republicanism
How Are People's Views Represented in Government?

The Framers of the Constitution wanted the people to have a voice in government. Yet the Framers also feared that public opinion might stand in the way of sound decision making. To solve this problem, they looked to **republicanism** as a model of government.

Republicanism is based on this belief: The people exercise their power by voting for their political representatives. According to the Framers, these lawmakers played the key role in making a republican government work. Article 4, Section 4, of the Constitution also calls for every state to have a "republican form of government."

Senator Barack Obama, Democrat of Illinois, addresses a 2005 town meeting in Carrollton, IL.

③ Federalism
How Is Power Shared?

The Framers wanted the states and the nation to become partners in governing. To build cooperation, the Framers turned to federalism. **Federalism** is a system of government in which power is divided between a central government and smaller political units, such as states. Before the Civil War, federalism in the United States was closely related to dual sovereignty, the idea that the federal government and the states each had exclusive power over their own spheres.

The Framers used federalism to structure the Constitution. The Constitution assigns certain powers to the national government. These are delegated powers. Powers kept by the states are reserved powers. Powers shared or exercised by national and state governments are known as concurrent powers.

Federalism

Powers delegated to the **NATIONAL GOVERNMENT**

Shared (concurrent) Powers

Powers reserved for the **STATE GOVERNMENTS**

The overlapping spheres of power bind the American people together.

❹ Separation of Powers
How Is Power Divided?

The Framers were concerned that too much power might fall into the hands of a single group. To avoid this problem, they built the idea of **separation of powers** into the Constitution. This principle means the division of basic government roles into branches. No one branch is given all the power. Articles 1, 2, and 3 of the Constitution detail how powers are split among the three branches.

Separation of Powers

Article 1	Article 2	Article 3
LEGISLATIVE BRANCH Congress makes laws.	**EXECUTIVE BRANCH** President enforces the law.	**JUDICIAL BRANCH** Supreme Court interprets the law.

❺ Checks and Balances
How Is Power Evenly Distributed?

Baron de Montesquieu, an 18th-century French thinker, wrote, "power should be a check to power." His comment refers to the principle of **checks and balances**. Each branch of government can exercise checks, or controls, over the other branches. Though the branches of government are separate, they rely on one another to perform the work of government.

The Framers included a system of checks and balances in the Constitution to help make sure that the branches work together fairly. For example, only Congress can pass laws. Yet the president can check this power by refusing to sign a law into action. In turn, the Supreme Court can declare that a law, passed by Congress and signed by the president, violates the Constitution.

Checks and Balances

EXECUTIVE BRANCH

JUDICIAL BRANCH

LEGISLATIVE BRANCH

Checks on President

Checks on Courts

Checks on President

Checks on Congress

Checks on Congress

Checks on Courts

6 Limited Government
How Is Abuse of Power Prevented?

The Framers restricted the power of government. Article 1, Section 9, of the Constitution lists the powers denied to the Congress. Article 1, Section 10, forbids the states to take certain actions.

The principle of **limited government** is also closely related to the "rule of law": In the American government everyone, citizens and powerful leaders alike, must obey the law. Individuals or groups cannot twist or bypass the law to serve their own interests.

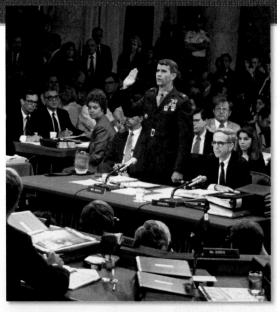

In mid-1987, Congress conducted a dramatic inquiry into the Iran-Contra affair. (*above*) Lieutenant Colonel Oliver North testifies before the hearings. North was found guilty of taking part in a cover-up.

7 Individual Rights
How Are Personal Freedoms Protected?

The first ten amendments to the Constitution shield people from an overly powerful government. These amendments are called the Bill of Rights. The Bill of Rights guarantees certain **individual rights**, or personal liberties and privileges. For example, government cannot control what people write or say. People also have the right to meet peacefully and to ask the government to correct a problem. Later amendments to the Constitution also advanced the cause of individual rights.

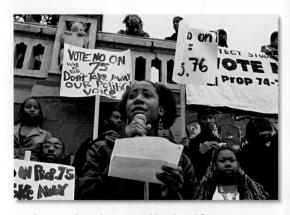

Students and teachers in Oakland, California, protest measures proposed in the 2005 election.

Seven Principles of the Constitution Assessment

MAIN IDEAS

1. What are the seven principles of government?
2. How does the Constitution reflect the principle of separation of powers?
3. Why did the Framers include a system of checks and balances in the Constitution?

CRITICAL THINKING

4. **Form Opinions** How do the rights and responsibilities of U.S. citizenship reflect American national identity?

Think about

• what it means to be an American
• the rights and responsibilities of U.S. citizens

The Constitution of the United States

⭐ ESSENTIAL QUESTION

How has our 220-year-old Constitution remained a living document?

Visitors hear a lecture on the Constitution at the National Archives Building, which also houses the Declaration of Independence and the Bill of Rights.

PREAMBLE. Purpose of the Constitution

We the people of the United States, in order to form a more perfect Union, establish justice, insure domestic tranquility, provide for the common defense, promote the general welfare, and secure the blessings of liberty to ourselves and our posterity, do ordain and establish this Constitution for the United States of America.

Goals of the Preamble

Preamble	Explanation	Examples
"Form a more perfect Union"	Create a nation in which states work together	• Interstate road network • U.S. coins, paper money
"Establish justice"	Make laws and set up courts that are fair	• Court system • Jury system
"Insure domestic tranquility"	Keep peace within the country	• National Guard • Federal marshals
"Provide for the common defense"	Safeguard the country against attack	• Army • Navy
"Promote the general welfare"	Contribute to the happiness and well-being of all the people	• Safety in the workplace • Aid to the poor
"Secure the blessings of liberty to ourselves and our posterity"	Make sure future citizens remain free	• Commission on Civil Rights • Federal Election Commission

CRITICAL THINKING

1. Which goal of the preamble do you think is most important? Why?
2. How does the preamble reflect the principle of popular sovereignty?

ARTICLE 1. The Legislature

▼ **KEY QUESTION** What is the main role of the legislative branch?

SECTION 1. Congress

All legislative powers herein granted shall be vested in a Congress of the United States, which shall consist of a Senate and House of Representatives.

SECTION 2. The House of Representatives

1. Elections The House of Representatives shall be composed of members chosen every second year by the people of the several states, and the **electors** in each state shall have the qualifications requisite for electors of the most numerous branch of the state legislature.

2. Qualifications No person shall be a Representative who shall not have attained to the age of twenty-five years, and been seven years a citizen of the United States, and who shall not, when elected, be an inhabitant of that state in which he shall be chosen.

3. Number of Representatives Representatives and direct taxes shall be apportioned among the several states which may be included within this Union, according to their respective numbers, which shall be determined by adding to the whole number of free persons, including those bound to service for a term of years, and excluding Indians not taxed, three-fifths of all other Persons. The actual **enumeration** shall be made within three years after the first meeting of the Congress of the United States, and within every subsequent term of ten years, in such manner as they shall by law direct. The number of Representatives shall not exceed one for every thirty thousand, but each state shall have at least one Representative; and until such enumeration shall be made, the state of New Hampshire shall be entitled to choose three, Massachusetts eight, Rhode Island and Providence Plantations one, Connecticut five, New York six, New Jersey four, Pennsylvania eight, Delaware one, Maryland six, Virginia ten, North Carolina five, South Carolina five, and Georgia three.

4. Vacancies When vacancies happen in the representation from any state, the executive authority thereof shall issue writs of election to fill such vacancies.

5. Officers and Impeachment The House of Representatives shall choose their Speaker and other officers; and shall have the sole power of **impeachment**.

SECTION 3. Congress

1. Numbers The Senate of the United States shall be composed of two Senators from each state, chosen by the legislature thereof, for six years; and each Senator shall have one vote.

BACKGROUND VOCABULARY

electors voters

enumeration an official count, such as a census

impeachment the process of accusing a public official of wrongdoing

Elections

Representatives are elected every two years. There are no limits on the number of terms a person can serve.

1. What do you think are the advantages of holding frequent elections of representatives?

Representation

Some delegates, such as Gouverneur Morris (*above*), thought that representation should be based on wealth as well as population. Others, such as James Wilson, thought representation should be based on population only. Ultimately, the delegates voted against including wealth as a basis for apportioning representatives.

2. How do you think the United States would be different today if representation were based on wealth?

2. Classifying Terms Immediately after they shall be assembled in consequence of the first election, they shall be divided as equally as may be into three classes. The seats of the Senators of the first class shall be vacated at the expiration of the second year, of the second class at the expiration of the fourth year, and of the third class at the expiration of the sixth year, so that one-third may be chosen every second year; ~~and if vacancies happen by resignation, or otherwise, during the recess of the legislature of any state, the executive thereof may make temporary appointments until the next meeting of the legislature, which shall then fill such vacancies.~~

3. Qualifications No person shall be a Senator who shall not have attained to the age of thirty years, and been nine years a citizen of the United States, and who shall not, when elected, be an inhabitant of that state for which he shall be chosen.

COMPARING Federal Office Terms and Requirements

Position	Term	Minimum Age	Residency	Citizenship
Representative	2 years	25	state in which elected	7 years
Senator	6 years	30	state in which elected	9 years
President	4 years	35	14 years in the U.S.	natural-born
Supreme Court Justice	unlimited	none	none	none

CRITICAL THINKING Why do you think the term and qualifications for a senator are more demanding than for a representative?

Impeachment

The House brings charges against the president. The Senate acts as the jury. The Chief Justice of the Supreme Court presides over the hearings.

3. How many presidents have been impeached?

4. Role of Vice President The Vice President of the United States shall be President of the Senate, but shall have no vote, unless they be equally divided.

5. Officers The Senate shall choose their other officers, and also a President **pro tempore**, in the absence of the Vice President, or when he shall exercise the office of President of the United States.

6. Impeachment Trials The Senate shall have the sole power to try all impeachments. When sitting for that purpose, they shall be on oath or affirmation. When the President of the United States is tried, the Chief Justice shall preside: and no person shall be convicted without the concurrence of two-thirds of the members present.

7. Punishment for Impeachment Judgment in cases of impeachment shall not extend further than to removal from office, and disqualification to hold and enjoy any office of honor, trust or profit under the United States; but the party convicted shall nevertheless be liable and subject to **indictment**, trial, judgment and punishment, according to law.

SECTION 4. **Congressional Elections**

1. Regulations The times, places and manner of holding elections for Senators and Representatives shall be prescribed in each state by the legislature thereof; but the Congress may at any time by law make or alter such regulations, except as to the places of choosing Senators.

2. Sessions The Congress shall assemble at least once in every year, ~~and such meeting shall be on the first Monday in December, unless they shall by law appoint a different day.~~

SECTION 5. **Rules and Procedures**

1. Quorum Each house shall be the judge of the elections, returns and qualifications of its own members, and a majority of each shall constitute a **quorum** to do business; but a smaller number may adjourn from day to day, and may be authorized to compel the attendance of absent members, in such manner, and under such penalties as each house may provide.

2. Rules and Conduct Each house may determine the rules of its proceedings, punish its members for disorderly behavior, and, with the concurrence of two-thirds, expel a member.

3. Congressional Records Each house shall keep a journal of its proceedings, and from time to time publish the same, excepting such parts as may in their judgment require secrecy; and the yeas and nays of the members of either house on any question shall, at the desire of one-fifth of those present, be entered on the journal.

4. Adjournment Neither house, during the session of Congress, shall, without the consent of the other, adjourn for more than three days, nor to any other place than that in which the two houses shall be sitting

SECTION 6. **Payment and Privileges**

1. Salary The Senators and Representatives shall receive a compensation for their services, to be ascertained by law, and paid out of the treasury of the United States. They shall in all cases, except treason, felony and breach of the peace, be privileged from arrest during their attendance at the session of their respective houses, and in going to and returning from the same; and for any speech or debate in either house, they shall not be questioned in any other place.

2. Restrictions No Senator or Representative shall, during the time for which he was elected, be appointed to any civil office under the authority of the United States, which shall have been created, or the emoluments whereof shall have been increased during such time; and no person holding any office under the United States, shall be a member of either house during his continuance in office.

Senate Rules

Senate rules allow for debate on the floor. Using a tactic called filibustering, senators give long speeches to block the passage of a bill. (*above*) Senator Strom Thurmond holds the filibustering record—24 hours, 18 minutes.

4. Why might a senator choose filibustering as a tactic to block a bill?

Connect *to* **Today**

Salaries Senators and representatives are paid $165,200 a year. The Speaker of the House is paid $212,100—the same as the vice president.

5. How do the salaries of members of Congress compare to those of adults—like teachers or famous sports figures?

SECTION 7. How a Bill Becomes a Law

1. Tax Bills All bills for raising **revenue** shall originate in the House of Representatives; but the Senate may propose or concur with amendments as on other Bills.

2. Lawmaking Process Every bill which shall have passed the House of Representatives and the Senate, shall, before it become a law, be presented to the President of the United States; if he approves he shall sign it, but if not he shall return it, with his objections to that house in which it shall have originated, who shall enter the objections at large on their journal, and proceed to reconsider it. If after such reconsideration two-thirds of that house shall agree to pass the bill, it shall be sent, together with the objections, to the other house, by which it shall likewise be reconsidered, and if approved by two-thirds of that house, it shall become a law. But in all such cases the votes of both houses shall be determined by yeas and nays, and the names of the persons voting for and against the bill shall be entered on the journal of each house respectively. If any bill shall not be returned by the President within ten days (Sundays excepted) after it shall have been presented to him, the same shall be a law, in like manner as if he had signed it, unless the Congress by their adjournment prevent its return, in which case it shall not be a law.

CONNECT TO GOVERNMENT *How a Bill Becomes a Law*

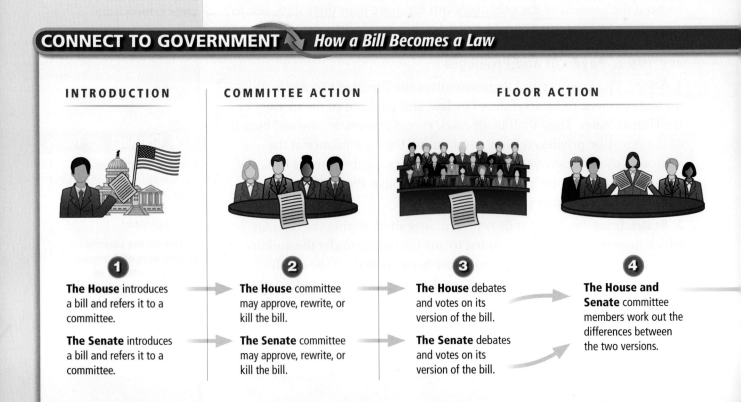

INTRODUCTION	COMMITTEE ACTION	FLOOR ACTION	
1	**2**	**3**	**4**
The House introduces a bill and refers it to a committee.	**The House** committee may approve, rewrite, or kill the bill.	**The House** debates and votes on its version of the bill.	**The House and Senate** committee members work out the differences between the two versions.
The Senate introduces a bill and refers it to a committee.	**The Senate** committee may approve, rewrite, or kill the bill.	**The Senate** debates and votes on its version of the bill.	

3. Role of the President Every order, resolution, or vote to which the concurrence of the Senate and House of Representatives may be necessary (except on a question of adjournment) shall be presented to the President of the United States; and before the same shall take effect, shall be approved by him, or being disapproved by him, shall be repassed by two-thirds of the Senate and House of Representatives, according to the rules and limitations prescribed in the case of a bill.

Activity

Creating a Play

1 Study the diagram below.

2 Work with a small group to create a presentation to teach an audience of younger students how a bill becomes a law.

• Assign the tasks of actor, illustrator, narrator, and scriptwriter.

• Develop a script.

• Gather props and rehearse your presentations.

3 Present the drama to a class of younger students.

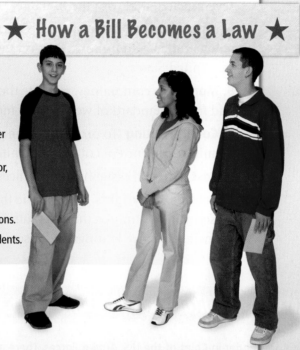

★ How a Bill Becomes a Law ★

FINAL APPROVAL **ENACTMENT**

5 Both houses of Congress pass the revised bill.

6 President vetoes the bill.
OR
President signs the bill.

7 Two-thirds majority vote of Congress is needed to approve a vetoed bill.

8 Bill becomes law.

SECTION 8. Powers Granted to Congress

1. Taxation The Congress shall have power to lay and collect taxes, duties, imposts and excises, to pay the debts and provide for the common defense and general welfare of the United States; but all duties, imposts and excises shall be uniform throughout the United States;

2. Credit To borrow money on the credit of the United States;

3. Commerce To regulate commerce with foreign nations, and among the several states, and with the Indian tribes;

4. Naturalization, Bankruptcy To establish a uniform rule of **naturalization**, and uniform laws on the subject of bankruptcies throughout the United States;

5. Money To coin money, regulate the value thereof, and of foreign coin, and fix the standard of weights and measures;

6. Counterfeiting To provide for the punishment of counterfeiting the securities and current coin of the United States;

7. Post Office To establish post offices and post roads;

8. Patents, Copyrights To promote the progress of science and useful arts, by securing for limited times to authors and inventors the exclusive right to their respective writings and discoveries;

COMPARING Military Responsibilities

The president is the Commander-in-Chief of the U.S. Armed Forces. There are five military branches—the Army, Marine Corps (USMC), Navy (USN), and Air Force (USAF), and the Coast Guard (USCG). The National Guard is the home based militia.

United States Army The largest branch of the U.S. armed forces, the U.S. Army has its roots in the Continental Army which was formed in June 1775. The army is responsible for land-based military operations. Motto: "Call to Duty."

U.S. Navy (USN) The branch of the U.S. armed forces responsible for naval operations. Unofficial motto: "*Non sibi sed patriae*" meaning "Not self but country."

U.S. Air Force (USAF) The largest and most technologically advanced air force in the world, USAF is trained for "offensive and defensive air operations." Unofficial motto: "No One Comes Close."

9. Federal Courts To constitute **tribunals** inferior to the Supreme Court;

10. International Law To define and punish piracies and **felonies** committed on the high seas, and offenses against the law of nations;

11. War To declare war, grant letters of marque and reprisal, and make rules concerning captures on land and water;

12. Army To raise and support armies, but no **appropriation** of money to that use shall be for a longer term than two years;

13. Navy To provide and maintain a navy;

14. Regulation of Armed Forces To make rules for the government and regulation of the land and naval forces;

15. Militia To provide for calling forth the **militia** to execute the laws of the Union, suppress insurrections and repel invasions;

16. Regulations for Militia To provide for organizing, arming, and disciplining the militia, and for governing such part of them as may be employed in the service of the United States, reserving to the states respectively the appointment of the officers, and the authority of training the militia according to the discipline prescribed by Congress;

Connect *to* Today

Declaring War Only Congress can declare war. Yet in the following "undeclared" wars, Congress bowed to the president's power to take military action and send troops overseas: Korean War (1950–1953), Vietnam War (1957–1975), Persian Gulf War (1991), and Kosovo crisis (1999).

6. Why do you think the Constitution sets limits on the president's power to make war?

U.S. National Guard

The National Guard is a component of the U.S. Army and USAF. National Guard units can be mobilized at any time to supplement regular armed forces.

U.S. Marine Corps (USMC) The marines have a multi-purpose role, including providing presidential protection and helicopter service. Marines also provide security for American embassies and consulates overseas. Motto: "*Semper Fidelis*" meaning "Always Faithful."

CRITICAL THINKING

1. **Form and Support Opinions** Women now serve in combat roles in the U.S. Armed Forces? Do you agree or disagree with this policy?

2. **Connect *to* Today** Under what circumstances do you think the president should call out the National Guard?

Residents of the District of Columbia elect a mayor and city council. However, Congress retains ultimate authority in the district and has veto power over the budget and legislative matters.

Habeas Corpus

A writ of habeas corpus is a legal order. It protects people from being held in prison or jail without formal charges of a crime. In 1992, the Supreme Court recognized that habeas corpus "is the [basic] instrument for safeguarding individual freedom."

7. How does habeas corpus help ensure fairness and justice?

Direct Tax

In 1913, the 16th Amendment allowed Congress to collect an income tax—a direct tax on the amount of money a person earns. Americans today pay much more in taxes than their ancestors would have imagined.

8. Why do you think the issue of taxes is so important to people?

17. District of Columbia To exercise exclusive legislation in all cases whatsoever, over such district (not exceeding ten miles square) as may, by cession of particular states, and the acceptance of Congress, become the seat of the government of the United States, and to exercise like authority over all places purchased by the consent of the legislature of the state in which the same shall be, for the erection of forts, magazines, arsenals, dockyards, and other needful buildings; and

Washington Monument   The White House

PENN.
N.J.
MD.
DEL.
VA.
⍟ Washington, D.C.

Supreme Court

The Capitol Building

18. Elastic Clause To make all laws which shall be necessary and proper for carrying into execution the foregoing powers, and all other powers vested by this Constitution in the government of the United States, or in any department or officer thereof.

SECTION 9. Powers Denied Congress

1. ~~Slave Trade The migration or importation of such persons as any of the states now existing shall think proper to admit, shall not be prohibited by the Congress prior to the year one thousand eight hundred and eight, but a tax or duty may be imposed on such importation, not exceeding ten dollars for each person.~~

2. Habeas Corpus The privilege of the writ of habeas corpus shall not be suspended, unless when in cases of rebellion or invasion the public safety may require it.

3. Illegal Punishment No **bill of attainder** or **ex post facto** law shall be passed.

4. Direct Taxes No capitation, ~~or other direct,~~ tax shall be laid, ~~unless in proportion to the census or enumeration herein before directed to be taken.~~

5. Export Taxes No tax or duty shall be laid on articles exported from any state.

6. No Favorites No preference shall be given by any regulation of commerce or revenue to the ports of one state over those of another: nor shall vessels bound to, or from, one state be obliged to enter, clear, or pay duties in another.

7. Public Money No money shall be drawn from the treasury, but in consequence of appropriations made by law; and a regular statement and account of the receipts and expenditures of all public money shall be published from time to time.

8. Titles of Nobility No title of nobility shall be granted by the United States: and no person holding any office of profit or trust under them shall, without the consent of the Congress, accept of any present, emolument, office, or title, of any kind whatever, from any king, prince, or foreign state.

SECTION 10. Powers Denied the States

1. Restrictions No state shall enter into any treaty, alliance, or confederation; grant letters of marque and reprisal; coin money; emit bills of credit; make anything but gold and silver coin a **tender** in payment of debts; pass any bill of attainder, ex post facto law, or law impairing the obligation of contracts, or grant any title of nobility.

2. Import and Export Taxes No state shall, without the consent of the Congress, lay any imposts or duties on imports or exports, except what may be absolutely necessary for executing its inspection laws; and the net produce of all duties and imposts, laid by any state on imports or exports, shall be for the use of the treasury of the United States; and all such laws shall be subject to the revision and control of the Congress.

3. Peacetime and War Restraints No state shall, without the consent of Congress, lay any duty of tonnage, keep troops or ships of war in time of peace, enter into any agreement or compact with another state, or with a foreign power, or engage in war, unless actually invaded, or in such imminent danger as will not admit of delay.

Titles of Nobility

The Framers disapproved of titles of nobility. The list of grievances in the Declaration of Independence included numerous examples of King George III's abuses of power. Symbols of these abuses included English titles of nobility, such as "king," "queen," and "duke." The Framers said clearly that there would be no such titles in the new republic.

9. How do TV news reporters address members of Congress and the president?

Article 1 Assessment

MAIN IDEAS

1. What is the main role of the legislative branch?
2. What role does the vice president of the United States play in the Senate?
3. Why are there more members in the House of Representatives than the Senate?
4. What is one of the powers denied to Congress?

CRITICAL THINKING

5. **Draw Conclusions** How does Article 1 show that the Constitution is a clearly defined yet flexible document?

   Think about
   • the powers of Congress
   • the "elastic clause"

BACKGROUND VOCABULARY

natural-born citizen a citizen born in the United States or a U.S. commonwealth, or to parents who are U.S. citizens living outside the country

affirmation a statement declaring that something is true

ARTICLE 2. The Executive

🔻 **KEY QUESTION** What is the chief purpose of the executive branch?

SECTION 1. The Presidency

1. Terms of Office The executive power shall be vested in a President of the United States of America. He shall hold his office during the term of four years, and, together with the Vice President, chosen for the same term, be elected, as follows:

2. Electoral College Each state shall appoint, in such manner as the Legislature thereof may direct, a number of electors, equal to the whole number of Senators and Representatives to which the State may be entitled in the Congress; but no Senator or Representative, or person holding an office of trust or profit under the United States, shall be appointed an elector.

CONNECT TO GOVERNMENT ➤ *Electoral College*

American voters do not choose their president directly. Members of a group called the Electoral College actually elect the president. Each state has electors. Together they form the Electoral College. In most states, the winner takes all. Except for Maine and Nebraska, all the electoral votes of a state go to one set of candidates.

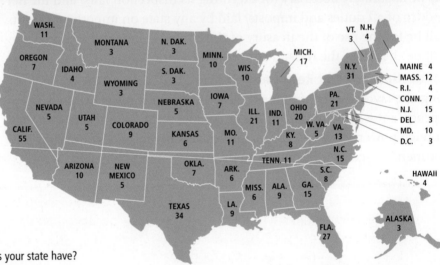

Number of electors for each state = total number of its senators and representatives

CRITICAL THINKING

1. Place How many electoral votes does your state have?

2. Draw Conclusions In which states would a presidential candidate campaign most heavily? Why?

---

3. Former Method of Electing President The electors shall meet in their respective states, and vote by ballot for two persons, of whom one at least shall not be an inhabitant of the same state with themselves. And they shall make a list of all the persons voted for, and of the number of votes for each; which list they shall sign and certify, and transmit sealed to the seat of the government of the United States, directed to the President of the Senate. The President of the Senate shall, in the presence of the Senate and House of Representatives, open all the certificates, and the votes shall then be counted. The person having the greatest number of votes shall be the President, if such number be a majority of the whole number of electors appointed; and if there be more than one who have such major-

ity, and have an equal number of votes, then the House of Representatives shall immediately choose by ballot one of them for President; and if no person have a majority, then from the five highest on the list the said House shall in like manner choose the President. But in choosing the President, the votes shall be taken by States, the representation from each state having one vote; a quorum for this purpose shall consist of a member or members from two-thirds of the states, and a majority of all the states shall be necessary to a choice. In every case, after the choice of the President, the person having the greatest number of votes of the electors shall be the Vice President. But if there should remain two or more who have equal votes, the Senate shall choose from them by ballot the Vice President.

4. Election Day The Congress may determine the time of choosing the electors, and the day on which they shall give their votes, which day shall be the same throughout the United States.

5. Qualifications No person except a **natural-born citizen**, or a citizen of the United States at the time of the adoption of this Constitution, shall be eligible to the office of President; neither shall any person be eligible to that office who shall not have attained to the age of thirty-five years, and been fourteen years a resident within the United States.

6. Succession In case of the removal of the President from office, or of his death, resignation, or inability to discharge the powers and duties of the said office, the same shall devolve on the Vice President, and the Congress may by law provide for the case of removal, death, resignation or inability, both of the President and Vice President, declaring what officer shall then act as President, and such officer shall act accordingly, until the disability be removed, or a President shall be elected.

7. Salary The President shall, at stated times, receive for his services, a compensation, which shall neither be increased nor diminished during the period for which he shall have been elected, and he shall not receive within that period any other emolument from the United States, or any of them.

8. Oath of Office Before he enter on the execution of his office, he shall take the following oath or **affirmation**: I do solemnly swear (or affirm) that I will faithfully execute the office of President of the United States, and will to the best of my ability, preserve, protect and defend the Constitution of the United States.

SECTION 2. Powers of the President

1. Military Powers The President shall be commander in chief of the Army and Navy of the United States, and of the militia of the several states, when called into the actual service of the United States; he may require the

Succession

Vice President Gerald Ford (*left*), next in the line of succession, takes the oath of office after the resignation of President Richard Nixon on August 9, 1974. Ford, like every U.S. president, promises to uphold the Constitution. The 25th Amendment sets up clearer procedures for presidential succession.

President's Salary

The president's yearly salary is $400,000. The president also gets special allowances, such as funds for travel expenses. Benefits include:

- living in a mansion, the White House
- vacationing at Camp David, an estate in Maryland
- using *Air Force One*, a personal jet plane

10. Why do you think the president needs to have a plane and a vacation spot?

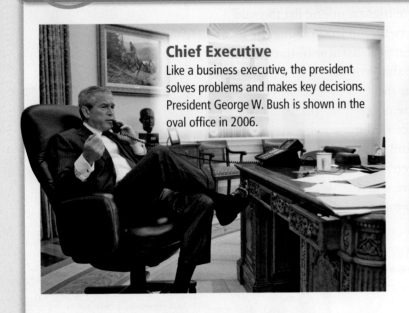

Chief Executive
Like a business executive, the president solves problems and makes key decisions. President George W. Bush is shown in the oval office in 2006.

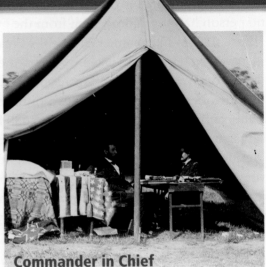

Commander in Chief
As a military leader, President Abraham Lincoln meets with General McClellan during the Civil War.

Head of a Political Party
President Andrew Jackson on his way to Washington, D.C. for his inauguration in 1829. Jackson was a leader of the Democratic-Republican Party—the forerunner of today's Democratic Party.

Chief Diplomat and Chief of State
As a foreign policy maker, President Ronald Reagan visits British Prime Minister Margaret Thatcher in 1984.

Legislative Leader
President Franklin D. Roosevelt signs the Social Security Act of 1935. All modern presidents have legislative programs they want Congress to pass.

CRITICAL THINKING

1. **Make Inferences** Why is it important that the commander in chief of the armed forces of the United States be a civilian (the president) rather than a military commander?

2. **Connect to Today** Why do you think the United States enjoys close relations with Britain?

opinion, in writing, of the principal officer in each of the executive departments, upon any subject relating to the duties of their respective offices, and he shall have power to grant **reprieves** and pardons for offenses against the United States, except in cases of impeachment.

2. Treaties, Appointments He shall have power, by and with the advice and consent of the Senate, to make treaties, provided two-thirds of the Senators present concur; and he shall nominate, and by and with the advice and consent of the Senate, shall appoint ambassadors, other public ministers and consuls, judges of the Supreme Court, and all other officers of the United States, whose appointments are not herein otherwise provided for, and which shall be established by law; but the Congress may by law vest the appointment of such inferior officers, as they think proper, in the President alone, in the courts of law, or in the heads of departments.

3. Vacancies The President shall have power to fill up all vacancies that may happen during the recess of the Senate, by granting commissions which shall expire at the end of their next session.

SECTION 3. Presidential Duties

He shall from time to time give to the Congress information of the State of the Union, and recommend to their consideration such measures as he shall judge necessary and expedient; he may, on extraordinary occasions, **convene** both houses, or either of them, and in case of disagreement between them, with respect to the time of adjournment, he may adjourn them to such time as he shall think proper; he shall receive ambassadors and other public ministers; he shall take care that the laws be faithfully executed, and shall commission all the officers of the United States.

SECTION 4. Impeachment

The President, Vice President and all civil officers of the United States shall be removed from office on impeachment for, and conviction of, treason, bribery, or other high crimes and **misdemeanors**.

BACKGROUND VOCABULARY

reprieves delays or cancellations of punishment

convene call together

misdemeanors violations of the law

Appointments

Recent presidents have used their power of appointment to add minorities and women to the Supreme Court. In 1967, President Lyndon Johnson appointed the first African-American justice, Thurgood Marshall. In 1981, President Ronald Reagan appointed the first woman, Sandra Day O'Connor.

11. What do you think influences a president's choice for a Supreme Court justice?

Connect to Today

State of the Union Major TV networks broadcast the State of the Union address to the whole nation. In this yearly message, the president urges Congress to achieve certain lawmaking goals. The president's speech also must gain the attention of TV viewers.

12. Why is the president's power to persuade an important political skill?

Article 2 Assessment

MAIN IDEAS

1. What is the chief purpose of the executive branch?
2. What are the requirements for becoming president?
3. How does the Constitution limit the president's power to make appointments and treaties?

CRITICAL THINKING

4. **Analyze Issues** Why do you think the Constitution states that the president must seek approval from the Senate for most political appointments and treaties?

Think about
- the abuse of power
- the will of the voters

inferior courts courts
with less authority than the
Supreme Court

appellate having power to
review court decisions

Federal Courts

The Judiciary Act of 1789, passed
by the first Congress, included
establishing a Supreme Court
with a chief justice and five
associate justices and other lower
federal courts.

**13. How many Supreme
Court justices are there
today?**

Judicial Power

Judicial power gives the Supreme
Court and other federal courts the
authority to hear certain kinds
of cases. These courts have the
power to rule in cases involving
the Constitution, national laws,
treaties, and states' conflicts.

**14. What federal cases have
you seen reported on TV?**

The Constitution actually
creates only one court—
the U.S. Supreme Court.
(*right*) The members of the
Supreme Court in 2006.

ARTICLE 3. The Judiciary

🔽 **KEY QUESTION** What is the main purpose of the judicial branch?

SECTION 1. Federal Courts and Judges

The judicial power of the United States shall be vested in one Supreme
Court, and in such **inferior courts** as the Congress may from time to time
ordain and establish. The judges, both of the Supreme and inferior courts,
shall hold their offices during good behavior, and shall, at stated times,
receive for their services a compensation, which shall not be diminished
during their continuance in office.

SECTION 2. The Courts Authority

1. General Authority The judicial power shall extend to all cases, in law
and equity, arising under this Constitution, the laws of the United States,
and treaties made, or which shall be made, under their authority;—to all
cases affecting ambassadors, other public ministers and consuls;—to all
cases of admiralty and maritime jurisdiction;—to controversies to which
the United States shall be a party;—to controversies between two or more
states;—between a state and citizens of another state;—between citizens of
different states;—between citizens of the same state claiming lands under
grants of different states, and between a state, or the citizens thereof, and
foreign states, citizens or subjects.

2. Supreme Court In all cases affecting ambassadors, other public ministers
and consuls, and those in which a state shall be party, the Supreme Court
shall have original jurisdiction. In all the other cases before mentioned, the
Supreme Court shall have **appellate** jurisdiction, both as to law and fact, with
such exceptions, and under such regulations, as the Congress shall make.

3. Trial by Jury The trial of all crimes, except in cases of impeachment, shall
be by jury; and such trial shall be held in the state where the said crimes shall
have been committed; but when not committed within any state, the trial
shall be at such place or places as the Congress may by law have directed.

COMPARING *Checks and Balances*

EXECUTIVE BRANCH (President)

CHECKS ON COURTS	CHECKS ON CONGRESS
• Appoints federal judges • Can grant reprieves and pardons for federal crimes	• Can veto acts of Congress • Can call special sessions of Congress • Can suggest laws and send messages to Congress

JUDICIAL BRANCH (Supreme Court)

CHECKS ON PRESIDENT	CHECKS ON CONGRESS
• Can declare executive acts unconstitutional • Judges, appointed for life, are free from executive control	• Judicial review—Can declare acts of Congress unconstitutional

LEGISLATIVE BRANCH (Congress)

CHECKS ON COURT	CHECKS ON PRESIDENT
• Can impeach and remove federal judges • Establishes lower federal courts • Can refuse to confirm judicial appointments	• Can impeach and remove the president • Can override veto • Controls spending of money • Senate can refuse to confirm presidential appointments and to ratify treaties

CRITICAL THINKING

1. Why is judicial review an important action of the Supreme Court?

2. Which check do you think is the most powerful? Why?

SECTION 3. Treason

1. Definition Treason against the United States shall consist only in levying war against them, or in adhering to their enemies, giving them aid and comfort. No person shall be convicted of treason unless on the testimony of two witnesses to the same overt act, or on confession in open court.

2. Punishment The Congress shall have power to declare the punishment of treason, but no attainder of treason shall work corruption of blood, or forfeiture except during the life of the person attained.

Article **3** Assessment

MAIN IDEAS

1. What is the main purpose of the judicial branch?

2. What is judicial review?

3. What are two kinds of cases that can begin in the Supreme Court?

CRITICAL THINKING

4. Draw Conclusions Why might the Supreme Court feel less political pressure than Congress in making judgments about the Constitution?

Think about

- the appointment of Supreme Court justices
- Congress members' obligation to voters

ARTICLE 4. Relations Among States

SECTION 1. State Acts and Records

Full faith and credit shall be given in each state to the public acts, records, and judicial proceedings of every other state. And the Congress may by general laws prescribe the manner in which such acts, records and proceedings shall be proved, and the effect thereof.

SECTION 2. Rights of Citizens

1. Citizenship The citizens of each state shall be entitled to all privileges and **immunities** of citizens in the several states.

2. Extradition A person charged in any state with treason, felony, or other crime, who shall flee from justice, and be found in another state, shall on demand of the executive authority of the state from which he fled, be delivered up, to be removed to the state having jurisdiction of the crime.

3. Fugitive Slaves No person held to service or labor in one state, under the laws thereof, escaping into another, shall, in consequence of any law or regulation therein, be discharged from such service or labor, but shall be delivered up on claim of the party to whom such service or labor may be due.

Extradition

Persons charged with serious crimes cannot escape punishment by fleeing to another state. They must be returned to the first state and stand trial there.

15. Why do you think the Framers included the power of extradition?

1 Form small groups to illustrate a chart showing the national, shared, and state powers.

2 Display the chart in your classroom.

COMPARING *Federal and State Powers*

Americans live under both national and state governments.

NATIONAL POWERS	SHARED POWERS	STATE POWERS
• Maintain military	• Collect taxes	• Establish local governments
• Declare war	• Establish courts	• Set up schools
• Establish postal system	• Regulate interstate commerce	• Regulate state commerce
• Set standards for weights and measures	• Regulate banks	• Make regulations for marriage
• Protect copyrights and patents	• Borrow money	• Establish and regulate corporations
	• Provide for the general welfare	
	• Punish criminals	

CRITICAL THINKING Evaluate What do you think is the purpose of dividing the powers between national and state governments?

SECTION 3. **New States**

1. Admission New states may be admitted by the Congress into this Union; but no new state shall be formed or erected within the jurisdiction of any other state; nor any state be formed by the junction of two or more states, or parts of states, without the consent of the legislatures of the states concerned as well as of the Congress.

2. Congressional Authority The Congress shall have power to dispose of and make all needful rules and regulations respecting the territory or other property belonging to the United States; and nothing in this Constitution shall be so construed as to prejudice any claims of the United States, or of any particular state.

SECTION 4. **Guarantees to the States**

The United States shall guarantee to every state in this Union a republican form of government, and shall protect each of them against invasion; and on application of the legislature, or of the executive (when the legislature cannot be convened) against domestic violence.

ARTICLE 5. **Amending the Constitution**

The Congress, whenever two-thirds of both houses shall deem it necessary, shall propose amendments to this Constitution, or, on the application of the legislatures of two-thirds of the several states, shall call a convention for proposing amendments, which, in either case, shall be valid to all intents and purposes, as part of this Constitution, when ratified by the legislatures of three-fourths of the several states, or by conventions in three-fourths thereof, as the one or the other mode of ratification may be proposed by the Congress; provided that no amendment which may be made prior to the year one thousand eight hundred and eight shall in any manner affect the first and fourth clauses in the ninth section of the first article; and that no state, without its consent, shall be deprived of its equal **suffrage** in the Senate.

Admission to Statehood

In 1998, Puerto Ricans voted against their island becoming the 51st state. A lawyer in Puerto Rico summed up a main reason: "Puerto Ricans want to have ties to the U.S., but they want to protect their culture and language." Also, as a U.S. commonwealth, Puerto Rico makes its own laws and handles its own finances

16. Do you think Puerto Rico should become a state? Why or why not?

Amending the Constitution

There are two ways to propose an amendment:

| **2/3** of each house of **Congress** vote to amend the Constitution* | **2/3** of **state legislatures** call for a national convention to amend the Constitution |

*All 27 amendments have been proposed by this method.

There are also two ways to ratify an amendment:

| **3/4** of state legislatures approve the amendment | **3/4** of states approve the amendment at state conventions |

CRITICAL THINKING Why do you think more votes are needed to ratify an amendment than to propose one?

Federal Supremacy

In 1957, the "supreme law of the land" was put to a test. The governor of Arkansas defied a Supreme Court order. The Court ruled that African-American students could go to all-white public schools. President Dwight D. Eisenhower then sent federal troops to protect the first African-American students to enroll in Central High School in Little Rock, Arkansas.

ARTICLE 6. Supremacy of the National Government

SECTION 1. Valid Debts

All debts contracted and engagements entered into, before the adoption of this Constitution, shall be as valid against the United States under this Constitution, as under the Confederation.

SECTION 2. Supreme Law

This Constitution, and the laws of the United States which shall be made in pursuance thereof; and all treaties made, or which shall be made, under the authority of the United States, shall be the supreme law of the land; and the judges in every state shall be bound thereby, anything in the constitution or laws of any state to the contrary notwithstanding.

SECTION 3. Loyalty to Constitution

The Senators and Representatives before mentioned, and the members of the several state legislatures, and all executive and judicial officers, both of the United States and of the several states, shall be bound by oath or affirmation to support this Constitution; but no religious test shall ever be required as a qualification to any office or public trust under the United States.

Members of the House of Representatives swear to support and defend the U.S. Constitution at the opening of the 109th Congress in 2005.

ARTICLE 7. **Ratification**

The **ratification** of the conventions of nine states shall be sufficient for the establishment of this Constitution between the states so ratifying the same. Done in convention by the **unanimous consent** of the states present, the seventeenth day of September in the year of our Lord one thousand seven hundred and eighty-seven and of the independence of the United States of America the twelfth. In witness whereof we have hereunto subscribed our names.

George Washington
President and deputy from Virginia

New Hampshire: *John Langdon, Nicholas Gilman*

Massachusetts: *Nathaniel Gorham, Rufus King*

Connecticut: *William Samuel Johnson, Roger Sherman*

New York: *Alexander Hamilton*

New Jersey: *William Livingston, David Brearley, William Paterson, Jonathan Dayton*

Pennsylvania: *Benjamin Franklin, Thomas Mifflin, Robert Morris, George Clymer, Thomas FitzSimons, Jared Ingersoll, James Wilson, Gouverneur Morris*

Delaware: *George Read, Gunning Bedford, Jr., John Dickinson, Richard Bassett, Jacob Broom*

Maryland: *James McHenry, Dan of St. Thomas Jenifer, Daniel Carroll*

Virginia: *John Blair, James Madison, Jr.*

North Carolina: *William Blount, Richard Dobbs Spaight, Hugh Williamson*

South Carolina: *John Rutledge, Charles Cotesworth Pinckney, Charles Pinckney, Pierce Butler*

Georgia: *William Few, Abraham Baldwin*

The Signers

The 39 men who signed the Constitution were wealthy and well educated. About half of them were trained in law. Others were doctors, merchants, bankers, and slaveholding planters. Missing from the list of signatures are the names of African Americans, Native Americans, and women. These groups reflected the varied population of the United States in the 1780s.

17. How do you think the absence of these groups affected the decisions made in creating the Constitution?

Articles 4–7 Assessment

MAIN IDEAS

1. What rights does Article 4 guarantee to citizens if they go to other states in the nation?

2. What are two ways of proposing an amendment to the Constitution?

3. What makes up "the supreme law of the land"?

CRITICAL THINKING

4. Form and Support Opinions Should the Framers of the Constitution have allowed the people to vote directly for ratification of the Constitution? Why or why not?

Think about

• the idea that the government belongs to the people

• the general public's ability to make sound political decisions

The Bill of Rights and Amendments 11–27

James Madison played a leading role in the creation of the U.S. Constitution.

In 1787, Thomas Jefferson sent James Madison a letter about the Constitution. Jefferson wrote, "I will now add what I do not like . . . [there is no] bill of rights." He explained his reasons: "A bill of rights is what the people are entitled to against every government on earth . . . and what no just government should refuse." Jefferson's disapproval is not surprising. In writing the Declaration of Independence, he spelled out basic individual rights that cannot be taken way. These are "life, liberty, and the pursuit of happiness." The Declaration states that governments are formed to protect these rights.

Several states approved the Constitution only if a list of guaranteed freedoms was added. While serving in the nation's first Congress, James Madison helped draft the Bill of Rights. In 1791, these first ten amendments became part of the Constitution.

AMENDMENTS 1–10. The Bill of Rights

▼ **KEY QUESTION** Why do some individual rights need special protection in the Constitution?

AMENDMENT 1. Religious and Political Freedom 1791

Congress shall make no law respecting an establishment of religion, or prohibiting the free exercise thereof; or **abridging** the freedom of speech, or of the press; or the right of the people peaceably to assemble, and to petition the Government for a redress of grievances.

The Five Freedoms

1. Freedom of Religion
2. Freedom of Speech
3. Freedom of the Press
4. Freedom of Assembly
5. Freedom to Petition

AMENDMENT 2. Right to Bear Arms 1791 A well-regulated militia, being necessary to the security of a free state, the right of the people to keep and bear arms, shall not be infringed.

AMENDMENT 3. Quartering Troops 1791 No soldier shall, in time of peace be quartered in any house, without the consent of the owner, nor in time of war, but in a manner to be prescribed by law.

AMENDMENT 4. Search and Seizure 1791 The right of the people to be secure in their persons, houses, papers, and effects, against unreasonable searches and seizures, shall not be violated, and no warrants shall issue, but upon probable cause, supported by oath or affirmation, and particularly describing the place to be searched, and the persons or things to be seized.

AMENDMENT 5. Rights of Accused Persons 1791 No person shall be held to answer for a capital, or otherwise infamous crime, unless on a presentment or indictment of a Grand Jury, except in cases arising in the land or naval forces, or in the militia, when in actual service in time of war or public danger; nor shall any person be subject for the same offense to be twice put in jeopardy of life or limb; nor shall be compelled in any criminal case to be a witness against himself, nor be deprived of life, liberty, or property, without **due process of law**; nor shall private property be taken for public use, without just compensation.

AMENDMENT 6. Right to a Speedy, Public Trial 1791 In all criminal prosecutions, the accused shall enjoy the right to a speedy and public trial, by an impartial jury of the State and district wherein the crime shall have been committed, which district shall have been previously ascertained by law, and to be informed of the nature and cause of the accusation; to be confronted with the witnesses against him; to have **compulsory process** for obtaining witnesses in his favor, and to have the assistance of **counsel** for his defense.

BACKGROUND VOCABULARY

abridging reducing

quartered given a place to stay

due process of law fair treatment under the law

compulsory process required procedure

counsel a lawyer

Legal Rights

In 1966, the Supreme Court made a decision based on the 5th and 6th Amendments. The outcome of this ruling is called "Miranda rights." Miranda rights protect suspects from giving forced confessions. Police must read these rights to a suspect they are questioning. For example:

- "You have the right to remain silent."

- "Anything that you say can and will be used against you in a court of law."

- "You have the right to an attorney."

(*left*) Demonstrators exercise their First Amendment rights of freedom of assembly and of speech at a rally in favor of immigration reform in 2006. (*above*) A journalist, utilizing freedom of the press, interviews a Hispanic family rallying for the same cause.

common law a system of law developed in England, based on customs and previous court decisions

bail money paid by arrested persons to guarantee they will return for trial

equity a system of justice not covered under common law

Members of the jury are expected to determine the guilt or innocence of a defendant in a court proceeding.

States Powers

The 10th Amendment gives the states reserved powers. Any powers not clearly given to the national government by the U.S. Constitution or denied to the states in Article I, Section 10, belong to the states. State constitutions sometimes assume authority in unexpected areas. For example, California's constitution sets rules for governing the use of fishing nets.

18. What are some common areas in which states have authority?

AMENDMENT 7. Trial by Jury in Civil Cases 1791 In suits at **common law**, where the value in controversy shall exceed twenty dollars, the right of trial by jury shall be preserved, and no fact tried by a jury, shall be otherwise reexamined in any court of the United States, than according to the rules of the common law.

AMENDMENT 8. Limits of Fines and Punishments 1791 Excessive **bail** shall not be required, nor excessive fines imposed, nor cruel and unusual punishments inflicted.

AMENDMENT 9. Rights of People 1791 The enumeration in the Constitution of certain rights shall not be construed to deny or disparage others retained by the people.

AMENDMENT 10. Powers of States and People 1791 The powers not delegated to the United States by the Constitution, nor prohibited by it to the States, are reserved to the States respectively, or to the people.

Bill of Rights Assessment

MAIN IDEAS

1. Why do some individual rights need special protection in the Constitution?

2. Which amendment protects your privacy?

3. Which amendments guarantee fair legal treatment?

4. Which amendment prevents the federal government from taking powers away from the states and the people?

CRITICAL THINKING

5. **Form and Support Opinions** The 4th, 5th, 6th, 7th, and 8th Amendments protect innocent people accused of crimes. Do you think these five amendments also favor the rights of actual criminals?

Think about

- criminals who go free if valuable evidence is found after their trials
- criminals released on bail

Amendments 11–27

🔻 **KEY QUESTION** How has the Constitution adapted to social changes and trends?

AMENDMENT 11. **Lawsuits Against States** 1795

Passed by Congress March 4, 1794. Ratified February 7, 1795. Proclaimed 1798.

Note: Article 3, Section 2, of the Constitution was modified by Amendment 11.

The Judicial power of the United States shall not be construed to extend to any suit in law or **equity**, commenced or prosecuted against one of the United States by citizens of another state, or by citizens or subjects of any foreign state.

AMENDMENT 12. **Election of Executives** 1804

Passed by Congress December 9, 1803. Ratified June 15, 1804.

Note: Part of Article 2, Section 1, of the Constitution was replaced by the 12th Amendment.

The electors shall meet in their respective states and vote by ballot for President and Vice-President, one of whom, at least, shall not be an inhabitant of the same state with themselves; they shall name in their ballots the person voted for as President, and in distinct ballots the person voted for as Vice-President, and they shall make distinct lists of all persons voted for as President, and of all persons voted for as Vice-President, and of the number of votes for each, which lists they shall sign and certify, and transmit sealed to the seat of the government of the United States, directed to the President of the Senate;—the President of the Senate shall, in the presence of the Senate and House of Representatives, open all the certificates and the votes shall then be counted;—the person having the greatest number of votes for President, shall be the President, if such number be a majority of the whole number of electors appointed; and if no person have such majority, then from the persons having the highest numbers not exceeding three on the list of those voted for as President, the House of Representatives shall choose immediately, by ballot, the President. But in choosing the President, the votes shall be taken by states, the representation from each state having one vote; a quorum for this purpose shall consist of a member or members from two-thirds of the states, and a majority of all the states shall be necessary to a choice. And if the House of Representatives shall not choose a President whenever the right of choice shall devolve upon them, ~~before the fourth day of March next following,~~ then the Vice-President shall act as President, as in the case of the death or other constitutional disability of the President. The person having the greatest number of votes as Vice-President, shall be the Vice-President, if such number be a majority of the whole number of Electors appointed, and if no person have a majority, then from the two highest numbers on the list, the Senate shall choose the Vice-President; a quorum for the purpose shall consist of two-thirds of the whole number of Senators, and a majority of the whole number shall be necessary to a choice. But no

Separate Ballots

The presidential election of 1800 ended in a tie between Thomas Jefferson and (*above*) Aaron Burr. At this time, the candidate with the most votes became president. The runner-up became vice-president. The 12th Amendment calls for separate ballots for the president and vice president. The vice president is specifically elected to the office, rather than being the presidential candidate with the second-most votes.

servitude being under the
authority of an owner or
master

naturalized granted
nationality

insurrection revolt against
authority

bounties rewards

Civil Rights Laws

The 14th Amendment laid the
groundwork for many civil rights
laws, such as the Americans
with Disabilities Act (1990). This
act gave people with mental
or physical disabilities "equal
protection of the laws." For
example, public places had to
be designed for wheelchair use.
Wider doors and ramps allow
people with disabilities to go
in and out of buildings, and
wheelchair lifts make public
buses accessible to people
with disabilities.

person constitutionally ineligible to the office of President shall be eligible
to that of Vice-President of the United States.

AMENDMENT 13. Slavery Abolished 1865

Passed by Congress January 31, 1865. Ratified December 6, 1865.

**Note: A portion of Article 4, Section 2, of the Constitution was superseded by the
13th Amendment.**

Section 1. Neither slavery nor involuntary **servitude**, except as a punishment for crime whereof the party shall have been duly convicted, shall
exist within the United States, or any place subject to their jurisdiction.

Section 2. Congress shall have power to enforce this article by appropriate
legislation.

AMENDMENT 14. Civil Rights 1868

Passed by Congress June 13, 1866. Ratified July 9, 1868.

**Note: Article 1, Section 2, of the Constitution was modified by Section 2 of the
14th Amendment.**

Section 1. All persons born or **naturalized** in the United States, and subject
to the jurisdiction thereof, are citizens of the United States and of the state
wherein they reside. No state shall make or enforce any law which shall
abridge the privileges or immunities of citizens of the United States; nor
shall any state deprive any person of life, liberty, or property, without due
process of law; nor deny to any person within its jurisdiction the equal
protection of the laws.

Section 2. Representatives shall be apportioned
among the several states according to their respective numbers, counting the whole number of
persons in each state, excluding Indians not taxed.
But when the right to vote at any election for the
choice of electors for President and Vice-President
of the United States, Representatives in Congress,
the executive and judicial officers of a state, or the
members of the legislature thereof, is denied to
any of the male inhabitants of such state, being
twenty-one years of age, and citizens of the United
States, or in any way abridged, except for participation in rebellion, or other crime, the basis of
representation therein shall be reduced in the proportion which the number of such male citizens
shall bear to the whole number of male citizens
twenty-one years of age in such state.

Section 3. No person shall be a Senator or Representative in Congress, or elector of President and Vice-President, or hold any office, civil or military, under the United States, or under any state, who, having previously taken an oath, as a member of Congress, or as an officer of the United States, or as a member of any state legislature, or as an executive or judicial officer of any state, to support the Constitution of the United States, shall have engaged in **insurrection** or rebellion against the same, or given aid or comfort to the enemies thereof. But Congress may, by a vote of two-thirds of each house, remove such disability.

Section 4. The validity of the public debt of the United States, authorized by law, including debts incurred for payment of pensions and **bounties** for services in suppressing insurrection or rebellion, shall not be questioned. But neither the United States nor any state shall assume or pay any debt or obligation incurred in aid of insurrection or rebellion against the United States, or any claim for the loss or emancipation of any slave; but all such debts, obligations and claims shall be held illegal and void.

Section 5. The Congress shall have power to enforce, by appropriate legislation, the provisions of this article.

AMENDMENT 15. Right to Vote 1870

Passed by Congress February 26, 1869. Ratified February 3, 1870.

Section 1. The right of citizens of the United States to vote shall not be denied or abridged by the United States or by any state on account of race, color, or previous condition of servitude.

Section 2. The Congress shall have power to enforce this article by appropriate legislation.

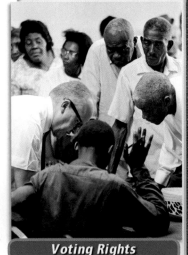

Voting Rights

The Voting Rights Act of 1965 extended the 15th Amendment. To qualify as voters, African Americans were no longer required to take tests proving that they could read and write. Also, federal examiners could help register voters. As a result, the number of African-American voters rose sharply. (*above*) Federal voter registrars enforce the Voting Rights Act in Canton, Miss. in 1965.

19. What effect do you think the Voting Rights Act had on candidates running for office?

COMPARING Reconstruction Amendments

The 13th, 14th, and 15th Amendments are often called the Reconstruction Amendments. They were passed after the Civil War during the government's attempt to rebuild the Union and to grant rights to recently freed African Americans.

EQUALITY

BALLOTS

13th Amendment 1865
- Ended slavery in the United States

14th Amendment 1868
- Defined national and state citizenship
- Protected citizens' rights
- Promised equal protection of the laws

15th Amendment 1870
- Designed to protect African Americans' voting rights

CRITICAL THINKING What problems did these amendments try to solve?

AMENDMENT 16. Income Tax 1913

Passed by Congress July 12, 1909. Ratified February 3, 1913.

Note: Article 1, Section 9, of the Constitution was modified by the 16th Amendment.

The Congress shall have power to lay and collect taxes on incomes, from whatever source derived, without apportionment among the several states, and without regard to any census or enumeration.

AMENDMENT 17. Direct Election of Senators 1913

Passed by Congress May 13, 1912. Ratified April 8, 1913.

Note: Article 1, Section 3, of the Constitution was modified by the 17th Amendment.

Section 1. The Senate of the United States shall be composed of two Senators from each state, elected by the people thereof, for six years; and each Senator shall have one vote. The electors in each state shall have the qualifications requisite for electors of the most numerous branch of the state legislatures.

Section 2. When vacancies happen in the representation of any state in the Senate, the executive authority of such state shall issue writs of election to fill such vacancies: Provided, that the legislature of any state may empower the executive thereof to make temporary appointments until the people fill the vacancies by election as the legislature may direct.

Section 3. This amendment shall not be so construed as to affect the election or term of any Senator chosen before it becomes valid as part of the Constitution.

AMENDMENT 18. Prohibition 1919

Passed by Congress December 18, 1917. Ratified January 16, 1919. Repealed by the 21st Amendment.

Section 1. After one year from the ratification of this article the manufacture, sale, or transportation of intoxicating liquors within, the importation thereof into, or the exportation thereof from the United States and all territory subject to the jurisdiction thereof for beverage purposes is hereby prohibited.

Section 2. The Congress and the several states shall have concurrent power to enforce this article by appropriate legislation.

Section 3. This article shall be inoperative unless it shall have been ratified as an amendment to the Constitution by the legislatures of the several states, as provided in the Constitution, within seven years from the date of the submission hereof to the states by the Congress.

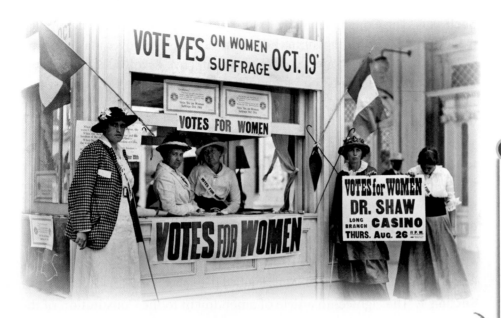

Connect *to* Today

The Equal Rights Amendment (ERA) In 1920, the 19th Amendment took effect, guaranteeing women the right to vote. Nevertheless, many women have continued to face discrimination in the United States. In 1923, the National Women's Party supported the passage of an equal rights amendment to protect women. Congress did not pass such an amendment until 1972. In 1982, however, the amendment died after it failed to be ratified by enough states to be added to the Constitution. As of the mid-2000s, the ERA was still not part of the U.S. Constitution.

21. Why do you think the 19th Amendment failed to create equality for women?

AMENDMENT 19. Woman Suffrage 1920

Passed by Congress June 4, 1919. Ratified August 18, 1920.

Section 1. The right of citizens of the United States to vote shall not be denied or abridged by the United States or by any state on account of sex.

Section 2. Congress shall have power to enforce this article by appropriate legislation.

AMENDMENT 20. "Lame Duck" Sessions 1933

Passed by Congress March 2, 1932. Ratified January 23, 1933.

Note: Article 1, Section 4, of the Constitution was modified by Section 2 of this amendment. In addition, a portion of the 12th Amendment was superseded by Section 3.

Section 1. The terms of the President and Vice-President shall end at noon on the 20th day of January, and the terms of Senators and Representatives at noon on the 3rd day of January, of the years in which such terms would have ended if this article had not been ratified; and the terms of their successors shall then begin.

Section 2. The Congress shall assemble at least once in every year, and such meeting shall begin at noon on the 3rd day of January, unless they shall by law appoint a different day.

Section 3. If, at the time fixed for the beginning of the term of the President, the President elect shall have died, the Vice-President elect shall become President. If a President shall not have been chosen before the time fixed for the beginning of his term, or if the President elect shall have failed to qualify, then the Vice-President elect shall act as President until a President shall have qualified; and the Congress may by law provide for the case wherein neither a President elect nor a Vice-President elect shall have qualified, declaring who shall then act as President, or the manner in which one who is to act shall be selected, and such person shall act accordingly until a President or Vice-President shall have qualified.

Section 4. The Congress may by law provide for the case of the death of any of the persons from whom the House of Representatives may choose a President whenever the right of choice shall have devolved upon them, and for the case of the death of any of the persons from whom the Senate may choose a Vice-President whenever the right of choice shall have devolved upon them.

Section 5. Sections 1 and 2 shall take effect on the 15th day of October following the ratification of this article.

Section 6. This article shall be **inoperative** unless it shall have been ratified as an amendment to the Constitution by the legislatures of three-fourths of the several states within seven years from the date of its submission.

AMENDMENT 21. **Repeal of Prohibition** 1933
Passed by Congress February 20, 1933. Ratified December 5, 1933.

Section 1. The eighteenth article of amendment to the Constitution of the United States is hereby repealed.

Section 2. The transportation or importation into any state, territory, or possession of the United States for delivery or use therein of intoxicating liquors, in violation of the laws thereof, is hereby prohibited.

Section 3. This article shall be inoperative unless it shall have been ratified as an amendment to the Constitution by conventions in the several states, as provided in the Constitution, within seven years from the date of the submission hereof to the states by the Congress.

AMENDMENT 22. **Limit on Presidential Terms** 1951
Passed by Congress March 21, 1947. Ratified February 27, 1951.

Section 1. No person shall be elected to the office of the President more than twice, and no person who has held the office of President, or acted as President, for more than two years of a term to which some other person was elected President shall be elected to the office of the President more than once. But this article shall not apply to any person holding the office of President when this article was proposed by the Congress, and shall not prevent any person who may be holding the office of President, or acting as President, during the term within which this article becomes operative from holding the office of President or acting as President during the remainder of such term.

Term Limits

George Washington set the tradition of limiting the presidency to two terms. Franklin Roosevelt broke this custom when he was elected president four terms in a row—1932, 1936, 1940, and 1944. His record-long presidency led to the 22nd Amendment. A two-term limit, written into the Constitution, checks the president's power.

President Roosevelt (*far right*) campaigns with farmers in Atlanta, Ga. before the 1932 election.

Section 2. This article shall be inoperative unless it shall have been ratified as an amendment to the Constitution by the legislatures of three-fourths of the several states within seven years from the date of its submission to the states by the Congress.

AMENDMENT 23. **Voting in District of Columbia** 1961

Passed by Congress June 16, 1960. Ratified March 29, 1961.

Section 1. The district constituting the seat of government of the United States shall appoint in such manner as Congress may direct: a number of electors of President and Vice-President equal to the whole number of Senators and Representatives in Congress to which the district would be entitled if it were a state, but in no event more than the least populous state; they shall be in addition to those appointed by the states, but they shall be considered, for the purposes of the election of President and Vice-President, to be electors appointed by a state; and they shall meet in the district and perform such duties as provided by the twelfth article of amendment.

Section 2. The Congress shall have power to enforce this article by appropriate legislation.

AMENDMENT 24. **Abolition of Poll Taxes** 1964

Passed by Congress August 27, 1962. Ratified January 23, 1964.

Section 1. The right of citizens of the United States to vote in any **primary** or other election for President or Vice-President, for electors for President or Vice-President, or for Senator or Representative in Congress, shall not be denied or abridged by the United States or any state by reason of failure to pay any poll tax or other tax.

Section 2. The Congress shall have power to enforce this article by appropriate legislation.

AMENDMENT 25. **Presidential Disability, Succession** 1967

Passed by Congress July 6, 1965. Ratified February 10, 1967.
Note: Article 2, Section 1, of the Constitution was affected by the 25th Amendment.

Section 1. In case of the removal of the President from office or of his death or resignation, the Vice-President shall become President.

Section 2. Whenever there is a vacancy in the office of the Vice-President, the President shall nominate a Vice-President who shall take office upon confirmation by a majority vote of both houses of Congress.

Section 3. Whenever the President transmits to the President pro tempore of the Senate and the Speaker of the House of Representatives his written declaration that he is unable to discharge the powers and duties of his office, and until he transmits to them a written declaration to the contrary, such powers and duties shall be discharged by the Vice-President as Acting President.

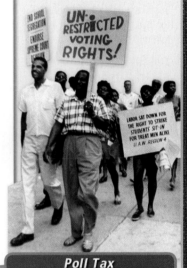

Poll Tax

The poll tax was aimed at preventing African Americans from exercising their rights. Many could not afford to pay this fee required for voting.

22. How do you think the 24th Amendment affected elections?

Line of Succession

On June 29, 2002, President George W. Bush underwent a medical procedure which required sedation. Bush declared himself temporarily unable to perform the duties of the presidency. Vice-President Dick Cheney acted as President for about two hours that day——until Bush notified in writing that he was resuming the powers and duties of the office.

23. What do you think can happen in a country where the rules for succession are not clear?

Who takes over if a president dies in office or is unable to serve? The top five in the line of succession follow:

- vice-president
- speaker of the house
- president pro tempore of the Senate
- secretary of state
- secretary of the treasury

24. Why should voters know the views of the vice-president?

Section 4. Whenever the Vice-President and a majority of either the principal officers of the executive departments or of such other body as Congress may by law provide, transmit to the President pro tempore of the Senate and the Speaker of the House of Representatives their written declaration that the President is unable to discharge the powers and duties of his office, the Vice-President shall immediately assume the powers and duties of the office as Acting President. Thereafter, when the President transmits to the President pro tempore of the Senate and the Speaker of the House of Representatives his written declaration that no inability exists, he shall resume the powers and duties of his office unless the Vice-President and a majority of either the principal officers of the executive department[s] or of such other body as Congress may by law provide, transmit within four days to the President pro tempore of the Senate and the Speaker of the House of Representatives their written declaration that the President is unable to discharge the powers and duties of his office. Thereupon Congress shall decide the issue, assembling within forty-eight hours for that purpose if not in session. If the Congress, within twenty-one days after receipt of the latter written declaration, or, if Congress is not in session, within twenty-one days after Congress is required to assemble, determines by two thirds vote of both houses that the President is unable to discharge the powers and duties of his office, the Vice-President shall continue to discharge the same as Acting President; otherwise, the President shall resume the powers and duties of his office.

Amendments Timeline

Use the key below to help you categorize the amendments.

- ■ Voting Rights
- ■ Overturned Supreme Court Decisions
- ■ Social Changes
- ■ Election Procedures and Conditions of Office

1791
Bill of Rights
Amendments 1–10

1798
Amendment 11
Protects state from lawsuits filed by citizens of other states or countries.

1804
Amendment 12
Requires separate electoral ballots for president and vice-president.

1865
Amendment 13
Bans slavery.

1868
Amendment 14
Defines American citizenship and citizens' rights.

1870
Amendment 15
Stops national and state governments from denying the vote based on race.

1791 | 1800 | 1850

AMENDMENT 26. 18-year-old Vote 1971

Passed by Congress March 23, 1971. Ratified July 1, 1971.

Note: Amendment 14, Section 2, of the Constitution was modified by Section 1 of the 26th Amendment.

Section 1. The right of citizens of the United States, who are eighteen years of age or older, to vote shall not be denied or abridged by the United States or by any state on account of age.

Section 2. The Congress shall have power to enforce this article by appropriate legislation.

AMENDMENT 27. Congressional Pay 1992

Passed by Congress September 25, 1789. Ratified May 7, 1992.

No law, varying the compensation for the services of the Senators and Representatives, shall take effect, until an election of Representatives shall have intervened.

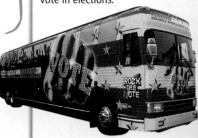

The Youth Vote

Members of the recording industry founded Rock the Vote. They urge young people to vote in elections.

Amendments 11–27 Assessment

MAIN IDEAS

1. How has the Constitution adapted to social changes and trends?
2. Which amendments affected the office of president?
3. Which pair of amendments shows the failure of laws to solve a social problem?
4. Which amendments corrected unfair treatment toward African Americans and women?

CRITICAL THINKING

5. **Summarize** What is the purpose of amending the Constitution?

Think about
- the purpose of the Constitution
- problems and issues that Americans have faced throughout U.S. history

---

1919
Amendment 18
Prohibits making, selling, and shipping alcoholic beverages.

1920
Amendment 19
Extends the vote to women.

1961
Amendment 23
Gives citizens of Washington, D.C., right to vote in presidential elections.

1933
Amendment 21
Repeals Amendment 18.

1964
Amendment 24
Bans poll taxes.

1971
Amendment 26
Gives 18-year-olds right to vote in federal and state elections.

1900   **1950**   **2000**

1913
Amendment 16
Allows Congress to tax incomes.

Amendment 17
Establishes direct election of U.S. senators.

1933
Amendment 20
Changes date for starting new Congress and inaugurating new president.

1951
Amendment 22
Limits terms president can serve to two.

1967
Amendment 25
Sets procedures for presidential succession.

1992
Amendment 27
Limits ability of Congress to increase its pay.

I'M AGAINST THE 3rd TERM
WASHINGTON WOULDN'T
GRANT COULDN'T
ROOSEVELT SHOULDN'T

Constitution Assessment

VOCABULARY

Briefly explain the significance of each of the following.

1. electors
2. impeachment
3. naturalization
4. felonies
5. bill of attainder
6. ex post facto law
7. suffrage
8. due process of law
9. servitude
10. primary

KEY IDEAS

1 Article 1 (pages 267–275)

11. What are the requirements for becoming a member of the House of Representatives and the Senate?

12. What are two military powers granted to Congress?

2 Articles 2–3 (pages 276–281)

13. How does the electoral college choose the president?

14. What are three powers of the president?

15. What are the two most important powers of the federal courts?

3 Articles 4–7 (pages 282–285)

16. How can the Constitution be changed?

17. If a state law and a federal law conflict, which law must be obeyed? Why?

18. How was the Constitution ratified?

4 Bill of Rights and Amendments 11–27 (pages 286–297)

19. What five freedoms are guaranteed in the First Amendment?

20. Which amendments extend voting rights to a broader range of Americans?

CRITICAL THINKING

21. **Drawing Conclusions** In a two-column chart, summarize the processes for changing the Constitution. Then use your completed chart to answer the questions below.

Proposing Amendments	Ratifying Amendments
1.	1.
2.	2.

   a. What role can citizens play in proposing amendments?

   b. What do you think are the main reasons for changing the Constitution?

22. **Make Inferences** Explain how the "elastic clause" in Article 1 gives Congress the authority to take action on other issues unknown to the Framers of the Constitution.

23. **Analyze Leadership** Think about the president's roles described in the Constitution. What qualities does a president need to succeed as a leader in so many different areas?

24. **Recognize Effects** How would you describe the impact of the 14th, 15th, and 16th Amendments on life in the United States?

25. **Citizenship** Suppose you and your family go on a road trip across several states. According to Article 4 of the Constitution, what citizens' rights do you have in the states you are visiting?

26. **Interpret Graphs** Read the graph below. What age group scored highest? Which scored lowest?

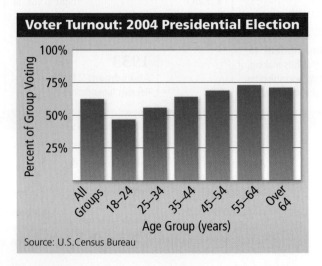

Voter Turnout: 2004 Presidential Election

Percent of Group Voting

Age Group (years): All Groups, 18–24, 25–34, 35–44, 45–54, 55–64, Over 64

Source: U.S. Census Bureau

☑ **TEST PRACTICE**

• **Online Test Practice @ ClassZone.com**
• **Test-Taking Strategies & Practice** at the front of this book

MULTIPLE CHOICE

Use the cartoon and your knowledge of U.S. history to answer question 1.

1. This cartoon shows two FBI officers carrying out their duties under the USA Patriot Act of 2001. The cartoon warns of too much power in the hands of

   A. the government

   B. the citizens

   C. young people

   D. libraries

Use the quotation and your knowledge of U.S. history to answer question 2.

❝ [The president] shall have power, by and with the advice and consent of the Senate, to make treaties, provided two-thirds of the Senators present concur; and he shall nominate, and by and with the advice and consent of the Senate, shall appoint ambassadors, other public ministers and consuls, judges of the Supreme Court, and all other officers of the United States . . . ❞

—U.S. Constitution, Art. 2, Sec. 2, part 2

2. The passage describes checks on the power of

   A. the president

   B. the judiciary

   C. the Senate

   D. the states

YOU BE THE HISTORIAN

27. **Make Inferences** How does the constitution reflect the fear of too strong a central government?

28. **Citizenship** Members of the electoral college elect the president. Would you support a campaign to choose the president by direct vote?

29. **Evaluate** The 15th, 19th, and 26th amendments give voting rights to specific groups. Why was it necessary for Congress to spell out these groups' rights in amendments?

30. **WHAT IF?** Suppose the 19th Amendment had been defeated. In what ways might this have affected American women?

31. **Connect _to_ Today** The Bill of Rights guarantees a defendant a speedy, public trial. Do you think this guarantee is being observed today?

32. **Writing** Report Use the Internet to research the U.S. Supreme Court. Write a brief report explaining the steps necessary towards becoming a Supreme Court justice.

 Answer the

ESSENTIAL QUESTION

How has our 220-year-old Constitution remained a living document?

Written Response Write a two-to three-paragraph response to the Essential Question. Be sure to consider the key ideas of each section as well as the principles of the U.S. Constitution. Use the Response rubric below to guide your thinking and writing.

Response Rubric

A strong response will include:

• discussion of the purpose for extablishing the U.S. Constitution

• analysis of the limits of power within the U.S Constitution

• explanation of the purposes for and the processes of amending the U.S. Constitution.

The Role of the Citizen

Citizens of the United States enjoy many basic rights and freedoms. Freedom of speech and religion are examples. These rights are guaranteed by the Constitution, the Bill of Rights, and other amendments to the Constitution. Along with these rights, however, come **responsibilities**. Obeying rules and laws, voting, and serving on juries are some examples.

Reason and **respect** are also important aspects of citizenship. Reason—considering perspectives, applying logical and analytical thought, and exercising good judgment—is an important part of developing positive character qualities. Respect—for one's self, for other people, and for the community—plays a key role in how you participate in society. These Three R's of Democratic Citizenship are listed below. As you read through this handbook, note how the Three R's impact all aspects of citizenship.

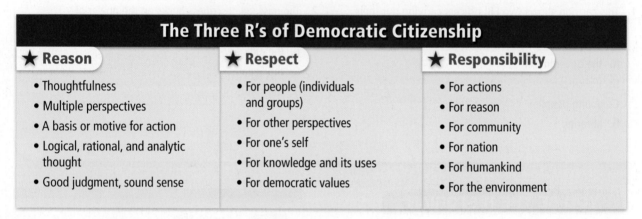

The Three R's of Democratic Citizenship

★ Reason

- Thoughtfulness
- Multiple perspectives
- A basis or motive for action
- Logical, rational, and analytic thought
- Good judgment, sound sense

★ Respect

- For people (individuals and groups)
- For other perspectives
- For one's self
- For knowledge and its uses
- For democratic values

★ Responsibility

- For actions
- For reason
- For community
- For nation
- For humankind
- For the environment

Active Citizenship

Active citizenship is not limited to adults. Younger citizens can help their communities become better places. The following pages will help you to learn about your rights and responsibilities. Knowing them will help you to become an active and involved citizen of your community.

The chart below lists five important ways *you* can be a model citizen. The examples in the pages that follow provide details about the five aspects of citizenship listed here.

How To Be a Model Citizen

1	2	3	4	5
Know your rights	Be responsible	Stay informed	Make good decisions	Take action in your community

The weather was sunny but cold on January 20, 1961—the day that John F. Kennedy became the 35th president of the United States. In his first speech as president, he urged all Americans to serve their country. Since then, Kennedy's words have inspired millions of Americans to become more active citizens.

❝ Ask not what your country can do for you—ask what you can do for your country! ❞

—John F. Kennedy

President John F. Kennedy urged all Americans to become active citizens and work to improve their communities.

What Is a Citizen?

A citizen is a legal member of a nation and pledges loyalty to that nation. A citizen has certain guaranteed rights, protections, and responsibilities. A citizen is a member of a community and wants to make it a good place to live.

Today in the United States there are a number of ways to become a citizen. The most familiar are citizenship by birth and citizenship by naturalization. All citizens have the right to equal protection under the law.

Citizenship by Birth A child born in the United States is a citizen by birth. Children born to U.S. citizens traveling or living outside the country are citizens. Even children born in the United States to parents who are not citizens of the United States are considered U.S. citizens. These children have dual citizenship. This means they are citizens of two countries—both the United States and the country of their parents' citizenship. At the age of 18, the child may choose one of the countries for permanent citizenship.

New U.S. citizens being sworn in on Ellis Island.

Citizenship by Naturalization A person who is not a citizen of the United States may become one through a process called naturalization. To become a naturalized citizen, a person must meet certain requirements.

- Be at least 18 years old. Children under the age of 18 automatically become naturalized citizens when their parents do.
- Enter the United States legally.
- Live in the United States for five years as a permanent resident prior to application.
- Read, write, and speak English.
- Show knowledge of American history and government.

The Naturalization Process

1. File an application.
2. Get fingerprints taken.
3. Be interviewed and take an examination.
4. Take an oath of allegiance.

The Role of the Citizen **301**

What Are Your Rights?

Citizens of the United States are guaranteed rights by the U.S. Constitution, state constitutions, and state and federal laws. All citizens have three kinds of rights:

1 **Basic Freedoms** Citizens' basic rights and freedoms are sometimes called **civil rights**. Some of these rights are personal, and others are political.

2 **Protection From Unfair Government Actions** The second category of rights is intended to protect citizens from unfair government actions.

3 **Equal Treatment Under the Law** The third category is the right to equal treatment under the law. The government cannot treat one individual or group differently from another.

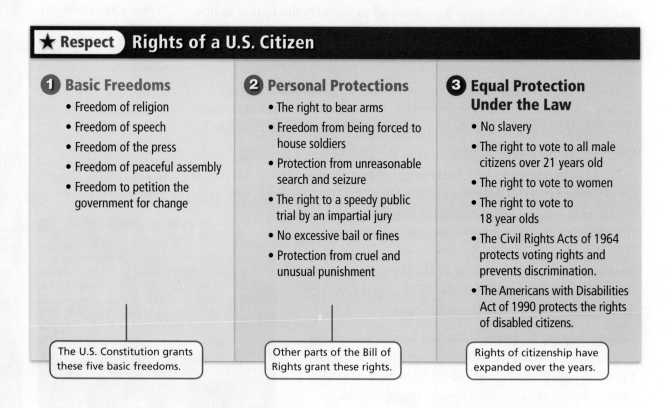

★ Respect **Rights of a U.S. Citizen**

1 Basic Freedoms
- Freedom of religion
- Freedom of speech
- Freedom of the press
- Freedom of peaceful assembly
- Freedom to petition the government for change

The U.S. Constitution grants these five basic freedoms.

2 Personal Protections
- The right to bear arms
- Freedom from being forced to house soldiers
- Protection from unreasonable search and seizure
- The right to a speedy public trial by an impartial jury
- No excessive bail or fines
- Protection from cruel and unusual punishment

Other parts of the Bill of Rights grant these rights.

3 Equal Protection Under the Law
- No slavery
- The right to vote to all male citizens over 21 years old
- The right to vote to women
- The right to vote to 18 year olds
- The Civil Rights Acts of 1964 protects voting rights and prevents discrimination.
- The Americans with Disabilities Act of 1990 protects the rights of disabled citizens.

Rights of citizenship have expanded over the years.

Limits to Rights The rights guaranteed to citizens have sensible limits. For example, the right to free speech does not allow a person to falsely shout, "Fire!" at a crowded concert. The government may place limits on certain rights to protect national security or to provide equal opportunities for all citizens. And rights come with responsibilities.

What Are Your Responsibilities?

For American democracy to work, citizens must carry out important responsibilities. There are two kinds of responsibilities—personal and civic. Personal responsibilities include taking care of yourself, helping your family, knowing right from wrong, and behaving in a respectful way.

Civic responsibilities are those that involve your government and community. They include obeying rules and laws, serving on juries, paying taxes, and defending your country when called upon. One of the most important responsibilities is voting. When you turn 18, you will have that right.

As a young person, you can be a good citizen in a number of ways. You might work with other people in your community to make it a fair and just place to live. Working for a political party or writing to your elected officials about issues that concern you are some other examples.

The chart below shows how responsibilities change with a citizen's age. Notice that all citizens share the responsibility to obey the laws of their communities.

★ **Responsibility** **Responsibilities of a U.S. Citizen**

UNDER 18
- Receive an education, either at school or at home.
- Take responsibility for one's behavior.
- Help one's family.

ALL AGES
- Obey rules and laws.
- Be tolerant of others.
- Pay taxes.
- Volunteer for a cause.
- Stay informed about issues.

OVER 18
- Vote.
- Serve on a jury.
- Serve in the military to defend the country.

Many citizens are required to serve on a jury to help ensure balance and fairness in our country's legal system.

Building Citizenship Skills

Good citizenship skills include staying informed, solving problems or making decisions, and taking action. Every citizen can find ways to build citizenship skills. By showing respect for the law and for the rights of others in your daily life, you promote democracy. You can also work to change conditions in your community to make sure all citizens experience freedom and justice.

How Do You Stay Informed?

Americans can sometimes feel that they have access to too much information. It may seem overwhelming. Even so, you should stay informed on issues that affect your life. Staying informed gives you the information you need to make wise decisions and helps you find ways to solve problems.

★ Responsibility Staying Informed

1 Watch, Listen, and Read

The first step in practicing good citizenship is to know how to find information that you need.

Sources of information include broadcast and print media and the Internet. Public officials and civic organizations are also good sources for additional information. Remember as you are reading to evaluate your sources.

2 Evaluate

As you become informed, you will need to make judgments about the accuracy of your news sources. You must also be aware of those sources' points of view and biases. (Bias is a one-sided presentation of an issue.)

You should determine if you need more information, and if so, where to find it. After gathering information, you may be ready to form an opinion or a plan of action to solve a problem.

3 Communicate

To bring about change in their communities, active citizens may need to contact public officials. In today's world, making contact is easy.

You can reach most public officials by telephone, voice mail, fax, or letter. Many public officials also have Internet pages or e-mail that encourages input from the public.

Teens from Stand, an Ohio youth group, with Ohio Governor Bob Taft and first lady Hope Taft.

How Do You Make Good Decisions?

Civic life involves making important decisions. As a voter, whom should you vote for? As a juror, should you find the defendant guilty or not guilty? As an informed citizen, should you support or oppose a proposed government action? Unlike decisions about which video to rent, civic decisions cannot be made by a process as easy as tossing a coin. Instead, you should use a problem-solving approach like the one shown in the chart below. Decision making won't always proceed directly from step to step. Sometimes it's necessary to backtrack a little. For example, you may get to the "Analyze the Information" step and realize that you don't have enough information to analyze. Then you can go back a step and gather more information.

★ Reason   Making Good Decisions

Problem-solving and decision-making involves many steps. This chart shows you how to take those steps. Notice that you may have to repeat some steps depending on the information you gather.

1 Identify the Problem
Decide what the main issues are and what your goal is.

2 Gather Information
Get to know the basics of the problem. Find out as much as possible about the issues.

3 Analyze the Information
Look at the information and determine what it reveals about solving the problem.

4 Consider Options
Think of as many ways as possible to solve the problem. Don't be afraid to include ideas that others might think of as unacceptable.

5 Choose a Solution
Choose the solution you believe will best solve the problem and help you reach your goal.

6 Implement the Solution
Take action or plan to take action on a chosen solution.

7 Evaluate the Solution
Review the results of putting your solution into action. Did the solution work? Do you need to adjust the solution in some way?

Conducting a survey is one way to gather information.

How Do You Take Action in Your Community?

Across the country many young people have come up with ways to make their communities better places to live. Thirteen-year-old Aubyn Burnside of Hickory, North Carolina, is just one example. Aubyn felt sorry for foster children she saw moving their belongings in plastic trash bags. She founded Suitcases for Kids. This program provides used luggage for foster children who are moving from one home to another. Her program has been adopted by other young people in several states. Below are some ways in which you can participate in your community.

★ Respect   Taking Action

1 Find a Cause

How can you become involved in your community? First, select a community problem or issue that interests you. Some ideas from other young people include starting a support group for children with cancer, publishing a neighborhood newspaper with children's stories and art, and putting on performances to entertain people in shelters and hospitals.

2 Develop Solutions

Once you have found a cause on which you want to work, develop a plan for solving the problem. Use the decision-making or problem-solving skills you have learned to find ways to approach the problem. You may want to involve other people in your activities.

3 Follow Through

Solving problems takes time. You'll need to be patient in developing a plan. You can show leadership in working with your group by following through on meetings you set up and plans you make. When you finally solve the problem, you will feel proud of your accomplishments.

Members of Clean & Green, a Los Angeles Conservation Corps program, help to renovate a city building.

Practicing Citizenship Skills

You have learned that good citizenship involves three skills: staying informed, making good decisions, and taking action. Below are some activities to help you improve your citizenship skills. By practicing these skills you can work to make a difference in your own life and in the lives of those in your community.

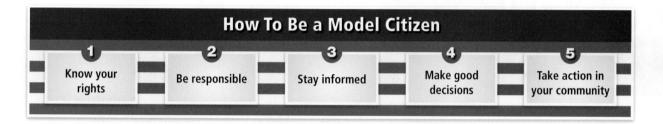

How To Be a Model Citizen

1. Know your rights
2. Be responsible
3. Stay informed
4. Make good decisions
5. Take action in your community

Stay Informed

▷ *Create a pamphlet or recruiting commercial*

Ask your school counselors or write to your state department of education to get information on state-run colleges, universities, or technical schools. Use this information to create a brochure or recruiting commercial showing these schools and the different programs and degrees they offer.

Keep in mind

What's there for me?
It may help you to think about what areas students are interested in and may want to pursue after graduation.

Where is it?
You may want to have a map showing where the schools are located in your state.

How can I afford it?
Students might want to know if financial aid is available to attend the schools you have featured.

Make Good Decisions

▷ *Create a game board or skit*

Study the steps on page 305. With a small group, develop a skit that explains the steps in problem solving. Present your skit to younger students in your school. As an alternative, create a game board that would help younger students understand the steps in making a decision.

Keep in mind

What do children this age understand?
Be sure to create a skit or game at an age-appropriate level.

What kinds of decisions do younger students make?
Think about the kinds of decisions that the viewers of your skit or players of the game might make.

How can I make it interesting?
Use visual aids to help students understand the steps in decision making.

Take Action

▷ *Create a bulletin board for your class*

Do some research on the Internet or consult the yellow pages under "Social Services" to find the names of organizations that have volunteer opportunities for young people. Call or write for more information. Then create a bulletin board for your class showing groups that need volunteer help.

Keep in mind

What kinds of jobs are they?
You may want to list the types of skills or jobs that volunteer groups are looking for.

How old do I have to be?
Some groups may be looking for younger volunteers; others may need older volunteers.

How do I get there?
How easy is it to get to the volunteer group's location?

Why It Matters Now

It was one thing for the founders to write a Constitution, another to make it work. Every decision made by the president and the Congress in the first 25 years of the Republic established a tradition of governance that continues to influence how we live today.

The history of liberty is a history of resistance.
The history of liberty is a history of limitations
of governmental power, not the increase of it.
—Woodrow Wilson

Launching a New Republic

1789–1800

ESSENTIAL QUESTION

What political traditions and tensions first appeared in the early years of the new republic?

CONNECT ⟳ Geography & History

How might the politics and geography of the United States have affected the choice of a capital?

Think about:

1 why two capitals preceded the final choice of Washington, D.C.

2 why the land forming the District of Columbia came from the states of Virginia and Maryland.

3 the geographic location of early settlement.

Washington's inaugural

Washington's medicine chest

1789

George Washington becomes the first president of the United States.

French Revolution in progress

1795 Pinckney's Treaty ratified.

▼

Effect U.S. southern border set at 31st parallel

1794 Battle of Fallen Timbers takes place.

▼

Effect Treaty of Greenville (1795) is signed.

Animated GEOGRAPHY & HISTORY
Early America *1776–1800*

Click here to preview the New Republic
@ClassZone.com

Claimed by both
U.S. and Britain

MAINE
(MASS.)

BRITISH CANADA

Montreal

VT.
Windsor N.H.
Exeter ★ ● Portsmouth
● Boston
Albany ★ MASS. ● Providence
CONN. ● Newport
New Haven ★ R.I.

Lake Ontario

NEW YORK

Lake Erie

Lake Huron

Lake Michigan

Mississippi River

✪ New York
(1785–1790)
PENNSYLVANIA
Philadelphia ★ Trenton
(1790–1800)
Lancaster ★ ✪ NEW JERSEY
Baltimore ★ Dover
Annapolis ★ DELAWARE
Washington, D.C. MARYLAND
(1800–Present-day)

INDIANA
TERRITORY

TERRITORY
NORTHWEST OF
OHIO RIVER

Ohio River

VIRGINIA
Richmond ★ ● Williamsburg

FRENCH LOUISIANA

★ Frankfort
KENTUCKY

APPALACHIAN MOUNTAINS

70°W
40°N
35°N

Raleigh ★
Knoxville ★ NORTH CAROLINA
TENNESSEE
Tennessee River

ATLANTIC
OCEAN

SOUTH CAROLINA

TERRITORY
SOUTH OF
OHIO RIVER

★ Columbia

● Charleston

Louisville ★
GEORGIA

✪ National capital
★ State capital

MISSISSIPPI
TERRITORY

● Savannah

30°N

Mississippi River

SPANISH FLORIDA ● St. Augustine

0   200   200 miles
0   100   200 kilometers

New Orleans ● Gulf of Mexico

85°W   80°W   75°W

1798 Alien and
Sedition Acts target
immigrants and
freedom of the press.

1800

1796 Federalists win
presidential election

▼

Effect John Adams
becomes president

(*top left*) John Adams'
birthplace in Braintree, Mass.

(*left*) John Adams

Convention of 1800
Thomas Jefferson is
elected president.

▶ Key Ideas

BEFORE, YOU LEARNED

A new Constitution, approved in 1788, served as a guide for the new republican government.

NOW YOU WILL LEARN

George Washington and his advisers faced many challenges during his Presidency.

▶ Vocabulary

TERMS & NAMES

Federal Judiciary (joo•DISH•ee•AIR•ee) **Act** 1789 law passed by the first Congress that set up lower federal courts

John Jay first chief justice of the U.S. Supreme Court

attorney general nation's top legal officer; today also the head of the Department of Justice

cabinet group of executive department heads that serve as the president's chief advisers

BACKGROUND VOCABULARY

inaugurate (in•AW•gyuh•rate) to formally swear in or induct into office

precedent (PRE•seh•dent) an example that becomes standard practice

tariff tax on imported goods

Visual Vocabulary
cabinet meeting

▶ Reading Strategy

Re-create the diagram shown at right. As you read and respond to the **KEY QUESTIONS**, use the diagram to list members of Washington's cabinet and their responsibilities.

 See Skillbuilder Handbook, page R6.

CATEGORIZE

Cabinet Member	Responsibilities
Hamilton	*managed the nation's money*
Jefferson	*oversaw foreign relations*

 GRAPHIC ORGANIZERS
Go to **Interactive Review** @ ClassZone.com

Washington's Presidency

 14.E.3 Compare the basic principles of the United States and its international interests (e.g., *territory, environment, trade, use of technology*).
14.F.3a Analyze historical influences on the development of political ideas and practices as enumerated in the Declaration of Independence, the United States Constitution, the Bill of Rights and the Illinois Constitution.

One American's Story

Charles Thomson had served as secretary of the Continental Congress in 1774. Now, on April 14, 1789, he came to Mount Vernon in Virginia with a letter for George Washington. Washington knew the reason for the visit. Thomson's letter was to tell him that he had been elected the nation's first president. Before giving Washington the letter, Thomson made a short speech.

George Washington— shown in a wax likeness—was a popular choice for first president of the new nation.

PRIMARY SOURCE

❝ I have now Sir to inform you that . . . your patriotism and your readiness to sacrifice . . . private enjoyments to preserve the happiness of your Country [convinced the Congress that you would accept] this great and important Office to which you are called not only by the unanimous votes of the Electors but by the voice of America. ❞

—Charles Thomson, quoted in *George Washington's Papers,*
at the Library of Congress 1741–1799

Washington accepted the honor and the burden of his new office. He would soon guide the nation through its early years.

Washington's New Government

🔻 **KEY QUESTION** How did Washington's presidency shape new political traditions?

Under the new Constitution, the first presidential election was held in 1789. Washington won, and traveled to New York City, the nation's capital, to be **inaugurated**, or formally sworn in, as president. On April 30, 1789 at Federal Hall, the inauguration took place. The runner-up, John Adams of Massachusetts, became Washington's vice-president. As the nation's first president, Washington knew that his every action would set a **precedent** —an example that becomes standard practice. Under the first president, many political institutions and traditions were established.

Congressional Decisions Washington took charge of a political system that was a bold experiment. No one knew if a government based on the will of the people could really work. The new government began to take shape in the summer of 1789. First, people argued over what to call Washington. Some suggested "His Excellency," but others argued that made the president sound as if he was a king. Finally, in keeping with the simplicity of a republic, Washington agreed to "Mr. President."

The writers of the Constitution had left many matters to be decided by Congress. For example, the Constitution created a Supreme Court but left it to Congress to decide on the details. What type of additional courts should there be and how many? What would happen if federal court decisions conflicted with state laws?

To help answer these questions, Congress passed a federal court system under the **Federal Judiciary** (joo•DISH•ee•AIR•ee) **Act** of 1789. This act gave the Supreme Court six members: a chief justice, or judge, and five associate justices. Over time, that number has grown to nine. The law also provided for less powerful federal courts. Washington appointed **John Jay**, the prominent lawyer and diplomat, as the first chief justice of the Supreme Court.

Assembling a Cabinet The Constitution also gave Congress the task of creating departments to help the president lead the nation. The president had the power to appoint the heads of these departments.

Congress created the departments: state, war, treasury, justice and postal service. The State Department dealt with relations with other countries. The War Department was in charge of the nation's defense. The Treasury Department was in charge of the nation's economy, or financial security.

George Washington's first cabinet

Washington chose talented people to run the departments. For secretary of war, he picked Henry Knox, a trusted general during the Revolution. For secretary of state, Washington chose Thomas Jefferson. He had been serving as U.S. minister to France. Washington chose the brilliant Alexander Hamilton to be secretary of the treasury. Hamilton was to manage the government's money. The secretary's ties to the president began during the war when he had served as one of Washington's aides. To advise the government on legal matters, Washington picked Edmund Randolph as **attorney general**.

These department heads and the attorney general made up Washington's **cabinet**. The Constitution made no mention of a cabinet, but Washington began the practice of calling his cabinet to advise him on official matters. Another high office, that of postmaster general, was not elevated to cabinet status until 1829.

▲ **EVALUATE** Explain how the decisions made by the first Congress created political traditions.

The Nation's Finances

KEY QUESTION What financial problems faced the new nation?

Washington assigned his secretary of the treasury, Alexander Hamilton, the task of straightening out the nation's finances. The most urgent money issue was the U.S. government's war debts.

War Debts During the Revolution, the United States had borrowed millions of dollars from France, Spain, and the Netherlands. The new nation was also in debt to private citizens, including soldiers who had received bonds—certificates that promised payment plus interest—as compensation for their services during the war. State governments also had wartime debts. By 1789, the national debt—foreign and domestic—totaled more than $52 million.

Most government leaders agreed that the nation must pay its debts to win the respect of both foreign nations and its own citizens. Hamilton saw that the new nation must assure other countries that it was responsible about money. These nations would do business with the United States if they saw that the country would pay its debts.

Hamilton's Political Views Hamilton believed in a strong central government. He thought the power of the national government should be stronger than that of the state governments. Hamilton also believed that government should encourage business and industry and that the nation's prosperity depended on the support of the nation's wealthy merchants and manufacturers. The government owed money to many of these rich men. By paying them back, Hamilton hoped to win their support for the new government.

Hamilton's Proposals In 1790, Hamilton presented his plan to Congress. He proposed three steps to improve the nation's finances and to strengthen the national government: 1) paying off all war debts, 2) raising government revenues, and 3) creating a national bank.

Hamilton also wanted the federal government to pay off the war debts of the states. However, sectional differences arose over repayment of state debts. Many Southern states resisted because they had already gone further

History Makers

Alexander Hamilton   1755–1804

Hamilton was one of the giants of American history. In his early twenties, he was a personal aide to General George Washington during the American Revolution. In the 1780s, he was a signer of the U.S. Constitution. He was one of the authors of a set of essays called *The Federalist* papers that persuaded Americans to ratify the Constitution.

As the first secretary of the treasury, Hamilton helped ensure the economic health of the new republic. His actions helped support his belief in a strong government and helped establish the executive branch as the most powerful branch of the government.

COMPARING *Leaders*

Compare Hamilton's leadership qualities to those of other American leaders mentioned in the chapter.

ONLINE BIOGRAPHY For more on Alexander Hamilton, go to the **Research & Writing Center** @ ClassZone.com

HOW BANKS WORK

Hamilton believed that a national bank could help the economy of the new nation. It would be funded by a partnership between the federal government and wealthy private investors. In that way, private money would be tied to the country's welfare.

DEPOSITS

LOANS

LOANS

DEPOSITS

If people want to buy something, like a house or a car, they ask the bank to lend them the money. But they have to pay back the money they borrow, plus interest. The interest rate is higher than the interest rate they get when they make a deposit.

Savers are loaning their money to the bank when they put it in a savings account. The bank pays them interest for using their money. The bank uses their money to make more money.

Businesses use loans to create new products and services. As they sell more, they hire more workers and raise wages.

PURCHASES

CRITICAL THINKING

1. **Analyze Point of View** Do you think that the people who feared a strong central government supported Hamilton's idea of a national bank? Why or why not?

2. **Make Inferences** What are some ways that banks make money?

towards paying off their debts. Hamilton asked Thomas Jefferson of Virginia to help him gain Southern support. They reached a compromise by agreeing that the southern states would support Hamilton's plan and back payment of state debts. In return, northerners would support locating the capital in the South. The location chosen was on the banks of the Potomac River.

Building a Strong Government To raise revenue, the secretary of the treasury favored **tariffs**, which are taxes on imported goods. Tariffs serve two purposes: raising money for the government and encouraging the growth of national business. Americans bought goods from overseas in large quantities, including hemp, steel, and molasses. Tariffs on these goods kept a steady income flowing to the government. Since tariffs made foreign goods more expensive, they encouraged people to buy American goods.

Hamilton also called for the creation of a national bank. It would give the government a safe place to keep money. It would also make loans to businesses and government. Most important, it would issue bank notes—paper money that could be used as currency.

Hamilton's Opponents Overall, Hamilton's plan was to strengthen the national government. Opponents of a national bank, including Jefferson and Madison, claimed that the bank would encourage an unhealthy partnership between the government and wealthy business interests. This angered Jefferson in particular. Those against the bank also argued that, since the Constitution does not mention a national bank, the government cannot create a national bank. They believed in the narrow or "strict" interpretation of the Constitution.

These differences began the debate among those who favored a "strict" interpretation of the Constitution, one in which the federal government has very limited powers, and a "loose" interpretation, which favors greater federal powers. Jefferson favored a strict interpretation, and Hamilton favored a broad or loose interpretation of the Constitution.

Hamilton's group used the so-called "Elastic Clause" of the Constitution (Article 1, Section 8, Number 18) to argue their case. This clause gives Congress the authority to do whatever is "necessary and proper" to carry out its specific powers, such as regulating commerce.

Washington backed Hamilton, and the Bank of the United States was established in 1791. Washington mostly tried to remain above the conflict between Hamilton and Jefferson and to encourage them to work together despite their basic differences. However, the formation of the two political factions, based on Hamilton's and Jefferson's opposing philosophies, laid the foundation for the American political factions that followed.

 CATEGORIZE List Hamilton's solutions for the nation's finances.

 Illinois Learning Standards *Review*

ONLINE QUIZ
For test practice, go to
Interactive Review @ ClassZone.com

TERMS & NAMES

1. Explain the importance of
- Federal Judiciary Act
- John Jay
- attorney general
- cabinet

USING YOUR READING NOTES

2. Categorize Complete the diagram you started at the beginning of the section.

Cabinet Member	Responsibilities
Hamilton	*managed the nation's money*
Jefferson	*oversaw foreign relations*

KEY IDEAS

3. What was the purpose of Washington's cabinet?

4. What were the three steps proposed by Hamilton for helping the nation's finances?

CRITICAL THINKING

5. Compare and Contrast How did Hamilton and Jefferson differ in their interpretation of the Constitution?

6. Make Inferences Why might merchants and manufacturers support a strong central government?

7. Connect *to* **Today** What organizational decisions made by the first Congress are still in effect today?

8. Writing Letter Imagine it's the 1790s. Write a letter to the editor that either supports or opposes Hamilton's plan for a national bank.

SECTION 2 Reading for Understanding

▶ Key Ideas

BEFORE, YOU LEARNED

George Washington faced many challenges during his presidency.

NOW YOU WILL LEARN

Washington established central authority at home and avoided war abroad

▶ Vocabulary

TERMS & NAMES

Battle of Fallen Timbers 1794 battle between Native Americans and American forces

Treaty of Greenville 1795 treaty in which 12 Native American tribes ceded control of much of Ohio and Indiana to the U.S. government

Whiskey Rebellion 1794 protest against the government's tax on whiskey by backcountry farmers

French Revolution revolution overthrowing the government in France that began in 1787 and ended in violence and mass executions

Jay's Treaty agreement that ended the dispute with Britain over American shipping during the French Revolution

Pinckney's (PINK•neez) **Treaty** 1795 treaty with Spain allowing U.S. commercial use of the Mississippi River

BACKGROUND VOCABULARY

cede surrender, or give up

REVIEW

Northwest Territory area bounded by the Ohio and Mississippi Rivers and the Great Lakes

neutral (NOO•truhl) not siding with any other country in dispute

▶ Reading Strategy

Re-create the diagram shown at right. As you read and respond to the **KEY QUESTIONS**, use the table to note important challenges and responses of the first U.S. government.

See Skillbuilder Handbook, page R3.

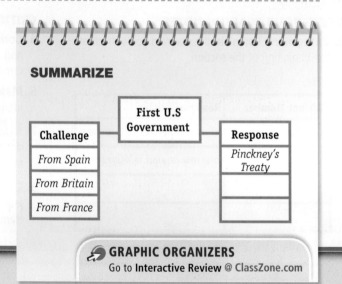

SUMMARIZE

First U.S Government

Challenge		Response
From Spain		*Pinckney's Treaty*
From Britain		
From France		

GRAPHIC ORGANIZERS
Go to **Interactive Review** @ ClassZone.com

Challenges to the New Government

14.E.3 Compare the basic principles of the United States and its international interests (e.g., *territory, environment, trade, use of technology*).

18.C.3b Explain how diverse groups have contributed to U.S. social systems over time.

One American's Story

Settlers moving west often met fierce resistance from Native Americans. In 1790 and 1791, for example, Chief Little Turtle of the Miami tribe of Ohio had won decisive victories against U.S. troops.

In 1794, the Miami again faced attack by American forces. Little Turtle warned his people about the troops led by General "Mad Anthony" Wayne.

PRIMARY SOURCE

❝ We have beaten the enemy twice under separate commanders. . . . The Americans are now led by a chief [Wayne] who never sleeps. . . . We have never been able to surprise him. . . . It would be prudent [wise] to listen to his offers of peace. ❞

—Little Turtle, quoted in *The Life and Times of Little Turtle*

Chief Little Turtle was willing to negotiate with U.S. leaders, but his tribal council voted for war.

While the council members weighed Little Turtle's warning, President Washington was making plans to secure, or to guard or protect, the western borders of the new nation.

Problems at Home

▼ **KEY QUESTION** How did two crises reveal the power of the national government?

Washington had always supported the idea of a strong national government. During his presidency, the government revealed its strength when dealing with a number of threatening situations.

Competing Claims to Territory Washington knew the nation needed peace to prosper. But trouble brewed in the Trans-Appalachian West, the land between the Appalachian Mountains and the Mississippi River. The source of conflict was competing claims for these lands. The 1783 Treaty of Paris had tried to resolve the claims. And some years later, Spain, Britain, the United States, and Native Americans all claimed parts of the area.

The strongest resistance to white settlement came from Native Americans in the **Northwest Territory**. This territory was bordered by the Ohio River to the south and Canada to the north. Native Americans in that territory hoped to unite to form an independent Native American nation. The British, who still held forts north of the Ohio River, supported Native Americans because they did not want to lose their access to trade in these territories.

Washington sent troops to the Northwest Territory to defend American interests. In 1790 this first federal army was no match for warriors led by Little Turtle. A second American force was defeated in 1791. Washington then formed another army and gave command to Revolutionary hero General Anthony ("Mad Anthony") Wayne.

Native Americans are Defeated On August 20, 1794, a force of around 2,000 Native Americans met Wayne's 1,000 troops near the future site of Toledo, Ohio. The Native Americans were easily defeated. The battlefield was covered with trees that had been struck down in a storm so the Americans called it the **Battle of Fallen Timbers**.

Native Americans were defeated by U.S. troops at the Battle of Fallen Timbers. They were disappointed when the British did not come to their aid.

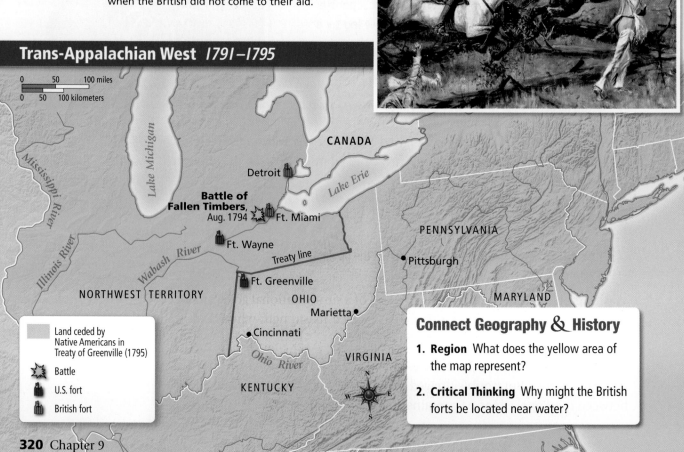

Trans-Appalachian West *1791–1795*

0   50   100 miles
0   50   100 kilometers

Mississippi River
Illinois River
Lake Michigan
CANADA
Detroit
Lake Erie
Battle of Fallen Timbers, Aug. 1794
Ft. Miami
Ft. Wayne
Wabash River
Treaty line
PENNSYLVANIA
Pittsburgh
Ft. Greenville
NORTHWEST TERRITORY
OHIO
Marietta
MARYLAND
Cincinnati
Ohio River
VIRGINIA
KENTUCKY

Land ceded by Native Americans in Treaty of Greenville (1795)
Battle
U.S. fort
British fort

Connect Geography & History

1. **Region** What does the yellow area of the map represent?

2. **Critical Thinking** Why might the British forts be located near water?

The Native Americans withdrew. The British, not wanting war with the United States, refused to help them. The Battle of Fallen Timbers crushed Native American hopes of keeping their land in the Northwest Territory. Twelve tribes signed the **Treaty of Greenville** in 1795. They agreed to **cede**, or surrender, much of present-day Ohio as well as numerous ports and outposts in Illinois, Michigan, and Indiana to the U.S. government.

Trouble in the Backcountry In spite of the United States' success at the Battle of Fallen Timbers, Washington soon found it necessary to put another army into the field. This was in response to a conflict over a new tax.

To raise revenue, Treasury Secretary Hamilton had pushed through Congress a tax to be levied specifically on the manufacture of whiskey. The tax hit small, backcountry farmers the hardest. One of their major crops was corn. But whiskey made from corn was more profitable than raw grain, so whiskey became central to the Backcountry economy. Having little money with which to buy goods, small farmers used whiskey like money to trade for other goods. As well, whiskey was one of the few local products suitable for transport to markets across the Appalachians. When the whiskey tax was enacted, outraged farmers from Pennsylvania to Georgia resisted.

Farmers Revolt In the summer of 1794, a group of farmers in western Pennsylvania staged the **Whiskey Rebellion** against the tax. One armed group attacked and burned the home of the regional tax collector. Others threatened an armed attack on Pittsburgh.

Most backcountry farmers had a long tradition of independent living and resistance to authority. And backcountry rebelliousness had helped defeat the British. That same rebelliousness was now seen as a threat to the new republic, and Washington and Hamilton needed to keep order. They looked upon the Whiskey Rebellion as an opportunity for the federal government to show it could enforce the law along the western frontier. Hamilton scolded the rebels for resisting the law.

PRIMARY SOURCE

❝ Such a resistance is treason against society, against liberty, against everything that ought to be dear to a free, enlightened, and prudent people. To tolerate it were to abandon your most precious interests. Not to subdue it were to tolerate it. ❞

—Alexander Hamilton, *The Works of Alexander Hamilton*

In October 1794, General Henry Lee, with Hamilton at his side, led an army of 13,000 soldiers into western Pennsylvania to put down the uprising. As news of the army's approach spread, the rebels fled. After much effort, federal troops rounded up a group of about 20 accused leaders. Washington had proved his point. He had shown that the government had the power and the will to enforce its laws. Meanwhile, events in Europe gave Washington a different kind of challenge.

▲ **SUMMARIZE** Describe how Washington dealt with two early crises.

Connecting History

Individual Rights vs. Majority Rule
The Whiskey Rebellion marked the first major challenge to the authority of the federal government. When the armed rebels gathered in Pittsburgh in 1794, they were angry not only about the whiskey tax but also about their underrepresentation in the state legislatures.

History *through* Art

The Women of Les Halles Marching to Versailles, 5th October 1789

by Jean-Francois Janinet

The work shows hungry, angry French women marching in support of the revolution. They are out to confront the French royal family who live in the palace of Versailles, about 15 miles (24 km) southwest of Paris, the capital of France.

CRITICAL VIEWING Why did the artist choose to portray some ordinary people of the revolution?

Problems Abroad

🔻 **KEY QUESTION** Why did events in Europe create problems for America?

The United States was now independent, but it remained tied to European nations by treaty and through trade. Britain was still the United States's biggest trading partner. France was allied with the United States by a treaty of 1778. When European nations went to war, Americans feared being dragged into the conflict.

Trouble in France In 1789, a financial crisis led the French people to rebel against their government. As in the American Revolution, the French revolutionaries demanded liberty and equality. At first, Americans supported the **French Revolution**. By 1792, however, the revolution had become very violent. Thousands were killed. Then, in 1793, the revolutionaries executed both the king and queen of France.

Other European monarchs believed the revolution threatened their own thrones by spreading outside of France. They joined in opposition to the revolution. France soon declared war on Britain, Holland, and Spain. Britain took the lead in the fight against France.

France and Britain at War War between France and Britain put the United States in an awkward position. France had backed America in the Revolution against the British. Also, many ordinary Americans saw France's revolution as proof that the American cause had been just.

Jefferson felt that a move to crush the French Revolution was an attack on liberty everywhere. But Hamilton argued that Britain was the United States' primary trading partner, and British trade was too vital to risk war. In April 1793, Washington declared that the United States would remain **neutral**, meaning it would not take sides. Congress then passed a law forbidding the United States to help either Britain or France.

Hamilton and Jefferson came to agree that entering a war was not in the new nation's interest. But Federalists attacked Jefferson for his support of France anyway. Jefferson was also tired of Washington's support of Hamilton's ideas. In 1793, Jefferson resigned as secretary of state.

Britain made it hard for the United States to remain neutral. The British were seizing the cargoes of American ships carrying goods from the French West Indies. Chief Justice John Jay went to England for talks about the seizure of U.S. ships. Jay also hoped to persuade the British to give up their forts on the northwest frontier.

Jay's Treaty During the talks in 1794, news came of the U.S. victory at the Battle of Fallen Timbers. Fearing another entanglement, the British agreed to leave the Ohio Valley by 1796. In what is called **Jay's Treaty**, the British also agreed to pay damages for U.S. vessels they had seized. Jay failed, however, to open up the profitable British Caribbean trade to Americans. Because of this, Jay's Treaty got through the House and Senate with great difficulty. Western settlers, for example, were angry that the British were still allowed to continue their fur trade on the American side of the U.S.-Canadian border. In spite of criticism, Jay's Treaty did help to reduce frontier tensions.

Like Jay, U.S. diplomat Thomas Pinckney helped reduce tensions along the frontier with the signing of **Pinckney's** (PINK•neez) **Treaty** of 1795. The United States won favorable terms with Spain in the peace treaty.

- Americans had the right to travel freely on the Mississippi River,
- U.S. goods could be stored at the port of New Orleans free of customs duties.
- Spain accepted the 31st parallel as the northern boundary of Florida and the southern boundary of the United States.

Together, Jay's Treaty and Pinckney's Treaty gave Americans a greater sense of security. With far less fear of European hostility, more Americans were moving west. But when Washington announced he would not run again for president, Americans were deeply divided over how the nation should be governed.

 ANALYZE Describe how crises in Europe created challenges for the new American government.

Illinois Learning Standards *Review*

⮑ **ONLINE QUIZ**
For test practice, go to
Interactive Review @ ClassZone.com

TERMS & NAMES

1. Explain the importance of:

- Battle of Fallen Timbers
- French Revolution
- Treaty of Greenville
- Jay's Treaty
- Whiskey Rebellion
- Pinckney's Treaty

USING YOUR READING NOTES

2. Summarize Complete the diagram you started at the beginning of the section.

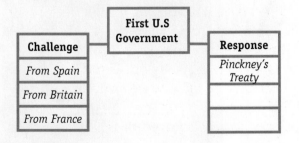

KEY IDEAS

3. Why did Washington consider it important to put down the Whiskey Rebellion?

4. How did the French Revolution create problems for the United States?

CRITICAL THINKING

5. Evaluate What were some of the advantages of the new nation remaining neutral?

6. Connect *to* Today The Whiskey Rebellion threatened civil order. What are some more current example of citizens threatening civil order in the belief that their cause is just?

7. Connect Economics & History How did Pinckney's Treaty protect American interests?

8. Geography/Art Map Make a map that shows a plan of the Battle of Fallen Timbers, or draw a scene from that battle.

NEW STYLES FOR A NEW NATION

The decade of the 1790s is often called the Federal period in the arts. During this time, Americans created art that expressed the attitudes, ideals, and hopes of their new nation.

A REVOLUTION IN FASHION

Clothing styles reflected the revolutionary political changes underway in America and France. Here, the old-style couple on the right is startled by the new fashions of youth. The ornate clothing and wigs of the aristocracy were on their way out, and a more relaxed, plainer style was on its way in.

ACHIEVEMENTS IN ART

Charles Willson Peale was America's greatest artist at this time. His work captured the informality and good humor of American culture. This painting of Peale's sons fooled even George Washington into thinking the stairs were real.

THE MODEL OF LIBERTY

The goddess of Liberty, who appeared on U.S. coins in 1795, was modeled on a famous woman of the Federal period—Anne Willing Bingham. Brilliant and highly educated, Bingham was a friend of Thomas Jefferson. Her world-famous intelligence, independent spirit, and beauty made her the perfect choice to represent liberty on America's new coins.

ABOLISHING SLAVERY

Many Americans in the early republic wanted to make America a place where "All men are created equal." Throughout the 1780s and '90s the Northern states slowly began abolishing slavery. The image shown here became an important symbol for the antislavery movement in America.

BACK TO THE FUTURE

Americans saw a link between their new republic and the ancient republic of Rome. Like the Romans, Americans had rebelled against a king and established a democracy. Architects began designing buildings for their new government using Roman forms to represent the nation's ideals of democracy and justice.

Massachusetts State House 1797

Virginia State Capitol 1789

Now look for pictures of other state capitols and identify the Roman forms you see.

Activity

Reveal the Romans!

Study the architectural forms below. Then identify Roman elements that you find in the American buildings on the left. (Some buildings might combine several Roman forms.)

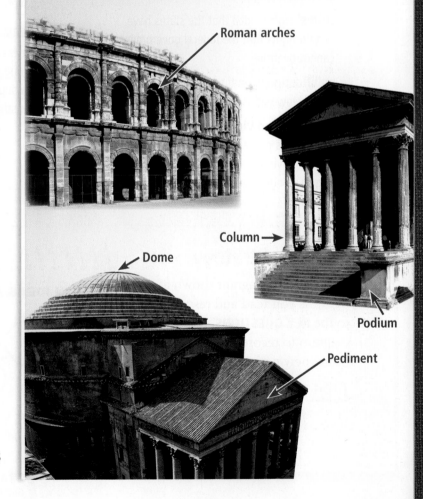

Roman arches

Column

Dome

Podium

Pediment

▶ Key Ideas

BEFORE, YOU LEARNED
Washington established central authority at home and avoided war overseas.

NOW YOU WILL LEARN
The Federalists dominated politics under the presidency of John Adams.

▶ Vocabulary

TERMS & NAMES

John Adams Second President of the United States

XYZ Affair 1797 incident in which French officials demanded a bribe from U.S. diplomats

Alien and Sedition Acts series of four laws enacted in 1798 to reduce the political power of recent immigrants

states' rights idea that the states have certain rights that the federal government cannot overrule

nullification idea that a state could cancel a federal law within the state

Kentucky and Virginia Resolutions Resolutions passed by Kentucky and Virginia in 1798 giving the states the right to declare acts of Congress null and void

BACKGROUND VOCABULARY

foreign policy relations with the governments of other nations

political party group of people that tries to promote its ideas and influence government

aliens immigrants who are not yet citizens

sedition stirring up rebellion against a government

REVIEW

Federalists people who supported a strong national government; and heirs to the supporters of the ratification of the Constitution

▶ Reading Strategy

Re-create the diagram shown at right. As you read and respond to the **KEY QUESTIONS**, use the diagram to record important events in the new nation.

 See Skillbuilder Handbook, page R4.

MAIN IDEAS AND DETAILS

rise of political parties

Federalist concerns

states' rights

GRAPHIC ORGANIZERS
Go to **Interactive Review** @ ClassZone.com

The Federalists in Charge

 14.D.3 Describe roles and influences of individuals, groups and media in shaping current Illinois and United States public policy (e.g., *general public opinion, special interest groups, formal parties, media*).
16.B.3a Describe how different groups competed for power within the colonies and how that competition led to the development of political institutions during the early national period.

One American's Story

Benjamin Banneker was born a free man at a time when most African Americans were enslaved. Largely self-educated, he became a surveyor, astronomer, and mathematician, and he published a yearly almanac. In 1790 Washington appointed him to the commission planning the new nation's capital.

Banneker was an exceptional example of what African Americans could achieve if released from the bondage of slavery and racism. In a letter to Jefferson, Banneker reminded him that "all men are created equal."

PRIMARY SOURCE

❝ [God] hath not only made us all of one flesh, but that he hath also, without partiality, afforded us all the same sensations and endowed us all with the same faculties; and that however variable we may be in society or religion, however diversified in situation or color, we are all of the same family, and stand in the same relation to him. ❞

—Benjamin Banneker, *letter to Thomas Jefferson 1791*

(*above*) Benjamin Banneker helped to survey the new capital of Washington, D.C.

Despite his efforts, Banneker was unable to change attitudes to slavery. However, Banneker will always be remembered as one of the outstanding Americans who helped launch the new republic.

Washington Retires

🔻 **KEY QUESTION** What dangers did President Washington warn against?

In 1796, President George Washington decided that two terms in office was enough. He wanted to return to Mount Vernon, his estate in Virginia. Throughout his eight years in office (1789–1797), he had tried to serve as a symbol of national unity. In large part, he succeeded.

Washington's Final Concerns During Washington's second term, opponents of Jay's Treaty, and other critics, led attacks on the president's policies. Thomas Paine, for example, called Washington "treacherous in private friendship . . . and a hypocrite in public life" because he failed to support the French Revolution. Washington saw such attacks as the outcome of political disagreements. In his farewell address, he warned that such differences could weaken the nation. Despite this advice, political differences became a part of American politics.

Americans listened more closely to Washington's parting words on **foreign policy**, or relations with the governments of other countries. He urged the nation's leaders to remain neutral and "steer clear of permanent alliances with any portion of the foreign world." He warned that agreements with foreign nations might work against U.S. interests.

Political Differences Continue Despite Washington's warnings against political differences, Americans were deeply divided over how the nation should be run. Hamilton and Jefferson had hotly debated the direction the new nation should take. But, after his frustrated resignation from public office in 1793, Jefferson returned to Virginia. During Washington's second term, Madison replaced Jefferson in the debates with Hamilton.

The two sides disagreed notably on how to interpret the Constitution and on economic policy. Hamilton favored the British and wanted to preserve good relations with them. He opposed the French Revolution. Jefferson and Madison supported it. Hamilton believed in a strong central government. Jefferson and Madison feared such a government might lead to tyranny. Hamilton wanted a United States in which trade, manufacturing, and cities grew. Jefferson and Madison pictured a rural nation of farmers.

Terence Kennedy's 1847 *Political Banner* combined several symbols of the young nation. **Would the banner have had greater appeal to Jefferson or Hamilton?**

Growth of Political Parties These differences on foreign and domestic policy led to the nation's first political parties. A **political party** is a group of people that tries to promote its ideas and influence government. It also backs candidates for office.

Together, Jefferson and Madison founded the Democratic-Republican Party. The party name reflected their strong belief in democracy and the republican system. Their ideas drew farmers' and workers' support to the new political party.

Jefferson and Madison's Democratic-Republican party eventually turned into the Democratic Party that is still active today. Hamilton and his friends formed the Federalist Party which reflected their belief in a strong national government. Many Northern merchants and manufacturers became **Federalists**, following the supporters of the ratification of the U.S. Constitution.

▲ **SUMMARIZE** List the dangers Washington warned about.

COMPARING ▸ Political Parties

FEDERALISTS

LEADERS:
Hamilton, Adams

SUPPORTERS:
lawyers, merchants, manufacturers, clergy

BELIEFS:
• strong national government
• loose construction of the Constitution
• favored national bank
• economy based on trade

Events in France not only affected politics in the United States, they influenced styles of clothing as well. Political differences could often be detected by observing different styles of dress and appearance.

powdered hair or wig

bow tie

broad coattails

breeches & stockings

buckles

loose hair

neckerchief

narrow coattails

trousers

laces

DEMOCRATIC-REPUBLICANS

LEADERS:
Jefferson, Madison

SUPPORTERS:
farmers, urban workers

BELIEFS:
• limited national government
• strict construction of the Constitution
• opposed national bank
• agricultural economy

CRITICAL THINKING **Compare and Contrast** Why might the Federalists be considered more supportive of business than the Democratic-Republicans?

John Adams's Administration

▼ **KEY QUESTION** What issues divided Americans during Adams' presidency?

In 1796, the United States held its first elections in which political parties competed. The Federalists picked vice-president **John Adams** as their candidate for president. The Democratic-Republicans chose Jefferson.

In the Electoral College, Adams received 71 votes and Jefferson 68. The Constitution stated that the runner-up should become vice-president. Therefore, the country had a Federalist president and a Democratic-Republican vice-president. Adams became president in 1797. His chief rival, Jefferson, was his vice-president.

Problems with France When Washington left office in 1797, relations between France and the United States were tense. With Britain and France still at war, the French began seizing and harassing U.S. ships. Within the year, France had looted more than 300 U.S. ships.

Some Federalists called for war with France, but Adams hoped talks would restore calm. He sent Charles Pinckney, Elbridge Gerry, and John

THE XYZ AFFAIR

"The Paris Monster" is the official title of this 1798 political cartoon satirizing the XYZ Affair. On the right, the five members of the French Directory, or ruling executive body, are shown demanding money. On the left, the Americans echo Charles Pinckney's actual reply: "No, no, not a sixpence!"

The French Directory is a five-headed monster demanding "Money, Money, Money!!"

The Americans answer, "Cease bawling, monster! We will not give you sixpence!"

CRITICAL THINKING Compare and Contrast How would you contrast the cartoon's depiction of the American representatives with its depiction of the French Directory?

See Skillbuilder Handbook, page R24.

Marshall to Paris. Arriving there, they requested a meeting with the French minister of foreign affairs. For weeks, they were ignored. Then three French agents—later referred to as X, Y, and Z—took the Americans aside to tell them the minister would hold talks. However, the talks would occur only if the Americans agreed to loan France $10 million and to pay the minister a bribe of $250,000. The American representatives refused.

Adams received a full report of what became known as the **XYZ Affair**. After Congress and an outraged public learned of it, "Millions for defense, not one cent for tribute!" became the popular slogan of the day. In 1798, Congress canceled its treaties with France and allowed U.S. ships to seize French vessels. Congress also set aside money to expand the armed forces.

The Alien and Sedition Acts Conflict with France made Adams and the Federalists popular with the public. Many Democratic-Republicans, however, were sympathetic to France. One Democratic-Republican newspaper called Adams "the blasted tyrant of America. Angered by criticism in a time of crisis, Adams blamed the Democratic-Republican newspapers and new immigrants, many of whom were sympathetic to the Democratic-Republicans. To silence their critics, the Federalist Congress passed the **Alien and Sedition Acts** in 1798. These acts targeted **aliens**, or immigrants who were not yet citizens.

One act increased the waiting period for U.S. citizenship from 5 to 14 years. Other acts gave the president the power to arrest suspicious aliens or deport them in wartime. Another act outlawed **sedition**, or stirring up rebellion against a government. Ten Democratic-Republican newspaper editors were convicted of opinions damaging to the government. With these acts, the Federalists clamped down on freedom of speech and the press and tried to silence their opposition.

The Kentucky and Virginia Resolutions Jefferson and Madison looked for a way to fight the Alien and Sedition Acts. They found it in a theory called **states' rights**—the idea that states have certain rights that the federal government cannot overrule. Madison's resolution was approved by the Virginia legislature. Jefferson's resolution was adopted by the Kentucky legislature. This idea of states' rights set a precedent for future conflicts in the nation between the states and the national government.

CONNECT to the Essential Question

What political traditions and tensions first appeared in the early years of the new republic?

PROBLEMS	SOLUTIONS
1789 Washington faces many challenges Authority of state and federal courts is in question	He creates first cabinet members Congress passes Federal Judiciary Act (1789).
1790 Nation's finances are in crisis	Hamilton sets up National bank.
1793 French Revolution in progress: France and Britain at war	U.S. declares neutrality in foreign affairs
1794 Conflict arises in the Northwest Britain seizes American ships.	(1795) Native Americans sign Treaty of Greenville. Jays' Treaty reduces U.S.—Britain border disputes
1795 U.S. challenges Spanish trade restrictions.	Pinckney's Treaty establishes 31st parallel as U.S. southern boundary
1796 Disagreements over interpretation of the Constitution	Two political parties develop: Federalist Party and Democratic-Republican Party.

CRITICAL THINKING Draw Conclusions How did the United States manage to stay out of overseas wars during this period?

The Kentucky Resolution, in particular, insisted on the principle of **nullification**, or the idea that a state could nullify, or cancel, any act of Congress that it considered unconstitutional. The **Kentucky and Virginia Resolutions** warned of the dangers that the Alien and Sedition Acts posed to a government of checks and balances as these checks and balances were guaranteed by the Constitution. Jefferson and Madison were not successful in overturning the acts while Adams was President. However, within two years the Democratic-Republicans won control of Congress, and they either reversed the acts or let them expire between 1800 and 1802.

Peace with France While Federalists and Democratic-Republicans battled at home, the United States made peace with France. Although war fever was high, Adams reopened talks with France. This time the two sides quickly signed the Convention of 1800, an agreement to stop all naval attacks. This treaty cleared the way for U.S. and French ships to sail the ocean in peace.

Adams's actions made him enemies among the Federalists. Despite this, he was proud of having saved the nation from bloodshed. In 1800, Adams became the first president to govern from the nation's new capital city, Washington, D.C. In 1800, however, he lost the presidential election to Thomas Jefferson.

 MAIN IDEAS & DETAILS Explain the issues that divided Americans during Adams' presidency.

 Illinois Learning Standards *Review*

ONLINE QUIZ
For test practice, go to
Interactive Review @ ClassZone.com

TERMS & NAMES

1. Explain the importance of:

- John Adams
- XYZ Affair
- Alien and Sedition Acts
- states' rights
- nullification
- Kentucky & Virginia Resolutions

USING YOUR READING NOTES

2. **Main Ideas and Details** Complete the diagram you started at the beginning of the section.

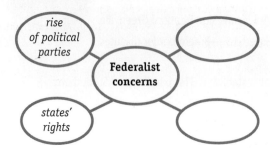

KEY IDEAS

3. What did Washington warn against before he left office?

4. What led to the rise of political parties?

5. Why did Congress pass the Alien and Sedition Acts?

CRITICAL THINKING

6. **Evaluate** Why was Washington's warning about political parties not heeded?

7. **Make Inferences** Why do you think so many merchants and manufacturers were Federalists?

8. **Draw Conclusions** How did the XYZ Affair show the young nation's growing confidence?

9. **Synthesize** How might the theory of states' rights undermine the federal government?

10. **Connect** *to* **Today** What are some issues that the two leading American political parties disagree on today?

11. **Writing** **Editorial** Imagine you are a newspaper editor in 1798. Write an editorial in favor of, or opposed to, the Alien and Sedition Acts.

Chapter Summary

1 **Key Idea**
George Washington and his advisers faced many challenges during his presidency.

2 **Key Idea**
Washington established central authority at home and avoided war abroad.

3 **Key Idea**
The Federalists dominated politics under the presidency of John Adams.

For detailed Review and Study Notes go to **Interactive Review** @ ClassZone.com

Name Game

Use the Terms & Names list to complete each sentence online or on your own paper.

1. In 1789, Congress passed the _____ to set up America's new court system.
   Federal Judiciary Act 🖑

2. Fighting over western territory in 1794, American troops clashed with Native Americans at the _____.

3. America's _____ dictates its relations and interactions with other countries.

4. _____ was the first chief justice of the United States Supreme Court.

5. The treaty that allowed Americans to use the Mississippi River was _____.

6. An exact or literal interpretation of the Constitution is called a _____.

7. Angry Pennsylvania farmers clashed with the American government during the _____.

8. The _____ in 1789 ended the monarchy in France.

9. The _____ restricted the political power of immigrants.

10. During the _____, French officials tried to bribe U.S. diplomats.

A. loose construction
B. Federal Judiciary Act
C. attorney general
D. strict construction
E. Battle of Fallen Timbers
F. Alien and Sedition Acts
G. foreign policy
H. John Jay
I. Whiskey Rebellion
J. Kentucky and Virginia Resolutions
K. French Revolution
L. Pinckney's Treaty
M. XYZ Affair
N. Treaty of Greenville
O. states' rights
P. nullification

Activities

CROSSWORD PUZZLE

Complete the online crossword to show what you know about the new republic.

ACROSS

1. _____ was the second American president.

GEOGAME

Use this online map to reinforce your understanding of early America, incuding the locations of important cities and geographic features. Drag and drop each place name in the list at its location on the map. A scorecard helps you keep track of your progress online.

Philadelphia

New York

District of Columbia

Ohio River

St. Augustine

District of Columbia 🖑

VOCABULARY

Explain the significance of each of the following.

1. Federal Judiciary Act
2. cabinet
3. nullification
4. Alien and Sedition Acts
5. French Revolution
6. John Jay
7. Attorney General
8. Whiskey rebellion
9. states' rights
10. Treaty of Greenville.

Choose the best answer from each pair.

11. This agreement ended the dispute with Britain over American shipping during the French Revolution. (Jay's Treaty / Pinckney's Treaty)

12. Which treaty ended a war with Native Americans? (Jay's Treaty / Treaty of Greenville)

13. Which law was passed in 1798 to reduce criticism of the government and limit the political activities of recent immigrants? (Alien and Sedition Acts / Federal Judiciary Act)

KEY IDEAS

1 Washington's Presidency (pages 312–317)

14. What questions about the judiciary were left open by the Constitution? How were they answered?

15. What financial problems did the new nation face?

16. How did Hamilton and Jefferson interpret the Constitution differently?

2 Challenges to the New Government (pages 318–323)

17. What did Washington do to secure the West?

18. What were the major arguments regarding taxation under the new government?

19. Why did Washington favor neutrality in the conflict between France and Britain?

3 The Federalists in Charge (pages 326–332)

20. Why did Washington oppose political parties?

21. Why did the Federalists pass the Alien and Sedition Acts?

CRITICAL THINKING

22. **Draw Conclusions** Why did Washington want both Thomas Jefferson and Alexander Hamilton to be among his closest advisers?

23. **Evaluate** Why did the federal government demonstrate its authority during the Whiskey Rebellion?

24. **Problems & Solutions** Create a chart to record the major problems and solutions faced by the leaders of the new nation.

Problems	Solutions
Need for executive aid and advice	Cabinet appointments
Government source of income	
Disputes with foreign nations	

25. **Draw Conclusions** Why do you think John Adams lost the presidential election of 1800?

26. **Causes and Effects** How did the French Revolution affect American politics?

27. **Citizenship** How did Washington's efforts to serve as a symbol of national unity help the new nation?

28. **Interpret Graphs** How much money did the government owe between 1789–1791?

Financial Problems *1789–1791*

Number of dollars (in millions)

80
70
60
50
40
30
20
10
0

Income   Expenses   Debts

Source: *Historical Statistics of the United States*

☑ **TEST PRACTICE**

- **Online Test Practice** @ ClassZone.com
- **Test-Taking Strategies & Practice** at the front of this book

DOCUMENT-BASED QUESTIONS

Part 1: Short Answer
Analyze each document and answer the questions that follow.

DOCUMENT 1

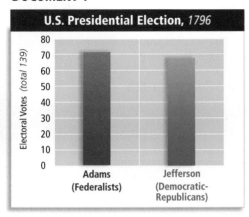

U.S. Presidential Election, 1796

Electoral Votes (total 139)

Adams (Federalists)

Jefferson (Democratic-Republicans)

1. How do the election results shown in the graph reflect the political divisions in the new nation?

DOCUMENT 2

PRIMARY SOURCE

❝ Let me now . . . warn you . . . against the harmful effects of the spirit of party. . . . This spirit, unfortunately . . . exists in different shapes in all governments . . . but in those of the popular form, it is seen in its greatest rankness and is truly their worst enemy. ❞

—George Washington, Farewell Address

2. Why might Washington's advice to avoid political parties be difficult to follow?

Part 2: Essay

3. Using information from the documents, your answers to the questions in Part 1 and your knowledge of U.S. history, write an essay that discusses the progression of the American two-party system.

YOU BE THE HISTORIAN

29. Problems and Solutions How might the farmers in the Whiskey Rebellion have expressed their disapproval of the whiskey tax while staying within the law?

30. Compare and Contrast What are some of the similarities and differences between the American Revolution and the French Revolution?

31. Evaluate How did the Virginia and Kentucky Resolutions challenge the authority of the federal government?

32. WHAT IF? What might have happened to immigrants and members of the press if the Alien and Sedition Acts had remained in effect?

33. Draw Conclusions Why did Native Americans demand negotiations with the United States over the Northwest Territory?

34. Connect to Today What are some examples of how people exercise their rights of free speech today?

 Answer the
ESSENTIAL QUESTION
What political traditions and tensions first appeared in the early years of the new republic?

Written Response Write a two or three paragraph response to the Essential Question. Be sure to consider the key ideas of each section, as well significant events that formed the political life of the new nation. Use the Rubric Response below to guide your thinking and writing.

Response Rubric
A strong response will

- discuss the precedents and challenges faced by Washington and Adams
- analyze the differences between Hamilton and Jefferson
- compare and contrast the Federalists and Democratic-Republicans

1. Jeffersonian Democracy

2. The Louisiana Purchase and Exploration

3. The War of 1812

The Jefferson Era

1800–1816

ESSENTIAL QUESTION

How did the events of the Jefferson Era strengthen the nation?

CONNECT ⟳ Geography & History

How might the United States have been changed by the purchase and exploration of western land?

Think about:

1 the amount of information about **physical features,** such as hills and lakes, in the West

2 how many **settlements** there were in the East

3 what **challenges** a nation might face in expanding its territory

George Catlin, *Buffalo Chase*

1800

Thomas Jefferson is elected president.

1804 Lewis and Clark explore the Louisiana Territory.

A page from Lewis's journal

Effect Expands knowledge of the American West.

1803 The United States purchases the Louisiana Territory.

Marbury v. *Madison* affirms the Supreme Court's power of judicial review.

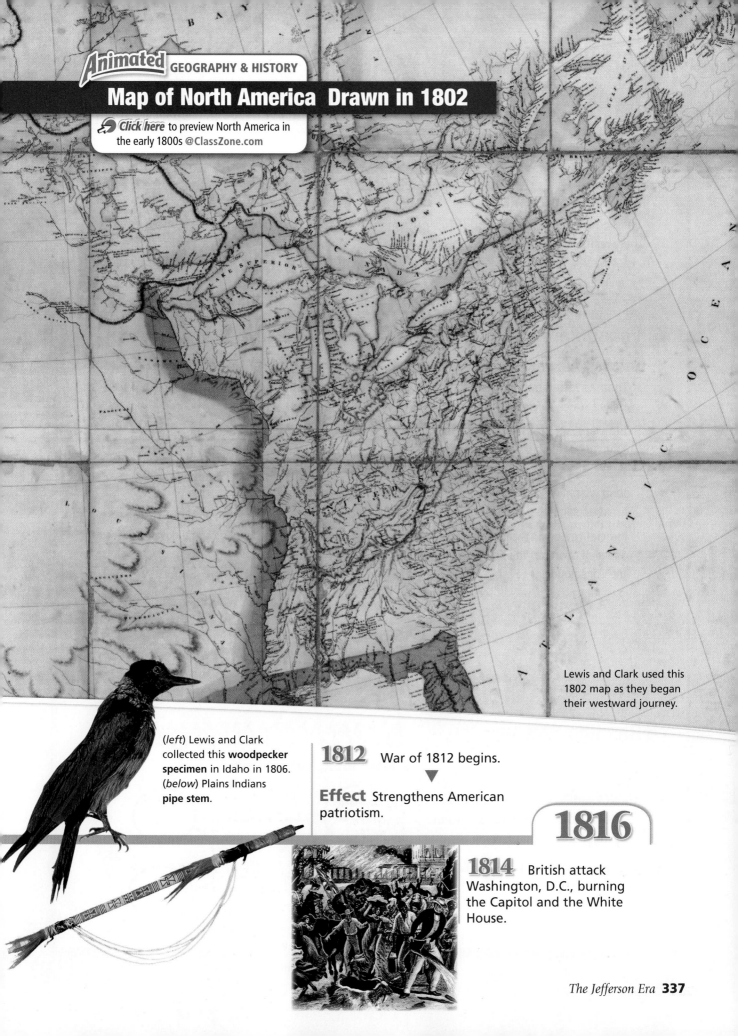

Map of North America Drawn in 1802

Click here to preview North America in the early 1800s @ClassZone.com

Lewis and Clark used this 1802 map as they began their westward journey.

(*left*) Lewis and Clark collected this **woodpecker specimen** in Idaho in 1806. (*below*) Plains Indians **pipe stem**.

1812 War of 1812 begins.

▼

Effect Strengthens American patriotism.

1816

1814 British attack Washington, D.C., burning the Capitol and the White House.

▶ Key Ideas

BEFORE, YOU LEARNED

The Federalists dominated politics under the presidency of John Adams.

NOW YOU WILL LEARN

After a tied election, Jefferson became president and the Democratic-Republicans reduced the power of the federal government.

▶ Vocabulary

TERMS & NAMES

Thomas Jefferson third president of the United States, elected in 1801

Judiciary Act of 1801 law that let President John Adams fill federal judgeships with Federalists

John Marshall chief justice of the Supreme Court appointed by President John Adams

judicial review principle that states that the Supreme Court has the final say in interpreting the Constitution

BACKGROUND VOCABULARY

radical person who takes extreme political positions

REVIEW

Federalist political party of Hamilton and Adams; supported a strong central government

Democratic-Republican Jefferson's political party; feared a strong central government

▶ Reading Strategy

Re-create the diagram shown at right. As you read and respond to the **KEY QUESTIONS**, use the boxes to show some of the changes made by Jefferson and his party.

 See Skillbuilder Handbook, page R4.

MAIN IDEAS AND DETAILS

repealed unpopular taxes

The Democratic-Republicans changed government policies.

GRAPHIC ORGANIZERS
Go to **Interactive Review** @ ClassZone.com

Jeffersonian Democracy

14.A.3 Describe how responsibilities are shared and limited by the United States and Illinois Constitutions and significant court decisions.
14.F.3a Analyze historical influences on the development of political ideas and practices as enumerated in the Declaration of Independence, the United States Constitution, the Bill of Rights and the Illinois Constitution.

One American's Story

During the election of 1800, supporters of President John Adams and challenger **Thomas Jefferson** fought for their candidates with nasty personal attacks. For instance, journalist James Callender published pamphlets that warned voters not to re-elect Adams.

PRIMARY SOURCE

❝ In the fall of 1796 . . . the country fell into a more dangerous juncture than almost any the old confederation ever endured. The tardiness and timidity of Mr. Washington were succeeded by the rancour [bitterness] and insolence [arrogance] of Mr. Adams. . . . Think what you have been, what you are, and what, under [Adams], you are likely to become. ❞

—James Callender, quoted in *American Aurora*

This campaign banner declared: "T. Jefferson President of the United States of America—John Adams no more."

Adams's defenders were just as vicious. Yet, in spite of the campaign's nastiness, the election ended with a peaceful transfer of power from one party to another.

A New Party Comes to Power

▼ **KEY QUESTION** How was the presidential election of 1800 resolved?

The 1800 election was a contest between two parties with different ideas about the role of government.

Election of 1800 The two parties contesting the election of 1800 were the **Federalists**, led by President John Adams, and the **Democratic-Republicans**, represented by Thomas Jefferson. Each party believed that the other was a threat to the Constitution and the American republic.

The Democratic-Republicans thought they were saving the nation from monarchy and oppression. They argued that the Alien and Sedition Acts passed by the Federalist congress in 1798 violated the Bill of Rights.

Meanwhile, the Federalists thought that the nation was about to be ruined by **radicals**—people who take extreme political positions. The Federalists remembered the violence of the French Revolution, in which radicals executed thousands in the name of liberty.

When election day came, the Democratic-Republicans won the presidency. Jefferson received 73 votes in the electoral college, and Adams earned 65. But there was a problem. Aaron Burr, whom the Democratic-Republicans wanted as vice president, also received 73 votes.

Breaking the Tie According to the Constitution, the House of Representatives had to choose between Burr and Jefferson. The Democratic-Republicans clearly wanted Jefferson to be president. However, the new House of Representatives, dominated by Jefferson's party, was not yet in office. Federalists still had a House majority, and their votes would decide the winner.

The Federalists were divided. Some feared Jefferson so much that they decided to back Burr. Others, such as Alexander Hamilton, considered Burr an unreliable man and urged the election of Jefferson.

TECHNOLOGY *of the* TIME

Thomas Jefferson had a passion for invention and technology. He also had classical tastes that are reflected in the look of our nation's capital and his plan of Monticello, his Virginia house (*below left*).

(*left*) Jefferson developed this **wheel cipher** to send and receive messages in secret code.

(*right*) Jefferson improved the design of this early **copy machine**. As he wrote with one pen, a second pen made an exact copy.

(*below right*) A reproduction of a **sundial** designed by Jefferson is in place on the North Terrace of Monticello. The equator is tilted at an angle based on the location's latitude, 38°1′N.

CRITICAL THINKING

1. **Make Generalizations** What do Jefferson's inventions tell about him?

2. **Connect *to* Today** What modern technology might appeal to Jefferson?

Hamilton did not like Jefferson, but he believed that Jefferson would do more for the good of the nation than Burr. "If there be a man in the world I ought to hate," he said, "it is Jefferson. . . . But the public good must be [more important than] every private consideration."

From February 11 to February 17, the House voted 35 times without a winner. Finally, Alexander Hamilton's friend James A. Bayard persuaded several Federalists not to vote for Burr. On the thirty-sixth ballot, Jefferson was elected president. Aaron Burr became vice president.

People were overjoyed by Jefferson's election. His many achievements and talents went beyond politics. He was a skilled violinist, amateur scientist, and devoted reader. His book collection later became the core of the Library of Congress. In addition, Jefferson's deep interest in the architecture of ancient Greece and Rome is reflected in the architecture of the nation's capital.

▲ **SUMMARIZE** Explain how the election of 1800 was resolved.

Jefferson and Democracy

▼ **KEY QUESTION** How did Jefferson's policies differ from those of the Federalists?

On inauguration day, no guards, no coach, not even a horse waited at the door for Thomas Jefferson. He strolled through Washington, D.C., accompanied by a few friends. As Americans would learn in the months to come, Jefferson's humble behavior on inauguration day reflected his ideas about government.

Jefferson's View of Government The new president's first order of business was to heal political wounds. He urged political enemies to unite as Americans.

PRIMARY SOURCE

❝ Let us, then, fellow-citizens, unite with one heart and one mind. . . . Every difference of opinion is not a difference of principle. . . . We are all Republicans, we are all Federalists. ❞

—Thomas Jefferson, First Inaugural Address

One way Jefferson sought to unify Americans was by promoting a common way of life. He wanted the United States to remain a nation of small independent farmers. Such a nation, he believed, would uphold the strong morals and democratic ideals he associated with country living. Jefferson also hoped that the enormous amount of land available in the United States would prevent Americans from crowding into cities, as so many people had in Europe.

Jefferson wanted to avoid having too much government. He believed that the power of the central government should be limited, and that the people should be enabled to govern themselves. Some of the changes he made during his presidency reflect these beliefs.

Connecting History

Change & Continuity
Americans' concerns about overcrowding grew during the first half of the eighteenth century. You will see this theme develop in later chapters when you study the emergence of industry and the effects of immigration.

The Jefferson Era **341**

Marbury v. Madison (1803)

KEY ISSUE   Judicial review

KEY PEOPLE
John Adams   president 1797–1801; appointed Federalists as judges
Thomas Jefferson president 1801–1809; Democratic-Republican
James Madison   secretary of state to President Jefferson
William Marbury   Federalist financier; appointed as justice by President Adams

History Makers

John Marshall
1755–1835

John Marshall was the fourth chief justice of the U.S. Supreme Court. Marshall set out to make the judiciary a force to be reckoned with.

In 1803, in the case of *Marbury* v. *Madison*, Marshall upheld the power of judicial review. Many other rulings during Marshall's tenure as chief justice also strengthened federal power over the states.

Jefferson and Madison were angry when Marshall claimed this power for the Court, but they could hardly fight his decision. After all, *Marbury* v. *Madison* was decided in their favor.

 ONLINE BIOGRAPHY

For more on John Marshall, go to the **Research & Writing Center** @ ClassZone.com

The Case

President John Adams appointed William Marbury to be a justice of the peace. However, Adams's term as president ended before the appointment papers were delivered to Marbury. After Thomas Jefferson took office, he named James Madison as secretary of state. Normally it would have been Madison's job to deliver appointment papers, but Jefferson ordered Madison not to deliver Marbury's papers.

Marbury then sued. He asked the Supreme Court to order Madison to deliver the papers.

The Court's Decision Marbury based his demand on two sections of the Judiciary Act of 1789. One section of that law created federal judgeships. Another section named the Supreme Court to settle disputes about certain judicial appointments.

The Supreme Court decided that the Judiciary Act was an invalid law. When Congress passed the Judiciary Act it gave a new power to the Supreme Court. But the Constitution does not allow Congress to do that. As Chief Justice John Marshall wrote, if the Constitution is to be the supreme law of the land, then any law contrary to the Constitution "is not law."

Historical Impact This was the first time the Supreme Court exercised the power of judicial review by overruling a law passed by Congress. Until this time, the Supreme Court was thought of as virtually powerless. That changed after Marshall proclaimed, "It is, emphatically, the province and the duty of the judicial department to say what the law is." Marshall's decision strengthened the Constitution's system of checks and balances by affirming an important power of the courts.

By upholding judicial review, Marshall helped to create a lasting balance among the three branches of government. The strength of this balance would be tested as the United States grew.

CRITICAL THINKING **Summarize** Explain how John Marshall strengthened the Supreme Court.

Jefferson and the Federalists Jefferson wanted the government to have less power than it had under the Federalists. He reduced the number of federal employees and the size of the military, and sought to end Federalist programs. Congress, now controlled by Democratic-Republicans, let the Alien and Sedition Acts end. Jefferson released prisoners convicted under the acts. Congress also ended many taxes, such as the unpopular whiskey tax.

Next, Jefferson made changes to Federalist financial policies. Alexander Hamilton had created a system that depended on a certain amount of public debt. Hamilton believed that people who were owed money by their government would make sure the government was run properly. But Jefferson opposed public debt. He used revenues from tariffs and land sales to reduce the amount of money owed by the government.

Conflict with the Courts Although Jefferson ended many Federalist programs, he had little power over the courts. Under the **Judiciary Act of 1801**, Adams had appointed as many Federalist judges as he could between the election of 1800 and Jefferson's inauguration. Because judges were appointed for life, Jefferson could do little about Federalist control of the courts.

Under Chief Justice **John Marshall**, the Supreme Court upheld federal authority and strengthened federal courts. In 1803, in *Marbury* v. *Madison*, Marshall affirmed the principle of **judicial review**—the final authority of the Supreme Court on the meaning of the Constitution. (See page 342.)

 COMPARE AND CONTRAST Explain how Jefferson's policies differed from those of the Federalists.

 Illinois Learning Standards *Review*

⮌ **ONLINE QUIZ**
For test practice, go to
Interactive Review @ ClassZone.com

TERMS & NAMES

1. Explain the significance of
   • Thomas Jefferson   • John Marshall
   • Judiciary Act of 1801   • judicial review

USING YOUR READING NOTES

2. **Main Ideas and Details** Complete the chart you started at the beginning of this section.

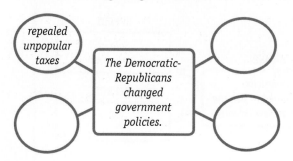

KEY IDEAS

3. What was unusual about the election of 1800?

4. Why did Jefferson seek unity between political parties?

5. What is the lasting importance of *Marbury* v. *Madison?*

CRITICAL THINKING

6. **Compare and Contrast** In what ways did the Federalists and Democratic-Republicans differ?

7. **Analyze Point of View** Why do you think Jefferson wished to promote a modest lifestyle?

8. **Causes and Effects** How did Adams's last-minute appointments affect the new president?

9. **Technology** Research Thomas Jefferson's interests. Design an Internet page about Jefferson that shows his inventions or a building he designed.

Reading for Understanding

▶ Key Ideas

BEFORE, YOU LEARNED

After a tied election, Jefferson became president and the Democratic-Republicans reduced the power of the federal government.

NOW YOU WILL LEARN

The nation doubled in size when Jefferson acquired the Louisiana Purchase.

▶ Vocabulary

TERMS & NAMES

Meriwether Lewis army captain appointed by President Jefferson to explore the Louisiana Territory and lands west to the Pacific Ocean

William Clark co-leader of the Lewis and Clark expedition

Sacagawea (sak•uh•juh•WEE•uh) Shoshone woman who assisted the Lewis and Clark expedition

Louisiana Purchase American purchase of the Louisiana Territory from France in 1803

Lewis and Clark expedition group that explored the Louisiana Territory and lands west; also known as the Corps of Discovery

Zebulon Pike leader of a southern expedition in the Louisiana Territory

BACKGROUND VOCABULARY

corps (kor) a number of people acting together for a similar purpose

Visual Vocabulary
William Clark (*left*) and Meriwether Lewis

▶ Reading Strategy

Re-create the diagram shown at right. As you read and respond to the **KEY QUESTIONS**, use the diagram to record important events and their effects. Add more boxes or start a new diagram as needed.

 See Skillbuilder Handbook, page R7.

CAUSES AND EFFECTS

CAUSE

Americans determined to use the port at New Orleans

EFFECT

Sale of Louisiana

EFFECT

GRAPHIC ORGANIZERS
Go to **Interactive Review** @ ClassZone.com

The Louisiana Purchase and Exploration

16.D.3a Describe characteristics of different kinds of communities in various sections of America during the colonial/frontier periods and the 19th century.

17.B.3a Explain how physical processes including climate, plate tectonics, erosion, soil formation, water cycle, and circulation patterns in the ocean shape patterns in the environment and influence availability and quality of natural resources.

One American's Story

In 1803, an expedition led by explorers **Meriwether Lewis** and **William Clark** set out to explore the American West. As they neared the Rocky Mountains, Lewis and Clark hired a French trapper to act as an interpreter with the Native Americans. He brought along his young wife, **Sacagawea**, a Shoshone Indian. Her knowledge of Native American languages and the land played an essential role in the expedition.

This detail from *Lewis and Clark* by N. C. Wyeth shows Sacagawea with Meriwether Lewis.

> **PRIMARY SOURCE**
>
> ❝ *The sight* of this Indian woman . . . [assured the Native Americans] of our friendly intentions. . . . No woman ever accompanied a war party in this quarter. ❞
>
> —William Clark, journal entry, October 19, 1805

Sacagawea did more than enable conversation and trade. Her presence led many tribes to believe that the explorers came in peace.

The Louisiana Purchase

▼ **KEY QUESTION** How did the United States acquire the Louisiana Purchase?

When Americans talked about the West in 1800, they meant the area between the Appalachian Mountains and the Mississippi River.

The West in 1800 By 1800, thousands of settlers were moving westward across the Appalachians. Many settled on land inhabited by Native Americans. Even so, several U.S. territories soon declared statehood. Kentucky and Tennessee became states by 1800, and Ohio entered the union in 1803.

Although the Mississippi River was then the western border of the United States, there was much activity farther west. France and Spain were negotiating for ownership of the Louisiana Territory—the vast region between the Mississippi River and the Rocky Mountains.

The Mississippi River and New Orleans As the number of westerners grew, so did their political influence. A vital issue for many farmers and merchants was the use of the Mississippi River. They used this highway of commerce to transport their products through the New Orleans port, across the Gulf of Mexico, and then to East Coast markets.

Although originally claimed by France, the port was turned over to Spain after the French and Indian War. In a secret treaty in 1800, Spain returned the port to France's powerful leader, Napoleon. Now Napoleon planned to colonize the American territory. This brought America close to war.

The United States Expands In 1802, before turning Louisiana over to France, Spain closed New Orleans to American shipping. Angry westerners called for war against both Spain and France. To avoid hostilities, Jefferson offered to buy New Orleans from France. He received a surprising answer. The French asked if the United States wanted to buy all of the Louisiana Territory—a tract of land even larger than the entire United States at that time.

A number of factors may have influenced Napoleon's offer. He was probably alarmed by America's determination to keep the port of New Orleans open. Also, his enthusiasm for a colony in America may have been lessened by events in Haiti, a French colony in the West Indies. There, a revolt led by Toussaint L'Ouverture (too•SAN loo•vehr•TOOR) had resulted in disastrous losses for the French. Another factor was France's costly war against Britain. America's money may have been more valuable to Napoleon than land.

Jefferson was thrilled by Napoleon's offer. However, the Constitution said nothing about the president's right to buy land. This troubled Jefferson, who believed in the strict interpretation of the Constitution. But he also believed in a republic of small farmers, and that required land. So, on April 30, 1803, the **Louisiana Purchase** was approved for $15 million—about three cents per acre. The size of the United States doubled. At the time, most Americans knew little about this territory. But that would soon change.

▲ **SUMMARIZE** Explain how the United States acquired the Louisiana Territory.

Exploring the Louisiana Territory

▼ **KEY QUESTION** What were some effects of exploring the Louisiana Territory?

Since 1802, Thomas Jefferson had planned an expedition to the Louisiana country. Now that the Louisiana Purchase had been made, learning about the territory became more important than ever.

The Lewis and Clark Expedition Jefferson chose a young officer, Captain Meriwether Lewis, to lead an exploration of the Louisiana country. Lewis asked Lieutenant William Clark, a mapmaker and outdoorsman, to help him oversee a volunteer force, or **corps**. They called it the Corps of Discovery, but it soon became known as the **Lewis and Clark expedition**.

Clark was accompanied by York, his African-American slave. York's hunting skills won him many admirers. The first black man that many Native Americans had seen, he became something of a celebrity among them.

Fort
Clatsop

Yakima Palouse   Shoshone

Lewis and Clark, 1806
Walla Walla

Nez
Perce

Flathead

Umatilla

OREGON
COUNTRY

Blackfoot

Assiniboine

Lewis's Return

Clark's Return

Columbia

R O C K Y

Snake R.

M O U N T A I N S

Colorado River

SPANISH TERRITORY

Crow

Yellowstone R.

Arikara

Teton

Cheyenne

Platte River

Pawnee

LOUISIANA PURCHASE
1803

Kansa

Mandan

Sioux

BRITISH
(Canada)

Mississippi R.

Lewis and Clark, 1804–1805

Missouri River

St. Louis

Arkansas River

Red River

Mississippi River

PACIFIC
OCEAN

TEXAS
(claimed by United States)

Kiowa
Encampment

Gulf of Mexico

Connect Geography & History
READING A ROUTE MAP

Route maps show the course of travel from one place to another. When reading a route map, use

- the labels on the map to reveal information about the map's subject and purpose
- the key to identify the direction of the route
- the legend to find the meaning of symbols and colors
- the scale to estimate distance.

1. **Movement** How can you tell which route the expedition took on its way to the Pacific?

2. **Critical Thinking** Why was St. Louis a logical starting point for the expedition?

| 0 | 100 | 200 miles |
| 0 | 100 | 200 kilometers |

The Journey Begins Lewis and Clark set out in the summer of 1803. By winter, they reached St. Louis. Located on the western bank of the Mississippi River, St. Louis would soon become the gateway to the West. But in 1803 it was a sleepy town. Lewis and Clark spent the winter there, waiting for the official transfer of Louisiana to the United States. In March 1804, the American flag flew over St. Louis for the first time.

West to the Ocean The expedition, which numbered about 40, left St. Louis in May of 1804. Jefferson had instructed them to explore the Missouri River in hopes of finding a water route across the continent. He also told them to establish good relations with Native Americans and to describe the landscape, plants, and animals they saw.

After reaching what is now North Dakota, the explorers spent the winter with the Mandan people. They also met British and Canadian trappers and traders, who were not happy to see them. The traders feared American competition in the trade in beaver fur—and they would be proved right.

In the spring of 1805, the expedition set out again. This time they were joined by Sacagawea, who was a Shoshone Indian. Her language skills—she knew sign language and several Native American languages—and her knowledge of geography would be of great value to Lewis and Clark.

ONLINE PRIMARY SOURCE

Hear the perspectives at the **Research & Writing Center** @ ClassZone.com

COMPARING *Perspectives*

President Thomas Jefferson sponsored Lewis and Clark's expedition to the West, where they met almost 50 tribes. In an 1806 speech, Jefferson described his goals for relations between the United States and Native Americans. From the Native American perspective, Kiowa Chief Satanta (c. 1830–1878) later described the impact of Jefferson's policies.

Jefferson Speaks

"My friends and children. We are descended from the old nations which live beyond the great water: but we and our forefathers have been so long here that we seem like you to have grown out of this land . . . you are all my children . . . we wish as a true father should do, that we may all live together as one household. "

—Thomas Jefferson, Speech to a Delegation of Indian Chiefs, January 4, 1806

Satanta Speaks

"I hear a great deal of good talk from the gentlemen the Great Father sends us . . . I have heard you intend to settle us on a reservation near the mountains. I don't want to settle. . . . A long time ago this land belonged to our fathers, but when I go up to the river I see camps of soldiers on its banks. These soldiers cut down my timber, they kill my buffalo and when I see that, my heart feels like bursting. "

—Satanta, Kiowa Chief, September 1876

CRITICAL THINKING

1. **Make Inferences** What did Jefferson want for Native Americans?

2. **Analyze** Why were the Native Americans resentful of the soldiers?

As they approached the Rocky Mountains, Sacagawea pointed out Shoshone lands. Lewis and a small party made their way overland. The chief recognized Sacagawea as his sister and traded horses to Lewis and Clark. This enabled the explorers to cross the mountains. The expedition continued on to the Columbia River, which leads to the Pacific Ocean. The group arrived at the Pacific Coast in November 1805 and returned to St. Louis in 1806.

Lewis and Clark brought back a wealth of valuable information. Though they learned that an all-water route across the continent did not exist, Americans received an exciting report of what lay to the west. More importantly, the expedition produced the first good maps of the Louisiana Territory.

Zebulon Pike and the Southern Route In 1806, an expedition led by explorer **Zebulon Pike** left St. Louis on a southerly route to find the sources of the Arkansas and Red rivers. The group entered Spanish territory and was arrested. The explorers were released in 1807 and returned to the United States.

Pike's group brought back valuable descriptions of the land it explored. Not all these descriptions were accurate, however. For example, Pike described the treeless Great Plains as a desert. This led many Americans to believe, mistakenly, that the Plains region was useless for farming.

Pike's Route 1806–1807

 CAUSES AND EFFECTS Describe some effects of exploring the Louisiana Territory.

Illinois Learning Standards *Review*

ONLINE QUIZ
For test practice, go to
Interactive Review @ ClassZone.com

TERMS & NAMES

1. Explain the importance of
- Louisiana Purchase
- Sacagawea
- Meriwether Lewis
- Zebulon Pike
- William Clark

USING YOUR READING NOTES

2. Causes and Effects Complete the diagram you started at the beginning of this section. Then create a diagram for each of the other main events in this section.

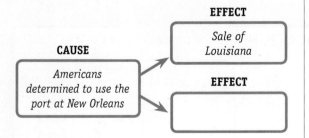

EFFECT

Sale of Louisiana

CAUSE

Americans determined to use the port at New Orleans

EFFECT

KEY IDEAS

3. Why was the Louisiana Purchase important to Jefferson?

4. Why were Lewis and Clark instructed to document the natural resources they found in their travels?

CRITICAL THINKING

5. Evaluate How did the Louisiana Purchase change the United States?

6. Make Inferences How might the information gathered by the explorers be useful to Jefferson?

7. Recognize Bias and Propaganda Read the quote by Jefferson on page 348. Is it propaganda? Explain.

8. **Connect** *to* **Today** Explorers still seek government funding for new expeditions. Where might today's explorers want to study?

9. **Writing** **Letter** Write a one-page letter from Jefferson to Lewis in which you describe your goals for the exploration of the Louisiana Territory.

American Landscapes

PACIFIC NORTHWEST Damp ocean winds help keep the coastal region green. East of the Cascades lie relatively dry highlands. The mountains of the region include more than a dozen major volcanoes.

SOUTHWEST For thousands of years, Native Americans have lived in the desert Southwest. Spanish settlement began here in 1598 and lasted to the 1840s. Explorer Zebulon Pike was arrested by Spanish authorities in the region in 1807.

ROCKY MOUNTAINS The majestic Rockies form the Continental Divide, which separates east-flowing and west-flowing rivers. Lewis and Clark crossed these mountains with the aid of Sacagawea, who obtained horses for them.

GREAT PLAINS The Plains region stretches from the foothills of the Rocky Mountains to the humid grasslands that lie west of the Mississippi River. It is mostly flat. At the time of the Lewis and Clark expedition, it was home to millions of bison.

GULF COAST The low, marshy region bordering the Gulf of Mexico is known as the Gulf Coast. Riverways and natural ports have long made commerce important here. The United States gained the valuable Lower Mississippi Valley in the 1803 Louisiana Purchase.

Pacific Northwest

Cascade Range

40°N

Sierra Nevada

Great Basin

Southwest

125°W

PACIFIC OCEAN

0 100 200 miles
0 100 200 kilometers

CROSS SECTION OF NORTH AMERICA (39°N)

Coast Ranges | Sierra Nevada | Rocky Mts. | Great Plains | Appalachian Mts.

Pikes Peak | Mississippi River

4,000 m — 13,100 ft
3,000 m — 9,800 ft
2,000 m — 6,600 ft
1,000 m — 3,300 ft
0 m — 0 ft

2,640 mi

115°W

Rocky Mountains

R O C K Y   M O U N T A I N S

G R E A T   P L A I N S

Great Plains

History Makers

Sacagawea   c. 1786–1812

A Shoshone Indian, Sacagawea was born in what
is now Idaho. When she was about 12 years old
she was kidnapped by the Hidatsa Sioux and
taken to what is now North Dakota. About four
years later she married a French trader, Toussaint
Charbonneau. Sacagawea and her husband traveled
with Lewis and Clark from 1804 to 1806. Their son
Jean Baptiste was born during the journey. When
the expedition reached Shoshone territory in the
Rocky Mountains, Sacagawea met her brother, Chief
Cameahwait. He agreed to trade the horses that the
explorers needed to cross the mountains.

CRITICAL THINKING Make Inferences How
might living in different cultures have helped
Sacagawea as a guide?

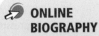 **ONLINE BIOGRAPHY**
For more on Sacagawea, go to the
Research & Writing Center
@ ClassZone.com

Connect Geography & History

1. **Region** Where are regions connected by water routes?
2. **Make Inferences** Which region would you expect to
   be the hardest to cross on foot? Why?

 See Geography Handbook, pages A8–A11.

Gulf Coast

Gulf of
Mexico

▶ Key Ideas

BEFORE, YOU LEARNED

After Jefferson acquired the Louisiana Purchase, the nation doubled in size.

NOW YOU WILL LEARN

The nation gained confidence and worldwide respect as a result of the War of 1812.

▶ Vocabulary

TERMS & NAMES

Embargo Act of 1807 law that forbade American ships from sailing to foreign ports and closed American ports to British ships

Tecumseh (tih•KUM•seh) Shawnee chief who sought to stop the loss of Native American land to white settlers

war hawk westerner who supported the War of 1812

Oliver Hazard Perry naval officer who led the U.S. victory over the British on Lake Erie in 1813

BACKGROUND VOCABULARY

tribute (TRIHB•yoot) payment in exchange for protection

impressment the act of seizing by force; between 1803 and 1812, the British impressed, or kidnapped, about 6,000 American sailors to work on British ships

coercion (ko•ER•shun) practice of forcing someone to act in a certain way by use of pressure or threats

Visual Vocabulary
impressment

▶ Reading Strategy

Re-create the diagram shown at right. As you read and respond to the **KEY QUESTIONS**, use the diagram to record important events in the order in which they occurred.

 See Skillbuilder Handbook, page R5.

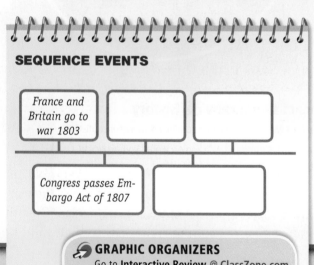

SEQUENCE EVENTS

France and Britain go to war 1803		

Congress passes Embargo Act of 1807	

🔹 **GRAPHIC ORGANIZERS**
Go to **Interactive Review** @ ClassZone.com

The War of 1812

14.E.3 Compare the basic principles of the United States and its international interests (e.g., *territory, environment, trade, use of technology*).
16.B.3d Describe ways in which the United States developed as a world political power.

One American's Story

From 1801 to 1805, the United States was at war with Tripoli, a state on the Barbary coast of North Africa. The war began because of attacks on American merchant ships by Barbary pirates. The United States had been paying protection money, or **tribute**, but the pasha (ruler) of Tripoli wanted more money.

In February 1804, President Thomas Jefferson sent U.S. Navy Lieutenant Stephen Decatur to destroy the U.S. ship *Philadelphia*, which was in the hands of Barbary pirates. Decatur set fire to the *Philadelphia* and then escaped under enemy fire. Later, he issued this rallying cry.

PRIMARY SOURCE

❝ Our country! In her [relationships] with foreign nations may she always be in the right; but our country, right or wrong. ❞

—Stephen Decatur, 1816

Stephen Decatur was a hero of the war between the United States and the North African state of Tripoli.

The conflict with Tripoli showed how hard it was for the United States to stay out of foreign affairs while its citizens were involved in overseas trade.

The Path to War

▼ **KEY QUESTION** What conflicts with other nations did the United States have in the early 1800s?

Jefferson wanted the United States to seek the friendship of all nations but have "entangling alliances with none." However, his desire to keep the United States out of conflict with other nations was doomed from the start. American merchants were engaged in trade all over the world. Besides, the United States had little control over the actions of foreign powers.

Problems with France and England War broke out between France and Great Britain in 1803. The United States tried to stay out of the war. But many American trading ships made stops in Europe. The British captured any ship bound for France, and the French stopped all ships bound for Britain.

Another conflict grew out of Britain's shortage of sailors. Life in the British navy was so bad at the time that few British citizens chose to join—and many deserted. To fill its need for sailors, Britain used the policy of **impressment**, or kidnapping, of American merchant sailors. Between 1803 and 1812, the British impressed about 6,000 Americans to work on British ships.

No More Trade   Instead of declaring war, Jefferson asked Congress to pass legislation that would stop all foreign trade. The president described his policy as "peaceable **coercion**." Coercion means forcing someone to act in a certain way by pressure or threats. Jefferson believed that the legislation would prevent further bloodshed.

In December, Congress passed the **Embargo Act of 1807**, which forbade American ships from sailing to foreign ports. The act also closed American ports to British ships. The policy harmed the United States more than it harmed France or Britain. American farmers lost key markets for their products. Shippers lost income, and many chose to violate the embargo by making false claims about where they were going.

The embargo became an issue in the election of 1808, which James Madison won. By then, Congress had repealed the act. Madison's solution to the problem was a law that allowed merchants to trade with any country except France and Britain. Trade with them would resume when they agreed to respect U.S. ships. This law was no more effective than the embargo.

Tecumseh and Native American Unity   British interference with American shipping and impressment of U.S. citizens made Americans angry. Many also believed the British were trying to stop American expansion in the Northwest by stirring up Native American resistance to frontier settlements.

Since the Battle of Fallen Timbers in 1794, Native Americans had continued to lose their land to white settlers. **Tecumseh**, a Shawnee chief, vowed to stop this. He believed that Native American tribes had to unite in order to protect their land. Events in 1809 proved him right. That September, William Henry Harrison, governor of the Indiana Territory, signed the Treaty of Fort Wayne with chiefs of the Miami, Delaware, and Potawatomi tribes. They agreed to sell more than three million acres of land. But Tecumseh declared the treaty void. He believed that the sale could go through only with the agreement of all tribes, not just some.

(*below right*) The Shawnee were defeated at the Battle of Tippecanoe. **How did the Battle of Tippecanoe affect Tecumseh's hopes for unity?**

Chief Tecumseh

Many Native Americans did answer Tecumseh's call for unity. But he was too late. In late 1811, while Tecumseh was away recruiting for his alliance, Harrison's forces defeated the Shawnee at the Battle of Tippecanoe. Following this defeat, Tecumseh sided with the British in Canada. Tecumseh's welcome in Canada increased anti-British feelings in the West.

▲ **SUMMARIZE** Explain what conflicts with other nations the United States had in the early 1800s.

The War of 1812

▼ **KEY QUESTION** What were the effects of the War of 1812?

By 1812, more and more Americans were calling for war against Britain for its role in helping Native Americans and its policy on the high seas. Those who supported war were called **war hawks**. Many of them came from the western part of the country. Those in the Northeast, which had business ties with Britain, were less eager for war. The American government wanted all Americans to feel that their country could protect them. Finally on June 18, 1812, President James Madison asked Congress to declare war on Britain.

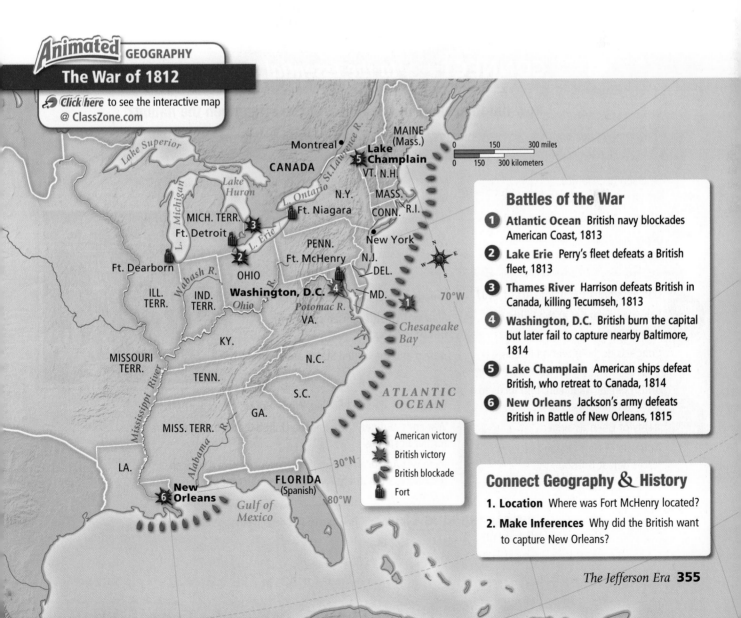

Animated GEOGRAPHY

The War of 1812

Click here to see the interactive map
@ ClassZone.com

Battles of the War

1 **Atlantic Ocean** British navy blockades American Coast, 1813

2 **Lake Erie** Perry's fleet defeats a British fleet, 1813

3 **Thames River** Harrison defeats British in Canada, killing Tecumseh, 1813

4 **Washington, D.C.** British burn the capital but later fail to capture nearby Baltimore, 1814

5 **Lake Champlain** American ships defeat British, who retreat to Canada, 1814

6 **New Orleans** Jackson's army defeats British in Battle of New Orleans, 1815

American victory
British victory
British blockade
Fort

Connect Geography & History

1. **Location** Where was Fort McHenry located?

2. **Make Inferences** Why did the British want to capture New Orleans?

The Jefferson Era **355**

The First Phase of the War The War of 1812 had two main phases. From 1812 to 1814, Britain concentrated on its war with France. It spent little energy on its conflict in North America, although it did send ships to blockade the American coast.

The American military was weak at the beginning of the war. Democratic-Republicans had reduced the size of the American armed forces. The U.S. Navy had only 16 warships. In spite of its small size, the U.S. Navy rose to the challenge. Ships such as the *Constitution* and the *United States* won stirring victories that boosted American confidence.

Triumph on Lake Erie The most important U.S. naval victory took place on Lake Erie. In September 1813, a small British force on the lake set out to attack a new fleet of American ships. Commodore **Oliver Hazard Perry**, who had taken charge of the fleet, sailed out to meet the enemy. Perry's ship, the *Lawrence*, flew a banner reading, "Don't give up the ship."

For two hours, the British and Americans exchanged cannon shots. Perry's ship was demolished and the guns put out of action. Under British fire, Perry grabbed the banner as he and four companions escaped and rowed to another ship. Commanding the second ship, Perry soon forced the British to surrender. In a message to General William Henry Harrison, commander

CONNECT *to the Essential Question*

How did the events of the Jefferson Era strengthen the nation?

EVENT	EFFECTS
1801–1804 Jefferson takes office; Democratic-Republicans in power	Many Federalist policies end, though Federalists retain control of Judiciary
Jefferson purchases Louisiana Territory	Doubles size of the United States
Lewis and Clark expedition charts important information about the West	Western settlement fever begins
1807–1812 Congress passes Embargo Act of 1807	American shipping and trade suffer
Shawnee defeated at the Battle of Tippecanoe	Shawnee chief Tecumseh sides with British in Canada
Congress declares war on Britain	Britain and the United States are at war
1814–1815 British defeat Napoleon, turn focus to war with the United States	British burn Capitol building, White House; attack Fort McHenry
Treaty of Ghent is signed	War ends, but news reaches the United States too late to prevent further hostilities
At Battle of New Orleans, Jackson's forces defeat British	Increases American patriotism; weakens Native American resistance; strengthens American manufacturing

CRITICAL THINKING **Synthesize** How would you describe the characteristics of the Jefferson Era?

of the Army of the Northwest, Perry wrote: "We have met the enemy and they are ours."

After General Harrison received Perry's note, he set out to attack the British. But when Harrison transported his army across Lake Erie to Detroit, he discovered that the British already had retreated into Canada. Harrison pursued the British and defeated their forces at the Battle of the Thames in October 1813. This American victory put an end to the British threat to the Northwest—and took the life of Tecumseh, who died in the battle, fighting for the British.

The Second Phase of the War The second phase of the War of 1812 began after the British defeated Napoleon in Europe in April 1814. Britain's army and navy were then free to attack the United States. In August 1814, President Madison and other officials fled Washington, D.C., as British forces neared the nation's capitol. Dolley Madison, the president's wife, stayed behind to rescue important objects from the White House. (See History Through Art at right.) She barely escaped before the British burned the White House and the Capitol building. The British then attacked Fort McHenry at Baltimore.

The commander of Fort McHenry had earlier requested a flag "so large that the British will have no difficulty in seeing it." Detained on a British ship, a Washington lawyer named Francis Scott Key watched the all-night battle. At dawn, Key saw that the flag was still flying. He expressed his pride in a poem that is now known as "The Star-Spangled Banner." It became the American national anthem.

Meanwhile, in the North, the British sent a force from Canada across Lake Champlain. Its goal was to push south and cut off New England. The plan failed when the American fleet defeated the British in the Battle of Lake Champlain in September 1814.

The Battle of New Orleans In the South, the British began to move against the strategically located port of New Orleans, in Louisiana. In December 1814, dozens of ships carrying some 7,500 British troops approached the coastline of Louisiana. To defend themselves, the Americans patched together an army under the

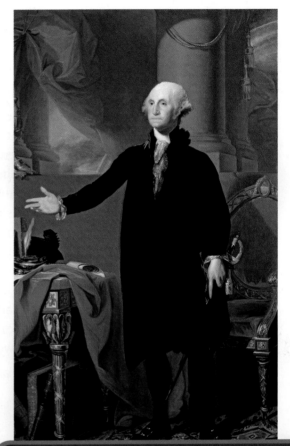

History *through* Art

George Washington, by Gilbert Stuart

As British troops closed in on Washington, D.C., in August 1814, most civilians fled the city. Even the 100 troops guarding the White House and First Lady Dolley Madison left. But Madison herself refused to leave until she had rescued one treasure: this full-length portrait of George Washington by renowned painter Gilbert Stuart. Madison was determined to save the painting or destroy it herself rather than let the British ruin it. When newly elected president James Monroe moved into the rebuilt White House in 1817, he restored this symbol of America to its rightful place.

CRITICAL VIEWING How does the artist show that Washington is an important person?

command of General Andrew Jackson. The British attacked Jackson's forces on January 8, 1815. American riflemen, who had protected themselves by building defenses out of earth, shot at advancing British troops. It was a great victory for Jackson. American casualties totaled 71, compared to Britain's 2,000.

The Battle of New Orleans made Jackson a hero. Nevertheless, the battle itself did not affect the course of the war. Slow mails from Europe had delayed news of the Treaty of Ghent, which had already ended the war. British and American diplomats had signed this treaty two weeks earlier. Americans, eager for an end to the fighting, welcomed the treaty.

The Legacy of the War The Treaty of Ghent showed that the War of 1812 had no clear winner. No territory changed hands, and trade disputes were left unresolved. Neither side made any significant gains. Still, the war had important consequences for America.

First, heroic exploits of men such as Jackson and Perry increased American patriotism. Second, the war broke the strength of Native Americans, who had sided with the British. Native American resistance was significantly weakened, especially in the South. Finally, when war interrupted trade, Americans were forced to make many of the goods they had previously imported. This encouraged the growth of American manufacturing.

The American victory also increased optimism about the nation's future. The United States had defended itself against one of the mightiest military powers of the era. For perhaps the first time, many Americans believed that their young nation would survive and prosper.

 SYNTHESIZE Explain how the War of 1812 led to changes in America.

 Illinois Learning Standards *Review*

 ONLINE QUIZ
For test practice, go to
Interactive Review @ ClassZone.com

TERMS & NAMES

1. Explain the importance of

- impressment
- war hawk
- Embargo Act of 1807
- Oliver Hazard Perry
- Tecumseh

USING YOUR READING NOTES

2. Sequence Events Complete the diagram you started at the beginning of this section.

KEY IDEAS

3. How did foreign powers affect American shipping?

4. Why did many Americans in the western part of the country support the war?

CRITICAL THINKING

5. Evaluate How did Jefferson use trade as a weapon prior to the start of the war?

6. Causes and Effects What effects did Native American unity have on the United States?

7. Connect *to* **Today** How do you think overseas trade affects America's relations with other nations today?

8. Writing Poem Use the Internet to research the U.S.S. *Constitution*. Write a poem or speech to commemorate one of its victories.

Chapter Summary

① Key Idea
After a tied election, Jefferson became president and the Democratic-Republicans reduced the power of the federal government.

② Key Idea
The nation doubled in size when Jefferson acquired the Louisiana Purchase.

③ Key Idea
The nation gained confidence and worldwide respect as a result of the War of 1812.

➲ For detailed Review and Study Notes go to **Interactive Review** @ ClassZone.com

Name Game

Use the Terms & Names list to identify each sentence online or on your own paper.

1. I helped to guide the Lewis and Clark expedition.
   Sacagawea 👆

2. This doubled the size of the United States.

3. President John Adams appointed me chief justice of the Supreme Court.

4. President Jefferson asked me to lead the Corps of Discovery.

5. This let President John Adams appoint many Federalist judges.

6. I was the third president of the United States.

7. This forbade U.S. ships from sailing to foreign ports.

8. I led the U.S. Navy to victory on Lake Erie.

9. I led a southern expedition in the Louisiana Territory.

10. This says the Supreme Court has the final say in interpreting the Constitution.

A. Thomas Jefferson
B. John Marshall
C. Meriwether Lewis
D. John Clark
E. Sacagawea
F. Zebulon Pike
G. impressment
H. judicial review
I. Oliver Hazard Perry
J. Judiciary Act of 1801
K. Embargo Act of 1807
L. Louisiana Purchase

Activities

CROSSWORD PUZZLE

Complete the online crossword puzzle to show what you know about the Jefferson era.

ACROSS
1. He fought to stop the loss of Native American land

FLIPCARD

Use the online flipcards to quiz yourself on the terms and names introduced in this chapter.

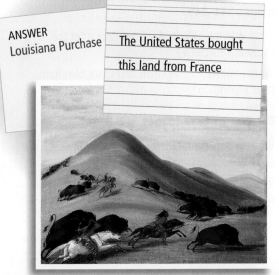

ANSWER
Louisiana Purchase

The United States bought this land from France

VOCABULARY

Explain the significance of each of the following.

1. Thomas Jefferson
2. Meriwether Lewis
3. Sacagawea
4. John Marshall
5. Tecumseh
6. William Clark
7. Oliver Hazard Perry
8. Zebulon Pike

Choose the term or name that does not belong in each group, and explain why.

9. Tecumseh, war hawk, Lewis and Clark expedition
10. impressment, judicial review, *Marbury* v. *Madison*
11. Judiciary Act of 1801, Embargo Act of 1807, Oliver Hazard Perry

KEY IDEAS

① Jeffersonian Democracy (pages 338–343)

12. Following the presidential election of 1800, how was the tie between Thomas Jefferson and Aaron Burr settled?
13. How did Jefferson imagine that Americans would live in the future?

② The Louisiana Purchase and Exploration (pages 344–349)

14. What was the extent of U.S. territory after the Louisiana Purchase?
15. What information did Lewis and Clark gain from their expedition?

③ The War of 1812 (pages 352–358)

16. What factors contributed to the outbreak of the War of 1812?
17. Where did the key conflicts in the second phase of the war take place?

CRITICAL THINKING

18. **Synthesize** Why did Jefferson take a stance on the issue of public debt?
19. **Analyze Point of View** The case of *Marbury* v. *Madison* was ruled in Jefferson's favor. Why, then, was he upset by the verdict?
20. **Evaluate** How did Jefferson think the American public could benefit from the information to be collected by Lewis and Clark?
21. **Sequence Events** In a chart like the one below, list the progression of the Lewis and Clark expedition.

22. **Causes and Effects** How did the expansion of the United States affect its foreign policy?
23. **Make Inferences** How do you think Thomas Jefferson's behavior as president might have affected the way later presidents viewed the office?
24. **Draw Conclusions** In the painting, Andrew Jackson rides a horse into the Battle of New Orleans. Why does the artist show Jackson on horseback?

Andrew Jackson at the Battle of New Orleans, 1815

DOCUMENT-BASED QUESTIONS

PART 1: Short Answer

Study each document carefully and answer the questions that follow.

DOCUMENT 1

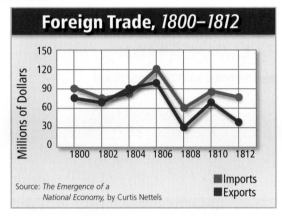

Foreign Trade, *1800–1812*

Source: *The Emergence of a National Economy*, by Curtis Nettels

■ Imports
■ Exports

1. Examine this graph that shows foreign trade between 1800 and 1812. What explains the dramatic drop in U.S. trade?

DOCUMENT 2

2. Note what "Ograbme" spells when written backward. What other clues tell you that this cartoon is about the embargo against Britain?

Part 2: Essay

3. Use information from the documents, your answer to the questions in Part 1, and your knowledge of U.S. history to write a short essay in which you explain the impact of the War of 1812 on the U.S. economy.

YOU BE THE HISTORIAN

25. **Make Inferences** Based on Zebulon Pike's mistaken descriptions, many Americans believed the Great Plains was a desert and useless for farming. What may have led to the idea that Native Americans east of the Mississippi should be moved to this region?

26. **Connect** *to* **Today** The Embargo Act of 1807 stopped American ships from going to foreign ports, and closed American ports to British ships. Suppose that an act were passed today that stopped international shipping. How would your life be affected? Use examples of items you use that are manufactured in other countries.

27. **Evaluate** Do you think that Tecumseh's confederacy helped or hurt the cause of Native Americans?

28. **Draw Conclusions** After the election of 1800, Congress passed the Twelfth Amendment, which required electors to cast separate ballots for president and vice president. Why was this change important for future elections?

Answer the
ESSENTIAL QUESTION
How did the events of the Jefferson Era strengthen the nation?

Written Response Write a two- to three-paragraph response to the Essential Question. As you consider the key ideas of each section, think about the most significant factors that contributed to the growth of the nation from 1800 to 1816. Use the Response Rubric to guide your thinking and writing.

Response Rubric
A strong response will
• describe Jefferson's views and changes in political policy
• explain the effects of the Louisiana Purchase
• analyze the impact of Jefferson's policies on foreign relations
• analyze the results of the War of 1812

National and Regional Growth

1800–1844

 ESSENTIAL QUESTION

What forces and events affected national unity and growth?

CONNECT 〰 **Geography & History**

How did geography affect regional growth?

Think about:

1 the rivers in the Northeast that powered the first textile mills

2 how a demand for cotton to supply Northeastern mills led to the spread of plantations in the South

3 how available farmland in the Midwest raised the need for better transportation routes

Steamboats speeded transportation on American waterways.

Portrait of Euphemia Toussaint, a free African American, c. 1825

1820 The Missouri Compromise balances the number of slave and free states.

▼

Effect Tension between the North and the South over slavery is temporarily eased.

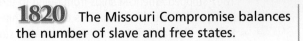

1800

Gabriel Prosser plans a slave rebellion in Virginia.

1807 Robert Fulton launches the first widely successful steamboat in America.

1812 War of 1812 disrupts U.S. shipping.

▼

Effect Americans start manufacturing more of their own goods.

Transportation Systems *1814*

Click here to explore the era of national and regional growth @ClassZone.com

Erie Canal

MAINE

VT.
N.H.

Albany
MASS.
Boston

Buffalo
N.Y.
R.I.
CONN.

WIS. TERR.

IOWA TERR.

MICH.

Lake Huron

Lake Michigan

Lake Ontario

Lake Erie

PA.

New York

Pittsburgh
N.J.
Philadelphia

OHIO

Baltimore
MD. DEL.
Washington, D.C.

ILL.

IND.

Cincinnati

Charleston
VA.

Richmond

MO.

St. Louis

Louisville
KY.

N.C.

ARK.

TENN.

S.C.

Charleston

MISS.

ALA.

GA.

ATLANTIC
OCEAN

FLA. TERR.

LA.

New Orleans

Gulf of Mexico

	Road
- - -	National Road
	Canal
+++++	Railroad

0   200   200 miles
0 100 200 kilometers

1823 The Monroe Doctrine is issued, warning European countries to stay out of the Americas.

▼

Effect United States is seen as world power.

1831 Nat Turner leads a slave rebellion in Virginia.

Early telegraph

1825 The Erie Canal is completed.

▼

Effect The canal creates a water route between New York City and the Great Lakes.

Barrel used on the Erie Canal

1844

A telegraph line connects Washington, D.C., and Baltimore.

Reading for Understanding

▶ Key Ideas

BEFORE, YOU LEARNED
The nation gained confidence and worldwide respect as a result of the War of 1812.

NOW YOU WILL LEARN
New industries and inventions changed the way people lived and worked in the early 1800s.

▶ Vocabulary

TERMS & NAMES

Industrial Revolution the economic changes of the late 1700s, when manufacturing replaced farming as the main form of work

Samuel Slater builder of the first water-powered textile mill in America

factory system method of production using many workers and machines in one building

Lowell mills textile mills located in the factory town of Lowell, Massachusetts

Robert Fulton inventor of America's first widely successful steamboat

Peter Cooper builder of America's first successful steam-powered locomotive

Samuel F. B. Morse inventor of the telegraph

BACKGROUND VOCABULARY

threshing machine a device that separates kernels of wheat from their husks

mechanical reaper a device that cuts grain

Visual Vocabulary
threshing machine

▶ Reading Strategy

As you read and respond to the **KEY QUESTIONS**, use a graphic organizer like the one shown to record important events in the order in which they occurred.

 See Skillbuilder Handbook, page R5.

SEQUENCE EVENTS

Samuel Slater builds mill in Rhode Island.

GRAPHIC ORGANIZERS
Go to **Interactive Review** @ ClassZone.com

Early Industry and Inventions

15.A.3b Explain the relationship between productivity and wages.
15.D.3c Explain how workers can affect their productivity through training and by using tools, machinery and technology.

One American's Story

Harriet Hanson Robinson began working in the textile mills in Lowell, Massachusetts, in 1835, when she was ten years old. At the time, there were few opportunities for girls and women to work outside the home, and Harriet was proud to earn a good wage. As an adult, Harriet described the life of the mill girls.

PRIMARY SOURCE

❝ Though the hours of labor were long, they were not overworked; they were obliged to tend no more looms and frames than they could easily take care of, and they had plenty of time to sit and rest. . . . They were treated with consideration by their employers, and there was a feeling of respectful equality between them. . . . In those days, there was no need of advocating the doctrine of the proper relation between employer and employed. *Help was too valuable to be ill-treated.* ❞

—Harriet Hanson Robinson, from *Loom and Spindle; or, Life Among the Early Mill Girls*

The textile industry employed young workers such as this unidentified mill girl, photographed holding a spindle (for spinning fibers).

Later, when laborers were more plentiful, the mill owners were able to cut wages, and life in the mills became much more difficult.

The Industrial Revolution

▼ **KEY QUESTION** How did the Industrial Revolution change the way Americans lived and worked?

After the War of 1812, Americans experienced a new kind of revolution. This was not a political revolution, but a change in the way that goods were produced. For centuries, people had made clothing, furniture, and other goods at home. Then, in late-18th-century Britain, factory machines started replacing hand tools. Soon large-scale manufacturing was producing huge quantities of goods. These changes are called the **Industrial Revolution**.

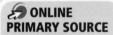

ONLINE PRIMARY SOURCE

Hear the perspectives at the **Research & Writing Center** @ ClassZone.com

Factories Rise in New England In America, the Industrial Revolution began in 1793, when the Englishman **Samuel Slater** built the first spinning mill in Pawtucket, Rhode Island. The year before, he had sailed to the United States, perhaps under a false name—it was illegal for British textile workers to leave the country. Britain did not want another nation to copy its machines for making thread and cloth. But Slater brought the secrets to America.

At first, Slater hired a small group of children and paid them a low wage. Later, he built a larger mill and employed whole families. As Slater influenced others to start mills, his family system of employment spread through Rhode Island, Connecticut, and southern Massachusetts.

New England was a good place to build factories. The mills needed water power, and New England had many fast-moving rivers. For transportation, it had ships and access to the ocean. The region also had a ready labor force of farmers who were tired of scraping together a living from stony fields.

The **factory system** brought many workers and machines together under one roof. People left their family farms and crowded into cities to take jobs in factories. They worked for wages on a set schedule. Their way of life changed—and not always for the better.

COMPARING *Perspectives*

LIFE IN THE MILLS

The Industrial Revolution swept England in the mid-1700s. Half a century later, America, too, began to be transformed from a land of small farmers to an industrial nation. In these excerpts, observers from America and England described what they saw on visits to America's then-new Lowell mills.

An American Speaks

❝ The din and clatter of these five hundred looms under full operation, struck us . . . as something frightful and infernal . . . The atmosphere of such a room . . . is charged with cotton filaments and dust, which, we were told, are very injurious to the lungs. On entering the room, although the day was warm, we remarked that the windows were down . . . [W]e found ourselves . . . in quite a perspiration. ❞

—*A Description of Factory Life by an Associationist,* 1846

An Englishman Speaks

❝ The rooms in which [the girls] worked were as well ordered as themselves. In the windows of some, there were green plants, which were trained to shade the glass; in all, there was as much fresh air, cleanliness, and comfort, as the nature of the occupation would possibly admit of. . . . I solemnly declare, that from all the crowd I saw . . . I cannot recall . . . one young face that gave me a painful impression . . . ❞

—Charles Dickens, *American Notes,* 1842

CRITICAL THINKING

1. **Make Inferences** What do you think working conditions were like in the mills in England?
2. **Recognizing Bias and Propaganda** Why might the two writers describe the same working conditions in such different ways?

Many Americans, such as Thomas Jefferson, did not want the United States to industrialize. But the War of 1812 brought growth to American industry. Because the British naval blockade kept imported goods from reaching U.S. shores, Americans had to manufacture their own goods. The blockade also stopped investors from spending money on shipping and trade. Instead, they invested in new American industries. Entrepreneurs built factories, starting in New England. These entrepreneurs and their region grew wealthier.

The Lowell Mills Hire Women In 1814, the U.S. textile industry took a leap forward when Francis Cabot Lowell built a factory in eastern Massachusetts. This factory spun raw cotton into yarn, and then wove the yarn into cloth on power looms. Lowell had seen power looms in English mills and had figured out how to build them.

Work at the early mills was guided by a bell schedule such as this one, which begins with a wake-up bell at 4:40 in the morning. **What does this schedule tell you about the workers' daily lives?**

The factory was so successful that Lowell's associates built a new factory town, Lowell, near the Merrimack and Concord rivers. The **Lowell mills**, textile mills in the town, brought another significant change as large numbers of women entered the workforce. Many were farm girls who lived in company-owned boardinghouses. In the early years, the Lowell girls' wages were high—between two and four dollars a week. Older women supervised the girls. Later, falling profits meant that wages dropped and working conditions worsened at the Lowell mills.

The Lowell mills and other early factories ran on water power. Factories built after the 1830s were run by more powerful steam engines. Because steam engines used coal and wood, not fast-moving water, these newer factories could be built away from rivers and beyond New England.

New Manufacturing Methods Spread New manufacturing methods changed work in other industries as well. In 1797, the U.S. government hired the inventor Eli Whitney to make 10,000 muskets for the army. Before this time, guns were made one at a time by a gunsmith. Each gun differed slightly. If a part broke, a new part had to be created to match the broken one.

Whitney sought a better way to make guns. In 1801, he went to Washington and laid out several piles of musket parts. He took a part from each pile and quickly assembled a musket. He had just demonstrated the use of interchangeable parts—parts that are exactly alike.

Machines that produced identical parts soon became standard. Interchangeable parts speeded up production, made repairs easy, and allowed the use of less-skilled workers.

▲ **SYNTHESIZE** Describe how the Industrial Revolution changed the way Americans lived and worked.

1765

▶ **1769**
Improved
Steam engine,
James Watt

c. 1786
Threshing machine, Andrew Meikle

1793
Cotton gin, Eli Whitney

▲ **c. 1803**
Locomotive,
Richard Trevithick

1807
Steamboat,
◀ Robert Fulton

1834 Reaper, Cyrus McCormick

1837 Telegraph, Samuel F. B. Morse
Steel plow, John Deere

1839
Photography, ▶
Louis Daguerre

1845

CRITICAL THINKING **Evaluate** Which of these inventions do you think had the greatest impact on life in the middle of the 19th century?

New Inventions Improve Life

🔻 **KEY QUESTION** How did new inventions improve American life?

New inventions improved transportation, communication, and production. They also quickened the pace of life.

Transportation and Communication Inventor **Robert Fulton** developed a steamboat that could move against the current or a strong wind. He launched the *Clermont* on the Hudson River in 1807. Its steam engine turned two side paddle wheels, which pulled the boat through the water. Many thought it looked silly and nicknamed it "Fulton's Folly," but it made the 300-mile round-trip from New York to Albany and back in a record 62 hours.

In 1811, a steamship first traveled down the Ohio and Mississippi rivers. However, its engine was not powerful enough to return upriver against the current. Henry Miller Shreve, a trader on the Mississippi, designed a steamship that could be powered up the Mississippi, against the current. In 1816, his boat launched a new era of transportation on the river.

Some cities, however, were not on rivers that could be navigated by steamship. Traders in these cities needed a way to ship goods. Steam-powered trains were the answer. English engineer Richard Trevithick had introduced the locomotive around 1803. In 1830, **Peter Cooper** built America's first successful steam-powered locomotive, called the *Tom Thumb*. By 1833, the 136-mile railroad track connecting Charleston and Hamburg, South Carolina, was the longest in the world.

Around 1837, **Samuel F. B. Morse** first demonstrated his telegraph. This machine sent long and short pulses of electricity along a wire. These pulses could be translated into letters spelling out messages. With the telegraph, it took only seconds to communicate with someone in another city. In 1844, the first long-distance telegraph line carried news from Baltimore to Washington, D.C., about who had been nominated for president. Telegraph lines spanned the country by 1861, bringing people closer as a nation.

Technology Improves Farming Other new inventions increased farm production. In 1837, blacksmith John Deere invented a lightweight plow with a steel cutting edge. Older cast-iron plows were designed for the relatively light and sandy soil of New England. But rich, heavy Midwestern soil clung to the bottom of these plows and slowed down farm work. Deere's new plow made preparing ground to plant crops much less work. As a result, more farmers began to move to the Midwest.

The **threshing machine** and the **mechanical reaper** were other inventions that improved agricultural production by making farm work quicker and more efficient. The threshing machine, which was invented around 1786 by Andrew Meikle of Scotland, mechanically separated kernels of wheat from husks. In 1831, Cyrus McCormick developed a reaper that cut ripe grain quickly and efficiently. McCormick patented his invention in 1834 and brought it to Europe in the 1850s.

New technologies linked regions and contributed to a feeling of national unity. With new farm equipment, Midwestern farmers grew food to feed Northeastern factory workers. In turn, Midwestern farmers became a market for Northeastern manufactured goods. The growth of Northeastern textile mills increased demand for Southern cotton, which, unfortunately, led to the expansion of slavery in the South.

▲ **MAIN IDEAS & DETAILS** Explain how new inventions improved American life.

 Illinois Learning Standards *Review*

 ONLINE QUIZ
For test practice, go to
Interactive Review @ ClassZone.com

TERMS & NAMES

1. Explain the importance of

- Industrial Revolution
- Robert Fulton
- Samuel Slater
- Peter Cooper
- factory system
- Samuel F. B. Morse
- Lowell mills

USING YOUR READING NOTES

2. Sequence Events Complete the diagram you started at the beginning of this section.

Samuel Slater builds mill in Rhode Island.

KEY IDEAS

3. Why was New England a good place to set up factories?

4. How were different regions of the United States linked economically?

CRITICAL THINKING

5. Summarize Explain how the use of interchangeable parts improved the manufacturing process.

6. Form and Support Opinions Samuel Slater and Francis Lowell both illegally brought industrial secrets to the United States. Do you think they were wrong to do this? Explain.

7. **Art** Use the library to find an image of one of the early inventions mentioned in this section. Draw a detailed picture of it. Then write a paragraph explaining how the invention worked.

🖱 **Click here** to see an American textile mill in operation @ ClassZone.com

The first textile mills in America ran on water power. Falling or flowing water powered the machinery through a system of gears and belts. Eventually, however, steam engines replaced water as the source of power for the mills.

🖱 **Click here** Early mills were built on deep, fast-moving rivers in the Northeast.

🖱 **Click here** The mills changed working life by bringing together many workers and machines in the same building.

🖱 **Click here** Many children worked at the early textile mills.

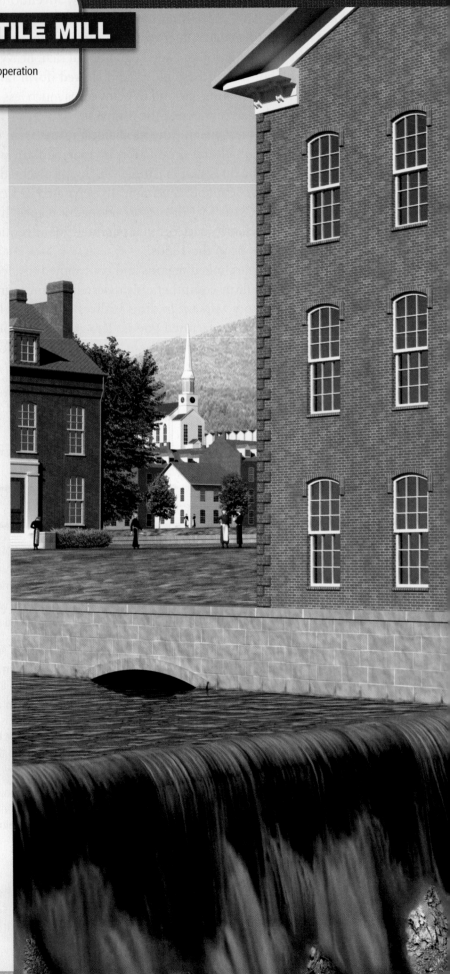

Long shafts distribute power to the machines on each floor.

Yarn is woven into cloth.

Carded fiber can be spun into yarn

Belts and pulleys transmit power to each floor.

Wool or cotton fiber must be carded, or disentangled.

A water turbine—a machine driven by water pressure—provides power to the belts and pulleys above.

Activity

Four Corners

1. Have a volunteer from the class write the following statement on the board: *Working at a textile mill was a good opportunity for young women in the 1800s.*

2. Ask another volunteer to write **Agree**, **Strongly Agree**, **Disagree**, and **Strongly Disagree** on four separate sheets of paper, and then tape each sheet in a different corner of your classroom.

3. Think about what you've read and studied about New England textile mills, including salaries, living quarters, working conditions, and the daily schedules of mill workers. Now go to the corner of the room that best represents your agreement or disagreement with the statement on the board.

4. Be prepared to use information from the chapter and the Animated History feature to defend the position or opinion you represent.

Reading for Understanding

▶ Key Ideas

BEFORE, YOU LEARNED

New industries and inventions changed the way people lived and worked in the early 1800s.

NOW YOU WILL LEARN

The invention of the cotton gin and the demand for cotton caused slavery to spread in the South.

▶ Vocabulary

TERMS & NAMES

cotton gin machine that made cleaning seeds from cotton faster

Eli Whitney inventor of the cotton gin

Nat Turner leader of an 1831 slave rebellion in Virginia

BACKGROUND VOCABULARY

spirituals religious folk songs

1 A hand crank turns a series of rollers.

2 A roller with wire teeth pulls the cotton through slots too narrow for the seeds.

3 The cotton seeds fall into a hopper.

4 A roller with brushes removes the cleaned cotton from the first roller.

5 The cleaned cotton leaves the gin.

Visual Vocabulary
cotton gin

▶ Reading Strategy

As you read and respond to the **KEY QUESTIONS**, use a graphic organizer like the one shown to note important events and their effects. Add boxes or start a new diagram as needed.

See Skillbuilder Handbook, page R7.

CAUSES AND EFFECTS

CAUSE

Eli Whitney invents the cotton gin.

EFFECT

EFFECT

GRAPHIC ORGANIZERS
Go to **Interactive Review** @ ClassZone.com

SECTION 2

Plantations and Slavery Spread

16.C.3b Explain relationships among the American economy and slavery, immigration, industrialization, labor and urbanization, 1700–present.
17.C.3b Explain how patterns of resources are used throughout the world.

One American's Story

Catherine Beale was born into slavery in 1838. In 1929, she recalled her childhood on a Southern plantation.

PRIMARY SOURCE

" We had to work in the field in the day and at night we had to pick out the seed before we went to bed. And we had to clean the wool, we had to pick the burrs and sticks out so it would be clean and could be carded and spun and wove. **"**

—Catherine Beale, quoted in *Slave Testimony*

Workers picking cotton in Texas

Catherine had to clean cotton by hand, probably because the plantation didn't have a **cotton gin**. This machine made cleaning cotton much faster. As a result, it became more profitable to grow cotton—and to own slaves.

The Cotton Boom

▼ **KEY QUESTION** How did the invention of the cotton gin change Southern life?

The Industrial Revolution increased the number of goods being produced. It also increased the demand for raw materials. In England, textile mills needed huge quantities of cotton to produce goods to sell throughout the British Empire. Cotton growers in the South wanted to meet this demand.

The Cotton Gin The short-fibered cotton that grew in most parts of the South was hard to clean by hand. A worker could clean just one pound of this cotton in a day. Then, in 1793, **Eli Whitney** invented a machine for cleaning cotton. With the new machine, one worker could clean as much as 50 pounds of cotton a day. The cotton gin helped set the South on a very different course of economic development than the North.

Slavery Expands From 1790 to 1860, cotton production increased more than a thousandfold, thanks in large part to the new cotton gin. Using slave labor, the South raised millions of bales of cotton each year for the textile mills of England and the American Northeast.

As cotton production grew, so did the demand for slavery. In 1808, it became illegal to import Africans for use as slaves. At the same time, however, the birth rate among the enslaved population already in the country began to increase rapidly. Between 1810 and 1840, the enslaved population in the South more than doubled.

Southern Support for Slavery Slavery divided white Southerners into those who held slaves and those who did not. Slaveholders with large plantations were the wealthiest and most powerful people in the South, but they were relatively few in number. Only about one-third of white families owned slaves in 1840. Of these slave-owning families, only about one-tenth had large plantations with 20 or more slaves.

Although most Southern farmers owned few or no slaves, many supported slavery anyway. They hoped to buy slaves someday, which would allow them to raise more cotton and earn more money.

🔺 **CAUSES AND EFFECTS** Explain how the cotton gin changed Southern life.

Connecting History

Human Rights

As slavery expanded in the South, an antislavery movement spread in the North. By the 1840s, the movement to abolish slavery had become a political force.

See Chapter 14, pages 465–468

African Americans in the South

🔻 **KEY QUESTION** What was life like for African Americans in the South?

By 1840, enslaved people formed about a third of the South's population.

Varied Conditions About half of enslaved people worked on plantations. Conditions could be cruel, as a former slave recalled decades later.

PRIMARY SOURCE

❝ The overseer was 'straddle his big horse at three o'clock in the mornin', roustin' the hands off to the field . . . . The rows was a mile long and no matter how much grass [weeds] was in them, if you [left] one sprig on your row they [beat] you nearly to death. ❞

—Wes Brady, quoted in *Remembering Slavery*

Not all enslaved people labored on plantations. In cities, some worked as domestic servants, skilled craftsmen, factory hands, and day laborers. Some were hired out and allowed to keep part of their earnings. But they were still enslaved—under the law, they were considered property.

In 1840, about 5 percent of African Americans in the South were free. They had either been born free, been freed by an owner, or bought their own freedom. Although they were not enslaved, they still faced many problems. Some states made them leave once they gained their freedom. Most states did not permit them to vote or to be educated. Many employers refused to hire them. But the biggest threat was the possibility of being captured and sold into slavery.

The Cotton Kingdom 1840

KENTUCKY

VIRGINIA
Norfolk

• Nashville
TENNESSEE

NORTH CAROLINA

ARKANSAS
Memphis •

• Atlanta

SOUTH
CAROLINA

MISSISSIPPI
ALABAMA

GEORGIA

Charleston •

• Jackson
Montgomery •

LOUISIANA
• Natchez

REPUBLIC
OF TEXAS

• Baton Rouge

New Orleans •

Gulf of Mexico

FLORIDA
TERRITORY

ATLANTIC
OCEAN

0 — 75 — 150 miles
0 — 75 — 150 kilometers

Cotton-growing areas in 1840

(left) Slave labor was the backbone of the cotton kingdom. (below) The seeds of the cotton plant are surrounded by soft, white fibers.

Connect Geography & History

1. **Human-Environment Interaction**
   Which six states had the largest areas devoted to growing cotton?

2. **Human-Environment Interaction**
   How far north was cotton grown?

CAUSE	EFFECTS

Whitney's cotton gin (short for "engine") made short-fibered cotton a commercially successful product. This changed Southern life in four important ways.

- Cotton plantations were no longer limited to Atlantic coastal states, where long-fibered cotton grew.
- Planters grew more cotton than other goods; cotton exports increased.
- Native Americans were driven off land that was taken to grow cotton.
- Slavery expanded, especially westward to new cotton plantations.

History Makers

Nat Turner   1800–1831

Nat Turner (above left) was born into slavery in Virginia. He learned to read as a child and became an enthusiastic reader of the Bible. Enslaved people gathered in forest clearings to listen to Turner's powerful sermons.

In 1831, Turner led a group of followers in killing about 55 white Virginians, starting with the family of his former owner. It was the bloodiest slave rebellion in American history. In an account of events that he dictated to Thomas R. Gray before his execution, Turner called himself a "prophet" and said that God had called him to commit his violent acts.

CRITICAL THINKING **Analyze Point of View** How did Turner justify his use of violence?

 ONLINE BIOGRAPHY For more on Nat Turner, go to the **Research & Writing Center** @ ClassZone.com

Families Under Slavery Perhaps the cruelest part of slavery was the sale of family members away from one another. Although some slaveholders would not part mothers from children, many did, causing unforgettable grief.

When enslaved families could manage to be together, they took comfort in family life. Enslaved people did marry each other, although their marriages were not legally recognized. They tried to raise children, while knowing that their children could be taken from them and sold at any time. Abolitionist Frederick Douglass, who was born into slavery, recalled visits from his mother, who lived 12 miles away.

PRIMARY SOURCE

❝ I do not recollect [remember] ever seeing my mother by the light of day. She was with me in the night. She would lie down with me, and get me to sleep, but long before I waked she was gone. **❞**

—Frederick Douglass, *Narrative of the Life of Frederick Douglass*

Douglass's mother resisted slavery by the simple act of visiting her child. Douglass later rebelled by escaping to the North. A small number of enslaved people rebelled in violent ways.

Slave Rebellions Armed rebellion by enslaved persons was an extreme form of resistance to slavery. Gabriel Prosser planned an attack on Richmond, Virginia, in 1800. In 1822, Denmark Vesey planned a revolt in Charleston, South Carolina. Both plots were betrayed and the leaders, as well as numerous followers, were hanged.

The most famous rebellion was led by **Nat Turner** in Southampton County, Virginia, in 1831. Beginning on August 21, Turner and 70 followers killed about 55 white men, women, and children. Most of Turner's men were captured when their ammunition ran out, and some were killed. After Turner was caught, he was tried and hanged.

Turner's rebellion spread fear in the South. Whites killed more than 200 African Americans in revenge. The state of Virginia considered ending slavery because of the upheaval, but the proposal was narrowly defeated. Some state legislatures, however, passed harsh laws that further limited the freedom of both free and enslaved African Americans. For African Americans in the South, the grip of slavery grew even tighter.

A Common Culture By the early 1800s, a distinctive African-American culture had emerged on Southern plantations. This common culture helped enslaved African Americans bond together and endure the brutal conditions of Southern plantation life.

Religion was a cornerstone of African-American culture in the South. Some slaveholders had tried to use religion to force enslaved people to accept mistreatment, emphasizing such Bible passages as "Servants, obey your masters." But enslaved people took their own messages from the Bible. They were particularly inspired by the book of Exodus, which tells of Moses leading the Hebrews out of bondage in Egypt. Many enslaved African Americans believed that this story offered a message of hope for their own people.

Enslaved people expressed their beliefs in **spirituals**—folk songs that were often religious in nature. Many spirituals voiced the desire for freedom. Sometimes, spirituals contained coded messages about a planned escape or an owner's unexpected return. African-American spirituals later had a strong influence on blues, jazz, and other forms of American music.

 COMPARE AND CONTRAST Compare the different conditions faced by African Americans in the South.

(*top*) *The Old Plantation*, late 1700s.
(*above*) Enslaved Africans brought the banjo to the American colonies.

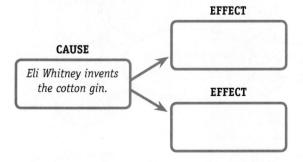

Illinois Learning Standards *Review*

ONLINE QUIZ
For test practice, go to
Interactive Review @ ClassZone.com

TERMS & NAMES

1. Explain the importance of
   - cotton gin
   - Nat Turner
   - Eli Whitney

USING YOUR READING NOTES

2. **Causes and Effects** Complete the diagram you started at the beginning of this section.

EFFECT

CAUSE

Eli Whitney invents the cotton gin.

EFFECT

KEY IDEAS

3. How did the invention of the cotton gin change Southern life?

4. What forms did resistance to slavery take?

CRITICAL THINKING

5. **Analyze Point of View** Why did many Southern farmers who owned no slaves support slavery?

6. **Connect Economics and History** The cotton gin made it possible to clean the same amount of cotton with fewer workers. Why did this result in an increased demand for slaves?

7. **Art** Choose an African-American spiritual. Write down and illustrate the lyrics, drawing any images or symbols used in the spiritual.

▶ Key Ideas

BEFORE, YOU LEARNED

The invention of the cotton gin and the demand for cotton caused slavery to spread in the South.

NOW YOU WILL LEARN

While patriotic pride increased national unity, tensions grew between the North and the South.

▶ Vocabulary

TERMS & NAMES

Henry Clay nationalist Representative from Kentucky

American System plan introduced in 1815 to make America economically self-sufficient

James Monroe fifth president of the United States, who proclaimed the Monroe Doctrine

Erie Canal waterway that connected New York City with Buffalo, New York

Missouri Compromise laws enacted in 1820 to maintain balance of power between slave and free states

Monroe Doctrine U.S. policy opposing European interference in the Western Hemisphere

BACKGROUND VOCABULARY

nationalism a feeling of pride, loyalty, and protectiveness toward one's country

protective tariff a tax on imported goods that protects a nation's businesses from foreign competition

sectionalism loyalty to the interests of one's own region or section of the country

Visual Vocabulary a contemporary lock on the Erie Canal

▶ Reading Strategy

As you read and respond to the **KEY QUESTIONS**, use a graphic organizer like the one shown to record main ideas and important details about factors that affected national unity in the early 1800s. Add ovals or start a new diagram as needed.

 See Skillbuilder Handbook, page R4.

MAIN IDEAS AND DETAILS

Nationalist feelings united the states

GRAPHIC ORGANIZERS
Go to **Interactive Review** @ ClassZone.com

Nationalism and Sectionalism

14.E.3 Compare the basic principles of the United States and its international interests (e.g., *territory, environment, trade, use of technology*).
16.C.3b Explain relationships among the American economy and slavery, immigration, industrialization, labor and urbanization, 1700–present.

One American's Story

The War of 1812 increased American nationalism. **Nationalism** is a feeling of pride, loyalty, and protectiveness toward your nation. Representative **Henry Clay** was a strong nationalist.

PRIMARY SOURCE

❝ Every nation should anxiously endeavor to establish its absolute independence, and consequently be able to feed and clothe and defend itself. If it rely upon a foreign supply that may be cut off . . . it cannot be independent. ❞

—Henry Clay, *The Life and Speeches of Henry Clay*

After the war, President James Madison supported Clay's plan to strengthen the country and unify its regions.

Nationalism Unites the Country

▼ **KEY QUESTION** What factors helped to promote national unity?

Henry Clay, U.S. representative from Kentucky

Madison wanted America to prosper by itself, without foreign products.

The American System In 1815, Madison presented a plan to Congress for making America economically self-sufficient. The plan—which Clay promoted as the **American System**—had three main actions.

1. Establish a **protective tariff**, a tax on imported goods that protects a nation's businesses from foreign competition. Congress passed a tariff in 1816. It made European goods more expensive and encouraged Americans to buy cheaper, American-made products.
2. Establish a national bank that would promote a single currency, making trade easier. (Most regional banks issued their own money.) In 1816, Congress set up the second Bank of the United States.
3. Improve the country's transportation systems, which were important for the economy. Poor roads made transportation slow and costly.

The Era of Good Feelings As nationalist feeling spread, people shifted their loyalty away from state governments and toward the federal government. Democratic-Republican **James Monroe** won the presidency in 1816 with a large majority of electoral votes. The Federalist Party provided little opposition to Monroe and soon disappeared. Political differences gave way to what one Boston newspaper called the Era of Good Feelings.

During the Monroe administration, several landmark Supreme Court decisions promoted national unity by strengthening the federal government. For example, in *McCulloch* v. *Maryland* (1819), the court ruled that a state could not tax a national bank. As Justice Marshall explained, "The power to tax involves the power to destroy."

Gibbons v. *Ogden* (1824) also strengthened the federal government. Two steamship operators fought over shipping rights on the Hudson River in New York and New Jersey. The Court ruled that interstate commerce could be regulated only by the federal government, not the state governments.

Historic Decisions of the SUPREME COURT

McCulloch v. Maryland (1819)

KEY ISSUE   federal supremacy vs. state powers
KEY PEOPLE   James McCulloch   cashier, Bank of the United States (Maryland branch)

The Case

The Second Bank of the United States was established by the U.S. Congress in 1816. The state of Maryland tried to put the bank out of business: it set a high tax on currency issued by the bank. When James McCulloch, the cashier at the Maryland branch, refused to pay the tax, Maryland sued him and the bank.

The Supreme Court ruled in favor of McCulloch and the Bank of the United States. It ruled that Congress had the right to establish the bank.

The court also ruled that the states do not have the right to tax the federal government. If the tax were allowed, it would give Maryland power over the federal government. In the ruling, John Marshall wrote that the framers of the Constitution did not intend to make the federal government subject to state powers. He cited the Supremacy Clause (Art. 6, Sec. 2): "This Constitution, and the laws of the United States . . . shall be the supreme law of the land."

CRITICAL THINKING

1. **Draw Conclusions** Why did John Marshall say that the power to tax "involves the power to destroy"?

2. **WHAT IF?** What do you think might have happened if *McCulloch* v. *Maryland* had been decided in Maryland's favor?

The Erie Canal

Transportation Links Cities In 1806, Congress had funded a road from Cumberland, Maryland, to Wheeling, West Virginia. By 1841, the National Road, the country's main east-west route, extended to Vandalia, Illinois.

Water transportation improved with the building of canals. The period from 1790 to 1855 is often called the Age of Canals. Completed in 1825, the massive **Erie Canal** created a water route between New York City and Buffalo, New York. The Erie Canal allowed farm products from the Great Lakes region to flow east, and people and manufactured goods from the East to flow west. Trade stimulated by the canal helped New York City to become the nation's largest city. Between 1820 and 1830, its population nearly doubled.

Improvements in railroads led to a decline in canal use. In 1830, about 23 miles of train track existed. By 1850, the number had climbed to 9,000.

▲ **SUMMARIZE** Describe the factors that helped to promote national unity.

Sectional Tensions Increase

▼ **KEY QUESTION** What factors increased sectional tension?

While nationalism grew, sectionalism threatened to tear the nation apart.

Sectional Interests **Sectionalism** is loyalty to the interests of a region or section of the country. By the early 1800s, economic changes had created divisions. The South relied on a plantation economy that used slavery. The Northeast focused on manufacturing and trade. In the West, settlers wanted cheap land. The interests of these sections were often in conflict.

Sectionalism became a major issue when Missouri applied for statehood in 1817. People in Missouri wanted to allow slavery in their state. At the time, the United States consisted of 11 slave states and 11 free states. Adding Missouri as a slave state would upset the balance of power in Congress.

The Missouri Compromise 1820–1821

OREGON COUNTRY
Claimed by U.S.
and Great Britain

NEW SPAIN
(Mexico)

PACIFIC
OCEAN

UNORGANIZED
TERRITORY

MICHIGAN TERRITORY

BRITISH TERRITORY

Claimed by U.S.
and Great Britain

MAINE
1820

VT.
N.H.
MASS.
NEW
YORK
R.I.
CONN.
PA.
N.J.
DEL.
MD.

ILL.
IND.
OHIO

MISSOURI
1821

36°30' Missouri Compromise Line

ARKANSAS
TERRITORY

KY.

VIRGINIA

N.C.

TENN.

S.C.

MISS.
ALA.
GA.

LA.

UNORGANIZED
TERRITORY

ATLANTIC
OCEAN

Gulf of Mexico

0 150 300 miles
0 150 300 kilometers

Free states and territories
Closed to slavery by
Missouri Compromise
Slave states and territories
Open to slavery by
Missouri Compromise
Other claimed areas

Connect Geography & History

1. **Region** How did the Missouri Compromise affect the amount of territory that was closed to slavery?

2. **Make Inferences** What concern might the Missouri Compromise have raised in slave states?

The Missouri Compromise Representatives in Congress argued over admitting the new state of Missouri as a slave state or a free state. Southerners claimed that the Constitution did not give Congress the power to ban slavery. They worried that if free states formed a majority in Congress, they would ban slavery altogether. Warned Representative Thomas Cobb of Georgia:

PRIMARY SOURCE

❝ If you persist, the Union will be dissolved. You have kindled a fire which . . . seas of blood can only extinguish. ❞

—Thomas Cobb, quoted in *Henry Clay: Statesman for the Union*

Meanwhile, Maine, which had been part of Massachusetts, also wanted statehood. Henry Clay suggested that Missouri be admitted as a slave state and Maine as a free state. Congress passed this plan, known as the **Missouri Compromise**, in 1820. It kept the balance of power in the Senate between the slave states and free states. It also called for slavery to be banned north of the parallel 36° 30', Missouri's southern border.

Amid these tensions, the Mason-Dixon Line, which formed the Maryland-Pennsylvania border, took on symbolic importance. The term "Mason-Dixon Line" came to be used for the division between slave states and free states, as well as the division between the North and the South.

▲ **SYNTHESIZE** Describe the factors that increased sectional tension.

National Boundaries and Foreign Affairs

▼ **KEY QUESTION** How were U.S. borders made more secure?

Nationalist feeling made Americans want to define the nation's borders. To do this, U.S. leaders had to reach agreements with Britain and Spain.

Settling Boundary Issues Two agreements improved relations between the United States and Britain. The Rush-Bagot Agreement (1817) limited each side's naval forces on the Great Lakes. In the Convention of 1818, the two countries set the 49th parallel as the U.S.-Canadian border as far west as the Rocky Mountains.

But U.S. relations with Spain were tense. The two nations disagreed on the boundaries of the Louisiana Purchase and the ownership of West Florida. Meanwhile, pirates and runaway slaves used Spanish-held East Florida as a refuge. In addition, the Seminoles of East Florida raided white settlements in Georgia to reclaim lost lands.

CONNECT to the Essential Question

What forces and events affected national unity and growth?

STRENGTHENING FORCES	WEAKENING FORCES
The Industrial Revolution fuels economic growth.	New industry and inventions lead to reliance on manufacturing in the North, and increased dependence on cotton and slavery in the South.
The American System encourages economic self-sufficiency.	
Supreme Court decisions strengthen the federal government.	Regional differences divide the nation among Northerners, Southerners, and Westerners.
Improvements in transportation and communication link cities and regions.	Although the Missouri Compromise keeps the balance of free and slave states, the issue of slavery continues to divide the nation.
The United States expands and defines its borders.	

CRITICAL THINKING **Compare and Contrast** In what ways did economic changes both strengthen and threaten national unity?

In 1817, U.S. General Andrew Jackson followed the Seminoles into Spanish territory and then captured two cities—Pensacola and Saint Marks—for the United States. Monroe ordered Jackson to withdraw but gave Spain a choice. It could either police the Floridas or turn them over to the United States. In the Adams-Onís Treaty of 1819, Spain handed Florida to the United States and gave up claims to the Oregon Country.

Connect *to the* **World**

Latin American Independence
Venezuelan-born Simón Bolívar was popularly known as the "George Washington of Latin America." When the Monroe Doctrine was issued, Bolívar was the dictator of Peru and already had led Venezuela, Colombia, Peru, and Ecuador to independence.

The Monroe Doctrine The nation felt threatened not only by sectionalism, but by other events in the Americas. In Latin America, several countries had successfully fought for independence from Spain and Portugal. Some European monarchies planned to help Spain and Portugal regain their colonies. U.S. leaders feared that this could put their own government in danger.

Russian colonies in the Pacific Northwest also concerned Americans. The Russians entered Alaska in 1784. By 1812, their trading posts reached almost to San Francisco.

In December 1823, Monroe issued a statement that became known as the **Monroe Doctrine**. (See Reading Primary Sources, page 385.) Monroe said that the Americas were closed to further colonization. He also warned that European efforts to reestablish colonies would be considered "dangerous to our peace and safety." Finally, he promised that the United States would stay out of European affairs. The Monroe Doctrine showed that the United States saw itself as a world power and protector of Latin America.

▲ **PROBLEMS AND SOLUTIONS** Describe how U.S. borders were made more secure.

Illinois Learning Standards *Review*

 ONLINE QUIZ
For test practice, go to
Interactive Review @ ClassZone.com

TERMS & NAMES

1. Explain the importance of
- Henry Clay
- American System
- James Monroe
- Erie Canal
- Missouri Compromise
- Monroe Doctrine

USING YOUR READING NOTES

2. Main Ideas and Details Complete the diagram you started at the beginning of this section.

Nationalist feelings united the states

KEY IDEAS

3. What were the three parts of the American System?

4. What was the main message of the Monroe Doctrine?

CRITICAL THINKING

5. Summarize How did the question of admitting Missouri to the Union divide the nation?

6. **Connect** *to* **Today** Think about the diagram you made of factors that contributed to American national unity in the early 1800s. Which of these factors are still important for national unity?

7. **Writing** **Editorial** Write an editorial giving your opinion of either the Missouri Compromise or the Monroe Doctrine. State how you believe it will affect the nation.

The Monroe Doctrine

SETTING THE STAGE On December 2, 1823, President Monroe gave a State of the Union address, part of which became known as the Monroe Doctrine. The "allied powers" he refers to are European monarchies that were threatening to help Spain regain its Latin American colonies.

The occasion has been judged proper for asserting, as a principle in which the rights and interests of the United States are involved, that the American continents, by the free and independent condition which they have assumed and maintain, are henceforth not to be considered as subjects for future colonization by any European powers. . . .

It was stated at the commencement of the last session that a great effort was then making in Spain and Portugal to improve the condition of the people of those countries, and that it appeared to be conducted with extraordinary moderation. It need scarcely be remarked that the result has been so far very different from what was then anticipated. . . . The citizens of the United States cherish sentiments the most friendly in favor of the liberty and happiness of their fellowmen on that side of the Atlantic. In the wars of the European powers in matters relating to themselves we have never taken any part, nor does it **comport**[1] with our policy so to do. It is only when our rights are invaded or seriously **menaced**[2] that we resent injuries or make preparation for our defense.

With the movements in this hemisphere we are of necessity more immediately connected, and by causes which must be obvious to all enlightened and impartial observers. The political system of the allied powers is essentially different in this respect from that of America. This difference proceeds from that which exists in their respective governments; and to the defense of our own, which has been achieved by the loss of so much blood and treasure, and matured by the wisdom of their most enlightened citizens, and under which we have enjoyed **unexampled felicity**,[3] this whole nation is devoted.

---

1. **comport:** agree with
2. **menaced:** threatened
3. **unexampled felicity:** the greatest happiness

No Future Colonies

Monroe declares that European countries may not start any new colonies in the Americas.

1. Why might it threaten the United States to have new European colonies nearby?

Neutrality Toward Europe

Monroe says that the United States will not take sides in European wars.

2. Why might the United States want to remain neutral toward conflicts in Europe?

che
event
ment
event
the 1
the ev
rules
In

A Different System

Monroe says that the United States will defend its republican form of government and would be threatened if Europeans set up monarchies in the Americas.

3. Why would U.S. citizens want their government to be a republic and not an absolute monarchy?

No Interference

Monroe warns that if Europeans invade the newly independent republics in Latin America, this would be considered hostile to the United States as well.

4. What would the United States have to fear if these republics were overthrown?

We owe it, therefore, to **candor**[4] and to the **amicable**[5] relations existing between the United States and those powers to declare that we should consider any attempt on their part to extend their system to any portion of this hemisphere as dangerous to our peace and safety.

With the existing colonies or dependencies of any European power we have not interfered and shall not interfere. But with the Governments who have declared their independence and maintained it, and whose independence we have, on great consideration and on just principles, acknowledged, we could not view any **interposition**[6] for the purpose of oppressing them, or controlling in any other manner their destiny, by any European power in any other light than as the manifestation of an unfriendly disposition toward the United States. In the war between those new Governments and Spain we declared our neutrality at the time of their recognition, and to this we have adhered, and shall continue to adhere, provided no change shall occur which, in the judgment of the competent authorities of this Government, shall make a corresponding change on the part of the United States indispensable to their security.

The late events in Spain and Portugal show that Europe is still unsettled. Of this important fact no stronger proof can be adduced than that the allied powers should have thought it proper, on any principle satisfactory to themselves, to have interposed by force in the internal concerns of Spain. To what extent such interposition may be carried, on the same principle, is a question in which all independent powers whose governments differ from theirs are interested, even those most remote, and surely none more so than the United States.

—James Monroe

----

4. **candor:** honesty and openness
5. **amicable:** friendly
6. **interposition:** interference

DOCUMENT-BASED QUESTIONS

Short Answer

1. How would staying neutral in European wars protect the United States?

2. How might the U.S. system of government be threatened if Europeans regained control of former colonies in the Americas?

Extended Answer

3. What does the Monroe Doctrine show about how the United States saw itself and wanted to be seen by other nations?

Chapter Summary

1 **Key Idea**
New industries and inventions changed the way people lived and worked in the early 1800s.

2 **Key Idea**
The invention of the cotton gin and the demand for cotton caused slavery to spread in the South.

3 **Key Idea**
While patriotic pride increased national unity, tensions grew between the North and the South.

For detailed Review and Study Notes go to **Interactive Review** @ ClassZone.com

Name Game

Use the list of terms and names to identify each sentence online or on your own paper.

1. I led a rebellion against slavery in Virginia in 1831. Nat Turner

2. I built a water-powered textile mill. _____

3. This connected New York City with Buffalo, New York, by water. _____

4. This policy opposed European interference in the Western Hemisphere. _____

5. The invention of this led to the expansion of slavery. _____

6. This was enacted in 1820 to keep a balance of power between slave states and free states. _____

7. I promoted the American System. _____

8. This is a feeling of pride, loyalty, and protectiveness toward one's country. _____

9. The telegraph is my invention. _____

10. I built America's first successful steam-powered locomotive. _____

A. Missouri Compromise
B. Erie Canal
C. Peter Cooper
D. Nat Turner
E. sectionalism
F. Monroe Doctrine
G. Henry Clay
H. nationalism
I. steamboat
J. Samuel F. B. Morse
K. Eli Whitney
L. Samuel Slater
M. cotton gin

Activities

CROSSWORD PUZZLE

Complete the online crossword puzzle to show what you know about the Industrial Revolution.

DOWN
1. The _____ made cleaning cotton faster

FLIPCARD

Use the online flipcards to quiz yourself on the terms and names introduced in this chapter.

Method of production that brought workers and machines together in one building.

ANSWER
factory system

VOCABULARY

Explain the significance of each of the following.

1. Samuel Slater
2. Industrial Revolution
3. Missouri Compromise
4. spirituals
5. cotton gin
6. Nat Turner
7. nationalism
8. sectionalism

Explain how the terms and names in each group are related.

9. Samuel F. B. Morse, Eli Whitney, interchangeable part
10. Monroe Doctrine, James Monroe, nationalism
11. mechanical reaper, threshing machine, cotton gin
12. Robert Fulton, Peter Cooper, Erie Canal
13. Henry Clay, protective tariff, American System
14. factory system, Industrial Revolution, Lowell mills

Robert Fulton

KEY IDEAS

1 Early Industry and Inventions (pages 364–369)

15. How did the War of 1812 cause economic changes in the United States?
16. How did interchangeable parts transform the manufacturing process?

2 Plantations and Slavery Spread (pages 372–377)

17. How did the rise in cotton production affect slavery?
18. What was family life like for enslaved people?

3 Nationalism and Sectionalism (pages 378–384)

19. How did the Erie Canal help the nation to grow?
20. How did the Missouri Compromise attempt to resolve a conflict between the North and the South?

CRITICAL THINKING

21. **Summarize** How did the Industrial Revolution change the way Americans worked?

22. **Causes and Effects** In a chart like the one shown, note new inventions discussed in the chapter and their effects on the United States. Then explain which inventions helped to link the nation, and how.

Invention	Effects
threshing machine	

23. **Form and Support Opinions** In your opinion, were free African Americans in the South truly free? Explain.

24. **Make Generalizations** What role did religion play in the system of slavery?

25. **Analyze Point of View** Why was it so important to Southerners to admit Missouri as a slave state?

26. **Connect Geography and History** How did geography affect the way each region developed?

27. **Analyze Primary Sources** This political cartoon shows European nations observing a naval blockade. Explain what the blockade represents as well as what nation caused it to exist, and why.

MULTIPLE CHOICE

Use the quotation and your knowledge of U.S. history to answer question 1.

PRIMARY SOURCE

❝ [The Missouri] question, like a fire bell in the night, awakened and filled me with terror. . . . A geographical line . . . once conceived and held up to the angry passions of men, will never be [erased]; and every new irritation will mark it deeper and deeper. ❞

—Thomas Jefferson, April 22, 1820

1. What did Jefferson fear the growth of?
   A. industry
   B. national unity
   C. sectional tensions
   D. European colonies

Read each question and choose the best answer.

2. Which invention had the greatest impact on the spread of slavery?
   A. cotton gin
   B. locomotive
   C. steamboat
   D. steel plow

3. Which was a result of the Missouri Compromise?
   A. Congress established a protective tariff.
   B. The Mason-Dixon Line divided slave states and free states.
   C. Slavery was banned from the Louisiana Territory.
   D. Maine was admitted to the Union as a free state.

4. What was the power source for the first textile mills in America?
   A. slave labor
   B. water
   C. coal
   D. mules and oxen

YOU BE THE HISTORIAN

28. **Evaluate** How did the Industrial Revolution affect the balance of power among American regions?

29. **Connect** *to* **Today** The steamboat and the telegraph were two of the most significant inventions of the early 1800s. What recent inventions have had a similar impact on life today?

30. **Make Inferences** What effect do you think armed rebellions by enslaved people, such as the uprising led by Nat Turner, had on the institution of American slavery?

31. **Form and Support Opinions** Consider what might have happened if the Missouri Compromise had not been passed, and explain whether you think the plan was a wise decision.

32. **Analyze Point of View** Does Marshall's opinion in *McCulloch* v. *Maryland* reflect a strict or a loose interpretation of the Constitution? Explain.

Answer the
ESSENTIAL QUESTION
What forces and events affected national unity and growth?

Written Response Write a two- to three-paragraph response to the Essential Question. Be sure to consider the key ideas of each section as well as economic changes in America during the early 1800s. Use the Response Rubric below to guide your thinking and writing.

Response Rubric
A strong response will

• describe the impact of the Industrial Revolution
• explain how new inventions affected the economy in different regions
• analyze the spread of slavery in South
• discuss the impact of nationalism and sectionalism

A Changing Nation

1824–1860

Why It Matters Now

Between 1810 and 1860, the nation had to face difficult questions about expansion, immigration, slavery, and the rights of minorities. America is still wrestling with the imperfect solutions of those crucial years in its early history.

Difficulty is the excuse history never accepts.
—Edward R. Murrow

CHAPTER 12

The Age of Jackson

1824–1840

1. Jacksonian Democracy and States' Rights
2. Jackson's Policy Toward Native Americans
3. Prosperity and Panic

 ESSENTIAL QUESTION

What impact did Andrew Jackson's presidency have on the nation?

CONNECT Geography & History

How did geography affect the settlement of the United States during this period?

Think about:

1 U.S. population growth

2 reasons why land might be considered valuable

3 the importance of rivers

Jackson's inauguration

1830 Indian Removal Act is passed.

Effect Thousands of Cherokees are forced west on the Trail of Tears.

1824

Sectional interests divide the Democratic-Republican Party in the 1824 election.

Effect John Quincy Adams is elected president.

1828 Andrew Jackson is elected president.

Settled Areas 1800–1830

Click here to explore the Age of Jackson
@ClassZone.com

Claimed by both
U.S. and Britain.

MAINE

MICHIGAN TERRITORY

VT.

N.H.

Albany MASS. Boston

NEW YORK

CONN. R.I.

UNORGANIZED
TERRITORY

PENNSYLVANIA N.J.

New York

Pittsburgh Philadelphia

OHIO MD. DEL.

Cincinnati Washington,
D.C.

ILLINOIS INDIANA

VIRGINIA ATLANTIC
OCEAN

MISSOURI

KENTUCKY

	Settled area, 1800
	Settled area, 1830
	Borders of 1830

NORTH
CAROLINA

TENNESSEE

SOUTH
CAROLINA

ARKANSAS
TERRITORY

Charleston

MISS. ALABAMA GEORGIA

MEXICO

Claimed
by U.S.

FLORIDA
TERR.

LOUISIANA

New Orleans

Gulf of Mexico

0   200   200 miles
0   100   200 kilometers

Mississippi River
Missouri River
Ohio River
Mississippi River

1832 Jackson vetoes charter
of the Bank of the United States.

Jackson is reelected.

1836 Martin
Van Buren is
elected president.

Harrison
campaign
poster

Wᴹ H. HARRISON,
OUR BRAVE DEFENDER.

1840

1834 Whig
Party is formed.

1837 Panic of
1837 occurs.

▼

Effect Many people
lose money and jobs.

William Henry
Harrison is elected
president.

Western settlers
clearing land

Reading for Understanding

▶ Key Ideas

BEFORE, YOU LEARNED

Forces and events in the early 19th century both strengthened and threatened national unity and growth.

NOW YOU WILL LEARN

Andrew Jackson's election to the presidency in 1828 opened a new era of popular democracy.

▶ Vocabulary

TERMS & NAMES

Andrew Jackson U.S. president from 1829–1837

John Quincy Adams 1824 presidential candidate favored by New Englanders

Jacksonian democracy the idea of widening political power to more of the people

spoils system the practice of giving government jobs to political backers

Tariff of Abominations 1828 law that significantly raised tariffs on raw materials and manufactured goods

John C. Calhoun Jackson's vice-president

doctrine of nullification idea that a state had the right to nullify, or reject, a federal law that it considers unconstitutional

BACKGROUND VOCABULARY

secede (SIH•SEED) to withdraw

REVIEW

states' rights the rights of the states to make decisions without interference from the federal government

Visual Vocabulary
John Quincy Adams

▶ Reading Strategy

As you read and respond to the **KEY QUESTIONS,** use a graphic organizer like the one shown to note the main ideas and important details. Create new diagrams as needed.

 See Skillbuilder Handbook, page R4.

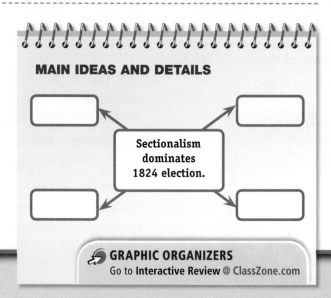

MAIN IDEAS AND DETAILS

Sectionalism dominates 1824 election.

GRAPHIC ORGANIZERS
Go to **Interactive Review** @ ClassZone.com

SECTION 1

Jacksonian Democracy and States' Rights

14.A.3 Describe how responsibilities are shared and limited by the United States and Illinois Constitutions and significant court decisions.
14.D.3 Describe roles and influences of individuals, groups and media in shaping current Illinois and United States public policy (e.g., *general public opinion, special interest groups, formal parties, media*).

One American's Story

Margaret Bayard Smith and her husband were central figures in the political and social life of Washington. Here Smith describes the lively scene at the presidential inauguration of **Andrew Jackson** on March 4, 1829.

PRIMARY SOURCE

❝ When the speech was over, and the President made his parting bow, the barrier that had separated the people from him was broken down and they rushed up the steps all eager to shake hands with him. . . . Country men, farmers, gentlemen, mounted and dismounted, boys, women, and children, black and white. Carriages, wagons, and carts all pursuing him to the President's house. ❞

—Margaret Bayard Smith, *The First Forty Years of Washington Society*

Margaret Bayard Smith wrote about life in the nation's capital in the first half of the 19th century.

Jackson's election to the presidency set the stage for an era of greater public involvement in government.

Sectionalism Changes Politics

▼ **KEY QUESTION** What political divisions appeared during the election of 1824?

By the 1820s, politics were increasingly dominated by sectionalism, or loyalty to the interests of a particular region of the country. In the election of 1824, these sectional interests tore apart the Democratic-Republican Party (the party of Thomas Jefferson). Four men competed to replace James Monroe as president. Their supporters were divided along sectional lines:

- New Englanders liked **John Quincy Adams**, Monroe's secretary of state.
- Westerners backed Henry Clay, "the Great Compromiser," and Andrew Jackson, a former military hero from Tennessee.
- Southerners supported Jackson and William Crawford of Georgia.

The Age of Jackson **395**

History Makers

Andrew Jackson   1767–1845

The son of Scots-Irish immigrants, Jackson grew up in the Carolina backcountry. Jackson's father died shortly before his birth, and his mother and two brothers died during the Revolutionary War. After the war, Jackson moved to Tennessee, built a successful law practice, and bought and sold land. After the War of 1812 broke out, he was appointed as a general in the army. His decisive win against the British at the Battle of New Orleans in 1815 brought him national recognition. He earned the nickname "Old Hickory" after soldiers claimed that he was "tough as hickory." Jackson's humble background, and his reputation as a war hero, helped make him president. Many saw his rise above hardship as an American success story.

CRITICAL THINKING

Connect *to* **Today**   Do you think Andrew Jackson would be a popular presidential candidate today? Record evidence to support your opinion as you read through this chapter.

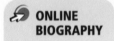 **ONLINE BIOGRAPHY**   For more on Andrew Jackson, go to the **Research & Writing Center** @ ClassZone.com

---

Adams Defeats Jackson in 1824   Jackson won the most popular votes in the election. But no candidate received a majority of electoral votes. According to the Constitution, the House of Representatives must choose the president when this happens.

Clay had come in fourth and threw his support to Adams, who then won. Because Adams later named Clay as his secretary of state, Jackson's supporters claimed that Adams gained the presidency by making a deal with Clay. Charges of a "corrupt bargain" followed Adams throughout his term.

Adams had many plans for his presidency. He wanted to build roads and canals, aid education and science, and regulate the use of natural resources. But Congress, led by Jackson supporters, defeated his proposals.

Jackson felt that the 1824 election had been stolen from him and that the will of the people had been ignored. He immediately set to work on gaining the presidency in 1828.

Over the next four years, the division in the Democratic-Republican Party between the supporters of Jackson and of Adams grew wider. Jackson claimed to represent the "common man." He said Adams represented a group of privileged, wealthy Easterners. This division eventually created two parties. The Democrats came from among the Jackson supporters, while the National Republicans grew out of the Adams camp.

▲ **SUMMARIZE**   Describe the political divisions that appeared before and after the 1824 election.

Jackson Redefines "Democracy"

▼ **KEY QUESTION**   How did American democracy change during Jackson's presidency?

Although the United States had been founded on democratic principles, only white male landowners could vote in many states. In the face of growing calls for reform, Andrew Jackson helped broaden American democracy by advocating the extension of voting rights to more of the population.

Voting Rights Expand   The election of 1828 again matched Jackson against Adams. It was a bitter campaign—both sides made vicious personal attacks. Even Jackson's wife, Rachel, became a target. During the campaign,

EXERCISING THE VOTE

The 1828 presidential election drew more than three times as many voters to the polls as the election of 1824. However, voting was limited to adult white males. Today, all citizens aged 18 and over are eligible to vote.

Citizens under the age of 18 can also participate in the election process. They can educate themselves about the issues, campaign for candidates they support, and practice casting their votes in mock, or pretend, elections. They can also urge eligible voters to cast their ballots, like the student shown here.

Hold a Mock Election.

1 Choose issues and candidates. You may focus on the national, state, or local level.

2 Campaign for the candidates or issues you support.

3 Set up a mock election in your classroom. Create a polling place, ballots, and other needed materials.

4 Prepare mock media reports on the election's outcome.

📖 See Citizenship Handbook, page 303.

Jackson crusaded against control of the government by the wealthy. He promised to look out for the interests of the common people. He also promoted the concept of majority rule. The idea of widening political power to more of the people and ensuring majority rule became known as **Jacksonian democracy**.

Actually, the practice of spreading political power had begun before Jackson ran for office. In the early 1800s, many states reduced restrictions on who could vote. This increased the number of voters. Despite the extension of voting rights, however, large segments of the population were still excluded. Women, the enslaved, and free African Americans still could not vote in most places.

Jackson Wins in 1828 The expansion of voting rights helped Jackson achieve an overwhelming win in the 1828 presidential election. Jackson's triumph was hailed as a victory for the common people. Large numbers of Western farmers as well as workers in the nation's cities supported him. Their vote put an end to the idea that government should be controlled by an educated elite.

Jackson's success in the election came at a high price. Shortly after he won, his wife died of a heart attack. Jackson believed that campaign attacks on her reputation had caused her death. She was a religious person who preferred a more private life. In fact, she had said that she "would rather be a doorkeeper

Jackson's presidency marked a dramatic shift in American politics. Although Jackson's Democrats had grown out of Jefferson's Democratic-Republican Party, ideas of democracy had changed.

JEFFERSONIAN DEMOCRACY	JACKSONIAN DEMOCRACY
Government by an educated few	More public involvement in government
Voting restricted to property owners	Voting expanded to all white males
Limited government	Limited government with a stronger executive branch

CRITICAL THINKING

1. **Draw Conclusions** Which president do you think exercised more power? Why?

2. **Compare and Contrast** What ideas did Jeffersonians and Jacksonians share in common?

in the house of God than . . . live in that palace at Washington."

The tragedy of his wife's death overshadowed Jackson's inauguration. But the capital was full of joy and excitement. Thousands of people attended the ceremony.

A throng followed Jackson to the White House. At the reception, people broke china and glasses as they grabbed for the food and drinks. The rowdiness finally drove Jackson to flee the White House. As Supreme Court Justice Joseph Story observed, "The reign of King Mob seemed triumphant."

A New Political Era Begins Jackson's inauguration began a new political era. In his campaign, he had promised to reform government. He started by replacing many government officials with his supporters. This practice of giving government jobs to political backers became known as the **spoils system**. The name comes from the statement "to the victor belong the spoils [possessions] of the enemy." Jackson defended the principle of "rotation in office," noting that it broke up one group's hold on government.

🔺 **CAUSE AND EFFECT** Explain how Jackson helped change American democracy.

Rising Sectional Differences

🔻 **KEY QUESTION** How did economic issues increase sectional tensions?

At the time of Jackson's inauguration, the country was being pulled apart by conflicts among its three main sections. Legislators from the Northeast, the South, and the West disputed three major economic issues:

- the sale of public lands in the West
- federal spending on internal improvements, such as roads and canals
- rising tariffs

Regional Interests Westerners wanted the federal government to sell public lands at low prices. They hoped to encourage settlement and give the section more political power. Northeasterners feared that cheap Western land might attract workers who were needed in Northeastern factories.

Better transportation routes would help bring food and raw materials to the Northeast and manufactured goods to Western markets. Southerners opposed federal spending on such projects because they were financed through tariffs.

Southerners Against Tariffs Tariffs made imported goods more expensive than American-made goods, which helped protect Northeastern factories from foreign competition. But Southern planters depended on trading cotton in exchange for foreign manufactured goods. Rising tariffs hurt the South's economy.

🔺 **MAIN IDEAS AND DETAILS** In what ways did economic issues increase sectional tensions?

Federal Government vs. the States

🔻 **KEY QUESTION** What issues were at stake in the debate over states' rights?

The issue of tariffs fueled the fires of a national debate that had been raging ever since the nation was formed. That debate was over the balance of power between federal and state governments. Some supported a strong federal government. Others defended **states' rights**, or the rights of the states to make decisions without interference from the federal government.

COMPARING → *Sectional Interests*

WESTERNERS
- Wanted Western lands sold at low prices
- Supported federal spending on internal improvements

NORTHEASTERNERS
- Wanted Western lands sold at higher prices
- Supported federal spending on internal improvements
- Supported high tariffs

SOUTHERNERS
- Opposed federal spending on internal improvements
- Opposed rising tariffs

CRITICAL THINKING **Connect** *to* **Today** The United States has free trade agreements with many foreign countries. In what ways can free trade both help and hurt American businesses?

The Nullification Crisis In 1828 Congress passed a bill that significantly raised tariffs on raw materials and manufactured goods. Southerners hated the tariff and called it the **Tariff of Abominations** (an abomination is a hateful thing). Southerners felt that the economic interests of the Northeast were determining national policy.

The Tariff of Abominations hit South Carolina especially hard because the state's economy was in a slump. Some leaders in the state even spoke of leaving the Union over the issue. **John C. Calhoun**, Jackson's vice-president, sympathized with the South Carolinians because he was one himself. However, he wanted to find a way to keep South Carolina from leaving the Union. His solution was the **doctrine of nullification**. A state, he said, had the right to nullify, or reject, a federal law that it considered unconstitutional. He believed that Congress had no right to impose a tariff that favored one section of the country over another.

The States' Rights Debate Calhoun's ideas increased controversy over the nature of the federal union. This would remain a major political issue until the Civil War resolved it almost 30 years later.

Senators Daniel Webster of Massachusetts and Robert Y. Hayne of South Carolina debated the doctrine of nullification. Hayne argued that nullification gave the states a lawful way to protest and maintain their freedom. In words that were printed and spread across the country, Webster argued that freedom and the Union go together.

John C. Calhoun led the fight for states' rights.

Daniel Webster spoke powerfully in favor of a strong Union.

PRIMARY SOURCE

❝ When my eyes shall be turned to behold for the last time the sun in heaven, may I not see him shining on the broken and dishonored fragments of a once glorious Union. . . . Liberty and Union, now and forever, one and inseparable! ❞

—Daniel Webster, a speech in the U.S. Senate, January 26, 1830

Jackson States His Position Although Jackson supported states' rights, he did not believe that the states should nullify federal law. But he kept his opinion to himself, until a dinner in honor of Thomas Jefferson's birthday. Jackson had learned that Calhoun planned to use the event to win support for nullification.

After dinner, Jackson was invited to make a toast. He stood up, looked directly at Calhoun, and stated bluntly, "Our Federal Union—it must be preserved." As Calhoun raised his glass, his hand trembled. Called on to make the next toast, Calhoun stood slowly and countered, "The Union— next to our liberty, the most dear; may we all remember that it can only be preserved by respecting the rights of the states and distributing equally the benefits and burdens of the Union." From that day, the two men were political enemies.

Henry Clay earned the nickname the "Great Compromiser" for his efforts to end sectional conflicts.

South Carolina Threatens to Secede Even though Jackson worked to limit the powers of the federal government, he was dedicated to preserving the Union. He asked Congress to reduce the tariffs, and Congress did so in 1832. Unsatisfied, South Carolina nullified the tariff acts of 1828 and 1832 and voted to build its own army. South Carolina's leaders threatened to **secede**, or withdraw from the Union, if the federal government tried to collect tariffs.

Jackson ran for reelection in 1832, this time without Calhoun as his running mate. After he won, he made it clear that he would use force to see that federal laws were obeyed and the Union preserved.

In the Senate, Henry Clay came forward with a compromise tariff in 1833. Congress quickly passed the bill, and the crisis ended. South Carolina remained in the Union.

 SUMMARIZE Identify the issues at stake in the state's rights debate.

Illinois Learning Standards *Review*

ONLINE QUIZ For test practice, go to **Interactive Review** @ ClassZone.com

TERMS & NAMES

1. Explain the importance of
   - Andrew Jackson
   - John Quincy Adams
   - Jacksonian democracy
   - spoils system
   - Tariff of Abominations
   - John C. Calhoun
   - doctrine of nullification

USING YOUR READING NOTES

2. **Main Ideas and Details** Complete the diagram you started at the beginning of this section. Then create a diagram for each other main idea in this section.

Sectionalism dominates 1824 election.

KEY IDEAS

3. What were the effects of the 1824 election?
4. What factors helped Jackson win the 1828 election?

CRITICAL THINKING

5. **Compare and Contrast** Why did Northeasterners and Southerners disagree over the issue of tariffs?

6. **Problems and Solutions** How was the nullification crisis resolved?

7. **WHAT IF?** What might have happened if states were allowed to nullify federal law?

8. **Connect** *to* **Today** Is the spoils system prevalent in government today?

9. **Math** Research the popular vote totals and percentages of the 1824 and 1828 elections. Then create comparison charts or graphs to display your findings.

▶ Key Ideas

BEFORE, YOU LEARNED

Andrew Jackson's election to the presidency in 1828 opened a new era of popular democracy.

NOW YOU WILL LEARN

During Jackson's presidency, Native Americans were forced to move west of the Mississippi River.

▶ Vocabulary

TERMS & NAMES

Sequoya (sih•KWOY•uh) a brilliant Cherokee who invented a writing system for the Cherokee language

Indian Removal Act 1830 law that called for the government to negotiate treaties requiring Native Americans to relocate west

Indian Territory an area to which Native Americans were moved covering what is now Oklahoma and parts of Kansas and Nebraska

Trail of Tears forced removal of the Cherokee from their homeland to Indian Territory

Osceola (AHS•ee•OH•luh) leader during the Second Seminole War

BACKGROUND VOCABULARY

assimilate to absorb into a culture

REVIEW

literacy the ability to read and write

Visual Vocabulary
Trail of Tears

▶ Reading Strategy

As you read and respond to the **KEY QUESTIONS,** use a graphic organizer like the one shown to list causes and effects of the forced removal of Native Americans from their homeland.

 See Skillbuilder Handbook, page R7.

CAUSES AND EFFECTS

CAUSES   EFFECTS

Forced removal of Native Americans

GRAPHIC ORGANIZERS
Go to **Interactive Review** @ ClassZone.com

Jackson's Policy Toward Native Americans

 14.C.3 Compare historical issues involving rights, roles and status of individuals in relation to municipalities, states and the nation.

One American's Story

In 1821, a brilliant Cherokee named **Sequoya** invented a writing system for the Cherokee language. Using this simple system, the Cherokees soon learned to read and write. A traveler in 1828 marveled at how many Cherokees had learned to read and write without schools or even paper and pens.

PRIMARY SOURCE

❝ I frequently saw as I rode from place to place, Cherokee letters painted or cut on the trees by the roadside, on fences, houses, and often pieces of bark or board, lying about the houses. ❞

—Anonymous traveler, quoted in the *Advocate*

Sequoya invented a writing system of 86 characters for the Cherokee language.

Sequoya hoped that by gaining **literacy**—the ability to read and write—his people could share the power of whites and keep their independence. But even Sequoya's invention could not save the Cherokees from the upheaval to come.

Native Americans Forced West

▼ **KEY QUESTION** Why did Jackson want native people moved to the West?

By the early 1800s, there were still many Native Americans living east of the Mississippi, despite the fact that white settlers had been pushing them westward for two hundred years. These remaining tribes were viewed by many whites as an obstacle to progress. They debated what to do with the native population.

Tribes of the Southeast Some whites hoped that Native Americans could **assimilate**, or be absorbed into white culture. Others wanted Native Americans to move. They believed this was the only way to avoid conflict over land. Also, many whites felt that Native Americans were "uncivilized" and did not want to live near them.

Traditional Creek belt

By the 1820s, about 100,000 Native Americans remained east of the Mississippi River. Most lived in the Southeast. The major tribes were the Cherokee, Chickasaw, Choctaw, Creek, and Seminole. Whites called them the Five Civilized Tribes because they had adopted many aspects of white culture. They held large areas of land in Georgia, the Carolinas, Alabama, Mississippi, and Tennessee.

More than any other Southeastern tribe, the Cherokee had adopted white customs, including their way of dressing. Cherokees owned prosperous farms and cattle ranches. From Sequoya, they acquired a written language, and they published their own newspaper, the *Cherokee Phoenix*. Some of their children attended missionary schools. In 1827, the Cherokees drew up a constitution based on the U.S. Constitution and founded the Cherokee Nation.

Jackson's Removal Policy Andrew Jackson had long supported a policy of moving Native Americans west of the Mississippi. He first dealt with moving the Southeastern tribes after the War of 1812. The federal government had ordered Jackson, then acting as Indian treaty commissioner, to make treaties with the Native Americans of the region.

Jackson believed that the government had the right to regulate where Native Americans could live. He viewed them as conquered subjects who lived within the borders of the United States. He thought Native Americans had two choices. They could either assimilate and become U.S. citizens, or they could move into western territories. They could not, however, have their own government within the nation's borders.

In 1828, gold was discovered on Cherokee land in Georgia. Now, not only settlers but also miners wanted to move the Cherokee. Many whites began to move onto Cherokee land. Georgia and other Southern states passed laws that gave them the right to take over Native American lands. When the Cherokee and other tribes protested, Jackson supported the states.

The Indian Removal Act Jackson asked Congress to pass a law that would require Native Americans to either move west or submit to state laws. Many Americans objected to Jackson's proposal. Massachusetts congressman Edward Everett warned against forcing Native Americans to a distant land, saying that the "inevitable suffering" would be "incalculable." Religious groups such as the Quakers also opposed moving Native Americans against their will. After heated debate, Congress passed the **Indian Removal Act** of 1830. The act called for the government to negotiate treaties that would require Native Americans to relocate west of the Mississippi.

▲ **CLARIFY** Explain why Jackson wanted Native Americans moved to the West.

The Trail of Tears

▼ **KEY QUESTION**   What were the effects of the Indian Removal Act?

Jackson immediately set out to enforce the law. He claimed his policy was "just and liberal" and would allow Native Americans to keep their way of life. Instead, his policy caused much hardship and forever changed relations between whites and Native Americans.

The Forced March   As whites invaded their homelands, many Native Americans saw no choice but to sign treaties. Under the treaties, Native Americans would exchange their current lands for lands in an area that covered what is now Oklahoma and parts of Kansas and Nebraska. This area came to be called **Indian Territory**.

Beginning in 1831, the Choctaw and other Southeast tribes were moved west. The Cherokees, however, appealed to the U.S. Supreme Court to protect their land from being seized by Georgia. In 1832, the Court, led by Chief Justice John Marshall, ruled that only the federal government, not the states, could make laws governing the Cherokees. This ruling meant that the Georgia laws did not apply to the Cherokee Nation. However, both Georgia and President Jackson ignored the Supreme Court. Jackson said, "John Marshall has made his . . . . let him enforce it."

Connecting History

Westward Expansion
By 1890, the western half of Indian Territory had opened up to white settlement as Oklahoma Territory. Native Americans tried to organize their remaining lands into the state of Sequoya. The federal government rejected this idea, and in 1907 the two territories formed the state of Oklahoma.

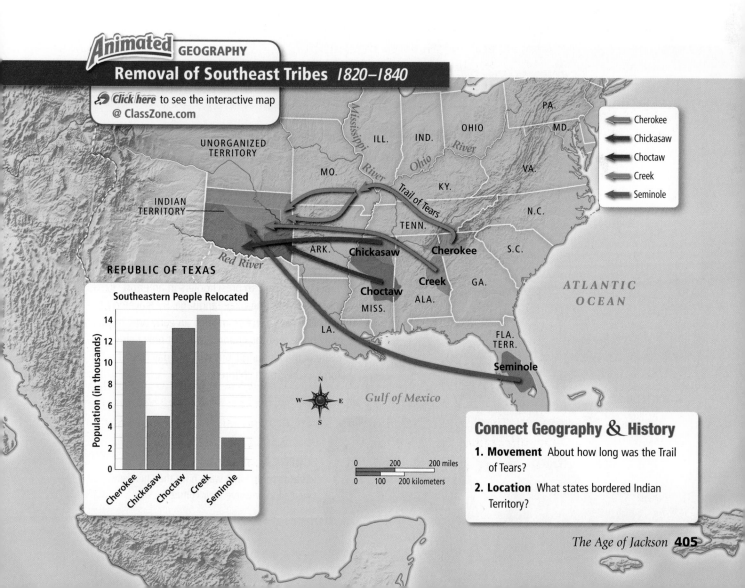

Animated GEOGRAPHY

Removal of Southeast Tribes *1820–1840*

Click here to see the interactive map @ ClassZone.com

Legend:
- Cherokee
- Chickasaw
- Choctaw
- Creek
- Seminole

Southeastern People Relocated

Bar chart — Population (in thousands) vs. tribe:
- Cherokee: 12
- Chickasaw: 5
- Choctaw: 13
- Creek: 14.5
- Seminole: 3

Connect Geography & History

1. **Movement**   About how long was the Trail of Tears?

2. **Location**   What states bordered Indian Territory?

The Age of Jackson   **405**

A small group of Cherokees gave up and signed a treaty. But most Cherokees, led by John Ross, opposed the treaty. Jackson refused to negotiate with these Cherokees.

In 1838, federal troops commanded by General Winfield Scott forced about 16,000 Cherokees into camps. Soldiers took people from their homes with nothing but the clothes on their backs. Over the fall and winter these Cherokees were forced to make the long journey west in the cold, rain, and snow. Many grew weak and ill. A quarter of the Cherokees died. The dead included John Ross's wife. One soldier never forgot what he witnessed.

PRIMARY SOURCE

❝ Murder is murder and somebody must answer. . . . Somebody must explain the four-thousand silent graves that mark the trail of the Cherokees to their exile. I wish I could forget it all, but the picture of six-hundred and forty-five wagons lumbering over the frozen ground with their Cargo of suffering humanity still lingers in my memory. **❞**

—John G. Burnett, quoted in *The Native Americans*,
edited by Betty and Ian Ballantine

This harsh journey of the Cherokee from their homeland to Indian Territory became known as the **Trail of Tears**.

CONNECT *To Today*

THE CHEROKEE NATION OF OKLAHOMA

As soon as the Cherokees arrived in Indian Territory in the 1830s, they set out to rebuild. They established schools, churches, and businesses. A new constitution was adopted and newspapers and periodicals began circulating.

Today the Cherokee Nation is a leader in education, business, and economic development in Oklahoma. The Cherokee Nation and its agencies employ over 3,000 people. Cherokee history and language continue to be taught in Cherokee schools. Recently, the Cherokee Nation began offering language immersion classes to preschoolers in an effort to preserve the Cherokee language. By teaching the classes in Cherokee at such an early age, many hope that the children will not only learn to speak the language, but will one day pass it along to their own children.

CRITICAL THINKING
Evaluate In what ways have the Cherokees worked to preserve their culture?

Native American Resistance Some Native Americans resisted relocation. In 1838, a Cherokee farmer named Tsali and his family struggled to escape as U.S. soldiers were taking them to a camp. Two soldiers were killed before Tsali fled with his family to the Great Smoky Mountains. There they found other Cherokees. According to Cherokee tradition, Tsali was assured by the U.S. Army that if he and his sons were found, the others could remain. They surrendered or were captured, and all except the youngest son were executed. This sacrifice allowed some Cherokees to stay in their homeland.

Osceola led the Seminole in the fight against removal.

In 1835, the Seminoles' refusal to leave Florida led to the Second Seminole War. One of the most important leaders in the war was **Osceola**. Hiding in the Everglades, Osceola and his band used surprise attacks to defeat the U.S. Army in many battles. In 1837, Osceola was tricked into capture when he came to peace talks during a truce. He later died in prison, but the Seminoles continued to fight. Some went deeper into the Everglades, where their descendants live today. Others moved west. The Second Seminole War ended in 1842.

Some Northern tribes also resisted relocation. In 1832, a Sauk chief named Black Hawk led a band of Sauk and Fox from Indian Territory back to their lands in Illinois. In the Black Hawk War, the Illinois militia and the U.S. Army crushed the uprising.

 CAUSES AND EFFECTS Describe the effects of the Indian Removal Act.

 Illinois Learning Standards *Review*

ONLINE QUIZ
For test practice, go to
Interactive Review @ ClassZone.com

TERMS & NAMES

1. Explain the importance of

- Sequoya
- Indian Removal Act
- Indian Territory
- Trail of Tears
- Osceola

USING YOUR READING NOTES

2. Causes and Effects Complete the diagram you started at the beginning of this section.

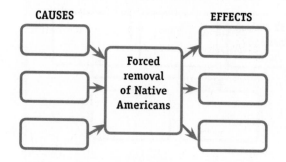

CAUSES   EFFECTS

Forced removal of Native Americans

KEY IDEAS

3. How did Americans react to Jackson's Native American policy?

4. Why were the Cherokees forced to move even though the Supreme Court ruled in their favor?

5. Describe how Native Americans resisted relocation.

CRITICAL THINKING

6. Main Ideas and Details In what ways had the Cherokee adapted to white culture?

7. Connect Geography & History How did the land in Indian Territory differ from the homelands of Southeastern Native Americans?

8. Writing Journal Write a journal entry as a Cherokee on the Trail of Tears. Include details about the traveling conditions and the people around you.

The Age of Jackson **407**

▶ Key Ideas

BEFORE, YOU LEARNED

During Jackson's presidency, Native Americans were forced to move west of the Mississippi River.

NOW YOU WILL LEARN

After Jackson left office, his policies caused the economy to collapse and affected the next election.

▶ Vocabulary

TERMS & NAMES

Martin Van Buren elected president in 1836 after serving as Jackson's vice-president

Panic of 1837 widespread fear about the state of the economy that spread after Van Buren took office

depression a severe economic slump

Whig Party political party formed by Henry Clay, Daniel Webster, and other Jackson opponents

William Henry Harrison Whig presidential candidate in 1840

John Tyler Harrison's running mate in the 1840 presidential election

BACKGROUND VOCABULARY

inflation an increase in prices and a decrease in the value of money

REVIEW

charter a written grant

Visual Vocabulary
William Henry Harrison

▶ Reading Strategy

As you read and respond to the **KEY QUESTIONS,** use a graphic organizer like the one shown to record important events in the order in which they happened.

 See Skillbuilder Handbook, page R5.

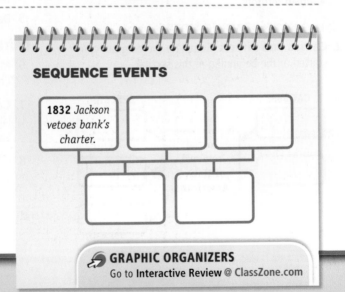

SEQUENCE EVENTS

| 1832 *Jackson vetoes bank's charter.* | | |

GRAPHIC ORGANIZERS
Go to **Interactive Review** @ ClassZone.com

Prosperity and Panic

15.A.3c Describe the relationship between consumer purchases and businesses paying for productive resources.
15.E.3b Explain how laws and government policies (e.g., *property rights, contract enforcement, standard weights/measurements*) establish rules that help a market economy function effectively.

One American's Story

Most of the nation prospered during Jackson's last years in office. However, shortly after his second term ended, the economy took a turn for the worse. Many people wanted the government to step in and help. Jackson's vice-president, **Martin Van Buren**, who succeeded Jackson as president, disagreed.

PRIMARY SOURCE

❝ All communities are apt to look to the Government for too much. . . . especially at periods of sudden embarrassment and distress. But this ought not to be. . . . [The framers of the Constitution] wisely judged that the less Government interferes with private pursuits, the better for the general prosperity. ❞

    —Martin Van Buren, from a letter to Congress dated September 4, 1837

Jackson and the Democrats opposed many forms of federal power.

Martin Van Buren served as president from 1837 to 1840. He ran unsuccessfully for reelection in 1840 and again in 1848.

Jackson Targets the National Bank

🔻 **KEY QUESTION** How did Jackson destroy the national bank?

The Second Bank of the United States was the most powerful bank in the country. Jackson declared war on the bank.

Mr. Biddle's Bank The bank's president, Nicholas Biddle, set policies that controlled the nation's money supply. Since the bank made loans to members of Congress, Biddle could influence these lawmakers. Jackson believed that the bank was corrupt and had too much power.

To operate, the bank needed a **charter**, or a written grant, from the federal government. In 1832, Biddle asked Congress to renew the bank's charter, even though it would not expire until 1836. He thought Jackson would agree to the renewal rather than risk angering his supporters. But Jackson took the risk.

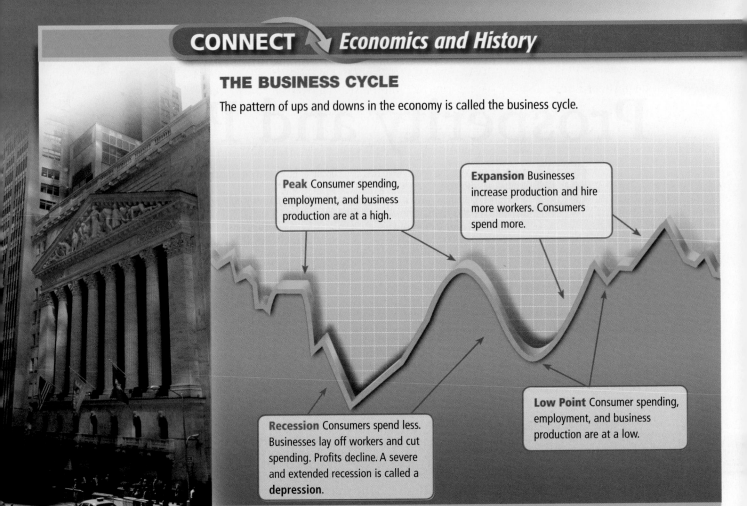

THE BUSINESS CYCLE

The pattern of ups and downs in the economy is called the business cycle.

Peak Consumer spending, employment, and business production are at a high.

Expansion Businesses increase production and hire more workers. Consumers spend more.

Recession Consumers spend less. Businesses lay off workers and cut spending. Profits decline. A severe and extended recession is called a **depression**.

Low Point Consumer spending, employment, and business production are at a low.

CRITICAL THINKING

Draw Conclusions In what ways can the amount people spend affect businesses?

Jackson's War on the Bank When Congress voted to renew the charter, Jackson vetoed the renewal. Although the Supreme Court had ruled that the bank was constitutional, Jackson argued that it was not. He said it was a monopoly that favored the few at the expense of the many.

The bank became the main issue in the presidential campaign of 1832. The National Republican candidate, Henry Clay, called Jackson a tyrant. The Democrats portrayed Jackson as a defender of the people. When he won reelection, Jackson took it as a sign of approval for his war on the bank.

Jackson set out to destroy the bank before its charter ended. He had government funds deposited in state banks. Biddle fought back by making it harder for people to borrow money. He hoped the resulting economic troubles would force Jackson to return government deposits to his bank. Instead, the people supported Jackson. Eventually the bank went out of business. Jackson had won the war, but the economy would suffer for it.

Prosperity to Panic Because Jackson's state banks made it easier to borrow money, many people took out loans. The economy boomed. But the banks issued too much paper money, and the rise in the money supply made each dollar worth less. **Inflation,** or an increase in prices and a decrease in the value of money, was the outcome. To fight inflation, Jackson issued an order that required people to pay in gold or silver for public lands.

Jackson left office proud of the nation's prosperity. But it was puffed-up prosperity. Like a balloon, it had little substance. Jackson's popularity helped Van Buren win the presidency in 1836. A few months after Van Buren took office, a panic, or widespread fear about the state of the economy, spread throughout the country. It became known as the **Panic of 1837**.

People began exchanging paper money for gold and silver. Banks quickly ran out of gold and silver. A **depression**, or severe economic slump, followed. Almost all factories in the East closed. Jobless workers had no way to buy food or pay rent. People went hungry and became homeless.

▲ **SUMMARIZE** Explain how Jackson destroyed the national bank.

CONNECT to the Essential Question

What impact did Andrew Jackson's presidency have on the nation?

EVENT	IMPACT
Election of 1828	Voting rights expand; Jackson's win hailed as victory for the common people
Tariff of Abominations	Sectional tensions grow over tariffs and states' rights; Jackson opposes nullification; South Carolina nullifies tariffs and threatens to secede
Indian Removal Act of 1830	Thousands of Native Americans are removed from their homeland; Cherokees suffer on the Trail of Tears
Bank War	Jackson drives the Second Bank out of business; inflation rises
Election of 1836	Jackson's popularity and the nation's prosperity help Vice-President Van Buren win the presidency

CRITICAL THINKING

1. **Form and Support Opinions** What do you think was the most important issue in Jackson's presidency? Why?

2. **Evaluate** In what ways did Jackson continue to affect politics after his presidency had ended?

The Birth of the Whigs

🔻 **KEY QUESTION** In what ways did the Whig Party differ from the Democrats?

Van Buren faced a new political party in his campaign for reelection in 1840. The **Whig Party** had been formed by Henry Clay, Daniel Webster, and other Jackson opponents. It was named after a British party that opposed royal power. The Whigs opposed the concentration of power in the chief executive—whom they mockingly called "King Andrew" Jackson.

This 1840 campaign banner shows a log cabin as a symbol of the frontier. The banner describes Harrison as "The Ohio Farmer" to set him apart from his wealthy opponent, Van Buren.

Political Beliefs The Whigs believed that Congress, not the president, represented the will of the people. They also blamed Van Buren—who objected to government "interference"—for not doing more to help the economy during the panic. In 1840 the Whigs chose **William Henry Harrison** of Ohio as a candidate for president and **John Tyler** as his running mate.

The Election of 1840 The Whigs nominated Harrison, the hero of Tippecanoe and the War of 1812, because of his military record and his lack of strong political views. During the campaign, the Whigs emphasized personalities rather than political issues. They portrayed Harrison as a frontiersman against the wealthy Van Buren. Harrison won the election but he died shortly after his inauguration, and John Tyler became president. The election of 1840 showed the importance of the West in American politics.

🔺 **COMPARE AND CONTRAST** Describe how the Whigs differed from the Democrats.

 Illinois Learning Standards *Review*

 ONLINE QUIZ
For test practice, go to
Interactive Review @ ClassZone.com

TERMS & NAMES

1. Explain the significance of
- Martin Van Buren
- Whig Party
- Panic of 1837
- William Henry Harrison
- depression
- John Tyler

USING YOUR READING NOTES

2. Sequence Events Complete the diagram to show the major events of this section.

1832 *Jackson vetoes bank's charter.*

KEY IDEAS

3. Why was Jackson against the Second Bank of the United States?

4. What was Nicholas Biddle's role in the bank war?

CRITICAL THINKING

5. Causes and Effects What role did Jackson's popularity play in the elections of 1836 and 1840?

6. **Connect** *to* **Today** The percentage of eligible voters who participate in elections today is much lower than it was during Jackson's time. In what ways do you think this influences elections today?

7. **Art** **Campaign Poster** Create a campaign poster representing either the Whig Party or the Democrats in the election of 1840.

Chapter Summary

1 **Key Idea**
Andrew Jackson's election to the presidency in 1828 opened a new era of popular democracy.

2 **Key Idea**
During Jackson's presidency, Native Americans were forced to move west of the Mississippi River.

3 **Key Idea**
After Jackson left office, his policies caused the economy to collapse and affected the next election.

For detailed Review and Study Notes go to **Interactive Review** @ ClassZone.com

Name Game

Use the Terms & Names list to identify each sentence online or on your own paper.

1. People accused me of making a deal with Henry Clay in the 1824 presidential election. John Quicy Adams

2. I felt that the 1824 election was stolen from me. _____

3. I was Jackson's vice president in his first term. _____

4. I invented a writing system for the Cherokee language. _____

5. South Carolina threatened to secede because of this. _____

6. I led the Seminoles in the fight against removal. _____

7. Shortly after Jackson left office, I spread fear about the state of the economy. _____

8. Many people blamed me for the depression during my presidency. _____

9. This name comes from a British party that opposed royal power. _____

10. I succeeded William Henry Harrison after he died in office. _____

A. Osceola
B. John Quincy Adams
C. John Tyler
D. Whig Party
E. Sequoya
F. Martin Van Buren
G. Andrew Jackson
H. Tariff of Abominations
I. inflation
J. Panic of 1837
K. spoils system
L. doctrine of nullification
M. John C. Calhoun

Activities

CROSSWORD PUZZLE

Complete the online crossword puzzle to show what you know about the Age of Jackson.

DOWN
10. 1840 Whig presidential candidate

GEOGAME

Use this online map to reinforce your understanding of the settlement of the United States, including the locations of areas settled between 1800 and 1830. Drag and drop each place name in the list at its location on the map. A scorecard helps you keep track of your progress online.

Missouri
Illinois
Indiana
Tennessee
Kentucky

More items online

VOCABULARY

Explain the significance of each of the following:

1. John Quincy Adams
2. Jacksonian democracy
3. spoils system
4. states' rights
5. Sequoya
6. Osceola
7. Whig Party
8. William Henry Harrison

Explain how the terms and names in each group are related.

9. Tariff of Abominations, John C. Calhoun, doctrine of nullification

10. Indian Removal Act, Indian Territory, Trail of Tears

11. Martin Van Buren, Panic of 1837, depression

12. Whig Party, William Henry Harrison, John Tyler

KEY IDEAS

1 Jacksonian Democracy and States' Rights (pages 394–401)

13. What changes in American democracy occurred during Jackson's presidency?

14. What issues divided Northeasterners, Southerners, and Westerners in the 1830s?

2 Jackson's Policy Toward Native Americans (pages 402–407)

15. Why did many whites want Native Americans to move west?

16. How did the Indian Removal Act affect Native Americans?

3 Prosperity and Panic (pages 408–412)

17. How did Jackson try to destroy the bank before its charter ended?

18. Describe the beliefs of the Whigs.

CRITICAL THINKING

19. **Compare and Contrast** Create a chart like the one below to show how Jackson portrayed himself against Adams in the 1828 election.

Jackson	Adams
Westerner	Easterner

20. **Summarize** How did nullification threaten the nation?

21. **Main Ideas and Details** How did the discovery of gold in Georgia affect policies toward Native Americans?

22. **Synthesize** How did Jackson's policy toward Native Americans show his belief in the power of the presidency?

23. **Causes and Effects** What were the effects of Jackson's war on the national bank?

24. **Draw Conclusions** Based on its economic effects, was Jackson's decision to end the national bank a good one?

25. **Evaluate** How does the campaign poster below portray William Henry Harrison?

Harrison campaign poster

ILLINOIS STANDARDS-BASED ASSESSMENT

TEST PRACTICE
- Online Test Practice @ ClassZone.com
- Test-Taking Strategies & Practice at the front of this book

MULTIPLE CHOICE

Use the cartoon and your knowledge of U.S. history to answer question 1.

BORN TO COMMAND.

KING ANDREW THE FIRST.

1. Why do you think Jackson is portrayed as a king?
   A. He came from a royal family.
   B. He supported a strong alliance with the British.
   C. Many people looked up to him.
   D. His opponents thought he had too much power.

Use the quotation and your knowledge of U.S. history to answer question 2.

PRIMARY SOURCE

❝All communities are apt to look to the Government for too much. Even in our own country, where its powers and duties are so strictly limited, we are prone to do so, especially at periods of sudden embarrassment and distress. But this ought not to be. . . . [The framers of the Constitution] wisely judged that the less Government interferes with private pursuits, the better for the general prosperity.❞

—Martin Van Buren, from a letter to Congress dated September 4, 1837

2. Why did Van Buren think the government did not need to help the economy during the depression?
   A. It would subject government leaders to embarrassment and distress.
   B. The economy would be better off without government interference.
   C. Any action taken should be made by Congress.
   D. It was the responsibility of the state governments.

YOU BE THE HISTORIAN

26. **Form and Support Opinions** Do you think Jackson was a champion of the common people? Why or why not?

27. **Recognize Bias and Propaganda** In what ways did Jackson's policy toward Native Americans reflect bias?

28. **Analyze Point of View** Do you think Jackson's use of power during his presidency contradicted his views as a proponent of limited government? Why or why not?

29. **WHAT IF?** What do you think would have happened if Congress had not passed the Indian Removal Act of 1830?

30. **Connect to Today** **Citizenship** In what ways do you think the changes that have occurred since Jackson's time in voter participation and voter eligibility affect government today?

 Answer the
ESSENTIAL QUESTION
What impact did Andrew Jackson's presidency have on the nation?

Written Response Write a two- or three-paragraph response to the Essential Question. Be sure to consider the key ideas of each section as well as the most significant factors that led to changes in the nation. Use the Response Rubric below to guide your thinking and writing.

Response Rubric
A strong response will
- analyze the democratic and political changes
- describe the relocation of Native Americans
- explain the effects of Jackson's policies

Manifest Destiny

1821–1853

ESSENTIAL QUESTION

How did westward expansion transform the nation?

CONNECT ↻ Geography & History

How might the geography and topography of the United States have affected westward expansion?

Think about:

1 the highest peak of the **Rocky Mountains**, in Central Colorado, is 14,431 feet high

2 how people traveled in the early 1800s

3 the distances covered

This mission, or settlement, is a legacy of Spanish rule.

Oxen yoke

1821

Mexico gains independence from Spain. Stephen Austin starts American settlement in Texas.

▼

Effect Settlers move to Texas from the United States.

1824 Jedediah Smith finds South Pass.

▼

Effect Pioneers move west on faster trails.

1836 Texas declares independence from Mexico.

▼

Effect Battle of the Alamo; Republic of Texas formed

U.S. military hat

1849 California gold rush

▼

Effect California enters the Union.

1853

This **trunk** was packed with precious possessions. Settlers seeking gold brought it with them to California.

1846 Oregon Territory acquired; war with Mexico begins.

▼

Effect 1848 Treaty of Guadalupe Hidalgo ends war with Mexico.

Manifest Destiny **417**

▶ Key Ideas

BEFORE, YOU LEARNED
President Jefferson moved the border of the United States westward with the purchase of the Louisiana Territory in 1803.

NOW YOU WILL LEARN
Thousands of adventurers and pioneers followed trails to the West to settle the land and make their fortunes.

▶ Vocabulary

TERMS & NAMES

Jedediah Smith explorer who opened up the West with the discovery of the South Pass

mountain men trappers and explorers who opened up the western pioneer trails

Jim Beckwourth legendary trapper who explored the West and opened up the fur trade

Santa Fe Trail trail that began in Missouri and ended in Santa Fe, New Mexico

Oregon Trail trail that ran westward from Independence, Missouri, to the Oregon Territory

Mormon member of a church founded by Joseph Smith in 1830

Brigham Young Mormon leader who moved his followers to Utah to practice their religion in peace

BACKGROUND VOCABULARY

land speculators (SPEC•yuh•LAY•tors) people who buy land in the hope that it will increase in value

converts people who accept a new religious belief

REVIEW VOCABULARY

rendezvous (RAHN•day•voo) meeting; from a French word meaning "present yourselves"

▶ Reading Strategy

Re-create the cluster diagram shown at right. As you read and respond to the **KEY QUESTIONS**, use the outer ovals to record important details about the trails west.

 See Skillbuilder Handbook, page R4.

MAIN IDEAS AND DETAILS

Jedediah Smith

Trails West

GRAPHIC ORGANIZERS
Go to **Interactive Review** @ ClassZone.com

Trails West

17.C.3c Analyze how human process influence settlement patterns including migration and population growth.
17.D.3a Explain how and why spatial patterns of settlement change over time.

One American's Story

In the 1824–1825 hunting season, trapper **Jedediah Smith** was leading a party through the Rocky Mountains when a grizzly bear attacked. The bear mauled Smith's face and partially tore off one ear. One hunter later remembered.

PRIMARY SOURCE

❝ [Smith] said, '[G]o for water and if you have a needle and thread get it out and sew up my wounds around my head.' . . . I told him I could do nothing for his ear. 'Oh, you must try to stitch it up some way or other,' said he. Then I put in my needle and stitched it through and through. ❞

—Jim Clyman, quoted in *The West*, by Geoffrey C. Ward

(*left*) Jedediah Smith was a true trailblazer, as shown in this desert scene by Frederic Remington. (*above*) Smith was most famous for exploring the Rockies.

Ten days after the attack, Jedediah Smith set out again. This time he found what he was looking for—a pass through the Rocky Mountains. Smith and other daring fur trappers and explorers were known as **mountain men**. They opened up the West by discovering the best trails through the Rockies. These trails were later used by thousands of pioneers who moved west. Smith died while leading a wagon train on the Santa Fe trail in 1831.

The Early Pioneers

▼ **KEY QUESTION** What motivated early pioneers to journey into the rugged west?

Mountain men were among the early pioneers who journeyed into the vast region, largely wilderness, that lay beyond the Rocky Mountains. These men survived by being tough and resourceful.

Mountain Men Open the West Mountain men roamed the Great Plains and the Far West, the regions between the Mississippi River and the Pacific Ocean, to trap animals for their furs. Some, like Jedediah Smith and

History Makers

James Beckwourth   1798–?1867

Not much is known about Jim Beckwourth's family history. At the age of 25, he joined a group of fur traders going west and in time became a daring mountain man. For several years, he lived with a Crow tribe and earned the warrior name, "Bloody Arm." Later, he worked as an army scout and gold prospector. In 1850, Beckwourth discovered a mountain pass across the Sierra Nevadas that enabled thousands of pioneers and gold seekers to reach northern California. This pass is still called Beckwourth Pass. The Western Pacific Railway later used this route as a gateway to the West.

CRITICAL THINKING Sequence Events How did Beckwourth's discovery of a mountain pass change the future of California and the nation?

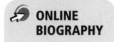 **ONLINE BIOGRAPHY**   For more on on James Beckwourth, go to the **Research & Writing Center @ ClassZone.com**

Jim Beckwourth, became famous for their adventures. Although perceived as rugged loners, the men connected economically to the businessmen who bought their furs.

One businessman, William Henry Ashley, created a trading arrangement called the **rendezvous** system. At a prearranged site, trappers met with traders from the East. There, trappers bought supplies and paid in furs. The rendezvous took place every year from 1825 to 1840, when silk came into fashion and the fur trade died out.

Many animals were killed off at the height of the fur trade. This forced trappers to search for new streams where beaver lived. The mountain men's explorations provided Americans with some of the earliest firsthand knowledge of the Far West. This knowledge, and the trails the mountain men blazed, helped later pioneers moving west.

For example, thousands of pioneers used the wide valley through the Rockies called South Pass. Smith learned of this pass, in present-day Wyoming, from Native Americans. Unlike the high northern passes used by Lewis and Clark, South Pass was low, so it got less snow than the higher passes. Also, because South Pass was wide and less steep, wagon trails could run through it.

The Lure of the West To many the West, with its vast stretches of land, offered a golden chance to make money. The Louisiana Purchase had doubled the size of the United States. Some Americans believed it was their right to take land away from Native Americans who inhabited the territory but did not own it.

People called **land speculators** bought huge areas of land. To speculate means to buy something in the hope that it will increase in value. If land value did go up, speculators divided their holdings into smaller sections. They made great profits by selling those sections to the thousands of settlers who dreamed of owning their own farms. Traders also traveled west. Manufacturers and merchants hoped to earn money by making and selling items to settlers and markets opening up in new communities. Others went to find jobs or to hide from the law.

SUMMARIZE Explain what motivated pioneers to undertake the hazardous journey into the rugged west.

Settling the West

▼ **KEY QUESTION** How did settlers make the difficult journey west?

The success of early pioneers convinced thousands of families and individuals to make the dangerous journey west. They traveled along a series of routes that led to New Mexico, Oregon, and Utah. Once in these places, the new pioneers claimed the land and established settlements.

The Santa Fe Trail In 1821, Mexico gained its independence from Spain. Lands in the Southwest that used to belong to Spain now belonged to Mexico. Spain had kept Americans out of these lands, but Mexico opened its borders to American traders.

One adventurer who took advantage of this new policy was Missouri trader William Becknell. In 1821 he left Missouri for the customary route to Santa Fe, capital of the Mexican province of New Mexico. He made a large profit because the New Mexicans were eager for goods. Back in Missouri, news spread that New Mexico was a place where traders could become rich.

The following year, Becknell left Missouri with a group of traders and pioneered a new route that became the **Santa Fe Trail.** Goods were hauled by covered wagons—rather than by pack animals. Becknell knew he could not haul wagons over the mountain pass he had used on his first trip. Instead, he found a cutoff, a shortcut that avoided steep slopes but it passed through a deadly desert to the south. As his traders crossed the burning sands, they ran out of water and were crazed by thirst. Finally, the traders found a stream

Along with tools, cooking supplies, and a hunting rifle, a tin of gunpowder was an essential item on an overland journey to the West.

Trails West 1850

Connect Geography & History

1. **Location** Which two trails share a portion of the same route?

2. **Analyze** Why do you think some of the trails run along rivers?

and pushed on to reach Santa Fe. Becknell returned home with another huge profit. Soon, hundreds of families were braving the cutoff to make the 800-mile journey from Missouri to Santa Fe, New Mexico.

Oregon Fever Hundreds of settlers began migrating west on the **Oregon Trail**, which ran from Independence, Missouri, to the Oregon Territory. Among the first settlers to cross the continent to Oregon were missionaries, such as Marcus and Narcissa Whitman in 1836. The Whitmans made few **converts** among the Native Americans, but their glowing reports of Oregon began to attract other American settlers to the region. American settlement eventually led to conflict between Britain and the United States because Oregon was jointly occupied by those two countries.

Daily Life   *On the Trail*

A Difficult Journey

For pioneers, the western lands held great hope. Following the trails promised new adventures. However, the journey was hazardous and filled with many challenges along the 2,000-mile route.

> **❝** The dust got deeper and deeper . . . Often it would lie in the road fully six inches deep, so fine that a person wading though it would scarcely leave a track. And when disturbed, such clouds! No words can describe it. **❞**
>
> —Ezra Meeker, pioneer

STRANGE BUT TRUE

A glass of water sometimes cost a lot of money on the trail.

Guess How Much!
$1 $5 $10 $20 $50 $100

Data File

WHO   350,000 pioneers between 1841 and 1867

WHAT   2,000 miles of trail across prairies, rivers, and mountains

WHERE   Missouri to Oregon. (There were many other trails including the Santa Fe trail and the Mormon Trail).

WHEN   early spring to avoid harsh winters

WHY   lure of available land and adventure

CHALLENGES OF THE TRAILS

- Wagon trains traveled from dawn to dusk with only a short break for a noontime meal, for nearly six months.
- Wagons were often overloaded with supplies, forcing family members, including children, to travel by foot.
- Children gathered firewood; when none was available they searched for dry buffalo dung.

ANSWER: $100

Amazing stories spread about Oregon—the sun always shone there and wheat grew as tall as six feet. Such stories lured many people to the 2,000-mile journey to Oregon. In 1843, nearly 1,000 people traveled from Missouri to Oregon. The next year, twice as many came. "The Oregon fever has broken out," observed the *National Intelligencer*, "and is now raging."

The Mormon Trail Most pioneers went west in search of wealth, but one large group migrated for religious reasons. Members of the Church of Jesus Christ of Latter-Day Saints, or **Mormons**, also moved west. The church was founded by Joseph Smith in upstate New York in 1830. The Mormons lived in close communities, worked hard, shared their goods, and prospered.

The Mormons also made enemies. Some saw the Mormon practice of polygamy—allowing a man more than one wife at a time—as immoral. Others objected to their policy of holding property in common.

In 1844, an anti-Mormon mob in Illinois killed Joseph Smith. **Brigham Young**, the next Mormon leader, moved his people out of the United States. His destination was Utah, then part of Mexico, where he hoped his people would be left in peace.

In 1847, about 148 Mormon pioneers followed part of the Oregon Trail to Utah. With about 1,700 who soon joined them, they built a new settlement by the Great Salt Lake called Salt Lake City. Because Utah has little rainfall, the Mormons built dams and canals. These structures caught water in the hills and carried it to the farms in the valleys below. During this same period, American settlers were also changing Texas.

 SUMMARIZE Explain how settlers made the difficult journey west.

Connecting History

Religion in Public Life
Today the Church of Jesus Christ of Latter-Day Saints thrives in Utah, where Mormons make up about 70 percent of the state's population.

Illinois Learning Standards *Review*

ONLINE QUIZ
For test practice, go to
Interactive Review @ ClassZone.com

TERMS & NAMES

1. Explain the importance of
- Jedediah Smith
- Jim Beckwourth
- Mountain Men
- Santa Fe Trail
- Oregon Trail
- Mormon
- Brigham Young

USING YOUR READING NOTES

2. Main Ideas and Details Complete the diagram you began at the beginning of this section.

KEY IDEAS

3. How did the mountain men open up the West for future settlement?

4. What were some of the reasons settlers chose to live in the West?

CRITICAL THINKING

5. Draw Conclusions Of all the hardships faced by people who went west, what do you think was the most challenging?

6. Analyze Causes and Effects How do you think the pioneers' needs affected the local economy of Missouri?

7. Draw Conclusions How did the early Mormon settlers adapt to the desert?

8. **Writing** Letter Research a pioneer from this section and either write a letter from his or her point of view to a friend or write a journal entry and illustrate it with sights from the journey.

HISTORY

Click here to see an animated version of wagon trains
@ ClassZone.com

American Trails West

Most of the trails west took pioneers over rugged mountain ranges and across rivers. The settlers often endured hunger and disease. Some Native American groups were friendly toward the settlers, other groups were hostile to settlers.

Click here Pioneers packed carefully for the challenges of the trail.

Click here Pioneers experienced varied climate conditions—such as the stark, dry, terrain of the desert.

Click here Pioneers had to clear the land to build a home for their families.

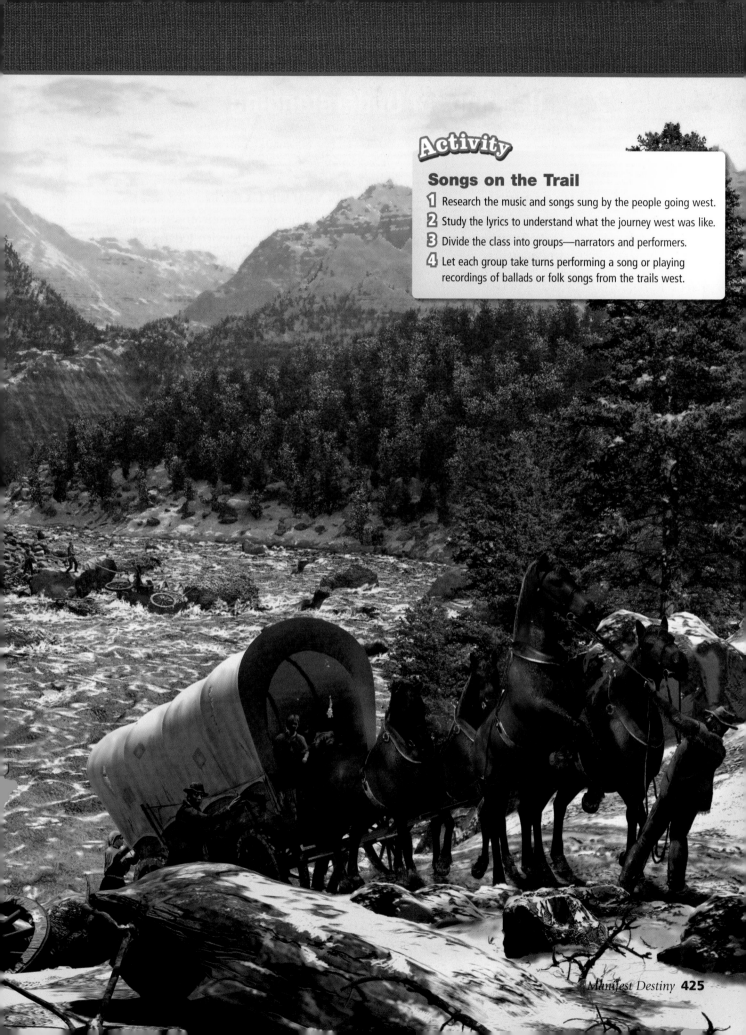

Songs on the Trail

1 Research the music and songs sung by the people going west.

2 Study the lyrics to understand what the journey west was like.

3 Divide the class into groups—narrators and performers.

4 Let each group take turns performing a song or playing recordings of ballads or folk songs from the trails west.

▶ Key Ideas

BEFORE, YOU LEARNED

Thousands of adventurers and pioneers followed trails to the West to make their fortunes and settle the land.

NOW YOU WILL LEARN

Conflicts between American settlers and the government of Mexico led Texas to revolt and win independence from Mexico in 1836.

▶ Vocabulary

TERMS & NAMES

Stephen F. Austin founded a colony for Americans in Spanish Texas

Tejanos (tay•HAH•nohs) people of Mexican heritage who consider Texas their home

Antonio López de Santa Anna Mexican president who led an army against Texas

Sam Houston commander of the Texas army at the Battle of San Jacinto; later elected president of the Republic of Texas

Juan Seguín (wahn seh•GEEN) a *Tejano* hero of the Texas Revolution

Battle of the Alamo battle between Texas and Mexico in 1836

Lone Star Republic nickname of the republic of Texas once free from Mexico

BACKGROUND VOCABULARY

Tejas (tay•HAHS) name the Spanish explorers gave present-day Texas

annex join or merge territory into an existing political unit such as a country or state

Visual Vocabulary
Lone Star Republic flag

▶ Reading Strategy

Re-create the diagram at right. As you read and respond to the **KEY QUESTIONS**, use the diagram to show important events leading to Texan independence.

 See Skillbuilder Handbook, page R5.

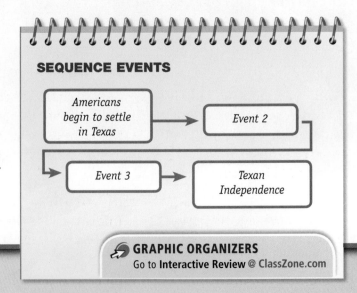

SEQUENCE EVENTS

Americans begin to settle in Texas → Event 2

Event 3 → Texan Independence

GRAPHIC ORGANIZERS
Go to **Interactive Review** @ ClassZone.com

The Texas Revolution

 14.E.3 Compare the basic principles of the United States and its international interests (e.g., territory, environment, trade, use of technology).
16.A.3b Make inferences about historical events and eras using historical maps and other historical sources.

One American's Story

In 1831, Mary Austin Holley visited her cousin Stephen F. Austin in Texas. She decided not to settle there, but published a widely read guide to the territory. Holley's guide was credited with bringing many settlers to Texas territory. Holley wrote approvingly of her cousin's vision.

PRIMARY SOURCE

❝ When, in the progress of years, the state of Texas shall take her place among the powerful empires of the American continent, her citizens will doubtless regard Col. Austin as their patriarch, and children will be taught to hold his name in reverence. . . . Col. Austin began the work, and was the first to open the wilderness. ❞

—Mary Austin Holley, *Texas: Observations Historical, Geographical and Descriptive* 1833

Mary Austin Holley

Stephen F. Austin's father, Moses Austin, had spent the last years of his life chasing a dream. He had hoped to found a colony for Americans in Spanish Texas. A week after his father's death in 1821, Stephen F. Austin was standing on Texas soil. His father's dream would become his destiny. Austin led the surge of American settlement in Texas.

Changes in Spanish Texas

🔻 **KEY QUESTION** How did American settlers cause problems in Texas?

Texas—the land the Spanish explorers called *Tejas* (tay•HAHS)—bordered the Louisiana Territory. *Tejas* had lush forests, plains, and rich soil, but relatively few settlers. When Austin arrived, fewer than 5,000 *Tejanos* (tay•HAH•nohs), people of Spanish heritage who thought of Texas as their home, lived in Texas.

American Settlers in Texas In 1820, to defend the land from hostile Native Americans, the Spanish government offered huge tracts of land to *empresarios*—people who agreed to find settlers for the land. When Spanish settlers did not respond to their offer of land, the Spanish agreed to let American Moses Austin start a colony there, provided the settlers followed Spanish law. Shortly after Stephen F. Austin arrived in Texas in 1821, Mexico successfully gained its independence from Spain. *Tejas* was now a part of the new nation of Mexico. With the change in government, the Spanish land grant given to Austin's father was worthless.

Stephen F. Austin traveled to Mexico City to persuade the new Mexican government to let him start his American colony. The Mexican government would consent only if the new settlers agreed to become Mexican citizens and members of the Roman Catholic Church.

Between 1821 and 1825, Austin attracted about 300 families to his new settlement. These original Texas settler families are known as the "Old Three Hundred." He demanded proof that each family head worked hard and did not use alcohol. The colony attracted more and more settlers. Some were looking for a new life, some were escaping from the law, and others were looking for a chance to grow rich. By 1830, the population had swelled to about 25,000, with Americans outnumbering the *Tejanos* six to one.

Rising Tensions in Texas As more Americans settled in Texas, tensions increased. Americans resented Mexican laws. They were unhappy that offi-

ONLINE
PRIMARY SOURCE

Hear the perspectives at the **Research & Writing Center** @ ClassZone.com

COMPARING *Perspectives*

By the 1820s, non-Mexican settlers were a growing presence in Texas. *Tejanos* were quickly outnumbered. Most of the American settlers refused to learn Spanish and resented the Mexican laws they were expected to honor. Different perspectives of the changes in Texas are quoted below.

Against Settlement

" The Americans . . . have taken possession of practically all the eastern part of Texas, in most cases without the permission of the authorities. They immigrate constantly, finding no one to prevent them, and take possession of the sitio [site] that best suits them without either asking leave or going through any formality other than that of building their homes.

" *attributed to Mexican soldier José María Sánchez, April 1828*

For Settlement

" My object, the sole and only desire of my ambitions since I first saw Texas, was to . . . settle it with an intelligent, honorable, and enterprising people. . . . Texas should be effectually, and fully, Americanized—that is—settled by a population that will harmonize with their neighbors on the East, in language, political principles, common origin, sympathy, and even interest. "

— *Stephen F. Austin, ca.1837*

CRITICAL THINKING **Make Inferences** Why do you think American settlers believed they could Americanize Texas?

cial documents were written in Spanish. Slave owners became angry when Mexico outlawed slavery in 1829. They wanted to maintain slavery so they could grow cotton. Austin persuaded the government to allow slave owners to keep their slaves.

On the other hand, the *Tejanos* found the Americans difficult to live with, too. *Tejanos* thought that the Americans believed they were superior and deserved special privileges. The Americans seemed unwilling to adapt to or to understand Mexican laws.

Responding to warnings of a possible revolution, the Mexican government cracked down on Texas. First, it closed the state to further American immigration. Next, it required Texans to pay taxes for the first time. Finally, to enforce these laws, the government sent more Mexican troops to Texas.

▲ **ANALYZE CAUSES AND EFFECTS** Explain how American settlers caused problems in Texas.

Texans Revolt Against Mexico

▼ **KEY QUESTION** What events led to Texas's independence from Mexico?

The actions of the Mexican government caused angry protests from Americans and many *Tejanos*. Some Texans talked about breaking away from Mexico. But Austin remained loyal to Mexico.

War Begins In 1833, Austin went to Mexico City to present a list of requested reforms to Mexican officials. The most urgent request was that Texas become a self-governing state within Mexico. Mexican president **General Antonio López de Santa Anna** agreed to most of the reforms. But Santa Anna then learned of a letter Austin had written. If his requests weren't met, wrote Austin, he would support breaking away from Mexican rule. This was rebellion! Santa Anna jailed Austin for almost a year. The furious Texans were ready to rebel.

(*left*) Mexican general Antonio López de Santa Anna liked to be known as the "Napoleon of the West."

Santa Anna sent more troops to Texas. In October 1835, Mexican soldiers marched to the town of Gonzales. They had orders to seize a cannon used by the Texans for protection against Native Americans. Texas volunteers had hung a flag over the big gun that said, "Come and Take It."

The Mexican troops failed to capture the cannon. In December, Texans drove Mexican troops out of an old mission in San Antonio called the Alamo that was used as a fortress. Angered by these insults, Santa Anna and 6,000 troops headed for Texas.

The Fight for the Alamo On March 1–2, 1836, Texans met at a settlement called Washington-on-the-Brazos to decide what to do about Santa Anna's troops. They decided to declare Texas a free and independent republic. **Sam Houston** was placed in command of the Texas army.

History Makers

Juan Seguín 1806–1890

Juan Seguín was a *Tejano* who wanted Texas to remain independent and not become part of the United States. He was a hero of the Battle of the Alamo. Seguín was elected to the Texas Senate in 1837 and was mayor of San Antonio twice. However, Seguín was often betrayed and harassed by American newcomers who mistrusted *Tejanos*. Finally he was forced to move to Mexico in 1842. In 1846–1848, Seguín fought against Americans in the War with Mexico.

CRITICAL THINKING Compare In what ways did the goals of Seguín and the Americans in Texas differ?

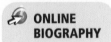 **ONLINE BIOGRAPHY** For more on Juan Seguín, go to the **Research & Writing Center** @ ClassZone.com

Juan Seguín (wahn seh•GEEN) led a band of 25 *Tejanos* in support of revolt. Also among the Texas volunteers were free African Americans, but the Texas army hardly existed. There were two small forces ready to stand up to Santa Anna's army. One was a company of some 300 to 400 men, led by James Fannin, stationed at Goliad, a fort in southeast Texas. The second was a company of about 180 volunteers at the Alamo. Headed by James Bowie and William Travis, this small force also included such famous frontiersmen as Davy Crockett.

On February 23, 1836, Santa Anna's troops surrounded San Antonio. The next day, Mexicans began their siege of the Alamo. Two nights later, Travis scrawled a message to the world: "The enemy has demanded surrender. . . . I have answered . . . with a cannon shot. . . . I shall never surrender or retreat." Juan Seguín, a *Tejano*, spoke Spanish, so he was chosen to carry the declaration through enemy lines. Seguín got the message through to other Texas defenders. But when he returned, he saw the Alamo in flames.

The Alamo's defenders held off the Mexican attack for 12 violent days. On the 13th day, Santa Anna ordered over 1,800 men to storm the fortress. The Texans met the attackers with a hailstorm of cannon and gun fire until the Texans ran out of ammunition. At day's end, all but seven Texans were dead and more than 1,000 Mexicans had fallen. The **Battle of the Alamo** was over.

The survivors were executed. A total of 183 Alamo defenders died. Only a few women and children were spared. Hundreds of Mexicans also perished. The slaughter shocked Texans—and showed them how hard they would have to fight for their freedom from Mexico.

Victory at San Jacinto With Santa Anna on the attack, Texans—both soldiers and settlers—fled eastward. Houston sent a message to the troops at Goliad, ordering them to retreat. They were captured by Mexican forces, who executed more than 300. But even in retreat and defeat, Houston's army doubled. Now it was a fighting force of 800 angry men. It included *Tejanos*, American settlers, and many free and enslaved African Americans.

In late April 1836, Houston surprised Santa Anna near the San Jacinto (san juh•SIN•toh) River. The Texans advanced screaming "Remember the Alamo!" and "Remember Goliad!"

In just 18 minutes, the Texans killed more than half of the Mexican army. Santa Anna had to sign a treaty giving Texas its freedom. With the Battle of San Jacinto, Texas was an independent nation.

Republic of Texas In December 1836, Texans raised the official flag of the independent nation of Texas, nicknamed the **Lone Star Republic**. Sam Houston was elected president.

Many Texans wanted to be part of the United States. In 1836 the Texas government asked Congress to **annex**, or join, Texas to the Union. Some Northerners objected. Some feared that Texas would allow slavery and upset the balance between free and slave states. Some opposed any expansion of slavery. Others feared that annexing Texas would lead to war with Mexico. In response Congress voted against annexation.

 SEQUENCE EVENTS Describe the events that led to Texas's independence from Mexico.

Texas Revolution 1836

Connect Geography & History

1. **Place** What geographic features marked the boundaries of the disputed territory?

2. **Clarify** What does the map show as a major disagreement left unresolved by the war?

Illinois Learning Standards *Review*

 ONLINE QUIZ
For test practice, go to
Interactive Review @ ClassZone.com

TERMS & NAMES

1. Explain the importance of
   - Stephen F. Austin
   - *Tejanos*
   - Sam Houston
   - Antonio López de Santa Anna
   - Juan Seguín
   - Battle of the Alamo
   - Lone Star Republic

USING YOUR READING NOTES

2. **Sequence** Complete the diagram you started at the beginning of this section. Then expand the diagram for each of the other important events in this section.

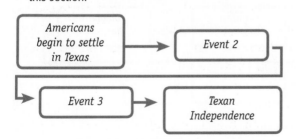

KEY IDEAS

3. How and why did Texas attract American settlers?

4. How did the Mexican government respond to the Texas rebellion?

CRITICAL THINKING

5. **Analyze Motives** Why do you think Stephen F. Austin thought it necessary to demand proof of settlers' high morals for his colony?

6. **Recognize Effects** How did losing the Battle of the Alamo serve as a turning point for Texas independence?

7. **Connect Economics & History** Why was Texas a magnet for land speculators and investors?

8. **Writing** **Speech** Write a one-page persuasive speech from Stephen F. Austin to the Mexican government asking for permission to form a colony in Texas.

Manifest Destiny **431**

▶ Key Ideas

BEFORE, YOU LEARNED

Conflicts between American settlers and the government of Mexico led Texans to revolt and win independence from Mexico in 1836.

NOW YOU WILL LEARN

Victory in a war with Mexico allowed Americans to expand the nation across the continent.

▶ Vocabulary

TERMS & NAMES

James K. Polk eleventh president of the United States who was committed to westward expansion

manifest destiny belief that the U.S. was meant to expand from coast to coast

Zachary Taylor U.S. general who led the battle over the disputed territory of the Rio Grande

Bear Flag Revolt rebellion by Americans in 1846 against Mexican rule of California

Treaty of Guadalupe Hidalgo (gwah•duh•L OOP•ay hih•DAHL•go) treaty that ended the War with Mexico

Mexican cession Mexican territory surrendered to the United States at the end of the war with Mexico

Visual Vocabulary
(*above left*) Original 1846 bear flag was replaced by (*above right*) state flag of California in 1911.

▶ Reading Strategy

Re-create a diagram like the one shown at right. As you read and respond to the **KEY QUESTIONS**, use boxes to show the sequence of events leading to war with Mexico.

 See Skillbuilder Handbook, page R5.

SEQUENCE EVENTS

manifest destiny → *Oregon Territory*

⤷ [ ] →

GRAPHIC ORGANIZERS
Go to **Interactive Review** @ ClassZone.com

The War with Mexico

14.E.3 Compare the basic principles of the United States and its international interests (e.g., *territory, environment, trade, use of technology*).
16.B.3d Describe ways in which the United States developed as a world political power.

One American's Story

Henry Clay sneered, "Who is **James K. Polk**?" Clay had just learned the name of the Democratic candidate who would run against him for president in 1844. However, Polk wasn't a complete unknown. He had served seven terms in Congress.

Polk was committed to national expansion. He vowed to annex Texas and take over Oregon. Americans listened and voted. When the votes were counted, Clay had his answer. James Knox Polk was the eleventh president of the United States. On the question of Texas, Polk said:

PRIMARY SOURCE

❝ To Texas, the reunion is important, because the strong protecting arm of our Government would be extended over her, and the vast resources of her fertile soil and genial climate would be speedily developed. ❞

—James K. Polk, *Inaugural Address*, 1845

James Polk's presidential campaign emphasized expansion of the United States.

Polk's ideas about expanding the country captured the attention of Americans. After his election Polk looked for ways to act on his agenda.

Americans Support Manifest Destiny

▼ **KEY QUESTION** How did belief in manifest destiny lead to friction overseas?

Land in the West held great promise for Americans. Although populated by Native Americans and Mexicans, American settlers viewed those lands as unoccupied. And Americans worried about claims by other nations.

Dispute over Oregon One country with whom the United States faced conflict was Great Britain. The United States and Britain shared control of the northwest Oregon Territory. Many Americans believed that it was their fate, or destiny, to expand the United States across the continent from ocean to ocean. In 1845, a newspaper editor, John O'Sullivan, gave a name to that belief. He called it **manifest destiny.**

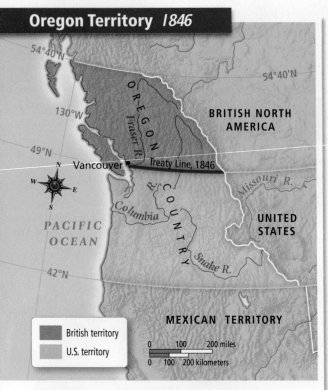

54°40'N

130°W

49°N

Vancouver

PACIFIC
OCEAN

42°N

O
R
E
G
O
N

Fraser R.

Columbia R.

Treaty Line, 1846

C
O
U
N
T
R
Y

Snake R.

54°40'N

BRITISH NORTH
AMERICA

Missouri R.

UNITED
STATES

MEXICAN TERRITORY

British territory

U.S. territory

0   100   200 miles

0   100   200 kilometers

Connect Geography & History

1. **Movement** Why was Oregon an attractive destination for settlers moving west?

2. **Compare** Refer to the map of Trails West on p. 421. How did the Oregon Trail contribute to the course of manifest destiny?

John O'Sullivan used the word *manifest* to mean *clear* or *obvious*. The word *destiny* means events sure to happen. Therefore, manifest destiny suggested that expansion was not only good but bound to happen—even if it meant pushing Mexicans and Native Americans out of the way.

PRIMARY SOURCE

❝ Our manifest destiny [is] to overspread the continent allotted [given] by Providence [God] for the free development of our yearly multiplying millions. ❞

—John O'Sullivan, *the Annals of America, Vol 7*

Since 1818, Oregon had been occupied jointly by the United States and Britain. By the 1840s, thousands of American settlers had moved into the Oregon Territory. In his campaign, Polk promised to take over all of Oregon. "Fifty-four forty or fight!" was one of his slogans. The parallel of 54°40'N latitude was the northern boundary of the shared Oregon Territory. After Polk's election in 1844, manifest destiny became government policy. The term "manifest destiny" was new, but not the idea.

Rather than fight for all of Oregon, however, Polk settled for half. In 1846, the United States and Great Britain agreed to divide Oregon at the 49th parallel. This agreement extended the boundary line already drawn between Canada and the United States. Today this line still serves as the border between much of the United States and Canada.

Troubles with Mexico Polk had good reason for settling with Britain over Oregon. By 1846, he had bigger troubles brewing with Mexico over Texas. In 1845, Congress admitted Texas as a slave state, despite Northern objections to the spread of slavery. However, Mexico still claimed Texas as its own. Mexico angrily viewed this **annexation**, or attachment, as an act of war.

To make matters worse, Texas and Mexico could not agree on the official border between them. Texas claimed the Rio Grande, a river south of San Antonio, as its southern boundary. Mexico insisted on the Nueces (noo•AY•sis) River (See the map on page 435.) as the Texas border. The difference in the distance between the two rivers was more than 100 miles at some points. Many thousands of square miles of territory were at stake.

Mexico said it would fight to defend its claim. Polk sent John Slidell, a Spanish-speaking ambassador, to offer Mexico up to $30 million for Texas, California, and New Mexico. But Slidell's diplomacy failed.

▲ **SEQUENCE EVENTS** Explain how belief in manifest destiny led to friction overseas.

The War with Mexico

▼ **KEY QUESTION** What events led to war with Mexico?

Giving up on diplomacy, Polk's next strategy was to force the issue. He purposefully ordered General **Zachary Taylor** to station 3,500 troops on the north bank of the Rio Grande, which was part of the disputed territory.

Polk Urges War On April 25, 1846, a Mexican unit crossed the Rio Grande and ambushed an American patrol. Polk sent a rousing war message to Congress, saying, "Mexico . . . has invaded our territory and shed American blood upon the American soil." Two days later, Congress declared war. The War with Mexico had begun.

Americans had mixed reactions to the war. In general, Southerners wanted to extend the territory open to slavery, while Northeners feared the expansion of slavery. Many also questioned the justice of men dying for territorial gain. Despite opposition, the United States plunged into war. In May 1846, General Zachary Taylor led troops into Mexico.

Capturing New Mexico and California Not long after the war began, U.S. General Stephen Kearny (KAHR•nee) left Kansas with orders to occupy New Mexico. Once there, Kearny persuaded the Mexican troops that he would withdraw. He took New Mexico without firing a shot. Then Kearny marched on to what is now California, which had fewer than 12,000 Mexican residents. The remainder of the force moved south toward Mexico.

Animated GEOGRAPHY

The War with Mexico 1846–1847

⟲ **Click here** to preview the War with Mexico @ ClassZone.com

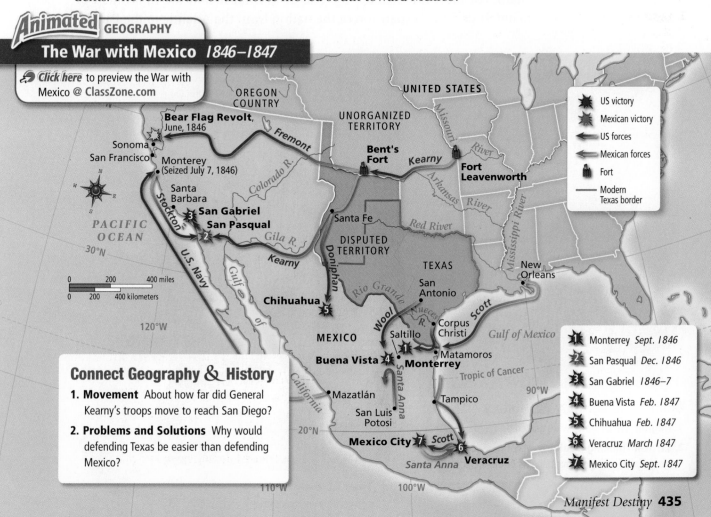

Connect Geography & History

1. **Movement** About how far did General Kearny's troops move to reach San Diego?

2. **Problems and Solutions** Why would defending Texas be easier than defending Mexico?

Legend:
- US victory
- Mexican victory
- US forces
- Mexican forces
- Fort
- Modern Texas border

Battle list:
1. Monterrey *Sept. 1846*
2. San Pasqual *Dec. 1846*
3. San Gabriel *1846–7*
4. Buena Vista *Feb. 1847*
5. Chihuahua *Feb. 1847*
6. Veracruz *March 1847*
7. Mexico City *Sept. 1847*

Connecting History

Not all war declarations have been as contentious as the war against Mexico. Representative Jeanette Rankin of Montana, the first woman in Congress and an avowed pacifist, was the only member of the House to vote against World War II.

Meanwhile, Americans in northern California staged a revolt and raised a crude flag featuring a grizzly bear. The revolt, known as the **Bear Flag Revolt**, was joined by explorer John C. Frémont. The rebels declared independence from Mexico and formed the Republic of California. U.S. troops joined forces with the rebels. Within weeks, American forces controlled all of California.

The Fighting in Mexico The defeat of Mexico proved more difficult. American forces invaded Mexico from two directions. Taylor battled his way south from Texas toward Monterrey in northern Mexico. On February 23, 1847, his 4,800 troops met Santa Anna's 15,000 Mexican soldiers near a ranch called Buena Vista. After two bloody days of fighting, Santa Anna retreated. The war in the north of Mexico was over.

In southern Mexico, Winfield Scott's forces landed at Veracruz on the Gulf of Mexico and made for Mexico City. Outside the capital, the Americans met fierce resistance. But Mexico City fell to Scott in September 1847. America had won the War with Mexico.

▲ **SEQUENCE EVENTS** Explain the events that led to the war with Mexico.

Impact of Victory

▼ **KEY QUESTION** What Mexican territory had the United States gained by 1853?

For Mexico, the war marked an ugly milestone in its relations with the United States. For the United States, the end of the war meant the fulfillment of manifest destiny—expansion of the nation from the Atlantic to the Pacific.

Growth of the United States *1783–1853*

OREGON COUNTRY
From Great Britain,
1846

Ceded to
Great Britain,
1818

Ceded by
Great Britain,
1818

CANADA

Ceded by Britain,
Webster-Ashburton Treaty,
1842

LOUISIANA PURCHASE
Bought from France, 1803

MEXICAN CESSION
From Mexico by Treaty of
Guadalupe Hidalgo, 1848

From Great Britain
by Treaty of Paris,
1783

ORIGINAL 13 COLONIES

GADSDEN
PURCHASE
Bought from
Mexico, 1853

PACIFIC
OCEAN

TEXAS ANNEXATION
Annexed independent republic, 1845

ATLANTIC
OCEAN

MEXICO

FLORIDA
CESSION
From Spain,
1819

1810   1813

Ceded by
Spain, 1818

Dates annexed
by United States

Gulf of Mexico

Modern U.S. boundaries shown

0   200   400 miles
0   200   400 kilometers

40°N
30°N
20°N
90°W
80°W

Connect Geography & History

1. **Region** Which states were gained by the Mexican cession?
2. **Critical Thinking Evaluate** What were some of the geographic and economic benefits of the Mexican cession?

From Sea to Shining Sea In February 1848, the war ended with the **Treaty of Guadalupe Hidalgo** (gwah•duh•LOOP•ay hih•DAHL•go). The loss was a bitter defeat. Many Mexicans felt that the United States had provoked the war in the hope of gaining Mexican territory. In this treaty Mexico

- recognized that Texas was part of the United States
- agreed to the Rio Grande as the border between the two nations
- gave up a vast region known as the **Mexican cession**— including Texas—amounting to almost one-half of present-day Mexico

In return the United States promised to protect the 80,000 Mexicans living in Texas and the Mexican cession. Some Mexicans, however, saw themselves as minorities in a nation with a strange language, culture, and legal system. Others taught new settlers how to develop the land for farming, ranching, and mining. Eventually, a rich new culture resulted from the blend of many cultures.

In 1853, Mexico sold one last strip of land, called the Gadsden Purchase, to the United States for $10 million. The U.S. wanted the land, now part of southern New Mexico and Arizona, for a southern transcontinental railroad. The United States now stretched "from sea to shining sea."

Frederic Remington painted this colorful portrait of a Mexican cowboy, *A Vaquero*, in the late nineteenth century.

 SUMMARIZE Describe the territory the United States gained from Mexico by 1853.

Illinois Learning Standards *Review*

ONLINE QUIZ
For test practice, go to **Interactive Review** @ ClassZone.com

TERMS & NAMES

1. Explain the importance of
   - James K. Polk
   - manifest destiny
   - Zachary Taylor
   - Bear Flag Revolt
   - Treaty of Guadalupe Hidalgo
   - Mexican cession

USING YOUR READING NOTES

2. **Sequence Events** Complete the diagram you started at the beginning of this section.

KEY IDEAS

3. Why did Britain and Mexico oppose American expansion?

4. How did the acquisitions of Oregon and the Mexican cession contribute to manifest destiny?

CRITICAL THINKING

5. **Analyze** Traveling along the Santa Fe Trail, General Kearny and his army sang songs like this one:

   ❝ Old Colonel Kearny, you can bet
   Will keep the boys in motion,
   Till Yankee Land include the sand
   On the Pacific Ocean. ❞

   How does this song support the idea of manifest destiny?

6. **Writing** **Political Cartoon** It is 1853. The Gadsden Purchase has just been completed. Create a political cartoon that comments on America's belief in manifest destiny.

▶ Key Ideas

BEFORE, YOU LEARNED

Victory in a War with Mexico allowed Americans to expand the country across the continent.

NOW YOU WILL LEARN

The discovery of gold in California in 1848 led to a population increase and statehood.

▶ Vocabulary

TERMS & NAMES

forty-niner person who went to California to find gold in 1849

Californios settlers of Spanish or Mexican descent who populated California

Mariano Vallejo a prosperous *Californio* who lost a lot of property after American settlement

James Marshall carpenter who discovered gold in California in 1848

California gold rush migration of thousands of settlers to California in search of gold

BACKGROUND VOCABULARY

migration movement of people from one country or locality to another

Visual Vocabulary
forty-niner

▶ Reading Strategy

Re-create the diagram shown at right. As you read and respond to the **KEY QUESTIONS**, use the chart to note important events and their effects. Add boxes or start a new diagram as needed.

 See Skillbuilder Handbook, page R7.

CAUSES AND EFFECTS

CAUSE

California gold rush

EFFECT

New settlers

EFFECT

> **GRAPHIC ORGANIZERS**
> Go to **Interactive Review** @ ClassZone.com

The California Gold Rush

17.C.3a Explain how human activity is affected by geographic factors.
17.C.3c Analyze how human process influence settlement patterns including migration and population growth.

One American's Story

Luzena Wilson said of the year 1849, "The gold excitement spread like wildfire." That year, **James Marshall** had discovered gold in California. Luzena's husband became a **forty-niner**—someone who went to California to find gold, starting in 1849. Luzena went to California with her husband. She found that women were rare in California. Shortly after she arrived, a miner offered her five dollars for her baked biscuits. Shocked, she just stared at him. He quickly doubled his offer and paid in gold. Finding she could make money by taking care of miners, Luzena opened a hotel. The gold rush boosted California's economy and changed the nation's history.

A Discovery Changes California

▼ **KEY QUESTION** What led to the rapid settlement in California?

Before the forty-niners came, California was populated by as many as 150,000 Native Americans and 6,000 *Californios*—settlers of Spanish or Mexican descent. Many *Californios* lived on huge cattle ranches.

The Rush for Gold On January 24, 1848, just one month before Mexico lost California to the United States, a carpenter named James Marshall made an important discovery. While building a sawmill in northern California, he saw a shiny stone in the nearby American River. He later said, "My eye was caught by a glimpse of something shining. . . . It made my heart thump for I felt certain it was gold." It was indeed. Marshall's discovery led to one of the greatest **migrations**—movements of persons from one country or locality to another—in American history, as thousands from all over the world poured into California to make their fortunes.

In 1849, people from all over California and the United States raced to the American River—starting the **California gold rush.** A gold rush occurs when large numbers of people move to a site where gold has been found.

These prospectors were residents of a mining camp in Auburn Ravine, California, in the mid-1800s.

Miners soon found gold in other streams flowing out of the Sierra Nevada. The military governor of California estimated that the region held enough gold to "pay the cost of the present war with Mexico a hundred times over." He sent this news to Washington with a box of gold dust as proof.

The following year thousands of gold seekers set out to make their fortunes. A forty-niner who wished to reach California from the East had a choice of three routes, all of them dangerous. 1) Sail 18,000 miles around South America and up the Pacific coast—enduring storms, seasickness, and spoiled food. 2) Sail to the narrow Isthmus of Panama, cross overland (and risk catching a deadly tropical disease), and then sail to California. 3) Travel the trails across North America—braving rivers, prairies, mountains, and all the hardships of the trail. Because the venture was so hard, most gold seekers were young men.

Mariano Vallejo (*inset*), a *Californio*, was the proud owner of a large California estate (*top*). **What major migration changed the *Californio* way of life?**

Changes for *Californios* James Marshall's discovery of gold in 1848 did little to improve the lot of the *Californios*. Before the gold rush, many *Californio* families had prospered when the Mexican government took away the land that once belonged to the Spanish missions in California.

One important *Californio* was **Mariano Vallejo**. He was a member of one of the oldest Spanish families in America, and owned 250,000 acres of land. Vallejo's nephew proudly described the heritage of the *Californios* as "the pioneers of the Pacific coast." The gold rush found *Californios* challenged by a new wave of pioneers.

The Gold Seekers About two-thirds of the forty-niners were Americans. Most of these were white men. However, Native Americans, free blacks, and enslaved African Americans also worked the mines.

Thousands of experienced miners came from Sonora in Mexico. Other foreign miners came from Europe, South America, Australia, and China. Most of the Chinese miners were peasant farmers who fled hardships in China. By the end of 1851, one of every ten immigrants was Chinese.

The Chinese would often take over sites that American miners had left because the easy gold was gone. Through steady, hard work, the Chinese made these "played-out" sites yield profits. Some Americans envied the success of the Chinese and made fun of their different customs. As the numbers of Chinese miners grew, American resentment toward them also increased.

The mining camps began as rows of tents along the streams flowing out of the Sierra Nevada. Gradually the tents gave way to rough wooden buildings that housed stores and saloons. Camp gossip told of miners who got rich overnight by finding eight-pound nuggets, but in reality, few miners got rich. Exhaustion, poor food, and disease all damaged the miners' health. Not only was acquiring gold brutally difficult, but the miners had to pay very high prices for basic supplies.

▲ **EVALUATE** Explain the events that led to fast settlement in California.

Final Impact of the Gold Rush

🔻 **KEY QUESTION** What was the final impact of the gold rush on California?

The gold rush peaked in 1852. While it lasted, about 250,000 people flooded into California. This huge migration caused economic growth that changed California permanently.

Opportunities and Turmoil By 1849, California had enough people to apply for statehood. It was admitted as a free state in 1850. Its constitution banned slavery, but it did not grant African Americans the right to vote.

For some people, California's statehood proved to be the opportunity of a lifetime. An enslaved woman, Nancy Gooch, gained her freedom because of the law against slavery. Then she worked to buy the freedom of her children in Missouri. Eventually, the Gooch family became so prosperous that they bought Sutter's sawmill, where James Marshall first found the gold that started California's gold rush.

The population explosion ruined many *Californios*. The newcomers did not respect *Californios* or their legal rights. In many cases, Americans seized their property. Mariano Vallejo lost all but 300 acres of his huge estate. Yet the Spanish heritage plays a prominent role in California culture today.

CONNECT *To Today*

ECONOMIC OPPORTUNITY

The discovery of gold brought tens of thousands of settlers west to find prosperity. Many newcomers chose to open businesses to meet the demands of what became a booming region.

Today, economic opportunity doesn't necessarily require people to move to another state, region, or country. Instead, many companies use the Internet to communicate with employees and customers at home and overseas. This practice is known as offshoring or outsourcing.

A number of large corporations outsource some or most of their work. Consequently, many overseas economies have ballooned since going into the offshore business. Huge western investments in outsourcing are bringing new prosperity to many developing nations. India is one example of successful offshoring. (*right*) Indian office workers work in a time zone 10.5 hours ahead of Eastern Standard Time. This means more time to conduct business.

CRITICAL THINKING

1. **Make Inferences** Why might a company hire workers in a different country and/or a different time zone?

2. **Evaluate** How might outsourced programs affect American education and the American workplace?

Native Americans and Foreigners Thousands of Native Americans died from diseases brought by the newcomers. Settlers killed thousands more. The impact on the environment also affected Native Americans' use of the land. Rivers that had been their waterways and fishing sites were diverted and polluted. Hunting grounds were taken over by settlers. By 1870, California's Native American population had fallen from 150,000 to about 58,000.

Once the easy-to-find gold was gone, American miners began to force Native Americans and miners such as Mexicans and Chinese out of the gold fields to reduce competition. This practice increased after California became a state in 1850.

Foreign Miners Tax One of the first acts of the California state legislature was to pass the Foreign Miners Tax, which imposed a tax of $20 a month on miners from other countries. That was more than most could afford to pay. As the tax collectors arrived in the camps, most foreigners left.

Driven from the mines, the Chinese opened shops, restaurants, and laundries. So many Chinese owned businesses in San Francisco that their neighborhood became known as Chinatown, as it still is today.

CONNECT to the Essential Question

How did westward expansion transform the nation?

EVENTS	EFFECTS
1820–1840 Westward trails move thousands to new territories	Native Americans are displaced
Austin and others colonize Texas	Earlier settlers are pushed aside
Texans revolt against Mexico	Republic of Texas is proclaimed
1841–1848 Texas annexed as a slave state	War with Mexico
Mexican cession	Almost 50% of Mexican territory is acquired by United States
1849–1853 California Gold Rush	California enters Union as a free state
U.S. transcontinental railroad planned	Gadsden Purchase completes expansion of the United States

CRITICAL THINKING Clarify Which event fulfilled the nation's "manifest destiny"?

Economic Effects of Statehood The port city of San Francisco grew to become a center of banking, manufacturing, shipping, and trade. Its population exploded from around 400 in 1845 to 35,000 in 1850. And, in response to increasing demand for food, Sacramento became the center of a rich farming region.

The population explosion also created a huge demand for water. California's complicated water system is a legacy of the inventiveness and skill of the forty-niners. The miners needed lots of water to pan for gold. (See chart at right.)

On a national level, California's application for statehood created turmoil. Before 1850, there were an equal number of free states and slave states. Southerners feared that because the statehood of California made free states outnumber slave states, Northerners might use their majority to abolish slavery. Conflict over this issue would threaten the very survival of the Union.

 CAUSES AND EFFECTS Describe the events that led to California statehood.

CALIFORNIA WATER RIGHTS

The forty-niners cleverly diverted water for their needs—laying the groundwork for the complex system of dams and canals serving California today. There are three basic categories of water rights in California: Riparian, Appropriative, and Public Trust uses.

RIPARIAN RIGHTS
allows a landowner to use the water flowing past his or her property; takes priority over other claims.

APPROPRIATIVE RIGHTS
allows use of water channelled well away from its original source; based on forty-niners' "finders keepers" law

PUBLIC TRUST DOMAIN
protects fish and wildlife; public recreation areas— such as parks, streams and lakes.

 Illinois Learning Standards *Review*

ONLINE QUIZ
For test practice, go to **Interactive Review** @ ClassZone.com

TERMS & NAMES
1. Explain the importance of
- forty-niner • *Californio* • Mariano Vallejo
- James Marshall • California Gold Rush

USING YOUR READING NOTES
2. Causes and Effects Complete the diagram you started at the beginning of this section.

KEY IDEAS
3. Why did the gold rush come to an end?

4. Why was California poised to upset the balance of the United States?

CRITICAL THINKING
5. Summarize What were some of the cultural conflicts caused by the influx of new settlers into California?

6. Evaluate What impact did the gold rush have on the people who lived in California before 1849?

7. Recognize Effects What effect did the gold rush have on the growth of California?

8. Writing Report Use the Internet to research women or foreign immigrants during the California gold rush. Write a brief report explaining how they created opportunities and shaped their new communities.

CALIFORNIA'S GOLD RUSH

Discovery of gold brought thousands of settlers to California from all over the world. What were some of the effects of rapid growth?

FORTY-NINERS

Water vastly eased the prospectors' work. At first, they waded in streams sloshing water around dirt and gravel in metal pans. Soon they were shoveling gravel into a sluice—a series of long boxes with ridges on the bottom. Rushing water carried lightweight materials along with it. Heavy gold sank to the bottom and was trapped between the ridges. Within two years, forty-niners were damming rivers and erecting simple storage reservoirs for the water so vital to their existence.

Teens in History

A YOUNG SETTLER

Elizabeth Keegan arrived in Marysville, California, on September 17, 1852. Two months later, she wrote to her brother and sister still back in St. Louis:

"See what gold can do (it) brings men from all nations here to this distance shore to make their fortune [and] many go home worse than when they came [but] others have wealth countless wealth . . ."

DIVERSITY

Many of the California migrants came to make their fortunes. Most were disappointed, but they stayed to establish thriving communities.

Chinese miner

Activity

Find the hidden words!

Find the ten words scrambled below—all are connected to the gold rush.

```
B Z R V H B N I H O N B
N T H I P U S V I Y E N
S M Q P V P A N I R G Z
X L M I N E R U L W O X
D A U S M O R G A L A C
C X X I F N E G E C N L
E X V I C O I E X U B O
R E L T T E S T I V N S
S A W M I L L M M I X A
C R O O W B B J U G P O
```

Chapter Summary

① Key Idea
Thousands of adventurers and pioneers followed trails to the West to settle the land and make their fortunes.

② Key Idea
Conflicts between American settlers and the government of Mexico led Texas to revolt and win independence from Mexico in 1836.

③ Key Idea
Victory in a war with Mexico allowed Americans to expand the nation across the continent.

④ Key Idea
The discovery of gold in California in 1848 led to a population increase and statehood.

For detailed Review and Study Notes go to **Interactive Review** @ **ClassZone.com**

Name Game

Use the Terms & Names list to complete each sentence online or on your own paper.

1. The Mormons settled in Utah for religious reasons.

2. _____ discovered the South Pass through the Rocky Mountains.

3. A person who went to California in search of gold was called a _____ .

4. The _____ was a route across the Rocky Mountains.

5. The victorious general at the Battle of the Alamo. _____

6. The _____ was a nickname for the republic of Texas.

7. _____ commanded the Texas Army at the battle of San Jacinto.

8. In the 1820s, people of Mexican heritage living in Texas were called _____ .

9. _____ was elected the eleventh president of the United States in 1844.

10. _____ was the belief that the United States was meant to expand from coast to coast.

A. Santa Fe Trail
B. *Tejanos*
C. Santa Anna
D. Jedediah Smith
E. Manifest Destiny
F. James K. Polk
G. Mormons
H. Jim Beckwourth
I. Forty-Niner
J. Sam Houston
L. California Gold Rush
M. Oregon Trail
N. Lone Star Republic
O. Zachary Taylor
P. Bear Flag Revolt

Activities

CROSSWORD PUZZLE

Use the online crossword puzzle to show what you know about western expansion.

ACROSS

1. _____ founded American colony in Spanish Texas.

FLIPCARD

Use the online flipcards to quiz yourself on the terms and names introduced in this chapter.

I was a *Tejano* who fought for Texan independence.

ANSWER
Juan Seguín

VOCABULARY

Explain the significance of each of the following.

1. Mexican cession
2. Sam Houston
3. James K. Polk
4. Brigham Young
5. Mariano Vallejo
6. James Marshall
7. Jedediah Smith
8. Stephen Austin
9. Zachary Taylor
10. Antonio López de Santa Anna

Choose the best answer from each pair.

11. Tensions resulted between these people and American settlers in Texas. (*Tejanos/Californios*)

12. This resulted in massive migration to California. (California Gold Rush/Treaty of Guadalupe Hidalgo)

13. American goal reached after post-war settlements with Mexico. (manifest destiny/Mexican cession)

14. William Becknell helped open this trail to pioneers. (Oregon Trail/Santa Fe Trail)

15. This American rebellion was against Mexican rule in California. (Bear Flag Revolt/Gadsden Purchase)

KEY IDEAS

1 Trails West 1810–1853 (pages 418–423)

16. What were three reasons why people moved west?

17. What were the three main trails that led to the West?

2 The Texas Revolution (pages 426–431)

18. Why were Texans unhappy with Mexican rule?

19. Why were the Battles of the Alamo and San Jacinto important to the Texas revolution?

3 The War with Mexico (pages 432–437)

20. What areas did the United States gain as a result of Americans' belief in manifest destiny?

21. What lands did the United States acquire as a result of the Treaty of Guadalupe Hidalgo?

4 The California Gold Rush (pages 438–443)

22. Who were four groups of forty-niners?

23. What were three ways California changed because of the gold rush?

CRITICAL THINKING

24. **Analyze Causes** How did Mexico's independence from Spain lead to changes in Texas?

25. **Make Inferences** Of the masses of pioneers moving west, in what ways was the Mormon migration unique?

26. **Distinguish Fact from Opinion** How do you think Americans considered Native Americans during the expansion period? How does this relate to the belief in manifest destiny?

27. **Compare and Contrast** Create a table to compare and contrast life in California before and after the Gold Rush.

	Before Gold Rush	After Gold Rush
population	*Native Americans & Californians*	*forty-niners & migrants*
economy	*agriculture*	

28. **Make Generalizations** Think about the leaders discussed in this chapter. What characteristics did they have that made them good leaders?

29. **Draw Conclusions** How did the War with Mexico and the California gold rush contributed to the cultural diversity of the United States?

30. **Interpret Graphs** In what year did the population of those living west of the Appalachian Mountains account for about half of the total U.S. population?

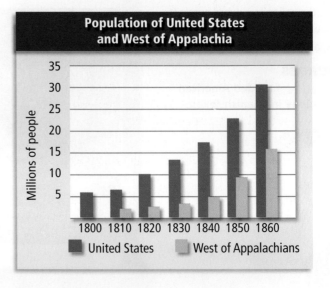

Population of United States and West of Appalachia

Millions of people

■ United States ■ West of Appalachians

✓ **TEST PRACTICE**

• **Online Test Practice** @ ClassZone.com
• **Test-Taking Strategies & Practice** at the front of this book

DOCUMENT-BASED QUESTIONS

PART 1: Short Answer

Analyze each document, and answer the questions that follow.

DOCUMENT 1

Settlement of Texas

Amarillo

Dallas

TEXAS

San Antonio · ★ Austin
Houston

Gulf of Mexico

Legend:
- Before 1800
- Between 1800 and 1850
- Between 1850 and 1890
- After 1890

1. When did Texas gain the largest expanse of territory?

DOCUMENT 2

PRIMARY SOURCE

❝ The determination of our slaveholding President to prosecute the war, and the probability of his success in wringing from the people men and money to carry it on, is made evident. . . . None seem willing to take their stand for peace at all risks; and all seem willing that the war should be carried on, in some form or other. ❞

—Frederick Douglass in *The North Star*, January 21, 1848

2. Why might Douglass have considered the War with Mexico a war against the free states?

Part 2: Essay

3. Using information from the documents, your answers to the questions in Part 1, and your knowledge of U.S. history, write an essay that discusses the American justification for manifest destiny.

YOU BE THE HISTORIAN

31. **Causes & Effects** Why, after the gold rush ended, did so many people choose to stay in California rather than return to their home state or country?

32. **What If?** Suppose the United States had lost the War with Mexico. How might this have changed the history of the territory gained from Mexico?

33. **Draw Conclusions** How did women and people of different racial, ethnic, or national groups contribute to the California gold rush?

34. **Summarize** How did the War with Mexico escalate the disagreement over slavery?

35. **Connect Geography & History** How did the opening of the West affect the economy of that region?

36. **Connect** *to* **Today** Large numbers of settlers moved west in the 1840s and after. What factors cause people to move from one part of the country to another today?

Answer the
ESSENTIAL QUESTION
How did westward expansion transform the nation?

Written Response Write a two- to three-paragraph response to the Essential Question. Be sure to consider the key ideas of each section as well as the most important factors that led to the expansion of the United States. Use the Response Rubric below to guide your thinking and writing.

Response Rubric
A strong response will include
• major discoveries and events that led to westward expansion
• discussion of manifest destiny and political issues
• analysis of key leaders
• knowledge of geography and territorial holdings

A New Spirit of Change

1830–1860

 ESSENTIAL QUESTION

How did immigration and social reform change the nation in the mid-1800s?

CONNECT ⟳ **Geography & History**

How did immigration affect America in the mid-1800s?

Think about:

1 how many immigrants came just from Germany and Ireland

2 the variety of cultures and beliefs they brought to America

3 where most immigrants settled—Northeastern cities and the Midwest

---

This early-19th-century image shows stagecoaches in lower Manhattan.

An Irish famine memorial in Westchester County, N.Y.

1840 The World Anti-Slavery Convention is held in London.

1830

1831 *The Liberator*, an abolitionist newspaper, begins publication.

1839 Mississippi passes the first U.S. law giving women rights to their own property and wages.

1843 Dorothea Dix asks the Massachusetts legislature to improve care for the mentally ill.

▼

Effect New laws create widespread changes in institutional care.

Click here to preview the Era of Reform @ClassZone.com

GERMANY
1,538,747

NORWAY and
SWEDEN
36,035

IRELAND
940,260

GREAT BRITAIN
339,303

*North
Sea*

*ATLANTIC
OCEAN*

FRANCE
199,195

SWITZERLAND
34,476

A 1978 stamp honoring
Harriet Tubman

Harriet Tubman

Black Heritage USA 13c

1848 Women demand
rights at the Seneca Falls
Convention.

Women's-rights advocate
Amelia Bloomer promoted
comfortable clothing for
women.

1860

1849 Harriet Tubman escapes
from slavery.

▼

Effect Tubman aids runaway
slaves on the Underground Railroad.

Abraham
Lincoln is
elected
president.

Reading for Understanding

▶ Key Ideas

BEFORE, YOU LEARNED

In colonial times, waves of immigrants created a diverse society in America.

NOW YOU WILL LEARN

In the mid-1800s, millions of Europeans came to the United States hoping to build a better life.

▶ Vocabulary

TERMS & NAMES

"push" factor a reason or force that causes people to leave their native land

"pull" factor a reason or force that causes people to choose to move to a new place

Know-Nothing Party political party in the United States during the 1850s that was against recent immigrants and Roman Catholics

Visual Vocabulary
Know-Nothing Party flag

BACKGROUND VOCABULARY

emigrant person who leaves a country

immigrant person who settles in a new country

steerage the cheapest deck on a ship

famine (FAM•ihn) severe food shortage leading to starvation

prejudice (PREHJ•uh•dihs) a negative opinion that is not based on facts

nativist native-born American who wanted to eliminate foreign influence

▶ Reading Strategy

Re-create the diagram shown at right. As you read and respond to the **KEY QUESTIONS**, use the center oval to record the main idea, and use the outer ovals to note important details. Add ovals or start a new diagram as needed.

 See Skillbuilder Handbook, page R4.

MAIN IDEAS AND DETAILS

abundant land

"pull" factors drew immigrants

🔊 **GRAPHIC ORGANIZERS**
Go to **Interactive Review** @ ClassZone.com

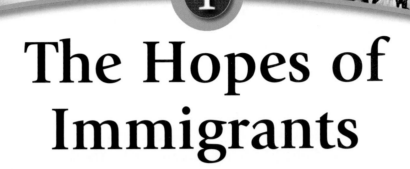

The Hopes of Immigrants

16.C.3b Explain relationships among the American economy and slavery, immigration, industrialization, labor and urbanization, 1700 present.
16.D.3a Describe characteristics of different kinds of communities in various sections of America during the colonial/frontier periods and the 19th century.

One American's Story

In 1830, English weaver John Downe became an **emigrant**, or person who leaves a country. Downe left England alone to work in New York, where he awaited his family's arrival.

PRIMARY SOURCE

❝ You will find a few inconveniences in crossing the Atlantic, but it will not be long, and when that is over, all is over, for I know you will like America.

America is not like England, for here no man thinks of himself as your superior. . . . This is a country where a man can stand as a man, and where he can enjoy the fruits of his own exertions [work], with rational liberty to its fullest extent. ❞

—John Downe, letter to his wife, August 12, 1830

The Bay and Harbor of New York, by Samuel B. Waugh

Emigrants—mainly from Europe—flocked to America during the mid-1800s. Like Downe, most left hoping to build a better life. After arrival in America, they became **immigrants**, or people who settle in a new country.

Patterns of Immigration

🔻 **KEY QUESTION** What attracted people to America in the mid-1800s?

Most immigrants endured hardships to reach America. Although some brought their families, many men, like Downe, went through the difficult journey alone. Most immigrants made the ocean voyage in **steerage**, the cheapest deck on a ship. In steerage, conditions were crowded and unhealthy. Many passengers became ill or died on the journey.

Why People Migrated What drew immigrants to America? Historians talk about **"push" factors** and **"pull" factors**. These forces push people out of their native land and pull them toward a new place. One push factor was population growth—a boom in population had made Europe overcrowded. Another push factor was crop failure. Poor harvests brought widespread hunger. Three main pull factors lured people to America:

- freedom
- economic opportunity
- abundant land

Germans Pursue Economic Opportunity The Germans were the largest immigrant group of the 1800s. They settled in cities as well as on farms and the frontier. Many were drawn to the fertile and newly available lands of Wisconsin, which was organized as a territory in 1836. Thousands more formed German-speaking communities in Texas.

Germans opened businesses as bakers, butchers, carpenters, printers, and tailors. Some, like John Jacob Bausch and Henry Lomb, achieved great success. In 1853, they started a firm to make eyeglasses and other lenses. Their company became the world's largest lens maker. Some German immigrants were Jews, many of whom worked as traveling salespeople. They brought pins, needles, pots—and news—to frontier homes and mining camps. In time, some opened their own stores. Many German Jews settled in cities.

German immigrants strongly influenced American culture. Many things we think of as originating in America came from Germany, such as kindergartens, gymnasiums, the Christmas tree, and the hamburger and frankfurter.

COMPARING *Push and Pull Factors*

The "push" factors of immigration pushed millions of people out of Europe and elsewhere in the 1800s. "Pull" factors drew many of them to the United States.

PULL FACTORS

- Tolerance and freedom
- New markets for artisans' skills
- Abundant and affordable land
- Opportunity to start over; healthy living

PUSH FACTORS

- Religious and political turmoil
- Artisans' jobs lost in Industrial Revolution
- Overcrowding caused by population growth
- Debt and hunger resulting from crop failures

CRITICAL THINKING

1. **Problems and Solutions** Many of the push factors were problems. Which pull factors were solutions to which problems?

2. **Make Inferences** Which pull factor probably attracted immigrants to the Midwest?

Immigrants Move Westward In the mid-1800s, public land in America was sold for $1.25 an acre. The promise of cheap land lured thousands of European immigrants, especially to territories in the Midwest.

Thousands of Scandinavians fled poverty in their homeland and moved to Minnesota and Wisconsin. Like Scandinavia, these states had forests, lakes, and cold winters. A high proportion of Scandinavian immigrants became farmers. Meanwhile, land shortages in Great Britain motivated thousands of British farmers to seek new opportunities in America. They, too, helped to make the Midwest a region known for farming. Many British artisans who felt squeezed out by the factory system also chose to emigrate.

The mid-1800s brought another major immigrant group: the Chinese. Most of the first Chinese immigrants went to California after the 1849 gold rush. By 1852, there were an estimated 25,000 Chinese in California. Most were miners, but some worked in agriculture and construction.

The Irish Flee Starvation Most Irish immigrants were Catholic. Protestant Britain had ruled Ireland for centuries—and controlled the Catholic majority by denying them rights. Irish Catholics could not vote, hold office, own land, or go to school. Because of the poverty produced by Britain's rule, some Irish had emigrated to America in the early 1800s.

In 1845, a disease attacked Ireland's main food crop, the potato. This caused a severe food shortage, or **famine** (FAM•in). The Irish Potato Famine killed 1 million people and forced many to emigrate. By 1855, an estimated 1.5 million people had left Ireland. Most went to North America, although some settled in Australia and Great Britain.

Connect *to the* **World**

The Potato Famine
In 1846, an Irish newspaper described famine victims "frantically rushing from their home and country, not with the idea of making fortunes in other lands, but to fly from a scene of suffering and death…"

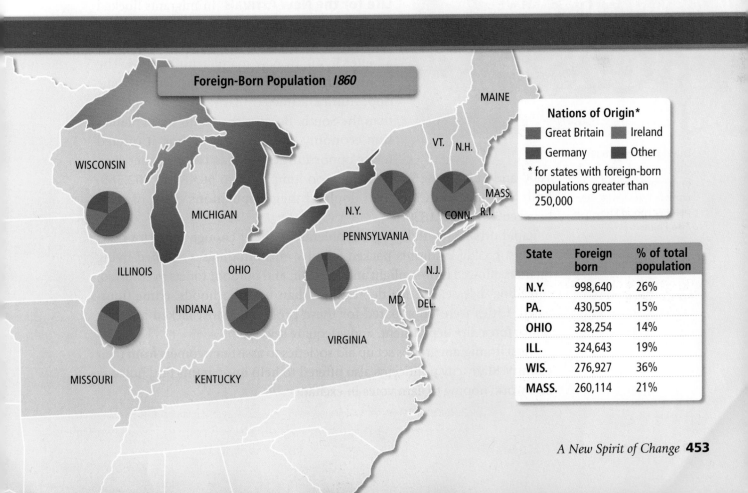

Foreign-Born Population *1860*

Nations of Origin*
Great Britain — Ireland
Germany — Other
* for states with foreign-born populations greater than 250,000

State	Foreign born	% of total population
N.Y.	998,640	26%
PA.	430,505	15%
OHIO	328,254	14%
ILL.	324,643	19%
WIS.	276,927	36%
MASS.	260,114	21%

In America, Irish farmers became city-dwellers. Arriving with little or no savings, many of these immigrants had to settle in the port cities where their ships had docked. By 1850, the Irish made up one-fourth of the population in Boston, New York, Philadelphia, and Baltimore.

The uneducated Irish immigrants came with few skills and had to take low-paying, back-breaking jobs. Irish women took in washing or worked as servants. The men built canals and railroads across America. So many Irish men died doing this dangerous work that people said there was "an Irishman buried under every [railroad] tie." The Irish competed with free African Americans for the jobs that nobody else wanted. Both groups had few other choices in America in the 1800s.

▲ **SUMMARIZE** Explain what attracted immigrants to America in the mid-1800s.

During the mid-1800s, thousands of new immigrants settled in the crowded New York City neighborhood known as Five Points.

America Adjusts to Immigrants

▼ **KEY QUESTION** What was life like for the new immigrants?

The huge numbers of immigrants caused overcrowding in the cities. This population explosion alarmed many Americans. However, some formed organizations to help immigrants adapt to their new country. Soon, like all immigrants before them, the new arrivals began to influence American society and culture.

Life for the New Arrivals Immigrants flocked to American cities. So did many native-born Americans, who left rural areas hoping to make a better living in new manufacturing jobs. The North, with its higher wages and greater economic opportunity, attracted many more immigrants than the South. Because the South was a plantation economy based on slave labor, it offered fewer opportunities for free laborers. Between 1800 and 1830, New York's population jumped from 60,489 to 202,589. Both St. Louis and Cincinnati doubled their populations every 10 years between 1800 and 1850.

Rapid urban growth brought problems. Without enough space for newcomers, greedy landlords packed tenants into buildings. Cramped living quarters allowed little sunlight and fresh air, and outdoor toilets overflowed, spreading disease. In such depressing urban neighborhoods, crime flourished. Cities were unprepared for these problems. Most lacked a public police force, fire department, and adequate sewers.

Most immigrant groups set up aid societies to assist newcomers from their country. Many city politicians also offered to help immigrants find housing and work, hoping to earn votes in exchange.

Opposition to Immigration Some native-born Americans believed that immigrants were too foreign to learn American ways. Others feared that immigrants might outnumber natives. Immigrants faced anger and **prejudice**—a negative opinion that is not based on facts. For example, some Protestants believed that Catholics threatened democracy. Those Protestants feared that the Pope, the head of the Roman Catholic Church, was plotting to overthrow democracy in America.

People who want to eliminate foreign influence are known as **nativists**. In the mid-1800s, some American nativists refused to hire immigrants and put up signs like "No Irish need apply." In cities such as New York and Boston, nativists formed a secret society. Members promised not to vote for Catholics or immigrants running for political office. If asked about their society, they said, "I know nothing about it."

In the 1850s, nativists started a political party called the **Know-Nothing Party**. It wanted to ban Catholics and the foreign-born from holding office. It also called for a cut in immigration and a 21-year-wait to become an American citizen. The Know-Nothings did get six governors elected. But their Northern and Southern branches couldn't agree on the issue of slavery, and they disappeared quickly as a national party.

A nineteenth-century advertisement for "Know Nothing Soap"
What might the Native Americans represent?

 MAKE GENERALIZATIONS Describe what life was like for new immigrants.

Illinois Learning Standards *Review*

ONLINE QUIZ
For test practice, go to
Interactive Review @ ClassZone.com

TERMS & NAMES

1. Explain the importance of
   - "push" factor
   - "pull" factor
   - Know-Nothing Party

USING YOUR READING NOTES

2. **Main Ideas and Details** Use the diagram you started at the beginning of the section to record details about immigration. Note which groups came and why, and where they settled.

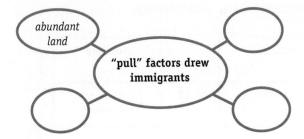

KEY IDEAS

3. What difficulties did immigrants face in the United States?

4. How did the arrival of immigrants affect U.S. cities?

CRITICAL THINKING

5. **Make Inferences** Why were immigrants willing to endure the hardships of coming to America?

6. **Analyze Primary Sources** In 1841, British novelist Charles Dickens described the huts in which some Irish railroad workers in New York lived:

   ❝ The best were poor protection from the weather; the worst let in the wind and rain . . . some had neither door nor window; some had nearly fallen down. ❞

   Do you think these immigrants were better off in America than in Ireland? Explain.

7. **Writing** Letter Research the Irish Potato Famine. Write a letter to friends in America that describes life in Ireland and why you want to join them in America.

▶ Key Ideas

BEFORE, YOU LEARNED

In the mid-1800s, millions of Europeans came to the United States hoping to build a better life.

NOW YOU WILL LEARN

A 19th-century religious revival launched movements to reform education and society.

▶ Vocabulary

TERMS & NAMES

Second Great Awakening renewal of religious faith in the 1790s and early 1800s

temperance movement campaign to stop the drinking of alcohol

Shaker member of a Christian sect that practiced communal living and did not allow marriage and childbearing

Horace Mann reformer who advocated improving education

Dorothea Dix reformer who was a pioneer in the movement for better treatment of the mentally ill

BACKGROUND VOCABULARY

labor union group of workers who band together to seek better working conditions

strike to stop work to demand better working conditions

REVIEW

evangelicalism the doctrine, or belief, that each person can experience a sudden conversion and experience a new spiritual relationship with God

▶ Reading Strategy

Re-create the problem-solution chart at right. As you read and respond to the **KEY QUESTIONS**, use the chart to organize the problems reformers identified in society and the solutions they proposed.

 See Skillbuilder Handbook, page R9.

PROBLEMS AND SOLUTIONS

Problem		Solution
heavy drinking	→	*temperance movement*

GRAPHIC ORGANIZERS
Go to **Interactive Review** @ ClassZone.com

Reforming American Society

14.D.3 Describe roles and influences of individuals, groups and media in shaping current Illinois and United States public policy (e.g., *general public opinion, special interest groups, formal parties, media*).

16.C.3b Explain relationships among the American economy and slavery, immigration, industrialization, labor and urbanization, 1700 present.

One American's Story

In the mid-1800s, many Americans had ideas for creating a better society in their new nation. Mary Lyon, the founder of Mount Holyoke Seminary in Massachusetts, advocated college-level education for women. Seeing the first building go up at her school gave Lyon a sense of awe.

Mary Lyon

PRIMARY SOURCE

❝ . . . The stones and brick and mortar speak a language which vibrates through my very soul. I have indeed lived to see the time when a body of gentlemen have ventured to lay the corner stone of an edifice [building] which . . . will be an institution for the education of females. . . . This will be an era in female education. ❞

—Mary Lyon, letter, October 7, 1836

In this section, you will learn how individuals like Lyon called on Americans to reform, or improve, themselves and their society.

A Spirit of Revival

▼ **KEY QUESTION** How did religion and philosophy encourage people to improve society?

In the early 19th century, a reform movement swept through American society. This movement was inspired mainly by a religious revival, like the one that had changed American life a century before.

The Second Great Awakening The renewal of religious faith in the 1790s and early 1800s is called the **Second Great Awakening**. Unlike Puritans, who believed that only some people would be saved, revivalist preachers insisted that anyone could choose salvation. This idea appealed to Americans' sense of optimism and equality, and offered a new interpretation of Christianity.

Revival meetings—emotionally charged events in which religious leaders hoped to attract followers—spread quickly across the country. Many groups, such as Baptists and Methodists, gained converts during this time. Settlers in the West eagerly awaited revivalist preachers like Peter Cartwright, who spent more than 60 years preaching on the frontier. In Eastern cities, Charles Grandison Finney held large revival meetings. He preached that selfishness was sin and that faith led people to help others.

The spread of evangelical ideas awakened a spirit of reform. Many people began to believe that they could help to right the wrongs of the world.

Temperance Heavy drinking was common in the early 1800s. One response to this problem was the **temperance movement**—a campaign to stop the drinking of alcohol. Some men spent most of their wages on alcohol, leaving their families poor. As a result, many women joined the movement.

Temperance workers handed out pamphlets urging people to stop drinking and gave plays dramatizing the evils of alcohol. They asked people to sign a pledge to not use alcohol. By 1838, a million had signed.

In 1851, Maine banned the sale of liquor. By 1855, 13 other states had passed similar laws. Most of these laws were later repealed. Still, the movement to ban alcohol remained strong, even into the 20th century.

Creating Ideal Societies Some people wanted society to start anew. They aimed to build an ideal society, called a utopia.

Religion led to some utopian experiments. The **Shakers** followed the beliefs of English immigrant Ann Lee, who preached that people should live in faith-centered communities. Shakers vowed not to marry or have children. They shared all their goods with each other and treated men and women as equals.

People called them Shakers because they shook with emotion during church services. Shakers set up communities in New York, New England, and on the frontier. Because they did not marry, Shakers depended on converts and adoption to keep their communities going. In the 1840s, Shakers had 6,000 members. In 2005, only four remained.

Not all utopian communities were based on religion. Two well-known experiments in communal living took place in New Harmony, Indiana, and Brook Farm, Massachusetts. However, these communities experienced conflicts and financial difficulties. They ended after only a few years.

▲ **EVALUATE** Explain how religion and philosophy encouraged people to try to improve society.

Temperance pledges often featured inspiring pictures and mottoes. **What does the main picture suggest about the benefits of giving up alcohol?**

Workers' Rights

▼ **KEY QUESTION** How did the labor movement try to improve working conditions?

Factory conditions were often unhealthy, and management could be unjust. By the 1830s, American workers had begun to demand improvements.

Factory Life Most factory workers labored 12 or 14 hours a day for six days a week. A typical workday began at five o'clock in the morning. It was not unusual for workers to spend most of the workday in dark, hot, crowded rooms with air so dirty that it was difficult to breathe. In the 1830s, many workers began to call for a ten-hour workday.

Hoping to increase profits, factory owners sometimes cut workers' pay and forced them to increase their pace. It was also legal to pay women and children lower wages than men in similar jobs. Partly for this reason, the majority of workers at the mills in Lowell, Massachusetts, were young women. Some of these women became active in the fight for workers' rights.

Organizing for Better Conditions The young women mill workers in Lowell, Massachusetts, started a **labor union**—a group of workers who band together to seek better working conditions. In 1836, the mill owners raised the rent of the company-owned boarding houses where the women lived. About 1,500 women went on **strike**, stopping work to demand better conditions. Eleven-year-old Harriet Hanson helped lead the strikers.

PRIMARY SOURCE

❝ I . . . started on ahead, saying, . . . 'I don't care what you do, I am going to turn out, whether anyone else does or not,' and I marched out, and was followed by the others. As I looked back at the long line that followed me, I was more proud than I have ever been since. ❞

—Harriet Hanson, quoted in Howard Zinn's *A People's History of the United States*

In 1835 and 1836, 140 strikes took place in the eastern United States alone. Some striking workers compared themselves to the American patriots who had fought for freedom in the Revolutionary War. In 1860, one group of workers began a strike on Washington's birthday.

Then the Panic of 1837 brought hard times economically. Jobs were scarce, and workers were afraid to cause trouble. The young labor movement fell apart. Even so, workers achieved a few goals. For example, in 1840 President Martin Van Buren ordered a ten-hour workday for government workers.

▲ **SUMMARIZE** Explain how the labor movement tried to improve working conditions.

Connect *to the* **World**

By the 1830s, a labor movement had gathered strength in Great Britain. Like the American labor movement, it sought better conditions and a shorter workday.

About 800 women shoemakers march during a strike in Lynn, Massachusetts, in 1860.

History Makers

Horace Mann 1796–1859

Mann is remembered as "the father of the American common [public] school." He believed that education was "the balance wheel of the social machinery." As secretary of the Massachusetts board of education, Mann advanced his cause by reporting to the state legislature, lecturing widely, and writing for various publications. His efforts raised awareness of the value of public education. They also led to dramatic changes in Massachusetts and across the country, with increased public spending on education, higher teacher salaries, better books for students, advanced teacher training, and—ultimately—a more educated population.

COMPARING Leaders

Compare and Contrast As you read through the chapter, look for other reform leaders. Compare Mann's efforts to promote his cause with those of other leaders in this chapter.

 ONLINE BIOGRAPHY For more on Horace Mann, go to the **Research & Writing Center** @ ClassZone.com

Social Reform

▼ **KEY QUESTION** What aspects of society did reformers try to change?

By the 1830s, the religious revival had sparked the rise of a reform movement. Social reformers campaigned to improve education, establish mental hospitals, and improve prisons.

Improving Education In the 1830s, Americans began to demand better schools. Massachusetts set up the first state board of education in 1837. Its leader, **Horace Mann**, called public education "the great equalizer" and argued for improving public educational opportunities. By 1850, most Northern states had opened public elementary schools.

Boston opened the first public high school in 1821. A few other Northern cities soon did the same. In addition, churches and other groups founded hundreds of private colleges in the following decades. Many were located in states carved from the Northwest Territory. These included Antioch and Oberlin Colleges in Ohio, Notre Dame in Indiana, and Northwestern University in Illinois.

Expanding Opportunities Women could not attend most colleges. An exception was Oberlin—the first college to accept women. From its founding in 1833, Oberlin admitted students regardless of race or sex. Until the late 1800s, however, it was rare for a woman to attend college.

African Americans also faced obstacles to getting an education. This was especially true in the South. Teaching an enslaved person to read was illegal in most of the Southern states. Enslaved African Americans who tried to learn to read were brutally punished. Even in the North, African-American children were barred from most public schools.

Few colleges accepted African Americans. The first African-American man to receive a college degree was Alexander Twilight in 1823. He later became a Vermont state legislator. Mary Jane Patterson was the first African-American woman to earn a college degree. She graduated from Oberlin in 1862 and became a teacher.

Care for the Needy Some reformers sought to improve care for society's most vulnerable members. In 1841 **Dorothea Dix**, a reformer from Boston, was teaching at a women's jail when she discovered that some women were locked up simply because they were mentally ill. Dix learned that the mentally ill often received no treatment, and that some were chained and beaten. Dix lectured widely in the United States and Europe to promote better care. Her efforts led to publicly funded mental hospitals in a number of states.

Some reformers worked to improve life for people with other disabilities. In 1817 in Hartford, Connecticut, educator Thomas H. Gallaudet started the first free school for deaf children in the United States. Reformer Samuel G. Howe directed the New England Asylum for the Blind (now the Perkins School for the Blind), which opened in Boston in 1832.

Reformers also tried to improve prisons. In the early 1800s, debtors, lifelong criminals, and children were put in the same cells. Reformers demanded that children go to special jails. They also called for adult prisoners to be rehabilitated, or prepared to live useful lives after their release.

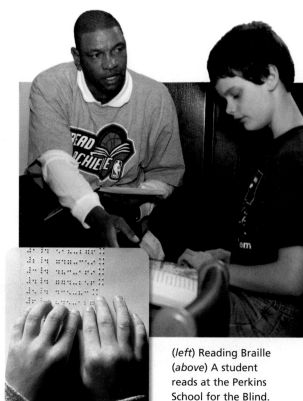

(*left*) Reading Braille
(*above*) A student reads at the Perkins School for the Blind.

 PROBLEMS AND SOLUTIONS List the problems in society that reformers worked to change.

Illinois Learning Standards *Review*

ONLINE QUIZ For test practice, go to **Interactive Review** @ ClassZone.com

TERMS & NAMES

1. Explain the importance of
   - Second Great Awakening
   - temperance movement
   - Shakers
   - Horace Mann
   - Dorothea Dix

USING YOUR READING NOTES

2. **Problems and Solutions** Complete the chart you started at the beginning of the section. Show the problems reformers identified in society and the solutions they proposed.

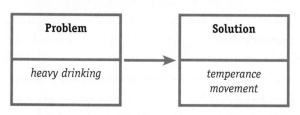

Problem		Solution
heavy drinking	→	*temperance movement*

KEY IDEAS

3. How did the Second Great Awakening influence the reform movement?

4. How did women contribute to social reform?

CRITICAL THINKING

5. **Main Ideas and Details** How did government work for better schools?

6. **Summarize** What obstacles faced women and African Americans who wanted an education?

7. **Causes and Effects** What factors might have caused utopian communities to fail?

8. **Art** Imagine you are a reformer in the mid-1800s. Choose one of the problems that you read about in this section and make a poster that encourages citizens to become involved and make positive changes.

Report to the Massachusetts Legislature

SETTING THE STAGE After traveling to several places where the mentally ill were kept in terrible conditions, Dorothea Dix wrote a report describing what she had seen. In 1843, she presented her report to lawmakers.

Advocate of the Helpless

In earlier times, the word *idiotic* did not mean "stupid." It was used to describe someone who was mentally disabled.

1. For what groups of people is Dix pleading for help?

History Makers

Dorothea Dix
1802–1887
Dix began teaching at 14 and opened her own school at 19. Later, she turned her skills as an educator toward improving society. Her bold activism earned her the nickname "Dragon Dix."

Gentlemen: . . . I come to present the strong claims of suffering humanity. I come to place before the Legislature of Massachusetts the condition of the miserable, the desolate, the outcast. I come as the **advocate**[1] of helpless, forgotten, insane, and idiotic men and women; of beings sunk to a condition from which the most unconcerned would start with real horror; of beings wretched in our prisons, and more wretched in our **almshouses**.[2] I must confine myself to a few examples, but am ready to furnish other and more complete details, if required.

I proceed, gentlemen, briefly to call your attention to the present state of insane persons confined within this **Commonwealth**,[3] in cages, closets, cellars, stalls, pens! Chained, naked, beaten with rods, and lashed into obedience.

I offer the following extracts from my notebook and journal.

Springfield: In the jail, one lunatic woman, furiously mad, a state **pauper**,[4] improperly situated, both in regard to the prisoners, the keepers, and herself. It is a case of extreme self-forgetfulness and oblivion to all the decencies of life … In the almshouse of the same town is a woman apparently only needing **judicious**[5] care and some well-chosen employment to make it unnecessary to confine her in solitude in a dreary unfurnished room. Her appeals for employment and companionship are most touching, but the mistress replied "she had no time to attend to her."

Lincoln: A woman in a cage. Medford: One idiotic subject chained, and one in a close stall for seventeen years. Pepperell: One often doubly chained, hand and foot; another violent; several peaceable now. Brookfield: One man caged, comfortable. Granville: One often closely confined, now losing the use of his limbs from want of exercise.

----

1. **advocate:** a person who promotes a cause.
2. **almshouses:** homes for poor people.
3. **Commonwealth:** a term used to refer to certain U.S. states; in this case, Massachusetts.
4. **pauper:** a person who lives on the state's charity.
5. **judicious:** wise and careful.

Charlemont: One man caged. Savoy: One man caged. Lenox: Two in the jail, against whose unfit condition there the jailer protests.

Dedham: The insane **disadvantageously**[6] placed in the jail. In the almshouse, two females in stalls, situated in the main building, lie in wooden bunks filled with straw; always shut up. One of these subjects is supposed curable. The overseers of the poor have declined giving her a trial at the hospital, as I was informed, on account of expense.

Besides the above, I have seen many who, part of the year, are chained or caged. The use of cages is all but universal. Hardly a town but can refer to some not distant period of using them; chains are less common; **negligences**[7] frequent; willful abuse less frequent than sufferings proceeding from ignorance, or want of consideration. I encountered during the last three months many poor creatures wandering reckless and unprotected through the country. . . . But I cannot **particularize**.[8] In traversing the state, I have found hundreds of insane persons in every variety of circumstance and condition, many whose situation could not and need not be improved; a less number, but that very large, whose lives are the saddest pictures of human suffering and degradation.

I give a few illustrations; but description fades before reality. . . .

Men of Massachusetts, I beg, I implore, I demand pity and protection for these of my suffering, outraged sex. . . . Become the benefactors of your race, the just guardians of the solemn rights you hold in trust. Raise up the fallen, **succor**[9] the desolate, restore the outcast, defend the helpless, and for your eternal and great reward receive the benediction, "Well done, good and faithful servants, become rulers over many things!"

----

6. **disadvantageously:** harmfully.

7. **negligences:** careless actions.

8. **particularize:** to name in detail.

9. **succor:** to help in a time of need.

I Have Seen Many

Notice that Dix cites evidence from many different towns.

2. Why do you think she includes so many specific details in her report?

Men of Massachusetts

When Dix says "Men of Massachusetts," she is still speaking to the members of the state legislature.

3. What does Dix want the Massachusetts Legislature to do?

DOCUMENT-BASED QUESTIONS

Short Answer

1. On what evidence did Dorothea Dix base her report about "suffering humanity"?

2. Whom did Dix ask to help improve the care of the mentally ill?

Extended Answer

3. What do Dix's efforts have in common with other social reform efforts discussed in this chapter?

▶ Key Ideas

BEFORE, YOU LEARNED

A 19th-century religious revival launched movements to reform education and society.

NOW YOU WILL LEARN

The social campaigns to gain freedom for enslaved persons and equality for women were closely linked.

▶ Vocabulary

TERMS & NAMES

abolition the movement to stop slavery

Frederick Douglass abolitionist and journalist who became an influential lecturer in the North and abroad

Sojourner Truth abolitionist and feminist who spoke against slavery and for the rights of women

Underground Railroad a series of escape routes used by slaves escaping the South

Harriet Tubman conductor on the Underground Railroad who led enslaved people to freedom

Elizabeth Cady Stanton reformer who helped organize the first women's rights convention

Seneca Falls Convention the first women's rights convention, held in Seneca Falls, New York

BACKGROUND VOCABULARY

suffrage the right to vote

Visual Vocabulary
Seneca Falls Convention

▶ Reading Strategy

Re-create the diagram shown at right. As you read and respond to the **KEY QUESTIONS**, use the diagram to note important issues and their effects. Add boxes or start a new diagram as needed.

 See Skillbuilder Handbook, page R7.

CAUSES AND EFFECTS

CAUSE

Slavery

EFFECT

Underground Railroad

EFFECT

↗ **GRAPHIC ORGANIZERS**
Go to **Interactive Review** @ ClassZone.com

Abolition and Women's Rights

14.C.3 Compare historical issues involving rights, roles and status of individuals in relation to municipalities, states and the nation.

14.D.3 Describe roles and influences of individuals, groups and media in shaping current Illinois and United States public policy (e.g., *general public opinion, special interest groups, formal parties, media*).

One American's Story

African-American poet and reformer Frances Ellen Watkins Harper often wrote about the suffering of enslaved persons, including enslaved mothers.

Frances Ellen Watkins Harper

PRIMARY SOURCE

❝ They tear him from her circling arms,
Her last and fond embrace.
Oh! never more may her sad eyes
Gaze on his mournful face.
No marvel, then, these bitter shrieks
Disturb the listening air:
She is a mother, and her heart
Is breaking in despair. ❞

—Frances Ellen Watkins Harper, "The Slave Mother"

Harper toured the North as an antislavery speaker. She also spoke out for women's rights and against racism. As this section explains, many individuals in the mid-1800s demanded equal rights for African Americans and women.

Abolitionists Protest Slavery

🔻 **KEY QUESTION** What methods did abolitionists use to fight against slavery?

In the late 1600s, the Quakers had been among the first to take a stand against slavery. However, **abolition**, the movement to end slavery, did not begin until the late 1700s. During the Revolution, Northern states began passing antislavery laws. By 1804, almost all the Northern states had abolished slavery, and Congress banned the importation of African slaves into the United States starting in 1807. Abolitionists then demanded a law ending slavery in the South, where the economy depended on slave labor. The stage was set for an emotional debate that would tear the nation apart.

Demanding an End to Slavery Abolitionists were bold in their statements and reactions to their beliefs were just as fierce. David Walker, a free African American in Boston, printed a pamphlet in 1829 urging slaves to revolt. Copies of the pamphlet appeared in the South. This angered slaveholders. Shortly afterward, Walker died; some believed he had been poisoned.

Some Northern whites also fought slavery. In 1831, William Lloyd Garrison began publishing an abolitionist newspaper, *The Liberator,* in Boston. Of his antislavery stand, he wrote, "I will not retreat a single inch—AND I WILL BE HEARD." Many hated his views. In 1835, a mob in Boston grabbed Garrison and dragged him toward a park to hang him. He was rescued by the mayor.

Two famous abolitionists were Southerners who grew up on a plantation. Sisters Sarah and Angelina Grimké believed that slavery was morally wrong. They moved to the North and spoke out against slavery, even though women at the time were not supposed to lecture in public. Theodore Weld, Angelina's husband, led a campaign to send antislavery petitions to Congress. Proslavery congressmen passed a gag rule to prevent the reading of petitions in Congress.

President John Quincy Adams ignored the gag rule and read the petitions. He also introduced an amendment to abolish slavery. Proslavery congressmen tried to stop him. Such efforts, however, weakened the proslavery cause by showing them to be opponents of free speech. Adams also defended a group of enslaved Africans who had rebelled on the slave ship *Amistad.* He successfully argued their case before the U.S. Supreme Court in 1841, and the Africans returned home immediately.

Eyewitness to Slavery Two powerful abolitionist speakers, **Frederick Douglass** and **Sojourner Truth**, spoke from their own experiences of having been enslaved. Douglass had a long career as a lecturer for the Massachusetts Anti-Slavery Society.

People who opposed abolition spread rumors that the brilliant speaker could never have been a slave. To prove them wrong, in 1845 Douglass published an autobiography that vividly narrated his slave experiences. Afterward, he feared recapture by his owner, so he left America for a two-year speaking tour of Great Britain and Ireland. When Douglass returned, he bought his freedom.

History Makers

Frederick Douglass   1818–1895

When lecturing on abolition, Douglass—an escaped slave—was often introduced as "a piece of property." Douglass was a popular and eloquent speaker who had few equals on the lecture circuit. Abolitionists welcomed his graphic descriptions of slave life as a way to publicize the injustice of slavery. As his popularity grew, Douglass began to introduce the topic of racial discrimination in the North. In addition to lecturing, Douglass published his autobiography and an abolitionist newspaper, *The North Star*. He said that in the North, people "are far wealthier than any plantation owner—they are rich with freedom."

CRITICAL THINKING

1. **Draw Conclusions** How might Douglass's life experiences have made him a persuasive speaker?

2. **Make Inferences** What did Douglass mean by Northerners being "rich with freedom"?

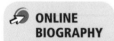

ONLINE BIOGRAPHY For more on Frederick Douglass, go to the **Research & Writing Center** @ ClassZone.com

Underground Railroad

UNORGANIZED TERRITORY

Legend:
- Free states
- Slave states
- Routes of the Underground Railroad

CANADA — Montreal — VT. — MAINE
Collingwood — NEW YORK — N.H. — Boston — MASS.
WISCONSIN — MICHIGAN — Niagara Falls — CONN.
MINN. — Detroit — Erie — New York City — R.I. — Brooklyn
IOWA — Chicago — PA. — N.J.
IND. — Sandusky — N.J.
ILL. — OHIO — MD. — DEL.
MISSOURI — Cincinnati — Ripley — Baltimore — Washington, D.C.
Evansville — Ohio River — VIRGINIA
KANSAS TERRITORY — Cairo — KENTUCKY
INDIAN TERRITORY — ARKANSAS — TENNESSEE — NORTH CAROLINA
TEXAS — Mississippi River — SOUTH CAROLINA
LA. — MISS. — ALABAMA — GEORGIA
New Orleans — Gulf of Mexico — FLORIDA

ATLANTIC OCEAN

0 100 200 miles
0 100 200 kilometers

Harriet Tubman (left) with people she helped to free

Connect Geography & History

Movement How might weather or time of year affect the movement along the Underground Railroad?

Sojourner Truth also began life enslaved, in New York State. In 1827, when she was about 30, Truth fled her owners and stayed with a Quaker family. She was originally called Isabella but changed her name in 1843 to reflect her life's work: to sojourn (stay temporarily in a place) and "declare the truth to the people." A bold and captivating speaker, Truth drew huge crowds.

The Underground Railroad Some brave abolitionists helped slaves escape to freedom along the **Underground Railroad**. Neither underground nor a railroad, the Underground Railroad was actually a series of aboveground escape routes from throughout the South up to the free North. On these routes, runaway slaves traveled on foot and by wagons, boats, and trains. They usually journeyed by night and hid by day in places called stations. Stables, attics, and cellars all served as stations. At his home in Rochester, New York, Frederick Douglass once housed 11 runaways at the same time.

The people who led the runaways to freedom were called conductors. The most famous was **Harriet Tubman**, who was born into slavery in Maryland. She escaped in 1849 when she learned that her owner was about to sell her. Tubman later described her feelings as she crossed into the free state of Pennsylvania: "I looked at my hands to see if I was the same person now that I was free. There was such a glory over everything."

After her escape, Harriet Tubman made 19 dangerous journeys to free enslaved persons. She carried medicine to quiet crying babies. Her enemies offered $40,000 for her capture, but no one ever caught her. "I never run my train off the track and I never lost a passenger," she proudly declared. Among the people she saved were her sister, brother, and parents.

Great Escapes Some escapes by enslaved persons became famous. In 1848, Ellen Craft disguised herself as a white man while her husband, William, pretended to be her slave. Together they traveled more than 1,000 miles, by train and steamboat, from slavery in Georgia to freedom in the North.

In 1849, Henry Brown had a white carpenter pack him in a box and ship him to Philadelphia. The box was two and one half feet deep, two feet wide, and three feet long. It bore the label "This side up with care." Nevertheless, Brown spent several miserable hours traveling head down. At the end of about 27 hours, "Box" Brown climbed out a free man in Philadelphia.

▲ **SUMMARIZE** List the methods abolitionists used to fight against slavery.

The Fight for Women's Rights

▼ **KEY QUESTION** What rights were women fighting for in the mid-1800s?

Some white abolitionist women had begun to realize that their own rights were extremely limited. In 1840, an incident at a major antislavery convention in London helped launch the U.S. movement for women's rights.

Women Reformers Face Barriers Lucretia Mott and **Elizabeth Cady Stanton** were two leading women abolitionists. Mott and Stanton were part of an American delegation that attended the World Anti-Slavery Convention in London in 1840. Although the women in the delegation had much to say, they were not allowed to participate in the convention or speak in public. Instead, they had to sit silent behind a heavy curtain.

To show his support, the famed abolitionist William Lloyd Garrison joined them. He said, "After battling so many long years for the liberties of African slaves, I can take no part in a convention that strikes down the most sacred rights of all women."

But most Americans agreed that women should stay out of public life. Women in the 1800s possessed few legal or political rights. Few could vote, sit on juries, or hold public office. Many laws treated women—especially married women—as children. Single women had some freedoms, such as being able to manage their own property. But in most states, a husband controlled any property his wife inherited and any wages she might earn.

The Seneca Falls Convention After the World Anti-Slavery Convention, Stanton and Mott decided it was time to demand not only freedom for enslaved people, but equality for women. They made up their minds to plan a convention for women's rights after they returned to the United States.

On July 19 and 20, 1848, Stanton and Mott headed the **Seneca Falls Convention** for women's rights in Seneca Falls, New York. It was the world's first convention on the rights of women. It attracted about 300 women and men, including the well-known abolitionist Frederick Douglass.

Before the meeting opened, a small group of planners discussed how they would present their ideas. The planners wrote a document modeled on the Declaration of Independence. They called it the Declaration of Sentiments and Resolutions. Just as the Declaration of Independence said that "All men are created equal," the Declaration of Sentiments stated that "All men and women are created equal." It went on to list several statements of opinion, or resolutions. Then it concluded with a demand for rights.

PRIMARY SOURCE

❝ Now, in view of this entire disenfranchisement [denying the right to vote] of one-half the people of this country, their social and religious degradation—in view of the unjust laws above mentioned, and because women do feel themselves aggrieved, oppressed, and fraudulently deprived of their most sacred rights, we insist that they have immediate admission to all the rights and privileges which belong to them as citizens of the United States. ❞

—Declaration of Sentiments and Resolutions, 1848

Every resolution won unanimous approval from the group except **suffrage**, or the right to vote. Some argued that the public would laugh at women if they asked for the vote. But Elizabeth Cady Stanton and Frederick Douglass fought for the resolution. They argued that the right to vote would give women political power that would help them win other rights. The resolution for suffrage won by a slim margin.

History Makers

Elizabeth Cady Stanton 1815–1902

Stanton (pictured with one of her children) had long known that the world could be unfair to women. Her father was a lawyer who had many women clients. Some faced poverty because laws gave a married woman's money to her husband, who could lose it to drink or gambling. Women who divorced often lost the right to see their children. As an adult, Stanton fought to change laws that affected women, and strongly believed that the ability to vote would help women to ensure their rights. Stanton was a persuasive lecturer and writer. During a career that lasted half a century, she recruited many to her cause.

CRITICAL THINKING

1. **Draw Conclusions** Why did Stanton want women to have more legal rights?
2. **Form and Support Opinions** Do you agree with Stanton about the importance of voting? Explain.

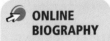 **ONLINE BIOGRAPHY** For more on Elizabeth Cady Stanton, go to the **Research & Writing Center** @ ClassZone.com

Continued Calls for Women's Rights The women's rights movement of the mid-1800s was ridiculed by many people. Newspaper cartoons and editorials often poked fun at women who wanted equal rights, and suffrage seemed far out of reach.

As women's rights activists continued their efforts, however, they began to see results. Susan B. Anthony, a skilled organizer from the temperance and abolitionist movements, played a key part in building the call for women's rights into a national movement. Anthony argued that women's suffrage would be the foundation on which women would achieve other legal rights. She believed that "there never will be complete equality until women themselves help to make laws and elect lawmakers."

Anthony was an outspoken advocate for equal pay for men and women. She also called for laws that would give married women the right to keep their own property and wages. In 1839, Mississippi passed the first such law. New York passed a property law in 1848 and a wages law in 1860. By 1865, 29 states had similar laws.

▲ **CAUSES AND EFFECTS** Explain what rights women fought for in the mid-1800s.

CONNECT *to the Essential Question*

How did immigration and social reform change the nation in the mid-1800s?

PROBLEM	SOLUTION
Overcrowding and lack of opportunity in Europe and elsewhere	Millions of immigrants settle in the United States
Poor working conditions	Workers form labor unions and go on strikes Schools founded for children with disabilities
Education for only the few	Public schooling becomes more widespread
Slavery in the South	Abolitionists demand an end to slavery Underground Railroad helps some enslaved people escape
Limited rights for women	Women demand rights to vote and to keep their own property and wages

CRITICAL THINKING **Causes and Effects** What long-term effects did these solutions have on American society?

A Changing Nation

▼ **KEY QUESTION** How did immigration, religious revival, and reform change the nation?

In the early and mid–19th century, America experienced dramatic social and cultural changes. These changes came from forces outside the country as well as from the religious and reform movements within its borders.

America Transformed Americans continued to adapt to their growing nation. Immigration had produced a far more diverse population, and cities were dramatically changed in size, culture, and economy. Some people felt threatened by the new face of America and fought to stop immigration. Others launched a reform movement, sparked by the religious revivals, that sought to take control of the forces of change. American reformers advocated such causes as temperance, education, and workers' rights. Soon, some women reformers began to fight for their own rights.

Meanwhile, the issue of slavery continued to tear the nation apart. As the abolitionist movement gathered strength in the North, the economy of the South continued to depend on slave labor—and millions of African Americans remained enslaved.

▲ **CAUSES AND EFFECTS** Explain how immigration, religious revival, and reform changed the nation.

 Illinois Learning Standards *Review*

 ONLINE QUIZ
For test practice, go to
Interactive Review @ ClassZone.com

TERMS & NAMES

1. Explain the importance of
- abolition
- Frederick Douglass
- Sojourner Truth
- Underground Railroad
- Harriet Tubman
- Elizabeth Cady Stanton
- Seneca Falls Convention

USING YOUR READING NOTES

2. Causes and Effects Complete the diagram you started at the beginning of this section. Then create a diagram for each of the other main issues in this section.

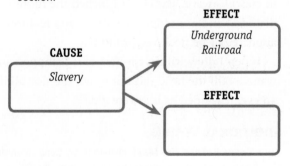

CAUSE

Slavery

EFFECT

Underground Railroad

EFFECT

KEY IDEAS

3. How did formerly enslaved persons participate in the abolitionist movement?

4. What barriers to equality did women face in the mid-1800s?

5. How did women abolitionists help to spark the fight for women's rights?

CRITICAL THINKING

6. Make Inferences Why did the women at the Seneca Falls Convention believe they should have rights?

7. Analyze Point of View Runaway slaves risked their lives for freedom. Why do you think some risked their lives and freedom again to help free others?

8. Draw Conclusions How did the Underground Railroad reflect a geographic division over slavery in America?

9. **Computer Science** Use the Internet to research the Quakers and their position on slavery. Design a web page that describes their position and how they helped people such as Sojourner Truth.

The True Confessions of Charlotte Doyle by Avi

The period in which *The True Confessions of Charlotte Doyle* takes place was one of significant developments in American literature. In the 1830s, several American thinkers including Ralph Waldo Emerson, a poet and essayist, developed a philosophical and literary movement that rejected traditional beliefs and authority in favor of the individual's intuition and insight. Transcendentalism, as this movement came to be called, was part of the romantic movement prominent in England and Germany at that time—a movement of style, literature, and thought that focused on emotional forms of expression.

Henry David Thoreau, another transcendentalist writer of the period, praised self-reliance and individual decision-making. Thoreau believed that people should reject the materialism and greed that, for many, had come to guide American life. In *Walden*, Thoreau puts his beliefs into practice as he writes of his life alone in the New England woods.

Themes of individualism appeared in the works of other writers of the period as well, including Nathaniel Hawthorne, Henry Wadsworth Longfellow, and later Louisa May Alcott, Herman Melville, and Walt Whitman.

The True Confessions of Charlotte Doyle takes place in this period of change in America and across the seas. Here, Charlotte Doyle, a thirteen-year-old American girl, confronts uncertainty in the dark hold of the ship that carries her across dangerous seas from England to America.

I was too frightened to cry out again. Instead I remained absolutely still, crouching in pitch blackness while the wash of ship sounds eddied about me, sounds now intensified by the frantic knocking of my heart. Then I recollected that Zachariah's dirk was still with me. With a shaking hand I reached into the pocket where I'd put it, took it out, and removed its wooden sheath which slipped through my clumsy fingers and clattered noisily to the floor.

"Is someone there?" I called, my voice thin, wavering.

No answer.

After what seemed forever I repeated, more boldly than before, *"Is someone there?"*

Still nothing happened. Not the smallest breath of response. Not the slightest stir.

Gradually, my eyes became accustomed to the creaking darkness. I could make out the ladder descending from the deck, a square of dim light above. From that point I could follow the line of the ladder down to where it plunged into the hold below. At that spot, at the edge of the hole, I could see the head more distinctly. Its eyes were glinting wickedly, its lips contorted into a grim, satanic smirk.

Horrified, I nonetheless stared back. And the longer I did so the more it dawned on me that the head had not in fact moved—not at all. The features, I saw, remained unnaturally fixed. Finally, I found the courage to edge aside my fear and lean forward—the merest trifle—to try and make out who—or what—was there.

With the dirk held awkwardly before me I began to crawl forward. The closer I inched the more distorted and grotesque grew the head's features. It appeared to be positively inhuman.

When I drew within two feet of it I stopped and waited. Still the head did not move, did not blink an eye. It seemed as if it were *dead*.

ADDITIONAL READING

Two Years Before the Mast Richard Henry Dana chronicles his adventures as a crewmember aboard two ships, the *Pilgrim* and the *Alert*, between 1833 and 1855.

Chapter Summary

① **Key Idea**
In the mid-1800s, millions of
Europeans came to the United
States hoping to build a better
life.

② **Key Idea**
A 19th-century religious revival
launched movements to reform
education and society.

③ **Key Idea**
The social campaigns to gain
freedom for enslaved persons
and equality for women were
closely linked.

 For detailed Review and Study Notes
go to **Interactive Review**
@ ClassZone.com

Name Game

Use the Terms & Names list to identify each
sentence online or on your own paper.

1. I lived in a community centered on religion.
   Shaker 🖑

2. I helped enslaved people reach freedom
   through the Underground Railroad.

3. This is a work stoppage to demand better
   conditions.

4. This is the right to vote.

5. I was opposed to recent immigrants.

6. Economic opportunity is an example of this.

7. I was an abolitionist speaker who chose my
   own name.

8. I worked toward better treatment of the
   mentally ill.

9. I worked toward improvements in public
   education.

10. This was the cheapest deck on a ship.

A. Horace Mann
B. Dorothea Dix
C. Elizabeth Cady Stanton
D. steerage
E. suffrage
F. strike
G. nativist
H. Sojourner Truth
I. Harriet Tubman
J. Shaker
K. "push" factor
L. "pull" factor
M. temperance movement

Activities

FLIPCARD

Use the online flip cards to quiz yourself on the
terms and names introduced in this chapter.

He escaped from slavery
and became a famous
abolitionist speaker and
newspaper publisher.

ANSWER
Frederick Douglass

CROSSWORD PUZZLE

Complete the online crossword puzzle to
show what you know about social change in
the early 1800s.

ACROSS
1. Harriet Tubman was
a _____ on the
Underground Railroad.

Harriet Tubman

Black Heritage USA 13c

VOCABULARY

Match the term on the left with its description on the right.

1. Know-Nothing Party
2. temperance movement
3. Second Great Awakening
4. Underground Railroad
5. Seneca Falls Convention

A. helped slaves escape
B. called for women's rights
C. opposed immigration
D. revived religious feeling
E. worked to stop the drinking of alcohol

Choose the term or name that does not belong in each group, and explain why.

6. Sojourner Truth, Horace Mann, Frederick Douglass

7. nativism, labor union, strike

8. steerage, suffrage, emigrant

Sojourner Truth

KEY IDEAS

1 The Hopes of Immigrants (pages 450–455)

9. What factors pushed emigrants out of Europe in the mid-1800s?

10. What was the Know-Nothing Party, and what was its stance on immigration?

2 Reforming American Society (pages 456–461)

11. What were the goals of people who fought for workers' rights?

12. How did reformers seek to improve educational opportunities?

3 Abolition and Women's Rights (pages 464–471)

13. How did the Underground Railroad operate?

14. What were the goals of the women's rights movement in the mid-1800s?

CRITICAL THINKING

15. **Synthesize** Why was America the destination for so many immigrants?

16. **Causes and Effects** How did the rapid increase in immigration during the mid-1800s cause conflicts in society?

17. **Make Generalizations** Why did many factory owners support the temperance movement?

18. **Causes and Effects** Create a chart to show the effects of educational reform in the mid-1800s. After you complete your chart, explain how these efforts have helped to make society more equal.

19. **Compare and Contrast** How were Frederick Douglass and Sojourner Truth similar as abolitionists?

20. **Make Inferences** Why do you think that some of the people who fought for abolition also fought for women's rights?

21. **Draw Conclusions** The cartoon below shows a husband and wife fighting over "who will wear the pants in the family"—that is, who will rule the household. What do the pants symbolize?

DOCUMENT-BASED QUESTIONS

PART 1: Short Answer

Analyze each document and answer the questions that follow.

DOCUMENT 1

1. This nineteenth-century painting shows a revival meeting. Note the figure on the left with the outstretched arms. What is he doing, and how would he have hoped to affect the crowd?

DOCUMENT 2

PRIMARY SOURCE

❝ What, to the American slave, is your Fourth of July? I answer: a day that reveals to him, more than all other days of the year, the gross injustice and cruelty to which he is the constant victim. To him, your celebration is a sham [something false]; . . . your sounds of rejoicing are empty and heartless; . . . ❞

—Frederick Douglass, 1852

2. Frederick Douglass gave this speech at a Fourth of July celebration in New York. Why does he say the sounds of the celebration are "empty and heartless"?

PART 2: Essay

3. In two or three short paragraphs, explain how individuals in the nineteenth century sought to influence their society. Use information from your answers to Part 1 and your knowledge of U.S. history.

YOU BE THE HISTORIAN

22. **Connect to Today** Which "pull" factors of the mid-1800s still attract new immigrants to the United States today?

23. **Analyze Point of View** Think of a person in this chapter who exercised leadership by standing up for an unpopular position. Why might this leader have been willing to take such a risk?

24. **Causes and Effects** What were the long-term effects of the nineteenth-century reform movement?

25. **Evaluate** How successful was the women's movement of the mid-1800s?

26. **Form and Support Opinions** Of the reform efforts you learned about in this chapter, which do you consider the most important? Explain.

 Answer the
ESSENTIAL QUESTION
How did immigration and social reform change the nation in the mid-1800s?

Written Response Write a two- to three-paragraph response to the Essential Question. Be sure to consider the key ideas of each section as well as the most significant problems that faced Americans in the mid-1800s. Use the Response Rubric below to guide your thinking and writing.

Response Rubric
A strong response will
• analyze factors that pulled immigrants to America
• evaluate the impact of social reform movements
• discuss the strategies of leading abolitionists
• describe the goals of the women's rights movement

A Nation Divided and Rebuilt

1846–1877

Why It Matters Now

The Civil War represented the greatest threat to the survival of the American republic in our history. Why we fought, how the Union won, and how we rebuilt the nation remain enduring matters of discussion and debate.

American history is longer, larger, more various, more beautiful, and more terrible than anything anyone has ever said about it.
—James Baldwin

1. Tensions Rise Between North and South

2. Slavery Dominates Politics

3. Lincoln's Election and Southern Secession

The Nation Breaking Apart

1846–1861

🔲 ESSENTIAL QUESTION

What issues and events shattered the nation's unity and led to civil war?

CONNECT ↻ Geography & History

How did geography and climate help create the nation's sectional division?

Think about:

1 the areas where cotton was grown

2 the difference between the climate of the South and that of the North

3 why cotton flourished in the South

Playing cards showing American generals in the War with Mexico

1846

War with Mexico

Wilmot Proviso introduced

1850 Compromise of 1850, including the Fugitive Slave Act, is passed.

▼

Effect Abolitionists defy the law by helping slaves escape.

1852 *Uncle Tom's Cabin* published

▼

Effect The novel increases tension between North and South.

MAINE

N.H.

VT.

Lowell
Boston

MASS.

NEW YORK

R.I.

CONN.

PENNSYLVANIA

New York

Philadelphia

N.J.

MICHIGAN

IOWA

OHIO

DELAWARE

Baltimore

MARYLAND

INDIANA

ILLINOIS

Cincinnati

MISSOURI

VIRGINIA

*ATLANTIC
OCEAN*

KENTUCKY

NORTH CAROLINA

TENNESSEE

ARKANSAS

SOUTH
CAROLINA

MISS.

ALABAMA

GEORGIA

TEXAS

LOUISIANA

FLORIDA

Gulf of Mexico

	Free States
	Territory closed to slavery
	Slave states
	Territory open to slavery
	Cotton Belt
•	Major manufacturing city

Major Industries

	Flour milling
	Fishing
	Ironworks and steelworks
	Lumber and timber
	Mining
	Textiles and clothing

0   100   200 miles
0   100   200 kilometers

Preston Brooks beats
Senator Sumner in Congress.

1860 Lincoln elected president

▼

Effect South Carolina secedes.

1857 The Supreme
Court rules on *Dred
Scott* v. *Sandford*.

1861

1854
Kansas-
Nebraska Act is
passed.

The Republican
Party is formed.

The Confederate
States of America is
formed.

Fugitive slaves escaping
from Maryland

The Nation Breaking Apart **479**

▶ Key Ideas

BEFORE, YOU LEARNED

The North and South tried to reach a compromise in their disagreements over slavery.

NOW YOU WILL LEARN

Rising anger over slavery increased tensions between the North and South and led to violence.

▶ Vocabulary

TERMS & NAMES

Wilmot Proviso 1846 proposal that outlawed slavery in any territory gained from the War with Mexico

Free-Soil Party political party dedicated to stopping the expansion of slavery

Stephen A. Douglas Illinois senator who backed the Compromise of 1850

Compromise of 1850 series of laws intended to settle the major disagreements between free states and slave states

Fugitive Slave Act 1850 law meant to help slaveholders recapture runaway slaves

Harriet Beecher Stowe abolitionist; author of *Uncle Tom's Cabin*

Uncle Tom's Cabin novel published by Harriet Beecher Stowe in 1852 that showed slavery as brutal and immoral

Kansas-Nebraska Act 1854 law that established the territories of Kansas and Nebraska and gave their residents the right to decide whether to allow slavery

BACKGROUND VOCABULARY

bickering petty quarreling

REVIEW

popular sovereignty a system in which issues are decided by the citizenry or voters

▶ Reading Strategy

Re-create the diagram shown at right. As you read and respond to the **KEY QUESTIONS**, use the diagram to note the difference between the economies of the North and South.

 See Skillbuilder Handbook, page R8.

COMPARE AND CONTRAST

Northern Economy	Southern Economy
	relied on plantation farming

 GRAPHIC ORGANIZERS
Go to **Interactive Review** @ ClassZone.com

Tensions Rise Between North and South

14.C.3 Compare historical issues involving rights, roles and status of individuals in relation to municipalities, states and the nation.
14.D.3 Describe roles and influences of individuals, groups and media in shaping current Illinois and United States public policy (e.g., *general public opinion, special interest groups, formal parties, media*).

One American Story

During the 1830s, a French government official named Alexis de Tocqueville (TOHK•vihl) traveled along the Ohio River. The river was the border between Ohio, a free state, and Kentucky, a slave state. Tocqueville noted what he saw on both sides of the river.

Alexis de Tocqueville

PRIMARY SOURCE

❝ The State of Ohio is separated from Kentucky just by one river; on either side of it the soil is equally fertile, and the situation equally favourable, and yet everything is different. Here [on the Ohio side] a population devoured by feverish activity, trying every means to make its fortune. . . . There [on the Kentucky side] is a people which makes others work for it and shows little compassion, a people without energy, mettle or the spirit of enterprise. . . . These differences cannot be attributed to any other cause but slavery. ❞

—**Alexis de Tocqueville,** *Journey to America*

Foreign observers were often surprised by the cultural and political division between North and South. This division was now widening.

North and South Follow Different Paths

🔻 **KEY QUESTION** How did the economies of the North and South differ?

The economies of the North and South had been developing differently ever since colonial times. Although both economies were mainly agricultural, there were more small farms in the North. The North had also developed more industry and commerce. By contrast, the Southern economy relied on plantation farming and slave labor rather than industry. The economic differences between the two sections began to divide the nation politically.

Industry and Immigration in the North The growing industries of the North attracted many immigrants to Northern cities. As the Northern cities grew, immigrants and Easterners were also moving west. They built farms in the new states carved out of the Northwest Territory. Most canals and railroads ran east and west, strengthening ties between Eastern and Midwestern states.

In the North, some abolitionists believed that slavery was immoral and should be ended immediately. But other Northern opponents of slavery took a different position. Some Northern workers opposed slavery because it was an economic threat to them. Because slaves did not work for pay, wage workers feared that enslaved labor would replace them.

Agriculture and Slavery in the South The Southern economy was mostly agricultural. A small class of wealthy planters dominated Southern politics and society. They made great profits from the labor of their slaves. Much of this profit came from trade. Planters relied on exports of cash crops, especially cotton, and invested in land and slaves instead of industry.

Most Southern whites were poor farmers who owned no slaves. Many of these people resented the powerful plantation owners. But some poor whites accepted slavery because it gave them a feeling of social superiority.

Connecting History

Expanding Liberty
In the late 1700s, slavery was gradually outlawed throughout the Northern states. However, as slavery declined in the North, it continued to spread in the South. *See Chapter 8, page 247.*

CONNECT *Economics and History*

INVESTMENT

The sectional differences between North and South increased partly through investment. Investment is when money is committed to a project in order to create a profit.

Northerners invested in new kinds of machinery that might save them money. This helped fuel the industrial boom in the North.

Southerners, in contrast, invested profits back into land and slaves. Thus, investment strengthened sectional differences: the North became more industrial and "modern" while the South remained agricultural.

North

factories   profit   more factories and machines

South

land and slaves   profit   more land and slaves

CRITICAL THINKING **Connect** *to* **Today** If you were an investor, in what new industries would you invest?

When Northern criticism of slavery increased, slaveholders defended their way of life. To justify slavery, most offered the openly racist argument that white people were superior to African Americans. Many also claimed that slavery helped slaves by introducing them to Christianity, as well as providing them with food, clothing, and shelter throughout their lives. In time, different attitudes to slavery brought the North and the South into conflict.

▲ **COMPARE AND CONTRAST** Compare the economies of the North and South.

Slavery and Territorial Expansion

▼ **KEY QUESTION** How did territorial expansion inflame sectional conflicts?

After the Missouri Compromise in 1820, political disagreements over slavery seemed to fade. However, the War with Mexico in 1846 brought the issue of slavery back to the forefront.

The Wilmot Proviso Many Northerners suspected that Southerners wanted to take territory from Mexico in order to extend slavery. They feared that this would upset the balance between free and slave states. To prevent this, Representative David Wilmot of Pennsylvania proposed a bill, known as the **Wilmot Proviso**, to outlaw slavery in any territory the United States might acquire from the War with Mexico.

But slaveholders believed that Congress had no right to prevent them from bringing slaves into any of the territories. The Constitution, they claimed, gave equal protection to the property rights of all U.S. citizens. The Wilmot Proviso divided Congress along sectional lines. The bill passed the House of Representatives. But Southerners prevented it from passing the Senate.

Even though the Wilmot Proviso never became law, it had important effects. It led to the creation of the **Free-Soil Party**, a political party dedicated to stopping the expansion of slavery. The party's slogan expressed its ideals—"Free Soil, Free Speech, Free Labor, and Free Men." The Free-Soil Party won ten seats in Congress in the election of 1848. More important, the party made slavery a key issue in national politics.

The Compromise of 1850 By 1848, the nation's leaders had begun to debate how to deal with slavery in the lands gained from the War with Mexico. The proposed addition of new states threatened the balance of power in Congress between North and South. Both sides worried about what would happen when California became a state.

The discovery of gold attracted so many people to California that there soon would be enough people to qualify for statehood. Most California residents wanted theirs to be a free state. But this would tip the balance of power in favor of the North. Southerners wanted to divide California in half, making the northern half a free state and the southern half a slave state.

In March 1850, California applied to be admitted as a free state. With California as a free state, slave states would become a minority in the Senate just as they were in the House.

Ribbon of the Free-Soil Party worn on supporters' clothing

IMAGES OF SLAVERY

Supporters of slavery argued that the enslaved were well fed, well clothed, and happy—much as they appear on this tobacco label below. However, the reality of slavery was very different, as the photograph at right reveals. Even the children of the enslaved were forced to labor long hours in dangerous and unhealthy conditions. Slaves suffered violent and cruel punishments. Many enslaved families were broken up when family members were sold to work on distant plantations.

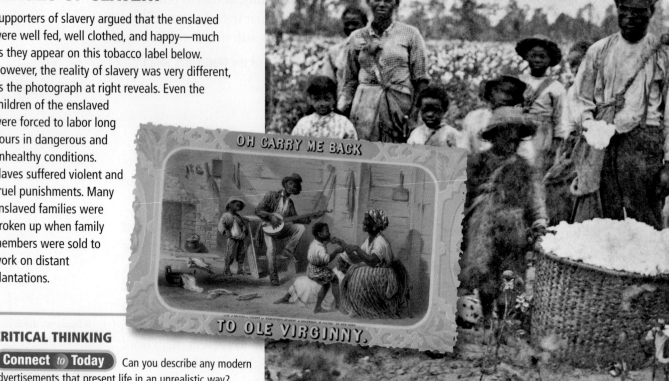

OH CARRY ME BACK

TO OLE VIRGINNY.

CRITICAL THINKING

Connect *to* **Today** Can you describe any modern advertisements that present life in an unrealistic way?

California could not gain statehood, however, without the approval of Congress. And Congress was divided over the issue. But statesmen sought compromise. Senator Henry Clay of Kentucky crafted a plan to settle the problem.

- To please the North, California would be admitted as a free state, and the slave trade would be abolished in Washington, D.C.
- To please the South, Congress would not pass laws regarding slavery for the rest of the territories won from Mexico, and Congress would pass a stronger law to help slaveholders.

People on both sides felt they had to give up too much in this plan. Others, tired of the sectional **bickering**, just wanted to preserve the Union.

The job of winning passage of the plan fell to Senator **Stephen A. Douglas** of Illinois. By the end of September, Douglas succeeded, and the plan, now known as the **Compromise of 1850**, became law.

Some people celebrated the compromise, believing that it had saved the Union. But the compromise would not bring peace. In the years that followed, sectional tensions continued to rise.

▲ **CAUSES AND EFFECTS** Explain how the Wilmot Proviso inflamed debate.

The Crisis Deepens

▼ **KEY QUESTION** How did the Fugitive Slave Act deepen the crisis?

The Compromise of 1850 was an attempt to calm the political situation. However, it contained one bill that heightened, rather than calmed, the crisis. That bill was called the **Fugitive Slave Act**.

The Fugitive Slave Act Under this law, accused fugitives could be held without an arrest warrant. They had no right to a jury trial. Instead, a federal commissioner ruled on each case.

Southerners backed the Fugitive Slave Act because they considered slaves to be property. But one aspect of the act especially enraged Northerners: it required them to help recapture runaway slaves. It also placed penalties on people who would not cooperate with the law. Southern slave catchers were allowed to roam the North. Sometimes they captured free African Americans.

The act drew more people to the abolitionist cause. Many decided to defy the act, even though this meant breaking the law.

Outrage Over the Act Abolitionist writer **Harriet Beecher Stowe** was outraged by the Fugitive Slave Act. Her anger inspired her to write *Uncle Tom's Cabin* in 1852. The novel presented the cruelty and immorality of slavery. The novel describes the escape of a slave named Eliza and her baby across the Ohio River.

PRIMARY SOURCE

❝ Eliza made her desperate retreat across the river just in the dusk of twilight. The gray mist of evening, rising slowly from the river, enveloped her as she disappeared up the bank, and the swollen current and floundering masses of ice presented a hopeless barrier between her and her pursuer. ❞

—Harriet Beecher Stowe, *Uncle Tom's Cabin*

Stowe's book was popular in the North. But white Southerners argued that the book presented a false picture of the South and slavery.

▲ **CAUSES AND EFFECTS** Explain how the Fugitive Slave Act affected the country.

History Makers

Harriet Beecher Stowe   1811–1896

Harriet Beecher Stowe came from a family of abolitionists. While Stowe and her family were living in Cincinnati, Ohio, they bravely sheltered slaves fleeing from the neighboring slave state of Kentucky. Outrage at the Fugitive Slave Act of 1850 led Stowe to write *Uncle Tom's Cabin*. This novel, published in 1852, revealed the cruelties of slavery. But it also went a step further—and showed the evil effects that slavery had on slaveholders themselves.

Uncle Tom's Cabin made Stowe famous. It was translated into more than 20 languages. Because of its popularity, it drew the world's attention to the injustice of slavery in the South.

CRITICAL THINKING **Draw Conclusions** Why was the novel so unpopular in the South?

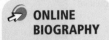 **ONLINE BIOGRAPHY** For more on Harriet Beecher Stowe, go to the **Research & Writing Center** @ ClassZone.com

Violence Erupts

KEY QUESTION Why did violence erupt in Kansas and Congress?

The Fugitive Slave Act and *Uncle Tom's Cabin* heightened tension between the North and South. As political tensions increased, the issue of slavery in the territories brought bloodshed to the West and even to Congress itself.

The Kansas-Nebraska Act In 1854, Senator Douglas drafted a bill to organize the Nebraska Territory. This bill became known as the **Kansas-Nebraska Act**. It proposed to divide the territory into two parts—Nebraska and Kansas.

To get Southern support for the bill, Douglas suggested that **popular sovereignty** should be used to decide whether a territory becomes either slave or free. Popular sovereignty is a system that allows residents to vote to decide an issue. Southerners liked the bill because people would be able to vote for slavery in territories where it had been banned by the Missouri Compromise. However, if the bill passed, it would mean the destruction of the Missouri Compromise.

The bill angered opponents of slavery, but it passed. Few people realized that the Kansas-Nebraska Act would soon turn Kansas into a violent and bloody battleground over the issue of slavery.

COMPARING *Free States, Slave States, and Territories*

Compromise of 1850

OREGON TERRITORY 1848
MINN. TERR. 1849
UNORGANIZED TERRITORY
UTAH TERRITORY 1850
CALIFORNIA 1850
NEW MEXICO TERRITORY 1850

Kansas-Nebraska Act *1854*

WASH. TERR.
OREGON TERR.
NEBRASKA TERRITORY 1854
KANSAS TERR. 1854

Free States
Territory closed to slavery
Slave states
Territory open to slavery

Senators debate the Compromise of 1850.

Connect Geography & History

1. **Place** How were the political divisions of the East carried into the West?

2. **Evaluate** Why would Northerners believe that slavery was spreading?

Bleeding Kansas During the election of March 1855, there were more proslavery than antislavery settlers in the Kansas Territory. After five thousand residents of neighboring Missouri came and voted illegally, the Kansas legislature was filled with proslavery representatives.

Antislavery settlers rejected the elected government. Settlers on both sides armed themselves. In May, a proslavery mob looted the town of Lawrence, Kansas. This attack was called the Sack of Lawrence.

In response, John Brown, an extreme abolitionist, led seven other men in a massacre of five of his proslavery neighbors. This attack is known as the Potawatomie Massacre, after the creek near where the victims were found. As news of the violence spread, civil war broke out in Kansas. It continued for three years, and the territory came to be called "Bleeding Kansas."

Violence in Congress In May 1856, Senator Charles Sumner of Massachusetts spoke against the proslavery forces in Kansas. In his speech, Sumner insulted A. P. Butler, a senator from South Carolina.

Preston Brooks, a relative of Butler, heard about Sumner's speech. He attacked Sumner, who was sitting at his desk in Congress. Brooks beat Sumner unconscious with his cane, causing severe injuries that disabled him for years.

Brooks was cheered in the South. But Northerners were shocked at the violence in the Senate. "Bleeding Kansas" and "Bleeding Sumner" became rallying cries for antislavery Northerners. In their anger over events, antislavery forces united to create a new political organization—the Republican Party.

SUMMARIZE Describe the events that led to violence in Kansas.

Illinois Learning Standards *Review*

 ONLINE QUIZ
For test practice, go to
Interactive Review @ ClassZone.com

TERMS & NAMES

1. Explain the importance of

- Wilmot Proviso
- Free-Soil Party
- Stephen A. Douglas
- Compromise of 1850
- Fugitive Slave Act
- Harriet Beecher Stowe
- *Uncle Tom's Cabin*
- Kansas-Nebraska Act

USING YOUR READING NOTES

2. Compare and Contrast Complete the diagram you started at the beginning of this section.

Northern Economy	Southern Economy
	relied on plantation farming

KEY IDEAS

3. What were two ways that the North and the South differed by the 1850s?

4. How did the War with Mexico provoke disagreements between the North and the South?

5. Why was the Kansas-Nebraska Act so controversial?

CRITICAL THINKING

6. Causes and Effects How did *Uncle Tom's Cabin* affect national politics?

7. Problems and Solutions What might have been done to prevent the violence in Kansas?

8. **Art** Research the architecture of the North and South in the 19th century. Then create a travel poster showing the kinds of houses a visitor might see in each section of the country.

Connect Geography & History

Land Use and Slavery

In 1850 cotton was the main cash crop of the lower South. But there was a problem: cotton exhausts the fertility of the soil. So planters had to abandon farmland and move west into new land. As planters moved west, they brought hundreds of thousands of enslaved people with them to farm the land.

One of the largest concentrations of cotton plantations was along the Mississippi River. The lower Mississippi offered excellent transportation for the crops. It also provided fertile soil for agriculture.

TENNESSEE

ARKANSAS

Mississippi River

ALABAMA

MISSISSIPPI

LOUISIANA

New Orleans

Cotton Production

45
30   In bales
15   per square
5   mile

New Orleans, the main port for shipments of cotton on the Mississippi River

In some places along the river, cranes were used to load cotton onto steamboats.

Enslaved people and their children shown outside the plantation slave cabins

Connect Geography & History

1. **Make Inferences** Why would this region of the South have had such a large African-American population?

2. **Draw Conclusions** Why did New Orleans become such an important city?

See Geography Handbook, pages A1–A17.

▶ Key Ideas

BEFORE, YOU LEARNED
Rising anger over slavery destroyed compromise between the North and South and led to violence.

NOW YOU WILL LEARN
The formation of the antislavery Republican Party further divided the country.

▶ Vocabulary

TERMS & NAMES

Republican Party political party formed in 1854 by opponents of slavery

John C. Frémont Republican presidential candidate in 1856

James Buchanan Democratic presidential candidate in 1856

Dred Scott v. Sandford 1856 Supreme Court case in which a slave, Dred Scott, sued for his freedom; the Court ruled against Scott

Roger B. Taney (TAW•nee) Supreme Court chief justice who wrote the majority opinion in the case of *Dred Scott* v. *Sandford*

Abraham Lincoln Illinois Republican who ran against Stephen A. Douglas in 1858

Harpers Ferry federal arsenal in Virginia; captured in 1859 during an antislavery revolt

REVIEW

Whig Party political party organized in 1834 to oppose the policies of Andrew Jackson

Know-Nothing Party anti-immigrant party formed in the 1850s

Visual Vocabulary
Harpers Ferry today

▶ Reading Strategy

Re-create the diagram shown at right. As you read and respond to the **KEY QUESTIONS**, use the center oval to record the main idea; use the outer ovals to note important details.

 See Skillbuilder Handbook, page R4.

MAIN IDEAS AND DETAILS

Detail

Detail

Main Idea
Slavery affected politics in the 1850s.

GRAPHIC ORGANIZERS
Go to **Interactive Review** @ ClassZone.com

Slavery Dominates Politics

14.C.3 Compare historical issues involving rights, roles and status of individuals in relation to municipalities, states and the nation.
16.B.3c Describe the way the Constitution has changed over time as a result of amendments and Supreme Court decisions.

One American's Story

She was only 13, but her story edged the nation closer to civil war. Emily Edmondson grew up in slavery in Washington, D.C. On April 15, 1848, Emily, her 15-year-old sister Mary, and four of her brothers joined more than 70 other slaves in an escape attempt. Hidden on board a ship, they sailed toward freedom in the North. However, their ship was pursued and captured. Despite a debate in Congress and a public outcry, Emily and her sister were shipped to New Orleans to be resold.

In New Orleans an outbreak of yellow fever forced slave traders to send the girls back to the safety of Virginia. It was then that the girls' parents contacted Harriet Beecher Stowe's brother, who was a famous abolitionist. He raised enough money to buy their freedom. Harriet Beecher Stowe arranged for the girls to attend Oberlin College. (In the photo at right, they appear in plaid dresses.)

Although Mary died young, Emily became a famous abolitionist. Her story motivated various antislavery groups to create the Republican Party—a party dedicated to the elimination of slavery.

Emily Edmondson (standing center behind table) with her sister (in plaid at far left) as well as Frederick Douglass and others at an abolitionist convention, 1850

Slavery and Political Division

🔻 **KEY QUESTION** How did the issue of slavery affect political parties?

As you have read, the Kansas-Nebraska Act allowed residents of a new territory to vote either for or against slavery. This act caused a political crisis for the **Whig Party**. The Whig party had been formed in 1834 to oppose the policies of Andrew Jackson. Now the act began to tear the party apart. Southern

Whigs supported the act. Northern Whigs opposed it. There was no room for compromise. As a result, the Whig Party split into two factions.

The Republican Party Forms Some of the Southern Whigs joined the Democratic Party. Others looked for leaders who supported slavery and the Union. The Northern Whigs, however, joined with other rivals and formed the **Republican Party**.

The Republican Party was both an antislavery party and a sectional party that sought to protect the interests of the North. Republicans not only used moral arguments against slavery, they also looked down on the South's agricultural system based on enslaved labor.

The Republicans quickly gained strength in the North. "Bleeding Kansas" was the key to the Republican rise. Many blamed the violence on the Democrats. With the 1856 elections nearing, Republicans seized the chance to gain seats in Congress and win the presidency.

The Republicans needed a strong presidential candidate in 1856 to strengthen their young party. They nominated **John C. Frémont**. Frémont was a handsome young hero known for his explorations in the West. He was nicknamed "the Pathfinder."

Republicans liked Frémont because he wanted California and Kansas admitted as free states. Also, he did not have a controversial political past. Even so, the Republican position on slavery was so unpopular in the South that Frémont's name did not appear on the ballot there.

Election of 1856 The Democrats nominated **James Buchanan** for the presidency in 1856. As ambassador to Great Britain, he had been in England since 1853 and had spoken neither for nor against the Kansas-Nebraska Act.

REPUBLICAN PARTY
• opposes expansion of slavery
• opposes Kansas-Nebraska Act

John Frémont

Northern interests
Abolitionists
Free Soil Party
Northern Whigs

DEMOCRATIC PARTY
• supports states' rights
• favors limited government

James Buchanan

Slavery supporters
Southern Whigs

Buchanan said little about slavery and claimed that his goal was to maintain the Union. Buchanan appealed to Southerners, especially to people in the upper South and the border states, and to Northerners who feared that Frémont's election could tear the nation apart.

The American Party, or **Know-Nothing Party**, an anti-immigrant party, nominated Millard Fillmore as presidential candidate in 1856. Fillmore had been president following the death of Zachary Taylor, from 1850 until 1853. But the Know-Nothings were divided over slavery and had little strength.

The 1856 presidential election turned into two separate races. In the North, it was Buchanan against Frémont. In the South, it was Buchanan against Fillmore. Buchanan won. He carried all the slave states except Maryland, where Fillmore claimed his only victory. Buchanan also won several Northern states, such as Pennsylvania and Illinois.

Although he lost the election, Frémont won 11 Northern states. These results showed two things. First, the Republican Party was a major force in the North. Second, slavery was dividing the nation along sectional lines.

🔺 **MAIN IDEAS & DETAILS** Explain how the issue of slavery affected political parties.

The Breaking Point

🔻 **KEY QUESTION** What events brought the nation to a crisis?

The argument over slavery was affecting not only Congressional politics. The slavery debate was forcing its way into another branch of government—the judiciary. In the mid-1850s, a legal case involving an enslaved man named Dred Scott reached the Supreme Court. The Supreme Court's decision in this case divided the country even further.

Article covering the Dred Scott case from *Frank Leslie's Illustrated Newspaper*

The Case of Dred Scott Scott had been an enslaved person in Missouri. However, he had lived for a time in free territories before being taken back to Missouri. After his owner's death, Dred Scott argued that he was a free man because he had lived in territories where slavery was illegal. Scott's wife and their two daughters also sued in court for their freedom. Scott's case, *Dred Scott v. Sandford*, reached the Supreme Court in 1856.

In 1857, the Court ruled against Scott. Chief Justice **Roger B. Taney** (TAW•nee) stated that Dred Scott was not a U.S. citizen. As a result, he could not sue in U.S. courts. Taney also ruled that Scott was bound by Missouri's slave code because he had lived in Missouri.

Taney also argued that banning slavery in the territories would violate slaveholders' property rights, protected by the Fifth Amendment. This meant that legislation such as the Missouri Compromise was unconstitutional.

Dred Scott v. Sandford (1857)

KEY ISSUE citizenship

KEY PEOPLE

Dred Scott	b. 1795, d. 1858; enslaved to John and Irene Emerson
John and Irene Emerson	"owners" of Dred and Harriet Scott; residents of Missouri
John Sanford	executor of the Emersons' estate (Sanford's name was misspelled "Sandford" by a court clerk)
Roger Taney	Chief justice of the Supreme Court (1836–1864)

History Makers

Roger Taney
1777–1864

Roger Taney was born in Maryland, the son of plantation owners. Personally, he abhorred slavery, and upon inheriting his family's plantation, he freed all his slaves.

In 1831 he became President Andrew Jackson's attorney general. In 1836 Taney was appointed chief justice in the Supreme Court.

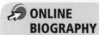 **ONLINE BIOGRAPHY**

For more on the life of Roger Taney, go to the **Research & Writing Center @ ClassZone.com**

The Case

John and Irene Emerson lived in Missouri. John worked for the military, so he traveled, and when he did he brought his slave Dred Scott with him. After the Emersons died, Dred Scott sued their estate for his freedom. Scott's lawyers argued that Scott became free when he lived with Emerson in Illinois—a free state—and in Wisconsin, which was made a free territory by the Missouri Compromise.

The Court's Decision The court protected and even expanded slavery. It said that, as a slave, Dred Scott was property. He was not a citizen; he would not be a citizen even if he were freed. He had no rights; he could not even file a lawsuit. The court also said that the Congress had no power to limit slavery, because any such limits would violate the Constitutional property rights of slaveholders.

Historical Impact The decision meant that the Missouri Compromise was void, because Congress could not limit slavery in the territories. Further, it seemed to imply that no state could be a free state because states could not prohibit their citizens from importing, owning, or buying and selling slaves.

Dred Scott thrilled slaveowners, while it outraged free-soilers and abolitionists. By deepening the sectional divide between North and South, the decision helped bring about the Civil War. Following the Civil War, the 14th Amendment to the U.S. Constitution was passed, undoing the Dred Scott decision.

CRITICAL THINKING

1. **Summarize** What was the basis of Scott's argument, and why did the Taney court disagree?

2. **Make Inferences** How did this decision bring the nation closer to civil war?

The Lincoln-Douglas Debate After the Dred Scott decision, the Republicans charged that the Democrats wanted to legalize slavery not only in all U.S. territories but in all the states. They used this charge to attack individual Democrats. Stephen A. Douglas, sponsor of the Kansas-Nebraska Act, was one of their main targets in 1858. That year, Illinois Republicans nominated **Abraham Lincoln** to challenge Douglas for his U.S. Senate seat. In his first campaign speech, Lincoln expressed the Northern fear that Southerners wanted to expand slavery to the entire nation. He laid the groundwork for his argument by using a phrase from the Bible.

PRIMARY SOURCE

❝ 'A house divided against itself cannot stand.' I believe this government cannot endure, permanently, half slave and half free. I do not expect the Union to be dissolved; I do not expect the house to fall; but I do expect it will cease to be divided. It will become all one thing, or all the other. **❞**

—Abraham Lincoln, Springfield, Illinois, June 16, 1858

Later in the year, the two men held debates across Illinois in front of large crowds. The Lincoln-Douglas debates are models of political debate.

CONNECT ↪ *To Today*

POLITICAL DEBATE

In the mid-19th century, large crowds listened to candidates debate the issues of the day. Lincoln debated Douglas seven times; thousands of people came to listen.

The first televised presidential debate, in 1960, featured candidates John F. Kennedy and Richard Nixon. Today, millions watch televised debates. These debates have strict rules—about the topics, the length of each debate and its closing arguments, and so forth. In contrast to the Lincoln-Douglas debates, today's live audiences are instructed not to applaud or make any noise while the debate is in progress.

Senator John Kerry (*standing*) debates President George W. Bush (*right, seated*) in a 2004 "town meeting" style debate.

CRITICAL THINKING
Make Generalizations What factors might influence your opinion of a candidate during a political debate?

REACHING COMPROMISE

Compromise comes when two people or groups each give way a little to settle their dispute. In the mid-19th century, the failure to compromise led to violence and eventually to a civil war in which hundreds of thousands of Americans died.

Today, negotiation and compromise—whether in government or business or in classrooms and on playgrounds—is just as important as it was in the 19th century. Educational programs under the names of peace education, conflict resolution, and negotiation teach compromising skills. The purpose of these programs is not just to resolve conflicts and prevent violence, but to develop skills for citizenship.

CRITICAL THINKING **Make Inferences** What factors lead to a successful compromise? Give an example of a time when you've compromised.

 See Citizenship Handbook, pages 300–307.

Activity

Discuss how to promote compromise in your school.

1 Respect yourself and encourage your friends to respect others.

2 Encourage your friends to be good observers.

3 Help your friends pause a moment if something angers them.

4 During disagreements, encourage others to keep from shouting.

5 Compromise is a form of bargaining. Next time you overhear a dispute, suggest ways that the two parties might reach an agreement.

The two men addressed the expansion of slavery. For Lincoln, slavery was "a moral, a social, and a political wrong." But he did not suggest that he wanted to end slavery where it existed. He argued only that slavery should not be expanded.

Douglas agreed that it was the national government's role to prevent the expansion of slavery. But he argued that popular sovereignty was the best way to address the issue because it was the most democratic method of doing so.

Popular sovereignty was a problem for Douglas. The Supreme Court decision in the Dred Scott case had made popular sovereignty unconstitutional. Why? It said that people could not vote to ban slavery, because doing so would take away slaveholders' property rights. (Slaves were considered property.) In a debate at Freeport, Illinois, Lincoln asked Douglas if he thought people in a territory who were against slavery could legally prohibit it—despite the Dred Scott decision.

Douglas replied that it did not matter what the Supreme Court might decide about slavery because "the people have the lawful means to introduce it or exclude it as they please." Douglas won reelection. Lincoln, despite his loss, became a national figure and strengthened his position in the Republican Party.

John Brown's Raid In 1859, John Brown, who had murdered proslavery Kansans three years before, added to the sectional tensions. Brown wanted to provoke a slave uprising. To do this, he planned to capture the weapons in the U.S. arsenal at **Harpers Ferry**, Virginia.

On October 16, 1859, Brown and 18 followers—13 whites and 5 blacks—captured the Harpers Ferry arsenal. Brown then sent out the word to rally and arm local slaves. But no slaves joined the fight. U.S. marines attacked Brown at Harpers Ferry. Some of his men escaped, but Brown and six others were captured, and ten men were killed.

John Brown Going to His Hanging, by Horace Pippin

Brown was tried for murder and betrayal of his country, or treason. He was also accused of conspiracy to cause a slave revolt. Brown was convicted and sentenced to hang. On the day he was hanged, abolitionists tolled bells and fired guns in his honor. Southerners were enraged by Brown's actions and horrified by Northern reactions to his death. As the nation headed toward the election of 1860, the issue of slavery had raised sectional tensions to the breaking point.

 SUMMARIZE Describe the events that brought the nation to a crisis.

Illinois Learning Standards *Review*

 ONLINE QUIZ
For test practice, go to
Interactive Review @ ClassZone.com

TERMS & NAMES

1. Explain the importance of

- Republican Party
- Roger B. Taney
- John C. Frémont
- Abraham Lincoln
- James Buchanan
- Harpers Ferry
- *Dred Scott* v. *Sandford*

USING YOUR READING NOTES

2. Main Ideas and Details Complete the diagram you started at the beginning of this section.

KEY IDEAS

3. Why was the Republican Party created?

4. What were the consequences of the Dred Scott decision for enslaved people?

5. How did John Brown's attack on Harpers Ferry increase tensions between the North and the South?

CRITICAL THINKING

6. Make Inferences How did the opinion in the Dred Scott case threaten the idea of popular sovereignty?

7. Draw Conclusions What did the Dred Scott decision reveal about Southern attitudes to slavery?

8. Writing **Speech** Imagine you are a candidate in the 1856 election. Write a speech explaining your political opinions.

▶ Key Ideas

BEFORE, YOU LEARNED

The formation of the antislavery Republican Party further divided the country.

NOW YOU WILL LEARN

The election of Abraham Lincoln as president in 1860 led seven Southern states to secede from the Union.

▶ Vocabulary

TERMS & NAMES

Confederate States of America confederation formed in 1861 by the Southern states after their secession from the Union

Jefferson Davis first president of the Confederate States of America

Crittenden Compromise compromise introduced in 1861 that might have prevented secession

BACKGROUND VOCABULARY

platform statement of beliefs

secede to withdraw

REVIEW

states' rights idea that the states have certain rights that the federal government cannot overrule

Visual Vocabulary
Jefferson Davis

▶ Reading Strategy

Re-create the diagram shown at right. As you read and respond to the **KEY QUESTIONS**, use the diagram to show why the Democratic Party broke apart.

 See Skillbuilder Handbook, page R6.

CATEGORIZE

Southern Democrats	Northern Democrats
wanted party to defend slavery	

 GRAPHIC ORGANIZERS
Go to **Interactive Review** @ ClassZone.com

Lincoln's Election and Southern Secession

14.B.3 Identify and compare the basic political systems of Illinois and the United States as prescribed in their constitutions.
14.D.3 Describe roles and influences of individuals, groups and media in shaping current Illinois and United States public policy (e.g., *general public opinion, special interest groups, formal parties, media*).

One American's Story

Mary Boykin Chesnut was born into wealth but died in poverty, one of the many victims of the political events that tore the nation apart.

Born in South Carolina in 1823, Mary grew up in a world of privilege and political power. At the age of 17 she married James Chesnut, a wealthy lawyer who became a senator. James supported slavery and resigned his senate seat at the news of Lincoln's election in 1860. Mary was also upset by this political event, and recorded the moment when she first heard the news.

Wedding photo of Mary and James Chesnut

PRIMARY SOURCE

❝ CHARLESTON, S.C., November 8, 1860. - Yesterday on the train, just before we reached Fernandina, a woman called out: "That settles the hash." Tanny touched me on the shoulder and said: "Lincoln's elected." "How do you know?" "The man over there has a telegram."

The excitement was very great. Everybody was talking at the same time. One, a little more moved than the others, stood up and said despondently: "The die is cast; no more vain regrets; sad forebodings are useless; the stake is life or death." ❞

—Mary Boykin Chesnut, *A Diary from Dixie*

For Mary Chesnut, Lincoln's election was a threat. Perhaps she foresaw the coming war that would take her from riches to poverty. But like the other Southerners on the train, she knew that Lincoln's election meant there could be no more compromise. Now there was no choice left but to fight.

The Election of 1860

▼ **KEY QUESTION** How did the 1860 election reveal the divisions in the country?

In April, the Democratic convention was held in Charleston, South Carolina. It was clear that Northern and Southern Democrats had very different ideas about slavery. The Democratic Party began to split along sectional lines.

The Split in the Democratic Party The Southerners wanted the party to defend slavery in the party's **platform**, or statement of beliefs. But Northerners wanted the platform to support popular sovereignty as a way of deciding whether a territory became a free state or a slave state. The Northerners won the platform vote, causing many Southern delegates to leave the convention before the Democrats chose a candidate for the presidential election.

The Democrats met again in Baltimore to choose a candidate. Northerners and Southerners remained at odds. Most Southerners left the meeting.

The Northern Democrats backed Stephen A. Douglas and his support for popular sovereignty. Meanwhile, proslavery Southern Democrats nominated vice president John Breckinridge of Kentucky.

The Republicans had already nominated Abraham Lincoln. Also in the race was a fourth party—the Constitutional Union Party. Its members had one aim—to preserve the Union. They nominated John Bell of Tennessee.

Animated GEOGRAPHY

Election of 1860

Click here to preview the Election of 1860 map @ ClassZone.com

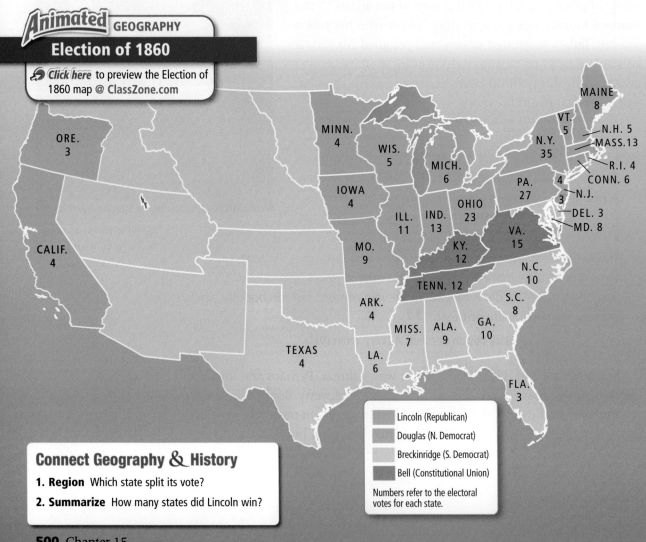

Legend:
- Lincoln (Republican)
- Douglas (N. Democrat)
- Breckinridge (S. Democrat)
- Bell (Constitutional Union)

Numbers refer to the electoral votes for each state.

Connect Geography & History

1. **Region** Which state split its vote?

2. **Summarize** How many states did Lincoln win?

FOOTRACE TO THE WHITE HOUSE

In this cartoon from 1860, the rival presidential candidates are competing in a footrace. As they race toward the White House, it is obvious which runner is going to win.

Bell:
"Bless my soul . . . I give up."

Breckinridge:
"That long legged Abolitionist is getting ahead of us after all."

Douglas:
"I never run so in my life."

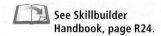
the White House

CRITICAL THINKING

1. **Make Inferences** What common symbol for a political campaign is used in the cartoon?

2. **Synthesize** What is the basic message of the cartoon?

See Skillbuilder Handbook, page R24.

Two Political Races The election of 1860 turned into two different races for the presidency—one in the North and one in the South. Lincoln and Douglas were the only candidates with much support in the North. Breckinridge and Bell competed for Southern votes.

Lincoln and Breckinridge were considered to have the most extreme views on slavery. Lincoln opposed the expansion of slavery into the territories. Breckinridge insisted that the federal government be required to protect slavery in any territory. Douglas and Bell were considered moderates because neither wanted the federal government to pass new laws on slavery.

The outcome of the election made it clear that the nation was tired of compromise. Lincoln defeated Douglas in the North. Breckinridge carried most of the South. Douglas and Bell managed to win only in the border states. Because the North had a larger population, Lincoln won the election.

Despite Lincoln's statements that he would do nothing to abolish slavery in the South, white Southerners did not trust him. Many were sure that he and the other Republicans would move to ban slavery. As a result, white Southerners saw the Republican victory as a threat to their way of life.

▲ **CATEGORIZE** Explain the divisions that affected political parties in 1860.

Southern States Secede

▼ **KEY QUESTION** How did seven Southern states justify their decision to secede?

Even before the election, Southerners had warned that if Lincoln won the presidency, Southern states would **secede**, or withdraw, from the Union.

The Confederate States of America Southerners based their arguments on **states' rights**, the idea that states have certain rights that the federal government cannot overrule. They argued that since the states had voluntarily joined the Union, they could voluntarily leave it.

On December 20, 1860, South Carolina became the first state to secede. Other states in the Deep South, where the economies depended on slavery and cotton production, also considered secession. Shortly after, Mississippi, Florida, Alabama, Georgia, Louisiana, and Texas joined South Carolina.

In early February 1861, the states that had seceded met in Montgomery, Alabama. They formed the **Confederate States of America**. The convention named **Jefferson Davis** president of the Confederacy.

The convention then drafted a constitution. The Confederate Constitution was modeled on the U.S. Constitution. But there were a few important differences. For example, the Confederate Constitution supported states' rights. It also protected slavery in the Confederacy, including any territories it might acquire.

Having formed its government, the Confederate states made plans to defend their separation from the Union. Some believed that war between the states could not be avoided. But everyone waited to see what the Union government would do in response.

The Union's Response Northerners considered the secession of the Southern states was unconstitutional. President James Buchanan argued against secession. He believed that the states did not have the right to withdraw from the Union because the federal government, not the state governments, was sovereign. If secession were permitted, the Union would become weak, like a "rope of sand." He believed that the U.S. Constitution was framed to prevent such a thing from happening.

In addition to these issues, secession raised the issue of majority rule. Southerners complained that Northerners intended to use their majority to force the South to abolish slavery. But Northerners responded that Southerners were not willing to live with the election results. As Northern writer James Russell Lowell wrote, "[The Southerners'] quarrel is not with the Republican Party, but with the theory of Democracy."

The Failure of Compromise With the states in the lower South forming a new government, some people continued to seek compromise. Senator John J. Crittenden of Kentucky proposed that slavery should be protected south of the line established in the Missouri Compromise, that Congress should not abolish slavery in a slave state, and that the federal government should compensate the owners of fugitive slaves. **The Crittenden Compromise** was presented to Congress in early 1861, but it was defeated in the Senate.

Connecting History

Federalism
Many Southerners claimed that their fight for independence from the federal government was an echo of America's fight to separate from British tyranny during the Revolutionary War.

Detail of secession banner with tree representing South Carolina

With the election of 1860, it was clear that attempts at compromise had failed. The issue of slavery had pulled the nation apart. Every Congressional attempt to reach a compromise only served to enrage one section of the country or the other. The following chart shows how the events and laws of these years brought the nation closer to civil war.

CONNECT to the Essential Question

What issues and events shattered the nation's unity and led to civil war?

	EVENT	NORTHERN REACTION	SOUTHERN REACTION
1846	**War with Mexico**	fear that slavery would expand into the territories won from Mexico	desire to extend slavery into territory taken from Mexico
1846	**Wilmot Proviso proposes that slavery be outlawed in territory taken from Mexico.**	support for Wilmot Proviso founding of Free-Soil Party dedicated to stopping expansion of slavery	Southerners fear that more free states will be created and upset the balance of power. Southern senators prevent passage of Wilmot Proviso
1850	**Compromise of 1850**	relief that California would be a free state outrage over Fugitive Slave Act	relief that Congress would not ban slavery from territories won from Mexico with the exception of California satisfaction with Fugitive Slave Act
1852	***Uncle Tom's Cabin* is published.**	The novel becomes highly popular.	Southerners believe the book gives a false impression of the South and slavery.
1854	**Kansas–Nebraska Act**	anger over repeal of Missouri Compromise, which banned slavery in some territories	support for popular sovereignty, which allowed people to vote for slavery in territories where Missouri Compromise had banned it
1854	**Whig Party splits over Kansas–Nebraska Act.**	Northern Whigs join other groups to form antislavery Republican Party.	Southern Whigs join Democrats.
1860	**Election of 1860**	satisfaction with election of Republican candidate Abraham Lincoln	Seven Southern states secede from Union.

CRITICAL THINKING Causes and Effects Why did this series of laws and events shatter the unity of the nation?

Lincoln's Inauguration With the hopes for compromise fading, Americans waited for Lincoln's inauguration. What would the new president do about the crisis? On March 4, Lincoln took the oath of office and gave his First Inaugural Address. He assured the South that he had no intention of abolishing slavery there. But he spoke forcefully against secession. Then he ended his speech with an appeal to friendship.

PRIMARY SOURCE

❝ We are not enemies, but friends. We must not be enemies. Though passion may have strained, it must not break our bonds of affection. The mystic chords of memory, stretching from every battle-field and patriot grave, to every living heart and hearthstone, all over this broad land, will yet swell the chorus of the Union, when again touched, as surely they will be, by the better angels of our nature. ❞

Abraham Lincoln, *First Inaugural Address*

Lincoln did not want to invade the South. But he would not abandon the government's forts that stood on Southern soil. These forts would soon need to be resupplied. Throughout March and into April, Northerners and Southerners waited anxiously to see what would happen next.

 SEQUENCE Explain how the Southern states justified secession.

 Illinois Learning Standards *Review*

ONLINE QUIZ
For test practice, go to
Interactive Review @ ClassZone.com

TERMS & NAMES

1. Explain the importance of
   - Confederate States of America
   - Jefferson Davis
   - Crittenden Compromise

USING YOUR READING NOTES

2. **Categorize** Complete the diagram you started at the beginning of this section.

Southern Democrats	Northern Democrats
wanted party to defend slavery	

KEY IDEAS

3. Who were the candidates in the 1860 presidential election, and what policies did each candidate support?

4. What attempts did the North and the South make to compromise? What were the results?

CRITICAL THINKING

5. **Analyze Point of View** Do you think the Southern states seceded to protect slavery or states' rights?

6. **Connect** *to* **Today** What can the events in this section teach us about compromise in the political process today?

7. **Writing** **News Article** Imagine you are a newspaper reporter covering the 1860 election. Write a short analysis of the election results for either Northern or Southern readers.

Chapter Summary

1 **Key Idea**
Rising anger over slavery increased tensions between the North and South and led to violence.

2 **Key Idea**
The formation of the antislavery Republican Party further divided the country.

3 **Key Idea**
The election of Abraham Lincoln as president in 1860 led seven Southern states to secede from the Union.

For detailed Review and Study Notes go to **Interactive Review** @ ClassZone.com

Name Game

Use the Terms & Names list to identify each sentence online or on your own paper.

1. I was the first president of the Confederacy. _____
   Jefferson Davis

2. This compromise of 1861 might have prevented secession. _____.

3. I am the Illinois senator who backed the Compromise of 1850. _____

4. I ran for President as a Democrat in 1856. _____

5. I wrote a novel about slavery. _____

6. I presided in the case of *Dred Scott* v. *Sandford*. _____

7. This party's slogan was "Free Soil, Free Speech, Free Labor, and Free Men." _____

8. This 1850 law was meant to help slaveholders recapture runaway slaves. _____

9. I was the Republican candidate in 1856. _____

10. This proposal was meant to outlaw slavery in new territories. _____

A. Harriet Beecher Stowe
B. Free-Soil Party
C. Roger B. Taney
D. Crittenden Compromise
E. Abraham Lincoln
F. James Buchanan
G. Wilmot Proviso
H. Jefferson Davis
I. Confederate States of America
J. Fugitive Slave Act
K. Stephen A. Douglas
L. John Frémont

Activities

CROSSWORD PUZZLE

Complete the online puzzle to show what you know about the buildup to the Civil War.

ACROSS
1. The election of this man frightened the Southern states.

GEOGAME

Use this online map to reinforce your understanding of the sectional divide. Drag and drop the labels to identify slave states and free states. A scorecard helps you keep track of your progress online.

slave state

free state

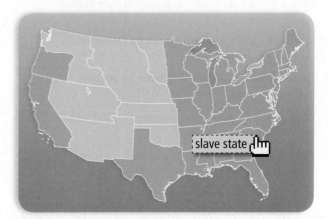

slave state

VOCABULARY

Explain the significance of each of the following.

1. Harriet Beecher Stowe
2. Stephen A. Douglas
3. Harpers Ferry
4. Jefferson Davis
5. Roger B. Taney
6. Abraham Lincoln
7. *Dred Scott* v. *Sandford*
8. James Buchanan
9. John C. Frémont

Explain how the terms and names in each group are related.

10. Stephen A. Douglas, Compromise of 1850, Kansas-Nebraska Act
11. Compromise of 1850, Fugitive Slave Act
12. James Buchanan, John C. Frémont
13. John Brown, Harpers Ferry
14. Free-Soil Party, Wilmot Proviso

KEY IDEAS

1 Tensions Rise Between North and South (pages 480–487)

15. In what ways did the North and the South differ in the 1840s?
16. How did Southerners react to the Wilmot Proviso?

2 Slavery Dominates Politics (pages 490–497)

17. What positions did Lincoln and Douglas take in their debates?
18. Why were Southerners so angry about John Brown's attack on Harpers Ferry?

3 Lincoln's Election and Southern Secession (pages 498–504)

19. What were the results of the election of 1860, and what did these results show?
20. Why did Southerners want to secede?

CRITICAL THINKING

21. **Compare and Contrast** What did the Compromise of 1850 and the Kansas-Nebraska Act have in common?
22. **Analyze Point of View** Why did Northerners and Southerners disagree about the Kansas-Nebraska Act?
23. **Evaluate** Which event do you think caused the most damage to the relationship between the North and the South?
24. **Compare and Contrast** Make a chart to compare the fears that people in each section of the country had about the other section's intentions.

Northern Fears	Southern Fears
slavery was expanding	

25. **WHAT IF?** What might have been done in the 1850s to prevent the Southern states from seceding?
26. **Draw Conclusions** Which sectional economy was better prepared for war—the industrial North or the agricultural South?
27. **Analyze Primary Sources** What does this poster tell you about how people in the North reacted to the Fugitive Slave Act?

DOCUMENT-BASED QUESTIONS

PART 1: Short Answer

Study each document carefully and answer the questions that follow.

DOCUMENT 1

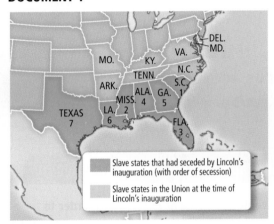

Slave states that had seceded by Lincoln's inauguration (with order of secession)

Slave states in the Union at the time of Lincoln's inauguration

1. Examine this map of secession. At the time of Lincoln's inauguration, where were the slave states that remained in the Union?

DOCUMENT 2

PRIMARY SOURCE

❝ In January next we shall take leave of the Union and shall construct with our Sister Cotton States a government for ourselves. Whether the other Slave States will join seems very uncertain at least for the present. The condition of affairs at the North since the election of an Abolitionist for President makes it necessary for us to get away as quickly as possible. ❞

—E. B. Heyward, South Carolina, Nov. 20, 1860

2. Why does the writer support secession?

Part 2: Essay

3. Using information from the documents, your answers to the questions in Part 1, and your knowledge of U.S. history, write a brief essay that discusses why the Southern states began seceding at the news of Lincoln's election victory.

YOU BE THE HISTORIAN

28. **Make Inferences** Why did the Confederate government's support of states' rights threaten its own unity?

29. **WHAT IF?** Suppose the Supreme Court had ruled in favor of Dred Scott in *Dred Scott* v. *Sandford*. How might this have changed American history?

30. **Make Generalizations** How far back in American history can you trace the economic difference between North and South?

31. **Draw Conclusions** Why do you think so many Americans supported slavery when it seemed to contradict Jefferson's words from the Declaration of Independence that "all men are created equal"?

32. **Connect** *to* **Today** **Citizenship** What are some of the social, political, and economic trends in modern American life that can traced back to the North-South conflict and secession?

 Answer the
ESSENTIAL QUESTION
What issues and events shattered the nation's unity and led to civil war?

Written Response Write a four-paragraph response to the Essential Question. Be sure to consider the key ideas of each section as well as the most significant factors that led to the split between North and South. Use the Response Rubric below to guide your thinking and writing.

Response Rubric
A strong response will

• analyze the differences between the Northern and Southern states
• discuss the major events that led to the split between North and South
• show why the process of compromise broke down

CHAPTER

16

1. War Erupts
2. Life in the Army
3. No End in Sight

Detail of a painting of Union general McClellan

The Civil War Begins

1861–1862

 ESSENTIAL QUESTION

What events, leaders, and strategies shaped the early years of war?

CONNECT ⟳ **Geography & History**

What geographic features would the Union have to seize in order to defeat the Confederacy?

Think about:

1 how goods and weapons were transported in the South, which did not have an extensive railway system

2 the way the Southern economy relied on exporting cotton by ship

3 the position of New Orleans, the South's largest city

1861 July: Confederacy sets up its capital in Richmond.

Recruitment posters

1861

April: Confederate attack on Fort Sumter

Detail of a painting of Bull Run

1861 July: First Battle of Bull Run

▼

Effect Lincoln realizes he must raise a national army.

508 Chapter 16

Animated GEOGRAPHY & HISTORY

The Early Years of the War 1861–1862

Click here to preview the early years of the Civil War @ClassZone.com

Rivers could act as barriers dividing regions.

N.J.

PA.

IOWA

OHIO

Washington, D. C. Union capital

MD.

DEL.

Potomac R.

ILL.

IND.

1st Bull Run

VA.

Richmond, VA. Confederate capital

MO.

KY.

Fort Henry

Cumberland River

N.C.

Fort Donelson

Tennessee River

Rivers were transportation routes.

Shiloh

TENN.

Mississippi River

A P P A L A C H I A N   M O U N T A I N S

ARK.

Mountains were difficult for armies to cross.

S.C.

Fort Sumter

MISS.

ALA.

GA.

TEX.

LA.

	Union states
	Confederate states
	Union victory
	Confederate victory
	Strategic river

New Orleans **3**

FLA.

Ships carried Southern cotton to markets worldwide.

Civil War bugle

Drum of New York Infantry

1862 **February:** Union general Grant captures Fort Henry and Fort Donelson.

1862

1862 **April:** New Orleans captured by Union forces

▼

Effect The Confederacy loses its most important city.

September: Battle of Antietam

▼

Effect 23,000 casualties; Lee retreats

The Civil War Begins **509**

▶ Key Ideas

BEFORE, YOU LEARNED

Southern states seceded from the Union after the election of Abraham Lincoln in 1860.

NOW YOU WILL LEARN

After more Southern states joined the Confederacy, fighting began on Confederate territory.

▶ Vocabulary

TERMS & NAMES

Fort Sumter Union fort in the harbor of Charleston, South Carolina

Confederacy nation formed by Southern states

Robert E. Lee Confederate general, commander of the Army of Northern Virginia

border states slave states that bordered states in which slavery was illegal

Anaconda Plan Union strategy to defeat the Confederacy

First Battle of Bull Run first major battle of the Civil War

Thomas J. Jackson Confederate general at Bull Run

BACKGROUND VOCABULARY

uprising rebellion

populous heavily populated

Visual Vocabulary
Attack on Fort Sumter

▶ Reading Strategy

Re-create the diagram shown at right. As you read and respond to the **KEY QUESTIONS**, use the diagram to note problems faced by the Union and the Southern states and how they were addressed.

 See Skillbuilder Handbook, page R9.

PROBLEMS AND SOLUTIONS

Problem	Solution
What to do about the federal forts located in the Confederacy?	

 GRAPHIC ORGANIZERS
Go to **Interactive Review** @ ClassZone.com

War Erupts

16.C.3b Explain relationships among the American economy and slavery, immigration, industrialization, labor and urbanization, 1700–present.
18.B.3a Analyze how individuals and groups interact with and within institutions (e.g., educational, military).

One American's Story

Like other South Carolinians, Emma Holmes got caught up in the passions that led her state to secede. In her diary, she wrote about South Carolina's attack on **Fort Sumter**, a federal fort on an island in Charleston's harbor.

PRIMARY SOURCE

❝ [A]t half past four this morning, the heavy booming of cannons woke the city from its slumbers. . . . Every body seems relieved that what has been so long dreaded has come at last and so confident of victory that they seem not to think of the danger of their friends. . . . With the telescope I saw the shots as they struck the fort and [saw] the masonry crumbling. ❞

—Emma Holmes, *The Diary of Miss Emma Holmes 1861–1866*

Emma Holmes

Many Southerners expected a short war that they would easily win. Northerners expected the same. In this section, you will learn how Americans slowly realized that the war would be long and difficult.

First Shots at Fort Sumter

▼ **KEY QUESTION** What did Lincoln do about the forts in Confederate territory?

As Southern states seceded from the Union, they took control of most of the federal forts located within their borders. President Abraham Lincoln wrestled with a decision that might provoke war—what should he do about the forts that remained under federal control?

Lincoln's Decision In Charleston Harbor, Robert Anderson's garrison in Fort Sumter was running out of supplies.

Lincoln faced a difficult decision. If he sent supplies, he risked war. If he surrendered the fort, he would be giving in to the rebels. Lincoln decided to send supply ships and notified the leaders of the **Confederacy**—the nation formed by Southern states. Confederate leaders decided to attack the fort before the supply ships arrived.

On April 12, 1861, the Confederates opened fire. After enduring 34 hours of shelling, Anderson surrendered. No one was killed defending the fort, but the attack on Fort Sumter marked the beginning of the Civil War.

Lincoln Calls Out the Militia Two days after the surrender of Fort Sumter, President Lincoln asked the Union states to provide 75,000 militiamen for 90 days to put down the **uprising**, or rebellion, in the South. Citizens of the North responded with enthusiasm to the call to arms. A New York woman wrote, "it seems as if we never were alive till now; never had a country till now."

In the upper South, however, state leaders responded with defiance. The governor of Kentucky said that the state would "furnish no troops for the wicked purpose of subduing her sister Southern states." In the weeks that followed, Virginia, North Carolina, Tennessee, and Arkansas voted to join the Confederacy.

▲ **PROBLEMS AND SOLUTIONS** Explain how Lincoln tried to solve the problem of the federal forts.

History Makers

Abraham Lincoln   1809–1865

Today Abraham Lincoln, shown above with his son, is regarded as a national hero. Yet when Lincoln became President, many people in the North did not think he was equal to the enormous task before him.

Lincoln surprised his critics with his vision and his ability to organize and lead the war effort. In the nation's worst crisis, he focused on winning the war and preserving the Union. Throughout the war, Lincoln inspired fellow Americans to "dare to do our duty as we understand it."

CRITICAL THINKING Make Inferences
Why would the ability to inspire people be important in a wartime leader?

 ONLINE BIOGRAPHY   For more on Abraham Lincoln, go to the **Research & Writing Center** @ ClassZone.com

Preparing For Battle

▼ **KEY QUESTION** What strategy did each side hope to pursue?

With Virginia on its side, the Confederacy had a better hope of victory. Virginia was rich and **populous**, or heavily populated. In July of 1861, the Confederacy moved its capital to Richmond.

Virginia was also the home of **Robert E. Lee**, a military leader who became the South's greatest general. When Virginia seceded, Lee resigned from the United States army and joined the Confederacy. Lee's support strengthened the Confederacy.

Choosing Sides After Virginia seceded, all eyes turned to the **border states**. The border states—Delaware, Maryland, Kentucky, and Missouri—were slave states that bordered states where slavery was illegal. Their location and resources were important to both sides.

All four states stayed in the Union. Later in the war, the Union gained territory when the western counties of Virginia broke away from the Confederacy and formed the state of West Virginia in 1863. West Virginia supported the Union. In the end, there were 24 states in the Union and 11 in the Confederacy.

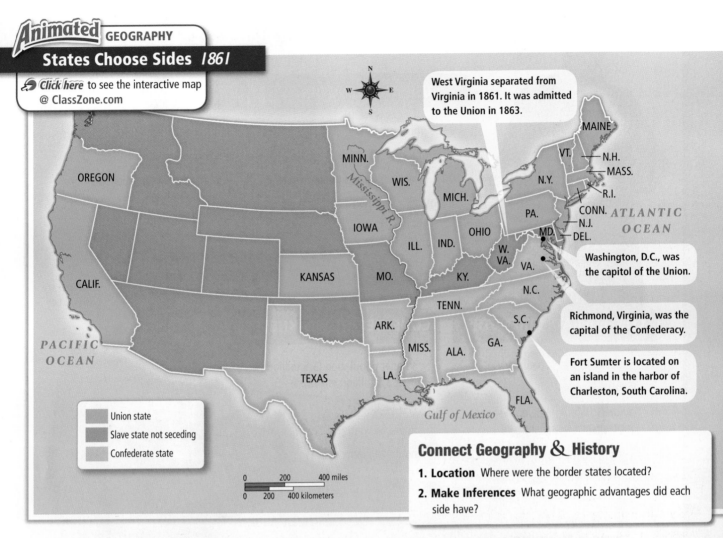

West Virginia separated from Virginia in 1861. It was admitted to the Union in 1863.

MAINE
VT.
N.H.
MASS.
R.I.
CONN.
N.J.
DEL.

MINN.
OREGON
WIS.
MICH.
N.Y.
PA.
IOWA
OHIO
ILL. IND.
W. VA.
MD.
VA.

Mississippi R.

CALIF.
KANSAS
MO.
KY.

N.C.
TENN.
S.C.
ARK.

PACIFIC OCEAN

TEXAS
MISS. ALA. GA.
LA.
FLA.

Gulf of Mexico

ATLANTIC OCEAN

Washington, D.C., was the capitol of the Union.

Richmond, Virginia, was the capital of the Confederacy.

Fort Sumter is located on an island in the harbor of Charleston, South Carolina.

Legend:
- Union state
- Slave state not seceding
- Confederate state

0   200   400 miles
0   200   400 kilometers

Connect Geography & History

1. **Location** Where were the border states located?
2. **Make Inferences** What geographic advantages did each side have?

Planning Strategies The Confederacy started off with a defensive strategy. Confederate leaders knew that support for the war in the North would weaken if the fighting went on for a long time. They also hoped that foreign dependence on their cotton exports would bring military aid from Great Britain and France. But both European nations had sufficient supplies of cotton. The South adopted a mix of defensive and offensive strategy, invading the North several times.

The Northern strategy was to invade and conquer the South. To do this they adopted the **Anaconda Plan**, developed by General Winfield Scott. This plan was designed to strangle the South's economy like a giant anaconda snake squeezing its prey. The plan called for

- a naval blockade of the South's coastline. In a blockade, armed forces block the traffic of goods or people.
- taking control of the Mississippi River. This would split the Confederacy in two.
- capturing Richmond, Virginia—the Confederate capital.

With Richmond only about 100 miles from Washington, Virginia became the site of many battles during the war.

▲ **CAUSES AND EFFECTS** Explain each side's strategy for winning the war.

The Civil War Begins **513**

COMPARING North and South

UNION STRENGTHS

large population (22 million)

85% of nation's factories

70% of the nation's railroad mileage

almost all the nation's naval vessels and shipyards

UNION WEAKNESSES

had to depend on long supply lines

fewer good military leaders

soldiers fighting an offensive war

Union general McClellan

Confederate general Lee

CONFEDERATE STRENGTHS

vast size of the Confederacy

good generals

soldiers fighting a defensive war to protect their homeland

CONFEDERATE WEAKNESSES

smaller population (5.5 million free; 3.5 million enslaved)

few factories

fewer railroads

no naval power

CRITICAL THINKING Draw Conclusions Which strength or weakness might have had the greatest effects?

First Battle of Bull Run

🔻 **KEY QUESTION** Why was the Union surprised by the outcome of Bull Run?

Many people in the North called for an immediate attack on Richmond. But to take Richmond, the Union army would first have to defeat the Confederate troops stationed at the town of Manassas, Virginia, near Washington, D.C. Many believed the battle, and the war, would be quickly won.

Intense Fighting On July 16, 1861, Union forces led by General Irvin McDowell marched to Manassas. They were joined there by hundreds of spectators from Washington who expected a quick and entertaining battle. Both soldiers and spectators were totally unprepared for what followed.

Union forces attacked the Confederates near the creek called Bull Run. In the North this battle is known as the **First Battle of Bull Run**. The Confederates, led by General Pierre Beauregard, were driven back. However, a regiment led

Fighting at Bull Run

by **Thomas J. Jackson** stopped the Union advance. Another officer saw Jackson and said, "There is Jackson standing like a stone wall!" From then on, Jackson was known as "Stonewall" Jackson.

Confederate forces launched a counter-charge while letting out a blood-curdling scream that became known as the "rebel yell." Frightened Union soldiers ran for their lives, along with scared and confused spectators.

The Confederate victory thrilled the South and shocked the North. Casualty figures reached around 2,700 for the Union and 2,000 for the Confederacy. It was obvious that this would be a deadly war.

Lessons of Bull Run The First Battle of Bull Run made three points clear:

- The fighting would be bloody.
- The war would not be over quickly.
- Southern soldiers would fight fiercely to defend the Confederacy.

After Bull Run, Lincoln realized the 90-day militias were no match for Confederate forces. He sent them home and called for a real army of 500,000 volunteers for three years. He also appointed George McClellan as commander of the Union army in the east.

 SUMMARIZE Explain why the Union was surprised by the outcome of Bull Run.

Illinois Learning Standards *Review*

🔁 **ONLINE QUIZ**
For test practice, go to
Interactive Review @ ClassZone.com

TERMS & NAMES

1. Explain the significance of

- Fort Sumter
- Confederacy
- Robert E. Lee
- border states
- Anaconda Plan
- First Battle of Bull Run
- Thomas J. Jackson

USING YOUR READING NOTES

2. Problems and Solutions Complete the diagram that you started at the beginning of this section.

Problem	Solution
What to do about the federal forts located in the Confederacy?	

KEY IDEAS

3. What were Lincoln's choices in regard to Fort Sumter?

4. Why were the border states important to both sides in the Civil War?

5. What kind of military strategy did each side develop?

CRITICAL THINKING

6. Evaluate Which side seemed better prepared for the conflict?

7. Draw Conclusions Why did the Confederacy adopt a defensive strategy?

8. Connect Economics and History How did the Union hope to damage the Southern economy?

9. Writing Description Imagine you were a spectator at Bull Run. Describe what you saw and explain how it changed your attitude toward the war.

▶ Key Ideas

BEFORE, YOU LEARNED
The Civil War began on Confederate territory.

NOW YOU WILL LEARN
Army life and new technology brought unexpected hardships to millions of soldiers.

▶ Vocabulary

TERMS & NAMES

the *Monitor* Union ironclad ship

the *Merrimack* Confederate ironclad ship, later renamed the *Virginia*

BACKGROUND VOCABULARY

enlist to join the armed forces

contractor private supplier

hygiene conditions and practices that promote health

Visual Vocabulary
The *Monitor* (below) clashes with the *Merrimack*, or *Virginia* (below left)

▶ Reading Strategy

Re-create the diagram shown at right. As you read and respond to the **KEY QUESTIONS**, use the boxes to show causes of important events. Create a new diagram for each event.

See Skillbuilder Handbook, page R7.

CAUSES AND EFFECTS

Cause
African Americans saw the war as a way to end slavery.

Effect
Many volunteered to fight.

Cause

Cause

🖱 **GRAPHIC ORGANIZERS**
Go to **Interactive Review** @ ClassZone.com

Life in the Army

16.A.3b Make inferences about historical events and eras using historical maps and other historical sources.
18.B.3a Analyze how individuals and groups interact with and within institutions (e.g., *educational, military*).

One American's Story

In 1862, Peter Vredenburgh, Jr., answered President Lincoln's call for an additional 300,000 soldiers. Nearly 26 years old, Vredenburgh became a major in the 14th Regiment New Jersey Volunteer Infantry. Less than two months after joining the regiment, he wrote a letter urging his parents to keep his 18-year-old brother from enlisting.

PRIMARY SOURCE

❝ I am glad that Jim has not joined any [regiment] and I hope he never will. I would not have him go for all my pay; it would be very improbable that we could both go through this war and come out unharmed. Let him come here and see the thousands with their arms and legs off, or if that won't do, let him go as I did the other day through the Frederick hospitals and see how little account a man's life and limbs are held in by others. ❞

—**Major Peter Vredenburgh, Jr., quoted in *Upon the Tented Field***

Major Peter Vredenburgh, Jr., was an officer in the Union army.

On September 19, 1864, Vredenburgh was killed in battle. He was only one of many young men unprepared for the horrors of the war.

Civilians Become Soldiers

🔻 **KEY QUESTION** Why did so many volunteer to fight?

Like Peter Vredenburgh, the majority of soldiers in the Civil War were between 18 and 30 years of age. But both the Confederate and Union armies had younger and older soldiers, whose ages ranged from 11 to 83. These soldiers came from cities, towns, and farms across America.

Joining Up On both sides volunteers rushed to **enlist**, or join the army. Many were farmers who had never been far from home. Some rode a train for the first time. German and Irish immigrants made up the largest ethnic groups.

(top) Soldiers off duty.
(inset) Union jacket
and cap.

How does the crisp, new jacket above compare to those in the larger photograph?

At the beginning of the war, African Americans wanted to fight. They saw the war as a way to end slavery. However, neither the North nor the South accepted African Americans into their armies—at first. But as the war dragged on, the North finally took African Americans into its ranks.

In all, about 2 million men served in the Union Army and less than 1 million fought for the Confederacy. Most were volunteers. They enlisted for many different reasons. Some fought out of loyalty to their state or country. They also sought excitement and glory. Some soldiers signed up to escape the boredom of their lives in the factory or on the farm. Still others joined for the money.

Turning Civilians Into Soldiers After enlisting, volunteers were sent to an army camp for training. They lived in tents and had drill sessions. In winter, the soldiers lived in log huts or in heavy tents positioned on a log base.

Union soldiers were issued blue uniforms. Confederate soldiers wore gray or yellowish-brown. Early in the war, Northern soldiers received clothing of very poor quality. **Contractors,** or private suppliers, often supplied shoddy goods. In the Confederacy, some states had trouble providing uniforms at all. Confederate soldiers sometimes lacked shoes. After battles needy soldiers took coats, boots, and other clothing from the dead.

As the war went on, food became scarce. When soldiers were on the march they were sometimes out of reach of supply trains and had to find food on their own.

▲ **CAUSES AND EFFECTS** Explain why men volunteered for the army.

A New Kind of War

▼ **KEY QUESTION** How was the Civil War different from previous conflicts?

For many soldiers, the experience of army life did not meet their expectations. Advances in military technology brought high casualties. Primitive medical techniques and filthy conditions helped spread disease.

Unhealthy Conditions Military camps were filthy and smelled from the odors of garbage and latrines. One Union soldier described a camp near Washington. In the camp, cattle were killed to provide the troops with meat.

PRIMARY SOURCE

❝ The hides and [waste parts] of the [cattle] for miles upon miles around, under a sweltering sun and sultry showers, would gender such swarms of flies, armies of worms, blasts of stench and oceans of filth as to make life miserable. ❞

—William Keesy, quoted in *The Civil War Infantryman*

Amputation kit
Why would equipment like this have helped increase casualties?

Not only were the camps filthy, but so were the soldiers. They often went weeks without bathing or washing their clothes. Their bodies, clothing, and bedding became infested with lice and fleas. Poor **hygiene**—or conditions and practices that promote health—resulted in widespread sickness. Doctors were unaware that dirt carried germs that caused disease. They performed surgery without washing their hands. Because of these conditions, more soldiers died from disease than on the battlefield.

Civil War Prison Camps The war was difficult for all soldiers, but prisoners had an especially hard time. At prison camps in both the North and the South, prisoners of war faced terrible conditions.

One of the worst prison camps in the North was in Elmira, New York. In just one year, more than 24 percent of Elmira's 12,121 prisoners died of sickness and exposure to severe weather.

Conditions were also horrible in the South. The camp with the worst reputation was in Andersonville, Georgia. Inmates had little shelter from the heat or cold. Drinking water came from a tiny creek that also served as a sewer. As many as 13,000 died at Andersonville from starvation, disease, and exposure.

Andersonville prison camp. A prisoner's meal might be little more than a single cracker.

CIVIL WAR TECHNOLOGY

The American Civil War brought startling changes to military warfare.

Railroads and Cannons

The North's superior railway system gave the Union a distinct advantage. Railways helped move millions of soldiers and supplies quickly and easily to strategic positions. Cannon could also be mounted on railcars, as in the photo above.

Ironclads

The ironclads transformed naval warfare. Powered by steam, and with their sides protected by iron plates, ironclads were fast and deadly. The Union churned them out in order to create an inland navy to control Southern rivers. Union ironclads like the one above played an important role in Grant's capture of Fort Henry.

Rifles and Grenades

The rifle and minié ball increased the range of accuracy from 100 to 400 yards. Defenders could shoot down lines of advancing troops. Grenades were thrown by hand and exploded on impact. The days of formal, linear warfare were over.

Trenches

Soldiers quickly learned to stay low to the ground in order to avoid rifle fire. The new weaponry encouraged soldiers to protect themselves by digging trenches. Massive trench systems were dug by both sides during the war.

CRITICAL THINKING **Make Inferences** Which aspect of military technology do you think had the most impact on the fighting?

Changes in Military Technology Improvements in the weapons of war had far-reaching effects. The new weaponry increased the number of casualties. It also changed battlefield strategies.

One change was the use of rifles and minié balls. A rifle is a gun with a grooved barrel that spins a bullet through the air. The minié ball is a bullet with a hollow base. The bullet expands upon firing to fit the grooves in the barrel. Rifles with minié balls could shoot farther and more accurately than old-fashioned muskets. As a result, mounted charges and assaults did not work as well. Defenders could shoot more of the attackers before they got close.

New technology also changed naval warfare. Ironclads were naval warships covered with iron. They were a vast improvement over conventional warships. Ironclads were faster and better-protected than wooden ships. A witness reported that an ironclad ship's prow cut through a wooden ship "as a knife goes through cheese."

In March 1862, off the coast of Virginia, a Union ironclad named **the _Monitor_**, fought **the _Merrimack_**, a Confederate ironclad renamed the _Virginia_. The day-long battle between the _Monitor_ and the _Merrimack_ ended in a draw. But the event became famous as the first battle in history between two ironclad ships.

Despite new technology and tactics, in the first two years of the war, neither side was able to defeat its enemy.

▲ **SUMMARIZE** Describe ways the Civil War differed from previous conflicts.

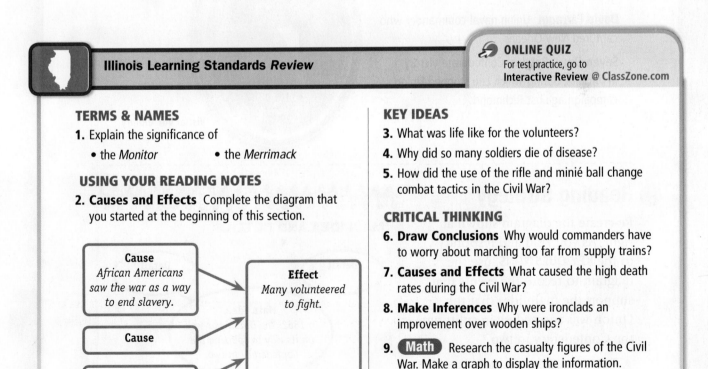

Illinois Learning Standards _Review_

🔁 **ONLINE QUIZ**
For test practice, go to
Interactive Review @ ClassZone.com

TERMS & NAMES

1. Explain the significance of
   • the _Monitor_   • the _Merrimack_

USING YOUR READING NOTES

2. Causes and Effects Complete the diagram that you started at the beginning of this section.

Cause
African Americans saw the war as a way to end slavery.

Cause

Cause

Effect
Many volunteered to fight.

KEY IDEAS

3. What was life like for the volunteers?

4. Why did so many soldiers die of disease?

5. How did the use of the rifle and minié ball change combat tactics in the Civil War?

CRITICAL THINKING

6. Draw Conclusions Why would commanders have to worry about marching too far from supply trains?

7. Causes and Effects What caused the high death rates during the Civil War?

8. Make Inferences Why were ironclads an improvement over wooden ships?

9. Math Research the casualty figures of the Civil War. Make a graph to display the information.

Reading for Understanding

▶ Key Ideas

BEFORE, YOU LEARNED

The Union defeat at the Battle of Bull Run shocked the North.

NOW YOU WILL LEARN

Both the Union and the Confederacy won important victories in the first years of the war.

▶ Vocabulary

TERMS & NAMES

George McClellan commander of Union army in the east

Ulysses S. Grant Union general who won battles in the west

Battle of Shiloh bloody battle in Tennessee won by Grant

William Tecumseh Sherman Union general at Battle of Shiloh

David Farragut Union naval commander who captured New Orleans

Seven Days' Battles Confederate victory in Virginia, during which Lee stopped Union campaign against Richmond

Battle of Antietam battle in Maryland that ended Lee's first invasion of the North

BACKGROUND VOCABULARY

plunder steal from, ransack

Visual Vocabulary
William Tecumseh Sherman

▶ Reading Strategy

Re-create the diagram shown at right. As you read and respond to the **KEY QUESTIONS**, use the diagram to record the events that support the main idea that the Union was succeeding in splitting the Confederacy in two.

 See Skillbuilder Handbook, page R4.

MAIN IDEA AND DETAILS

Detail   Detail

Main Idea
In 1862, the Union was well on its way to splitting the Confederacy in two.

GRAPHIC ORGANIZERS
Go to **Interactive Review** @ ClassZone.com

No End in Sight

14.D.3 Describe roles and influences of individuals, groups and media in shaping current Illinois and United States public policy (e.g., *general public opinion, special interest groups, formal parties, media*).
18.B.3a Analyze how individuals and groups interact with and within institutions (e.g., educational, military).

One American's Story

Twenty-year-old Sarah Morgan was living in the river town of Baton Rouge, Louisiana, when the Yankee gunships arrived. The Union navy had already captured New Orleans. Now Union ships were sailing deep into Confederate territory. When the gunships began shelling the town, the Morgans fled their home.

PRIMARY SOURCE

Sarah Morgan

❝ As we stood in the door, four or five shells sailed over our heads at the same time, seeming to make a perfect corkscrew of the air—for it sounded as though it went in circles. . . . I [stayed] behind to lock the door, with this new music in my ears. . . . I had heard Jimmy laugh about the singular sensation produced by the rifled balls spinning around one's head, and [here] I heard the same peculiar sound, ran the same risk, and was equal to the rest of the boys, for was I not in the midst of flying shells, in the middle of a bombardment? I think I was rather proud of it. ❞

—Sarah Morgan, *The Civil War Diary of a Southern Woman*

Sarah Morgan had rejoiced at the news of Confederate victories in the east. Now she remained defiant as the Union gained control of the Mississippi River in the west.

Union Victories in the West

▼ **KEY QUESTION** In 1862, how close did the Union come to achieving its goals?

In the summer of 1861, President Lincoln gave **George McClellan** command of the Union army in the East. The army had recently been defeated at Bull Run. Within months, McClellan restored the soldiers' confidence and organized and trained an army that could defeat the Confederates. Although McClellan prepared his army well, he seemed reluctant to attack the Southern capital at

Richmond. Instead, he kept drilling his troops. Lincoln, growing impatient, said that McClellan had "the slows." Meanwhile, another Union general was winning victories in the west.

Grant Opens Up the South That victorious Union general in the west was **Ulysses S. Grant**. In civilian life, he had failed at many things. But Grant had a simple strategy of war: "Find out where your enemy is. Get at him as soon as you can. Strike at him as hard as you can, and keep moving on."

In February 1862, Grant made a bold move to take Tennessee. Using ironclad gunboats, Grant's forces captured two Confederate river forts. These were Fort Henry on the Tennessee and Fort Donelson on the nearby Cumberland. (See map **A**) The seizure of Fort Henry opened up a river highway into the heart of the South. Union gunboats could now travel by river as far as northern Alabama. A week later, Union troops marched into Nashville.

Battle of Shiloh

The Battle of Shiloh After Grant's river victories, Albert S. Johnston, Confederate commander on the Western front, ordered a retreat to Corinth, Mississippi. Grant followed. By early April, Grant's troops had reached Pittsburg Landing on the Tennessee River. There he waited for more troops from Nashville. Johnston, however, decided to attack before Grant gained reinforcements. Marching his troops north

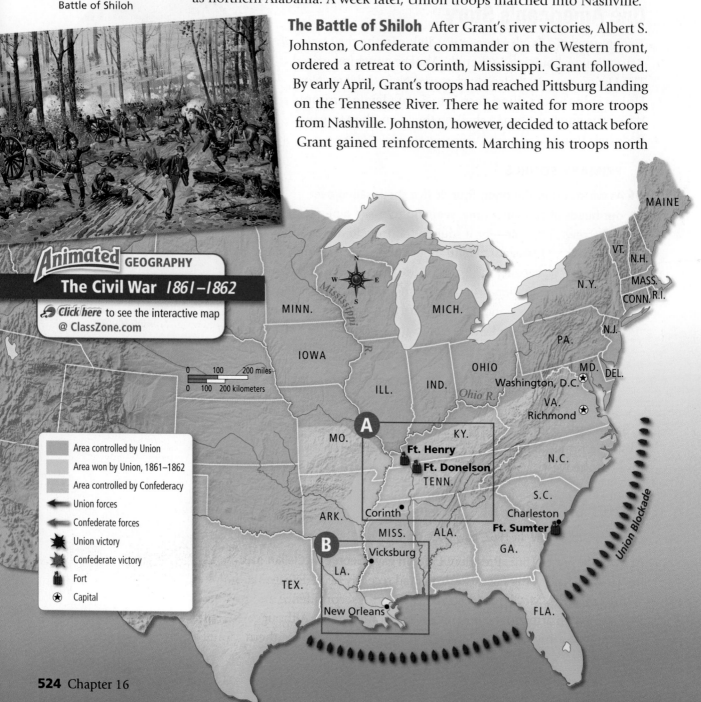

Animated GEOGRAPHY

The Civil War *1861–1862*

Click here to see the interactive map
@ ClassZone.com

0   100   200 miles
0   100   200 kilometers

Area controlled by Union
Area won by Union, 1861–1862
Area controlled by Confederacy
Union forces
Confederate forces
Union victory
Confederate victory
Fort
Capital

from Corinth on April 6, 1862, Johnston surprised the Union forces near Shiloh Church. The Battle of Shiloh in Tennessee turned into the fiercest fighting the Civil War had yet seen. (See map **B** below.)

Commanders on each side rode into the thick of battle to rally their troops. One Union general, **William Tecumseh Sherman**, had three horses shot out from under him. General Johnston was killed, and the command passed to General Pierre Beauregard. By the end of the day, each side believed that dawn would bring victory.

That night, there was a terrible thunderstorm. Lightning lit up the battlefield, where dead and dying soldiers lay in water and mud. During the night, Union boats ferried fresh troops to Grant's camp. Grant then led an attack at dawn and forced the exhausted Southern troops to retreat.

The cost of the Union victory was staggering. Union casualties at Shiloh numbered over 13,000, about one-fifth of the 65,000 who had fought. The Confederates lost nearly 11,000 out of 41,000 soldiers. Describing the piles of mangled bodies, General Sherman wrote home, "The scenes on this field would have cured anybody of war." In the North, people were horrified at the slaughter. Members of Congress criticized Grant for the high casualties and urged Lincoln to replace him. But Lincoln replied, "I can't spare this man—he fights."

Connect Geography & History

1. **Location** Where were Grant's early victories?

2. **Make Inferences** How might the fall of New Orleans have affected Southern trade?

The Fall of New Orleans The spring of 1862 brought other bad news for the Confederacy. On April 25, a Union fleet led by Admiral **David Farragut** captured New Orleans, the largest city in the South. (See map **B** on page 525.) Rebel gunboats tried to ram the Union warships and succeeded in sinking one. Farragut's ships had to run through cannon fire and then dodge burning rafts in order to reach the city.

The fall of New Orleans was a heavy blow to the South. Mary Chesnut of South Carolina, the wife of an aide to President Davis, wrote in her diary, "New Orleans gone—and with it the Confederacy. Are we not cut in two?" Indeed, after the victories of General Grant and Admiral Farragut, only a 150-mile stretch of the Mississippi remained in Southern hands. The Union was well on its way to achieving its goal of cutting the Confederacy in two. But guarding the remaining stretch of the river was the heavily armed Confederate fort at Vicksburg, Mississippi.

▲ **MAIN IDEAS & DETAILS** Explain how close the Union came to achieving its goals in 1862.

Southern Success in the East

▼ **KEY QUESTION** In 1862, how close did the South come to victory?

As New Orleans fell in the spring of 1862, McClellan was slowly advancing up a peninsula between the York and James rivers in Virginia. His goal during this Peninsula Campaign was to try to capture the Confederate capital at Richmond. McClellan got so close that his soldiers could see the church steeples in the city. But just as Union forces grew confident of victory, the situation in the East changed dramatically.

Lee's Victories In June 1862, Robert E. Lee took charge of the Army of Northern Virginia and proceeded to turn the situation around. Lee sent Jeb Stuart and his cavalry, or soldiers on horseback, to spy on McClellan. With about 1,200 men, Stuart rode around the whole Union army in a few days and reported its position back to Lee. Lee then attacked McClellan's army. The two sides clashed for a week, from June 25 to July 1, 1862, in what became known as the **Seven Days' Battles**.

Again, the number of casualties was horrific, with 15,849 for the Union and around 20,000 for the Confederacy. Although the Confederate Army of Northern Virginia suffered heavier losses, McClellan's army was forced to retreat. The Union plan to capture Richmond had failed.

Battles in the East *1862*

Map legend:
- Controlled by Union
- Controlled by Confederacy
- ← Union forces
- ← Confederate forces
- ✦ Union victory
- ✦ Confederate victory

Labeled on map: PENNSYLVANIA, Antietam Sept. 1862, Harpers Ferry, McClellan, Lee, Burnside, MARYLAND, Washington, D.C., Pope, 2nd Bull Run Aug. 1862, Shenandoah Valley, Chancellorsville May 1863, Fredericksburg Dec. 1862, Rappahannock R., Chesapeake Bay, VIRGINIA, Lee, James R., Richmond, McClellan, Seven Days June-July 1862, Monitor & Merrimack March 1862 (indecisive), NORTH CAROLINA, Potomac R.

Connect Geography & History

1. **Location** How far is Washington from Richmond?
2. **Draw Conclusions** Why was there so much military activity in Virginia?

In late August, the Confederates won a second victory at Bull Run, and Union troops withdrew to Washington. Within just a few months, Lee had ended the Union threat in Virginia. He had also renewed Confederate hopes of winning the war. After the Confederate defeats in the West, Lee's victories were welcome news for the South.

Lee Invades the North Riding his recent wave of victories, General Lee decided to invade the Union. He wrote to tell President Davis of his plan. Lee thought it was a crucial time, with the North at a low point. Without waiting for Davis's response, Lee crossed the Potomac with his army and invaded Maryland in early September 1862. With this invasion, Lee reversed the previous Southern strategy of fighting a purely defensive war.

Lee had several reasons for taking the war to the North:

- He hoped a victory in the North might force Lincoln into peace talks.
- The invasion would give Virginia farmers a rest from the war during harvest season.
- The Confederates could **plunder**, or steal from, Northern farms for food.
- Lee hoped the invasion would show that the Confederacy could indeed win the war, which might convince European nations to side with the South.

By this time, both Britain and France were leaning toward recognizing the Confederacy as a separate nation. They were impressed by Lee's military successes, and their textile industries needed Southern cotton.

Fighting to a Draw at Antietam Soon after invading Maryland, Lee drew up a plan for his campaign in the North. A Confederate officer accidentally left a copy of Lee's battle plans wrapped around three cigars at a campsite. When Union troops passed by the abandoned campsite, a Union soldier stumbled on the plans. The captured plans gave McClellan a chance to stop Lee and his army.

McClellan went on the attack, though he moved slowly as always. On September 17, 1862, at Antietam Creek near Sharpsburg, Maryland, McClellan's army clashed with Lee's. The resulting **Battle of Antietam** was the bloodiest day in American history. A Confederate officer later described the battle.

History *through* Art

The Peninsula Campaign

Somewhere in Virginia, two soldiers in McClellan's army await orders. A young artist named Winslow Homer caught the moment. Homer was an artist/correspondent for the magazine *Harper's Weekly*. Here he created a different kind of war painting. Instead of showing us a heroic battle scene, Homer gives us a glimpse into the life of ordinary soldiers serving under McClellan during the Peninsula Campaign.

Soldiers in the Peninsula Campaign spent a lot of time waiting for orders. McClellan's reluctance to attack the enemy frustrated Lincoln. This scene captures the endless wait for the fighting to start.

CRITICAL VIEWING

1. **Make Inferences** What does the painting convey about army life?
2. **Draw Conclusions** What does the painting reveal about McClellan's Peninsula Campaign?

CONNECT ➤ *To The Essential Question*

What events, leaders, and strategies shaped the early years of the war?

Effect on the Union	BATTLE OR EVENT	Effect on the Confederacy
	1861	
	APRIL	
Lincoln calls out the militia.	Fort Sumter in Charlestown harbor surrenders to the Confederacy.	Virginia, North Carolina, Tennessee, and Arkansas join the Confederacy.
Union loses a great military leader.	Robert E. Lee resigns from the Union army and joins the Confederate army.	Confederate army gains its most important general.
	JULY	
Northerners are shocked by the Union defeat. Lincoln realizes that he must raise an army.	First Battle of Bull Run, Virginia: Confederate victory	Southerners are encouraged by their victory.
	1862	
	FEBRUARY	
Grant opens up a river highway into the heart of the South. Over half of Tennessee is now in Union hands.	Union general Ulysses S. Grant captures Fort Henry and Fort Donelson in Tennessee.	Confederate defenses are dramatically weakened.
	APRIL	
Despite the loss of 13,000 men, the Union is now in control of important Confederate territory. Grant continues advance toward the Mississippi River.	Battle of Shiloh in Tennessee: Union victory	Confederacy loses 11,000 men. As Grant marches south, Southerners fear that the Confederacy will be split in two.
Union gets closer to its goal of splitting the Confederacy in two.	New Orleans is captured by Union forces.	South loses its most important city. Only a 150-mile stretch of the Mississippi River remains in Confederate hands.
	JUNE–JULY	
McClellan forced to retreat from his attack on the Confederate capital at Richmond.	During the Seven Days' Battles, Lee attacks Union general McClellan in Virginia.	Lee ends the Union threat to Virginia.
	SEPTEMBER	
Despite the high number of casualties, Northerners are encouraged that Lee's invasion has been stopped.	23,000 Americans die at the Battle of Antietam in Maryland.	Lee is forced to retreat from his invasion of Union territory.

CRITICAL THINKING Compare and Contrast In the first two years of the war, which side seemed closer to achieving its strategic goals?

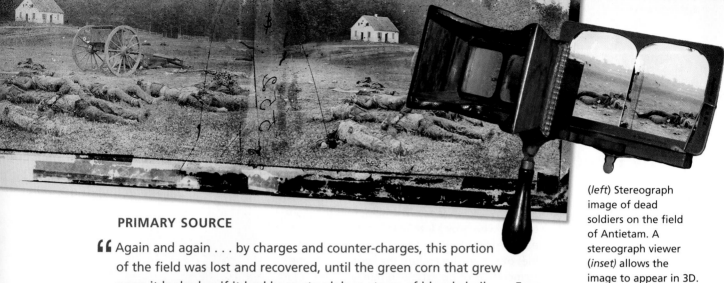

(*left*) Stereograph image of dead soldiers on the field of Antietam. A stereograph viewer (*inset*) allows the image to appear in 3D.

PRIMARY SOURCE

❝ Again and again . . . by charges and counter-charges, this portion of the field was lost and recovered, until the green corn that grew upon it looked as if it had been struck by a storm of bloody hail. . . . From sheer exhaustion, both sides, like battered and bleeding athletes, seemed willing to rest. ❞

—John B. Gordon, quoted in *Voices of the Civil War*

After fighting all day, neither side had gained any ground by nightfall. The only difference was that about 23,000 men were dead or wounded. Lee, who lost as much as one-quarter of his fighting force, withdrew to Virginia. The cautious McClellan did not follow, missing a chance to finish off the crippled Southern army. Lincoln was so frustrated that he fired McClellan in November 1862.

 CAUSES AND EFFECTS Explain how close the South came to victory in 1862.

 Illinois Learning Standards *Review*

🔁 **ONLINE QUIZ**
For test practice, go to
Interactive Review @ ClassZone.com

TERMS & NAMES

1. Explain the significance of:
   - George McClellan
   - David Farragut
   - Ulysses S. Grant
   - Seven Days' Battles
   - Battle of Shiloh
   - Battle of Antietam
   - William Tecumseh Sherman

USING YOUR READING NOTES

2. **Main Idea and Details** Complete the diagram that you started at the beginning of this section.

> Detail
>
> Detail
>
> **Main Idea**
> *In 1862, the Union was well on its way to splitting the Confederacy in two.*

KEY IDEAS

3. Why were Union victories in the West and the fall of New Orleans significant to the Union cause?

4. Why did Lee go on the offensive against the North?

5. How did the South's fortunes change after Lee took command of the Army of Northern Virginia?

CRITICAL THINKING

6. **Make Inferences** What does Lee's invasion of the North suggest about his qualities as a general and a leader?

7. **Draw Conclusions** Why was Southern cotton not reaching the factories of Europe?

8. **Causes and Effects** Why did Lincoln fire McClellan?

9. **Writing** **Letter** Imagine you are a Confederate soldier. Write a letter home about Robert E. Lee and his victories in the east.

Connect to Literature

Across Five Aprils
by Irene Hunt

Irene Hunt's acclaimed historical novel, *Across Five Aprils*, captures the
emotions, events, and people of the Civil War era. The book tells the story
of Jethro Creighton, a boy of nine who grows into manhood during the four
long years of civil war in the United States. Hunt depicts the savagery of
battle as well as the difficulties of those who endure the conflict at home.
In this scene, Jethro listens to members of his extended family—Wilse, Matt,
John, and Bill—debate the issue of slavery and its effects on the Union. Here
Jethro's cousin, Wilse Graham, responds to a question about whether slaves
in the South should be freed.

"Well then, I'll ask you this: if tomorrow every
slave in the South had his freedom and come up
North, would yore abolitionists git the crocodile
tears sloshed out of their eyes so they could take the
black man by the hand? Would they say, 'We'll see
that you git good-payin' work fitted to what you're
able to do—we'll see that you're well housed and
clothed—we want you to come to our churches
and yore children to come to our schools—why, we
danged near fergit the difference in the colors of our
skins because we air so almighty full of brotherly
love!' Would it be like that in yore northern cities,
Cousin John?"

"It ain't like that fer the masses of white people
in our northern cities—nor in the southern cities
either. And yet, there ain't a white man, lean-bellied
and hopeless as so many of them are, that would
change lots with a slave belongin' to the kindest
master in the South."

Then Bill spoke for the first time, his eyes still on
the yellow light of the lamp.

"Slavery, I hate. But it is with us, and them that
should suffer fer the evil they brought to our shores
air long dead. What I want us to answer in this year
of 1861 is this, John: does the trouble over slavery
come because men's hearts is purer above the
Mason-Dixon line? Or does slavery throw a shadder
over greed and keep that greed from showin' up
quite so bare and ugly?"

Wilse Graham seemed to leap at Bill's question.
"You're right, Cousin Bill. It's greed, not slavery,
that's stirrin' up this trouble. And as fer human
goodness—men's hearts is jest as black today as in
the Roman times when they nailed slaves to crosses
by the hunderd and left 'em there to point up a
lesson."

Matt Creighton shook his head. "Human nature
ain't any better one side of a political line than on
the other—we all know that—but human nature,
the all-over picture of it, *is* better than it was a
thousand—five hundred—even a hundred years
ago. There is an awakenin' inside us of human
decency and responsibility. If I didn't believe that,
I wouldn't grieve fer the children I've buried; I
wouldn't look for'ard to the manhood of this
youngest one."

Jethro felt as if he were bursting with the tumult
inside him. The thought of war had given him a
secret delight only a matter of hours before . . .

Suddenly he was deeply troubled. He groped
towards an understanding of something that was far
beyond the excitement of guns and shouting men;
but he could not find words to define what he felt,
and that lack left him in a turmoil of frustration.

ADDITIONAL READING

Carrying the Flag, by Gordon C. Rhea Mr. Rhea tells the amazing
story of Private Charles Whilden, an unlikely hero of the Confederacy.

To Be a Slave, by Julius Lester Julius Lester presents a wealth
of slave narratives that provide important insight into the lives of
enslaved African Americans in the early years of America. Paintings by
Tom Feelings capture the brutality of the slave experience.

Chapter Summary

1) Key Idea
After more Southern states joined the Confederacy, fighting began on Confederate territory.

2) Key Idea
Army life and new technology brought unexpected hardships to millions of soldiers.

3) Key Idea
Both the Union and the Confederacy won important victories in the first years of the war.

For detailed Review and Study Notes go to **Interactive Review** @ **ClassZone.com**

Name Game

Use the Terms & Names list to identify each sentence online or on your own paper.

1. I was the Confederacy's greatest general.
   Robert E. Lee

2. This Union ironclad fought the *Merrimack*. ____

3. I was a Union general who won battles in the west. ____

4. I was the commander of the Union army in the east. ____

5. This plan was meant to strangle the Confederacy. ____

6. I captured New Orleans. ____

7. This was the first major battle of the Civil War. ____

8. I was a Confederate general at Bull Run. ____

9. During these battles, Lee prevented a Union attack on Richmond. ____

10. The attack on this Union fort marked the beginning of the Civil War. ____

A. Anaconda Plan
B. Thomas J. Jackson
C. *Monitor*
D. George McClellan
E. Seven Days' Battles
F. Fort Sumter
G. Robert E. Lee
H. William Tecumseh Sherman
I. First Battle of Bull Run
J. Ulysses S. Grant
K. Battle of Shiloh
L. David Farragut

Activities

CROSSWORD PUZZLE

Complete the online crossword puzzle to show what you know about the early years of the Civil War.

ACROSS
1. _____ was a very cautious Union general.

GEOGAME

Use this online map to reinforce your understanding of the first years of the Civil War, including the locations of important battles and geographic features. Drag and drop each place name in the list at its location on the map. A scorecard helps you keep track of your progress online.

Mississippi River

Shiloh

New Orleans

Bull Run

Tennessee River

More items online.

New Orleans

VOCABULARY

Explain the significance of each of the following.

1. William Tecumseh Sherman
2. Battle of Antietam
3. George McClellan
4. Ulysses S. Grant
5. Robert E. Lee
6. the *Monitor* and the *Merrimack*
7. First Battle of Bull Run
8. Fort Sumter
9. Confederacy
10. Anaconda Plan
11. Battle of Shiloh
12. David Farragut

Match each military commander on the left with a battle on the right and explain the role he played in that battle.

13. Grant
14. Sherman
15. Lee
16. McClellan
17. Farragut
18. Jackson
19. Johnston

A. Battle of Shiloh
B. Battle of Antietam
C. Seven Days' Battles
D. New Orleans
E. First Battle of Bull Run

KEY IDEAS

1 War Erupts (pages 510–515)

20. What did the South need to do to win the war?
21. What did the Battle of Bull Run reveal about the future battles of the Civil War?

2 Life in the Army (pages 516–521)

22. Why did so many people volunteer to fight in the Civil War?
23. How did the use of rifles and minié balls change military tactics?

3 No End in Sight (pages 522–529)

24. What part of the Union strategy did Grant accomplish in 1862? How did he do it?
25. Why did Congressmen criticize Grant and why did Lincoln like him?

CRITICAL THINKING

26. **Evaluate** Which side came out of the Battle of Shiloh in worse condition? Explain your answer.
27. **Draw Conclusions** Why do you think Confederate forces attacked Fort Sumter when they did?
28. **Make Inferences** What did the Union hope to gain by damaging the Southern economy?
29. **Compare and Contrast** Compare and contrast the Union with the Confederacy by filling in this chart.

	Union	Confederacy
Reasons for Fighting	*to preserve the Union*	
Advantages		
Disadvantages		
Military Strategy		
Battle Victories		

30. **Causes and Effects** Why did the introduction of ironclad warships have such an impact on naval warfare?
31. **Draw Conclusions** Why did the North have such difficulty in capturing Richmond, Virginia?
32. **Make Inferences** What changes in military technology might have surprised new recruits?
33. **Connect Geography and History** Study the map below. Why didn't McClellan take a land route to attack Richmond?

DOCUMENT-BASED QUESTIONS

PART 1: Short Answer

Analyze each document and answer the questions that follow.

DOCUMENT 1

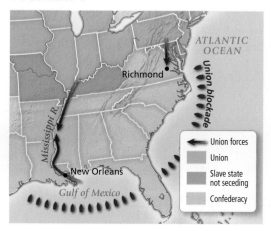

1. Examine this map of the Anaconda Plan. By 1862, which parts of the plan had been successful?

DOCUMENT 2

PRIMARY SOURCE

❝[S]oon as I feel that my army is well organized and well disciplined and strong enough, I will advance and force the Rebels to a battle on a field of my own selection. A long time must elapse before I can do that.❞

—General George McClellan, quoted in
Civil War Journal: The Leaders

2. What reason does General McClellan give for his slowness in attacking Confederate forces?

Part 2: Essay

3. Using the information from the documents, your answers to the questions in Part 1, and your knowledge of U.S. history, write an essay that describes the success of the Anaconda Plan in the early years of the war.

YOU BE THE HISTORIAN

34. WHAT IF? In what ways might history have been changed if Lincoln had ordered Major Anderson to turn Fort Sumter over to the Confederacy?

35 Causes and Effects How do you think the Civil War affected the lives of civilians who were not in the war zone?

36. Compare and Contrast In what ways was the South's strategy in 1861–1862 like the American army's strategy during the American Revolution?

37. Evaluate What does the presence of picnickers at the Battle of Bull Run reveal about civilians' attitude to the war?

38. Make Generalizations Why is an invading army usually at a disadvantage in a conflict?

39. Analyze Point of View What does Lincoln's admiration for Grant reveal about Lincoln?

 Answer the
ESSENTIAL QUESTION
What events, leaders, and strategies shaped the early years of the war?

Written Response Write a four–paragraph response to the Essential Question. Be sure to consider the key ideas of each section as well as the most significant facts that helped determine your answer. Use the Response Rubric below to guide your thinking and writing.

Response Rubric
A strong response will

• describe each side's strengths and weaknesses
• evaluate how close each side came to achieving its strategic goals
• explain the long-term effects of the events of the first two years of the war

The Tide of War Turns

1863–1865

1. The Emancipation Proclamation
2. War Affects Society
3. The North Wins
4. The Legacy of the War

The Freedman by John Quincy Adams Ward

ESSENTIAL QUESTION
In what ways did the Civil War transform the nation?

CONNECT → **Geography & History**

How did the Union make use of Southern geography in order to defeat the Confederacy?

Think about:

1 Union victories during the first two years of the war

2 the strength of the Union navy

3 the destructive Union march through Georgia

1863 May
Siege of Vicksburg begins.

1863

January Lincoln issues the Emancipation Proclamation.

▼

Effect Slaves are declared free in Confederate territory.

1863 **July** Battle of Gettysburg takes place.
July Vicksburg falls.

▼

Effect The tide of war turns in favor of the North.

Animated GEOGRAPHY & HISTORY

The Confederacy Falls 1863–1865

Click here to preview the final years of the Civil War @ClassZone.com

Ohio River

MD.

N.J.

DEL.

Washington, D.C.

W. VA.

MO.

Richmond

KY.

VA.

Nashville

TENN.

N.C.

Raleigh

ARK.

Grant

Chattanooga

Sherman

Columbia

Grant

S.C.

MISS.

Atlanta

GA.

Sherman

ALA.

Savannah

Vicksburg

LA.

Union blockade

Mobile Bay

Farragut

FLA.

	Controlled by the Union
	Won by the Union
	Controlled by the Confederacy
←	Union forces
✸	Union victory
—+—	Railroad

1864 **March** General Grant is appointed commander of all Union armies.

1864 **November** Union general Sherman begins his March to the Sea.

▼

Effect Southern resources are destroyed; Southern morale sinks.

Lee Surrendering at Appomattox by Thomas Lovell

1865

April Lee surrenders at Appomattox Court House.

The Tide of War Turns **535**

▶ Key Ideas

BEFORE, YOU LEARNED

Abolitionists had been fighting to end slavery for many decades before the Civil War began.

NOW YOU WILL LEARN

The Emancipation Proclamation promised freedom to slaves in the Confederacy and allowed African Americans to join the Union army.

▶ Vocabulary

TERMS & NAMES

Emancipation Proclamation document issued by Lincoln that declared that all slaves in Confederate-held territory were free

54th Massachusetts Volunteers regiment of African-American soldiers that gained fame for its courageous assault on Fort Wagner, South Carolina

BACKGROUND VOCABULARY

emancipate to free

Commander-In-Chief the President in his role as commander of all armed forces

liberation the act of setting someone free

prolong to lengthen (in time)

REVIEW

Battle of Antietam bloody battle in Maryland that ended Lee's first invasion of the North

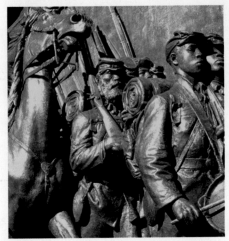

Visual Vocabulary detail of a sculpture of the 54th Massachusetts Volunteers

▶ Reading Strategy

Re-create the diagram shown at right. As you read and respond to the **KEY QUESTIONS**, use the diagram to note the effects of the Emancipation Proclamation.

 See Skillbuilder Handbook, page R7.

CAUSES AND EFFECTS

Effect on War Aims
Purpose of war expands—to liberating the enslaved as well as preserving the Union.

Emancipation Proclamation

Effect on African Americans

Effect on Southern Economy

GRAPHIC ORGANIZERS
Go to **Interactive Review** @ ClassZone.com

The Emancipation Proclamation

14.C.3 Compare historical issues involving rights, roles and status of individuals in relation to municipalities, states and the nation.
14.D.3 Describe roles and influences of individuals, groups and media in shaping current Illinois and United States public policy (e.g., *general public opinion, special interest groups, formal parties, media*).

One American's Story

During the Civil War, abolitionists such as Frederick Douglass continued their campaign against slavery. Douglass urged President Lincoln to **emancipate**, or free, all enslaved Americans.

PRIMARY SOURCE

❝ To fight against slaveholders, without fighting against slavery, is but a half-hearted business, and paralyzes the hands engaged in it. . . . Fire must be met with water. . . . War for the destruction of liberty [by the South] must be met with war for the destruction of slavery. ❞

—Frederick Douglass, quoted in *Battle Cry of Freedom*

Frederick Douglass

For Douglass there was now a practical as well as a moral purpose for ending slavery. If the Union promised to end slavery, millions of enslaved Americans might help the Union cause. Urged on by Douglass and others, Lincoln decided to act.

A War of Liberation

▼ **KEY QUESTION** How did the Emancipation Proclamation affect the war effort?

Arguments over the issue of slavery had brought the nation to war. Now the war was forcing Americans to resolve the slavery question once and for all.

Abolitionists Demand Action In parts of the South, slavery began collapsing early in the war. As Union armies swept through Confederate territory, thousands of enslaved people escaped from the plantations.

Meanwhile, abolitionists were pressuring the government to act. They realized that the war provided an opportunity to destroy slavery forever. Lincoln hesitated for several reasons. Although he did not like slavery, he feared that he did not have the constitutional power to abolish slavery in every state.

Most importantly, Lincoln's priority was to preserve the Union. "If I could save the Union without freeing any slave I would do it," he declared. "If I could save it by freeing all the slaves I would do it; and if I could save it be freeing some and leaving others alone, I would also do that."

In his struggle to keep the Union together, Lincoln did not want to anger the border states, the four slave states that remained in the Union. He also knew that many in the North opposed emancipation.

By the summer of 1862, however, Lincoln had decided in favor of emancipation. The war was taking a terrible toll. If freeing the slaves helped weaken the South, then he would do it. Lincoln waited for a moment when the Union was in a position of strength. After General Lee's forces were stopped at the **Battle of Antietam**, Lincoln felt confident enough to act.

The Emancipation Proclamation On January 1, 1863, Lincoln issued the **Emancipation Proclamation**, which declared that all slaves in Confederate-held territory were free.

PRIMARY SOURCE

❝ On the first day of January, in the year of our Lord one thousand eight hundred and sixty-three, all persons held as slaves within any State or designated part of a State, the people whereof shall then be in rebellion against the United States, shall be then, thenceforward, and forever free. ❞

—Abraham Lincoln, from the *Emancipation Proclamation*

The proclamation made a great impact on the public, but it freed few slaves. The Union army could enforce the proclamation only in the Confederate territory under its control. Most slaves lived in areas far removed from the Union army and remained under the control of plantation owners.

Scene of the Emancipation Proclamation being read in a slave cabin. **Why didn't the artist show the Proclamation being read outside, in daylight?**

FREEDOM TO THE SLAVE

Political cartoons are images that carry a political message. Older political cartoons, especially those from the 18th and 19th centuries, are often very detailed. First read the words in the banner. Then study the cartoon in order to understand its meaning.

The image shows enslaved African Americans gaining their liberty from a Union soldier as the Union army passes by. On the left-hand side, the cartoonist has imagined what will happen after slavery ends.

freed slaves entering a school

a newspaper, symbolizing literacy

CRITICAL THINKING

1. **Make Inferences** What does the cartoonist suggest will happen after the abolition of slavery?

2. **Synthesize** What is the overall meaning of the cartoon?

 See Skillbuilder Handbook, page R24.

"Freedom to the Slave" printed in Philadelphia 1863

Why, critics asked, did Lincoln free slaves only in the South? Lincoln believed that the Constitution did not give him the authority to free all slaves. But because freeing slaves in the South weakened the Confederacy, the proclamation could be seen as a military action. According to the Constitution, the President is **Commander-in-Chief** of all armed forces. In this role, Lincoln claimed the military authority to issue the proclamation.

Although the Emancipation Proclamation did not free many enslaved people at the time, it added a great moral purpose to the Union cause. The Northern goal was no longer simply to preserve the Union. The Civil War was now being fought to free millions of Americans from slavery. The conflict had become a war of **liberation**.

Response to the Proclamation Abolitionists were thrilled that Lincoln had finally issued the Emancipation Proclamation. "We shout for joy that we live to record this righteous decree," wrote Frederick Douglass. Still, many believed the law should have gone further. They were upset that Lincoln had not freed *all* enslaved people, including those in the border states.

Other people in the North, especially Democrats, were angered by the president's decision. A majority of Northern Democrats opposed emancipat-

Connecting History

Expanding Liberty
During the Revolutionary War, the British had also tried to weaken their opponents by offering to free the enslaved. *See Chapter 7, page 196.*

ing even Southern slaves. They claimed that the proclamation would only **prolong**, or lengthen, the war by further angering the South. A newspaper man in Ohio called Lincoln's proclamation "monstrous, impudent, and heinous . . . insulting to God as to man."

Most Union soldiers welcomed emancipation. One officer noted that, although few soldiers were abolitionists, most were happy "to destroy everything that . . . gives the rebels strength."

White Southerners reacted angrily to the proclamation. Although it had no effect in areas outside the reach of Northern armies, many slaves began escaping to Union lines. At the same time that these slaves deprived the Confederacy of labor, they also began to provide the Union with soldiers.

▲ **CAUSES AND EFFECTS** Describe how the Emancipation Proclamation affected the war.

Fighting for Freedom

▼ **KEY QUESTION** How did African-American soldiers contribute to the Union cause?

In addition to freeing slaves, the Emancipation Proclamation declared that African-American men willing to fight "will be received into the armed service of the United States." Determined to destroy slavery, African-American soldiers brought renewed intensity to the Union cause.

African-American Soldiers Frederick Douglass had argued for the recruitment of African-American soldiers since the start of the war. He believed that military service would be the first step to full citizenship. Douglass declared, "Once [you] let the black man get upon his person the brass letters, U.S. . . . there is no power on earth which can deny that he has earned the right to citizenship."

Recruitment poster to attract African-American volunteers
Why would an image like this have attracted volunteers?

COME AND JOIN US BROTHERS.

PUBLISHED BY THE SUPERVISORY COMMITTEE FOR RECRUITING COLORED REGIMENTS
1210 CHESTNUT ST. PHILADELPHIA.

Before the proclamation, the federal government had discouraged the enlistment of African Americans, and only a few regiments were formed. Once the restriction was lifted, African Americans rushed to join the army. Most of these African Americans came from the South. By war's end, about 180,000 black soldiers wore the blue uniform of the Union army.

African-American soldiers were organized in 166 all-black regiments, usually led by white officers. They were paid less than white soldiers. Despite these obstacles, African Americans showed great courage on the battlefield and wore their uniforms with pride. More than one regiment insisted on fighting without pay rather than accepting lower pay.

African-American soldiers were determined to destroy slavery, gain self-respect, and prove they deserved equal treatment. Many white officers started out with racist views about their soldiers. After seeing these soldiers' determination and courage on the battlefield, many of these officers changed their minds.

Middle school students, dressed in period uniforms, portray life in the 54th Massachusetts Volunteers.

The 54th Massachusetts The **54th Massachusetts Volunteers** was one of the first African-American regiments organized in the North. The soldiers of the 54th—which included two sons of Frederick Douglass—soon made the regiment one of the most famous of the Civil War.

The 54th Massachusetts earned its greatest glory in July 1863, when it led a heroic attack on Fort Wagner in South Carolina. The soldiers' bravery made them famous and increased African-American enlistment.

Soldiers in African-American regiments faced grave dangers if captured. The Confederate government threatened to execute them or return them to slavery rather than make them prisoners of war.

The Emancipation Proclamation was one sign that the war was bringing dramatic change to both North and South. As the fighting continued, it was clear that the war was changing American society in unexpected ways.

 SUMMARIZE Describe the contributions of African-American soldiers to the Union cause.

Illinois Learning Standards *Review*

ONLINE QUIZ For test practice, go to **Interactive Review @ ClassZone.com**

TERMS & NAMES

1. Explain the importance of
   • Emancipation Proclamation
   • 54th Massachusetts Volunteers

USING YOUR READING NOTES

2. **Causes and Effects** Complete the chart that you started at the beginning of this section.

Emancipation Proclamation
→ **Effect on War Aims** *Purpose of war expands—to liberating the enslaved as well as preserving the Union.*
→ **Effect on African Americans**
→ **Effect on Southern Economy**

KEY IDEAS

3. Why was the Emancipation Proclamation limited in scope?

4. How did African Americans help the Union cause?

CRITICAL THINKING

5. **Causes and Effects** How did the Emancipation Proclamation change the role of African Americans in the Civil War?

6. **Make Inferences** Why would African-American Union soldiers face greater danger than white Union soldiers?

7. **Draw Conclusions** Why do you think that Lincoln waited until the Union was in a position of strength before issuing the Emancipation Proclamation?

8. **Math** Research the number of free and enslaved people in each Confederate state. Then calculate the percentage of slaves in each of those states.

Reading for Understanding

▶ Key Ideas

BEFORE, YOU LEARNED

The Civil War took millions of men from their homes, disrupting life in both North and South.

NOW YOU WILL LEARN

As the war dragged on, social, economic, and political change affected both the Union and the Confederacy.

▶ Vocabulary

TERMS & NAMES

Copperheads Northern Democrats who favored peace with the South

writ of *habeas corpus* law that prevents the government from holding citizens without formal charges

Clara Barton Civil War nurse who later founded the American Red Cross

BACKGROUND VOCABULARY

conscription military draft

income tax tax on earnings

greenback paper money introduced during the Civil War

REVIEW

inflation increase in prices and decrease in value of money

Visual Vocabulary
greenback

▶ Reading Strategy

Re-create the diagram shown at right. As you read and respond to the **KEY QUESTIONS**, use the center box to record the main idea; use the outer ovals to note important details. Add circles or start a new diagram as needed.

 See Skillbuilder Handbook, page R4.

MAIN IDEAS AND DETAILS

Detail — **Main Idea** *Disagreements emerged in both the Union and the Confederacy.* — Detail

🌀 **GRAPHIC ORGANIZERS**
Go to **Interactive Review** @ ClassZone.com

War Affects Society

 14.C.3 Compare historical issues involving rights, roles and status of individuals in relation to municipalities, states and the nation.
15.D.3a Explain the effects of increasing and declining imports and exports to an individual and to the nation's economy as a whole.

One American's Story

On April 4, 1863, a Southern woman named Agnes came upon a group of hungry women and children marching through the streets of the Confederate capital of Richmond, Virginia. The crowd was joined by others angered by the shortage of food.

PRIMARY SOURCE

❝ The crowd now rapidly increased, and numbered, I am sure, more than a thousand women and children. It grew and grew until it reached the dignity of a mob—a bread riot. ❞

— Agnes, quoted in *Reminiscences of Peace and War*

The mob broke into shops and stole food and other goods. When President Jefferson Davis appeared, the crowd hissed at him. As the Civil War moved into its third year, American society in both the North and the South began cracking under the strain of war.

A Divisive Time

🔻 **KEY QUESTION** What disagreements emerged inside both the Union and the Confederacy?

The fight between the North and the South was not the only conflict of the Civil War. Even within the Union and the Confederacy, disagreements raged.

Disagreements About the War Some Southern areas opposed secession. The western counties of Virginia had few plantations or slaves. In 1863, these counties seceded from Virginia and formed a new state—West Virginia. West Virginia then joined the Union.

Disagreements over the war also arose in the North. Lincoln's main opponents were the **Copperheads**, Northern Democrats who favored peace with the South. (A copperhead is a poisonous snake that strikes without warning.) Lincoln had protesters arrested. He also suspended the **writ of habeas corpus**, which prevents the government from holding citizens without formal charges.

Illustration of a food riot in the South, from a Northern magazine

Slaves escaping from Southern plantations. **Why would wartime conditions have allowed enslaved people to escape?**

Slaves Undermine the Confederacy Enslaved people did their best to weaken the Confederacy. Slaves slowed their work or stopped working altogether. When planters fled advancing Union armies, slaves often refused to join their former "masters." In defiance, they stayed behind, waiting to greet or join the Union armies. One Union officer described a common sight.

PRIMARY SOURCE

❝ It was very touching to see the vast numbers of colored [African-American] women following after us with babies in their arms, and little ones like our Anna clinging to their tattered skirts. One poor creature, while nobody was looking, hid two boys, five years old, in a wagon, intending, I suppose that they should see the land of freedom if she couldn't. ❞

—Union officer, quoted in *Sherman: Fighting Prophet*

After the Emancipation Proclamation, the number of slaves fleeing Southern plantations greatly increased.

The Draft Laws As enthusiasm for the war declined, both the North and the South began passing laws of **conscription**, also known as the draft. These laws required men to serve in the military.

In the South, planters with more than 20 slaves were not required to serve in the army. In both the Union and Confederacy, the rich could pay substitutes to serve in their place. This caused widespread resentment.

The draft was extremely unpopular. In July 1863, anger over the draft and simmering racial tensions led to the four-day-long New York City draft riots. Irish-Americans and others destroyed property and attacked African Americans on the streets. Over 1000 people were killed or wounded. Union troops were brought to the city to put down the uprising.

▲ **MAIN IDEAS & DETAILS** Describe the disagreements that emerged in both the Union and the Confederacy.

Economic and Social Change

▼ **KEY QUESTION** What economic and social changes were caused by the war?

In the North and the South, the war brought economic and social change. In the North, free African Americans were now serving in the Union military. Women were taking over jobs in factories and hospitals. At the same time, poverty and hunger spread through the Union and the Confederacy. The suffering was worse in the South.

Economic Effects of the War Food shortages were very common in the South. Many farmers were in the army and unable to harvest crops. Transportation was disrupted, preventing food from reaching markets. Additionally, both the Confederate and invading Union armies seized food.

Another problem in the South was **inflation**. Inflation is an increase in the cost of goods and a decrease in the value of money. Over the course of the war, prices rose steadily in the South. Inflation in the North was much lower, but prices still rose faster than wages, making life harder for working people.

During the war, the federal government passed two important economic measures. In 1861, it established the first **income tax**—a tax on earnings. The following year, the government issued a new paper currency, known as

COMPARING Northern and Southern Inflation

During the Civil War, inflation affected both the North and the South. Inflation occurs when prices rise and the purchasing power of money falls. Wartime inflation was especially severe in the Confederacy, where basic necessities became outrageously expensive.

Wartime Price Increases

Source: Gallman, *1994*

FOOD PRICES IN THE SOUTH, 1864

$6.00 Dozen Eggs

$6.25 Pound of Butter

$10.00 Quart of Milk

$12.00 Pound of Coffee

$18.00 Confederate Soldier's Monthly Pay

CRITICAL THINKING **Draw Conclusions** How long would it take a soldier to earn enough to buy some of the items shown above?

greenbacks because of their color. The new currency helped the Northern economy by ensuring that people had money to spend. It also helped the federal government to pay for the war.

Women Aid the War Effort With so many men away at war, women in both the North and the South assumed more responsibilities. Women plowed fields and ran farms and plantations. They also took over office and factory jobs that had previously been done only by men.

Thousands of women, such as **Clara Barton**, served on the front lines as volunteer workers and nurses. Susie King Taylor was an African-American woman who wrote an account of her experiences as a volunteer with an African-American regiment. She asked her readers to remember that "many lives were lost,—not men alone but noble women as well."

Relief agencies allowed women to work gathering supplies, washing clothes, and cooking food for soldiers. Also, nursing became a respectable profession for many women. By the end of the war, around 20,000 nurses had worked in Union and Confederate hospitals. Southern women were also active as nurses and as volunteers on the front.

CONNECTING History

WARS AND SOCIAL CHANGE

During the Civil War, many people were presented with opportunities for freedom or advancement. This situation was not unique to the Civil War. In fact, throughout American history, long, deadly wars have helped bring about dramatic social change.

1700s

1775–1783
The Revolutionary War
allowed African Americans to serve in the military.

1800s

1861–1865
The Civil War
freed enslaved people; allowed more women to enter the workforce and take on jobs traditionally done by men.

1900s

1939–1945
World War II
helped desegregate some factories and temporarily created more opportunities for women.

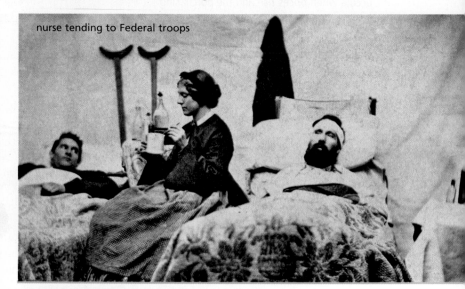
nurse tending to Federal troops

CRITICAL THINKING

1. **Make Inferences** Why would wartime situations offer more opportunities for women?

2. **Summarize** Why do wars help cause social change?

As in the American Revolution, some women on both sides disguised themselves as men and enlisted. One was an Illinois woman named Jennie Hodgers. She served in a Union regiment as Albert Cashier.

Women also played a key role as spies in both the North and the South. Harriet Tubman served as a spy for Union forces in South Carolina. The most famous Confederate spy was Belle Boyd. Although she was arrested six times, she continued her work through much of the war.

War Transforms Society With millions of men absent from their homes and workplaces, the war transformed Northern and Southern societies. In the North, opportunities opened up for those who had traditionally been kept out of public life. Women became active in the war effort and staffed hospitals in large numbers. African Americans gained more rights as several states began repealing discriminatory laws.

In the South, ordinary people began to resent the burden they were forced to bear. Small farmers, reduced to poverty by the war, were growing bitter. Many questioned why they were asked to fight a war for rich slaveowners. As the war dragged on, social resentment, inflation, and food shortages began to destroy Southern morale.

Woman Soldier in 95th Ill.

ALBERT D. J. CASHIER
OF
COMPANY G, 95TH ILLINOIS REGIMENT
Photographed November, 1864

ALBERT D. J. CASHIER
OF
COMPANY G, 95TH ILLINOIS REGIMENT
Photographed July, 1913

Albert Cashier (Jenny Hodgers) was one of hundreds of women who disguised themselves as men in order to fight in the war.

▲ **SUMMARIZE** Describe the economic and social changes caused by the war.

Illinois Learning Standards *Review*

🔁 **ONLINE QUIZ**
For test practice, go to
Interactive Review @ ClassZone.com

TERMS & NAMES

1. Explain the importance of
   - Copperheads
   - Clara Barton
   - writ of *habeus corpus*

USING YOUR READING NOTES

2. **Main Ideas and Details** Complete the diagram that you started at the beginning of this section.

Detail — **Main Idea** *Disagreements emerged in both the Union and the Confederacy.* — Detail

KEY IDEAS

3. Why were people in the western counties of Virginia against secession?

4. What hardships did civilians suffer during the war?

CRITICAL THINKING

5. **Connect Economics and History** Why do you think the economy of the South suffered more during the war than that of the North?

6. **Make Generalizations** Why do you think both sides introduced a draft?

7. **Writing** **Newspaper Article** Suppose you are a journalist for a foreign newspaper. Write an article describing war-time conditions in both the Confederacy and the Union.

▶ Key Ideas

BEFORE, YOU LEARNED

General Robert E. Lee caused the Union many difficulties in the east.

NOW YOU WILL LEARN

After a series of Southern victories, the North began winning battles that led to the defeat of the Confederacy.

▶ Vocabulary

TERMS & NAMES

Battle of Gettysburg battle in 1863 in Pennsylvania when Union forces stopped a Confederate invasion of the North

George Pickett Confederate general who fought at Gettysburg

Pickett's Charge failed assault on Union positions on final day of Battle of Gettysburg

Siege of Vicksburg the surrounding of the city of Vicksburg, Mississippi, by Union forces

Sherman's March to the Sea Union general Sherman's destructive march across Georgia

Appomattox Court House town in Virginia where Lee surrendered to Grant

BACKGROUND VOCABULARY

dislodge remove

Visual Vocabulary monument on the site of the Battle of Gettysburg

▶ Reading Strategy

Re-create the diagram shown at right. As you read and respond to the **KEY QUESTIONS**, use the diagram to show the effects of Union victories at Gettysburg and Vicksburg.

 See Skillbuilder Handbook, page R7.

CAUSES AND EFFECTS

Cause
Union victories at Gettysburg and Vicksburg

Effect
Union victory at Vicksburg splits the Confederacy in two.

Effect

Effect

GRAPHIC ORGANIZERS
Go to **Interactive Review** @ ClassZone.com

The North Wins

 14.D.3 Describe roles and influences of individuals, groups and media in shaping current Illinois and United States public policy (e.g., *general public opinion, special interest groups, formal parties, media*).
18.B.3a Analyze how individuals and groups interact with and within institutions (e.g., *educational, military*).

One American's Story

Tillie Pierce was 15 years old when war came to her doorstep in Gettysburg, Pennsylvania. On July 2, 1863, the second day of the battle, Tillie and her family tried to flee. She later wrote about her memories of the epic battle that took place around her home.

PRIMARY SOURCE

❝ Hardly had we arrived at our supposed place of refuge, when we were told to hurry back to where we came from . . . So there was no alternative but to retrace our steps about as fast as we came.

During the whole of this wild goose chase, the cannonading had become terrible! . . . Occasionally a shell would come flying over Round Top and explode high in the air over head. It seemed as though the heavens were sending forth peal upon peal of terrible thunder directly over our heads; while at the same time, the very earth beneath our feet trembled. ❞

—Tillie Pierce, quoted in *War Between Brothers*

Tillie Pierce

Tillie Pierce spent the next few days helping care for wounded Union soldiers. Little did she realize that the battle she had just witnessed would be the turning point of the war.

Union Victories at Gettysburg and Vicksburg

🔻 **KEY QUESTION** Why were the battles of Gettysburg and Vicksburg so significant?

In 1863 the war in the east seemed to be going well for the Confederacy. Confident after a series of victories at Fredericksburg and Chancellorsville, Virginia, General Lee decided to invade the North. It was a fatal mistake.

Lee Invades the North For Lee, the victory at Chancellorsville came at a high price. In the confusion after the battle, Confederate guards accidentally shot Confederate General Stonewall Jackson, who died a week later.

After Chancellorsville, Lee decided to head north once again. He hoped that a victory in Union territory would fuel Northern discontent and bring calls for peace. He also hoped that a Southern victory would lead European nations to recognize the Confederacy as an independent nation.

In late June 1863, Lee crossed into southern Pennsylvania. At the town of Gettysburg the Confederates stumbled upon Union troops. Both sides called for reinforcements, and on July 1, the **Battle of Gettysburg** began.

The Battle of Gettysburg The fighting raged for three days. On the rocky hills and fields around Gettysburg, 90,000 Union troops under the command of General George Meade clashed with 75,000 Confederates.

During the struggle, Union forces tried to hold their ground on Cemetery Ridge, just south of town, while rebel soldiers tried to **dislodge**, or remove, them. (See map on facing page.) At times, the air seemed full of bullets. "The balls [were] whizzing so thick," said one Texan, "that it [looked] like a man could hold out a hat and catch it full."

The turning point came on July 3, when General **George Pickett** mounted a direct attack on the middle of the Union line. It was a deadly mistake. Some 15,000 rebel troops charged up the ridge into heavy Union fire. One soldier recalled "bayonet thrusts, sabre strokes, pistol shots . . . men going down on their hands and knees, spinning round like tops . . . ghastly heaps of dead men."

Pickett's Charge, as this attack came to be known, was a failure. The Confederates retreated and waited for a counterattack. But once again, Lincoln's generals failed to completely defeat Lee's army. The furious Lincoln wondered when he would find a general to defeat Lee once and for all.

Even so, the Union rejoiced over the victory at Gettysburg. Lee's hopes for a Confederate victory in the North were crushed. The North suffered 23,000 casualties, or about one quarter of the army, but Southern losses were even greater. Over one-third of Lee's army, 28,000 men, lay dead or wounded. Sick at heart, Lee led his army back to Virginia.

Although the war would last two years longer, the South never recovered from its defeat at Gettysburg.

Reenactors portray the Battle of Gettysburg.

Gettysburg

Culp's Hill

Rock Creek

Willoughby Run

Seminary Ridge

Confederate forces

2 On July 2, Confederate troops attacked at this point, but were stopped.

Cemetery Ridge

3 On July 3, having failed to advance on the Union flanks, Lee decided to attack the Union Center.

PICKETT'S CHARGE

Union forces under Meade

Union line, July 3

1 On July 2, Confederate troops attacked here. Although they had some success, Union forces drove them back.

Little Round Top

Big Round Top

N
W E
S

| 0 | 1 Mile |
| 0 | 1 Kilometer |

- - - Confederate positions
➤➤ Confederate troop movements
- - Union positions
— Roads

Connect Geography & History

1. **Place** What advantage did Union forces gain by fighting on higher ground?

2. **Make Inferences** Why would the arch-shaped Union troop formation have given the Union an advantage?

The Siege of Vicksburg On July 4, 1863, the day after Pickett's Charge, the Union received more good news. Confederate troops at Vicksburg in Mississippi had surrendered to General Ulysses S. Grant.

The previous year, Grant had won important victories in the West that opened up the Mississippi River and allowed Union troops to travel deep into the South. Vicksburg was the last major Confederate stronghold on the river. Grant had begun his attack on Vicksburg in May 1863. When direct attacks failed, he settled in for a long siege.

During the **Siege of Vicksburg**, Grant's troops surrounded the city and prevented the delivery of food and supplies. Eventually, the Confederates ran out of food. The civilian population moved into caves to protect themselves from the constant bombardment. After nearly a month and a half, the city surrendered.

The Union victory fulfilled a major part of the Anaconda Plan. The North had taken New Orleans in April 1862. With the Union now in complete control of the Mississippi River, the South was split in two.

With the victories at Vicksburg and Gettysburg, the tide of war turned in favor of the North. In General Grant, President Lincoln found a man who might be able to defeat General Lee.

▲ **CAUSES AND EFFECTS** Explain how the Union victories at Gettysburg and Vicksburg affected the course of the war.

Connect *to the* **World**

Crucial Decisions
After Gettysburg and Vicksburg, the British government dropped discussion of recognizing the Confederacy.

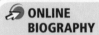 **ONLINE BIOGRAPHY**

For more on Grant and Lee go to the **Research & Writing Center** @ ClassZone.com

History Makers Civil War Generals

Ulysses S. Grant 1822–1885

When the Civil War broke out, Ulysses S. Grant was quickly promoted through the ranks and proved to be a brilliant general. Highly focused and cool under fire, Grant won the first major Union victories of the war. Grant was willing to attack Lee's army, even if the costs were high. He told one of his generals, "Wherever Lee goes, there you will go also."

Robert E. Lee 1807–1870

In General Robert E. Lee, the Confederacy found an unlikely hero. Lee opposed slavery and secession. He did not want to fight the Union, but felt he had to defend his home state of Virginia. "I did only what my duty demanded," Lee said. "I could have taken no other course without dishonor."

During the Seven Days' Battles Lee forced the Union army away from Richmond. After this, his reputation began to rise. By the end of the war, Lee inspired respect and devotion in the South and fear in the North.

COMPARING *Leaders*

What qualities did Grant have that helped him defeat Lee?

Vicksburg and Sherman's March 1863–1864

MD.
Washington, D.C.
OHIO
Ohio R.
ILLINOIS
INDIANA
Chancellorsville,
May 1863
WEST
VIRGINIA
Cold Harbor,
June 1864
Richmond
MISSOURI
KENTUCKY
VIRGINIA
35°N
Mississippi R.
Durham Station,
April 1865
Raleigh
Nashville,
Dec. 1864
NORTH CAROLINA
ARKANSAS
TENNESSEE
Chattanooga,
Nov. 1863
Grant
SOUTH
CAROLINA
Sherman
Wilmington
ATLANTIC
OCEAN
Chickamauga,
Sept. 1863
Atlanta,
July 20, 22, 28
Sept. 2, 1864
Columbia
75°W
MISSISSIPPI
ALABAMA
Sherman
Charleston
Union blockade
Vicksburg,
May–July 1863
Montgomery
Savannah,
occupied Dec. 1864
30°N
GEORGIA
Controlled by Union
Won by Union, 1863–1864
Controlled by Confederacy
Union forces
Union victory
Confederate victory
LOUISIANA
New Orleans
FLORIDA
80°W
Gulf of Mexico
90°W
85°W

Connect Geography & History

1. **Movement** How did Sherman's march further divide the Confederacy?
2. **Make Inferences** In what ways was Sherman's march an economic attack?

The Confederacy Falls

▼ **KEY QUESTION** How did Grant's new strategy defeat the Confederacy?

In March 1864, President Lincoln gave General Grant command of all Union armies. Grant then called for all Union forces to coordinate their attacks. Grant would pursue Lee's army in Virginia, while Union forces under General William Tecumseh Sherman pushed through the Deep South.

Sherman Takes Atlanta Battling southward from Tennessee, Sherman took Atlanta in September 1864. Sherman's victory affected the 1864 election. Northerners were tired of war, and Peace Democrats—who had nominated George McClellan—stood a chance of winning on an antiwar platform. But with Sherman's success, Northerners could sense victory. The President won reelection. (See page 564 for Lincoln's Second Inaugural Address.)

In November 1864, Sherman burned Atlanta and set out on a terrifying march to the sea. Sherman's army cut a path of destruction across Georgia that was 60 miles wide and 300 miles long. Sherman waged total war: a war not only against enemy troops, but against everything that supported

Grant's Virginia Campaign 1864–1865

Union forces
Confederate forces
Union victory
Confederate victory

Washington, D.C.
MARYLAND

Wilderness,
May 5–6, 1864
Fredericksburg

Spotsylvania,
May 8–19, 1864

VIRGINIA

Rappahannock R.

James River

Cold Harbor,
June 3, 1864

Richmond

Appomattox
Court House,
Apr. 9, 1865
Lee surrenders
to Grant

Petersburg,
June 1864–Apr. 1865

The fall of Richmond

Connect Geography & History

1. **Movement** Why did the opposing forces circle Richmond?
2. **Make Inferences** Why did Lee turn to the West?

the enemy. His troops tore up railroad lines, destroyed crops, and burned and looted towns. He reached the coast at Savannah in December 1864, then marched north into the Carolinas. His goal was to join Grant's troops in Virginia.

Sherman's March to the Sea, as it was called, tore into the heart of the Confederacy. Sherman's march also increased the size of the Union army—in Georgia alone more than 19,000 former slaves left plantations and followed the Union army to freedom.

Grant's Virginia Campaign In Virginia, Grant pursued Lee's army. Grant had a brutal plan for ending the war: to keep attacking Lee despite the number of casualties that Union forces might suffer. The Union armies could replace fallen soldiers, but the South was running out of men and supplies.

In the Virginia campaign, Lee showed his genius for strategy. Lee's army lacked sufficient manpower and supplies. But Lee excelled at maneuvering his army to fight and then escaping to fight another day. It took Grant a year to corner and defeat Lee.

At the Battle of the Wilderness in May 1864, Union and Confederate forces fought in a tangle of trees and brush so thick that they could barely see each other. Grant suffered over 17,000 casualties, but he pushed on. "Whatever happens," he told Lincoln, "we will not retreat."

At Spotsylvania and Cold Harbor, the fighting continued. Again, the losses were staggering. Grant's attack in June, at Cold Harbor, cost him 7,000 casualties, most in the first few minutes of battle. Some Union troops were so sure they would die in battle that they pinned their names and addresses to their jackets so their bodies could be identified later.

In June 1864, Grant's armies arrived at Petersburg, just south of Richmond. Unable to break through the Confederate defenses, the Union forces dug trenches and settled in for a nine-month-long siege.

Richmond Falls At the beginning of April 1865, Lee realized he could hold out no longer. He sent Davis a note advising the government to leave Richmond. Lee hoped to move his army to food supplies and so prolong the war.

On April 2, the Confederate government fled Richmond. Confederate leaders burnt anything that could be of use to the enemy. The fires spread, and the city was in flames when Union forces arrived on April 3, 1865.

Lincoln visited Richmond to see the prize that the Union had pursued for four years. Most white residents stayed indoors. African Americans cheered the president of the United States who had led the fight for freedom.

Surrender at Appomattox From Richmond and Petersburg, Lee fled west, while Grant followed in pursuit. Lee wanted to continue fighting, but he knew that his situation was hopeless. He sent a message to General Grant that he was ready to surrender.

On April 9, 1865, Lee and Grant met in the small Virginia town of **Appomattox Court House** to arrange the surrender. Grant later wrote that his joy at that moment was mixed with sadness.

Grant offered generous terms of surrender. After laying down their arms, the Confederates could return home in peace, taking their private possessions and horses with them. Grant also fed the hungry Confederate soldiers.

The Civil War was ending. The conflict had changed the country forever.

SUMMARIZE Explain Grant's strategy for ending the war.

 Illinois Learning Standards *Review*

 ONLINE QUIZ
For test practice, go to
Interactive Review @ ClassZone.com

TERMS & NAMES

1. Explain the importance of
   - Battle of Gettysburg
   - George Pickett
   - Pickett's Charge
   - Siege of Vicksburg
   - Appomattox Court House
   - Sherman's March to the Sea

USING YOUR READING NOTES

2. **Causes and Effects** Complete the diagram that you started at the beginning of this section.

KEY IDEAS

3. Why was the Battle of Gettysburg important?

4. How did the victory at Vicksburg fulfill a part of the Union strategy?

5. How did Sherman's victory at Atlanta affect the election of 1864?

CRITICAL THINKING

6. **Evaluate** How was Sherman's March to the Sea different from other military campaigns in the Civil War?

7. **Draw Conclusions** Why do you think Grant gave generous terms of surrender to Lee?

8. **Make Inferences** Why was the Confederacy unable to stop Sherman's campaign?

9. **Writing** **Description** Suppose that you lived on a farm overlooking the battlefield at Gettysburg. Describe what you saw during the battle.

NAVAL ACTION AT VICKSBURG

 Click here to see an animated version of the Union strategy at Vicksburg @ ClassZone.com

The Struggle for Vicksburg

On April 16, 1863, the Union fleet steamed down the Mississippi past Vicksburg. As the enemy ships sailed south, the Confederate defenders of Vicksburg opened fire. The missiles failed to stop the Union fleet.

General Grant's brilliant strategy to capture Vicksburg had begun.

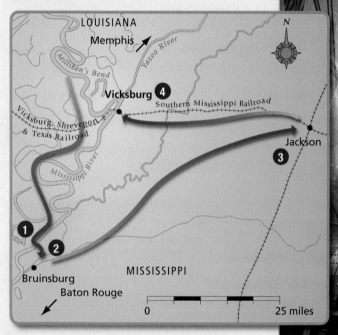

LOUISIANA
Memphis
Millikenâ€™s Bend
Yazoo River
Vicksburg **4**
Southern Mississippi Railroad
Vicksburg, Shreveport & Texas Railroad
Mississippi River
Jackson
3
1
2
Bruinsburg
Baton Rouge
MISSISSIPPI
N
0   25 miles

1 As his fleet sailed south, Grant moved his army down the west bank of the Mississippi.

2 **Next,** He marched north east. The Confederates could not understand why he was cutting himself off from his supplies on the river.

3 **Next,** Grant sent forces to conquer Jackson and turned west. He defeated a Confederate force sent from Vicksburg to stop him.

4 **Finally,** When Grant reached the massive fortifications around Vicksburg, he decided to starve the city into surrender. He surrounded the city with fortifications of his own. The Siege of Vicksburg lasted about six weeks. The city surrendered to the Union on July 4.

Activity

Sharing Perspectives

1 As a class, divide into 2 groups representing (a) the Confederate defenders and civilians of Vicksburg, and (b) the Union attackers.

2 Read about the siege of Vicksburg on pages 552 and 556–557.

3 Discuss how your group would have experienced the siege. For instance: How might a siege affect civilians? In what ways would life be different inside and outside the city?

4 Prepare a brief presentation or skit to present your group's perspective.

CRITICAL THINKING

1. **Draw Conclusions** Why do you think the Confederates in Vicksburg were confused by Grant's strategy?

2. **Make Inferences** How did Grant turn the Vicksburg defenses into a trap for the city's defenders?

▶ Key Ideas

BEFORE, YOU LEARNED
During the Civil War, important social, economic, and political changes took place.

NOW YOU WILL LEARN
The Civil War transformed the nation.

▶ Vocabulary

TERMS & NAMES

Walt Whitman poet who wrote about the Civil War

Ford's Theatre Washington, D.C. theater where Lincoln was shot

John Wilkes Booth Confederate supporter who assassinated Abraham Lincoln

Thirteenth Amendment Constitutional amendment that ended slavery

BACKGROUND VOCABULARY
ratify approve

Visual Vocabulary
Ford's Theatre

▶ Reading Strategy

Re-create the diagram shown at right. As you read and respond to the **KEY QUESTIONS**, use the diagram to categorize what Americans lost and gained because of the war.

 See Skillbuilder Handbook, page R6.

CATEGORIZE

Losses	Gains
	Union preserved

 GRAPHIC ORGANIZERS
Go to **Interactive Review** @ ClassZone.com

The Legacy of the War

14.C.3 Compare historical issues involving rights, roles and status of individuals in relation to municipalities, states and the nation.
14.D.3 Describe roles and influences of individuals, groups and media in shaping current Illinois and United States public policy (*e.g., general public opinion, special interest groups, formal parties, media*).

One American's Story

Walt Whitman is one of America's greatest poets. Whitman was 41 when the war began, which was too old to serve in the army. Whitman volunteered as a nurse and cared for wounded soldiers at hospitals in Washington, D.C. Whitman wrote many poems about the Civil War. These lines were written after the death of President Lincoln.

PRIMARY SOURCE

❝ This dust was once the man,
 Gentle, plain, just and resolute, under whose cautious hand,
 Against the foulest crime in history known in any land or age,
 Was saved the Union of these States. ❞

—Walt Whitman, *This Dust Was Once the Man*

Walt Whitman

Whitman's poem expresses the grief that followed Lincoln's assassination—five days after Lee's surrender. For many Americans, the terrible costs of the war prevented the celebration of victory.

Costs of the War

▼ **KEY QUESTION** What were the losses and gains of the war?

With the defeat of the Confederacy, the Union of the United States had been preserved, but at a terrible cost.

Terrible Losses The Civil War was the deadliest war in American history. In four years, around 620,000 soldiers died: 360,000 from the Union and 260,000 from the Confederacy. Another 275,000 Union soldiers and about 100,000 Confederate soldiers were wounded. Many suffered health problems for the rest of their lives.

Both the North and the South spent enormous sums of money. Years later, the government was still paying interest on loans taken out during the war.

The photographs of the Civil War altered the way people thought about warfare. For centuries, artists showed battle as a heroic, glorious adventure. The invention of photography changed this misconception. For the first time civilians saw the results of battle. The pictures of contemporary photographers revealed the horrors, rather than the heroism, of war.

Photograph of Gettysburg by Timothy O'Sullivan

Battle of Cedar Creek
by Kurz and Allison

CRITICAL THINKING

1. **Make Inferences** Why did so many traditional images of war show the moment before a battle?

2. **Draw Conclusions** How might photographs have changed civilians' attitudes to war?

The South in Ruins The war brought economic disaster to the South. Farms and plantations were destroyed. About 40 percent of the South's livestock was killed, and 50 percent of its farm machinery was wrecked. Factories were demolished, and thousands of miles of railroad tracks were torn up.

Before the war, the South accounted for 30 percent of the nation's wealth. After the war it accounted for only 12 percent. Long after the Northern economy began to rebound, the South remained locked in poverty. The economic gap between the North and the South would last for decades.

Lincoln's Assassination Although the war was over, one final disaster was yet to come. On April 14, 1865, five days after Lee's surrender, President Lincoln was shot while watching a play at **Ford's Theatre** in Washington, D.C. His attacker was **John Wilkes Booth**, a Confederate supporter. Booth escaped from the theater but was pursued and killed by troops 11 days later.

The wounded Lincoln was carried to a house nearby. Doctors tried to save him, but the bullet in his brain could not be removed. The next morning, April 15, 1865, the president died. He was the first American president to be assassinated. At the news of his death, many Americans wept in the streets.

▲ **CATEGORIZE** List the losses and gains of the war.

The Nation Transformed

 KEY QUESTION What changes did the war bring about?

The Civil War brought the most sweeping change to America since the Revolution. Socially and economically, the Civil War created a new nation.

A New Nation The war settled an old argument about states' rights—now it was clear that the states did not have the power to secede. The United States was recognized as a union rather than as a loose federation of states.

The war also caused the national government to expand. Along with a new paper currency and income tax, the government established a new federal banking system. It funded railroads, gave western land to settlers, and provided for state colleges.

CONNECT to the Essential Question

In what ways did the Civil War transform the nation?

Economic Change
- Income tax is introduced.
- New national paper currency is introduced.
- Industry begins to replace farming as the basis of the national economy.
- Southern slavery-based economy is destroyed.
- Factory production increases.

Civil War transforms the nation

Social Change
- Slavery is abolished; millions are freed.
- African Americans serve in the military.
- Conscription is introduced.
- Women become active in nursing.

Political Change
- Federal government grows more powerful.
- Triumph of idea of United States as a union, rather than a loose federation of states.

Changes in Warfare
- Modernized rifle and minié ball gives advantage to defender.
- New weaponry increases number of casualties on battlefield.
- Ironclads make wooden warships obsolete.

CRITICAL THINKING **Draw Conclusions** Which changes continue to affect life today?

The war destroyed a Southern economic system based on slavery and replaced it with paid labor. In the North, industries such as steel, petroleum, food processing, and manufacturing grew rapidly. By the late 1800s, industry had begun to replace farming as the basis of the national economy.

The Thirteenth Amendment But the greatest effect of the war was the freeing of millions of enslaved Americans. One of those was Booker T. Washington, who became a famous educator and reformer. He recalled a Union officer coming to his plantation to read the Emancipation Proclamation.

PRIMARY SOURCE

❝After the reading we were told that we were all free, and could go when and where we pleased. My mother, who was standing by my side, leaned over and kissed her children, while tears of joy ran down her cheeks. She explained to us what it all meant, that this was the day for which she had been so long praying, but fearing that she would never live to see.❞

—Booker T. Washington, *Up from Slavery*

In January 1865, Congress passed a constitutional amendment to end slavery. The **Thirteenth Amendment** was **ratified**, or approved, by 27 states, including 8 in the South. Slavery was now banned in the United States.

The country faced difficult challenges after the war. The South had to be brought back into the Union. Four million former slaves had to be integrated into national life. After four years of destruction, Americans turned their energies to rebuilding their nation.

 SUMMARIZE List changes brought about by the Civil War.

 Illinois Learning Standards *Review*

⟳ **ONLINE QUIZ**
For test practice, go to
Interactive Review @ ClassZone.com

TERMS & NAMES

1. Explain the importance of
- Walt Whitman
- John Wilkes Booth
- Ford's Theatre
- Thirteenth Amendment

USING YOUR READING NOTES

2. Categorize Complete the diagram you started at the beginning of this section.

Losses	Gains
	Union preserved

KEY IDEAS

3. What long-term effect did the war have on the South?

4. What economic changes did the war bring to the nation?

CRITICAL THINKING

5. Analyze Point of View What do you think former slaveowners thought about the Thirteenth Amendment?

6. Connect *to* **Today** In what ways are the effects of the Civil War still being felt today?

7. Math Graph Research the casualty figures for the Civil War. Make a graph showing the deaths for the North and the South in each year of the war.

The Gettysburg Address (1863)

SETTING THE STAGE On November 19, 1863, officials gathered in Gettysburg, Pennsylvania. They were there to dedicate a national cemetery on the ground where the decisive Battle of Gettysburg had taken place nearly five months earlier. Following the ceremony's main address, which lasted nearly two hours, President Lincoln delivered his Gettysburg Address in just two minutes. In this famous speech, Lincoln expressed his hopes for the nation.

Four**score**[1] and seven years ago our fathers brought forth on this continent a new nation, conceived in liberty, and dedicated to the proposition that all men are created equal.

Now we are engaged in a great civil war, testing whether that nation, or any nation so conceived and so dedicated, can long endure. We are met on a great battlefield of that war. We have come to dedicate a portion of that field as a final resting-place for those who here gave their lives that this nation might live. It is altogether fitting and proper that we should do this.

But, in a larger sense, we cannot dedicate . . . we cannot **consecrate**[2] . . . we cannot hallow . . . this ground. The brave men, living and dead, who struggled here, have consecrated it far above our poor power to add or **detract**.[3] The world will little note nor long remember what we say here, but it can never forget what they did here. It is for us, the living, rather, to be dedicated here to the unfinished work which they who fought here have thus far so nobly advanced. It is rather for us to be here dedicated to the great task remaining before us . . . that from these honored dead we **take increased devotion to**[4] that cause for which they **gave the last full measure of devotion**[5]; that we here highly resolve that these dead shall not have died **in vain**[6]; that this nation, under God, shall have a new birth of freedom; and that government of the people, by the people, for the people, shall not perish from the earth.

Fighting for a Cause

Different people fought for different causes during the Civil War. Sometimes, the causes for which people fought changed over the course of the war.

1. What cause is Lincoln referring to in the Gettysburg Address?

Lincoln's Modesty

Lincoln claimed that what he said at Gettysburg would not be long remembered. However, the address soon came to be recognized as one of the best speeches of all time.

2. What features of Lincoln's address make it so memorable?

---

1. **score** a group of twenty
2. **consecrate** declare as sacred
3. **detract** take away from
4. **take increased devotion to** work harder for
5. **gave the last full measure of devotion** sacrificed their lives
6. **in vain** for nothing

Second Inaugural Address (1865)

SETTING THE STAGE President Lincoln delivered his Second Inaugural Address just before the end of the Civil War. In this excerpt, he recalled the major cause of the war and vowed to fight for the restoration of peace and unity.

Slavery in Territories

Before the Civil War, Northern states wanted to prohibit slavery in territories that would eventually become new states. Southern states fought to expand slavery, fearing that outlawing it would threaten slavery where it already existed.

1. **Why did the Southerners fear that prohibiting slavery in new territories might threaten slavery where it already existed?**

Malice Toward None

As Northerners became more confident in victory, many wanted to punish Southerners, whom they blamed for the war. Lincoln, however, urged citizens to care for one another and work for a just and lasting peace.

2. **Why do you think that Lincoln believed it would be wiser for Americans not to place blame or seek revenge on one another?**

One-eighth of the whole population were colored slaves. . . . These slaves constituted a peculiar and powerful interest. All knew that this interest was, somehow, the cause of the war. To strengthen, perpetuate, and extend this interest was the object for which the **insurgents**[1] would rend the Union, even by war; while the government claimed no right to do more than to restrict the territorial enlargement of it. Neither party expected for the war, the magnitude, or the duration, which it has already attained. Neither anticipated that the cause of the conflict might cease with, or even before, the conflict itself should cease. Each looked for an easier triumph, and a result less fundamental and astounding. Both read the same Bible, and pray to the same God; and each invokes His aid against the other. . . . Fondly do we hope—fervently do we pray—that this mighty **scourge**[2] of war may speedily pass away. Yet, if God wills that it continue until all the wealth piled by the **bondsman's**[3] two hundred and fifty years of **unrequited**[4] toil shall be sunk, and until every drop of blood drawn with the lash, shall be paid by another drawn with the sword, as was said three thousand years ago, so still it must be said, "the judgments of the Lord are true and righteous altogether."

With malice toward none; with charity for all; with firmness in the right as God gives us to see the right, let us strive on to finish the work we are in; to bind up the nation's wounds; to care for him who shall have borne the battle, and for his widow, and his orphan—to do all which may achieve and cherish a just and lasting peace, among ourselves and with all nations.

----

1. **insurgents** one that revolts against civil authority

2. **scourge** a source of suffering and devastation

3. **bondsman** enslaved person

4. **unrequited** not paid for

DOCUMENT–BASED QUESTIONS

Short Answer

1. Why might President Lincoln have begun the Gettysburg Address by noting that the country was "dedicated to the proposition that all men are created equal"?

2. According to Lincoln's Second Inaugural Address, why did the Confederacy go to war?

Extended Answer

3. In 1865, if the South had asked to rejoin the Union without ending slavery, do you think Lincoln would have agreed? Use statements from the two documents and your knowledge of U.S. history to support your position.

Chapter Summary

1 **Key Idea**
The Emancipation Proclamation promised freedom to slaves in the Confederacy and allowed African Americans to join the Union army.

2 **Key Idea**
As the war dragged on, social, economic, and political change affected both the Union and the Confederacy.

3 **Key Idea**
After a series of Southern victories, the North began winning battles that led to the defeat of the Confederacy.

4 **Key Idea**
The Civil War transformed the nation.

For detailed Review and Study Notes go to **Interactive Review** @ **ClassZone.com**

Name Game

Use the list of terms and names to identify each sentence online or on your own paper.

1. I shot Abraham Lincoln. John Wilkes Booth

2. I was a poet who wrote about the Civil War. ____

3. This constitutional amendment ended slavery. ____

4. This was a famous regiment of African Americans. ____

5. I was a nurse who founded the American Red Cross. ____

6. This battle stopped a Confederate invasion of the North. ____

7. We were Northern Democrats who favored peace with the South. ____

8. This document freed all slaves in Confederate territory. ____

9. I was a Confederate general who fought at Gettysburg. ____

10. This law prevents the government from holding citizens without a trial. ____

A. Thirteenth Amendment

B. Clara Barton

C. Emancipation Proclamation

D. John Wilkes Booth

E. writ of habeas corpus

F. Battle of Gettysburg

G. 54th Massachusetts Volunteers

H. Copperheads

I. George Pickett

J. Walt Whitman

K. Siege of Vicksburg

L. Pickett's Charge

Activities

FLIPCARD

Use the online flipcards to quiz yourself on the terms and names introduced in this chapter.

Theater in Washington, D.C., where Lincoln was shot.

ANSWER
Ford's Theatre

GEOGAME

Use this online map to reinforce your understanding of the final years of the Civil War, including the locations of important battles and geographic features. Drag and drop each place name in the list at its location on the map. A scorecard helps you keep track of your progress online.

Nashville

Chattanooga

Richmond

Vicksburg

Raleigh

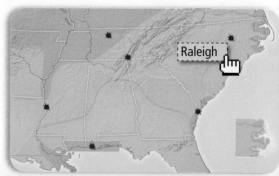

Raleigh

More items online

VOCABULARY

Match the term or name on the left with an item on the right.

1. Clara Barton   **A.** Battle of Gettysburg
2. John Wilkes Booth   **B.** American Red Cross
3. Copperheads   **C.** ended slavery
4. Thirteenth Amendment   **D.** Northern Democrats
5. George Pickett   **E.** assassinated President

Explain how the terms in each group are related.

6. Battle of Antietam, Emancipation Proclamation

7. George Pickett, Battle of Gettysburg, Pickett's Charge

8. 54th Massachusetts Volunteers, Emancipation Proclamation

9. Thirteenth Amendment, Emancipation Proclamation

KEY IDEAS

1 The Emancipation Proclamation (pages 536–541)

10. What impact was the Emancipation Proclamation meant to have on the Confederacy?

11. In what ways did African-American soldiers aid the war effort?

2 War Affects Society (pages 542–547)

12. How did enslaved people help undermine the Confederacy?

13. What economic changes did the war bring about?

3 The North Wins (pages 548–555)

14. Why were the Union victories at Gettysburg and Vicksburg a turning point in the war?

15. What was Grant's strategy for defeating Lee?

4 The Legacy of the War (pages 558–562)

16. What were some of the positive results of the war?

17. How did the war change the federal government?

CRITICAL THINKING

18. **Make Inferences** How do you think the assassination of President Lincoln affected the nation?

19. **Categorize** Describe the difference between the tactics of Grant and Lee during the Virginia campaign.

Grant	Lee
determined to keep attacking Lee	

20. **Problems and Solutions** How did Grant help bring the war to an end?

21. **Draw Conclusions** Why do you think Lincoln waited until the Union was in a strong position before he issued the Emancipation Proclamation?

22. **Make Inferences** Why did the federal government expand its powers during the Civil War?

23. **Causes and Effects** How did Sherman's victory in Atlanta affect the election of 1864?

24. **Make Generalizations** At what point did the Civil War become a war of liberation?

25. **Draw Conclusions** Study the casualty charts below. Approximately how many soldiers were wounded in the war?

Union and Confederate Casualties

■ Union Casualties   ■ Confederate Casualties

Source: *Encyclopedia of American History* and *Battle Cry of Freedom: The Civil War Era* by James McPherson

TEST PRACTICE

• **Online Test Practice** @ ClassZone.com
• **Test-Taking Strategies & Practice** at the front of this book

DOCUMENT-BASED QUESTIONS

PART 1: Short Answer

Study each document carefully and answer the questions that follow.

DOCUMENT 1

1. Examine this picture called *A Ride for Liberty* by Eastman Johnson. What messages might this painting have conveyed to people who saw it during the war?

DOCUMENT 2

PRIMARY SOURCE

" The war now being waged in this land is a war for and against slavery; and that it can never be effectually put down till one or the other of these vital forces is completely destroyed.

—Frederick Douglass, quoted in *Passages to Freedom*

2. According to Frederick Douglass, why was the Civil War fought?

Part 2: Essay

3. Using information from the documents, your answers to the questions in Part 1, and your knowledge of U.S. history, write an essay that discusses how the Civil War became a fight against slavery.

YOU BE THE HISTORIAN

26. **Draw Conclusions** Do you think Sherman's tactics were justified? Explain your answer.

27. **WHAT IF?** How might the course of the Civil War have changed if Lincoln had not issued the Emancipation Proclamation?

28. **Causes and Effects** Discuss the impact that Grant and Sherman had on the outcome of the Civil War.

29. **Connect** *to* **Today** What political, social, and economic issues of the Civil War are still relevant today?

30. **Causes and Effects** Why did the Union win the war?

31. **Problems and Solutions** What great national questions were settled by the Civil War?

32. **Draw Conclusions** Why did Confederates believe they might win the war?

Answer the
ESSENTIAL QUESTION

In what ways did the Civil War transform the nation?

Written Response Write a four-paragraph response to the Essential Question. Be sure to consider the key ideas of each section as well as the most significant forces that transformed the nation. Use the Response Rubric below to guide your thinking and writing.

Response Rubric

A strong response will

• discuss the social and economic transformation brought by the end of slavery
• analyze the effects of four years of war
• describe the increases in the powers of the federal government

CHAPTER 18

1. Rebuilding the Union

2. Reconstruction and Daily Life

3. The End of Reconstruction

Reconstruction

1865–1877

ESSENTIAL QUESTION

How did a deeply divided nation move forward after the Civil War?

CONNECT ↻ Geography & History

How might the Civil War have affected the economy of the South?

Think about:

1 how most of the war was fought in the South, including major battles in Virginia, Tennessee, Georgia, and Mississippi

2 how the amount of Southern farmland before the war compares with the amount after the war

3 what happened to the region's main system of labor—slavery

Lincoln's funeral train left Washington, D.C., on April 21, 1865, and arrived in Springfield, Illinois, on May 3.

1868 President Johnson impeached and later acquitted by a single vote

A ticket to Johnson's impeachment proceedings

1865

Lincoln assassinated; Johnson becomes president.
▼
Effect Johnson pardons white Southerners.

1866 Fourteenth Amendment
▼
Effect Former slaves become citizens.

1870 Fifteenth Amendment
▼
Effect African-American men get the vote.

Farmland in the South

Click here to preview the Reconstruction years in the South @ClassZone.com

VIRGINIA
31.1*   18.1

TENNESSEE
20.7   19.6

NORTH CAROLINA
23.8   19.8

ARKANSAS
9.6   7.6

SOUTH CAROLINA
16.2   12.1

TEXAS
25.3   18.4

MISSISSIPPI
15.8   13.1

ALABAMA
19.1   15.0

GEORGIA
26.7   23.6

LOUISIANA
9.3   7.0

FLORIDA
2.9   2.4

Farmland in former Confederate States (*in millions of acres*)

1860   1870

* 1860 data include West Virginia.

Hiram Revels (*far left*), the first African-American U.S. senator, with six U.S. representatives

During Reconstruction, federal troops were stationed in the South.

1877

1871 Congress passes anti-Klan legislation.

1873 Financial panic begins depression.

1876 Supreme Court rules that the Fifteenth Amendment does not give everyone the right to vote.

▼

Effect Southern states stop African Americans from voting.

Federal troops leave the South.

▼

Effect Reconstruction ends.

▶ Key Ideas

BEFORE, YOU LEARNED

The Civil War promoted industry and economic growth in the North, but left the South in ruins.

NOW YOU WILL LEARN

During Reconstruction, the president and Congress fought over how to rebuild the South.

▶ Vocabulary

TERMS & NAMES

Radical Republican congressman who favored using federal power to rebuild the South and promote African-American rights

Reconstruction period from 1865 to 1877 in which the U.S. government attempted to rebuild Southern society and governments

Freedmen's Bureau federal agency set up to help former enslaved people

Andrew Johnson Democrat who became president after Lincoln was assassinated

black codes laws that limited the freedom of former enslaved people

Fourteenth Amendment constitutional amendment that made all people born in the U.S. (including former slaves) citizens

scalawag white Southerner who supported Radical Reconstruction

carpetbagger Northerner who went to the South after the Civil War to participate in Reconstruction

BACKGROUND VOCABULARY

amnesty official pardon

civil rights rights granted to all citizens

impeach to formally accuse the president of misconduct in office

REVIEW

veto (VEE•to) to prevent from becoming law

▶ Reading Strategy

As you read and respond to the **KEY QUESTIONS**, use a graphic organizer like the one shown to compare presidential and Congressional Reconstruction. Record the goals of each plan in the columns. Circle any shared goals.

 See Skillbuilder Handbook, page R8.

COMPARE AND CONTRAST

Presidential Reconstruction	Congressional Reconstruction
	promote civil rights for freed people

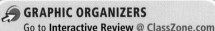

GRAPHIC ORGANIZERS
Go to **Interactive Review** @ ClassZone.com

Rebuilding the Union

14.C.3 Compare historical issues involving rights, roles and status of individuals in relation to municipalities, states and the nation.
16.B.3c Describe the way the Constitution has changed over time as a result of amendments and Supreme Court decisions.

One American's Story

After the Civil War, Pennsylvania congressman Thaddeus Stevens became a leader of the **Radical Republicans**. This group of congressmen favored using federal power to promote full citizenship for freed African Americans.

PRIMARY SOURCE

❝ We have turned, or are about to turn, loose four million slaves without a hut to shelter them or a cent in their pockets. . . . if we leave them to the legislation of their late masters, we had better have left them in bondage. ❞

—Thaddeus Stevens, the *Congressional Globe*, December 18, 1865

Radical Republicans wanted to make the South a region of small farms, free schools, and equality for all citizens.

Thaddeus Stevens was a passionate opponent of slavery and a strong supporter of the rights of African Americans.

Presidential Reconstruction

🔻 **KEY QUESTION** Why did presidential Reconstruction fail under Johnson?

Soon after the war ended, the nation began a process called **Reconstruction**. It lasted from 1865 to 1877. During Reconstruction, the federal government faced the challenge of rebuilding Southern society and governments.

Reconstruction Under Lincoln In his Second Inaugural Address, in March 1865, President Lincoln promised to reunify the nation "with malice [harm] toward none, with charity for all." Lincoln wanted to treat the South with respect. His plan included pardoning Confederate officials. It also called for allowing the Confederate states to send representatives to Congress.

Congress established the **Freedmen's Bureau**—a federal agency set up to assist former enslaved people. The Freedmen's Bureau set up schools and hospitals for African Americans and distributed clothes, food, and fuel.

Reconstruction Under Johnson When Lincoln was killed, Vice-President **Andrew Johnson** became president. Johnson believed that Reconstruction was the job of the president, not Congress. His policies were based on Lincoln's goals. He insisted that the new state governments ratify the Thirteenth Amendment, which banned slavery in the United States. He also insisted that they accept the supreme power of the federal government.

Johnson offered **amnesty**, or official pardon, to most white Southerners. He promised that their property would be returned to them. However, they had to pledge loyalty to the United States. At first, the large plantation owners, top military officers, and ex-Confederate leaders were not included in this offer. But most of them, too, eventually won amnesty.

Johnson's Failure Congress was not in session when Johnson became president in April 1865. Congress did not reconvene until December. During these eight months, the Southern states rebuilt. As they did so, they set up new state governments that were very much like the old ones. Some states flatly refused to ratify the Thirteenth Amendment. "This is a white man's government," said the governor of South Carolina, "and intended for white men only."

Johnson required only that the Southern states meet the conditions of his Reconstruction plan. His main goal was to have the Southern states readmitted to the Union as quickly as possible. He did not attempt to meet the needs of formerly enslaved people by helping them to gain land, voting rights, or equal protection under the law. Johnson believed the states should have the right to address these matters on their own. This was a relief to many white Southerners.

Southern states passed laws, known as **black codes**, that limited the freedom of formerly enslaved people. These laws were simply updated versions of the rules that had governed Southern African Americans during slavery. In Mississippi, for instance, one law said that African Americans had to have written proof of employment. Anyone without such proof could be arrested or imprisoned. African Americans were forbidden to meet in unsupervised groups or carry guns. Because the black codes were so much like slave codes, many people in the North suspected that white Southerners were trying to bring back the "old South."

▲ **CAUSES AND EFFECTS** Explain what caused the failure of presidential Reconstruction.

History Makers

Andrew Johnson   1808–1875

Andrew Johnson came from humble beginnings. His first career was as a tailor; his wife taught him to write and do arithmetic. In 1857, he was elected to the U.S. Senate from Tennessee. Although he was a Democrat and a former slaveholder, Johnson remained loyal to the Union. As president, he called for a mild program for bringing the South back into the Union. In particular, he let states decide whether to give voting rights to freed African Americans. Johnson's policies led to a break with the Radical Republicans in Congress and, finally, to his impeachment trial. (See page 575.)

CRITICAL THINKING

1. **Analyze Point of View** Why would many white Southerners have welcomed Johnson's decision on voting rights?

2. **Analyze Point of View** Why might Johnson have chosen not to punish the South?

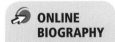
ONLINE BIOGRAPHY For more on Andrew Johnson, go to the **Research & Writing Center** @ ClassZone.com

Congressional Reconstruction

▼ **KEY QUESTION** What were the goals of Congressional Reconstruction?

When Congress finally met again in December 1865, its members first refused to seat representatives from the South. Many of these Southern representatives had been Confederate leaders only months before.

Congress States Its Intentions Congress exercised its Constitutional right to decide whether its members are qualified to hold office. It set up a committee to study conditions in the South and decide whether the Southern states should be represented. By taking such action, Congress let the president know that it planned to play a major role in Reconstruction.

Republicans outnumbered Democrats in both houses of Congress. Within the Republican Party, however, opinions differed as to how involved Congress should be in Reconstruction. Moderate Republicans supported the states' right to govern themselves. Radical Republicans wanted the federal government to play an active role in remaking Southern politics and society. Led by Thaddeus Stevens and Massachusetts senator Charles Sumner, the group demanded full and equal citizenship for African Americans.

Civil Rights for African Americans Urged on by the Radicals, Congress passed a bill promoting **civil rights**—those rights granted to all citizens. The Civil Rights Act of 1866 said that all people born in the United States (except Native Americans) were citizens. It also stated that all citizens were entitled to equal rights regardless of their race.

"The First Vote," by Alfred R. Waud, appeared on the cover of *Harper's Weekly* on November 16, 1867.

Republicans were shocked when Johnson chose to **veto** the bill, or stop it from becoming law. Johnson argued that federal protection of civil rights would lead to "centralization" of the government. He was also against giving African Americans full citizenship. Two-thirds of the House and two-thirds of the Senate voted to override the veto, and the bill became law.

Republicans wanted equality to be protected by the Constitution itself, and proposed an amendment in 1866. The **Fourteenth Amendment** stated that all people born or naturalized in the United States were citizens, had the same rights, and were to be granted "equal protection of the laws." However, the amendment did not specifically give African Americans the vote. Instead, it declared that any state that kept African Americans from voting would lose representatives in Congress. This meant that the Southern states would have less power if they did not grant black men the vote.

First district
Second district
Third district
Fourth district
Fifth district
1868 Date state readmitted to the Union

VIRGINIA
1870

NORTH CAROLINA
1868

TENNESSEE
(not in a military district)
1866

SOUTH CAROLINA
1868

ARKANSAS
1868

MISS.
1870

ALABAMA
1868

GEORGIA
1870

ATLANTIC OCEAN

TEXAS
1870

LOUISIANA
1868

FLORIDA
1868

Gulf of Mexico

N W E S

0   150   300 miles
0   150   300 kilometers

Connect Geography & History

1. **Place** Which former Confederate state was not assigned to a military district? Why not?

2. **Compare and Contrast** Which states were the first to be readmitted to the Union? Which states were the last to be readmitted?

Under the Reconstruction Acts, the U.S. army governed states in the Southern military districts.

Radical Reconstruction Johnson refused to support the Fourteenth Amendment. So did every former Confederate state except Tennessee. Moderate and Radical Republicans were outraged. The two groups joined forces and passed the Reconstruction Acts of 1867. This began a phase, known as Radical Reconstruction, in which Congress controlled Reconstruction.

The Reconstruction Acts divided the South into five military districts. They also said that before Southern states could rejoin the Union, they must:

1. approve new state constitutions that gave the vote to all adult men, including African Americans.
2. ratify the Fourteenth Amendment.

▲ **SUMMARIZE** Summarize Congressional goals for Reconstruction.

The Impact of Reconstruction

▼ **KEY QUESTION** What were the effects of Congressional Reconstruction?

After the Reconstruction Acts, Southern voters chose delegates to draft state constitutions. Delegates—all Republicans—came from three groups.

Constitutional Delegates Many of the Republicans were white farmers, many of them poor, who were angry at planters for starting what they called the "rich man's war." Some Democrats called these delegates **scalawags** (scoundrels) for going along with Radical Reconstruction.

The second group of delegates were known as **carpetbaggers**—white Northerners who rushed to the South after the war. Many Southerners accused them, often unfairly, of seeking only wealth or political power.

African Americans made up the third group of delegates. Of these, half had been free before the war. Most were teachers or other skilled workers.

New Southern Governments The new constitutions written by these delegates gave the vote to all adult males. By 1870, voters in all the Southern states had approved their new constitutions. As a result, former Confederate states were let back into the Union and allowed to send representatives to Congress.

During Reconstruction, nearly 700 African Americans served in Southern state legislatures, and 16 served as Southern U.S. congressmen. These included two senators: Hiram Revels and Blanche Bruce, both of Mississippi.

Johnson Is Impeached Johnson fought many changes made by Radical Republicans. His conflicts with Congress brought a showdown. In 1867, Congress passed the Tenure of Office Act, which prohibited the president from firing government officials without Senate approval. In February 1868, Johnson fired his secretary of war over disagreements about Reconstruction. Three days later, the House **impeached** the president, or formally accused him of improper conduct while in office.

The case moved to the Senate for a trial. If Johnson were convicted, he would have to leave office. In the end, Johnson was acquitted by a single vote. But much work remained to be done in rebuilding the South.

Carpetbaggers—Northerners who went South after the Civil War—were named for a type of luggage, made from old carpet, that was popular at the time.

▲ **CAUSES AND EFFECTS** Identify the effects of Congressional Reconstruction.

 Illinois Learning Standards *Review*

 ONLINE QUIZ
For test practice, go to
Interactive Review @ ClassZone.com

TERMS & NAMES

1. Explain the importance of

- Radical Republican
- black codes
- Reconstruction
- Fourteenth Amendment
- Freedmen's Bureau
- scalawag
- Andrew Johnson
- carpetbagger

USING YOUR READING NOTES

2. Compare and Contrast Complete the chart to show the goals of presidential and Congressional Reconstruction.

Presidential Reconstruction	Congressional Reconstruction
	promote civil rights for freed people

KEY IDEAS

3. How did President Andrew Johnson treat the South during Reconstruction?

4. Why did Congress decide to take a larger role in Reconstruction?

5. What conditions did the Southern states meet in order to rejoin the Union?

CRITICAL THINKING

6. Compare and Contrast How were the black codes similar to the old slave codes?

7. Draw Conclusions Did the Fourteenth Amendment truly protect African-American men's right to vote? Explain.

8. Evaluate Do you think the House was justified in impeaching President Johnson? Why or why not?

9. Writing Speech Research an African American who served in Congress during Reconstruction. Write a speech about his accomplishments.

▶ Key Ideas

BEFORE, YOU LEARNED

During Reconstruction, the president and Congress fought over how to rebuild the South.

NOW YOU WILL LEARN

As the South rebuilt, millions of freed African Americans worked to improve their lives.

▶ Vocabulary

TERMS & NAMES

freedmen's school school set up to educate newly freed African Americans

sharecropping system under which landowners gave poor farmers seed, tools, and land to cultivate in exchange for part of their harvest

Ku Klux Klan secret group that used violence to try to restore Democratic control of the South and keep African Americans powerless

BACKGROUND VOCABULARY

lynch to kill by hanging without due process of law

REVIEW

plantation large farm that raises cash crops

Visual Vocabulary
freedmen's school

▶ Reading Strategy

Re-create the diagram shown here. As you read and respond to the **KEY QUESTIONS**, use the center box to record the main idea; use the outer ovals to note important details. Add ovals or start a new diagram as needed.

 See Skillbuilder Handbook, page R4.

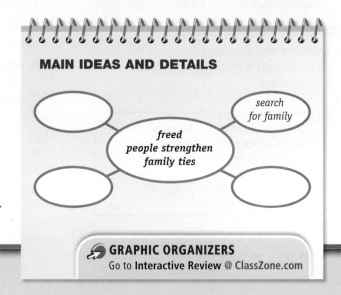

MAIN IDEAS AND DETAILS

search for family

freed people strengthen family ties

GRAPHIC ORGANIZERS
Go to **Interactive Review** @ ClassZone.com

SECTION
2

Reconstruction and Daily Life

14.C.3 Compare historical issues involving rights, roles and status of individuals in relation to municipalities, states and the nation.
14.D.3 Describe roles and influences of individuals, groups and media in shaping current Illinois and United States public policy (e.g., *general public opinion, special interest groups, formal parties, media*).

One American's Story

After emancipation, many African Americans went in search of family members separated from them by slavery. One observer described a Virginia search party in a letter to an African-American newspaper.

PRIMARY SOURCE

❝ Aged women and grayhaired men journeyed to Virginia from far-off Georgia hoping to . . . meet sons and daughters whom they bade farewell at the auction block. Many had the good fortune to find those they sought, and their greetings were pathetic [heartbreaking] beyond description. ❞

—B., *The New National Era*, July 23, 1874

Freed people on the South Carolina plantation of former Confederate general Thomas Drayton

Some former slaves walked hundreds of miles to find loved ones. Many placed advertisements in newspapers or with the Freedmen's Bureau.

Responding to Freedom

🔻 **KEY QUESTION** How did formerly enslaved people first respond to freedom?

Most African Americans' first reaction to freedom was to leave the **plantations**, the large farms that had raised cash crops using slave labor.

Leaving Plantations Some former slaves went looking for economic opportunity, while others traveled just because they could—they no longer needed passes to travel. Freedom also allowed African Americans to strengthen their family ties. For the first time, they could marry legally and raise families, knowing that their children could not be sold.

Education
American education had boomed in the mid–19th century, thanks to the efforts of reformers in both state governments and private organizations.
See Chapter 14, p. 460.

Freedmen's Schools With freedom, African Americans no longer had to work for an owner's benefit. They could now work to provide for their families. To reach their goal of economic independence, however, most had to learn to read and write. Children and adults flocked to **freedmen's schools,** which were set up to educate newly freed African Americans.

Such schools were started by the Freedmen's Bureau, Northern missionary groups, and African-American organizations. Freed people in cities held classes in warehouses, billiard rooms, and former slave markets. In rural areas, classes were held in churches and private homes. Children who went to school often taught their parents to read at home.

By 1869, more than 150,000 African-American students were attending 3,000 schools. Almost 20 percent of the South's African-American adults could read. Many white Southerners, however, worked against African Americans' efforts to educate themselves. White racists even killed teachers and burned freedmen's schools in some parts of the South. Despite these violent attacks, African Americans kept working toward an education.

▲ **SYNTHESIZE** Explain how freedom changed the lives of formerly enslaved people.

CONNECT ↝ *To Today*

RICHMOND, VIRGINIA

During the Civil War, Richmond was the capital of the Confederate States of America. In April 1865, the South faced defeat as Union troops approached the city. The retreating Confederates blew up Richmond's gunpowder supplies in a shattering explosion. Most of the business district and many residential areas were destroyed by fire.

Richmond quickly rebuilt after the war, aided by money from the tobacco industry, of which the city was a hub. Today, Richmond is the capital city of Virginia.

(*right*) A statue of Confederate general Robert E. Lee on Richmond's Monument Avenue. The street was built in the 1880s to honor Civil War veterans. (*inset*) Richmond, April 1865

CRITICAL THINKING

1. Make Inferences Why would the Confederates destroy their own supplies?

2. Evaluate What are the advantages and disadvantages of rebuilding a city?

Working the Land

▼ **KEY QUESTION** What prevented formerly enslaved people from making greater economic advances?

More than anything else, freed people wanted land. To them, land meant economic independence. As one freedman said, "Give us our own land and we take care of ourselves, but without land, the old masters can hire us or starve us, as they please."

Forty Acres and a Mule As the Civil War ended, General Sherman suggested that abandoned land in the coastal South be split into 40-acre parcels and given to freedmen. The army also had extra mules that Sherman wanted to loan. The rumor then spread that all freedmen would get 40 acres and a mule. Most freed people thought they deserved at least that much. Said one freedman:

PRIMARY SOURCE

❝ Our wives, our children, our husbands, [have] been sold over and over again to purchase the lands we now [locate] upon; for that reason we have a divine right to the land. . . . And [then] didn't we clear the land, and raise [the] crops [of] corn, of cotton, of tobacco, of rice, of sugar, of everything? And then didn't . . . cities in the North grow up on the cotton and the sugars and the rice that we made! . . . I say they have grown rich, and my people are poor. ❞

—Bayley Wyat, quoted in *Reconstruction: America's Unfinished Revolution*

In the end, however, most freedmen received no land. Those who did often had to return it later to its former owners—planters who were pardoned by President Johnson.

Radical Republicans Thaddeus Stevens and Charles Sumner pushed for land reform. Stevens proposed a plan that would have taken land from plantation owners and given it to freed people. He argued that civil rights meant little without economic independence. But many other Republicans were against the plan. They believed that civil and voting rights for African Americans were enough, and that the plantation owners had the right to keep their land. As a result, Congress did not pass the plan.

Picking cotton on a Southern plantation, 1870

COMPARING *Southern Agriculture*

	Cotton (bales)	Corn (bushels)	Hay (tons)
1850	2.5 million	240 million	718,997
1860	5.3 million	283 million	1.1 million
1870	3.1 million	179 million	474,739
1880	5.9 million	249 million	699,200

(Source: *Historical Statistics of the States of the United States*)

CRITICAL THINKING Make Inferences What effects of the Civil War explain the drop in agricultural production in Southern states?

The Contract System After the Civil War, planters needed workers to raise cotton—still the South's main cash crop. Without their own land, many African Americans accepted contracts for plantation work.

The contract system was far better than slavery. African Americans were paid for their labor and could decide whom to work for. But even the best contracts paid very low wages. Some landowners abused or cheated workers. As a result, many African Americans turned to sharecropping.

The Economics of Sharecropping In the **sharecropping** system, farmers rented land on credit. The landowner provided tools and seed. At harvest time, farmers gave a share of their crops to the landowner as payment.

The sharecropping system had serious problems. Farmers wanted to grow food to feed their families, but landowners forced them to grow cash crops, such as cotton. Meanwhile, most farmers had to buy food, clothing, and other goods on credit—often at inflated prices. By the time they had shared their crops with the landowner and paid their debts, sharecroppers usually had little or no money left. Without money or land of their own, most sharecroppers had no hope of escaping poverty.

▲ **CAUSES AND EFFECTS** Identify the factors that held back the economic advancement of formerly enslaved people.

COMPARING ▸ *The Contract System and Sharecropping*

CONTRACT SYSTEM

- earn wages
- choose whom to work for

SHARECROPPING

- earn portion of harvest
- supervise own work

DRAWBACKS

- low wages
- often cheated by landowner

BENEFITS

- families stay together
- landowner provides land, tools, seed

DRAWBACKS

- landowner decides what to grow
- farmers often must buy goods on credit from landowner

CRITICAL THINKING **Form and Support Opinions** Which do you think offered farmers a better chance of escaping poverty: the contract system or sharecropping? Why?

Violent Racism

🔻 **KEY QUESTION** What were the goals of the Ku Klux Klan?

African Americans in the South faced serious problems besides poverty—including violent racism. Many planters and former Confederate soldiers did not want African Americans to have equal rights.

The Ku Klux Klan In 1866, racism in the South spurred the rise of a terrorist group called the **Ku Klux Klan**. Its members came from all walks of life, from poor farmers to former Confederate officers. The Klan's goals were to restore Democratic control of the South and keep former slaves powerless. By 1868, the Klan existed in nearly every Southern state.

The Klan attacked African Americans and white Republicans. Klansmen rode on horseback and dressed in robes and hoods that hid their faces. They beat and tortured people and burned schools, churches, and homes. They even **lynched** some victims—killed them by hanging without a trial as punishment for a supposed crime.

Targets of the Klan had little protection. Military governors in the South often ignored the violence. President Johnson had appointed most of these authorities, and they were against Reconstruction.

The Klan's violence served the Democratic Party. As Klansmen kept Republicans away from the polls, the Democrats' power increased.

🔺 **SUMMARIZE** Describe the goals of the Ku Klux Klan.

(*top*) A former slave trader and Confederate general, Nathan Bedford Forrest led the Klan from 1867 to 1869. (*bottom*) an 1866 Klan flag.

Illinois Learning Standards *Review*

🔁 **ONLINE QUIZ**
For test practice, go to
Interactive Review @ ClassZone.com

TERMS & NAMES

1. Explain the importance of:
- freedmen's school
- Ku Klux Klan
- sharecropping

USING YOUR READING NOTES

2. Main Ideas and Details Give details about the ways in which newly freed African Americans worked to strengthen family ties.

search for family

freed people strengthen family ties

KEY IDEAS

3. How did newly freed African Americans work to improve their lives?

4. Why did many African Americans move from the contract system to sharecropping?

5. How did the Ku Klux Klan benefit the Democratic Party?

CRITICAL THINKING

6. Connect Economics and History How did the sharecropping system affect African Americans' efforts to achieve economic independence?

7. Problems and Solutions What problems did formerly enslaved people face in their efforts to improve their lives?

8. Writing **Journal** Write a journal entry from the point of view of a sharecropper who was a former contract worker. Describe a day in the life of this person.

▶ Key Ideas

BEFORE, YOU LEARNED

As the South rebuilt, millions of newly freed African Americans worked to improve their lives.

NOW YOU WILL LEARN

As white Southerners regained power in Congress, Reconstruction ended, as did African-American advances toward equality.

▶ Vocabulary

TERMS & NAMES

Fifteenth Amendment constitutional amendment that stated that citizens could not be stopped from voting "on account of race, color, or previous condition of servitude"

Panic of 1873 financial panic in which banks closed and the stock market crashed

Compromise of 1877 agreement that decided the 1876 presidential election

BACKGROUND VOCABULARY

stock market place where shares of ownership in companies are bought and sold

depression time of low business activity and high unemployment

compromise settlement of differences in which each side gives up something it wants

REVIEW

Ulysses S. Grant former Union general

electoral votes votes made by the members of the Electoral College, which elects the president and vice president

amendment formal alteration or addition to the U.S. Constitution

Visual Vocabulary
Panic of 1873

▶ Reading Strategy

Re-create the diagram shown here. As you read and respond to the **KEY QUESTIONS**, use the diagram to note important events and their effects. Add boxes or start a new diagram as needed.

 See Skillbuilder Handbook, page R7.

CAUSES AND EFFECTS

CAUSE

Congress passes anti-Klan bill

EFFECT

federal marshals arrest Klansmen

EFFECT

GRAPHIC ORGANIZERS
Go to **Interactive Review** @ ClassZone.com

The End of Reconstruction

14.C.3 Compare historical issues involving rights, roles and status of individuals in relation to municipalities, states and the nation.
15.A.3d Describe the causes of unemployment (e.g., *seasonal fluctuation in demand, changing jobs, changing skill requirements, national spending*).

One American's Story

Robert B. Elliott was elected to the U.S. Congress from South Carolina in 1871. A brilliant orator, he gave a famous speech to Congress in favor of the Civil Rights Act of 1875, which outlawed racial segregation in public services such as restaurants, hotels, and transportation.

PRIMARY SOURCE

❝ The passage of this bill will determine the civil status, not only of the negro but of any other class of citizens who may feel themselves discriminated against. It will form the capstone of that temple of liberty begun on this continent. ❞

—**Robert B. Elliott, quoted in** *The Glorious Failure*

In 1877, federal troops left the South. White Southerners quickly took back control of the region, and African Americans lost many hard-earned gains. Even the Civil Rights Act of 1875 was overturned within a decade.

Protecting African-American Rights

🔻 **KEY QUESTION** How did the Republican Party try to advance civil rights for African Americans?

In 1868, the Republican candidate, former Union general **Ulysses S. Grant**, won the presidency. The Republican Party seemed stronger than ever.

Grant's Victory Grant won with 214 **electoral votes**—votes in the Electoral College, which elects the president and vice president. His Democratic opponent received only 80. In the popular count, however, Grant had a majority of only about 305,000 votes. He would not have had this majority without the freedmen's vote. Despite attacks by the Klan, about 500,000 African Americans voted in the South, and most cast their ballots for Grant.

On January 6, 1874, U.S. Representative Robert B. Elliott argued for "equal rights and equal public privileges for all classes of American citizens." This demand was made law in the Civil Rights Act of 1875.

The Fifteenth Amendment After Grant's win, Radical Republicans feared that Southern states might try to keep African Americans from voting in future elections. In addition, some states outside the South still prohibited African-American men from voting. To protect African-American suffrage, Radical Republican leaders proposed a constitutional **amendment**—a formal change or addition to the U.S. Constitution.

The **Fifteenth Amendment** stated that citizens could not be stopped from voting "on account of race, color, or previous condition of servitude." (This amendment, like the Fourteenth Amendment, did not apply to Native Americans on tribal lands.) The amendment was ratified in 1870.

The amendment did not apply to women. This made many white women angry, especially those who had fought to end slavery. Suffragist Elizabeth Cady Stanton was opposed to the idea of uneducated immigrants and freedmen "who cannot read the Declaration of Independence . . . making laws for . . . women of wealth and education." But most African-American women, including suffragist Frances E. W. Harper, felt it was important for African Americans to gain voting rights, even if that meant only men at first.

COMPARING *Political Representation*

AFRICAN AMERICANS AND WOMEN IN CONGRESS

(*left*) Jeannette Rankin, elected in 1916, and (*right*) Shirley Chisholm, elected in 1968

These graphs show the number of African Americans and women who served in the U.S. Congress from 1866 onward.

Sources: CRS Report for Congress: Black Members of the United States Congress: 1870–2005; *Women of Congress* by Rep. Marcy Kaptur; Center for American Women and Politics

CRITICAL THINKING

1. **Draw Conclusions** What happened to African-American representation in Congress after Reconstruction ended?

2. **Make Generalizations** Who made advances in representation more quickly after 1916, African Americans or women?

Grant Fights the Klan Despite gaining the vote, African Americans in the South continued to be terrorized by the Ku Klux Klan. In 1871, President Grant asked Congress to pass a tough law against the Klan. Joseph Rainey, a black congressman from South Carolina, had received death threats from the Klan. He urged his fellow lawmakers to support the bill.

PRIMARY SOURCE

> ❝ When myself and colleagues shall leave these Halls and turn our footsteps toward our southern home we know not but that the assassin may await our coming. Be it as it may we have resolved to be loyal and firm, and if we perish, we perish! I earnestly hope the bill will pass. ❞

—Joseph Rainey, quoted in *The Trouble They Seen*

This cartoon from *Puck* magazine shows Grant weighed down by corruption in his administration. **How was Grant burdened by his employees?**

Congress approved the anti-Klan bill. Federal marshals then arrested thousands of Klansmen. Klan attacks on African-American voters declined. As a result, the 1872 presidential election was both fair and peaceful in the South. Grant won a second term.

▲ **PROBLEMS AND SOLUTIONS** Identify the ways Republicans tried to advance rights for African Americans.

Reconstruction Weakens

▼ **KEY QUESTION** How did Reconstruction lose its strength?

Under President Grant, support for the Republicans and their pro–African-American attitude toward Reconstruction weakened. One major cause of this loss of support was scandal in Grant's administration.

Scandal in the Republican Party President Grant did not choose his advisers well. He put his former army friends and his wife's relatives in government positions. Many of these people were unqualified. Some Grant appointees took bribes. Grant's private secretary, for instance, was involved with whiskey distillers who wanted to avoid paying taxes. Grant's secretary of war, General William Belknap, left office after people accused him of taking bribes.

Such scandals angered many Republicans. In 1872, some Republican officials broke away and formed the new Liberal Republican Party. The Republicans, no longer unified, became less able to impose tough Reconstruction policies on the South.

This cartoon by Thomas Nast dramatizes the Panic of 1873: a sudden explosion hits Wall Street, New York's financial center. **What does the image suggest about the effects of the Panic?**

The Panic of 1873 In 1873, political corruption and quarreling gave way to a more serious problem. Several powerful Eastern banks ran out of money after making bad loans. Worried that the banks would lose their money, people made withdrawals. In the **Panic of 1873**, banks across the land closed. The **stock market** (a place where shares of ownership in companies are bought and sold) temporarily collapsed. The panic caused an economic **depression**, a time of low business activity and high unemployment.

The depression, which lasted about five years, touched nearly all parts of the economy. By 1875, more than 18,000 companies had folded and half a million workers had lost their jobs. Many Americans blamed the crisis on the Republicans—the party in power. As a result, Democrats won victories in the 1874 congressional and state elections. In the middle of the depression, Americans grew tired of hearing about the South's problems. The nation was losing interest in Reconstruction.

Civil Rights Reversals To make matters worse for the Republicans, the Supreme Court began to undo some of the progress that had been made for civil rights. In an 1876 case, *U.S.* v. *Cruikshank*, the Court ruled that the federal government could not punish individuals who violated the civil rights of African Americans. Only the states had that power, the Court declared. Southern state officials often would not punish those who attacked African Americans. As a result, violence against them increased.

In the 1876 case *U.S.* v. *Reese*, the Court ruled in favor of white Southerners who barred African Americans from voting. The Court stated that the Fifteenth Amendment did not give everyone the right to vote—it merely listed the grounds on which states could not deny the vote. In other words, states could prevent African Americans from voting for other reasons. States later imposed poll taxes and unfair literacy tests to restrict the vote. These Court decisions weakened Reconstruction and blocked African-American efforts to gain full equality.

▲ **CAUSES AND EFFECTS** Explain what caused Reconstruction to weaken.

Reconstruction Ends

▼ **KEY QUESTION** What finally led to the end of Reconstruction?

The final blow to Reconstruction came with the 1876 presidential election. In the election, the Democrats chose Samuel J. Tilden, governor of New York. The Republicans nominated Rutherford B. Hayes, governor of Ohio. The election's result forced a **compromise**—a settlement in which both parties gave up some things they wanted. The Republicans gave up the most.

Compromise of 1877 Victory in the 1876 presidential election depended on three Southern states—South Carolina, Louisiana, and Florida. The votes in those states were so close that both sides claimed victory. A commission of Republicans and Democrats made a deal. Under the **Compromise of 1877**, Republican Rutherford Hayes became president. But the terms were a blow to Republican Reconstruction in the South:

- The government would remove federal troops from the South.
- The government would provide land grants and loans for the construction of railroads linking the South to the West Coast.
- Southern officials would receive federal funds for construction and improvement projects.
- Hayes would appoint a Democrat to his cabinet.
- The Democrats promised to respect African Americans' rights.

Connecting History

Presidential Elections
The election of 1876 was not the first to be disputed. The election of 1800 had resulted in a tie, which was broken by a compromise in the House of Representatives. *See Chapter 10, pp. 337–339.*

CONNECT to the Essential Question

How did a deeply divided nation move forward after the Civil War?

PROBLEM	PRESIDENTIAL SOLUTIONS	CONGRESSIONAL SOLUTIONS
State governments led by former Confederates	Asked Southern states to ratify the Thirteenth Amendment and accept the supreme power of the federal government Offered amnesty and return of property to Confederates who pledged loyalty to the federal government ✓ SUCCESS	Set up commission to study conditions in the South and determine if Southern states should be allowed representation in U.S. Congress ✓ SUCCESS
Resistance to granting civil rights to formerly enslaved people	Asked Congress to pass anti–Ku Klux Klan legislation ✓ SOME SUCCESS	Passed Civil Rights Act of 1866 Proposed Fourteenth and passed Fifteenth Amendments Passed anti–Ku Klux Klan legislation ✓ SOME SUCCESS
Formerly enslaved people needing education and employment	None ✗ FAILURE	Freedmen's Bureau ✓ SOME SUCCESS

CRITICAL THINKING Make Inferences Why might Reconstruction be considered a time in which the presidency was weak?

Abolitionist Wendell Phillips was against the compromise. He doubted that the South would respect African Americans' rights. "The whole soil of the South is hidden by successive layers of broken promises," he said. "To trust a Southern promise would be fair evidence of insanity."

After the 1876 presidential election, Republican Reconstruction in the South collapsed. The Democrats returned to power.

The Legacy of Reconstruction Historians still argue about the success of Reconstruction. The government did achieve its most important goal—the reunification of the nation. However, Reconstruction's effect on African Americans is less straightforward.

African Americans' legal situation changed greatly during Reconstruction. Slavery was outlawed, and African-American men gained the vote and ability to hold office. But the federal government did not enforce the spirit of the Fourteenth and Fifteenth Amendments. In fact, the Supreme Court's rulings in favor of states' rights practically reversed these two amendments. Meanwhile, African Americans continued to face widespread violence and prejudice. White intimidation prevented many African Americans from taking part in politics. Lack of land ownership and economic opportunity meant that most African Americans continued to live in poverty and as second-class citizens.

 SYNTHESIZE Explain how Reconstruction ended.

A statue of educator Booker T. Washington at Hampton University, one of several historically black colleges founded during Reconstruction

---

 ONLINE QUIZ
For test practice, go to
Interactive Review @ ClassZone.com

Illinois Learning Standards *Review*

TERMS & NAMES

1. Explain the importance of
- Fifteenth Amendment
- Compromise of 1877
- Panic of 1873

USING YOUR READING NOTES

2. Causes and Effects Complete the diagram you started at the beginning of this section. Then create a diagram for each of the other main events in this section.

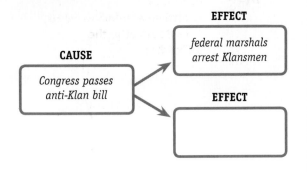

CAUSE

Congress passes anti-Klan bill

EFFECT

federal marshals arrest Klansmen

EFFECT

KEY IDEAS

3. What did the Fifteenth Amendment declare?

4. What effect did scandals in the Grant administration have on the Republican Party?

5. What concessions did the Republicans make in the Compromise of 1877?

CRITICAL THINKING

6. Analyze Point of View Why did the Fifteenth Amendment anger some white women?

7. Causes and Effects Why did the Supreme Court's decisions in favor of states' rights hurt African-American advances toward equality?

8. Draw Conclusions Why do you think the Republicans were willing to agree to the Compromise of 1877, even though they knew it would weaken Reconstruction?

9. **Writing** **Essay** Research the presidential election of 2000. Write a one-page essay comparing and contrasting the settlement to that election with that of the presidential election of 1876.

Chapter Summary

1 Key Idea
During Reconstruction, the president and Congress fought over how to rebuild the South.

2 Key Idea
As the South rebuilt, millions of freed African Americans worked to improve their lives.

3 Key Idea
As white Southerners regained power in Congress, Reconstruction ended, as did African-American advances toward equality.

For detailed Review and Study Notes go to **Interactive Review** @ ClassZone.com

Name Game

Use the Terms & Names list to identify each sentence online or on your own paper.

1. I was a farmer who rented land on credit.
   sharecropper

2. I believed in using Congressional power to rebuild the South.

3. This caused high unemployment.

4. This was set up by Congress to help formerly enslaved people.

5. This used violence to try to restore Democratic control of the South.

6. I was a white Southerner who supported Reconstruction.

7. This stated that citizens could not be stopped from voting on the basis of race.

8. This was a reason that formerly enslaved people had limited legal rights.

9. This was a time in which the U.S. government tried to rebuild Southern society.

10. This removed federal troops from the South.

A. Radical Republican
B. Freedmen's Bureau
C. Fourteenth Amendment
D. Fifteenth Amendment
E. Panic of 1873
F. Compromise of 1877
G. carpetbagger
H. Ku Klux Klan
I. black codes
J. scalawag
K. Reconstruction
L. sharecropper

Activities

FLIPCARD

Use the online flip cards to quiz yourself on the terms and names introduced in this chapter.

This president was impeached and later acquitted by a single vote.

ANSWER
Andrew Johnson

CROSSWORD PUZZLE

Complete the online crossword puzzle to show what you know about Reconstruction.

ACROSS
1. Northerner who moved to the South after the Civil War

VOCABULARY

Explain the significance of each of the following.

1. Fifteenth Amendment
2. freedmen's school
3. black codes
4. Fourteenth Amendment
5. amnesty
6. Compromise of 1877
7. carpetbagger

Identify the term that does not belong in each group, and explain why.

8. stock market, Radical Republican, civil rights
9. depression, Panic of 1873, carpetbagger
10. Andrew Johnson, Fifteenth Amendment, amnesty

KEY IDEAS

① Rebuilding the Union (pages 570–575)

11. Under the Reconstruction Acts of 1867, what was asked of Southern states before rejoining the Union?

12. Why was Andrew Johnson impeached?

② Reconstruction and Daily Life (pages 576–581)

13. What was a freedmen's school?

14. Why did Congress not pass a land-reform plan?

③ The End of Reconstruction (pages 582–588)

15. Why did Republicans lose power in the government?

16. During Reconstruction, how did the Supreme Court weaken African Americans' civil rights?

CRITICAL THINKING

17. **Synthesize** Why was Reconstruction needed?

18. **Compare and Contrast** How did President Johnson's ideas about Reconstruction differ from those of the Radical Republicans?

19. **Make Inferences** What years included in the chart brought the greatest increase in the national debt? Why might this have been?

National Debt *1861–1869*

*millions of dollars

(Source: U.S. Department of the Treasury)

20. **Summarize** What impact did the Reconstruction Acts of 1867 have on the South?

21. **Analyze Point of View** Why did African Americans want their own land?

22. **Causes and Effects** How did the Panic of 1873 affect Reconstruction?

23. **Main Ideas and Details** What demands did Southern Democrats make in the Compromise of 1877? What did Republicans gain from the Compromise?

24. **Problems and Solutions** Fill in a table like the one shown to identify the major problems of Reconstruction and how the government attempted to solve them.

PROBLEMS	PROPOSED SOLUTIONS
State governments led by former Confederates	
Resistance to granting civil rights to former enslaved people	
Large numbers of former enslaved people needing education and employment	

✓ **TEST PRACTICE**

• **Online Test Practice** @ ClassZone.com
• **Test-Taking Strategies & Practice** at the front of this book

MULTIPLE CHOICE

Use the map and your knowledge of U.S. history to answer question 1.

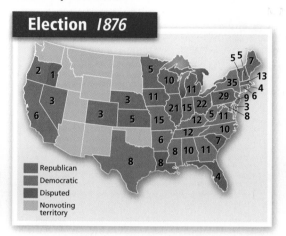

Election *1876*

Republican
Democratic
Disputed
Nonvoting territory

1. What regions voted mostly Republican?

   A. the North and East

   B. the North and West

   C. the South and East

   D. the South and West

Use the quotation and your knowledge of U.S. history to answer question 2.

PRIMARY SOURCE

❝ It is a matter of regret to me that it is necessary at this day that I should rise in the presence of an American Congress to advocate a bill which simply asserts equal rights and equal public privileges for all classes of American citizens. ❞

—**U.S. Representative Robert Elliott of South Carolina**

2. Why was it "a matter of regret" to Robert Elliott that he had to speak in support of this bill?

   A. He wanted Congress to compromise on the bill.

   B. The failures of Reconstruction filled him with regret.

   C. Supporting the bill could cause him to lose his job.

   D. He believed all Americans should already have equal rights.

YOU BE THE HISTORIAN

25. **Make Generalizations** How did Reconstruction change the lives of most formerly enslaved people?

26. **WHAT IF?** If the Ku Klux Klan had not existed, how might Reconstruction have been different?

27. **Causes and Effects** How did government corruption and misconduct make an impact on Reconstruction?

28. **Citizenship** How did the Fifteenth Amendment promote citizenship for African Americans? How was the amendment limited?

29. **Draw Conclusions** What lasting gains did African Americans make during Reconstruction?

30. **Form and Support Opinions** Do you think African Americans were better off in 1877 than they had been in 1865? Why?

Answer the
ESSENTIAL QUESTION
How did a deeply divided nation move forward after the Civil War?

Written Response Write a two- to three-paragraph response to the Essential Question. Consider the key ideas of each section along with the major successes and failures of Reconstruction. Use the Response Rubric below to guide your thinking and writing.

Response Rubric
A strong response will

• compare presidential and Congressional Reconstruction

• explain the obstacles to Reconstruction

• identify the major successes and failures of Reconstruction

• analyze how those successes and failures affected American society

America Transformed

1860–1920

Why It Matters Now

The industrialization of the United States in the
60 years after the Civil War made America a world
power. But not without a price. The era is also
notable for efforts to humanize the U.S. industrial
system, to make it work not just for the most
privileged members of our society but for everyone.

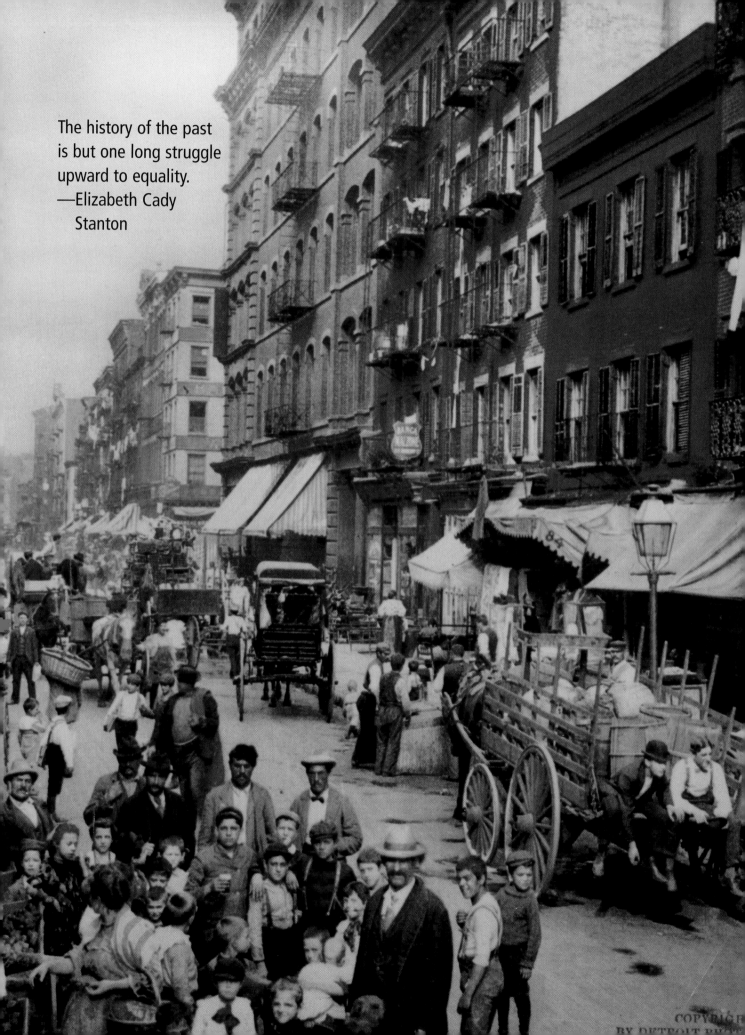

The history of the past is but one long struggle upward to equality.
—Elizabeth Cady Stanton

Growth in the West

1860–1900

 ESSENTIAL QUESTION

How did the nation change as a result of westward movement after the Civil War?

CONNECT ⟲ **Geography & History**

How might U.S. geography have affected western settlement?

Think about:

1 the advantages of being on a coastal area or waterway

2 how the population density in desert areas, such as the Southwest, compares with the population density in areas with greater rainfall, such as the Midwest

3 the obstacles presented by mountains in the West

A replica of a Central Pacific steam engine

This railroad advertisement shows a route in the outline of a chair.

1862 Congress passes Homestead Act.

▼

Effect Offer of free land encourages western settlement.

1869 The transcontinental railroad is completed.

▼

Effect Western settlement increases.

1860

Abraham Lincoln is elected president.

1864 Colorado militia kill peaceful Native Americans in Sand Creek Massacre.

1876 Native Americans triumph at Battle of the Little Bighorn.

▼

Effect U.S. steps up military action.

Click here to preview western expansion @ClassZone.com

Persons per sq mi		Cities	
Over 90	▨	☐	Over 1 million
19–90	▨	◉	500,000 to 1 million
2–18	▨	●	200,000 to 500,000
Under 2	☐		

WASH.

MAINE

MONT.

NORTH DAKOTA

VT. N.H.

ORE.

MINN.

N.Y. Boston

IDAHO

Minneapolis

WIS.

MASS. CONN. R.I.

SOUTH DAKOTA

MICH.

Buffalo

WYO.

Milwaukee

Detroit

Jersey City — New York

NEV.

IOWA Chicago

Cleveland

Newark — N.J.

Pittsburgh

PA.

Philadelphia

San Francisco

UTAH

NEBR.

OHIO

Baltimore

UTAH

ILL. IND. Cincinnati

W. VA.

DEL.

MD.

Washington, D.C.

CALIF.

COLO.

KANS.

St. Louis

KY.

Louisville

VA.

ARIZONA TERR.

NEW MEXICO TERR.

OKLA. TERR.

UNORG. TERR.

MO.

TENN.

N.C.

S.C.

ARK.

MISS. ALA.

GA.

TEXAS

LA.

New Orleans

FLA.

N
W E
S

0   150   300 miles
0   150   300 kilometers

A vaquero (cowhand)
in New Mexico Territory

1892 Populist Party is founded to support rights of farmers and laborers.

1900

1887 The Dawes Act distributes reservation land to individuals.

Sioux moccasins, circa 1895

1896 William McKinley wins presidential election.

▼

Effect Populist Party collapses.

Reading for Understanding

▶ Key Ideas

BEFORE, YOU LEARNED

As white Southerners regained power, Reconstruction ended in 1877.

NOW YOU WILL LEARN

A railroad, completed in 1869, spanned the continent and helped to open the way for settlers in the West.

▶ Vocabulary

TERMS & NAMES

transcontinental railroad railroad that spanned the U.S. continent

Great Plains the area from the Missouri River to the Rocky Mountains

frontier parts of the West that were occupied mainly by Native Americans, rather than settlers

BACKGROUND VOCABULARY

solar time time based on calculations of the sun's passage across the sky

standard time the time zones devised by railroad companies

Visual Vocabulary
Great Plains

▶ Reading Strategy

Re-create the diagram shown at right. As you read and respond to the **KEY QUESTIONS**, use the diagram to note the effects of building the transcontinental railroad. Add boxes or start a new diagram as needed.

 See Skillbuilder Handbook, page R7.

CAUSES AND EFFECTS

Cause
Transcontinental railroad completed

Effect
Linked economies of East and West

Effect

GRAPHIC ORGANIZERS
Go to **Interactive Review** @ ClassZone.com

Railroads Transform the Nation

15.C.3 Identify and explain the effects of various incentives to produce a good or service.
15.E.3b Explain how laws and government policies (e.g., property rights, contract enforcement, standard weights/measurements) establish rules that help a market economy function effectively.

One American's Story

Ah Goong was one of many Chinese workers on the western railroads in the late 1800s. In some places, workers had to blast rock from a cliff wall. Lightweight Chinese workers were lowered in baskets hundreds of feet to the blasting site. Years later, Ah Goong's granddaughter imagined his work.

PRIMARY SOURCE

❝ Swinging near the cliff, Ah Goong . . . dug holes, then inserted gunpowder and fuses. . . . He struck match after match and dropped the burnt matches over the sides. At last his fuse caught; he waved, and the men above pulled hand over hand hauling him up, pulleys creaking. ❞

—Maxine Hong Kingston, *China Men*

Thousands of Chinese immigrants helped to build the transcontinental railroad.

The building of the transcontinental railroad changed American life. It speeded economic growth and helped open the West to settlers.

Railroads Link East and West

🔻 **KEY QUESTION** How was the first transcontinental railroad built?

For years, Americans had talked about building a **transcontinental railroad**—one that would connect the Atlantic and Pacific coasts. Such a railroad would encourage people to settle in the West and develop its economy.

Help from the Government In 1862, Congress gave the task of building the railroad to two companies: the Union Pacific and the Central Pacific. The Central Pacific was to start in Sacramento, California, and build east. The Union Pacific was to start in Omaha, Nebraska, and build west.

The federal government lent the railroad companies millions of dollars. It also passed legislation that gave them grants of public land along the track. The railroad companies could then sell the land to raise money.

Railroads of the Transcontinental Era 1865–1900

PACIFIC TIME ZONE

MOUNTAIN TIME ZONE

CENTRAL TIME ZONE

EASTERN TIME ZONE

Seattle

Portland

Butte

Great Northern

Northern Pacific

Minneapolis

N.Y. Central

Boston

Southern Pacific

Central Pacific

Union Pacific

Chicago

Cleveland

New York

Salt Lake City

Pennsylvania

Washington, D.C.

San Francisco

Denver & Rio Grande

Denver

Kansas City

St. Louis

Illinois Central

Atlantic & Pacific

Memphis

Southern

Los Angeles

Albuquerque

Atchison, Topeka & Santa Fe

Atlanta

PACIFIC OCEAN

Southern Pacific

Texas & Pacific

Fort Worth

New Orleans

ATLANTIC OCEAN

Standard time zones were adopted by railroads in 1883

0   150   300 miles

0 150 300 kilometers

Connect Geography & History

1. **Region** Why were there more railroads in the eastern half of the country than in the western half?

2. **Draw Conclusions** What do you think each of the time zones was named for?

3. **Make Inferences** Note whether more tracks run north to south, or east to west. What is a likely reason for this?

This golden spike was used in the ceremony that marked the completion of the railroad.

Immigrants Lay the Track Building the railroads was hard, dangerous work. Many of the workers hired by the railroad companies were immigrants with few other choices of work. In the West, the Central Pacific railroad hired many Chinese workers, who faced widespread discrimination. More than 10,000 Chinese men worked on the Central Pacific.

The Union Pacific hired workers from a variety of backgrounds. Many of its workers were Irish immigrants. After 1865, many former soldiers from both the North and the South also worked on the railroad.

Joining the Railroads In May 1869, the Central Pacific and the Union Pacific met in Utah at Promontory Summit. The Central Pacific had crossed California's rugged Sierra Nevada Mountains and laid about 700 miles of track. The Union Pacific had laid more than 1,000 miles, mostly across the **Great Plains**—the area from the Missouri River to the Rocky Mountains.

Hundreds of railroad workers, managers, and journalists gathered for a ceremony. A band played and a golden spike was hammered to honor the completion of the railroad. The transcontinental railroad was complete. By 1895, four more railroad lines were built spanning the United States.

⬤ **CAUSES AND EFFECTS** Explain the roles of the government and immigrants in building the transcontinental railroad.

The Impact of the Railroads

▼ **KEY QUESTION** How did the transcontinental railroad change America?

The railroads changed many things in people's lives—even timekeeping.

Railroad Time Before the railroads, each community determined its own time, based on calculations about the sun's travels. This system was called "**solar time**." Solar time caused problems for people who scheduled trains crossing a long distance. It also confused railroad travelers, who had to ask, "Is the train arriving at 2:00 our time or their time?" To solve this problem, the railroad companies set up **standard time**. This system divided the United States into four time zones. (See the map on page 598.)

Movement to the Frontier The transcontinental railroad brought settlers to the **frontier**—the parts of the West (mostly in the Great Plains) that were occupied mainly by Native Americans. Trains were a lifeline for settlers. They brought lumber, food, and other necessities. They also brought settlers and miners who laid claim to Native American land. In this way, the railroads helped weaken the Native American hold on the West.

Railroads also linked the nation economically. From the West, trains carried raw materials such as lumber, livestock, and grain eastward. These materials were processed in midwestern cities such as Chicago. From eastern cities, in turn, came manufactured goods, which were sold to westerners.

▲ **SYNTHESIZE** Explain how the transcontinental railroad changed America.

This nineteenth-century railroad conductor's watch shows the time in different zones.

Illinois Learning Standards *Review*

🖙 **ONLINE QUIZ**
For test practice, go to
Interactive Review @ ClassZone.com

TERMS & NAMES

1. Explain the importance of
   - transcontinental railroad
   - frontier
   - Great Plains

USING YOUR READING NOTES

2. **Causes and Effects** Complete the diagram you started at the beginning of the section. Then create a diagram for each of the main events in this section.

KEY IDEAS

3. How was the transcontinental railroad financed?
4. Why did the country need a standard time?

CRITICAL THINKING

5. **Analyze Point of View** Why would the federal government have wanted a transcontinental railroad to be built?

6. **Synthesize** How did the railroads benefit the economy?

7. **Connect** *to* **Today** What changes created by the railroads are part of the business world today?

8. **Writing** **Letter** Suppose that you were one of the workers who helped build the railroads. Write a one-page letter to a family member explaining how your work will help to transform the nation.

▶ Key Ideas

BEFORE, YOU LEARNED

A railroad, completed in 1869, spanned the continent and helped to open the way for settlers in the West.

NOW YOU WILL LEARN

The mining and cattle industries contributed to population growth in western territories.

▶ Vocabulary

TERMS & NAMES

vaquero (vah•KAIR•oh) Spanish term for cowhand

long drive journey that takes cattle by foot to a railway

vigilante (vij•uh•LAN•tee) person who takes the law into his or her own hands

buffalo soldier name Native Americans gave to African-American soldiers in the West

Mexicano (may•hi•KAH•noh) Spanish word for a person of Mexican heritage; a Spanish-speaking person in the Southwest whose ancestors had come from Mexico

Anglo English-speaking settler in the Southwest

BACKGROUND VOCABULARY

lode deposit of mineral buried in rock

boomtown town that experiences sudden growth in population or economic activity

REVIEW

black codes laws passed by Southern states that limited the freedom of formerly enslaved people

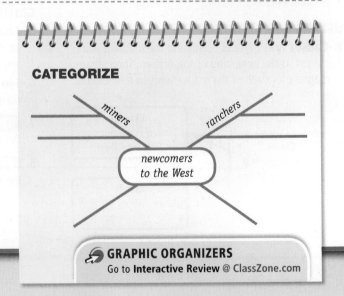

Visual Vocabulary
buffalo soldier

▶ Reading Strategy

Re-create the diagram shown at right. As you read and respond to the **KEY QUESTIONS**, use the main branches to note facts about categories of newcomers in the West. Add stems to record important details in each category.

 See Skillbuilder Handbook, page R6.

CATEGORIZE

miners   ranchers

newcomers
to the West

🖱 **GRAPHIC ORGANIZERS**
Go to **Interactive Review** @ ClassZone.com

Miners, Ranchers, and Cowhands

15.C.3 Identify and explain the effects of various incentives to produce a good or service.
16.E.3b Describe how the largely rural population of the United States adapted, used and changed the environment after 1818.

One American's Story

Nat Love was born into slavery in Tennessee in 1854. After the Civil War, he became one of thousands of African Americans who journeyed west. Love's horse-taming skills landed him a job as a cowhand. He became well known for his expert horsemanship and rodeo riding and roping. In his 1907 autobiography, Love offered a lively but exaggerated account of his life.

PRIMARY SOURCE

❝ I carry the marks of fourteen bullet wounds on different parts of my body, most any one of which would be sufficient to kill an ordinary man. . . . Horses were shot from under me, men killed around me, but always I escaped with a trifling wound at the worst. ❞

—Nat Love, *The Life and Adventures of Nat Love*

Few cowhands led lives as exciting as that described by Love. However, they all helped to open a new chapter in the history of the American West.

This photograph of Nat Love, the most famous African-American cowhand, appeared in his autobiography. He captioned it "In my fighting clothes."

Gold and Silver in the Mountains

▼ **KEY QUESTION** How did mining affect western settlement during the late 1800s?

The discovery of precious metals in the Rockies helped draw settlers west.

Mining in the West Western gold and silver strikes, or discoveries, brought crowds of fortune seekers. The hope of striking it rich drew Americans from across the nation, as well as prospectors from all over the world. "Gold fever" attracted miners from Europe, South America, Mexico, and China.

In 1859, as many as 100,000 miners raced to what is now Colorado after gold was discovered in the mountains near Pikes Peak. The mining camp that grew up nearby became the town of Denver.

A silver bar

Also in 1859, prospectors hit "pay dirt" in what came to be called the Comstock Lode in western Nevada. (A **lode** is a deposit of valuable mineral buried in layers of rock.) From 1859 to 1880, the Comstock Lode produced at least $300 million in silver and gold.

Bonanza barons, the lucky miners who became instant millionaires, built mansions in nearby Virginia City, Nevada. (The term *bonanza* refers to an especially rich mineral deposit.) Virginia City became a **boomtown**—a town that has a sudden burst of economic activity or population growth. Its population jumped from 3,000 in the 1860s to more than 30,000 in the 1870s. By 1876, the town had an opera house, several theaters, and more than 100 saloons. The writer Mark Twain described the excitement of life there.

PRIMARY SOURCE

❝ The sidewalks swarmed with people. . . . So great was the pack, that buggies frequently had to wait half an hour for an opportunity to cross the principal street. . . . Money was as plenty as dust; every individual considered himself wealthy . . . ❞

—Mark Twain, *Roughing It*

Other major strikes took place in the Black Hills of the Dakota Territory in 1874, at Cripple Creek in Colorado in 1891, and in Canada's Yukon Territory in 1896.

The Rush Ends Unfortunately, few prospectors became rich. Most left, disappointed and poor. Large mining companies moved in after surface mines no longer yielded gold and silver. Only they could buy the heavy equipment needed to take the precious metals from underground. Soon, paid workers in company mines replaced independent prospectors. The work was hard and dangerous. Dust caused lung problems, and deadly cave-ins could trap miners hundreds of feet below the surface.

By the 1890s, the mining boom was over. Many mines closed because the costs had become too high, while the precious metals were becoming sparse. Jobless workers moved elsewhere, and once-thriving communities became ghost towns. Still, the mining boom had long-lasting effects in the West. Nevada, Colorado, and South Dakota all grew so rapidly that they soon gained statehood.

▲ **SYNTHESIZE** Describe how mining affected western settlement in the late 1800s.

The Cattle Industry

🔻 **KEY QUESTION** What caused the rise and fall of the cattle industry?

While miners searched for gold and silver, a new breed of settler—the rancher—was turning the cattle industry into big business in the West. Before the railroads extended to the Great Plains, most ranchers had small herds and few employees. But rapid growth in the cattle industry greatly increased the need for cowhands, also known as cowboys or "buckaroos."

Vaqueros and Cowhands The first cowhands, or **vaqueros**, as they were known in Spanish, came from Mexico with the Spaniards in the 1500s. They settled in the Southwest. The vaqueros helped Spanish, and later Mexican, ranchers manage their herds.

American cowhands learned how to round up, rope, brand cattle, and ride from the vaqueros. The vaqueros also had a strong influence on how cowhands dressed. American cowhands adapted the vaqueros' saddle, spurs, lariat (which they used to rope a calf or steer), and chaps—seatless leather pants, worn over regular trousers, that protect the legs from scrub brush and cactus. In addition, a number of terms used in American ranching are borrowed from the Spanish, such as *corral*, *rodeo*, and the word *ranch* itself.

A diverse group of men—and a few women—worked as cowhands. About a third of all cowhands in the West were Mexican or African American. Many Mexican cowhands were descendants of the first vaqueros. Like Nat Love, some African-American cowhands had been born into slavery. They came west at the end of Reconstruction in response to the **black codes**—laws in the South that put restrictions on the freedom of formerly enslaved people. Also among the cowhands were large numbers of former Confederate and Union soldiers.

Daily Life

THE COWHAND'S GEAR

Although the cowhand is now an American icon, his distinctive look owes much to Spanish ranchers in Mexico. The cowboy boot, for example, came to Mexico from Spain. Its design reflects Spanish traditions of decorative leather work, but is also practical—a narrow toe allows the boot to slip easily into a stirrup, which the high heel can then hook for stability.

Unlike American settlers, Mexican ranchers had years of experience working on horseback on the open range. On their feet, they wore metal spurs (far right) to control their horses. Wide-brimmed hats helped to protect them from sun and weather during long hours spent outdoors.

CRITICAL THINKING

1. **Make Inferences** Why do you think cowhands have remained popular in American culture?

2. **Summarize** How did the dress of cowhands reflect the meeting of cultures in the West?

The Long Drive In the 1860s, the extension of railroad lines from Chicago and St. Louis into Kansas brought big changes to the cattle industry. A live-stock dealer named Joseph McCoy realized that railroads could bring cattle from Texas to cities in the East. All that had to be done was for cowhands to drive Texas cattle to stockyards in Abilene, Kansas. From there, the beef could be shipped by rail. This practice came to be called the **long drive**.

McCoy's plan made cattle ranching very profitable. Cattle fed on the open range for a year or two and cost the rancher nothing. The rancher then hired cowhands to round up the cattle and take them to Abilene. Over time, cow-hands followed specific trails. The principal trail was the Chisholm Trail, which stretched from San Antonio, Texas, to Abilene, Kansas. From 1867 to 1884, about 4 million cattle were driven to market on this trail.

The End of the Long Drives For about 20 years, the cattle industry boomed. The long drives grew shorter as the railroads extended farther into Texas. But by 1886, several developments brought the boom to an end.

First, the price of beef dropped sharply as the supply increased in the 1880s. Then came a new invention: barbed wire. As more settlers moved to the Great Plains, they fenced their lands with barbed wire. The open range disappeared, and cowhands could no longer pass freely over trails. Finally, in the harsh winter of 1886–1887, thousands of cattle froze to death. Many ranchers were put out of business or forced to downsize.

▲ **CAUSES AND EFFECTS** Explain why the cattle industry grew and then declined.

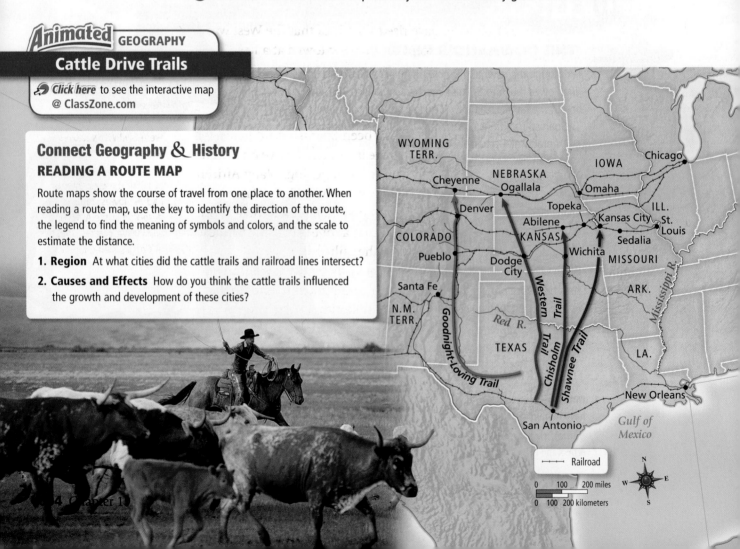

Animated GEOGRAPHY

Cattle Drive Trails

Click here to see the interactive map
@ ClassZone.com

Connect Geography & History
READING A ROUTE MAP

Route maps show the course of travel from one place to another. When reading a route map, use the key to identify the direction of the route, the legend to find the meaning of symbols and colors, and the scale to estimate the distance.

1. **Region** At what cities did the cattle trails and railroad lines intersect?

2. **Causes and Effects** How do you think the cattle trails influenced the growth and development of these cities?

Railroad

0   100   200 miles

0 100 200 kilometers

The Myth and Reality of the Wild West

The "Bandit Queen" Belle Starr, a famous horse thief. Belle once said of herself, "I regard myself as a woman who has seen much of life."

▼ **KEY QUESTION** How were the myth and reality of the West different?

In American myth, westerners spent their days riding horses on the open range. Popular novels and movies described a world in which white settlers became heroes, often by fighting Native Americans.

The Wild West Legends of the West often suggest that it was lawless. It is true that at first, rapidly growing cow towns had no local governments and no law officers to handle fights that broke out between cowhands.

Outlaws such as John Wesley Hardin, "Billy the Kid," and Jesse James became famous across America. A woman named Belle Starr, the "Bandit Queen," was a legendary horse thief. In some places, citizens formed **vigilante** groups to protect themselves. Vigilantes were people who took the law into their own hands. They caught suspected criminals and punished them without a trial. Vigilante justice sometimes consisted of hanging suspects from the nearest tree or shooting them on the spot.

Reports of this kind of violence gave rise to the idea that the West was a wild place, but the truth was that except for in a few towns at a few times, the West was no wilder than anyplace else. As towns became settled, citizens typically elected a local sheriff.

The Real West The myth of the Old West overlooked the contributions of many peoples. Large parts of the region had been Spanish-dominated for centuries, and Hispanic influence helped shape its culture. Native Americans and African Americans played important roles in ranching. Many African Americans also served in the U.S. Army in the West, where Native Americans nicknamed them "**buffalo soldiers**"—a term of honor, inspired by their short, curly hair, that compared their fighting spirit to that of the buffalo. Chinese immigrants were essential to the building of the railroads.

Western legends often emphasized the attacks by Native Americans on soldiers or settlers. But the misunderstandings and broken treaties that led to the conflicts were usually ignored in popular stories.

Historians also note that the image of the self-reliant westerner who tames the wild frontier ignores the important role played by the government in western settlement. Settlers could not have forced Native Americans off the land without the help of the army. The government also aided in the building of the railroads and offered free land that drew settlers to the West.

▲ **COMPARE AND CONTRAST** Explain how the real West differed from the myth of the Wild West.

Connecting History

American Spirit
Most of the buffalo soldiers were Civil War veterans who had been organized into six all-black regiments in 1866. These regiments had the lowest rates of desertion in the Army and earned the greatest number of Congressional Medals of Honor.

Population Growth

▼ **KEY QUESTION** What led to population growth in western cities and the Southwest?

Parts of the West seemed to grow overnight. While some cities prospered, however, most of the region remained sparsely settled.

Mining Centers and Railroad Hubs Denver, Colorado, is just one of the western cities that grew up quickly after a gold or silver rush. Miners who flocked to the "Pikes Peak" gold rush of 1859 stopped in Denver to buy supplies. Not even a town in 1857, Denver was the capital of Colorado Territory by 1867. A decade later, it became the capital of the state of Colorado. The decision by Denver citizens to build a railroad to link their city with the transcontinental railroad had contributed to the boom. In 1860, it had about 2,600 residents. By 1890, it had nearly 107,000.

The railroads brought rapid growth to a number of western towns. Omaha, Nebraska, began to flourish as a meat-processing center for cattle ranches in the area. Des Moines grew into a bustling transportation hub in central Iowa. Portland, Oregon, became a regional market for fish, grain, and lumber.

COMPARING *Population of Western Cities*

Some of today's most important western cities sprung up during the last half of the nineteenth century. Others, however, like Virginia City, Nevada (below left), went from boomtown in the 1870s to ghost town by the early 1900s.

CITY	1860	1890
Denver, Colorado	4,749	106,713
Des Moines, Iowa	3,965	50,093
Kansas City, Missouri	4,418	132,716
Omaha, Nebraska	1,883	140,452
Portland, Oregon	2,874	46,385

Sources: *Population Abstract of the United States, 1999*

CRITICAL THINKING

1. **Compare and Contrast** Which city had the largest increase in numbers of people from 1860 to 1890?

2. **Make Generalizations** Which cities had similar rates of growth?

Growth in the Southwest For centuries the Southwest had been home to people of Spanish descent whose ancestors had come from Mexico. These Spanish speakers thought of themselves as Mexican and **Mexicanos**.

In the 1840s, both the annexation of Texas and Mexico's defeat in the Mexican War brought much of the Southwest under the control of the United States. Soon after, many English-speaking white settlers—called **Anglos** by the Mexicanos—began arriving. These settlers were drawn to the Southwest by opportunities in ranching, farming, and mining. Their numbers grew in the 1880s and 1890s, as railroads connected the region with the rest of the country.

The increase of Anglos in the Southwest caused Mexicanos to lose economic and political power and land. Mexicanos claimed their land through grants from Spain and Mexico. But American courts did not usually recognize these grants. One Mexicano remarked that "the North Americans . . . consider us unworthy to form with them one nation and one society." It was only in New Mexico Territory that Hispanic society survived despite Anglo-American settlement.

Mexicanos in Colorado grinding coffee, c. 1890.

 CAUSES AND EFFECTS Explain the causes of population growth in western cities and the Southwest.

Illinois Learning Standards *Review*

ONLINE QUIZ
For test practice, go to
Interactive Review @ ClassZone.com

TERMS & NAMES

1. Explain the importance of
   - vaquero
   - long drive
   - vigilante
   - buffalo soldier
   - Mexicano
   - Anglo

USING YOUR READING NOTES

2. **Categorize** Complete the diagram you started at the beginning of this section.

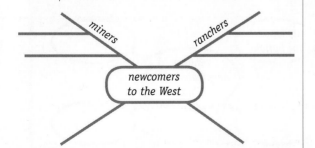

miners   ranchers

newcomers
to the West

KEY IDEAS

3. What effect did gold and silver strikes have on small towns?

4. What did cowhands learn from vaqueros?

5. What was the purpose of the long drive?

CRITICAL THINKING

6. **Summarize** What role did miners play in the settlement of the West?

7. **Problems and Solutions** Why did vigilante groups arise in some areas?

8. **Causes and Effects** What factors led to the development of western cities?

9. **Science** Use the Internet to research how metallic ore deposits form in rock, and how these deposits are mined. Explain your findings in labeled diagrams.

▶ Key Ideas

BEFORE, YOU LEARNED

The mining and cattle industries contributed to population growth in western territories.

NOW YOU WILL LEARN

Native Americans of the Great Plains fought to maintain their way of life as settlers poured onto their lands.

▶ Vocabulary

TERMS & NAMES

Sand Creek Massacre 1864 attack in which as many as 200 Cheyenne were killed by the Colorado militia

Sitting Bull Sioux chief who led the attack on Custer at the Battle of the Little Bighorn

George A. Custer commander of U.S. troops at the Battle of the Little Bighorn

Visual Vocabulary
George A. Custer

Battle of the Little Bighorn 1876 battle in which Sioux and Cheyenne killed an entire force of U.S. troops

Dawes Act 1887 law that distributed reservation land to individual Native American owners

Wounded Knee Massacre mass killing by U.S. soldiers of as many as 300 unarmed Sioux at Wounded Knee, South Dakota, in 1890

BACKGROUND VOCABULARY

nomadic characterized by moving from place to place

REVIEW

reservation land set aside by the U.S. government for Native American tribes

▶ Reading Strategy

Re-create the diagram shown at right. As you read and respond to the **KEY QUESTIONS**, use the center box to record the main idea, and use the outer ovals to note important details. Add ovals or start a new diagram as needed.

 See Skillbuilder Handbook, page R4.

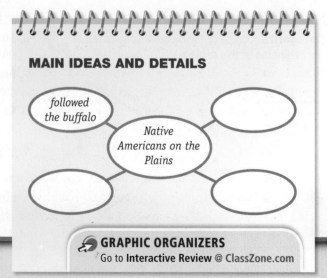

MAIN IDEAS AND DETAILS

followed the buffalo

Native Americans on the Plains

GRAPHIC ORGANIZERS
Go to **Interactive Review** @ ClassZone.com

Native Americans Fight to Survive

14.C.3 Compare historical issues involving rights, roles and status of individuals in relation to municipalities, states and the nation.
16.D.3a Describe characteristics of different kinds of communities in various sections of America during the colonial/frontier periods and the 19th century.

One American's Story

Buffalo Bird Woman was a Hidatsa who lived almost 100 years. She was born around 1839 in a Native American village on the Knife River. The federal government later forced her family onto a **reservation**—land set aside for Native American tribes. In old age, Buffalo Bird Woman looked back on her early years.

PRIMARY SOURCE

❝ Sometimes at evening I sit, looking out on the . . . Missouri [River]. . . . In the shadows I seem . . . to see our Indian village, with smoke curling upward from the earth lodges; and in the river's roar I hear the yells of the warriors, the laughter of . . . children as of old. **❞**

—Buffalo Bird Woman, quoted in *Native American Testimony*

Buffalo Bird Woman

As white settlers claimed Native American lands, Plains peoples fought a losing battle to save both their lands and their way of life.

Native Americans on the Plains

🔻 **KEY QUESTION** What was life like for Native Americans on the Great Plains?

Before the arrival of Europeans in the 1500s, most Native American tribes on the Great Plains lived in villages along rivers and streams. They tended crops of beans, squash, and corn. Hunters stalked deer and elk, as well as the vast buffalo herds that inhabited the region.

Horses and Buffalo In the early 1500s, the Spanish brought the first horses to the Great Plains. The arrival of horses changed how the Plains peoples lived. By the late 1700s, most Plains tribes kept their own herds of horses. Hunters traveled far from their villages on horseback in search of buffalo, which were central to the lives of Plains tribes.

Plains tribes ate buffalo meat and used its hide for clothing and tepees. They made its bones and horns into tools. Buffalo chips (dried manure) were used for fuel. Plains tribes followed the buffalo herds, developing a way of life that was **nomadic**—characterized by moving from place to place.

Broken Promises In the 1830s, the U.S. government had forced Native Americans of the Southeast to move onto the Great Plains. White settlers believed the Plains region was too dry for farming. But by the 1850s, some settlers who were crossing the Plains to Oregon and California saw possibilities for farming and ranching there. They pressured the government to take lands from Native Americans and make them available for settlers.

In 1851, the government called the Sioux, Cheyenne, Arapaho, and other Plains tribes together near Fort Laramie in present-day Wyoming. In the First Treaty of Fort Laramie (1851), government officials set boundaries for tribal lands. Many Plains tribes signed the treaty—they saw no other choice.

▲ **SUMMARIZE** Describe Native American life on the Great Plains in the early 1800s.

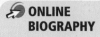

ONLINE BIOGRAPHY

For more on these leaders, go to the **Research & Writing Center** @ ClassZone.com

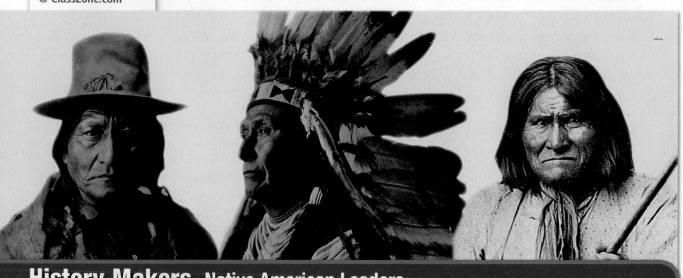

History Makers Native American Leaders

Sitting Bull c. 1831–1890

Sitting Bull was a Sioux war chief and spiritual leader. He fought U.S. troops over rights to Sioux land in several battles, most famously at the Little Bighorn. He remained an outspoken critic of the U.S. government until the end of his life.

Chief Joseph 1840–1904

Faced with forced removal, Nez Perce chief Joseph prepared to leave his land peacefully. But three young men massacred a group of whites. Fearing reprisal, Joseph helped lead a legendary retreat over four months and more than 1,000 miles.

Geronimo c. 1829–1909

Apache leader Geronimo fought settlers on his land for more than 25 years—all the while avoiding permanent capture by the U.S. and Mexican armies. In 1886, he became the last Native American leader to formally surrender to the U.S. government.

CRITICAL THINKING

1. **Compare and Contrast** What did these three leaders have in common?
2. **Analyze Point of View** How do you think these three leaders viewed the U.S. government?

Native Americans Resist

🔻 **KEY QUESTION** How did Native Americans resist white efforts to take their land?

Some Sioux resisted signing the Laramie Treaty. They chose to fight for their land.

Bloodshed on the Plains In 1864, Colorado militia opened fire on a peaceful Cheyenne village along Sand Creek. As many as 200 Cheyenne men, women, and children were killed in what became known as the **Sand Creek Massacre**.

The Plains tribes responded with attacks on settlements and soldiers. The government sought to end the fighting. In 1868, the Second Treaty of Fort Laramie gave tribes a large reservation in the Black Hills of South Dakota. Then, in 1874, white prospectors found gold in the Black Hills. Miners flooded onto Sioux land. Two Sioux chiefs, **Sitting Bull** and Crazy Horse, united to push back the intruders.

PRIMARY SOURCE

❝ We did not give our country to you; you stole it. You come here to tell lies; when you go home, take them with you. ❞

—Sitting Bull

By the 1870s, the Cheyenne decided to fight back, too. On June 25, 1876, the Seventh Cavalry of the United States, commanded by Lieutenant Colonel **George A. Custer**, confronted several thousand Sioux and Cheyenne near the Little Bighorn River in Montana. In the **Battle of the Little Bighorn**, Custer and all of his men were killed.

History *through* Art

Battle of the Little Big Horn

A Lakota Sioux chief, Kicking Bear (c. 1846–1904) fought in the Battle of the Little Bighorn. He made this painting of it more than twenty years later at the request of artist Frederic Remington. White Americans had great curiosity about the battle, but no U.S. soldiers had survived to describe it. In Kicking Bear's painting, Custer is on the left, wearing yellowish buckskins. The ghost-like figures in the upper left, behind the bodies of the soldiers, represent the spirits of the dead. The figures in the middle are the Sioux chiefs Sitting Bull, Rain-in-the-Face, Crazy Horse, and Kicking Bear.

CRITICAL VIEWING How does Kicking Bear's painting show the viewer the result of the battle?

In response, the government stepped up military action. Little Bighorn would be the last major Native American victory. In 1877, Crazy Horse surrendered, and Sitting Bull and his followers fled to Canada. In 1881, Sitting Bull surrendered and was eventually sent to a reservation.

Conflict in the Northwest and Southwest The Nez Perce (nehz PURS) lived in Idaho, eastern Oregon, and Washington. In the 1860s, the government took their land and forced them onto a reservation in Idaho. A group of Nez Perce led by Chief Joseph resisted, and in 1877 fled to seek refuge in Canada. Over four months, they crossed more than 1,000 miles with army troops in pursuit. When the army caught up, Chief Joseph was forced to surrender, saying, "I will fight no more, forever."

In the Southwest, both the Navajos and Apaches fought being removed to reservations. U.S. troops ended Navajo resistance in Arizona in 1863 by burning Navajo homes and crops. Most Navajos were forced to take what they called the "Long Walk," a brutal journey of 300 miles to a reservation in eastern New Mexico. Hundreds died on the way.

In the 1870s and 1880s, a group of Apache led by Geronimo resisted being relocated to a reservation. They raided settlements across the Southwest. Geronimo was captured several times but always managed to escape. In 1886, he finally surrendered and was sent to prison. He said, "Once I moved about like the wind. Now I surrender."

▲ **MAIN IDEAS & DETAILS** Describe how Native Americans resisted white settlement.

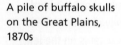

A pile of buffalo skulls on the Great Plains, 1870s

A Way of Life Ends

▼ **KEY QUESTION** What caused the end of Plains peoples' traditional way of life?

While white settlers moved westward, Plains peoples struggled to remain free.

The End of the Buffalo Newcomers threatened the buffalo upon which Plains tribes depended. Once, up to 60 million buffalo had roamed the Plains. But hired hunters killed buffalo to feed railroad crews and supply eastern factories with leather. Beginning in the 1870s, hunters killed at least 1 million buffalo a year. By the 1880s, the buffalo were dying out and most Plains peoples were being forced onto reservations.

Forced Assimilation Some whites believed that assimilation—adopting the dominant culture— was the way for Native Americans to survive. The **Dawes Act** of 1887 was intended to encourage Native Americans to farm alongside settlers. It divided tribal lands into plots for each family.

In the end, the Dawes Act did little to benefit Native Americans. Not all wanted to be farmers. Those who did lacked the tools and money to be successful. Over time, many sold their land for a fraction of its real value to white land promoters or settlers.

The U.S. government also sent many Native American children to boarding schools in an effort to assimilate or "Americanize" them. The children were dressed in European-style clothes, learned English, and typically spent part of the day farming or doing other manual labor. Many were kept away from their families for years at a time. Disease was rampant, and hundreds died.

Wounded Knee Massacre With their cultures under attack and their lands disappearing, some Native Americans turned to a prophet named Wovoka. He described a hopeful vision of a new age in which whites would leave the West and the buffalo would return.

A key part of Wovoka's teachings was a ceremony called the Ghost Dance. When Sioux gathered for a Ghost Dance in 1890, white officials thought they were preparing for war. On December 29, at Wounded Knee Creek in South Dakota, troops opened fire, killing more than 200 Sioux men, women, and children in what became known as the **Wounded Knee Massacre**. It was the last armed conflict with Native Americans in the West.

A shirt worn in the Ghost Dance ceremony

 CAUSES AND EFFECTS Explain the events that ended the Plains Indians' traditional way of life.

Illinois Learning Standards *Review*

 ONLINE QUIZ
For test practice, go to
Interactive Review @ ClassZone.com

TERMS & NAMES

1. Explain the importance of
- Sand Creek Massacre
- Battle of the Little Bighorn
- Sitting Bull
- Dawes Act
- George A. Custer
- Wounded Knee Massacre

USING YOUR READING NOTES

2. Main Ideas & Details Complete the diagram you started at the beginning of the section. Include key events and note their importance.

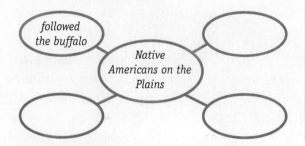

KEY IDEAS

3. How was the buffalo important to Native Americans on the Great Plains?

4. What caused conflict between Native Americans and settlers on the Great Plains?

CRITICAL THINKING

5. Causes and Effects How did the Battle of the Little Bighorn affect U.S. government policy?

6. Analyze Point of View Why do you think Chief Joseph, Crazy Horse, Sitting Bull, and Geronimo chose to surrender? What other choices might they have made?

7. Form and Support Opinions What do you think was the most important factor in bringing about the end of the Plains peoples' way of life? Explain.

8. Art Draw two pictures of Native American life on the Plains that contrast life before and after the flood of settlers.

Native American Land Losses

Native Americans were the sole inhabitants of the Great Plains for thousands of years. In the 1850s, the U.S. government began to take possession of Plains land and set aside specific areas for different tribes. This brought conflicts with Native Americans, who did not believe that the land could be bought and sold. Said Sioux chief Crazy Horse: "One does not sell the land people walk on."

(*clockwise from upper left*)
Omaha calumet (ceremonial pipe); Sioux/Arapaho storage bag; Sioux moccasins; Haida basket

Native American Lands *1819*

SPANISH
MEXICO

40°N

30°N

90°W   80°W

▆ Land reserved for Native Americans

The U.S. government laid claim to the Great Plains mainly to satisfy settlers' demands for farmland. "Are we then to give up [our ancestors'] sacred graves to be plowed for corn?" Sioux chief Red Cloud asked before an 1866 battle with U.S. troops. But Native Americans were severely outnumbered. By the 1890s, nearly all had been forced onto reservations.

Native American Lands 1894

Nez Perce
Blackfoot
Chippewa
Shoshone
Cheyenne
ROCKY
Missouri River
Mississippi
40°N
Sioux
Arapaho
Shoshone
GREAT PLAINS
Ute
Colorado
River
Ohio
River
Ute
Navajo
Hopi
Pawnee
Arapaho
Cheyenne
Cherokee
Creek
Apache
Choctaw
Apache
Comanche
Kiowa
Chickasaw
80°W
30°N
Rio Grande
MOUNTAINS

0   150   300 miles
0   150   300 kilometers

■ Land reserved for Native Americans

Connect Geography & History

1. **Movement** What was the major change that took place in the West between 1819 and 1894?

2. **Draw Conclusions** Why might the U.S. government setting boundaries for tribal lands have led to conflict between Native Americans and settlers?

See Geography Handbook, pages A14–A17.

Reading for Understanding

▶ Key Ideas

BEFORE, YOU LEARNED

Native Americans of the Great Plains fought to maintain their way of life as settlers poured onto their lands.

NOW YOU WILL LEARN

A wave of farmers moved to the Plains in the 1800s and faced many economic problems.

▶ Vocabulary

TERMS & NAMES

Homestead Act 1862 law that offered 160 acres free to anyone who agreed to live on and improve the land for five years

Exodusters name for African Americans who settled on the Great Plains

sodbusters name for pioneer farmers on the Great Plains

Grange organization formed in 1867 to meet the social needs of farm families

Populist Party political party formed in 1890s that wanted a policy that would raise crop prices

gold standard a policy under which the government backs every dollar with a certain amount of gold

William Jennings Bryan Democratic and Populist candidate for President in 1896 who advocated a policy of free silver

BACKGROUND VOCABULARY

sod the top layer of prairie soil that contains thick, tightly tangled grass roots

---

▶ Reading Strategy

Re-create the diagram shown at right. As you read and respond to the **KEY QUESTIONS**, use the diagram to record significant events in the order in which they occurred.

 See Skillbuilder Handbook, page R5.

SEQUENCE EVENTS

Homestead Act 1862

GRAPHIC ORGANIZERS
Go to **Interactive Review** @ ClassZone.com

Farm Economics and Populism

15.A.3a Explain how market prices signal producers about what, how and how much to produce.

16.E.3b Describe how the largely rural population of the United States adapted, used and changed the environment after 1818.

One American's Story

From 1865 to 1900, about 800,000 Swedes left their homeland in northern Europe. Most, like Olaf Olsson, were drawn to America by the promise of land. Shortly after he arrived in 1869, Olsson wrote home to tell friends and family about the opportunities that awaited them.

PRIMARY SOURCE

❝ We do not dig gold with pocket knives, we do not expect to become . . . rich in a few days or in a few years, but what we aim at is to own our own homes. . . . The advantage which America offers is not to make everyone rich at once, without toil and trouble, but . . . that the poor . . . can work up little by little. **❞**

—Olaf Olsson, quoted in *The Swedish Americans*

The hope of land ownership motivated settlers such as the McCarty family in Custer County, Nebraska.

Many immigrants and native-born Americans shared Olsson's optimism about the hope of possessing their own land.

The Great Land Giveaway

🔻 **KEY QUESTION** How did the federal government encourage western settlement?

Millions of farmers saw the Great Plains as an incredible opportunity.

Free Land Attracts Farmers For years, many Americans had been asking their government to make western land available. But people in the South feared that a westward migration would create more nonslave states. In 1862, after the South had left the Union, the government answered the call for free land by passing the **Homestead Act**. This law offered 160 acres of free land to anyone who agreed to live on and improve the land for five years.

Those who took advantage of the Homestead Act were called homesteaders. Many European immigrants became homesteaders. So did some African Americans from the South who went westward to escape violence and poverty, especially after Reconstruction ended in 1877. They compared themselves to the Hebrews in the biblical book of Exodus who escaped slavery in Egypt and called themselves **Exodusters**.

Railroads Profit from Free Land From 1850 to 1871, the government gave millions of acres of public land to the railroads to promote railroad expansion. The railroads resold much of the land to settlers. This made the railroad companies rich and supplied new customers for railroad services. The railroads' sales pitch worked. In the 1860s, so many Swedes and Norwegians settled in Minnesota that a local editor wrote, "It seems as if the Scandinavian Kingdoms were being emptied into this state."

▲ **ANALYZE POINT OF VIEW** Explain the appeal of the Homestead Act.

Farm Life on the Frontier

▼ **KEY QUESTION** What was life like for farmers on the frontier?

Farmers on the Plains quickly found that life there was not easy. Winter brought deep snows. In spring, melting snow caused flooding. Then came summer, with its harsh winds and soaring temperatures. To make matters worse, wood and water were in short supply.

A Shortage of Wood and Water Because the Plains were nearly treeless, farmers had to find other building material for their cabins and fuel for their fireplaces. They built homes from blocks of **sod**—the top layer of prairie soil that contains thick, tightly tangled grass roots. These farmers were called **sodbusters**. For fuel, they burned corncobs or "cow chips" (dried manure). In some places, they had to dig wells more than 280 feet deep. Blizzards, prairie fires, tornadoes, grasshoppers, and drought added to the miseries of life.

Lives of Women Women played a central role in settling the frontier. They worked beside men on the farm. They had to make by hand many of the items their families wore, ate, and used. Before schools were established, women taught their children. Many were also skilled in offering medical care—from snakebites to broken limbs.

Connecting History

Expanding Liberty
The Homestead Act was a well-timed opportunity for enslaved African Americans. It took effect the same day President Lincoln issued the Emancipation Proclamation, which abolished slavery: January 1, 1863.

The Shores family of Custer County, Nebraska, with sod buildings. **What do you think it would be like to live in a sod house?**

Although most went west with their families, thousands of women claimed land on their own. Most such women were in their twenties and had never been married, but others were older—even in their sixties. Some women homesteaders were divorced or widowed; some were single mothers. Like the men who homesteaded, many were motivated by the dream of owning their own land. It is estimated that about 5 percent of claims for public land were filed by women, though in some areas the figure was much higher.

Western women gained legal rights more quickly than women in the East. In 1869, Wyoming Territory became the first state or territory to grant women the right to vote. In 1870, it became the first to allow women to serve on juries. By the 1890s, women could vote in Utah, Colorado, and Idaho.

Improvements in Farming New inventions helped Plains farmers meet some of the challenges of frontier life. A steel plow invented by John Deere in 1837 and improved upon by James Oliver in 1868 sliced through the tough sod of the prairie. Windmills adapted to the Plains pumped water from deep wells to the surface. Barbed wire allowed farmers to fence in land and livestock. Reapers made the harvesting of crops much easier, and threshers helped farmers to separate grain or seed from straw.

These inventions also made farm work more efficient. From 1860 to 1890, farmers doubled their production of wheat.

▲ **MAIN IDEAS & DETAILS** Describe what life was like for frontier farmers.

Connecting History

Rights & Responsibilities
Although some western women could vote in state and local elections, none could vote in federal elections until 1920, when the 19th Amendment secured voting rights for all American women.

CONNECT To Today

FARMING: THEN & NOW

The first settlers struggled to break up the soil of the Great Plains, which was held together by tall prairie grasses. Early farm machinery was pulled by horses or by hand.

Modern-day farming has much more powerful equipment, such as the harvester shown here. Farm machines are often computerized. Sometimes, a worker can remotely operate a plow or tractor.

The agricultural cycle is still reflected in today's nine-month school schedule. This schedule dates from a time when most Americans participated in farming. School was dismissed for the summer so that children could help with farm work.

CRITICAL THINKING

1. **Evaluate** What are some of the advantages of modern-day farming?

2. **Compare and Contrast** What does modern-day farming have in common with farming long ago?

Farmers Organize

▼ **KEY QUESTION** What economic problems did farmers face?

In the 1870s, farmers in the West and South watched with alarm as prices for their crops dropped lower and lower. One reason for lower prices was overproduction. Farmers were able to grow more food more easily because additional farmland had been opened up, and machines had improved.

The Problems of Farmers Not only were farmers receiving less money for their crops, but they also had to spend more to run a farm. Farming machinery was expensive, and railroads were charging higher rates to ship crops to market. As a result, farmers, angry over lower profits, began to organize to seek solutions to their problems.

In 1867, farmers had formed a group called the **Grange**, officially known as the Patrons of Husbandry. Its main purpose at first had been to meet the social needs of farm families. However, as economic conditions got worse, Grange members, known as Grangers, took action. They formed cooperatives—organizations that are owned and run by their members. The cooperatives bought grain elevators and sold crops directly to merchants. This allowed farmers to keep more of their profits.

CONNECT ↻ Economics and History

SUPPLY AND DEMAND

In the 1870s, Plains farmers experienced hard times, some of which followed big harvests. How did good harvests create hard times? The answer is the law of supply and demand.

The amount of goods available for sale is the **supply**. The willingness and ability of consumers to spend money for goods is called **demand**. The law of supply and demand says that when supply increases or demand decreases, prices fall. By contrast, when supply decreases and demand rises, prices rise.

Population grows.
Demand rises.

Prices go up.

Farmers plant more.
Supply increases.

Prices go down.

CRITICAL THINKING

1. **Summarize** Explain why consumers would buy more of a product when the price is lower, and less when the price is higher.

2. **Causes and Effects** Suppose that in the 1870s, farmers had found an additional new market for their supplies. Would this have been likely to drive prices up or down? Why?

Farmers Demand Action Farmers also began to demand action from the government. Grangers asked states to regulate railroad freight rates and storage charges. Illinois, Minnesota, Wisconsin, Iowa, and Missouri did so. In 1877, the Supreme Court backed the farmers in their fight against the railroads. In *Munn* v. *Illinois*, the Court ruled that states and the federal government could regulate the railroads because this business served the public interest.

The Rise of Populism In the early 1890s, several farm groups joined together to form a new political party called the **Populist Party**, or People's Party.

The Populists wanted the government to adopt a "free silver" policy, or the unlimited coining of silver. Since silver was plentiful, more money would be put in circulation. They believed that increasing the money supply would cause inflation. Inflation, in turn, would result in rising prices. Higher prices for crops would help farmers pay back the money that they had borrowed to improve their farms.

Opponents of free silver wanted to keep the **gold standard**. Under the gold standard, the government backs every dollar with a certain amount of gold. Since the gold supply is limited, fewer dollars are in circulation, and inflation is less likely.

In the 1892 presidential election, the Populist Party called for a free silver policy, government ownership of railroads, and other reforms. The Populist candidate, James B. Weaver, lost to Grover Cleveland. But he won more than a million votes—a good showing for a third-party candidate.

The Election of 1896 Four years later, the Populists joined the Democratic Party in supporting **William Jennings Bryan** for president. Bryan urged the Democratic convention to support free silver.

History Makers

William Jennings Bryan   1860–1925

A Midwest native, William Jennings Bryan was nicknamed "the Great Commoner" because he embraced the causes of farmers and other working people. He championed their interests against the power of big business and the banks.

Bryan served two terms in Congress and made three unsuccessful bids for the presidency. He was an influential speaker and political leader for more than 30 years, even after leaving elective office. Many reforms that he fought for, such as an eight-hour workday and woman suffrage, later became law.

CRITICAL THINKING

1. **Make Inferences** How did the reforms Bryan fought for reflect his concern for working people?

2. **Connect *to* Today** What public figures today have some of the same qualities as Bryan?

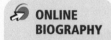 **ONLINE BIOGRAPHY**   For more on William Jennings Bryan, go to the **Research & Writing Center** @ ClassZone.com

PRIMARY SOURCE

❝ Burn down your cities and leave our farms, and your cities will spring up again as if by magic; but destroy our farms and the grass will grow in the street of every city in the country. . . . [We] . . . answer . . . their demand for a gold standard by saying . . . : You shall not press down upon the brow of labor this crown of thorns. You shall not crucify mankind upon a cross of gold. ❞

—William Jennings Bryan, "Cross of Gold" speech

In the election of 1896, money issues mattered much more to voters than they had in the previous election. The nation had suffered through an economic crisis—the Panic of 1893. The Republican candidate, William McKinley, favored the gold standard. He warned that "free silver" would mean higher prices for food and other goods.

On election day, farmers in the South and the West voted overwhelmingly for Bryan. But McKinley, who was backed by industrialists, bankers, and other business leaders, won the East and the election by about half a million votes. This election was the beginning of the end for the Populist Party.

▲ **PROBLEMS AND SOLUTIONS** Explain how the Populist Party sought to address the economic problems faced by farmers.

CONNECT to the Essential Question

How did the nation change as a result of westward movement after the Civil War?

Transcontinental railroad built	Mining and cattle industries develop	U.S. government takes Native American lands	Congress passes the Homestead Act
Economies of East and West linked	Miners, ranchers, and cowhands settle in the West and Southwest	U.S. army and Native Americans clash in bloody battles	Settlers claim western land
Frontier settlement increases	Mexicanos lose economic and political power	Buffalo herds are destroyed; nomadic ways of Plains Indians end	Plains becomes farming region
Standard time established	Mining centers and cow towns grow into western cities	Native Americans forced onto reservations	Farmers become political force

CRITICAL THINKING **Summarize** How did the population of the West change during the late 1900s? How did the U.S. government help to create this change?

The Closing of the Frontier

🔻 **KEY QUESTION** What events symbolized the frontier's closing?

By 1890, fenced fields had replaced the open frontier.

The Oklahoma Land Rush The last lands not claimed by settlers were in the area called Indian Territory. At the blast of a starting gun on April 22, 1889, thousands rushed to claim 2 million acres that had been inhabited by Native Americans. In May 1890, the area became Oklahoma Territory.

In 1890, 17 million people lived between the Mississippi and the Pacific. That year, the Census Bureau declared that the frontier no longer existed.

Historians' View of the Frontier Many people believed that the frontier was what had made America unique. In 1893, historian Frederick Jackson Turner wrote an influential essay on the frontier, saying "The existence of an area of free land, . . . and the advance of American settlement westward, explain American development." To Turner, the frontier had meant opportunity.

But many historians today think that Turner gave too much importance to the frontier in shaping an American character. They point out that the United States remains a land of opportunity long after the frontier's closing.

🔺 **SUMMARIZE** Describe the events that symbolized the closing of the frontier.

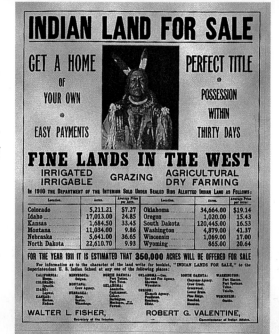

This poster advertised the sale of Native American lands by the U.S. government.

Illinois Learning Standards *Review*

🔁 **ONLINE QUIZ**
For test practice, go to
Interactive Review @ ClassZone.com

TERMS & NAMES

1. Explain the importance of
   - Homestead Act
   - Exoduster
   - sodbuster
   - Grange
   - Populist Party
   - gold standard
   - William Jennings Bryan

USING YOUR READING NOTES

2. **Sequence Events** Complete the diagram to show the most important events of this section.

Homestead Act 1862

KEY IDEAS

3. What attracted European immigrants and African Americans to the West?

4. How did new inventions help farmers meet the challenges of the Plains?

5. What were the goals of the Populist Party?

CRITICAL THINKING

6. **Summarize** What steps did farmers take to seek solutions to their problems?

7. **Compare and Contrast** What were the arguments for and against "free silver"?

8. **Evaluate** Reread the quote from the essay by Frederick Jackson Turner, above. What did he mean by "an area of free land"? Was it really free?

9. **Writing** **Report** Research sod houses. Write a short report that explains how prairie grass held the sod together, and list the advantages and disadvantages of building with sod.

THE WILD WEST

America's fascination with the idea of the "Wild West" began even before the frontier closed. Why did the West capture the popular imagination?

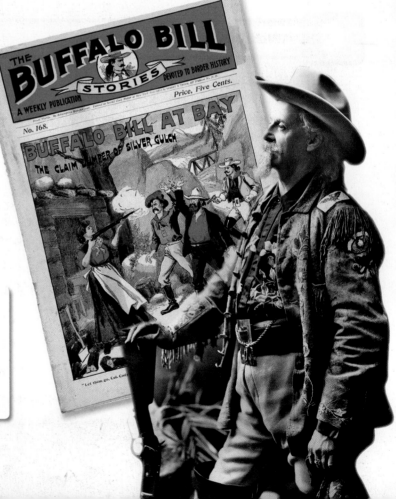

THE PONY EXPRESS

From April 1860 to October 1861, the Pony Express carried mail by relay. Riders switched horses at stations 10 or 15 miles apart on a route covering nearly 2,000 miles. All riders had to weigh less than 125 pounds; the youngest was only 11 years old.

BUFFALO BILL'S WILD WEST

William "Buffalo Bill" Cody (below right), a buffalo hunter turned showman, dramatized legends of the West in his Wild West Show of the 1880s. The show brought reenactments of frontier life across the country and to Europe. Marksman Annie Oakley (above) was a star attraction. She could shoot a dime in the air from 90 feet away.

Activity

Make a WANTED poster!

Research one of the outlaws mentioned on page 605, or another outlaw who became part of western legend. Create a WANTED poster for the person. Include images, quotes, and infamous deeds.

Chapter Summary

1 **Key Idea**
A railroad, completed in 1869, spanned the continent and helped to open the way for settlers in the West.

2 **Key Idea**
The mining and cattle industries contributed to population growth in western territories.

3 **Key Idea**
Native Americans on the Great Plains fought to maintain their way of life as settlers poured onto their lands.

4 **Key Idea**
A wave of farmers moved to the Plains in the 1800s and faced many economic problems.

For detailed Review and Study Notes go to **Interactive Review** @ ClassZone.com

Name Game

Use the Terms & Names list to identify each sentence online or on your own paper.

1. In the mid-1800s, this part of the West was occupied mainly by Native Americans.
   frontier

2. I taught American cowhands how to rope and ride.

3. This was invented by the railroad companies.

4. I took the law into my own hands.

5. I was given this nickname by Native Americans in the West.

6. This brought cattle on foot to railway centers.

7. I was an African American who settled on the Great Plains.

8. I built my home from the dense soil of the Plains.

9. This allowed settlers to get free western land.

10. I was defeated at the Battle of the Little Bighorn.

A. vaquero
B. vigilante
C. buffalo soldier
D. Sitting Bull
E. frontier
F. long drive
G. Exoduster
H. sodbuster
I. Dawes Act
J. vaquero
K. standard time
L. George A. Custer
M. Homestead Act

Activities

FLIPCARD

Use the online flipcards to quiz yourself on the terms and names introduced in this chapter.

> Native Americans in this region followed the buffalo herds.
>
> ANSWER
> Great Plains

GEOGAME

Use this online map to reinforce your knowledge of the locations of western cities, especially railroad hubs that boomed in the late 1800s. Drag and drop each city name in the list at its location on the map. A scorecard helps you keep track of your progress online.

Chicago

Omaha

St. Louis

Kansas City

Minneapolis

More items online

VOCABULARY

Explain the significance of each of the following.

1. transcontinental railroad
2. vaquero
3. boomtown
4. sodbusters
5. Wounded Knee Massacre
6. standard time
7. long drive
8. lode
9. Dawes Act
10. gold standard

Explain how the terms and names in each group are related.

11. Sitting Bull, George Custer, Battle of the Little Bighorn
12. Grange, Populist Party, William Jennings Bryan
13. Homestead Act, frontier, Exodusters

KEY IDEAS

① Railroads Transform the Nation (pages 596–599)

14. How did the government encourage the building of the first transcontinental railroad?

15. How did the railroad affect the frontier?

② Miners, Ranchers, and Cowhands (pages 600–607)

16. What economic opportunities drew large numbers of people to the West beginning in the 1860s?

17. What ended the boom in the cattle business?

③ Native Americans Fight to Survive (pages 608–613)

18. Why did the U.S. government take land from Native Americans on the Great Plains?

19. What were the results of the Battle of the Little Bighorn?

④ Farm Economics and Populism (pages 616–623)

20. What problems in the 1890s led farmers to take political action?

21. Why was the Oklahoma Land Rush significant?

CRITICAL THINKING

22. **Causes and Effects** What were the main reasons that settlers moved to the West?

23. **Compare and Contrast** Fill in the chart comparing the building of the Union Pacific and Central Pacific railroads. Which workers do you think had the more difficult route? Why?

Railroad	Route	Workers	Physical Challenges
Union Pacific			
Central Pacific			

24. **Summarize** How did U.S. government policy toward Native Americans change as white settlers moved westward?

25. **Form and Support Opinions** What do you think would be the most difficult challenge in starting a new life on the Great Plains? Explain.

26. **Make Inferences** This image from 1873 depicts the benefits of membership in the Grange. What does the central image suggest about how being part of the Grange might affect an individual farmer?

TEST PRACTICE

• **Online Test Practice** @ ClassZone.com
• **Test-Taking Strategies & Practice** at the front of this book

DOCUMENT-BASED QUESTIONS

Part 1: Short Answer

Analyze each document, and answer the questions that follow.

DOCUMENT 1

1. Briefly tell what the people shown in the painting are doing and why.

DOCUMENT 2

PRIMARY SOURCE

❝Do not misunderstand me, but understand me fully with reference to my affection for the land. I never said the land was mine to do with as I chose. The one who has the right to dispose of it is the one who has created it. I claim a right to live on my land, and accord you the privilege to live on yours.❞

—Chief Joseph (Nez Perce)

2. Summarize Chief Joseph's beliefs about land ownership. How did they contrast with the beliefs of the U.S. government?

PART 2: Essay

3. In two or three short paragraphs, explain how western settlement changed the lives of Native Americans. Use information from your answers to Part 1 and your knowledge of U.S. history.

YOU BE THE HISTORIAN

27. **Form and Support Opinions** Which groups of people do you think benefited most from western settlement? Which groups did not benefit? Explain.

28. **Analyze Point of View** Chief Joseph said, "It makes my heart sick when I remember all the good words and broken promises." What did he mean by this?

29. **Compare and Contrast** How did the lives of western settlers during the late 1800s compare with the myth of the Wild West?

30. **Make Inferences** Why do you think women in the West were the first women to gain the right to vote?

31. **Connect** *to* **Today** Choose a western city from a map of the United States. How might its location have contributed to its growth?

 Answer the
ESSENTIAL QUESTION
How did the nation change as a result of westward movement after the Civil War?

Written Response Write a two- or three-paragraph response to the Essential Question. Be sure to consider the key ideas of each section as well as events that encouraged western settlement. Use the Rubric Response below to guide your thinking and writing.

Response Rubric
A strong response will

• discuss events that opened the West to settlers
• explore the role of the mining and cattle industries
• explain how the U.S. government encouraged western settlement
• analyze the effects of settlement on Native Americans

CHAPTER 20

Industrialization and Immigration

1860–1914

 ESSENTIAL QUESTION

What new problems and opportunities developed as America became an industrial power?

CONNECT Geography & History

How did immigration affect industrialization in the United States?

Think about:

1 where immigrants settled

2 the location of the nation's main industrial areas

Immigrants often lived in the same neighborhood as others from their home country.

Statue of Liberty

1882 Congress passes the Chinese Exclusion Act.

1860

U.S. population reaches 31,443,321.

Announcement for the demonstration that turned into the Haymarket Affair

Attention Workingmen!

MASS-MEETING

TO-NIGHT, at 7:30 o'clock,

1886 Haymarket Affair occurs.

▼

Effect Opposition to unions increases.

CANADA

MAINE

VT.

N.H.

WISCONSIN

MICHIGAN

NEW YORK

MASS. Boston

MINN.

Milwaukee

Detroit

Buffalo

R.I.

CONN.

IOWA

Chicago

Cleveland

PENN.

New York

Ellis Island

40°N

70°W

N.J.

OHIO

Philadelphia

ILLINOIS

INDIANA

Pittsburgh

DEL.

St. Louis

Cincinnati

Baltimore

MD.

MISSOURI

W. VA.

VIRGINIA

KENTUCKY

NORTH CAROLINA

0   50   100 miles

0   50   100 kilometers

ARKANSAS

SOUTH CAROLINA

West Coast Port of Entry

Industrial areas, 1860

Additional industrial areas, 1900

• Major industrial city

⚓ Immigrant port of entry

GEORGIA

Angel Island San Francisco

40°N

NEVADA

CALIFORNIA

MISS.

ALABAMA

ATLANTIC OCEAN

PACIFIC OCEAN

30°N

120°W

FLORIDA

80°W

(*left*) John D. Rockefeller
(*right*) Andrew Carnegie

Historic San Francisco streetcar

1914

World War I begins in Europe.

1894
Pullman Strike

▼

Effect Trains stop until the strike ends.

1896
Plessy v. *Ferguson*

Thomas Edison's fireside phonograph

1910
Immigration Center on Angel Island opens.

▶ Key Ideas

BEFORE, YOU LEARNED

Millions of farmers moved to the Plains in the late 1800s and faced economic problems.

NOW YOU WILL LEARN

New inventions and corporations created the Gilded Age of industrial growth and great wealth for a few.

▶ Vocabulary

TERMS & NAMES

Lewis Latimer African-American inventor who played a key role in improving practical electrical lighting

Thomas Edison inventor of the electric light bulb and many other devices

Alexander Graham Bell inventor of the telephone

John D. Rockefeller founder of the Standard Oil Trust

robber baron a business leader who became wealthy through dishonest methods

Andrew Carnegie built U.S. steel industry

Gilded Age late 1800s era of fabulous wealth

BACKGROUND VOCABULARY

patents government documents giving an inventor the exclusive right to make and sell an invention for a specific number of years

corporation a business owned by investors who buy part of it through shares of stock

monopoly business that gains control of an industry by eliminating other competitors

trust a legal body created to hold stock in many companies, often within an industry

business cycle the pattern of good and bad economic times

shareholder an investor who buys part of a company through shares of stock

depression a period of low economic activity

▶ Reading Strategy

Re-create the diagram shown at right. As you read and respond to the **KEY QUESTIONS**, use the diagram to record new inventions and the ways that they changed American life. Add boxes or start a new diagram as needed.

 See Skillbuilder Handbook, page R4.

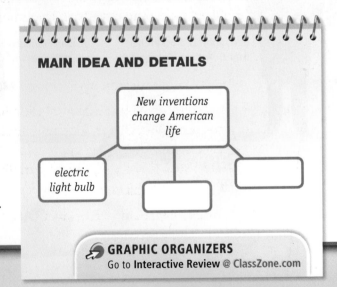

MAIN IDEA AND DETAILS

New inventions change American life

electric light bulb

GRAPHIC ORGANIZERS
Go to **Interactive Review** @ ClassZone.com

America Enters the Industrial Age

15.B.3b Explain the effects of choice and competition on individuals and the economy as a whole.
16.C.3c Describe how economic developments and government policies after 1865 affected the country's economic institutions including corporations, banks and organized labor.

One American's Story

Lewis Latimer learned the trade of mechanical drawing after serving in the Union Navy in the Civil War. He worked with inventor Thomas Edison and played a key role in improving practical electric lighting.

PRIMARY SOURCE

❝ I had qualified myself to take charge of producing the carbons for the lamps, when I was not drawing, and worked through the day helping to make the lamps and at night locating them in stores and offices... These were strenuous times, and we made long hours each day. At the factory by seven in the morning, and after the day's work somewhere running lamps until twelve o'clock or later at night. ❞

—Lewis Latimer, *1911 Logbook*

Lewis Latimer

Latimer held many **patents** as an inventor. A patent is a government document that gives an inventor the exclusive right to make and sell an invention for a number of years. Inventors such as Latimer and Edison developed new technologies during the years of the Industrial Revolution.

The Industrial Revolution Continues

▼ **KEY QUESTION** What new inventions changed life in the 1800s?

During the early to mid-1800s, an industrial revolution had been underway in America. Factory machines began to replace hand tools. In some parts of the country, large-scale manufacturing began to replace farming. However, it was not until the late 1800s that a surge in industrialization, the process of developing industry, changed the nation dramatically.

Causes of Growth There were many factors that caused industrial growth in the United States after the Civil War.

The New Steel Industry The steel industry contributed to America's industrial growth. In the 1850s, William Kelly in the United States and Henry Bessemer in England independently developed what became known as the Bessemer steel process. This new process used much less coal than the older process used. Because the Bessemer steel process cut the cost of steel, the nation's steel output increased by more than 350 times between 1867 and 1900. Factories began to make plows, barbed wire, nails, and beams for buildings. Throughout the late 1800s, steel was also used for rails to expand the railroads.

Edison and Electricity The electric power industry also grew during the late 1800s. The inventor who found many ways to use electricity was **Thomas Edison**. In 1876, Edison opened a laboratory in Menlo Park, New Jersey. He employed Lewis Latimer and many other assistants. Edison's laboratory invented so many things that Edison received more than 1,000 U.S. patents, more than any other inventor.

One of Edison's most famous inventions was practical electric lighting. Other inventors had already created electric lights, but they were too bright and unstable for home use. Edison figured out how to make a safe, steady light bulb. He also invented a system to deliver electricity to buildings.

(*below*) Market Street, San Francisco, 1900

Causes of Growth 1860–1900

Growing Population
The U.S. population more than doubled. Over 14 million immigrants were part of this growth.

Improved Transportation
Raw materials and finished products could be shipped longer distances more quickly with
- steamboats
- canals
- railroads

Natural Resources
America was able to produce a variety of goods using its vast resources of
- forests
- copper
- water
- silver
- coal
- gold
- iron

New Inventions
Industry was able to produce goods more efficiently with new machines and processes.

Government Support
States and the federal government used land grants, subsidies, and tariffs to help business grow.

Investment Capital
Hoping to share in the thriving economy, banks and wealthy people lent businesses money.

CRITICAL THINKING Causes and Effects How did new technology affect industrial growth?

U.S. Patents Issued 1860–1909

Thousands (y-axis: 0, 50, 100, 150, 200, 250, 300, 350)

| 1860-69 | 1870-79 | 1880-89 | 1890-99 | 1900-09 |

Source: *Historical Statistics of the United States*

CRITICAL THINKING Analyze Graphs Based on the information in the graph, what can you conclude about the process of invention during the late 1800s?

By 1882, Edison had installed the first permanent commercial central power system in New York City. Electric lighting slowly replaced gaslights.

Bell and the Telephone After years of experiments, **Alexander Graham Bell**, an accomplished inventor, invented the telephone in 1876. Bell's breakthrough was the result of an accident. He was adjusting the transmitter in the laboratory and his assistant, Thomas Watson, was in another room with the receiver. Bell reportedly spilled acid on himself and said, "Mr. Watson, come here. I want you." Watson burst into the laboratory, exclaiming that he had heard Bell's words through the receiver.

New Industries New inventions often became the basis of new industries that changed American life. The telephone industry grew rapidly after the invention of the telephone. By 1880, more than 50,000 telephones had been sold. The invention of the switchboard allowed more people to connect to a telephone network. Women commonly worked in the new job of switchboard operator. The typewriter also opened jobs for women. Christopher Latham Sholes helped invent the first practical typewriter in 1867.

The sewing machine created changes in industry, too. Elias Howe first patented the sewing machine in 1846. Isaac Singer also patented a sewing machine in 1851 and continued to improve it. It became a bestseller and led to a new industry. In factories, people produced ready-made clothes. Instead of being fitted to each buyer, clothes came in standard sizes and popular styles. Increasingly, people bought clothes instead of making their own.

Other inventors also helped industry advance. African-American inventor Granville T. Woods patented devices to improve telephone and telegraph systems. Margaret Knight invented machines for the packaging and shoe making industries.

▲ **MAIN IDEAS & DETAILS** Identify new inventions that changed American life.

(*top*) Thomas Edison and his safe, steady light bulb (*bottom*) Alexander Graham Bell and one of his telephones
Why was 1876 an important year for both inventors?

Corporations Gain Power

🔻 **KEY QUESTION** How did corporations affect business competition?

In the decades following the Civil War, the American business world was thoroughly reorganized. This reorganization changed the way businesses were managed and financed. It also appeared to threaten business competition and the free market.

Businesses Become Corporations Until the late 1800s, most businesses were owned directly by one person or by a few partners. Then advances in technology made many business owners want to buy new equipment. To raise money, they turned their businesses into **corporations**. A corporation is a business owned by **shareholders**, investors who buy part of the company through shares of stock. In the late 1800s, few laws regulated corporations. This led to the growth of a few powerful corporations that dominated American industry.

Rockefeller and the Oil Industry The oil industry, led by **John D. Rockefeller**, began to grow in the late 1800s. Rockefeller built his first refinery in 1863. He decided that the best way to make money was to put his competitors

---

CONNECT ➤ *Economics and History*

THE CORPORATION

The 1882 Supreme Court decision, *San Mateo County* v. *Southern Pacific Railroad*, gave corporations the same rights enjoyed by all people living in the United States. The court based its decision on the Fourteenth Amendment.

Corporations have several advantages over privately-owned businesses:

- Corporations can raise large amounts of money by selling stock.

- A corporation limits the risks to its shareholders.

- A corporation continues to exist after its founders die.

- Corporations are better able to run large operations such as the Standard Oil refinery shown on the right.

SHAREHOLDERS
- Own shares of the corporation
- Elect board of directors
- Vote on corporate policies

BOARD OF DIRECTORS
- Appoints officers
- Sets corporate policies

REPORTS TO SHAREHOLDERS

OFFICERS OF CORPORATION
- Are employees of the corporation
- Manage daily operations

REPORT TO BOARD OF DIRECTORS

REPORT TO SHAREHOLDERS

CRITICAL THINKING

1. **Compare and Contrast** How are corporations different from privately owned businesses?

2. **Draw Conclusions** Which corporate group has the most control over a corporation?

out of business. A company that wipes out its competitors and controls an industry is a **monopoly**. Rockefeller bought other refineries. He made deals with railroads to carry his oil at a lower rate than his competitors' oil. He also built and purchased his own pipelines to carry oil.

One of Rockefeller's most famous moves to end competition was to develop the **trust** in 1882. A trust is a legal body created to hold stock in many companies, often in the same industry. Other oil companies joined Rockefeller's Standard Oil Trust. By 1880, the trust controlled 95 percent of all oil refining in the United States and was able to set a high price for oil. Consumers had to pay Standard Oil's high price because they couldn't buy oil from anyone else. As head of Standard Oil, Rockefeller earned millions of dollars. He became known as a **robber baron**, a business leader who uses dishonest methods to grow rich.

Political cartoons of (*left*) John D. Rockefeller and (*below*) Andrew Carnegie
Why did Rockefeller become known as a robber baron?

Carnegie and the Steel Industry Andrew Carnegie, unlike Rockefeller, tried to beat his competition in the steel industry by making the best and cheapest product. To do so, he sought to control all the processes related to the manufacture of steel. He bought iron mines as well as the ships and railroads that carried iron ore to his mills. Carnegie's company dominated the U.S. steel industry from 1889 to 1901, when he sold it to J.P. Morgan, the nation's top banker, for $480 million.

Carnegie and Rockefeller became multimillionaires. They were also philanthropists, or people who give large sums of money to charities. Rockefeller donated money to the University of Chicago and Rockefeller University in New York. Carnegie also gave money to universities, and he built hundreds of public libraries. During his life, Rockefeller gave away more than $500 million. Carnegie gave away more than $350 million.

The Business Cycle In the second half of the 19th century American industry experienced ups and downs. This pattern of good and bad times is called the **business cycle**. During very good times, called booms, people buy more, and some invest in business. As a result, industries and businesses grow. During very bad times, called busts, spending and investing decrease. Industries lay off workers and make fewer goods. Businesses may shrink, or even close. Such a period of extremely low economic activity is a **depression**.

In the late 1800s there were two harsh depressions. The depression of 1873 lasted five years. At its height, three million people were out of work. During the depression that began in 1893, thousands of businesses failed, including more than 150 railroads. Even with these economic lows, industries in the United States grew between 1860 and 1900. The amount of manufactured goods increased six-fold during these years.

▲ **CAUSES AND EFFECTS** Explain how corporations affected business competition.

Economic Growth Brings Wealth and Poverty

▼ **KEY QUESTION** What inequalities emerged in the late 19th century?

Industrialization raised living standards in America and brought great wealth to business owners. The richest Americans celebrated and often flaunted their fortunes by spending them—on mansions filled with fine furniture, antiques, and art. However, the economic growth of this time did little to help minorities, factory workers, and many in the South.

The Gilded Age The rags-to-riches stories of people such as Rockefeller and Carnegie inspired many Americans to believe that they, too, could grow rich. Horatio Alger wrote popular stories about poor boys who worked hard

COMPARING *Life in the Gilded Age*

RICH AND POOR

During the Gilded Age, the wealthiest Americans lived in palace-like mansions, while the poorest families lived in small, cramped apartments.

CRITICAL THINKING Compare and Contrast How do these two images reflect the distance between rich and poor in the United States during the Gilded Age?

and became successful. These stories hid an important truth, however. Most people who made millions had not been raised in poverty. Many belonged to the upper classes, attended college, and began their careers with the advantage of money or family connections.

Writers Mark Twain and Charles Warner named the era the **Gilded Age**. To gild is to coat an object with gold leaf. The name has a deeper meaning, however. Just as gold leaf can disguise an object of lesser value, the wealth of a few masked society's problems, including corrupt politics and widespread poverty. In 1890, the average income for 11 million of the nation's 12 million families was $380, well below the poverty line.

Gilded pottery figure, 1900

The South Remains Agricultural Most of the industrial growth during the late 1800s took place in the North. Compared with the North's economy, the South's economy grew slowly after the Civil War. Industry did grow in some areas, such as Birmingham, Alabama, and southern Virginia, but most of the South remained agricultural. The price of cotton, the South's main crop, was very low. Sharecroppers made little money from selling cotton and had a hard time paying what they owed. At the same time that southern sharecroppers struggled to break free of debt, workers in the industrial North also faced injustices.

▲ **SUMMARIZE** Describe the inequalities that emerged during the Gilded Age.

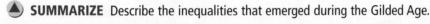

🔲 **Illinois Learning Standards** *Review*

🔗 **ONLINE QUIZ**
For test practice, go to
Interactive Review @ ClassZone.com

TERMS & NAMES

1. Explain the importance of
   - Lewis Latimer
   - Thomas Edison
   - Alexander Graham Bell
   - John D. Rockefeller
   - robber baron
   - Andrew Carnegie
   - Gilded Age

USING YOUR READING NOTES

2. **Main Ideas & Details** Complete the diagram you started at the beginning of this section. Then write a one-sentence summary of the most important points.

New inventions change American life

electric light bulb

KEY IDEAS

3. How did new inventions change life in the late 1800s?

4. How did John D. Rockefeller become so powerful in the oil industry?

5. Why did Mark Twain and Charles Warner call the late 1800s the Gilded Age?

CRITICAL THINKING

6. **Causes and Effects** How did the growth in population and immigration affect industrial growth in the United States?

7. **Compare and Contrast** How were Rockefeller's methods for building Standard Oil different from Carnegie's in building his steel company?

8. **Connect** *to* **Today** What inventions and industries have done the most to change life in the United States recently?

The Steel Industry

In the late 1800s, the steel and steel-products industries began to boom in the Great Lakes region. The natural resources used to make steel—coal, oil, iron ore, and limestone—were abundant. Trains, rivers, and lakes connected the region to markets in the East and South and brought in raw materials from the West. The map shows the resources of the Great Lakes and how transportation by rail and water joined regions. The steps in the steel production process are shown below.

Lake Superior

MINNESOTA

Duluth

WISCONSIN

St. Paul

Minneapolis

Mining
- Iron ore
- Limestone
- Coal
- Iron and steel works

Transportation
- Canal
- Railroad
- Shipping

0   50   100 miles
0   50   100 kilometers

1. Transporting Raw Materials

Iron ore, limestone, and coal were used to make a form of iron called pig iron. Raw materials were carried by ship and train from mines to iron and steel works.

2. Converting Iron to Steel

Steel is iron that has most of its impurities removed to make it stronger. Starting in 1856, steel workers turned iron into steel in pear-shaped Bessemer converters. In the 1900s, the Bessemer process began to be replaced with the open hearth process.

Lake Huron

Lake Ontario

Lake Michigan

Lake Erie

CONN.

NEW YORK

ONTARIO

Buffalo

New York

NEW JERSEY

PENNSYLVANIA

Philadelphia

MICHIGAN

Detroit

DELAWARE

Cleveland

Toledo

Pittsburgh

MARYLAND

Milwaukee

OHIO

VIRGINIA

Columbus

WEST VIRGINIA

Chicago

Gary

INDIANA

Indianapolis

Cincinnati

ILLINOIS

St. Louis

3. Casting Products

After steel was purified, liquid steel was poured into a ladle and cast into molds. Steel products, such as railroad rails and steel girders, helped industries and cities grow.

Connect Geography & History

1. **Region** What advantages did the Great Lakes region have that helped it become highly industrialized?

2. **Human-Environment Interaction** How did the development of railroads add to the region's advantages?

See Geography Handbook, pages A8–A9.

▶ Key Ideas

BEFORE, YOU LEARNED

New inventions and corporations created the Gilded Age of industrial growth and great wealth for a few.

NOW YOU WILL LEARN

Immigration and industrialization spurred the rapid growth of America's cities.

▶ Vocabulary

TERMS & NAMES

Ellis Island New York Harbor immigration station for European immigrants

Angel Island San Francisco Bay immigration station for Asian immigrants

melting pot a place where cultures blend

assimilation process of blending into society by adopting the dominant culture

Chinese Exclusion Act 1882 law which banned Chinese immigration

Jane Addams urban reformer

Hull House settlement house founded by Jane Addams in Chicago

social gospel movement reforms based on Christian values

Tammany Hall New York City political machine

BACKGROUND VOCABULARY

urbanization growth of cities resulting from industrialization

sweatshop place where workers labor long hours under poor conditions for low wages

tenements run-down and overcrowded apartment houses

slum neighborhood with overcrowded and dangerous housing

political machine organization that controls a local government

▶ Reading Strategy

Re-create the diagram shown at right. As you read and respond to the **KEY QUESTIONS**, use the diagram to identify causes of urban growth. Add boxes or start a new diagram as needed.

 See Skillbuilder Handbook, page R7.

CAUSES AND EFFECTS

CAUSES

EFFECT

Urban growth

🔄 **GRAPHIC ORGANIZERS**
Go to **Interactive Review** @ ClassZone.com

Immigration and Modern Urban Growth

 16.C.3b Explain relationships among the American economy and slavery, immigration, industrialization, labor and urbanization, 1700–present.
16.E.3c Describe the impact of urbanization and suburbanization, 1850–present, on the environment.

One American's Story

In 1907, 10-year-old Edward Corsi left Italy to come to America. After two weeks at sea, he saw the Statue of Liberty.

PRIMARY SOURCE

❝ This symbol of America . . . inspired awe in the hopeful immigrants. Many older persons among us, burdened with a thousand memories of what they were leaving behind, had been openly weeping. . . . Now somehow steadied, I suppose, by the concreteness of the symbol of America's freedom, they dried their tears. ❞

—Edward Corsi, *In the Shadow of Liberty*

Edward Corsi was one of millions of immigrants who came to the United States in the years between 1890 and 1920. Most of these immigrants settled in America's growing cities.

A young immigrant

Industrialization Changes Cities

🔻 **KEY QUESTION** How did industry and new inventions change society?

New materials and inventions helped speed industrial growth. This growth caused far-reaching changes in American society.

The Population Shifts to Cities The Industrial Revolution changed not just how people worked, but also where they worked. Since colonial days, most Americans had lived and worked in rural areas. In the late 1800s, more and more people moved to cities to find jobs.

Industries were drawn to cities that offered good transportation and plentiful workers. Increasing numbers of factory jobs became available in cities, followed by more workers to fill those jobs. The growth of cities that resulted from these changes is called **urbanization**.

Skyscrapers In the late 1800s, a new type of building called the skyscraper helped cities absorb millions of people. Skyscrapers looked tall enough to scrape the sky. They increased the amount of housing and workspace available within cities.

One invention that made it possible to build skyscrapers was the electric elevator. Before the 1860s, buildings were rarely more than four stories high because many people didn't want to climb more stairs than that. In 1889, Otis Elevator Company installed the first electric elevator. Buildings could now be more than a few stories tall.

The use of steel also helped engineers construct taller buildings. In 1885, the Home Insurance Building in Chicago boasted an iron and steel skeleton that could hold the immense weight of the skyscraper's floors and walls. The building climbed to ten stories. Skyscrapers changed city skylines forever.

Streetcars and Suburbs Just as electricity changed the way people lived inside buildings, it also changed the way they traveled around cities. Before industrialization, people walked or used horse-drawn vehicles to travel over land. But by 1900, electric streetcars in American cities were carrying more than 5 billion passengers a year.

CONNECT To History

CHINESE IMMIGRATION

Between 1849 and 1882, tens of thousands of Chinese immigrants came to America.

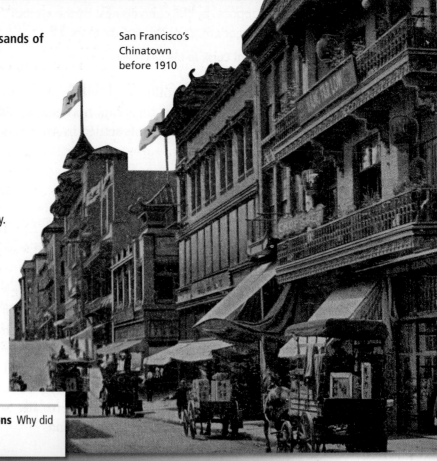

San Francisco's Chinatown before 1910

▶ **1849**
California Gold Rush attracts fortune-seekers who have heard that California is a "Gold Mountain."

▶ **1851–1864**
Taiping Rebellion in China causes widespread death, destruction and poverty.

▶ **1877–1878**
Drought in China ruins farms, creating hardship for millions.

▶ **1882**
Chinese Exclusion Act stops immigration of Chinese workers for 10 years; bans Chinese from U.S. citizenship.

CRITICAL THINKING Draw Conclusions Why did Chinese immigrants leave China?

By allowing workers to live further away from their jobs, public transportation helped new suburbs develop. It also helped cities expand. Some suburbs wanted to merge with the city that they bordered in order to be served by the city's transportation system. In 1889, Chicago annexed several suburbs and more than doubled its population and area.

▲ **CAUSES AND EFFECTS** Explain how industry and new inventions changed society.

The New Immigrants

▼ **KEY QUESTION** Who were the new immigrants and where did they settle in the United States?

Until the 1890s, most immigrants to the United States had come from northern and western Europe. But after 1896, immigrants came mainly from southern and eastern Europe, including southern Italy, Poland, and Russia. This later group became known as the "new immigrants."

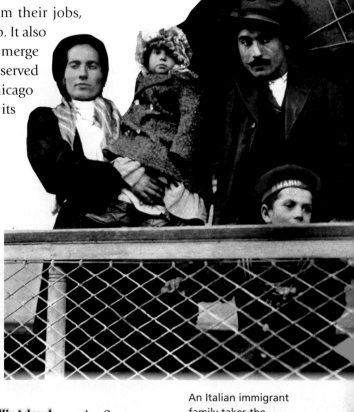

An Italian immigrant family takes the Ellis Island ferry to Manhattan in 1905. **What process did immigrants go through on Ellis Island?**

New Arrivals For most European immigrants, **Ellis Island** was the first stop. There, they were processed before they could enter the United States. First, they had to pass a physical examination. Those with serious health problems were sent home. Immigrants who passed the physical were then asked for their name, occupation, and financial situation. In 1910, Asian immigrants began to land at **Angel Island** in San Francisco Bay. In Angel Island's filthy buildings, most Chinese immigrants were held for weeks. Many Mexican immigrants entered the United States through Texas.

Finding Work and Housing American cities such as New York, Boston, Philadelphia, and Chicago attracted immigrants with the promise of jobs. Newer immigrants looked for people from the old country to help them find jobs and housing. People with similar ethnic backgrounds often moved to the same neighborhoods. As a result, ethnic neighborhoods with names like "Little Italy" and "Chinatown" became common in American cities.

While European immigrants settled mostly in the East and Midwest, Asian immigrants settled mostly in the West. Many Chinese immigrants worked on the railroads. Others settled in western cities. Japanese immigrants first came to Hawaii in 1868 to work on sugar plantations. Others settled on the mainland where they commonly fished, farmed, or worked in mines.

Immigrants from Mexico came to the Southwest. Mexican immigration increased after 1910 when revolution in that country forced many people to flee. Many Mexican immigrants found work on ranches in California and Texas or in Arizona copper mines.

▲ **MAIN IDEA & DETAILS** Explain where the "new immigrants" came from and where they settled in America.

Reactions to Immigration

▼ **KEY QUESTION** What did native-born Americans fear about immigration?

Immigrants were eager to become part of their new country. However, many native-born Americans regarded immigrants as a threat.

Americanization and Prejudice Some Americans have described the United States as a **melting pot,** or a place where cultures blend. The new immigrants blended into American society as earlier immigrants had. This process of blending into society is called **assimilation**. To assimilate, new immigrants studied English and how to be American citizens.

Many workers began to assimilate in order to get and retain work. Employers and labor unions both tried to "Americanize" immigrant workers by offering classes in citizenship and English. Yet, at the same time that immigrants were learning about America, they were also changing America. Immigrants did not give up their cultures completely. Bits and pieces of immigrant languages, foods, and music worked their way into the rest of American culture.

Despite their efforts to assimilate, immigrants faced prejudice from native-born Americans. Many Protestants feared the arrival of Catholics and Jews. Other native-born Americans thought immigrants would not fit into demo-

(*below*) New American citizens swear to uphold the Constitution at their citizenship ceremony in New York City, 2005.

CONNECT *Citizenship and History*

BECOMING A CITIZEN

Immigrants to the U.S. in 1900 as today went through the following naturalization process to become citizens:

- Declare an intention to become a U.S. citizen
- Renounce allegiance to foreign country
- Live in the United States for a specified period of time
- Petition the court to become a citizen
- Swear oath to uphold the U.S. Constitution

Today the process is more complex. Applicants need also to be able to read and write English, pass a test about the principles of U.S. government and the Constitution, and undergo a background check, among other requirements.

How Does Someone Become a Citizen?

1 In a small group, discuss what questions you would ask those seeking to become U.S. citizens.

2 Discuss the naturalization process. How has it changed since 1900? Why do you think it has changed?

 See Citizenship Handbook, pages 300–301.

cratic society because they would be controlled by politicians. Such prejudices led some native-born Americans to push for restrictions on the numbers of new immigrants.

Restrictions on Immigration Many native-born Americans also feared they would have to compete with immigrants for jobs. Immigrants often took whatever jobs they could get, working for long hours, low wages, and in unsafe conditions. Many found jobs in **sweatshops**—hot, crowded, dangerous factories—for about ten dollars a week.

Some Americans worried that there would not be enough jobs for everyone. These fears led to increased opposition to immigration. In 1882, Congress began to pass laws to restrict immigration. They placed taxes on new immigrants and banned specific groups, such as convicts and people with mental illness. Nonwhites faced deeper prejudice than European immigrants, and Asians faced some of the worst. In 1882, Congress passed the **Chinese Exclusion Act**. It banned Chinese immigration for ten years.

Immigration and Racism The Chinese Exclusion Act was not the only example of prejudice in America around 1900. Chinese immigrants who came to the West in the 1800s also faced severe discrimination. Chinese laborers received lower wages than whites for the same work. Sometimes, Chinese workers faced violence. In 1885, white workers in Rock Springs, Wyoming, refused to work in the same mine as Chinese workers. The whites stormed through the Chinese part of town, killing 28 Chinese people.

At the same time, Mexicans and African Americans who came to the American Southwest were forced into peonage. In this system of labor, people are forced to work until they have paid off debts. Congress outlawed peonage in 1867, but some workers were still forced to work to repay debts. In 1911, the U.S. Supreme Court declared such labor to be the same as peonage. As a result, the Court struck down such forms of labor as a violation of the Thirteenth Amendment.

▲ **SUMMARIZE** Describe what native-born Americans feared about immigration.

(*top*) Many Jewish immigrants lived on Hester Street on New York's Lower East Side. (*bottom*) A pushcart vendor sells goods on Mulberry Street. **How did immigrants change American culture?**

Problems of Urbanization

▼ **KEY QUESTION** What problems were caused by urbanization?

The growing population of the cities led to overcrowding and disease. Soon political organizations and reformers were working to improve conditions.

History Makers

Jane Addams   1860–1935

Founding Hull House would have assured Jane Addams' place in history. Her remarkable career extended much further, however. She was also a leader in the women's suffrage movement. She was a founder of the National Association for the Advancement of Colored People (NAACP) and the American Civil Liberties Union (ACLU). She also founded the Women's International League of Peace and Freedom and served as its president from 1919 until 1935. In 1931, she became the first American woman to be awarded the Nobel Peace Prize for her work in promoting world peace. (She shared the prize with Nicholas Murray Butler.)

CRITICAL THINKING What obstacles do you think Jane Addams faced in her work promoting justice and peace?

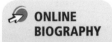 **ONLINE BIOGRAPHY**   For more on Jane Addams, go to the **Research & Writing Center** @ ClassZone.com

Urban Disasters and Slums The concentration of people in cities increased the danger of disaster because people and buildings were packed closely together. For example, in 1906, a powerful earthquake rocked San Francisco, destroying the central business district and killing about 700 people.

Natural disasters were not the only danger for city dwellers. Poverty and disease also threatened lives. Many people lived in **tenements,** run-down and overcrowded apartment houses. Old buildings, landlord neglect, poor design, and little government control led to dangerous conditions in many tenements. Inadequate garbage pick-up also caused problems. Tenants sometimes dumped their smelly garbage into the narrow air shafts between tenements.

Many tenements had no running water. Residents had to collect water from a faucet on the street. The water could be heated for bathing, but it was often unsafe for drinking. Sewage flowed in open gutters and threatened to spread disease among tenement dwellers.

A neighborhood with such overcrowded, dangerous housing was called a **slum**. The most famous example was New York City's Lower East Side, but every city had slums.

Reformers Attack Urban Problems Many Americans were disgusted by poverty and slums. Urban reformers fought for changes that would solve these problems. Some reformers opened settlement houses to help immigrants and the poor improve their lives. Settlement houses offered daycare, education, and health care to needy people in slums.

Many settlement house founders were educated middle-class women. **Jane Addams**, an urban reformer and suffrage leader, founded Chicago's **Hull House** in 1889 with Ellen Gates Starr. Hull House became a model for other settlement houses. In 1893, Lillian D. Wald founded the Henry Street Settlement House in New York.

Some reformers were inspired by the **social gospel movement**, which was based on Christian values and led by Protestant ministers. The movement worked for labor reforms, such as abolishing child labor.

Political Machines Run Cities Political machines were another type of organization that addressed the problems of the city. A **political machine** is an illegal gang that influences enough votes to control a local government. Political machines gained support by trading favors for votes. Machine bosses gave jobs, cash, or food to supporters. In return, supporters voted for the machine. Political machines did many other illegal things. They broke rules to win elections. They demanded bribes and used extortion, or threats, to affect government actions.

The most famous political machine was **Tammany Hall** in New York City. It was led by William Marcy Tweed. Along with his greedy friends, "Boss" Tweed stole enormous amounts of money from the city.

Despite such corruption, political machines did a number of good things. They built parks, sewers, schools, roads, and orphanages in many cities. Machine politicians often helped immigrants get settled by helping them find jobs or homes. Many immigrants gratefully supported the political machine after this kind of help.

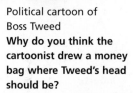

Political cartoon of Boss Tweed
Why do you think the cartoonist drew a money bag where Tweed's head should be?

▲ **PROBLEMS AND SOLUTIONS** Describe the problems caused by urbanization.

Illinois Learning Standards *Review*

🔁 **ONLINE QUIZ**
For test practice, go to
Interactive Review @ ClassZone.com

TERMS & NAMES

1. Explain the importance of

- Ellis Island
- Angel Island
- melting pot
- assimilation
- Chinese Exclusion Act
- Jane Addams
- Hull House
- social gospel movement

USING YOUR READING NOTES

2. Causes and Effects Complete the diagram you started at the beginning of this section. Make a new diagram to list other causes and their effects.

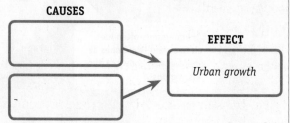

CAUSES

EFFECT

Urban growth

KEY IDEAS

3. How did streetcars change cities?

4. Why did many immigrants move to cities?

5. What was the Chinese Exclusion Act?

6. How did political machines and immigrants help each other?

CRITICAL THINKING

7. Causes and Effects How did industrial growth affect immigration?

8. Draw Conclusions How did urbanization change American society and politics?

9. Compare and Contrast Compare the challenges faced by the new immigrants from Europe to challenges faced by Asian immigrants.

10. **Art** **Political Cartoon** Draw a political cartoon that shows a reformer's solution to an urban problem in the late 19th century.

Click here to explore Ellis Island @ ClassZone.com

Gateway to America

Between 1892 and 1954, 12 million immigrants passed through the Ellis Island Immigration Station. Some immigrants stayed on Ellis Island for days or even weeks if they failed their health exams. Others waited for family members or money to arrive before they could travel to the mainland.

Click here Ferries took immigrants from piers on the mainland to Ellis Island.

Click here In the station cafeteria, immigrants could have their first taste of ice cream and other American dishes.

Click here After waiting for hours to be inspected, immigrants still had to wait in long lines to leave Ellis Island.

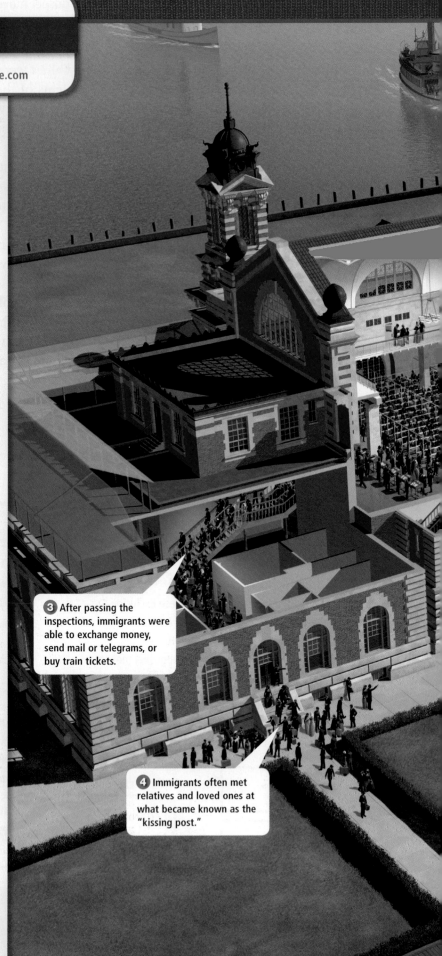

③ After passing the inspections, immigrants were able to exchange money, send mail or telegrams, or buy train tickets.

④ Immigrants often met relatives and loved ones at what became known as the "kissing post."

⑤ Immigrants who had to stay overnight were assigned to separate dormitories for men and women.

② Although lines were long, the inspection itself usually lasted only three to five minutes.

① Doctors examined immigrants as they headed upstairs to the Great Hall.

Activity

The Immigrant Experience

What did new immigrants need to do once they arrived in America?

1 Prepare for your role as an immigrant who has just arrived on Ellis Island, or volunteer to take one of the following roles: legal inspector, doctor, appeals judge, cook, nurse, or translator.

2 Set up an "Ellis Island Immigration Center" in your classroom. Take your place in the center, depending on your role.

3 Play your role as the class walks through the immigration process.

▶ Key Ideas

BEFORE, YOU LEARNED

Immigration and industrialization spurred the rapid growth of America's modern cities.

NOW YOU WILL LEARN

Segregation and discrimination against African Americans was commonplace in the years after the Civil War.

▶ Vocabulary

TERMS & NAMES

Jim Crow laws enacted in Southern states designed to separate white and black people

segregation the separation of races

Ida B. Wells African-American journalist who led the fight against lynching

Plessy v. Ferguson 1896 Supreme Court case that upheld the legality of segregation

Booker T. Washington African-American leader who did not believe in challenging segregation

W. E. B. Du Bois African-American leader who fought against segregation and for equal rights and who helped found the NAACP

NAACP National Association for the Advancement of Colored People

REVIEW

literacy the ability to read and write

lynch to kill by hanging without due process of the law

▶ Reading Strategy

Re-create a diagram like the one shown at right. As you read and respond to the **KEY QUESTIONS**, fill in the diagram. Add more fact boxes or create a new diagram as needed.

 See Skillbuilder Handbook, page R3.

SUMMARIZE

Jim Crow laws

Discrimination Against African Americans

GRAPHIC ORGANIZERS
Go to **Interactive Review** @ ClassZone.com

Discrimination Against African Americans

14.C.3 Compare historical issues involving rights, roles and status of individuals in relation to municipalities, states and the nation.
16.B.3c Describe the way the Constitution has changed over time as a result of amendments and Supreme Court decisions.

An American Story

African-American sisters Sarah and Elizabeth Delany grew up in North Carolina in the early 20th century. Almost 100 years later, they described their first taste of racial discrimination, or different treatment on the basis of race.

PRIMARY SOURCE

❝ We were about five and seven years old. . . . Mama and Papa used to take us to Pullen Park . . . and that particular day, the trolley driver told us to go to the back. We children objected loudly, because we always liked to sit in the front. . . . But Mama and Papa just gently told us to hush and took us to the back. ❞

— Sarah L. Delany and A. Elizabeth Delany, *Having Our Say*

Sisters Elizabeth and Sarah Delany

As you will read in this section, racial discrimination was common throughout the United States in the late 1800s and early 1900s.

Racism Causes Discrimination

🔻 **KEY QUESTION** How did racism affect African Americans?

In America, many whites considered themselves superior to Asians, Native Americans, Latin Americans, and African Americans. Racist beliefs inspired acts of violence and racial discrimination. Some of the most widespread discrimination was directed against African Americans.

A History of Racism Racist attitudes toward African Americans had existed in America since the introduction of slavery. In colonial times, the low social rank held by slaves led many whites to assume that whites were superior to blacks. Reconstruction was a brief period when African Americans began to achieve equal rights in the South. However, when Reconstruction ended in 1877, white Southerners struck back sharply.

Segregation and Jim Crow Laws Whites weakened African-American political power by restricting their voting rights. Southern states passed laws that set up **literacy**, or reading, tests and poll taxes to prevent African Americans from voting. White officials made sure that blacks failed literacy tests by giving unfair exams. For example, white officials sometimes gave blacks tests written in Latin. Poll taxes kept many blacks from voting because they didn't have enough money to pay the tax.

Such laws threatened to prevent poor and uneducated whites from voting, too. To keep them from losing the vote, several Southern states added grandfather clauses to their constitutions. Grandfather clauses stated that a man could vote if he or an ancestor, such as a grandfather, had been eligible to vote before 1867. Before that date, most African Americans, free or enslaved, did not have the right to vote. Whites could use the grandfather clause to protect their voting rights. Blacks could not.

In addition to voting restrictions, African Americans faced **Jim Crow** laws. "Jim Crow" was a character in minstrel shows that made fun of African Americans. Jim Crow laws were meant to enforce **segregation**, or separation, of white and black people in public places. As a result, separate schools, trolley seats, and rest rooms were common in the South.

Journalist Ida B. Wells worked to end lynching. **Besides lynching, what else did whites do to keep African Americans from challenging segregation?**

Violence Increases Besides discrimination, African Americans in the South also faced violence. The Ku Klux Klan, which first appeared during Reconstruction, used terror and violence to keep blacks from challenging segregation. Between 1885 and 1900, more than 1,500 African Americans were **lynched**, or hanged without due process of the law.

Ida B. Wells, an African-American journalist from Memphis, led the fight against lynching. After three of her friends were lynched in 1892, she mounted an antilynching campaign in her newspaper. When whites called for Wells herself to be lynched, she moved to Chicago and continued her work against lynching.

Like Wells, some blacks moved north to escape discrimination. Although public facilities there were not segregated by law, Northern whites still discriminated against blacks. Blacks could not get housing in white neighborhoods and usually were denied good jobs. Anti-black feelings among whites sometimes led to violence. In 1908, whites in Springfield, Illinois, attacked blacks who had moved there. The whites lynched two blacks within a half mile of Abraham Lincoln's former home.

Plessy v. Ferguson African Americans resisted segregation, but they had little power to stop it. In 1892, Homer Plessy, an African American, sued a railroad company, arguing that segregated seating violated his Fourteenth Amendment right to "equal protection of the laws." The Supreme Court ruled that "separate but equal" facilities did not violate the Fourteenth Amendment. This decision allowed Southern states to maintain segregated institutions. The separate facilities were not equal. White-controlled governments and companies allowed the facilities for African Americans to decay. African Americans would have to organize to fight for equality.

▲ **CAUSES AND EFFECTS** Explain how racism affected African Americans.

A white train passenger harasses an African-American passenger for sitting in the white section of the train.

Historic Decisions of the SUPREME COURT

Plessy v. Ferguson *(1896)*

KEY ISSUE   Segregation in public facilities
KEY PEOPLE Homer Plessy   African-American shoemaker and activist
                John Ferguson   district court judge

The Case

In 1892, a group of African Americans arranged to challenge Louisiana's Separate Car Act, which legalized segregated seating on trains. They asked African-American shoemaker Homer Plessy to sit in a whites-only train car. As the challengers had expected, railroad officials arrested Plessy. In district court, Plessy's lawyer argued that segregated seating violated Plessy's rights to equal protection. Judge Ferguson ruled against Plessy, stating that Louisiana had the right to make its own laws for railroad travel within the state. Plessy appealed the decision to the U.S. Supreme Court.

The Court's Decision In 1896, the Supreme Court upheld Judge Ferguson's original ruling. Justice Henry B. Brown wrote that although segregation treated the races differently, it did not treat one race as legally inferior or unequal.

Historical Impact The *Plessy* ruling made "separate but equal" the law of the land. In fact, separate facilities were never equal. African Americans received inferior treatment. African-American school buildings were often poorly maintained. Teachers were not paid the same as teachers in white schools. There were fewer books and materials for students. Supreme Court Justice John Marshall Harlan wrote the only dissenting opinion in *Plessy* v. *Ferguson*. He warned that the "thin disguise" of separate but equal facilities would fool no one, "nor atone for the wrong this day done."

CRITICAL THINKING

1. **Causes and Effects** What effect did the Supreme Court's ruling on *Plessy* v. *Ferguson* have on segregation laws?

2. **Analyze Point of View** What do you think Justice Harlan meant when he said that the "thin disguise" of separate-but-equal facilities would fool no one?

African Americans Organize

▼ **KEY QUESTION** What two approaches did African-American leaders take in the face of segregation?

African Americans faced discrimination and violence with determination and courage. Two different leaders emerged from the African-American community. They had different ideas about how to respond to the problems faced by African Americans.

ONLINE BIOGRAPHY

For more on Washington and Du Bois go to the **Research & Writing Center** @ ClassZone.com

Two Leaders Booker T. Washington was an early leader in the effort to achieve equality. In 1881, he founded the Tuskegee Institute in Alabama to help African Americans learn teaching or trades as well as patience, enterprise, and thrift. Washington believed that this type of education would help African Americans gain their advancement through economic security. In

History Makers African-American Leaders

Booker T. Washington 1856–1915

Between 1895 and 1915, Washington was one of the nation's most prominent African-American educators and reformers. His position of compromise on segregation, known as the Atlanta Compromise, was embraced by moderate whites and most African Americans at the time. Many African Americans considered Washington their unofficial spokesperson. They looked to his self-help autobiography, *Up from Slavery*, as a guide for their own advancement.

W. E. B. Du Bois 1868–1963

In his 1903 essay collection, *The Souls of Black Folk*, Du Bois criticized the principles of the Atlanta Compromise and challenged Washington's leadership. Du Bois helped form the Niagara Movement, and in 1909, the National Association for the Advancement of Colored People (NAACP). Both groups demanded full civil and political rights for African Americans. As an NAACP board member and editor of its magazine, *The Crisis*, Du Bois was able to shape public opinion in the African-American community.

COMPARING *Leaders*

Draw Conclusions Which leader was more effective in advancing African-American civil rights? Explain your answer.

exchange for economic security, he thought that African Americans should not openly challenge segregation. He thought that whites and blacks could work together yet live separate social lives. Washington's position on segregation became known as the Atlanta Compromise.

W. E. B. Du Bois, a sociology professor, disagreed strongly with Booker T. Washington. He believed African Americans should fight against segregation. He also thought that industrial training would limit African Americans to inferior jobs. Instead, he pushed for higher education for the most able African Americans, which he called the "Talented Tenth." They were teachers, ministers, and professionals who would lead the struggle for equal rights.

In 1909, Du Bois, Jane Addams, and other reformers founded the National Association for the Advancement of Colored People, or the **NAACP**. The NAACP played a major role in ending segregation in the 20th century.

NAACP members march in Greenville, South Carolina, 2003.

 SUMMARIZE Explain why Du Bois and Washington disagreed about segregation.

 Illinois Learning Standards *Review*

ONLINE QUIZ
For test practice, go to
Interactive Review @ ClassZone.com

TERMS & NAMES

1. Explain the importance of
- Jim Crow
- segregation
- Ida B. Wells
- *Plessy* v. *Ferguson*
- Booker T. Washington
- W. E. B. Du Bois
- NAACP

USING YOUR READING NOTES

2. Summarize Complete the diagram you started at the beginning of the section. Add more fact boxes or create a new diagram as needed.

KEY IDEAS

3. How did Southerners keep African Americans from political power?

4. How did Ida Wells lead the fight against lynching?

5. What was the Atlanta Compromise?

CRITICAL THINKING

6. Make Inferences How do you think Jim Crow laws and the Ku Klux Klan kept African Americans from claiming their rights as American citizens?

7. Draw Conclusions Why did reformers form the NAACP?

8. **Connect** *to* **Today** Even though racial discrimination is against the law, do you think it is still a part of American society today? Explain.

▶ Key Ideas

BEFORE, YOU LEARNED

Segregation and discrimination against African Americans was commonplace in the years after the Civil War.

NOW YOU WILL LEARN

As business leaders guided industrial expansion, workers organized to gain their rights.

▶ Vocabulary

TERMS & NAMES

Knights of Labor an organization of workers from all trades formed after the Civil War

socialism system in which the state controls the economy

Haymarket Affair 1886 union protest

Samuel Gompers labor leader, founder of the American Federation of Labor (AFL)

American Federation of Labor (AFL) a national organization of labor unions founded in 1886 by Samuel Gompers

Homestead Strike violent strike at Andrew Carnegie's Homestead, Pennsylvania, steel mills in 1892

Pullman Strike nationwide railway strike that spread throughout the rail industry in 1894

Eugene V. Debs American Railway Union leader jailed in Pullman strike in 1894

BACKGROUND VOCABULARY

anarchist person who believes in a society that has no government at all

Visual Vocabulary
Haymarket Affair

▶ Reading Strategy

Re-create the diagram shown at right. As you read and respond to the **KEY QUESTIONS**, use the diagram to note major events in the labor movement between the Civil War and the 1900s. Add more boxes as needed.

 See Skillbuilder Handbook, page R5.

SEQUENCE

Soldiers return from war.
1865

GRAPHIC ORGANIZERS
Go to **Interactive Review** @ ClassZone.com

The Labor Movement

 16.C.3c Describe how economic developments and government policies after 1865 affected the country's economic institutions including corporations, banks and organized labor.
16.D.3b Describe characteristics of different kinds of families in America during the colonial/frontier periods and the 19th century.

One American's Story

In 1867, Mary Harris Jones lost her husband and four children to yellow fever. Moving to Chicago, Jones started a dressmaking business. When she lost all she owned in the great Chicago fire of 1871, she found a cause to fight for.

PRIMARY SOURCE

❝From the time of the Chicago fire I . . . decided to take an active part in the efforts of the working people to better the conditions under which they worked and lived.❞

— **Mary Harris Jones,** *Autobiography of Mother Jones*

Jones became an effective labor leader who organized meetings, gave speeches, and helped strikers. Workers loved her so much that they called her Mother Jones.

Workers Organize

🔻 **KEY QUESTION** Why did workers organize?

As industrialization expanded, standards of living generally improved. However, workers suffered from dangerous conditions in the factories, low wages, and long hours. To improve conditions, workers began to organize.

Poor Working Conditions Workers faced a long list of problems. Among them were:

- 10–12-hour days
- no sick days
- unsafe and unhealthy working conditions
- low pay
- dull, repetitive jobs

Many business owners of the late 1800s ran their factories as cheaply as possible. Many omitted safety equipment to save money. For example, railroads would not buy air brakes or automatic train-car couplers even though about 30,000 railroad workers were injured and 2,000 killed every year.

Mother Jones won the love of working people by fighting for their rights.

Adults and children work in a food-processing factory.

In the 1880s, the average weekly wage was less than ten dollars. This barely paid a family's expenses. To get by, whole families worked, including young children. If a worker missed work due to illness or had unexpected bills, the family usually went into debt.

Workers often had little direct contact with business owners, who kept their distance from workers and their grievances. Workers began to feel that only other working people could understand their troubles. Discontented workers formed labor unions—groups of workers that negotiated with business owners to obtain better wages and working conditions.

Early Unions The first labor unions began in the mid-1800s but did not win many improvements for workers. After the Civil War, some unions formed national organizations such as the **Knights of Labor**. This was a loose federation of workers from different trades. Unlike many unions, the Knights of Labor allowed women and, after 1878, African-American workers to join.

Beginning in 1873, the United States fell into an economic depression. Over the next four years, millions of workers took pay cuts, and about one-fifth lost their jobs. In July 1877, the Baltimore and Ohio (B & O) Railroad declared a 10 percent wage cut. In response, B & O workers in Martinsburg, West Virginia, refused to run the trains. Workers in other cities joined in, throwing the country into turmoil. This work stoppage grew into the Railroad Strike of 1877. President Rutherford B. Hayes called out federal troops. Before the two-week strike ended, dozens of people had been killed.

The strike did not prevent the railroad pay cut, but it showed how angry American workers had become. In 1884–1885, railroaders went on strike again, this time against the Union Pacific and two other railroads. The strikers, members of the Knights of Labor, gained nationwide attention when they won their strike. Hundreds of thousands of workers joined the union.

Racism and the Unions Unions and industry leaders alike had racist policies. Many unions tried to exclude African-American workers from joining. Chinese laborers received lower wages than whites for the same work and sometimes faced violence from white coworkers. During strikes, industry leaders hired Chinese workers and other minorities who would work for less money than white workers.

▲ **SUMMARIZE** Explain why workers organized.

The Struggle Between Business and Labor

▼ **KEY QUESTION** How did business leaders react to workers' demands?

The growth of labor unions frightened many business leaders. In the last decades of the 1800s, conflicts between business and labor grew bitter.

Union Setbacks Powerful unions could threaten business leaders' profits and their near-complete control of industry. In business leaders' fights with unions, they tried to portray union leaders as people with extreme, un-American ideas. They blamed the labor movement on socialists and anarchists. Socialists believe in **socialism**, a social system in which the means of producing and distributing goods is owned collectively or by a centralized government. **Anarchists** believe in anarchy, the abolition of all governments.

Business and government leaders tried to break union power. In Chicago in 1886, the McCormick Harvester Company locked out striking union members and hired strikebreakers to replace them. On May 3, union members, strikebreakers, and police clashed. One union member died.

The next day, union leaders called a protest meeting at Haymarket Square. As police moved in to end the meeting, an unknown person threw a bomb.

ANALYZING *Political Cartoons*

This cartoon, which appeared in 1883 before the Union Pacific strike of 1884–1885, draws a sharp comparison between powerful monopolies and the lowly working man.

Capitalists cheer for Monopoly.

Monopoly wears armor and wields a lance.

Monopoly's horse has train wheels instead of legs.

Workers cheer on Labor.

Labor rides a scrawny horse and has only a short hammer for a weapon.

"THE TOURNAMENT OF TODAY—A SET-TO BETWEEN LABOR AND MONOPOLY."

CRITICAL THINKING

1. **Draw Conclusions** Which side seems more likely to win? Explain your answer.

2. **Analyze** What point is the cartoonist trying to make about monopolies?

See Skillbuilder Handbook, page R24.

It killed 7 police and wounded about 60 people. The police then fired on the crowd, killing several people and wounding about 100 people. This conflict was called the **Haymarket Affair**. Afterward, the Chicago police arrested hundreds of union leaders, socialists, and anarchists. Opposition to unions increased and union membership dropped rapidly.

The Homestead and Pullman Strikes In 1886, the same year as the Haymarket Affair, **Samuel Gompers**, a labor leader, helped found a national organization of unions called the **American Federation of Labor** (AFL). He served as AFL president for 37 years. The AFL used negotiations, strikes, and boycotts to achieve its aims. By 1904 it had about 1.7 million members.

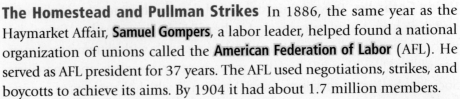

CONNECT to the Essential Question

What new problems and opportunities developed as America became an industrial power?

DEVELOPMENT	OPPORTUNITIES	PROBLEMS
Industrialization	• Provided job opportunities • Modern and efficient products • Leisure	• Pollution • Unhealthy, unsafe working conditions • Dull, repetitive jobs
Urban growth	• New leisure activities • People from different cultures lived in same communities	• Tenements and slums • Corruption and political machines
Segregation and discrimination	• Greater perceived opportunities for whites	• Injustice against African Americans and other non-whites • Betrayal of the promise of equality and freedom for all Americans
Immigration	• Cultural diversity • Millions of people took jobs and purchased goods in a growing economy	• Discrimination • Corruption from political machines
Corporations gain power	• Corporations raised large amounts of money by selling stock • Corporations turned inventions into new products	• Corporations turned into monopolies • Labor conflicts and strikes

CRITICAL THINKING **Analyze** What were some of the benefits of immigration?

Gompers' AFL had success, but national labor conflicts grew more bitter. In 1892 Andrew Carnegie reduced wages at his steel mills in Homestead, Pennsylvania. The union organized what became known as the **Homestead Strike**, so the company locked union workers out of the mills and hired nonunion labor as well as 300 armed guards. On July 6, a battle between the guards and the locked-out workers left ten people dead. The Pennsylvania state militia escorted the nonunion workers to the mills. After four months, the strike collapsed, breaking the union.

Workers lost another dispute in 1894. In that depression year, many railroad companies went bankrupt. To stay in business, the Pullman Palace Car Company cut workers' pay 25 percent. However Pullman did not lower the rent it charged workers to live in company housing. After rent was deducted from their pay, many Pullman workers took home almost nothing.

The Pullman workers began the **Pullman Strike**, a strike which spread throughout the rail industry in 1894. When the Pullman Company refused to negotiate, American Railway Union president **Eugene V. Debs** called on all U.S. railroad workers to refuse to handle Pullman cars. Rail traffic in much of the country stopped. President Grover Cleveland called out federal troops, which ended the strike. Debs was put in jail.

Political cartoon of Eugene V. Debs, American Railway Union President and leader of the Pullman Strike.

 CAUSES AND EFFECTS Describe how business leaders reacted to workers' demands.

 ONLINE QUIZ
For test practice, go to
Interactive Review @ ClassZone.com

Illinois Learning Standards *Review*

TERMS & NAMES

1. Explain the importance of the following

- Knights of Labor
- American Federation of Labor (AFL)
- socialism
- Homestead Strike
- Haymarket Affair
- Pullman Strike
- Samuel Gompers
- Eugene V. Debs

USING YOUR READING NOTES

2. Sequence Complete the diagram you started at the beginning of the section. Which events were setbacks for labor?

Soldiers return from war.

1865

KEY IDEAS

3. What injustices did American workers face in the last decades of the 1800s?

4. What happened in the Pullman Strike?

5. What organization did Samuel Gompers lead?

CRITICAL THINKING

6. Main Idea & Details What was significant about the Railroad Strike of 1877?

7. Draw Conclusions Why do you think the government usually sided with industry in its struggle with early labor unions?

8. Problems and Solutions What were some of the ways that the American Federation of Labor tried to solve workers' problems?

9. Writing Article Write a newspaper article that tells the story of the Haymarket Affair in your own words.

Key Ideas

BEFORE, YOU LEARNED

As business leaders guided industrial expansion, workers organized to gain rights.

NOW YOU WILL LEARN

Industrialization and new technology created a mass culture in the United States.

Vocabulary

TERMS & NAMES

mass culture common culture experienced by a large number of people

Joseph Pulitzer newspaper publisher, owner of the *New York World*

William Randolph Hearst newspaper publisher, owner of *New York Morning Journal*

vaudeville live entertainment that featured song, dance, and comedy

ragtime type of music that blended African-American songs and European musical forms

BACKGROUND VOCABULARY

leisure freedom from time-consuming duties

consumer person who buys something

Visual Vocabulary
vaudeville

Reading Strategy

Re-create the diagram shown at right. As you read and respond to the **KEY QUESTIONS**, use the diagram to identify the effect of immigration on publishing and education. Add more boxes or create a new diagram as needed.

See Skillbuilder Handbook, page R7.

CAUSES AND EFFECTS

CAUSE → EFFECT/CAUSE

Immigration →

EFFECT/CAUSE → Publishing expands

EFFECT

GRAPHIC ORGANIZERS
Go to **Interactive Review** @ ClassZone.com

Society and Mass Culture

16.D.3b Describe characteristics of different kinds of families in America during the colonial/frontier periods and the 19th century.
16.E.3c Describe the impact of urbanization and suburbanization, 1850–present, on the environment.

One American's Story

Schools around 1900 were very different from present-day schools. Classes were large. Most learning was done by memorization and repetition.

PRIMARY SOURCE

❝ I learned arithmetic and penmanship and spelling—every misspelled word written ten times or more, traced painfully and carefully in my blankbook . . . In this same way I learned how to read in English, learned geography and grammar . . . Most learning was done in unison. You recited to the teacher standing at attention. ❞

— Leonard Covello, *The Heart Is the Teacher*

A student in the back row stands to recite a lesson at a New York City grammar school, c. 1870.

Discipline was a key goal of education in the 1800s. In this section, you will learn how education also helped create an American **mass culture**—a common culture experienced by large numbers of people.

Education and Publishing Expand

▼ **KEY QUESTION** What caused education and publishing to expand?

In the late 19th century, industrialization and urbanization created a new kind of society. Urban populations grew, and industrialization helped create cheaper goods and more **leisure**, or freedom from time-consuming duties. Public education also expanded and more students learned to read.

Changes in Schooling Immigration caused enormous growth in American schools. To teach citizenship and English to immigrants, new city and state laws required children to attend school. Between 1880 and 1920, the number of children attending school more than doubled.

Literacy Increases The growth of education increased the number of American readers. Reading became more popular and led to the growth of publishing, the industry that produces books, magazines, and newspapers. Americans read large numbers of novels. Dime novels were especially popular. They sold for ten cents each and told exciting tales.

Americans also read more newspapers. Tough competition pushed newspaper publishers to try all sorts of gimmicks to outsell their rivals. For example, **Joseph Pulitzer**, owner of the *New York World*, and **William Randolph Hearst**, owner of the *New York Morning Journal*, were fierce competitors. They filled their pages with dramatic stories and special features, such as comics.

🔺 **CAUSES AND EFFECTS** Explain why education and publishing expanded in the late 19th century.

Pleasures of the Consumer Society

🔻 **KEY QUESTION** How did Americans spend their leisure time in the late 1800s?

In the late 1800s, American **consumers** could buy new products and experience new forms of entertainment. Movies, music, sports, and advertising combined to shape modern American mass culture.

Daily Life

Fun at Coney Island

In the late 19th century, New York City's Coney Island was the nation's most famous amusement park. It was known for its plush seaside hotels, boardwalk, hot dogs, roller coasters, rides, and many other amusements. In 1884, fun seekers could ride the nation's first roller coaster, the Switchback Railway, for a nickel. One immigrant woman said Coney Island "is just like what I see when I dream of heaven!" Indeed, Coney Island's Dreamland park opened in 1904.

CRITICAL VIEWING **Analyze** Based on the pictures above, what kind of leisure activities did people take part in when they went to Coney Island?

Modern Advertising and New Products The rise of modern advertising in newspapers had a wide influence on American life. Advertising made people aware of new products and of places where they could buy them. Department stores were a new type of store that sold everything from clothing to furniture to hardware. People who did not live near a department store could use mail-order catalogs to order goods.

Mass Culture Leisure activities also changed. Cities had new parks, where city dwellers could stroll wooded walkways, ride bikes, and play sports. Amusement parks had shops, food vendors, and exciting rides such as roller coasters. Between 1876 and 1915, Philadelphia, Chicago, St. Louis, and San Francisco hosted world's fairs. Visitors were drawn to foods, shows, and amusements.

Ragtime music program

Baseball was the most popular sport, but racial discrimination kept African-American baseball players out of baseball's American and National Leagues. African Americans formed their own teams in the Negro leagues. Other forms of live entertainment included **vaudeville**, a mixture of song, dance, and comedy. **Ragtime**, a type of music that blended African-American songs and European musical forms, also became popular.

 MAIN IDEAS & DETAILS Describe how Americans spent their leisure time in the late 1800s.

Illinois Learning Standards *Review*

ONLINE QUIZ
For test practice, go to
Interactive Review @ ClassZone.com

TERMS & NAMES

1. Explain the importance of:
   - mass culture
   - Joseph Pulitzer
   - William Randolph Hearst
   - vaudeville
   - ragtime

USING YOUR READING NOTES

2. **Analyzing Causes** Complete the diagram you started at the beginning of this section. Add more boxes or start a new diagram as needed.

KEY IDEAS

3. What were the connections between newspapers, advertising, and mass culture?

4. What were some of the new forms of entertainment that Americans began to enjoy in the late 1800s?

CRITICAL THINKING

5. **Compare and Contrast** What is the difference between vaudeville and ragtime?

6. **Cause and Effect** How did urbanization change leisure activities?

7. **Connect to Today** What leisure activities from the end of the 1800s are still popular today?

8. **Writing** Postcard Write a postcard to a friend describing some of the amusements at Coney Island in the late 1800s.

Dragonwings by Laurence Yep

From 1900 to 1914, close to 30,000 Chinese immigrants made the difficult journey to the United States to seek employment and a new life. In *Dragonwings*, Laurence Yep brings that era to life through the experiences of Moon Shadow, a young Chinese boy new to America. As Moon Shadow struggles to find his place in the new land, he grapples with conflicts involving traditional Chinese values, the authority of the police, and mainstream American culture. In this scene, Moon Shadow recalls his early desire to know more about America, where his father has gone to seek work. Based on what he has heard of this distant country, Moon Shadow describes America as both "the land of the Golden Mountain" and "the demon land."

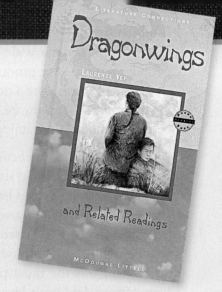

Ever since I can remember, I had wanted to know about the Land of the Golden Mountain, but my mother had never wanted to talk about it. All I knew was that a few months before I was born, my father had left our home in the Middle Kingdom, or *China*, as the white demons call it, and traveled over the sea to work in the demon land. There was plenty of money to be made among the demons, but it was also dangerous. My own grandfather had been lynched about thirty years before by a mob of white demons almost the moment he had set foot on their shores.

Mother usually said she was too busy to answer my questions. It was a fact that she was overworked, for Grandmother was too old to help her with the heavy work, and she had to try to do both her own work and Father's on our small farm. The rice had to be grown from seeds, and the seedlings transplanted to the paddies, and the paddies tended and harvested. Besides this, she always had to keep one eye on our very active pig to keep him from rooting in our small vegetable patch. She also had to watch our three chickens, who loved to wander away from our farm.

Any time I brought up the subject of the Golden Mountain, Mother suddenly found something going wrong on our farm. Maybe some seedlings had not been planted into their underwater beds properly, or perhaps our pig was eating the wrong kind of garbage, or maybe one of our chickens was dirtying our doorway. She always had some good excuse for

not talking about the Golden Mountain. I knew she was afraid of the place, because every chance we got, she would take me into the small temple in our village and we would pray for Father's safety, though she would never tell me what she was afraid of. It was a small satisfaction to her that our prayers had worked so far. Mother was never stingy about burning incense for Father.

I was curious about the Land of the Golden Mountain mainly because my father was there. I had, of course, never seen my father. And we could not go to live with him for two reasons. For one thing, the white demons would not let wives join their husbands on the Golden Mountain because they did not want us settling there permanently. And for another thing, our own clans discouraged wives from leaving because it would mean an end to the money the husbands sent home to their families—money which was then spent in the Middle Kingdom. The result was that wives stayed in the villages, seeing their husbands every five years or so if they were lucky—though sometimes there were longer separations, as with Mother and Father.

ADDITIONAL READING

The Chinese American Family Album, by Dorothy and Thomas Hoobler. Period photos and original documents let Chinese immigrants speak for themselves.

To the Golden Mountain: The Story of the Chinese Who Built the Transcontinental Railroad, by Lila Perl. Chinese immigrants join the gold rush, build a railroad, and endure the Exclusion Act.

Chapter Summary

① Key Idea
New inventions and corporations created the Gilded Age of industrial growth and great wealth for a few.

② Key Idea
Immigration and industrialization spurred the rapid growth of America's cities.

③ Key Idea
Segregation and discrimination against African Americans was commonplace in the years after the Civil War.

④ Key Idea
As business leaders guided industrial expansion, workers organized to gain their rights.

⑤ Key Idea
Industrialization and new technology created a mass culture in the United States.

For detailed Review and Study Notes go to **Interactive Review** @ ClassZone.com

Name Game

Use the Terms & Names list to complete each sentence online or on your own paper.

1. I invented the telephone. ____
   Alexander Graham Bell

2. Standard Oil was my company. ____

3. ____ looked tall enough to scrape the sky.

4. In 1910, Asian immigrants began to land on ____ in San Francisco.

5. I was a journalist who worked to end lynching. ____

6. I challenged Louisiana's Separate Cars Act. ____

7. I founded the American Federation of Labor. ____

8. The ____ was an 1886 union protest.

9. ____ featured a popular mixture of song, dance, and comedy.

10. I disagreed with Booker T. Washington about segregation. ____

A. Ida B. Wells
B. Homer Plessy
C. W. E. B. Du Bois
D. Alexander Graham Bell
E. Ellis Island
F. Skyscrapers
G. Vaudeville
H. Joseph Pulitzer
I. Angel Island
J. Ragtime
K. John D. Rockefeller
L. Mother Jones
M. Samuel Gompers
N. Haymarket Affair
O. Thomas Edison

Activities

CROSSWORD PUZZLE

Complete the online puzzle to show what you know about industrialization and immigration.

ACROSS
1. I started the Standard Oil Trust. ____

FLIPCARD

Use the online flipcards to quiz yourself on the terms and names introduced in this chapter.

Ellis Island was our first stop before entering the United States.

ANSWER
The new immigrants

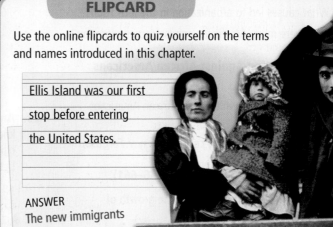

VOCABULARY

Match the name in the left-hand column with a phrase on the right.

1. Lewis Latimer
2. Jane Addams
3. Booker T. Washington
4. Samuel Gompers
5. Joseph Pulitzer

a. labor leader
b. African-American inventor
c. social reformer, founder of Hull House
d. newspaper owner
e. African-American educator

Explain how the terms and names in each group are related.

6. Ida B. Wells, W. E. B. Du Bois, NAACP
7. Ellis Island, Angel Island, Chinese Exclusion Act
8. Knights of Labor, Haymarket Affair, Homestead Strike

Ida Wells

KEY IDEAS

1 **America Enters the Industrial Age (pages 630–637)**

9. How did Edison's inventions change industry?
10. What advantages does a corporation have over a privately owned business?

2 **Immigration and Modern Urban Growth (pages 640–641)**

11. What causes led to urbanization in the late 1800s?
12. Why were many Americans opposed to immigration?

3 **Discrimination Against African Americans (pages 650–655)**

13. How did Southern whites keep African Americans from voting?
14. What was decided in the case of *Plessy* v. *Ferguson*?

4 **The Labor Movement (pages 656–661)**

15. Why did business owners resist the growth of unions?
16. What was the American Federation of Labor (AFL)?

5 **Society and Mass Culture (pages 662–665)**

17. How did immigration affect American education?
18. How did Americans use leisure in the years around 1900?

CRITICAL THINKING

19. **Causes and Effects** How did abundant natural resources and new means of transportation affect the growth of industry in the United States?

20. **Make Generalizations** What obstacles did immigrants face in trying to make a life in the United States?

21. **Analyze Point of View** What social and historical factors do you think caused Booker T. Washington to take the approach to segregation that he did?

22. **Draw Conclusions** How did the great wealth of some business leaders affect workers' attitudes towards joining unions?

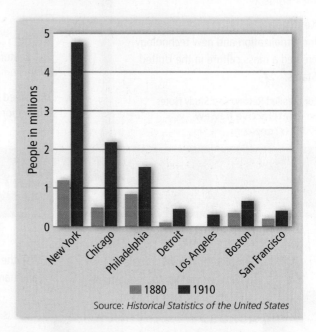

Source: *Historical Statistics of the United States*

23. **Analyze Graphs** Use the graph and your knowledge of American history to explain why most cities more than or nearly doubled in population between 1880 and 1910.

TEST PRACTICE
- **Online Test Practice @ ClassZone.com**
- **Test-Taking Strategies & Practice** at the front of this book

DOCUMENT-BASED QUESTIONS

PART 1: Short Answer

Analyze each document, and answer the questions that follow.

DOCUMENT 1

1. What was this political cartoon trying to say about Standard Oil's practices as a corporation?

DOCUMENT 2

PRIMARY SOURCE

❝ . . . I believe it is my duty to make money and still more money and to use the money I make for the good of my fellow man according to the dictates of my conscience. ❞

—John D. Rockefeller

2. In what ways did Rockefeller and Andrew Carnegie use their money for the public good?

PART 2: Essay

3. In two or three short paragraphs, explain the impact that John D. Rockefeller and Andrew Carnegie had on the daily lives of Americans during the late 1800s and early 1900s.

YOU BE THE HISTORIAN

24. Causes and Effects How did the growth of public transportation in cities lead to the leisure activities that became popular in American cities?

25. Draw Conclusions How did inventions in the period from 1870–1910 change American life?

26. Causes and Effects Why did immigrants settle in cities?

27. Compare and Contrast Compare and contrast the experiences of newly arrived immigrants in American cities with the experiences of African Americans who moved to northern cities in the Great Migration.

28. **Connect** *to* **Today** What political changes have improved working conditions for American workers over the last 100 years?

Answer the
ESSENTIAL QUESTION
What new problems and opportunities developed as America became an industrial power?

Written Response Write a two- to three-paragraph response to the Essential Question. Consider the key ideas of each section and the impact that industrial growth had on workers. Use the rubric below to guide your writing.

Response Rubric
A strong response will

- discuss the struggle for power between business owners and workers
- evaluate the impact of industrialization on immigration
- analyze the way inventions and industry changed American life

1. Roosevelt and Progressivism

2. Taft and Wilson As Progressives

3. Women Win New Rights

The Progressive Era

1890–1920

 ESSENTIAL QUESTION

How did Americans benefit from progressive reforms?

CONNECT Geography & History

Why do you think some states allowed woman suffrage before other states?

Think about:

1 the location of most of the states that did not have woman suffrage

2 what the Western states have in common

Suffragist marching

Theodore Roosevelt helped preserve the wilderness in the West.

1890

Congress passes Sherman Antitrust Act.

▼

Effect Enables government to prevent one company from controlling an entire industry.

1901 President William McKinley is assassinated.

▼

Effect Vice President Theodore Roosevelt becomes president.

1903 Wisconsin becomes the first state to have a direct primary.

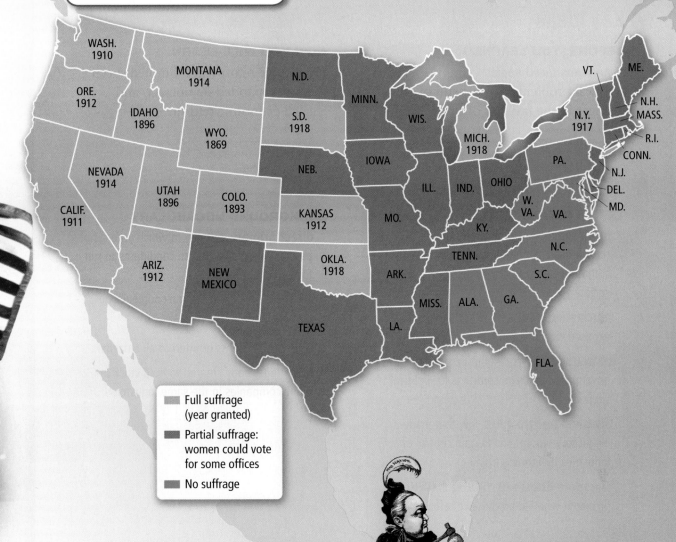

WASH.
1910

MONTANA
1914

N.D.

ORE.
1912

IDAHO
1896

WYO.
1869

S.D.
1918

MINN.

WIS.

ME.

VT.

N.H.

N.Y.
1917

MASS.

NEVADA
1914

UTAH
1896

COLO.
1893

NEB.

IOWA

MICH.
1918

PA.

R.I.

CONN.

N.J.

CALIF.
1911

ARIZ.
1912

NEW
MEXICO

KANSAS
1912

MO.

ILL.

IND.

OHIO

W.
VA.

VA.

DEL.

MD.

KY.

OKLA.
1918

ARK.

TENN.

N.C.

S.C.

TEXAS

LA.

MISS.

ALA.

GA.

FLA.

Full suffrage
(year granted)

Partial suffrage:
women could vote
for some offices

No suffrage

Prohibitionist Carry Nation

1906 Roosevelt
signs the Pure Food
and Drug Act.

1912 Woodrow
Wilson is elected
president.

1919 Eighteenth
Amendment outlaws
alcohol.

1920

Ayer's Sarsaparilla

Has Cured Others
Will Cure You
The Superior Medicine

The Pure Food and
Drug Act made it
illegal for advertisers
to make false claims
about food and drugs.

1914 Congress passes
Clayton Antitrust Act.

▼

Effect Encourages
competition among businesses.

Nineteenth
Amendment
grants women
the right to vote.

▶ Key Ideas

BEFORE, YOU LEARNED
Americans faced social, economic, and political problems as the result of rapid changes in the last half of the 1800s.

NOW YOU WILL LEARN
Progressive reformers promoted social welfare, expanded democracy, and created economic reform.

▶ Vocabulary

TERMS & NAMES

progressivism (pruh•GREHS•ih•VIHZ•uhm) reform movements that sought to raise living standards and correct wrongs in American society

muckraker (MUHK•RAYK•er) writer who exposed corruption in American society

patronage (PA•truh•nihj) exchanging government jobs and contracts for political support

Sherman Antitrust Act law that made it illegal for corporations to gain control of industries by forming trusts

Theodore Roosevelt (ROH•zuh•VEHLT) president who led progressive reforms

BACKGROUND VOCABULARY

direct primary primary in which voters, not party conventions, choose candidates to run for public office

conservation controlling resource usage

REVIEW

civil rights rights granted to all citizens

trust legal body created to hold stock in many companies in the same industry

---

▶ Reading Strategy

Re-create the diagram shown here. As you read and respond to the **KEY QUESTIONS**, use the diagram to list details about each type of progressive reform. Add ovals or start a new diagram as needed.

 See Skillbuilder Handbook, page R4.

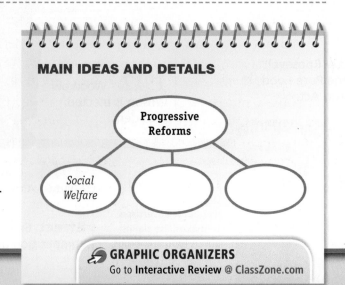

MAIN IDEAS AND DETAILS

Progressive Reforms

Social Welfare

GRAPHIC ORGANIZERS
Go to **Interactive Review** @ ClassZone.com

Roosevelt and Progressivism

15.B.3b Explain the effects of choice and competition on individuals and the economy as a whole.

16.C.3c Describe how economic developments and government policies after 1865 affected the country's economic institutions including corporations, banks and organized labor.

One American's Story

Nellie Bly worked as a reporter. In 1887, she faked mental illness so that she could become a patient at a women's asylum (uh•SY•luhm) in New York. Afterward, Bly wrote a newspaper article about what she had witnessed. She described being forced to take ice cold baths.

PRIMARY SOURCE

❝ My teeth chattered and my limbs were goose-fleshed and blue with cold. Suddenly I got, one after the other, three buckets of water over my head—ice-cold water, too, into my eyes, my ears, my nose, and my mouth. **❞**

—Nellie Bly, quoted in *Nellie Bly: Daredevil, Reporter, Feminist*

Bly reported that nurses choked and beat patients. Shortly after her stories appeared, conditions at the asylum improved.

Nellie Bly

The Rise of Progressivism

🔻 **KEY QUESTION** What problems did reformers seek to solve?

Bly was not the only one who wanted to correct society's wrongs. By the end of the 19th century and the beginning of the 20th century, Americans faced many problems as a result of the rapid growth of cities and industry. To attack these problems, some Americans organized political and social reform movements that came to be grouped under the label **progressivism**. Progressive reformers shared at least one of three basic goals: to promote social welfare; to expand democracy; and to create economic reform.

Writers Expose Corruption The progressive movement was helped by a new group of journalists who emerged around 1900. These journalists were called **muckrakers** because they tried to discover muck, or corruption, in society. The muckrakers fueled public demand for reform.

Promoting Social Reform Social reformers wanted to help the poor, the unemployed, immigrants, and workers. Some reformers started community centers that provided educational and employment services to immigrants and the poor. They also promoted minimum wage laws, limits on working hours, and help for the unemployed. Prohibitionists were reformers who worked to prevent the manufacture, sale, and transport of alcohol. The prohibitionists expanded the temperance movement of the 1800s.

Expanding Democracy Progressives wanted qualified workers to get government jobs based on their merits. Instead, officials often handed out jobs in exchange for political support. This practice was called **patronage**. The Pendleton Civil Service Act of 1883 forced candidates for some government jobs to pass an exam. The act also prevented officials from firing workers for political reasons.

Progressives thought officials would be more responsive to voters' interests if voters were directly involved in the government. In 1903, Wisconsin became the first state to have a **direct primary**, in which voters could choose candidates for public office. In Oregon, progressives pushed for direct primaries and three other democratic reforms:

- **Initiative** Voters may directly propose laws.
- **Referendum** Voters can approve proposed laws.
- **Recall** Elected officials can be voted out of office.

CONNECT *Citizenship and History*

COMMUNITY SERVICE

Since the United States began, citizens have shared concerns about their communities. Many citizens, such as Jane Addams, have identified problems and helped to solve them.

Eighth-grader Kelli Collins reads to first graders as part of National Youth Service Day, 2004.

Young citizens help their communities solve problems, too. National and Global Youth Service Day is a yearly event during which millions of students around the world design and lead service projects. Projects have included helping the elderly, protecting the environment, and providing food for the hungry. In Roswell, New Mexico, Kelli Collins and other middle school students read to first-graders regularly as part of a literacy project.

Activity

How do you help your community?

1. In a small group, think about needs within your community. Make a list of those needs and choose one need to work on.

2. Gather information about the need.

3. After you gather information, brainstorm solutions. Create a plan to carry out one solution.

4. Present the need and your plan to the class.

 See Citizenship Handbook, page 306.

Creating Economic Reform Progressive reformers wanted to limit the power of big business and regulate its activities. By the late 1800s, business leaders in some major industries had formed **trusts**. The businesses in a trust worked together to cut prices and squeeze out competitors. Then the trust would raise prices and make larger profits.

The **Sherman Antitrust Act** of 1890 made it illegal for corporations to gain control of industries by forming trusts. However, the government did not enforce the law at first. Enforcement required a strong president.

▲ **PROBLEMS AND SOLUTIONS** Identify problems that progressive reformers wanted to solve.

Theodore Roosevelt's Square Deal

▼ **KEY QUESTION** What was Roosevelt's square deal?

Young **Theodore Roosevelt** led daring exploits in Cuba during the Spanish-American War. He returned a hero and became governor of New York in 1898. Only two years later, in 1900, Roosevelt became vice-president under William McKinley during McKinley's second term as president. However, McKinley died just six months later. In 1901, at the age of 42, Roosevelt became the youngest president the nation had ever had.

Roosevelt—A Born Reformer Roosevelt entered politics when he was just 23 years old and quickly became known for fighting corrupt political machines in New York. When Roosevelt became president, he turned his fight against corruption into a policy. Roosevelt felt government's purpose was to ensure fairness, or a "square deal," for workers, consumers, and big business.

PRIMARY SOURCE

❝ When I say I believe in a square deal I do not mean, and nobody who speaks the truth can mean, that he believes it possible to give every man the best hand. . . . All I mean is that there shall not be any crookedness in the dealing. ❞

—**Theodore Roosevelt, speech on April 5, 1905**

History Makers

Theodore Roosevelt   1858–1919

Theodore Roosevelt was one of the most popular, controversial, and important presidents of the United States. Roosevelt was the first reformer president of the modern era. Many Americans, politicians and citizens alike, were afraid of the federal government gaining too much power. Not Roosevelt—he said, "I believe in a strong executive; I believe in power." He used the power of the presidency to strengthen business regulation, support labor unions, promote social welfare, and conserve natural resources and wilderness. He also made the United States a major force in international affairs in the Western Hemisphere, Europe, and the Far East.

CRITICAL THINKING

Connect to Today   How do you think Theodore Roosevelt would address today's problems with the environment and conservation?

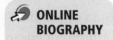
ONLINE BIOGRAPHY   For more on Theodore Roosevelt, go to the **Research & Writing Center** @ ClassZone.com

Roosevelt began his reforms against "crookedness" by enforcing the Sherman Antitrust Act. Roosevelt was not against big business. However, he thought that industries should be regulated for the public good and he opposed any trust that he thought worked against the national interest.

At the end of 1901, the nation's railroads were run by only a few companies. The power of railroads continued to grow. It was not surprising, therefore, that one of Roosevelt's first targets was the railroads. He used the Sherman Antitrust Act to dissolve a railroad trust. Roosevelt also broke up the Standard Oil Company and a tobacco trust. During Roosevelt's presidency, the government filed suit against 44 corporations for antitrust violations.

Protecting Consumers Roosevelt became concerned about the meat-packing industry after reading Upton Sinclair's (UHP•tuhn sihn•KLAIR) *The Jungle*. The novel describes a packing plant in which dead rats end up in the sausage. Sinclair originally wanted to expose the poor sanitary conditions in which the meat-packers worked. Roosevelt launched an investigation of the meat-packing industry. In 1906, he signed the Meat Inspection Act. This act created a government meat inspection program. Roosevelt also signed the Pure Food and Drug Act. This law banned the sale of impure foods and medicines.

Conserving Natural Resources Roosevelt was a strong crusader for **conservation**—controlling how America's natural resources were used. Roosevelt preserved 194 million acres of public lands, including the Grand Canyon in Arizona, California's Muir Woods, and the country's first wildlife refuge at Pelican Island, Florida. He also created the U.S. Forest Service.

🔺 **EVALUATE** Name the accomplishments of Roosevelt's square deal.

Grand Canyon National Park, Arizona
What effect did Roosevelt's conservation policies have on the Grand Canyon?

Roosevelt's Civil Rights Dilemma

🔻 **KEY QUESTION** What was Roosevelt's civil rights dilemma?

While Roosevelt tried to win a square deal for most Americans, he did not push for civil rights for African Americans. However, he personally felt that everyone should be treated fairly based on merit, regardless of race.

A Man of His Time Roosevelt, like other people of his time, did not believe in African-American suffrage. Yet some of his views on race relations were different from those of the average American. He believed that given the same opportunities as white Americans, African Americans would achieve equality. During Roosevelt's first term as president, he appointed African Americans to Southern political offices, and denounced lynching.

Fierce Opposition On October 16, 1901, Roosevelt invited Booker T. Washington, founder of the Tuskegee (tuhs•KEE•gee) Institute, to stay for dinner after meeting at the White House. No other president had invited an African American to the White House. But Roosevelt decided to break precedent.

While African Americans saw the dinner as a great step towards racial equality, it angered many Southerners. Many Northern newspapers supported the dinner, while a newspaper in Memphis, Tennessee called the dinner an "outrage." Roosevelt told Washington that he did not care what his critics said. Privately, the president worried that the dinner had hurt his chances for re-election. He never asked an African American to a White House dinner again.

Although Roosevelt was re-elected, he did no more to advance civil rights for African Americans. Roosevelt made no statement on the Atlanta race riot of 1906. He also discharged a large group of African American soldiers for allegedly conspiring to protect fellow African American soldiers wrongly accused of murder in Brownsville, Texas.

Booker T. Washington dined with President Theodore Roosevelt at the White House. **Why was the dinner supported by some people and condemned by others?**

 MAIN IDEAS & DETAILS Explain Roosevelt's civil rights dilemma.

Illinois Learning Standards *Review*

ONLINE QUIZ
For test practice, go to
Interactive Review @ ClassZone.com

TERMS & NAMES

1. Explain the importance of

- progressivism
- muckraker
- patronage
- Sherman Antitrust Act
- Theodore Roosevelt

USING YOUR READING NOTES

2. Main Ideas and Details Complete the diagram you started at the beginning of this section. Then write a one-sentence summary of the most important points of this section.

KEY IDEAS

3. How did progressives seek to expand democracy?

4. Explain how Theodore Roosevelt used his presidential power to further progressive reforms.

CRITICAL THINKING

5. Analyze Primary Sources What did Theodore Roosevelt mean when he said he believed in a "square deal"?

6. Connect *to* **Today** In what ways do the reforms that President Roosevelt promoted affect your life today?

7. Writing News Story In the role of a muckraker, write a short news story about a need in your community.

The Progressive Era **677**

▶ Key Ideas

BEFORE, YOU LEARNED

Progressive reformers promoted social welfare, expanded democracy, and created economic reform.

NOW YOU WILL LEARN

Progressive reforms continued under Presidents William Howard Taft and Woodrow Wilson.

▶ Vocabulary

TERMS & NAMES

William Howard Taft Republican elected president in 1908

Sixteenth Amendment amendment that gave Congress the power to create income taxes

Seventeenth Amendment amendment that provided for direct election of U.S. senators

Bull Moose Party progressive political party in 1912 presidential election

Clayton Antitrust Act legislation that strengthened the Sherman Antitrust Act's power

Federal Reserve Act law that created the modern banking system

BACKGROUND VOCABULARY

revenue income

REVIEW

socialism system in which the state controls the economy

William Jennings Bryan Democratic candidate in 1908 presidential election

segregation racial separation

Visual Vocabulary
Bull Moose
Party buttons

▶ Reading Strategy

Re-create the diagram shown here. As you read and respond to the **KEY QUESTIONS**, use the diagram to compare and contrast the progressive reform efforts of Presidents Taft and Wilson.

 See Skillbuilder Handbook, page R8.

COMPARE AND CONTRAST

Taft	Wilson
• *antitrust*	• *antitrust*

 GRAPHIC ORGANIZERS
Go to **Interactive Review** @ ClassZone.com

Taft and Wilson As Progressives

14.D.3 Describe roles and influences of individuals, groups and media in shaping current Illinois and United States public policy (e.g., *general public opinion, special interest groups, formal parties, media*).
16.B.3c Describe the way the Constitution has changed over time as a result of amendments and Supreme Court decisions.

One American's Story

During the Progressive Era, many Americans became disturbed by the problems caused by capitalism. Some even turned to **socialism**. This is a system in which the state controls the economy. Labor leader Eugene V. Debs (See Chapter 20, page 661) became a socialist while serving time in prison for his role in an 1894 labor strike.

Debs ran for president in 1900, 1904, 1908, 1912, and 1920. In his 1908 campaign, he urged American workers to consider what competition was like in a capitalist system.

Eugene V. Debs (*right*) was the Socialist candidate for president five times. This button is from his 1912 campaign.

PRIMARY SOURCE

❝ Competition was natural enough at one time, but do you think you are competing today? . . . Against whom? Against Rockefeller? About as I would if I had a wheelbarrow and competed with the Santa Fe [railroad] from here to Kansas City. ❞

—Eugene V. Debs, from a speech given in Girard, Kansas

Taft and Progressivism

🔻 **KEY QUESTION** How did Taft continue Roosevelt's progressive policies?

In the 1908 election, Debs and Democrat **William Jennings Bryan** ran against Republican **William Howard Taft**. Neither candidate stood much of a chance against Taft. Roosevelt had handpicked Taft to carry on his own progressive policies.

Taft As Roosevelt's Heir Taft continued Roosevelt's attack on trusts. During four years in office, Taft pursued almost twice as many antitrust suits as Roosevelt had in nearly eight years. Although Taft's policies angered conservationists, he made democratic, social welfare, and economic reforms.

Two Progressive Amendments Two of the major progressive achievements under President Taft were constitutional amendments. The **Sixteenth Amendment** was passed in 1909 and ratified in 1913. It gave Congress the power to create federal income taxes. Before this, the Constitution did not allow federal taxes on an individual's income. This amendment was intended to spread the cost of running the government among more people. The income tax soon became an important source of federal revenue.

The **Seventeenth Amendment** gave voters the right to elect senators directly. Formerly, state legislatures had chosen U.S. senators. Under this system, many senators gained their positions through corrupt bargains. The Seventeenth Amendment gave people a more direct voice in the government.

▲ **SUMMARIZE** Summarize the progressive policies achieved under President Taft.

Wilson and Progressivism

▼ **KEY QUESTION** What did Wilson contribute to the progressive movement?

During Taft's presidency, a split developed between Taft and other progressive Republican leaders. Many of these leaders supported Theodore Roosevelt, who entered the 1912 presidential race as a candidate for the new, progressive **Bull Moose Party**. The Democrats chose Woodrow Wilson (WUD•roh WIHL•suhn), governor of New Jersey, as their candidate. With Republicans deeply divided, Wilson won the election.

Connecting History

Judicial Power
During the Civil War era, Congress instituted temporary federal income taxes until 1872. In 1894, the Supreme Court ruled that aspects of federal income taxes were unconstitutional.

CONNECT ⟳ *Economics & History*

TYPES OF TAXES

Today, federal, state, and local governments use tax revenues to pay for the services that they provide. The income tax is only one of several taxes governments use to raise money.

SALES TAXES
Sellers collect state sales taxes from consumers when they buy retail goods and services.

INCOME TAXES
Individuals pay a percentage of their earnings, and corporations pay a percentage of their profits. With a graduated income tax, larger incomes are taxed at higher rates than smaller incomes.

PROPERTY TAXES
People who own property, such as a house or land, pay property taxes. Governments often use property taxes to pay for services such as schools.

ESTATE TAXES
When a person dies and leaves behind property, taxes are charged against part of the value of the dead person's property, or estate, before it passes on to heirs.

CRITICAL THINKING

1. **Categorize** What kinds of taxes do businesses pay?
2. **Compare and Contrast** How do sales taxes differ from income taxes?

Wilson's Economic Reforms At Wilson's urging, Congress passed the **Clayton Antitrust Act** of 1914. The new law further prohibited monopolies and business practices that lessened competition. A business, for example, could no longer buy a competitor's stock. The Clayton Act gave the government more power to regulate trusts. In addition, the Clayton Act allowed labor unions to expand and legalized strikes.

Under Wilson, Congress also reformed the nation's financial system. In 1913, the **Federal Reserve Act** created the modern banking system, led by the Federal Reserve Board (the "Fed"). The Fed oversees 12 regional Federal Reserve Banks and makes sure that money is distributed where it is most needed. These are bankers' banks that serve consumer banks. The Federal Reserve Act created a more flexible currency system by allowing banks to control the money supply. To raise money, the Fed lowers the interest rate that it charges member banks. These banks then borrow more from the Fed, and thus have more money to lend to people and businesses.

Wilson's Failure in Civil Rights While Roosevelt's attitude toward African Americans was progressive for his time, Wilson's was not. Wilson was from the South. He personally believed in **segregation**—the practice of keeping whites and African Americans apart. In his presidential campaign, Wilson spoke of his "willingness and desire to deal with [African Americans] fairly and justly." After he was elected, however, Wilson approved segregation in the federal government. During his presidency, white Southerners gained the most federal support they had had since the Civil War.

 COMPARE AND CONTRAST Compare Wilson and Roosevelt as progressives.

 Illinois Learning Standards *Review*

 ONLINE QUIZ
For test practice, go to
Interactive Review @ ClassZone.com

TERMS & NAMES

1. Explain the importance of

- William Howard Taft
- Bull Moose Party
- Sixteenth Amendment
- Clayton Antitrust Act
- Seventeenth Amendment
- Federal Reserve Act

USING YOUR READING NOTES

2. Compare and Contrast Complete the diagram you started at the beginning of the section. Then answer the following question: Who was more effective at reforming society, Taft or Wilson?

Taft	Wilson
• *antitrust*	• *antitrust*

KEY IDEAS

3. What was the purpose of the Sixteenth Amendment?

4. How did the Clayton Antitrust Act change business?

CRITICAL THINKING

5. Make Inferences Why did progressive presidents do little to advance African Americans' civil rights?

6. Evaluate What was the most important progressive reform achieved under Presidents Taft and Wilson? Explain.

7. **Writing** **Speech** Use the library or the Internet to learn more about the Bull Moose Party. Then write a presidential campaign speech from the point of view of a Bull Moose Party member endorsing Theodore Roosevelt in the 1912 election.

Reading for Understanding

▶ Key Ideas

BEFORE, YOU LEARNED

Progressive reforms continued under Presidents William Howard Taft and Woodrow Wilson.

NOW YOU WILL LEARN

During the Progressive Era, women became leaders in reform movements and won the right to vote.

▶ Vocabulary

TERMS & NAMES

Carry A. Nation fought for prohibition

prohibition (PROH•uh•BIHSH•uhn) legal ban on the production, possession, and sale of alcohol

Eighteenth Amendment constitutional amendment enacting Prohibition

Susan B. Anthony fought for woman suffrage

Carrie Chapman Catt president of National American Woman Suffrage Association

Nineteenth Amendment constitutional amendment that gave women the vote

BACKGROUND VOCABULARY

settlement house community center providing help to immigrants and the poor

REVIEW

Jane Addams founded Hull House

suffrage right to vote

Visual Vocabulary Carry Nation cartoon

▶ Reading Strategy

Re-create the diagram shown here. As you read and respond to the **KEY QUESTIONS**, use the diagram to record the causes and effects of women's changing roles in society.

 See Skillbuilder Handbook, page R7.

CAUSE AND EFFECT

CAUSE

New Technology

CAUSE

EFFECT

Homemakers have more time.

GRAPHIC ORGANIZERS
Go to **Interactive Review** @ ClassZone.com

Women Win New Rights

14.C.3 Compare historical issues involving rights, roles and status of individuals in relation to municipalities, states and the nation.
14.D.3 Describe roles and influences of individuals, groups and media in shaping current Illinois and United States public policy (e.g., *general public opinion, special interest groups, formal parties, media*).

One American's Story

In the 1890s, Lillian Wald was teaching a home nursing class at a school for immigrants in New York City. One day a child asked Wald to help her sick mother. Following the child home, Wald was shocked by what she saw.

PRIMARY SOURCE

❝ Over broken asphalt, over dirty mattresses and heaps of refuse we went. The tall houses reeked with rubbish. . . . There were two rooms and a family of seven not only lived here but shared their quarters with boarders. ❞

—Lillian Wald, quoted in *Always a Sister*

Inspired to help such poor immigrants, Wald founded the Nurses' Settlement. This was later called the Henry Street Settlement. The Settlement aimed to help children, families, and the poor by providing nurses' training, educational programs for the community, youth clubs, and children's summer camps. It also opened one of New York City's earliest playgrounds.

Lillian Wald

New Roles for Women

▼ **KEY QUESTION** How did women's lives change in the late 1800s?

At the turn of the century, middle-class women were looking for new roles outside the home. At the same time, middle-class homes were changing. Families were becoming smaller as women had fewer children. New products and inventions reduced some of the work of homemaking, which was done mostly by women and servants.

New Industries and Technology Factories now produced soap, clothing, canned food, and other goods that had been homemade. New technology, such as indoor running water and vacuum cleaners, made it possible for homemakers to wash clothes, clean, and cook in less time and with less effort than before.

New Opportunities Charlotte Perkins Gilman was an influential writer on women's rights. She wanted to free women from housework to pursue new opportunities. In *Concerning Children* (1900) and *The Home* (1903), she proposed that families live in large apartments. These would have centralized nurseries and a staff devoted to cooking, cleaning, and child-care. According to Gilman, this support would free women to work outside the home.

Some women who took jobs outside of the home worked as telephone operators, store clerks, and typists. Those with a college education could enter fields such as teaching and nursing. Women who could afford to were expected to quit their jobs when they married. In 1890, approximately 30 percent of women between the ages of 20 and 24 worked outside the home. However, only about 15 percent between the ages of 25 and 44 did so.

▲ **CAUSES AND EFFECTS** Explain what led middle-class women's lives to change in the Progressive Era.

COMPARING *The Growth of Women's Rights*

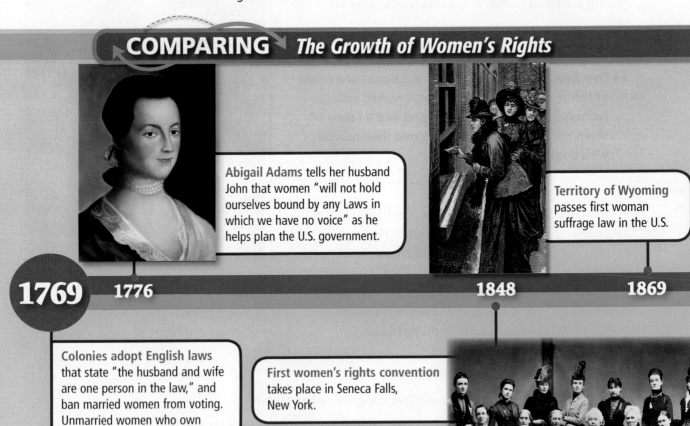

Abigail Adams tells her husband John that women "will not hold ourselves bound by any Laws in which we have no voice" as he helps plan the U.S. government.

Territory of Wyoming passes first woman suffrage law in the U.S.

1769   1776   1848   1869

Colonies adopt English laws that state "the husband and wife are one person in the law," and ban married women from voting. Unmarried women who own property can vote in most colonies.

First women's rights convention takes place in Seneca Falls, New York.

Women and Progressivism

▼ **KEY QUESTION** On what social problems did Jane Addams and other women work?

The social reforms that many middle-class, college-educated women took part in were focused on helping people. These reforms included the establishment of **settlement houses**—community centers that provided help to immigrants and the poor—and working to pass prohibition.

Jane Addams and Hull House Jane Addams (See History Maker on page 646) was a good example of a progressive female leader. After graduating from college, Addams sought a meaningful way to participate in society. A visit to a settlement house in a London slum inspired her to start a similar program in Chicago aided by her friend Ellen Gates Starr.

With donations from wealthy Chicagoans, Addams and Starr opened Hull House in a poor, immigrant neighborhood. Hull House served as an information bureau for new immigrants. It also helped the unemployed find jobs. It offered a kindergarten, a day nursery, after-school youth clubs, health clinics, and citizenship classes. Many of the programs were run by the young women residents. Hull House workers also pressured politicians for improved city services for the neighborhood.

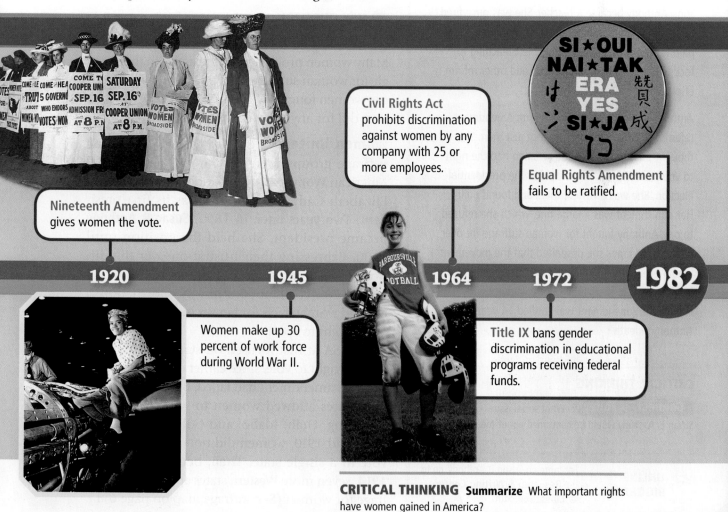

Civil Rights Act prohibits discrimination against women by any company with 25 or more employees.

Equal Rights Amendment fails to be ratified.

Nineteenth Amendment gives women the vote.

1920   **1945**   **1964**   **1972**   **1982**

Women make up 30 percent of work force during World War II.

Title IX bans gender discrimination in educational programs receiving federal funds.

CRITICAL THINKING **Summarize** What important rights have women gained in America?

These programs were run by a group of young men and women residents and volunteers. The residents of Hull House received no salary and had to pay for their room and board.

Prohibition Another prominent, but controversial, progressive leader was **Carry A. Nation**. She campaigned for **prohibition**—a ban on the production and sale of alcohol. Nation had once been married to an alcoholic. Tall and strong, she adopted dramatic methods in her opposition to alcoholic beverages. In the 1890s, she smashed saloons with a hatchet. She was often arrested. Although some people criticized Nation, her efforts helped bring about passage in 1919 of the **Eighteenth Amendment**, which made Prohibition the law of the land.

🔺 **MAIN IDEAS & DETAILS** Name the social problems on which progressive women worked.

Suffrage for Women

🔻 **KEY QUESTION** How did women finally obtain the right to vote?

Many women progressives were active in the struggle for woman **suffrage**, or the right to vote. American women fought longer for the right to vote than they did for any other reforms.

Women Unite In 1890, two separate woman suffrage groups merged to form the National American Woman Suffrage Association (NAWSA). Elizabeth Cady Stanton served as its first president. Two years later, in 1892, **Susan B. Anthony** became president. She held the position until 1900. Expressing their frustration over the difficulty of gaining suffrage, Stanton and Anthony wrote, "Words can not describe the indignation... a proud woman feels for her sex in [being deprived of the right to vote]."

NAWSA at first focused on state campaigns to win the right to vote, since earlier efforts at passing a federal amendment had failed. But by 1896, only four states allowed women to vote. These were Wyoming, Utah, Idaho, and Colorado. Between 1896 and 1910, women did not gain the right to vote in a single state. Then, between 1910 and 1914, seven more Western states approved full suffrage for women (See suffrage map on page 671).

History Makers

Susan B. Anthony   1820–1906

Susan B. Anthony was born into a Quaker family in Massachusetts. Quakers believe in the equality of men and women, and Anthony's father made sure his daughters received the same education as his sons. Anthony became a teacher. She was once fired for complaining about earning less than a man was paid for the same work. Anthony left teaching to focus full-time on women's rights and other reform efforts.

Anthony noticed that the Fourteenth Amendment referred to citizens as persons, not just men. She thought this could mean that women had the right to vote. In 1872, Anthony voted in the presidential election. She was arrested, tried, and found guilty. Her punishment was a large fine, which she refused to pay. Anthony fought for woman suffrage for over 45 years. At times she despaired that the movement would ever succeed. But she never gave up hope. In her last speech, she said, "Failure is impossible." The Nineteenth Amendment was ratified 14 years after Anthony's death.

CRITICAL THINKING

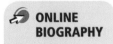 What social issues do you think Susan B. Anthony would be concerned about today? Why?

🌀 **ONLINE BIOGRAPHY** For more on Susan B. Anthony, go to the **Research & Writing Center** @ ClassZone.com

The Nineteenth Amendment The Western successes turned the tide in favor of woman suffrage. The United States' entry into World War I in 1917 pushed the nation to take the final step. During the war, membership in NAWSA reached 2 million. **Carrie Chapman Catt**, president of NAWSA, supported President Wilson and volunteered NAWSA's services to the government in case it entered the war. She may have believed

CONNECT to the Essential Question

How did Americans benefit from progressive reforms?

	PROBLEM	SOLUTION
POLITICAL	Government officials respond to special interests instead of public interests	direct primary, initiative, referendum
	Corrupt politicians	recall, Pendleton Civil Service Act, Seventeenth Amendment
	Women lack equal rights	Nineteenth Amendment grants women the right to vote
ECONOMIC	Unfair business practices	Sherman Antitrust Act, Clayton Antitrust Act
	Unhealthy food and medicines	Meat Inspection Act, Pure Food and Drug Act
	Loss of wilderness and nature due to the spread of industry	T. Roosevelt creates Forest Service, establishes wildlife refuges, national parks, and national monuments
	Lack of government funds	Sixteenth Amendment creates income tax
	Unstable banking system	Federal Reserve Act
SOCIAL	Alcoholism	Eighteenth Amendment bans production and sale of alcohol
	Poverty, poor healthcare, and lack of education among immigrants and the working class	settlement houses

Ayer's Sarsaparilla

Has Cured Others Will Cure You The Superior Medicine

CRITICAL THINKING **Evaluate** Which progressive reform produced the greatest benefit for Americans?

Progressive Amendments

16th	Federal income tax
17th	Senators elected by people rather than state legislatures
18th	Manufacture, sale, or transport of alcohol prohibited
19th	Woman suffrage

that by helping President Wilson with the war effort, she could ask for his support of woman suffrage. President Wilson urged the Senate to pass a woman suffrage amendment. He called its passage "vital to the winning of the war."

In 1918, the House gave women full voting rights by passing the **Nineteenth Amendment**. The Senate approved the amendment in 1919. For the final state campaigns, women staged marches, parades, and rallies. In 1920, the states ratified the Nineteenth Amendment and made it law.

PRIMARY SOURCE

❝ The right of citizens of the United States to vote shall not be denied or abridged by the United States or by any State on account of sex. ❞

—The Nineteenth Amendment to the U.S. Constitution

Charlotte Woodard had attended the first women's rights convention in 1848 at Seneca Falls as a teenager. In 1920, the 91-year-old Woodard voted in a presidential election for the first time.

▲ **SEQUENCE EVENTS** List the order of events that led to woman suffrage.

 Illinois Learning Standards *Review*

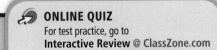 **ONLINE QUIZ**
For test practice, go to
Interactive Review @ ClassZone.com

TERMS & NAMES

1. Explain the importance of

- Carry A. Nation
- prohibition
- Eighteenth Amendment
- Susan B. Anthony
- Carrie Chapman Catt
- Nineteenth Amendment

USING YOUR READING NOTES

2. Causes and Effects Complete the diagram of causes and effects you started at the beginning of this section. Then decide which cause had the greatest impact on women's lives.

KEY IDEAS

3. How did women's roles in society expand in the Progressive Era?

4. In what ways did settlement houses serve their communities?

5. What voting rights did women have prior to 1920?

CRITICAL THINKING

6. Compare and Contrast Compare the struggle for woman suffrage to African Americans' struggle for equal rights.

7. Make Inferences How did technological advances and social reform movements affect poor women?

8. Writing Report Research the history of woman suffrage in a country such as Australia, India, or South Africa. Write a brief report on your findings.

Chapter Summary

1 **Key Idea**
Progressive reformers promoted social welfare, expanded democracy, and created economic reform.

2 **Key Idea**
Progressive reforms continued under Presidents William Howard Taft and Woodrow Wilson.

3 **Key Idea**
During the Progressive Era, women became leaders in reform movements and won the right to vote.

For detailed Review and Study Notes go to **Interactive Review** @ ClassZone.com

Name Game

Use the Terms & Names list to complete each sentence online or on your own paper.

1. As president, I was a strong supporter of conserving natural resources. Theodore Roosevelt.

2. The 20th century movement to correct societal problems was called ____.

3. Ratified in 1913, the ____ enabled Congress to levy and collect income taxes.

4. In the 1912 election, progressive Republican leaders formed the ____.

5. Writers who exposed corruption and wrong-doing were known as ____.

6. As Roosevelt's successor as president, I continued to challenge big business in America. ____

7. Exchanging jobs for political support, or ____, was popular during the 1870s and 1880s.

8. As an advocate for equality between men and women, I fought for women's suffrage for over 45 years. ____

9. Passed by the House in 1918, the ____ gave women in America the right to vote.

10. The ____ made it illegal for corporations to control industries.

A. Sherman Antitrust Act

B. Theodore Roosevelt

C. Seventeenth Amendment

D. Progressivism

E. William Howard Taft

F. Sixteenth Amendment

G. Clayton Antitrust Act

H. muckrakers

I. Federal Reserve Act

J. Patronage

K. Susan B. Anthony

L. Carrie Chapman Catt

M. Bull Moose Party

N. Prohibition

O. Nineteenth Amendment

Activities

CROSSWORD PUZZLE

ACROSS
1. I helped improve conditions at a women's asylum (two words).

FLIPCARD

Use the online flip cards to quiz yourself on the terms and names introduced in this chapter.

I signed the Pure Food and Drug Act of 1906 while I was president.

ANSWER
Theodore Roosevelt

VOCABULARY

Write the term or name that correctly fills in the blank in each of the following sentences.

1. Upton Sinclair wrote a novel describing the _____ industry.

2. _____ was the first state to establish a direct primary.

3. In 1914 Congress passed the _____ to regulate trusts and help organized labor.

4. _____ was the second president of the National American Woman Suffrage Association.

5. The states ratified the _____ in 1920, giving women the vote.

For each of the following pairs, explain the impact that the person had on the event.

6. Theodore Roosevelt; Meat Inspection Act

7. Woodrow Wilson; Federal Reserve Act

8. Carry A. Nation; prohibition

KEY IDEAS

1 **Roosevelt and Progressivism (pages 672–677)**

9. What were three goals that progressive reformers shared?

10. What reforms were part of Roosevelt's square deal?

2 **Taft and Wilson As Progressives (pages 678–681)**

11. In what areas did Taft achieve a more progressive record than Roosevelt?

12. What happened to African Americans' civil rights during Wilson's presidency?

3 **Women Win New Rights (pages 682–688)**

13. How did women work for change in the late 1800s?

14. What organization played an important role in obtaining woman suffrage?

CRITICAL THINKING

15. **Make Inferences** How might the 1912 presidential election have been different if some Republicans had not left their party to form the Progressive Party?

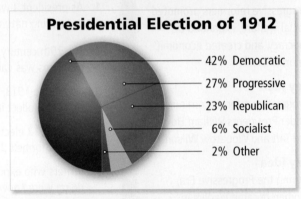

Presidential Election of 1912

- 42% Democratic
- 27% Progressive
- 23% Republican
- 6% Socialist
- 2% Other

16. **Evaluate** Which president do you think was most effective—Roosevelt, Taft, or Wilson? Why?

17. **Analyze Point of View** Why might women at the turn of the century have considered suffrage a cause worth devoting their lives to?

18. **Problems and Solutions** Explain whether you think Hull House was an effective solution to poverty.

19. **Analyze Political Cartoons** Look at the political cartoon below. The words on the peoples' chests read "R.R. Trust," "Oil Trust," and "Everything in General." Explain what Roosevelt is doing in the cartoon below.

NO MOLLY-CODDLING HERE

TEST PRACTICE

• **Online Test Practice** @ ClassZone.com
• **Test-Taking Strategies & Practice** at the front of this book

DOCUMENT-BASED QUESTIONS

PART 1: Short Answer

Analyze each document, and answer the questions that follow.

DOCUMENT 1

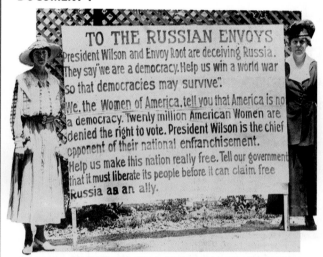

1. Read the sign above. Why do these women believe that the United States is not a democracy?

DOCUMENT 2

PRIMARY SOURCE

❝The Settlement . . . is an experimental effort to aid in the solution of the social and industrial problems which are engendered by the modern conditions of life in a great city. . . It is an attempt to relieve, at the same time, the over accumulation at one end of society and the destitution at the other . . .❞

—Jane Addams, quoted in *Twenty Years at Hull House*

2. What were some of the problems that Jane Addams and other settlement house workers tried to solve?

PART 2: Essay

3. In two or three short paragraphs, explain why women were essential to the progressive movement. Use information from your answers to Part I and your knowledge of U.S. history.

YOU BE THE HISTORIAN

20. WHAT IF? How do you think the United States might be different today if Theodore Roosevelt had not made the conservation efforts he did?

21. Causes and Effects Susan B. Anthony never married, and disapproved of suffragist leaders who did. Why do you think Anthony saw marriage as incompatible with the cause of woman suffrage?

22. Analyze Point of View Prior to the Sixteenth Amendment, the federal government was financed by taxes on imports, inheritances, and the sale of various goods. How do you think Americans reacted to the income tax?

23. Predict Do you think prohibition had the potential to succeed? Why or why not?

24. Make Inferences Why did the fight for woman suffrage last so long?

Answer the

ESSENTIAL QUESTION

How did Americans benefit from Progressive reforms?

Written Response Write a two- or three-paragraph response to the Essential Question. Be sure to consider the key ideas of each section as well as the most significant changes in the lives of Americans at the turn of the century. Use the Response Rubric below to guide your thinking and writing.

Response Rubric

A strong response will

• describe the three basic goals of progressives
• explain how changes affected Americans of differing social classes
• discuss contributions by specific individuals
• analyze the role of government in reform

CHAPTER

22

1. Imperialism in the Pacific

2. The Spanish-American War

3. Expanding Interests in Asia and Latin America

Becoming a World Power

1880–1914

 ESSENTIAL QUESTION

How did America's growing power affect its relationships with other nations?

CONNECT ↪ **Geography & History**

How might the geography of the United States have affected its desire to become a world power?

Think about:

1 the location of the newly acquired territory of Alaska

2 the continent on which most European colonies were located

3 the country with the largest expanse of colonial territory

Alaskan totem pole

1880

1884
Congress officially makes Alaska U.S. territory (following U.S. purchase of Alaska from Russia in 1867).

1893
American planters overthrow Hawaii's Queen Liliuokalani.

▼

Effect U.S. annexes Hawaii.

sugar cane

1898 Spanish-American War begins.

▼

Effect Spain cedes Puerto Rico, Guam, and the Philippines.

ASIA

ALASKA

NORTH AMERICA

UNITED STATES

CHINA

JAPAN

FRENCH INDOCHINA

PACIFIC OCEAN

Midway Is.

Wake I.

Johnston Atoll

Hawaii

Philippine Is.

Guam

Howland I.

Palmyra Atoll

Baker I.

Jarvis I.

AUSTRALIA

American Samoa

Route of "The Great White Fleet"

NEW ZEALAND

Ship going through the Panama Canal

1904

Roosevelt Corollary is established.

▼

Effect Allows U.S. interference in Latin American domestic affairs.

1914

Panama Canal opens.

1899 U.S. Open Door Policy favors foreign traders in China.

▼

Effect 1900 Boxer Rebellion breaks out in China.

Detail of Chinese print of Boxer Rebellion.

▶ Key Ideas

BEFORE, YOU LEARNED

In the Progressive era, Americans reformed government and expanded rights for women.

NOW YOU WILL LEARN

The United States took its first steps in becoming a world power by acquiring Alaska and Hawaii.

▶ Vocabulary

TERMS & NAMES

Queen Liliuokalani (lee•LEE•oo•oh•kah•LAH•nee) first and only reigning Hawaiian queen

imperialism policy by which stronger nations extend their economic, political, or military control over weaker nations

William Seward Secretary of State under presidents Lincoln and Andrew Johnson; purchased Alaska from Russia in 1867

Pearl Harbor Hawaiian port; granted by 1887 treaty to the United States for use as a refueling station for U.S. ships

REVIEW VOCABULARY

manifest destiny belief that the United States was meant to expand from coast to coast

missionary person sent to another country by a church to spread its faith

Visual Vocabulary
William Seward

▶ Reading Strategy

Re-create the diagram at right. As you respond to the **KEY QUESTIONS**, use the outer boxes to fill in details that support the main idea.

 See Skillbuilder Handbook, page R4.

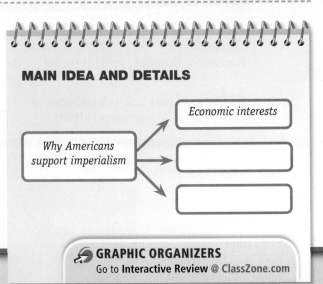

MAIN IDEA AND DETAILS

Why Americans support imperialism → *Economic interests*

⊖ GRAPHIC ORGANIZERS
Go to **Interactive Review** @ ClassZone.com

Imperialism in the Pacific

14.E.3 Compare the basic principles of the United States and its international interests (e.g., *territory, environment, trade, use of technology*).
16.B.3d Describe ways in which the United States developed as a world political power.

One American's Story

In 1893, American sugar planters in Hawaii, supported by a U.S. naval gunboat, overthrew the Hawaiian government of **Queen Liliuokalani** (lee•LEE•oo•oh•kah•LAH•nee). The proud monarch was forced to surrender.

PRIMARY SOURCE

❝ I had informed President Harrison ...of the ... assistance given by the forces of the United States ship *Boston* ... through which ... my government had been overthrown. I had asked that justice should be done, and that the rights of my people should be restored. President Harrison chose to set aside my statement and petition. **❞**

— Queen Liliuokalani, *Hawaii's Story by Hawaii's Queen (1898)*

The U.S. ambassador to Hawaii reported that "The Hawaiian pear is now fully ripe, and this is the golden hour for the United States to pluck it." The annexation of Hawaii was only one of the goals of America's empire builders in the late 19th century.

Queen Lydia Liliuokalani was the first and only reigning queen of Hawaii.

America Becomes an Imperial Power

🔻 **KEY QUESTION** Why did some Americans support imperialist policies?

Americans had always sought to expand the size of their nation. Throughout the 19th century, they believed it was their **manifest destiny** to push American control westward to the Pacific coast. Once this goal had been achieved, Americans began to look overseas for additional sources of wealth.

Reasons for U.S. Expansion By the late 1800s, many American leaders wanted the United States to join the imperialist powers of Europe and establish colonies overseas. **Imperialism** is the policy by which stronger nations extend their economic, political, or military control over weaker nations.

Becoming a World Power **695**

COMPARING Characteristics of American Imperialism

ECONOMIC	MILITARY	CULTURAL
Maintain industrial prosperity	Show foreign powers the strength of U.S. power	Belief in cultural superiority of industrialized nations
Acquire raw materials from new markets	Build strong U.S. navy to protect shipping lanes.	Belief in cultural inferiority of nonindustrial societies
Find new markets for sale of American goods.	Establish U.S. military bases overseas	Belief in need to spread democracy and Christianity

CRITICAL THINKING Make Inferences Why might economic and military interests go hand in hand?

European nations had been establishing colonies for centuries. In the late 19th century, for example, Africa became a major area of European expansion. Most Americans gradually came to approve of the idea of expansion overseas (See the chart above).

Supporters of expansionism argued that it would increase the nation's financial prosperity, strengthen the nation militarily, and spread democratic ideas. They also firmly believed in the superiority of western culture.

▲ **MAIN IDEAS & DETAILS** List the main reasons that American leaders supported imperialism.

American Expansionism

▼ **KEY QUESTION** Why did America want to acquire Alaska and Hawaii?

With American territory now stretching between two oceans, America was well placed to extend its influence in the Pacific. Through purchase and annexation, the nation began expanding beyond its shores.

America Acquires Alaska A strong backer of expansion was **William Seward**, Secretary of State under Abraham Lincoln and Andrew Johnson. Seward made his biggest move in 1867 when he arranged for the purchase of Alaska from Russia. Congress officially annexed Alaska in 1884.

Seward was widely criticized for the $7.2-million deal. Newspapers called Alaska "Seward's Icebox." Even so, the purchase of the territory turned out to be a bargain. For about two cents an acre, the United States had acquired a land rich in timber, minerals and, as it turned out, oil.

The Annexation of Hawaii In the early 1800s, American **missionaries** had moved to Hawaii to convert the local population to Christianity. Some of the missionaries' descendants started sugar plantations. By the late 1800s, wealthy American planters dominated Hawaii's economy.

In 1891, Queen Liliuokalani became the leader of Hawaii. Believing that American planters had too much influence, she moved to limit their power. Around the same time, U.S. trade laws changed to favor sugar grown in the United States.

Connecting History

Imperialism
Throughout his career, William Seward continued to pursue new territory. Before he retired in 1869, he considered acquiring the Hawaiian Islands, although that did not happen until 1898.

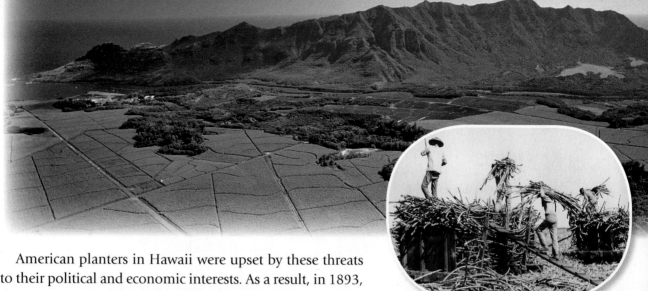

American planters in Hawaii were upset by these threats to their political and economic interests. As a result, in 1893, the planters staged a revolt. With the help of U.S. Marines, they overthrew the queen and set up their own government. They then asked to be annexed by the United States.

U.S. leaders already understood the value of the islands. In 1887, they had pressured Hawaii to allow a U.S. base at **Pearl Harbor,** the kingdom's best port. The base became an important refueling station for American merchant and military ships bound for Asia.

Thus, when President Benjamin Harrison received the planters' request, he gave his approval. But before the Senate could act on the issue, Grover Cleveland became president. He did not approve of the planters' actions and withdrew the treaty. Hawaii would not be annexed until 1898.

(*above*) Workers harvest sugar cane in Hawaii around 1900, set against a landscape of sugar cane fields today.

▲ **SUMMARIZE** Explain the U.S. acquisition of Alaska and interest in Hawaii.

Illinois Learning Standards *Review*

🔁 **ONLINE QUIZ**
For test practice, go to
Interactive Review @ ClassZone.com

TERMS & NAMES

1. Explain the importance of
- Queen Liliuokalani
- imperialism
- William Seward
- Pearl Harbor

USING YOUR READING NOTES

2. Main Ideas and Details Complete the chart you started at the beginning of this section.

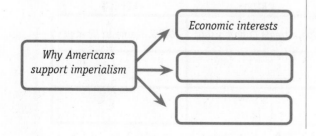

Why Americans support imperialism → *Economic interests*

KEY IDEAS

3. How did William Seward contribute to U.S. expansion?

4. Why did American planters in Hawaii stage a revolt in 1893?

CRITICAL THINKING

5. Make Inferences How did time prove that the purchase of Alaska was farsighted?

6. WHAT IF? What might have happened to Hawaii if President Cleveland's wishes had been respected by subsequent U.S. administrations?

7. Writing Diary Imagine that you are a native Hawaiian in the 1890's. Write a one-or-two-paragraph entry in your diary about the actions of the United States.

▶ Key Ideas

BEFORE YOU LEARNED
The United States took its first steps in becoming a world power by acquiring Alaska and Hawaii.

NOW YOU WILL LEARN
The United States went to war with Spain and gained colonies in the Caribbean and the Pacific.

▶ Vocabulary

TERMS & NAMES

yellow journalism style of journalism that exaggerates and sensationalizes the news

U.S.S. *Maine* U.S. warship that exploded off Havana, Cuba, on February 15, 1898

Spanish-American War 1898 war that began when the United States demanded Cuba's independence from Spain

George Dewey U.S. naval officer who defeated the Spanish fleet during the Spanish-American War

Rough Riders members of the First U.S. Volunteer Cavalry, organized by Theodore Roosevelt during the Spanish-American War

Platt Amendment agreement claiming the United States' right to intervene in Cuban affairs

Anti-Imperialist League group of influential Americans who believed the United States should not deny other people the right to govern themselves

Visual Vocabulary explosion of the U.S.S. *Maine*

▶ Reading Strategy

Re-create the diagram shown at right. As you respond to the **KEY QUESTIONS**, use the diagram to show the important events of the Spanish-American War.

 See Skillbuilder Handbook, page R7.

CAUSES AND EFFECTS

CAUSE	EFFECT
Spain treats Cuba harshly	*U.S.S.* Maine *to Havana*

 GRAPHIC ORGANIZERS
Go to **Interactive Review** @ ClassZone.com

The Spanish-American War

14.D.3 Describe roles and influences of individuals, groups and media in shaping current Illinois and United States public policy (e.g., *general public opinion, special interest groups, formal parties, media*).

16.B.3d Describe ways in which the United States developed as a world political power.

One American's Story

José Martí, a poet and journalist, was forced to leave Cuba in the 1870s. In those years, Cuba was a Spanish colony, and he had spoken out for independence. Martí later described the terrible conditions the Cuban people suffered under Spanish rule.

PRIMARY SOURCE

❝ Cuba's children . . . suffer in indescribable bitterness as they see their fertile nation enchained and also their human dignity stifled . . . all for the necessities and vices of the [Spanish] monarchy. **❞**

— José Martí quoted in *José Martí, Mentor of the Cuban Nation*

Sculpture of José Marti in Central Park, New York City.

In New York City, Martí began to plan a Cuban revolt against Spain that began in 1895. Martí's lifelong struggle for Cuban independence made him a symbol of liberty throughout Latin America. But U.S. disapproval of Spain's treatment of Cubans led to the Spanish-American War.

American Interests in Cuba

▼ **KEY QUESTION** How did Americans respond to the Cuban Revolution?

When the first English colonies were established in America, Spain had a worldwide empire. This empire grew until it covered most of the Americas, including land that became part of the United States. But, by the 1890's, Spanish power was crumbling, and only a few of its colonies remained. Among them were the Philippine Islands in the Pacific and the Caribbean islands of Cuba and Puerto Rico. (See the maps on pages 702 and 703.) Many of the inhabitants of these colonies had begun to demand independence.

Cubans Rebel Against Spain Cubans had unsuccessfully revolted against Spain several times. In 1895, anger over poor economic conditions came to a boiling point, and the Cubans rebelled again against Spanish rule. José Martí, who helped to organize the rebellion from New York, went back to Cuba. He was killed in a skirmish with Spanish troops shortly after his return, but the revolt continued.

Spain treated the rebels and other Cubans harshly. Many Cubans were forced from their homes and placed in camps guarded by Spanish troops. Thousands died of starvation and disease.

Yellow Journalism The revolt in Cuba caused alarm in the United States. Business leaders were concerned because the fighting disrupted U.S. trade with Cuba. Most Americans, however, became outraged when the press began to describe the brutality of Spanish officials. Two New York City newspapers, in particular, stirred up people's emotions.

The New York *World*, owned by Joseph Pulitzer, and the New York *Journal*, owned by William Randolph Hearst, were battling for customers. Both owners were able to attract readers by printing stories that described—and often exaggerated—news about Spanish cruelty. This sensational style of writing was known as **yellow journalism**. It was named after *The Yellow Kid*, a popular comic strip that ran in both newspapers.

The Yellow Kid was the first comic strip in America. This edition was published in 1897.

America Declares War William McKinley, the U.S. president in 1898, did not want war. "I have been through war," he told a friend. "I have seen the dead piled up, and I do not want to see another." But American public opinion forced McKinley to take action. He demanded that Spain halt its harsh treatment of Cubans.

Riots had broken out in Havana, the Cuban capital. In January 1898, McKinley sent the battleship, **U.S.S. *Maine*** to Havana to protect U.S. citizens. On February 15, the *Maine* exploded and sank. Two hundred and sixty-six American sailors died. No one knows what caused the explosion. Many historians today believe that it was an accident. Most Americans blamed Spain. "Remember the *Maine*!" became a call to arms.

On April 20, 1898, President McKinley signed a congressional resolution that called for Cuba's independence and demanded a withdrawal of Spanish forces. Spain responded by breaking off diplomatic relations with the United States. The stage was set for war.

▲ **CAUSES AND EFFECTS** Explain the American response to the Cuban Revolution.

This photo shows several cannons overlooking the Bay of Havana on the coast of Cuba.

The Battles for the Philippines and Cuba

🔻 **KEY QUESTION** What was the outcome of the Spanish-American War?

In 1898, America went to war against Spain to fight for Cuban freedom. But the first major battle of the **Spanish-American War** took place in the Philippine Islands—a Spanish colony in the Pacific Ocean—on the other side of the world. Many Filipinos, as the inhabitants of the islands are called, had also revolted against Spanish rule in the 1890's.

The War in the Philippines On April 30, 1898 the American fleet in the Pacific steamed to the Philippines. American Commodore **George Dewey** had the support of the head of the Filipino rebel forces, Emilio Aguinaldo (eh•MEE•lyoh AH•gee•NAHL•doh).

The next morning, May 1, Dewey gave the command to open fire on the Spanish fleet at Manila, the Philippine capital. In seven hours, Dewey's men had destroyed the Spanish fleet. About 380 Spanish sailors were dead or wounded. No Americans died. U.S. troops, aided by Filipino rebels, took control of Manila in August.

Dewey became an instant hero in the United States. Some babies born at the time of the victory in Manila Bay were named for him, and a chewing gum called "Dewey's Chewies" became popular.

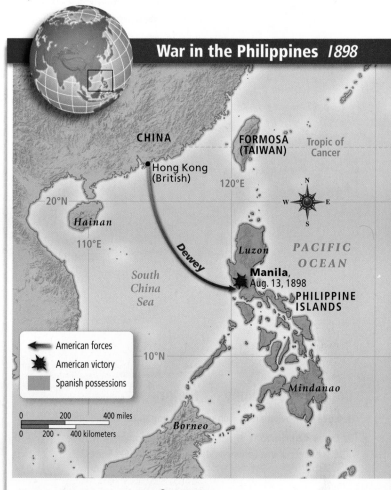

War in the Philippines *1898*

American forces
American victory
Spanish possessions

Connect Geography & History

1. **Movement** Where was Dewey's fleet before it steamed toward the Philippines?

2. **Make Inferences** Why might the geographic location of the Philippines be of interest to American imperialists?

The War in the Caribbean When the Spanish-American War began, the U.S. Army had only 28,000 men. Within four months, over 200,000 more joined up. Among the new recruits was Theodore Roosevelt, who had resigned from the U.S. Navy Department to volunteer.

Roosevelt helped to organize the First U.S. Volunteer Cavalry. This unit was nicknamed the **Rough Riders**. Its recruits included cowboys, miners, college students, New York policemen, athletes, and Native Americans.

In June, the Rough Riders and about 15,000 other soldiers, including four regiments that were African American, gathered in Tampa, Florida. They then set out for Santiago, a Spanish stronghold in southern Cuba. (See the map on page 702.) When the Rough Riders arrived, their dark-blue wool uniforms were too hot for the Cuban climate. Also, many of the soldiers came down with tropical diseases. Even so, they fought their way toward Santiago.

War in the Caribbean 1898

Legend:
- American forces
- Spanish forces
- American victory
- U.S. naval blockade
- Spanish possessions

0   150   300 miles
0   150   300 kilometers

ATLANTIC OCEAN

Gulf of Mexico
Tampa
FLORIDA
30°N
U.S.S. Maine sunk, Feb. 1898
BAHAMAS (Br.)
Havana
CUBA
San Juan Hill, July 1
Santiago
Guantánamo
PUERTO RICO
JAMAICA (Br.)
20°N
Spanish fleet destroyed, July 3
HAITI DOMINICAN REPUBLIC
Caribbean Sea
Guanica, July 25
From Spain, May 19
70°W
80°W

Connect Geography & History

1. **Location** Where does Cuba lie in relation to the United States?
2. **Draw Conclusions** Given its geographic location, why were the islands of the Caribbean of value to the United States?

In order to gain control of Santiago's port, American troops had to capture San Juan Hill. (See map on this page.) They attacked the Spanish on July 1. African-American soldiers from the Tenth Cavalry began to drive the Spanish back. Roosevelt and the Rough Riders joined them as they rushed forward and captured the hill.

Two days later, American ships destroyed Spain's fleet as it tried to escape Santiago Harbor. On July 17, the city surrendered. A week later, U.S. forces took Puerto Rico. Finally, on August 12, 1898, Spain signed a truce. To U.S. Secretary of State John Hay, it had been "a splendid little war." For Spain, four centuries of glory had come to an end.

Although Americans had declared war to secure Cuba's independence, U.S. leaders began demanding that Spain also give up its other colonies. At the Treaty of Paris in 1898, the former Spanish colonies of Cuba, Puerto Rico, Guam, and the Philippines came under U.S. control. Now the United States had to decide how much independence it would allow its new territories.

▲ **SUMMARIZE** Explain the outcome of the Spanish-American War.

The New American Empire

▼ **KEY QUESTION** How did Americans view their nation's new power?

One of the most challenging questions for U.S. leaders after the war was what to do with the Philippines. Filipinos had fought alongside Americans during the Spanish-American War and believed that Spain's defeat would bring them independence. But President McKinley, in the spirit of imperialism, decided that the Philippines should become an American colony. Disappointed, Filipinos, led by Emilio Aguinaldo, began to fight against their new colonial rulers. American troops were not able to put down the Filipino rebellion until 1902.

Cuba and Puerto Rico Cuban independence was granted by the Treaty of Paris, but Cuba remained under the control of the U.S. military. The American position was that rapid withdrawal might jeopardize Cuban stability.

Cuba was forced to add the **Platt Amendment** to its constitution. This gave the United States the right to intervene in Cuban affairs anytime there was a threat to "life, property, and individual liberty." Cuba also had to allow a U.S. naval base at Guantánamo Bay.

Puerto Rico became an American territory. The United States set up a government and appointed the top officials. Puerto Ricans were allowed little say in their own affairs. In 1917 the United States would agree to make Puerto Rico a self-governing territory and grant U.S. citizenship to all Puerto Ricans.

The Anti-Imperialist League U.S. treatment of Spain's former colonies after the Spanish-American War disappointed many people in the United States. Several influential Americans, including former president Grover Cleveland, businessman Andrew Carnegie, reformer Jane Addams, and writer Mark Twain, joined with others to form the **Anti-Imperialist League**. Members of the League believed that Americans should not deny other people the right to govern themselves.

PRIMARY SOURCE

❝ We hold that the policy known as imperialism is hostile to liberty. . . . We regret that it has become necessary in the land of Washington and Lincoln to reaffirm that all men, of whatever race or color, are entitled to life, liberty, and the pursuit of happiness. ❞

—from the Platform of the *American Anti-Imperialist League*

The voice of the Anti-Imperialist League was lost, however, in the roar of popular approval of the Spanish-American War. Many Americans hoped that their nation would surpass the glory of the old Spanish empire.

▲ **COMPARE AND CONTRAST** Explain the different sides Americans took regarding the nation's new power.

Illinois Learning Standards *Review*

⤷ **ONLINE QUIZ**
For test practice, go to
Interactive Review @ ClassZone.com

TERMS & NAMES

1. Explain the importance of:

- U.S.S. *Maine*
- yellow journalism
- Spanish-American War
- George Dewey
- Rough Riders
- Platt Amendment
- Anti-Imperialist League

USING YOUR READING NOTES

2. Causes and Effects Re-create the cause-and-effect diagram from the beginning of this section.

CAUSE	EFFECT
Spain treats Cuba harshly	*U.S.S.* Maine *to Havana*

KEY IDEAS

3. What role did New York City newspapers play in the outbreak of the Spanish-American War?

4. What happened to the Philippines after the war?

CRITICAL THINKING

5. Make Inferences How did the United States betray its democratic principles by adding the Platt Amendment to Cuba's constitution?

6. **Connect** *to* **Today** Give examples of how modern newspapers might impact political events by using "yellow journalism" tactics.

7. **Writing** Script Research the Rough Riders. Write a television news script covering a major Rough Rider battle.

Global Expansion

By the end of the nineteenth century, many European powers had established prosperous settlements along the coast of China. They also had carved out spheres of influence—areas where each nation claimed special rights and economic privilege. As a result, American leaders adopted these ideas as the bedrock of U.S. foreign policy:

- the growth of the U.S. economy depended on exports
- the United States had a right to intervene abroad to keep foreign markets open
- the closing of an area to American products, citizens, or ideas threatened U.S. survival
- refueling posts in the Pacific for the U.S. Navy were essential to U.S. security

These goals led to the establishment of U.S. military bases in the Pacific.

RUSSIA

140°E

160°E

40°N

PACIFIC OCEAN

JAPAN

Shanghai

CHINA

Hong Kong

20°N

WAKE ISLAND
annexed by United States for military purposes

GUAM
ceded to United States by Spain: became U.S. naval base

Wake I. (1899)

Manila

Philippine Islands (1898)

PHILIPPINES
ceded by Spain: withdrew U.S. bases in 1945.

Guam (1898)

FRENCH INDOCHINA

Caroline Islands

Marshall Islands

0° Equator

DUTCH EAST INDIES

British

French

German

U.S.

⊙ Ports open to U.S. trade before 1911

(1867) Date of U.S. possession

BRITISH NEW GUINEA

INDIAN OCEAN

| 0 | 500 | 1,000 miles |
| 0 | 500 | 1,000 kilometers |

120°E

AUSTRALIA

New Caledonia

Alaska Purchased
from Russia
(1867)

180°

60°N

140°W

160°W

Aleutian Islands

PACIFIC
OCEAN

UNITED STATES

San Francisco

Midway I.
(1867)

HAWAIIAN ISLANDS
Hawaii gives U.S. exclusive
rights to build a base in
Pearl Harbor.

Tropic of Cancer

Hawaiian Islands
(1898)

*Johnston
Atoll*

"Guano Act"
Islands (1856)

Palmyra Atoll

Howland I.
Baker I.

Jarvis I.

In 1907, Theodore Roosevelt sent a fleet of 16 battleships on
a 14-month long voyage around the world to demonstrate
that the United States was a world-class naval power. Since
the voyage of this "Great White Fleet," U.S. Navy ships have
been painted gray.

0° Equator

AMERICAN SAMOA
U.S. coaling station and
naval base.

P   o   l   y   n   e   s   i   a

*Western
Samoa*

French Polynesia

**American
Samoa (1899)**

Connect Geography & History

1. **Location** What geographic features of the
   Pacific Islands would make them of particular
   interest to the U.S. Navy?

2. **Evaluate** Why do you think American bases
   in the Pacific would be beneficial to the
   United States?

 See Geography Handbook, page A2.

▶ Key Ideas

BEFORE, YOU LEARNED

The United States went to war with Spain and won colonies in the Caribbean and the Pacific.

NOW YOU WILL LEARN

The United States expanded its influence in China and in Latin America, and built the Panama Canal.

▶ Vocabulary

TERMS & NAMES

sphere of influence areas where foreign nations claimed special rights and economic privileges

Open Door Policy U.S. policy proposed in 1899 which stated that no single country should have a monopoly on trade with China

Boxer Rebellion 1900 nationalist uprising in China

Panama Canal canal through the Isthmus of Panama that connects the Atlantic and Pacific

Roosevelt Corollary United States claim of right to interfere in the affairs of Latin American countries

BACKGROUND VOCABULARY

malaria infectious disease spread by mosquitoes

REVIEW

Monroe Doctrine policy of U.S. opposition to any European interference in the Western Hemisphere

Visual Vocabulary
member of Boxer Rebellion

▶ Reading Strategy

Re-create the diagram shown at the right. As you respond to the **KEY QUESTIONS**, use the diagram to record the important events in the order in which they occurred.

 See Skillbuilder Handbook, page R5.

SEQUENCE EVENTS

Open Door Policy →

Revolution in Panama →

GRAPHIC ORGANIZERS
Go to **Interactive Review** @ ClassZone.com

Expanding Interests in Asia and Latin America

14.E.3 Compare the basic principles of the United States and its international interests (e.g., *territory, environment, trade, use of technology*).
16.B.3d Describe ways in which the United States developed as a world political power.

One American's Story

In 1852, President Millard Fillmore sent Commodore Matthew Perry on a mission to open Japan to U.S. trade. For over two centuries, Japan's rulers had kept the country closed to most foreigners. Perry wanted to break Japan's traditional policy.

PRIMARY SOURCE

❝ [I was determined] to adopt an entirely contrary plan of proceedings from that of all others who had . . . visited Japan on the same errand [to open up trade]: to demand as a right and not to [ask] as a favor those acts of courtesy which are due from one civilized nation to another. ❞

—Commodore Matthew Perry, *Personal Journal*

Under the threat of force, Japan signed a treaty in 1854 giving American ships access to its ports. This was the start of U.S. involvement in Asia.

A Power in the Pacific

🔻 **KEY QUESTION** What steps increased American influence in East Asia and the Pacific?

When Commodore Perry opened Japan to U.S. trade in the 1850s, he also opened the nation to Western ideas. Because of this, Japan began to modernize and soon emerged as a world power. In the 1890s, Japan demonstrated its strength in a successful war against China. After the war, Japan as well as the major European powers expanded their **spheres of influence**. These were areas where foreign nations claimed special rights and economic privileges. Like other Western nations, the United States also wanted to trade with China.

Commodore Matthew Perry as portrayed by a 19th century Japanese artist

Becoming a World Power **707**

The United States and China By the late 1890s, France, Germany, Britain, Japan, and Russia had established prosperous settlements along the coast of China. They also claimed exclusive rights to railroad construction and mining development in the nation's interior.

The competition for spheres of influence worried U.S. leaders who wanted access to China's markets and resources. In 1899, Secretary of State John Hay asked nations involved in the region to follow an **Open Door Policy.** This policy stated that no single country should have a monopoly on trade with China. Eventually, most of the nations accepted Hay's proposal.

Many Chinese people were not pleased by the presence of foreigners. One group, called the "Boxers," was angered by the privileges given to foreigners and the disrespect they showed toward Chinese traditions. In 1900, Chinese resentment led to a violent uprising known as the **Boxer Rebellion.** The rebellion was put down by an international force from eight nations, including Americans. About 230 foreigners and thousands of Chinese Christians and rebels were killed as a result of the Boxer Rebellion.

America Secures the Philippines As the Boxer Rebellion raged in China, American forces were still struggling to put down the independence movement in the Philippines. In 1902, they succeeded. Senator Albert Beveridge from Indiana, a supporter of imperialism boasted, "The Philippines are ours forever. And just beyond the Philippines are China's [unlimited] markets. We will not retreat from either. . . . The power that rules the Pacific is the power that rules the world."

Many Americans looked forward to the profits promised by Asian markets and resources. Others saw a chance to extend U.S. democracy in the region. The Philippines would provide a base for these activities.

Now that the Philippines were firmly under American control, the United States possessed a chain of islands in the Pacific that included Hawaii and Guam. Never before had America owned territories in such distant regions. The United States now had to find a way to help protect its Pacific empire, and allow ships from its east coast to gain easier access to the Far East.

🔺 **SEQUENCE** List in chronological order the events that led to increasing U.S. influence in East Asia and the Pacific.

U.S. Interests in Latin America

🔻 **KEY QUESTION** Why did the United States get involved in Latin America?

As the U.S. economy continued to grow, easy access to the Pacific became vital. For that reason, U.S. leaders proposed a canal to connect the Pacific and Atlantic oceans.

The Panama Canal A canal connecting the Atlantic and Pacific would mean that U.S. ships would not have to travel around the coast of South America. Such a canal would greatly reduce travel time for commercial and military transport. The Spanish-American War, fought in both oceans, also made clear the need for such a shortcut.

Connect to the World

Imperialism
The Boxers' real name was I-ho ch'üan, or "Righteous and Harmonious fists," from which the term "Boxers" came. The Boxers opposed Christianity, the Chinese power structure, and foreigners. Most of its members were young peasant men.

TECHNOLOGY *of the* PANAMA CANAL

Click here to explore the technology of the Panama Canal @ ClassZone.com

The Panama Canal begins and ends at sea level but rises to 85 feet above sea level at Panama's Gatun Lake. (See inset map.) Why doesn't the lake empty into the sea?

1. With the left gate open and the right gate closed, a ship enters the lock.

2. The gate closes and water is pumped out. As the water level lowers, the ship is lowered with it. When the water level in the chamber reaches the level of the canal, the right gate opens.

3. The ship can also be raised by pumping water into the lock.

CRITICAL THINKING

1. **Draw Conclusions** Why did the United States want a shorter route between the Atlantic and Pacific oceans?

2. **Connect** *to* **Today**

   Why is there less need for the Panama Canal today?

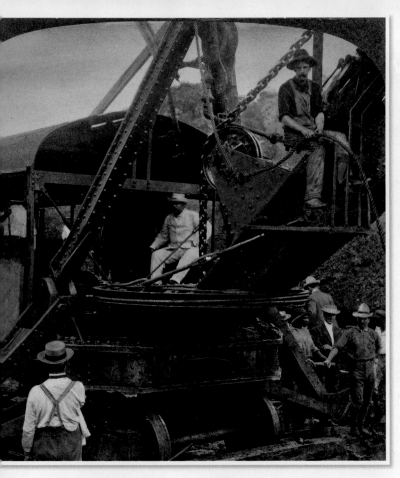

The best spot for a canal was the Isthmus of Panama. It was part of Colombia, but Colombia was unwilling to give up this land. Ignoring Colombia's right to control its territory, President Roosevelt sent the U.S. Navy to support a revolution on the isthmus. Out of this revolution the new nation of Panama was created in 1903.

The Panamanian leaders granted the United States rights to a ten-mile-wide strip of land called the Canal Zone. There the United States would build the **Panama Canal**, the shortcut that would connect the Atlantic and Pacific.

Some people in Latin America and the United States opposed Roosevelt's actions. They believed that he had interfered in Colombia's affairs in order to cheat it out of land. In 1921, the U.S. finally paid Colombia $25 million for the loss of Panama.

Theodore Roosevelt (in white suit) operates a steamshovel during the construction of the Panama Canal. **Why was Roosevelt's visit important?**

Building the Panama Canal Building the canal was a huge challenge. The land was swampy and full of mosquitoes that carried the organism that causes **malaria**—an infectious disease marked by cycles of chills and fever.

In spite of the challenges, the project moved forward. When Roosevelt visited Panama in 1906, he described the building of the canal.

PRIMARY SOURCE

❝ Steam shovels are hard at it; scooping huge masses of rock and gravel and dirt previously loosened by the drillers and dynamite blasters, loading it on trains which take it away. . . . They are eating steadily into the mountain cutting it down and down. . . . It is an epic feat. ❞

—Theodore Roosevelt, *from a letter sent to his son*

More than 44,000 workers, including many black West Indians, labored on the canal. The Panama Canal opened in 1914. It cost between $350–$380 million to build, and was then the most expensive construction project in the world. More than 5,500 canal workers died from diseases or accidents.

U.S. Involvement in Latin America The Panama Canal was only one sign of U.S. involvement in Latin America. As the U.S. economy continued to grow, so did U.S. interest in the resources of their southern neighbors.

Businesses in the United States found that they could cheaply buy food and raw materials, such as bananas, coffee, and copper from Latin America. They shipped these goods to the United States and sold them for higher prices.

U.S. companies also bought large amounts of land in the region for farming and mining. As economic interests drew the United States deeper into Latin American affairs, U.S. leaders became concerned about political stability in the region. They worried that instability might tempt European nations to intervene in the region.

Policing the Hemisphere During his presidency, Theodore Roosevelt made it clear that the United States would remain the dominant power in the Western Hemisphere. He summed up his foreign policy toward the region when he said: "Speak softly and carry a big stick." Roosevelt was warning that the United States would use military force if its interests were threatened.

Roosevelt reminded European powers of the **Monroe Doctrine**—the policy that barred European nations from intervening in Latin America. In 1905, he added the **Roosevelt Corollary.** It authorized the United States to act as a "policeman" in the region. That is, U.S. leaders would now intervene in Latin America's domestic affairs when they believed that such action was necessary to maintain stability.

CONNECT to the Essential Question

How did America's growing power affect its relationships with other nations?

1867
U.S. Purchases Alaska

1914
Panama Canal Opens
Improves international commerce.
Increases U.S. naval power.

IMPERIALISM
- **Economic Competition**
- **Belief in Cultural Superiority**
- **Military Competition**

1898
U.S. Annexes Hawaii

1905
Roosevelt Corollary
Asserts right of the U.S. to exercise police power in the Western Hemisphere.

1898
Spanish–American War
Cuba gains independence from Spain.
U.S. gains Puerto Rico, Guam, and the Philippine islands.

1899
Open Door Policy
U.S. secures trading rights in China.

CRITICAL THINKING Causes and Effects
What were some of the long-term effects of U.S. overseas expansion?

In 1905, the United States used the Roosevelt Corollary to justify taking control of the Dominican Republic's finances. This was after the Dominican Republic failed to pay its foreign debts. A year later, when a revolt threatened Cuba's government, the policy was used to send troops there.

Later presidents expanded on Roosevelt's "big stick diplomacy." William Howard Taft urged American businesses to invest in Latin America. Taft promised military action if anything or anyone threatened these investments. He kept his word. In 1912, when Nicaraguan citizens revolted against their leader, Taft sent marines to Nicaragua to put down a revolt against the pro-American president.

President Taft's successor, Woodrow Wilson, also intervened in Latin America. In 1914 a revolution in Mexico began to threaten U.S. interests, Wilson sent a fleet to Veracruz after American sailors were arrested. Two years later, in 1916, he sent troops to Mexico when a Mexican revolutionary named Pancho Villa (PAHN•choh VEE•yah) raided New Mexico and killed 17 Americans in the town of Columbus.

Americans rarely questioned U.S. actions in Latin America. They saw their nation as a good police officer maintaining peace and preventing disorder. However, many Latin Americans did not agree. They saw the United States as a greedy imperial power that cared only about its own interests. This mistrust continues to trouble U.S. relations with its neighbors.

▲ **ANALYZE CAUSES** Why did America expand its involvement in Latin America?

Illinois Learning Standards *Review*

 ONLINE QUIZ
For test practice, go to
Interactive Review @ ClassZone.com

TERMS & NAMES

1. Explain the importance of
- sphere of influence
- Panama Canal
- Open Door Policy
- Roosevelt Corollary
- Boxer Rebellion

USING YOUR READING NOTES

2. Sequence Events Complete the diagram that you started at the beginning of this section.

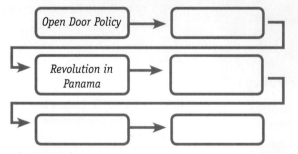

KEY IDEAS

3. What caused the Boxer Rebellion?

4. What events made the building of the Panama Canal so important to the United States?

CRITICAL THINKING

5. Make Inferences Why was the United States interested in the political stability of Latin America?

6. **Connect** *to* **Today** Why do you think the Panama Canal has more commercial than military importance today?

7. **Math** Using the Internet or library resources, find out the dimensions of the Panama Canal. Then write a short report on how much time and distance was saved by ships after the construction of the canal.

Chapter Summary

1 **Key Idea**
The United States took its first steps in becoming a world power by acquiring Alaska and Hawaii.

2 **Key Idea**
The United States went to war with Spain and won colonies in the Caribbean and the Pacific.

3 **Key Idea**
The United States expanded its influence in China and in Latin America, and built the Panama Canal.

For detailed Review and Study Notes go to **Interactive Review** @ ClassZone.com

Name Game

Use the Terms & Names list to complete each sentence online or on your own paper.

1. _____ is the policy by which strong nations extend control over weaker territories. imperialism

2. _____ was responsible for America's acquisition of Alaska in 1867.

3. In 1898, the _____ exploded and sank off the coast of Cuba.

4. The _____ was opposed to foreign presence in China.

5. _____ were members of the first U.S. Volunteer Cavalry.

6. The _____ was fought over Cuba's right to independence.

7. Construction of the _____ facilitated trade between the U.S. and Latin America.

8. In 1902, the U.S. insisted that Cuba add the _____ to its new constitution.

9. Reporting that sensationalized the news was known as _____

10. In 1898, the U.S. proposed an _____ to promote unrestricted trade with China.

A. U.S.S *Maine*
B. Boxer Rebellion
C. Open Door Policy
D. George Dewey
E. William Seward
F. Anti-Imperialist League
G. Roosevelt Corollary
H. Platt Amendment
I. Rough Riders
J. Panama Canal
K. Imperialism
L. Yellow Journalism
M. Sphere of Influence
N. Spanish-American War
O. Queen Liliuokalani

Activities

CROSSWORD PUZZLE

Complete the online crossword to show what you know about American imperialism.

ACROSS

1. _____ _____ is grown on Hawaiian plantations.

FLIPCARD

Use the online flip cards to quiz yourself on the terms and names introduced in this chapter.

Led U.S. trade expedition to Japan in 1850s.

ANSWER: Matthew Perry

VOCABULARY

Choose the correct answer.

1. Commodore George Dewey was (the leader of the Rough Riders/the hero of the Battle of Manila Bay).

2. Queen Liliuokalani was the ruler of (Alaska/Hawaii).

3. William Seward purchased (Alaska/Hawaii) from Russia.

4. The Rough Riders fought in (Cuba/Panama).

5. The Boxer Rebellion took place in (China/the Philippines).

Explain how the terms and names in each group are related.

6. yellow journalism, U.S.S. *Maine*, Spanish-American War

7. Platt Amendment, Panama Canal, Roosevelt Corollary

8. sphere of influence, William Seward, imperialism

KEY IDEAS

1 Imperialism in the Pacific (pages 694–697)

9. Why did Americans become interested in overseas expansion in the late 1800s?

10. How did the public react when William Seward negotiated the purchase of Alaska in 1867?

11. Why did the United States take an interest in Hawaii?

2 The Spanish-American War (pages 698–703)

12. How did the Spanish-American War begin?

13. What territories did the United States take as a result of its victory over the Spanish?

3 Expanding Interests in Asia and Latin America (pages 706–712)

14. Why did U.S. leaders want access to Asian markets after the Spanish-American War?

15. Why was there an interest in building a canal across Latin America?

16. How were the Latin American policies of Roosevelt, Taft, and Wilson similar?

CRITICAL THINKING

17. **Draw Conclusions** How did U.S. economic interests in Latin America influence the foreign policy of the United States?

18. **Form and Support Opinions** How did the presence of foreigners in China contribute to the Boxer Rebellion?

19. **Categorize** Use a chart like the one below to record details about U.S. involvement in Asia and Latin America.

Asia	Latin America
Filipino independence defeated	*Panama Canal constructed*

20. **Summarize** What political difficulty faced U.S. leaders who wanted to build the Panama Canal?

21. **Evaluate** Do you think the United States was justified in going to war with Spain? Explain your answer.

22. **Synthesize** How did the building of the Panama Canal support United States efforts to become a world power?

23. **Analyze Leadership** What qualities made Theodore Roosevelt an effective leader?

24. **Interpret Graphs** Read the graph below. When did U.S. exports first outnumber U.S. imports?

U.S. Trade Expansion *1865–1915*

Dollars (in millions)

■ EXPORTS   ■ IMPORTS

Source: *Historical Statistics of the United States*

ILLINOIS STANDARDS-BASED ASSESSMENT

 TEST PRACTICE
- **Online Test Practice** @ ClassZone.com
- **Test-Taking Strategies & Practice** at the front of this book

DOCUMENT-BASED QUESTIONS

PART 1: Short Answer

Analyze each document, and answer the questions that follow.

DOCUMENT 1

1. This cartoon is about the relationship between the United States and Cuba in the late 19th century. What is the point of view of the cartoonist?

DOCUMENT 2

❝ How long are the Spaniards to drench Cuba with the blood and tears of her people? . . . How long shall American citizens, arbitrarily arrested while on peaceful and legitimate errands, be immured [held] in foul Spanish prisons without trial? . . .

How long shall the United States sit idle and indifferent within sound and hearing of . . . murder? How long? ❞

—Joseph Pulitzer, New York *World*, February 13, 1897

2. What was the probable intent of this example of "yellow journalism"?

PART 2: Essay

3. Using information from the documents, your answers to the questions in Part 1, and your knowledge of U.S. history, write an essay that discusses the American justification of imperialism.

YOU BE THE HISTORIAN

25. Draw Conclusions How do you think manifest destiny set the stage for American imperialism at the end of the 19th century?

26. Compare and Contrast How did U.S. expansion at the end of the 19th century compare and contrast with expansion that occurred earlier?

27. Connect Economics & History How did the U.S. purchase of Alaska protect America's future interests?

28. WHAT IF? How might history have been different if the United States had given the Philippines its independence after the Spanish-American War?

29. Citizenship How might the activities of the Anti-Imperialist League have helped to remind citizens of their democratic responsibilities?

30. Connect *to* **Today** The "yellow journalism" of major newspapers influenced U.S. foreign policy at the turn of the century. How does modern media, such as television, shape public opinion today?

 Answer the

ESSENTIAL QUESTION

How did America's growing power affect its relationships with other nations?

Written Response Write a two-to-three-paragraph response to the Essential Question. Be sure to consider the key ideas of each section as well as the most significant factors that affected America's relationships with other nations.

Response Rubric

A strong response will

- discuss major events that led to the growth of American power
- explain the importance of strong leadership
- evaluate how the use of American power impacted other nations
- analyze how the use of American power influenced public opinion in America

War and the Jazz Age

1914–1929

Why It Matters Now

Despite the continuing dominance of isolationist thinking in the years between 1880 and 1930, international events drew America ever more fully into world affairs. The period was a prelude to America's later emergence as the world's greatest power.

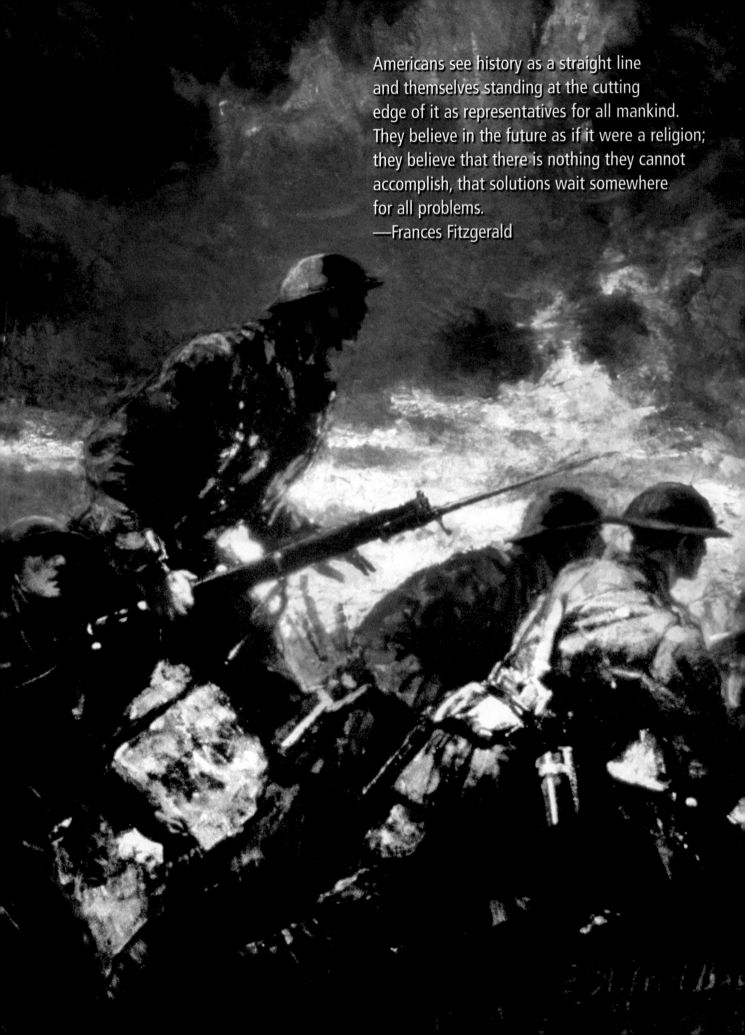

Americans see history as a straight line
and themselves standing at the cutting
edge of it as representatives for all mankind.
They believe in the future as if it were a religion;
they believe that there is nothing they cannot
accomplish, that solutions wait somewhere
for all problems.
—Frances Fitzgerald

World War I and Its Legacy

1914–1920

 ESSENTIAL QUESTION

How did World War I impact America and transform Europe?

I WANT YOU FOR U.S. ARMY
NEAREST RECRUITING STATION

CONNECT Geography & History

Why did so many countries participate in World War I?
Think about:

1 where most of the fighting took place

2 which nations did most of the fighting

Archduke Franz Ferdinand and his wife are murdered in Sarajevo on June 28, 1914.

An American soldier throws a hand grenade in Aneauvau, France, on March 15, 1918.

1915 A German U-boat sinks the *Lusitania*.

▼

Effect Americans turn against Germany.

1916 The battles of Verdun and the Somme claim millions of lives.

1914

Serbian separatist assassinates Austro-Hungarian Archduke Franz Ferdinand.

▼

Effect World War I begins.

1917 Zimmerman telegram is intercepted.
America declares war against Central Powers.

Europe Divided 1914

Click Here to explore World War I
@ClassZone.com

ATLANTIC OCEAN

60°N

NORWAY

North Sea

SWEDEN

DENMARK

Baltic Sea

GREAT BRITAIN ⑥ ⑧

50°N

London •

NETH.

• Berlin

BELG.

GERMANY ④ ⑤

RUSSIA ③

Paris •

LUX.

FRANCE ⑧

SWITZ.

Vienna • ② ⑦

AUSTRIA-HUNGARY

ITALY

①

Sarajevo •

ROMANIA

Black Sea

SERBIA

PORTUGAL

• Madrid

MONTENEGRO

BULGARIA

SPAIN

40°N

Rome •

ALBANIA

OTTOMAN EMPIRE

SPANISH MOROCCO

GREECE

Mediterranean Sea

0°

10°E

20°E

30°E

Allies

Central Powers

Neutral nations

Neutral nations later aligned with Allies

0   200   400 miles
0   200   400 kilometers

STEPS TO WAR

① **JUNE 28** Archduke Franz Ferdinand is assassinated.

② **JULY 28** Austria-Hungary declares war on Serbia.

③ **JULY 30** Russia (Serbia's ally) mobilizes armed forces.

④ **AUGUST 1** Germany (Austria-Hungary's ally) declares war on Russia.

⑤ **AUGUST 3** Germany declares war on France (Russia's ally); prepares to invade Belgium.

⑥ **AUGUST 4** Britain, having pledged to protect Belgium, declares war on Germany.

⑦ **AUGUST 6** Austria-Hungary declares war on Russia.

⑧ **AUGUST 12** France and Britain declare war on Austria-Hungary.

Signing the Treaty of Versailles

Armistice poppy flower

1918 Armistice is declared on November 11, 1918.

▼

Effect World War I ends.

1919 Treaty of Versailles is signed.

▼

Effect Allied powers punish Germany; new nations are formed.

1920

Italian-born anarchists Sacco and Vanzetti are arrested during the Red Scare.

Reading for Understanding

▶ Key Ideas

BEFORE, YOU LEARNED

By the early 1900s, America exerted its influence in East Asia, the Pacific region, and Latin America.

NOW YOU WILL LEARN

After the outbreak of World War I, the United States eventually joined the Allies to fight against the Central Powers.

▶ Vocabulary

TERMS & NAMES

Central Powers the World War I alliance of Germany, Austria-Hungary, the Ottoman Empire, and Bulgaria

Allies the World War I alliance of Great Britain, France, Russia, Italy, Serbia, and others

nationalism pride in and loyalty to nation

militarism policy of making military power a primary goal of a nation

trench warfare warfare in which soldiers dug into deep trenches across the battlefield

U-boat German submarine

Zimmermann telegram telegram telling the German ambassador to ask Mexico to declare war on the United States

REVIEW

Woodrow Wilson president of the United States during World War I

communism single-party political system in which the government controls and plans the economy with the goal of common ownership of all property

Visual Vocabulary
U-Boat

▶ Reading Strategy

Re-create the diagram shown at right. As you read and respond to the **KEY QUESTIONS**, use the diagram to note important causes of World War I. Add boxes or start a new diagram as needed.

 See Skillbuilder Handbook, page R7.

CAUSES AND EFFECTS

Causes		Effect
Imperialism	→	
	→	*World War I*
	→	
	→	

🔵 **GRAPHIC ORGANIZERS**
Go to **Interactive Review** @ ClassZone.com

War Breaks Out in Europe

14.E.3 Compare the basic principles of the United States and its international interests (e.g., *territory, environment, trade, use of technology*).
16.B.3d Describe ways in which the United States developed as a world political power.

One American's Story

Alan Seeger was a young American poet who moved to Paris shortly before World War I. When war broke out, he joined the French Foreign Legion. In July 1916, he died on the first day of the First Battle of the Somme (SAHM), one of the bloodiest battles of the war. He wrote a letter to a friend before the battle.

PRIMARY SOURCE

❝ We go up to the attack tomorrow. This will probably be the biggest thing yet. We are to have the honor of marching in the first wave. . . . I am glad to be going in the first wave. If you are in this thing at all it is best to be in to the limit. And this is the supreme experience. ❞

—Alan Seeger, quoted in *Letters and Diary of Alan Seeger*, June 28, 1916

Alan Seeger

Alan Seeger was one of millions who died in World War I, the most destructive conflict the world had ever seen.

The Great War Begins

🔻 **KEY QUESTION** What events and factors helped cause World War I?

On June 28, 1914 a Serbian man assassinated Archduke Franz Ferdinand in the city of Sarajevo (SAIR•eh•YAY•voh). The archduke was the heir to the throne of Austria-Hungary. Soon, Austria declared war on Serbia. One by one, the other nations of Europe joined in. World War I had begun.

European nations had divided into two opposing alliances. The **Central Powers** were made up of Austria-Hungary, Germany, the Ottoman Empire, and Bulgaria. They faced the Allied Powers, or **Allies**, consisting of Serbia, Russia, France, Great Britain, Italy, and seven other countries that actively fought in the war.

Causes of World War I A single action, the assassination of the archduke, started World War I. The conflict had many underlying causes, however.

1. **Imperialism** Britain, France, Germany, and Italy competed for colonies in Africa and Asia. Germany had fewer colonies than Britain and France, and felt it deserved more colonies to provide it with resources and to buy its goods.

2. **Nationalism** Many Europeans embraced **nationalism**, strong feelings of pride, loyalty, and protectiveness toward their own countries. They wanted to prove that their nations were the best.

3. **Militarism** The policy of making military power a primary goal of a nation is called **militarism**. In the decades before the war, the major powers built up their armies and navies.

4. **Alliances** In 1914, a tangled network of competing alliances bound European nations together. An attack on one nation forced its allies to come to its aid. Any small conflict could become a larger war.

Stalemate in the Trenches When the war began in August, most people on both sides assumed it would be over within a few months. The war continued much longer than that, however. Germany invaded Belgium on its way to France and reached the Marne River, 30 miles from Paris. There the French, supported by the British, stopped the German advance. Instead of one side quickly defeating the other, the two sides slaughtered one another for more than three years. The soldiers were fighting a new kind of war called **trench warfare**. (See Animated History on pages 726–727.) Both sides dug a dense network of trenches from the English Channel coast to Switzerland.

When battles did take place, they cost many thousands of lives. The First Battle of the Somme, in 1916, resulted in more than 1.2 million casualties. British dead or wounded numbered over 400,000. German losses totaled over 600,000, and the number of French killed reached nearly 200,000. Despite this, the Allies advanced the trench line only about five to seven miles.

German soldiers wait in a trench, 1915.
What does the placement of the soldiers' weapons suggest about trench warfare?

A War of New Technology New technology made trench warfare especially deadly. Quick-firing artillery turned the area between opposing trenches into a no man's land too dangerous to occupy above ground. Soldiers who left the trenches to attack enemy lines rushed into a hail of bullets from enemy machine guns that could fire 600 bullets per minute. Poison gas, used by both sides, burned and blinded soldiers. Later in the war, the tank, a British invention, smashed through barbed wire, cleared paths through no man's land between enemy lines, and crossed trenches.

World War I was also the first major conflict in which airplanes were used in combat. By 1917, fighter planes fought each other far above the trenches. Manfred von Richthofen (man•frehd•vahn•RIKT•HO•fehn), known as the Red Baron, was Germany's top ace. An ace was an aviator who had downed five or more enemy aircraft. Von Richthofen shot down over 80 enemy planes before he was killed in action on April 21, 1918.

At sea, the Germans used submarines, which they called **U-boats**, to block trade. U-boats were equipped with both guns and torpedoes. German U-boats sank over 10 million tons of Allied shipping.

▲ **CAUSES AND EFFECTS** List the causes of World War I.

America's Path to War

▼ **KEY QUESTION** What events brought America into the war?

When the war started in 1914, American president **Woodrow Wilson** announced a policy of neutrality (noo•TRAL•IH•tee), refusing to take sides in the war. Many Americans were reluctant to become involved in a European conflict. However, over time, a series of events shifted public opinion to support the Allied cause.

The Sinking of the *Lusitania* In the fall of 1914, Britain set up a naval blockade of German ports, seizing all goods bound for Germany. In response, German submarines sank all Allied merchant ships they encountered off the British coast. In May 1915, a German U-boat torpedoed the British passenger ship *Lusitania* (Loo•sih•TAY•nee•uh), killing 1,198 people, including 128 Americans. The Germans thought that the ship was carrying military supplies—and it was carrying some arms. The sinking turned many Americans against Germany.

President Wilson kept the United States neutral. He demanded that the German government halt unrestricted submarine warfare, and it agreed. In the election of 1916, the Democratic Party's campaign slogan, "He kept us

(*above*) Allied uniform with gas mask

(*below*) The British passenger ship *Lusitania* sinks following a German U-boat attack.

out of war," appealed to voters. Wilson won reelection.

Germany, desperate to defeat Britain, resumed unrestricted submarine warfare on February 1, 1917. Its military leaders knew this action would bring the United States into the war, but they hoped to win the war before the Americans arrived.

The next month, the **Zimmermann telegram** dealt another blow to German-American relations. In it, Arthur Zimmermann, the German foreign minister, directed the German ambassador in Mexico to propose that Mexico join the Germans. In exchange, Germany would help Mexico get back its "lost" territories of Texas, New Mexico, and Arizona. The telegram was discovered by the British, who passed it on to U.S. officials. Americans were furious.

Debate in Congress In March 1917, German submarines sank three American ships. Americans had had enough. On April 2, 1917, President Woodrow Wilson asked Congress for a declaration of war.

Congress debated the resolution for three days. Most members were in favor. Some members, such as Representative Jeannette Rankin of Montana and Robert La Follette of Wisconsin, raised strong objections. Senator George Norris of Nebraska said Wilson wanted war because Wall Street financiers

ONLINE PRIMARY SOURCE

Hear the perspectives at the **Research & Writing Center** @ ClassZone.com

COMPARING *Perspectives*

OPINIONS OF THE WAR

One way to gauge the change in public opinion of the war is to examine the lyrics of two hit songs from the time. One from 1915, when a majority of Americans favored neutrality, is called, "I Didn't Raise My Boy To Be A Soldier." Two years later, as America marched off to war, "Over There" was a hit song.

I Didn't Raise My Boy To Be A Soldier

Ten million soldiers to the war
    have gone,
Who may never return again.
Ten million mothers' hearts
    must break,
For the ones who died in vain.
Head bowed down in sorrow in her
    lonely years,
Heard a mother murmur thro' her tears

Words by Alfred Bryan, music by Al Piantadosi

Over There

Johnnie get your gun, get your gun,
    get your gun,
Take it on the run, on the run,
    on the run,
Hear them calling you and me;
Ev'ry son of Liberty
Hurry right away, no delay, go today,
Make your daddy glad to have had
    such a lad
Tell your sweetheart not to pine,
To be proud her boy's in line.

Words and music by G. M. Cohan

CRITICAL THINKING Compare and Contrast Compare the perspectives of the two songs, paying particular attention to family elements referred to in the lyrics.

had loaned money to the Allies. If the Allies lost, they might not be able to repay the loans. Despite opposing voices, Congress voted to go to war.

Revolution in Russia Events in Russia made U.S. entry into the war more urgent for the Allies. By 1917, military failures, food shortages, and soaring inflation led to riots and strikes by angry workers in Russia. In March 1917, Czar Nicholas II was forced to step down. A temporary government continued the unpopular war until November. In that month the Bolsheviks, a communist group led by Vladimir Ilich Lenin (VLAH•deh•meer•EEL•yich•LEH•nin), took power. **Communism** is a political system in which a single party holds power and the state controls the economy with the goal of common ownership of all property.

The war had devastated Russia. Lenin began peace talks with Germany. In March 1918, Russia withdrew from the war by signing the Treaty of Brest-Litovsk (BREHST•lih•TOFSK). German troops could now turn from Russia to the Western front. The Allies urged the American troops to come quickly.

 CAUSES AND EFFECTS Describe events that brought America into World War I.

This 1917 Russian revolution poster reads, "You—still not a member of the cooperative, sign up immediately!"

Illinois Learning Standards *Review*

ONLINE QUIZ
For test practice, go to
Interactive Review @ ClassZone.com

TERMS & NAMES

1. Explain the importance of the following:

- Central Powers
- Allies
- nationalism
- militarism
- trench warfare
- U-boat
- Zimmermann telegram

USING YOUR READING NOTES

2. Causes and Effects Complete the diagram you started at the beginning of this section. Then create a diagram for each of the other main ideas.

Causes   Effect

Imperialism → World War I

KEY IDEAS

3. How did nationalism help cause World War I?

4. How did World War I differ from previous wars?

5. Why did the United States enter World War I?

CRITICAL THINKING

6. Causes and Effects Why did the Germans sink the *Lusitania*?

7. Analyze Point of View What events changed Americans' opinions about supporting the Allies?

8. WHAT IF? Do you think Congress would have voted to go to war if the Germans hadn't sent the Zimmermann telegram? Explain your answer.

9. **Writing** **Letter** Write a letter to a member of Congress that explains why Americans should either support the Allied cause or remain neutral.

Click here to explore World War I trench warfare
@ ClassZone.com

Life in the Trenches

Cramped trenches full of mud, rats, and rotting corpses were the only protection that soldiers on the 450-mile Western Front had. Unless soldiers were on patrol or charging the enemy, they stayed in the trenches for weeks at a time.

Click here Soldiers went to the front lines without much food or water.

Click here These machine gunners wore masks for protection from poison gas.

Click here Barbed wire was just one of the many deadly obstacles in no man's land.

Activity

Go Over the Top!

1. Divide into two "platoons," one on either side of the room. Build "trench lines" out of desks and chairs.

2. One platoon should lay out a "no man's land" of obstacles, while the other platoon plans a surprise" charge."

3. "Troops" on each side of the room should then describe what their actions or reactions might be during a charge.

▶ Key Ideas

BEFORE, YOU LEARNED
After the outbreak of World War I, the United States eventually joined the Allies to fight against the Central Powers.

NOW YOU WILL LEARN
The war required sacrifice for Americans at home and changed their daily lives.

▶ Vocabulary

TERMS & NAMES

American Expeditionary Forces (EK•speh •DISH•uh•nair•ee) the American army that fought in Europe in World War I

General John J. Pershing commander of American forces in Europe in World War I

war bonds a low-interest loan by civilians to the government meant to be repaid in a number of years

War Industries Board managed the buying and distributing of war materials; set goals for production, ordered construction of new factories and with the president's approval, also set prices.

Committee on Public Information government organization that produced propaganda to build support for the war

Espionage Act (ESS•PEE•eh•nazh) 1917 law that set heavy fines and long prison terms for antiwar activities

Sedition Act (seh•DISH•un) 1918 law that made it illegal to criticize the government

BACKGROUND

propaganda opinions expressed for the purpose of influencing the actions of others

Visual Vocabulary
propaganda poster

▶ Reading Strategy

Re-create the diagram shown at right. As you read and respond to the **KEY QUESTIONS**, use the center box to record the main idea; use the outer ovals to note important details. Add ovals or start a new diagram as needed.

 See Skillbuilder Handbook, page R4.

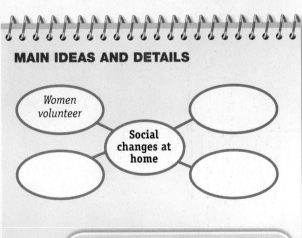

MAIN IDEAS AND DETAILS

Women volunteer

Social changes at home

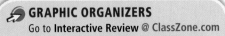

GRAPHIC ORGANIZERS
Go to **Interactive Review** @ ClassZone.com

America Prepares for War

14.D.3 Describe roles and influences of individuals, groups and media in shaping current Illinois and United States public policy (e.g., *general public opinion, special interest groups, formal parties, media*).

14.E.3 Compare the basic principles of the United States and its international interests (e.g., *territory, environment, trade, use of technology*).

One American's Story

Helen Burrey (1892–1987) was one of the first Army nurses to go to France in 1917. She worked on trains evacuating wounded soldiers from the battlefields.

PRIMARY SOURCE

❝ The third [trip] was to a small town outside of Chateau-Thierry. It was after dark when we got there and we immediately started to load our train with patients that had been gassed. At the height of our work, we had an alarm of the enemy airplanes which meant all lights out and we had to work in the dark getting as many patients under shelter as possible. We loaded our train without keeping count of the patients that could walk. After the train pulled out and we got to a place of safety, the lights were turned on and we found we had patients everywhere, in the berths, on the seats and crowded in the aisle. ❞

—Helen Burrey, quoted in the *Official History* of *the Red Cross*, 1920

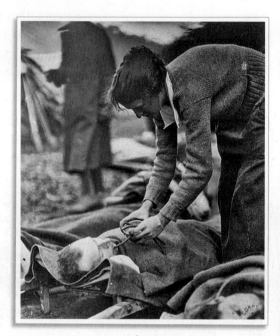

Helen Burrey

American nurses like Burrey volunteered to help wounded soldiers. They and millions of other Americans served their country during World War I.

Raising an Army and a Navy

🔻 **KEY QUESTION** What social changes did the war effort help bring about?

The U.S. Army in 1917 was not ready for war on the scale being waged in Europe. American military forces consisted of about 200,000 soldiers, many of them recent recruits. Because so many people were needed for the war effort, the government began a draft. It was also forced to adopt policies that led to great social change.

Connecting History

A draft system of choosing people for forced military service was first used in the United States during the Civil War. The draft caused riots.

The Selective Service Act In May 1917, Congress passed the Selective Service Act. This act required all males between the ages of 21 and 30 to sign up for military service. By the end of 1918, nearly 3 million men had been drafted.

About 2 million American soldiers went to France. They served as the **American Expeditionary Forces** (EK•speh•DISH•uh•nair•ee), or AEF, under **General John J. Pershing**. British commanders asked the U.S. government to have AEF troops join existing French and British combat units. Pershing refused, and Wilson supported him. Wilson believed that having "distinct and separate" American combat units would guarantee the United States a major role in the peace talks when the war ended.

Around 400,000 African Americans served in the armed forces. More than half of them served in France. As they had at home, African-American troops overseas faced discrimination. However, it came from white American soldiers rather than European allies. At first, the Army used African-American troops as laborers only and refused to let them participate in combat. Responding to pressure from African-American groups, the military eventually created two African-American combat divisions.

Women Volunteer Nearly 40,000 American women also served in World War I. Some volunteered for overseas duty with the American Red Cross. Women were also allowed to serve in the military as non-combatants. The Navy, desperate for clerical workers, took about 12,000 female volunteers.

ONLINE PRIMARY SOURCE

For more on women in the military, go to the **Research & Writing Center** @ ClassZone.com

CONNECT To Today

Silver Star medal

WOMEN IN THE MILITARY

During World War I, over 35,000 women entered the military. Most were nurses. Over 250 women served in the U.S. Army Signal Corps as bilingual operators connecting soldiers to officers behind the lines.

Today there are over 200,000 women on active duty in the U.S. armed forces and 1.6 million women veterans. Whether they are fighter pilots, commanding officers, or enlisted soldiers, women have distinguished themselves in combat. National Guard Sergeant Leigh Ann Hester is one of them. She is the first woman since World War II to receive the Silver Star, which she earned for her bravery during an ambush in Iraq.

CRITICAL THINKING **Compare and Contrast** How do women's roles in the military today compare to their roles during World War I?

Sergeant Leigh Ann Hester

The Marine Corps accepted 305 female recruits, known as Marinettes. Over 1,000 women like Helen Burrey went overseas for the Army. Many became nurses. Women also worked as interpreters, operated switchboards, entertained troops, and drove AEF ambulances.

▲ **MAIN IDEAS & DETAILS** List some of the social changes that the war effort helped to create.

The Government Mobilizes the Population

▼ **KEY QUESTION** How did American civilians contribute to the war effort?

The scale of the conflict in Europe was overwhelming. To fight such a war, the government began to mobilize the entire civilian population to help with the war effort.

Civilians Raise Money and Economize To prepare for war, the government needed money. World War I cost the United States $35.5 billion. Americans helped pay more than $20 billion by buying **war bonds**. War bonds were low-interest loans by civilians to the government, meant to be repaid in a number of years. To sell the bonds, officials held Liberty Loan drives.

Civilians economized by conserving scarce resources. Children rolled bandages and collected tin cans, paper, toothpaste tubes, and cherry pits. The pits were burned and made into charcoal for gas mask filters. Women's groups came together in homes and churches to knit socks and sweaters and sew hospital gowns. People planted "victory gardens" in backyards and vacant lots to become more self-reliant so that more food could be sent to soldiers. Patriotic citizens also saved food by observing wheatless or meatless days when they ate no bread or no meat. To save gas, they stopped their Sunday pleasure drives. The government limited civilian use of steel and other metals.

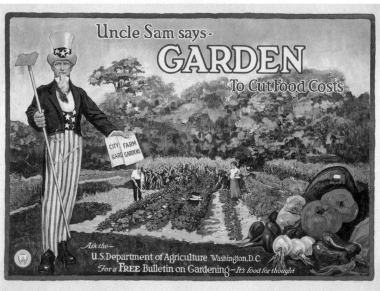

Victory garden poster
Why did Americans plant victory gardens?

Controlling the Economy and Information The war effort led to more government control of the economy. In 1917, President Wilson set up the **War Industries Board** to produce needed war supplies. The board had great power. It managed the buying and distributing of war materials. It also set production goals, ordered construction of new factories, and controlled wages and prices. Another government agency, the National War Labor Board, settled conflicts between workers and factory owners.

Schenck v. United States (1919)

Historic Decisions of the SUPREME COURT

KEY ISSUE Freedom of speech during wartime
KEY PEOPLE Charles T. Schenck, socialist war protester
Justice Oliver Wendell Holmes Jr., Supreme Court justice.

The Case

Charles T. Schenck was a socialist who was against American participation in World War I. Schenck printed leaflets that called the draft a crime and urged people to work for the repeal of the Selective Service Act. Schenck was arrested and convicted for violating the Espionage Act by trying to block military recruitment. He appealed his conviction to the United States Supreme Court. Schenck had argued that the Espionage Act violated his First Amendment right to free speech.

HISTORICAL IMPACT On March 3, 1919, in a unanimous decision, the Court upheld Schenck's conviction. Justice Oliver Wendell Holmes, Jr., wrote the Court's opinion, saying that the right of free speech was not protected when it created "a clear and present danger" to the nation's interests. Schenck's pamphlet, Holmes charged, endangered the U.S. war effort and therefore did not merit protection under the First Amendment. Schenck served time in federal prison for his offense.

CRITICAL THINKING **Form and Support Opinions** Explain whether you agree or disagree with the Court's opinion in Schenck v. United States.

To rally citizen support, Wilson created the **Committee on Public Information**. The committee produced **propaganda**, opinions expressed for the purpose of influencing the actions of others. The committee sold the war through posters, pamphlets, and movies.

Attacks on Civil Liberties and Dissent Patriotic propaganda did much to win support for the war. However, its anti-German, anti-foreign focus also fueled prejudice. Suddenly people distrusted anything German. A number of towns with German names changed their names. Berlin, Iowa, was renamed Lincoln. German shepherd owners called their pets "police dogs."

On June 15, 1917, Congress passed the **Espionage Act** (ESS•pee•eh•nazh). The **Sedition Act** (seh•DISH•un) followed in May 1918. These laws set heavy fines and long prison terms for such antiwar activities as encouraging draft resisters. U.S. courts tried several thousand pacifists, socialists, and other war critics. At least 1,000 went to jail. Socialist Party leader Eugene Debs gave a speech arguing that the war was fought by poor working men for the profit of wealthy business owners. For this talk, a judge sentenced Debs to ten years in prison.

The government ignored complaints that the rights of Americans were being trampled. In the 1919 decision in *Schenck* v. *United States*, the Supreme Court upheld the Espionage Act. Charles T. Schenck (SHEHNK), convicted of distributing pamphlets against the draft, had argued that the Espionage Act violated his right to free speech. Justice Oliver Wendell Homes, Jr. wrote the Court's opinion:

PRIMARY SOURCE

❝ When a nation is at war, many things that might be said in time of peace are such a hindrance to its effort that their utterance will not be endured so long as men fight. ❞

—Supreme Court Justice Oliver Wendell Holmes, Jr.

The Supreme Court declared that free speech, guaranteed by the First Amendment, could be limited, especially in wartime.

 MAIN IDEAS & DETAILS Explain how Americans at home contributed to the war effort.

Justice Oliver Wendell Holmes, Jr.

Illinois Learning Standards *Review*

🔁 **ONLINE QUIZ**
For test practice, go to
Interactive Review @ ClassZone.com

TERMS & NAMES

1. Explain the importance of
- American Expeditionary Force
- General John J. Pershing
- war bonds
- War Industries Board
- Committee on Public Information
- Espionage Act
- Sedition Act

USING YOUR READING NOTES

2. Main Idea and Details Complete the diagram you started at the beginning of this section. Then create a diagram for each of the other main ideas.

KEY IDEAS

3. Why did Congress pass the Selective Service Act in 1917?

4. Why did Americans buy war bonds?

5. What did the Committee on Public Information do?

CRITICAL THINKING

6. Draw Conclusions How do you think the government's use of propaganda affected Americans' ability to form their own thoughts about the war and government policy?

7. Compare and Contrast Compare the way African-American troops were treated by other American troops to how they were treated by European troops.

8. Writing **Speech** Give a speech in which you explain whether or not free speech should be limited when the United States is at war.

Reading for Understanding

▶ Key Ideas

BEFORE, YOU LEARNED

The war required sacrifice for Americans at home and changed their daily lives.

NOW YOU WILL LEARN

U.S. forces helped the Allies win World War I.

▶ Vocabulary

TERMS & NAMES

Eddie Rickenbacker (RICK•ehn•BAHK•er) the American "ace of aces"

Belleau Wood (beh•LOH) site of American victory in France in 1918

Second Battle of the Marne battle that was the turning point of the war

Alvin York Tennessee-born soldier whose action in the Argonne Forest made him an American hero

BACKGROUND VOCABULARY

convoy a guard that accompanies and protects ships or troops

armistice (AR•mih•stiss) an end to the fighting

epidemic outbreak of a contagious disease that spreads rapidly and widely

Visual Vocabulary
convoy

▶ Reading Strategy

Re-create the diagram shown at right. As you read and respond to the **KEY QUESTIONS**, use the diagram to place events in the proper sequence.

 See Skillbuilder Handbook, page R5.

SEQUENCE EVENTS

Belleau Wood

Armistice

GRAPHIC ORGANIZERS
Go to **Interactive Review** @ ClassZone.com

Pushing the Germans Back

16.B.3d Describe ways in which the United States developed as a world political power.
18.B.3a Analyze how individuals and groups interact with and within institutions (e.g., *educational, military*).

One American's Story

Eddie Rickenbacker (RICK•ehn•BAHK•er) was America's most famous flying ace. He was one of the first Americans to get a look at the trenches from the cockpit of an airplane.

PRIMARY SOURCE

❝ [T]here appeared to be nothing below me but old battered trenches . . . and billions of shell holes. . . . Not a tree, a fence . . . nothing but . . . ruin and desolation. The awfulness of the whole thing was truly appalling. ❞

—Eddie Rickenbacker, *Fighting the Flying Circus*

The United States sent Rickenbacker and other U.S. soldiers to Europe after declaring war on the Central Powers and joining the Allies in 1917.

Flying ace Eddie Rickenbacker

American Troops Enter the War

🔻 **KEY QUESTION** How did American troops help the Allies win the war?

By the time the first American troops arrived in France in June 1917, the Allies had been at war for almost three years. The small force of 14,000 "Yanks" boosted the morale of the battle-weary Allies. Almost a year would pass before the bulk of the American troops landed in Europe.

American Ships Make a Difference In the first years of the war, German U-boat attacks on supply ships were a serious threat to the Allied war effort. American Rear Admiral William S. Sims convinced the Allies to adopt a system of protection. In a **convoy** system, a heavy guard of destroyers escorted merchant ships across the Atlantic in groups. Begun in May 1917, this strategy quickly reduced the rate of lost ships.

U.S. General John J. Pershing inspects French troops in Boulogne, France on June 13, 1917. **What was General Pershing's role in World War I?**

Another American tactic helped protect the Allies from the U-boat menace. Beginning in 1918, the Allies laid a barrier of 70,000 mines in the North Sea. The minefield made U-boat access to the North Atlantic almost impossible.

Just in Time With Russia out of the war, in March 1918 the Germans launched an offensive to end the war before the Americans arrived in force. Within two months, they had smashed through the French lines, reaching the Marne River only 50 miles from Paris. By midsummer 1918, there would be one million fresh American troops ready to fight.

Americans Take Cantigny On May 28, American soldiers attacked the French town of Cantigny, which was occupied by the Germans. The soldiers advanced into the town, blasting enemy soldiers out of trenches. Within two hours, the Yanks had taken control of Cantigny (kahn•tee•NYEE). The American victory lifted Allied morale.

In June 1918, the Germans moved against the town of Château-Thierry (shah•TOH•tye•REE) to the southeast of Cantigny and northeast of Paris. The Americans counterattacked on June 3–4 and halted the German advance on Paris. Next, General Pershing and the AEF set out to retake **Belleau Wood** (beh•LOH). This was a forest near the Marne River well defended by German troops. American soldiers succeeded, but at a horrific cost. One unit lost 380 of its 400 men.

The Turning Point The **Second Battle of the Marne** was the turning point of the war. It began in the summer of 1918 with a German drive against the French line. During three days of heavy fighting, about 85,000 Americans helped the Allies halt the German advance. The Allies then took the initiative and forced the Germans back.

By early September, the Germans had lost all the territory they had gained since the spring. September 26, 1918, marked the beginning of the final Meuse-Argonne (myooz•ahr•GAHN) offensive. Around 1.2 million U.S. soldiers took part in a massive drive to push back the German line between the Argonne Forest and the Meuse River. The war's final battle left 26,000 Americans dead. But by November, the Germans were retreating.

The Meuse-Argonne offensive made a hero of American soldier **Alvin York**. Sergeant York had refused to bear arms because of his religious beliefs, until his superiors changed his mind. In October 1918, in the Argonne Forest, York

London

GREAT BRITAIN

10°E   60°N

NETHERLANDS

Brussels

BELGIUM

Lille

Amiens

1

Paris

3   4

2

5

Metz

FRANCE

ARGONNE FOREST

English Channel

Somme

Seine

Marne

Meuse

Rhine

LUXEMBOURG

GERMANY

0°   50°N   N   W   E   S

0   50   100 miles
0   50   100 kilometers

Allies

Central Powers

Neutral nations

Deepest German advance, July

Allied drive, late summer and autumn

Armistice line, November 11

Allied victories, 1918

1 **Cantigny**, May

2 **Château-Thierry**, May

3 **Belleau Wood**, June

4 **2nd Battle of the Marne**, summer

5 **Meuse-Argonne**, autumn

Connect Geography & History
READING A MILITARY MAP

Military maps show opponents, the movement of forces, where battles happened, and, in some cases, alliances. When reading a military map, use

- the scale to estimate distance
- the key to identify alliances
- the key to identify battles and battlefronts

1. Location Which battle occurred closest to the Armistice line?

2. Movement In what two directions did the Allied drives move?

(*left*) Gas and flame attack at St. Mihiel, France, 1918

(*below*) German anti-aircraft machine gun crew wearing gas masks in gas zone

Nine members of the African-American 369th Infantry Regiment, each wearing the French *Croix de Guerre* medal, return to the United States in 1919 aboard the *SS Stockholm*.

attacked German machine gunners, killing 25 of them. Other German soldiers surrendered, and York returned to the U.S. lines with 132 captives.

Over 100 African-Americans were also recognized for their battlefield valor. For their service under French commanders, soldiers from the 369th regiment were awarded the *Croix de Guerre* and the Legions of Merit, two of France's highest military awards. The 369th spent more continuous time on the front lines than any other American unit. Another American hero was pilot Eddie Rickenbacker. He won fame as the U.S. "ace of aces" for shooting down a total of 26 enemy planes.

▲ **SEQUENCE EVENTS** List the steps U.S. troops took to help the Allies win the war.

The War Comes to an End

▼ **KEY QUESTION** What were the human costs of World War I and the 1918 flu epidemic?

Although the Germans were losing ground on the Western Front, they still controlled vast areas of land across Europe. However, with 10,000 Americans landing in France every day, the Germans knew that the Allies would win.

Germany Stops Fighting Before the defeat of the Meuse-Argonne, German General Erich Ludendorff advised his government to seek an **armistice** (AR•mih•stiss), an end to fighting. In early November, Germany's navy mutinied. Its allies Austria and Bulgaria had already dropped out. On November 9, the Kaiser stepped down. Two days later Germany agreed to an armistice. On November 11, 1918, at 11:00 A.M.—the 11th hour of the 11th day of the 11th month—all fighting ceased.

About 8.5 million soldiers died in the war, and about 21 million were

About 8.5 million soldiers died in the war, and about 21 million were wounded. One British soldier summed up the war's tragic costs.

PRIMARY SOURCE

❝ The sufferings of the men at the Front, of the wounded whose flesh and bodies are torn in a way you cannot conceive; the sorrow of those at home. . . . What a cruel and mad diversion of human activity! ❞

—William John Mason, quoted in *The Lost Generation of 1914*

There were fewer military deaths than civilian deaths during the war, however. An estimated 13 million civilians in Europe, Asia, and Africa died in the war from starvation and disease.

The Flu Epidemic of 1918 In 1918 and 1919, a deadly flu epidemic swept the globe. Worldwide, more than 20 million people died of the flu, including some 550,000 Americans. The flu had no known cure. Everywhere, schools and other public places shut down to limit the flu's spread. Soldiers in trenches were also at risk for catching it. In some AEF units, one-third of the troops died from the flu.

 CAUSES AND EFFECTS Name the human costs of World War I and the 1918 flu epidemic.

Military Deaths in World War I*

Lives lost (in millions) — France, Britain, Russia, Germany, Austria-Hungary, U.S.

*Not all countries are listed.   Source: *Over There*, by Byron Farwell

CRITICAL THINKING Analyze Graphs About how many European military deaths were there during World War I?

Illinois Learning Standards *Review*

ONLINE QUIZ
For test practice, go to
Interactive Review @ ClassZone.com

TERMS & NAMES

1. Explain the importance of
  • Eddie Rickenbacker
  • Second Battle of the Marne
  • Belleau Wood
  • Alvin York

USING YOUR READING NOTES

2. Sequence Events Complete the diagram you started at the beginning of this section. Then create a diagram that places other war events in sequence.

KEY IDEAS

3. What was the convoy system?

4. What happened at Cantigny?

5. How did American troops impact Germany's decision to surrender?

CRITICAL THINKING

6. Draw Conclusions Why do you think Sergeant Alvin York's actions made him a hero?

7. Problems and Solutions Why were German U-boats a problem for the Allies?

8. (**Connect** *to* **Today**) How might your life change if a deadly flu epidemic swept the United States today?

9. (**Art**) Create a piece of art that shows the accomplishments of Eddie Rickenbacker, Sergeant Alvin York, or the 369th regiment.

▶ Key Ideas

BEFORE, YOU LEARNED
U.S. forces helped the Allies win World War I.

NOW YOU WILL LEARN
The war left Americans divided over foreign policy and domestic issues.

▶ Vocabulary

TERMS & NAMES

Fourteen Points President Woodrow Wilson's goals for peace after World War I

League of Nations an organization set up after World War I to settle international conflicts

Treaty of Versailles (ver•SYE) the 1919 treaty that ended World War I

reparations (REHP•eh•RAY•shunz) money that a defeated nation pays for the destruction it caused in other countries

Great Migration the movement of African Americans from the South to northern cities between 1910–1920

Red Scare in 1919–1920 a fearful reaction that the United States was threatened by a Communist revolution

Palmer raids raids carried out by federal agents and police against radicals at the direction of U.S. Attorney-General A. Mitchell Palmer

▶ Reading Strategy

Recreate the diagram shown at right. As you read and respond to the **KEY QUESTIONS,** use the diagram to note important events and their effects. Add boxes or start a new diagram as needed.

 See **Skillbuilder Handbook, page R7.**

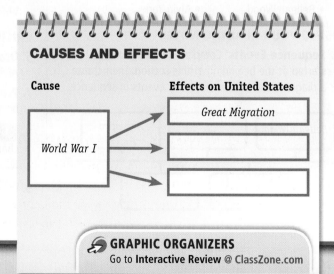

CAUSES AND EFFECTS

Cause

Effects on United States

World War I

Great Migration

GRAPHIC ORGANIZERS
Go to **Interactive Review** @ ClassZone.com

The Legacy of World War I

 14.C.3 Compare historical issues involving rights, roles and status of individuals in relation to municipalities, states and the nation.
14.D.3 Describe roles and influences of individuals, groups and media in shaping current Illinois and United States public policy (e.g., *general public opinion, special interest groups, formal parties, media*).

One American's Story

Wayne DeSilvey (deh•SIL•vee) was a young soldier from Harrisburg, Pennsylvania. During the war, he served as a bugler in the 112th Infantry Division. De Silvey was wounded and gassed in an attack on November 11, 1918, the last day of the war. Here he describes his return to America with other U.S. troops.

American veterans and citizens at a peace celebration, 1919

PRIMARY SOURCE

❝ March 24, 1919 Entered N.Y. Harbor. Mayor Committee of Welcome came to meet us & band began to play "Home Sweet Home." Crowd began to cheer. As we steamed up the Bay, we all crowded to one side of the boat, almost upsetting the boat. . . . Passed the Statue of Liberty & such whooping & cheering one never heard. ❞

—Bugler Wayne DeSilvey, 112th Infantry Regiment, AEF, in his diary

DeSilvey spent several months in Europe and two days in a hospital in New York City before being discharged from the army and returning home to Harrisburg. He eventually died from the effects of the gassing. People on both sides of the war wanted to prevent such losses from happening again.

Woodrow Wilson's Plans for Peace

🔻 **KEY QUESTION** How did Woodrow Wilson hope to achieve world peace?

President Woodrow Wilson hoped to prevent a conflict like World War I from ever happening again. So, in January 1918, ten months before the war ended, Wilson told Congress about his radical new plan for peace. His speech became known as the **Fourteen Points**. (See Reading Primary Sources

History Makers

Woodrow Wilson   1856–1924

Woodrow Wilson, born in Virginia, was the first Southerner to become president since the Civil War. Wilson was committed to progressive policies such as banking reform and antitrust regulation, but was reluctant to support woman suffrage, and allowed racial segregation in federal agencies. Wilson won the 1919 Nobel Peace Prize for creating the League of Nations. After becoming ill during his cross-country speaking tour to promote the Treaty of Versailles, Wilson suffered a stroke on October 2, 1919, from which he never fully recovered.

CRITICAL THINKING Analyze Leadership Why do you think the ability to compromise is an important skill for political leaders?

ONLINE BIOGRAPHY   For more on Woodrow Wilson, go to the **Research & Writing Center** @ ClassZone.com

Connect Geography & History

1. **Region** What new nations were created after the Treaty of Versailles?

2. **Region** In what part of Europe were most of the new nations located?

Wilson's Fourteen Points Wilson's plan called for smaller military forces, an end to secret treaties, freedom of the seas, free trade, and changes in national boundaries. Most of these changes gave independence to peoples whom Austria-Hungary or the Ottoman Empire had ruled.

For Wilson, the fourteenth point mattered most. He called for a new association of nations called the **League of Nations**, whose purpose would be to peacefully settle disputes. Wilson firmly believed that acceptance of his Fourteen Points by the warring parties would bring about what he called a "peace without victory."

Treaty of Versailles Wilson led the U.S. delegation to the peace conference in France. The leaders of Britain, France, and Italy did not share Wilson's vision of "peace without victory." They wanted Germany to pay heavily for the war.

The **Treaty of Versailles** (ver•SYE) forced Germany to accept full blame for the war. Germany was stripped of its colonies and its military was limited to 100,000. It was also burdened with $33 billion in **reparations**, (REHP•eh•RAY•shunz)

Postwar Europe 1919

money that a defeated nation pays for the destruction caused by a war. The treaty divided up the empires of Austria-Hungary and the Ottomans. It created Czechoslovakia (CHEK•eh•slo•VAHK•ee•uh) and recognized Poland's independence.

Wilson managed to include the League of Nations in the treaty. He returned home to seek Senate approval for the treaty, but the Republican-run Senate was dead set against it. Senator Henry Cabot Lodge kept delaying a vote on the treaty. Lodge and his supporters offered to accept the treaty only if major changes were made in the League. Wilson refused to compromise. As a result, the United States did not ratify the treaty. The League of Nations was formed without the United States.

The Treaty of Versailles failed to make Europe "safe for democracy." In the next decades, Germany's economic burdens and resentment of the treaty would grow. The treaty planted the seeds of World War II, an even more deadly conflict that would yet again change the face of Europe.

▲ **MAIN IDEA & DETAILS** Explain how President Wilson thought world peace could be achieved.

African Americans wait in a segregated seating area at the Union Railroad Depot in Jacksonville, Florida. **Why did the Great Migration take place during the war?**

The War and Social Change

▼ **KEY QUESTION** What social changes did the war help bring about?

The massive mobilization of soldiers and civilians led to sweeping changes in American life—both during the war and after it ended. Some of these changes caused years of social conflict.

New Jobs and the Great Migration The war also provided new opportunities for African Americans. Northern factories gearing up for war were suddenly willing to hire workers they had once rejected. Throughout the South, African Americans heeded the call. Between 1910 and 1920, about 500,000 African Americans moved north to such cities as New York, Chicago,

Detroit, Cleveland, and St. Louis. This movement became known as the **Great Migration**. African Americans also left to escape the bigotry, poverty, and racial violence of the South.

Women Take On "Men's Work" As with the Civil War, new jobs opened for women during World War I. With millions of men serving in the military, women replaced male workers in steel mills, ammunition factories, and assembly lines on the home front. Women served as streetcar conductors and elevator operators. After the war, women workers were laid off to create positions for returning veterans. Many women found that they enjoyed their work, however, and continued to look for jobs after the war.

Strikes and the Red Scare Labor conflicts divided Americans after the war when the nation had a number of strikes. Federal regulators had kept workers' wages low during the war. Workers expected a postwar wage increase, but did not get one. In February 1919, more than 55,000 workers in Seattle, Washington held a peaceful general strike to demand better wages. The shutdown paralyzed the city.

CONNECT to the Essential Question

How did World War I impact America and transform Europe?

United States

- Increased involvement in world affairs during the war
- Women move into the work place and win suffrage
- Great Migration
- Civilian participation in war effort
- Stifling of dissent with Espionage and Sedition Acts
- Strikes and social turmoil
- Acclaim for African-American soldiers
- Racial tension and violence
- Withdrawal from world leadership with Senate rejection of Treaty of Versailles

Europe

- Destruction of land and cities
- Deaths of millions of young men
- Millions of civilian deaths
- Breakup of empires
- Independence for Czechoslovakia
- Formation of League of Nations
- German resentment at Treaty of Versailles which led to World War II

CRITICAL THINKING

1. **Compare and Contrast** Where did most of the war's destruction take place?

2. **Analyze** Which changes happened as a result of civilian participation in the war effort?

The strikes sparked fears of a communist revolution like the one that toppled the Russian czar. In 1919–1920, this fear created a reaction called the **Red Scare**. Public fear was heightened by the discovery of mail bombs sent to government officials. Many believed the bombs were the work of anarchists, radicals who do not believe in any form of government.

In January 1920, Attorney General A. Mitchell Palmer ordered a raid of the homes and headquarters of suspected radicals, people who use extreme measures to bring about change. Palmer's agents arrested at least 6,000 people without search warrants in what became known as the **Palmer raids**.

The Red Scare was not only anti-radical but also anti-foreign. Two Italian-born anarchists, Nicola Sacco (NEE•koh•lah•SAHK•koh)and Bartolomeo Vanzetti (bar•tah•loh•MAY•oh•van•ZEHT•tee), were arrested for killing two men in an armed robbery. Despite claiming innocence, they were found guilty and executed.

Bartolomeo Vanzetti (*left*) and Nicola Sacco
What effect did the Red Scare have on Sacco and Vanzetti?

Racial Conflict Racial tensions increased after the war and the Great Migration. White vigilantes lynched African Americans before mobs. In most cases, the victims had been arrested on false evidence. In the northern cities, whites and blacks competed for factory jobs. Simmering resentments over housing, jobs, and segregation exploded during the summer of 1919. Over 20 race riots flared in cities around the country.

CAUSES AND EFFECTS List social changes that developed after the war.

 Illinois Learning Standards *Review*

ONLINE QUIZ
For test practice, go to
Interactive Review @ ClassZone.com

TERMS & NAMES

1. Explain the importance of:
   - Fourteen Points
   - League of Nations
   - Treaty of Versailles
   - reparations
   - Great Migration
   - Red Scare
   - Palmer raids

USING YOUR READING NOTES

2. **Causes and Effects** Complete the diagram you started at the beginning of this section. Then create a diagram for each of the other main events.

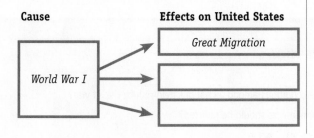

Cause

Effects on United States

World War I

Great Migration

KEY IDEAS

3. What were some of Woodrow Wilson's ideas for achieving world peace?

4. How did World War I affect African Americans?

CRITICAL THINKING

5. **Analyze Point of View** Why do you think Wilson refused to compromise in the battle over ratifying the Treaty of Versailles?

6. **Causes and Effects** Explain the effect that postwar labor strikes had on American society.

7. **Connect** *to* **Today** What international organization today is most like the League of Nations? How are the roles of the two organizations similar?

8. **Writing** Research Report Use the Internet to research women's work during and after the war. Write a brief report explaining how women's work changed during this time.

Reading Primary Sources

The Fourteen Points

SETTING THE STAGE Nine months after the United States entered World War I, President Wilson gave a speech to Congress in which he proposed 14 ways to reduce the risk of war in the future. The proposals became known as the "Fourteen Points."

Open Covenants

Wilson's first point tries to solve one of the problems that caused World War I—secret agreements between nations.

1. How might public agreements between nations prevent war?

Fairness

Wilson appeals to fairness, balance, and impartiality in settling competing claims.

2. What was unusual about Wilson's call for an impartial adjustment of colonial claims?

A World Organization

Wilson proposes that nations join a formal organization to protect one another.

3. Why did Wilson believe that such an organization would benefit the world?

All the peoples of the world are in effect partners . . . , and for our own part we see very clearly that unless justice be done to others it will not be done to us. The program of the world's peace, therefore, is our program; and that program, . . . as we see it, is this:

[1] Open **covenants**[1] of peace, openly arrived at, after which there shall be no private international understandings of any kind but diplomacy shall proceed always frankly and in the public view.

[2] Absolute freedom of navigation upon the seas . . . in peace and in war. . . .

[3] The removal, so far as possible, of all economic barriers and the establishment of an equality of trade conditions among all the nations. . . .

[4] Adequate guarantees given and taken that national **armaments**[2] will be reduced. . . .

[5] A free, open-minded, and absolutely impartial adjustment of all colonial claims, based upon . . . the principal that . . . the interests of the populations concerned must have equal weight with the . . . claims of the government whose title is to be determined.

[6–13: These eight points deal with specific boundary changes.]

[14] A general association of nations must be formed under specific covenants for the purpose of affording mutual guarantees of political independence and territorial **integrity**[3] to great and small states alike.

—Woodrow Wilson

----

1. **covenants:** binding agreements

2. **armaments:** weapons and supplies of war

3. **integrity:** the condition of being whole or undivided; completeness

DOCUMENT-BASED QUESTIONS

Short-Answer

1. Why would equality of trade conditions among all nations help reduce risk of war?

2. Why did Wilson think that armaments should be reduced?

Extended Answer

3. Explain how Wilson's Fourteen Points might reduce the risk of war between nations.

Chapter Summary

1 **Key Idea**
After the outbreak of World War I, the United States eventually joined the Allies to fight against the Central Powers.

2 **Key Idea**
The war required sacrifice for Americans at home and changed their daily lives.

3 **Key Idea**
U.S. forces helped the Allies win World War I.

4 **Key Idea**
The war left Americans divided over foreign policy and domestic issues.

For detailed Review and Study Notes go to **Interactive Review** @ ClassZone.com

Name Game

Use the Terms & Names list to complete each sentence online or on your own paper.

1. The _____ were Woodrow Wilson's goals for peace.
   Fourteen Points

2. African Americans moved from the South to northern cities during the _____.

3. Germany was part of this alliance during the war. _____

4. I commanded American forces during World War I. _____

5. This was the turning point of World War I. _____

6. My action in the Argonne Forest made me a hero.

7. Germany agreed to an _____ on November 11, 1918.

8. I was the American president during World War I. _____

9. The Allies and Germans signed the _____ after the war.

10. My assassination sparked the war. _____

A. General Pershing
B. Treaty of Versailles
C. Second Battle of the Marne
D. Fourteen Points
E. Sergeant Alvin York
F. armistice
G. Great Migration
H. Allies
I. League of Nations
J. Woodrow Wilson
K. Central Powers
L. Austria-Hungary
M. Belleau Wood
N. Archduke Franz Ferdinand
O. Red Baron

Activities

CROSSWORD PUZZLE

Complete the online puzzle to show what you know about World War I.

ACROSS

1. **American World War I flying ace Eddie _____.**

GEOGAME

Use this online map to reinforce your understanding of the sequence of events that led to World War I. Drag and drop each event on the list at its location on the map. A score card helps you keep track of your progress online.

Archduke Franz Ferdinand is assassinated

Austria-Hungary declares war on Serbia.

Russia mobilizes armed forces

VOCABULARY

Match the term or name in the left hand column with its definition or identification in the right.

1. American Expeditionary Forces
2. militarism
3. convoy
4. Allies
5. Zimmermann telegram

A. Great Britain, France, Russia
B. told German ambassador to ask Mexico to declare war on the United States
C. guard that protects ships
D. American army in Europe
E. making military power a primary goal

Explain how the terms and names in each group are related.

6. War Bonds, War Industries Board, Committee on Public Information
7. Alvin York, Eddie Rickenbacker
8. Fourteen Points, League of Nations, Treaty of Versailles

KEY IDEAS

① War Breaks Out in Europe (pages 720–725)

9. What was trench warfare?
10. Why did the German sinking of the *Lusitania* make Americans angry?

② America Prepares for War (pages 728–733)

11. What military jobs did women do during World War I?
12. How did civilians help aid the war effort?

③ Pushing the Germans Back (pages 734–739)

13. How did U.S. ships help the Allies in World War I?
14. Which battle was the turning point of World War I?

④ The Legacy of World War I (pages 740–745)

15. What were Wilson's plan for peace?
16. Why did the Senate reject the Treaty of Versailles?

CRITICAL THINKING

17. **Analyzing Leadership** Woodrow Wilson was reelected in 1916 campaigning on his keeping America out of war. A month after being inaugurated for a second term, he asked Congress for a declaration of war. Do you think Wilson showed leadership by changing his mind? Explain.

18. **Causes and Effects** How did America's entry into World War I and the Russian Revolution influence the outcome of the war?

19. **Compare and Contrast** How did Wilson's goals of making the world safe for democracy contrast with his actions at home during the war?

Use the images below and your knowledge of U.S. history to answer questions 20 and 21.

20. **Problems and Solutions** Why did Americans buy war bonds during World War I?

21. **Recognize Bias and Propaganda** What images and words did the posters use to persuade viewers to buy war bonds?

"SHALL WE BE MORE TENDER WITH OUR DOLLARS THAN WITH THE LIVES OF OUR SONS?" *McAdoo*
SECRETARY OF THE TREASURY

BUY A LIBERTY BOND

WE DEPEND ON YOU

YOU buy a Liberty Bond TO-DAY I'LL do the rest

ONLY BUYERS OF LIBERTY BONDS WEAR THIS BUTTON

MULTIPLE CHOICE

Read questions 1–3 and choose the best answer.

1. What did the Germans use to attack Allied shipping during World War I?

   A. U-boats

   B. convoys

   C. the *Lusitania*

   D. trench warfare

2. Sacco and Vanzetti were arrested during the _____

   A. Red Scare

   B. Palmer raids

   C. Espionage Act

   D. Great Migration

3. Which of the following was an underlying cause of World War I?

   A. Sedition Act

   B. European alliances

   C. Zimmermann telegram

   D. The Fourteen Points

The German Embassy placed the following notice near an advertisement for the *Lusitania*. Use the notice and your knowledge of U.S. history to answer question 4.

PRIMARY SOURCE

❝ NOTICE! TRAVELLERS intending to embark on the Atlantic voyage are reminded that. . . vessels flying the flag of Great Britain, or any of her allies, are liable to destruction. . .❞

—Imperial German Embassy, April 22, 1915

4. In the notice, the German embassy tells travelers

   A. to sail on German ships

   B. British ships might be sunk

   C. the war will not affect their safety

   D. to ignore all warnings from Germany

YOU BE THE HISTORIAN

22. **WHAT IF?** How might the course of the war been affected if Germany had been successful in getting Mexico to declare war on the United States?

23. **Causes and Effects** How did World War I help cause the Russian Revolution?

24. **Evaluate** If Woodrow Wilson thought the League of Nations was the most important point of the Treaty of Versailles, what do you think he should have done to insure ratification of the treaty?

25. **Analyze** How did the events in the United States immediately following World War I influence the fate of the Treaty of Versailles in the U.S. Senate?

26. **Connect** *to* **Today** How effective do you think the United Nations would be today if the United States withdrew as a member nation?

 Answer the
ESSENTIAL QUESTION
How did World War I impact America and transform Europe?

Written Response Write a two- to three-paragraph response to the Essential Question. Be sure to consider the key ideas of each section as well as the significant changes the war made to Americans at home and the international standing of the United States in the world.

Response Rubric
A strong response will

• discuss the social changes brought on by the war

• evaluate Wilson's political leadership at home and abroad

• analyze how the achievements of African Americans inspired a racist reaction

CHAPTER 24

1. Postwar Economics and Politics

2. The Jazz Age and Popular Culture

3. The Harlem Renaissance

The Roaring Twenties

1919–1929

 ESSENTIAL QUESTION

How did American society change during the 1920s?

CONNECT Geography & History

What economic activities helped drive U.S. prosperity in the 1920s?

Think about:

1 population growth and migration

2 why cities became leading economic centers

3 the importance of transportation

This 1920s magazine cover captures the carefree spirit of the decade.

Women vote in their first national election in 1920.

Warren G. Harding

1919

United States moves to a peacetime economy.

1920 Prohibition takes effect.

Warren G. Harding is elected president.

1923 Harding dies in office.

▼

Effect Calvin Coolidge becomes president. U.S. economy booms.

Personal Income in the U.S. *1927*

Click here to explore the Roaring Twenties @ClassZone.com

CANADA

WASHINGTON $185

MONTANA $112

NORTH DAKOTA $63

MINNESOTA $129

MAINE $150

OREGON $188

IDAHO $84

SOUTH DAKOTA $63

WISCONSIN $174

VT. $136

N.H. $174

MASS. $320

WYOMING $150

IOWA $96

MICHIGAN $250

NEW YORK $542

R.I. $252

CONN. $309

NEVADA $255

UTAH $119

NEBRASKA $115

ILLINOIS $319

INDIANA $124

OHIO $195

PENNSYLVANIA $249

N.J. $343

Washington, D.C. $433

DEL. $432

CALIFORNIA $423

COLORADO $165

KANSAS $103

MISSOURI $169

KENTUCKY $81

W. VA. $101

VIRGINIA $82

MARYLAND $279

ARIZONA $115

NEW MEXICO $78

OKLAHOMA $112

ARKANSAS $49

TENNESSEE $82

NORTH CAROLINA $70

SOUTH CAROLINA $39

MISS. $47

ALABAMA $63

GEORGIA $66

TEXAS $132

LOUISIANA $112

FLORIDA $209

MEXICO

ATLANTIC OCEAN

Gulf of Mexico

Per Capita Income, 1927

Under $100
$101 to $200
$201 to $300
Over $300

Louis Armstrong brought jazz from its birthplace in New Orleans to the North in the 1920s.

1924 Coolidge is elected.
▼
Effect Influence of business grows.

1927 Charles Lindbergh makes first solo flight across the Atlantic.

1929

1925 Jazz Age and Harlem Renaissance are in full swing.
▼
Effect American culture changes dramatically.

UNITED STATES POSTAGE
LINDBERGH AIR MAIL
NEW YORK
10 CENTS 10

► Key Ideas

BEFORE, YOU LEARNED

The devastation of World War I and the turmoil of 1919 changed life in America in significant ways.

NOW YOU WILL LEARN

During the 1920s, most Americans were eager for a "return to normalcy" and prosperity.

► Vocabulary

TERMS & NAMES

Warren G. Harding 29th president, served from 1921–1923 with a focus on peace abroad and prosperity at home

assembly line manufacturing using a conveyor belt to move materials to workers who stay in one place to work

installment buying paying for items in small monthly payments

Teapot Dome Scandal corruption by a Harding cabinet member, who took bribes to allow oil drilling on public lands

Calvin Coolidge 30th president, served from 1923–1929 with a pro-business aim

laissez-faire economics theory that business, if free of government regulation, will act in ways that benefit the nation

BACKGROUND VOCABULARY

credit arrangement for delayed payment of a loan or purchase

REVIEW

tariff tax on imported goods

► Reading Strategy

Re-create the diagram shown at right. As you read and respond to the **KEY QUESTIONS**, use the diagram to record important events in the order in which they occurred.

 Skillbuilder Handbook, page R5.

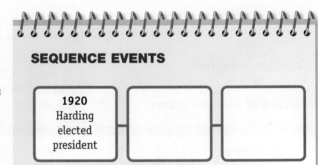

SEQUENCE EVENTS

1920 Harding elected president		

 GRAPHIC ORGANIZERS
Go to **Interactive Review** @ ClassZone.com

Postwar Economics and Politics

 15.C.3 Identify and explain the effects of various incentives to produce a good or service.
16.C.3c Describe how economic developments and government policies after 1865 affected the country's economic institutions including corporations, banks and organized labor.

One American's Story

From 1908 to 1927, the Ford Motor Company sold over 15 million Model T cars, making owner Henry Ford one of the world's first billionaires. The Model T sold well because it was very affordable. To keep costs down, Ford used new manufacturing methods and sold the Model T in just one color—black.

PRIMARY SOURCE

❝ I will build a car for the great multitude. It will be large enough for the family, but small enough for the individual to run and care for. It will be constructed of the best materials. . . . But it will be so low in price. . . . ❞

—Henry Ford, quoted in *My Life and Work*, 1922

Henry Ford stands with one of his first Model Ts (right) and his 10 millionth.

However, by the mid-1920s, Ford's rival, Alfred Sloan of General Motors, saw that Americans wanted more stylish cars. Sloan began producing new models to meet these changing demands. His motto was: "A car for every purse and purpose." In 1927, Ford stopped producing Model Ts—and General Motors became the nation's leading car maker. The car symbolized American freedom, ingenuity, and prosperity in the 1920s.

America After World War I

🔻 **KEY QUESTION** What did Warren G. Harding offer Americans as president?

The 1920s did not get off to a roaring start. As you learned, 1919 had been a tumultuous year, with strikes, race riots, and the Red Scare. The U.S. postwar economy also struggled, putting many people out of work. Fairly or not, many Americans blamed Europe, immigrants—and President Woodrow Wilson—for this instability.

Postwar Politics During the 1920 presidential campaign, the Republican nominee, **Warren G. Harding**, a U.S. senator from Ohio, promised a "return to normalcy." Harding supported lower taxes and less government regulation over business. He also rejected Wilson's call to join the League of Nations.

Harding's pro-business, isolationist stances appealed to many Americans. As a result, he won the 1920 election—the first in which women could vote. Harding then chose a pro-business cabinet to help him lower taxes and balance the budget.

Connecting History

Women's Suffrage
Women gained the right to vote in 1920 with the passage of the 19th Amendment.

A Protective Tariff After World War I, many European countries had large war debts. America's economy was also struggling to change from a war economy to a peacetime one. Congress saw its main duty as protecting "the home market for American labor, agriculture, and industry." As a result, it passed the Fordney-McCumber Tariff in 1922, which President Harding signed into law. This **tariff** set the highest level of taxes on foreign goods in U.S. history to date. It made imported goods very expensive and enabled U.S. companies to keep their prices high.

▲ **PROBLEMS AND SOLUTIONS** How did Harding's policies address the concerns of Americans in the early 1920s?

Mixed Industrial Success

▼ **KEY QUESTION** What economic developments affected life in the 1920s?

Harding's policies helped the economy grow rapidly during the 1920s. Americans had more money to spend than ever before.

The appeal of modern conveniences like this new refrigerator grew in the 1920s.

Roots of Prosperity In 1913, the United States established an income tax. To help pay for the war, the maximum tax rate was raised to 67 percent in 1917. In 1924, the maximum rate was reduced to 46 percent, and then to 25 percent in 1925. These income tax cuts helped create prosperity.

Cheap fuel also powered the new prosperity. In urban areas, electric power reached nearly every home. As a result, new consumer products—such as electric vacuum cleaners, washers, toasters, and fans—became more popular and created new jobs. But rural areas saw little economic growth.

The Transportation Industry Henry Ford wanted to make a car—the Model T—that most people could afford. To speed up production and lower costs, Ford used an **assembly line** in which materials move along a conveyor belt while workers stay in one place. Workers add parts or do one specific job as the belt moves past them. Assembly lines and modern manufacturing processes enabled Ford to lower costs and increase productivity.

23,121,000

6,679,000

1919   1929

Source: *U.S. Census Bureau*

CRITICAL THINKING Form and Support Opinions
Why do you think car registrations rose so much in the 1920s?

Car makers employed hundreds of thousands of workers to meet the growing demand. Assembly line work was hard and dangerous.

PRIMARY SOURCE

❝ The machine that I am on goes at such a terrific speed that I can't help stepping on it in order to keep up with it. The machine is my boss. ❞

—anonymous auto worker, 1920s

The 1920s also marked the birth of the airline industry. Many former military pilots found new uses for old warplanes, working as crop dusters, stunt fliers, and flight instructors. In 1918, the Post Office Department began airmail service. Transatlantic flights by Charles A. Lindbergh in 1927 and Amelia Earhart in 1928 helped to promote the idea of commercial air travel.

Economic Problems New manufacturing processes turned out products faster and cheaper. Consumer demand for these products grew. To pay for these products, especially cars, consumers relied on **credit**, a way to delay paying for a purchase. Installment buying was one form of credit that grew popular in the 1920s. **Installment buying** allowed consumers to pay for cars and purchases in small monthly payments.

Although the Harding years were generally prosperous, some economic problems remained or grew worse. Many industries protected by tariffs, such as drugs, steel, and mining, faced little or no competition. As a result, big companies regained monopoly control over many markets—and many prices rose sharply. At the same time, better machinery allowed farmers to produce more food than the nation needed, driving food prices down.

Government policies favored corporate interests over social progress. For example, the income gap between the rich and most Americans reached its widest point in history to date. Many Americans—about half—lived in poverty. Further, the practice of allowing investors to buy stocks on credit caused stock prices to rise rapidly.

🔺 **SUMMARIZE** Name developments that affected life in the 1920s.

The assembly line helped auto workers work efficiently, helping keep car costs low.
What would be some disadvantages to working on an assembly line?

Coolidge Takes Over

🔻 **KEY QUESTION** What challenges did Calvin Coolidge face as president?

Some members of Harding's cabinet were unqualified, and even corrupt. Their actions largely ruined his presidency.

Teapot Dome The worst scandal involved Secretary of the Interior Albert Fall. Oil executives bribed Fall to give them access to oil-rich government land in Teapot Dome, Wyoming, and other areas. News of this deal resulted in the **Teapot Dome Scandal**. Fall became the first cabinet member imprisoned for committing a crime while in office.

Some historians think that corruption charges led to Harding's sudden death on August 2, 1923. Americans mourned the loss of their president, but these scandals shocked them. Because Harding died in office, his vice-president, **Calvin Coolidge**, became president.

Laissez-Faire Economics Coolidge moved quickly to clean up the scandals. His efforts limited the political damage to his party. In the 1924 national elections, Coolidge and the Republican Congress retained power by promising to further strengthen pro-business policies.

(*below*) New York stockbrokers examine stock prices printed on tickertape. Stock prices show the value of an individual's or company's investments—a key part of a free enterprise system.

CONNECT 🔄 *Economics and History*

GOVERNMENT AND CAPITALISM

The United States has a free-enterprise economic system, also known as capitalism. In a free-enterprise system, corporations and individuals have the right to make most economic choices. Government plays a limited, but important, role as the examples in the chart below show.

Ensuring Fair Competition	Protecting Health and Safety	Providing Services	Ensuring Stability
• preventing fraud • barring monopolies	• labor laws • building codes • environmental protection laws	• building and repairing highways • defending the country	• regulating banks • coining money

CRITICAL THINKING **Make Generalizations** In your own words, define the role of government in capitalism.

Coolidge agreed with the theory of **laissez-faire economics**, which stated that business, if left unregulated by the government, would act in ways that would benefit the nation. In 1925 Coolidge stated his belief that "the chief business of the American people is business." Under Coolidge, American corporations prospered, and so did many individuals.

Coolidge also believed that government should not address social and economic problems. For example, Congress passed a bill that would have helped struggling farmers, but Coolidge vetoed it.

Prosperity Labor-saving appliances and shorter working hours gave Americans more leisure time. Higher wages also gave them more money to spend on leisure activities. By the end of the 1920s, Americans were buying more than 100 million movie tickets each week. Americans also spent time listening to the radio and attending sporting events. In 1929, they spent about $4 billion on entertainment alone—a 100 percent jump in a decade.

But not all Americans prospered. Many, especially small farmers, African Americans, and other ethnic minorities, faced more limited choices. Still, Americans in general wanted more fun—and were willing to pay for it.

Talking pictures—or "talkies"—transformed the movie industry in the late 1920s.

 EVALUATE How did Calvin Coolidge respond to the challenges that faced him when he assumed the presidency in 1923?

 Illinois Learning Standards *Review*

ONLINE QUIZ
For test practice, go to
Interactive Review @ ClassZone.com

TERMS & NAMES

1. Explain the importance of

- Warren G. Harding
- Teapot Dome Scandal
- assembly line
- Calvin Coolidge
- installment buying
- laissez-faire economics

USING YOUR READING NOTES

2. Sequence Events Complete the diagram you started at the beginning of this section.

KEY IDEAS

3. Why were American voters eager to "return to normalcy" in 1920?

4. What were Harding's and Coolidge's policies toward business?

CRITICAL THINKING

5. Draw Conclusions Why did Coolidge act quickly to clean up the scandals of Harding's presidency?

6. **Technology/Art** **1920s Ad** Use the library or the Internet to find magazine advertisements of household products that were offered in the 1920s. Design your own ad for one of these products.

▶ Key Ideas

BEFORE, YOU LEARNED

During the 1920s, most Americans were eager for a "return to normalcy" and prosperity.

NOW YOU WILL LEARN

Changes in the roles of women and in popular culture led to new attitudes and lifestyles, but also to conflicts in society.

▶ Vocabulary

TERMS & NAMES

flapper a young woman eager to try the latest fashion, dance, or fad

Jazz Age name for the 1920s, because of the popularity of jazz—a new type of American music that combined African rhythms, blues, and ragtime

Visual Vocabulary
flapper

mass media communications that reach a large audience

popular culture movies, fashions, songs, slang, and other expressions of culture that appeal to many people

Prohibition legal ban on alcohol imposed by the Eighteenth Amendment

speakeasies nightclubs that illegally served alcohol

BACKGROUND VOCABULARY

fundamentalism belief that every word of the Bible is literally true

evolution scientific theory of how life forms developed over millions of years

▶ Reading Strategy

Re-create the diagram shown at right. As you read and respond to the **KEY QUESTIONS**, use the diagram to record important events and their effects. Add boxes or start a new diagram as needed

 Skillbuilder Handbook, page R7.

CAUSES AND EFFECTS

CAUSE

More rights and freedoms for women

EFFECT

EFFECT

GRAPHIC ORGANIZERS
Go to **Interactive Review** @ ClassZone.com

The Jazz Age and Popular Culture

15.D.3c Explain how workers can affect their productivity through training and by using tools, machinery and technology.
16.B.3c Describe the way the Constitution has changed over time as a result of amendments and Supreme Court decisions.

One American's Story

Many young American women in the 1920s called themselves **flappers**. They were eager to try new fashions, dances, and fads. With their independent attitudes, flappers helped usher in a new modern age. One of the most famous flappers of the time was Zelda Fitzgerald. Zelda wrote, painted, danced, traveled, and more.

Two spirited young flappers kick up their heels atop a downtown Chicago hotel.

PRIMARY SOURCE

❝ The flapper awoke from her lethargy [boredom] . . . and went into the battle. . . . [S]he refused to be bored chiefly because she wasn't boring. She was conscious that the things she did were the things she had always wanted to do. ❞

—Zelda Fitzgerald, "Eulogy on the Flapper"

Many young women admired Zelda for living life on her own terms. In so doing, Zelda Fitzgerald helped inspire them to break from tradition.

Daily Life in the Twenties

🔻 **KEY QUESTION** How did U.S. culture change during the 1920s?

Whether it was called the Roaring Twenties or the **Jazz Age**, the 1920s was a time to celebrate the new and the modern. Jazz music, a mix of African rhythms, ragtime, and blues, captured the carefree spirit of these times. Young people wanted fun and freedom—and to dance to jazz's lively beat. They rebelled against the values that had led to World War I.

New Roles for Women During the 1920s, women had more personal freedom than ever before. They drove cars, played sports, and attended college. Growing prosperity opened up more job opportunities for women, although they were still generally limited to certain jobs.

Women typists in a 1920s office.
How does this office compare with a modern office?

Most often, women college graduates became teachers, nurses, and social workers. Others worked as factory laborers, office secretaries, and store clerks.

The 19th Amendment had ensured women the right to vote, and in 1924 two were elected governors—Nellie Tayloe Ross in Wyoming and Miriam "Ma" Ferguson in Texas. But the growing independence of women often clashed with traditional society. One young woman described her generation's struggles in a popular magazine.

PRIMARY SOURCE

❝ We are the Younger Generation. The war tore away our spiritual foundations and challenged our faith. We are struggling to regain our equilibrium [balance]. . . . Help us. . . . Work with us! ❞

—Ellen Welles Page, "A Flapper's Appeal to Parents"

Women in the 1920s had more control over their lives than ever before. This led to new attitudes toward marriage. Men and women started to view marriage as more of a partnership. However, women still did most of the housework and child rearing.

Mass Media Several types of **mass media**, or communications that reach a large audience, gained importance in the 1920s. Movies presented a world of glamour few people could otherwise experience. Movies also spread **popular culture**—songs, dances, fashion, and even slang expressions.

Radio also changed American culture. The number of households with radios jumped from about 60,000 in 1922 to 10 million in 1929. Radio made athletes such as Babe Ruth, Bobby Jones, and Babe Didrikson Zaharias national heroes. Listening to common radio shows and music also helped to unite Americans.

Belief and Controversy A religious movement called **fundamentalism** gained many followers, and political power, during the 1920s. Fundamentalists believed that every word of the Bible was literally true. They objected to public schools teaching **evolution**, the scientific theory that living things developed over millions of years from earlier and simpler forms of life. They felt it contradicted the biblical account of creation.

Fundamentalists succeeded in banning the teaching of evolution in three states. In 1925, John Scopes, a biology teacher, broke the law in Tennessee to test whether it could be enforced. His trial attracted national attention. Scopes was found guilty, but the Tennessee Supreme Court reversed the decision. Controversy over the teaching of evolution continues today.

Prohibition The 18th Amendment, banning the manufacture and sale of alcohol, went into effect in 1920. Many people saw the amendment, commonly called **Prohibition**, as a victory of small-town Protestants over

---

Connecting History

Rise of African-American Newspapers
The 1920s saw African American newspapers grow in influence across the country. Some papers even encouraged people in the South to move north. This "push" helped fuel more movement to the North as a continuation of the Great Migration.

city dwellers. Supporters felt that Prohibition would promote morality and health. But many people resented this government interference. Those who wanted alcohol had ways to get it. Some went to **speakeasies**, nightclubs that were supplied with alcohol by criminals called bootleggers.

As a result, Prohibition helped organized crime grow. By the late 1920s, most Americans considered Prohibition a failure. It would eventually be repealed by the 21st Amendment in 1933.

Despite the best efforts of law enforcement officials (above), they weren't able to stop the flow of alcohol by bootleggers.

 SUMMARIZE What key changes took place in the United States in the 1920s?

 Illinois Learning Standards *Review*

ONLINE QUIZ
For test practice, go to
Interactive Review @ ClassZone.com

TERMS & NAMES

1. Explain the importance of
- flapper
- popular culture
- Jazz Age
- Prohibition
- mass media
- speakeasies

USING YOUR READING NOTES

2. Causes and Effects Complete the diagram you started at the beginning of this section.

EFFECT

CAUSE

More rights and freedoms for women

EFFECT

KEY IDEAS

3. How did life change for women in the 1920s?

4. What was the 18th Amendment, and how did it affect life in the 1920s?

CRITICAL THINKING

5. Summarize Describe two ways that religious beliefs had an impact on life in the United States during this period.

6. Draw Conclusions How did mass media help to unite the country?

7. Writing Editorial Imagine that you are a newspaper editor in the 1920s. Write an editorial that either calls for repealing Prohibition or for keeping it.

▶ Key Ideas

BEFORE, YOU LEARNED

Changes in the roles of women and in popular culture led to new attitudes and lifestyles, but also to conflicts in society.

NOW YOU WILL LEARN

After World War I, African Americans confronted new challenges and made great contributions to American culture.

▶ Vocabulary

TERMS & NAMES

Marcus Garvey leader who called for a return to Africa to form a separate nation there

Harlem Renaissance a burst of African-American culture in the 1920s and 1930s

Langston Hughes Harlem Renaissance poet

Lost Generation Americans who became disillusioned with society after World War I

expatriate (ehk•SPAY•tree•IHT) a citizen of one country who lives in another country

BACKGROUND VOCABULARY

materialistic putting value on material things above intellectual or spiritual things

REVIEW

Ku Klux Klan racist group that used violence to keep former slaves powerless and America "racially and morally pure"

NAACP (National Association for the Advancement of Colored People) group formed in 1909 to protect the rights of African Americans

Visual Vocabulary
Marcus Garvey

▶ Reading Strategy

Re-create the graphic organizer shown here. As you read and respond to the **KEY QUESTION**, use the graphic organizer to record the section's main ideas. Add ovals or start a new diagram as needed.

 Skillbuilder Handbook, page R4.

MAIN IDEAS AND DETAILS

Harlem Renaissance revives African-American culture

GRAPHIC ORGANIZERS
Go to **Interactive Review** @ ClassZone.com

The Harlem Renaissance

14.C.3 Compare historical issues involving rights, roles and status of individuals in relation to municipalities, states and the nation.
14.D.3 Describe roles and influences of individuals, groups and media in shaping current Illinois and United States public policy (e.g., *general public opinion, special interest groups, formal parties, media*).

One American's Story

Zora Neale Hurston was born in Alabama in 1891. Like many African-American writers and artists of the time, she made her way to New York City's Harlem neighborhood.

PRIMARY SOURCE

❝ [W]anting to be in New York, I decided to go there and try to get back in school in that city. So the first week of January, 1925, found me in New York with $1.50, no job, no friends and a lot of hope. ❞

—**Zora Neale Hurston**, *Dust Tracks on a Road*

Hurston studied anthropology and incorporated her research of African-American folklore into her writing. For Hurston, as for many other African Americans in the 1920s, New York was the center for learning and culture—and the place to make their mark on American society.

Zora Neale Hurston based much of her writing, including her book *Mules and Men*, on African-American folklore.

Rising Expectations for African Americans

🔻 **KEY QUESTION** What did African Americans do to confront racism in the 1920s?

The 1920s brought changes to the lives of many African Americans. To find better jobs, people had begun moving to northern cities in the early 1900s. This Great Migration and the jobs that people held in industries during World War I raised their expectations for a better life.

Confronting Racism In the North, African Americans gained some economic and political power. But they still faced discrimination in jobs and housing. Rising tensions with whites had led to race riots in 1919. During the 1920s, the arrival of hundreds of thousands more African Americans to Northern cities increased tensions even more.

One result was the rebirth of the **Ku Klux Klan**. The Klan called for a "racially and morally pure" America. By 1924, the Klan claimed about five million members. It tried to influence national, state, and local politics by using violence against African Americans and others.

Marcus Garvey Daily threats and racial discrimination made some lose faith in America. As a result, **Marcus Garvey**, founder of the Universal Negro Improvement Association, or UNIA, gained support. Garvey felt that black people were kept powerless everywhere. The only solution, in Garvey's view, was for people of African descent to unite and establish their own nation in Africa: "We are looking toward political freedom on the continent of Africa, the land of our fathers."

Garvey spread his vision, rallying hundreds of thousands of people from all over the world to join his cause. In 1920, UNIA delegates met in New York City for a convention at which Garvey named himself president of a future nation in Africa. In the end, however, Garvey's vision failed. Few migrated to Africa, not even Garvey himself. But Garvey had given African Americans dignity and pride, setting an example for future political movements.

The NAACP Founded in 1909 in New York City, the **NAACP** (National Association for the Advancement of Colored People) worked for the enforcement of the civil and voting rights of African Americans. It also worked to end segregation and to make people aware of crimes against African Americans. The NAACP published a magazine, *Crisis*, which became one of the most important African-American publications in the country. But the NAACP was unable to get Congress to help African Americans fight against discrimination.

▲ **COMPARE AND CONTRAST** Describe how the UNIA and the NAACP responded to racism in the 1920s.

(*top*) Jazz and blues great Bessie Smith, 1923 (*bottom*) *Church on Lenox Avenue* (ca. 1930), William H. Johnson

The Harlem Renaissance

▼ **KEY QUESTION** How did Harlem become a center of African-American culture?

Military service and work in war industries had given African Americans a new sense of freedom. They migrated to many cities, but it was New York City that became the unofficial capital of black America.

The Rise of Harlem In the 1920s, Harlem, a neighborhood on New York's West Side, was the world's largest black urban community. In the late 1800s it had been developed as a community for wealthy whites. The developers thought people would move away from the congestion of the city. They built elegant apartment buildings and homes on tree-lined streets. But they erected too many buildings in Harlem, which caused real estate prices to fall.

An African-American businessman, Philip Payton, Jr., saw an opportunity. He started to buy up the inexpensive buildings and sell them to African Americans who lived in other neighborhoods in New York City. The Great Migration brought many more African Americans to Harlem. By 1920, most Harlem residents were African Americans.

Soon Harlem produced a burst of cultural activity known as the **Harlem Renaissance**, which began in the 1920s and lasted into the 1930s. It was called a renaissance because it symbolized a rebirth of hope and culture for African Americans.

A Cultural Center Harlem became home to writers, musicians, singers, painters, sculptors, and scholars. There they were able to exchange ideas and develop their creativity. They also worked with organizations such as the NAACP and the National Urban League to fight racism. In fact, many leading activists in these organizations also wrote fiction, essays, poetry, and plays. Their works became regular features in the NAACP's *Crisis* and *Opportunity*, the magazine of the National Urban League.

Les Fétiches (1938), Lois Mailou Jones. Jones (1905–1998) was an African-American painter who used African themes in her work. She taught at Howard University.

ONLINE PRIMARY SOURCE

Hear the perspectives at the **Research & Writing Center** @ ClassZone.com

COMPARING *Perspectives*

Langston Hughes and Zora Neale Hurston explored similar themes in their writings—love, life, beauty, and justice. Although both wrote about race, Hughes believed it should be a focus of his work while Hurston claimed her individuality as her focus.

Langston Hughes and Zora Neale Hurston

Langston Hughes

❝Most of my poems are racial in theme and treatment, derived from the life I know. In many of them I try to grasp and hold some of the meanings and rhythms of jazz. . . . [Y]et after every reading I answer questions like these from my own people: Do you think Negroes should always write about Negroes? . . . What makes you do so many jazz poems?❞

—*The Negro Artist and the Racial Mountain* (1926)

Zora Neale Hurston

❝I do not belong to the sobbing school of Negrohood who hold that nature somehow has given them a lowdown dirty deal and whose feelings are all hurt about it. Even in the helter-skelter skirmish that is my life, I have seen that the world is to the strong. . . . At certain times I have no race, I am *me*.❞

—*How It Feels to Be Colored Me* (1928)

CRITICAL THINKING **Compare and Contrast** What is the main difference between Hughes's and Hurston's perspectives?

Among Harlem's residents were poets **Langston Hughes**, James Weldon Johnson, and Countee Cullen and novelists Claude McKay and Zora Neale Hurston. Hughes became one of Harlem's leading writers.

Jazz spread from its birthplace in New Orleans to other parts of the country and made its way into the nightclubs of Harlem. These nightclubs featured popular jazz musicians such as Louis Armstrong and Duke Ellington, and singers such as Bessie Smith. Harlem's most famous nightclub, the Cotton Club, made stars of many African-American performers, but only white customers were allowed into the club.

The Lost Generation For some, the decade after World War I was not a time of celebration, but a time of deep despair. They had seen Progressive ideals end in a senseless war. Filled with resentment, they saw little hope for the future. They were called the **Lost Generation**.

Many of them found freedom and tolerance in Paris. The French capital became a gathering place for American **expatriates**, people who choose to live in a country other than their own. Among the American expatriates living in Paris was the young novelist Ernest Hemingway. Driving an ambulance during World War I had shown him the war's worst side. Hemingway's early novels, *The Sun Also Rises* and *A Farewell to Arms*, reflected the despair that followed the war.

CONNECT to the Essential Question

How did American society change during the 1920s?

CHANGE	IMPACT
Pro-business stance of Harding and Coolidge	Many Americans experience great prosperity.
The assembly line	New, cheaper products flood the market.
New roles for women	More women work; views on marriage change.
Mass media	Radio and the movies bring Americans closer together as a nation.
Harlem Renaissance	African-American culture changes American music and other popular culture.
The Lost Generation	People question America's values.

CRITICAL THINKING **Causes and Effects** Which factor played the greatest role in how America changed during the 1920s? Explain and justify your answer.

F. Scott Fitzgerald and his wife, Zelda, lived the whirlwind life of the Jazz Age—fast cars, nightclubs, wild parties, and stays in Paris. His masterpiece, *The Great Gatsby*, is a tragic story of wealthy New Yorkers whose lives spin out of control. The novel—and the real-life tragedies of the Fitzgeralds— show the dark side of the Roaring Twenties.

Sinclair Lewis was another member of the Lost Generation. He wrote *Babbitt*, a novel that satirized, or made fun of, the American middle class and its **materialistic** concerns.

F. Scott Fitzgerald and Zelda Fitzgerald were one of the most famous celebrity couples of the 1920s.

PRIMARY SOURCE

❝ It's the fellow with four to ten thousand a year . . . and an automobile and a nice little family in a bungalow . . . that makes the wheels of progress go round! . . . That's the type of fellow that's ruling America today; in fact, it's the ideal type to which the entire world must tend. ❞

—Sinclair Lewis, *Babbitt*

Lewis could not know at the time that the social values and materialistic lifestyles he criticized would not last much longer. The soaring economy that brought prosperity in the 1920s came to a crashing halt in the 1930s.

 SUMMARIZE How did Harlem become a cultural center in the 1920s?

 Illinois Learning Standards *Review*

ONLINE QUIZ
For test practice, go to
Interactive Review @ ClassZone.com

TERMS & NAMES

1. Explain the importance of
   - Marcus Garvey
   - Lost Generation
   - Harlem Renaissance
   - expatriate
   - Langston Hughes

USING YOUR READING NOTES

2. **Main Ideas and Details** Complete the diagram you started at the beginning of this section.

KEY IDEAS

3. Why was Harlem called the unofficial capital of black America?

4. What actions did African-American organizations take to counter racism in the 1920s?

CRITICAL THINKING

5. **Summarize** Why were the writers and artists of the Lost Generation disillusioned?

6. **Make Inferences** Why do you think so many African Americans responded to Marcus Garvey's ideas?

7. **Writing** **Analysis** Zora Neale Hurston was raised in the rural South, and Langston Hughes was raised in the Midwest and Northeast. Write a brief analysis explaining what role their backgrounds may have played in their views.

THE JAZZ AGE

The Jazz Age was named after the style of music that became widely popular during the 1920s. What contributions to culture were being made at the time?

CLARA BOW

Bow was perhaps Hollywood's top silent pictures star—and America's leading flapper—until the "talkies" (movies with sound) all but ended her career.

BABE RUTH

Ruth's home run blasts and larger-than-life personality made him the most famous sports star of the 1920s.

DUKE ELLINGTON

Ellington blended elements of blues, jazz, and popular songs into classics such as *Mood Indigo*.

AIMEE SEMPLE MCPHERSON

McPherson used radio to become a leading religious preacher in the 1920s.

Activity

Pop Culture: 20s Style

1 Choose a person who was popular during the 1920s.

2 Design a visual on his or her life and work.

3 Use styles and themes from this era in your visual.

4 Present your visual to the class.

Chapter Summary

① Key Idea
During the 1920s, most Americans were eager for a "return to normalcy" and prosperity.

② Key Idea
Changes in the roles of women and in popular culture led to new attitudes and lifestyles, but also to conflicts in society.

③ Key Idea
After World War I, African Americans confronted new challenges and made great contributions to American culture.

For detailed Review and Study Notes go to **Interactive Review** @ ClassZone.com

Name Game

Use the Terms & Names list to complete each sentence online or on your own paper.

1. _____ is the theory that business, if free of government regulation, will act in ways that benefit the nation.
   laissez-faire economics

2. _____ is a way of purchasing that allows people to pay for items in small monthly payments.

3. When _____ served as president, he focused on peace abroad and prosperity at home.

4. The ban on alcohol was called _____.

5. The belief that every word in the Bible is literally true is called _____.

6. A _____ loved to try the latest fashion, dance, or fad.

7. An _____ is a citizen of one country who lives in another.

8. _____ was a Harlem Renaissance poet.

9. _____ wanted to lead African Americans back to Africa so that they could form a separate nation there.

10. The organization formed in 1909 to protect the rights of African Americans is the _____.

A. Prohibition
B. flapper
C. expatriate
D. Marcus Garvey
E. Lost Generation
F. NAACP
G. assembly line
H. fundamentalism
I. laissez-faire economics
J. Calvin Coolidge
K. popular culture
L. installment buying
M. Langston Hughes

Activities

CROSSWORD PUZZLE

Complete the online cross word puzzle to show what you know about the Roaring Twenties.

DOWN
1. 30th president, served from 1923–1929. Calvin _____

FLIPCARD

Use the interactive flipcards to study the 1920s.

manufacturing technique that uses a conveyor belt to move materials to workers who stay in one place

ANSWER
assembly line

VOCABULARY

Explain the significance of each of the following.

1. Calvin Coolidge
2. Marcus Garvey
3. Prohibition
4. assembly line
5. Harlem Renaissance
6. fundamentalism
7. laissez-faire economics
8. Langston Hughes
9. Lost Generation
10. Jazz Age

Explain how the terms and names in each group are related.

11. Warren G. Harding, Calvin Coolidge, Teapot Dome Scandal

12. mass media, flapper, popular culture

13. Ku Klux Klan, Marcus Garvey, National Association for the Advancement of Colored People (NAACP)

Calvin Coolidge

KEY IDEAS

1 **Postwar Economics and Politics (pages 752–757)**

14. What was Warren Harding's view of the League of Nations?

15. Which factors contributed to prosperity in the 1920s?

2 **The Jazz Age and Popular Culture (pages 758–761)**

16. What types of mass media became popular in the 1920s?

17. Explain why Prohibition was not a success.

3 **The Harlem Renaissance (pages 762–767)**

18. What was Marcus Garvey's plan for dealing with discrimination against blacks?

19. Why did Harlem's Cotton Club benefit only a few African Americans and not others?

CRITICAL THINKING

20. **Make Inferences** Would Coolidge have been more likely to support or oppose the 18th Amendment? Explain your answer.

21. **Causes and Effects** Fill in the effects caused by each of the events shown in the Cause boxes.

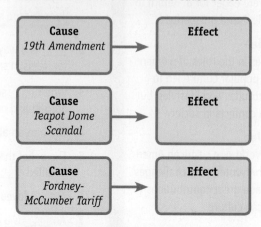

Cause	Effect
Cause 19th Amendment	**Effect**
Cause Teapot Dome Scandal	**Effect**
Cause Fordney-McCumber Tariff	**Effect**

22. **Summarize** How did the jazz music style develop?

23. **Causes and Effects** Why did the members of the Lost Generation leave the country during the 1920s?

24. **Compare and Contrast** What are the strengths and weaknesses of a laissez-faire economic policy?

25. **Make Inferences** Read the graph below. Why would the leading job category for women in 1920 be "domestic"?

Women's Employment 1920

- 25.6% DOMESTIC
- 22.6% MANUFACTURING & MECHANICAL
- 16.6% CLERICAL
- 12.7% AGRICULTURE
- 11.9% PROFESSIONAL
- 7.9% TRADE
- 2.6% TRANSPORTATION & COMMUNICATION

Source: Grace Hutchins, *Women Who Work*

DOCUMENT-BASED QUESTIONS

Study each document carefully and answer the questions that follow.

DOCUMENT 1

1. This image is the cover to sheet music from the 1920s. What does it tell you about the KKK's views on being an American?

DOCUMENT 2

 We shall march out, yes, as black American citizens, as black British subjects, as black French citizens, as black Italians or as black Spaniards, but we shall march out with a greater loyalty, the loyalty of race. We shall march out in answer to the cry of our fathers, who cry out to us for the redemption of our own country, our motherland, Africa. **"**

—Marcus Garvey, speech, November 25, 1922

2. How does this quote support Marcus Garvey's view that African Americans should form a separate nation?

PART 2: Essay

3. Using information from the documents, your answers to the questions in Part 1, and your knowledge of U.S. history, write a brief essay that discusses the various responses of African Americans to American society in the 1920s.

YOU BE THE HISTORIAN

26. Form and Support Opinions What effect did the Fordney-McCumber Tariff likely have on European countries in the 1920s?

27. Draw Conclusions What do you think was the most important technology of the 1920s? Explain and justify your answer.

28. Evaluate Why did women's roles in society change so significantly in the 1920s?

29. WHAT IF? What do you think might have happened if the 18th Amendment had not been ratified?

30. **Connect to Today** Name some ways the Harlem Renaissance still influences American culture today.

Answer the

ESSENTIAL QUESTION

How did American society change during the 1920s?

Written Response Write a two- to three-paragraph response to the Essential Question. Be sure to consider the key ideas of each section as well as the most significant economic, political, and social changes that occurred. Use the Response Rubric below to guide your thinking and writing.

Response Rubric

A strong response will

- summarize government policies that promoted prosperity, such as lowering the income tax rate
- analyze changing cultural values, including the role of women in society
- discuss the increased expectations of African Americans

Why It Matters Now

The Depression and World War II tested America at home and abroad
to a greater extent than at any other time since the Civil War. The New
Deal response to the nation's economic collapse created a safety net of
programs that many Americans hold dear to this day. America's defeat
of Nazism, Fascism, and Japanese militarism in World War II represented
a landmark moment in the triumph of democracy in the 20th century.
And the onset of the Cold War after 1945 tested anew America's ability
to meet a new world challenge in the form of communist competition.

History and experience tell us
that moral progress comes not in
comfortable and complacent times,
but out of trial and confusion.
—Gerald R. Ford

The Great Depression and the New Deal

1929–1940

ESSENTIAL QUESTION

How did the government react to the crisis of the Great Depression?

CONNECT Geography & History

How were different regions of the United States impacted by the Great Depression?

Think about:

1. how the Great Depression affected people living on the east and west coasts

2. how people living in the Dust Bowl were forced to move in search of work

3. the role of the natural environment and weather in economics and recovery

---

WHY CAN'T YOU GIVE MY DAD A JOB?

Child tries to help his father find employment.

STAGE BROADWAY SCREEN

VARIETY 25¢

WALL ST. LAYS AN EGG

1929

U.S. stock market crashes. Great Depression begins.

$100 WILL BUY THIS CAR MUST HAVE CASH LOST ALL ON THE STOCK MARKET

Bankrupt man selling car

1931 Over 8 million Americans are unemployed.

1932 Military removes veterans seeking bonuses from Washington.

Effect Americans turn against Hoover. Franklin D. Roosevelt is elected president.

1933 States ratify 20th Amendment. Presidential inauguration date moved to January.

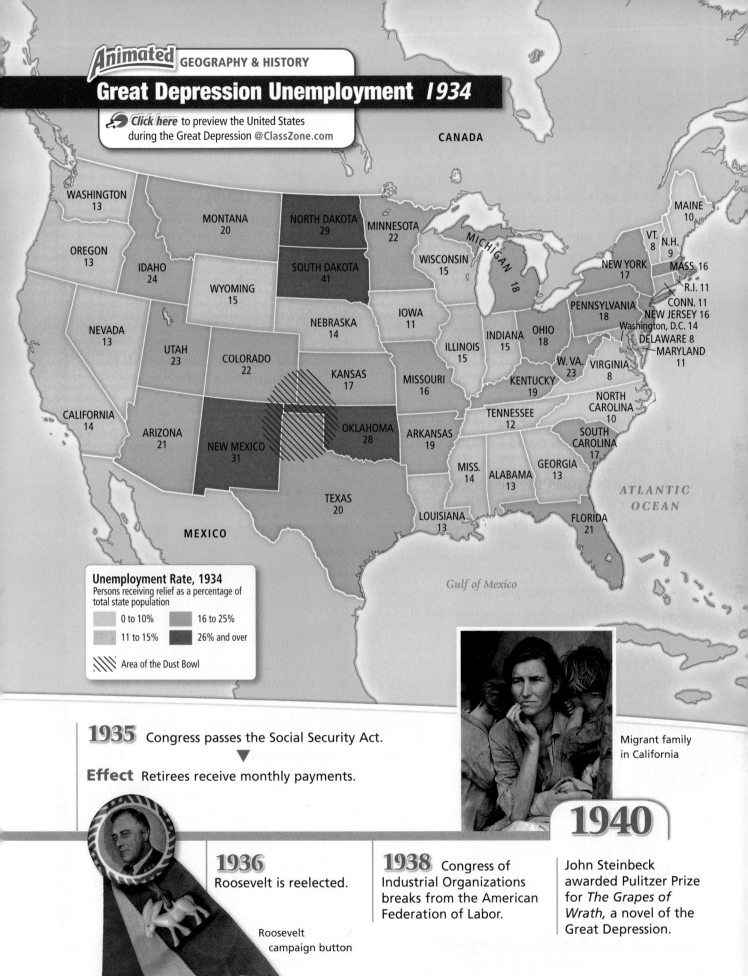

CANADA

WASHINGTON 13

MONTANA 20

NORTH DAKOTA 29

MINNESOTA 22

MICHIGAN 18

MAINE 10

OREGON 13

IDAHO 24

SOUTH DAKOTA 41

WISCONSIN 15

VT. 8
N.H. 9

NEW YORK 17

MASS. 16
R.I. 11

WYOMING 15

NEBRASKA 14

IOWA 11

PENNSYLVANIA 18

CONN. 11
NEW JERSEY 16

NEVADA 13

UTAH 23

COLORADO 22

ILLINOIS 15

INDIANA 15

OHIO 18

Washington, D.C. 14
DELAWARE 8
MARYLAND 11

CALIFORNIA 14

ARIZONA 21

NEW MEXICO 31

KANSAS 17

OKLAHOMA 28

MISSOURI 16

ARKANSAS 19

KENTUCKY 19

W. VA. 23

VIRGINIA 8

NORTH CAROLINA 10

TENNESSEE 12

SOUTH CAROLINA 17

TEXAS 20

MISS. 14

ALABAMA 13

GEORGIA 13

ATLANTIC OCEAN

LOUISIANA 13

FLORIDA 21

MEXICO

Gulf of Mexico

Unemployment Rate, 1934
Persons receiving relief as a percentage of total state population

0 to 10%	16 to 25%
11 to 15%	26% and over

////// Area of the Dust Bowl

1935 Congress passes the Social Security Act.
▼
Effect Retirees receive monthly payments.

Migrant family in California

1940

1936
Roosevelt is reelected.

Roosevelt campaign button

1938 Congress of Industrial Organizations breaks from the American Federation of Labor.

John Steinbeck awarded Pulitzer Prize for *The Grapes of Wrath,* a novel of the Great Depression.

Reading for Understanding

▶ Key Ideas

BEFORE, YOU LEARNED

The Roaring Twenties was a time of great prosperity for many Americans.

NOW YOU WILL LEARN

When the prosperity of the 1920s collapsed, President Herbert Hoover struggled to address the country's economic problems.

▶ Vocabulary

TERMS & NAMES

Herbert Hoover Republican president who failed to halt the Great Depression

Stock Market Crash of 1929 plunge in stock market prices that marked the beginning of the Great Depression

Great Depression the serious and world-wide economic decline of the 1930s

Bonus Army World War I veterans who came to Washington seeking early payment of bonuses for wartime service

BACKGROUND VOCABULARY

speculation buying and selling risky items in the hope of making a quick profit

public works government-funded projects to assist individuals, families, and communities in need

REVIEW

credit arrangement for delaying payment of a loan or purchase

economic depression severe economic slump

Visual Vocabulary Herbert Hoover

▶ Reading Strategy

Re-create the diagram shown at right. As you read and respond to the **KEY QUESTIONS**, use the diagram to record the differences between wealthy Americans, the middle class, and the poor.

 See Skillbuilder Handbook, page R8.

COMPARE AND CONTRAST

Rich	Middle Class	Poor
able to buy luxury items	forced to buy goods on credit	forced to buy goods on credit
invested heavily in the stock market		

GRAPHIC ORGANIZERS
Go to **Interactive Review** @ ClassZone.com

Economic Collapse

15.A.3c Describe the relationship between consumer purchases and businesses paying for productive resources.
15.A.3d Describe the causes of unemployment (e.g., *seasonal fluctuation in demand, changing jobs, changing skill requirements, national spending*).

One American's Story

Gordon Parks was a well-known photographer, author, and filmmaker who grew up in the 1920s. As a 16-year-old, he worked as a busboy at the exclusive Minnesota Club. There, prosperous club members spoke of the strong economy. Parks expected a bright future—he hoped to graduate from high school and begin a career. Then came the stock market crash of October 1929.

Gordon Parks

PRIMARY SOURCE

❝ I couldn't imagine such financial disaster touching my small world; it surely concerned only the rich. But by the first week of November . . . I was without a job. All that next week I searched for any kind of work that would prevent my leaving school. Again it was 'We're firing, not hiring.' . . . I went to school and cleaned out my locker, knowing it was impossible to stay on. **❞**

—Gordon Parks, *A Choice of Weapons*

The crash of 1929 crushed the dreams of Parks and millions of other Americans. The "Roaring Twenties" had suddenly gone silent.

The Myth of Prosperity

▼ **KEY QUESTION** How did 1920s prosperity affect different social groups?

In 1928, Secretary of Commerce **Herbert Hoover** became the Republican candidate for president. Americans believed Hoover when he predicted growing prosperity in the next decade. Few people recognized that serious economic problems were threatening the "roar" in the Roaring Twenties.

Problems in Business The prosperity of the 1920s hid the fact that some basic industries were in serious trouble. Many industries—such as railroads, textile mills, and mining—had improved efficiency and begun to produce more goods. But the income of middle-class and poor people didn't rise enough for them to purchase the additional products. Many items went unsold and piled up in warehouses. Unless businesses sold their products, they couldn't pay for materials, salaries, equipment, or shipping.

Farmers also faced difficult times. Due in part to advances in technology—such as improvements in motorized machinery, irrigation methods, and motor fuels—farmers produced more crops than they could sell. The increased supply caused lower food prices. Low prices and high rates of debt for new machinery made farmers vulnerable to changes in the economy.

The Illusion of Wealth The vast wealth of America's richest citizens hid the fact that many people were struggling just to get by. Although fancy cars and modern appliances were the latest fads, most Americans could not afford such luxuries. Rather, the vast majority of people in the 1920s had only small incomes and little savings.

Making matters worse, many Americans could not find steady work. In particular, African Americans had high jobless rates. Regardless, many consumers continued to buy goods on **credit**, an arrangement for delaying payment on a purchase. This caused many people to acquire large debts.

Yet the stock market still showed promise as prices kept climbing. As a result, many Americans rushed to buy stocks. Increasingly, investors bought on **speculation**, buying and selling risky stocks in the hope of making a quick profit. In addition, investors often borrowed money to buy more stocks. But this was a dangerous strategy. When stock prices fell, borrowers couldn't repay their loans. Due to their debt, many Americans risked bankruptcy.

▲ **COMPARE & CONTRAST** Explain how 1920s prosperity affected rich and poor.

COMPARING *Economic Data 1920–1929*

Throughout the 1920s, the stock market rose to new heights. Believing the future looked bright, many Americans spent their money on stocks and luxury items.

Stock Market Prices

Dollars per share

300
250
200
150
100
50
0

1920   1922   1924   1926   1928
Year

Consumer Spending

Billions of dollars

10
8
6
4
2
0

1920   1922   1924   1926   1928
Year

CRITICAL THINKING

1. **Analyze Graphs** How much did consumer spending increase between 1920 and 1929?

2. **Recognize Effects** How did the rise in stock prices relate to increased consumer spending?

The Crash and the Great Depression

▼ **KEY QUESTION** What caused the crash of 1929 and the Great Depression?

After only eight months in office, President Herbert Hoover watched helplessly as the country fell into the worst **economic depression**, or financial slump, in United States history.

Economic Crisis The fragile American economy worsened considerably when a massive financial panic led to the **Stock Market Crash of 1929.** During a mere two-month period, stocks on the New York Stock Exchange went from being worth a fortune to being almost worthless. As a result, investors tried desperately to sell their stocks before going bankrupt.

On the worst day of the crash—October 29—stock prices fell so sharply that people referred to the day as "Black Tuesday." On that day, some stocks fell more than 75 percent. Millions of ordinary Americans lost their entire life savings in a matter of hours.

But the stock market crash was only the first in a series of devastating events. In the following five months, thousands of banks were forced to close, having literally run out of money.

With little or no cash in their pockets, people could not afford to purchase goods and everyday products. In addition, businesses laid off, or fired, millions of workers. Many Americans were now unemployed.

The Great Depression The United States had experienced economic depressions before. But the **Great Depression** of the 1930s was the worst economic crisis in the nation's history. It also affected millions of others around the globe. Many European countries had borrowed money from U.S. banks to rebuild after World War I. When the American economy failed, so did Europe's.

The depression held its grip on America and the world for over a decade, from its beginning in October 1929 to America's entry into World War II in 1941. During this period, millions experienced starvation, homelessness, and extreme suffering.

▲ **CAUSES AND EFFECTS** Explain what caused Black Tuesday, bank closings, and mass unemployment.

CONNECT — Cause and Effect

TROUBLING SIGNS Although the 1920s were seemingly prosperous, there were many signs of the coming crisis. Key industries struggled and products went unsold. Farmers faced growing debts. And Americans used credit to make purchases beyond their means.

September 23, 1929
Stock prices reach a high point.

September 1929

2	3	4	5	6	7
9	10	11	12	13	14
15	16	17	18	19	20	21
22	**23**	24	25	26	27	28
29	30				

October 23, 1929
Stock prices drop sharply, after period of decline.

October 1929

1	2	3	4	5
7	8	9	10	11	12
13	14	15	16	17	18	19
20	21	22	**23**	**24**	25	26
27	28	**29**	30	31	

October 24, 1929
People panic and sell their stocks to avoid going bankrupt.

October 29, 1929
Stock market crashes on Black Tuesday.

THE GREAT DEPRESSION SETS IN

Panicked Americans withdraw life savings from banks.

Banks run out of money and are forced to close.

Cash becomes scarce and people stop buying goods.

Businesses close or lay off workers.

Unemployment and homelessness soar.

CRITICAL THINKING **Evaluate** What was the most significant cause of the Great Depression?

Bonus Army members outside their shack, 1932 **Why did Bonus Army members camp in Washington, D.C.?**

Hoover Loses the Nation's Trust

▼ **KEY QUESTION** Why did the American people lose faith in Hoover?

As unemployment, hunger, and homelessness grew, many Americans blamed President Hoover and looked to him to end their hard times. But the Republican Hoover did not want to increase the government's role in the economy, nor did he believe in government aid to the needy. Instead, Hoover encouraged churches and private charities to aid people in need. He also met with business leaders and persuaded them to voluntarily maintain wage rates.

Eventually, Hoover decided that voluntary efforts weren't enough. In 1932 he supported creation of the Reconstruction Finance Corporation, a government-funded organization that would give loans directly to banks and railroads. He also approved **public works** projects—government-funded construction that would create jobs as well as addressing other community needs. The most famous project was one Hoover had been working for since 1922, when he was Secretary of Commerce: the Boulder Dam (today called Hoover Dam) in Nevada, a massive development to supply three states with cheap hydro-powered electricity. (See pages 782–783.) Yet these measures were "too little, too late" to save Hoover's presidency. He could not escape a reputation as a "do-nothing" president.

The Bonus Army Many World War I veterans had been promised a bonus for their wartime service. The bonuses were not due until after 1940. But the depression hit veterans as hard as anyone. In the summer of 1932, the **Bonus Army** of an estimated 15,000 veterans poured into Washington, D.C., to appeal to Congress for early payment. Congress, facing its own financial problems, rejected early payment. Feeling angry and defeated, much of the Bonus Army left the capital and returned home. Thousands of others, however, stayed to protest.

By late July, the remaining Bonus Army was camped in a "Hooverville"—a village of huts, shacks, and other temporary residences—on the outskirts of Washington, D.C. Angered by their protest, General Douglas MacArthur decided to drive out the Bonus Army. His troops threw tear gas, fired shots, and prodded the veterans with bayonets. In the skirmish, one veteran was shot to death. A witness described the event:

Bonus Army members clash with authorities.

PRIMARY SOURCE

❝ I saw in a news reel the tanks, the cavalry, and the gas-bomb throwers running those wretched Americans out of our capital. I was so raging mad I could have torn the theater down. ❞

—Evalyn Walsh McLean, *Father Struck It Rich*

Americans were outraged, and many blamed President Hoover for the attack. Hoover's increasing unpopularity led to his defeat in the 1932 presidential election. Rejecting Hoover's policies, Americans elected the Democratic candidate—New York State governor Franklin Delano Roosevelt (or FDR, as he was known). As president, FDR's first goal would be to rebuild Americans' hope for the future and their trust in government.

▲ **SEQUENCE EVENTS** Describe how the nation lost trust in Hoover.

Illinois Learning Standards *Review*

 ONLINE QUIZ
For test practice, go to
Interactive Review @ ClassZone.com

TERMS & NAMES

1. Explain the importance of
- Herbert Hoover
- Stock Market Crash of 1929
- Great Depression
- Bonus Army

USING YOUR READING NOTES

2. Compare and Contrast Complete the diagram from the beginning of this section.

Rich	Middle Class	Poor
able to buy luxury items	forced to buy goods on credit	forced to buy goods on credit
invested heavily in the stock market		

KEY IDEAS

3. What were the risks of buying goods on credit and stocks on margin?

4. What caused thousands of banks to fail?

5. Why did Hoover become unpopular?

CRITICAL THINKING

6. Analyze Point of View In a 1928 campaign speech, presidential candidate Herbert Hoover said, "We shall soon . . . be in sight of the day when poverty will be banished from this nation." Explain why Hoover believed this.

7. Synthesize Why do you think the economic depression that began on Black Tuesday came to be called the Great Depression?

8. Writing **Letter** As a young person hit by the Depression, write a letter to Hoover. Describe your circumstances and why you have lost faith in him.

HISTORY

BUILDING THE BOULDER DAM

Click here to see the Boulder Dam public works project come to life @ ClassZone.com

Hoover's Public Works

In 1929, President Herbert Hoover approved the Boulder Canyon Project Act. Employing over 5000 people, the dam was created to provide hydro-powered electricity to three states.

Click here Before construction started, engineers diverted the Colorado River around the dam site by blasting four large tunnels through the canyon walls.

Click here To enable construction, workers built a complex system of metal and wooden scaffolding.

Click here Once completed in 1936, the Boulder Dam was 726 feet high and 1,244 feet long.

Activity

Construct a Model Dam!

1. In a cookie pan, use clay to construct a model river canyon. Pour water in the river and observe the flow.

2. Use the clay to construct a dam across the river. Pour water behind the dam and observe how the river reacts.

3. In groups, make inferences about how the Boulder Dam affected the Colorado River canyon.

Think about:

- how nearby communities were affected by the rising water

- how the size of the river below the dam changed

- how development can impact the environment

▶ Key Ideas

BEFORE, YOU LEARNED

During the 1930s President Herbert Hoover struggled to address the country's economic problems.

NOW YOU WILL LEARN

President Franklin D. Roosevelt launched an aggressive program to fight the Great Depression.

▶ Vocabulary

TERMS & NAMES

Franklin Delano Roosevelt Democratic president who created the New Deal to counter the effects of the Great Depression

First New Deal 1933–1935 program created by President Roosevelt to fight the Depression

Twentieth Amendment constitutional amendment moving presidential inauguration from March to January

Hundred Days March 9 to mid-June 1933 congressional session in which many laws designed to fight the Depression were passed

fireside chats series of radio talks in which FDR explained his policies in a casual style

Second New Deal 1935–1937 extension of Roosevelt's First New Deal

Social Security Act law creating fund for assisting retired workers and the unemployed

BACKGROUND VOCABULARY

deficit spending using borrowed money to fund government programs

REVIEW

socialism economic system in which members of a society own businesses equally

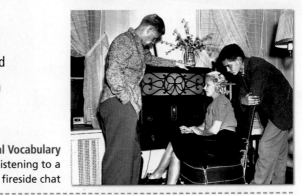

Visual Vocabulary listening to a fireside chat

▶ Reading Strategy

Re-create the diagram shown at the right. As you respond to the **KEY QUESTIONS**, use the diagram to record the main goals of the First New Deal. You may add additional branches.

 See Skillbuilder Handbook, page R4.

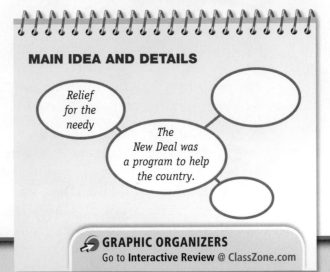

MAIN IDEA AND DETAILS

Relief for the needy

The New Deal was a program to help the country.

🔧 **GRAPHIC ORGANIZERS**
Go to **Interactive Review** @ ClassZone.com

Roosevelt and the New Deal

 14.D.3 Describe roles and influences of individuals, groups and media in shaping current Illinois and United States public policy (e.g., *general public opinion, special interest groups, formal parties, media*).

15.E.3b Explain how laws and government policies (e.g., *property rights, contract enforcement, standard weights/measurements*) establish rules that help a market economy function effectively.

One American's Story

During the 1932 presidential campaign, FDR had offered few specifics about how he would solve the nation's problems. But voters appreciated his upbeat campaign speeches and great personal charm. Roosevelt's inaugural speech showed his serious side. It also displayed his trademark optimism.

PRIMARY SOURCE

❝ So, first of all, let me assert my firm belief that the only thing we have to fear is fear itself—nameless, unreasoning, unjustified terror which paralyzes needed efforts to convert retreat into advance. ❞

—Franklin Delano Roosevelt, *Inaugural Address*

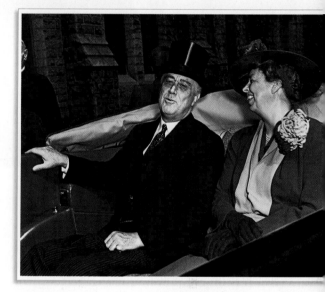

Franklin Delano Roosevelt and Eleanor Roosevelt

FDR's words reassured Americans and gave them hope that their country could prosper once again.

Roosevelt Takes Charge

▼ **KEY QUESTION** What were the goals of the New Deal?

During his campaign, FDR created a comprehensive program to fight the Great Depression. He called it the "New Deal." There were two New Deals. In the **First New Deal**, which lasted from 1933 to 1935, FDR focused his programs on relief, recovery, and reform in America.

The Waiting Period The country had to endure a frustrating four-month wait from the November election to Roosevelt's inauguration in March. The **Twentieth Amendment**, which moved the inauguration date to January, was ratified too late for Roosevelt. As he waited, FDR consulted his brain trust—a group of economists and professors who had advised him during his campaign. They studied the nation's problems and recommended solutions.

The Hundred Days On March 4, 1933, **Franklin Delano Roosevelt** was finally inaugurated as the 32nd president. With the help of Congress, he set to work immediately. The session of Congress lasting from March 9 to mid-June 1933 is called the **Hundred Days**.

Roosevelt took three immediate steps that boosted public confidence. First, he declared a bank holiday—a temporary shutdown of all banks. Second, he promised that only the banks that were in good shape would be allowed to reopen. And third, FDR communicated directly with the public through **fireside chats**, a series of radio talks in which he explained his policies in a warm, casual style.

Roosevelt gave the first fireside chat on March 12, 1933. It was the day before banks reopened. FDR told Americans it was safer to "keep your money in a reopened bank than under the mattress." The next day, people deposited more money into banks than they withdrew.

During the Hundred Days, FDR sent many new bills to Congress. These bills had three major goals—to bring relief to the needy, recovery for agriculture and industry, and reforms to the economy. (The chart on page 788 lists programs of the first hundred days of FDR's First New Deal and explains what those programs accomplished.)

Responses to the New Deal Some critics thought the New Deal went too far. In programs such as the Tennessee Valley Authority (TVA), government-run enterprises competed with private businesses. This caused many people to view New Deal programs as a form of **socialism**, an economic system in which members of a society own businesses equally.

Other critics charged that the New Deal didn't go far enough. Louisiana senator Huey Long suggested a program he called "Share the Wealth," under which every family would be guaranteed a decent income. Another critic, Francis Townsend, wanted every American over age 60 to receive a $200 pension, or sum of money paid regularly, every month.

In the 1934 congressional elections, voters had a chance to react to these criticisms. But, indicating their support for Roosevelt, voters sided with FDR and sent even more Democrats to Congress.

▲ **MAIN IDEAS & DETAILS** Describe the goals of the New Deal.

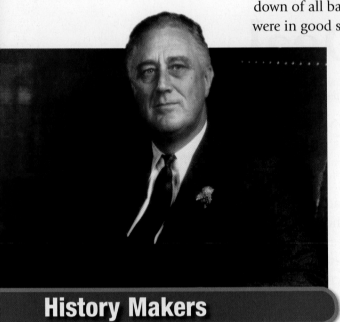

History Makers

Franklin Delano Roosevelt 1882–1945

When Franklin Delano Roosevelt was 39 years old, he contracted the debilitating disease polio, which left him paralyzed from the waist down. With the support of his wife Eleanor, however, Roosevelt refused to give up. Instead, he made himself into a strong and optimistic leader.

Perhaps because of his own physical challenges, Roosevelt was determined to help people in need. Roosevelt's New Deal enacted numerous programs to bring relief to the unemployed, the elderly, the poor, and the homeless. Although raised in social and economic privilege, Roosevelt produced far-reaching social reforms to help those less fortunate.

CRITICAL THINKING Make Inferences
Why might FDR's illness have influenced his thinking about people in need?

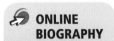 **ONLINE BIOGRAPHY**   For more on Franklin Delano Roosevelt go to the **Research & Writing Center** @ ClassZone.com

NEW DEALS FOR YOUTHS

During the Great Depression, many youths lost their part-time and after-school jobs. As a result, some could not afford to pay for college. Others got into trouble with the law. One person who recognized the severity of this problem was Eleanor Roosevelt, who pushed her husband to address the situation. In 1935 FDR created the National Youth Administration (NYA). This agency provided technical training and part-time jobs for youths in America.

Today, America's youths continue to be important to many presidents. In 1993, President Clinton established AmeriCorps. This program places volunteers throughout the country to assist people in need. In 2003, President Bush nearly doubled AmeriCorps' enrollment to more than 70,000 volunteers annually.

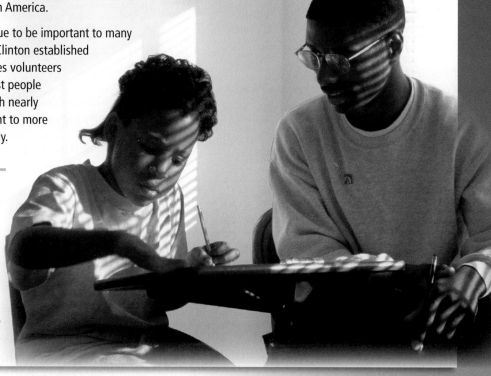
Americorps volunteer tutors student.

CRITICAL THINKING

1. **Evaluate** Some critics thought the NYA took away the ability of young people to solve problems on their own. Do you agree?

2. **Summarize** What is the double purpose of modern programs, such as AmeriCorps?

Roosevelt's Second New Deal

▼ **KEY QUESTION** How did the Social Security Act reflect Roosevelt's goals in the Second New Deal?

Despite some critics of the New Deal, most Americans greatly supported Roosevelt's efforts. Roosevelt was so encouraged by this support that, in 1935, he launched the **Second New Deal**. It lasted until 1937.

Social Reforms The Second New Deal focused on social reform. (See the chart on page 788.) In August 1935, Congress passed one of the most important bills of the century: the **Social Security Act**—dedicated largely to important social issues such as unemployment and retirement.

The act stated that while a person worked, a small amount of each paycheck would go to the Social Security fund in the Treasury. Employers would match their employees' contributions. Then, when a person retired from work, he or she would receive a monthly payment from the fund.

Another part of the act helped disabled, low-income elderly people not eligible for Social Security and low-income families with dependents.

FIRST NEW DEAL, 1933

FERA (Federal Emergency Relief Program)
Provided federal money for relief projects to the roughly 13 million unemployed

PWA (Public Works Administration)
Created jobs by having people build public works, such as highways and bridges

AAA (Agricultural Adjustment Administration)
Regulated farm production and promoted soil conservation

CCC (Civilian Conservation Corps)
Hired young men to work on other conservation projects, such as planting trees

FDIC (Federal Deposit Insurance Corporation)
Protected money of depositors in insured banks

NRA (National Recovery Act)
Regulated industry and raised wages and prices

SECOND NEW DEAL, 1935

WPA (Works Project Administration)
Established national works programs to create jobs

REA (Rural Electrification Administration)
Brought electricity to rural areas

Wagner Act
Protected labor's right to form unions and set up a board to hear labor disputes

Social Security Act
Provided workers with unemployment insurance and retirement benefits

Men working in the CCC

CRITICAL THINKING
Make Generalizations How did New Deal programs help America's workers?

The act also gave a small monthly payment to the unemployed while they looked for work. Explaining the act, FDR stated:

PRIMARY SOURCE

❝ We have tried to frame a law which will give some measure of protection to the average citizen and to his family against the loss of a job and against poverty-ridden old age. ❞

—Franklin D. Roosevelt, quoted in *Promises to Keep*

Roosevelt political button, 1936

FDR's Reelection In 1936, the Democrats nominated Roosevelt for a second term. Business leaders opposed his reelection because they thought that government power was increasing at their expense. But an alliance of working-class Americans supported FDR. The alliance included African Americans, who until then had remained loyal to the Republican Party—the party of Lincoln, who had freed enslaved people during the Civil War. However, FDR's programs to help the poor convinced many African Americans to vote Democrat. On election day, FDR won every state except Maine and Vermont.

🔺 **CAUSES AND EFFECTS** Explain how the Social Security Act reflected Roosevelt's goals in the Second New Deal.

The New Deal Slows Down

🔻 **KEY QUESTION** What led to the slowdown of the Second New Deal?

From the high point of his 1936 victory, Roosevelt's presidency took a downward turn. One of the reasons was a struggle between FDR and the Supreme Court.

Roosevelt and the Supreme Court Most of the nine justices of the Supreme Court did not support FDR's programs. They believed, as did many of Roosevelt's critics, that FDR's programs gave the federal government too much power in controlling the nation's economy. Using the power of judicial review (see Chapter 10), in 1935 the Court struck down laws that it believed gave the federal government too much power. These actions threatened to destroy the New Deal.

In 1937, FDR asked Congress to pass a bill allowing him to add six justices to the Supreme Court. If approved, FDR planned to appoint justices who shared his ideas about increasing the government's role in ending the Great Depression. This would give him the majority he needed to save his programs from being overturned. Both Republicans and Democrats harshly criticized FDR's court-packing bill. They said it interfered with the system of checks and balances that were set up by the U.S. Constitution. Congress agreed and voted it down.

ANALYZING *Political Cartoons*

In 1937, FDR's proposal to add six justices to the Supreme Court earned him many critics. Both Republicans and Democrats in Congress insisted that FDR's plan violated the Constitution. In the cartoon below, the artist depicts FDR's struggle with Congress.

FDR trying to steer a reluctant donkey with the word "Congress" written on it

The donkey is the symbol of the Democratic party.

Political cartoonists used FDR's buggy as a symbol of his presidency.

CRITICAL THINKING

1. **Make Inferences** What does the cartoon say about FDR's relationship with Democrats in Congress?

2. **Draw Conclusions** Why is the donkey resisting FDR?

3. **Synthesize** What is the basic meaning of the cartoon?

 See Skillbuilder Handbook, page R24.

In the end, however, Roosevelt did achieve his goal of a more sympathetic Court. Between 1937 and 1941, retirements and deaths of Supreme Court justices allowed Roosevelt to name eight new judges to the bench. But the president may have lost more than he won. His attempt to pack the Supreme Court with allies damaged his image and gave ammunition to his critics.

A Downward Turn Roosevelt's problems continued into 1937, when he made a grave miscalculation. Like many others, FDR had severe doubts about the use of **deficit spending**, or using borrowed money to fund government programs. As a result, in 1937 Roosevelt decided to reduce the deficit by cutting back on his New Deal programs. He believed the nation had sufficiently recovered its economic health. But FDR was wrong. And the results for the nation were disastrous.

In no time, the economy spiraled downward as the amount of goods produced by industry fell and unemployment rose once again. So bad was this downturn that the economy would not recover fully again until the United States entered World War II in 1941. The war at last provided the hundreds of thousands of jobs needed to end the Great Depression.

 CAUSES AND EFFECTS Describe the key events that caused the slowdown of the Second New Deal.

 Illinois Learning Standards *Review*

⮫ **ONLINE QUIZ**
For test practice, go to
Interactive Review @ ClassZone.com

TERMS & NAMES

1. Explain the importance of
   - Franklin Delano Roosevelt
   - fireside chats
   - First New Deal
   - Second New Deal
   - Twentieth Amendment
   - Social Security Act
   - Hundred Days

USING YOUR READING NOTES

2. **Main Ideas and Details** Complete the diagram you started at the beginning of this section. Record the main goals of the First New Deal. Create a second chart to record the goals of the Second New Deal.

Relief for the needy

The New Deal was a program to help the country.

KEY IDEAS

3. In what ways did Roosevelt give Americans hope?

4. How did FDR succeed in winning a second term?

CRITICAL THINKING

5. **Analyze Point of View** Why did people criticize FDR and his New Deal policies?

6. **Make Inferences** Why might the Social Security Act be considered one of the most important achievements of the New Deal?

7. **Form and Support Opinions** Do you agree with Congress's decision to stop FDR's Court-packing bill? Explain.

8. **Evaluate** How successful was FDR in addressing the Great Depression, and why?

9. **Math** **Graph** One of the New Deal programs was the Agricultural Adjustment Administration. It used the economic theory of supply and demand to help farmers. Use books or the Internet to research both the AAA and supply and demand. Create a graph to show how the AAA's regulation of supply and demand helped farmers.

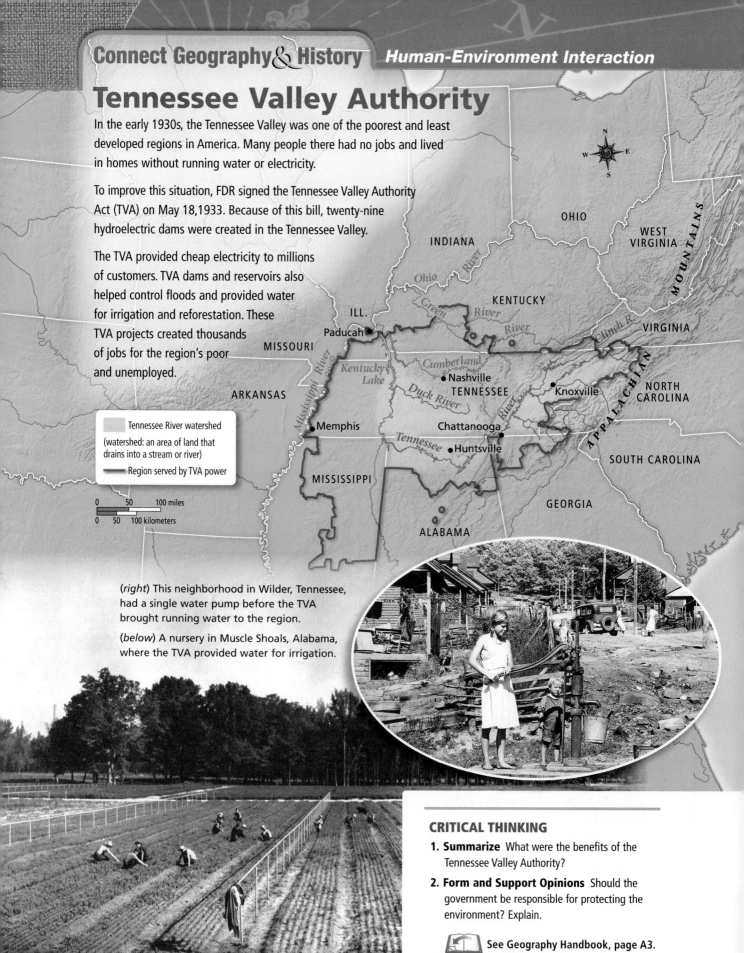

Tennessee Valley Authority

In the early 1930s, the Tennessee Valley was one of the poorest and least developed regions in America. Many people there had no jobs and lived in homes without running water or electricity.

To improve this situation, FDR signed the Tennessee Valley Authority Act (TVA) on May 18, 1933. Because of this bill, twenty-nine hydroelectric dams were created in the Tennessee Valley.

The TVA provided cheap electricity to millions of customers. TVA dams and reservoirs also helped control floods and provided water for irrigation and reforestation. These TVA projects created thousands of jobs for the region's poor and unemployed.

Map labels: OHIO, INDIANA, WEST VIRGINIA, KENTUCKY, VIRGINIA, ILL., Paducah, MISSOURI, MOUNTAINS, Clinch R., Green River, Ohio River, Cumberland River, Kentucky Lake, Nashville, TENNESSEE, Knoxville, NORTH CAROLINA, Duck River, APPALACHIAN, ARKANSAS, Memphis, Chattanooga, Tennessee River, Huntsville, SOUTH CAROLINA, MISSISSIPPI, GEORGIA, ALABAMA, Mississippi River, Kentucky River

Map legend:
- Tennessee River watershed (watershed: an area of land that drains into a stream or river)
- Region served by TVA power

0   50   100 miles
0   50   100 kilometers

(*right*) This neighborhood in Wilder, Tennessee, had a single water pump before the TVA brought running water to the region.

(*below*) A nursery in Muscle Shoals, Alabama, where the TVA provided water for irrigation.

CRITICAL THINKING

1. **Summarize** What were the benefits of the Tennessee Valley Authority?

2. **Form and Support Opinions** Should the government be responsible for protecting the environment? Explain.

    See Geography Handbook, page A3.

The Great Depression and the New Deal   **791**

▶ Key Ideas

BEFORE, YOU LEARNED

In 1933, President Franklin D. Roosevelt launched an aggressive program to fight the Great Depression.

NOW YOU WILL LEARN

The Great Depression and the policies of the New Deal forever changed American society and government.

▶ Vocabulary

TERMS & NAMES

Dust Bowl region including parts of Kansas, Oklahoma, Texas, Colorado, and New Mexico in which farms were damaged by dust storms

Eleanor Roosevelt wife of FDR who helped him monitor New Deal programs and became a strong voice for women and minorities

Congress of Industrial Organizations (CIO) labor union; included skilled and unskilled workers; open to women and minorities

American Federation of Labor (AFL) largest labor union; more selective than CIO

BACKGROUND VOCABULARY

sit-down strike union tactic in which workers stayed idle in a plant rather than walking out

Liberal someone who favors federal government action to bring about social and economic reform

Conservative someone who favors restricted policies in social and economic reform

Visual Vocabulary
Dust Storm, circa 1930

▶ Reading Strategy

Re-create the diagram shown at right. As you read and respond to the **KEY QUESTIONS**, use the diagram to record how the Great Depression affected the American people. Add boxes as needed.

 See Skillbuilder Handbook, page R7.

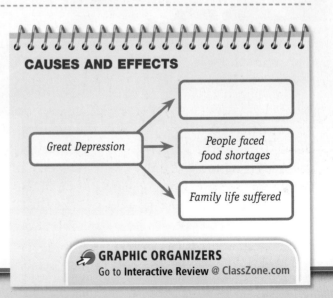

CAUSES AND EFFECTS

Great Depression

People faced food shortages

Family life suffered

GRAPHIC ORGANIZERS
Go to **Interactive Review** @ ClassZone.com

Effects of the Depression and New Deal

14.D.3 Describe roles and influences of individuals, groups and media in shaping current Illinois and United States public policy (e.g., *general public opinion, special interest groups, formal parties, media*).

15.A.3d Describe the causes of unemployment (e.g., *seasonal fluctuation in demand, changing jobs, changing skill requirements, national spending*).

One American's Story

Dynamite Garland's father had worked for the railroad. When the Great Depression struck, Dynamite's father lost his job, and her family moved into a rent-free garage.

PRIMARY SOURCE

❝ We had a coal stove, and we had to each take turns, the three of us kids, to warm our legs. It was awfully cold when you opened those garage doors.
. . . In the morning, we'd get out and get some snow and put it on the stove and melt it and wash around our faces. ❞

—Dynamite Garland, quoted in *Hard Times*

Living Through Hard Times

🔻 **KEY QUESTION** What hardships did the Great Depression bring to Americans?

Child living in Oklahoma City Shacktown by Dorothea Lange.

During the Great Depression, few people escaped financial hardships. But farmers, particularly those on the Great Plains, were especially hard hit.

The Dust Bowl In the early 1930s, a drought hit the Great Plains and lasted for several years. A journalist wrote, "The only movement in the down-driving heat was the dead withering of the dry blighted leaves on the twigs." Even before then, farming and grazing practices had damaged the land by destroying the natural grasses whose roots anchored the soil.

Winds picked up dirt from the dry, exposed fields. During dust storms, day turned into night as walls of dust filled the air and hid the sun. Dust damaged farms across a 150,000-square-mile region called the **Dust Bowl**, which covered parts of Kansas, Oklahoma, Texas, Colorado, and New Mexico. It was years until rain and new farming methods finally brought relief.

Dust Bowl Migration *1930–1940*

Migrants from Texas move to California in 1937.

Area of severe damage
Other areas damaged by dust storms
Migration route

0   200   400 miles
0   200   400 kilometers

Connect Geography & History

1. **Place** Which states suffered the most damage as a result of the dust storms?
2. **Movement** Why did families living in the Dust Bowl migrate west?

With their crops buried under layers of dirt, ruined farmers loaded their belongings onto trucks and set off with their families to find work. Many drove west. They had heard that California's farms needed workers. Because many came from Oklahoma, they were sometimes called "Okies."

By 1940, about 2.5 million people fleeing the Dust Bowl had made their way to California and other Pacific coast states. But as the newcomers poured in, California farm towns quickly became overcrowded.

The Unemployed Not just in the Dust Bowl but all over the country, families suffered. Even after the recovery measures of the New Deal, unemployment remained high. In 1936, for example, 9 million people had no jobs.

Without work, families couldn't afford to buy food. Bread lines fed the hungry. In 1931, New York's 82 bread lines served an average of 85,000 small meals a day, usually consisting of bread with soup or stew. Men, women, and children waited in these lines for their daily food. Some fainted from hunger while they waited.

In addition, many people lost their homes during these difficult times. Thousands of homeless people sought shelter under bridges and overpasses. One woman remembered "people living in old, rusted out car bodies. . . . There were people living in shacks made of orange crates. One family with a whole lot of kids were living in a piano box."

Impact on Women and Children Children had to grow up fast during the Great Depression. To add to their family's income, boys worked after school or even dropped out of school. Often girls had to stay home to look after younger children. Sometimes teenagers who failed to find jobs ran away from home to avoid burdening their families. By late 1932, perhaps a quarter million teens roamed the country. They snuck onto freight trains, begged for food, and lived in squatter camps along the railroad tracks.

Family life suffered as many unemployed men felt a loss of status. They sometimes became irritable and quarreled with their families. Working women came under pressure to give up their jobs to jobless men. In fact, some New Deal projects would hire a woman only if her husband had a job. Even so, poverty forced many women to work as servants or at other low-paying jobs that men didn't want.

Tenement Flats
by Millard Sheets

🔺 **CAUSES AND EFFECTS** Describe the hardships the Great Depression brought to Americans.

Culture in the 1930s

🔻 **KEY QUESTION** How did American culture reflect the Great Depression?

During the Great Depression, Americans sought relief in many ways. Some expressed their desperation through literature, photography, and painting works of art. Others escaped from the misery of their lives through the magic of motion pictures and radio.

Art and Entertainment The Works Progress Administration (WPA) helped writers find employment. Freed from economic worries, they wrote creatively in their spare time. The result was many significant works of literature. John Steinbeck was one such writer. His novel *The Grapes of Wrath* (1939) tells of Okies evicted from their farms.

Motion pictures and radio were also important—and very popular—industries in the 1930s. Even though these were difficult times for most Americans, many thought that 25 cents to see a film was money well spent. In the 1930s, historical epics such as *Gone with the Wind* (1939)

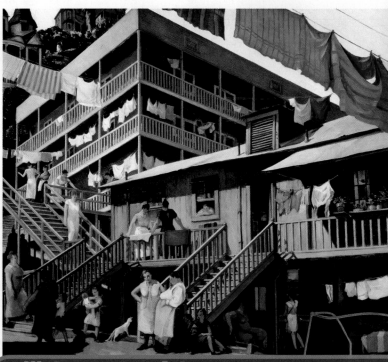

History *through* Art

Tenement Flats

by Millard Sheets

Due to financial hardships during the 1930s, many Americans moved to low-rent apartment buildings called tenements. There, people often lived in small, dirty, unheated, and crowded apartments.

In this painting titled "Tenement Flats," artist Millard Sheets portrays a typical apartment building of the 1930s. Sheets created this painting in 1934 under the Public Works of Art Project (PWAP), that provided economic relief to artists.

CRITICAL VIEWING Make Generalizations What does the painting tell you about life in tenement neighborhoods?

and musicals like *The Wizard of Oz* (1939) were crowd favorites. As a result, many motion picture actors, directors, and executives prospered during the Great Depression, enjoying "the golden age of cinema."

Radio, too, was popular. Once a family owned a radio, the entertainment it provided was free. In addition to enjoying comedy shows, families also listened to President Roosevelt's fireside chats.

History Makers

Eleanor Roosevelt   1884–1962

In 1905, Eleanor Roosevelt married her distant cousin, Franklin Delano Roosevelt. Despite her privileged upbringing, Eleanor was committed to several social causes.

From the start, Eleanor Roosevelt dedicated herself to her husband's causes. As first lady, Mrs. Roosevelt was an active political ally. Often she traveled the country to promote New Deal programs on her husband's behalf.

Even after her husband's death, Mrs. Roosevelt remained an inspired social reformer. She fought for human rights, child welfare, housing reform, and equal rights for women and minorities. By the time of her death in 1962, Eleanor Roosevelt had become one of the most influential women of the 20th century.

COMPARING *Leaders*

How do Eleanor Roosevelt's contributions compare to those of other First Ladies?

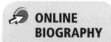

ONLINE BIOGRAPHY   For more on Eleanor Roosevelt, go to the **Research & Writing Center** @ ClassZone.com

▲ **SUMMARIZE** Explain the ways American culture reflected the Depression.

Changes in American Society

▼ **KEY QUESTION** How did New Deal policies impact American society?

FDR's policies offered some opportunities to minorities. However, for the most part, these gains were modest, and minority groups were among those hardest hit by the Depression.

Opportunities for Women Throughout FDR's presidency, First Lady **Eleanor Roosevelt** acted as her husband's "eyes and ears." Often, she traveled on his behalf. She visited coal mines, work camps, and hospitals to find out how programs were working. Then she told the president what she learned and made suggestions.

In March 1933, Eleanor Roosevelt began to hold regular press conferences for women reporters. At these meetings, the first lady introduced the women who ran New Deal programs. During Roosevelt's presidency, more women held government positions than ever before. In 1933, the president named Frances Perkins secretary of labor. This appointment made her the first female cabinet officer.

Minorities and the New Deal Under FDR, African Americans played a bigger role in government than ever before. FDR had a group of African-American advisers, called his "Black Cabinet."

Though he included African Americans in government, FDR failed to back some civil rights bills. In spite of this, African Americans remained loyal to the president because of his efforts to help the poor and end unemployment.

At the same time, many Mexican Americans were also affected by FDR's economic reforms. As the economy worsened, some American farmers blamed Mexican immigrants who had taken their jobs. As a result, the federal government deported some immigrants back to Mexico. Many of those who were forced to leave, however, were legal U.S. citizens. Upon being deported, they argued that their rights as U.S. citizens were ignored.

Unions Gain Strength Some minorities joined a new union, the **Congress of Industrial Organizations** (CIO). Previously, the country's largest labor organization was the **American Federation of Labor** (AFL). It was open only to skilled workers, such as plumbers and electricians. The CIO, however, included both skilled and unskilled workers and was also open to women and minorities.

To improve working conditions, some labor organizations used a **sit-down strike** as a bargaining tactic. Instead of walking off their jobs, striking workers remained idle. This prevented factory owners from hiring strikebreakers. In addition, the Wagner Act, passed in 1935, gave unions the ability to negotiate better working conditions. The growing strength of labor unions was just one legacy of the New Deal.

▲ **SYNTHESIZE** Summarize the New Deal's impact on American society.

Historic Decisions of the SUPREME COURT

NLRB v. Jones & Laughlin Steel Corp. (1937)

KEY ISSUE The role of the U.S. Government in regulating labor relations and union practices

The Case

In 1935, Congress established the National Labor Relations Board (NLRB). This agency was created to regulate labor practices and working conditions.

The following year, the NLRB charged the Jones and Laughlin Steel Corporation with "unfair labor practices" for intimidating union organizers. In 1936, the case went to the Supreme Court to determine if a congressional agency had the authority to regulate labor relations.

HISTORICAL IMPACT In 1937, the Supreme Court ruled in favor of the NLRB. This had a major impact on American business. First, it allowed unions to grow throughout the country. Second, it broadened the power of Congress by confirming its right to regulate corporations.

CRITICAL THINKING

1. **Make Inferences** Why did some people oppose the government's involvement in labor relations?

2. **Causes and Effects** Why did unions grow as a result of the Court's decision?

Legacies of the New Deal

▼ **KEY QUESTION** What are some of the legacies of Roosevelt's New Deal?

Roosevelt's New Deal transformed American society. In the past, Americans had looked to local and state government for help. Under the New Deal, however, the federal government took on a greater role in social reform.

A Larger Role for Government President Roosevelt's presidency had two major effects upon the role of government. First, FDR greatly increased the power of the president's office. During FDR's administration, the White House became the center of government. More than other early 20th-century presidents, Roosevelt proposed bills and programs for Congress to consider instead of waiting for Congress to act.

Second, Roosevelt expanded the federal government. The New Deal established numerous government agencies and organizations to promote government social programs.

CONNECT ⟳ to the Essential Question

How did the government react to the crisis of the Great Depression?

HOOVER'S SOLUTION	PROBLEM	ROOSEVELT'S SOLUTION
Encouraged volunteer relief efforts	**Homelessness and poverty**	Created programs for social relief
Reduced federal spending Raised taxes	**Federal government in debt**	Reduced deficit spending
Funded public works projects that created jobs	**High Unemployment**	Created Public Works Administration Protected laborers' rights Passed Social Security Act to provide unemployment benefits
Did not offer a solution	**Loss of confidence in stock market and banks**	Created SEC to monitor and regulate the stock market Created FDIC to protect money in banks
Reconstruction Finance Corporation	**Government blamed for worsening economy**	Conducted fireside chats to explain policies Increased role of the federal government as protector of public welfare Increased power of the presidency

CRITICAL THINKING Evaluate Did the government do enough to end the Great Depression?

An Ongoing Political Debate Many issues that arose during FDR's presidency continue to influence American politics. For example, **Liberals** and **Conservatives** still argue about whether federal or local government should be responsible for various reform programs. A political liberal favors government action to bring about social and economic reform. A conservative favors fewer government controls and more individual freedom in economic matters.

New Deal Programs Today Despite these lingering disagreements, a number of FDR's New Deal programs remain important today. For example, Social Security—created during the Second New Deal in 1935—still provides retirement and healthcare benefits to millions of Americans. In fact, all Americans who are legally employed must register for Social Security.

In addition, the Federal Deposit Insurance Corporation (FDIC) continues to operate today. This agency insures bank deposits up to $100,000 and replaces the deposits if banks should fail.

The Securities and Exchange Commission (SEC)—created in 1934—continues to monitor the stock market. It makes sure companies and individuals follow fair practices for buying and selling stocks. Both the FDIC and SEC were established after the Stock Market Crash in 1929 and continue to protect American investors today.

▲ **SUMMARIZE** Describe the legacies of Roosevelt's New Deal.

Connecting History

The Role of Government
Debate over the federal government's role in social and economic reform began in the 1780s. Then, Federalists battled Anti-Federalists over the strength of the national government.

 Illinois Learning Standards *Review*

 ONLINE QUIZ
For test practice, go to
Interactive Review @ ClassZone.com

TERMS & NAMES

1. Explain the importance of

- Dust Bowl
- Eleanor Roosevelt
- American Federation of Labor (AFL)
- Congress of Industrial Organizations (CIO)

USING YOUR READING NOTES

2. Causes and Effects Use the diagram to record how the Great Depression affected the American people.

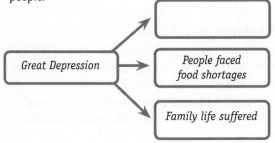

Great Depression →

People faced food shortages

Family life suffered

KEY IDEAS

3. Why were movies popular during the Depression?

4. What was FDR's "Black Cabinet"?

5. How do some of today's political issues date back to the Depression?

CRITICAL THINKING

6. Make Generalizations Why did New Deal programs include funding to support the arts and culture?

7. Compare and Contrast How did Eleanor Roosevelt's early views about the role of women in society contrast with her later views?

8. Evaluate Overall, do you think that minorities gained more under Roosevelt than they had before?

9. Writing Editorial As first lady, Mrs. Roosevelt wrote a newspaper column in which she tried to get support for her programs. Write an editorial about a policy you'd like to see changed in your school or community. State the problem with the policy clearly and provide sound solutions that support your views.

Roll of Thunder, Hear My Cry by Mildred Taylor

Set in segregated Mississippi during the Great Depression, this book develops characters first introduced in Taylor's novel *Song of the Trees*. Through the saga of the Logans, readers come to understand the hardships faced by black families during the Great Depression, a period of financial depression and severe unemployment in the 1930s. Cassie Logan, the main character in *Roll of Thunder, Hear My Cry*, suffers under the crushing oppression of segregation—the separation of groups of people by custom or by law—in the 1930s South. In this scene, Cassie and her brothers, Stacey, Christopher-John, and Little Man, and neighbors T.J. and Claude Avery experience the cruel reality of segregation's inequality as they walk to school.

We were nearing the second crossroads, where deep gullies lined both sides of the road and the dense forest crept to the very edges of high, jagged, clay-walled banks. Suddenly, Stacey turned. "Quick!" he cried. "Off the road!" Without another word, all of us but Little Man scrambled up the steep right bank into the forest.

"Get up here, Man," Stacey ordered, but Little Man only gazed at the ragged red bank sparsely covered with scraggly brown briars and kept on walking. "Come on, do like I say."

"But I'll get my clothes dirty!" protested Little Man.

"You're going to get them a whole lot dirtier you stay down there. Look!"

Little Man turned around and watched saucer-eyed as a bus bore down on him spewing clouds of red dust like a huge yellow dragon breathing fire. Little Man headed toward the bank, but it was too steep. He ran frantically along the road looking for a foothold and, finding one, hopped onto the bank, but not before the bus had sped past enveloping him in a scarlet haze while laughing white faces pressed against the bus windows.

Little Man shook a threatening fist into the thick air, then looked dismally down at himself.

"Well, ole Little Man done got his Sunday clothes dirty," T.J. laughed as we jumped down from the bank. Angry tears welled in Little Man's eyes but he quickly brushed them away before T.J. could see them.

"Ah, shut up, T.J.", Stacey snapped.

"Yeah, shut up, T.J.", I echoed.

"Come on, Man," Stacey said, "and next time do like I tell ya."

Little Man hopped down from the bank. "How's come they did that, Stacey, huh?" he asked, dusting himself off. "How's come they didn't even stop for us?"

"'Cause they like to see us run and it ain't our bus," Stacey said, balling his fists and jamming them tightly into his pockets.

"Well, where's our bus?" demanded Little Man.

"We ain't got one."

ADDITIONAL READING

Growing Up in the Great Depression 1929 to 1941 by Amy Ruth This book shows how young people and their families coped with life during the Great Depression.

The Great Depression by Don Nardo Provides a good perspective on the Great Depression from different points of view.

The Great Depression by Stewart Ross Good illustrated study of the worldwide economic depression of the 1930s.

Chapter Summary

① Key Idea
When the prosperity of the 1920s collapsed, President Herbert Hoover struggled to address the country's economic problems.

② Key Idea
Franklin D. Roosevelt launched an aggressive program to fight the Great Depression.

③ Key Idea
The Great Depression and the policies of the New Deal forever changed American society and government.

↪ For detailed Review and Study Notes go to **Interactive Review** @ ClassZone.com

Name Game

Use the **Terms and Names** list to complete each sentence online or on your own paper.

1. The massive worldwide economic decline of the 1930s is known as the ▸ Great Depression 🖱

2. The congressional session lasting from March to June 1933 was known as the ____.

3. Many Americans lost faith in my presidency during the Great Depression. ____

4. In 1935, Congress passed the ____ to assist retired workers and the unemployed.

5. I defeated Herbert Hoover in 1932 to become the thirty-second president of the United States.

6. The ____ marked the beginning of the Great Depression in America.

7. In the 1930s, a drought caused the Great Plains region to become known as the ____.

8. The ____ was the 1933 to 1935 program created by President Roosevelt to fight the Depression.

9. I was an advocate for women and minorities, as well as First Lady. ____

10. Open only to skilled workers, the ____ was the country's largest labor union.

A. Second New Deal
B. American Federation of Labor
C. Social Security Act
D. Congress of Industrial Organizations
E. Herbert Hoover
F. Dust Bowl
G. First New Deal
H. Twentieth Amendment
I. Eleanor Roosevelt
J. Stock Market Crash of 1929
K. Franklin Delano Roosevelt
L. Hundred Days
M. Buying on Margin
N. Great Depression

Activities

CROSSWORD PUZZLE

Complete the online crossword puzzle to show what you know about the Great Depression.

ACROSS
1. Veterans who protested in Washington were known as _____.

GEOGAME

Use this online map to reinforce your understanding of the Great Depression, including the locations of key events and groups. Drag and drop each name in the list at its location on the map. A scorecard helps you keep track of your progress online.

Tennessee Valley Authority

Boulder Dam

Bonus Army

New York Stock Exchange

"Okies" destination

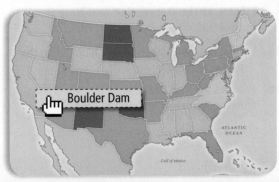

More items online

VOCABULARY

Match each cause on the left with an effect on the right.

1. Dust Bowl
2. Stock Market Crash of 1929
3. Hundred Days
4. Social Security Act
5. Bonus Army

A. Banks failed
B. Americans turned against Hoover
C. Destroyed farms
D. Restored public confidence
E. Created pensions for the needy

Explain how the terms and names in each group are related.

6. speculation, buying on margin, Great Depression
7. Franklin Delano Roosevelt, First New Deal, public works
8. Second New Deal, Congress of Industrial Organizations, sit-down strike

KEY IDEAS

1 Economic Collapse (pages 776–781)

9. Why did stock prices fall so quickly during the Stock Market Crash of 1929?

10. Who did President Hoover think should help the needy?

2 Roosevelt and the New Deal (pages 784–790)

11. What were "fireside chats," and how did they affect the nation?

12. Why didn't President Roosevelt propose many new programs in his second term?

3 Effects of the Depression and New Deal (pages 792–799)

13. Why were farmers hit especially hard during the Great Depression?

14. How did the New Deal change the role of the federal government in American life?

CRITICAL THINKING

15. **Evaluate** What do you think was President Hoover's most successful response to the Depression? Why?

16. **Compare and Contrast** Compare Hoover's response to the Great Depression with FDR's actions.

17. **Analyze Cause and Effect** Review the economic problems that led to the Depression. Are there any similar problems in the economy today? Explain.

18. **Make Inferences** Why were Mexican Americans deported and their rights as U.S. citizens ignored in the 1930s?

19. **Make Judgments** Did FDR's policies truly "fix" the Great Depression? Why or why not?

20. **Analyze** What does the graph below show about unemployment during the first half of the 1920s? How did unemployment change after 1928?

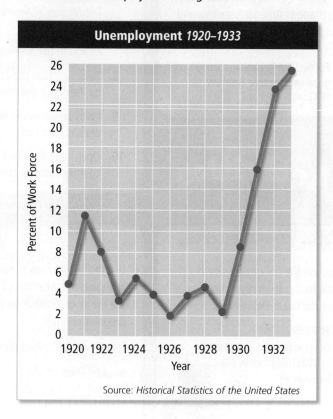

Unemployment 1920–1933

Source: *Historical Statistics of the United States*

DOCUMENT-BASED QUESTIONS

PART 1: Short Answer

Use the photograph, the primary source quotation, and your knowledge of U.S. history to answer the following questions.

DOCUMENT 1

1. Dorothea Lange's 1936 photo, "Migrant Mother," is probably the most famous image of the Great Depression. What does it tell you about the time period?

DOCUMENT 2

PRIMARY SOURCE

❝ I saw and approached the hungry and desperate mother . . . She told me her age, that she was thirty-two. She said that they had been living on frozen vegetables from the surrounding fields, and birds that the children killed. She had just sold the tires from her car to buy food. There she sat in that lean-to tent with her children huddled around her, and seemed to know that my pictures might help her, and so she helped me. There was a sort of equality about it. ❞

—Dorothea Lange, in *Popular Photography*, 1960

2. Why do you think the migrant mother believed Lange's pictures would help her?

Part 2: Essay

3. In two paragraphs explain how the work of artists and writers benefited society during the Great Depression.

YOU BE THE HISTORIAN

21. **Form and Support Opinions** Based on his responses to the Great Depression, how would you rank FDR among America's presidents? Explain.

22. **WHAT IF?** What do you think might have happened to the economy in the 1930s if FDR had not instituted the New Deal?

23. **Make Judgments** Do you think the long-term impact of the federal government's increased involvement in people's lives has been positive or negative? Explain.

24. **Form and Support Opinions** Over time, which view do you think has had the strongest effect on the American system of government: Herbert Hoover's "do-nothing" approach or FDR's belief in the ability of the federal government to assist its citizens? Why?

25. **Evaluate** Which program was the most important achievement of the New Deal?

 Answer the
ESSENTIAL QUESTION
How did the government react to the crisis of the Great Depression?

Written Response Write a two- to three-paragraph response to the Essential Question. Be sure to consider the key ideas of each section along with the actions of the government and individuals. Use the Response Rubric below to guide your thinking and writing.

Response Rubric
A strong response will

• discuss the effects of hardships
• analyze the role of the government in helping people
• include the responses of different types of people, including artists, to the Great Depression
• demonstrate an understanding of the lasting effects of the New Deal

The Rise of Dictators and World War II

1931–1945

ESSENTIAL QUESTION

How did World War II transform America and the world?

CONNECT ▶ **Geography & History**

How did the rise of dictators lead to World War II?

Think about:

1️⃣ the location of the Axis countries in 1936

2️⃣ the areas controlled by the Axis countries in 1941

W HITLER · ANNO · PACE CIVILTÀ LAVORO · XVI · W MVSSOLINI

This 1938 poster celebrates the pact between dictators Adolf Hitler and Benito Mussolini.

German "Tiger" tank, 1944

1935 Congress passes the Neutrality Act. Italy invades Ethiopia.

1937 Japan invades China.

1931

Japan invades Manchuria.

Japanese military flag

1936 Hitler and Mussolini form the Rome-Berlin Axis.

UNITED
STATES

CANADA

ARCTIC
OCEAN

Hawaii (U.S.)
**Pearl Harbor
attack**, 1941

180°

PACIFIC
OCEAN

JAPAN

MANCHURIA

KOREA

150°E

ATLANTIC
OCEAN

60°N

BRITAIN   FIN.

30°W

U.S.S.R.

FRANCE   GER.

POL.

ITALY

CHINA

LIBYA

INDIA

FRENCH WEST AFRICA

DUTCH
EAST INDIES

90°E

0°

ETHIOPIA

	Axis countries
-----	German controlled area
-----	Italian controlled area
-----	Japanese controlled area
	1931 borders

1939   Germany invades Poland.

▼

Effect Britain and France declare
war on Germany.

U.S. Marines
raising the flag
on Mt. Suribachi,
Iwo Jima

LOOSE
LIPS

1941   Japan bombs
Pearl Harbor.

▼

Effect United States
declares war on Japan.

MIGHT
Sink Ships

1944
D-Day invasion

1945

U.S. drops atomic
bombs on Hiroshima
and Nagasaki.

▼

Effect Japan
surrenders.

The Rise of Dictators and World War II **805**

Reading for Understanding

▶ Key Ideas

BEFORE, YOU LEARNED
The Great Depression and the policies of the New Deal forever changed American society and government.

NOW YOU WILL LEARN
The rise of dictators led to World War II.

▶ Vocabulary

TERMS & NAMES

Benito Mussolini Italian Fascist dictator

fascism political philosophy that advocates a strong nationalistic dictatorship

Adolf Hitler German dictator, Nazi Party head

Joseph Stalin Communist dictator of the Soviet Union c.1924–1953

Axis the Rome-Berlin Axis, the alliance between Mussolini and Hitler, later joined by Japan

Neville Chamberlain Prime Minister of Great Britain, made Munich Agreement with Hitler

appeasement meeting demands of a hostile power in order to avoid war

blitzkrieg German "lightning war" tactics

Lend-Lease Act allowed the United States to lend weapons to allies

Pearl Harbor U.S. naval base attacked by Japanese forces on December 7, 1941

BACKGROUND VOCABULARY

Hideki Tojo (HEE•deh•kee TOH•joh) Prime Minister of Japan 1941–1944

infamy evil fame or reputation

Visual Vocabulary
Joseph Stalin

▶ Reading Strategy

Re-create the diagram shown here. As you read and respond to the **KEY QUESTION**, use the diagram to identify causes that brought dictators to power.

 See Skillbuilder Handbook, page R7.

CAUSES AND EFFECTS

Cause
Economic problems

Effect
Dictators seize power

GRAPHIC ORGANIZERS
Go to **Interactive Review** @ ClassZone.com

Steps to War

14.E.3 Compare the basic principles of the United States and its international interests (e.g., *territory, environment, trade, use of technology*).
16.B.3d Describe ways in which the United States developed as a world political power.

One American's Story

George Messersmith was a U.S. diplomat in Austria in the 1930s. What he saw happening in Germany worried him.

PRIMARY SOURCE

❝ The National Socialist regime in Germany is based on a program of ruthless force, which program has for its aim, first, the enslavement of the German population to a National Socialist social and political program, and then to use the force of these 67 million people for the extension of German political and economic sovereignty over South-Eastern Europe—thus putting it into a position to dominate Europe completely. ❞

—**George Messersmith, in *The Making of the Second World War***

Messersmith's predictions would prove true. In the coming years, Germany and its allies threw the world into war.

The Rise of Dictators

🔻 **KEY QUESTION** What brought dictators to power?

By the mid-1930s, dictators, or absolute rulers, had seized control in several countries—Italy, Germany, Japan, and the Soviet Union. Their rise to power was due to the economic and political conditions created by World War I.

The Bitter Legacy of World War I The treaties that ended World War I had not resolved the issues that caused the war. Japan and Italy had helped to win the war, but both were dissatisfied with the treaties. Of the losing countries, Germany was treated most severely. Meanwhile, the war had left the economies of Europe in ruins. Countries on both sides emerged from the war heavily in debt. There was some economic growth in the 1920s, but the world economy collapsed because of the Great Depression in the United States and Europe in the 1930s. Mass unemployment caused widespread unrest. Many Europeans turned to new leaders to solve these problems.

Adolf Hitler salutes the crowd at a 1927 National Socialist (Nazi) Party rally in Nuremberg, Germany. George Messersmith predicted that the Nazi regime would dominate Europe.

Dictators Seize Power One new leader was **Benito Mussolini**, who came to power in Italy in 1922. Mussolini began a political movement known as **fascism** (FASH•iz•uhm). Fascists preached an extreme form of patriotism and nationalism that was often linked to racism. In 1925, he became dictator and took the title *Il Duce* (eel•DOO•chay), or "the Leader."

In Germany, **Adolf Hitler** led the fascist National Socialist German Workers' Party, or Nazi Party. The Nazis attracted supporters by preaching German racial superiority. After elections in 1932, Hitler was appointed chancellor of Germany. He then overthrew the constitution and took control of the government. He called himself *der Führer* (dear•FYUR•uhr), or "the Leader."

In the Soviet Union, the Communists tightened their grip on power during the 1920s and 1930s. **Joseph Stalin** took power in 1924 after the death of Vladimir I. Lenin, who had led the Communist takeover of Russia in 1917. Under Stalin, the government tried to control every aspect of life in the nation. It crushed any form of opposition.

While dictators gained power in Europe, the military increased its power in Japan. In 1941, former army officer **Hideki Tojo** became Prime Minister. As the war progressed, he assumed virtual dictatorial powers.

▲ **CAUSES AND EFFECTS** Describe what brought dictators to power.

Dictators Expand Their Territory

▼ **KEY QUESTION** How did dictators demonstrate their power in the 1930s?

In the 1930s dictators in Europe and Japan seized territory and threatened democratic governments. Little was done to stop them.

Axis Aggression Italy, Germany, and Japan sought new territory. (See "Policies of Aggression" time line on page 809.) In 1936, Hitler and Mussolini formed an alliance called the Rome-Berlin Axis, which became known as the **Axis**. Japan joined the Axis in 1940.

In 1938, Hitler invaded Austria, home to mostly German-speaking peoples. Many residents of Austria and Germany welcomed the unification. After taking over Austria, Hitler set his sights on the Sudetenland, a region of Czechoslovakia where many people of German descent lived. Czechoslovakia did not want to give up the region, however. France and the Soviet Union pledged their support to Czechoslovakia if Germany attacked. Suddenly, Europe teetered on the brink of another war.

Appeasement at Munich British Prime Minister **Neville Chamberlain** met with Hitler in Munich, Germany. They reached an agreement: Germany would gain control of the Sudetenland and Hitler promised to stop seeking more territory. The Munich Agreement was part of the British and French policy of **appeasement**, meeting Germany's demands in order to avoid war. Chamberlain announced that he had achieved "peace in our time." Others, such as Winston Churchill, strongly disagreed with appeasement. He warned, correctly, that Hitler would not stop with the Sudetenland.

▲ **DRAW CONCLUSIONS** Explain how dictators' actions threatened peace.

NORWAY

SWEDEN

FINLAND

• Leningrad

North Sea

DENMARK

Baltic Sea

ESTONIA

LATVIA

LITHUANIA

EAST PRUSSIA

• Moscow

GREAT BRITAIN

Liverpool

Hull

NETHERLANDS

Manchester
London

Berlin •

• Warsaw

U.S.S.R.
(SOVIET UNION)

IRELAND

Bristol

Rotterdam

BELG.

GERMANY

POLAND

Plymouth

Dunkirk

LUX.

CZECHOSLOVAKIA

Extent of Axis advance, 1941

Southampton

Paris •

• Munich

AUSTRIA

HUNGARY

Stalingrad •

ATLANTIC OCEAN

FRANCE

SWITZ.

ROMANIA

Extent of Axis advance, 1940

VICHY FRANCE

ITALY

YUGOSLAVIA

• Belgrade

Black Sea

BULGARIA

Rome •

ALBANIA

PORTUGAL

SPAIN

GREECE

TURKEY

...nean Sea

	Axis, 1939
	Axis-controlled, 1941
	Allies
	Neutral
←	Axis advances
✸	Cities severly damaged by bombing

0   250   500 miles
0   250   500 kilometers

N
W   E
S

Connect Geography & History

1. **Movement** In which direction did the Germans attack in 1940? in 1941?

2. **Place** Which European nations were neutral in World War II?

Policies of Aggression

Japan conquers Manchuria in northern China.

Italy invades Ethiopia in Africa.

Japan invades China.

Germany conquers Czechoslovakia.

German *blitzkrieg* in Poland starts World War II.

Germany invades the Soviet Union.

1931

1935

1937

1939

1941

1936

1938

1940

Hitler moves troops into the Rhineland on French border.

Mussolini and Hitler form Rome-Berlin Axis.

Germany invades Austria.

Germany invades Denmark, Norway, Belgium, and France.

Germany bombs Great Britain.

World War II Begins

▼ **KEY QUESTION** What events led to World War II?

Hitler soon broke his promise. In March 1939, German troops conquered the rest of Czechoslovakia. The *Führer* then said he would seize Polish territory. Britain and France warned that an attack on Poland would mean war.

Germany Starts the War In August 1939, Germany and the Soviet Union agreed not to attack each other. Germany then invaded Poland on September 1, 1939. Great Britain and France declared war on Germany two days later. World War II had begun.

German forces drove deep into Poland using a new method of warfare called *blitzkrieg*, or "lightning war," which stressed speed and surprise in the use of tanks, troops, and planes. In less than a month, Poland fell. In April 1940, Hitler conquered Denmark and overran Norway. Next, Germany launched a *blitzkrieg* against Belgium and the Netherlands.

Allies Under Attack British and French troops could do little to stop the advancing Germans. As nation after nation surrendered, British soldiers and other Allied troops retreated to the French seaport of Dunkirk on the English Channel. Under heavy German bombardment, Allied vessels evacuated nearly 340,000 British, French, and Belgian troops.

In June 1940, Germany invaded France. In less than two weeks, France surrendered. Hitler expected Britain to seek peace after France fell. The British had no intention of quitting, however. Hitler soon made plans to invade Britain. To do so, he needed to destroy Britain's Royal Air Force (RAF). In the summer and fall of 1940, the German air force, or *Luftwaffe* (LUFT•vahf•eh), fought the RAF and bombed London and other civilian targets during the Battle of Britain. The RAF was able to hold off the *Luftwaffe*. Despite constant bombing, the British people did not surrender.

Buildings destroyed by bombing in London near Trafalgar Square, 1942
Which nation's forces bombed London during the Battle of Britain?

Despite his partnership with Stalin, Hitler feared Stalin's ambitions in Europe. He also wanted Soviet wheat and oil fields to help sustain his military machine. In June 1941, his forces invaded the Soviet Union. They inflicted heavy casualties on Soviet troops until December 1941, when the harshest winter in decades stopped the Nazi advance.

In 1941, Congress approved the **Lend-Lease Act**, which Roosevelt had supported. The act allowed the United States to lend or lease resources and equipment to the Allies. The United States sent Great Britain, the Soviet Union, and other Allies about $50 billion worth of goods.

Japan Attacks Pearl Harbor In 1940, Japan had joined the Axis alliance. Then, in 1941, Hideki Tojo came to power, and Japan became even more warlike. The Tojo government planned to conquer the Dutch East Indies, a source of oil, and other Asian territories. In the eyes of Japan's rulers, only the U.S. Navy stood in their way. On December 7, 1941, Japanese warplanes bombed the huge American naval base at **Pearl Harbor** in Hawaii. The attack came as a complete surprise. About 2,400 Americans—both servicemen and civilians—died. Many U.S. warplanes and ships were destroyed or damaged, leaving the U.S. fleet devastated.

President Roosevelt asked Congress to declare war on Japan. He called December 7, 1941 "a date that will live in infamy." The nation quickly united behind him. On December 11, Japan's allies Germany and Italy declared war on the United States.

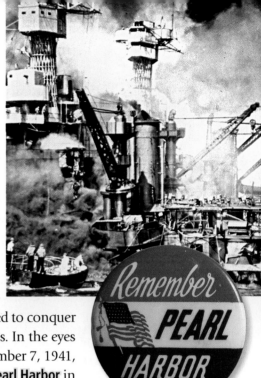

(*top*) U.S.S. *West Virginia* and U.S.S. *Tennessee* under attack at Pearl Harbor. (*bottom*) Pearl Harbor button.

 SEQUENCE EVENTS Describe the events that led to World War II.

ONLINE QUIZ
For test practice, go to
Interactive Review @ ClassZone.com

Illinois Learning Standards *Review*

TERMS AND NAMES

1. Explain the importance of the following:

- Benito Mussolini
- fascism
- Adolf Hitler
- Joseph Stalin
- Axis
- Neville Chamberlain
- appeasement
- *blitzkrieg*
- Lend-Lease Act
- Pearl Harbor

USING YOUR READING NOTES

2. Causes and Effects Complete the diagram you started at the beginning of this section. Add more boxes to show more causes or create a new chart if needed.

KEY IDEAS

3. Which dictators helped cause World War II?

4. What event brought the United States into the war?

CRITICAL THINKING

5. Synthesize Why do you think dictators were able to gain such power and threaten other countries?

6. Evaluate What role was played by the nonaggression pact between Germany and the Soviet Union in the start of World War II?

7. Writing Letter Write a letter to President Roosevelt explaining why the United States should or should not enter World War II.

▶ Key Ideas

BEFORE, YOU LEARNED

The rise of dictators in Europe and Asia led to World War II.

NOW YOU WILL LEARN

Americans at home made great contributions to the Allied victory.

▶ Vocabulary

TERMS & NAMES

War Production Board government agency set up during World War II to coordinate the production of military equipment and supplies

A. Philip Randolph African-American labor leader active during World War II

braceros Mexican workers hired to perform farm labor during World War II

Tuskegee Airmen famous segregated unit of African-American pilots

Rosie the Riveter a character who symbolized women in manufacturing jobs

Japanese-American internment the removal of Japanese Americans from the West to prison camps during World War II

Nisei (NEE•say) Japanese Americans born in the United States

BACKGROUND VOCABULARY

gross national product total value of all the goods and services produced by a nation during a year

rationing the distribution of scarce resources and products

REVIEW

war bonds loans that the government promised to repay with interest

▶ Reading Strategy

Re-create the diagram shown here. As you read and respond to the **KEY QUESTIONS**, use the center oval to record the main idea. Use the outer ovals to note important details.

 See Skillbuilder Handbook, page R4.

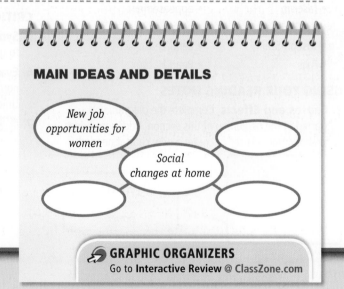

MAIN IDEAS AND DETAILS

New job opportunities for women

Social changes at home

GRAPHIC ORGANIZERS
Go to **Interactive Review** @ ClassZone.com

The Home Front

14.C.3 Compare historical issues involving rights, roles and status of individuals in relation to municipalities, states and the nation.

15.E.3b Explain how laws and government policies (e.g., *property rights, contract enforcement, standard weights/measurements*) establish rules that help a market economy function effectively.

One American's Story

During World War II, Margaret Hooper took a job as an "incoming inspector" at an aircraft plant. She often described her work in her letters to a friend serving with the Pacific fleet.

PRIMARY SOURCE

❝ Gosh, we have been working hard at work lately. Just rushed to death and never getting through. Our production schedule has been doubled and still we work harder and put out more all the time. . . . ❞

—Margaret Hooper, quoted in *Since You Went Away*

Americans like Hooper worked together on the home front to help achieve an Allied victory.

American defense worker riveting a warplane

Supporting the War Effort

▼ **KEY QUESTION** What social changes did the war bring about?

The effort to defeat the Axis powers took more than just soldiers. American forces needed planes, tanks, weapons, parachutes, and other supplies. As in World War I, the war effort brought about social change.

Wartime Production During World War II, the government set up an agency called the **War Production Board** (WPB) to coordinate the production of military equipment and supplies. Under the guidance of the WPB, factories churned out materials around the clock. By 1945, the country had built about 300,000 aircraft and 75,000 ships. The United States was producing 60 percent of all Allied ammunition.

With so many factories in need of workers, jobs became easy to find. In effect, the war ended the Great Depression. During the war, the country's yearly **gross national product** (GNP) rose to new heights. The GNP is the total value of all the goods and services produced by a nation during a year. Between 1939 and 1945, the U.S. GNP soared from $90.5 billion to nearly $212 billion.

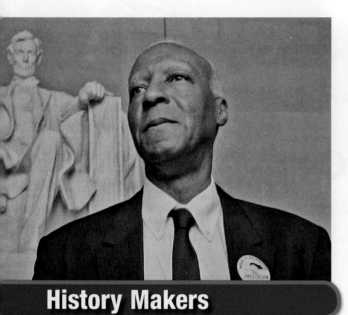

History Makers

A. Phillip Randolph (1889–1979)

Randolph moved to Harlem as a young man and attended City College. In 1925 he organized railroad sleeping car porters into a union, the Brotherhood of Sleeping Car Porters. On trains, sleeping cars had attendants called porters who were mostly African Americans. Randolph's union won gains for workers from the Pullman Company. During World War II, he became a leader for civil rights for all African Americans when his efforts led President Roosevelt to outlaw discrimination in defense industries. After the war, Randolph helped lead the fight against Jim Crow laws in the South. In 1963, he was one of the leaders of the March on Washington for civil rights, along with Dr. Martin Luther King, Jr.

CRITICAL THINKING What obstacles do you think African-American workers faced in their struggle for improved working conditions and pay?

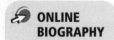 **ONLINE BIOGRAPHY** For more on A. Philip Randolph, go to the **Research & Writing Center** @ ClassZone.com

As the armed forces' needs for materials grew, Americans found that some goods became scarce. For example, American auto makers did not produce any cars between 1942 and 1945. Instead, they built tanks, jeeps, and airplanes. Items such as gasoline, tires, shoes, meat, and sugar were also in short supply. To divide these goods among its citizens, the government used a system of **rationing**, or giving families a fixed amount of a certain item.

The war was expensive. To help pay the cost, the government raised income taxes and sold **war bonds**. These bonds were loans that the government promised to repay with interest. Movie stars promoted bonds, and Americans bought enough bonds to raise billions of dollars for the war.

Opportunities and Tensions for Minorities The war created new job opportunities for minorities. More than 1 million African Americans worked in the defense industry during the war. Many of them migrated from the South to fill these jobs, most of which were located on the West Coast and in the North. The inflow of African Americans often inflamed racial tensions. In 1943, a race riot broke out in Detroit. Thirty-four people were killed before federal troops restored order.

On paper, at least, African Americans had equal rights in some workplaces. **A. Philip Randolph**, an African-American labor leader, helped to achieve these rights in 1941. Randolph threatened to lead an African-American protest march for better jobs through Washington, D.C. To prevent the march, President Roosevelt issued Executive Order 8802. It outlawed discrimination in defense industries working for the federal government.

About 40,000 Native Americans worked in the nation's war industries. Tens of thousands of Hispanics—people with ancestors from Spanish-speaking lands—also joined the country's war-related laborers. Included in this group were thousands of Mexicans workers known as *braceros*. The U.S. government requested the *braceros'* help because the nation faced a shortage of farm workers during the war years. By mid-1945, more than 120,000 *braceros* worked on farms throughout the country. Meanwhile, Mexican Americans struggled against prejudice and sometimes violence. In 1943, riots erupted in Los Angeles after American servicemen attacked Mexican Americans. These riots became known as the Zoot Suit Riots for the bold, broad-shouldered zoot suits that some young Mexican American men wore.

Minorities also aided the war effort by serving in the armed forces. About one million African Americans served in the armed services. Because of racial prejudice, they served in segregated units. One such unit was the **Tuskegee Airmen**, African-American pilots and crew members who served with honor in North Africa and Europe. More than 300,000 Mexican Americans also fought in the war.

Opportunities for Women With so many men fighting overseas, the demand for women workers rose sharply. In 1940, about 14 million women worked—about 25 percent of the nation's labor force. By 1945, that number grew to more than 19 million—roughly 30 percent of the work force. Women worked in munitions factories, shipyards, and offices. Much of the nation welcomed the growing numbers of women into the workplace. The country promoted "**Rosie the Riveter**"—an image of a strong woman hard at work at an arms factory—as its symbol for its new group of wage earners.

More than 300,000 women served in the U.S. armed forces. Many worked for the Women's Army Corps (WAC) as mechanics, drivers, and clerks. Others joined the Army and Navy Nurse Corps. Thousands of women performed important noncombat duties in the U.S. Navy and Coast Guard.

▲ **SUMMARIZE** Describe the social changes brought about by the war.

CONNECT *Citizenship and History*

MILITARY SERVICE

Many Americans believe that military service is a civic duty, and they honor those who have risked their lives for liberty. During World War II, more than 2.5 million African Americans registered for the draft to fight for an ideal of democratic freedom that still did not fully include them.

Almost one million African-American soldiers served their country even though they were restricted to segregated units, usually as laborers. There were some exceptions. The Army Air Corps started training African Americans in 1941. In 1942, the Coast Guard began to integrate its ship crews. President Harry S. Truman ordered an end to military segregation in 1948. The armed forces began to desegregate during the Korean War, from 1950 to 1953.

Colonel Benjamin O. Davis, Jr., commander of the Tuskegee Airmen

Activity

1 Interview someone you know who lived through World War II.

2 Ask the following questions: What did you do during the war? How did your decision affect your life?

3 Share the person's responses with your class.

 See Citizenship Handbook, page 303.

The Internment of Japanese-Americans

▼ **KEY QUESTION** What happened to Japanese-Americans after Pearl Harbor?

In the aftermath of the Japanese attack on Pearl Harbor, a growing number of Americans directed their anger toward people of Japanese ancestry.

Sent to Internment Camps In response to the anti-Japanese hysteria that grew after Pearl Harbor, President Roosevelt signed Executive Order 9066 in February 1942. The order allowed for the removal of Japanese and Japanese Americans from the Pacific Coast. This action came to be known as the **Japanese-American internment**. More than 110,000 men, women, and children were rounded up. They were forced to sell their homes and possessions, leave their jobs, and move to prison-like camps. About two-thirds of the people interned were *Nisei*, Japanese Americans born in the United States.

Fred Korematsu was convicted of defying Executive Order 9066 by refusing to leave his home. In 1944, Korematsu appealed his conviction to the Supreme Court. He argued that the order was unconstitutional because it was based on race. The Court, however, ruled that the order was based on military necessity and was constitutional. Korematsu's conviction stood.

The nation's fear of disloyalty from Japanese Americans was unfounded.

> 🔊 **ONLINE PRIMARY SOURCE**
>
> Hear the perspectives at the **Research & Writing Center** @ ClassZone.com

---

COMPARING ▶ *Perspectives*

JAPANESE-AMERICAN INTERNMENT

Sue Kunitomi Embry

Many Americans thought Japanese-American internment was necessary to protect national security. Fewer Americans viewed it as a racist, fear-driven reaction against loyal Americans whose only crime was to look like the enemy.

Some internees, such as Sue Kunitomi Embry, felt that being interned would help Japanese Americans prove their patriotism:

"I had a neighbor who said . . . 'You know, we're American Citizens, and we really could fight this thing.' . . . I just had the feeling that this was something the whole community was going to go through because . . . we're loyal, and we'll do whatever we need to do in order to help the war effort. "

General John DeWitt was in charge of the Western Defense Command. He testified to Congress for the need for internment:

"I don't want any of them (people of Japanese descent) here. They are a dangerous element. There is no way to determine their loyalty. . . . It makes no difference whether he is an American citizen, he is still a Japanese. American citizenship does not necessarily determine loyalty."

CRITICAL THINKING

1. **Analyze Points of View** Why did most Americans feel that Japanese-American internment camps were necessary during World War II?

2. **Form an Opinion** Do you think that the United States government ever has the right to suspend Americans' civil rights? Explain your answer.

Many of the camp internees raised the American flag each morning. Thousands of young men in the camps volunteered to fight for the United States. The all-*Nisei* units, the 442nd Infantry and the 100th Infantry, fought in Europe. They were among the most highly decorated units in the war. One member, Daniel Inouye, showed extreme courage. After being wounded, he led his platoon in an attack in Italy. He lost an arm in the attack, but earned the Distinguished Service Cross for his bravery.

△ SUMMARIZE Explain what happened to Japanese-Americans after Pearl Harbor.

(*top*) Japanese Americans under arrest after Pearl Harbor
(*inset*) Internees who were released, such as Ruth Asawa, carried War Relocation Authority identification cards.

 Illinois Learning Standards *Review*

 ONLINE QUIZ
For test practice, go to
Interactive Review @ ClassZone.com

TERMS & NAMES

1. Explain the importance of the following:
   - War Production Board
   - A. Philip Randolph
   - *braceros*
   - Tuskegee Airmen
   - Rosie the Riveter
   - Japanese-American internment
   - *Nisei*

USING YOUR READING NOTES

2. **Main Ideas and Details** Complete the diagram you started at the beginning of the section. Then create a new diagram for each main idea in this section.

New job opportunities for women

Social changes at home

KEY IDEAS

3. Why were certain goods rationed during the war?
4. Why were Japanese-Americans sent to internment camps?

CRITICAL THINKING

5. **Compare and Contrast** Compare and contrast what happened to many American women during the war with what happened to African-American men.

6. **Summarize** How did fear and prejudice factor into the decision to send Japanese-Americans to internment camps?

7. **Art** **Poster** Make a poster that promotes the wartime service of the Tuskegee Airmen, women workers, or the *braceros*.

8. **Connect** *to* **Today** Which World War II-era laws and government programs still affect Americans today?

▶ Key Ideas

BEFORE, YOU LEARNED
Americans at home made great
contributions to the Allied victory.

NOW YOU WILL LEARN
The Allies defeated the Axis powers in
Europe and Africa.

▶ Vocabulary

TERMS & NAMES

D-Day Allied invasion of France on June 6,
1944

General Erwin Rommel German commander
in North Africa

General Dwight D. Eisenhower Supreme
Allied Commander in Europe

Stalingrad Soviet city where the German
army was forced to surrender after a battle
that lasted for months

Battle of the Bulge final German assault in
December 1944 in Ardennes region of Belgium
and Luxembourg

Yalta Conference conference where Allies
planned the post-war world

Holocaust Nazi German crime of killing more
than 11 million Jews and other persecuted
peoples in concentration camps

BACKGROUND VOCABULARY

anti-Semitism prejudice against Jews

Visual Vocabulary
Yalta Conference

▶ Reading Strategy

Re-create the diagram shown here.
As you read and respond to the
KEY QUESTIONS, use the diagram
to record important events in the
order that they occurred.

 See Skillbuilder Handbook, page R5.

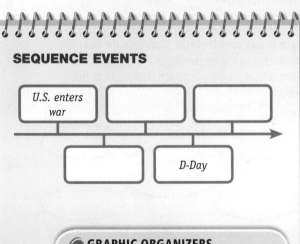

SEQUENCE EVENTS

U.S. enters
war

D-Day

GRAPHIC ORGANIZERS
Go to **Interactive Review** @ ClassZone.com

War in Africa and Europe

14.E.3 Compare the basic principles of the United States and its international interests (e.g., *territory, environment, trade, use of technology*).
16.B.3d Describe ways in which the United States developed as a world political power.

One American's Story

On June 6, 1944, more than 150,000 Allied soldiers crossed the English Channel to the coast of Normandy in northern France. Major John R. Armellino was the commanding officer of one of the first units to land.

PRIMARY SOURCE

❝ Many men were cut down as they left the craft. Those who reached the shore started running across the beach through heavy machine-gun crossfire, mortars, and artillery fire. ❞

—Major John R. Armellino (Ret.)

This Allied invasion of France became known as **D-Day**. It was the largest seaborne invasion in history. By the end of the month, 850,000 Allied troops had poured into France.

On D-Day, photographer Robert Capa was struggling to get ashore while under heavy fire from German defenses when he took this picture of American troops landing on Omaha Beach. The photograph is blurry because Capa could not stand still to take it.

Allied Advances

🔻 **KEY QUESTION** How did the Allies turn the tide in Europe and North Africa?

The Japanese attack on Pearl Harbor pulled the United States into World War II. Now, the nation had to build up its armed forces quickly. Millions of Americans enlisted. Millions more were drafted, or selected for military service. Under the Selective Service Act of 1940, all men between the ages of 21 and 35 had to register for military service.

The Fight for North Africa The Allies began making plans to invade Europe. The Americans wanted to land in France as soon as possible. Stalin agreed. But Churchill thought the Allies were unprepared for such an invasion. He convinced the Americans that the Allies should first drive the Germans out of North Africa in order to gain control of the Mediterranean and open the way to invade Europe through Italy.

History Makers

Dwight D. Eisenhower (1890–1969)

"Ike," as he was known to his soldiers, excelled at leadership. As Supreme Commander of the Allied forces, he was able to harness the different abilities and egos of outstanding generals and hammer out campaigns that were both brilliant and efficient. Eisenhower rose through the ranks on the strengths of his organizational abilities, and his leadership emerged in the crucible of wartime. After the war, he served as the Military Governor of the U.S. Occupation Zone of Germany. In 1952 he was elected President of the United States.

CRITICAL THINKING Why was organizational skill important for a person in Eisenhower's position?

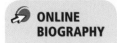 **ONLINE BIOGRAPHY** For more on Dwight D. Eisenhower, go to the **Research & Writing Center** @ ClassZone.com

Since the summer of 1940, Britain had been battling Axis forces for control of northern Africa—especially Egypt. Without Egypt, the British would lose access to the Suez Canal. The canal was the shortest sea route to Asia and the Middle Eastern oil fields. British troops in northern Africa faced a tough opponent in Germany's **General Erwin Rommel**. Rommel's skills had earned him the nickname "The Desert Fox." He commanded Germany's Afrika Korps, including two powerful tank divisions. In June 1942, Rommel's tanks pushed the British lines to the Egyptian town of El Alamein. The Desert Fox was just 200 miles from the Suez Canal.

The British stopped Rommel's advance at El Alamein and then forced the Germans to retreat. Allied troops, under the command of American **General Dwight D. Eisenhower**, landed in northern Africa in November 1942. They advanced toward Rommel's army in Tunisia. In February 1943, the two sides clashed. The inexperienced Americans were pushed back by Rommel's forces. However, the Allies regrouped and continued attacking. In May, the Axis powers in northern Africa surrendered. The Allies now could set up bases from which to attack southern Europe.

Invasion of Italy The Allies invaded the Italian island of Sicily in July 1943. (See map on page 821.) Allied and Axis forces engaged in a month of bitter fighting. American nurse June Wandrey remembered trying to help one wounded 18-year-old soldier.

PRIMARY SOURCE

❝ He looked up at me trustingly, sighed and asked, "How am I doing, Nurse?" . . . I put my hands around his face, kissed his forehead and said, "You are doing just fine, soldier." He smiled sweetly and said, "I was just checking up." Then he died. Many of us shed tears in private. ❞

—June Wandrey, quoted in *We're in This War, Too*

The Allies forced the Germans out of Sicily and then swept into Italy. By this time, Italians had turned on Mussolini, and officials had imprisoned him. Although he escaped, the new Italian government surrendered to the Allies in September 1943.

▲ **SUMMARIZE** Describe how the Allies turned the tide in North Africa and Europe.

Germany On the Defensive

▼ **KEY QUESTION** What events helped put Germany on the defensive?

For three years Hitler's troops had won battles and occupied other nations with lightning speed. However, the German advance into the Soviet Union ended in disaster for the German army.

German Retreat from Russia In September 1942, German forces attacked the Russian city of **Stalingrad**, an important industrial center. The Soviet army fiercely defended the city. As winter approached, the German commander begged Hitler to let him retreat, but Hitler refused.

Fighting continued through the winter. Soviet troops drove tanks across the frozen landscape and launched a massive counterattack that trapped the Germans and cut off their food and supplies. Many thousands of Nazi soldiers froze or starved to death. In February 1943, the remaining German troops surrendered.

Each side had suffered staggering losses. It was not apparent at the time, but the German defeat at Stalingrad was the turning point of the war. Soviet troops began to push the German Army westward out of the Soviet Union and back towards Germany.

World War II in Europe and Africa 1942–1945

1942 • British forces stop the German advance at El Alamein.

1943 • German troops surrender at Stalingrad.
• Allies invade Sicily. Italy surrenders.

1944 • Allies invade Normandy; liberate Paris.
• Hitler launches the Battle of the Bulge.

1945 • Allied forces advance on Berlin.
• Germany surrenders on May 7.

Connect Geography & History

1. **Place** Identify the places where the Allies had to make an invasion from the sea.

2. **Evaluate** Why was the Soviet victory in Stalingrad so crucial to the defeat of Germany?

Legend:
- Axis
- Axis controlled, 1942
- Allies
- Neutral
- ← Allied advances
- ✸ Major Allied victories

June 6, 1944: D-Day Hitler soon had other things to worry about in the West. Hitler felt sure that the Allies would attack at Calais (ca•LAY), the narrowest point on the English Channel separating England and France. In June 1944, the Allies' plan to invade France began. The plan, Operation Overlord, was commanded by General Eisenhower, the Supreme Allied Commander in Europe. On June 6, shortly after midnight, Allied paratroopers and glider-borne forces landed behind German lines in Normandy, a region of northern France. Then, in the early morning, more than 5,000 ships and landing craft carried more than 150,000 American, British, and Canadian soldiers across the Channel to Normandy. This historic assault became known as D-Day, and was the largest land-sea-air operation in history. Although the size and location of the attack surprised the German forces positioned along the beach, more than 10,000 Allied soldiers were killed or wounded as they attempted to move inland. By day's end, however, the Allies had secured the beaches.

The Allies Gain Ground By the end of June 1944, 850,000 Allied troops had poured into France. They moved inland toward Paris, battling German troops along the way. On August 25, Allied forces freed the French capital.

D-Day on Omaha Beach

From concrete fortifications and machine gun nests above the beach, German soldiers pinned down American forces in the early hours of the Allied invasion of Normandy.

As they fought to retake the rest of France from the Germans, General George S. Patton, commander of the Third Army under General Omar Bradley, led the way to the German frontier. During this time, many American heroes emerged. One of them was Audie Murphy, the most decorated U.S. soldier of World War II. In January 1945, when German troops attacked Murphy's unit in France, he climbed on a burning tank destroyer and used its machine gun to kill or wound about 50 enemy troops. The U.S. government awarded him the Medal of Honor, the nation's highest military award.

As Allied forces advanced through Europe from the west, Soviet troops were beating back Hitler's army in the east. In December 1944, Hitler launched a final assault, the **Battle of the Bulge**. German troops pushed back Allied forces in the Ardennes region of Belgium and Luxembourg before U.S. forces regrouped and defeated them. The battle's human toll was costly, with about 120,000 German casualties and about 80,000 Americans casualties.

▲ **SUMMARIZE** Identify the events that put Germany on the defensive.

D-Day Sea Invasion Map

London
GREAT BRITAIN   Dover
Southampton   Strait of Dover
Portland   Calais
Dartmouth   Allied Forces
50°N
English Channel   Cherbourg
4°W   2°W   FRANCE
Axis-controlled

0 30 60 miles
0 30 60 kilometers

The Allies divided the Normandy coast into five sectors for Operation Overlord. From west to east, the sectors were code-named Utah (American), Omaha (American), Gold (British), Juno (Canadian), and Sword (British).

The Rise of Dictators

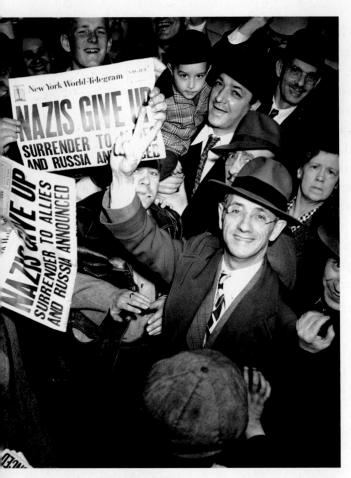

Americans celebrated Victory in Europe Day on May 8, 1945.

The War Ends in Europe

▼ **KEY QUESTION** What crimes did the Allies discover as they advanced toward Berlin?

By early 1945, the Germans were retreating every-where. As the Americans and British advanced from the west, the Russians raced toward the German capital from the east.

Planning the Postwar World In February 1945, Allied leaders met in the Soviet resort of Yalta. Attending the **Yalta Conference** were the "Big Three" as they were called—Roosevelt, Churchill, and Stalin. During the conference, these leaders made plans for the end of the war and the future of Europe.

Stalin promised to declare war on Japan after Germany surrendered. The three leaders also agreed to establish a postwar international peace-keeping organization. In addition, they discussed the type of governments that would be set up in Eastern Europe after the war.

By the time of the Yalta Conference, President Roosevelt was in poor health. In April 1945, just months after being sworn in for a fourth term, the president died. Roosevelt's vice-president, Harry S. Truman, succeeded him and continued the war effort.

Germany Surrenders In late April 1945, the Russians reached Berlin. Deep inside his air-raid bunker, Adolf Hitler sensed the end was near. On April 30, the man who had conquered much of Europe committed suicide.

On May 2, the Soviet Army captured Berlin. Five days later, German leaders officially signed an unconditional surrender at General Eisenhower's head-quarters in France. The Allies declared the next day, May 8, as V-E Day, or Victory in Europe Day. The war in Europe was finally over.

The Horrors of the Holocaust As the Allies fought toward Berlin, they made a shocking discovery. Scattered throughout German-occupied Europe were concentration camps where Jews and people of other persecuted groups had been murdered.

The world soon learned of the horrifying events that took place behind German lines during the war. In what has become known as the **Holocaust**, the Nazis killed about 6 million Jewish men, women, and children—almost two-thirds of the Jews in Europe. The Nazis also killed millions of people of other ethnic groups, including Gypsies (or Roma), Russians, and Poles, as well as political prisoners and homosexuals. An estimated 11 million people were killed in all.

The roots of the Holocaust lay in Adolf Hitler's intense hatred of Jews. He had preached that the Jews were inferior to Germans, and he blamed them for Germany's troubles. After becoming leader of Germany, Hitler had enforced **anti-Semitism**, prejudice against Jews, by denying them many of their rights.

Soon after war broke out, Germany's anti-Semitic policies took an even darker turn. In a policy decision labeled "The Final Solution," Nazi leaders set out to murder every Jew under German rule. To accomplish this evil scheme, the Germans built huge facilities known as concentration camps. Officials crammed Jews into railroad boxcars and sent them to these camps. They forced able-bodied people to work. All others were slaughtered.

On reaching the camps, the advancing Allies were outraged by what they saw. The Allies would eventually bring German leaders to trial for what they had done. First, however, they had to defeat the Japanese.

 MAIN IDEAS & DETAILS Identify crimes the Allies discovered as they advanced towards Berlin.

(*top*) Child prisoners of Auschwitz just after liberation, 1945
(*bottom*) Under Hitler's government, Jews were forced to wear this yellow Star of David badge that identified them as Jewish.

Illinois Learning Standards *Review*

 ONLINE QUIZ
For test practice, go to
Interactive Review @ ClassZone.com

TERMS & NAMES

1. Explain the importance of the following:

- D-Day
- General Erwin Rommel
- General Dwight D. Eisenhower
- Stalingrad
- Battle of the Bulge
- Yalta Conference
- Holocaust

USING YOUR READING NOTES

2. Sequence Events Complete the chart that you started at the beginning of the section. Add boxes as needed to include events, or create a new chart.

U.S. enters war

D-Day

KEY IDEAS

3. How did victory in North Africa help the Allies in invading southern Europe?

4. Why were the Germans surprised on D-Day?

5. What was Auschwitz?

CRITICAL THINKING

6. Analyze Why do you think Hitler refused to allow his army to retreat from Stalingrad?

7. WHAT IF? How might the outcome of the war have changed if the D-Day invasion had not been successful?

8. Writing Biography Use the Internet and other library resources to research someone who was part of the D-Day invasion or who survived the Holocaust. Use your research to write a short biography of that person.

The Rise of Dictators and World War II **825**

▶ Key Ideas

BEFORE, YOU LEARNED
The Allies defeated the Axis powers in Europe and Africa.

NOW YOU WILL LEARN
After early losses, the Allies defeated the Japanese in the Pacific.

▶ Vocabulary

TERMS & NAME

Battle of Midway U.S. victory over Japanese off Midway Island that proved to be the turning point of the war

island hopping Allied strategy in Pacific of invading selected islands, and using them as bases to advance closer to Japan

Guadalcanal first U.S. land victory over the Japanese, 1943

Manhattan Project top-secret government project to develop the atomic bomb

Hiroshima Japanese city that was hit with the first atomic bomb on August 6, 1945

BACKGROUND VOCABULARY

Code Talkers Navajo Indians recruited by the U.S. Marine Corps to transmit messages in the Navajo language

kamikaze (KAH•mih•KAH•zee) Japanese suicide pilot

Visual Vocabulary
Code Talkers

▶ Reading Strategy

Re-create the diagram shown here. As you read and respond to the **KEY QUESTIONS**, use the diagram to compare and contrast Japanese and American fighting tactics.

 See Skillbuilder Handbook, page R8.

COMPARE AND CONTRAST

Japanese	American
	• *island hopping*

 GRAPHIC ORGANIZERS
Go to **Interactive Review** @ ClassZone.com

War in the Pacific

14.E.3 Compare the basic principles of the United States and its international interests (e.g., *territory, environment, trade, use of technology*).
16.B.3d Describe ways in which the United States developed as a world political power.

One American's Story

In April 1942, more than 70,000 Filipino and American troops surrendered to the Japanese on the Bataan Peninsula in the Philippines. From there, the Japanese marched the soldiers over 65 miles to a prison camp. On the way, about 10,000 prisoners died from shootings, beatings, or starvation. This tragedy became known as the Bataan Death March. American Sergeant Sidney Stewart was there.

PRIMARY SOURCE

❝ The sun beat down on my throbbing head. I thought only of bringing my feet up, putting them down, bringing them up. Along the road the jungle was a misty green haze, swimming before my sweat-filled eyes. The hours dragged by, and a great many of the prisoners reached the end of their endurance. . . .They fell by the hundreds in the road. . . . There was a crack of a pistol and the shot rang out across the jungle. There was another shot, and more shots, and I knew that, straggling along behind us, was a clean-up squad of Japanese, killing their helpless victims. . . . I gritted my teeth. 'Oh, God, I've got to keep going. I can't stop. I can't die like that'. ❞

—Sidney Stewart, quoted in *Give Us This Day*

Filipino and American troops on the Bataan Death March

Allied and Japanese forces would fight on for three more years in the Pacific before the Allies emerged victorious.

Fighting the Japanese Empire

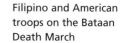 **KEY QUESTION** How did the Allies stop the Japanese advance?

Japan's expanding empire threatened American possessions in the Pacific Ocean. Upon entering the war, the United States was forced to fight on two fronts. While some troops crossed the Atlantic to fight in Europe and North Africa, others were sent to fight the Japanese in the Pacific.

Marines fighting hidden Japanese forces in the jungles of Bougainville in the Solomon Islands, November, 1943
What territories and nations did Japanese forces invade and conquer?

Japanese Conquests At the same time as the attack on Pearl Harbor, Japanese forces launched attacks throughout the Pacific. By Christmas, Japan controlled Hong Kong, Thailand, and the U.S. islands of Guam and Wake.

The Japanese also pushed further into Southeast Asia, attacking Malaya and Burma. Great Britain, which ruled these lands and Hong Kong, fought back. But British forces proved to be no match for the Japanese invaders. Japan conquered the region within a few months.

It took Japan longer to conquer the Philippines. They invaded the islands in December 1941 and pushed the Allied forces from the capital city of Manila onto the Bataan Peninsula. American and Filipino troops, led by U.S. General Douglas MacArthur, then fought the Japanese to a standstill for several months.

As fighting raged in the Philippines, the Allies feared that the Japanese might invade Australia. President Roosevelt ordered MacArthur to withdraw to Australia in March 1942. Upon reaching Australia, MacArthur promised, "I shall return." Shortly after MacArthur left, the Japanese mounted an offensive. The U.S. troops on Bataan surrendered and endured the brutal Bataan Death March. The situation looked bleak for the Allies.

The Allies Turn the Tide at Midway In the spring of 1942, the Allies began to turn the tide against the Japanese. The push began in April, with a daring air raid on Japanese cities, including Tokyo. Lieutenant Colonel James Doolittle led 16 bombers in the attack. Doolittle's raid caused little damage, but it shocked Japan's leaders and boosted the Allies' morale.

In May, the U.S. Navy clashed with Japanese forces in the Coral Sea off Australia. For the first time in naval history, enemy ships fought a battle without seeing each other. Instead, war planes launched from aircraft carriers fought the battle. Neither side won a clear victory in the Battle of the Coral Sea. However, the Americans had successfully blocked Japan's push toward Australia.

The opposing navies clashed again in June off the island of Midway in the central Pacific. The U.S. Navy destroyed four Japanese carriers and at least 250 planes. America lost one carrier and about 150 planes. The **Battle of Midway**, in June 1942, was a turning point in the war.

▲ **MAIN IDEA & DETAILS** Explain how the Allies stopped the Japanese advance.

U.S.S.R.
(SOVIET UNION)

ALASKA
(U.S.)

60°N

150E°   165E°   180°   165°W

Attu,
June 1942

Aleutian Islands

Kiska,
June 1942

45°N

Kuril Islands

PACIFIC
OCEAN

MONGOLIA   MANCHURIA

Beijing

KOREA

Nagasaki,
Aug. 9, 1945

JAPAN
Tokyo

CHINA

Nanking

Hiroshima,
Aug. 6, 1945

Battle of Midway,
June 1942

30°N

Pearl Harbor,
Dec. 1941

TAIWAN

Okinawa,
April–June
1945

Iwo Jima,
Feb.–Mar. 1945

Tropic of Cancer

*Hawaiian Islands
(U.S.)*

BURMA

Hong
Kong

*Mariana
Islands*

Wake I.

15°N

THAILAND

INDOCHINA

PHILIPPINES

Guam,
July–Aug. 1944

Saipan,
June–July 1944

*Marshall
Islands*

N
W   E
S

MALAYA
Singapore

Leyte Gulf,
Oct. 1944

Caroline Islands

Equator

Tarawa,
Nov. 1943

0°

*Gilbert
Islands*

DUTCH
EAST INDIES

NEW
GUINEA

*Solomon
Islands*

0   500   1,000 miles
0   500 1,000 kilometers

Coral Sea,
May 1942

Guadalcanal,
Aug. 1942–Feb. 1943

Coral Sea

15°S

Legend:
- Japanese empire, 1931
- Japanese gains by 1942
- Allies
- ← Allied advances
- ▪▪▪ Extent of Japanese expansion
- 💥 Allied victory
- ✶ Japanese victory
- ☁ Atomic bombing

AUSTRALIA

Connect Geography & History

1. **Location** Why did Japanese leaders want to expand their empire?

2. **Analyzing Maps** Which battles took place closest to the Japanese mainland?

The Allies Gain the Upper Hand

🔻 **KEY QUESTION** How was the United States able to make progress in the Pacific?

After the Battle of Midway, the Americans went on the attack to liberate the lands Japan had conquered. Rather than attempt to retake every Japanese-held island, American military leaders decided to invade islands that were not heavily defended by the Japanese. The Americans could then use the captured islands to stage further attacks. This strategy was known as **island hopping**.

General Douglas MacArthur (center) led Allied troops in the Pacific.

Progress in the Pacific Most of the Allied progress in the Pacific was made by American troops. They gained their first major land victory against the Japanese on the island of **Guadalcanal**. U.S. Marines marched ashore in August 1942. Six months of bitter fighting followed. In February 1943, the Americans finally won the battle. Playing a role in this victory—and in many others throughout the Pacific—was a group of Navajo Indians. To keep Japanese intelligence from breaking American codes, the U.S. military had begun using the Navajo language to transmit important messages. The Marines recruited over 400 Navajos to serve as **Code Talkers**.

A *kamikaze* makes an unsuccessful attempt to fly his plane into an American ship.

In October 1944, Allied forces invaded the Philippines. The effort included a massive three-day naval battle off the Philippine island Leyte (LAY•tee). The Allies won the battle, which left Japan's navy so badly damaged that it was no longer a threat. Allied forces came ashore and liberated Manila in March 1945. Three years after leaving the Philippines, General MacArthur had returned as promised.

Although they lost the fight in the Philippines, the Japanese increased their use of a new weapon—the *kamikaze*, or suicide pilot. *Kamikazes* filled their planes with explosives and crashed them into Allied warships. Many Japanese pilots volunteered for these suicide missions but they couldn't stop Allied advances.

Iwo Jima and Okinawa By the end of 1944, with Japan's defenses weakened, the Allies began bombing Japan. To succeed, however, they had to establish bases closer to the mainland. They chose the Japanese-held islands of Iwo Jima and Okinawa. In February 1945, U.S. Marines invaded Iwo Jima. In late February, American soldiers planted the U.S. flag at the top of Iwo Jima's Mount Suribachi, signaling their victory, though fighting continued for several days afterward. In April, they invaded Okinawa. In the several months it took the U.S. Marines to conquer both islands, more than 18,000 U.S. men died. Japanese deaths exceeded 120,000.

▲ **SUMMARIZE** Describe the progress made by U.S. troops in the Pacific.

Atomic Weapons End the War

▼ **KEY QUESTION** Why did the United States decide to drop the atomic bomb?

In the summer of 1945, Japan continued to fight. The Allies planned to invade Japan in November 1945. American military leaders feared that the invasion might cost between 200,000 and 1,000,000 American casualties. Therefore, American officials considered the use of an atomic bomb.

The Manhattan Project Shortly after entering the war, the United States had set up the **Manhattan Project** in 1942. This was a top-secret program to build an atomic bomb. Led by American physicist J. Robert Oppenheimer, the project team worked for three years to construct the weapon.

Soon after scientists and military officials successfully tested the bomb, President Truman told Japan that if it did not surrender, it faced destruction. The Japanese refused to give in. On August 6, 1945, the B-29 bomber *Enola Gay* dropped

The ruins of Hiroshima after August 6, 1945

an atomic bomb on the industrial city of **Hiroshima**. The explosion killed more than 75,000 people and turned five square miles into a wasteland. Still, the Japanese refused to surrender. On August 9, the United States dropped a second atomic bomb on Nagasaki, killing another 40,000. On August 14, Japan surrendered. September 2, 1945, Japanese and Allied leaders met aboard the U.S. battleship *Missouri* in Tokyo Bay. There, Japanese officials signed an official letter of surrender. The war was over.

 DRAW CONCLUSIONS Explain why the United States dropped atomic bombs on Japanese cities.

Illinois Learning Standards *Review*

 ONLINE QUIZ
For test practice, go to
Interactive Review @ ClassZone.com

TERMS & NAMES

1. Explain the importance of the following:
- Battle of Midway
- island hopping
- Guadalcanal
- Manhattan Project
- Hiroshima

USING YOUR READING NOTES

2. Compare and Contrast Complete the chart that you started at the beginning of the section.

Japanese	American
	• *island hopping*

KEY IDEAS

3. Why did President Roosevelt have General MacArthur withdraw from the Philippines?

4. Why was Guadalcanal an important victory?

5. What happened in Nagasaki on August 9, 1945?

CRITICAL THINKING

6. Compare and Contrast What different challenges did the United States face fighting in the Pacific versus fighting in Europe?

7. Form an Opinion Did President Truman make the right decision to use atomic bombs against the Japanese? Explain your answer.

8. Connect *to* **Today** How do atomic weapons impact the balance of military power in the world today?

The Rise of Dictators and World War II **831**

▶ Key Ideas

BEFORE, YOU LEARNED
After early losses, the Allies defeated the Japanese in the Pacific.

NOW YOU WILL LEARN
World War II had deep and lasting effects on the United States and the world.

▶ Vocabulary

TERMS & NAMES

Marshall Plan U.S. plan developed by George C. Marshall to help boost the economies of European nations after the war

Potsdam Conference Allies' meeting in Potsdam, Germany, to plan the end of the war

Nuremberg trials war crime trials of Nazi leaders in Nuremberg, Germany

United Nations international peacekeeping body founded by 50 nations in April 1945

G.I. Bill of Rights government bill that paid for veterans' education and living expenses

REVIEW

communism single-party political system in which the government controls and plans the economy with the goal of common ownership of all property

Visual Vocabulary
United Nations building in New York

▶ Reading Strategy

Re-create the diagram shown here. As you read and respond to the **KEY QUESTION**, use the diagram to identify the costs of World War II.

 See Skillbuilder Handbook, page R7.

CAUSES AND EFFECTS

World War II → _millions of soldiers died_

GRAPHIC ORGANIZERS
Go to **Interactive Review** @ ClassZone.com

The Legacy of World War II

14.E.3 Compare the basic principles of the United States and its international interests (e.g., *territory, environment, trade, use of technology*).
16.B.3d Describe ways in which the United States developed as a world political power.

One American's Story

When the end of the war came, Elliot Johnson was excited. He was finally going home. However, one of his captains told the troops that it might not be so easy.

PRIMARY SOURCE

❝ 'You guys are anxious to get home and put this all behind you,' he said. 'But you don't understand how big a part of your life this has been. You'll put it all behind you for about ten years, and then someday you'll hear a marching band. You'll pick up the beat and it will all come back to you and you'll be right back here on the parade ground marching again.' And he was right. ❞

—Elliot Johnson, quoted in *The Homefront*

From the soldiers who survived it to families who lost a loved one, World War II affected millions of people in the United States and around the world.

Members of the Fourth Infantry Division return from Europe aboard the *Hermitage*.

Worldwide Destruction

🔻 **KEY QUESTION** What were the costs of the war?

No war has caused as much death and destruction as World War II. When peace returned, cities all over the world lay in ruins and millions had died.

The War's Human Cost Although specific statistics will never be known, the human cost on both sides was immense. About 20 million soldiers were killed, and millions more were wounded. The Soviet Union suffered the greatest losses, with estimates of about 8 million military deaths and another 5 million soldiers wounded. More than 400,000 American soldiers died and more than 600,000 were wounded.

Civilian casualties also numbered in the millions. Both the Allied and Axis powers had fought a war without boundaries. They bombed cities and destroyed villages. Again, the Soviet Union experienced the worst losses. An estimated 7 to 12 million Soviet citizens died. China, under attack from Japan in the 1930s, lost about 10 million civilians.

The war created a huge wave of refugees. They included orphans, prisoners of war, survivors of concentration camps, and those who fled advancing armies. After the war, 21 million refugees, most starving and homeless, tried to put their lives back together amid the ruins of Europe and Asia.

Economic Winners and Losers The war left many of the world's economies in ruins. Only the United States—where no major battles were fought except for Pearl Harbor—came out of the war with a strong economy. The wartime boom in industry had pulled the nation out of the Great Depression. After the war, the U.S. economy kept growing.

U.S. forces occupied Japan for several years after the war. During that time, they created programs to help Japan's economy recover. In 1948, Congress approved Secretary of State George C. Marshall's plan to help boost European economies. Under the **Marshall Plan**, the United States gave more than $13 billion to help the nations of Europe get back on their feet.

▲ **SUMMARIZE** Describe the costs of World War II.

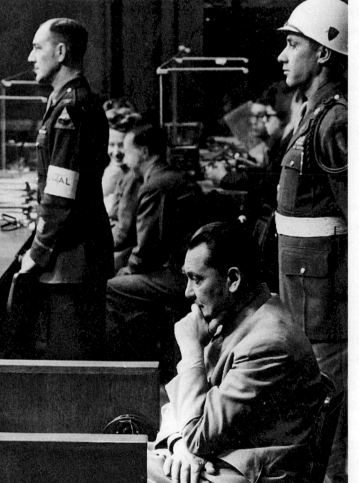

Hermann Göring, shown here seated on the witness stand at Nuremberg, created and headed the GESTAPO—the Nazi secret police—which persecuted, imprisoned, enslaved, and murdered political and racial "undesirables."
What were the Nazis' "crimes against humanity?"

Attempts at World Peace

▼ **KEY QUESTION** What did the international community do to protect world peace?

After the war, the international community took steps to ensure that such a conflict would never happen again.

The Nuremberg Trials In July 1945, the Allies held the **Potsdam Conference** to plan the war's end. They decided to put German war criminals on trial at the **Nuremberg trials**, which opened that November in Germany. The original 24 defendants included some of Hitler's top officials. They were charged with crimes against humanity for the Nazis' murder of millions of Jews and others. The U.S. chief counsel spelled out why the trial was needed.

PRIMARY SOURCE

". . . these prisoners . . . are living symbols of racial hatreds, of terrorism and violence, and of the arrogance and cruelty of power."

—**Robert H. Jackson,** *The Nürnberg Case*

INTERNATIONAL CRIMINAL COURT

On July 17, 1998, 120 nations created the first independent and permanent International Criminal Court, or ICC, by adopting a treaty called the Rome Statute. The Rome Statute describes the ICC's goals, structure, rules, and jurisdiction, or the crimes it may prosecute. The ICC's goals are to promote the rule of law and make sure serious international crimes are punished. Under the Rome Statute, these crimes include genocide, war crimes, aggression, and crimes against humanity such as torture, slavery, and apartheid.

Although the ICC is independent, it works with the United Nations, national governments, and citizens to investigate and prosecute international crimes. In recent years, the ICC has investigated crimes in Uganda, the Democratic Republic of the Congo, and the Darfur region of Sudan.

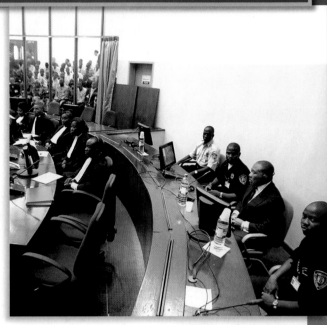

In 2006, the Special Court for Sierra Leone used ICC facilities at the Hague for the war crimes trial of former Liberian president Charles Taylor.

CRITICAL THINKING

1. **Main Ideas and Details** What are the goals of the International Criminal Court?
2. **Compare and Contrast** What does the ICC have in common with the United Nations?

After nearly a year-long trial, 19 of the defendants were found guilty. Twelve were sentenced to death. Over 130 others were found guilty in later trials. The Nuremberg trials upheld an important idea: people are responsible for their actions, even in wartime.

The Creation of the United Nations The war also helped to establish the principle that nations must work together in order to secure world peace. The outbreak of World War II demonstrated the weakness of the League of Nations, the international peacekeeping body created after the First World War. The League was weak in large part because the United States had refused to join out of a strong desire to stay out of foreign affairs. Toward the end of World War II, President Roosevelt urged Americans not to turn their backs on the world again.

The country listened. In April 1945, delegates from 50 nations—including the United States—met in San Francisco to discuss creating a new international peace organization. In June, all 50 nations approved the charter creating the new peacekeeping body known as the **United Nations**, or UN.

▲ **PROBLEMS AND SOLUTIONS** Describe what nations did to protect world peace.

Changes in America and the World

▼ **KEY QUESTION** What changes did the war bring about?

The war radically altered the world. Not only were economies ruined and lives lost, but many nations experienced social change. The war also helped the spread of **communism**, which America would oppose in the years ahead.

Changes in American Society With millions of veterans back home, competition for jobs and education increased dramatically. The government responded by passing the **G. I. Bill of Rights,** or G. I. Bill, which paid for returning soldiers' schooling and gave them a living allowance. More than 8 million veterans went to school under the G. I. Bill.

The return of so many veterans also created great demand for housing. The Truman administration addressed the country's housing shortage. However, many Americans had to live in crowded urban slums or in country shacks.

CONNECT ⟳ to the Essential Question

How did World War II transform America and the world?

U.S. CHANGES	GLOBAL CHANGES	
• 400,000+ soldiers dead	• About 20 million soldiers dead	• U.S. creates Marshall Plan to help European economies recover
• 600,000+ soldiers wounded	• Millions of soldiers wounded	• United Nations replaces League of Nations
• Japanese Americans arrested and interned	• Millions of civilians killed or wounded in Holocaust or bombings	• German war criminals tried at Nuremberg
• New job opportunities during the war for women and minorities	• Jews and other groups interned in Nazi concentration camps	• Communism spreads
• Millions of Americans move to the West Coast and cities to take war-related jobs	• Communities destroyed by bombing in Europe and Asia	• United Nations creates new nation of Israel
• Strong economy keeps growing	• 21 million refugees, many starving and homeless	• Soviet Union becomes world power
• As veterans return home, competition increases for jobs, education, and housing; many women are fired from their wartime jobs.	• Economies in Europe and Asia shattered	• Atomic age begins
• More than 8 million veterans return to school under G. I. Bill of Rights	• U.S. forces occupy Japan, create economic recovery programs	

CRITICAL THINKING **Compare and Contrast** How did World War II's effects on America compare to the war's effects on the rest of the world?

Returning veterans found an America that had changed. During the war, millions of Americans had moved to find war-related jobs in California and the cities. By war's end, hundreds of thousands of African Americans had moved from the South to Northern cities. There, they lived in overcrowded ghettos and experienced prejudice. However, many also found economic opportunity.

International Tensions Although many countries worked together toward lasting peace, tensions still lingered after the war. In response to the Holocaust, the United Nations created the new nation of Israel in 1948 as a homeland for the Jews in Palestine. Many Arabs in Palestine violently opposed Israel. Fighting broke out as neighboring Arab nations attacked the new nation. The Israeli-Palestinian conflict continues to this day and remains an obstacle to peace in the Middle East.

The United States was concerned with the rise of the Soviet Union. Despite huge losses, the Soviet Union emerged from World War II as a great power. During the war, Stalin had promised to promote democracy in Soviet-occupied Eastern Europe. Instead, he forced the occupied countries to live under Communist regimes and wanted to spread communism. The United States wanted to halt it. This would lead to future conflict.

Finally, the end of the war marked the beginning of the atomic age. The atomic bombs dropped on Japan were a powerful new weapon, one that increased tensions between the United States and the Soviet Union.

 SUMMARIZE Explain what changes were brought about by the war.

Illinois Learning Standards *Review*

🔄 **ONLINE QUIZ**
For test practice, go to
Interactive Review @ ClassZone.com

TERMS & NAMES

1. Explain the importance of
- Marshall Plan
- United Nations
- Potsdam Conference
- G.I. Bill of Rights
- Nuremberg Trials

USING YOUR READING NOTES

2. Causes and Effects Complete the chart you started at the beginning of this section. Add more boxes to show more effects or create a new chart if needed.

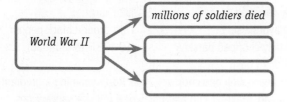

World War II → millions of soldiers died

KEY IDEAS

3. What happened in Japan after the war?

4. Who was put on trial at the Nuremberg Trials?

5. Why was the United Nations created?

CRITICAL THINKING

6. Analyze Why was it in the interest of the United States to spend billions of dollars on the Marshall Plan?

7. Draw Conclusions Why do you think Arab nations attacked the new nation of Israel?

8. **Science** **Research and Form an Opinion** Use the Internet and library resources to find out more about the problems and benefits of using atomic energy. Then write a short essay explaining whether or not nations should use atomic energy as an energy source. Support your opinion with facts you have researched.

American Spirit

Do with less— so they'll have enough!

RATIONING GIVES YOU YOUR FAIR SHARE

A NATION UNITES

Americans on the home front united behind the war effort. What effect did the war have on daily life?

> " Use it up. Wear it out. Make it do. Or do without. "
> —War Advertising Council slogan

Teens in History

GARDENING FOR VICTORY

In December 1941, Americans young and old became citizen gardeners to help the war effort as part of the National Victory Garden Program. Students at Jane Addams High School in Portland, Oregon, earned physical culture credits for working in their school's victory garden. By the summer of 1943, almost 20 million victory gardens produced a third of America's vegetables.

RATIONING

The U.S. Office of Price Administration began its rationing program on May 5, 1942, with a 28-stamp "Sugar Book." The government created ten different rationing programs, including coffee, butter and other fats, canned and frozen goods, red meat, gasoline, oil, and metal.

Activity

Make a Victory Sandwich

Magazines printed recipes and menus to help families eat nourishing meals while wartime rationing was in effect.

Victory Sandwiches

2.5 cups cooked string beans, finely chopped	1/4 t dried thyme
2 T mayonnaise	1/2 t salt
2 T finely chopped parsley	1/8 t ground black pepper
1/4 t dried basil	(10-12 slices of bread)

Drain beans well and chop very fine. Add remaining ingredients and blend. Makes 1 cup and fills 5 or 6 full-size sandwiches.

—from Joanne Lamb Hayes, *Grandma's Wartime Kitchen: World War II and the Way We Cooked.*

Chapter Summary

1 Key Idea
The rise of dictators led to World War II.

2 Key Idea
Americans at home made great contributions to the Allied victory.

3 Key Idea
The Allies defeated the Axis powers in Europe and Africa.

4 Key Idea
After early loses, the Allies defeated the Japanese in the Pacific.

5 Key Idea
World War II had deep and lasting effects on the United States and the world.

For detailed Review and Study Notes go to **Interactive Review** @ ClassZone.com

Name Game

Match each sentence with the correct term or name.

1. I convinced the president to desegregate the defense industry. _____ A. Philip Randolph

2. The Germans used _____, or "lightning war" attacks.

3. Italians called me *Il Duce*. _____

4. Our segregated combat unit included fighter pilots. _____

5. We used the Navajo language as a code. _____

6. The United States dropped atomic bombs on Hiroshima and _____ .

7. Germans called me *der Führer*. _____

8. I was the British prime minister who appeased Hitler during the Munich crisis. _____

9. I was a symbol for women who worked in defense industries. _____

10. The "Big Three" met at the _____ to plan Europe's future and the end of the war.

A. Lend-Lease Act
B. Neville Chamberlain
C. General Hideki Tojo
D. Rosie the Riveter
E. Adolf Hitler
F. Benito Mussolini
G. Tuskegee Airmen
H. Nagasaki
I. Yalta Conference
J. Nisei
K. A. Philip Randolph
L. Dwight D. Eisenhower
M. *kamikaze*
N. Code Talkers
O. *blitzkrieg*

Activities

CROSSWORD PUZZLE

Complete the online crossword puzzle to show what you know about World War II.

ACROSS
1. General _____ was the Supreme Allied Commander in Europe.

GEOGAME

Use this online map to reinforce your knowledge of World War II in Europe, including alliances and major battles. Drag and drop each name or event at its location on the map. A scorecard helps you keep track of your progress online.

blitzkrieg
Stalingrad
Battle of the Bulge
El Alamein
Omaha Beach

More place names online

VOCABULARY

Match the term or name in the left hand column with its definition or identification in the right.

1. Holocaust
2. Dwight D. Eisenhower
3. Joseph Stalin
4. island hopping
5. Manhattan Project

A. Nazi German crime of killing millions of people
B. developed atomic bomb
C. Allied strategy in the Pacific
D. Supreme Allied Commander in Europe
E. Soviet dictator

Explain what the terms and names in each group have in common.

6. Battle of Midway, Guadalcanal, Hiroshima
7. War Production Board, Rosie the Riveter, rationing
8. Stalingrad, D-Day, Battle of the Bulge

KEY IDEAS

1 Steps to War (pages 806–811)

9. Why did Hitler attack the Soviet Union?
10. Explain how the United States became involved in the war.

2 The Home Front (pages 812–817)

11. In what ways did Americans at home contribute to the war effort?
12. Why did the nation put thousands of Japanese Americans in internment camps during the war?

3 War in Africa and Europe (pages 818–825)

13. Why did the Allies invade North Africa?
14. What did the Allies accomplish on D-Day?

4 War in the Pacific (pages 826–831)

15. How did the Allies turn the tide in the Pacific?
16. What happened at Hiroshima in 1945?

5 The Legacy of World War II (pages 832–837)

17. What happened to the relationship between the United States and the Soviet Union after the war?
18. What were the Nuremberg trials?

CRITICAL THINKING

19. **Problems and Solutions** What problem did the Code Talkers help the Allies solve?

20. **Causes and Effects** How did dictators help cause World War II?

21. **Analyze Charts** Study the chart below. How do the United States' losses compare to those of the other countries?

World War II Military Casualties *1939–1945*

COUNTRY	DEAD	WOUNDED
Soviet Union	8,668,400	14,685,593
Germany	3,250,000	7,250,000
China	2,220,000	1,761,335
Japan	2,565,878	326,000
United States	407,318	671,801
U.K. (Great Britain)	403,195	369,267
France	245,000	390,000
Italy	380,000	225,000

22. **Compare and Contrast** Compare the effect of the war on the American economy with the war's effect on other countries' economies.

23. **Analyze Political Cartoons** Study the cartoon and caption below. What is the cartoonist suggesting that America's war industry should do?

"Listen, maestro . . . If you want to get real harmony, use the black keys as well as the white!"

TEST PRACTICE

• **Online Test Practice @ ClassZone.com**
• **Test-Taking Strategies & Practice** at the front of this book

MULTIPLE CHOICE

Use the photo and your knowledge of U.S. history to answer question 1.

1 The photo above shows that during World War II, many Japanese-Americans were

A. able to stay in their own homes.

B. sent to German concentration camps.

C. forced to move to U.S. internment camps.

D. able to use the island hopping strategy to defeat their enemies.

Read questions 2–3 and choose the best answer.

2 How did World War II lead to one of the largest population shifts in U.S. history?

A. The loss of loved ones led people to move in with their families.

B. American citizens were forced to leave their homes for Europe.

C. People moved to states with military bases and factories for better jobs.

D. People moved to the middle of the country to escape wars on both coasts.

3 How did physical geography contribute to Germany's defeat in World War II?

A. There were too few rivers to transport German supplies.

B. Large bodies of water stood between Germany and its enemies.

C. German soldiers could not cross the mountain ranges along Germany's borders.

D. Soviet troops were able to drive tanks across the frozen ground at Stalingrad during the winter of 1942–1943.

YOU BE THE HISTORIAN

24. **Form an Opinion** Describe President Truman's rationale for using atomic weapons in Japan. Explain why you either agree or disagree with his decision.

25. **WHAT IF?** Suppose Neville Chamberlain's strategy of appeasement had succeeded. How would this have affected the United States?

26. **Analyze Leadership** What was General Eisenhower's most effective contribution to the war effort?

27. **Evaluate** Which battle do you think was the most important turning point of the war? Explain.

28. **Causes and Effects** How did the U.S. government's actions during World War II affect Americans' civil rights?

 Answer the
ESSENTIAL QUESTION
How did World War II transform America and the world?

Written Response Write a two- to three-paragraph response to the essential question. Be sure to consider the key ideas of each section.

Response Rubric
A strong response will

• describe the post-war world

• explain the challenges faced by nations most affected by the war

• analyze American actions and leadership during and after the war

• explain the effects of American leadership on the postwar world

CHAPTER

27

1. Peacetime Adjustments and the Cold War

2. The Korean War and McCarthyism

3. American Life in the Fifties

The Cold War and the American Dream

1945–1960

 ESSENTIAL QUESTION

How did the Cold War and domestic changes in the postwar years affect the nation?

CONNECT ➤ Geography & History

How did geography affect world relations at the end of World War II?

Think about:

1 the division of Eastern and Western Europe

2 the neighboring countries of the Soviet Union

3 the location and size of the United States compared to the Soviet Union

The television became a common household item in the postwar years.

1945

World War II ends.
▼
Effect Stalin installs pro-Soviet governments throughout Eastern Europe.

1947 The U.S. announces the Truman Doctrine and Marshall Plan.

The Berlin Airlift

1948 President Harry S. Truman is reelected.

1948 The Soviet Union blockades Berlin.
▼
Effect Truman responds with the Berlin airlift.

Europe after World War II *1949*

🚀 *Click here* to explore the Cold War
@ClassZone.com

Communist
Non-Communist

0   150   300 miles
0 150 300 kilometers

60°N

NORWAY

FINLAND

SWEDEN

North Sea

Baltic Sea

• Moscow

DENMARK

SOVIET UNION

UNITED KINGDOM

IRELAND

NETHERLANDS

London •

50°N

• Berlin   Warsaw •

EAST GERMANY   POLAND

BELGIUM

WEST GERMANY   CZECHOSLOVAKIA

• Paris
LUXEMBOURG

ATLANTIC
OCEAN

SWITZERLAND   AUSTRIA   HUNGARY

FRANCE

ROMANIA

Black Sea

YUGOSLAVIA   BULGARIA

Adriatic Sea

ITALY

PORTUGAL

• Rome   ALBANIA   TURKEY

SPAIN

40°N

GREECE

0°   10°E

Mediterranean Sea

20°E

1950 North Korea invades South Korea.

▼

Effect The U.S. leads UN troops in the Korean War until the cease-fire in 1953.

1954 U.S. Senate holds Army-McCarthy hearings.

Sputnik, the world's first space satellite

1960

1952 Dwight D. Eisenhower is elected president.

1957 The Soviet Union launches *Sputnik*.

John F. Kennedy is elected president.

I LIKE IKE

Eisenhower campaign button

▶ **Key Ideas**

BEFORE, YOU LEARNED
World War II had deep and lasting effects on the United States and the world.

NOW YOU WILL LEARN
The end of World War II led to prosperity and a new kind of war against communism.

▶ **Vocabulary**

TERMS & NAMES

Harry S. Truman U.S. president from 1945 to 1953

Fair Deal social reforms proposed by Truman; built on Roosevelt's New Deal

Cold War conflict between the United States and Soviet Union following World War II

Truman Doctrine policy promising aid to countries fighting to maintain democracies

NATO North Atlantic Treaty Organization, a military alliance that included Canada, the United States, and ten European nations

BACKGROUND VOCABULARY

containment policy to stop the spread of communism

REVIEW

New Deal programs proposed by President Franklin Roosevelt to help solve problems caused by the Depression

Visual Vocabulary Harry S. Truman

▶ **Reading Strategy**

Recreate the diagram shown at right. As you read and respond to the **KEY QUESTIONS**, use the diagram to identify economic and social effects of World War II.

 See Skillbuilder Handbook, page R7.

CAUSES AND EFFECTS

CAUSE

End of World War II

EFFECT

EFFECT

EFFECT

⟳ **GRAPHIC ORGANIZERS**
Go to **Interactive Review** @ ClassZone.com

Peacetime Adjustments and the Cold War

 14.E.3 Compare the basic principles of the United States and its international interests (e.g., *territory, environment, trade, use of technology*).
15.A.3a Explain how market prices signal producers about what, how and how much to produce.

One American's Story

In 1946 Harold Russell won an Academy Award for best supporting actor in the film *The Best Years of Our Lives*. Russell played an amputee adjusting to civilian life after World War II, a role he knew well. Russell had lost both hands in an explosion and was fitted with hooks.

PRIMARY SOURCE

❝ I was all right. My problem was to make the people I met feel at ease. I just acted myself and didn't sulk in corners hiding the hooks. When my neighborhood friends saw I was okay and laughing they said to themselves, "Why should we feel sorry for him? He's getting along better than we are." ❞

—Harold Russell, quoted in *Life*, December 16, 1946

Sergeant Harold Russell received an additional Academy Award for "bringing hope and courage to his fellow veterans."

Millions of returning soldiers like Russell had to restart their lives after the war ended.

Peacetime Economics and Politics

🔽 **KEY QUESTION** How did the U.S. economy and political climate change after World War II?

The United States had spent the years 1941–1945 fighting World War II. Now, the country was at peace.

Peacetime Adjustments As defense industries began changing over to make goods for peacetime, most reduced their workforce. Factories closed, and thousands of workers—mostly women—were laid off. In addition, more than 10 million returning veterans flooded the job market. These veterans won out over female workers in the competition for jobs. Many women returned to jobs in more traditional fields, such as nursing or teaching.

MEDIAN FAMILY INCOME

Half of all families have an annual income above the median and half have income below it.

$3,500
$3,300
$3,100
$2,900
$2,700
$2,500

1945   1950

CONSUMER PRICE INDEX

The Consumer Price Index is a measure of the change in cost of the goods and services most commonly bought by consumers.

26
24
22
20
18
16

1945   1950

Source: *Statistical Abstract of the United States, U.S. Bureau of Labor Statistics.*

CRITICAL THINKING Analyze What did income and price levels in 1950 reveal about the U.S. economy?

The Postwar Economy Instead of slowing down, as many feared, the postwar economy boomed. People wanted to start families, buy new homes, and purchase goods they had put off buying during the war. Increased demand for goods led to skyrocketing prices.

Government-guaranteed housing loans for veterans under the G.I. Bill helped spur the demand for new houses. Businessman William Levitt met this demand by using assembly-line techniques to mass-produce houses and sell them cheaply. In 1947, he built Levittown on Long Island, New York. Three years later, the farmland had been transformed by more than 17,000 new homes.

Labor Unrest and Reaction During the war, labor unions agreed not to strike or seek pay raises. To keep up with rising prices, however, more than 4 million union workers went on strike for better pay in 1946. During a railroad strike, President **Harry S. Truman** threatened to draft workers into the army to run the trains. The strike was settled before he carried out his threat.

Steps on Civil Rights African Americans, especially veterans, hoped for greater equality after the war. But most found that little had changed. In the South, African Americans trying to vote were threatened and even murdered. In response, Truman created a civil rights commission. He also issued an order against racial segregation and discrimination in the military. His actions began the federal government's effort to deal with racial issues.

Reelection and the Fair Deal Few political experts believed Truman would win the 1948 presidential election. To campaign, Truman traveled by train across the country and blasted the "do-nothing" Republican Congress for blocking many of his proposals. His strategy worked. Truman won in an upset over Republican candidate Thomas Dewey. Truman then proposed the **Fair Deal**, an extension of FDR's **New Deal**. It called for new housing and employment projects and an end to racial discrimination in hiring. But Congress fought against it, and few measures passed.

▲ **SUMMARIZE** Explain how the United States changed after World War II.

America Fights a Cold War

▼ **KEY QUESTION** How did the Cold War affect the United States and Europe?

In addition to challenges at home, Truman also faced major problems abroad. The United States and Soviet Union were allies during World War II. However, as victory neared, the two world powers increasingly distrusted one another.

Origins of the Cold War The future of Eastern Europe was the most divisive issue. The Soviets occupied the Eastern European states that they had freed from Nazi rule. Soviet leader Joseph Stalin had promised to allow free elections in those states. However, at the final wartime conference in Potsdam, Germany, Stalin's true intentions became clear. When the war ended, Stalin installed pro-Soviet governments throughout Eastern Europe.

As tensions mounted between the capitalist Western democracies and the communist Soviet Union, each side suspected the other of trying to dominate world affairs. The resulting **Cold War** set the United States and Soviet Union against each other. Although the two nations never directly met on the battlefield, the threat of deadly conflict would last for decades. Britain's Winston Churchill warned the world of Soviet power in 1946.

PRIMARY SOURCE

❝ From Stettin in the Baltic to Trieste in the Adriatic, an iron curtain has descended across the Continent. Behind that line lie all the . . . states of Central and Eastern Europe. . . . All these . . . populations . . . lie in the Soviet sphere, and all are subject . . . not only to Soviet influence but to . . . increasing . . . control from Moscow. ❞

—Winston Churchill, "Iron Curtain" speech in Fulton, Missouri

The Berlin Airlift The European nation in which the Cold War almost turned hot was Germany. In 1945, the Allies agreed to a temporary division of Germany into four zones controlled by the Soviet Union, France, Great Britain, and the United States. Western powers merged their zones and planned to unite them as West Germany. Stalin feared a united Germany would threaten the Soviet Union and decided to take action.

The Division of Berlin *1945*

Occupation Zone
- British
- French
- Soviet
- U.S.

EAST GERMANY

Havel R.

East Berlin

West Berlin

Spree R.

EAST GERMANY

0   4   8 miles
0   4   8 kilometers

North Sea · Berlin · EAST GERMANY · WEST GERMANY

Connect Geography & History

1. **Location** Which nation's zone shared the longest border with the Soviet zone?

2. **Make Inferences** How do you think the division of Berlin affected its residents?

In 1961, the Berlin Wall was built to prevent East Germans from fleeing to West Germany. As communism began to fall in 1989, the wall was torn down.

Berlin, Germany's former capital, lay within the eastern zone held by the Soviet Union. However, the city had been divided into East and West Berlin. In 1948, Stalin's forces blocked access to Berlin. Truman responded by approving a huge airlift of food, fuel, and equipment into the city. For nearly a year, more than 270,000 U.S. and British flights carried supplies to Berlin. In 1949, Stalin gave up the blockade. Germany had been divided into communist East Germany and democratic West Germany.

The Politics of Containment Truman's main strategy in the Cold War was **containment**, or stopping the spread of communism through military and nonmilitary ways. The **Truman Doctrine** promised aid to people fighting to maintain democracy. One of Truman's actions, the Marshall Plan, aimed to prevent the spread of communism by reviving war-torn economies in Europe. Offering $13 billion in aid, the plan helped western and southern European countries rebuild.

Alarm over Communist control of Eastern Europe led to the formation of the North Atlantic Treaty Organization (**NATO**) in 1949. This alliance included the United States, Canada, and ten Western European nations. In 1955, the Soviet Union and Eastern European nations countered by forming the Warsaw Pact.

▲ **CAUSES AND EFFECTS** Explain the relationship between Soviet actions in Eastern Europe and the formation of NATO.

CONNECT ↝ To Today

FOREIGN AID

By the end of World War II, much of Europe had been destroyed. When Truman's secretary of state George C. Marshall announced the Marshall Plan for European aid in 1947, he said, "Our policy is directed not against any country or doctrine, but against hunger, poverty, desperation, and chaos."

The United States has continued to help countries around the world ever since. In some cases, it responds to natural disasters, such as the severe earthquake that rocked South Asia in 2004. The United States also provides aid to promote democracy, land reform, and economic change. It funds child survival and health programs and has contributed nearly $6 billion to fight HIV/AIDS.

CRITICAL THINKING Make Generalizations What benefits might the United States gain by helping other countries?

A young girl in Afghanistan carries water in a U.S. government aid agency can.

The Cold War at Home

 KEY QUESTION How did fear of communism affect people in the United States?

Many Americans feared that communism would spread inside the United States. Two famous spy trials confirmed such fears.

Americans on Trial Alger Hiss, a former State Department official, was accused of passing military information to the Soviet Union. He was jailed for lying under oath in 1950. Ethel and Julius Rosenberg, members of the American Communist Party, were convicted of passing atomic secrets to the Russians. They were executed in 1953.

Uncovering "Un-American Activities" In 1947, Truman ordered 4 million government workers to undergo loyalty checks. Loyalty boards forced several thousand government workers to resign.

The House Un-American Activities Committee (HUAC) began targeting people in the movie industry. Many careers were ruined through black-lists—unofficial lists of suspected Communists. Fear of communism would spread throughout America in the early 1950s.

 MAKE GENERALIZATIONS Explain how fear of communism affected people in the United States.

Connect to the World

In 1950, physicist Klaus Fuchs was arrested in Britain and confessed to providing information about the atomic bomb to the Soviets. The Rosenbergs were charged in connection with this case.

Illinois Learning Standards *Review*

ONLINE QUIZ
For test practice, go to
Interactive Review @ ClassZone.com

TERMS & NAMES

1. Explain the importance of
- Harry S. Truman
- Fair Deal
- Cold War
- Truman Doctrine
- NATO

USING YOUR READING NOTES

2. Causes and Effects Complete the diagram you started at the beginning of this section. Then create a diagram for the other main ideas in this section.

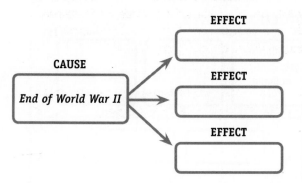

CAUSE

End of World War II

EFFECT

EFFECT

EFFECT

KEY IDEAS

3. How did Soviet leaders expand their influence immediately after World War II?

4. How did World War II affect the hopes and expectations of African Americans?

CRITICAL THINKING

5. Causes and Effects Why did labor unions go on strike in 1946?

6. Analyze Point of View Reread the quotation by Winston Churchill on p. 847. What does he mean by an "iron curtain"?

7. Connect to Today How do you think the fear of communism after World War II compares to the fear of terrorism today?

8. Writing Letter Imagine that you are a resident of Berlin in 1949. Write a letter to a relative describing recent events and your hope for the city's future.

▶ Key Ideas

BEFORE, YOU LEARNED

The end of World War II led to prosperity and a new kind of war against communism.

NOW YOU WILL LEARN

The Cold War and the Korean War produced a wave of anticommunist sentiment.

▶ Vocabulary

TERMS & NAMES

Joseph McCarthy senator who accused many Americans of having Communist ties

38th parallel line of latitude dividing North and South Korea

Korean War conflict involving U.S.-led UN forces against North Korea and China

arms race competition between the United States and the Soviet Union to develop more destructive weapons

H-bomb hydrogen bomb

space race competition between the United States and the Soviet Union to lead in space exploration

BACKGROUND VOCABULARY

brinkmanship (BREENK•MIHN•ship) policy of going to the brink of war to combat communism

Visual Vocabulary Joseph McCarthy

▶ Reading Strategy

Re-create the diagram shown at right. As you read and respond to the **KEY QUESTIONS**, use the diagram to record important events of the Cold War and the Korean War in the order in which they occurred.

 See Skillbuilder Handbook, page R5.

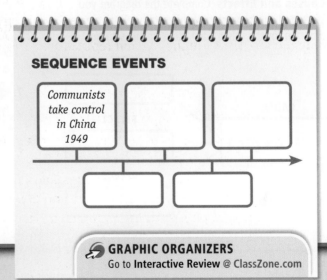

SEQUENCE EVENTS

Communists take control in China 1949

GRAPHIC ORGANIZERS
Go to **Interactive Review** @ ClassZone.com

The Korean War and McCarthyism

 14.D.3 Describe roles and influences of individuals, groups and media in shaping current Illinois and United States public policy (e.g., *general public opinion, special interest groups, formal parties, media*).
14.E.3 Compare the basic principles of the United States and its international interests (e.g., *territory, environment, trade, use of technology*).

One American's Story

Senators Margaret Chase Smith and **Joseph McCarthy** were both members of the Republican Party. But when McCarthy began crusading against alleged Communist conspirators in the U.S. government, Smith spoke out against him.

PRIMARY SOURCE

❝ Those of us who shout the loudest about Americanism in making character assassinations are all too frequently those who . . . ignore some of the basic principles of Americanism: The right to criticize; The right to hold unpopular beliefs; The right to protest; The right of independent thought. The exercise of these rights should not cost one single American citizen his reputation or his right to a livelihood nor should he be in danger of losing his reputation or livelihood merely because he happens to know someone who holds unpopular beliefs. ❞

—Margaret Chase Smith, "Declaration of Conscience" speech, U.S. Senate, 1950

Senator Margaret Chase Smith

Although McCarthy's allegations were unsubstantiated, thousands of people did lose their livelihoods and reputations as a result of his claims.

The Cold War Heats Up in Korea

🔽 **KEY QUESTION** What events led to the Korean War, and what was its outcome?

In 1949, the Chinese Communist Party, led by Mao Zedong, defeated the Nationalists in a civil war in China. The Nationalists, led by Chang Kai-shek, fled to Taiwan, an island off the coast of mainland China. Many Americans were shocked by the fall of the Nationalists and blamed the State Department for failing to stop the revolution. American fear of communism grew. Events in Korea contributed to this fear.

Conflict Erupts in Korea After World War II, Korea, a former Japanese colony, was divided at the **38th parallel**, or line of latitude. Aided by the Soviet Union, a Communist government came to power in North Korea. The United States supported a non-communist government in South Korea.

In June 1950, North Korean forces crossed the 38th parallel into South Korea. President Truman saw this move as a threat to his containment policy. The United States asked the United Nations (UN) to stop the Communists. In the conflict that became known as the **Korean War**, the UN supplied soldiers from sixteen nations. U.S. troops made up most of the UN force, which was led by World War II hero General Douglas MacArthur.

Initially, the North Koreans pushed through to Pusan at the tip of the Korean peninsula. Then MacArthur executed a daring plan that landed his troops behind North Korean lines at the port of Inchon.

General MacArthur directs the Inchon invasion on September 15, 1950.

China Enters the Conflict Surrounded, North Korean forces retreated back across the 38th parallel. UN forces pushed them northward toward the Yalu River, the boundary with Communist China. Chinese leaders saw the UN forces as a threat. They warned that a further UN advance would force them to enter the war. MacArthur's troops

COMPARING *Phases of the Korean War*

North Korea Invasion, 1950

CHINA
Yalu River
NORTH KOREA
40°N
Prewar Boundary
Sea of Japan (East Sea)
38°N
Seoul
Yellow Sea
SOUTH KOREA
Pusan
35°N
JAPAN

UN Offensive, 1950

CHINA
Yalu River
NORTH KOREA
40°N
Sea of Japan (East Sea)
38°N
Inchon • Seoul
Yellow Sea
SOUTH KOREA
Pusan
35°N
JAPAN
30°N

0   100   200 miles
0   100   200 kilometers

Chinese Offensive, 1950

CHINA
Yalu River
NORTH KOREA
40°N
Sea of Japan (East Sea)
38°N
• Seoul
Yellow Sea
SOUTH KOREA
Pusan
35°N
JAPAN

Stalemate and Armistice, 1953

CHINA
Yalu River
NORTH KOREA
40°N
Sea of Japan (East Sea)
Panmunjom
Armistice Line (DMZ)
Seoul •
38°N
SOUTH KOREA
Yellow Sea
Pusan
35°N
JAPAN
30°N

- ▢ Area occupied by Communist forces
- ▢ Area occupied by UN forces
- ← Movement of Communist forces
- ← Movement of UN forces

Connect Geography & History

1. **Movement** In the first map, which forces moved south toward Pusan?

2. **Summarize** Compare the first map with the last and summarize changes caused by the war.

ignored the warning. On November 25, 1950, hundreds of thousands of Chinese soldiers entered North Korea. By early 1951, the two sides were again deadlocked along the 38th parallel.

MacArthur requested permission to blockade China's coastline and bomb China. Truman refused. He feared it would draw the Soviet Union into the conflict. MacArthur disagreed and criticized Truman publicly. As president, Truman was commander in chief of the armed forces. He fired General MacArthur and ordered him to return to the United States.

War Ends in Stalemate Truman began truce talks in July 1951, which dragged on through the 1952 presidential campaign. The Republican candidate, Dwight D. Eisenhower, criticized the unpopular war. Ike, as voters called him, promised a speedy end to the conflict. He won the election in a landslide victory against Democratic candidate Adlai Stevenson.

Eisenhower made good on his campaign promise. He compromised with the North Koreans and Chinese to end the war, but warned them privately that he was ready to use nuclear weapons. The two Koreas remained split at the 38th parallel. Americans felt frustrated by the indecisive war.

▲ **SUMMARIZE** Explain the outcome of the Korean War.

McCarthy and Communism

▼ **KEY QUESTION** How did Senator Joseph McCarthy gain political power?

Senator Joseph McCarthy and other politicians exploited Americans' frustrations over the government's efforts to contain communism.

Charges Without Proof In February 1950, McCarthy declared that he had a list of 205 State Department officials who belonged to the Communist Party. These charges were never proven, but his claims launched a hunt for Communists that wrecked the careers of thousands of people. The term *McCarthyism* now refers to reckless charges against innocent citizens.

Army-McCarthy Hearings In 1954, the Senate held the nationally televised hearings. During these hearings, McCarthy accused the U.S. Army of "coddling Communists." Joseph Welch, the Army counsel, spoke out when McCarthy made charges against a member of Welch's law firm.

PRIMARY SOURCE

❝ Until this moment, Senator, I think I never really gauged your cruelty or your recklessness. . . . . You have done enough. Have you no sense of decency, sir, at long last? Have you left no sense of decency? ❞

—Joseph Welch, Army-McCarthy hearings, June 9, 1954

Americans watching the exchange were shocked. The Senate condemned McCarthy's conduct, and he eventually faded from public view.

▲ **MAKE INFERENCES** Explain why McCarthy lost political power.

The Cold War Around the World

▼ **KEY QUESTION** How did the Cold War affect other countries around the world?

Like Truman, President Eisenhower waged the Cold War. But he favored a more aggressive stand against communism.

H-bomb test, Nevada, 1957

The Arms Race Eisenhower's secretary of state, John Foster Dulles, rejected Truman's containment policy. He announced that the United States would go to the brink of war to combat communism, a policy known as **brinkmanship**.

In 1949, Americans learned that the Soviet Union had produced an atomic bomb using information stolen by Soviet spies. The two nations became locked in an **arms race**, developing weapons with more destructive power. In 1952, the United States built a hydrogen bomb, or **H-bomb**. By 1955, the Soviets tested their own H-bomb. Fear led both sides to build up huge stockpiles of nuclear weapons.

Foreign Intrigues The United States and the Soviet Union both worked to help allies and weaken enemies. In 1953 in Iran, the U.S. Central Intelligence Agency (CIA) helped to topple a leader whom they thought might

TECHNOLOGY *of the* TIME

TECHNOLOGY AND FEAR

World War II inspired many technological innovations, including advances in transportation and medicine. But the war and the Cold War that followed also produced inventions that frightened people.

Sputnik The launch of *Sputnik* worried Americans. It meant that the Soviets had a guided missile capable of reaching the United States in less than an hour.

H-Bomb The H-bomb was even more destructive than the atomic bomb. Civil defense agencies encouraged people to "duck and cover" or hide in "fallout shelters" in the event of an attack. The photograph here shows students taking cover during a disaster drill in 1962.

U-2 Spy Plane This U.S. plane could take detailed pictures from the sky without detection—the government could watch people without their knowledge.

CRITICAL THINKING

Connect *to* **Today**   In what ways is technology related to fears of terrorism today?

seek Soviet aid. In 1954, the CIA trained an army that overthrew Guatemala's president because he was believed to favor communism.

The Suez Canal in Egypt, which connected the Mediterranean and the Red Sea, became the center of another conflict. In 1956, Britain and the United States withdrew their aid from Egypt because of its ties with the Soviet Union. Egypt reacted by seizing the canal, which France and Britain owned. France, Britain, and Israel then invaded Egypt. The Soviet Union threatened to help Egypt. The crisis ended when the UN imposed a cease-fire.

The Space Race In 1957, the two superpowers began a **space race**. The Soviet Union stunned the world by launching *Sputnik*, the world's first space satellite. American scientists scrambled to catch up. Congress responded to the Soviet success by setting aside billions of dollars for space research.

The U-2 Incident Eisenhower suggested easing Cold War tensions with the Soviet Union through face-to-face talks. However, two weeks before a meeting with Soviet Premier Nikita Khrushchev, the Soviets shot down an American U-2 spy plane over the Soviet Union. Eisenhower denied the aircraft was spying until he learned that the pilot had been captured. Khrushchev demanded an apology. When Eisenhower refused, the talks collapsed.

Connect *to the* **World**

Nikita Khrushchev rose to power after the death of Stalin in 1953. He attacked Stalin's "brutality" and "abuse of power," and favored more peaceful relations between the Communist and non-Communist world. He was removed from power in 1964.

▲ **MAIN IDEAS & DETAILS** Identify ways in which the United States and Soviet Union competed with one another.

 Illinois Learning Standards *Review*

 ONLINE QUIZ
For test practice, go to
Interactive Review @ ClassZone.com

TERMS & NAMES

1. Explain the importance of
   - Joseph McCarthy
   - 38th parallel
   - Korean War
   - arms race
   - H-bomb
   - space race

USING YOUR READING NOTES

2. **Sequence Events** Complete the diagram you started at the beginning of this section. Then explain which event you think is most important.

KEY IDEAS

3. Why did war break out in Korea? How did it end?

4. Why was Senator Joseph McCarthy able to gain so much political power in the 1950s?

CRITICAL THINKING

5. **Causes and Effects** Why did China enter the Korean War?

6. **Compare and Contrast** How was Truman's policy of containment similar to Eisenhower's policy of brinkmanship? How was it different?

7. **Connect** *to* **Today** How do you think the arms race of the 1950s compares with the economic competition of nations today?

8. **Writing** Article Write a newspaper article announcing the surprise launch of *Sputnik* in 1957. Describe the U.S. reaction and the reasons for it.

from Speech at Wheeling, West Virginia

SETTING THE STAGE In February 1950, Joseph McCarthy made headlines across the country when he claimed that Communists were shaping policy in the U.S. government.

57 Cases

According to news reports of this speech, McCarthy claimed to have a list of 205 Communists or Communist loyalists in government. In the text of the speech that was released to the Congressional Record two weeks later, that number had reduced to 57. McCarthy's list was never shown or proven to exist.

1. Why do you think the number changed?

Sermon on the Mount

McCarthy refers to Secretary of State Dean Acheson's public statement that he would not "turn [his] back on Alger Hiss" after Hiss was charged with providing information to the Soviets and found guilty of lying under oath.

2. According to McCarthy, how has Acheson affected the American people?

Today we are engaged in a final, all-out battle between communistic **atheism**[1] and Christianity. The modern champions of communism have selected this as the time, and ladies and gentlemen the chips are down—they are truly down. . . . In my opinion the State Department, which is one of the most important government departments, is thoroughly infested with communists. . . . I have in my hand 57 cases of individuals who would appear to be either card carrying members or certainly loyal to the Communist Party, but who nevertheless are still helping to shape our foreign policy. . . . One of the important reasons for the graft, the corruption, the dishonesty, the disloyalty, the treason in high government positions—one of the most important reasons why this continues—is a lack of moral uprising on the part of the 140 million American people. In the light of history, however, it is not hard to explain. It is the result of an emotional hangover and a temporary moral lapse which follows every war. . . . However, the morals of our people have not been destroyed. They still exist. This cloak of numbness and apathy has only needed a spark to rekindle them. Happily, this spark has finally been supplied. As you know, very recently the Secretary of State proclaimed his loyalty to a man guilty of what has always been considered as the most abominable of all crimes—of being a traitor to the people who gave him a position of great trust. The Secretary of State, in attempting to justify his continued devotion to the man who sold out the Christian world to the atheistic world, referred to Christ's Sermon on the Mount as a justification and reason therefore. . . . When this pompous diplomat in striped pants, with a phony British accent, proclaimed to the American people that Christ on the Mount endorsed communism, high treason, and betrayal of a sacred trust, the blasphemy was so great that it awakened the dormant **indignation**[2] of the American people. He has lighted the spark which is resulting in a moral uprising and will end only when the whole sorry mess of twisted warped thinkers are swept from the national scene so that we may have a new birth of national honesty and decency in government.

----

1. atheism: rejection of a belief in a god or gods

2. indignation: anger

from **See It Now**

SETTING THE STAGE In March 1954, newscaster Edward Murrow devoted the entire half hour of his *See It Now* program to an attack on Senator McCarthy.

It is necessary to investigate before legislating, but the line between investigating and persecuting is a very fine one and the junior Senator from Wisconsin has stepped over it repeatedly. His primary achievement has been in confusing the public mind, as between the internal and the external threats of Communism. We must not confuse **dissent**[1] with disloyalty. We must remember always that accusation is not proof and that conviction depends upon evidence and due process of law. We will not walk in fear, one of another. We will not be driven by fear into an age of unreason, if we dig deep in our history and our doctrine, and remember that we are not descended from fearful men—not from men who feared to write, to speak, to associate and to defend causes that were, for the moment, unpopular. . . .

As a nation we have come into our full inheritance at a tender age. We proclaim ourselves, as indeed we are, the defenders of freedom, wherever it continues to exist in the world, but we cannot defend freedom abroad by deserting it at home.

The actions of the junior Senator from Wisconsin have caused alarm and dismay amongst our allies abroad, and given considerable comfort to our enemies. And whose fault is that? Not really his. He didn't create this situation of fear; he merely exploited it—and rather successfully.

----

1. dissent: difference of opinion

Confusing the Public

McCarthy made charges against respected military officials and politicians, famous writers and artists, and average Americans such as an Army dentist and a cleaning woman at the Pentagon.

3. Why was it hard for people to defend themselves against McCarthy's accusations?

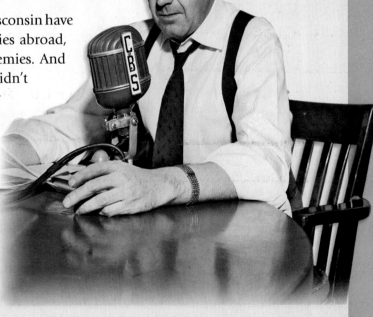

Edward R. Murrow

DOCUMENT–BASED QUESTIONS

Short Answer

1. How does McCarthy explain the "corruption" and "dishonesty" in government?

2. Whom does Murrow blame for the results of McCarthy's actions?

Extended Answer

3. Explain the different points of view about how Americans should react to the threats of communism.

Key Ideas

BEFORE, YOU LEARNED

The Cold War and the Korean War produced a wave of anticommunist sentiment.

NOW YOU WILL LEARN

Economic growth and the Cold War caused many changes in American society.

Vocabulary

TERMS & NAMES

rock 'n' roll musical style based on rhythm and blues that became popular in the 1950s

baby boom a sharp increase in the U.S. birthrate following World War II

suburbs residential areas surrounding a city

sunbelt warmer states in the southern and southwestern United States

BACKGROUND VOCABULARY

conform to agree with the beliefs and ideas of the majority

REVIEW

consumer a person buying goods or using services

Visual Vocabulary
consumers

Reading Strategy

Re-create the diagram shown at right. As you read and respond to the **KEY QUESTIONS**, use the diagram to record important changes that took place in the 1950s.

 See Skillbuilder Handbook, page R4.

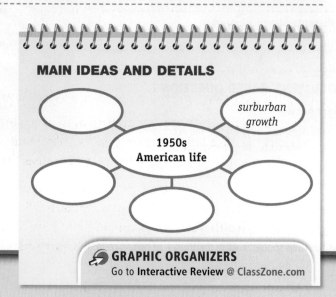

MAIN IDEAS AND DETAILS

surburban growth

1950s American life

GRAPHIC ORGANIZERS
Go to **Interactive Review** @ ClassZone.com

American Life in the Fifties

15.C.3 Identify and explain the effects of various incentives to produce a good or service.
16.E.3c Describe the impact of urbanization and suburbanization, 1850–present, on the environment.

One American's Story

Ruth Brown was one of many African-American artists who influenced popular music in the 1950s. She adopted a style called "rhythm and blues," which at first sold mostly to African Americans. As the sound became more popular, white singers covered, or copied, her songs. The white singers made more money and gained more fame.

PRIMARY SOURCE

❝ Rhythm and blues was getting ready to be called rock and roll. It had become interesting enough; white kids were starting to pay attention to it. And then on the scene came Alan Freed. . . . Elvis Presley. . . . Jerry Lee Lewis. But we already had Jackie Wilson. . . . Bo Diddley. . . . B. B. King. We had it all in place. . . . and we didn't get the media exposure. I never got to do *The Ed Sullivan Show*. ❞

—Ruth Brown, quoted in *She's a Rebel*, 1992

Nicknamed "Miss Rhythm," Ruth Brown was elected to the Rock and Roll Hall of Fame in 1993.

The rise of **rock 'n' roll** music was one of the many changes in American society during the 1950s.

The American Dream in the Fifties

▼ **KEY QUESTION** How did American life change during the 1950s?

When Eisenhower ran for president, he promised to steer a middle course. His decisions in office helped foster a period of growth and prosperity that allowed many people to achieve what they viewed as the American dream.

Prosperity Fifties Style Eisenhower disliked government spending, but he kept most New Deal programs. He expanded Social Security and created the Department of Health, Education, and Welfare. He increased the minimum wage for workers and even backed some new programs.

One new program was the Highway Act of 1956, which spent $32 billion to build 41,000 miles of roads around the country. This act marked the beginning of the interstate highway system still in place today.

In the postwar period, many people dreamed of living a more comfortable, secure life. A prosperous economy encouraged them to buy new goods, get married, start families, and move to new areas.

Baby Boomers Swell the Suburbs During the 1950s, the U.S. population grew by almost 30 million people. This growth was mostly an effect of the **baby boom**, a sharp increase in the U.S. birthrate after World War II.

The baby boom spurred the growth of **suburbs**, residential areas surrounding a city. Families left crowded city apartments for larger, single-family homes. Irving, Texas, a suburb of Dallas, was typical. It grew from 2,600 residents in 1950 to over 45,000 in 1960. Shopping centers, movie theaters, and restaurants sprouted up on what used to be farmland. As suburbs grew, car sales exploded. The number of registered automobiles in the United States grew from about 28 million in 1946 to over 60 million by 1960.

The 1950s saw another change in living patterns. A surge of Americans moved from the north and east to the south and west. This movement to the **sunbelt** increased the population of the warmer states. By 1970, California surpassed New York as the most populous state.

Soviet missiles on display in Moscow.

CONNECT to the Essential Question

How did the Cold War and domestic changes in the postwar years affect the nation?

Tensions between capitalist and communist countries spark the start of the Cold War.

The U.S. and the U.S.S.R. are locked in an arms race.

North Korea invades South Korea.

Events Abroad

1945   1946   1947   1949   1950

Events at Home

Millions of workers go on strike to keep up with rising consumer prices.

The baby boom spurs the demand for new houses and suburbs.

Senator McCarthy's accusations and government loyalty checks contribute to heightened fears of communism.

Consumerism For millions of white Americans, life in the suburbs was the American dream. The advertising industry helped convince **consumers** that the American dream meant buying new products. Television and magazine ads pictured ideal homes with modern conveniences such as washing machines, vacuum cleaners, televisions, and high-fidelity record players.

Social Conformity Some critics worried that Americans were being forced to fit into a suburban lifestyle. They argued that people felt pressured to **conform**—that is, to go along with the beliefs and ideas of the majority.

Popular magazines, films, and television programs praised women for their roles as homemakers. *Time* magazine called women the "keeper[s] of the suburban dream." But not all women felt fulfilled in this role. Most job opportunities for women were limited to nursing, teaching, and office work.

Allen Ginsberg and Jack Kerouac led a group of poets and writers who resisted what they saw as the shallowness and conformity of American society. Known as "beatniks," their followers filled coffeehouses to hear their heated attacks on "square" society.

▲ **MAIN IDEAS & DETAILS** Describe suburban life in the 1950s.

Owning a car was part of the suburban lifestyle.

The Korean War ends with Korea still divided.

The United States and the Soviet Union begin a space race.

The U-2 incident ruins efforts to ease tensions.

1953   **1955**   **1957**   **1960**

Rock 'n' roll and television emerge as prominent forms of popular culture.

Most households have a television and at least one car.

CRITICAL THINKING **Categorize** What events on the time line were related to the economic prosperity of the 1950s?

Those Left Behind

🔻 **KEY QUESTION** What groups were left out of the prosperity of the 1950s?

Not everyone prospered in the 1950s. Some lived in poverty in cities that lacked basic services.

Neglected Cities In 1957, about one out of every five Americans lived in poverty, many in the nation's cities. In his book *The Other America* (1962), Michael Harrington called attention to the forgotten poor. As well-to-do Americans headed for the suburbs, shops and businesses moved with them. Fewer people remained in the city to pay taxes for services such as garbage collection, firefighting, and road repair. Cities began to decay without proper care and maintenance. Often those most affected by urban decay were African Americans and Latinos.

The Forgotten Poor In the 1950s, immigration from Mexico increased greatly. Many Mexicans crossed the border illegally. Others came through the government-sponsored *bracero*, or temporary worker, program. *Braceros* found jobs on farms in the Southwest and Midwest. They earned low wages and endured difficult living and working conditions. Still, when the program ended, many stayed on illegally. Employers took advantage of them, and many worked even longer hours for lower pay.

🔺 **CAUSES AND EFFECTS** Explain how the growth of suburbs affected cities.

Elvis Presley and Fats Domino helped define rock 'n' roll music in the 1950s.

A New Generation of Americans

🔻 **KEY QUESTION** What cultural aspects influenced Americans in the 1950s?

Some Americans enjoyed economic prosperity, while others struggled to meet basic needs. All were a part of a rapidly changing society.

Rock 'n' Roll Teenagers fell head over heels for a new form of entertainment—rock 'n' roll music. In 1955, Bill Haley and His Comets hit it big with "Rock Around the Clock." By the mid-1950s, Chuck Berry, Little Richard, Fats Domino, and other black musicians enjoyed the spotlight with white rockers such as Jerry Lee Lewis. But the largest fan club belonged to Elvis Presley. With such songs as "Heartbreak Hotel" and "Don't Be Cruel," he became known as the king of rock 'n' roll. His onstage bumps and shakes delighted teenagers.

Television In the 1950s, Hollywood produced numerous westerns, musicals, and romances. However, movie theater attendance plummeted as more and more people stayed home to watch TV. By 1960, nine out of ten households owned a set—up from only one out of ten in 1950. Children enjoyed such programs as *Lassie*, *The Lone Ranger*, *The Howdy Doody Show*, and *The Mickey Mouse Club*.

One of the most popular shows of the decade was the situation comedy (sitcom) *I Love Lucy*. It starred Lucille Ball as the zany wife of bandleader Desi Arnaz. At the time, most Fifties sitcoms featured cheerful moms who kept the house spotless while the dads worked to support the family. These shows did not necessarily reflect reality; rather, they represented an ideal of the American family at that time.

A Youthful President In 1960, John F. Kennedy, a Democratic senator from Massachusetts, ran for president against Richard Nixon, Eisenhower's vice president. One of Kennedy's campaign promises was to "get this country moving again" after the Eisenhower years. Kennedy and Nixon participated in the first televised presidential debates. Kennedy's energy, confidence, and insight into the power of television (he spoke directly at the camera during the debates) helped him win one of the closest presidential elections in U.S. history.

Television hero the Lone Ranger on his horse, Silver.

▲ **COMPARE AND CONTRAST** Compare aspects of 1950s culture with today's.

 Illinois Learning Standards *Review*

⮎ **ONLINE QUIZ**
For test practice, go to
Interactive Review @ ClassZone.com

TERMS & NAMES

1. Explain the importance of
   - rock 'n' roll
   - baby boom
   - suburbs
   - sunbelt

USING YOUR READING NOTES

2. **Main Ideas and Details** Complete the diagram you started at the beginning of this section. Then choose one change and write a paragraph about it.

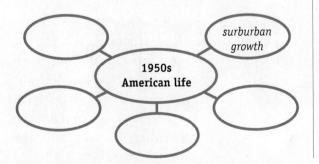

KEY IDEAS

3. How did the population change during the 1950s?

4. What were some effects of the growth of the suburbs?

CRITICAL THINKING

5. **Causes and Effects** How did television impact American life in the 1950s?

6. **Make Inferences** Why do you think so many people moved to the sunbelt during the 1950s?

7. **Connect** *to* **Today** What aspects of 1950s popular culture are still relevant today?

8. **Math** **Graph** Use the Internet or library resources to create a graph that shows U.S. population growth between 1945 and 1960.

Cities and Suburbs

By the end of World War II, many cities were plagued by overcrowding and poor sanitation. In 1950, Pittsburgh, Pennsylvania, became one of the first cities in the nation to attempt "urban renewal" by tearing down neglected buildings and redeveloping city neighborhoods. Known as the "Pittsburgh Renaissance," the program had some major success. An entire section of the downtown was cleared to make way for Gateway Center, a series of stainless steel office buildings, and the 36-acre, riverfront Point State Park.

But some areas of the city continued to suffer. Those who could afford to moved to new suburbs. The demolition of more than 1,300 buildings in the Lower Hill District forced out 8,000 people. As families relocated, racial divisions became worse. New highways further isolated and divided some neighborhoods. Today, a section of Lower Hill remains a parking lot rather than a planned cultural center.

Pittsburgh, Pennsylvania 1950–1960

PENNSYLVANIA
● Pittsburgh

ALLEGHENY CENTER
EAST ALLEGHENY
NORTH SHORE
STRIP DISTRICT
Allegheny River
Ohio River
Point State Park
Gateway Center
DOWNTOWN
LOWER HILL DISTRICT
UPTOWN
Monongahela River
MT. WASHINGTON
SOUTH SIDE FLATS

0 0.1 0.2 miles
0 0.1 0.2 kilometers

— New highway or road

Connect Geography & History

WHAT IF? Suppose you are a city planner in Pittsburgh during the 2000s. What changes would you suggest to help improve the city?

 See Geography Handbook, pp. A14–A17.

Gateway Center under construction in 1951 (*right*) and today (*below*).

Chapter Summary

① Key Idea
The end of World War II led to prosperity and a new kind of war against communism.

② Key Idea
The Cold War and the Korean War produced a wave of anti-communist sentiment.

③ Key Idea
Economic growth and the Cold War caused many changes in American society.

For detailed Review and Study Notes go to **Interactive Review** @ ClassZone.com

Name Game

Use the Terms and Names list to complete each sentence online or on your own paper.

1. I won an upset victory in 1948 to get reelected as president. _____ Harry S. Truman

2. I led the Chinese Communists to victory over the Nationalists. _____

3. I led investigations which falsely charged many people of having Communist ties. _____

4. This began after the Soviet Union launched *Sputnik* in 1957. _____

5. President Eisenhower used this aggressive policy to challenge communism around the world. _____

6. Truman's _____ called for new housing.

7. Many people moved here during the 1950s. _____

8. Teenagers made this popular during the 1950s. _____

9. This includes the U.S. and Western European countries. _____

10. This divided North and South Korea before and after the Korean War. _____

A. Harry S. Truman
B. Fair Deal
C. containment
D. NATO
E. Korean War
F. Mao Zedong
G. 38th parallel
H. Joseph McCarthy
I. brinksmanship
J. arms race
K. space race
L. suburbs
M. rock 'n' roll

Activities

FLIPCARD

Senator who accused many Americans of having Communist ties

ANSWER
Joe McCarthy

GEOGAME

Use this online map to reinforce your understanding of world relations at the end of World War II, including the locations of Communist and non-Communist countries. Drag and drop each place name in the list at its location on the map. A scorecard helps you keep track of your progress online.

East Germany

West Germany

Austria

Hungary

Yugoslavia

Yugoslavia

Explain the significance of each of the following:

1. Harry S. Truman
2. Fair Deal
3. Cold War
4. 38th parallel
5. Korean War
6. Joseph McCarthy
7. space race
8. rock 'n' roll

Explain how the terms and names in each group are related.

9. containment, Truman Doctrine, NATO

10. brinkmanship, arms race, H-bomb

11. baby boom, suburbs, sunbelt

KEY IDEAS

1 **Peacetime Adjustments and the Cold War (pages 844–849)**

12. How was the Fair Deal related to the New Deal and how effective was it?

13. Describe the Berlin airlift and how it was related to Truman's containment policy.

2 **The Korean War and McCarthyism (pages 850–855)**

14. How did the results of the civil war in China later affect the Korean War?

15. How did the Cold War affect U.S. and Soviet relations with other countries?

3 **American Life in the Fifties (pages 858–863)**

16. Describe the changes that took place in and around cities during the 1950s.

17. Describe the movement and growth of the U.S. population during the 1950s.

18. **Summarize** Why did prices rise quickly after World War II?

19. **Causes and Effects** What led to the demand for new homes in the postwar years, and what was the result of this demand?

20. **Causes and Effects** Why did the United States and other nations organize NATO?

21. **Sequence Events** Create a sequence chart to organize the main events of the Korean War in the order in which they happened.

22. **Make Inferences** Why were Americans frustrated by the outcome of the Korean War?

23. **Draw Conclusions** Why was Senator McCarthy able to gain and keep so much political power during the early 1950s?

24. **Summarize** What problems did cities face at the end of the 1950s?

25. **Interpret Graphs** Study the graph below. Describe the changes in the Consumer Price Index during the period shown.

Consumer Price Index *1945–1960*

Source: *U.S. Bureau of Labor Statistics*

☑ **TEST PRACTICE**

- **Online Test Practice @ ClassZone.com**
- **Test-Taking Strategies & Practice** at the front of this book

MULTIPLE CHOICE

Use the quotation and your knowledge of U.S. history to answer question 1.

SECONDARY SOURCE

❝ During the McCarthy era . . . the domestic Communist menace was exaggerated, largely for political purposes, as the Soviet Union itself was growing steadily weaker, not stronger, in its military, economic, and political competition with the United States. . . . Then as now, nuclear weapons . . . did raise the terrifying prospect . . . of extinguishing "any life on earth." They still do. ❞

—Haynes Johnson *The Age of Anxiety*, 2005

1 According to the author, during the McCarthy era, the Soviet Union was

A. much stronger than before

B. not as dangerous as it appeared

C. ready to invade the United States

D. about to abandon nuclear weapons

Use the cartoon and your knowledge of U.S. history to answer question 2.

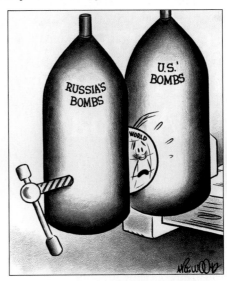

2 According to the cartoon, how does the rest of the world feel about the arms race?

A. angry   **C.** proud

B. excited   **D.** worried

YOU BE THE HISTORIAN

26. **WHAT IF?** Suppose Truman had accepted MacArthur's proposal to blockade and bomb China during the Korean War. How do you think the war and its effects would have changed?

27. **Form and Support Opinions** Was communism or McCarthyism a greater threat to the American way of life? Explain and justify your opinion.

28. **Analyze Point of View** Why do you think African-American veterans of World War II were especially disappointed with their opportunities after the war?

29. **Draw Conclusions** How did changes in the postwar years affect the role of women in American society?

30. **Evaluate** Do you think the popularity of television has had a positive or negative effect on American life? Explain and justify your opinion.

31. **Make Generalizations** Why do you think people who grew up during the Depression and World War II were so attracted to the new American dream?

 Answer the

ESSENTIAL QUESTION

How did the Cold War and domestic changes in the postwar years affect the nation?

Written Response Write a three paragraph response to the Essential Question. Be sure to consider the key ideas of each section as well as significant factors that affected the nation. Use the Response Rubric below to guide your thinking and writing.

Response Rubric

A strong response will

- identify factors that affected the nation during the period
- describe economic and social changes during the postwar years and their effects
- discuss the effects of the Cold War

Tensions at Home and Abroad

1954–present

Why It Matters Now

The years since 1954 demonstrate at home and abroad that democracy is never a finished enterprise. Struggles for social equality and against external dangers have become fixed challenges to the fulfillment of the American Dream.

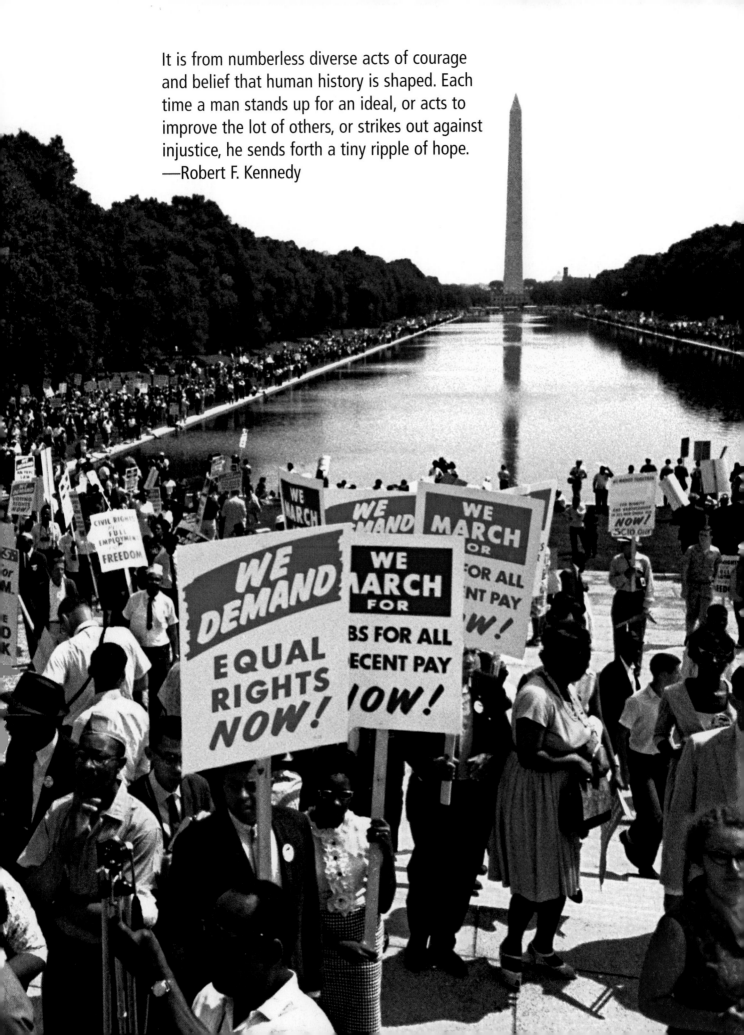

It is from numberless diverse acts of courage and belief that human history is shaped. Each time a man stands up for an ideal, or acts to improve the lot of others, or strikes out against injustice, he sends forth a tiny ripple of hope.
—Robert F. Kennedy

The Civil Rights Era

1954–1975

1. Reconstruction and Jim Crow

2. The Modern Civil Rights Movement

3. Kennedy, Johnson, and Civil Rights

4. The Equal Rights Struggle Expands

 ESSENTIAL QUESTION

How did Americans respond to discrimination during the civil rights era?

CONNECT ⟳ **Geography & History**

How might the geography of the United States have affected the civil rights movement?

Think about:

1 how population is included in the study of geography. Geography also plays a role in where people live

2 how from 1954 to 1975, groups across America organized to gain the civil rights they had been denied

3 why school segregation during this time was permitted in many parts of America

Coretta and Martin Luther King lead a march to Montgomery in 1965.

Rosa Parks on a bus in Montgomery, Alabama, after the Supreme Court ruled that segregation was illegal on city buses.

1963 The March on Washington takes place.

▼

Effect Unites many people who call for passage of civil rights laws. Kennedy is assassinated; Johnson becomes president.

1954

The Supreme Court decides *Brown v. Board of Education*.

1955 Rosa Parks is arrested for refusing to give up her bus seat.

▼

Effect The Montgomery bus boycott begins.

1964 Congress passes the Civil Rights Act of 1964.

U.S. School Segregation *1952*

Click here to explore the Civil Rights Era
@ClassZone.com

CANADA

WASHINGTON

MONTANA

NORTH DAKOTA

MINNESOTA

MICHIGAN

MAINE

OREGON

IDAHO

SOUTH DAKOTA

WISCONSIN

VT.
N.H.

NEW
YORK

MASS.

WYOMING

IOWA

PENNSYLVANIA

R.I.
CONN.

N.J.

NEVADA

NEBRASKA

OHIO

Washington, D.C.

DELAWARE

UTAH

ILLINOIS

INDIANA

MARYLAND

CALIFORNIA

COLORADO

KANSAS

MISSOURI

KENTUCKY

W. VA.

VIRGINIA

NORTH
CAROLINA

ARIZONA

NEW MEXICO

OKLAHOMA

ARKANSAS

TENNESSEE

SOUTH
CAROLINA

MISS.

ALABAMA

GEORGIA

ATLANTIC
OCEAN

TEXAS

LOUISIANA

FLORIDA

MEXICO

Gulf of Mexico

Segregation required
Segregation permitted
Segregation prohibited
No specific legislation, or local option

Source: Murray, Pauli.
State's Laws on Race and Color, 1951

Members of AIM protest anti-Indian
legislation in Washington, D.C.

1975

1965 Congress passes the
Voting Rights Act.

▼

Effect Many more African
Americans register to vote.

1970 *La Raza Unida*
is founded.

1968 Dr. Martin
Luther King, Jr. is
assassinated.

A Freedom Rider bus
burns in Alabama.

1972 Members of AIM—the American
Indian Movement—occupy the Bureau of
Indian Affairs.

Equal Rights Amendment fails to get ratified.

▶ Key Ideas

BEFORE, YOU LEARNED
The Cold War and the Korean War produced a wave of anticommunist sentiment.

NOW YOU WILL LEARN
Between the 1870s and the 1950s, African Americans lost many of the civil rights they had gained during Reconstruction.

▶ Vocabulary

REVIEW

segregation (seh•greh•GA•shun) separation, especially of races

civil rights rights granted to all citizens

black codes laws passed by Southern states that limited the freedom of former slaves

Plessy v. Ferguson 1896 case in which the Supreme Court ruled that separation of the races in public accommodations was legal

Jim Crow laws laws meant to enforce separation of white and black people in public places in the South

National Association for the Advancement of Colored People (NAACP) a civil rights organization

BACKGROUND VOCABULARY

infringe (ihn•FRINJ) to violate

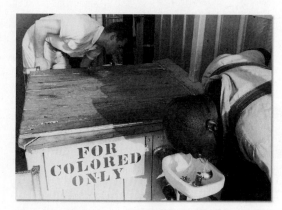

Visual Vocabulary
segregation

▶ Reading Strategy

Re-create the diagram shown here. As you read and respond to the **KEY QUESTION**, use the diagram to record events in chronological order that you find in the section. Create new boxes as needed.

 Skillbuilder Handbook, page R5.

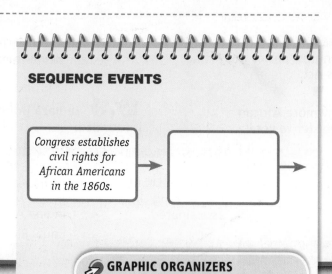

SEQUENCE EVENTS

Congress establishes civil rights for African Americans in the 1860s. → →

GRAPHIC ORGANIZERS
Go to **Interactive Review** @ ClassZone.com

REVIEW

Reconstruction and Jim Crow

14.C.3 Compare historical issues involving rights, roles and status of individuals in relation to municipalities, states and the nation.

16.B.3c Describe the way the Constitution has changed over time as a result of amendments and Supreme Court decisions.

One American's Story

From the late 1870s through the 1960s, Jim Crow laws in the South enforced racial **segregation**. T. R. Davidson, an African American in 1940s North Carolina, felt the effects of Jim Crow.

PRIMARY SOURCE

❝ [Y]ou always had to make a special effort . . . to find out the places where you could go, where you wouldn't be embarrassed or refused service. So, if you were in a strange place, no matter what part of the country it was, you had to say, 'Where do they serve black people?' ❞

—T. R. Davidson, "Eyewitness to Jim Crow"

T.R. Davidson studied at the Tuskegee Institute and became a flight instructor.

Segregation and the lack of civil rights made life much more difficult for African Americans.

Civil Rights Won and Lost

🔻 **KEY QUESTION** How were African Americans' civil rights violated in the decades following Reconstruction?

After the Civil War, enslaved African Americans were not only freed, but their **civil rights** were established by three amendments to the Constitution.

Civil Rights Gains of Reconstruction The process of Reconstruction created intense political conflict. Southern states resisted actions by Congress to ensure the civil rights of African Americans. In December 1865, the Thirteenth Amendment was ratified, banning slavery. In response, Southern states passed the **black codes**. Congress then passed the Civil Rights Act of 1866, which stated that all persons born in the United States (except Native Americans, who were not taxed) were citizens and had equal rights, regardless of their race.

Congress also proposed the Fourteenth Amendment, which prohibited states from **infringing** on the rights of citizens, including the right to vote.

A state could not deny any citizen "the equal protection of the laws." This became the foundation of the modern civil rights movement.

In 1869, despite resistance from southern states, Congress proposed the Fifteenth Amendment, which prohibited states from discriminating against voters based on "race, color, or previous condition of servitude."

The Supreme Court Reacts While Congress advanced the civil rights of African Americans, the Supreme Court reversed many civil rights African Americans had gained during Reconstruction.

Rulings Reversing Civil Rights for African Americans	
1873 Slaughterhouse cases	The 14th Amendment is weakened because most civil rights are ruled to be state, rather than federal rights.
1876 *U.S. v. Cruikshank*	State governments are given the power to let violators of African-Americans' civil rights go unpunished.
1876 *U.S. v. Reese*	While states cannot deny the vote for reasons of "race, color, or previous condition of servitude," they can deny it for any other reason they choose, such as failure to pass a literacy test or to pay a poll tax.
1883 Civil Rights Cases	While states cannot deny equal protection to citizens, individuals such as hotel, restaurant, and other business owners are free to discriminate.
1896 *Plessy* v. *Ferguson*	Segregation practices which had begun earlier throughout the South are given a legal basis to continue and spread.

In 1876, in *U.S. v. Cruikshank*, the Court ruled that only the states, not the federal government, could punish those who violated the civil rights of African Americans. In a landmark case in 1896, ***Plessy v. Ferguson***, the Supreme Court upheld a Louisiana law segregating African Americans from whites in railroad cars, stating that no civil rights were violated because the accommodations were "separate but equal."

🔺 **ANALYZE CAUSES AND EFFECTS** Explain how African Americans' civil rights were violated in the decades following Reconstruction.

The Fight Against Injustice

🔻 **KEY QUESTION** How did African Americans react to discrimination and segregation?

As African Americans suffered from more racist policies and discrimination, they began organizing to win back their civil rights.

Life Under Jim Crow After the Supreme Court rulings, racism and discrimination in the South spread. **Jim Crow laws**, which had begun to be adopted in various settings in the late 1870s, became systematized and widespread.

The purpose of Jim Crow laws was to segregate races. African Americans could not attend the same schools as whites or sit in the same sections in restaurants or other public places. Buses followed the "separate but equal" standard established by *Plessy* v. *Ferguson*, but schools, for example, were markedly inferior for African Americans.

Another purpose of Jim Crow was intimidation. In Mississippi in 1875, white people shot African-American voters. During that same period, the right of African Americans to vote was denied legally when states made them take special "tests" or charged them poll taxes.

While racial discrimination was especially intense in the South, blacks settling in the North were often resented by whites. Lynchings occurred in the Midwest, and race riots erupted in Chicago in 1919 and Tulsa in 1921.

Calls for Justice and Equality Grow Despite outbreaks of violence, the North offered a better life for African Americans. The period from 1916 to 1919 is the first wave of what is called "The Great Migration." During that migration, more than a half million African Americans moved north to such cities as Chicago, Detroit, and New York.

African Americans in the North united. In 1909, African-American leaders and white activists formed the **National Association for the Advancement of Colored People (NAACP)**, which brought attention to discrimination against African Americans.

World Wars I and II also strengthened African Americans' awareness of their civil rights. After fighting against racism in Europe, they were no longer willing to accept it at home.

Lynching, the illegal execution of a person by a mob, became a serious problem.

 FIND MAIN IDEAS List ways that African Americans reacted to discrimination and segregation.

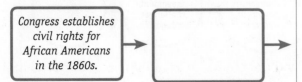

Illinois Learning Standards *Review*

ONLINE QUIZ
For test practice, go to
Interactive Review @ ClassZone.com

TERMS & NAMES

1. Explain the importance of

- segregation
- civil rights
- black codes
- *Plessy* v. *Ferguson*
- Jim Crow laws
- The National Association for the Advancement of Colored People (NAACP)

USING YOUR READING NOTES

2. Sequence Events Complete the sequence diagrams you created while reading this section.

> Congress establishes civil rights for African Americans in the 1860s. → □ →

KEY IDEAS

3. What did the Fourteenth Amendment declare?

4. What did the Supreme Court rule in *Plessy* v. *Ferguson*?

CRITICAL THINKING

5. Recognize Effects What was the effect of the Supreme Court rulings during and immediately after Reconstruction?

6. **Writing** Report Use the Internet to research the NAACP. Write a brief report explaining its role in campaigning to end segregation in schools and other public places.

▶ Key Ideas

BEFORE, YOU LEARNED

Between the 1870s and the 1950s, African Americans lost many of the civil rights they had gained during Reconstruction.

NOW YOU WILL LEARN

Changes after World War II helped African Americans make progress in their struggle for equality.

▶ Vocabulary

TERMS & NAMES

integrate to open to people of all races or ethnic groups

Thurgood Marshall NAACP legal counsel and the first African-American Supreme Court Justice

Brown v. Board of Education of Topeka 1954 case in which the Supreme Court ruled that "separate but equal" education for black and white students was unconstitutional

Montgomery bus boycott 1955 protest action to end segregation on buses in Montgomery, Alabama

Martin Luther King, Jr. an influential leader of the civil rights era, assassinated in 1968

Southern Christian Leadership Conference (SCLC) organization that coordinated non-violent civil rights protests across the South

sit-in protest in which people sit in a place and refuse to move until their demands are met

Student Nonviolent Coordinating Committee (SNCC) organization created to give young people a greater role in the civil rights movement

BACKGROUND VOCABULARY

grassroots group of ordinary people who come together at a local level for a cause

activism direct action taken to support or oppose a social or political goal

▶ Reading Strategy

As you read and respond to the **KEY QUESTIONS**, use a graphic organizer like the one shown to record main ideas and details about the modern civil right movement. Add ovals or start a new diagram as needed.

 Skillbuilder Handbook, page R4.

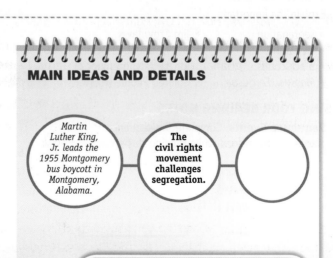

MAIN IDEAS AND DETAILS

Martin Luther King, Jr. leads the 1955 Montgomery bus boycott in Montgomery, Alabama.

The civil rights movement challenges segregation.

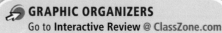

GRAPHIC ORGANIZERS
Go to **Interactive Review** @ ClassZone.com

The Modern Civil Rights Movement

14.C.3 Compare historical issues involving rights, roles and status of individuals in relation to municipalities, states and the nation.

16.B.3c Describe the way the Constitution has changed over time as a result of amendments and Supreme Court decisions.

One American's Story

On December 1, 1955, in Montgomery, Alabama, Rosa Parks boarded a bus to ride home from work. Along the way, a group of white people boarded. The bus driver ordered Parks and a few other African Americans to give up their seats to the white people and move to the back of the bus. All of them except Parks obeyed.

PRIMARY SOURCE

❝ The driver of the bus saw me still sitting there, and he asked was I going to stand up. I said, 'No.' He said, 'Well, I'm going to have you arrested.' Then I said, 'You may do that.' ❞

—Rosa Parks, *Rosa Parks: My Story*

Parks was arrested, and this event would spark a movement that began to tear down segregation in America.

The Montgomery Sheriff's Department photographed Rosa Parks after her arrest.

Court Decisions and Grassroots Organizing

🔻 **KEY QUESTION** How did civil rights supporters challenge segregation?

As you have read, African Americans had been fighting for equality since the Civil War. Their goals included full political rights, better job opportunities, and an end to segregation. But before World War II, they had little success. This situation changed in the 1950s. A series of Supreme Court decisions and a popular **grassroots** movement—one that was locally organized by ordinary citizens—helped expand the civil rights of all Americans.

Brown* Overturns *Plessy The NAACP, the oldest civil rights organization in the United States, benefited from these changes. Before the war, it had established a fund to pay for legal challenges to segregation. Even so, the "separate but equal" doctrine remained in effect well into the 1950s. This doctrine had been established by the *Plessy* v. *Ferguson* case in 1896.

In the early 1950s, African Americans in several states sued to **integrate**, or end segregation, in public schools. Until this time, white-controlled school boards had provided white children with better schoolhouses and newer books and equipment than they had provided to black children. Schools were separate, but they were unequal in the service they provided. **Thurgood Marshall**, the NAACP counsel, led the legal team that challenged the segregation laws in the courts.

In the early 1950s, the Supreme Court took on the issue by accepting the case of ***Brown v. Board of Education of Topeka***. On May 17, 1954, Chief Justice Earl Warren delivered the Court's historic opinion:

PRIMARY SOURCE

❝ We conclude that in the field of public education the doctrine of 'separate but equal' has no place. Separate educational facilities are inherently unequal. **❞**

—**CHIEF JUSTICE EARL WARREN**, *Brown* v. *Board of Education of Topeka*

Thurgood Marshall's arguments had prevailed. The Court overturned *Plessy* v. *Ferguson*, striking down the "separate but equal" doctrine and declaring that the nation's public schools should be integrated.

Although the Brown decision was limited to public schools, many people hoped that it would eventually end segregation in other public facilities. In the meantime, civil rights supporters assumed that African-American children would receive the same educational opportunities as white children. But the Supreme Court did not say how desegregation was to occur until a year later.

At that time, the Court ordered public schools to desegregate "with all deliberate speed." This ruling, which was known as *Brown II*, actually gave segregated school districts more time to desegregate. Some communities, such as Washington, D.C., desegregated quickly. But in most places, white-controlled schools bitterly resisted desegregation.

Protesters wave to an empty bus during the Montgomery Bus Boycott.

Montgomery Bus Boycott In 1955, about six months after the *Brown II* decision, Rosa Parks was arrested for refusing to give up her seat on a city bus. News of her arrest quickly spread from the NAACP and members of her church to other African-American churches and local groups. Along with the news came a call to action: "If Negroes did not ride the buses, they [the buses] could not operate. We are, therefore, asking every Negro to stay off the buses Monday in protest of the arrest and trial." This protest became known as the **Montgomery bus boycott**. A boycott is a form of political **activism**, or direct action taken to support or oppose a social or political goal.

Brown v. Board of Education of Topeka 1954

KEY ISSUE   School desegregation

KEY PEOPLE   Linda Brown   seven-year-old student in Topeka, Kansas
              Thurgood Marshall   Brown's attorney; employed by NAACP
              Earl Warren   Chief Justice, U.S. Supreme Court, 1953–1969

History Makers

Thurgood Marshall
1908–1993

In 1930, Thurgood Marshall was denied admission to the segregated University of Maryland Law School. Five years later, Marshall won his first major civil rights case, forcing the same law school to open its doors to African Americans. In 1940, he was appointed chief counsel for the NAACP and went on to win 29 of the 32 cases he argued before the Supreme Court. One of the most prominent cases was the landmark *Brown* v. *Board of Education of Topeka*. In 1967, President Johnson appointed Marshall to be the first African-American Supreme Court justice. He served with distinction for 24 years.

Connect *to* Today Research the life of a present day Supreme Court Justice. Compare his or her approach to law with that of Thurgood Marshall.

The Case

In September 1950, Linda Brown was refused enrollment at her neighborhood grade school. Topeka, like many other school systems at the time, operated separate schools for "the two races"—blacks and whites. Linda was an African American, and the school was for whites only. Linda was required to attend a school farther away from her home. The Browns filed suit against the school board, demanding that Linda be allowed to attend the neighborhood school.

The Court's Decision The Fourteenth Amendment requires "equal protection" of the laws. But the Supreme Court had ruled in *Plessy* v. *Ferguson* (1896) that "separate but equal" facilities for blacks and whites were permissible. Chief Justice Warren, however, pointed out that Plessy had involved transportation, not education. He stressed the importance of education in society:

"It is doubtful that any child may reasonably be expected to succeed in life if he is denied the opportunity for education."

Warren went on to suggest that segregation denied African-American children that opportunity. He concluded:

"In the field of public education the doctrine of 'separate but equal' has no place. Separate educational facilities are inherently unequal."

Historical Impact The *Brown* decision marked a turning point in the civil rights movement. Despite the initial resistance to desegregation (some 10 years after the decision many Southern school districts were still segregated), *Brown* helped to change Americans' views on equality in education. As important, it provided the basis for most of the civil rights laws passed in the late 1950s and 1960s.

CRITICAL THINKING **Summarize** Explain how the Supreme Court's ruling in *Brown* strengthened the civil rights of all Americans.

History Makers

Martin Luther King, Jr.
1929–1968

King was only twenty-six years old when he became leader of the Montgomery bus boycott. Although he was young, King's extraordinary courage, intelligence, and speaking abilities made him the ideal leader for the civil rights movement. His belief in love and nonviolence was in stark contrast to the hatred and violence African Americans continued to suffer in the Jim Crow South.

King learned about nonviolence by studying writers and thinkers such as Mohandas Gandhi. He came to believe that only love could convert people to the side of justice. He described the power of nonviolent resisters: "We will soon wear you down by our capacity to suffer. So in winning the victory . . . we will win you in the process."

WHAT IF?
How do you think history would have been different if Dr. King had not been assassinated in 1968?

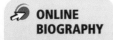 **ONLINE BIOGRAPHY**   For more on Martin Luther King, Jr., go to the **Research & Writing Center** @ ClassZone.com

That evening, local NAACP leaders held a meeting to decide whether to continue the boycott. A 26-year-old Baptist minister from Atlanta, Georgia, **Dr. Martin Luther King, Jr.**, spoke plainly yet eloquently to the group.

PRIMARY SOURCE

❝There comes a time that people get tired. We are here this evening to say to those who have mistreated us so long that we are tired—tired of being segregated and humiliated; tired of being kicked about by the brutal feet of oppression.❞

—Martin Luther King, Jr.,
quoted in *Stride Toward Freedom*

The church members decided to continue the boycott despite the numerous hardships involved. It went on for 13 months—months during which Montgomery's black community remained united in the fight against injustice. Boycotters organized car pools or simply walked. King and other leaders endured death threats, bombings, and jailings. The violent reactions of whites to the nonviolent boycott gained the attention of the national media.

Meanwhile, the Montgomery bus segregation law had been challenged in court. On November 13, 1956, the Supreme Court ruled that the law was unconstitutional. The ruling was a turning point for Africa Americans and a significant victory for the emerging civil rights movement. African Americans once again boarded the buses in Montgomery. This time they sat wherever they pleased.

The boycott had several important results. First, it ended segregation on Montgomery buses. Second, it led to the founding of the **Southern Christian Leadership Conference (SCLC)**. The SCLC soon coordinated nonviolent civil rights protests across the South. Third, the boycott set Dr. King on a path that would make him one of the best-known civil rights leaders of his day.

🔺 **SUMMARIZE** Describe how civil rights' supporters challenged segregation.

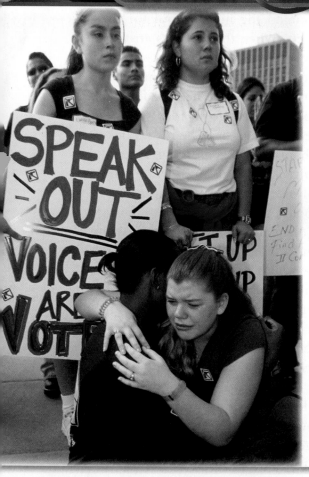

POLITICAL PROTEST

The First Amendment to the Constitution guarantees "the right of the people peaceably to assemble, and to petition the government for a redress of grievances." Political protests can take many forms, such as sit-ins, boycotts, marches, rallies, and demonstrations. As you will see, young people often play a vital part in protesting injustice.

Activity

Organize to Fight Injustice

1 Learn as much as you can about the issue you are concerned about.

2 Write letters or email elected officials explaining your position.

3 Find and join a group that shares your views. You can form a local chapter of a national organization, if none exists.

4 Participate in marches, vigils, demonstrations, or rallies organized by a recognized group.

 See Citizenship Handbook, pp. 306–307

Emotions run high at a protest against gun violence in Austin, Texas.

Civil Rights Supporters Face Violence

🔻 **KEY QUESTION** How did segregationists try to stop integration?

Civil rights victories upset many Southern whites. Segregationists fought back against African Americans and civil rights organizations. The Ku Klux Klan used beatings, arson, and murder to threaten African Americans who pursued their civil rights. Many whites organized groups known as White Citizens Councils to prevent desegregation. The opposition of whites to desegregation became known as "massive resistance."

Showdown in Little Rock Massive resistance threatened the desegregation of schools in Little Rock, Arkansas, in 1957. Following the *Brown* case, the Little Rock school board made plans to integrate. It called for nine African-American students to enroll at Central High School in September 1957. They became known as "the Little Rock Nine."

Segregationists tried to stop the integration of the school. Governor Orval Faubus of Arkansas sided with the segregationists. On September 3, he ordered National Guard troops to prevent the nine students from entering the school the next morning.

Elizabeth Eckford makes her way through a hostile mob while attempting to enter Central High School in Little Rock in 1957.

Eight of the students had been informed that someone would drive them to the high school for their safety. When the students arrived at the school, the National Guard troops turned them away. The family of the ninth student, Elizabeth Eckford, had no telephone, so word of the plan never reached her. She rode a bus to school alone that morning. When she arrived, a mob of angry white people followed her toward the school's doors.

She saw a guard let some white students pass, so she went to him. But he would not move. Later Eckford wrote, "When I tried to squeeze past him, he raised his bayonet. . . . Somebody started yelling, 'Lynch her! Lynch her!'" Finally, a white woman guided Eckford away and took her home.

For three weeks, Faubus refused to allow the African-American students into the school—even after meeting with President Dwight Eisenhower. The president did not want to force the governor to obey the law, but he eventually realized that it was his only choice.

On September 24, Eisenhower ordered the 101st Airborne Division into Little Rock. The Little Rock Nine rode to school escorted by jeeps armed with machine guns. Paratroopers lined the streets and protected the students as they entered Central High.

Sit-Ins Energize the Movement Victories like the one in Little Rock encouraged civil rights supporters to continue their fight. In February 1960, four African-American college students began a sit-in to desegregate a lunch counter at a store in Greensboro, North Carolina. A **sit-in** is a protest in which people sit and refuse to move until their demands are met. The students sat at the lunch counter and ordered coffee. The waitress refused to serve them because they were African Americans.

That first day, the students stayed for about an hour. They came back each day that week and brought more protesters. By Thursday, there were more than 100 protesters, including some whites. In the following weeks, thousands of protesters took part in sit-ins across the South.

As the sit-ins spread, segregationists began to abuse the protesters. They covered the protesters with ammonia and itching powder. Acid was also thrown. They yelled at them, beat them, and burned them with cigarettes. Some protesters went to jail. But other protesters came forward to replace them. The sit-ins were an effective protest tactic. They eventually forced many stores with lunch counters to serve African Americans.

John Salter, Joan Trumpaurer, and Anne Moody stage a sit-in at Woolworth's lunch counter in Jackson, Mississippi, May 28, 1963; Photo by Fred Blackwell.

Robert Moses, a young teacher who later became a leader of SNCC, was inspired by the protesters he saw in newspaper photos. He said, "Before, the Negro in the South had always looked on the defensive, cringing. This time they were taking the initiative. . . . It made me realize that for a long time I had been troubled by the problem of being a Negro and at the same time being an American. This was the answer."

CRITICAL VIEWING How might this photo affect people differently from the photo of Elizabeth Eckford on page 882?

Many civil rights leaders saw the success of the sit-ins and supported an organization for young people. Out of this movement, the **Student Nonviolent Coordinating Committee (SNCC)** was formed. Through SNCC, SCLC, and other groups, the civil rights movement increased the pressure for change in the 1960s.

 FIND MAIN IDEAS Describe how segregationists tried to stop integration.

 Illinois Learning Standards *Review*

ONLINE QUIZ
For test practice, go to
Interactive Review @ ClassZone.com

TERMS & NAMES

1. Explain the importance of

- integrate
- Thurgood Marshall
- *Brown* v. *Board of Education of Topeka*
- Montgomery bus boycott
- Martin Luther King, Jr.
- SCLC
- sit-in
- SNCC

USING YOUR READING NOTES

2. Main Ideas and Details Complete the diagram you created at the beginning of this section with details from the text.

> *Martin Luther King, Jr. leads the 1955 Montgomery bus boycott in Montgomery, Alabama.*

> **The civil rights movement challenges segregation.**

KEY IDEAS

3. What role did Thurgood Marshall play in challenging segregation?

4. What happened when African-American students tried to enter Central High School in Little Rock in 1957?

CRITCAL THINKING

5. WHAT IF? What might have happened if *Brown* v. *the Board of Education of Topeka* had been decided in favor of the Board of Education of Topeka?

6. Connect *to* **Today** What issues cause people to engage in protests today?

7. Writing How did the tactics used by civil rights protesters differ from the response of many Southern whites? Write a paragraph comparing and contrasting their methods.

▶ Key Ideas

BEFORE, YOU LEARNED

Changes after World War II helped African Americans make progress in their struggle for equality.

NOW YOU WILL LEARN

The civil rights movement led to the end of legal segregation.

▶ Vocabulary

TERMS & NAMES

Freedom Rides protests against segregation on interstate busing in the South

Congress of Racial Equality (CORE) organization that planned Freedom Rides

March on Washington huge civil rights demonstration in Washington, D.C., in 1963

Civil Rights Act of 1964 law banning segregation in public places and creating the Equal Employment Opportunity Commission

Freedom Summer 1964 voter-registration drive for Southern blacks

Voting Rights Act 1965 law banning literacy tests and other laws that kept blacks from registering to vote

Great Society President Johnson's programs to help the poor, elderly, and women

Malcolm X African-American activist killed in 1965

BACKGROUND VOCABULARY

disenfranchised (DISS•ehn•FRAN•chyzd) people deprived of legal rights, especially the right to vote

Visual Vocabulary Malcolm X

▶ Reading Strategy

Re-create the diagram shown at right. As you read and respond to the **KEY QUESTION** use the diagram at the right to record significant civil rights events in the order in which they occurred.

 Skillbuilder Handbook, page R5.

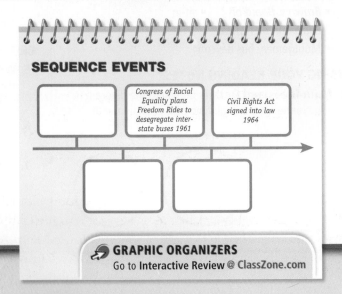

SEQUENCE EVENTS

| | Congress of Racial Equality plans Freedom Rides to desegregate interstate buses 1961 | Civil Rights Act signed into law 1964 |

GRAPHIC ORGANIZERS
Go to **Interactive Review** @ ClassZone.com

Kennedy, Johnson, and Civil Rights

14.C.3 Compare historical issues involving rights, roles and status of individuals in relation to municipalities, states and the nation.

14.D.3 Describe roles and influences of individuals, groups and media in shaping current Illinois and United States public policy (e.g., *general public opinion, special interest groups, formal parties, media*).

One American's Story

Jim Zwerg joined a Freedom Ride in May 1961. **Freedom Rides** were protests against segregation on interstate buses in the South. During the rides, whites would sit in the back of a bus. African Americans would sit in the front and refuse to move. At bus terminals along the route, black riders would try to use "whites only" facilities. A mob attacked Zwerg's group.

PRIMARY SOURCE

❝ I was knocked to the ground. I remember being kicked in the spine and hearing my back crack, and the pain. I fell on my back and a foot came down on my face. . . . I went unconscious and I woke up in the hospital. I was informed that I had been unconscious for a day and a half. One of the nurses told me that another little crowd were going to try and lynch me. **❞**

—**Jim Zwerg, from a radio interview**

Jim Zwerg recovers in a Montgomery hospital.

The many, many people who participated in Freedom Rides and other forms of protest opened the doors to change in government and society.

The Movement Gains Strength

▼ **KEY QUESTION** How did ordinary people help bring about change?

In the early 1960s, Congress was reluctant to act on civil rights issues. However, ordinary people throughout America were joining the civil rights movement. They traveled from all parts of the country to support African Americans in the South. As this grassroots movement intensified its protests, politicians were forced to get involved.

Kennedy and Civil Rights In 1960 Americans elected a new president. Although civil rights was not the main issue in the campaign, it played an important role. The Democrats nominated John F. Kennedy, a senator from Massachusetts. The Republicans nominated Vice-President Richard Nixon

The Civil Rights Era **885**

of California. Though the candidates had similar positions on many issues, Kennedy won in a very close election.

Southern Democrats supported segregation. Kennedy did not want to anger them because they could weaken his presidency and prevent his reelection. However, civil rights activists continued to pressure the federal government. In May 1961, the **Congress of Racial Equality (CORE)** staged Freedom Rides to desegregate buses traveling between states. Despite attacks by segregationists along the route, the freedom riders would not give up. Kennedy sent federal marshals to protect the riders. Four months later, the federal government issued an order to integrate all interstate bus facilities.

Protests in Birmingham In the early 1960s, the civil rights movement gained strength. African Americans in Birmingham, Alabama, wanted to integrate public facilities and gain better job and housing opportunities. Local civil rights leaders invited Dr. King and SCLC to join the protests.

Birmingham presented an opportunity for protesters. They knew that Eugene "Bull" Connor, the city's Public Safety Commissioner, would use violence to stop the protests. They also knew that the sight of segregationists attacking nonviolent protesters would increase the pressure for change.

Animated HISTORY

TECHNOLOGY *of the* TIME

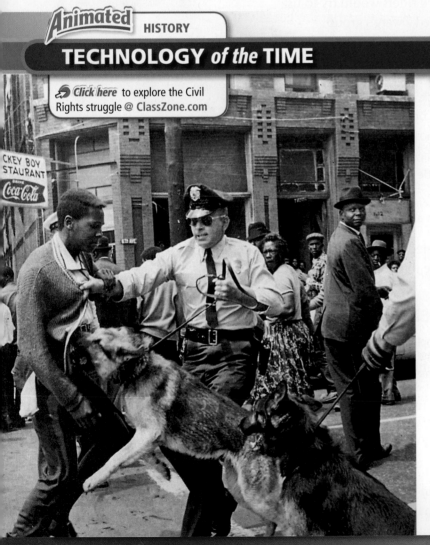

Click here to explore the Civil Rights struggle @ ClassZone.com

THE POWER OF IMAGES

As the events in the civil rights movement unfolded, newspapers and television—a technology that was changing how the nation viewed the civil rights movement—showed agonizing and wrenching scenes from the struggle.

Many Americans were affected by images of peaceful demonstrators subjected to violence by angry whites—including police—in ways that the printed word could not convey.

This photograph shows a police dog attacking a 17-year-old demonstrator in 1963. President Kennedy was forced to acknowledge the violence after the photo appeared on the front page of the *New York Times*.

CRITICAL THINKING

Form and Support Opinions Are television viewers and newspaper readers today as moved by scenes of injustice as they were in the time of the civil rights movement? Support your answer.

The demonstrations began in April 1963. The police arrested and held Dr. King. From jail, he wrote a defense of the protests.

PRIMARY SOURCE

❝ I guess it is easy for those who have never felt the stinging darts of segregation to say, 'Wait.' . . . [But] there comes a time when the cup of endurance runs over, and men are no longer willing to be plunged into an abyss [a bottomless pit] of injustice. ❞

—Martin Luther King, Jr., "Letter from Birmingham Jail"

The SCLC recruited children to join the Birmingham marches. The police used dogs and firehoses on them. People across the nation who watched the events on television were horrified. Soon Birmingham's white leaders agreed to desegregate lunch counters, remove segregation signs, and employ more African Americans in downtown stores.

🔺 **SUMMARIZE** Summarize how people in the civil rights movement helped bring about change.

The High Water Mark, 1963–1965

🔻 **KEY QUESTION** What did the Civil Rights Act and the Voting Rights Act achieve?

The Birmingham protests, a march on Washington, and a voter registration drive helped move civil rights legislation through Congress.

The March on Washington The events in Birmingham caused many Americans to support passage of new laws to protect the civil rights of all American citizens.

On August 28, 1963, about 250,000 people joined Martin Luther King, Jr., in the **March on Washington**. The high point of the demonstration came when King delivered his "I Have a Dream" speech. (For a selection from King's speech, see page 901.) During this speech, he spoke these famous words:

PRIMARY SOURCE

❝ I have a dream that my four little children will one day live in a nation where they will not be judged by the color of their skin but by the content of their character. ❞

—Martin Luther King, Jr., from "I Have a Dream"

The March on Washington united many groups that all called for passage of civil rights laws. President Kennedy promised his support.

New Civil Rights Laws Tragically, President Kennedy did not live long enough to fulfill this promise. On November 22, 1963, Kennedy and Vice-President Lyndon Baines Johnson went to Texas to campaign. As the motorcade passed through Dallas, thousands of people greeted the president. Suddenly, shots rang out. President Kennedy was hit and died within an hour.

Lyndon Johnson was sworn in as president, and he promised to continue Kennedy's policies. Johnson argued that "no memorial oration or eulogy

History Makers

Fannie Lou Hamer   1917–1977

Until Fannie Lou Hamer was 44, she worked as a sharecropper in rural Mississippi. That ended in 1962, when civil rights workers came to her county to help register voters. Within a year, she had been thrown off her land and badly beaten for trying to register to vote and for helping others to do the same. She helped found a group that challenged the all-white delegation to the Democratic National Convention in 1964. Hamer spoke to a national television audience, detailing the savage resistance of whites to her cause. "Is this America?" she asked, provoking an outpouring of support nationwide.

CRITICAL THINKING

Connect *to* **Today**   What might be some reasons today for people to ask Fannie Lou Hamer's question, "Is this America?"

could more eloquently honor President Kennedy's memory than the earliest possible passage of the civil rights bill." The nation's grief led to broad support for the bill.

In July the **Civil Rights Act of 1964** was signed into law. The law banned segregation in public places, such as hotels and theaters. It also created the Equal Employment Opportunity Commission to prevent job discrimination. Segregation officially became illegal throughout the United States.

Fighting for Voting Rights Southern states had long used literacy tests, poll taxes, and violence to prevent African Americans from voting. The Civil Rights Act of 1964 barred states from using different voting standards for blacks and whites. In the same year, the states ratified the Twenty-Fourth Amendment. It outlawed poll taxes. Even so, many African Americans still found it difficult to vote. They lobbied Congress to pass a stronger voting rights law.

In 1964, SNCC organized a voter-registration drive for Southern blacks. It was called **Freedom Summer**. It brought Northern college students into Mississippi to work with SNCC organizers. These young volunteers endured much mistreatment while performing their work. Some were even killed. Still, they helped add many African Americans to the voter-registration roles.

Early in 1965, King and SCLC organized voter-registration drives in Selma, Alabama, including a protest march to Montgomery. On March 7, as the marchers crossed a bridge at the edge of Selma, state troopers on horseback attacked them. Americans watched as the violence was broadcast on national television. Pressure for federal action rose.

African American Voter Registration in the South 1960–1971

Percent of registered voters in black voting-age population

29% 1960   58% 1970

Source: *Statistical Abstract of the United States, 1972*

VIRGINIA 59% 23%

59% 75%

TENNESSEE 59%

88%

38%

75% ARKANSAS

59% 39% N.C.

16%

58% S.C.

70%

5%

MISS. 60%

14% ALABAMA

29% GEORGIA

54%

75%

35%

TEXAS

31% LA.

57% 39% FLORIDA

Connect Geography & History

Compare and Contrast
Which state had the lowest percentage of black voters in 1960? Which had the highest?

President Johnson told Alabama Governor George Wallace that he would not tolerate any more violence. When the march to Montgomery resumed, the president sent troops to protect it. He also used the public's anger to push for action on voting rights.

On August 6, 1965, Johnson signed the **Voting Rights Act** into law. It banned literacy tests and other laws that kept people from registering to vote. It also sent federal officials to register voters. Within months, the number of black registered voters in Selma and throughout Dallas County rose from 383 to about 8,000.

▲ **PROBLEMS AND SOLUTIONS** Discuss what the Civil Rights Act and the Voting Rights Act achieved.

The Focus Shifts

▼ **KEY QUESTION** What happened to the civil rights movement in the late 1960s?

After President Johnson signed the Voting Rights Act into law, the focus of the civil rights movement began to shift to economic issues. However, disagreements over goals caused division within the movement.

Johnson and the Great Society Shortly after taking office, Johnson asked Americans to seek a "great society [that] demands an end to poverty and racial injustice." His program was called the **Great Society**. It provided a series of measures to help the poor, the elderly, women, and the disenfranchised—people deprived of the right to vote. It also included legislation to promote education, end discrimination, and protect the environment.

Many of these programs passed and still exist today, such as Medicare and Medicaid. Medicare provides health insurance for senior citizens, while Medicaid provides medical care for the poor.

In addition, Congress passed the Elementary and Secondary School Act, which provided new federal funds for education.

Congress also strengthened the 1960 Clean Water and 1963 Clean Air acts. It passed legislation to protect endangered species and to preserve millions of acres of wilderness.

Divisions in the Civil Rights Movement In the late 1960s, civil rights leaders disagreed about what steps to take next. The SCLC and other organizations wanted to expand the nonviolent struggle. But other groups wanted the movement to become more aggressive.

The Great Society

Civil Rights Act (1964)
Outlawed discrimination in public places, created the Equal Employment Opportunity Commission, and barred states from using different standards for voter registration for whites and blacks.

Voting Rights Act (1965)
Banned literacy tests and used federal registrars to register voters.

Medical Care Act (1965)
Established Medicare and Medicaid programs to assist the aged and the poor with medical care.

Elementary and Secondary School Act (1965)
Provided federal aid to education.

Department of Housing and Urban Development (1965)
Formed to administer federal housing.

Wilderness Preservation Act (1964) Set aside over nine million acres for national forest lands.

Department of Transportation (1966) Created to deal with national air, rail, and highway transportation.

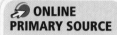
Some African Americans had begun to reject nonviolence and cooperation with whites. In 1966, SNCC's black members forced white members out of the organization. Stokely Carmichael, the leader of SNCC, began to call for "black power." He and others wanted black people to create their own organizations under their own control to fight racism.

The Nation of Islam, a branch of Islam founded in the United States, also urged African Americans to separate from whites. The Nation was led by Elijah Muhammad, but its most popular figure was **Malcolm X**. By the mid-1960s, Malcolm X had rejected the separatist ideas of the Nation of Islam—although he remained a devout Muslim. During a trip to Mecca, in Saudi Arabia, he saw Muslims of all races treat each other as equals. He envisioned a world where all races could live together in peace. But he had little time to spread his new message. In 1965, he was assassinated by members of the Nation of Islam.

In 1966, Dr. King and the SCLC joined protests in Chicago. In the North, laws didn't deny African Americans their civil rights—white people simply discriminated against them. Whites would not sell property in certain areas to

ONLINE PRIMARY SOURCE

Hear the perspectives at the **Research & Writing Center** @ ClassZone.com

COMPARING *Perspectives*

Martin Luther King, Jr. and Malcolm X shared the same goals but had different ideas of how to achieve them. These quotes reflect both their areas of agreement and disagreement.

Martin Luther King, Jr., Speaks

❝Mankind must evolve for all human conflict a method which rejects revenge, aggression, and retaliation. The foundation of such a method is love. ❞
—*December 11, 1964*

❝ . . . I always had a deep affection for Malcolm and felt he had a great ability to put his finger on the existence and the root of the problem. ❞
—*telegram to Betty Shabazz, after the murder of Malcolm X*

Malcolm X Speaks

❝And I feel that when the law fails to protect Negroes from whites' attack then those Negroes should use arms, if necessary, to defend themselves.... I firmly believe that Negroes have the right to fight against these racists, by any means that are necessary. ❞
—*Autobiography of Malcolm X*

❝Dr. King wants the same thing I want. Freedom. ❞
—*television interview, April 4, 1964*

CRITICAL THINKING

1. **Analyze Primary Sources** What are some of the words used by Dr. King that reinforce his overall message? What words reinforce Malcolm X's message?

2. **Draw Conclusions** What events during the civil rights movement might have caused Malcolm X to fight "by any means that are necessary"?

African Americans, and some employers refused to hire African-American workers.

In spite of the protests, most white Chicagoans were no more interested in desegregation than Southern whites had been. Chicago mayor Richard J. Daley made only a few changes before SCLC abandoned its campaign.

African Americans in Chicago and other U.S. cities grew frustrated with their lack of political power and economic opportunity. Their frustration led to a series of riots in the late 1960s. Nationwide, 164 riots broke out in the first nine months of 1967. Then, on April 4, 1968, Martin Luther King, Jr., was assassinated in Memphis, Tennessee. African-American neighborhoods across the country exploded in anger. About 40 people died in the rioting.

People point towards the source of gunfire that killed Martin Luther King, Jr., who lies at their feet.

 ANALYZE CAUSES AND EFFECTS Explain what happened to the civil rights movement in the late 1960s.

 Illinois Learning Standards *Review*

 ONLINE QUIZ
For test practice, go to
Interactive Review @ ClassZone.com

TERMS & NAMES

1. Explain the importance of

- Freedom Rides
- Congress of Racial Equality (CORE)
- March on Washington
- Civil Rights Act of 1964
- Freedom Summer
- Voting Rights Act
- Great Society
- Malcolm X

USING YOUR READING NOTES

2. Sequence Complete the sequence chart you started at the beginning of this section with details from the text.

Congress of Racial Equality plans Freedom Rides to desegregate interstate buses 1961

Civil Rights Act signed into law 1964

KEY IDEAS

3. Why did civil rights workers believe that Birmingham, Alabama, was a good place to protest?

4. How did civil rights workers fight to improve African-American voting rights?

CRITICAL THINKING

5. What was the cause of disagreement among civil rights leaders in the late 1960s?

6. Evaluate Why do you think the March on Washington became such an important event in the civil rights movement?

7. Connect *to* Today The NAACP and the SCLC are still active today. How might their work today be different from their work in the 1960s?

8. Writing Imagine that you are a reporter covering the March on Washington and that Dr. King has just delivered his "I Have a Dream" speech. Describe the scene.

FIGHTING FOR JUSTICE

The civil rights movement required the courage and sacrifices of ordinary Americans. How did their actions help end injustice?

TRIGGERING OUTRAGE

Three months before the Montgomery Bus Boycott, Mamie Till-Mobley *(right)* held an open-casket funeral for her son Emmett *(left)*, who was murdered by white racists. Thousands attended the service, and the media shocked the world by publishing images of the boy's mutilated corpse. Public outcry intensified following the acquittal of Till's accused murderers, who openly admitted to the crime.

❝ I am so thankful for the bravery and courage Mamie demonstrated when she shared her only child with the world. The news of Emmett's death caused many people to participate in the cry for justice and equal rights, including myself. **❞**

—Rosa Parks, in praise for Mamie Till-Mobley's memoir, *Death of Innocence: The Story of the Hate Crime That Changed America*

▲ ENDURING HARDSHIP

Thousands of bus boycotters walked miles each day to work or school. Others rode in organized car pools. During the Tallahassee bus boycott of 1955–1956, the state attorney general ruled that the car pools violated state law. Car pool drivers were arrested and fined.

▼ FACING HARASSMENT AND INTIMIDATION

Many demonstrators across the country faced arrest and intimidation in their fight for justice, as shown in this photograph taken in Nashville, Tennessee, on April 27, 1964.

RISKING LIVES ▶

Many civil rights workers lost their lives in the fight for justice. Andrew Goodman, James Earl Chaney, and Michael Henry Schwerner helped register voters in Mississippi during Freedom Summer. The Federal Bureau of Investigation circulated this poster after their disappearance. The FBI later discovered that the young men had been murdered by members of the Ku Klux Klan.

▲ MARCHING

Marching was one way people supported the civil rights movement. One example is the five-day, 54-mile civil rights march from Selma to Montgomery, Alabama. Two weeks earlier the march had been forcibly blocked by state troopers in a day remembered as "Bloody Sunday." What began as a protest by a few hundred ended with thousands gathered outside the Alabama state capitol to demand justice.

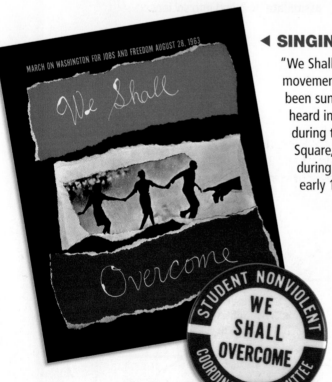

◀ SINGING FOR FREEDOM

"We Shall Overcome" became an anthem of the civil rights movement in the 1960s. Its simple yet empowering lyrics have been sung in dozens of languages across the globe. The tune was heard in Germany as the Berlin Wall came down in 1989–1990, during the 1989 pro-democracy demonstrations in Tiananmen Square, China, and by resisters of racial injustice in South Africa during the later years of the apartheid era, which ended in the early 1990s.

Activity

Express Your Thoughts

1 Work with a partner to find out more about one of the topics discussed on these pages.

2 Use your findings to write a song or poem to express your feelings about the fight for justice during the civil rights movement.

Reading for Understanding

▶ Key Ideas

BEFORE, YOU LEARNED

The civil rights movement led to the end of legal segregation.

NOW YOU WILL LEARN

The African-American struggle for equality inspired other groups in their fight for civil rights.

▶ Vocabulary

TERMS & NAMES

Dolores Huerta Mexican-American union organizer and negotiator

César Chávez Mexican-American union organizer and leader

National Congress of American Indians (NCAI) organization founded in 1944 to promote rights of Native Americans

Betty Friedan women's rights leader and author of *The Feminine Mystique*

National Organization for Women (NOW) organization founded in 1966 to get women good jobs at equal pay

Equal Rights Amendment (ERA) amendment proposed that would give equality of rights regardless of sex

BACKGROUND VOCABULARY

Latinos people in the United States who trace their origins to Latin American countries and cultures

abridged shortened

REVIEW

assimilate to blend into society

▶ Reading Strategy

Re-create the spider diagram shown at right. As you read and respond to the **KEY QUESTIONS**, use the main branches to categorize facts about the different groups' struggles for civil rights. Add stems to record important details in each category.

 Skillbuilder Handbook, page R6.

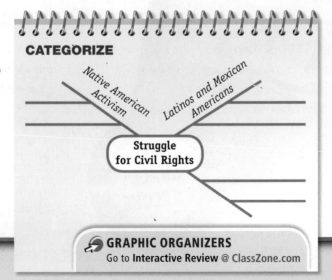

CATEGORIZE

Native American Activism

Latinos and Mexican Americans

Struggle for Civil Rights

GRAPHIC ORGANIZERS
Go to **Interactive Review** @ ClassZone.com

The Equal Rights Struggle Expands

14.C.3 Compare historical issues involving rights, roles and status of individuals in relation to municipalities, states and the nation.

14.D.3 Describe roles and influences of individuals, groups and media in shaping current Illinois and United States public policy (e.g., *general public opinion, special interest groups, formal parties, media*).

One American's Story

During the first half of the twentieth century, efforts by farm workers to organize labor unions had been suppressed by farm owners. In the 1950s and 1960s, Mexican-American activists continued to organize, inspired by African Americans in the civil rights movement. **Dolores Huerta** was teaching the children of farm workers in California when she realized what her contribution could be.

PRIMARY SOURCE

❝ I couldn't stand seeing kids come to class hungry and needing shoes. I thought I could do more by organizing farm workers than by trying to teach their hungry children. ❞

—Dolores Huerta, *Biography of Dolores Huerta*

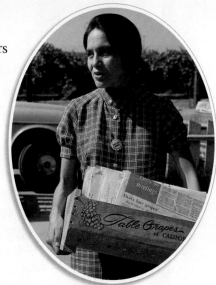

Dolores Huerta during a grape pickers' strike in 1968.

Huerta went on to help found the first farm workers' union in 1962. She became the union's chief negotiator for contracts, guaranteeing farm workers fair wages, benefits, and humane working conditions.

Other Minorities Organize

▼ **KEY QUESTION** How did other minorities fight for civil rights?

The civil rights movement sent shock waves through American society. Many people reconsidered issues of equality and discrimination and became politically involved in their communities. The civil rights movement encouraged other minorities in their fight for equal rights.

Mexican Americans Unite **Latinos** trace their roots to Spanish-speaking Latin American countries. The Latino population in the United States is extremely diverse. It includes people from many places, including Mexico, Puerto Rico, Cuba, and Central and South America. Each group has its own social and political concerns. For example, Mexican Americans are concerned about immigration and citizenship. Puerto Ricans are already U.S. citizens; therefore immigration issues aren't their primary concern.

The Civil Rights Era **895**

History Makers

César Chávez   1927–1993

César Chávez's 25-day fast in 1965 brought national attention to the conditions of farmworkers. The following year, he led a 250-mile "Pilgrimage" from Delano, California, to the state capitol in Sacramento. Under Chávez's leadership the UFW won such benefits as rest periods, toilets in the fields, and a ban on spraying pesticides while workers are in the fields.

Dolores Huerta   b. 1930

A former elementary school teacher, Dolores Huerta began working as a labor organizer after teaching the children of poor, migrant farm workers in central California. Since then, she has served as a union leader, a political delegate, and a successful lobbyist of both state and national governments. Since 2002, the Organizing Institute of the Dolores Huerta Foundation has been providing needy communities with training in organizing and leadership.

CRITICAL THINKING Evaluate What actions show Chávez's and Huerta's dedication to helping people?

 ONLINE BIOGRAPHY For more on César Chávez and Dolores Huerta, go to the **Research & Writing Center** @ ClassZone.com

Like African Americans, Mexican Americans united to fight for equality. In the 1950s, **César Chávez**, a Mexican-American farm worker and labor organizer, began working with Dolores Huerta to create a labor union. Chávez had been inspired by the nonviolent tactics of Gandhi and Martin Luther King, Jr. In 1962, Chávez and Huerta founded what would become the United Farm Workers Organizing Committee (UFWOC). In 1965, when California's grape growers refused to recognize the union, Chávez launched a nationwide grape boycott. The boycott succeded, and in 1970 Huerta negotiated a favorable contract between grape growers and the UFWOC.

The farm workers' struggle inspired Mexican Americans in cities to organize. In 1968, students in Los Angeles walked out of classes to press their demands for reform in the school system. They wanted better facilities, more courses on Mexican-American topics, and more Mexican-American teachers. At first, school authorities had protesters arrested. Later, they admitted to the poor conditions, and many reforms were eventually made. In 1970, Mexican Americans formed *La Raza Unida* (lah RAH•sah oo•NEE•dah), meaning the united people, to elect Mexican Americans to public office and to advocate for better jobs, pay, housing, and education.

Native American Activism As the United States grew, Native American groups suffered the loss of their lands and the massive killing of their people. Surviving Native Americans had been relocated onto reservations, where they lived in poverty. From the late 1800s until the mid-1900s, many Native American children were taken from reservations to attend "Indian schools." There Native American languages, clothing, and other expressions of culture were forbidden, and children were taught to **assimilate**, or blend into white society.

In the 1950s, the Bureau of Indian Affairs began a "termination policy" that ended federal protection of assets held by Native American tribes. Responsibility for providing services to Native Americans was given to state governments. The bureau also sold to developers 1.6 million acres of land that belonged to Native Americans.

NATIVE AMERICAN RIGHTS AND STATUS

Native American groups have worked to gain increased civil rights and status. Their struggle continues today. During the 1960s and 1970s, many people joined in protesting for more self-determination and advancement.

▶ **1924**—Snyder Act extends citizenship to all Indians born in the U.S.

▶ **1934**—Indian Reorganization Act encourages Indian self-government by decreasing federal control

▶ **1944**—The National Congress of American Indians is founded

▶ **1946**—The Indian Claims Commission is founded to receive land claims from Indian tribes.

▶ **1968**—The American Indian Movement (AIM) is founded.

▶ **1973**—AIM occupies Wounded Knee for 71 days in protest for Native American causes

▶ **1975**—The Indian Self-Determination and Education Assistance Act gives tribal governments more control

Native Americans unite to promote social change.

CRITICAL THINKING **Make Inferences**
In what ways can protesting bring about social change?

Native Americans united to protest the termination policy. The **National Congress of American Indians (NCAI)**—founded in 1944 to promote the "common welfare" of Native Americans—led the protests. Under pressure, the federal government changed the policy in 1958. These protests inspired a new generation of Native American activists to fight for their rights. By the 1960s, Native Americans were the least prosperous and least healthy of all ethnic groups in the United States. Their unemployment rate was ten times the national average. Poverty and disease made their life expectancy twenty years shorter than the national average.

In 1961 more than 400 people from dozens of tribes met in Chicago. They issued the Declaration of Indian Purpose. In it, they demanded the "right to choose our own way of life" and the "responsibility of preserving precious heritage."

In 1968, the American Indian Movement (AIM) was founded. AIM demanded rights for people on reservations and recognition of tribal laws. In 1972 AIM members occupied the Bureau of Indian Affairs in Washington, D.C.

In the early 1970s, Native Americans protested for more federal aid. The Indian Self-Determination and Education Assistance Act of 1975 gave tribal governments more control over social programs, law enforcement, and education. Through other court victories, Native Americans won back some of their land. They also went to court over rights to water, hunting, and fishing on what was once Native American land.

▲ **SUMMARIZE** Summarize how other minorities fought for civil rights.

The Women's Movement Revives

🔻 **KEY QUESTION** What did the Women's Movement hope to achieve?

Connecting History

Seneca Falls Conference

The women's movement in the United States traces its origins to an 1848 meeting organized by Elizabeth Cady Stanton and Lucretia Mott in Seneca Falls, N.Y.

The American women's movement began in the mid-19th century. After decades of fighting for equal rights, a victory was achieved in 1920 when women gained the right to vote. Despite this achievement, women were still excluded from many jobs, and they had limited legal rights.

Discrimination and Limited Rights During World War II, almost seven million women filled jobs left open by servicemen. When the soldiers began coming home, however, many women lost their jobs.

In the 1960s, women continued to demand equal rights. Early in the decade, women faced discrimination in many businesses. For example, there were few female police officers; the military also limited jobs for women.

Women also had limited legal rights. Married women, for example, faced problems in signing contracts, selling property, and getting credit. A woman could lose her job if she became pregnant. Society pressured women to quit their jobs when they married.

History Makers Women's Rights Leaders

Betty Friedan 1921–2006

In the late 1950s, Betty Friedan was a housewife and mother. She was also a journalist and graduate of Smith College. She began a survey of her college classmates and found many of them experienced "a strange stirring, a sense of dissatisfaction, a yearning..." The result of her survey eventually led her to write *The Feminine Mystique*, which would become one of the most important books in the feminist movement.

Bella Abzug 1920–1998

Elected in 1970, Bella Abzug began three terms representing her New York City district in the U.S. Congress. She took on a wide range of issues, including the Equal Rights Amendment. Abzug once said: "Women have been trained to speak softly and carry a lipstick. Those days are over."

Gloria Steinem b. 1934

After graduating from college, Gloria Steinem became a journalist to fight social injustice. In 1972 she helped to found *Ms. Magazine*, the first magazine to reflect a feminist point of view. Steinem has written five books and has continued to promote women's rights.

COMPARING LEADERS

Compare the career of one of the women profiled here to another 20th-century leader. What impact did each person have on national events or culture?

In a 1963 book, **Betty Friedan** described the problems women faced:

PRIMARY SOURCE

❝ We can no longer ignore that voice within women that says: 'I want something more than my husband and my children and my home. ❞

—Betty Friedan, *The Feminine Mystique*

Friedan's words helped give direction to a movement for women's liberation. In 1966, Friedan helped found the **National Organization for Women (NOW)**. NOW's goals included helping women get good jobs and equal pay.

According to NOW's charter, in 1966 fewer than 4 percent of lawyers and 1 percent of federal judges were women. Also, "full-time women workers today earn on the average only 60 percent of what men earn." As of 2006, women still only earned about 76 percent as much as men.

Part of the problem has been identified as the "glass ceiling"—an invisible barrier that keeps women, no matter how talented, from receiving the same promotions as equally-qualified men. In fact, in 2005 only 8 of the 500 largest corporations in the country were led by women.

CONNECT To The Essential Question

How did Americans respond to discrimination during the civil rights era?

AFRICAN AMERICANS' STRUGGLE FOR CIVIL RIGHTS

1954 *Brown* v. *Board of Education of Topeka* overturns "separate but equal" doctrine for public schools

1955 Rosa Parks refuses to give up her bus seat: civil rights movement begins.

1957 Federal troops enforce integration of school in Little Rock Arkansas.

1961 Freedom Rides

1963 Protests in Birmingham, Alabama; March on Washington

1964 Civil Rights Act; Freedom Summer; voter registration begins.

1965 Voting Rights Act

(above) Rosa Parks; *(below)* AIM march

EQUAL RIGHTS EXPAND

1958 National Congress of American Indians forces government to protect land and assets of Native Americans.

1966 National Organization of Women founded

1968 National Council of La Raza and MALDEF, the Mexican American Legal Defense and Education Fund, are founded.

1968 American Indian Movement founded

1972 Higher Education Act, also called Title IX, outlaws discrimination against women in schools.

1975 Indian Self-Determination Act gives tribal governments more control over social programs.

CRITICAL THINKING How did African Americans' struggle for civil rights affect civil rights for other groups?

A NOW member protests outside the U.S. Supreme Court.

The Movement's Impact In response to women's groups, Congress passed the **Equal Rights Amendment (ERA)** in 1972 and sent it to the states for ratification. The proposed amendment stated that "Equality of rights under the law shall not be denied or **abridged** (shortened) by the United States or any State on account of sex." Supporters argued that it would protect women against discrimination and help them achieve equality with men, including equal opportunity for jobs, pay, and education.

For the amendment to be added to the Constitution, 38 of the 50 states had to ratify it. By the 1982 deadline, only 35 states had ratified the amendment. The amendment faced well-organized opposition. Phyllis Schlafly, ERA's most famous opponent, argued that the amendment would destroy American families and that the problems of women were not the government's business.

Other reforms reduced some of the inequality between women and men. The Civil Rights Act of 1964 covered many areas where discrimination occurred, but some inequalities remained. The Higher Education Act of 1972, sometimes called "Title IX," outlawed discrimination against women in schools, including colleges that receive federal funds. For example, many large universities spent far more money on men's sports programs than on women's. Title IX made it against the law to do so.

 FIND MAIN IDEAS Explain what the women's movement achieved.

Illinois Learning Standards *Review*

 ONLINE QUIZ
For test practice, go to
Interactive Review @ ClassZone.com

TERMS & NAMES

1. Explain the importance of
- Dolores Huerta
- César Chávez
- National Congress of American Indians (NCAI)
- Betty Friedan
- National Organization for Women (NOW)
- Equal Rights Amendment (ERA)

USING YOUR READING NOTES

2. Categorize Complete the diagram you started at the beginning of the section. Add lines as necessary.

KEY IDEAS

3. How did Mexican Americans organize to promote reforms?

4. What was the Declaration of Indian Purpose?

5. How did Betty Friedan help to launch the women's liberation movement?

CRITICAL THINKING

6. Summarize What were conditions like for Native Americans in the 1960s in comparison with other minority groups?

7. Connect *to* Today How do the jobs that women hold today reflect changes won in the civil rights era?

8. Writing Pamphlet Research one of the groups mentioned in this section. Create a pamphlet explaining that group's goals.

I Have a Dream

SETTING THE STAGE On August 28, 1963, Martin Luther King Jr., delivered a moving speech at the March on Washington. In it, he shared his dream of equality for all.

I am happy to join with you today in what will go down in history as the greatest demonstration for freedom in the history of our nation.

Five score years ago, a great American, in whose symbolic shadow we stand today, signed the Emancipation Proclamation. . . . But one hundred years later, the Negro still is not free. One hundred years later, the life of the Negro is still sadly crippled by the manacles[1] of segregation and the chains of discrimination.

So we've come here today to dramatize a shameful condition. . . .

I say to you today, my friends, that even though we face the difficulties of today and tomorrow, I still have a dream. It is a dream deeply rooted in the American dream.

I have a dream that one day this nation will rise up and live out the true meaning of its creed[2]—we hold these truths to be self-evident that all men are created equal.

I have a dream that my four little children will one day live in a nation where they will not be judged by the color of their skin but by the content of their character.

I have a dream today!

This is our hope. This is the faith that I will go back to the South with. . . .

With this faith we will be able to work together, to pray together, to struggle together, to go to jail together, to stand up for freedom together, knowing that we will be free one day. This will be the day, this will be the day when all of God's children will be able to sing with new meaning "My country 'tis of thee, sweet land of liberty, of thee I sing. Land where my fathers died, land of the Pilgrim's pride, from every mountainside, let freedom ring!" And if America is to be a great nation this must become true.

And when this happens, when we allow freedom to ring, when we let it ring from every village and every hamlet, from every state and every city, we will be able to speed up that day when all of God's children, black men and white men, Jews and Gentiles,[3] Protestants and Catholics, will be able to join hands and sing in the words of the old Negro spiritual, "Free at last, free at last. Thank God Almighty, we are free at last."

Martin Luther King, Jr.

Five Score Years

King refers to Abraham Lincoln. He specifically mentions the Emancipation Proclamation and uses the phrase "Five score years ago" to remind his listeners of the Gettysburg Address.

1. Why do you think King would refer to Lincoln?

Go to Jail Together

Dr. King—who was arrested 30 times for civil rights activities—says that people will be ready to go to jail together.

2. Why do you think civil rights workers were willing to go to jail?

----

1. **manacle:** handcuff
2. **creed:** statement of belief
3. **Gentile:** Non-Jewish person

An Open Letter

SETTING THE STAGE In a 1969 letter, César Chávez denied accusations that he had used violence to win decent wages and better benefits for farm workers.

Our Cause

Farm workers were excluded from the National Labor Relations Act of 1935—the law that gives most Americans the right to organize a union. Chávez wanted lawmakers to allow farm workers to organize unions.

1. Why do you think farm workers wanted to organize a union?

Our Strikers

During the civil rights era, protesters often received extensive training before participating in marches, demonstrations, and sit-ins. Chávez explains that farm workers were also trained for the struggle.

2. Why might training for nonviolent protest be necessary?

Today . . . we remember the life and sacrifice of Martin Luther King, Jr., who gave himself totally to the nonviolent struggle for peace and justice. In his letter from Birmingham Jail, Dr. King describes better than I could our hopes for the strike and boycott: "Injustice must be exposed, with all the tension its exposure creates, to the light of human conscience and the air of national opinion before it can be cured." For our part, I admit that we have seized upon every tactic and strategy consistent with the morality of our cause to expose that injustice and thus to heighten the sensitivity of the American conscience so that farmworkers will have without bloodshed their own union and the dignity of bargaining with their agribusiness[1] employers. . . .

Our strikers here in Delano[2] and those who represent us throughout the world are well trained for this struggle. . . . they have been taught not to lie down and die or to flee in shame, but to resist with every ounce of human endurance and spirit. To resist not with retaliation in kind but to overcome with love and compassion, with ingenuity[3] and creativity, with hard work and longer hours, with stamina and patient tenacity,[4] with truth and public appeal, with friends and allies, with mobility and discipline, with politics and law, and with prayer and fasting. They were not trained in a month or even a year; after all, this new harvest season will mark our fourth full year of strike and even now we continue to plan and prepare for the years to come. . . .

We shall overcome and change it not by retaliation or bloodshed but by a determined nonviolent struggle carried on by those masses of farm-workers who intend to be free and human.

César E. Chávez

----

1. **agribusiness:** farming as a large-scale business operation
2. **Delano:** a farming city in California
3. **ingenuity:** imagination or cleverness
4. **tenacity:** persistence

DOCUMENT-BASED QUESTIONS

1. From what "shameful condition" does King want people to free themselves?
2. **Extended Response** How do you think these documents reflect the continuing struggle by many Americans for civil rights and justice?

Chapter Summary

① Key Idea
Between the 1870s and the 1950s, African Americans lost many of the civil rights they had gained during Reconstruction.

② Key Idea
Changes after World War II helped African Americans make progress in their struggle for equality.

③ Key Idea
The civil rights movement led to the end of legal segregation.

④ Key Idea
The African-American struggle for equality inspired other groups in their fight for civil rights.

⟶ For detailed Review and Study Notes go to **Interactive Review** @ ClassZone.com

Name Game

Use the Terms and Names list to complete each sentence online or on your own paper.

1. I was an African-American activist who advocated fighting injustice by any means necessary. _____
   Malcolm X ⟶

2. This 1965 law banned literacy tests and other laws that kept blacks from registering to vote. _____

3. It is not easy for groups to _____ , or to blend into society.

4. Some people hold a _____ to protest and refuse to move until their demands are met.

5. I helped organize unions and acted as a negotiator for farmers. _____

6. I was the first African-American Supreme Court Justice. _____

7. To _____ means to violate.

8. People who are deprived of their right to vote are _____ .

9. I was very influential leader of the civil rights era who led the March on Washington. _____

10. I authored the book *The Feminine Mystique*. _____

A. Dr. Martin Luther King, Jr.

B. Dolores Huerta

C. segregation

D. Malcolm X

E. Betty Friedan

F. Montgomery Bus Boycott

G. infringe

H. assimilate

I. Voting Rights Act

J. sit-in

K. disenfranchised

L. integrate

M. Thurgood Marshall

Activities

CROSSWORD PUZZLE

Complete the online crossword puzzle to show what you know about the civil rights era.

ACROSS

1. _____ gave the "I Have a Dream" speech.

GEOGAME

Use this online map to reinforce your understanding school segregation across the country in 1952. Drag and drop each place name in the list at its location on the map. A scorecard helps you keep track of your progress online.

Iowa

Mississippi

Wyoming

Alabama

More places online

Mississippi ⟶

ATLANTIC OCEAN

Gulf of M

VOCABULARY

Explain the significance of the following:

1. *Brown* v. *Board of Education of Topeka*
2. Montgomery bus boycott
3. Martin Luther King, Jr.
4. March on Washington
5. Civil Rights Act of 1964
6. Voting Rights Act
7. Great Society
8. César Chávez
9. National Congress of American Indians (NCAI)
10. Equal Rights Amendment (ERA)

Explain how the terms and names in each group are related.

11. Jim Crow laws, segregation, black codes
12. Thurgood Marshall, integrate, *Brown* v. *Board of Education of Topeka*
13. Freedom Rides, Freedom Summer, March on Washington

KEY IDEAS

① Reconstruction and Jim Crow (pages 872–875)

14. Which branches of government blocked progress for civil rights during Reconstruction?
15. What led African Americans to migrate North after Reconstruction?

② The Modern Civil Rights Movement (pages 876–883)

16. What factors helped give strength to the demands of the civil rights movement?
17. How did white people react to civil rights protests?

③ Kennedy, Johnson, and Civil Rights (pages 884–891)

18. What factors made it difficult for Kennedy to act on civil rights?
19. What effects did Johnson's Great Society legislation have?

④ The Equal Rights Struggle Expands (pages 894–900)

20. How did farm workers participate in the equal rights movement?
21. What kinds of discrimination did women challenge during the civil rights era?

CRITICAL THINKING

22. **Compare and Contrast** Create a table to compare and contrast the status of African Americans in the South during and after slavery. After you fill in your table, name two obstacles that blocked progress in the improvement of African Americans' lives after slavery.

During Slavery	After Slavery

23. **Synthesize** What issues led Betty Friedan to write *The Feminine Mystique*?

24. **Analyze** What qualities do you think made Martin Luther King, Jr. an effective leader?

25. **Make Generalizations** How did participants in the civil rights movement advance the democratic ideals of the United States?

26. **Interpret Graphs** Read the graph below. Compare the poverty rates of whites and nonwhites in 1962 and in 1974. What can you infer about the civil rights movement's impact on economic opportunities for nonwhites by the mid-1970s?

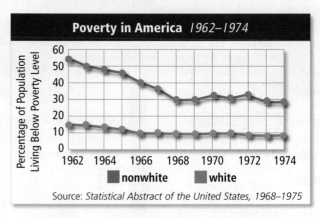

Poverty in America *1962–1974*

Source: *Statistical Abstract of the United States, 1968–1975*

27. **Causes and Effects** What was "massive resistance" and what effect did it have on African American civil rights?

DOCUMENT-BASED QUESTIONS

PART 1: Short Answer

Analyze each document and answer the questions that follow.

DOCUMENT 1

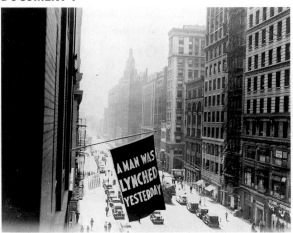

1. This 1938 photo shows a flag hanging from the NAACP headquarters in New York. The NAACP flew flags reporting lynchings until it was threatened with loss of its lease. What effect do you think this flag had on people who saw it? What effect might this photograph have had when it was first published?

DOCUMENT 2

PRIMARY SOURCE

❝ We consider the underlying fallacy . . . to consist in the assumption that the enforced separation of the two races stamps the colored race with the badge of inferiority. If this be so, it is not by reason of anything found in the act, but solely because the colored race chooses to put that construction upon it. ❞

2. Supreme Court Justice Henry Brown states above that separating the races does not imply that one race is inferior to the other. He says that if "the colored races," wants to see it that way, it's their choice. How do the Justice's words show his bias?

PART 2: Essay

Write an essay that discusses the challenges that faced the civil rights movement and the ways leaders and ordinary people faced those challenges.

YOU BE THE HISTORIAN

28. **Make Inferences** Why do you think people continued to participate in the civil rights movement even though they faced violence and terror?

29. **Make Generalizations** In what ways do you think the lives of Americans today might differ from the lives of Americans who lived before the civil rights movement?

30. **WHAT IF?** Suppose Rosa Parks had given up her seat on the bus. How might this have changed the course of the civil rights movement? Explain your answer.

31. **Connect Geography and History** What impact did migration to the North by African Americans have on the development of the civil rights movement?

32. **Connect to Today** How has your study of the civil rights era influenced your decision about the ways in which you would act to change injustices in society?

Answer the
ESSENTIAL QUESTION
How did Americans respond to discrimination during the civil rights era?

Written Response Write a two- to three-paragraph response to the Essential Question. Be sure to consider the key ideas of each section as well as the most significant factors that led to the civil rights movement and the progress it achieved. Use the Response Rubric below to guide your thinking and writing.

Response Rubric
A strong response will

• discuss the conditions that led to the fight for civil rights
• analyze key events
• discuss key groups, movements, and leaders,
• explain the importance of participating in democratic processes such as voting and protesting
• cover all the minority groups

1. Cold War Roots of the Conflict
2. War Expands in Vietnam
3. Conflicts at Home
4. The Vietnam War Ends

The Vietnam War Years

1954–1975

 ESSENTIAL QUESTION

What were the causes and effects of America's involvement in the Vietnam War?

CONNECT ⟶ **Geography & History**

How might the location of Vietnam have affected the course of the war?

Think about:

1. how Vietnam covers a surface area of 128,000 square miles—making it roughly the size of the state of New Mexico

2. how Vietnam is bordered by Cambodia, China, and Laos

3. how all of Vietnam's major cities are situated along the Pacific coast

---

1954

Vietnam is divided into North and South.

▼

Effect United States sends economic aid to South Vietnam.

1960
John F. Kennedy is elected president.

The Kennedy family in 1960

1962 Cuban missile crisis occurs

▼

Effect Fear that communism might spread increases

1963
Kennedy is assassinated; Lyndon B. Johnson becomes president

CHINA

TAIWAN

Macao
(Port.)

Hong Kong
(Br.)

Red River

BURMA

Hanoi

Gulf of Tonkin

LAOS

NORTH VIETNAM

Hainan

20°N

| French Indochina 1945–1954 |

Rangoon

Vientiane

N
W — E
S

Mekong River

THAILAND

0   200   400 miles
0   200   400 kilometers

South China Sea

Bangkok

CAMBODIA

SOUTH VIETNAM

PHILIPPINES

Manila

Andaman Sea

10°N

Phnom Penh

Saigon

Gulf of Thailand

MALAYA

BRUNEI

BRITISH NORTH BORNEO

SARAWAK

100°E

Kuala Lumpur

110°E

120°E

Singapore

I N D O N E S I A

Equator 0°

NIXON FOR PRESIDENT

1969 campaign button

1971 Twenty-sixth Amendment is ratified

▼

A nineteen-year-old voter in the 1972 presidential election

1969 Richard M. Nixon becomes president.

Effect Voting age is lowered from 21 to 18

1975

1968 Tet offensive occurs

▼

Effect More U.S. citizens begin to question the war in Vietnam.

1973 United States withdraws from Vietnam.

War ends after Communists take over South Vietnam.

An American P.O.W. returns to his family.

The Vietnam War Years **907**

▶ Key Ideas

BEFORE, YOU LEARNED
The end of World War II led to prosperity and a new kind of war against communism.

NOW YOU WILL LEARN
The United States intensified its military and political interests in Southeast Asia.

▶ Vocabulary

TERMS & NAMES

French Indochina French-ruled colony made up of Vietnam, Laos, and Cambodia

Ho Chi Minh (HO•CHEE•MIHN) revolutionary founder of the Indochinese Communist Party

domino theory belief that if a country fell to communism, nearby countries would follow

Ngo Dinh Diem (ING•AH•DIHN•DEE•EM) leader of South Vietnam

Bay of Pigs invasion failed U.S. attempt to overthrow Cuba's Communist leader

Cuban missile crisis 1962 confrontation between the United States and the Soviet Union caused by Soviet nuclear missiles in Cuba

Viet Cong South Vietnamese who fought to overthrow the Diem government and reunite the country under Communist rule

Ho Chi Minh Trail secret route used by North Vietnamese to send troops and supplies to the Viet Cong

REVIEW

communism system of government in which the state plans and controls the economy

guerrillas small bands of fighters who weaken the enemy with surprise raids and hit-and-run attacks

▶ Reading Strategy

Re-create the diagram shown at right. As you read and respond to the **KEY QUESTIONS**, use the diagram to sequence the important events of this section.

📖 See Skillbuilder Handbook, page R5.

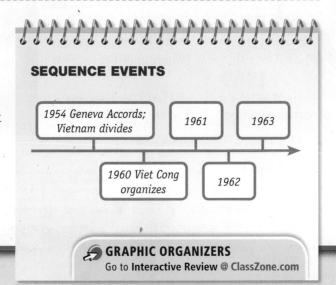

SEQUENCE EVENTS

1954 Geneva Accords; Vietnam divides → 1961 → 1963

1960 Viet Cong organizes → 1962

GRAPHIC ORGANIZERS
Go to **Interactive Review** @ ClassZone.com

Cold War Roots of the Conflict

14.E.3 Compare the basic principles of the United States and its international interests (e.g., *territory, environment, trade, use of technology*).
16.B.3d Describe ways in which the United States developed as a world political power.

One American's Story

Edward Lansdale, a U.S. military intelligence officer, went to South Vietnam in June 1954. His mission was to stop **communism** from spreading through Vietnam. He would try to do this by helping the non-Communist government of South Vietnam resist being taken over by Communist North Vietnam. He believed the United States could defeat communism with generous economic and military aid.

PRIMARY SOURCE

❝ We have too much to lose to consider . . . withdrawing. We have no other choice but to win here or face an increasingly grim future . . . I would like to see our efforts here geared as completely as possible to the operating philosophy of helping the Vietnamese to help themselves. . . . in a struggle with the Communists. ❞

—Edward G. Lansdale, *Major Problems in the History of the Vietnam War*, ed. Robert J. McMahon

Edward G. Lansdale

Lansdale was too optimistic. He did not anticipate that U.S. involvement in Vietnam would grow into the longest war the United States ever fought—and one in which it failed.

Vietnamese Fight for Independence

🔻 **KEY QUESTION** How did the Vietnamese organize against foreign rule?

For decades before the United States became involved, the Vietnamese had been fighting foreign rule. From the late 1800s until World War II, France ruled Vietnam as part of its colony of **French Indochina**. The colony also included neighboring Laos (LOWS) and Cambodia. (See the map on page 911.) During this period, France increased its wealth by exporting rice and rubber from Vietnam. But Vietnamese peasants lost their land and grew poor.

Vietnamese Revolt Against Foreign Rule The Vietnamese never accepted French rule. Various groups of nationalists wanted Vietnam to become an independent nation, and staged revolts against the French. In 1930, a revolutionary leader named **Ho Chi Minh** (HO•CHEE•MIHN) united three Communist groups to form the Indochinese Communist Party (ICP). This new party called for an independent Vietnam controlled by peasants and other workers.

The ICP organized protests by peasants against the French government. The French responded by arresting suspected Communists and executing a number of leaders.

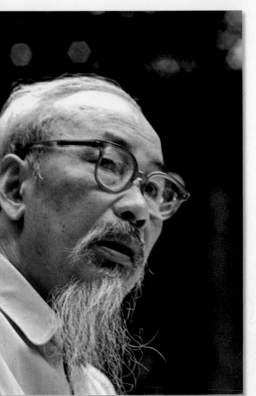

(*above*) Ho Chi Minh fought (*far right*) French troops in Vietnam.

Viet Minh is Formed In 1940, during World War II, Japan took over Indochina. The next year, Ho Chi Minh secretly returned to Vietnam. Under his direction, the ICP joined with other nationalists to form the Viet Minh. The Viet Minh trained soldiers to make Vietnam free of all foreign rulers. Because Japan was an enemy of the United States in World War II, the U.S. government aided the Viet Minh in their fight against the Japanese.

After the Japanese surrendered to the Allies in August 1945, Ho Chi Minh declared Vietnam's independence. But France tried to regain control of Vietnam. Ho sought a peaceful solution to the conflict with France.

PRIMARY SOURCE

❝ If they force us into war, we will fight. The struggle will be atrocious [terrible], but the Vietnamese people will suffer anything rather than renounce [give up] their freedom. ❞

—Ho Chi Minh, quoted in *Vietnam: A History* by Stanley Karnow

In 1946, war broke out between the Viet Minh and France. The French bombed Haiphong (HY•FAWNG), and the Viet Minh attacked Hanoi (HUH•NOY).

🔺 **SUMMARIZE** Explain the ways that the Vietnamese organized against foreign rule.

America Enters the Conflict

🔻 **KEY QUESTION** How did United States become involved in Vietnam?

As France fought to hold on to power in Vietnam, the United States struggled against the Soviet Union in the Cold War. President Truman followed a policy of containment, working to prevent the spread of communism in Western Europe. Then, in late 1949, the Communists took over in China. Many people in the United States began to fear the communist threat.

Truman and Eisenhower Aid the French U.S. leaders now felt they had to stop the spread of communism in Asia, as well as in Europe. When France asked the United States for aid to help them fight the Viet Minh, the United States agreed. In addition to wanting to stop communism, U.S. leaders needed French support in opposing the Soviets in Europe.

The United States entered the conflict in Vietnam in 1950, when President Truman offered $15 million in military aid to the French. After Dwight D. Eisenhower became president in 1953, he continued aiding the French.

Both Truman and Eisenhower used the **domino theory** to explain the need to support anti-Communists in Vietnam. According to this theory, if a country fell to communism, nearby countries would also topple, like a row of dominoes standing on end. U.S. leaders feared that if Vietnam became Communist, the rest of Southeast Asia would follow.

Vietnam Divides into North and South Even with about $3 billion in American aid, France could not defeat the Viet Minh. In May 1954, France met with the Viet Minh for peace talks in Geneva, Switzerland. The two sides reached an agreement called the Geneva Accords. This agreement divided Vietnam into North and South along the 17th parallel, or at 17°N latitude. Surrounding this line was a demilitarized zone, or DMZ.

The Geneva Accords provided for a temporary division of Vietnam pending a nationwide election to be held in the summer of 1956. Until then, the truce allowed for separate governments in the North and the South. Ho Chi Minh and the Communists controlled North Vietnam. **Ngo Dinh Diem**, an anti-Communist, became prime minister and, later, president of South Vietnam.

Ho Chi Minh was a popular leader, while Diem had little support from the people of South Vietnam. As a result, Diem refused to hold national elections in 1956. President Eisenhower supported him, later saying, "If the elections had been held in 1956, Ho Chi Minh would have won 80 percent of the vote." Eisenhower sent more aid to the Diem government. U.S. advisers described their mission as "nation-building."

▲ **CAUSES AND EFFECTS** Describe why the United States became involved in Vietnam.

Vietnam 1959–1975

Connect Geography & History

1. **Location** What country lies along the northern border of North Vietnam?

2. **Make Inferences** How might North Vietnam's location have enabled it to get aid from its ally, China?

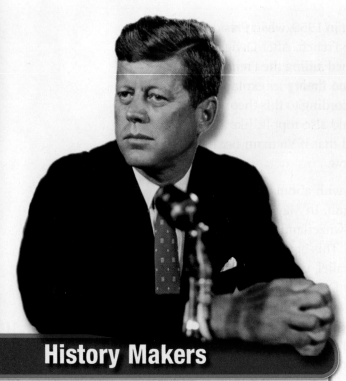

History Makers

John F. Kennedy   1917–1963

In 1960, 43-year-old John F. Kennedy, a Roman Catholic, became the youngest U.S. president ever elected. No one believed that a Roman Catholic could be elected president. But by emphasizing his belief in the importance of separation of church and state, Kennedy won over voters of all faiths. His poise, good looks, and command of the new medium of television also helped. As president, he succeeded in inspiring the public, as when he told the nation, "Ask not what your country can do for you—ask what you can do for your country."

Many Americans regard the Cuban missile crisis as Kennedy's finest moment of leadership. This conflict brought the United States to the brink of nuclear war. Kennedy considered bombing the Soviet missile sites in Cuba and invading the country. He decided it was safer to blockade Cuba and keep bargaining with Soviet leader Nikita Khrushchev.

CRITICAL THINKING Do you think Kennedy's leadership qualities would be of value today? In what circumstances?

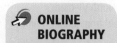 **ONLINE BIOGRAPHY**   For more on John F. Kennedy, go to the **Research & Writing Center** @ ClassZone.com

Fear of Communism Shapes U.S. Policy

🔻 **KEY QUESTION** What world events influenced U.S. policy in Vietnam?

When John F. Kennedy became president in 1960, Cold War crises convinced him to keep supporting the fight against communism in Vietnam.

Kennedy Faces Communist Threats Responding to perceived communist threats, Kennedy ordered the **Bay of Pigs invasion** in April 1961. An army of Cuban exiles, trained by the United States, invaded Cuba. They planned to overthrow the country's Communist leader, Fidel Castro. Cuban troops easily crushed the invasion, humiliating the United States.

Then in June 1961, the Soviet Union threatened to close off Western access to West Berlin because so many East Germans were fleeing there to escape communism. Tensions rose when Kennedy insisted on West Berlin's independence.

In August, the Soviet Union and East Germany built the Berlin Wall, a heavily guarded barrier dividing free West Berlin from Communist East Berlin and East Germany. The wall, which made it harder for East Germans to flee, became a symbol of Communist oppression.

Showdown with Cuba The **Cuban missile crisis** in October 1962 was Kennedy's most serious confrontation with the Soviets. Fidel Castro and Soviet leader Nikita Khrushchev believed the United States planned another attack on Cuba. The United States learned that the Soviets had put nuclear missiles in Cuba. These missiles could reach U.S. cities within minutes. Kennedy weighed his choices. "The greatest danger of all," he told the country, "would be to do nothing." In a frightening showdown between the two superpowers, the Soviets agreed to remove the missiles, and the United States promised not to invade Cuba.

These Cold War crises fed U.S. fears that the Soviet Union might become the strongest world power. In this climate of fear and suspicion, the United States made a greater effort to contain communism in Asia by sending more money and military advisers to South Vietnam.

Diem Receives More U.S. Aid In spite of increasing U.S. aid, Diem did not establish a democratic government in South Vietnam. Instead, his corrupt government held on to power. In the countryside he let landlords take back land given to peasants. In addition, he jailed, tortured, and killed opponents. Diem's policies drove many people to join the Communists.

In 1960, dissatisfied South Vietnamese joined with South Vietnamese Communists to form the National Liberation Front. Diem ridiculed the group by calling them the **Viet Cong**, for Vietnamese Communists. This name became the commonly used term for the group.

The Viet Cong fought to overthrow the Diem government and reunite the country under Communist rule. North Vietnam supported the Viet Cong, sending soldiers and supplies along a network of paths called the **Ho Chi Minh Trail**. This supply line wove through the jungles and mountains of neighboring Laos and Cambodia.

The Diem Government Falls By late 1963, the United States had more than 16,000 military personnel in Vietnam. As U.S. aid increased, so did South Vietnamese opposition to Diem. American officials told Diem to make political, economic, and military reforms. But Diem stubbornly refused.

The Kennedy administration lost faith in Diem. With U.S. support, a military coup overthrew Diem on November 1, 1963. Against Kennedy's wishes, the coup's leaders killed Diem. In a terrible and unrelated turn of events, President Kennedy was assassinated three weeks later. Vice President Lyndon Johnson became president. He deepened U.S. involvement in the Vietnam War.

▲ **SEQUENCE EVENTS** Explain how world events affected U.S. policy in Vietnam.

 Illinois Learning Standards *Review*

 ONLINE QUIZ
For test practice, go to
Interactive Review @ ClassZone.com

TERMS & NAMES

1. Explain the importance of

- French Indochina
- Ho Chi Minh
- domino theory
- Ngo Dinh Diem
- Bay of Pigs invasion
- Cuban missile crisis
- Viet Cong
- Ho Chi Minh Trail

USING YOUR READING NOTES

2. Sequence Events Complete the diagram(s) you started at the beginning of this section.

KEY IDEAS

3. What were Ho Chi Minh's goals for Vietnam?

4. How did the Cold War affect American decisions regarding Vietnam?

CRITICAL THINKING

5. Analyze Causes Why did the Vietnamese reject French rule?

6. Evaluate How did U.S. support of the Diem government involve a conflict of values?

7. **Connect *to* Today** How does America's involvement in Vietnam connect to U.S. foreign policy today?

8. **Speech** Write a short speech that President Kennedy might have made to the American people to gain their support for increasing aid to Vietnam.

Reading for Understanding

▶ Key Ideas

BEFORE, YOU LEARNED

The United States intensified its military and political interests in Southeast Asia.

NOW YOU WILL LEARN

The United States sent ground troops to Vietnam expecting victory, but soldiers soon grew frustrated.

▶ Vocabulary

TERMS & NAMES

guerrilla warfare surprise attacks by small bands of fighters

Gulf of Tonkin Resolution 1964 legislation that gave President Johnson the power to use military force in Vietnam

escalation policy of increasing military involvement in Vietnam

William Westmoreland general in command of U.S. forces in South Vietnam

Tet offensive surprise Communist attack on U.S. and South Vietnamese forces in 1968; further weakened American support for the war

BACKGROUND VOCABULARY

napalm jellied gasoline that burns violently; used to destroy vegetation and as a weapon

Agent Orange chemical that kills plants; used in Vietnam to expose Viet Cong hideouts

Visual Vocabulary napalm

▶ Reading Strategy

Re-create the diagram shown at right. As you read and respond to the **KEY QUESTIONS**, use the diagram to show key military tactics and weapons of the Viet Cong and Americans.

 See Skillbuilder Handbook, page R3.

SUMMARIZE

	Viet Cong	U.S.
Tactics	*surprise attacks*	*large-scale bombing*
Weapons		

GRAPHIC ORGANIZERS
Go to **Interactive Review** @ ClassZone.com

War Expands in Vietnam

14.E.3 Compare the basic principles of the United States and its international interests (e.g., *territory, environment, trade, use of technology*).
16.B.3d Describe ways in which the United States developed as a world political power.

One American's Story

After dropping out of college, Stan Goff was drafted and sent to Vietnam. He became a machine gunner with the 196th Light Infantry Brigade. Infantry troops are foot soldiers who engage the enemy, often at close range. Goff's company rode armored personnel carriers (heavy vehicles with treads, similar to tanks) deep into the countryside to engage the Viet Cong.

PRIMARY SOURCE

❝ When you had thirty-five mechanized vehicles, you had to figure this . . . was a huge thing—like a wagon train. . . . Of course, they knew we were coming. ❞

—Stanley Goff, *Brothers: Black Soldiers in the Nam*

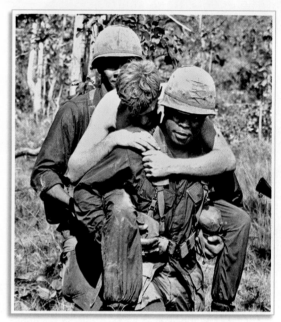

A soldier wounded in battle in South Vietnam is rescued by soldiers of the 1st Cavalry Division.

Because the Viet Cong could not match American firepower, they relied on **guerrilla warfare**, or surprise attacks by small bands of fighters. Yet when the United States began sending combat troops to Vietnam, the military tried to apply traditional methods of fighting. The Viet Cong proved an elusive enemy.

Direct Military Involvement Begins

▼ **KEY QUESTION** What led to increased U.S. military involvement in Vietnam?

South Vietnam did not seem strong enough to resist a Communist takeover on its own. The assassination of President Diem in 1963 brought chaos to South Vietnam. One ineffective leader after another headed the government. By 1964, combined Viet Cong and North Vietnamese Army (NVA) forces controlled much of the South Vietnamese countryside.

The Gulf of Tonkin Resolution In the summer of 1964, Johnson's military advisers made plans to bomb North Vietnam. Johnson wanted to pressure

Ho Chi Minh to stop supporting the Viet Cong. At first, no bombing could start unless Congress approved the plan, but a shooting incident off the coast of North Vietnam spurred Congress to give its approval.

The U.S. destroyer Maddox had been patrolling in the Gulf of Tonkin when North Vietnamese torpedo boats fired on it. Two days later, on August 4, the Maddox and another destroyer reported a second possible attack.

Despite doubts about the second incident, Johnson asked Congress to pass the **Gulf of Tonkin Resolution**. This gave the president the power to use military force in Vietnam. All but two senators voted for the resolution. The "yes" vote in the House was unanimous.

Johnson Sends Troops In March 1965, Johnson began the sustained bombing of North Vietnam. At about the same time, he sent the first combat ground troops to Vietnam. Their numbers grew from 75,000 in the middle of 1965 to 184,000 by the end of 1965.

This policy of **escalation**, or increasing military involvement in Vietnam, continued over the next few years. General **William Westmoreland**, the commander of U.S. forces in South Vietnam, asked for more and more troops. By the end of 1968 there were more than 536,000 American military personnel in South Vietnam.

▲ **SEQUENCE EVENTS** Explain the escalation of U.S. military involvement in Vietnam.

A Different Kind of War

▼ **KEY QUESTION** How did American forces try to defeat the Viet Cong?

Many people in the United States thought that, with their superior weapons, U.S. ground forces would quickly defeat the Viet Cong and drive them out of the villages. Many conditions frustrated U.S. soldiers, however. First of all, they could wage only a limited war, partly because the government feared drawing China into the conflict.

U.S. Disadvantages Most U.S. soldiers in Vietnam were young and inexperienced. The average soldier was 19 and served a one-year tour of duty. Officers served even shorter tours. By the time soldiers and officers had gained enough experience, their tours of duty were over.

History Makers

Lyndon Baines Johnson   1908–1973

Before becoming John F. Kennedy's vice president, Lyndon Johnson had a long career in Congress—11 years in the House and 12 years in the Senate. He earned a reputation as a brilliant politician who could get things done. He used his skills to pass the first civil rights legislation of the 20th century, in 1957. In 1963, President Johnson calmed the public and provided effective leadership in the turmoil following John F. Kennedy's assassination.

As a young man, he taught for a year in a school at which many students lived in poverty. He never forgot the struggles of these children and their families. As president, Johnson presented his vision for a "Great Society," one in which there would be "abundance and liberty for all."

COMPARING *Leaders*

Compare Johnson's leadership with that of John F. Kennedy. How were they similar? How were they different?

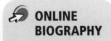

ONLINE BIOGRAPHY For more on Lyndon Baines Johnson, go to the **Research & Writing Center @ ClassZone.com**

The Vietnam War differed from World War II in that there was no front-line. The Viet Cong mixed with the general population and operated everywhere. Even a shoeshine boy on a city street corner might toss a grenade into an army bus carrying American soldiers. U.S. Marine Captain E.J. Banks described his frustration: "You never knew who was the enemy and who was the friend. . . . The enemy was all around you."

Guerrilla Warfare The style of fighting in Vietnam also differed from that in World War II. Viet Cong guerrillas would suddenly emerge from networks of underground tunnels to fight. Then they would disappear back into the tunnels. They riddled the countryside and jungles with land mines and booby traps, such as bamboo stakes hidden in covered pits. They hung grenades from trees and hid them in bushes.

Even the land and climate of Vietnam proved difficult. The heat was suffocating and the rain almost constant. Soldiers sweated through tangled jungles. After wading through flooded rice paddies, they had to pick leeches off their feet and legs.

Additionally, the Viet Cong were a very dedicated enemy. They took heavy losses, built up their ranks again, and kept on fighting year after year because they believed in their cause. An American journalist, who interviewed Viet Cong prisoners noted, "They see the war entirely as one of defense of their country against the invading Americans, who, in turn, are seen merely as successors to the French."

COMPARING *Warfare Tactics*

In Vietnam, both sides fought a war of attrition—trying to kill as many enemy troops as possible and destroy as many bases and supplies as they could. The guerrilla tactics of the Communist forces were highly effective in this type of war.

United States

66 [Westmoreland's] idea was to go after people and kill them in great number. . . . However, one of the basic problems was that the North Vietnamese had an almost bottomless pit of people with the determination to outlast the Americans. 99

—General Bernard Trainor, U.S. Marines

North Vietnam

66 . . . to fight the Americans, you had to get close to them. . . . to attack them while they were on the move, or at night when they were stationed together. So our tactics were different from theirs. 99

—Colonel Huong Van Ba, North Vietnamese Army (NVA)

CRITICAL THINKING Draw Conclusions
What did General Trainor regard as the North Vietnamese advantage in warfare tactics?

U.S. marine NVA soldier

American Strategies One of the strengths of the Viet Cong was their ability to hide in the jungle and in underground tunnels. To reveal and destroy Viet Cong hideouts, American troops used chemicals that ruined the landscape. Over wide areas, U.S. planes dropped bombs of **napalm**, jellied gasoline that burns violently. Planes also sprayed **Agent Orange**, a chemical that kills plants, over the jungles.

Such chemicals helped destroy the hideouts and food supplies of the Viet Cong. But in the process, they also harmed innocent Vietnamese villagers. Later, people learned that Agent Orange harmed U.S. soldiers as well. Veterans exposed to it have suffered from skin diseases and cancers.

Search-and-destroy missions were another American war tactic that terrorized Vietnamese villagers. In such missions, soldiers hunted Viet Cong and burned or bombed villages thought to be sheltering them.

These destructive methods defeated the purpose of "winning the hearts and minds" of the villagers and turning them against communism. Even if the tactics did clear a village of Viet Cong temporarily, the Viet Cong usually returned later.

▲ **SUMMARIZE** Describe how the U.S. forces tried to defeat the Viet Cong.

(*below right*) A U.S. tank rolls into Saigon during the Tet Offensive.

Tet Offensive *January 30 and 31, 1968*

CHINA

Major battle
National capital

Red River
Hanoi
20°N
LAOS   NORTH VIETNAM   Gulf of Tonkin   Hainan
Vientiane
Demilitarized Zone (DMZ)
Quang Tri
Hue
Khesanh   Da Nang
Hoi An
Mekong River   Quang Ngai
15°N
THAILAND   Kontum
Pleiku   Qui Nhon
Ho Chi Minh Trail
Bangkok   CAMBODIA   Banmethuot
South China Sea
SOUTH VIETNAM   Nha Trang
Phnom Penh
Gulf of Thailand   Bien Hoa
Saigon
Vinh Long   Ben Tre
10°N
Can Tho   *Mekong Delta*

0   100   200 miles
0   100   200 kilometers
105°E   110°E

Tet: A Turning Point

🔻 **KEY QUESTION** How did the Tet offensive affect the course of the war?

By the end of 1967, neither side was close to victory. Despite this stalemate, U.S. military officials claimed that they would soon win the war. Then an unexpected turn of events changed the situation completely.

Connect Geography & History

1. **Human-Environment Interaction** How did the Ho Chi Minh Trail make the Tet offensive possible?

2. **Make Inferences** What does the number and location of attacks suggest about South Vietnam's security?

The Tet Surprise On January 30 and 31, 1968, the Communists launched the **Tet offensive**. This was a surprise attack on U.S. military bases and more than 100 cities and towns in South Vietnam. It came during Tet, the Vietnamese celebration of the lunar new year.

In preparation for the offensive, the Viet Cong smuggled weapons into South Vietnamese cities. Soldiers dressed in civilian clothes entered the cities on buses, on motorcycles, and on foot. No one could tell them apart from the war refugees fleeing the countryside or visitors coming for the holiday.

The Viet Cong fought to take over the cities during the offensive. They killed not only enemy soldiers but also government officials, schoolteachers, doctors, and priests. The Tet offensive was a military defeat for the Communists. They gained no cities and lost 45,000 soldiers.

U.S. Doubts Grow But the attack stunned Americans. General Westmoreland had recently suggested that victory was in sight. The Tet offensive raised doubts that this was true. A "credibility gap" was growing between the government's claims and what the public saw was really happening.

Tet also made many people in the United States question the wisdom of the U.S. mission in Vietnam. To retake some cities, troops had to almost level them with bombing. Speaking of the city of Ben Tre, a U.S. major said, "It became necessary to destroy the town in order to save it." The quote spoke for what many considered the senselessness of the war, and it motivated some U.S. citizens, especially young people, to publicly protest the war.

▲ **RECOGNIZE EFFECTS** Explain how the Tet offensive changed the course of the war.

 Illinois Learning Standards *Review*

 ONLINE QUIZ
For test practice, go to
Interactive Review @ ClassZone.com

TERMS & NAMES

1. Explain the importance of

- guerrilla warfare
- Gulf of Tonkin Resolution
- escalation
- William Westmoreland
- Tet offensive

USING YOUR READING NOTES

2. Summarize Complete the diagram you started at the beginning of this section.

	Viet Cong	U.S.
Tactics	surprise attacks	large-scale bombing
Weapons		

KEY IDEAS

3. What made fighting the war so frustrating for American soldiers?

4. Why did the Tet offensive make Americans doubt they could win the war?

CRITICAL THINKING

5. Analyze Point of View Were the Viet Cong right to see the Americans "merely as successors to the French"? Why or why not?

6. Compare and Contrast Compare and contrast the American and Viet Cong approaches to fighting the war.

7. Draw Conclusions How was the Tet offensive a success for the Viet Cong, even though they lost many fighters and gained no cities?

8. Writing Letter Imagine that you are an American soldier serving in Vietnam. Write a brief letter to your family describing your experiences.

▶ Key Ideas

BEFORE, YOU LEARNED

The United States sent ground troops to Vietnam expecting victory, but soldiers soon grew frustrated.

NOW YOU WILL LEARN

As the war escalated, it divided American society.

▶ Vocabulary

TERMS & NAMES

counterculture movement of mostly young Americans who had become disillusioned with the Vietnam War and injustices in society

doves U.S. citizens who opposed the Vietnam War

hawks U.S. citizens who supported the Vietnam War

Richard Nixon Republican president elected in 1968

Vietnamization strategy for withdrawing U.S. troops and turning the ground fighting over to the South Vietnamese

Cambodia country bordering Vietnam

BACKGROUND VOCABULARY

commune a place where people or families live together and share everything

Visual Vocabulary doves' banner

▶ Reading Strategy

Re-create the diagram shown at right. As you read and respond to the **KEY QUESTIONS**, use the chart to list the effects of the Vietnam War on America.

 See Skillbuilder Handbook, page R7.

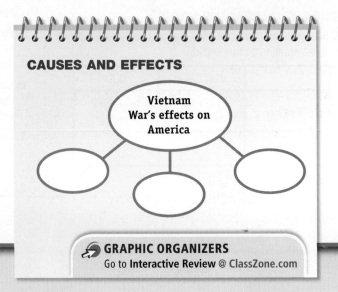

CAUSES AND EFFECTS

Vietnam War's effects on America

GRAPHIC ORGANIZERS
Go to **Interactive Review** @ ClassZone.com

Conflicts at Home

14.C.3 Compare historical issues involving rights, roles and status of individuals in relation to municipalities, states and the nation.
14.D.3 Describe roles and influences of individuals, groups and media in shaping current Illinois and United States public policy (e.g., *general public opinion, special interest groups, formal parties, media*).

One American's Story

A student journalist took Mary Ann Vecchio's picture as she knelt by a dead student at Kent State University in Ohio. The dead youth was Jeffrey Glenn Miller, one of four students killed by the National Guard during an antiwar demonstration on May 4, 1970. Later, Vecchio said

PRIMARY SOURCE

❝ I couldn't believe that people would kill . . . just because he demonstrated against the Vietnam War. ❞

—Mary Ann Vecchio Gillum, conference at Emerson College, April 23, 1995

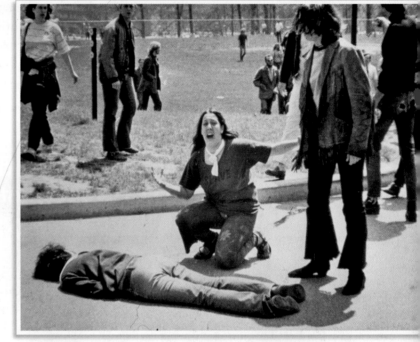

Kent State University, May 4, 1970

Mary Ann Vecchio was just 14 when she became a symbol of anguish over the Vietnam War. Growing opposition to the war led to deep divisions in American society.

The Growing Antiwar Movement

🔻 **KEY QUESTION** Why did so many Americans oppose the war?

As the war escalated in the mid-1960s, antiwar feeling grew among Americans at home. Religious leaders, civil rights leaders, teachers, students, journalists, and others opposed the war for a variety of reasons.

Protests Grow Some protesters believed that the United States had no business involving itself in another country's civil war. Others believed that the methods of fighting the war were immoral. Still others thought that the costs to American society were too high.

College students formed a large and vocal group of protesters. Many opposed the draft, which required young men to serve in the military. In protests nationwide, young men burned their draft cards. About 50,000 people staged such a protest in front of the Pentagon on October 21, 1967.

Opponents of the draft pointed out its unfairness. Most draftees were poor. Middle- and upper-class youths could delay being drafted by enrolling in college. They also sought advice from draft counselors, doctors, and lawyers to help them avoid service. Certain medical conditions or religious beliefs, for example, could keep them out of the military.

Links to Civil Rights Another unfair aspect of the draft was the high number of African Americans called to serve. African Americans made up about 10 percent of combat troops in Vietnam. In 1965, they accounted for 20 percent of U.S. army combat deaths. Yet they were only 13.5 percent of the military-age population in the United States.

For this and other reasons, the antiwar movement became linked with the civil rights movement. In 1967, civil rights leader Martin Luther King, Jr., spoke out against the Vietnam War. King was concerned that the war took money away from antipoverty programs.

▲ **SUMMARIZE** Explain why so many Americans opposed the Vietnam War.

CONNECTING History

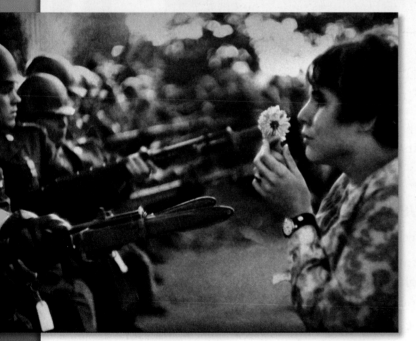

An antiwar protester confronts the National Guard outside the Pentagon in 1967.

WAR PROTESTS

During the Vietnam War the country was deeply divided between those who supported the war and those who opposed it. Americans had been divided in earlier wars as well—the nineteenth century war with Mexico and World War I are two examples. The ideas of past antiwar protesters influenced the U.S. antiwar movement of the 1960s–1970s.

Civil disobedience, or the deliberate breaking of a law, was supported by the ideas of Henry David Thoreau, an influential writer of the mid nineteenth-century. Thoreau was a pacifist, meaning he was opposed to war or violence as a means of resolving disputes. Some of the young men who refused to report for military duty and burned their draft cards during the Vietnam War liked to quote Thoreau's ideas.

CRITICAL THINKING Make Connections Thoreau's values and ideals of justice emphasized the necessity of practicing civil disobedience. How do those values express the American spirit of justice today?

The War Divides American Society

🔻 **KEY QUESTION** How did the Vietnam War divide Americans?

The war helped turn some young people against traditional society. This movement, called the **counterculture**, rejected the middle-class lifestyle of consumerism and corporate influence. Members of the counterculture, or hippies, wanted to create a new society based on peace and love. Many joined **communes**, places where people or families live together and share everything.

A Divided Country By 1967, it was clear that the Vietnam War was dividing Americans into two camps. Even within families, people took opposite sides. Those who opposed the war were called **doves**. Those who supported it were known as **hawks**. Supporters of the war staged marches of their own. Believing that antiwar protesters were unpatriotic, they popularized such slogans as "America—love it or leave it." Because draftees tended to be poor, working class, or minorities, many doves belonged to these groups.

Some Americans were angry that the cost of the war drew money away from social programs. The normal generation gap, or differences in values, between the older and younger generations, widened in the 1960s.

🔺 **SUMMARIZE** Explain how the Vietnam War created divisions in American society.

This sign represents the hawk philosophy.

Vietnam Overwhelms American Politics

🔻 **KEY QUESTION** How did the war affect American politics?

The Tet offensive that began in early 1968 became a turning point in the war. Tet made Americans doubt that they could win the war. The news media reflected the public's growing discontent with the state of affairs.

A Change in Leadership Walter Cronkite, a respected TV news anchorman, visited Vietnam in February. He concluded that the United States was not winning the war but was in a deadlock.

PRIMARY SOURCE

❝ [The] only rational way out, then, will be to negotiate, not as victors, but as an honorable people who lived up to their pledge to defend democracy, and did the best they could. ❞

—Walter Cronkite, *A Reporter's Life*

Johnson took Cronkite's words to heart. "If I've lost Cronkite, I've lost middle America," he reportedly said. In addition, after Tet, Johnson changed his war policy. He refused, for example, General Westmoreland's request for 206,000 more troops. Then, on March 31, 1968, Johnson said that he would would seek to bargain for peace. In the same speech, he announced that he would not run for another term as president.

Johnson's domestic policies had been largely successful. He helped create programs to assist the poor and the elderly, and to protect civil rights.

Connecting History

Technology
The Vietnam War was the first "television war"—it was broadcast each night on the evening news. After the war, General Westmoreland charged that television and other media coverage had hurt U.S. efforts in Vietnam. Television continues to influence public opinion on world conflicts today.

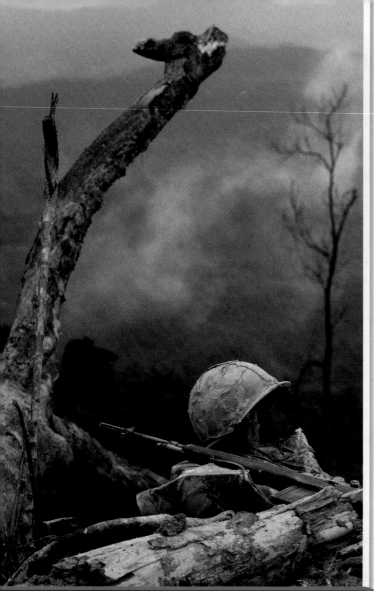

History through Art

The Aftermath of Battle

British photojournalist Larry Burrows took this picture in 1966. It shows a Marine's helmet and rifle on Hill 484, in the northernmost part of South Vietnam. The photo was taken in the aftermath of a battle fought as part of Operation Prairie. The military wanted to stop North Vietnamese troops from using this area to enter South Vietnam. Because the North Vietnamese held the high ground, the fighting was intense. U.S. troops suffered heavy casualties and there were several "friendly fire" incidents.

CRITICAL VIEWING Do you think the photographer's decision not to show a casualty is effective? Why or why not?

But Vietnam overshadowed his accomplishments at home. Johnson lost the support of liberal Democrats, civil rights leaders, and intellectuals. The war destroyed this "New Deal coalition" that had supported large-scale government programs since the 1930s.

Nixon Promises Results That summer, the Democratic National Convention in Chicago reflected the country's turmoil. Democrats chose Hubert Humphrey, Johnson's vice-president, as their nominee. Outside the convention hall, TV cameras showed police clubbing antiwar demonstrators and bystanders. The chaos helped Republican candidate **Richard Nixon** win the 1968 presidency. In his campaign, Nixon promised to restore law and order and "bring an honorable end to the war in Vietnam."

Nixon was determined not to let the same thing happen to him as had happened to Johnson. He promised his supporters, "I'm going to stop that war. Fast." But Nixon did not follow through with his promise, and the war dragged on.

Morale Sinks As the Vietnam War went on, it wore down American soldiers. They fought hard, but many were losing faith that the United States could win the war. The South Vietnamese government did not have the loyalty of the people. In addition, the South Vietnamese army was racked by desertions. American soldiers asked why they were fighting a war the Vietnamese did not want to fight themselves.

The low morale of U.S. forces in Vietnam became clear when news of the My Lai (MEE•LY) massacre broke in 1969. The incident happened on March 16, 1968. A U.S. platoon led by Lieutenant William Calley, Jr., rounded up and shot between 400 and 500 unarmed civilians, mostly women, children, and old men. A U.S. helicopter pilot rescued some civilians by threatening to fire on the soldiers. To Americans, My Lai represented a horrifying breakdown in morality and discipline in the armed forces.

"Peace With Honor" In Spring 1969, Nixon announced his strategy of **Vietnamization**. It called for gradually withdrawing U.S. forces and turning the ground fighting over to the South Vietnamese. Nixon promised to withdraw 25,000 of the 543,000 U.S. ground troops in Vietnam by the end of the year.

Although U.S. troops began coming home in 1969, Nixon was not willing to simply retreat. He wanted "peace with honor" for the United States. Nixon thought he could force the North Vietnamese to negotiate a peace settlement.

Widening the War In 1969, Nixon began secret bombing raids of **Cambodia**, a country bordering Vietnam. This bombing was meant to stop North Vietnamese troops and supplies from moving along the Ho Chi Minh Trail. And in 1970, Nixon said that he had sent American troops into Cambodia to attack Communist camps. Many people grew angry when they learned that the government had widened the war and hidden its actions.

Public anger and distrust of the government grew after Daniel Ellsberg released the Pentagon Papers to the *New York Times* in 1971. Ellsberg had helped research and write these secret Defense Department papers. They showed that the four previous presidential administrations had not been honest with the public about U.S. involvement and goals in Vietnam.

▲ **CAUSES AND EFFECTS** Describe how the war in Vietnam affected American politics at home and abroad.

 Illinois Learning Standards *Review*

 ONLINE QUIZ
For test practice, go to
Interactive Review @ ClassZone.com

TERMS & NAMES

1. Explain the significance of
- counterculture
- doves
- hawks
- Richard Nixon
- Vietnamization
- Cambodia

USING YOUR READING NOTES

2. Causes and Effects Complete the diagram you started at the beginning of the section.

Vietnam War's effects on America

KEY IDEAS

3. What were the reasons that young people in particular opposed the war?

4. Why did Lyndon Johnson decide not to run for reelection as president?

CRITICAL THINKING

5. Make Generalizations Why did less privileged people feel that they carried a larger share of the burden of the Vietnam War than did wealthier U.S. citizens?

6. Cause and Effects How did the Vietnam War play a part in turning the United States in a more conservative political direction?

7. Writing Journal Take the part of a hawk or a dove. Write a brief journal entry explaining the reasons why you either support the war or oppose it.

Key Ideas

BEFORE, YOU LEARNED

As the Vietnam War escalated, it divided American society.

NOW YOU WILL LEARN

The Vietnam War had lasting effects in the United States and Southeast Asia.

Vocabulary

TERMS & NAMES

Twenty-sixth Amendment Constitutional amendment passed in 1971 that lowered the voting age from 21 to 18

War Powers Act legislation passed in 1973 to limit the president's war-making powers

BACKGROUND VOCABULARY

ambush an unexpected attack from a hidden position

Visual Vocabulary
Button and bag used to show support for the Twenty-sixth Amendment.

Reading Strategy

Re-create the diagram shown at right. As you read and respond to the **KEY QUESTIONS**, use the chart to sequence the events that led to the end of the Vietnam War.

 See Skillbuilder Handbook, page R5.

SEQUENCE EVENTS

Nixon is reelected

GRAPHIC ORGANIZERS
Go to **Interactive Review** @ ClassZone.com

The Vietnam War Ends

14.E.3 Compare the basic principles of the United States and its international interests (e.g., *territory, environment, trade, use of technology*).

14.F.3a Analyze historical influences on the development of political ideas and practices as enumerated in the Declaration of Independence, the United States Constitution, the Bill of Rights and the Illinois Constitution.

One American's Story

Dolia Gonzalez raised her son, Alfredo "Freddy" Gonzalez, as a single parent. The two were close. Dolia said, "I think Freddy knew he wouldn't live a long time, so he wanted to spend time with me." Freddy enlisted in the Marines right out of high school. He served one tour of duty in Vietnam in 1966–1967 and did not plan to go back. However, after a group of men he had served with died in an **ambush**—an unexpected attack from a hidden position—Freddy felt it was his duty to return. He was killed in the Tet offensive during his second tour of duty. The death of her only child was hard for Dolia to accept.

Marine Sergeant Alfredo (Freddy) Gonzalez won the Medal of Honor for bravery in Vietnam.

PRIMARY SOURCE

❝ Before he [Freddy] died he sent me a letter and said he was going to come back and take care of me and build a big house for us to live in. He never got that chance. ❞

—Dolia Gonzalez, newspaper interview

By the time President Richard Nixon took office, almost 35,000 Americans had died in Vietnam. The public looked to Nixon to bring the troops home.

America Withdraws

🔻 **KEY QUESTION** In what ways did the war change America?

In the 1972 presidential election, the Vietnam War was again a major issue. Promising that peace was at hand, Nixon was reelected by a landslide.

Peace Agreement On January 27, 1973, in Paris, the United States and South Vietnam agreed to a cease-fire with North Vietnam and the Viet Cong. The United States agreed to withdraw all its troops. On March 29, the last U.S. combat troops left Vietnam. For the United States, the war was over.

But for the Vietnamese, the war continued. In 1975, North Vietnam launched a massive invasion of South Vietnam. The American government sent money to help the south Vietnamese , but no troops. On April 30 of that year, Communist forces captured Saigon, which they renamed Ho Chi Minh City. The war then ended. Many Vietnamese fled and succeeded in resettling in the United States. By 2000, the Vietnamese-American community was 1.2 million-strong .

The Vietnam War caused terrible destruction and suffering. More than 1.5 million North and South Vietnamese died in the conflict. American bombing and chemical spraying caused lasting damage to farmland and forests. In addition, the war left Southeast Asia highly unstable, which led to further war in Cambodia.

Legacy of the War at Home The Vietnam War also took a heavy toll on American soldiers. About 58,000 died, and more than 300,000 were wounded. Returning soldiers often had recurring nightmares and other stress-related problems. To make things worse, they came home to a public that, in many instances, treated them coldly.

The war also had far-reaching political effects in the United States. The **Twenty-sixth Amendment**, passed in 1971, lowered the voting age from 21 to 18. Its supporters argued that anyone old enough to be drafted should be allowed to vote. Then, in 1973, the government ended the draft, which had stirred so much antiwar sentiment.

CONNECT to the Essential Question

What were the causes and effects of America's involvement in the Vietnam War?

EVENTS	EFFECTS
1954 Vietnam is divided into North and South.	U.S. sends economic aid to South Vietnam.
1962 Cuban Missile Crisis	Increases fear that communism might spread
1964 Congress passes Gulf of Tonkin Resolution	Escalation of U.S. involvement in Vietnam
1968 Tet offensive	Americans divide on the outcome of the War
1969–1970 Nixon announces Vietnamization	U.S. begins to withdraw combat troops
1971 Twenty-sixth Amendment ratified	Lowers voting age from 21 to 18
1973 Paris Peace Accord	U.S. involvement in Vietnam War ends
1973 Congress passes War Powers Act	Limits president's ability to wage war
1975 Communists invade South Vietnam	War ends after Communists take over

(Row groupings labeled: 1950s, 1960s, 1970s)

CRITICAL THINKING Make Inferences What were some long-term effects of the Vietnam War?

Since Vietnam, the United States has been less willing to get involved in overseas wars. In 1973, Congress passed the **War Powers Act**, which limits the president's war-making powers. The president must report to Congress within 48 hours if troops have been sent into a hostile situation without a declaration of war. In addition, the troops may remain there for no longer than 90 days unless Congress approves the president's actions or declares war.

Military tactics have changed as a result of Vietnam. For example, the U.S. armed forces prefer to enter into battle only with "overwhelming force." This approach, applied in the 1990 Gulf War (See Chapter 30), is intended to limit the number of American casualties.

Politicians also keep in mind the lessons of Vietnam—especially the effect of the war on President Johnson's career. In the build-up to the 2003 American invasion of Iraq, some politicians expressed the fear that such a conflict could turn into another Vietnam.

Finally, the war made many U.S. citizens distrust government leaders, who sometimes misled the public about actions in Vietnam. American confidence in government was at a very low point. Many Americans believed that their government should think twice before deciding whether or not to intervene in the affairs of other nations.

The Vietnam Veterans Memorial was unveiled in Washington, D.C., in 1982. For many Vietnam veterans, visiting the memorial is a healing experience.

▲ **SEQUENCE EVENTS** Sequence the ways in which Vietnam changed America.

Illinois Learning Standards *Review*

🔁 **ONLINE QUIZ**
For test practice, go to
Interactive Review @ ClassZone.com

TERMS & NAMES

1. Explain the importance of
- Twenty-sixth Amendment
- War Powers Act

USING YOUR READING NOTES

2. Sequence Events Complete the diagram you started at the beginning of this section.

> Nixon is reelected

KEY IDEAS

3. How did the Vietnam War end?

4. What are the major ways in which the war affected Southeast Asia and the United States?

CRITICAL THINKING

5. Citizenship Would you have supported changing the voting age from 21 to 18? Why or why not?

6. Form & Support Opinions What is your opinion of the way the United States ended its involvement in Vietnam? Explain.

7. Make Inferences Why did the Vietnam War influence Congress to pass the War Powers Act?

8. **Writing** **Editorial** Write an editorial for a leading newspaper explaining why you think the Vietnam War Memorial is a symbol of national unity.

Fallen Angels
by Walter Dean Myers

During the Vietnam War, tens of thousands of young American men graduated from high school and went directly into basic training, then on to the steaming jungles of Vietnam as combat infantrymen. In *Fallen Angels* Walter Dean Myers, a veteran himself, conveys the uncertainty, danger, and tragedy of the war through the story of Richard Perry, a young African-American soldier from Harlem, New York. In this scene Perry recalls his decision to go into the army rather than to college, as well as his commitments to his mother and to his younger brother, Kenny.

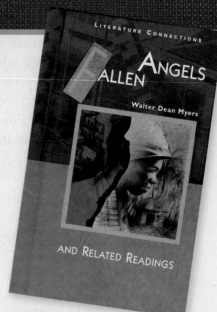

LITERATURE CONNECTIONS
FALLEN ANGELS
Walter Dean Myers
AND RELATED READINGS

I finished high school, but I hadn't gone to the graduation exercises. It just hadn't made sense anymore.

"You can go to City College," the guidance counselor had said. "Your grades are good enough."

I told her I'd think about it. What I was thinking about was that I had to get up every morning and dry the clothes I had washed the night before by putting them on the oven door, to have something to wear to high school. How was I going to get the clothes for college? How was I going to get clothes for Kenny so he would stay in school? Mama had said that she'd see to it that Kenny stayed in school if I sent the money for clothes for him. I wasn't saving any money, the way I figured I would when I first got into the army, but I figured that might come later if I made sergeant.

I thought of writing a letter to Kenny. He would dig getting a letter from Nam. I remembered once he was involved with a pen-pal program and got a letter from some kid in Logan, West Virginia. He had looked at me with his wide, bright eyes and smiled like he couldn't believe the great thing that had happened to him. The night before I left for the army we had sat and talked about what we were going to do in the future. No matter what I said, I knew he was sorry that I was leaving.

"Richie," he had said before he went to sleep, "when you get to Vietnam, I hope you guys win."

The Monarchs, the neighborhood team I played for, had just lost a tournament the week before. It had bothered me a lot. I had done well, and Kenny had said that it wasn't my fault. I had given him a big speech about basketball being a team sport, and that my doing well didn't matter.

"Either the team wins or the team loses," I had said.

I had wanted to win badly. I knew I was going into the army, but for me that was a kind of defeat. My plans, maybe just my dreams really, had been to go to college, and to write like **James Baldwin**.[1] All the other guys in the neighborhood thought I was going to college. I wasn't, and the army was the place I was going to get away from all the questions. I wanted to win the tournament, to walk away from the streets I had been raised in with my head high, a winner.

ADDITIONAL READING

And One for All, Theresa Nelson, New York: Orchard, 1989. Three young people are torn between conflicting loyalties over the Vietnam War.

Voices from Vietnam, Barry Denenberg, NY: Scholastic, 1995. A collection of quotations from soldiers, politicians, celebrities, and reporters about the difficulty of understanding the Vietnam War.

---

1. **James Baldwin**: (1924–1987) American writer and civil rights advocate.

Chapter Summary

1 Key Idea
The United States intensified its military and political interests in Southeast Asia.

2 Key Idea
The United States sent ground troops to Vietnam expecting victory, but soldiers soon grew frustrated.

3 Key Idea
As the war escalated, it divided American society.

4 Key Idea
The Vietnam War had lasting effects in the United States and Southeast Asia.

For detailed Review and Study Notes go to **Interactive Review** @ **ClassZone.com**

Name Game

Use the Terms & Names list to complete each sentence online or on your own paper.

1. The _____ was a confrontation between the United States and the Soviet Union in 1962.
   Cuban missile crisis

2. A term used to describe the South Vietnamese people who attempted to unite the country under Communist rule was _____.

3. _____ is a method of fighting that relies on surprise attacks by a small band of fighters.

4. The surprise attack on the U.S. military bases and 100 cities and towns in South Vietnam was the _____.

5. 1964 legislation that gave President Johnson the power to use military force in Vietnam is the _____.

6. A term used to describe Americans who opposed the Vietnam War is _____.

7. _____ is a term used to describe Americans who supported the Vietnam War.

8. _____ was a movement of disillusioned young Americans over the injustices in society.

9. Passed in 1971, the _____ lowered the voting age from 21 to 18.

10. Legislation passed in 1973 that limits the presidents war-making power is the _____.

A. War Power Act
B. Tet offensive
C. counterculture
D. Vietnamization
E. Cuban missile crisis
F. Twenty-sixth Amendment
G. Gulf of Tonkin Resolution
H. guerrilla warfare
I. Bay of Pigs invasion
J. hawks
K. Viet Cong
L. French Indochina
M. Cambodia
N. doves
O. domino theory

Activities

CROSSWORD PUZZLE

Complete the online crossword to show what you know about the Vietnam War.

ACROSS
1. Nixon's strategy for ending the war was called _____.

FLIPCARD

Use the online flipcards to quiz yourself on the terms and names introduced in this chapter.

The president who was assassinated in 1963.

ANSWER:
John F. Kennedy

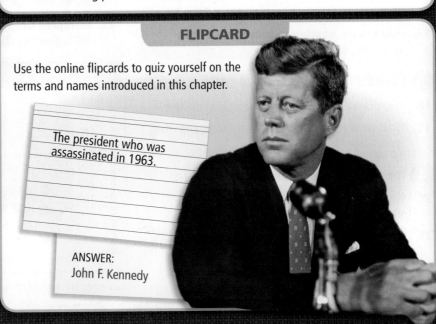

VOCABULARY

Explain the significance of each of the following:

1. French Indochina
2. Ho Chi Minh
3. Cambodia
4. Ngo Dinh Diem
5. Viet Cong
6. Ho Chi Minh Trail
7. domino theory
8. doves
9. hawks
10. Twenty-sixth Amendment

Place the items and/or events in each group below in chronological order.

11. escalation, Gulf of Tonkin Resolution, Cuban Missile Crisis

12. Vietnamization, Tet offensive, War Powers Act

13. Bay of Pigs invasion, credibility gap, Twenty-sixth Amendment

KEY IDEAS

1 Cold War Roots of the Conflict (pages 908–913)

14. Why did the United States decide to support France in its fight against the Viet Minh?

15. What decisions about Vietnam were laid out in the 1954 Geneva Accords?

2 War Expands in Vietnam (pages 914–919)

16. What kept U.S. troops from defeating the Viet Cong?

17. How was the Tet offensive both a defeat and a victory for the Communists?

3 Conflicts at Home (pages 920–925)

18. Why did many Americans protest against the war?

19. What types of people tended to be doves, and what types tended to be hawks?

4 The Vietnam War Ends (pages 926–929)

20. What policies did President Nixon pursue in Vietnam?

21. What long-term political effects did the Vietnam War have on the United States?

CRITICAL THINKING

22. **Compare** Create a table to compare and contrast the Vietnam policy for each of the following presidents: Truman, Eisenhower, Kennedy, and Johnson.

President	Vietnam Policy
Harry S. Truman	economic aid to France
Dwight D. Eisenhower	
John F. Kennedy	

23. **Make Decisions** In the early years of the war, would you have been a hawk or a dove? Why?

24. **Compare & Contrast** Compare and contrast the fighting methods of the U.S. troops with those of the Viet Cong.

25. **Evaluate** How would you evaluate President Johnson's leadership during the Vietnam War and his decision not to seek a second term as president?

26. **Analyze Motives** Why do you think President Nixon's desire for "peace with honor" was so strong?

27. **Make Inferences** How might involvement in Vietnam have affected the reputation of the United States among other nations? Why?

28. **Interpret Graphs** In which year did the U.S. have the highest number of troops in Vietnam?

U.S. Military in Vietnam

Source: Stanley I. Kutler, *Encyclopedia of the Vietnam War*

MULTIPLE CHOICE

Use the cartoon and your knowledge of U.S. history to answer question 1.

Things the POWs tell

1. This cartoon shows Lady Liberty listening to the stories told by U.S. prisoners of war (POWs) on their return from Vietnam. What can you infer from Lady Liberty's tears?

   A. the POWs were ill treated   C. the POWs were poor

   B. the POWs were healthy   D. the POWs were wealthy

Use the quotation and your knowledge of U.S. history to answer question 2.

PRIMARY SOURCE

❝The poor in general have the worst health. . . . But most poor and working-class kids . . . had to rely on army doctors to pronounce them unfit for military service, . . . They were cattle calls. . . . people who had legitimate ailments under the written regulations put forth by the Selective Service System were approved for military service. ❞

—James Lafferty, quoted in *Patriots: The Vietnam War Remembered from All Sides* by Christian Appy

2. The writer of this article had been a draft counselor during the Vietnam War. What was his opinion of the draft?

   A. unfair to the military   C. unfair to the disadvantaged

   B. unfair to students   D. unfair to the privileged

YOU BE THE HISTORIAN

29. **WHAT IF?** Suppose the United States had never sent money or troops to Vietnam. How do you think Vietnam's history would be different? Explain.

30. **Make Inferences** Why do you think the American public treated soldiers returning from Vietnam differently than they had treated World War II veterans?

31. **Form & Support Opinions** Why do you think so many people find the Vietnam Veterans Memorial in Washington, D.C., so powerful?

32. **Connect** *to* **Today** The draft ended in 1973. How might having an all-volunteer military affect politicians' decisions as to whether or not to send troops into harm's way?

33. **Make Judgments** Do you think American society was stronger or weaker after the war? Explain and justify your opinion.

 Answer the

ESSENTIAL QUESTION

What were the causes and effects of America's involvement in the Vietnam War?

Written Response Write a two- to three-paragraph response to the Essential Question. Be sure to consider the key ideas of each section as well as the most significant factors that led to the American withdrawal from Vietnam. Use the Response Rubric below to guide your thinking and writing.

Response Rubric

A strong response will

- discuss U.S. foreign relations in the 1950s and 1960s
- analyze the role of the South Vietnamese government in the war
- explain how the war affected Americans' views of government

America in a Changing World

1969–2006

ESSENTIAL QUESTION

How have America's strengths helped us to face the challenges of the past four decades?

1. Nixon, Watergate, and Years of Doubt

2. Conservatives Reshape Politics

3. America Enters a New Millennium

CONNECT → Geography & History

How do geography and technology affect America's role in the world?

Think about:

1 how communications and transportation technologies have changed in the last century

2 U.S. commercial and political interests around the world

3 how humans and our technologies have affected the environment

WOODSTOCK MUSIC & ART FAIR presents AN AQUARIAN EXPOSITION in WHITE LAKE, N.Y.

3 DAYS of PEACE & MUSIC

WITH

AUGUST 15, 16, 17.

In August 1969, the Woodstock Music and Art Fair drew nearly 500,000 participants.

RONALD REAGAN PRESIDENT 1980

1972
President Nixon visits China.

1973
Last troops leave Vietnam.

1974
Nixon resigns as president.

1980
Ronald Reagan elected president.

1969

First moonwalk

(from left) Vice-President Ford, Betty Ford, Pat Nixon, and President Nixon

1979
Iranians overrun U.S. Embassy and take American hostages.

An IBM personal computer, 1981

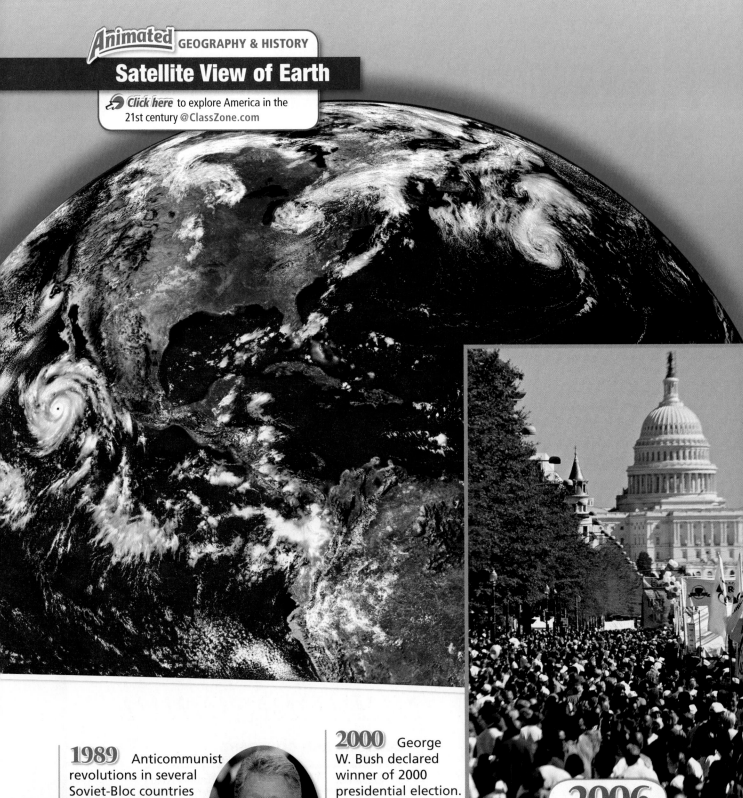

1989 Anticommunist
revolutions in several
Soviet-Bloc countries

1991
Persian
Gulf War

President
George H. W. Bush

President
Bill Clinton

2000 George
W. Bush declared
winner of 2000
presidential election.

2001 Terrorists
attack World Trade
Center and the Pentagon.

Effect U.S.-led coalition
invades Afghanistan.

2006

Three hundred
millionth American
born.

▶ Key Ideas

BEFORE, YOU LEARNED

The Vietnam War had lasting effects in the United States and Southeast Asia.

NOW YOU WILL LEARN

President Richard M. Nixon governed a divided nation and faced a political scandal that forced him to resign.

▶ Vocabulary

TERMS & NAMES

Richard M. Nixon U.S. president elected in 1968 on a promise to restore law and order

Watergate scandal illegal actions by President Nixon and his aides to cover up crimes related to Nixon's re-election campaign

Organization of Petroleum Exporting Countries (OPEC) nations, mostly in the Middle East, that cut oil shipments to the United States in 1973

Camp David Accords 1978 peace treaty between Egypt and Israel

REVIEW

inflation an increase in the price of goods and services and a decrease in the value of money

Visual Vocabulary
Camp David Accords: Egyptian premier Anwar Sadat, President Jimmy Carter, and Israeli prime minister Menachem Begin

▶ Reading Strategy

Re-create the diagram shown at right. As you read and respond to the **KEY QUESTIONS**, use the diagram to note what problems presidents Nixon, Ford, and Carter faced in America and abroad.

 See Skillbuilder Handbook, page R8.

COMPARE AND CONTRAST

President	Problems faced	Solutions tried
Nixon	social unrest	
Ford		
Carter		

 GRAPHIC ORGANIZERS
Go to **Interactive Review** @ ClassZone.com

Nixon, Watergate, and Years of Doubt

14.D.3 Describe roles and influences of individuals, groups and media in shaping current Illinois and United States public policy (e.g., *general public opinion, special interest groups, formal parties, media*).

15.D.3a Explain the effects of increasing and declining imports and exports to an individual and to the nation's economy as a whole.

One American's Story

President **Richard M. Nixon** was re-elected by a landslide. However, *Washington Post* reporters uncovered evidence that several Nixon campaign workers had engaged in illegal activities—and that Nixon had covered up for the White House's involvement. Under strong opposition from the White House, editors at the *Post* published what they had learned. The nation was stunned. Years later Katharine Graham, former publisher of the *Post*, recalled the magnitude of the scandal that came to be called **Watergate**.

PRIMARY SOURCE

❝ I have often been credited with courage for backing our editors in Watergate. The truth is that I never felt there was much choice. . . . By the time the story had grown to the point where the size of it dawned on us, we had already waded deeply into its stream. Once I found myself in the deepest water in the middle of the current, there was no going back. ❞

—Katharine Graham, in *Personal History*

Katharine Graham

Crowds began waiting outside the *Post*'s offices in the morning to get the latest news on the scandal. By the middle of 1974, the Watergate scandal had led the nation into one of its greatest political crises.

The Nation Confronts Domestic Problems

🔻 **KEY QUESTION** What problems did America face at the time Nixon took office?

As president, Richard M. Nixon wanted to focus on foreign policy and leave domestic issues to his cabinet. But he became president at a time when America was being torn apart by inflation, racial problems, and conflict over the war in Vietnam.

Connecting History

Dissent & Diversity

In the late 1960s, the Vietnam War divided Americans more sharply than any other issue. Protesters took to the streets in Washington, D.C., and rallied in cities and on college campuses across the nation.

"Restoring Law and Order" During the presidential campaign, Nixon had promised an end to the social unrest and rioting of the late 1960s. One way to achieve his goal, Nixon thought, was to appoint more conservative justices to the Supreme Court. As president, Nixon used all the powers of the federal government to "crack down" on crime and protest. He directed the Central Intelligence Agency and the Federal Bureau of Investigation to investigate some of his political enemies. Nixon later excused any illegal acts by claiming they were needed for the nation's security.

A Troubled Economy Under the Johnson administration, the government had spent huge amounts of money on programs to aid the poor and on fighting the Vietnam War. But taxes were not raised to cover these expenses. As a result, the government spent more money than it collected in taxes. This practice is called deficit spending.

Nixon had won the presidency as a conservative. He promised to shrink the federal government, end Johnson's Great Society programs, and turn many government activities over to the states. But both houses of Congress were controlled by the Democrats. As a result, Nixon took a more moderate approach at first. But he did veto many spending bills passed by the Democratic Congress, including cuts to Great Society programs.

CONNECT To Economics

INFLATION

Inflation is a rise in prices across the economy. When the price of milk goes up, that's a price increase; when the prices of food, energy, housing, appliances, electronics, and health care all go up, that's inflation.

In the 1970s, a major cause of inflation was rising oil prices. Oil is used in many basic ways across the economy, such as to produce heat and electricity, and as gasoline to power vehicles. Thus, the rising price of oil affected most businesses. These businesses increased their prices in order to cover their higher costs.

Retail Motor Gasoline Prices (gal.)*

1950	1960	1970	1980	1990	2000
$ 0.27	$ 0.31	$ 0.36	$ 1.19	$ 1.16	$ 1.51
THIS SALE $	THIS SALE $	THIS SALE $	THIS SALE $	THIS SALE $	THIS SALE $
1.000	1.000	1.000	1.000	1.000	1.000
GALLON	GALLON	GALLON	GALLON	GALLON	GALLON

*1950–1980: leaded regular;
1990–2000: unleaded regular
Source: U.S. Dept. of Energy

CRITICAL THINKING

1. **Compare and Contrast** What is the difference between a price increase and inflation?

2. **Summarize** Why do rising oil prices have such a widespread effect on the economy?

Deficit spending put a great deal of money into circulation in the late 1960s. At the same time, the economy began to slow down. By 1970, the economy had gone into a recession. With the recession, fewer goods were produced. The increase in the money supply and the decrease in products to buy caused inflation. (See Connect to Economics, page 938.)

Inflation created problems for all Americans, but especially the poor. One mother said, "I used to be able to go to the store with $50 and come back with six or seven bags of groceries. Now I'm lucky if I come back with three." When Nixon took office in 1969, the inflation rate was about 5 percent. That was twice the rate it had been earlier in the decade. At the same time, unemployment rose from about 3 percent in 1969 to 6 percent in 1971.

Then, in 1973, the economy was jolted by the actions of the **Organization of Petroleum Exporting Countries (OPEC)**, a worldwide cartel, or business group. OPEC raised its prices and cut its shipments of oil to the United States. In a few months, gas prices quadrupled. Inflation and unemployment soared to new heights.

▲ **PROBLEMS AND SOLUTIONS** Describe how Nixon tried to solve the problems America faced.

Nixon Eases Cold War Tensions

▼ **KEY QUESTION** What were some of Nixon's foreign-policy goals?

Nixon's main foreign-policy goal was world stability. During his 1968 presidential campaign, Nixon pledged to end the Vietnam War quickly and honorably. It took four years to negotiate a cease-fire with the North Vietnamese.

Nixon's most important success came in dealings with the People's Republic of China. He had long opposed the Communists, who took power in China in 1949. But Nixon believed a nation of a billion people could not be ignored. He asked national security advisor Henry Kissinger to find a way to improve relations with China, even though they knew many Americans would be opposed. Kissinger arranged for Nixon to visit China in February 1972. This trip led to the opening of diplomacy and trade with the Chinese.

History Makers

Richard M. Nixon   1913–1994

Richard M. Nixon served two terms in the U.S. House of Representatives, where he earned a reputation for being a fierce opponent of communism. From 1953 to 1961 he served as Dwight D. Eisenhower's vice-president. During this time he gained experience in foreign affairs by making trips to Latin America and the Soviet Union.

In 1960, Nixon won the Republican nomination for president, but lost the election. In 1962, he lost the race for governor of California. Most observers thought his career was over. He bounced back, however, and won the presidency in 1968.

COMPARING *Leaders*

As you read about Nixon's presidency, look for examples of his leadership. Compare his leadership qualities with those of the presidents who followed him.

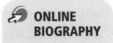 **ONLINE BIOGRAPHY**   For more on Richard M. Nixon, go to the **Research & Writing Center** @ ClassZone.com

Nixon and his inner circle (*insets, clockwise from top left*): former attorney general John Mitchell; chief domestic adviser John Ehrlichman; White House counsel John Dean; and chief of staff H. R. Haldeman

Nixon's China trip affected U.S. relations with the Soviet Union. The Soviets were having conflicts with China and feared closer relations between the United States and China. They invited Nixon to Moscow in May 1972. As a result, Soviet-American relations improved. Later that year, the two nations signed the Strategic Arms Limitation Treaty (SALT) of 1972, which limited the number of each country's nuclear weapons, easing fears of nuclear war.

▲ **EVALUATE** Discuss how effectively Nixon pursued his foreign-policy goals.

Watergate Brings Down Nixon

▼ **KEY QUESTION** What events led to Nixon's resignation?

Nixon wanted to win the 1972 presidential election by a landslide so that he could help Republicans take back control of Congress. To ensure this land-slide victory, some people working for him engaged in illegal activities.

The Watergate Scandal Comes to Light These activities were first discovered on June 17, 1972. Five men were caught breaking into Democratic Party headquarters in the Watergate office-apartment complex in Washington, D.C. The burglars had cameras and listening devices for the telephones. All five were linked to Nixon's Committee to Re-elect the President. Nixon may not have known in advance about the break-in. But in less than a week, he ordered a cover-up of any White House connection to the burglary.

The cover-up involved lies told by Nixon and his aides, payments to the Watergate burglars and others to lie, and the use of the CIA to halt an FBI investigation of Watergate. These illegal actions to cover up the Watergate break-in and related crimes became known as the Watergate scandal.

The break-in stayed on the back pages of most newspapers through the 1972 campaign. But in February 1973, the Senate began an investigation.

The Scandal Explodes The Senate Watergate investigation began with the questioning of members of the re-election committee and White House staff. Within six weeks, the investigation was closing in on the president's closest advisers: H. R. Haldeman, Nixon's chief of staff; John Ehrlichman, Nixon's chief domestic adviser; and John Mitchell, Nixon's former attorney general and head of his re-election committee.

Under oath, John Dean, one of the president's attorneys, testified to the Senate that the president had been involved in the cover-up. But Nixon said to the country, "I am not a crook." It was Dean's word against Nixon's until mid-July. Then a White House aide revealed that Nixon had been taping conversations in his office. A long battle over the tapes began in the courts.

In the spring of 1974, the House Judiciary Committee began an impeachment inquiry. Nixon did not give the committee his tapes, but he did release edited transcripts. In July, both Democrats and Republicans on the committee approved three articles of impeachment.

Nixon Resigns On August 5, a federal judge ordered the president to release full transcripts of the tapes. The tapes proved with certainty that Nixon himself had abused his presidential power to stop the FBI from investigating the break-in. On August 9, 1974, Richard Nixon became the first U.S. president to resign from office.

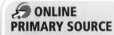

ONLINE PRIMARY SOURCE

Hear the perspectives at the **Research & Writing Center** @ ClassZone.com

---

COMPARING *Perspectives*

THE MEANING OF WATERGATE

Historians still debate the effects of the Watergate scandal. Some believe that public awareness of corruption in government has permanently damaged trust in democracy. Others believe that the outcome proved that the American legal system works.

Watergate as Tragedy

❝ I used to think that the Civil War was our country's greatest tragedy, but . . . there were some redeeming features in the Civil War . . . some spirit of sacrifice and heroism. . . . I see no redeeming features in Watergate. ❞

—*Sam Ervin, Chair of Senate Watergate Committee*

Watergate as Lesson

❝ From Watergate we learned what generations before us have known; our Constitution works. And during Watergate years it was interpreted again so as to reaffirm that no one— absolutely no one—is above the law. ❞

—*Leon Jaworski, Watergate Prosecutor*

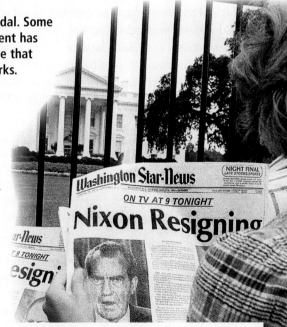

CRITICAL THINKING Form and Support Opinions How do you think Watergate affected the average American's view of government?

Watergate was one of the worst political scandals in the nation's history. Eventually, 40 members of the Nixon administration were indicted or served prison terms for crimes connected to Watergate. Many Americans lost faith in the government and its leaders. This lack of confidence weakened the government, especially the president. The next two presidents—Gerald Ford and Jimmy Carter—worked hard to restore the presidency.

▲ **SEQUENCE EVENTS** Outline the events leading to Nixon's resignation.

The Ford and Carter Presidencies

▼ **KEY QUESTION** What challenges faced presidents Ford and Carter?

At the same time as Watergate was coming to light, it became known that Spiro Agnew had accepted bribes as governor of Maryland and continued taking them as Nixon's vice-president. Not wanting to face impeachment, Agnew resigned in October 1973. Nixon then nominated House Speaker Gerald Ford of Michigan as the new vice-president. When Nixon resigned, Ford became the country's first unelected president.

Ford Takes Over Gerald Ford inherited a presidency that had suffered through the years not only of Watergate but also of Vietnam, a troubled economy, and a hotly divided public. During his first weeks in office, Ford set out to restore confidence in the presidency. He tried to reassure Americans that the turmoil of the Nixon years was behind them.

However, within a month, Ford lost the support of many Americans when he pardoned Richard Nixon for any crimes he may have committed while in office. It had been Ford's hope to spare the country the pain of an impeachment trial. But many people felt strongly that Nixon should be tried in a court.

In 1976, Ford was challenged for the presidency by Democrat Jimmy Carter, governor of Georgia. Carter campaigned as a Washington outsider. He promised honesty in government and support for human rights throughout the world.

Historic Decisions of the SUPREME COURT

Regents v. Bakke (1978)

KEY ISSUE affirmative action

KEY PEOPLE Allan Bakke, medical school applicant

Regents of the University of California, state-appointed group that runs the state universities

The Case

A medical school admissions quota ensured that 16 out of 100 admitted students were racial minorities. The goal was to assure a diverse student body. Bakke, a white applicant, was denied admission. His lawsuit charged that the university had excluded him because of his race. He claimed that affirmative action was "reverse discrimination" in violation of the XIVth Amendment.

THE VERDICT AND ITS IMPACT The court partially agreed with Bakke. It said that the state's goal of diversity could be a factor in admissions. But it also said that strict quotas were discriminatory and illegal.

The ruling was difficult to understand, even for lawyers, and the court was highly divided. As a result, affirmative action law remains unsettled.

CRITICAL THINKING **Draw Conclusions** In the Bakke case, the justices issued six separate opinions. Also, the voting on the two central issues was 5–4. Why would a divided Supreme Court opinion cause problems?

Carter as President Americans hoped that Carter would bring fresh ideas to the presidency. But being a Washington outsider made political life difficult for him.

A point of conflict arose early in 1977, when shortages of oil and natural gas forced many schools and businesses to close. Carter proposed a national energy program to cut dependence on oil imports and to promote alternative energy sources, such as coal and nuclear and solar energy. Congress passed some of the measures, but Americans did not like the sacrifices they were asked to make. And when OPEC again sharply raised oil prices, inflation surged beyond 10 percent and unemployment rose.

On inauguration day, Jimmy and Rosalynn Carter walked to the White House rather than taking the traditional limousine. **Why might Carter have chosen to walk to the White House?**

Carter had more success in accomplishing his foreign-policy goals. He wanted to end the long-standing conflict with Panama over the Panama Canal. Under treaties signed in 1977, the United States agreed to transfer the canal to Panama on December 31, 1999. Carter also tried to reduce tensions in the Middle East. In 1978, he helped to negotiate the **Camp David Accords**. Under these agreements, Egypt and Israel signed the first peace treaty between Israel and an Arab nation, thus ending 30 years of conflict.

▲ **CAUSES AND EFFECTS** Describe the impact of the challenges that faced presidents Ford and Carter.

Illinois Learning Standards *Review*

 ONLINE QUIZ
For test practice, go to
Interactive Review @ ClassZone.com

TERMS & NAMES

1. Explain the importance of
   - Richard M. Nixon
   - OPEC
   - Watergate scandal
   - Camp David Accords

USING YOUR READING NOTES

2. **Compare and Contrast** Complete the diagram you started at the beginning of this section. Then decide which president you think faced the most difficult issues.

President	Problems faced	Solutions tried
Nixon	social unrest	
Ford		
Carter		

KEY IDEAS

3. What economic concerns did Nixon face?
4. What were the causes of the Watergate scandal?
5. What successes did Carter have with foreign policy?

CRITICAL THINKING

6. **Evaluate** Why were the tapes made in Nixon's office so important to the Watergate investigation?
7. **Causes and Effects** What were the events that caused Nixon to resign?
8. **Draw Conclusions** In 1976, why do you think voters elected Carter rather than Ford?
9. **Writing** Letter Suppose that it is 1973 and Ford has just pardoned Nixon. Write a letter to your local newspaper that explains whether you think Ford made a good decision.

Animated HISTORY
THE SPACE PROGRAM

Click here to see an animated version of the first moonwalk @ ClassZone.com

On July 20, 1969, Apollo 11 astronauts Neil Armstrong and Edwin "Buzz" Aldrin made the first moonwalk. They placed a plaque that read, "Here Men From Planet Earth First Set Foot Upon the Moon. July 1969 A.D. We Came in Peace For All Mankind."

Click here A third astronaut, Michael Collins, piloted the command module.

Click here After eight days in space, the crew splashed down in the Pacific Ocean.

Click here The three astronauts were quarantined for 21 days.

Activity

Moon Plaque

1 Suppose that you are an astronaut who is preparing to make a lunar landing. Design a plaque that you will leave on the moon. Tell why you went there and why your trip was important.

2 Present your design to the class. Describe how you would like to see your plaque displayed on the moon.

► Key Ideas

BEFORE, YOU LEARNED
President Richard M. Nixon governed a divided nation and faced a political scandal that forced him to resign.

NOW YOU WILL LEARN
During the 1980s, conservatives reshaped U.S. domestic policy, and world events influenced U.S. foreign policy.

► Vocabulary

TERMS & NAMES

Iran-Contra affair scandal in which the United States sold weapons to Iran and gave the money to Contra rebels in Nicaragua

Persian Gulf War 1990–1991 war in which the United States and the United Nations drove Iraq out of Kuwait

North American Free Trade Agreement (NAFTA) 1993 agreement that limited tariffs on trade among the United States, Mexico, and Canada

BACKGROUND VOCABULARY

entitlements government programs that guaranteed certain benefits to citizens

Kosovo (KAW•suh•VOH) province of southern Serbia that is inhabited mostly by people of Albanian descent

Visual Vocabulary
flags of NAFTA nations

► Reading Strategy

Re-create the diagram shown at right. As you read and respond to the **KEY QUESTIONS**, record world events affecting America in the order in which they occurred.

 See Skillbuilder Handbook, page R5.

SEQUENCE EVENTS

Iran hostage crisis begins 1979

Reagan elected president 1980

GRAPHIC ORGANIZERS
Go to **Interactive Review** @ ClassZone.com

Conservatives Reshape Politics

14.E.3 Compare the basic principles of the United States and its international interests (e.g., *territory, environment, trade, use of technology*).
15.E.3b Explain how laws and government policies (e.g., *property rights, contract enforcement, standard weights/measurements*) establish rules that help a market economy function effectively.

One American's Story

The U.S.-backed Shah of Iran was overthrown in a 1979 revolution led by Ayatollah Ruholla Khomeini. Khomeini's anti-American statements incited action against the United States. An Iranian mob seized the U.S. embassy in Tehran, Iran, taking 66 Americans captive. Some were soon released, but more than 50 would be held hostage for over a year.

Among those taken hostage was Ambassador Bruce Laingen. Later, Laingen recalled what helped him and others endure their 444 days in captivity.

PRIMARY SOURCE

❝ In a situation like that . . . . you tell yourself, 'Hey . . . Christmas? They wouldn't hold 53 Americans hostage through Christmas and thus demonstrate to world opinion how heartless a regime this is.' Well, Thanksgiving and Christmas came, New Year's came, St. Patrick's came, birthdays came. Second Thanksgiving, second Christmas even. We lived on hope. ❞

—Bruce Laingen

Jimmy Carter's presidency had seen many troubles before the hostage crisis. Now, disapproval of Carter grew.

The Reagan Revolution

🔽 **KEY QUESTION** How did government policy change under President Reagan?

Besides the hostage crisis, economic troubles seemed to show Carter's ineffectiveness. In 1980, millions of Democrats turned to Carter's Republican opponent, former California governor Ronald Reagan. Reagan was elected by an electoral vote of 489 to 49 for Carter.

After his release, Bruce Laingen was greeted at home by yellow balloons and ribbons. (The color yellow has long been associated with waiting for troops to return.)

America in a Changing World **947**

History Makers

Ronald Reagan   1911–2004

Before entering politics, Ronald Reagan had been an actor for nearly 30 years. He began his political career as president of the Screen Actors Guild, where he earned a reputation as a staunch opponent of communism. In 1966, he made the first of two successful bids for governor of California.

A skilled campaigner and gifted speaker, Reagan swept the 1980 presidential election. In 1984, he won a second term with the highest-ever popular vote and the highest-ever electoral college vote. One reason for Reagan's appeal was his strong optimism at a time when many Americans felt uncertain.

CRITICAL THINKING Draw Conclusions Why might it be important for a leader to convey a sense of optimism?

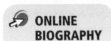
ONLINE BIOGRAPHY For more on Ronald Reagan, go to the **Research & Writing Center** @ ClassZone.com

Reagan's Conservative Goals In his 1981 inaugural address, President Reagan outlined his goals to solve the nation's "economic ills." He declared, "In this present crisis, government is not the solution to our problem; government is the problem." Reagan pursued the following conservative goals.

1. **Lower Taxes.** Reagan preached supply-side economics. This theory held that if taxes were lower, people would save more money. Banks could loan that money to businesses, which could invest in ways to improve productivity. The supply of goods would increase, driving down prices. At Reagan's urging, Congress lowered income taxes by 25 percent over three years.

2. **Deregulation.** The president deregulated, or eased restrictions on, many industries. Reagan believed that business would grow more rapidly if government interfered with it less. He also fought to end or weaken many programs, such as affirmative action and environmental protections.

3. **Smaller Government.** Reagan claimed that government bureaucracies were both ineffective and inefficient. He tried to shrink the government by expanding the use of private contractors to perform government business.

4. **A Conservative Supreme Court.** President Reagan named three conservative judges to the Supreme Court. One of them, Sandra Day O'Connor, was the first woman to sit on the nation's highest court.

5. **Cutting Entitlements.** Reagan and other conservatives believed that **entitlements**— programs that guaranteed benefits, such as AFDC—made people dependent on government and unable to help themselves. In this view, cutting welfare was not only practical, it was a moral duty.

At first, inflation rose and unemployment stayed high. But by 1983, they both decreased, and business boomed. Even so, Reagan's policies created a problem. Because of the tax cut, the federal government took in less money and had to resort to deficit spending. As a result, the national debt doubled from 1981 to 1986.

A Tough Anti-Communist Stand Although he wanted to shrink the government, Ronald Reagan believed that military force was an essential protection against a communist takeover of the world. To compete militarily with the Soviet Union, he began the most expensive arms buildup in history. It cost more than $2 trillion.

In 1985, Mikhail Gorbachev became the leader of the Soviet Union. He and Reagan met four times to discuss improving U.S.-Soviet relations and easing the threat of nuclear war. They signed the Intermediate-Range Nuclear Forces (INF) Treaty in 1987. Under that treaty, the two countries agreed to destroy all of their medium-range missiles.

The Reagan administration also decided to support the anti-Communist side in several conflicts, including two Central American civil wars. In El Salvador, the United States backed the government against Communist-led rebels. In Nicaragua, the United States secretly provided aid to anti-Communist rebels known as Contras.

President Reagan with Mikhail Gorbachev

This aid resulted in a scandal, known as the **Iran-Contra affair**. In 1986, Americans learned that the U.S. government had sold weapons to Iran in exchange for help in freeing American hostages in the Middle East. The money from these sales went to the Contras. This action violated a law that barred the U.S. government from funding the rebels. President Reagan claimed he never knew about the deal. But investigators concluded that he should have kept better track of what his administration was doing.

 COMPARE AND CONTRAST Describe how the goals of government changed under President Reagan.

A New Era in Foreign Relations

▼ **KEY QUESTION** What shocking events occurred around the world in the 1980s?

Despite the Iran-Contra scandal and the growing national debt, Reagan and his administration remained popular. In 1988, Reagan's vice-president, George H. W. Bush, ran for president and won. During his presidency, dramatic foreign events took place.

The End of the Cold War In 1989, several Eastern European countries ended Communist rule. This angered hard-line Communists in the Soviet Union. In August 1991, a group of them tried to take over the Soviet government. Boris Yeltsin, a Russian reform leader, fought the takeover attempt and won.

Unlike Gorbachev, who wanted to reform communism, Yeltsin and others wanted to get rid of it. One by one, the republics that made up the Soviet Union declared their independence. In December 1991, Yeltsin and the leaders of these nations joined in a loose alliance called the Commonwealth of Independent States (CIS). The Soviet Union, once a superpower, was gone. Its breakup marked the end of the Cold War.

Connect *to the* **World**

A New Era
Yeltsin became Russia's first democratically elected president. He said about the breakup of the Soviet Union, "Today is the last day of an era past."

THE COLD WAR

At the close of World War II, the Soviets began to build an "iron curtain" around Eastern Europe. The East-West divide set the stage for the Cold War: an era of conflict, distrust, and military standoff. The fight against Communism powerfully influenced U.S. politics and policy for nearly five decades.

1945 Potsdam Conference divides Europe.

1948 Berlin Airlift begins.

1949 Western nations form NATO.

1956 Soviet tanks crush revolt in Hungary.

1962 Cuban Missile Crisis

1968 Soviets put down uprising in Czechoslovakia.

1972 U.S. and Soviet Union sign SALT 1 treaty.

1989 East Germany opens Berlin Wall.

The fall of the Berlin Wall

The Berlin Airlift

Churchill, Truman, and Stalin at Potsdam

(*above*) Kennedy placed a naval blockade on Cuba. (*right*) Soviet tanks roll into Czechoslovakia.

CRITICAL THINKING

1. **Synthesize** How long did the Cold War last?

2. **Connect Geography & History** What was the symbolic significance of the fall of the Berlin Wall?

The Persian Gulf War A crisis also erupted in the Middle East. In August 1990, Iraq invaded neighboring Kuwait—a major supplier of oil. The United States, led by Bush, and the United Nations (UN) organized a group of 39 nations to free Kuwait by fighting the **Persian Gulf War**. In mid-January 1991, UN forces began bombing Iraqi military targets. A month later, UN ground forces moved into Kuwait and drove the Iraqis out of that country.

The war boosted Bush's popularity, and he seemed certain to be re-elected. Then the economy stalled. By the spring of 1992, the unemployment rate had climbed to around 7 percent—a six-year high. Americans began to think that Bush was good at foreign policy but ineffective at home. In November, they elected his Democratic opponent, Arkansas governor Bill Clinton.

🔺 **CAUSES AND EFFECTS** Explain how events around the world affected America.

Clinton Fights a Republican Congress

🔻 **KEY QUESTION** What fights broke out between President Clinton and Congress?

One of Clinton's first acts as president was to try to reform the health-care system. This was just one issue over which he clashed with Congress.

Conflicts Over Domestic Issues Clinton appointed his wife, Hillary Rodham Clinton, to head a task force to design a national health-care plan. Conservative opponents criticized the plan as costing too much, while liberals criticized it for not going far enough. Congress chose not to vote on any health-care plan. But it did pass a law allowing workers to keep insurance when they change jobs.

The **North American Free Trade Agreement (NAFTA)** won passage in 1993, supported by both the president and some members of both parties. NAFTA lifted tariffs in an effort to increase trade among Mexico, Canada, and the United States. Critics of the treaty claimed America would lose jobs to Mexico, where wages were lower and workplace safety and environmental regulations were looser.

Republican congressman Newt Gingrich of Georgia was one of Clinton's most vocal opponents. In part because of Gingrich's rhetoric, Republicans won control of both houses of Congress in the 1994 elections. In 1995, Gingrich became the new Speaker of the House.

President Clinton and Newt Gingrich

After the 1994 elections, conflict between Congress and the president intensified. President Clinton—and other Democrats—opposed budget cuts to programs providing for basic needs. When Clinton rejected Congress's budgets, government agencies were forced to shut down twice in late 1995. Finally, Clinton and Congress reached a compromise on the budget.

Democrats and Republicans did work together to pass a welfare reform bill—a long-time conservative goal. The bill ended a guarantee of aid to needy families. It also cut the length of time people could receive benefits.

Clinton Impeached In 1996, Clinton was re-elected. But his second term in office was marked by scandals. Information emerged that Clinton had had an improper relationship with a White House intern. In addition, he allegedly had lied about it under oath.

When the charges became public in January 1998, the president denied them. Later, he admitted to the relationship but denied lying under oath. In December 1998, the House of Representatives impeached President Clinton. In general, Republicans voted for impeachment while Democrats voted against it. In spite of the charges, Clinton remained popular. In January 1999, the Senate held its trial of President Clinton and acquitted him. Clinton finished his second term with three successive years of budget surpluses. But partisan divisions continued to hold up needed legislation.

CONNECT　Citizenship and History

WRITING TO GOVERNMENT OFFICIALS

Every year, thousands of Americans write to government officials to share their thoughts on important public issues. In the late 1990s, a letter-writing campaign led to renewal of the Water Resources Development Act. The bill authorized more than $7 billion to protect and restore Florida's Everglades. Signing the bill, President Clinton said, "Preserving our environment and restoring its wonders are for our common good."

Even though you're not old enough to vote, and even if you are not a citizen, you can still write to government officials about issues that concern you.

(*top left*) President Clinton signs the Water Resources Development Act.
(*left*) Students visit the Everglades.

Write a Persuasive Letter

1 Make sure you know the facts before you write.

2 Decide whether your issue is federal, state, or local. Then, find the name and address of the correct representative or other official at a government Web site.

3 In your letter, state clearly what action you want, and explain your reasons fully.

4 Use respectful language, and proofread carefully.

 See Citizenship Handbook, pages 300–307.

War in Kosovo Despite his troubles in Washington, Clinton still had to act as a world leader. In 1999, he led a group of nations in dealing with a crisis in Yugoslavia. The European country of Yugoslavia had been created after World War I. It contained many ethnic and religious groups that were often in conflict with one another.

Within the Yugoslav republic of Serbia was a region called **Kosovo** that was inhabited mostly by people of Albanian descent. The Kosovars sought independence, but the Serbs opposed them. A vicious war broke out over Kosovo. The Serbian government tried to drive the Albanians out of Kosovo by using violence and murder.

In March 1999, North Atlantic Treaty Organization (NATO) military forces began bombing Serbia. This was the first time that NATO had intervened with an independent nation's treatment of its own citizens. In June 1999, the Serbs withdrew from Kosovo. Since then, Kosovo has been administered by a United Nations peacekeeping mission called UNMIK (UN Interim Administration Mission in Kosovo).

In February 2003, the country of Yugoslavia became a federation known as Serbia and Montenegro. This federation dissolved when Montenegro achieved independence in June 2006. The following month, Serbian and Kosovar leaders met for the first time to discuss the future of Kosovo.

▲ **SUMMARIZE** Describe the conflicts between President Clinton and Congress.

Illinois Learning Standards *Review*

 ONLINE QUIZ
For test practice, go to
Interactive Review @ ClassZone.com

TERMS & NAMES

1. Explain the significance of
- Iran-Contra affair
- NAFTA
- Persian Gulf War

USING YOUR READING NOTES

2. Sequence Events Complete the diagram you started at the beginning of this section. Discuss which event you think was most important, and why.

Iran hostage crisis begins 1979

Reagan elected president 1980

KEY IDEAS

3. How did Reagan improve the economy?

4. Why did Clinton have conflicts with Congress?

5. What was the goal of NAFTA?

CRITICAL THINKING

6. Causes and Effects What caused the Iran-Contra affair?

7. Compare and Contrast How did Gorbachev and Yeltsin differ in their attitudes toward communism?

8. Citizenship How is writing to government officials a kind of political participation?

9. Problems and Solutions How did international powers respond to the war in Kosovo?

10. **Math** Research U.S. military spending during the last five years of the Cold War and the first five years after its end. Then calculate the average annual military spending for each period.

▶ Key Ideas

BEFORE, YOU LEARNED

During the 1980s, conservatives reshaped U.S. domestic policy, and world events influenced U.S. foreign policy.

NOW YOU WILL LEARN

The United States faces great challenges in the 21st century.

▶ Vocabulary

TERMS & NAMES

George W. Bush 43rd president of the United States

9/11 hijackings 2001 terrorist plot to crash jets into New York's World Trade Center, the Pentagon, and the White House

al-Qaeda (al•KAY•duh) terrorist group of radical Islamist fundamentalists

BACKGROUND VOCABULARY

coalition alliance

insurgent one who rebels or revolts

REVIEW

baby boom a sharp increase in the U.S. birthrate following World War II

Visual Vocabulary
baby boom

The American Baby Boom

Live births (in millions)

Source: *Historical Statistics of the United States*

▶ Reading Strategy

As you read and respond to the **KEY QUESTIONS**, use a graphic organizer like the one shown to record main ideas and important details about challenges affecting America since 2000. Add ovals or start a new diagram as needed.

 See Skillbuilder Handbook, page R4.

MAIN IDEAS AND DETAILS

2000 election very close

vote recount in Florida

GRAPHIC ORGANIZERS
Go to **Interactive Review** @ ClassZone.com

America Enters a New Millennium

14.E.3 Compare the basic principles of the United States and its international interests (e.g., *territory, environment, trade, use of technology*).

15.D.3c Explain how workers can affect their productivity through training and by using tools, machinery and technology.

One American's Story

Florida voter Valerie Buford-Wells was shocked when she went to her polling place on November 7, 2000.

PRIMARY SOURCE

❝ They said that my name was not on the list [of registered voters] and I could not vote. ❞

—Valerie Buford-Wells

How could this be? She had voted in the last election and lived at the same address for 20 years. But Buford-Wells was not alone. Tens of thousands of Floridians claimed there were problems with the voting process.

Valerie Buford-Wells

A Monumental Election

▼ **KEY QUESTION** What was unique about the 2000 presidential election?

The 2000 election was one of the closest in history. The leaders in the race were Vice-President Al Gore, a Democrat, and Texas governor **George W. Bush**, a Republican, the son of former president George H. W. Bush.

Questionable Events As the day of November 7 moved into night, it became clear that the candidate who won Florida would win the most electoral votes—and the presidency. Gore led the nationwide popular vote by more than 300,000 votes. But Bush led in Florida by a few hundred votes.

The vote was so close in Florida that recounts were required. In addition, voters in some counties said that confusing ballots caused them to vote for the wrong candidate. Some voting machines did not work correctly, in some cases counting more votes in a precinct than there were residents. And thousands of voters were turned away because state officials had deleted their names from the rolls. Valerie Buford-Wells joined in a lawsuit filed by the NAACP charging that elections officials had denied her the right to vote.

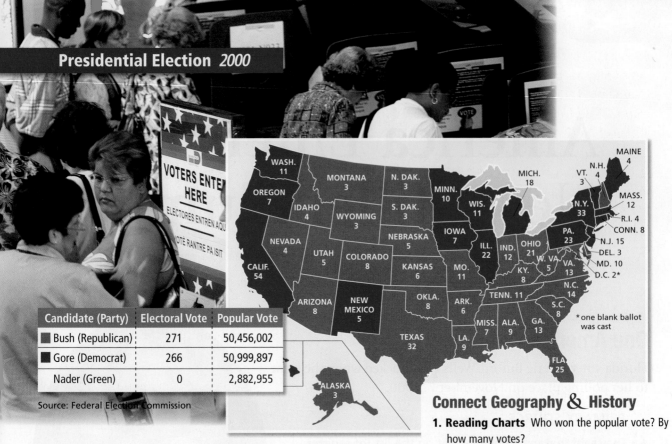

VOTERS ENTE
HERE

ELECTORES ENTREN AQU

OTE RANTRE PA ISIT

Candidate (Party)	Electoral Vote	Popular Vote
■ Bush (Republican)	271	50,456,002
■ Gore (Democrat)	266	50,999,897
Nader (Green)	0	2,882,955

Source: Federal Election Commission

* one blank ballot was cast

Connect Geography & History

1. Reading Charts Who won the popular vote? By how many votes?

2. Draw Conclusions What is the least number of states required to win the presidency?

The Gore campaign asked for manual (hand) recounts of ballots in four Florida counties. The Bush campaign sued to stop them. The battle reached the U.S. Supreme Court, which on December 12 voted five to four to stop the recounts. The majority argued that there was no way to be sure the votes would be recounted in the same way in all counties. With the recounts stopped, the original counts became official. Florida's electoral votes, and the presidency, went to Bush.

▲ **SUMMARIZE** Summarize the events of the 2000 election.

Responding to Terrorism

▼ **KEY QUESTION** How has terrorism affected U.S. policies?

Bush tried to put the election behind him and begin governing. On September 11, 2001, the president and the nation faced a new challenge.

The 9/11 Hijackings On the morning of September 11, 2001, 19 terrorists hijacked four airplanes heading from East Coast airports to California. The hijackers crashed two of the jets into the twin towers of the World Trade Center in New York City. Another was crashed into the Pentagon near Washington, D.C. The fourth jet crashed in an empty field after passengers courageously fought the hijackers. Everyone on all four planes died.

Some 3,000 people were killed in the **9/11 hijackings**. Americans could no longer view terrorism as something that happened in other countries. With the overwhelming support of Congress and the American people, the Bush administration shifted its energy and attention to fighting terrorists.

Fighting Terrorism In October 2001, the U.S. led forces from several nations in an attack on Afghanistan. The Afghan government harbored Osama bin Laden and his **al-Qaeda** terrorist network, which was believed responsible for the 9/11 attacks. In 2002, the U.S.-led **coalition**, or alliance, broke up the al-Qaeda network in Afghanistan. Bin Laden, however, remained at large.

Also in October 2001, President Bush signed into law a bill allowing the government to detain foreigners suspected of terrorism for seven days without charging them with a crime. He also created the Department of Homeland Security, a government body to coordinate anti-terrorism efforts. In addition, the federal government became more involved in aviation security.

President
George W. Bush

The United States Invades Iraq In 2003, Bush expanded the war to Iraq. Bush claimed that Iraqi president Saddam Hussein was supporting al-Qaeda and supplying terrorists with biological, chemical, and nuclear weapons, together labeled weapons of mass destruction (WMD).

The UN conducted weapons inspections of Iraq in November 2002, but Iraq did not fully cooperate. The United States and Great Britain ended diplomacy with Iraq, ordered Hussein to leave the country, and began air strikes of Iraqi military and intelligence installations. In March 2003, U.S. and British forces invaded Iraq. Within a month, Iraq's forces were defeated.

No WMD were ever found. Nevertheless, many Iraqis were overjoyed to be free from Hussein's dictatorial rule. As of December 2006, Iraq had a new republican constitution and a new government, and Hussein had been convicted and sentenced to death by an Iraq court. The U.S. military continued to occupy the country and to train police and military troops. Meanwhile, U.S. troops and unarmed Iraqi citizens faced daily attacks from **insurgents**, or rebels. By the end of 2006, more than 2,900 U.S. troops had been killed, and well over 50,000 Iraqis.

The government stepped up its involvement in airport security after the September 11 attacks.

PROBLEMS AND SOLUTIONS Tell how the United States has addressed the problem of terrorism.

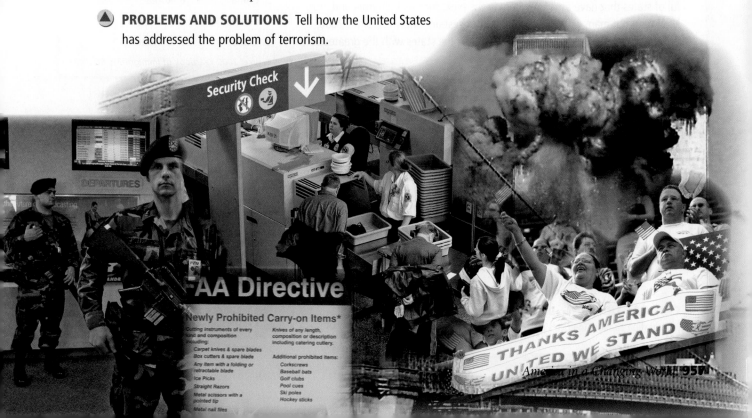

Security Check

DEPARTURES

FAA Directive

Newly Prohibited Carry-on Items*

Cutting instruments of every
kind and composition
including:
  Carpet knives & spare blades
  Box cutters & spare blade
  Any item with a folding or
  retractable blade
  Ice Picks
  Straight Razors
  Metal scissors with a
  pointed tip
  Metal nail files

Knives of any length,
composition or description
including catering cutlery.

Additional prohibited items:
  Corkscrews
  Baseball bats
  Golf clubs
  Pool cues
  Ski poles
  Hockey sticks

THANKS AMERICA
UNITED WE STAND

Challenges to Face, Strengths to Build On

🔻 **KEY QUESTION** How will America change in the years ahead?

Besides terrorist attacks and two wars, the United States faced other great challenges in the early years of this century. How the country continues to address these challenges will shape the lives of the coming generations.

America's Changing Population America is still feeling the effects of the **baby boom**, the sharp increase in the U.S. birthrate following World War II, on demographic changes. In addition, improvements in diet and health care, plus the decline of cigarette smoking, have increased Americans' life expectancy to about 77 years. The Census Bureau predicts that by 2030 the elderly will make up almost 20 percent of the population.

Countering this trend of aging is the fact that almost half of all new immigrants are under age 35. Unlike the immigrants of the 20th century, more than twice as many of today's immigrants come from Asia as from Europe, and an even greater number come from Latin America. Additionally, there are an estimated 10.5 million immigrants in the country illegally.

CONNECTING 🔗 History

IMMIGRATION TODAY

Through the 1960s, most U.S. immigrants came from Europe. This changed after the Immigration and Nationality Act of 1965 expanded immigration for Asians and Latin Americans. The act also gave priority to refugees, drawing Cubans, Vietnamese, and newcomers from war-torn countries.

Where immigrants settle has changed as well. Most still live in the handful of states that have attracted them in the past, such as California and New York, but many are now settling in the West and Midwest. Since 2000, South Dakota and Colorado have been among the states with the greatest increase in the number of immigrants.

Top Countries of Birth for Immigrants Admitted in 2005	
1. Mexico	6. Vietnam
2. India	7. Dominican Republic
3. China	8. Korea
4. Philippines	9. Colombia
5. Cuba	10. Ukraine

Source: *2005 Yearbook of Immigration Statistics*

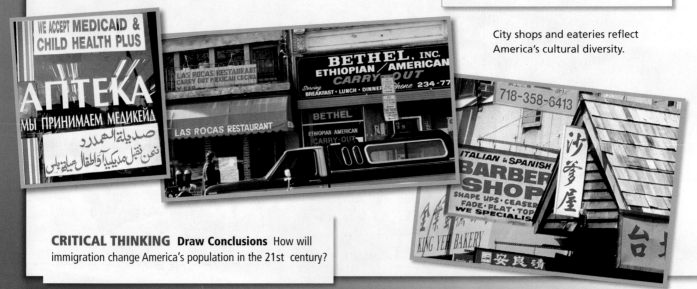

City shops and eateries reflect America's cultural diversity.

CRITICAL THINKING **Draw Conclusions** How will immigration change America's population in the 21st century?

Immigrants now make up about 12.4 percent of America's population. As earlier immigrants did, many newcomers today came seeking economic opportunity and, in some cases, political freedom. Recent immigrants have brought many talents and skills to the United States. High-tech industries, such as those located in Silicon Valley, California, have especially benefited from their contributions.

Technology and Daily Life Advances in technology have changed everyday life in America. By the end of the 20th century, a wide range of institutions, from hospitals to airports to banks, relied upon computers to perform essential tasks. Computer use also grew in homes and schools. By 2003, more than 60 percent of U.S. households had a personal computer.

The Internet has linked computer users around the world. Developed in the late 1960s by the U.S. Department of Defense, the Internet soon spread to universities. In the 1990s, it boomed in popularity among the general public. Now millions of Americans use the Internet daily, not only for work but for activities that range from shopping for groceries to getting the news.

Cellular phones have also transformed communication by allowing people to carry their phones anywhere. In 1985, about 340,000 Americans were cell phone subscribers. By 2005, that number had risen to more than 207,000,000.

A Global Economy Technology has helped to build a more global economy—one in which countries around the world are linked through business. Via the Internet, companies on different continents do business as though they are in the same city. Trade and investment among nations has expanded, and the economies of various countries are more closely linked.

Computers have changed not just industries but also the lives of individual workers. Technology has given people access to far more information than ever before, which has improved productivity in many industries. Workers share information through computer networks. Laptops and cell phones have enabled increasing numbers of people to work at home or in multiple locations.

TECHNOLOGY *of the* TIME

1969
early Internet

1969

1975
VCR (videocasette recorder)

1981
IBM personal computer introduced

laptop hits the market

1982
CD (compact disk)

1983
U.S. cellular phone system

1991
World Wide Web revealed to the public

1993
PDA (personal digital assistant)

1998
MP3 player

1999
DVD (digital versatile disk) with audio

2004
mass-market VoIP (voiceover Internet protocol) services

2006

CRITICAL THINKING **Make Decisions** Which of these inventions has had the greatest impact on your daily life?

How have America's strengths helped us to face the challenges of the past four decades?

CHALLENGES TO FACE		STRENGTHS TO BUILD ON
• Huge, growing national debt—over $8.5 trillion as of August 2006; increasing by $1.66 billion each day • How to compete with cheap labor abroad, decrease reliance on imports, and preserve jobs	ECONOMY	• Participation in free trade agreements (NAFTA, WTO) • Leadership in Group of Eight economic summit • History of technical and social innovation
• Dependence on imported oil • Dependence on automobiles • President Bush rejects world agreement on preventing global warming (Kyoto protocol)	ENERGY AND ENVIRONMENT	• Many natural resources including minerals and energy sources • EPA has authority to protect the environment
• 2000 and 2004 national elections marred by charges of fraud • Hostility and mistrust between "liberals" and "conservatives"	GOVERNMENT AND POLITICS	• Representative government with popular elections • Government based on a written Constitution and Bill of Rights
• Terrorists threaten America and American interests at home and abroad • Nuclear weapons in unfriendly nations • Ongoing war in Iraq	INTERNATIONAL AFFAIRS	• Over 860 military installations in 46 foreign countries • World's largest military power • World's largest economy • Permanent member of UN Security Council
• Aging "baby boom" population • Health care costs growing faster than inflation; over 46 million without health insurance • About half a million people each year immigrate illegally	SOCIETY	• Free, public education available nationwide • Acknowledged world leader in higher education • Attractive to immigrants—about 1 million annually

CRITICAL THINKING Form and Support Opinions What do you think is America's greatest strength today? Why?

As NAFTA critics had warned, however, the global economy caused problems for some U.S. workers. To cut costs, some businesses moved their operations to countries where wages are lower. Yet America continues to attract immigrants looking for jobs, freedom, and a better life.

The New America Today America is a very different nation from the one founded in 1776. Democratic rights have expanded to include more and more people. Immigration, entrepreneurship, technology, and social reform have shaped a nation that the Founders would barely recognize. Yet the principles they relied on—equal rights, liberty, republicanism, individual responsibility, and freedom of conscience—continue to guide our nation's history and form the American identity.

Now the responsibility for interpreting and preserving these values and for recreating America is becoming yours. What will you do with it?

 PREDICT Explain how you think America will change in the upcoming decades.

Illinois Learning Standards *Review*

 ONLINE QUIZ
For test practice, go to
Interactive Review @ ClassZone.com

TERMS & NAMES

1. Explain the importance of
- George W. Bush
- al-Qaeda
- 9/11 hijackings

USING YOUR READING NOTES

2. Main Ideas and Details Complete the diagram you started at the beginning of this section.

KEY IDEAS

3. Why did the United States invade Iraq?

4. In what parts of the world were most recent U.S. immigrants born?

CRITICAL THINKING

5. Main Ideas and Details In the 2000 election, what were some of the controversial aspects of the voting process in Florida?

6. Connect Economics and History What problems has the global economy caused for U.S. workers?

7. Form and Support Opinions What do you think is America's greatest challenge today? Why?

8. Writing Essay Write a short essay that predicts the effects of new technology on American life 20 years from now. Describe how businesses, schools, and communications might change.

American Spirit

TEENS MAKING HISTORY

Millions of teen volunteers have made a difference in their communities—and the world. Here are a few ways that American teens have used their time to help put ideas into action.

MAKING CONNECTIONS

(right) A teen volunteer for Hands On Miami connects with an elder in her community. The Florida service organization includes a special division led and staffed by volunteers aged 13 to 17.

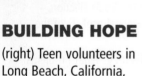

TAKING CHARGE

(left) Not all volunteers work through an organization; some launch their own projects. After Hurricane Katrina, a teenager in Lexington, Kentucky, helped lead a home-grown fundraising effort to support the Red Cross.

BUILDING HOPE

(right) Teen volunteers in Long Beach, California, lend a hand with Habitat for Humanity. The international organization, which constructs affordable homes, has its own youth program. Habitat believes that "young people are today's builders and tomorrow's leaders."

Activity

Peer Interview

1 Choose a cause that interests you. Use the Internet to find a local or national organization where volunteers support this cause.

2 Take notes about the organization's goals and how volunteers help to advance them.

3 Find a partner and interview each other about the organizations you researched.

Chapter Summary

① Key Idea
President Richard M. Nixon
governed a divided nation and
faced a political scandal that
forced him to resign.

② Key Idea
During the 1980s, conservatives
reshaped U.S. domestic policy,
and world events influenced U.S.
foreign policy.

③ Key Idea
The United States faces great
challenges in the 21st century.

⇨ For detailed Review and Study Notes
go to **Interactive Review**
@ ClassZone.com

Name Game

Use the Terms & Names list to complete each
sentence online or on your own paper.

1. I am the 43rd president
of the United States. ___   `George W. Bush` 🖑

2. In the 1970s, nations in this group cut oil shipments
to the United States. ___

3. Under the ___ , Egypt and Israel ended their conflict.

4. This guaranteed certain benefits to citizens. ___

5. In 1977, I proposed a national energy program. ___

6. The U.S. funded Nicaraguan rebels in the ___ .

7. This agreement sought to increase trade among
Canada, Mexico, and the United States. ___

8. This was a 2001 terrorist plot to crash jets into New
York's World Trade Center. ___

9. This is a region in the republic of Serbia. ___

10. During the ___ , 39 nations fought to free Kuwait.

A. OPEC
B. insurgent
C. entitlement
D. Camp David
Accords
E. George W. Bush
F. Iran-Contra affair
G. al-Qaeda
H. Persian Gulf War
I. NAFTA
J. entitlements
K. 9/11 hijackings
L. Kosovo
M. Jimmy Carter

Activities

CROSSWORD PUZZLE

Complete the online crossword
puzzle to show what you know about
America in a changing world.

ACROSS
1. Katharine ___ was
publisher of the
Washington Post
at the time Nixon
resigned.

FLIPCARD

Use the online flipcards to quiz
yourself on the terms and names
introduced in this chapter.

This scandal led to
Nixon's resignation

ANSWER
Watergate

Washington Star-News
NIGHT FINAL
LATE STOCKS/SPORTS
ON TV AT 9 TONIGHT
Nixon Resigning

Washington Star-News
ON TV AT 9 TONIGHT
Nixon Resign

VOCABULARY

Match the president with the event that took place during his term in office.

1. George H. W. Bush
2. George W. Bush
3. Jimmy Carter
4. Bill Clinton
5. Richard M. Nixon
6. Ronald Reagan

A. signing of NAFTA
B. Camp David Accords
C. Iran-Contra Affair
D. Watergate scandal
E. 9/11 hijackings
F. Persian Gulf War

7. **List the following presidents in the order they held office. Then circle the ones who were elected to a second term.**

George H. W. Bush
George W. Bush
Jimmy Carter
Bill Clinton
Gerald Ford
Richard M. Nixon
Ronald Reagan

President Carter

KEY IDEAS

1 **Nixon, Watergate, and Years of Doubt**
(pages 936–943)

8. What event was at the heart of the Watergate scandal?

9. What were Carter's successes in foreign relations?

2 **Conservatives Reshape Politics**
(pages 946–953)

10. What were President Reagan's beliefs about communism?

11. How successful was President Clinton in working with Congress? Why?

3 **America Enters a New Millennium**
(pages 954–961)

12. What role did the Supreme Court play in deciding the 2000 election?

13. What event made terrorism a major issue in America?

CRITICAL THINKING

14. **Problems and Solutions** What problems did the nation face when Nixon took office, and how did he seek to address them?

15. **Sequence Events** What events led to the breakup of the Soviet Union?

16. **Summarize** What caused the violence in Kosovo, and what was the outcome?

17. **Causes and Effects** Make a chart like the one shown. Use it to record the effects of the September 11 attacks.

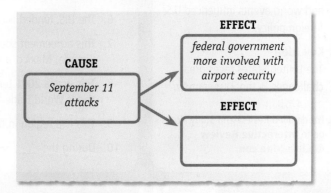

18. **Causes and Effects** Why did George W. Bush win the 2000 election even though he had fewer popular votes than Gore?

19. **Main Ideas and Details** What factors have contributed to a projected increase in America's elderly population?

20. **Analyze Primary Sources** This 1973 political cartoon shows an audiotape crushing the White House. Identify the event the cartoon represents and explain the significance of the audiotape.

✓ TEST PRACTICE

• **Online Test Practice** @ ClassZone.com
• **Test-Taking Strategies & Practice** at the front of this book

MULTIPLE CHOICE

Use the photograph and your knowledge of U.S. history to answer question 1.

1. This 2002 photograph shows U.S. troops. Where are they?

   A. Afghanistan   **C.** Kosovo

   B. Iraq   **D.** Kuwait

Use the quotation and your knowledge of U.S. history to answer question 2.

SECONDARY SOURCE

" There is no other country on Earth that is configured like ours. Every other nation is there because of race, religion, language, ethnicity, or geography. We are here only because we agreed to subscribe to the words on four pieces of paper—the U.S. Constitution. "

—Ken Burns, quoted in *The West*

2. According to the passage, what is unique about the way the United States was founded?

   A. It is an ethnically diverse nation.

   B. Americans share no single religious creed.

   C. It was founded on the ideals of its Constitution.

   D. Americans believe strongly in democracy and freedom.

YOU BE THE HISTORIAN

21. **Evaluate** Do you think that Ford made a good decision in pardoning Nixon? Why?

22. **WHAT IF?** Suppose the hostages in Iran had been released before the 1980 presidential campaign. How might this have affected the outcome of the election?

23. **Form and Support Opinions** What do you think was the stronger force shaping U.S. politics from 1981 to 2006: economics or foreign affairs? Why?

24. **Citizenship** Think about the issues related to energy and the environment that America faces today. What actions do you think ordinary citizens can take to help their nation confront these challenges?

25. **Connect** *to* **Today** What traditions and ideals do all Americans share, regardless of whether they were born in the United States or another nation?

26. **Draw Conclusions** How has the United States become more democratic since its founding in 1776?

 Answer the
ESSENTIAL QUESTION
How have America's strengths helped us to face the challenges of the past four decades?

Written Response Write a two- to three-paragraph response to the Essential Question. Be sure to consider the key ideas of each section. Use the Response Rubric below to guide your thinking and writing.

Response Rubric
A strong response will

• identify America's strengths

• summarize economic and political challenges America has faced, at home and abroad

• discuss some of the ways recent presidents have sought to address the challenges facing the nation

Reference Section

American HISTORY

Table of Contents

Reading and Critical Thinking

Reading Maps, Graphs, and Other Visuals

Research, Writing, and Presentation Skills

Using the Internet

1.1 Taking Notes with Graphic Organizers

Defining the Skill

When you **take notes**, you write down the important ideas and details of a paragraph, passage, or chapter. A chart or an outline can help you organize your notes to use in the future.

Applying the Skill

The following passage describes President Washington's cabinet. Use the strategies listed below to help you take notes on the passage.

How to Take and Organize Notes

Strategy 1 Look at the title to find the main topic of the passage.

Strategy 2 Identify the main ideas and details of the passage. Then summarize the main idea and details in your notes.

Strategy 3 Identify key terms and define them. The term *cabinet* is shown in boldface type and highlighted; both techniques signal that it is a key term.

Strategy 4 In your notes, use abbreviations to save time and space. You can abbreviate words such as *department (dept.)*, *secretary (sec.)*, *United States (U.S.)*, and *president (pres.)* to save time and space.

---

1 WASHINGTON'S CABINET

2 The Constitution gave Congress the task of creating departments to help the president lead the nation. The **2** president had the power to appoint the heads of these departments, which became his **3** **cabinet**.

Congress created three departments. Washington chose talented people to run them. **2** For secretary of war, he picked Henry Knox, a trusted general during the Revolution. **2** For secretary of state, Washington chose Thomas Jefferson. He had been serving as ambassador to France. The State Department oversaw U.S. foreign relations. For secretary of the treasury, Washington turned to the brilliant **2** Alexander Hamilton.

Make a Chart

Making a chart can help you take notes on a passage. The chart below contains notes from the passage you just read.

Item	Notes
1. **3** cabinet	heads of **4** depts; **4** pres. appoints heads
a. War Dept.	Henry Knox; **4** sec. of war; former Revolutionary War general
b. State Dept.	Thomas Jefferson; sec. of state; oversees relations between **4** U.S. and other countries
c. Treasury Dept.	Alexander Hamilton; sec. of the treasurey

Practicing the Skill

Turn to Chapter 3, Section 3, "The Southern Colonies." Read "The Region of the South" on page 81, and use a graphic organizer to take notes on the passage.

1.2 Summarizing

Defining the Skill

When you **summarize**, you restate a paragraph, passage, or chapter in fewer words. You include only the main ideas and most important details. It is important to use your own words when summarizing.

Applying the Skill

The passage below tells about Harriet Tubman, a prominent member of the Underground Railroad. She helped runaway slaves to freedom. Use the strategies listed below to help you summarize the passage.

How to Summarize

Strategy ❶ Look for topic sentences stating the main idea. These are often at the beginning of a section or paragraph. Briefly restate each main idea—in your own words.

Strategy ❷ Include key facts and any numbers, dates, amounts, or percentages from the text.

Strategy ❸ After writing your summary, review it to see that you have included only the most important details.

HARRIET TUBMAN

❶ One of the most famous conductors on the Underground Railroad was Harriet Tubman. ❷ Born into slavery in Maryland, the 13-year-old Tubman once tried to save another slave from punishment. The angry overseer fractured Tubman's skull with a two-pound weight. She suffered fainting spells for the rest of her life but did not let that stop her from working for freedom. When she was 25, Tubman learned that her owner was about to sell her. Instead, ❷ she escaped.

After her escape, ❷ Harriet Tubman made 19 dangerous journeys to free enslaved persons. The tiny woman carried a pistol to frighten off slave hunters and medicine to quiet crying babies. Her enemies offered $40,000 for her capture, but ❷ no one caught her. "I never run my train off the track and I never lost a passenger," she proudly declared. Among the people she saved were her parents.

Write a Summary

You can write your summary in a paragraph. The paragraph at right summarizes the passage you just read.

❸ Harriet Tubman was one of the most famous conductors on the Underground Railroad. She had been a slave, but she escaped. She later made 19 dangerous journeys to free other slaves. She was never captured.

Practicing the Skill

Turn to Chapter 6, Section 2, "Colonial Resistance Grows." Read "The Boston Massacre" on pages 163–164, and write a paragraph summarizing the passage.

1.3 Finding Main Ideas

Defining the Skill

The **main idea** is a statement that summarizes the main point of a speech, an article, a section of a book, or a paragraph. Main ideas can be stated or unstated. The main idea of a paragraph is often stated in the first or last sentence. If it is the first sentence, it is followed by sentences that support that main idea. If it is the last sentence, the details build up to the main idea. To find an unstated idea, you must use the details of the paragraph as clues.

Applying the Skill

The following paragraph describes the role of women in the American Revolution. Use the strategies listed below to help you identify the main idea.

How to Find the Main Idea

Strategy ① Identify what you think may be the stated main idea. Check the first and last sentences of the paragraph to see if either could be the stated main idea.

Strategy ② Identify details that support that idea. Some details explain the main idea. Others give examples of what is stated in the main idea.

WOMEN IN THE REVOLUTION

① Many women tried to help the army. Martha Washington and other wives followed their husbands to army camps. ② The wives cooked, did laundry, and nursed sick or wounded soldiers. ② A few women even helped to fight. ② Mary Hays earned the nickname "Molly Pitcher" by carrying water to tired soldiers during a battle. ② Deborah Sampson dressed as a man, enlisted, and fought in several engagements.

Make a Chart

Making a chart can help you identify the main idea and details in a passage or paragraph. The chart below identifies the main idea and details in the paragraph you just read.

Main Idea: Women helped the army during the Revolution.

Detail: They cooked and did laundry
Detail: They nursed the wounded and sick soldiers
Detail: They helped to fight.
Detail: One woman, Molly Pitcher, carried water to soldiers during battles.

Practicing the Skill

Turn to Chapter 5, Section 2, "Roots of American Democracy." Read "Parliament and Colonial Government" on page 139, and create a chart that identifies the main idea and the supporting details.

1.4 Sequencing Events

Defining the Skill

Sequence is the order in which events follow one another. By being able to follow the sequence of events through history, you can get an accurate sense of the relationships among events.

Applying the Skill

The following passage describes the sequence of events involved in Britain's plan to capture the Hudson River valley during the American Revolution. Use the strategies listed below to help you follow the sequence of events.

How to Find the Sequence of Events

Strategy ① Look for specific dates provided in the text. If several months within a year are included, the year is usually not repeated.

Strategy ② Look for clues about time that allow you to order events according to sequence. Words such as *day*, *week*, *month*, or *year* may help to sequence the events.

> **BRITAIN'S STRATEGY**
>
> Burgoyne captured Fort Ticonderoga in ① July 1777. From there, it was 25 miles to the Hudson River, which ran to Albany. ② Burgoyne took three weeks to reach the Hudson. On ① August 3, Burgoyne received a message from Howe. He would not be coming north, Howe wrote, because he had decided to invade Pennsylvania to try to capture Philadelphia and General Washington. "Success be ever with you," Howe's message said. But General Burgoyne needed Howe's soldiers, not his good wishes. Howe did invade Pennsylvania. In ① September 1777, he defeated —but did not capture—Washington at the Battle of Brandywine.

Make a Time Line

Making a time line can help you sequence events. The time line below shows the sequence of events in the passage you just read.

July 1777: Burgoyne captures Fort Ticonderoga.

August 3, 1777: Howe writes that he will not join Burgoyne.

Three weeks after the capture of Fort Ticonderoga: Burgoyne reaches the Hudson.

September 1777: Howe defeats Washington at Brandywine.

Practicing the Skill

Turn to Chapter 8, Section 1, "The Confederation Era." Read "The Articles Are Ratified" on page 237, and make a time line showing the sequence of events in that passage.

1.5 Categorizing

Defining the Skill

To **categorize** is to sort people, objects, ideas, or other information into groups, called categories. Historians categorize information to help them identify and understand patterns in historical events.

Applying the Skill

The following passage contains information about the reasons people went west during the mid-1800s. Use the strategies listed below to help you categorize information.

How to Categorize

Strategy ① First, decide what kind of information needs to be categorized. Decide what the passage is about and how that information can be sorted into categories. For example, find the different motives people had for moving west.

Strategy ② Then find out what the categories will be. To find why many different groups of people moved west, look for clue words such as *some*, *other*, and *another*.

Strategy ③ Once you have chosen the categories, sort information into them. Of the people who went west, which ones had which motives?

THE LURE OF THE WEST

① People had many different motives for going west. ② One motive was to make money. ② *Some* people called speculators bought huge areas of land and made great profits by selling it to thousands of settlers. ② *Other* settlers included farmers who dreamed of owning their own farms in the West because land was difficult to acquire in the East. ② *Another* group to move west was merchants. They hoped to earn money by selling items that farmers needed. Finally, ② *some* people went west for religious reasons. These people included ② missionaries, who wanted to convert the Native Americans to Christianity, and Mormons, who wanted a place where they could practice their faith without interference.

Make a Chart

Making a chart can help you categorize information. You should have as many columns as you have categories. The chart below shows how the information from the passage you just read can be categorized.

③

Motives	Money	Land	Religion
Groups	• speculators • merchants	• farmers	• missionaries • Mormons

Practicing the Skill

Turn to Chapter 14, Section 3, "Reforming American Society." Read "Social Reform" on page 460, and make a chart in which you categorize the changes happening in elementary, high school, and college education.

1.6 Analyzing Causes and Effects

Defining the Skill

A **cause** is an action in history that makes something happen. An **effect** is the historical event that is the result of the cause. A single event may have several causes. It is also possible for one cause to result in several effects. Historians identify cause-and-effect relationships to help them understand why historical events took place.

Applying the Skill

The following paragraph describes events that caused changes in Puritan New England. Use the strategies listed below to help you identify the cause-and-effect relationships.

How to Analyze Causes and Recognize Effects

Strategy ❶ Ask why an action took place. Ask yourself a question about the title and topic sentence, such as, "What caused changes in Puritan society?"

Strategy ❷ Look for effects. Ask yourself, "What happened?" (the effect). Then ask, "Why did it happen?" (the cause). For example, What caused the decline of Puritan religion in New England?

Strategy ❸ Look for clue words that signal causes, such as *cause* and *led to*.

Strategy ❹ One way to practice recognizing effects is to make predictions about the consequences that will result from particular actions. Then, as you read, look to see if your predictions were accurate.

---

❶ **CHANGES IN PURITAN SOCIETY**

❶ The early 1700s saw many changes in New England society. ❷ One of the most important changes was the gradual decline of the Puritan religion in New England. There were a number of reasons for that decline.

❸ One *cause* of this decline was the increasing competition from other religious groups. Baptists and Anglicans established churches in Massachusetts and Connecticut, where Puritans had once been the most powerful group. ❸ Political changes also *led to* a weakening of the Puritan community. In 1691, a new royal charter for Massachusetts granted the vote based on property ownership instead of church membership.

Make a Diagram

Using a diagram can help you understand causes and effects. The diagram below shows two causes and an effect for the passage you just read.

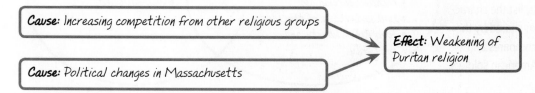

Cause: Increasing competition from other religious groups → **Effect:** Weakening of Puritan religion

Cause: Political changes in Massachusetts →

Practicing the Skill

Turn to Chapter 4, Section 2, "The Southern Colonies: Plantations and Slavery." Read "Expansion of Plantations Brings Resistance" on pages 106–107, and make a diagram about the causes and effects of slave resistance.

1.7 Comparing and Contrasting

Defining the Skill

Comparing means looking at the similarities and differences between two or more things. **Contrasting** means examining only the differences between them. Historians compare and contrast events, personalities, behaviors, beliefs, and situations in order to understand them.

Applying the Skill

The following paragraph describes the American and British troops during the Revolutionary War. Use the strategies listed below to help you compare and contrast these two armies.

How to Compare and Contrast

Strategy ① Look for two aspects of the subject that may be compared and contrasted. This passage compares the British and American troops to show why the Americans won the war.

Strategy ② To contrast, look for clue words that show how two things differ. Clue words include *by contrast*, *however*, *except*, and *yet*.

Strategy ③ To find similarities, look for clue words indicating that two things are alike. Clue words include *both*, *like*, *as*, and *similarly*.

> **WHY THE AMERICANS WON**
>
> ① By their persistence, the Americans defeated the British even though they faced many obstacles. The Americans lacked training and experience. They were often short of supplies and weapons. ② *By contrast*, the British forces ranked among the best trained in the world. They were experienced and well-supplied professional soldiers. ② *Yet*, the Americans also had advantages that enabled them to win. These advantages over the British were better leadership, foreign aid, a knowledge of the land, and motivation. Although ③ *both* the British and the Americans were fighting for their lives, ② the Americans were also fighting for their property and their dream of liberty.

Make a Venn Diagram

Making a Venn diagram will help you identify similarities and differences between two things. In the overlapping area, list characteristics shared by both subjects. Then, in the separate ovals, list the characteristics of each subject not shared by the other. This Venn diagram compares and contrasts the British and American soldiers.

American Soldiers:
- lacked experience and training
- short of supplies and weapons
- had better leadership
- received foreign aid
- had knowledge of the land
- fought for liberty and property

Both: fought for their lives

British Soldiers:
- best trained in the world
- experienced
- well-supplied

Practicing the Skill

Turn to Chapter 5, Section 1, "Early American Culture." Read "Life of the Young" on pages 129–130, and make a Venn diagram showing the similarities and differences between the roles of boys and girls in colonial America.

1.8 Identifying Problems and Solutions

Defining the Skill

Identifying problems means finding and understanding the difficulties faced by a particular group of people during a certain time. **Solutions** are the actions people took to remedy those problems. By studying the solutions to problems in the past, you can learn ways to solve problems today.

Applying the Skill

The following paragraph describes problems that the Constitutional Convention faced on the issues of taxation, representation, and slavery. Use the strategies listed below to help you identify the Founders' solutions to these problems.

How to Identify Problems and Solutions

**Strategy ① Look for the diffi-
culties, or problems, people faced.**

**Strategy ② Consider how
the problem affected people
with different points of view.
For example, the main problem
described here was how to count
the population of each state.**

**Strategy ③ Look for solutions
people tried to deal with each
problem. Think about whether
the solution was a good one for
people with differing points of
view.**

> **SLAVERY AND THE CONSTITUTION**
>
> Because the House of Representatives would have members based on the population of each state, ① the delegates had to decide who would be counted in that population. The Southern states had many more slaves than the Northern states. ② Southerners wanted the slaves to be counted as part of the general population for representation but not for taxation. ② Northerners argued that slaves were not citizens and should not be counted for representation but should be counted for taxation. ③ The delegates decided that three-fifths of the slave population would be counted for both purposes: representation and taxation.

Make a Chart

Making a chart will help you identify and organize information about problems and solutions. The chart below shows problems and solutions included in the passage you just read.

① Problem	② Differing Points of View	③ Solution
Northerners and Southerners couldn't agree on how to count population because of slavery in the South.	*Southerners wanted slaves counted for representation but not for taxation. Northerners wanted slaves counted for taxation but not for representation.*	*Delegates decided that three-fifths of the slave population should be counted.*

Practicing the Skill

Turn to Chapter 8, Section 2, "Creating the Constitution." Read "Some Challenges of the Convention" on pages 245–246, and make a chart that details the problems faced by the delegates at the Constitutional Convention and the solutions they agreed on.

1.9 Making Inferences

Defining the Skill

Inferences are ideas that the author has not directly stated. **Making inferences** involves reading between the lines to interpret the information you read. You can make inferences by studying what is stated and using your common sense and previous knowledge.

Applying the Skill

The passage below describes the strengths and weaknesses of the North and the South as the Civil War began. Use the strategies listed below to help you make inferences from the passage.

How to Make Inferences

Strategy ❶ Read to find statements of facts and ideas. Knowing the facts will give you a good basis for making inferences.

Strategy ❷ Use your knowledge, logic, and common sense to make inferences that are based on facts. Ask yourself, "What does the author want me to understand?" For example, from the facts about population, you can make the inference that the North would have a larger army than the South. See other inferences in the chart below.

ADVANTAGES OF THE NORTH AND THE SOUTH

The North had more people and resources than the South. ❶ The North had about 22 million people. ❶ The South had roughly 9 million, of whom about 3.5 million were slaves. In addition, ❶ the North had more than 80 percent of the nation's factories and almost all of the shipyards and naval power. The South had some advantages, too: ❶ able generals, such as Robert E. Lee, ❶ and the advantage of fighting a defensive war. Soldiers defending their homes have more will to fight than invaders do.

Make a Chart

Making a chart will help you organize information and make logical inferences. The chart below organizes information from the passage you just read.

❶ Stated Facts and Ideas	❷ Inferences
The North had about 22 million people. The Confederacy had about 9 million.	The North would have a larger army than the South.
The North had more factories, naval power, and shipyards.	The North could provide more weapons, ammunition, and ships for the war.
The Confederacy had excellent generals.	The Confederacy had better generals, which would help it overcome other disadvantages.
The Confederacy was fighting a defensive war	Confederate soldiers would fight harder because they were defending their homes and families.

Practicing the Skill

Turn to Chapter 12, Section 1, "Jacksonian Democracy and States' Rights." Read "Voting Rights Expand" on pages 396–397, and use a chart like the one above to make inferences about Jacksonian democracy.

1.10 Making Generalizations

Defining the Skill

To **make generalizations** means to make broad judgments based on information. When you make generalizations, you should gather information from several sources.

Applying the Skill

The following three passages contain different views on George Washington. Use the strategies listed below to make a generalization about these views.

How to Make Generalizations

Strategy 1 Look for information that the sources have in common. These three sources all discuss George Washington's ability as a military leader.

Strategy 2 Form a generalization that describes Washington in a way that all three sources would agree with. State your generalization in a sentence.

> ### WASHINGTON'S LEADERSHIP
>
> **1** Washington learned from his mistakes. After early defeats, he developed the strategy of dragging out the war to wear down the British. **1** Despite difficulties, he never gave up.
>
> *—Creating America*
>
> **1** [Washington] was no military genius. . . . But he was a great war leader. Creating an army out of unpromising material, he kept it in being against great odds.
>
> *—The Limits of Liberty*
>
> **1** [Washington] certainly deserves some merit as a general, that he . . . can keep General Howe dancing from one town to another for two years together, with such an army as he has.
>
> *—The Journal of Nicholas Cresswell, July 13, 1777*

Make a Chart

Using a chart can help you make generalizations. The chart below shows how the information you just read can be used to generalize about people's views of Washington.

1 *Washington kept the army together.*

1 *Washington kept the enemy guessing.*

2 **Generalization:** *Although Washington made mistakes, he was a good military leader.*

1 *Washington learned from his mistakes.*

Practicing the Skill

Turn to Chapter 16, Section 1, "War Erupts." Read "Planning Strategies" on page 513. Also read "Comparing North and South" on page 514. Then, use a chart like the one above to make generalizations about the two sides on the eve of the Civil War.

1.11 Drawing Conclusions

Defining the Skill

Drawing conclusions means analyzing what you have read and forming an opinion about its meaning. To draw conclusions, look at the facts and then use your own common sense and experience to decide what the facts mean.

Applying the Skill

The following passage presents information about the Intolerable Acts and the colonists' reactions to them. Use the strategies listed below to help you draw conclusions about those acts.

How to Draw Conclusions

Strategy 1 Read carefully to identify and understand all the facts, or statements, that can be proven true.

Strategy 2 List the facts in a diagram and review them. Use your own experiences and common sense to understand how the facts relate to each other.

Strategy 3 After reviewing the facts, write down the conclusion you have drawn about them.

THE INTOLERABLE ACTS

1 In 1774, Parliament passed a series of laws to punish the Massachusetts colony and serve as a warning to other colonies.

1 These laws were so harsh that colonists called them the **Intolerable Acts**. One of the acts closed the port of Boston. Others banned committees of correspondence and allowed Britain to house troops wherever necessary.

In 1773, Sam Adams had written, "I wish we could arouse the continent." **1** The Intolerable Acts answered his wish. Other colonies immediately offered Massachusetts their support.

Make a Diagram

Making a diagram can help you draw conclusions. The diagram below shows how to organize facts and inferences to draw a conclusion about the passage you just read.

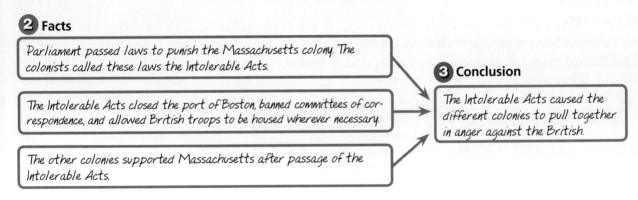

2 Facts

Parliament passed laws to punish the Massachusetts colony. The colonists called these laws the Intolerable Acts.

The Intolerable Acts closed the port of Boston, banned committees of correspondence, and allowed British troops to be housed wherever necessary.

The other colonies supported Massachusetts after passage of the Intolerable Acts.

3 Conclusion

The Intolerable Acts caused the different colonies to pull together in anger against the British.

Practicing the Skill

Turn to Chapter 3, Section 2, "New England Colonies." Read "Puritans Persecute Quakers" on page 71, and use the diagram above as a model to draw conclusions about Puritans' beliefs.

1.12 Making Decisions

Defining the Skill

Making decisions involves choosing between two or more options or courses of action. In most cases, decisions have consequences, or results. Sometimes decisions may lead to new problems. By understanding how historical figures made decisions, you can learn how to improve your decision-making skills.

Applying the Skill

The following passage describes Lincoln's decisions regarding federal forts after the Southern states seceded. Use the strategies listed below to help you analyze his decisions.

How to Make Decisions

Strategy 1 Identify a decision that needs to be made. Think about what factors make the decision difficult.

Strategy 2 Identify possible consequences of the decision. Remember that there can be more than one consequence to a decision.

Strategy 3 Identify the decision that was made.

Strategy 4 Identify actual consequences that resulted from the decision.

> ### FIRST SHOTS AT FORT SUMTER
>
> **1** Lincoln had to decide what to do about the forts in the South that remained under federal control. A Union garrison still held Fort Sumter, but it was running out of supplies. **2** If Lincoln supplied the garrison, he risked war. **2** If he withdrew the garrison, he would be giving in to the rebels. **3** Lincoln informed South Carolina that he was sending supply ships to Fort Sumter. **4** Confederate leaders decided to prevent the federal government from holding on to the fort by attacking before the supply ships arrived. No one was killed, but **4** the South's attack on Fort Sumter signaled the beginning of the Civil War.

Make a Flow Chart

A flow chart can help you identify the process of making a decision. The flow chart below shows the decision-making process in the passage you just read.

1 *Decision to Be Made:* What should Lincoln do about the federal forts within the borders of the seceded states? Should Lincoln supply the garrison or withdraw it?

2 *Possible Consequences:* Supply the garrison and risk war.

2 *Possible Consequences:* Withdraw the garrison and give in to the rebels.

3 *Decision Made:* Supply the garrison.

4 *Actual Consequence:* The Confederates attacked the fort. This attack began the Civil War.

Practicing the Skill

Turn to Chapter 12, Section 2, "Jackson's Policy Toward Native Americans." Read "Native American Resistance" on page 407, and make a flow chart to identify a decision and its consequences described in that section.

1.13 Evaluating

Defining the Skill

To **evaluate** is to make a judgment about something. Historians evaluate the actions of people in history. One way to do this is to examine both the positives and negatives of a historical action, then decide which is stronger—the positive or the negative.

Applying the Skill

The following passage describes Susan B. Anthony's fight for women's rights. Use the strategies listed below to evaluate how successful she was.

How to Evaluate

Strategy ① Before you evaluate a person's actions, first determine what that person was trying to accomplish.

Strategy ② Look for statements that show the positive, or successful, results of Anthony's actions. Did she achieve her goals?

Strategy ③ Also look for statements that show the negative, or unsuccessful, results of her actions. Did she fail to achieve something she tried to do?

Strategy ④ Write an overall evaluation of the person's actions.

SUSAN B. ANTHONY

① Susan B. Anthony was a skilled organizer who fought for women's rights. **②** She successfully built the women's movement into a national organization. An outspoken advocate for equal pay for men and women, she called for laws that would give married women the right to keep their own property and wages. **②** Mississippi passed the first such law in 1839. New York passed a property law in 1848 and a wages law in 1860. **③** Anthony also wanted to win the vote for women but failed to convince lawmakers to pass this reform in her lifetime. This reform did go through in 1920, 14 years after her death.

Make a Diagram for Evaluating

Using a diagram can help you evaluate a person's actions and decisions. The diagram below shows how the information from the passage you just read can be organized.

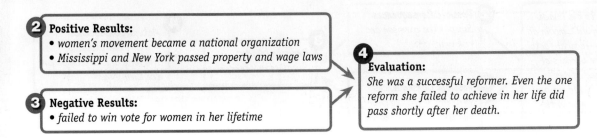

② Positive Results:
• *women's movement became a national organization*
• *Mississippi and New York passed property and wage laws*

③ Negative Results:
• *failed to win vote for women in her lifetime*

④ Evaluation:
She was a successful reformer. Even the one reform she failed to achieve in her life did pass shortly after her death.

Practicing the Skill

Turn to Chapter 2, Section 3, "The Spanish and Native Americans." Read "The Columbian Exchange" on pages 44–45, and make a diagram in which you evaluate whether the Columbian Exchange had mainly a positive or negative impact on the world.

1.14 Analyzing Point of View

Defining the Skill

Analyzing point of view means looking closely at a person's arguments to understand the reasons behind that person's beliefs. The goal of analyzing a point of view is to understand a historical figure's thoughts, opinions, and biases about a topic.

Applying the Skill

The following passage describes the Panic of 1837 and two politicians' points of view about it. Use the strategies listed below to help you analyze their points of view.

How to Analyze Point of View

Strategy ❶ Look for statements that show you a person's view on an issue. Van Buren said he believed the economy would improve if he took no action. Clay thought the government should do something.

Strategy ❷ Use information about people to validate them as sources and understand their differences. What do you know about Clay and Van Buren that might explain their biases and disagreements?

Strategy ❸ Write a summary that explains why different people took different positions on the issue.

THE PANIC OF 1837

The Panic of 1837 caused severe hardship. People had little money, so manufacturers had few customers for their goods. Almost 90 percent of factories in the East closed. Jobless workers could not afford food or rent. Many people went hungry. ❶ Whig senator Henry Clay wanted the government to do something to help the people. ❶ President Van Buren, a Democrat, disagreed. He believed that the economy would improve if left alone. He argued that "the less government interferes with private pursuits the better for the general prosperity." Many Americans blamed Van Buren for the Panic, though he had taken office only weeks before it started.

Make a Diagram

Using a diagram can help you analyze points of view. The diagram below analyzes the views of Clay and Van Buren in the passage you just read.

❷ **Clay**
• *Whig*
• *Argues government should help the people*

❷ **Van Buren**
• *Democrat*
• *Argues the economy should be left alone to fix itself*

❸ *Clay is attacking Van Buren because he's in a different party. He does not want Van Buren reelected in 1840.*

Practicing the Skill

Turn to the Reading Primary Sources on pages 255 and 256. Read the selections by James Madison and George Mason. Use their language, information from other sources, and information about each man to validate them as sources. Then make a diagram to analyze their different points of view on the Constitution.

1.15 Distinguishing Fact from Opinion

Defining the Skill

Facts are events, dates, statistics, or statements that can be proved to be true. **Opinions** are the judgments, beliefs, and feelings of a writer or speaker. By distinguishing fact from opinion, you will be able to think critically when a person is trying to influence your own opinion.

Applying the Skill

The following passage tells about the Virginia Plan for legislative representation offered at the Constitutional Convention of 1787. Use the strategies listed below to help you distinguish facts from opinions.

How to Recognize Facts and Opinions

**Strategy ① Look for specific information that can be proved or checked for accuracy.

**Strategy ② Look for assertions, claims, and judgments that express opinions. In this case, one speaker's opinion is expressed in a direct quotation.

**Strategy ③ Think about whether statements can be checked for accuracy. Then, identify the facts and opinions in a chart.

> ### ANTIFEDERALIST VIEWS
>
> ① Antifederalists published their views about the Constitution in newspapers and pamphlets. ① They thought the Constitution took too much power away from the states and did not protect the rights of the people. They charged that the Constitution would destroy American liberties. As one Antifederalist wrote, ② "It is truly astonishing that a set of men among ourselves should have had the [nerve] to attempt the destruction of our liberties."

Make a Chart

The chart below analyzes the facts and opinions from the passage above.

Statement	③ Can It Be Proved?	③ Fact or Opinion
Antifederalists published their views in newspapers and pamphlets.	Yes. Check newspapers and other historical documents.	Fact
They thought the Constitution took too much power away from the states.	Yes. Check newspapers and other historical documents.	Fact
It is astonishing that some Americans would try to destroy American liberties.	No. This cannot be proved. It is what one speaker believes.	Opinion

Practicing the Skill

Turn to Chapter 11, Section 3, "Nationalism and Sectionalism." Read "The Missouri Compromise" on page 382, and make a chart in which you analyze key statements to determine whether they are facts or opinions.

1.16 Analyzing Primary Sources

Defining the Skill

Primary sources are materials written or made by people who lived during historical events and witnessed them. When you **analyze** primary sources, you interpret them, or decide what they tell you about history. Analyzing primary sources will help deepen your understanding of historical events.

Applying the Skill

The following passage is from a magazine article written by an African American who taught formerly enslaved persons in South Carolina. Use the strategies listed below to analyze it.

How to Analyze Primary Sources

Strategy 1 Use the information in the document to make inferences about daily life at the time it was written.

Strategy 2 Look for evidence that will tell you what the author's purpose may have been, and who was her intended audience.

Strategy 3 Identify the author of the primary source and note when it was written. Consider what important historical events were occurring at this time.

PRIMARY SOURCE

1 Many of the grown people are desirous of learning to read. It is wonderful how a people who have been so long crushed to the earth, so imbruted [treated cruelly] as these have been . . . can have so great a desire for knowledge, and such a capability for attaining it. 2 One cannot believe that the haughty Anglo Saxon race, after centuries of such an experience as these people have had, would be very much superior to them.

3 —Charlotte Forten, "Life on the Sea Islands," 1864

Make a Chart

Making a chart will help you analyze information from primary sources. The chart below provides an analysis of the passage you just read.

Author: Charlotte Forten	
Type of source: magazine article	**Title:** "Life on the Sea Islands"
Date: 1864	**Historical events:** Civil War
Author's purpose: Gain support for education of former enslaved persons	
Audience: Whites, free African Americans	
What it tells you about history: Enslaved African Americans were prevented from getting an education, but after they were freed, they eagerly pursued education.	

Practicing the Skill

Turn to Chapter 11, Section 1, "Early Industry and Inventions." Read "Time Table of the Holyoke Mills" on page 367, and analyze the poster to understand the historical context in which it was written.

1.17 Recognizing Bias and Propaganda

Defining the Skill

Bias is a one-sided presentation of an issue. **Propaganda** is communication that aims to influence people's opinions, emotions, or actions. Propaganda is not always factual. Rather, it uses prejudicial language or striking symbols to sway people's emotions. Modern advertising often uses propaganda. By thinking critically, you can avoid being swayed by bias and propaganda.

Applying the Skill

The following political cartoon shows Andrew Jackson dressed as a king. Use the strategies listed below to help you understand how it works as propaganda.

How to Recognize Bias and Propaganda

Strategy 1 Identify the aim, or purpose, of the cartoon. Point out the subject and explain the point of view.

Strategy 2 Identify those images on the cartoon that viewers might respond to emotionally and identify the emotions.

Strategy 3 Think critically about the cartoon. What facts has the cartoon ignored?

Make a Chart

Making a chart will help you think critically about a piece of propaganda. The chart below summarizes the information from the anti-Jackson cartoon.

1	**Identify Purpose**	*The cartoon portrays Jackson negatively by showing him as a king.*
2	**Identify Emotions**	*The cartoonist knows that Americans like democracy. So he portrays Jackson as a king because kings are not usually supporters of democracy. He also shows Jackson standing on a torn U.S. Constitution—another thing that Americans love.*
3	**Think Critically**	*The cartoon shows Jackson vetoing laws. But it ignores the fact that those actions were not against the Constitution. The president has the power to veto legislation. In this case, Jackson was exercising the power of the presidency, not acting like a king.*

Practicing the Skill

Turn to Chapter 6, Section 2, "Colonial Resistance Grows," and look at Paul Revere's etching of the Boston Massacre on page 164. Use a chart like the one above to think critically about the etching as an expression of bias or as an example of propaganda.

1.18 Synthesizing

Defining the Skill

Synthesizing means bringing together information to create an overall picture of a topic. Historians use synthesis to understand the importance of historical events. Like detectives, they look for "clues" such as facts, explanations, and conclusions. The historian then combines this information with his or her own knowledge to understand the event.

Applying the Skill

The following passage presents information about agriculture in the Americas prior to 1500. Use the strategies listed below to help you synthesize the information.

How to Synthesize

Strategy ❶ Read the entire passage carefully. Then reread, looking for facts, explanations, conclusions, and other important clues.

Strategy ❷ Record the important information in a web. Then review the evidence, looking for the larger idea that ties these pieces of information together.

Strategy ❸ Bring together the information you have gathered to create an overall picture of the subject.

AGRICULTURE IN THE AMERICAS

❶ The first Americans hunted animals and gathered wild seeds, nuts, and berries. ❶ In time, people started to plant the seeds they found. This was the beginning of agriculture. By trial and error, people learned which seeds grew the best crops.

Knowledge of agriculture spread throughout the Americas. ❶ Having a stable food supply changed the way people lived. ❶ Once they no longer had to travel to find food, they built permanent villages. ❶ Farmers were able to produce large harvests, so that fewer people needed to farm. Some people began to practice other crafts, such as weaving or making pottery. A few people became religious leaders. Slowly, some cultures grew complex and became civilizations.

Make a Web

Making a web can help you synthesize. The web at the right shows how to organize the facts, examples, and conclusions needed to synthesize the information in the above passage.

❷ Early Americans were hunters and gatherers.

❷ Farming produced a stable food supply.

❷ People built villages because they did not have to travel to find food.

❸ **Synthesis:** When cultures changed from hunting and gathering to agriculture, it made possible the development of civilizations.

❷ Agriculture began when people planted the seeds they gathered.

❷ People who didn't farm practiced other crafts, and cultures became more complex.

Practicing the Skill

Turn to Chapter 15, Section 1, "Tensions Rise Between North and South." Read "North and South Follow Different Paths" on page 481, and make a web to synthesize the economic factors that contributed to the division between North and South.

2.1 Reading Maps

Defining the Skill I

Maps are representations of features on the earth's surface. Historical maps often show political features, such as national borders, and physical features, such as bodies of water. Reading maps requires identifying map elements and using math skills.

Applying the Skill

The following map shows the Battle of Yorktown during the Revolution. Use the strategies listed below to help you identify the elements common to most maps.

How to Read a Map

Strategy ① Read the title. This identifies the main idea of the map.

Strategy ② Look for the grid of lines on the map. These numbered lines are the lines of latitude (horizontal) and longitude (vertical). They indicate the location of the area on the earth.

Strategy ③ Read the map key. It is usually in a box. This will give you the information you need to interpret the symbols or colors on the map.

Strategy ④ Use the scale and the pointer, or compass rose, to determine distance and direction.

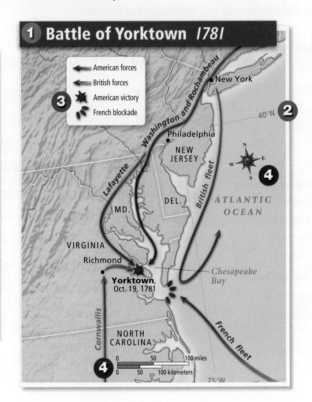

Make a Chart

A chart can help you organize information given on maps. The chart below summarizes information about the map you just studied.

Title	Battle of Yorktown, 1781
Location	between latitude 40°N and 35°N, just east of longitude 80°W
Map Key Information	blue = American forces, red = British forces
Scale	approx. 3/4 in. = 100 miles; approx. 1/2 in. = 100 km
Summary	British forces led by Cornwallis were trapped by American troops and a French naval blockade.

Practicing the Skill

Turn to Chapter 3, Section 4, "The Middle Colonies." Read the map entitled "American Colonies, 1740" on page 86, and make a chart to identify information on the map.

Defining the Skill II

Special-purpose maps help people focus on a particular aspect of a region, such as economic development in the South. These kinds of maps often use symbols to indicate information.

Applying the Skill

The following special-purpose map indicates the exports of the Southern colonies. Use the strategies listed below to help you identify the information shown on the map.

How to Read a Special-Purpose Map

Strategy 1 Read the title. It tells you what the map is intended to show.

Strategy 2 Read the legend. This tells you what each color and symbol stands for. This legend shows the exports that were produced in various Southern colonies.

Strategy 3 Look for the places on the map where the symbol appears. These tell you the places where the goods were produced.

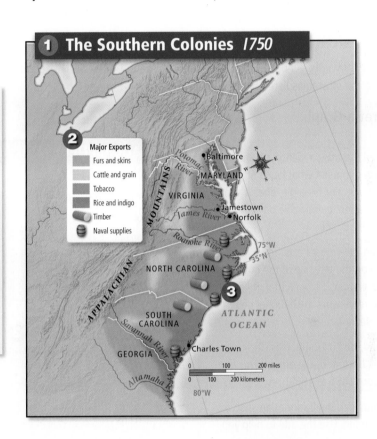

1 The Southern Colonies 1750

2 Major Exports
- Furs and skins
- Cattle and grain
- Tobacco
- Rice and indigo
- Timber
- Naval supplies

Make a Chart

A chart can help you understand special-purpose maps. The chart below shows information about the special-purpose map you just studied.

	Furs and skins	Cattle and grain	Tobacco	Rice and indigo	Timber	Naval stores
Maryland	x	x	x			
Virginia	x	x	x			
North Carolina	x	x	x	x	x	x
South Carolina	x	x		x	x	x
Georgia	x			x		

Practicing the Skill

Turn to Chapter 8, Section 2, "Creating the Constitution." Look at the special-purpose map entitled "Slave Poplulation, 1790" on page 246, and make a chart that shows information about the population of slaves soon after the Constitution was ratified.

2.2 Reading Graphs and Charts

Defining the Skill I

Graphs use pictures and symbols, instead of words, to show information. Graphs are created by taking information and presenting it visually. The graph on this page takes numerical information on the national debt and presents it as a bar graph. There are many different kinds of graphs. Bar graphs, line graphs, and pie graphs are the most common. Bar graphs compare numbers or sets of numbers. The length of each bar shows a quantity. It is easy to see how different categories compare on a bar graph.

Applying the Skill

The bar graph below shows the amount of the national debt in the United States between 1861 and 1869. Use the strategies listed below to help you interpret the graph.

How to Interpret a Graph

Strategy ① Read the title to identify the main idea of the graph. Ask yourself what kinds of information the graph shows. For example, does it show chronological information, geographic patterns and distributions, or something else?

Strategy ② Read the vertical axis (the one that goes up and down) on the left side of the graph. This one shows the amount of the debt in millions of dollars. Each bar represents the national debt during a particular year.

Strategy ③ Read the horizontal axis (the one that runs across the bottom of the graph). This one shows each year from 1861 to 1869.

Strategy ④ Summarize the information shown in each part of the graph. Use the title to help you focus on what information the graph is presenting.

① National Debt *1861–1869*

*millions of dollars   ③ (Source: U.S. Department of the Treasury)

Write a Summary

Writing a summary will help you understand the information in the graph. The paragraph to the right summarizes the information from the bar graph.

④ The national debt of the United States rose sharply during the years of the Civil War. In 1861 the country owed about $100 million, but by 1865 its debt had surpassed $2.5 billion. The debt peaked in 1866, when it totalled approximately $2.75 billion. By 1869, the U.S. had decreased the national debt by about $200 million.

Practicing the Skill

Turn to Chapter 4, Section 2, "The Southern Colonies: Plantations and Slavery." Look at the graph entitled "Slave Populations" on page 105, and write a paragraph in which you summarize what you learned from it.

Defining the Skill II

Charts, like graphs, present information in a visual form. Charts are created by organizing, summarizing, and simplifying information and presenting it in a format that makes it easy to understand. Tables and diagrams are examples of commonly used charts.

Applying the Skill

The chart below shows a comparison between the Virginia and New Jersey plans for government. Use the strategies listed below to help you interpret the information in the chart.

How to Interpret a Chart

Strategy ① Read the title. It will tell you what the chart is about. Ask yourself what kinds of information the chart shows. For example, does it show chronological information, geographic patterns and distributions, or something else?

Strategy ② Read the labels to see how the information in the chart is organized. In this chart, it is organized by plan and branch of government.

Strategy ③ Study the data in the chart to understand the facts that the chart intends to show.

Strategy ④ Summarize the information shown in each part of the chart. Use the title to help you focus on what information the chart is presenting.

COMPARING *Plans for Government*

	VIRGINIA PLAN	NEW JERSEY PLAN
Legislative branch	Two (branches) houses: representation determined by state population or wealth	One house: one vote for each state, regardless of size
	Lower House: elected by the people Upper House: elected by lower house	Elected by state legislatures
Executive branch	Appointed by Legislature	Appointed by Legislature
Judicial branch	Appointed by Legislature	Appointed by Executive

Write a Summary

Writing a summary can help you understand the information given in a chart. The paragraph to the right summarizes the information in the chart "Comparing Plans for Government."

④ The chart compares the Virginia Plan for government with the New Jersey Plan. It focuses on each plan's approach to how the three branches of government should be formed. The main difference between them was in the legislature, with the Virginia Plan calling for two houses and the New Jersey Plan arguing for one house.

Practicing the Skill

Turn to Chapter 8, Section 1, "The Confederation Era." Study the chart entitled "Powers Granted and Denied Congress" on page 236, and write a paragraph in which you summarize what you learned from it.

2.3 Analyzing Political Cartoons

Defining the Skill

Political cartoons are cartoons that use humor to make a serious point. Political cartoons often express a point of view on an issue better than words do. Understanding signs and symbols will help you to interpret political cartoons.

Applying the Skill

The cartoon below shows Abraham Lincoln and the other candidates running for the presidency in 1860. Use the strategies listed below to help you understand the cartoon.

How to Interpret a Political Cartoon

Strategy ❶ Identify the subject by reading the title of the cartoon and looking at the cartoon as a whole.

Strategy ❷ Identify important symbols and details. The cartoonist uses the image of a running race to discuss a political campaign. The White House is the finish line.

Strategy ❸ Interpret the message. Why is Lincoln drawn so much taller than the other candidates? How does that make him the fittest candidate?

Make a Chart

Making a chart will help you summarize information from a political cartoon. The chart below summarizes the information from the cartoon above.

Subject	*"A Political Race" (The Election of 1860)*
Symbols and Details	*Running is a symbol for a political campaign. Lincoln is the tallest and fastest candidate.*
Message	❸ *Lincoln is pulling ahead of the other candidates in the campaign for the presidency.*

Practicing the Skill

Turn to Chapter 18, Section 3, "The End of Reconstruction." Look at the political cartoon on page 585 showing a cartoonist's view of corruption in the Grant administration. Use a chart like the one above and the strategies outlined to interpret the cartoon.

2.4 Creating a Map

Defining the Skill

Creating a map involves representing geographical information. When you draw a map, it is easiest to use an existing map as a guide. On the map you draw, you can show geographical information. You can also show other kinds of information, such as data on climates, population trends, resources, or routes. Often, this data comes from a graph or a chart.

Applying the Skill

Below is a map that a student created to show information about the number of slaves in 1750. Read the strategies listed below to see how the map was created.

How to Create a Map

Strategy ① Select a title that identifies the geographical area and the map's purpose. Include a date in your title.

Strategy ② Draw the lines of latitude and longitude using short dashes.

Strategy ③ Create a key that shows the colors.

Strategy ④ Draw the colors on the map to show information.

Strategy ⑤ Draw a compass rose and scale.

① **Slave Population of the Southern Colonies, 1750**

- less than 300,000
- 300,000–400,000
- 400,000–450,000
- Over 450,000

Practicing the Skill

Make your own map. Turn to page 90 in Chapter 3 and study the graph entitled "Population of the 13 Colonies, 1650–1750." Use the strategies described above to create a map that shows population growth in the three colonial regions between 1650 and 1750. You can use the map on page 86 of that chapter as a guide.

2.5 Creating a Model

Defining the Skill

When you **create a model**, you use information and ideas to show an event or a situation in a visual way. A model might be a poster or a diagram that explains how something happened. Or, it might be a three-dimensional model, such as a diorama, that depicts an important scene or situation.

Applying the Skill

The following sketch shows the early stages of a model of three ways that people could have traveled from the eastern United States to California during the gold rush. Use the strategies listed below to help you create your own model.

How to Create a Model

Strategy ❶ Gather the information you need to understand the situation or event. In this case, you need to be able to show the three routes and their dangers.

Strategy ❷ Visualize and sketch an idea for your model. Once you have created a picture in your mind, make an actual sketch to plan how it might look.

Strategy ❸ Think of symbols you may want to use. Since the model should give information in a visual way, think about ways you can use color, pictures, or other visuals to tell the story.

Strategy ❹ Gather the supplies you will need and create the model. For example, you will need a globe and art supplies, such as yarn, for this model.

Strategy ❺ Write and answer a question about the California gold rush, as shown in the model.

The California Gold Rush
Dangerous Routes West

Wagon:
Dangers from hardships of the trail, mountains, rivers

Boat/overland:
Dangers from tropical sickness

Boat:
Dangers from sickness, storms, spoiled food

Practicing the Skill

Turn to Chapter 13 and read the Animated History called "American Trails West" on pages 424–425. Follow the steps above to create a model of a covered wagon.

3.1 Formulating Historical Questions

Defining the Skill

Formulating historical questions means asking questions about events and trends in history. These questions might ask how or why something happened, why someone acted a certain way, or how different conditions might have changed an event. To decide if a historical question is reasonable, ask yourself (1) whether the answer is important or not, and (2) if enough information exists to answer it.

Applying the Skill

The following passage describes the Boston Tea Party. Use the strategies listed below to help you formulate questions about this historical event.

How to Formulate Questions

Strategy 1 First ask about the basic facts of the event using the questions Who, What, When, Where, Why, and How.

Strategy 2 Think about where the event fits into the sequence of history. What events led up to it? What were its results?

Strategy 3 Formulate a central question about the event. Make sure it is neither too narrow nor too broad and can be answered from the sources available.

THE BOSTON TEA PARTY

In 1773, British Parliament passed the Tea Act. The Tea Act gave the British East India Company control over the American tea trade. Colonists would have to pay a tax on this regulated tea.

Protests against the Tea Act took place all over the colonies. One such protest occurred in Boston. The Sons of Liberty, a secret society that opposed the British, organized what came to be known as the Boston Tea Party.

On the evening of December 16, 1773, a group of men disguised as Native Americans boarded three tea ships docked in Boston Harbor. They destroyed 342 chests of tea. Many colonists rejoiced at the news. They believed that Britain would now see how strongly colonists opposed taxation without representation.

The Boston Tea Party aroused fury in Britain. In 1774, Parliament passed a series of laws to punish the Massachusetts colony. The British reaction fanned the flames of rebellion in the 13 colonies.

Make a Web

Making a web will help you formulate historical questions. In the web shown here, the center oval asks a central question about the event. More narrow questions—ones that help explore the broader question—are noted in the outer ovals.

1 Who participated?

2 How did other colonists react?

3 How did colonists in Boston protest the Tea Act?

1 What actions did they take?

2 What were the effects of the protest?

Practicing the Skill

Turn to Chapter 4, Section 1, "New England: Commerce and Religion." Read "Harvesting the Sea" on page 96, and make a web of narrow and broad historical questions about New England's coastal commerce.

3.2 Identifying and Using Primary and Secondary Sources

Defining the Skill

Primary sources are materials written or made by people who lived during historical events and witnessed them. They can be letters, journal entries, speeches, autobiographies, artwork, government documents, census surveys, or financial records. **Secondary sources** are materials written by people who did not participate in an event. History books are secondary sources.

Applying the Skill

The following passage contains both a primary source and a secondary source. Use the strategies listed below to help you read them.

How to Identify and Use Primary and Secondary Sources

Strategy 1 Distinguish secondary sources from primary sources. The first paragraph is a secondary source that explains something about the primary source in the next paragraph.

Strategy 2 Analyze the primary source and consider why the author produced it. Consider what the document was supposed to achieve and who would read it.

Strategy 3 Identify the author of the primary source and note when and where it was written.

> **1** The core idea of the Declaration is based on the philosophy of John Locke that people have unalienable rights that government cannot take away. Jefferson stated this belief in what was to become the Declaration's best-known passage.
>
> **2** We hold these truths to be self-evident, that all men are created equal, that they are endowed by their Creator with certain unalienable Rights, that among these are Life, Liberty and the pursuit of Happiness.
>
> **3** —Thomas Jefferson, *The Declaration of Independence*, 1776

Make a Chart

Making a chart will help you summarize information from primary sources and secondary sources. The chart below summarizes the information from the passage you just read.

Author	*Thomas Jefferson*
Document	*The Declaration of Independence*
Notes on Primary Source	*The Declaration says that "all men are created equal" and that people have "unalienable rights." These rights include life, liberty, and the pursuit of happiness.*
Notes on Secondary Source	*Jefferson based his ideas on those of John Locke. Locke had written about rights that governments could not take away from the people.*

Practicing the Skill

Turn to Chapter 6, Section 3, "The Road to Lexington and Concord." Read "British Control Begins to Slip" on page 172, and make a chart like the one above to summarize the information in the primary source and the secondary source.

3.3 Using a Database

Defining the Skill

Using a database allows you to find and retrieve information on a specific topic quickly and easily. By selecting keywords from your topic, you can search a database for related materials and sort them by date, format, or relevance.

Databases for Historical Research

- The Archival Research Catalog (ARC) – a database of many historic documents, photographs, maps, and other artifacts in the collection of the National Archives in Washington, D.C.
- The University of Virginia Library's Historical Census Browser – an easy-to-use online database of population and housing data from 1790 to 1960.

Applying the Skill

The image below shows a screen from a database of materials related to the Battle of Gettysburg. Use the strategies listed below to help you use the database.

How to Use a Database

Strategy ❶ You can broaden or narrow your search of the database. For example, if your search produced too few materials, you can search using more general keywords or a larger date range.

Strategy ❷ The title of the item alone will rarely give you enough information to judge whether or not it will be useful to you. Read all the fields.

Strategy ❸ Many valuable sources of information, including some newspapers and magazines, are not available in digital format. To view some materials, you may have to go to the library.

❶ **Database results for search terms "Civil War" AND "Gettysburg"**

❷ Title	Collection	Date	Available Formats
Battle of Gettysburg	maps	August 11, 1864	• original • digital
Rebel Sharpshooter	photographs	July 5, 1863	• original
Letters	documents	June 1861–1906	• original
Military service records	documents	1890–1912	❸ • original • microfilm
Casualty lists	data files	1861–1865	• original • digital
Union military orders	documents	1861–1865	• original
Diagrams of Confederate positions	engineering drawings	1861–1876	• original

Practicing the Skill

Turn to Chapter 12, Section 2, "Jackson's Policy Toward Native Americans." Read "Trail of Tears" on pages 405–406. Then go to the Archival Research Catalog on the Internet and search the database for "Trail of Tears." Compile the results in a table like the one above.

3.4 Paraphrasing

Defining the Skill

When you **paraphrase**, you restate a sentence, paragraph, or passage in your own words. Unlike a summary, which includes only the most important ideas, a paraphrase includes all information and is about the same length as the original. When paraphrasing, you change the structure of the sentence, as well as individual words.

Applying the Skill

The passage below describes the development of the idea of manifest destiny in the mid-1800s. Use the strategies listed below to help you paraphrase the passage.

How to Paraphrase

Strategy **1** Think about the ideas that each sentence is trying to communicate. Then express the same ideas in your own words.

Strategy **2** In addition to using different vocabulary, you must use your own sentence structures. Do not copy the grammar of the original.

Strategy **3** Paraphrasing is useful in research papers to avoid cluttering your report with too many quotations. But remember always to cite your source, even for a paraphrase.

MANIFEST DESTINY

Many Americans believed that the United States was destined to stretch across the continent from the Atlantic Ocean to the Pacific Ocean. In 1845, a newspaper editor name John O'Sullivan gave a name to that belief. O'Sullivan wrote, "Our manifest destiny [is] to overspread and possess the whole of the continent which Providence [God] has given us for the development of the great experiment of liberty. . . ." Manifest destiny suggested that expansion was not only good but bound to happen—even if it meant pushing Mexicans and Native Americans out of the way. After James K. Polk's election in 1844, manifest destiny became government policy.

—John Q. Author, in *A History Book*

Write a Paraphrase

Write your paraphrase in the same form as the original. The following paragraph paraphrases the passage above.

The idea that the United States was meant to cover the continent from the east coast to the west coast was a common one among Americans. Newspaper editor John O'Sullivan coined the term "manifest destiny" in 1845. **1** O'Sullivan believed that God wanted Americans to spread their system of government all across the continent. According to manifest destiny, the widespread growth of America was both positive and unstoppable. **2** The fact that Mexicans and Native Americans were already occupying parts of the continent did not matter. The U.S. government officially pursued manifest destiny after Polk became president in 1844. **3** Source: A History Book, by John Q. Author

Practicing the Skill

Turn to Chapter 1, Section 2, "Societies of Africa." Read "One African's Story" on page 11, and paraphrase the section in your own words.

3.5 Outlining

Defining the Skill

An **outline** is a summary of the information you plan to include in a written piece, and how you plan to structure it. A topic outline begins with a shortened version of the thesis statement. Roman numerals identify the major parts of the essay, followed by key ideas and supporting details listed with letters and Arabic numerals. Ways to organize your ideas include chronological order, cause-and-effect, and order of degree.

Applying the Skill

The outline shown here is a plan for a report on the Lewis and Clark expedition. Use the strategies listed below to help you create an outline.

How to Outline

Strategy ① Write a possible title for the essay, along with your thesis statement, at the top of your outline.

Strategy ② The body of the essay is where you discuss the points that support your thesis. List each main point after a capital letter.

Strategy ③ List supporting details below each main point with Arabic numerals. In general, there should be at least two details that support each main idea. If you have only one detail for a main idea, you may need more research.

① **The Accomplishments of the Lewis and Clark Expedition**

Thesis statement: The Lewis and Clark expedition made important contributions to the expansion of the U.S. in the 19th century.

　I. Introduction
② II. **Body:** Three goals accomplished by the Lewis and Clark expedition
　　A. Increased knowledge of the geography of the American West
③　　1. Learned there was no all-water route across the continent
　　　2. Made more accurate maps than had previously existed of areas west of St. Louis
　　B. Established good relations with Native Americans
③　　1. Guidance of Sacagawea and the Shoshone
　　　2. Assistance of the Nez Perce
　　C. Discovered natural resources
③　　1. Navigated Missouri, Clearwater, Snake, and Columbia Rivers
　　　2. Sketched edible plants and animals
　III. Conclusion

Practicing the Skill

Prepare an outline for an essay called "The Impact of the Emancipation Proclamation on the Civil War." Refer to Chapter 17, Section 1, "The Emancipation Proclamation" on pages 537–540, as a resource for your outline.

3.6 Forming and Supporting Opinions

Defining the Skill

When you **form opinions**, you interpret and judge the importance of events and people in history. You should always **support your opinions** with facts, examples, and quotes.

Applying the Skill

The following passage describes events that followed the gold rush. Use the strategies listed below to form and support your opinions about the events.

How to Form and Support Opinions

Strategy 1 Look for important information about the events. Information can include facts, quotations, and examples.

Strategy 2 Form an opinion about the event by asking yourself questions about the information. For example, How important was the event? What were its effects?

Strategy 3 Support your opinions with facts, quotations, and examples. If the facts do not support the opinion, then rewrite your opinion so it is supported by the facts.

THE IMPACT OF THE GOLD RUSH

By 1852, the gold rush was over. **1** While it lasted, about 250,000 people flooded into California. **1** This huge migration caused economic growth that changed California. **1** The port city San Francisco grew to become a center of banking, manufacturing, shipping, and trade. **1** However, the gold rush ruined many *Californios*. *Californios* are the Hispanic people of California. The newcomers did not respect *Californios*, their customs, or their legal rights. **1** In many cases, Americans seized their property.

Native Americans suffered even more. **1** Thousands died from diseases brought by the newcomers. **1** Miners hunted down and killed thousands more. **1** By 1870, California's Native American population had fallen from 150,000 to only about 30,000.

Make a Chart

Making a chart can help you organize your opinions and supporting facts. The following chart summarizes one possible opinion about the impact of the gold rush.

2 Opinion	*The effects of the gold rush were more negative than positive.*
3 Facts	*Californios were not respected, and their land was stolen.* *Many Native Americans died from diseases, and others were killed by miners.* *Their population dropped from 150,000 to about 30,000.*

Practicing the Skill

Turn to Chapter 11, Section 3, "Nationalism and Sectionalism." Read "The Monroe Doctrine" on page 385, and form your own opinion about the United States' reaction to European colonialism. Make a chart like the one above to summarize your opinion and the supporting facts and examples.

3.7 Essay

Defining the Skill

An **essay** is a written presentation consisting of (1) a thesis, and (2) an argument supported by details and evidence. A thesis is a statement that answers the question you are exploring in your essay. The argument explains why you believe your thesis is true. An argument is based on accurate evidence (facts, examples, statistics, etc.) from which you draw logical conclusions that help prove your thesis.

Applying the Skill

The page shown here is from an essay on the role of the cotton gin in the growth of slavery. Analyze the writer's use of these strategies in the essay.

How to Write an Essay

Strategy ① Use the introduction to state your thesis and provide important background information.

Strategy ② The body of the essay is where you present your argument. Often, you can present each point of your argument in a separate paragraph.

Strategy ③ Fill out each paragraph with details and evidence that support the main point.

Practicing the Skill

Turn to Chapter 11, Section 1, "Early Industry and Inventions." Read "One American's Story" on page 365, "The Lowel Mills Hire Women" on page 367, and "Comparing Perspectives" on page 366. Then, write an essay around a thesis statement about the working conditions for women in the Lowell mills.

THE COTTON GIN AND THE GROWTH OF SLAVERY

① A warm climate and fertile soil made the southern states ideal for agriculture. In the late 1700s, cash crops such as tobacco, indigo, rice, and sugar cane were grown on plantations using enslaved labor. The demand for that labor grew dramatically after new technology made cotton the dominant cash crop in the South. Eli Whitney's invention of the cotton gin in 1793 led to an increase in the use of slave labor in the United States at the end of the 18th century.

② Separating seeds and other debris from cotton fibers by hand was slow and very expensive. Whitney's gin made the cleaning process fast and easy. Sold at a lower price, cotton became the most commonly used fiber in textile production. As the demand for cotton grew, so did the demand for labor in the form of slaves.

Many plantations that had grown tobacco, rice, or indigo switched to cotton. From the increased profits on cotton, plantation owners could purchase more slaves. If soiled by storms, cotton was worthless. So many laborers were needed to pick cotton quickly before bad weather could destroy the crop.

Cotton could be grown on smaller plots than sugar cane and still make a profit. As a result, more people began to farm, more land was cultivated, and more labor was needed. **③** In Georgia, for example, from 1790 to 1810 (a period during which the cotton gin was invented), the number of slaves increased 104 percent.

3.8 Constructed Response

Defining the Skill

A **constructed response** requires you to write your own answer to a question, rather than to make a choice among provided answers. A constructed-response item consists of an "exhibit"—a document or artifact, such as a quotation, map, drawing, or photograph—and a series of questions about the exhibit and related history. Often, the answer can be found within the exhibit, but some questions require your own knowledge of the subject.

Applying the Skill

Shown here are three sample constructed-response items along with answers. Use the strategies listed below to help you answer constructed-response questions.

How to Answer Constructed-Response Questions

Strategy ① Unless the directions specify otherwise, you do not need to write your answers in complete sentences.

Strategy ② Look for clues to answer a question. One clue for the second question is in the exhibit—the date the magazine was published (1845). The second clue is in the question itself, which provides a description of the Industrial Revolution.

Strategy ③ The third question requires you to synthesize your own knowledge about the Industrial Revolution with information in the exhibit. This response refers to specific details in the exhibit and compares them to the student's own knowledge about factory work in the 1800s.

1. Who wrote the articles published in the *Lowell Offering*?

   ① young women who worked in factories

2. At the time the *Lowell Offering* was published, **②** what movement was replacing hand tools with machines, and farming with manufacturing?

   the Industrial Revolution

3. Does the cover illustration accurately reflect the daily lives of young women employed in factories? Why or why not?

   ③ No. In the illustration, the girl is standing in a wooded area holding a book, which makes her daily life look peaceful and leisurely, when factory girls actually worked 12-hour days in noisy, crowded mills.

Practicing the Skill

Turn to Chapter 9, Section 3, "The Federalists in Charge." Read the excerpt of the letter from Benjamin Banneker to Thomas Jefferson on page 327, and formulate a constructed response to the following question: Why do you think Banneker wrote these words to Jefferson?

3.9 Extended Response

Defining the Skill

An **extended response** is a detailed answer to a complex question about an exhibit or topic. It requires more time and thought to answer than a constructed response. Many extended-response questions ask you to write an essay on a given topic, using information from the exhibit and your own knowledge.

Applying the Skill

Shown here is a sample extended-response item along with its answer. Use the strategies listed below to help you answer extended-response questions.

How to Answer Extended-Response Questions

Strategy 1 Carefully read or study the exhibit and the question that follows.

Strategy 2 Take notes or diagram important information on a separate sheet of paper.

Strategy 3 Create a rough outline for your essay on a separate sheet of paper. Then use the outline to write your answer.

Read the passage about religion in some of the colonies. How did these colonies' ideas of religious tolerance help shape attitudes about diversity in the United States today?

RELIGIOUS TOLERATION IN THE COLONIES

William Penn founded Pennsylvania in 1681 when King Charles II gave him a large piece of land in America as repayment for debts to his family. Penn, a Quaker, organized his colony to provide a safe haven for Quakers and other persecuted peoples. Lord Baltimore founded Maryland in 1632 to create a refuge for Roman Catholics fleeing persecution in England. To attract other settlers besides Catholics, Maryland passed the Toleration Act in 1649. Like William Penn and Lord Baltimore, James Oglethorpe also wanted to help people persecuted for their religion, especially Protestants. He founded the Georgia colony, where all religions were welcome.

In response to religious persecution in Europe in the 1600s, the colonies of Pennsylvania, Maryland, and Georgia each offered settlers religious freedom. Whether to provide a safe haven for persecuted people or to attract more settlers, the founders of these colonies believed it important not to exclude anyone from living there based on religion. The ideas of religious tolerance in the Middle and Southern Colonies helped shape attitudes toward religious diversity in the United States today.

Those who had been persecuted for their beliefs in Europe greatly valued the freedom of religion they found in the colonies, where people of many faiths often lived side-by-side. As America developed from individual colonies into a nation, the freedom to worship became an expectation of society. Many states refused to ratify the U.S. Constitution until the founders agreed to add a Bill of Rights, the first of which protected religious freedom.

The toleration that started in the colonies extends today in the United States. . . .

Practicing the Skill

Turn to Chapter 17, Section 2, "War Affects Society." Read "Economic and Social Change" on pages 545–547, and formulate an extended response to the following question: What impact did the Civil War have on American society?

3.10 Creating a Multimedia Presentation

Defining the Skill

Movies, CD-ROMs, television, and computer software are different kinds of media. To **create a multimedia presentation**, you need to collect information in different media and organize them into one presentation.

Applying the Skill

Use the strategies listed below to help you create your own multimedia presentation.

How to Create a Multimedia Presentation

Strategy ① Identify the topic of your presentation and decide which media are best for an effective presentation. For example, you may want to use slides or posters to show visual images of your topic. Or, you may want to use CDs or audiotapes to provide music or spoken words.

Strategy ② Research the topic in a variety of sources. Images, text, props, and background music should reflect the historical period of the event you choose.

Strategy ③ Write the script for the oral portion of the presentation. You could use a narrator and characters' voices to tell the story. Primary sources are an excellent source for script material. Make sure the recording is clear so that the audience will be able to understand the oral part of the presentation.

Strategy ④ Videotape the presentation. Videotaping the presentation will preserve it for future viewing and allow you to show it to different groups of people.

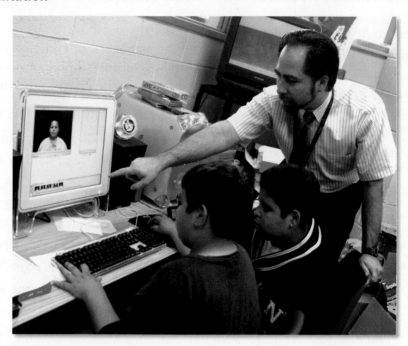

③

> **Narrator**
> Lee's plan on July 3 was to attack the middle of the Union line along Cemetery Ridge with 15,000 Confederate soldiers. But General Longstreet disagreed with Lee's strategy.
>
> **Longstreet**
> It is my opinion that no 15,000 men ever arrayed for battle can take that position.
>
> **Narrator**
> Lee refused to change his mind. He wanted to see the battle—and the war—end that day.
>
> **Pickett**
> [to Longstreet] General, shall I advance?
>
> **Narrator**
> Longstreet, foreseeing disaster, could not speak. He only bowed to Pickett in a silent order of "Advance".
>
> **Pickett**
> [shouting] Charge the enemy and remember old Virginia!

Practicing the Skill

Turn to Chapter 16, "The Civil War Begins." Choose a topic from the chapter, and use the strategies listed above to create a multimedia presentation about it.

4.1 Using a Search Engine

Defining the Skill

A **search engine** is a computer program that looks for, gathers, and reports information available on the Internet. Using a search engine helps you find such information quickly and easily. By entering key words into a search engine, you will generate a list of Web pages and sites that contain those words.

Applying the Skill

Shown here is a list of results from a search for information on Harriet Tubman's work on the Underground Railroad. Use the strategies listed below to get better results when you search the Internet.

How to Use a Search Engine

Strategy 1 Be specific when searching to get more relevant information. Use quotation marks around exact phrases that you want the engine to search for as a whole. Narrow your search with plus and minus signs. For example, to include Harriet Tubman in your search but exclude Levi Coffin, you would enter "+Tubman –Coffin" in the search box.

Strategy 2 The brief excerpt that appears under the title is actual text from the page. Read it carefully for clues as to whether or not the site contains useful information. The first result, for example, shows a quotation from Tubman, which might indicate that there are more pirmary sources on the Web site.

Strategy 3 Read the title of the Web site. Although a site might meet the search criteria, sometimes you can tell by reading the title that it will not be useful. The third result, for example, is a quiz that probably will not help your research.

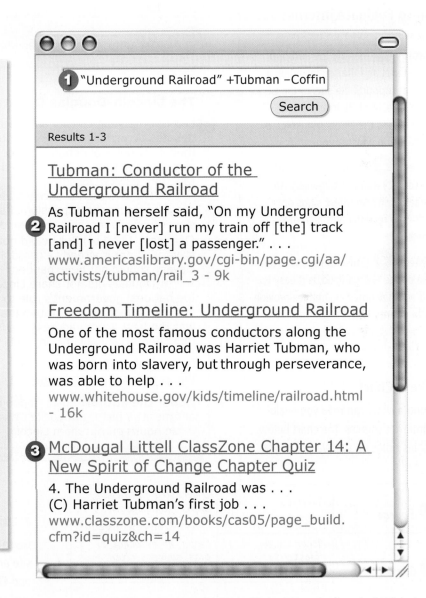

1 "Underground Railroad" +Tubman –Coffin

Search

Results 1-3

Tubman: Conductor of the Underground Railroad

2 As Tubman herself said, "On my Underground Railroad I [never] run my train off [the] track [and] I never [lost] a passenger." . . .
www.americaslibrary.gov/cgi-bin/page.cgi/aa/activists/tubman/rail_3 - 9k

Freedom Timeline: Underground Railroad

One of the most famous conductors along the Underground Railroad was Harriet Tubman, who was born into slavery, but through perseverance, was able to help . . .
www.whitehouse.gov/kids/timeline/railroad.html - 16k

3 **McDougal Littell ClassZone Chapter 14: A New Spirit of Change Chapter Quiz**

4. The Underground Railroad was . . .
(C) Harriet Tubman's first job . . .
www.classzone.com/books/cas05/page_build.cfm?id=quiz&ch=14

Practicing the Skill

Turn to Chapter 3, Section 2, "New England Colonies," and read about Anne Hutchinson on page 70. Then look for Web sites about Hutchinson and her trial using an Internet search engine. Jot down the three sites that you feel provide the best information.

4.2 Evaluating Internet Sources

Defining the Skill

Evaluating Internet sources will help you decide if the information you find online is trust-worthy. Reliable Internet sources generally:

- are created by a credible author, with the backing of an educational institution or government agency;
- have content that is well-researched and free from bias with sources cited.

Applying the Skill

Shown here is a Web page about the Lincoln-Douglas debates. Use the strategies listed below to help you evaluate Internet sources.

How to Evaluate Internet Sources

Strategy ① Identify the author of the material and the organization, if any, that supports the site. In the example here, the URL includes ".edu," which means the site is sponsored by an educational institution.

Strategy ② Examine the content for accuracy and thoroughness. Are sources cited? Are there signs of bias? How recently was it created or updated?

Strategy ③ Consider how well the page or site is organized. Is it easy to read and navigate? Do images provide useful information?

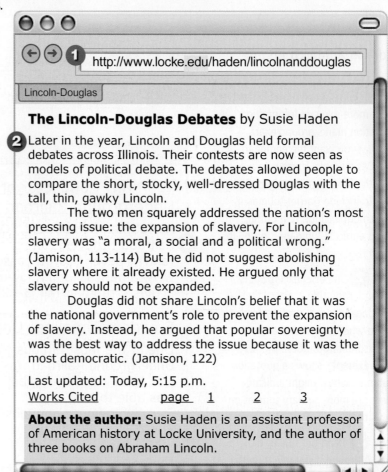

① http://www.locke.edu/haden/lincolnanddouglas

Lincoln-Douglas

The Lincoln-Douglas Debates by Susie Haden

② Later in the year, Lincoln and Douglas held formal debates across Illinois. Their contests are now seen as models of political debate. The debates allowed people to compare the short, stocky, well-dressed Douglas with the tall, thin, gawky Lincoln.

The two men squarely addressed the nation's most pressing issue: the expansion of slavery. For Lincoln, slavery was "a moral, a social and a political wrong." (Jamison, 113-114) But he did not suggest abolishing slavery where it already existed. He argued only that slavery should not be expanded.

Douglas did not share Lincoln's belief that it was the national government's role to prevent the expansion of slavery. Instead, he argued that popular sovereignty was the best way to address the issue because it was the most democratic. (Jamison, 122)

Last updated: Today, 5:15 p.m.

Works Cited   page   1   2   3

About the author: Susie Haden is an assistant professor of American history at Locke University, and the author of three books on Abraham Lincoln.

Make a Chart

Making a chart can help you evaluate Internet sources. The chart below contains notes on the Web page you just read.

① Source	Author	University professor, expert on Lincoln
	Sponsor	Locke University (.edu)
② Content	Accuracy & objectivity	Good, no evidence of bias, sources cited
	Thoroughness	Good
	Up-to-date	Yes
③ Style & Functionality	Organization	Clear
	Legibility	Good, easy to read
	Ease of navigation	Yes, links provided to each page of site

Practicing the Skill

Go to the Library of Congress Web site and find the exhibition on Lewis and Clark. Use the above strategies to evaluate the exhibition's reliability as a historical source about the Corps of Discovery. Create a chart like the one here to organize your evaluation.

4.3 Recognizing Bias

Defining the Skill

Bias is the presentation of only one side of an issue. A biased source is not objective: it exhibits a point of view influenced by its author's emotions or personal preferences. Bias can also appear in the form of advertising to try to persuade you to patronize a product or service. Recognizing bias will help you evaluate whether or not a source is reliable.

Applying the Skill

Shown here is a Web page about Thomas Jefferson's first term as president. Use the strategies listed below to identify words and tone that indicate bias.

How to Recognize Bias

Strategy 1 Read the Web page carefully, looking for evidence of the author's point of view. Note places where the author expresses a personal opinion. Consider word choice.

Strategy 2 Think critically about the text. Decide whether or not it seems balanced. Does it present both sides of an argument?

Strategy 3 Use the evidence you have gathered to judge whether or not the material is biased.

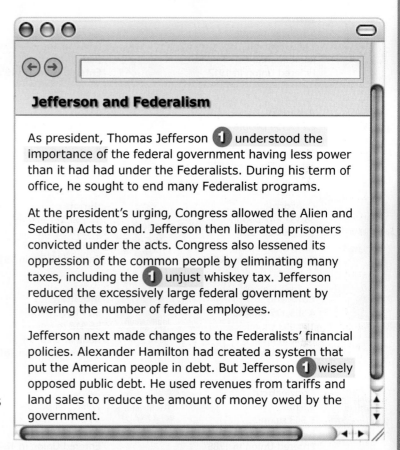

Jefferson and Federalism

As president, Thomas Jefferson **1** understood the importance of the federal government having less power than it had had under the Federalists. During his term of office, he sought to end many Federalist programs.

At the president's urging, Congress allowed the Alien and Sedition Acts to end. Jefferson then liberated prisoners convicted under the acts. Congress also lessened its oppression of the common people by eliminating many taxes, including the **1** unjust whiskey tax. Jefferson reduced the excessively large federal government by lowering the number of federal employees.

Jefferson next made changes to the Federalists' financial policies. Alexander Hamilton had created a system that put the American people in debt. But Jefferson **1** wisely opposed public debt. He used revenues from tariffs and land sales to reduce the amount of money owed by the government.

Make a Chart

Making a chart will help you recognize bias in online materials. The chart below shows how bias appears in the Web site.

1 Evidence of Point of View	Author shows his own belief ("the importance of") that the federal government needed to have less power. Word choice: *unjust, wisely*
2 Think Critically	Makes all Federalist policies sound bad. Does not tell Hamilton's "side of the story."
3 Bias	Biased in favor of Jefferson and small government. Author's purpose is to persuade reader that Federalism is bad.

Practicing the Skill

Search the Web for an article about an event or figure in American history. Using the above strategies, create a chart to identify any instances of bias in the content of the article. If you notice bias, consider how it could be written more objectively.

Facts About the States

Alabama
4,557,808 people
52,218 sq. mi.
Rank in area: 30
Entered Union in 1819

Florida
17,789,864 people
59,909 sq. mi.
Rank in area: 22
Entered Union in 1845

Louisiana
4,523,628 people
49,650 sq. mi.
Rank in area: 31
Entered Union in 1812

Alaska
663,661 people
616,240 sq. mi.
Rank in area: 1
Entered Union in 1959

Georgia
9,072,576 people
58,970 sq. mi.
Rank in area: 24
Entered Union in 1788

Maine
1,321,505 people
33,738 sq. mi.
Rank in area: 39
Entered Union in 1820

Arizona
5,939,292 people
113,998 sq. mi.
Rank in area: 6
Entered Union in 1912

Hawaii
1,275,194 people
6,641 sq. mi.
Rank in area: 43
Entered Union in 1959

Maryland
5,600,388 people
12,297 sq. mi.
Rank in area: 42
Entered Union in 1788

Arkansas
2,779,154 people
53,178 sq. mi.
Rank in area: 29
Entered Union in 1836

Idaho
1,429,096 people
83,570 sq. mi.
Rank in area: 14
Entered Union in 1890

Massachusetts
6,398,743 people
9,240 sq. mi.
Rank in area: 44
Entered Union in 1788

California
36,132,147 people
158,854 sq. mi.
Rank in area: 3
Entered Union in 1850

Illinois
12,763,371 people
57,914 sq. mi.
Rank in area: 25
Entered Union in 1818

Michigan
10,120,860 people
96,716 sq. mi.
Rank in area: 11
Entered Union in 1837

Colorado
4,665,177 people
104,093 sq. mi.
Rank in area: 8
Entered Union in 1876

Indiana
6,271,973 people
36,418 sq. mi.
Rank in area: 38
Entered Union in 1816

Minnesota
5,132,799 people
86,938 sq. mi.
Rank in area: 12
Entered Union in 1858

Connecticut
3,510,297 people
5,543 sq. mi.
Rank in area: 48
Entered Union in 1788

Iowa
2,966,334 people
56,271 sq. mi.
Rank in area: 26
Entered Union in 1846

Mississippi
2,921,088 people
48,282 sq. mi.
Rank in area: 32
Entered Union in 1817

Delaware
843,524 people
2,396 sq. mi.
Rank in area: 49
Entered Union in 1787

Kansas
2,744,687 people
82,276 sq. mi.
Rank in area: 15
Entered Union in 1861

Missouri
5,800,310 people
69,704 sq. mi.
Rank in area: 21
Entered Union in 1821

District of Columbia
550,521 people
68 sq. mi.
Created 1790

Kentucky
4,173,405 people
40,409 sq. mi.
Rank in area: 37
Entered Union in 1792

Montana
935,670 people
147,042 sq. mi.
Rank in area: 4
Entered Union in 1889

Sources: U.S. Census Bureau, *American Factfinder* online: 2005 Population Estimates. *CIA World Factbook* online.
Encyclopaedia Britannica Almanac 2006. *Rand McNally Goode's World Atlas,* 20th ed., 2000.

Nebraska
1,758,787 people
77,353 sq. mi.
Rank in area: 16
Entered Union in 1867

Ohio
11,464,042 people
44,825 sq. mi.
Rank in area: 34
Entered Union in 1803

Texas
22,859,968 people
267,256 sq. mi.
Rank in area: 2
Entered Union in 1845

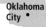

Nevada
2,414,807 people
110,560 sq. mi.
Rank in area: 7
Entered Union in 1864

Oklahoma
3,547,884 people
69,898 sq. mi.
Rank in area: 20
Entered Union in 1907

Utah
2,469,585 people
84,898 sq. mi.
Rank in area: 13
Entered Union in 1896

New Hampshire
1,309,940 people
9,282 sq. mi.
Rank in area: 46
Entered Union in 1788

Oregon
3,641,056 people
97,126 sq. mi.
Rank in area: 9
Entered Union in 1859

Vermont
623,050 people
9,614 sq. mi.
Rank in area: 45
Entered Union in 1791

New Jersey
8,717,925 people
8,214 sq. mi.
Rank in area: 47
Entered Union in 1787

Pennsylvania
12,429,616 people
46,055 sq. mi.
Rank in area: 33
Entered Union in 1787

Virginia
7,567,465 people
42,328 sq. mi.
Rank in area: 35
Entered Union in 1788

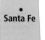

New Mexico
1,928,384 people
121,589 sq. mi.
Rank in area: 5
Entered Union in 1912

Rhode Island
1,076,189 people
1,231 sq. mi.
Rank in area: 50
Entered Union in 1790

Washington
6,287,759 people
70,634 sq. mi.
Rank in area: 18
Entered Union in 1889

New York
19,254,630 people
54,077 sq. mi.
Rank in area: 27
Entered Union in 1788

South Carolina
4,255,083 people
31,190 sq. mi.
Rank in area: 40
Entered Union in 1788

West Virginia
1,816,856 people
24,230 sq. mi.
Rank in area: 41
Entered Union in 1863

North Carolina
8,683,242 people
52,670 sq. mi.
Rank in area: 28
Entered Union in 1789

South Dakota
775,933 people
77,116 sq. mi.
Rank in area: 17
Entered Union in 1889

Wisconsin
5,536,201 people
65,498 sq. mi.
Rank in area: 23
Entered Union in 1848

North Dakota
636,677 people
70,699 sq. mi.
Rank in area: 19
Entered Union in 1889

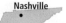

Tennessee
5,962,959 people
42,143 sq. mi.
Rank in area: 36
Entered Union in 1796

Wyoming
509,294 people
97,813 sq. mi.
Rank in area: 10
Entered Union in 1890

United States: *Major Dependencies*

- American Samoa—62,700 people; 90 sq. mi.
- Guam—165,000 people; 217 sq. mi.
- Commonwealth of Puerto Rico—3,898,000 people; 5,324 sq. mi.
- Virgin Islands of the United States—109,000 people; 171 sq. mi.
- Midway Islands—no indigenous inhabitants; 6.2 sq. mi.
- Wake Island—no indigenous inhabitants; 6.5 sq. mi.

Presidents of the United States

Here are some little-known facts about the presidents of the United States:

- First president born in the new United States: **Martin Van Buren** (eighth president)
- Only president who was a bachelor: **James Buchanan**
- First left-handed president: **James A. Garfield**
- Largest president: **William H. Taft** (6 feet 2 inches, 332 pounds)
- Youngest president: **Theodore Roosevelt** (42 years old)
- Oldest president: **Ronald Reagan** (77 years old when he left office in 1989)
- First president born west of the Mississippi River: **Herbert Hoover** (born in West Branch, Iowa)
- First president born in the 20th century: **John F. Kennedy** (born May 29, 1917)

1 George Washington
1789–1797
No Political Party
Birthplace: Virginia
Born: February 22, 1732
Died: December 14, 1799

2 John Adams
1797–1801
Federalist
Birthplace: Massachusetts
Born: October 30, 1735
Died: July 4, 1826

3 Thomas Jefferson
1801–1809
Democratic-Republican
Birthplace: Virginia
Born: April 13, 1743
Died: July 4, 1826

4 James Madison
1809–1817
Democratic-Republican
Birthplace: Virginia
Born: March 16, 1751
Died: June 28, 1836

5 James Monroe
1817–1825
Democratic-Republican
Birthplace: Virginia
Born: April 28, 1758
Died: July 4, 1831

6 John Quincy Adams
1825–1829
Democratic-Republican
Birthplace: Massachusetts
Born: July 11, 1767
Died: February 23, 1848

7 Andrew Jackson
1829–1837
Democrat
Birthplace: South Carolina
Born: March 15, 1767
Died: June 8, 1845

8 Martin Van Buren
1837–1841
Democrat
Birthplace: New York
Born: December 5, 1782
Died: July 24, 1862

9 William H. Harrison
1841
Whig
Birthplace: Virginia
Born: February 9, 1773
Died: April 4, 1841

10 John Tyler
1841–1845
Whig
Birthplace: Virginia
Born: March 29, 1790
Died: January 18, 1862

11 James K. Polk
1845–1849
Democrat
Birthplace: North Carolina
Born: November 2, 1795
Died: June 15, 1849

12 Zachary Taylor
1849–1850
Whig
Birthplace: Virginia
Born: November 24, 1784
Died: July 9, 1850

13 Millard Fillmore
1850–1853
Whig
Birthplace: New York
Born: January 7, 1800
Died: March 8, 1874

14 Franklin Pierce
1853–1857
Democrat
Birthplace: New Hampshire
Born: November 23, 1804
Died: October 8, 1869

15 James Buchanan
1857–1861
Democrat
Birthplace: Pennsylvania
Born: April 23, 1791
Died: June 1, 1868

16 Abraham Lincoln
1861–1865
Republican
Birthplace: Kentucky
Born: February 12, 1809
Died: April 15, 1865

17 Andrew Johnson
1865–1869
Democrat
Birthplace: North Carolina
Born: December 29, 1808
Died: July 31, 1875

18 Ulysses S. Grant
1869–1877
Republican
Birthplace: Ohio
Born: April 27, 1822
Died: July 23, 1885

19 Rutherford B. Hayes
1877–1881
Republican
Birthplace: Ohio
Born: October 4, 1822
Died: January 17, 1893

20 James A. Garfield
1881
Republican
Birthplace: Ohio
Born: November 19, 1831
Died: September 19, 1881

21 Chester A. Arthur
1881–1885
Republican
Birthplace: Vermont
Born: October 5, 1829
Died: November 18, 1886

22 24 Grover Cleveland
1885–1889, 1893–1897
Democrat
Birthplace: New Jersey
Born: March 18, 1837
Died: June 24, 1908

23 Benjamin Harrison
1889–1893
Republican
Birthplace: Ohio
Born: August 20, 1833
Died: March 13, 1901

25 William McKinley
1897–1901
Republican
Birthplace: Ohio
Born: January 29, 1843
Died: September 14, 1901

26 Theodore Roosevelt
1901–1909
Republican
Birthplace: New York
Born: October 27, 1858
Died: January 6, 1919

27 William H. Taft
1909–1913
Republican
Birthplace: Ohio
Born: September 15, 1857
Died: March 8, 1930

28 Woodrow Wilson
1913–1921
Democrat
Birthplace: Virginia
Born: December 28, 1856
Died: February 3, 1924

29 Warren G. Harding
1921–1923
Republican
Birthplace: Ohio
Born: November 2, 1865
Died: August 2, 1923

Presidents of the United States

30 Calvin Coolidge
1923–1929
Republican
Birthplace: Vermont
Born: July 4, 1872
Died: January 5, 1933

31 Herbert C. Hoover
1929–1933
Republican
Birthplace: Iowa
Born: August 10, 1874
Died: October 20, 1964

32 Franklin D. Roosevelt
1933–1945
Democrat
Birthplace: New York
Born: January 30, 1882
Died: April 12, 1945

33 Harry S. Truman
1945–1953
Democrat
Birthplace: Missouri
Born: May 8, 1884
Died: December 26, 1972

34 Dwight D. Eisenhower
1953–1961
Republican
Birthplace: Texas
Born: October 14, 1890
Died: March 28, 1969

35 John F. Kennedy
1961–1963
Democrat
Birthplace: Massachusetts
Born: May 29, 1917
Died: November 22, 1963

36 Lyndon B. Johnson
1963–1969
Democrat
Birthplace: Texas
Born: August 27, 1908
Died: January 22, 1973

37 Richard M. Nixon
1969–1974
Republican
Birthplace: California
Born: January 9, 1913
Died: April 22, 1994

38 Gerald R. Ford
1974–1977
Republican
Birthplace: Nebraska
Born: July 14, 1913
Died: December 26, 2006

39 James E. Carter, Jr.
1977–1981
Democrat
Birthplace: Georgia
Born: October 1, 1924

40 Ronald W. Reagan
1981–1989
Republican
Birthplace: Illinois
Born: February 6, 1911
Died: June 5, 2004

41 George H. W. Bush
1989–1993
Republican
Birthplace: Massachusetts
Born: June 12, 1924

42 William J. Clinton
1993–2001
Democrat
Birthplace: Arkansas
Born: August 19, 1946

43 George W. Bush
2001– 2008
Republican
Birthplace: Connecticut
Born: July 6, 1946

Gazetteer

A gazetteer is a dictionary of geographical terms and place names. This Gazetteer identifies important places and geographical features in this book. Entries include a short description, often followed by page numbers. Arabic numbers refer to a text page on which the entry is discussed; numbers in italics refer to a map where the place appears. In addition, some entries include rounded-off geographical coordinates.

Afghanistan nation in Central Asia. Capital: Kabul. *A24–A25*

Africa world's second largest continent.

Alabama 22nd state. Capital: Montgomery. *A34–A35*

Alamo Texas mission in San Antonio captured by Mexico in 1836. (29°N 98°W) *431*

Alaska 49th state. Capital: Juneau. *A34–A35*

Antarctica continent at the South Pole.

Antietam Maryland creek; site of bloodiest day's fighting in the Civil War. (39°N 77°W) *526*

Appalachian Mountains mountain range running from Alabama into Canada. *A36–A37*

Appomattox Court House town near Appomattox, Virginia, where Lee surrendered to Grant on April 9, 1865. (37°N 79°W) *554*

Arizona 48th state. Capital: Phoenix. *A34–A35*

Arkansas 25th state. Capital: Little Rock. *A34–A35*

Asia world's largest continent.

Atlantic Ocean ocean forming east boundary of the United States.

Australia island country between Indian and Pacific ocean; Capital: Canberra. Also the world's smallest continent. *A24–A25*

Austria-Hungary one of the Central Powers in World War I; after the war, divided into smaller countries. *719*

Aztec Empire region of what is now Mexico, once under Aztec control.

Backcountry identification for former undeveloped region beginning in the Appalachian Mountains and extending west. *118*

Baltimore Maryland city on Chesapeake Bay. (39°N 77°W)

Bay of Pigs (Bahía de Cochinos) inlet on south coast of Cuba; site of 1961 ill-fated, U.S.-backed Cuban invasion attempt.

Beringia former land bridge connecting Asia with North America and now under waters of Bering Strait. (66°N 169°W).

Berlin capital of Germany; divided into East and West Berlin, 1948–1989. (53°N 13°E) *847*

Boston capital of Massachusetts; site of early colonial unrest and conflict. (42°N 71°W) *38, 96*

Bull Run stream 30 miles southwest of Washington, D.C.; site of first land battle of Civil War. (39°N 78°W)

Bunker Hill hill now part of Boston; its name misidentifies Revolutionary War battle fought at nearby Breed's Hill. (42°N 71°W) *190*

Cahokia Illinois Mound Builders site; village taken from British by Clark in 1778. (39°N 90°W) *209*

California 31st state. Capital: Sacramento. *A34–A35*

Canada nation sharing northern U.S. border. Capital: Ottawa. *A28*

Caribbean Sea expanse of the Atlantic Ocean between the Gulf of Mexico and South America. *A30–A31*

Central America area of North America between Mexico and South America. *A30–A31*

Charleston as Charles Town, largest Southern colonial city; South Carolina site of first Civil War shots, at offshore Fort Sumter. (33°N 80°W) *80*

Charlestown former town, now part of Boston; site of both Bunker and Breed's hills. (42°N 71°W) *190*

Chesapeake Bay inlet of the Atlantic Ocean, located in Virginia and Maryland. *A36–A37*

Chicago large Illinois city on Lake Michigan. (42°N 88°W)

China large nation in Asia. Capital: Beijing. *A24–A25*

Colorado 38th state. Capital: Denver. *A34–A35*

Concord Massachusetts town and site of second battle of the Revolutionary War. (42°N 71°W)

Confederate States of America nation formed by 11 Southern states during the Civil War. Capital: Richmond, Virginia. *509*

Connecticut 5th state. Capital: Hartford. *A34–A35*

Cuba Caribbean island south of Florida. Capital: Havana. *A24–A25*

Delaware 1st state. Capital: Dover. *A34–A35*

District of Columbia (D.C.) self-governing federal district between Virginia and Maryland, made up entirely of the city of Washington, the U.S. capital. (39°N 77°W)

Dominican Republic nation sharing the island of Hispaniola with Haiti. Capital: Santo Domingo. *A24–A25*

Eastern Hemisphere the half of the world that includes Europe, Africa, and Asia. *A6*

El Salvador Central American nation. Capital: San Salvador. *A24–A25*

England southern part of Great Britain. *A24–A25*

English Channel narrow waterway separating Great Britain from France. *823*

Erie Canal all-water channel dug out to connect the Hudson River with Lake Erie. *363, 381*

Europe second smallest continent, actually a peninsula of the Eurasian landmass.

Florida 27th state. Capital: Tallahassee. *A34–A35*

Fort McHenry fort in Baltimore harbor where 1814 British attack inspired U.S. national anthem. (39°N 77°W) *355*

Fort Sumter fort in Charleston, South Carolina, harbor where 1861 attack by Confederates began the Civil War. (33°N 80°W) *509, 524*

Fort Ticonderoga fort in New York on Lake Champlain; site of battles during French and Indian War and the Revolutionary War. (44°N 73°W) *145, 178, 200*

France nation in western Europe; it aided America in the Revolutionary War. Capital: Paris. *A24–A25*

Gadsden Purchase last territory (from Mexico, 1853) added to continental United States. *A38–A39*

Georgia 4th state. Capital: Atlanta. *A34–A35*

Germany nation in central Europe; once divided into West and East Germany, 1949–1990. Capital: Berlin. *A24–A25, 742, 847*

Gettysburg Pennsylvania town and site of 1863 Civil War victory for the North that is considered the war's turning point. (40°N 77°W) *551*

Ghana first powerful West African trading empire. *14*

Great Britain European island nation across from France; it consists of England, Scotland and Wales. *A24–A25*

Great Lakes five connected lakes—Ontario, Erie, Huron, Michigan, and Superior—on the U.S. border with Canada. *A24–A25*

Great Plains vast grassland region in the central United States. *A36–A37*

Guam Pacific island, possession of United States. *A24–A25, 829*

Gulf of Mexico body of water forming southern U.S. boundary from east Texas to west Florida. *A30–A31*

Haiti nation sharing the island of Hispaniola with Dominican Republic. Capital: Port-au-Prince. *A30–A31*

Harlem neighborhood of New York City, home to large African-American community since 1910s. *764–766*

Harpers Ferry village today in extreme eastern West Virginia where John Brown raided stored U.S. weapons in 1859. (39°N 78°W)

Hawaii 50th state. Capital: Honolulu. *A34–A35*

Hiroshima Japanese city destroyed by U.S. atomic bomb dropped to end World War II. (34°N 132°E) *829*

Hispaniola West Indies island (shared today by Dominican Republic and Haiti) that Columbus mistook for Asia. *A30–A31*

Hudson River large river in eastern New York. *113, 200*

Idaho 43rd state. Capital: Boise. *A34–A35*

Illinois 21st state. Capital: Springfield. *A34–A35*

Indiana 19th state. Capital: Indianapolis. *A34–A35*

Indian Territory area, mainly of present-day Oklahoma, that in the 1800s became land for relocated Native Americans. *405*

Iowa 29th state. Capital: Des Moines. *A34–A35*

Iran Middle East nation. Capital: Tehran. *A24–A25, 947*

Iraq Middle East nation whose 1990 invasion of Kuwait led to the Persian Gulf War. Capital: Baghdad. *A24–A25, 947*

Ireland island country west of England whose mid-1800s famine caused more than one million people to emigrate to America. Capital: Dublin. *A24–A25*

Israel Jewish nation in the Middle East. Capital: Jerusalem. *A24–A25*

Italy nation in southern Europe. Capital: Rome. *A24–A25*

Jamestown community in Virginia that was the first permanent English settlement in North America. *59, 80*

Japan island nation in east Asia. Capital: Tokyo. *A24–A25, 829*

Kansas 34th state. Capital: Topeka. *A34–A35*

Kentucky 15th state. Capital: Frankfort. *A34–A35*

Kosovo province of the Yugoslavian republic of Serbia.

Kuwait tiny, oil-rich Middle East nation. Capital: Kuwait City. *947*

Latin America region made up of Mexico, Caribbean Islands, and Central and South America, where Latin-based languages of Spanish, French, or Portuguese are spoken. *A30–A31*

Lebanon Middle East country on the Mediterranean coast. Capital: Beirut. *A24–A25*

Lexington Massachusetts town and site of first Revolutionary War battle in 1775. (42°N 71°W)

Little Bighorn River Montana site of Sioux and Cheyenne victory over Custer. (46°N 108°W)

Little Rock capital of Arkansas and site of 1957 school-desegregation conflict.

Los Angeles 2nd largest U.S. city, on California's coast.

Louisiana 18th state. Capital: Baton Rouge. *A34–A35*

Louisiana Purchase land west of the Mississippi River purchased from France in 1803. *347, 436*

Lowell Massachusetts city built in early 1800s as planned factory town. (43°N 71°W)

Maine 23rd state. Capital: Augusta. *A34–A35*

Mali early West African trading empire succeeding Ghana empire. *14*

Maryland 7th state. Capital: Annapolis. *A34–A35*

Massachusetts 6th state. Capital: Boston. *A34–A35*

Mexico nation sharing U.S. southern border. Capital: Mexico City. *A30–A31*

Michigan 26th state. Capital: Lansing. *A34–A35*

Middle East eastern Mediterranean region that includes countries such as Iran, Iraq, Syria, Kuwait, Jordan, Saudi Arabia, Israel, and Egypt.

Minnesota 32nd state. Capital: St. Paul. *A34–A35*

Mississippi 20th state. Capital: Jackson. *A34–A35*

Mississippi River second longest U.S. river, south from Minnesota to the Gulf of Mexico.

Missouri 24th state. Capital: Jefferson City. *A34–A35*

Missouri River longest U.S. river, east from the Rockies to the Mississippi River.

Montana 41st state. Capital: Helena. *A34–A35*

Montgomery Alabama capital and site of 1955 African-American bus boycott. (32°N 86°W)

Nagasaki Japanese port city, one-third of which was destroyed by U.S. atomic bomb dropped to end World War II. (33°N 130°E) *829*

Nebraska 37th state. Capital: Lincoln. *A34–A35*

Nevada 36th state. Capital: Carson City. *A34–A35*

New England northeast U.S. region made up of Maine, New Hampshire, Vermont, Massachusetts, Rhode Island, and Connecticut. *72*

New France first permanent French colony in North America. *38*

New Hampshire 9th state. Capital: Concord. *A34–A35*

New Jersey 3rd state. Capital: Trenton. *A34–A35*

New Mexico 47th state. Capital: Santa Fe. *A34–A35*

New Netherland early Dutch colony that became New York in 1664. *38*

New Orleans Louisiana port city at mouth of the Mississippi River. *355*

New Spain former North American province of the Spanish Empire, made up mostly of present-day Mexico and the southwest United States. *42*

New York 11th state. Capital: Albany. *A34–A35*

New York City largest U.S. city, at the mouth of the Hudson River; temporary U.S. capital, 1785–1790.

Nicaragua Central American nation. Capital: Managua. *A24–A25*

Normandy region of northern France where Allied invasion in 1944 turned tide of World War II.

North America continent of Western Hemisphere north of Panama-Colombia border.

North Carolina 12th state. Capital: Raleigh. *A34–A35*

North Dakota 39th state. Capital: Bismarck. *A34–A35*

North Korea Communist country in Asia, bordering eastern China. Capital: Pyongyang. *852*

North Vietnam northern region of Vietnam, established in 1954; reunified with South Vietnam in 1975 after Vietnam War. *911*

Northwest Territory U.S. land north of the Ohio River to the Great Lakes and west to the Mississippi River; acquired in 1783. *240, 320*

Ohio 17th state. Capital: Columbus. *A34–A35*

Ohio River river that flows from western Pennsylvania to the Mississippi River.

Oklahoma 46th state. Capital: Oklahoma City. *A34–A35*

Oregon 33rd state. Capital: Salem. *A34–A35*

Oregon Country former region of northwest North America claimed jointly by Britain and the United States until 1846. *347, 434*

Oregon Trail pioneer wagon route from Missouri to the Oregon Territory in the 1840s and 1850s. *421*

Pacific Ocean world's largest ocean, on the west coast of the United States.

Panama Canal ship passageway cut through Panama in Central America, linking Atlantic and Pacific oceans. (8°N 80°W) *709*

Paris capital city of France. (49°N 2°E)

Pearl Harbor naval base in Hawaii; site of surprise Japanese aerial attack in 1941. (21°N 158°W) *805*

Pennsylvania 2nd state. Capital: Harrisburg. *A34–A35*

Persian Gulf waterway between Saudi Arabia and Iran, leading to Kuwait and Iraq. *947*

Philadelphia large port city in Pennsylvania; U.S. capital, 1790–1800. (40°N 76°W) *113*

Philippine Islands Pacific island country off the southeast coast of China. Capital: Manila. *701*

Plymouth town on Massachusetts coast and site of Pilgrim landing and colony. (42°N 71°W) *69*

Poland central European republic on the Baltic coast. Capital: Warsaw. (52°N 21°E) *A24–A25, 742*

Portugal nation in southwestern Europe; leader in early oceanic explorations. Capital: Lisbon. *A24–A25, 30*

Potomac River river separating Virginia from Maryland and Washington, D.C.

Puerto Rico Caribbean island that has been U.S. territory since 1898. *A30–A31*

Quebec major early Canadian city; also a province of eastern Canada. *38*

Rhode Island 13th state. Capital: Providence. *A34–A35*

Richmond Virginia capital that was also the capital of the Confederacy. (38°N 77°W)

Rio Grande river that forms part of the border between the United States and Mexico. *435*

Roanoke Island island off the coast of North Carolina; 1585 site of the first English colony in the Americas. (36°N 76°W) *59*

Rocky Mountains mountain range in the western United States and Canada. *A36–A37*

Russia large Eurasian country, the major republic of the former Soviet Union (1922–1991). Capital: Moscow. *A24–A25*

St. Augustine oldest permanent European settlement (1565) in the United States, on Florida's northeast coast. (30°N 81°W) *38*

St. Lawrence River Atlantic-to-Great Lakes waterway used by early explorers of mid-North America. *38*

St. Louis Missouri city at the junction of the Missouri and Mississippi rivers. (39°N 90°W) *363*

San Antonio Texas city and site of the Alamo. (29°N 99°W) *431*

San Francisco major port city in northern California. (38°N 123°W)

San Salvador West Indies island near the Bahamas where Columbus first landed in the Americas. (24°N 74°W)

Santa Fe Trail old wagon route from Missouri to Santa Fe in Mexican province of New Mexico. *421*

Scotland northern part of the island of Great Britain. *A24–A25*

Serbia republic, part of the former Yugoslavia. Capital: Belgrade. *A24–A25*

Sierra Nevada mountain range near the Pacific coast.

Songhai early West African trading empire succeeding Mali empire. *12*

South America continent of Western Hemisphere south of Panama-Colombia border.

South Carolina 8th state. Capital: Columbia. *A34–A35*

South Dakota 40th state. Capital: Pierre. *A34–A35*

South Korea East Asian country bordering North Korea. Capital: Seoul. *852*

South Vietnam southern region of Vietnam, established in 1954; reunified with North Vietnam in 1975 after Vietnam War. *911*

Soviet Union (U.S.S.R.) country created in 1922 by joining Russia and other republics; in 1991, broken into independent states. *843*

Spain nation in southwestern Europe; early empire builder in the Americas. Capital: Madrid. *A24–A25, 30*

Tennessee 16th state. Capital: Nashville. *A34–A35*

Tennessee Valley area of Appalachian Mountains drained by the Tennessee River. *791*

Tenochtitlán Aztec Empire capital; now site of Mexico City. *30*

Texas 28th state. Capital: Austin. *A34–A35*

Timbuktu city and trading center of ancient Mali. *14*

Utah 45th state. Capital: Salt Lake City. *A34–A35*

Valley Forge village in southeast Pennsylvania and site of Washington's army camp during winter of 1777–1778. (40°N 75°W) *193, 207, 208*

Vermont 14th state. Capital: Montpelier. *A34–A35*

Vicksburg Mississippi River site of major Union victory (1863) in Civil War. (32°N 91°W) *553, 556*

Vietnam country in Southeast Asia; divided into two regions (1954–1975), North and South, until end of Vietnam War. Capital: Hanoi. *A24–A25, 907, 911*

Virginia 10th state. Capital: Richmond. *A34–A35*

Washington 42nd state. Capital: Olympia. *A34–A35*

Washington, D.C. capital of the United States since 1800; makes up whole of District of Columbia (D.C.). (39°N 77°W) *274*

West Africa region from which most Africans were brought to the Americas.

Western Hemisphere the half of the world that includes the Americas. *A6*

West Indies numerous islands in the Caribbean Sea, between Florida and South America. *A30–A31*

West Virginia 35th state. Capital: Charleston. *A34–A35, 513*

Wisconsin 30th state. Capital: Madison. *A34–A35*

Wounded Knee South Dakota site that was scene of 1890 massacre of Sioux. (43°N 102°W)

Wyoming 44th state. Capital: Cheyenne. *A34–A35*

Yorktown Virginia village and site of American victory that sealed British defeat in Revolutionary War. (37°N 77°W) *216*

English Glossary

38th parallel line of latitude dividing North and South Korea (p. 850)

54th Massachusetts Volunteers regiment of African-American soldiers that gained fame for its courageous assault on Fort Wagner, South Carolina (p. 536)

9/11 hijackings 2001 terrorism plot to crash jets into New York's World Trade Center, the Pentagon, and the White House (p. 954)

A

abolition the movement to stop slavery (p. 464)

abridged shortened (p. 894)

Act of Toleration Maryland law that forbade religious persecution (p. 76)

activism direct action taken to support or oppose a social or political goal (p. 876)

Agent Orange chemical that kills plants; used in Vietnam to expose Viet Cong hideouts (p. 914)

al Qaeda (al•KAY•duh) terrorist group of radical Islamist fundamentalists (p. 954)

Alamo, Battle of the battle between Texas and Mexico in 1836 (p. 426)

Albany Plan of Union first formal proposal to unite the colonies (p. 142)

Alien and Sedition Acts series of four laws enacted in 1798 to reduce the political power of recent immigrants (p. 326)

aliens immigrants who are not yet citizens (p. 326)

alliance people or nations involved in a pact or treaty (p. 26)

Allies the World War I alliance of Great Britain, France, Russia, and others (p. 720)

ally (AL•eye) a country that agrees to help another country achieve a common goal (p. 204)

ambush an unexpected attack from a hidden position (p. 926)

amendment addition to a document (p. 248)

American Expeditionary (EK•speh•DISH•uh•nair•ee) **Force** the American army that fought in Europe in World War I (p. 728)

American Federation of Labor (AFL) a national organization of labor unions founded in 1886 by Samuel Gompers (pp. 656, 792)

American System plan introduced in 1815 to make America economically self-sufficient (p. 378)

amnesty official pardon (p. 570)

Anaconda Plan Union strategy to defeat the Confederacy (p. 510)

anarchist person who believes in anarchism or a society that has no government at all (p. 656)

Angel Island San Francisco Bay immigration station for Asian immigrants (p. 640)

Anglo English-speaking settler in the Southwest (p. 600)

annex join or merge territory into an existing political unity such as a country or state (p. 426)

Antietam, Battle of battle in Maryland that ended Lee's first invasion of the North (p. 522)

Antifederalists people who opposed ratification of the Constitution (p. 248)

Anti-Imperialist League group of influential Americans who believed the United States should not deny other people the right to govern themselves (p. 698)

anti-Semitism prejudice against Jews (p. 818)

Appalachian Mountains mountain range stretching from eastern Canada south to Alabama (p. 116)

appeasement meeting demands of a hostile power in order to avoid war (p. 806)

Appomattox Court House town in Virginia where Lee surrendered to Grant (p. 548)

apprentice (a•PREN•tis) one who is learning a trade from an experienced craftsperson (p. 126)

armistice (AR•mih•stiss) an end to fighting (p. 734)

arms race competition between the United States and the Soviet Union to develop more destructive weapons (p. 850)

arsenal place where weapons are kept (p. 234)

Articles of Confederation plan for national government ratified in 1781 (p. 234)

artillery cannon and large guns (p. 176)

artisans skilled craftspeople, such as blacksmiths and cabinet makers (p. 110)

assembly line manufacturing using a conveyor belt to move materials to workers who stay in one place to work (p. 752)

assimilate to absorb into a culture (p. 402)

assimilation the process of blending into society (p. 640)

attorney general nation's top legal officer; today also the head of the Department of Justice (p. 312)

Axis the Rome-Berlin Axis; the alliance between Mussolini and Hitler (p. 806)

Aztec Native American civilization that spread through what is now Mexico (p. 4)

B

baby boom a sharp increase in the U.S. birthrate following World War II (p. 858)

Backcountry the far western edges of the colonies (p. 94)

Bacon's Rebellion 1676 rebellion in Virginia (p. 102)

banish to force someone to leave a place (p. 66)

Bay of Pigs invasion failed U.S. attempt to overthrow Cuba's Communist leader (p. 908)

Bear Flag Revolt rebellion by Americans in 1846 against Mexican rule of California (p. 432)

Belleau (be•LOW) **Wood** site of American victory in France in 1918 (p. 734)

bickering petty quarreling (p. 480)

Bill of Rights first ten amendments to the U.S. Constitution (p. 248)

black codes laws passed by Southern states that limited the freedom of former slaves (pp. 570, 872)

Black Death deadly disease that spread through Europe in the 14th century (p. 16)

blitzkrieg German "lightning war" tactics (p. 806)

Bonus Army World War I veterans who came to Washington seeking early payment of bonuses for wartime service (p. 776)

boomtown town that experiences sudden growth in population or economic activity (p. 600)

border states slave states that bordered states in which slavery was illegal (p. 510)

Boston Massacre incident in 1770 in which British troops fired on and killed American colonists (p. 160)

Boston Tea Party incident in 1773, when colonists protested British policies by boarding British ships and throwing their cargoes of tea overboard (p. 160)

Boxer Rebellion 1900 nationalist uprising in China (p. 706)

boycott refusal to buy (p. 156)

braceros Mexican workers hired to perform farm labor during World War II (p. 812)

brinkmanship (BREENK•MIHN•ship) policy of going to the brink of war to combat communism (p. 850)

Brown v. Board of Education of Topeka 1954 case in which the Supreme Court ruled that "separate but equal" education for black and white students was unconstitutional (p. 876)

buffalo soldier name Native Americans gave to African-American soldiers in the West (p. 600)

Bulge, Battle of the December 1944 German assault in Ardennes region of Belgium and Luxembourg (p. 818)

Bull Moose Party progressive political party in 1912 presidential election (p. 678)

Bull Run, First Battle of first major battle of the Civil War (p. 510)

business cycle the pattern of good and bad economic times (p. 630)

cabinet group of Executive department heads that serve as the President's chief advisers (p. 312)

California Gold Rush migration of thousands of settlers to California in search of gold (p. 438)

Californios settlers of Spanish or Mexican descent who populated California (p. 438)

Cambodia country bordering Vietnam (p. 920)

Camp David Accords 1978 peace treaty between Egypt and Israel (p. 936)

carpetbagger Northerner who went to the South after the Civil War to help with Reconstruction (p. 570)

cash crops crops raised to be sold for money (p. 102)

Catholics Christian followers of the Roman Catholic Church (p. 16)

cede surrender, or give up (p. 318)

Central Powers the World War I alliance of Germany, Austria-Hungary, the Ottoman Empire, and Bulgaria (p. 720)

Charles Town, Battle of British siege of Charles Town (Charleston), South Carolina, in May 1780, in which the Americans suffered their worst defeat of the war (p. 212)

charter written contract giving the right to establish a colony (p. 60)

checks and balances the ability of each branch of government to exercise checks, or controls, over the other branches (p. 242)

Chinese Exclusion Act 1882 law which banned Chinese immigration (p. 640)

citizen person owing loyalty to and entitled to protection of a state or nation (p. 234)

civil rights rights granted to all citizens (p. 570)

Civil Rights Act of 1964 law banning segregation in public places and creating the Equal Employment Opportunity Commission (p. 884)

civilization complex society in which people share key characteristics such as language and religion (p. 4)

clans large groups of families that claim a common ancestor (p. 116)

Clayton Antitrust Act legislation that strengthened the Sherman Antitrust Act's power (p. 678)

coalition alliance (p. 954)

Code Talkers Navajo Indians recruited by the U.S. Marine Corps to transmit messages in the Navajo language (p. 826)

coercion (ko•ER•shun) practice of forcing someone to act in a certain way by use of pressure or threats (p. 352)

Cold War conflict between the United States and Soviet Union following World War II (p. 844)

Columbian Exchange transfer of plants, animals and diseases between the Western and Eastern hemispheres (p. 40)

Commander-In-Chief the President in his role as commander of all armed forces (p. 536)

committee of correspondence organization formed to exchange information about British policies and American resistance (p. 160)

Committee on Public Information government organization that produced propaganda to build support for the war (p. 728)

common shared land where public activities took place (p. 94)

commune a place where people or families live together and share everything (p. 920)

communism political system in which the government controls and plans the economy with the goal of common ownership of all property (p. 720)

compromise settlement of differences in which each side gives up something it wants (p. 582)

Compromise of 1850 series of laws intended to settle the major disagreements between free states and slave states (p. 480)

Compromise of 1877 agreement that decided the 1876 presidential election (p. 582)

Conestoga wagons covered wagons introduced by German immigrants (p. 110)

Confederate States of America confederation formed in 1861 by the Southern states after their secession from the Union (p. 498)

Confederation Congress national legislative body formed by the Articles of Confederation (p. 234)

conform to agree with the beliefs and ideas of the majority (p. 858)

congregation a group of people who belong to the same church (p. 66)

Congress of Industrial Organizations (CIO) labor union; included skilled and unskilled workers; open to women and minorities (p. 792)

Congress of Racial Equality (CORE) organization that planned Freedom Rides (p. 884)

conquistador (kahn•KEES•tuh•dawr) Spanish soldier that explored the Americas and claimed land for Spain (p. 26)

conscription military draft (p. 542)

conservation controlling resource usage (p. 672)

Conservative someone who favors restricted policies in social and economic reform (p. 792)

Constitutional Convention 1787 meeting at which the U.S. Constitution was created (p. 242)

consumer person who buys something (p. 662)

containment policy to stop the spread of communism (p. 844)

Continental Army America's Patriot army during the Revolutionary War (p. 176)

contractor private supplier (p. 516)

converts people who accept a new religious belief (p. 418)

convoy a guard that accompanies and protects ships or troops (p. 734)

Copperheads Northern Democrats who favored peace with the South (p. 542)

corporation a business owned by investors who buy part of it through shares of stock (p. 630)

corps (kor) a number of people acting together for a similar purpose (p. 344)

cotton gin machine that made cleaning seeds from cotton faster (p. 372)

counterculture movement of mostly young Americans who had become disillusioned with the Vietnam War and injustices in society (p. 920)

credit arrangement for delayed payment of a loan or purchase (p. 752)

Crittenden Compromise compromise introduced in 1861 that might have prevented secession (p. 498)

Cuban missile crisis 1962 confrontation between the United States and the Soviet Union caused by Soviet nuclear missiles in Cuba (p. 908)

Daughters of Liberty organization of colonial women formed to protest British policies (p. 160)

Dawes Act 1887 law that distributed reservation land to individual Native American owners (p. 608)

D-Day Allied invasion of France on June 6, 1944 (p. 818)

Declaration of Independence document that declared American independence from Britain (p. 176)

deficit spending using borrowed money to fund government programs (p. 784)

denomination distinct religious group (p. 110)

depression a severe economic slump (pp. 408, 582)

desert (duh•ZERT) to leave military duty without permission (p. 204)

direct primary primary in which voters, not party conventions, choose candidates to run for public office (p. 672)

disenfranchised (DISS•ehn•FRAN•chyzd) people deprived of legal rights, especially the right to vote (p. 884)

dislodge remove (p. 548)

disputes (dis•PYOOTS) disagreements (p. 222)

dissenter (dih•SEHN•tuhr) a person who disagrees with an official church (p. 66)

diversity variety (p. 76)

doctrine of nullification idea that a state had the right to nullify, or reject, a federal law that it considers unconstitutional (p. 394)

domino theory belief that if a country fell to communism, nearby countries would follow (p. 908)

doves Americans who opposed the Vietnam War (p. 920)

Dred Scott v. *Sandford* 1856 Supreme Court case in which a slave, Dred Scott, sued for his freedom; the court ruled against Scott (p. 490)

Dust Bowl region including parts of Kansas, Oklahoma, Texas, Colorado, and New Mexico in which farms were damaged by dust storms (p. 792)

duties taxes placed on imported goods (p. 160)

Eighteenth Amendment constitutional amendment enacting Prohibition (p. 682)

electoral votes votes made by members of the Electoral College, which elects the president and vice president (p. 582)

elite highest-ranking social group (p. 76)

Ellis Island New York Harbor immigration station for European immigrants (p. 640)

emancipate to free (p. 536)

Emancipation Proclamation document issued by Lincoln that declared that all slaves in Confederate territory were free (p. 536)

Embargo Act of 1807 law that forbade American ships from sailing to foreign ports and closed American ports to British ships (p. 352)

emigrant person who leaves a country (p. 450)

encomienda grant of Native American slave labor (p. 40)

English Bill of Rights 1689 laws protecting the rights of English subjects and Parliament (p. 136)

Enlightenment philosophical movement stressing human reason (p. 126)

enlist to join the armed forces (p. 516)

entitlements government programs that guaranteed certain benefits to citizens (p. 946)

epidemic outbreak of a contagious disease that spreads rapidly and widely (p. 734)

Equal Rights Amendment (ERA) amendment proposed that would give equality of rights regardless of sex (p. 894)

Erie Canal waterway that connected New York City with Buffalo, New York (p. 378)

escalation policy of increasing military involvement in Vietnam (p. 914)

Espionage (ESS•PEE•eh•nazh) **Act** 1917 law that set heavy fines and long prison terms for antiwar activities (p. 728)

evolution scientific theory of how life forms developed over millions of years (p. 758)

executive branch government department that enforces laws (p. 242)

Exodusters name for African Americans who settled on the Great Plains (p. 616)

expatriate (ehk•SPAY•tree•IHT) a citizen of one country who lives in another country (p. 762)

export to send abroad for trade or sale (p. 40)

F

factory system method of production using many workers and machines in one building (p. 364)

Fair Deal social reforms proposed by Truman; built on Roosevelt's New Deal (p. 844)

fall line the point at which waterfalls prevent large boats from moving farther upriver (p. 116)

Fallen Timbers, Battle of 1794 battle between Native Americans and American forces (p. 318)

famine (FAM•ihn) severe food shortage leading to starvation (p. 450)

fascism political philosophy that advocates a strong nationalistic dictatorship (p. 806)

Federal Judiciary (joo•DISH•ee•ER•ee) **Act** 1789 law passed by the first Congress that set up lower Federal courts (p. 312)

Federal Reserve Act law that created the modern banking system (p. 678)

federalism system of government in which power is shared between the national (or federal) government and the states (p. 248)

The Federalist papers ratification essays published in New York newspapers (p. 248)

Federalists people who supported ratification of the Constitution (p. 248)

Fifteenth Amendment constitutional amendment that stated citizens could not be stopped from voting "on account of race, color, or previous condition of servitude" (p. 582)

fireside chats series of radio talks in which FDR explained his policies in a casual style (p. 784)

First Continental Congress meeting of delegates from most of the colonies, called in reaction to the Intolerable Acts (p. 168)

First New Deal 1933–1935 program created by President Roosevelt to fight the Depression (p. 784)

flapper a young woman eager to try the latest fashion, dance, or fad (p. 758)

Ford's Theatre theater in Washington, D.C. where Lincoln was shot (p. 558)

foreign policy relations with the governments of other nations (p. 326)

Fort Sumter a Union fort in the harbor of Charleston, South Carolina (p. 510)

forty-niner person who went to California to find gold in 1849 (p. 438)

Founders people who helped create the U.S. Constitution (p. 242)

Fourteen Points President Woodrow Wilson's goals for peace after World War I (p. 740)

Fourteenth Amendment constitutional amendment that made all people born in the U.S. (including former slaves) citizens (p. 570)

Freedman's Bureau federal agency set up to help former enslaved people (p. 570)

freedmen's school school set up to educate newly freed African Americans (p. 576)

Freedom Rides protest against segregation on interstate busing in the South (p. 884)

Freedom Summer 1964 voter-registration drive for Southern blacks (p. 884)

Free-Soil Party a political party dedicated to stopping the expansion of slavery (p. 480)

French and Indian War war of 1754–1763 between Britain, France, and their allies for control of North America (p. 142)

French Indochina French-ruled colony made up of Vietnam, Laos, and Cambodia (p. 908)

French Revolution revolution overthrowing the government in France that began in 1787 and ended in violence and mass executions (p. 318)

frontier parts of the West that were occupied mainly by Native Americans, rather than settlers (p. 596)

Fugitive Slave Act an 1850 law to help slaveholders recapture runaway slaves (p. 480)

Fundamental Orders of Connecticut document that has been called the first written constitution in America (p. 66)

fundamentalism belief that every word of the Bible is literally true (p. 758)

G

G.I. Bill of Rights government bill that paid for veterans' education and living expenses (p. 832)

galleon sailing ship (p. 34)

Gettysburg, Battle of battle in 1863 in Pennsylvania when Union forces stopped a Confederate invasion of the North (p. 548)

Ghana West African kingdom that prospered between A.D. 700 and 1000 (p. 10)

Gilded Age late 1800s era of fabulous wealth (p. 630)

Glorious Revolution events of 1688–1689, during which the English Parliament invited William and Mary to replace James II as monarchs (p. 136)

gold standard a policy under which the government backs every dollar with a certain amount of gold (p. 616)

Grange organization formed in 1867 to meet the social needs of farm families (p. 616)

grassroots group of ordinary people who come together at a local level for a cause (p. 876)

Great Awakening Christian religious movement (p. 126)

Great Compromise agreement to establish a two-house national legislature, with all states having equal representation in one house and each state having representation based on its population in the other house (p. 242)

Great Depression the serious and worldwide economic decline of the 1930's (p. 776)

great famine a widespread food shortage that killed thousands of Europeans (p. 16)

Great Migration (17th Century) the movement of tens of thousands of English settlers to New England during the 1630s (p. 66)

Great Migration (20th Century) the movement of African Americans from the South to northern cities between 1910–1920 (p. 740)

Great Plains the area from the Missouri River to the Rocky Mountains (p. 596)

Great Society President Johnson's programs to help the poor, elderly, and women (p. 884)

greenback paper money introduced during the Civil War (p. 542)

Greenville, Treaty of 1795 treaty in which 12 Native American tribes ceded control of much of Ohio and Indiana to the U.S. government. (p. 318)

gross national product total value of all the goods and services produced by a nation during a year (p. 812)

Guadalcanal first U.S. land victory over the Japanese, 1943 (p. 826)

Guadalupe Hidalgo (gwah•duh•LOOP•ay hih•DAHL•go), **Treaty of** treaty that ended the War with Mexico (p. 432)

guerillas (guh•RIL•uhz) small bands of fighters who weaken the enemy with surprise raids and hit-and-run attacks (p. 194)

guerrilla warfare surprise attacks by small bands of fighters (p. 914)

Gulf of Tonkin Resolution 1964 legislation that gave President Johnson the power to use military force in Vietnam (p. 914)

H

hacienda large farm or estate (p. 40)

Hamdan v. Rumsfeld 2006 Supreme Court decision requiring humane treatment of military prisoners (p. 954)

Harlem Renaissance a burst of African American culture in the 1920s and 1930s (p. 762)

Harpers Ferry a federal arsenal in Virginia captured in 1859 during an antislavery revolt (p. 490)

hawks Americans who supported the Vietnam War (p. 920)

Haymarket Affair 1886 union protest (p. 656)

H-bomb hyroden bomb (p. 850)

headright land grant given to one who could pay his or her way to the colonies (p. 60)

heritage tradition (p. 136)

Hiroshima Japanese city that was hit with the first atomic bomb on August 6, 1945 (p. 826)

Ho Chi Minh Trail secret route used by North Vietnamese to send troops and supplies to the Viet Cong (p. 908)

Holocaust Nazi German crime of killing more than 11 million Jews and other persecuted peoples in concentration camps (p. 818)

Homestead Act 1862 law that offered 160 acres free to anyone who agreed to live on and improve the land for five years (p. 616)

Homestead Strike violent strike at Andrew Carnegie's Homestead, Pennsylvania, steel mills in 1892 (p. 656)

House of Burgesses the Virginia assembly, which was the first representative assembly in the American colonies (p. 60)

Huguenots French Protestants (p. 76)

Hull House settlement house founded by Jane Addams in Chicago (p. 640)

Hundred Days March 9 to mid-June 1933 Congressional session in which many laws to fight the Depression were passed (p. 784)

hygiene conditions and practices that promote health (p. 516)

I

immigrant person who settles in a new country (p 450)

impeach to formally accuse the president of misconduct in office (p. 570)

imperialism policy by which stronger nations extend their economic, political, or military control over weaker nations (p. 694)

impressment the act of seizing by force; between 1803 and 1812, the British impressed, or kidnapped, about 6,000 American sailors to work on British ships (p. 352)

inaugurate (in•AW•gyuh•rate) to formally swear in or induct into office (p. 312)

Inca Native American civilization that developed in what is now Peru (p. 4)

income tax tax on earnings (p. 542)

indentured servant one who worked for a set time without pay in exchange for a free passage to America (p. 60)

Indian Removal Act 1830 law that called for the government to negotiate treaties requiring Native Americans to relocate west (p. 402)

Indian Territory an area to which Native Americans were moved that covered what is now Oklahoma and parts of Kansas and Nebraska (p. 402)

indigo plant that produces a deep blue dye (p. 102)

Industrial Revolution the economic changes of the late 1700s, when large-scale manufacturing replaced farming as the main form of work (p. 364)

infamy evil fame or reputation (p. 806)

inflation an increase in prices and a decrease in the value of money (p. 408)

infringe (ihn•FRINJ) to violate (p. 872)

installment buying paying for items in small, monthly payments (p. 752)

insurgent one who rebels or revolts (p. 954)

integrate to open to people of all races or ethnic groups (p. 876)

Intolerable Acts series of laws, known in Britain as the Coercive Acts, meant to punish Massachusetts and clamp down on resistance in other colonies (p. 168)

investor person who puts money into a project to earn a profit (p. 60)

Iran-Contra affair 1986 scandal in which the United States sold weapons to Iran and gave the money to Contra rebels in Nicaragua (p. 946)

Islam religion that teaches there is one God, named Allah, and Muhammad is his prophet (p. 10)

island hopping Allied strategy in Pacific of invading selected islands, and using them as bases to advance closer to Japan (p. 826)

J

Jacksonian democracy the idea of widening political power to more of the people (p. 394)

Jamestown the first permanent English settlement in North America (p. 60)

Japanese-American internment the removal of Japanese Americans from the West to prison camps during World War II (p. 812)

Jay's Treaty agreement that ended the dispute with Britain over American shipping during the French Revolution (p. 318)

Jazz Age name for the 1920s, because of the popularity of jazz — a new type of American music that combined African rhythms, blues, and ragtime (p. 758)

Jim Crow laws enacted in Southern states designed to separate white and black people (p. 650)

joint-stock company company funded by a group of investors (p. 60)

judicial branch government department that interprets laws (p. 242)

judicial review principle that states that the Supreme Court has the final say in interpreting the Constitution (p. 338)

Judiciary Act of 1801 law that let President John Adams fill federal judgeships with Federalists (p. 338)

K

kamikaze (KAH•mih•KAH•zee) Japanese suicide pilot (p. 826)

Kansas-Nebraska Act 1854 law that established the territories of Kansas and Nebraska and gave their residents the right to decide whether to allow slavery (p. 480)

Kentucky and Virginia Resolutions Resolutions passed by Kentucky and Virginia in 1798 giving the states the right to declare acts of Congress null and void (p. 326)

King Philip's War 1675–1676 Native American uprising against the Puritan colonies (p. 94)

Knights of Labor an organization of workers from all trades formed after the Civil War (p. 656)

Know-Nothing Party political party in the United States during the 1850s that was against recent immigrants and Roman Catholics (p. 450)

Kongo Central African kingdom that ruled during the 1400s (p. 10)

Korean War conflict involving U.S.-led UN forces against North Korea and China (p. 850)

Kosovo (KAW•suh•VOH) province of southern Serbia that is inhabited mostly by people of Albanian descent (p. 946)

Ku Klux Klan secret group that used violence to try to restore Democratic control of the South and keep African-Americans powerless (p. 576)

L

labor union group of workers who band together to seek better working conditions (p. 456)

laissez-faire economics theory that business, if free of government regulation, will act in ways that benefit the nation (p. 752)

Land Ordinance of 1785 law that established a plan for dividing the federally owned lands west of the Appalachian Mountains (p. 234)

land speculators (SPEC•yuh•LAY•tors) people who buy land in the hope that it will increase in value (p. 418)

Latinos people in the United States who trace their origins to Latin American countries and cultures (p. 894)

League of Nations an organization set up after World War I to settle international conflicts (p. 740)

legislative branch government department that makes laws (p. 242)

leisure freedom from time-consuming duties (p. 662)

Lend-Lease Act allowed the United States to lend weapons to allies (p. 806)

levy impose or raise a tax (p. 234)

Lewis and Clark expedition group that explored the Louisiana Territory and lands west; also known as the Corps of Discovery (p. 344)

Lexington and Concord first battles of the Revolutionary War (p. 168)

Liberal someone who favors federal government action to bring about social and economic reform (p. 792)

liberation the act of setting someone free (p. 536)

literacy the ability to read and write (p. 126)

Little Bighorn, Battle of the 1876 battle in which the Sioux and Cheyenne killed an entire force of U.S. troops (p. 608)

lode deposit of mineral buried in rock (p. 600)

Lone Star Republic nickname of the Republic of Texas once free from Mexico (p. 426)

long drive journey that takes cattle by foot to a railway (p. 600)

Lost Generation Americans who became disillusioned with society after World War I (p. 762)

Louisiana Purchase American purchase of the Louisiana Territory from France in 1803 (p. 344)

Lowell mills textile mills located in the factory town of Lowell, Massachusetts (p. 364)

Loyalists Americans who supported the British (p. 168)

lynch to kill by hanging without due process of law (p. 576)

M

Magna Carta charter of English political and civil liberties (p. 136)

majority rule system of government in which more than one half of a group holds the power to make decisions binding the entire group (p. 248)

malaria infectious disease spread by mosquitoes (p. 706)

Mali West African kingdom that ruled from about 1200 to 1400 (p. 10)

Manhattan Project top-secret government project to develop the atomic bomb (p. 826)

manifest destiny belief that the U.S. was meant to expand from coast to coast (p. 432)

March on Washington huge civil rights demonstration in Washington, D.C., in 1963 (p. 884)

maroon runaway or fugitive slave (p. 48)

Marshall Plan U.S. plan developed by George C. Marshall to help boost the economies of European nations after the war (p. 832)

mass culture common culture experienced by a large number of people (p. 662)

mass media communications that reach a large audience (p. 758)

materialistic putting value on material things above intellectual or spiritual things (p. 762)

Maya ancient Native American civilization of Mesoamerica (p. 4)

Mayflower Compact document that helped establish the practice of self-government (p. 66)

mechanical reaper a device that cuts grain (p. 364)

melting pot a place where cultures blend (p. 640)

mercantilism (MUR•kuhn•tee•LIHZ•uhm) economic system that increased money in a country's treasury by creating a favorable balance of trade (pp. 26, 60)

mercenary (MUR•suh•NAIR•ee) a professional soldier hired to fight for a foreign country (p. 194)

Merrimack Confederate ironclad ship, later renamed the *Virginia* (p. 516)

Mesoamerica region that stretches from modern-day Mexico to Nicaragua (p. 4)

Mexican cession Mexican territory surrendered to the United States at the end of the war with Mexico (p. 432)

Mexicano (may•hi•KAH•noh) Spanish word for a person of Mexican heritage; a Spanish-speaking person in the Southwest whose ancestors had come from Mexico (p. 600)

middle passage middle leg of the triangular trade route that brought captured Africans to the Americas to serve as slaves (p. 48)

Midway, Battle of U.S. victory over Japanese off Midway Island that proved to be the turning point of the war (p. 826)

migrate to move from one region to another (p. 4)

migration movement of people from one country or locality to another (p. 438)

militarism policy of making military power a primary goal of a nation and using that power to achieve national aims (p. 720)

militia a force of armed civilians pledged to defend their community (p. 168)

Minutemen group of armed civilians, trained to be ready to fight "at a minute's warning" (p. 168)

mission settlement created by the Spanish church in order to convert Native Americans to Christianity (p. 40)

missionary person sent by the Church to convert Native Americans to Christianity (p. 26)

Missouri Compromise laws enacted in 1820 to maintain balance of power between slave and free states (p. 378)

Monitor Union ironclad ship (p. 516)

monopoly business that gains control of an industry by eliminating other competitors (p. 630)

Monroe Doctrine U.S. policy opposing European interference in the Western Hemisphere (p. 378)

Montgomery bus boycott 1955 protest action to end segregation on buses in Montgomery, Alabama (p. 876)

Mormon member of a church founded by Joseph Smith in 1830 (p. 418)

mountain men trappers and explorers who opened up the western pioneer trails (p. 418)

muckraker (MUHK•RAYK•er) writer who exposed corruption in American society (p. 672)

Muslim follower of the religion of Islam (p. 10)

N NAACP National Association for the Advancement of Colored People (p. 650)

napalm jellied gasoline that burns violently; used to destroy vegetation and as a weapon (p. 914)

National Congress of American Indians (NCAI) organization founded in 1944 to promote rights of Native Americans (p. 894)

National Organization for Women (NOW) organization founded in 1966 to get women good jobs at equal pay (p. 894)

nationalism a feeling of pride, loyalty, and protectiveness towards one's country (pp. 378, 720)

nativist native-born American who wanted to eliminate foreign influence (p. 450)

NATO North Atlantic Treaty Organization, a military alliance that included Canada, the United States, and ten European nations (p. 844)

Navigation Acts laws passed by the English government to ensure that England made money from its colonies' trade (p. 94)

Ndongo Central African kingdom that ruled during the 1400s (p. 10)

neutral (NEW•truhl) not favoring any one side (p. 194)

New France first permanent French settlement in North America (p. 34)

New Jersey Plan proposal for a legislature in which each state would have one vote (p. 242)

New Netherland first permanent Dutch colony in North America (pp. 34, 82)

Nineteenth Amendment constitutional amendment that gave women the vote (p. 682)

Nisei (NEE•say) Japanese Americans born in the United States (p. 812)

nomadic characterized by moving from place to place (p. 608)

nondenominational not favoring any particular religion (p. 222)

nonsedentary societies people who move continually in search of food (p. 4)

North American Free Trade Agreement (NAFTA) 1993 agreement that limited tariffs on trade among the United States, Mexico, and Canada (p. 946)

North Atlantic current clockwise ocean current that flows between Northern Europe and the Caribbean Sea (p. 16)

Northwest Ordinance law that described how the Northwest Territory was to governed (p. 234)

Northwest Territory lands northwest of the Appalachians, covered by the Land Ordinance of 1785 (p. 234)

nullification idea that a state could cancel a federal law within the state (p. 326)

Nuremberg trials war crime trials of Nazi leaders in Nuremberg, Germany (p. 832)

O Open Door Policy U.S. policy proposed in 1899 which stated no single country should have a monopoly on trade with China (p. 706)

Oregon Trail trail that ran westward from Independence, Missouri, to the Oregon Territory (p. 418)

Organization of Petroleum Exporting Countries (OPEC) nations, mostly in the Middle East, that cut oil shipments to the United States in 1973 (p. 936)

outposts (OWT•posts) military bases, usually located on the frontier (p. 222)

overseers people who watch over and direct the work of slaves (p. 102)

Pacifist (PAS•uh•fist) someone who is opposed to all war (p. 194)

pact formal agreement; a bargain (p. 142)

Palmer Raids raids carried out by federal agents and police against radicals at the direction of U.S. Attorney-General, A. Mitchell Palmer (p. 740)

Panama Canal canal through the Isthmus of Panama that connects the Atlantic and Pacific (p. 706)

Panic of 1837 widespread fear about the state of the economy that spread after Van Buren took office (p. 408)

Panic of 1873 financial panic in which banks closed and the stock market crashed (p. 582)

Paris, Treaty of (1763) treaty that ended the war between France and Britain (p. 142)

Paris, Treaty of (1783) the 1783 treaty that ended the Revolutionary War (p. 222)

Parliament England's chief lawmaking body (p. 136)

patents government documents giving an inventor the exclusive right to make and sell an invention for a specific number of years (p. 630)

Patriots Americans who sided with the rebels (p. 168)

patronage (PA•truh•nihj) exchanging government jobs and contracts for political support (p. 672)

patroon person rewarded with a large land grant for bringing 50 settlers to New Netherland (p. 82)

Pearl Harbor Hawaiian port; granted by 1887 treaty to the United States for use as a refueling station for U.S. ships (pp. 694, 806)

persecute (PUR•sih•KYOOT) to mistreat (p. 66)

Persian Gulf War 1990–1991 war in which the United States and the United Nations drove Iraq out of Kuwait (p. 946)

Philadelphia settlement on the Delaware River that became the fastest growing city in the colonies (p. 110)

Pickett's Charge failed assault on Union positions on final day of Battle of Gettysburg (p. 548)

Piedmont the broad plateau that lies at the foot of the Blue Ridge Mountains of the Appalachian range (p. 116)

Pilgrims Separatist group that traveled to America to gain religious freedom (p. 66)

Pinckney's (PINK•neez) **Treaty** 1795 treaty with Spain allowing Americans to use the Mississippi River and to store goods in New Orleans (p. 318)

plantation large farm that raises cash crops (p. 40)

platform statement of beliefs (p. 498)

Platt Amendment agreement stating the United States' right to intervene in Cuban affairs (p. 698)

Plessy v. *Ferguson* 1896 Supreme Court case that upheld the legality of segregation (p. 650)

plunder steal from, ransack (p. 522)

political machine organization that controls a local government (p. 640)

political party group of people that tries to promote its ideas and influence government (p. 326)

Pontiac's Rebellion Native American revolt against the British colonies (p. 142)

popular culture movies, fashions, songs, slang, and other expressions of culture that appeal to many people (p. 758)

Populist Party political party formed in 1890s that wanted a policy that would raise crop prices (p. 616)

populous heavily populated (p. 510)

Potsdam Conference Allies' meeting in Potsdam, Germany, to plan the end of World War II (p. 832)

precedent (PRE•seh•dent) an example that becomes standard practice (p. 312)

prejudice (PREHJ•uh•dihs) a negative opinion that is not based on facts (p. 450)

printing press device that mechanically printed pages by pressing inked forms onto paper, invented in about 1455 (p. 16)

privateer (pry•vuh•TEER) a privately owened ship that has been granted permission by a wartime government to attack an enemy's merchant ships (p. 204)

Proclamation of 1763 British declaration that forbade colonists from settling west of the Appalachians (p. 142)

progressivism (pruh•GREHS•ih•VIHZ•uhm) reform movements that sought to raise living standards and correct wrongs in American society (p. 672)

Prohibition legal ban on alcohol imposed by the Eighteenth Amendment (p. 758)

prohibition (PROH•uh•BIHSH•uhn) legal ban on the production, possession, and sale of alcohol (p. 682)

prolong to lengthen (in time) (p. 536)

prominent important and well known (p. 136)

proprietary colony colony governed by a single owner, or proprietor (p. 76)

protective tariff a tax on imported goods that protects a nation's businesses from foreign competition (p. 378)

Protestants Christian group that broke away from the Catholic Church (p. 16)

public works government-funded projects to assist individuals, families, and communities in need (p. 776)

Pueblo Native Americans who built great mud-brick cities (p. 4)

"pull" factor a reason or force that causes people to choose to move to a new place (p. 450)

Pullman Strike nationwide railway strike that spread throughout the rail industry in 1894 (p. 656)

Puritans English dissenters who wanted to reform the Church of England (p. 66)

"push" factor a reason or force that causes people to leave their native land (p. 450)

Quakers group of Protestant dissenters (p. 66)

Quartering Act act requiring the colonists to quarter, or house, British soldiers and provide them with supplies (p. 156)

Quebec, Battle of battle that led to the British victory in the French and Indian War (p. 142)

R

racism belief that some people are inferior because of their race (p. 48)

Radical Republican congressman who favored using federal power to rebuild the South and promote African-American rights (p. 570)

radical person who takes extreme political positions (p. 338)

ragtime music that blended African-American songs and European musical forms (p. 662)

ratification act of official confirmation (p. 234)

ratify approve (p. 558)

rationing the distribution of scarce resources and products (p. 812)

Reconstruction period from 1865 to 1877, in which the U.S. government attempted to rebuild the Southern society and governments (p. 570)

Red Scare fearful reaction in 1919-1920 that the United States was threatened by a Communist revolution (p. 740)

redoubt (re•DOWT) a small fort (p. 212)

Reformation movement that divided the church between Catholics and Protestants (p. 16)

region distinct area of land (p. 76)

Renaissance a time of increased interest in art and learning in Europe (p. 16)

rendezvous (RAHN•day•voo) a meeting (p. 194)

reparations (REHP•eh•RAY•shunz) money that a defeated nation pays for the destruction caused by war (p. 740)

republic state, country or nation in which people elect representatives to govern (p. 234)

Republican Party political party formed in 1854 by opponents of slavery (p. 490)

reservation land set aside by the U.S. government for Native American tribes (p. 608)

revenue income (p. 678)

robber baron a business leader who became wealthy through dishonest methods (p. 630)

rock 'n' roll musical style based on rhythm and blues that became popular in the 1950s (p. 858)

Roosevelt Corollary United States' claim of right to interfere in the affairs of Latin American countries (p. 706)

Rough Riders members of the First U. S. Volunteer Cavalry, organized by Theodore Roosevelt during the Spanish-American War (p. 698)

royal colony colony ruled by the king's appointed officials (p. 60)

S

Sahara a large desert in Northern Africa (p. 10)

Sand Creek Massacre 1864 attack in which as many as 200 Cheyenne were killed by the Colorado militia (p. 608)

Santa Fe Trail trail that began in Missouri and ended in Santa Fe, New Mexico (p. 418)

Saratoga (sair•uh•TOH•guh), **Battles of** a series of conficts in 1777 near Albany, New York (p. 194)

savanna flat grassland with abundant wildlife, thorny bushes and scattered trees (p. 10)

scalawag white Southerner who supported Radical Reconstruction (p. 570)

Scots-Irish the name give to people from the borderlands of Scotland and England and from the region of northern Ireland (p. 116)

secede (sih•SEED) to withdraw (pp. 394, 498)

Second Battle of the Marne battle that was the turning point of the war (p. 734)

Second Continental Congress America's government during the Revolutionary War (p. 176)

Second Great Awakening renewal of religious faith in the 1790s and early 1800s (p. 456)

Second New Deal 1935-1937 extension of Roosevelt's First New Deal (p. 784)

sectionalism loyalty to the interests of one's own region or section of the country (p. 378)

sedentary societies people who settled in permanent villages or towns (p. 4)

Sedition (seh•DISH•un) **Act** 1918 law that made it illegal to criticize the government (p. 728)

sedition stirring up rebellion against a government (p. 326)

segregation (seh•greh•GA•shun) the separation of races (pp. 650, 872)

semisedentary societies people who settled in villages or towns but moved every few years in search of food (p. 4)

Seneca Falls Convention a women's rights convention held in Seneca Falls, New York (p. 464)

settlement house community center providing help to immigrants and the poor (p. 682)

Seven Days' Battles Confederate victory during which Lee stopped the Union campaign against Richmond (p. 522)

Seventeenth Amendment amendment that provided for direct election of U.S. senators (p. 678)

Shaker member of a Christian sect that practiced communal living and did not allow marriage and childbearing (p. 456)

sharecropping system under which landowners gave poor farmers seed, tools, and land to cultivate in exchange for part of their harvest (p. 576)

shareholder an investor who buys part of a company through shares of stock (p. 630)

Shays's Rebellion uprising of Massachusetts farmers who wanted debt relief (p. 234)

Sherman Antitrust Act law that made it illegal for corporations to gain control of industries by forming trusts (p. 672)

Sherman's March to the Sea Union General Sherman's destructive march across Georgia (p. 548)

Shiloh, Battle of bloody battle in Tennessee won by Grant (p. 522)

siege when enemy forces surround a town or city in order to force it to surrender (p. 176)

Siege of Vicksburg the surrounding of the city of Vicksburg, Mississippi, by Union forces (p. 548)

sit-down strike union tactic in which workers stayed idle in plant rather than walking out (p. 792)

English Glossary **R57**

sit-in protest in which people sit in a place and refuse to move until their demands are met (p. 876)

Sixteenth Amendment amendment that gave Congress the power to create income taxes (p. 678)

slash-and-burn process of clearing land by cutting down and burning trees (p. 4)

slave codes law passed to regulate the treatment of slaves (p. 48)

slave someone who is captured for use in forced, unpaid labor (p. 10)

slavery practice of one person being owned by another (p. 48)

slum neighborhood with overcrowded and dangerous housing (p. 640)

smallpox highly infectious and often fatal disease (p. 142)

smuggling importing or exporting goods illegally (p. 94)

social gospel movement reforms based on Christian values (p. 640)

Social Security Act law creating fund for assisting retired workers and the unemployed (p. 784)

socialism system in which the state controls the economy (p. 656)

society group of people with common interests, customs and way of life (p. 4)

sod the top layer of prairie soil that contains thick, tightly tangled grass roots (p. 616)

sodbusters name for pioneer farmers on the Great Plains (p. 616)

solar time time based on the calculations of the sun's passage across the sky (p. 596)

Sons of Liberty secret society formed to opposed British policies (p. 156)

South Atlantic current counter clockwise current that flows between Africa and South America (p. 16)

Southern Christian Leadership Conference (SCLC) organization that coordinated non-violent civil rights protests across the South (p. 876)

space race competition between the United States and the Soviet Union to lead in space exploration (p. 850)

Spanish Armada large fleet of ships sent to invade England and restore Catholicism (p. 34)

Spanish-American War 1898 war that began when the United States demanded Cuba's independence from Spain (p. 698)

speakeasy nightclub that illegally served alcohol (p. 758)

speculate to buy as an investment (p. 156)

speculation buying and selling risky items in the hope of making a quick profit (p. 776)

sphere of influence areas where foreign nations claimed special rights and economic privileges (p. 706)

spirituals religious folk songs (p. 372)

spoils system the practice of giving government jobs to political backers (p. 394)

Stalingrad Soviet city where German army was forced to surrender after a battle that lasted for months (p. 818)

Stamp Act law requiring all legal and commercial documents to carry and official stamp showing that a tax had been paid (p. 156)

standard time the time zones devised by railroad companies (p. 596)

states' rights the idea that the states have certain rights that the federal government cannot overrule (p. 326)

steerage the cheapest deck on a ship (p. 450)

Stock Market Crash of 1929 plunge in stock market prices that marked the beginning of the Great Depression (p. 776)

stock market place where shares of ownership in companies are bought and sold (p. 582)

Stono Rebellion 1739 slave rebellion in South Carolina (p. 102)

strategy (STRA•tuh•jee) an overall plan of action (p. 194)

strike to stop work to demand better working conditions (p. 456)

Student Nonviolent Coordinating Committee (SNCC) organization created to give young people a greater role in the civil rights movement (p. 876)

subsistence farming producing just enough food for one's needs (p. 94)

suburbs residential areas surrounding a city (p. 858)

suffrage the right to vote (p. 464)

Sugar Act law placing a tax on sugar, molasses, and other products shipped to the colonies (p. 156)

sunbelt warmer states in the southern and southwestern United States (p. 858)

sweatshop place where workers labored long hours under poor conditions for low wages (p. 640)

T

Tammany Hall New York City political machine (p. 640)

Tariff of Abominations 1828 law that significantly raised tariffs on raw materials and manufactured goods (p. 394)

tariff tax on imported goods (p. 312)

Teapot Dome Scandal corruption by a Harding cabinet member, who took bribes to allow oil drilling on public lands (p. 752)

Tejanos (tay•HAH•nohs) people of Mexican heritage who consider Texas their home (p. 426)

Tejas (tay•HAHS) name the Spanish explorers gave present-day Texas (p. 426)

temperance movement campaign to stop the drinking of alcohol (p. 456)

tenements run-down and overcrowded apartment houses (p. 640)

Tet offensive surprise Communist attack on U. S. and South Vietnamese forces in 1968; further weakened American support for the war (p. 914)

Thirteenth Amendment Constitutional amendment that ended slavery (p. 558)

Three-Fifths Compromise agreement that three-fifths of a state's slave population would be counted for representation and taxation (p. 242)

threshing machine a device that separates kernels of wheat from their husks (p. 364)

Tidewater flat land along the coast (p. 76)

tolerance acceptance of different opinions (p. 66)

Tordesillas (tawr•day•SEEL•yahs)**, Treaty of** 1494 treaty in which Spain and Portugal agreed to divide lands of the Western hemisphere between them and move the Line of Demarcation to the west (p. 26)

Townshend Acts acts passed by Parliament in 1767 to tax imports in the colonies (p. 160)

Trail of Tears forced removal of the Cherokee from their homeland to Indian Territory (p. 402)

transcontinental railroad railroad that spanned the U.S. continent (p. 596)

trench warfare warfare in which soldiers dug into deep trenches across the battlefield (p. 720)

triangular trade complex system of transatlantic exchange of slaves, rum, sugar, and molasses (p. 94)

tribute (TRIHB•yoot) payment in exchange for protection (p. 352)

Truman Doctrine policy primising aid to countries fighting to maintain democracies (p. 844)

trust a legal body created to hold stock in many companies, often within an industry (p. 630)

Tuskegee Airmen famous segregated unit of African American pilots (p. 812)

Twentieth Amendment Constitutional amendment moving presidential inauguration from March to January (p. 784)

Twenty-sixth Amendment Constitutional amendment passed in 1971 that lowered the voting age from 21 to 18 (p. 926)

U.S.S. *Maine* a U.S. warship that exploded off of Havana, Cuba, on February 15, 1898 (p. 698)

U-Boat German submarine (p. 720)

Uncle Tom's Cabin novel published by Harriet Beecher Stowe in 1852 that showed slavery as brutal and immoral (p. 480)

Underground Railroad a series of escape routes used by slaves escaping the South (p. 464)

United Nations international peacekeeping body founded by 50 nations in April, 1945 (p. 832)

uprising rebellion (p. 510)

urbanization growth of cities resulting from industrialization (p. 640)

Valley Forge site in southeast Pennsylvania where Washington and his army camped in the winter of 1777–1778 (p. 204)

vaquero (vah•KAIR•oh) Spanish term for cowhand (p. 600)

vaudeville live entertainment that featured song, dance and comedy (p. 662)

Versailles (ver•SYE)**, Treaty of** the 1919 treaty that ended World War I (p. 740)

veto (VEE•to) to prevent from becoming law (p. 570)

Viet Cong South Vietnamese who fought to overthrow the Diem government and reunite the country under Communist rule (p. 908)

Vietnamization strategy for withdrawing American troops and turning the ground fighting over to the South Vietnamese (p. 920)

vigilante (vij•uh•LAN•tee) person who takes the law into his or her own hands (p. 600)

Virginia Plan proposal for a two-house legislature with representation according to each state's population or wealth (p. 242)

Virginia Statute for Religious Freedom statement of religious liberty, written by Thomas Jefferson (p. 222)

Voting Rights Act 1965 law banning literacy tests and other laws that kept blacks from registering to vote (p. 884)

war bonds a low interest loan by civilians to the government meant to be repaid in a number of years (p. 728)

war hawk westerner who supported the War of 1812 (p. 352)

War Industries Board managed the buying and distributing of war materials; set goals for production, also set prices (p. 728)

War Powers Act legislation passed in 1973 to limit the president's war-making powers (p. 926)

War Production Board government agency set up during World War II to coordinate the production of military equipment and supplies (p. 812)

Watergate scandal illegal actions by President Nixon and his aides to cover up crimes related to Nixon's reelection campaign (p. 936)

Whig Party political party formed by Henry Clay, Daniel Webster, and other Jackson opponents (p. 408)

Whiskey Rebellion a 1794 protest against the government's tax on whiskey by backcountry farmers (p. 318)

Wilderness Road a trail into Kentucky (p. 204)

Wilmot Proviso 1846 proposal that outlawed slavery in any territory gained from the War with Mexico (p. 480)

Wounded Knee Massacre mass killing by U.S. soldiers of as many as 300 unarmed Sioux at Wounded Knee, South Dakota, in 1890 (p. 608)

writ of habeas corpus law that prevents the government from holding citizens without formal charges (p. 542)

writs of assistance search warrants used to enter homes or businesses to search for smuggled goods (p. 160)

XYZ Affair 1797 incident in which French officials demanded a bribe from U.S. diplomats (p. 326)

Yalta Conference conference where Allies planned the post-war world (p. 818)

yellow journalism style of journalism that exaggerates and sensationalizes the news (p. 698)

Yorktown, Battle of final battle of the war, in which French and American forces led by George Washington defeated British General Cornwallis (p. 212)

Zimmerman telegram telegram telling the German ambassador to ask Mexico to declare war on the United States (p. 720)

Spanish Glossary

38th parallel [paralelo 38] *s.* línea que separa Corea del Norte y Corea del Sur (pág. 850)

54th Massachussets Volunteers [voluntarios del regimiento 54° de Massachussets] *s.* regimiento de soldados afro-americanos que se hicieron famosos por su coraje en el asalto a Fort Wagner, Carolina del Sur (pág. 536)

9/11 hijackings [secuestros del 11/9] *s.* conspiración terrorista del 2001 para estrellar aviones comerciales contra el World Trade Center de Nueva York, el Pentágono y la Casa Blanca (pág. 954)

Abolition [abolición] *s.* movimiento para acabar con la esclavitud (pág. 464)

abridged [abreviado] *adj.* acortado (pág. 894)

Act of Toleration [Acta de Tolerancia] *s.* ley de Maryland que prohibía la persecución religiosa (pág. 76)

activism [activismo] *s.* acción directa que se toma para apoyar u oponerse a una meta política o social (pág. 876)

Agent Orange [Agente Naranja] *s.* producto químico que mata plantas, usado en Vietnam para descubrir los escondites del Viet Cong (pág. 914)

al Qaeda [al Qaeda] *s.* grupo terrorista de fundamentalistas islámicos radicales (pág. 954)

Alamo, Battle of the [batalla de El Álamo] *s.* batalla entre Texas y México, 1836 (pág. 426)

Albany Plan of Union [Plan de Unión de Albano] *s.* primera propuesta formal para unir las colonias (pág. 142)

Alien and Sedition Acts [Actas de Extranjeros y de Sedición] *s.* serie de cuatro leyes promulgadas en 1798 para reducir el poder político de los inmigrantes recién llegados (pág. 326)

aliens [extranjeros] *s.* inmigrantes que no son aún ciudadanos (pág. 326)

alliance [alianza] *s.* pacto o tratado en el que hay pueblos o naciones involucradas (pág. 26)

Allies [Aliados] *s.* la alianza de Gran Bretaña, Francia, Rusia y otros países durante la Primera Guerra Mundial (pág. 720)

ally [aliado] *s.* un país que accede a ayudar a otro país para lograr un objetivo común (pág. 204)

ambush [emboscada] *s.* ataque inesperado desde una posición oculta (pág. 926)

amendment [enmienda] *s.* adjunto hecho a un documento (pág. 248)

American Expeditionary Forces [Fuerzas Expedicionarias Estadounidenses] *s.* ejército estadounidense que luchó en Europa en la Primera Guerra Mundial (pág. 728)

American Federation of Labor, AFL [Federación Americana del Trabajo] *s.* organización sindical nacional fundada en 1886 (pág. 792)

American System [Sistema Americano] *s.* plan introducido en 1815 para convertir a EE.UU. en un país económicamente autosuficiente (pág. 378)

amnesty [amnistía] *s.* perdón oficial (pág. 570)

Anaconda Plan [Plan Anaconda] *s.* estrategia de la Unión para derrotar a la Confederación (pág. 510)

anarchist [anarquista] *s.* persona que cree en una sociedad que no tiene ningún gobierno (pág. 656)

Angel Island [*Angel Island*] *s.* estación de inmigración en la Bahía de San Francisco para los inmigrantes asiáticos (pág. 640)

Anglo [anglo] *s.* colono de habla inglesa asentado en el Suroeste (pág. 600)

annex [anexar] *v.* unir o agregar territorio a una unidad política ya existente, tal como un país o un estado (pág. 426)

Antietam, Battle of [batalla de Antietam] *s.* batalla en Maryland que terminó con la primera invasión de Lee en el Norte (pág. 522)

Antifederalists [antifederalistas] *s.* personas que se oponían a la ratificación de la Constitución (pág. 248)

Anti-Imperialist League [Liga Anti-imperialista] *s.* grupo de estadounidenses influyentes que opinaban que Estados Unidos no debían negar a otros pueblos el derecho a autogobernarse (pág. 698)

anti-Semitism [antisemitismo] *s.* prejuicio contra los judíos (pág. 818)

Appalachian Mountains [Montes Apalaches] *s.* cadena montañosa que se extiende desde el este de Canadá hasta Alabama (pág. 116)

appeasement [contemporización] *s.* acceder a las demandas de una potencia hostil para evitar la guerra (pág. 806)

Appomattox Court House [Appomattox Court House] *s.* ciudad de Virginia donde Lee se rindió a Grant (pág. 548)

apprentice [aprendiz] *s.* alguien que está aprendiendo un oficio con un artesano con experiencia (pág. 126)

armistice [armisticio] *s.* fin de una lucha (pág. 734)

arms race [carrera armamentista] *s.* competencia entre Estados Unidos y la Unión Soviética para desarrollar armas más destructivas (pág. 850)

arsenal [arsenal] *s.* donde se guardan armas (pág. 234)

Articles of Confederation [Artículos de la Confederación] *s.* plan para el gobierno nacional ratificado en 1781 (pág. 234)

artillery [artillería] *s.* cañones y armas grandes (pág. 176)

artisans [artesanos] *s.* personas especializadas en algún oficio (pág. 110)

assembly line [cadena de ensamblaje] *s.* manufacturación que emplea una cinta transportadora para llevar materiales a los trabajadores que permanecen en su puesto (pág. 752)

assimilate [asimilar] *v.* absorber una cultura (pág. 402)

assimilation [asimilación] *s.* el proceso de integrarse en una sociedad (pág. 640)

attorney general [fiscal general] *s.* el máximo funcionario legal de la nación; hoy en día también el jefe del Departamento de Justicia (pág. 312)

Axis [eje] *s.* Eje Roma-Berlín; la alianza entre Mussolini y Hitler (pág. 806)

Aztec [azteca] *s.* civilización de indígenas americanos que se propagó en lo que hoy es México (pág. 4)

Baby boom [*baby boom*] *s.* un aumento brusco en la tasa de natalidad de EE.UU. después de la Segunda Guerra Mundial (pág. 858)

backcountry [*backcountry*] *s.* las partes más lejanas hacia el Oeste de las colonias (pág. 94)

Bacon's Rebellion [Rebelión de Bacon] *s.* rebelión que tuvo lugar en Virginia en 1676 (pág. 102)

banish [desterrar] *v.* obligar a alguien a abandonar un lugar (pág. 66)

Bay of Pigs invasion [invasión de Bahía de Cochinos] *s.* intento estadounidense fallido de derrocar al líder comunista de Cuba (pág. 908)

Bear Flag Revolt [Revuelta de la Bandera del Oso] *s.* rebelión estadounidense contra el gobierno mexicano de California en 1846 (pág. 432)

Belleau Wood [bosque de Belleau] *s.* sitio de la victoria estadounidense en Francia en 1918 (pág. 734)

bickering [riña] *s.* pelea de poca importancia (pág. 480)

Bill of Rights [Declaración de Derechos] *s.* las primeras diez enmiendas a la Constitución de EE.UU. (pág. 248)

black codes [*black codes*] *s.* leyes aprobadas por los estados del Sur que limitaban la libertad de los antiguos esclavos (pág. 570, 872)

Black Death [muerte negra] *s.* enfermedad mortal que se extendió por Europa en el siglo XIV (pág. 16)

blitzkrieg [*blitzkrieg*] *s.* tácticas alemanas de "guerra relámpago" (pág. 806)

Bonus Army [*Bonus Army*] *s.* veteranos de la Primera Guerra Mundial que fueron a Washington buscando el temprano pago de primas por sus servicios en tiempos de guerra (pág. 776)

boomtown [ciudad de crecimiento rápido] *s.* pueblo que tiene una explosión repentina de población o de actividad económica (pág. 600)

border state [estados de la frontera] *s.* estados esclavistas que tenían frontera con otros estados en los que la esclavitud era ilegal (pág. 510)

Boston Massacre [masacre de Boston] *s.* incidente en el que las tropas británicas abrieron fuego y mataron a colonos norteamericanos en 1770 (pág. 160)

Boston Tea Party [Motín del té en Boston] *s.* incidente que tuvo lugar en 1773 cuando los colonos protestaron contra la política británica abordando barcos británicos y arrojando sus cargas de té por la borda (pág. 160)

Boxer Rebellion [Rebelión Bóxer] *s.* levantamiento nacionalista en China en 1900 (pág. 706)

boycott [boicot] *v.* negarse a comprar (pág. 156)

braceros [braceros] *s.* trabajadores mexicanos contratados para trabajar en granjas durante la Segunda Guerra Mundial (pág. 812)

brinkmanship [política arriesgada] *s.* política de ir al borde de la guerra para combatir el comunismo (pág. 850)

Brown vs. ***Board of Education of Topeka*** *s.* caso de 1954 por el cual la Corte Suprema sentenció que la educación "igual pero por separado" de estudiantes blancos y negros era inconstitucional (pág. 876)

buffalo soldier [soldado búfalo] *s.* nombre que los indígenas norteamericanos dieron a los soldados afroamericanos en el Oeste (pág. 600)

Bulge, Battle of the [batalla de las Ardenas] *s.* asalto alemán en diciembre de 1944 en la región de las Ardenas, perteneciente a Bélgica y Luxemburgo (pág. 818)

Bull Moose Party [Partido del Alce] *s.* partido político progresista de las elecciones presidenciales de 1912 (pág. 678)

Bull Run, First Battle of [primera batalla de Bull Run] *s.* primera gran batalla de la Guerra Civil (pág. 510)

business cycle [ciclo económico] *s.* patrón de buenos y malos tiempos para la economía (pág. 630)

Cabinet [gabinete] *s.* grupo de miembros del Ejecutivo que sirven como principales asesores al Presidente (pág. 312)

California Gold Rush [fiebre del oro californiana] *s.* emigración de miles de colonos a California en busca de oro (pág. 438)

Californios *s.* colonos de ascendencia española o mexicana que poblaron California (pág. 438)

Cambodia [Camboya] *s.* país que hace frontera con Vietnam (pág. 920)

Camp David Accords [Acuerdos de Camp David] *s.* tratado de paz de 1978 entre Egipto e Israel (pág. 936)

carpetbagger [*carpetbagger*] *s.* residentes en el Norte que fueron al Sur después de la Guerra Civil para ayudar con la Reconstrucción (pág. 570)

cash crops [cultivo comercial] *s.* cultivo destinado a ser vendido a cambio de dinero (pág. 102)

Catholics [católicos] *s.* cristianos seguidores de la Iglesia Católica Romana (pág. 16)

cede [ceder] *v.* rendirse o capitular (pág. 318)

Central Powers [Potencias Centrales] *s.* alianza de Alemania, el imperio austro-húngaro, el imperio otomano y Bulgaria durante la Primera Guerra Mundial (pág. 720)

Charles Town, Battle of [batalla de Charles Town] *s.* asedio británico a Charles Town (Charleston), Carolina del Sur, en mayo de 1780, en el que los norteamericanos sufrieron su peor derrota en la guerra (pág. 212)

charter [carta] *s.* contrato por escrito que otorga el derecho a establecer una colonia (pág. 60)

checks and balances [sistema de equilibrio de poderes] *s.* capacidad de cada rama del gobierno para ejercer control sobre las otras (pág. 242)

Chinese Exclusion Act [Acta de Exclusión de Chinos] *s.* ley de 1882 que prohibía la inmigración china (pág. 640)

citizen [ciudadano] *s.* persona que debe lealtad a un estado o nación y que tiene derecho a su protección (pág. 234)

civil rights [derechos civiles] *s.* derechos otorgados a todos los ciudadanos (pág. 570)

Civil Rights Act of 1964 [Acta de Derechos Civiles de 1964] *s.* ley que prohibió la segregación en los lugares públicos y creó la Comisión para la Igualdad de Oportunidades en el Empleo (pág. 884)

civilization [civilización] *s.* sociedad compleja en la que el pueblo comparte rasgos clave como el lenguaje y la religión (pág. 4)

clans [clanes] *s.* grupos grandes de familias que dicen tener un ancestro común (pág. 116)

Clayton Antitrust Act [Acta Antitrust Clayton] *s.* ley que reforzó la efectividad del Acta Antitrust de Sherman (pág. 678)

coalition [coalición] *s.* alianza (pág. 954)

Code Talkers [*Code Talkers*] *s.* indígenas navajo reclutados por el cuerpo de marines de EE.UU. para transmitir mensajes en lengua navajo (pág. 826)

coercion [coerción] *s.* obligar a alguien a actuar de cierta manera mediante el uso de presión o amenazas (pág. 352)

Cold War [guerra fría] *s.* conflicto entre Estados Unidos y la Unión Soviética tras la Segunda Guerra Mundial (pág. 844)

Columbian Exchange [intercambio colombino] *s.* traslado de animales, plantas y enfermedades entre los hemisferios oriental y occidental (pág. 40)

Commander-In-Chief [comandante en jefe] *s.* rol que ejerce el Presidente como comandante de todas las fuerzas armadas (pág. 536)

committee of correspondence [comité de correspondencia] *s.* organización formada para intercambiar información sobre la política británica y la resistencia norteamericana (pág. 160)

Committee on Public Information [Comité de Información Pública] *s.* organización gubernamental que producía propaganda para conseguir apoyo a la guerra (pág. 728)

common [campo comunal] *s.* tierra compartida donde tenían lugar las actividades públicas (pág. 94)

commune [comuna] *s.* lugar donde personas o familias viven juntas y comparten todas sus cosas (pág. 920)

communism [comunismo] *s.* sistema político en el que el gobierno controla la economía para llevar a cabo la posesión común de toda propiedad (pág. 672)

compromise [concesión] *s.* acuerdo por el que cada lado cede algo de lo que reclama (pág. 582)

Compromise of 1850 [Concesión de 1850] *s.* serie de leyes cuyo objetivo era poner fin a los desacuerdos más graves entre los estados libres y los estados esclavistas (pág. 480)

Compromise of 1877 [Concesión de 1877] *s.* acuerdo por el que se decidieron las elecciones presidenciales de 1876 (pág. 582)

Conestoga wagons [carromatos conestoga] *s.* carromatos cubiertos introducidos por los inmigrantes alemanes (pág. 110)

Confederate States of America [Estados Confederados de América] *s.* confederación formada por los estados del Sur en 1861 después de abandonar la Unión (pág. 498)

Confederation Congress [Congreso de la Confederación] *s.* cuerpo nacional legislativo formado por Artículos de la Confederación (pág. 234)

conform [ajustarse] *v.* estar de acuerdo con las creencias e ideas de la mayoría (pág. 858)

congregation [congregación] *s.* grupo de personas que pertenecen a la misma iglesia (pág. 66)

Congress of Industrial Organizations, CIO [Congreso de Organizaciones Industriales] *s.* organización sindical que incluía a trabajadores manuales y cualificados, abierto a las mujeres y a las minorías (pág. 792)

Congress of Racial Equality, CORE [Congreso para la Igualdad Racial] *s.* organización que planificaba los *Freedom Rides* (viajes por la libertad) (pág. 884)

conquistador [conquistador] *s.* soldado español que exploró las Américas reclamando tierra para España (pág. 26)

conscription [conscripción] *s.* reclutamiento militar (pág. 542)

conservation [conservación] *s.* control del uso de los recursos (pág. 672)

Conservative [conservador] *s.* alguien a favor de restringir las reformas económicas y sociales (pág. 792)

Constitutional Convention [Convención Constitucional] *s.* reunión de 1787 en la que se creó la Constitución de Estados Unidos (pág. 242)

consumer [consumidor] *s.* persona que compra algo (pág. 662)

containment [contención] *s.* política para frenar la expansión del comunismo (pág. 844)

Continental Army [Ejército Continental] *s.* ejército patriota norteamericano durante la Guerra de Independencia (pág. 176)

contractor [contratista] *s.* suministrador privado (pág. 516)

converts [conversos] *s.* personas que adoptan una nueva creencia religiosa (pág. 418)

convoy [*convoy*] *s.* guardia que acompaña y protege barcos o tropas (pág. 734)

Copperheads [*copperheads*] *s.* demócratas del Norte que estaban a favor de la paz con el Sur (pág. 542)

corporation [corporación] *s.* negocio que es propiedad de inversores que compran su parte en acciones de bolsa (pág. 630)

corps [cuerpo] *s.* un grupo de personas que actúan juntas por una meta común (pág. 344)

cotton gin [despepitadora de algodón] *s.* máquina que limpiaba las semillas de algodón más rápido (pág. 372)

counterculture [contracultura] *s.* movimiento formado principalmente por jóvenes estadounidenses desilusionados por la guerra de Vietnam y las injusticias sociales (pág. 920)

credit [crédito] *s.* previsión para el pago retrasado de un préstamo o una compra (pág. 752)

Crittenden Compromise [Concesión de Crittenden] *s.* concesión introducida en 1861 que podría haber evitado la secesión (pág. 498)

Cuban missile crisis [crisis de los misiles cubanos] *s.* confrontación en 1962 entre Estados Unidos y la Unión Soviética provocada por la existencia de misiles nucleares soviéticos en Cuba (pág. 908)

Daughters of Liberty [Hijas de la Libertad] *s.* organización que formaron las mujeres de las colonias para protestar contra la política británica (pág. 160)

Dawes Act [Acta de Dawes] *s.* ley de 1887 que distribuyó las tierras de las reservas entre propietarios indígenas (pág. 608)

D-Day [día-D] *s.* invasión aliada a Francia el 6 de junio de 1944 (pág. 818)

Declaration of Independence [Declaración de Independencia] *s.* documento que declaró la independencia estadounidense de Gran Bretaña (pág. 176)

deficit spending [gasto deficitario] *s.* usar dinero prestado para invertir en programas del gobierno (pág. 784)

denomination [denominación] *s.* determinado grupo religioso (pág. 110)

depression [depresión] *s.* un declive económico severo (pág. 408, 582)

desert [desertar] *v.* abandonar el ejército sin permiso (pág. 204)

direct primary [primarias directas] *s.* primarias en las que los votantes, no las convenciones de los partidos, eligen a los candidatos que compiten por puestos públicos (pág. 672)

disenfranchised [*disenfranchised*] *adj.* personas privadas de derechos legales, en especial del derecho al voto (pág. 884)

dislodge [sacar] *v.* quitar (pág. 548)

disputes [disputa] *s.* desacuerdos (pág. 222)

dissenter [disidente] *s.* persona en desacuerdo con una iglesia oficial (pág. 66)

diversity [diversidad] *s.* variedad (pág. 76)

doctrine of nullification [doctrina de la anulación] *s.* idea de que un estado tiene el derecho a anular, o rechazar, una ley federal que considera inconstitucional (pág. 394)

domino theory [efecto dominó] *s.* creencia en que si un país caía en el comunismo, los países cercanos le seguirían (pág. 908)

doves [palomas] *s.* estadounidenses contrarios a la guerra de Vietnam (pág. 920)

Dred Scott* vs. *Sandford [Dred Scott contra Sandford] *s.* caso de 1856 en la Corte Suprema en que un esclavo, Dred Scott, fue a juicio para pedir su libertad; la corte falló contra Scott (pág. 490)

Dust Bowl [Cuenca de Polvo] *s.* región en el centro de EE.UU. donde las granjas fueron dañadas por tormentas de polvo (pág. 792)

duties [impuestos] *s.* arancel que se pone a los productos de importación (pág. 160)

Eighteenth Amendment [Enmienda Decimoctava] *s.* enmienda constitucional que puso en práctica la Prohibición (pág. 682)

electoral votes [votos electorales] *s.* votos hechos por el Colegio Electoral, quien elige al presidente y vicepresidente (pág. 582)

elite [élite] *s.* grupo social de más alto rango (pág. 76)

Ellis Island [Ellis Island] *s.* estación de inmigración en la Bahía de Nueva York para emigrantes europeos (pág. 640)

emancipate [emancipar] *v.* liberar (pág. 536)

Emancipation Proclamation [Proclama de Emancipación] *s.* documento promulgado por Lincoln en el que declaraba la libertad de todos los esclavos en territorio Confederado (pág. 536)

Embargo Act of 1807 [Acta de Embargo de 1807] *s.* ley que prohibía a los barcos estadounidenses navegar a puertos extranjeros y cerraba los puertos estadounidenses a los barcos británicos (pág. 352)

emigrant [emigrante] *s.* persona que deja un país (pág. 450)

encomienda [encomienda] *s.* concesión del trabajo de los indígenas norteamericanos esclavizados (pág. 40)

English Bill of Rights [Declaración Inglesa de Derechos] *s.* leyes de 1689 que protegían los derechos de los súbditos ingleses y de su Parlamento (pág. 136)

Enlightenment [Ilustración] *s.* movimiento filosófico que subrayaba la razón humana (pág. 126)

enlist [alistarse] *v.* unirse a las fuerzas armadas (pág. 516)

entitlements [privilegios] *s.* programas gubernamentales que garantizan ciertos beneficios a los ciudadanos (pág. 946)

epidemic [epidemia] *s.* brote de una enfermedad contagiosa que se extiende rápida y ampliamente (pág. 734)

Equal Rights Amendment, ERA [Enmienda para la Igualdad de Derechos] *s.* enmienda propuesta para la igualdad de derechos sin importar el sexo (pág. 894)

Erie Canal [Canal de Erie] *s.* vía de agua que conectaba la Ciudad de Nueva York con Buffalo (pág. 378)

escalation [escalada] *s.* política de aumentar la presencia militar en Vietnam (pág. 914)

Espionage Act [Acta de Espionaje] *s.* ley de 1917 que fijaba graves multas y largas sentencias de prisión para las actividades contra la guerra (pág. 728)

evolution [evolución] *s.* teoría científica acerca de cómo las formas de vida se han desarrollado durante millones de años (pág. 758)

executive branch [poder ejecutivo] *s.* departamento del gobierno que hace cumplir las leyes (pág. 242)

Exodusters [*Exodusters*] *s.* nombre que se le daba a los afro-americanos que se asentaban en las Grandes Llanuras (pág. 616)

expatriate [expatriado] *s.* ciudadano de un país que vive en otro país (pág. 762)

export [exportar] *v.* enviar al extranjero para el comercio o la venta (pág. 40)

Factory system [*factory system*] *s.* método de producción que utilizaba a trabajadores y máquinas en un mismo edificio (pág. 364)

Fair Deal [Trato Justo] *s.* reformas sociales propuestas por Truman; basadas en el Nuevo Trato (pág. 844)

fall line [línea de descanso] *s.* punto en el que las cataratas impiden a los barcos grandes seguir navegando río arriba (pág. 116)

Fallen Timbers, Battle of [batalla de Fallen Timbers] *s.* lucha entre los indígenas norteamericanos y las fuerzas estadounidenses (pág. 318)

famine [hambruna] *s.* escasez grave de alimentos que resulta en el hambre (pág. 450)

fascism [fascismo] *s.* filosofía política que aboga por una dictadura nacionalista fuerte (pág. 806)

Federal Judiciary Act of 1789 [Acta de la Judicatura Federal] *s.* ley de 1789 aprobada por el primer Congreso que estableció las cortes federales menores (pág. 312)

Federal Reserve Act [Acta de la Reserva Federal] *s.* ley que creaba el sistema bancario moderno (pág. 678)

federalism [federalismo] *s.* sistema de gobierno en el cual el poder es compartido entre el gobierno nacional (o federal) y los estados (pág. 248)

The Federalist **papers** [The Federalist *papers*] *s.* ensayos de ratificación publicados en los periódicos de Nueva York (pág. 248)

Federalists [federalistas] *s.* personas que apoyaban la ratificación de la Constitución (pág. 248)

Fifteenth Amendment [Enmienda Decimoquinta] *s.* enmienda constitucional que establecía que no se podía impedir de votar a los ciudadanos "por motivos de raza, color, o haber sido esclavos" (pág. 582)

fireside chats [charlas junto a la chimenea] *s.* serie de conversaciones radiofónicas en las que FDR explicaba su política de manera informal (pág. 784)

First Continental Congress [Primer Congreso Continental] *s.* reunión de delegados de casi todas las colonias convocada como reacción a las Actas Intolerables (pág. 168)

First New Deal [Primer Nuevo Trato] *s.* programa creado entre 1933 y 1935 por el presidente Roosevelt para luchar contra la Depresión (pág. 784)

flapper [*flapper*] *s.* mujer joven dispuesta a probar la última moda, baile o tendencia (pág. 758)

Ford's Theatre [Teatro Ford] *s.* teatro en Washington, D.C., donde Lincoln fue asesinado (pág. 558)

foreign policy [política exterior] *s.* relaciones con los gobiernos de otras naciones (pág. 326)

Fort Sumter [*Fort Sumter*] *s.* fuerte de la Unión en el puerto de Charleston, Carolina del Sur (pág. 510)

forty-niner [minero del 49] *s.* persona que fue a California buscando oro en 1849 (pág. 438)

Founders [padres fundadores] *s.* personas que ayudaron a redactar la Constitución de EE.UU. (pág. 242)

Fourteen Points [Catorce Puntos] *s.* objetivos para la paz del presidente Woodrow Wilson tras la Primera Guerra Mundial (pág. 740)

Fourteenth Amendment [Enmienda Decimocuarta] *s.* enmienda constitucional que convirtió en ciudadanos a todas las personas nacidas en EE.UU. (incluidos los antiguos esclavos) (pág. 570)

Freedmen's Bureau [Agencia Federal de Libertos] *s.* agencia federal establecida para ayudar a los antiguos esclavos (pág. 570)

freedmen's school [escuelas para libertos] *s.* escuelas creadas para educar a los afro-americanos recién liberados (pág. 576)

Freedom Rides [Viajes por la libertad] *s.* protesta contra la segregación en los autobuses interestatales en el Sur (pág. 884)

Freedom Summer [Verano de libertad] *s.* campaña para el registro de votantes negros en el Sur en 1964 (pág. 884)

Free-Soil Party [Partido del Suelo Libre] *s.* partido político dedicado a frenar la expansión de la esclavitud (pág. 480)

French and Indian War [Guerra franco-indígena] *s.* guerra entre Bretaña, Francia, y sus aliados de 1754 a 1763 por el control de Norteamérica (pág. 142)

French Indochina [Indochina francesa] *s.* colonia constituída por Vietnam, Laos y Camboya y gobernada por Francia (pág. 908)

French Revolution [Revolución Francesa] *s.* revolución derrocando el gobierno de Francia que comenzó en 1787 y terminó en violencia y ejecuciones (pág. 318)

frontier [frontera] *s.* partes del Oeste que fueron ocupadas principalmente por indígenas norteamericanos, en vez de colonos (pág. 596)

Fugitive Slave Act [Acta del Esclavo Fugitivo] *s.* ley de 1850 que permitía a los propietarios de esclavos capturar a los esclavos huidos (pág. 480)

Fundamental Orders of Connecticut [Órdenes Fundamentales de Connecticut] *s.* documento que ha sido considerado la primera constitución escrita en Norteamérica (pág. 66)

fundamentalism [fundamentalismo] *s.* creencia de que cada palabra de la Biblia es verdad literalmente (pág. 758)

G

G.I. Bill of Rights [Declaración de Derechos de los G.I.] *s.* ley gubernamental que pagaba la educación y los gastos de los veteranos (pág. 832)

galleon [galeón] *s.* barco para la navegación (pág. 34)

Gettysburg, Battle of [batalla de Gettysburg] *s.* batalla de 1863 en Pennsylvania donde las fuerzas de la Unión evitaron una invasión Confederada del Norte (pág. 548)

Ghana [Ghana] *s.* reino de África Occidental que prosperó entre 700 y 1000 d. C. (pág. 10)

Gilded Age [Edad Dorada] *s.* época de fabulosa riqueza a finales del siglo XIX (pág. 630)

Glorious Revolution [Revolución Gloriosa] *s.* eventos sucedidos entre 1688 y 1689, por los cuales el Parlamento inglés invitó a William y Mary a reemplazar a James II como monarca (pág. 136)

gold standard [patrón oro] *s.* política bajo la cual el gobierno respalda cada dólar con una cierta cantidad de oro (pág. 616)

Grange [*Grange*] *s.* organización formada en 1867 para satisfacer las necesidades de las familias de agricultores (pág. 616)

grassroots [organización de base] *adj.* grupo de personas comunes que se unen por una causa a nivel local (pág. 876)

Great Awakening [Gran Despertar] *s.* movimiento religioso cristiano (pág. 126)

Great Compromise [Gran Concesión] *s.* acuerdo para establecer una legislatura nacional con dos cámara en la que todos los estados tienen la misma representación en una cámara y en la otra su representación se basa en la población (pág. 242)

Great Depression [Gran Depresión] *s.* el grave declive de la economía mundial alrededor de 1930 (pág. 776)

great famine [gran hambruna] *s.* generalizada escasez de alimentos que mató a miles de europeos (pág. 16)

Great Migration, 17th Century [Gran Migración, siglo XVII] *s.* movimiento de miles de colonos ingleses a Nueva Inglaterra durante la década de 1630 (pág. 66)

Great Migration, 20th Century [Gran Migración, siglo XX] *s.* movimiento de afro-americanos desde el Sur hacia las ciudades del Norte entre 1910 y 1920 (pág. 740)

Great Plains [Grandes Llanuras] *s.* área situada entre el río Missouri y las Montañas Rocosas (pág. 596)

Great Society [Gran Sociedad] *s.* programas del presidente Johnson para ayudar a los pobres, los ancianos y las mujeres (pág. 884)

greenback [*greenback*] *s.* papel moneda introducido durante la Guerra Civil (pág. 542)

Greenville, Treaty of [Tratado de Greenville] *s.* tratado firmado en 1795 por el que 12 tribus indígenas norteamericanas cedían el control de la mayor parte de Ohio e Indiana al gobierno de EE.UU. (pág. 318)

gross national product [producto nacional bruto] *s.* valor total de todos los bienes y servicios producidos por una nación a lo largo de un año (pág. 812)

Guadalcanal [Guadalcanal] *s.* primera victoria terrestre de EE.UU. sobre Japón, 1943 (pág. 826)

Guadalupe Hidalgo, Treaty of [Tratado de Guadalupe Hidalgo] *s.* tratado de 1848 que puso fin a la Guerra con México (pág. 432)

guerrillas [guerillas] *s.* pequeñas bandas de combatientes que debilitan al enemigo con rebatos y de golpe y fuga (pág. 194, 908)

guerrilla warfare [guerra de guerrilla] *s.* rebatos realizados por pequeños grupos de combatientes (pág. 914)

Gulf of Tonkin Resolution [Resolución del Golfo de Tonkin] *s.* legislación de 1964 que dio al presidente Johnson poder para usar la fuerza militar en Vietnam (pág. 914)

H

hacienda [hacienda] *s.* granja o propiedad grande (pág. 40)

Hamdan* vs. *Rumsfeld [Hamdan contra Rumsfeld] *s.* decisión de 2006 de la Corte Suprema que obliga al trato humanitario de los prisioneros militares (pág. 954)

Harlem Renaissance [Renacimiento de Harlem] *s.* explosión de cultura afro-americana en las décadas de 1920 y 1930 (pág. 762)

Harpers Ferry [Harpers Ferry] *s.* arsenal federal en Virginia, capturado en 1859 durante una revuelta antiesclavista (pág. 490)

hawks [*halcones*] *s.* estadounidenses que apoyaron la guerra de Vietnam (pág. 920)

Haymarket Affair [asunto Haymarket] *s.* protesta sindical en 1886 (pág. 656)

H-bomb [bomba H] *s.* bomba de hidrógeno (pág. 850)

headright [*headright*] *s.* tierra entregada a las personas que podían pagar, por sus propios medios, su viaje hacia las colonias (pág. 60)

heritage [herencia] *s.* tradición (pág. 136)

Hiroshima [Hiroshima] *s.* primera ciudad japonesa en ser alcanzada por una bomba atómica el 6 de agosto de 1945 (pág. 826)

Ho Chi Minh Trail [Ruta de Ho Chi Minh] *s.* ruta secreta usada por Vietnam del Norte para enviar tropas y suministros al Viet Cong (pág. 908)

Holocaust [holocausto] *s.* crimen de los Nazis por el que asesinaron a 11 millones de judíos y otros pueblos en campos de concentración (pág. 818)

Homestead Act [Acta de Heredades] *s.* ley de 1862 por la que se ofrecían 160 acres de terreno gratis a quien quisiera vivir en él y mejorarlo durante cinco años (pág. 616)

Homestead Strike [huelga de haciendas] *s.* huelga violenta en la hacienda de Andrew Carnegie, en los molinos de acero de Pensilvania, en 1892 (pág. 656)

House of Burgesses [Cámara de los Burgueses] *s.* asamblea de Virginia; la primera asamblea representativa en las colonias norteamericanas (pág. 60)

Huguenots [hugonotes] *s.* protestantes franceses (pág. 76)

Hull House [Casa Hull] *s.* centro comunitario fundado por Jane Addams en Chicago (pág. 640)

Hundred Days [Cien Días] *s.* sesión del Congreso entre el 9 de marzo y mitad de junio de 1933 durante la cual se aprobaron múltiples leyes para combatir la Depresión (pág. 784)

hygiene [higiene] *s.* condiciones y prácticas que favorecen la salud (pág. 516)

Immigrant [inmigrante] *s.* persona que se asienta en un país nuevo (pág. 450)

impeach [encausar] *v.* acusar formalmente al presidente de mala conducta durante su mandato (pág. 570)

imperialism [imperialismo] *s.* política por la cual naciones más fuertes extienden su control económico, político y militar sobre naciones más débiles (pág. 694)

impressment [leva] *s.* acto de tomar por la fuerza; entre 1803 y 1812, los británicos aprisionaron, o secuestraron, a 6.000 marineros norteamericanos para que sirvieran en la marina británica (pág. 352)

inaugurate [investir] *v.* jurar un cargo formalmente o hacerlo jurar (pág. 312)

Inca [inca] *s.* civilización indígena americana que se desarrolló en lo que hoy en día es Perú (pág. 4)

income tax [impuesto sobre la renta] *s.* impuesto sobre las ganancias (pág. 542)

indentured servant [sirviente por contrato] *s.* persona que trabajaba por un plazo fijado sin cobrar a cambio de un pasaje gratis a América (pág. 60)

Indian Removal Act [Acta de Traslado de Indios] *s.* ley de 1830 que obligaba al gobierno a negociar tratados para forzar a los indígenas norteamericanos a trasladarse al oeste (pág. 402)

Indian Territory [Territorio Indio] *s.* área a la que fueron trasladados los indígenas norteamericanos, que cubría lo que en la actualidad es Oklahoma y partes de Kansas y Nebraska (pág. 402)

indigo [índigo] *s.* planta que produce un tinte azul oscuro (pág. 102)

Industrial Revolution [Revolución Industrial] *s.* cambios económicos a finales del siglo XVIII por los que la fabricación a gran escala reemplazó a la agricultura como forma principal de empleo (pág. 364)

infamy [mala reputación] *s.* mala fama (pág. 806)

inflation [inflación] *s.* aumento de los precios y disminución del valor del dinero (pág. 408)

infringe [infringir] *v.* violar (pág. 872)

installment buying [pago a plazos] *s.* pagar bienes en pequeños pagos mensuales (pág. 752)

insurgent [insurgente] *s.* persona que se rebela o subleva (pág. 954)

integrate [integrar] *v.* abrirse a personas de todas razas o grupos étnicos (pág. 876)

Intolerable Acts [Actas Intolerables] *s.* serie de leyes, conocidas en Gran Bretaña como Actas Coercitivas, dirigidas a castigar a Massachussets y a contener la resistencia de las otras colonias (pág. 168)

investor [inversor] *s.* persona que pone dinero en un proyecto para obtener beneficios (pág. 60)

Iran-Contra affair [asunto Irán-Contra] *s.* escándalo de 1986 en el que Estados Unidos vendió armas a Irán y dio dinero a rebeldes de la Contra en Nicaragua (pág. 946)

Islam [Islam] *s.* religión que enseña que hay un solo Dios, llamado Alá, y Mahoma es su profeta (pág. 10)

island hopping [saltar islas] *v.* estrategia Aliada en el Pacífico que consistía en invadir determinadas islas y usarlas como base para avanzar hacia Japón (pág. 826)

Jacksonian democracy [democracia Jacksoniana] *s.* idea de ampliar el poder político a una parte mayor del pueblo (pág. 394)

Jamestown [Jamestown] *s.* primer asentamiento inglés permanente en Norteamérica (pág. 60)

Japanese-American internment [internamiento de japoneses-americanos] *s.* traslado de japoneses americanos del Oeste a campos de prisioneros durante la Segunda Guerra Mundial (pág. 812)

Jay's Treaty [Tratado de Jay] *s.* acuerdo que puso fin a la disputa con Gran Bretaña sobre la navegación de barcos norteamericanos durante la Revolución Francesa (pág. 318)

Jazz Age [Edad del Jazz] *s.* nombre adjudicado a la década de 1920, debido a la popularidad del jazz: un nuevo tipo de música norteamericana que combinaba los ritmos africanos, el blues y el ragtime (pág. 758)

Jim Crow [*Jim Crow*] *s.* leyes promulgadas en los estados del Sur con el propósito de separar a blancos y negros (pág. 650)

joint-stock company [compañía de acciones compartidas] *s.* compañía fundada por un grupo de inversores (pág. 60)

judicial branch [poder judicial] *s.* departamento del gobierno que interpreta las leyes (pág. 242)

judicial review [control judicial] *s.* principio que afirma que la Corte Suprema tiene la última palabra en la interpretación de la Constitución (pág. 338)

Judiciary Act of 1801 [Acta de la Judicatura de 1801] *s.* ley que permitió al presidente John Adams elegir a los nuevos jueces entre los Federalistas (pág. 338)

Kamikaze *s.* piloto suicida japonés (pág. 826)

Kansas-Nebraska Act [Acta de Kansas-Nebraska] *s.* ley de 1854 que estableció los territorios de Kansas y Nebraska y otorgó a sus residentes el derecho a permitir o no la esclavitud (pág. 480)

Kentucky and Virginia Resolutions [Resoluciones de Kentucky y Virginia] *s.* resoluciones aprobabas por Kentucky y Virginia en 1798 que daban a los estados el derecho a anular actas del Congreso (pág. 326)

King Philip's War [Guerra de rey Philip] *s.* levantamiento indígena norteamericano (1675-1676) contra las colonias Puritanas (pág. 94)

Knights of Labor [Caballeros del Trabajo] *s.* organización de trabajadores de todos los oficios formada tras la Guerra Civil (pág. 656)

Know-Nothing Party [Partido No-Sé-Nada] *s.* partido político formado en Estados Unidos durante la década de 1850 en contra de los nuevos inmigrantes y los católicos romanos (pág. 450)

Kongo [Congo] *s.* reino de África Central que gobernó en el siglo XV (pág. 10)

Korean War [guerra de Corea] *s.* conflicto que implicó a fuerzas de Naciones Unidas lideradas por EE.UU. contra Corea del Norte y China (pág. 850)

Kosovo [Kosovo] *s.* provincia al sur de Serbia habitada en su mayoría por personas de origen albanés (pág. 946)

Ku Klux Klan [Ku Klux Klan] *s.* grupo secreto que utilizaba la violencia para intentar devolver el control a los Demócratas en el Sur y mantener sin poder a los afro-americanos (pág. 576)

labor union [organización sindical] *s.* grupos de trabajadores que se asocian para buscar condiciones mejores de trabajo (pág. 456)

laissez-faire economics [*laissez-faire*] *s.* teoría que propugna que la economía, cuando no interviene el gobierno, actuará de forma beneficiosa para la nación (pág. 752)

Land Ordinance of 1785 [Ordenanza de la Tierra de 1785] *s.* ley que establecía un plan para dividir los territorios que poseía el gobierno federal al oeste de los Montes Apalaches (pág. 234)

land speculators [especuladores urbanísticos] *s.* personas que compran tierra esperando que aumente de valor (pág. 418)

Latinos [latinos] *s.* personas en Estados Unidos cuyos orígenes están en los países y culturas latinoamericanos (pág. 894)

League of Nations [Liga de Naciones] *s.* organización creada tras la Primera Guerra Mundial para solucionar conflictos internacionales (pág. 740)

legislative branch [poder legislativo] *s.* departamento del gobierno que elabora las leyes (pág. 242)

leisure [ocio] *s.* libertad de obligaciones exigentes (pág. 662)

Lend-Lease Act [Acta de Préstamo y Arriendo] *s.* ley que permitía a Estados Unidos prestar armas a sus aliados (pág. 806)

levy [gravar] *v.* imponer o recaudar un impuesto (pág. 234)

Lewis and Clark expedition [expedición de Lewis y Clark] *s.* grupo que exploró el Territorio de Luisiana y las tierras al oeste; también conocido como Cuerpo de Descubrimiento (pág. 344)

Lexington and Concord [Lexington y Concord] *s.* primeras batallas de la Guerra de Independencia (pág. 168)

Liberal [liberal] *s.* persona que está a favor de la acción del gobierno federal para lograr reformas económicas y sociales (pág. 792)

liberation [liberación] *s.* acto de dar la libertad (pág. 536)

literacy [alfabetización] *s.* saber leer y escribir (pág. 126)

Little Bighorn, Battle of the [batalla de Little Bighorn] *s.* batalla de 1876 en la que los sioux y los cheyenne mataron a una tropa de EE.UU. (pág. 608)

lode [filón] *s.* depósito mineral enterrado en la roca (pág. 600)

Lone Star Republic [República de la Estrella Solitaria] *s.* apodo de Texas tras separarse de México (pág. 426)

long drive [*long drive*] *s.* viaje que lleva al ganado a pie hasta el ferrocarril (pág. 600)

Lost Generation [Generación Perdida] *s.* personas que se desilusionaron con la sociedad tras la Primera Guerra Mundial (pág. 762)

Louisiana Purchase [Compra de Luisiana] *s.* compra estadounidense del Territorio francés de Luisiana en 1803 (pág. 344)

Lowell mills [hilanderías de Lowell] *s.* fábricas de tejidos en la ciudad industrial de Lowell, Massachusetts (pág. 364)

Loyalists [leales] *s.* norteamericanos que apoyaban a los británicos (pág. 168)

lynch [linchar] *v.* condenar a una persona a la horca sin seguir ningún proceso legal (pág. 576)

Magna Carta [Carta Magna] *s.* carta de libertades civiles y políticas de Inglaterra (pág. 136)

majority rule [gobierno de la mayoría] *s.* sistema en el que más de la mitad de un grupo tiene poder para tomar decisiones por todo el grupo (pág. 248)

malaria [malaria] *s.* enfermedad contagiosa que propagan los mosquitos (pág. 706)

Mali [Malí] *s.* reino de África Occidental que predominó entre 1200 y 1400 (pág. 10)

Manhattan Project [Proyecto Manhattan] *s.* proyecto de alto secreto del gobierno para desarrollar la bomba atómica (pág. 826)

manifest destiny [destino manifiesto] *s.* creencia de que EE.UU. estaban destinados a expandirse de costa a costa (pág. 432, 706)

March on Washington [Marcha a Washington] *s.* gran manifestación por los derechos civiles en Washington, D.C., en 1963 (pág. 884)

maroon [cimarrón] *s.* esclavo huido o fugitivo (pág. 48)

Marshall Plan [Plan Marshall] *s.* plan estadounidense desarrollado por George C. Marshall para estimular la economía en Europa tras la guerra (pág. 832)

mass culture [cultura de masas] *s.* cultura común que comparte un grupo grande de personas (pág. 662)

mass media [medios de comunicación] *s.* medios que llegan a una gran audiencia (pág. 758)

materialistic [materialista] *adj.* que valora lo material por encima de lo espiritual o lo intelectual (pág. 762)

Maya [maya] *s.* antigua civilización indígena de Mesoamérica (pág. 4)

Mayflower Compact [Convenio del Mayflower] *s.* documento que ayudó a establecer el gobierno autónomo (pág. 66)

mechanical reaper [cosechadora mecánica] *s.* máquina que corta el grano (pág. 364)

melting pot [crisol de culturas] *s.* lugar donde se mezclan las culturas (pág. 640)

mercantilism [mercantilismo] *s.* sistema económico que aumenta las divisas del tesoro de un país al crear una balanza comercial favorable (pág. 26, 60)

mercenary [mercenario] *s.* soldado profesional contratado para servir a un país extranjero (pág. 194)

Merrimack [Merrimack] *s.* acorazado Confederado, rebautizado después como *Virginia* (pág. 516)

Mesoamerica [Mesoamérica] *s.* región que se extiende desde lo que hoy es México hasta Nicaragua (pág. 4)

Mexican cession [cesión mexicana] *s.* territorio mexicano que se entregó a Estados Unidos al final de la guerra con México (pág. 432)

Mexicano [mexicano] *s.* persona de herencia mexicana (pág. 600)

middle passage [paso central] *s.* parte media de la ruta del comercio triangular que llevaba africanos capturados a las Américas para servir (pág. 48)

Midway, Battle of [batalla de Midway] *s.* victoria estadounidense sobre los japoneses cerca de la isla de Midway que se convirtió en el momento decisivo de la guerra (pág. 826)

migrate [migrar] *v.* trasladarse de una región a otra (pág. 4)

migration [migración] *s.* movimiento de personas desde una localidad a otra (pág. 438)

militarism [militarismo] *s.* política por la cual el poder militar es el principal objetivo de una nación y se usa para alcanzar metas nacionales (pág. 720)

militia [milicia] *s.* fuerza de civiles armados que juran defender su comunidad (pág. 168)

Minutemen [soldados al minuto] *s.* grupo de civiles armados, preparados para luchar un minuto después de ser avisados (pág. 168)

mission [misión] *s.* asentamiento creado por la iglesia española para convertir a los indígenas al cristianismo (pág. 40)

missionary [misionero] *s.* persona enviada por la Iglesia para a los indígenas convertir al cristianismo (pág. 26)

Missouri Compromise [Compromiso de Missouri] *s.* leyes promulgadas en 1820 para mantener el equilibrio de poderes entre los estados esclavistas y los libres (pág. 378)

Monitor [Monitor] *s.* acorazado de la Unión (pág. 516)

monopoly [monopolio] *s.* negocio que toma el control de una industria eliminando a sus competidores (pág. 630)

Monroe Doctrine [doctrina Monroe] *s.* política de EE.UU de oponerse a la injerencia europea en el hemisferio occidental (pág. 378)

Montgomery bus boycott [boicot a los autobuses de Montgomery] *s.* acción de protesta que tuvo lugar en 1955 para acabar con la segregación en los autobuses de Montgomery, Alabama (pág. 876)

Mormon [mormón] *s.* miembro de una iglesia fundada por Joseph Smith en 1830 (pág. 418)

mountain men [hombres de la montaña] *s.* tramperos y exploradores que abrieron senderos de pioneros en el Oeste (pág. 418)

muckracker [escarbador] *s.* escritor que destapaba la corrupción de la sociedad estadounidense (pág. 672)

Muslim [musulmán] *s.* seguidor del Islam (pág. 10)

N

NAACP [ANPPC] *s.* Asociación Nacional para el Progreso de las Personas de Color (pág. 650)

napalm [napalm] *s.* gasolina gelatinosa de combustión violenta; se usa para destruir vegetación y como arma (pág. 914)

National Congress of American Indians, NCAI [Congreso Nacional de Indígenas Estadounidenses] *s.* organización fundada en 1944 para promover los derechos de los indígenas estadounidenses (pág. 894)

National Organization for Women, NOW [Organización Nacional para las Mujeres] *s.* organización fundada en 1966 para conseguir buenos trabajos para las mujeres pagados igual que a los hombres (pág. 894)

nationalism [nacionalismo] *s.* sentimiento de orgullo, lealtad y protección hacia el país propio (pág. 672)

nativist [nativista] *s.* persona nacida en EE.UU. que quería eliminar la influencia extranjera (pág. 450)

NATO [OTAN] *s.* Organización del Tratado del Atlántico Norte, alianza militar que incluye a Canadá, Estados Unidos y diez naciones de Europa (pág. 844)

Navigation Acts [Actas de Navegación] *s.* leyes aprobadas por el gobierno inglés para asegurarse de que Inglaterra obtenía dinero del comercio de sus colonias (pág. 94)

Ndongo [Ndongo] *s.* reino de África Central que predominó en el siglo XVI (pág. 10)

neutral [neutral] *adj.* que no está a favor de ningún bando (pág. 194)

New France [Nueva Francia] *s.* primer asentamiento permanente francés en Norteamérica (pág. 34)

New Jersey Plan [Plan de New Jersey] *s.* propuesta de una legislatura en la que cada estado tendría un voto (pág. 242)

New Netherland [Nueva Holanda] *s.* primera colonia holandesa permanente en Norteamérica (pág. 34, 82)

Nineteenth Amendment [Enmienda Decimonovena] *s.* enmienda constitucional que dio el voto a las mujeres (pág. 682)

Nisei [*nisei*] *s.* americanos de origen japonés nacidos en Estados Unidos (pág. 812)

nomadic [nómada] *adj.* que se caracteriza por trasladarse de un lugar a otro (pág. 608)

nondenominational [aconfesional] *adj.* que no está a favor de ninguna religión concreta (pág. 222)

nonsedentary societies [sociedades nómadas] *s.* personas que se trasladaban continuamente buscando alimentos (pág. 4)

North American Free Trade Agreement, NAFTA [Tratado de Libre Comercio de Norteamérica] *s.* acuerdo de 1993 por el que se limitaban los aranceles comerciales entre Estados Unidos, México y Canadá (pág. 946)

North Atlantic current [corriente del Atlántico Norte] *s.* corriente oceánico que circula en el sentido de las agujas del reloj entre Europa y el mar Caribe (pág. 16)

Northwest Ordinance [Ordenanza de la Tierra del Noroeste] *s.* ley que describía cómo se gobernaría el Territorio del Noroeste (pág. 234)

Northwest Territory [Territorio del Noroeste] *s.* tierras al noroeste de los Apalaches, cubiertas por la Ordenanza de la Tierra de 1785 (pág. 234)

nullification [anulación] *s.* idea de que un estado puede cancelar una ley federal dentro de ese estado (pág. 326)

Nuremberg trials [juicio de Nuremberg] *s.* juicio por crímenes de guerra a los líderes nazi en Nuremberg, Alemania (pág. 832)

O

Open Door Policy [política de puertas abiertas] *s.* política de EE.UU. propuesta en 1899 por la cual ningún país debería tener el monopolio del comercio con China (pág. 706)

Oregon Trail [Ruta de Oregón] *s.* ruta que iba hacia el oeste desde Independence, Missouri, al Territorio de Oregón (pág. 418)

Organization of Petroleum Exporting Countries, OPEC [Organización de Países Exportadores de Petróleo] *s.* naciones, en su mayoría de Oriente Medio, que recortaron la exportación de petróleo a Estados Unidos en 1973 (pág. 936)

outposts [puesto fronterizo] *s.* bases militares, situadas generalmente en la frontera (pág. 222)

overseers [capataces] *s.* personas que vigilan y dirigen el trabajo de los esclavos (pág. 102)

P

pacifist [pacifista] *s.* alguien que se opone a todas las guerras (pág. 194)

pact [pacto] *s.* acuerdo formal; trato (pág. 142)

Palmer Raids [redadas de Palmer] *s.* redadas llevadas a cabo por agentes federales y de la policía contra radicales por orden del fiscal general del estado, A. Mitchell Palmer (pág. 740)

Panama Canal [Canal de Panamá] *s.* canal que atraviesa el istmo de Panamá y conecta los océanos Atlántico y Pacífico (pág. 706)

Panic of 1837 [pánico de 1837] *s.* temor extendido sobre el estado de la economía tras la toma de posesión de Van Buren (pág. 408)

Panic of 1873 [Pánico de 1873] *s.* pánico financiero que provocó el cierre de los bancos y que la bolsa se desplomara (pág. 582)

Paris, Treaty of, 1763 [Tratado de París, 1763] *s.* tratado que puso fin a la guerra entre Francia e Inglaterra (pág. 142)

Paris, Treaty of, 1783 [Tratado de París, 1783] *s.* tratado que puso fin a la Revolución (pág. 222)

Parliament [Parlamento] *s.* el organismo legislativo más importante de Inglaterra (pág. 136)

patents [patentes] *s.* documentos del gobierno que otorga a un inventor el derecho en exclusiva de fabricar y vender un invento durante un número específico de años (pág. 630)

Patriots [Patriotas] *s.* estadounidenses que se pusieron del lado de los rebeldes (pág. 168)

patronage [patrocinio] *s.* intercambiar puestos en el gobierno y contratos a cambio de apoyo político (pág. 672)

patroon [encomendero holandés] *s.* persona a quien se recompensaba con un gran lote de terreno por llevar 50 colonos a Nueva Amsterdam (pág. 82)

Pearl Harbor *s.* puerto hawaiano; cedido por un tratado en 1887 a Estados Unidos como estación para aprovisionar de combustible sus barcos (pág. 694, 806)

persecute [perseguir] *v.* maltratar (pág. 66)

Persian Gulf War [guerra del Golfo Pérsico] *s.* guerra entre 1990 y 1991 en la que EE.UU. y las Naciones Unidas expulsaron a Irak de Kuwait (pág. 946)

Philadelphia [Filadelfia] *s.* asentamiento en el río Delaware que se convirtió en la ciudad de mayor crecimiento de las colonias (pág. 110)

Pickett's Charge [carga de Pickett] *s.* asalto fallido a posiciones de la Unión el último día de la batalla de Gettysburg (pág. 548)

Piedmont [Piedmont] *s.* la amplia llanura que queda a los pies de las montañas Blue Ridge en los Apalaches (pág. 116)

Pilgrims [peregrinos] *s.* grupo separatista que viajó a Norteamérica para conseguir libertad religiosa (pág. 66)

Pinckney's Treaty [Tratado de Pinckney] *s.* tratado de 1795 por el que España permitió a los norteamericanos usar el río Mississippi y almacenar mercancías en Nueva Orleáns (pág. 318)

plantation [plantación] *s.* granja de gran tamaño donde hay cultivos comerciales (pág. 40)

platform [plataforma] *s.* declaración de creencias (pág. 498)

Platt Amendment [Enmienda Platt] *s.* acuerdo que afirmaba el derecho de los Estados Unidos de intervenir en los asuntos cubanos (pág. 698)

Plessy vs. Ferguson *s.* caso de 1893 en la Corte Suprema que ratificó la legalidad de la segregación (pág. 650)

plunder [saquear] *v.* robar, piratear (pág. 522)

political machine [maquinaria política] *s.* organización que controla un gobierno local (pág. 640)

political party [partido político] *s.* grupo de personas que intentan promover sus ideas e influir en el gobierno (pág. 326)

Pontiac's Rebellion [rebelión de Pontiac] *s.* revuelta indígena norteamericana contra las colonias británicas (pág. 142)

popular culture [cultura popular] *s.* películas, modas, canciones, jerga y otras expresiones culturales que utiliza mucha gente (pág. 758)

popular sovereignty [soberanía popular] *s.* sistema de gobierno regido por el pueblo (pág. 244)

Populist Party [Partido Populista] *s.* partido político formado en la década de 1890 a favor del aumento del precio en los cultivos (pág. 616)

populous [populoso] *adj.* muy poblado (pág. 510)

Potsdam Conference [Conferencia de Potsdam] *s.* rreunión de los Aliados en Potsdam (Alemania) para planear el final de la Segunda Guerra Mundial (pág. 832)

precedent [precedente] *s.* ejemplo que se convierte en práctica habitual (pág. 312)

prejudice [prejuicio] *s.* opinión negativa que no se basa en datos (pág. 450)

printing press [imprenta] *s.* máquina que imprimía páginas de forma mecánica y que se inventó alrededor de 1455 (pág. 16)

privateer [corsario] *s.* barco de propiedad privada a cuyo dueño se ha concedido permiso para atacar a barcos mercantes enemigos en tiempo de guerra (pág. 204)

Proclamation of 1763 [Proclamación de 1763] *s.* declaración británica que prohibió a los colonos asentarse al oeste de los Apalaches (pág. 142)

progressivism [progresismo] *s.* movimientos reformistas que buscaban mejorar las condiciones de vida y corregir los males de la sociedad estadounidense (pág. 672)

prohibition [prohibición] *s.* entredicho legal impuesto en la producción, posesión y venta de alcohol (pág. 682)

Prohibition [Prohibición] *s.* prohibición legal sobre el alcohol impuesta por la Enmienda Decimoctava (pág. 758)

prolong [prolongar] *v.* alargarse en el tiempo (pág. 536)

prominent [prominente] *adj.* importante y muy conocido (pág. 136)

proprietary colony [colonia propietaria] *s.* colonia gobernada por un solo propietario (pág. 76)

protective tariff [arancel proteccionista] *s.* impuesto sobre productos importados que protege los negocios de una nación frente a la competencia extranjera (pág. 378)

Protestants [protestantes] *s.* grupo cristiano que se separó de la Iglesia Católica (pág. 16)

public works [obras públicas] *s.* proyectos financiados por el gobierno para ayudar a individuos, familias o comunidades necesitadas (pág. 776)

Pueblo [pueblo] *s.* indígenas norteamericanos que construyeron grandes ciudades de adobe (pág. 4)

"pull" factor [factor de atracción] *s.* razón o fuerza que hace a la gente mudarse a un nuevo lugar (pág. 450)

Pullman Strike [huelga Pullman] *s.* huelga nacional de ferrocarriles que se extendió por la industria del ferrocarril en 1894 (pág. 656)

Puritans [puritanos] *s.* disidentes ingleses que querían reformar la Iglesia de Inglaterra (pág. 66)

"push" factor [factor de repulsión] *s.* razón o fuerza que hace a la gente abandonar su país de origen (pág. 450)

Quakers [cuáqueros] *s.* grupo de disidentes protestantes (pág. 66)

Quartering Act [Acta de Alojamiento] *s.* acta que obligaba a los colonos a alojar a soldados británicos y a proporcionarles suministros (pág. 156)

Quebec, Battle of [batalla de Quebec] *s.* batalla que condujo a la victoria británica en la Guerra Franco-Indígena (pág. 142)

racism [racismo] *s.* creencia de que algunas personas son inferiores debido a su raza (pág. 48)

radical [radical] *s.* persona que toma posiciones políticas extremas (pág. 338)

Radical Republican [republicano radical] *s.* congresista a favor de usar el poder federal para reconstruir el Sur y promover los derechos de los afroamericanos (pág. 570)

ragtime [*ragtime*] *s.* música que mezclaba las canciones afro-americanas y el estilo musical europeo (pág. 662)

ratification [ratificación] *s.* acto de confirmación oficial (pág. 234)

ratify [ratificar] *v.* aprobar (pág. 558)

rationing [racionamiento] *s.* distribución de productos y recursos que escasean (pág. 812)

Reconstruction [Reconstrucción] *s.* período entre 1865 y 1877 en el que el gobierno de EE.UU. intentó reconstruir la sociedad y el gobierno del Sur (pág. 570)

Red Scare [terror rojo] *s.* temor generado entre 1919 y 1920 de que una revolución comunista amenazaba a Estados Unidos (pág. 740)

redoubt [reducto] *s.* pequeño fuerte (pág. 212)

Reformation [Reforma] *s.* movimiento que dividió a la iglesia en católicos y protestantes (pág. 16)

region [región] *s.* área de tierra definida (pág. 76)

Renaissance [Renacimiento] *s.* época en la que aumentó el interés por el arte y el conocimiento en Europa (pág. 16)

rendezvous [*rendezvous*] *s.* encuentro (pág. 194)

reparations [reparaciones] *s.* dinero que una nación derrotada paga por la destrucción causada durante la guerra (pág. 740)

republic [república] *s.* estado, país o nación en donde la gente elige representantes para el gobierno (pág. 234)

Republican Party [Partido Republicano] *s.* partido político formado en 1854 por opositores a la esclavitud (pág. 490)

reservation [reservación] *s.* tierra reservada por el gobierno de EE.UU. para las tribus de indígenas norteamericanos (pág. 608)

revenue [renta] *s.* ingresos (pág. 678)

robber baron [*robber baron*] *s.* líder económico que se hizo muy rico mediante métodos deshonestos (pág. 630)

rock 'n' roll [*rock 'n' roll*] *s.* estilo musical basado en el ritmo y el blues que se hizo popular en la década de 1950 (pág. 858)

Roosevelt Corollary [corolario de Roosevelt] *s.* reivindicación de EE.UU. para intervenir en los asuntos de los países latinoamericanos (pág. 706)

Rough Riders [*Rough Riders*] *s.* miembros del Primer Regimiento de Voluntarios de Caballería de EE.UU., organizado por Theodore Roosevelt durante la Guerra Hispanoamericana (pág. 698)

royal colony [colonia real] *s.* colonia gobernada por funcionarios nombrados por el rey (pág. 60)

S

Sahara [Sahara] *s.* gran desierto en el norte de África (pág. 10)

Sand Creek Massacre [masacre de Sand Creek] *s.* ataque en 1864 en el que unos 200 cheyenne fueron asesinados por la milicia de Colorado (pág. 608)

Santa Fe Trail [Ruta de Santa Fe] *s.* ruta que comenzaba en Missouri y terminaba en Santa Fe, Nuevo México (pág. 418)

Saratoga, Battles of [batallas de Saratoga] *s.* serie de conflictos en 1777 cerca de Albany, Nueva York (pág. 194)

savanna [sabana] *s.* pradera llana con abundante vida animal, arbustos espinosos y árboles dispersos (p. 10)

scalawag [*scalawag*] *s.* hombre blanco del Sur que apoyó la Reconstrucción de los radicales (pág. 570)

Scots-Irish [escoceses-irlandeses] *s.* nombre dado a la gente que proviene de las tierras en la frontera de Escocia e Inglaterra o de la región de Irlanda del Norte (pág. 116)

secede [separarse] *v.* retirarse (pág. 394, 498)

Second Battle of the Marne [segunda batalla del Marne] *s.* batalla que se convirtió en el momento decisivo de la guerra (pág. 734)

Second Continental Congress [Segundo Congreso Continental] *s.* gobierno de Norteamérica durante la Guerra de Independencia (pág. 176)

Second Great Awakening [Segundo Gran Despertar] *s.* renovación de la fe religiosa a finales del siglo XVIII y principios del XIX(pág. 456)

Second New Deal [Segundo Nuevo Trato] *s.* ampliación entre 1935 y 1937 del primer Nuevo Trato de Roosevelt (pág. 784)

sectionalism [seccionalismo] *s.* lealtad a los intereses de la propia región o sección del país (pág. 378)

sedentary societies [sociedades sedentarias] *s.* personas que se asentaban en pueblos o ciudades estables (pág. 4)

sedition [sedición] *s.* provocar una rebelión contra un gobierno (pág. 326)

Sedition Act [Acta de Sedición] *s.* ley de 1918 que ilegalizó las críticas al gobierno (pág. 728)

segregation [segregación] *s.* separación racial (pág. 650)

semisedentary societies [sociedades semi-sendentarias] *s.* personas que se asentaba en pueblos o ciudades pero se trasladaban a los pocos años en busca de alimentos (pág. 4)

Seneca Falls Convention [Convención de Seneca Falls] *s.* convención a favor de los derechos de las mujeres celebrada en Seneca Falls, Nueva York (pág. 464)

settlement house [casa de asistencia] *s.* centro comunitario que proporcionaba ayuda a los inmigrantes y a los pobres (pág. 682)

Seven Days' Battles [batallas de los Siete Días] *s.* victoria Confederada en la que Lee detuvo la campaña de la Unión contra Richmond (pág. 522)

Seventeenth Amendment [Enmienda Decimoséptima] *s.* enmienda que proveyó la elección directa de los senadores estadounidenses (pág. 678)

Shaker [*Shaker*] *s.* miembro de una secta cristiana que vivía en comuna y no permitía el matrimonio o tener hijos (pág. 456)

sharecropping [aparcería] *s.* sistema mediante el cual los propietarios daban a los granjeros pobres semillas, herramientas y tierras para cultivar a cambio de parte de sus cosechas (pág. 576)

shareholder [accionista] *s.* inversor que compra parte de una compañía en acciones de bolsa (pág. 630)

Shays's Rebellion [rebelión de Shays] *s.* levantamiento de los granjeros de Massachusetts que querían la cancelación de sus deudas (pág. 234)

Sherman Antitrust Act [Acta Antitrust de Sherman] *s.* ley que ilegalizó el control de las industrias por parte de las corporaciones mediante la formación de trusts (pág. 672)

Sherman's March to the Sea [marcha al mar de Sherman] *s.* marcha destructiva del general Sherman a través de Georgia (pág. 548)

Shiloh, Battle of [batalla de Shiloh] *s.* batalla sangrienta en Tennessee que ganó Grant (pág. 522)

siege [asediar] *v.* cuando las fuerzas enemigas rodean un pueblo o ciudad para obligarla a rendirse (pág. 176)

Siege of Vicksburg [asedio de Vicksburg] *s.* rendición de la ciudad de Vicksburg, Mississippi, a las tropas de la Unión (pág. 548)

sit-down strike [huelga de brazos caídos] *s.* táctica sindical por la que los trabajadores quedaban ociosos en la fábrica en lugar de marcharse (pág. 792)

sit-in [sentada] *s.* protesta en la que la gente se sienta en un lugar y se niega a marcharse hasta que se satisfacen sus peticiones (pág. 876)

Sixteenth Amendment [Enmienda Decimosexta] *s.* enmienda que dio al Congreso poderes para establecer impuestos sobre la renta (pág. 678)

slash-and-burn [tala y quema] *s.* proceso de limpiar la tierra cortando y quemando árboles (pág. 4)

slave [esclavo] *s.* alguien que es capturado para usarlo en trabajos forzados sin cobrar (pág. 10)

slave codes [códigos de esclavos] *s.* ley aprobada para regular el trato a los esclavos (pág. 48)

slavery [esclavitud] *s.* práctica por la que una persona pertenece a otra (pág. 48)

slum [barriada] *s.* vecindario superpoblado y con edificios peligrosos (pág. 640)

smallpox [viruela] *s.* enfermedad altamente contagiosa y a menudo mortal (pág. 142)

smuggling [contrabandear] *v.* importar o exportar productos de forma ilegal (pág. 94)

social gospel movement [movimiento de evangelización social] *s.* reformas basadas en los valores cristianos (pág. 640)

Social Security Act [Acta de Seguridad Social] *s.* ley que creaba un fondo para auxiliar a los trabajadores jubilados y a los desempleados (pág. 784)

socialism [socialismo] *s.* sistema en el que el estado controla la economía (pág. 656)

society [sociedad] *s.* grupo de gente con intereses, costumbres y formas de vida comunes (pág. 4)

sod [terrón] *s.* primera capa del suelo de la pradera que tiene raíces gruesas y enredadas (pág. 616)

sodbusters [*sodbusters*] *s.* nombre de los granjeros pioneros en las Grandes Llanuras (pág. 616)

solar time [hora solar] *s.* hora basada en los cálculos del movimiento del sol por el cielo (pág. 596)

Sons of Liberty [Hijos de la Libertad] *s.* sociedad secreta formada para oponerse a las políticas británicas (pág. 156)

South Atlantic current [corriente del Atlántico Sur] *s.* corriente que circula en sentido contrario a las agujas del reloj entre África y América del Sur (pág. 16)

Southern Christian Leadership Conference, SCLC [Conferencia de Líderes Cristianos del Sur] *s.* organización que coordinaba las protestas no violentas por los derechos civiles en todo el Sur (pág. 876)

space race [carrera espacial] *s.* competencia entre Estados Unidos y la Unión Soviética para liderar la exploración del espacio (pág. 850)

Spanish Armada [Armada española] *s.* gran flota enviada para invadir Inglaterra y restaurar el catolicismo (pág. 34)

Spanish-American War [Guerra Hispanoamericana] *s.* guerra de 1898 que comenzó cuando EE.UU. exigió a España la independencia de Cuba (pág. 698)

speakeasy [*speakeasy*] *s.* club nocturno donde se servía alcohol de forma ilegal (pág. 758)

speculate [especular] *v.* comprar como inversión (pág. 156)

speculation [especulación] *s.* comprar y vender artículos arriesgados con la esperanza de obtener beneficios rápidos (pág. 776)

sphere of influence [esfera de influencia] *s.* áreas donde las naciones extranjeras demandan derechos especiales y privilegios económicos (pág. 706)

spirituals [espirituales] *s.* canciones religiosas populares (pág. 372)

spoils system [sistema de despojos] *s.* práctica de dar puestos en el gobierno a los partidarios políticos (pág. 394)

Stalingrad [Stalingrado] *s.* ciudad soviética donde el ejército alemán fue obligado a rendirse tras una batalla que duró meses (pág. 818)

Stamp Act [Acta del Timbre] *s.* ley que exigía que todos los documentos legales y comerciales llevaran un sello oficial demostrando que se había pagado un impuesto (pág. 156)

standard time [hora estándar] *s.* zonas horarias ideadas por las compañías de ferrocaril (pág. 596)

states' rights [derechos estatales] *s.* idea de que los estados tienen ciertos derechos que el gobierno federal no puede denegar (pág. 326)

steerage [tercera clase] *s.* la cubierta más barata de un barco (pág. 450)

stock market [bolsa de valores] *s.* lugar donde se compran y venden las acciones de las compañías (pág. 582)

Stock Market Crash of 1929 [quiebra de la Bolsa de 1929] *s.* desplome de los precios de las acciones que marcó el inicio de la Gran Depresión (pág. 776)

Stono Rebellion [Rebelión de Stono] *s.* rebelión de esclavos en 1739 en Carolina del Sur (pág. 102)

strategy [estrategia] *s.* plan general de acción (pág. 194)

strike [huelga] *s.* dejar de trabajar para exigir mejores condiciones laborales (pág. 456)

Student Nonviolent Coordinating Committee, SNCC [Comité de Coordinación No Violenta de Estudiantes] *s.* organización creada para dar a los jóvenes un papel mayor en el movimiento por los derechos civiles (pág. 876)

subsistence farming [agricultura de subsistencia] *s.* producir sólo alimentos para consumo propio (pág. 94)

suburbs [suburbios] *s.* áreas residenciales que rodean una ciudad (pág. 858)

suffrage [sufragio] *s.* derecho al voto (pág. 464)

Sugar Act [Acta del Azúcar] *s.* ley que creaba un impuesto sobre el azúcar, la melaza y otros productos enviados por barco a las colonias (pág. 156)

sunbelt [*sunbelt*] *s.* estados más cálidos al sur y el suroeste de los Estados Unidos (pág. 858)

sweatshop [maquiladora] *s.* lugar donde se trabaja muchas horas, en malas condiciones y por poco dinero (pág. 640)

Tammany Hall [Tammany Hall] *s.* maquinaria política en Nueva York (pág. 640)

tariff [arancel] *s.* impuesto sobre productos importados (pág. 312)

Tariff of Abominations [Arancel de las Abominaciones] *s.* ley de 1828 que aumentaba significativamente los aranceles de las materias primas y de los productos manufacturados (pág. 394)

Teapot Dome Scandal [escándalo del Teapot Dome] *s.* caso de corrupción en un miembro del gabinete Harding, quien tomó sobornos para permitir que las petroleras perforaran en tierras públicas (pág. 752)

Tejanos [Tejanos] *s.* gente de herencia mexicana que consideran Texas su hogar (pág. 426)

Tejas [Tejas] *s.* nombre designado por los exploradores españoles a la tierra que hoy día es Texas (pág. 426)

temperance movement [movimiento de la moderación] *s.* campaña para evitar el consumo de alcohol (pág. 456)

tenements [casa de vecindario] *s.* apartamentos superpoblados y deteriorados (pág. 640)

Tet offensive [ofensiva del Tet] *s.* ataque sorpresa comunista sobre tropas estadounidenses y de Vietnam del Sur en 1968; debilitó aún más el apoyo de los estadounidenses a la guerra (pág. 914)

Thirteenth Amendment [Enmienda Decimotercera] *s.* enmienda que puso fin a la esclavitud (pág. 558)

Three-Fifths Compromise [Concesión de los Tres Quintos] *s.* acuerdo por el que los tres quintos de la población de un estado esclavista se contarían para la representación y los impuestos (pág. 242)

threshing machine [trilladora] *s.* máquina que separa los granos de trigo de la paja (pág. 364)

Tidewater [agua de marea] *s.* zona de llanuras costeras (pág. 76)

tolerance [tolerancia] *s.* aceptación de distintas opiniones (pág. 66)

Tordesillas, Treaty of [Tratado de Tordesillas] *s.* tratado de 1494 por el cual España y Portugal acordaron repartirse las tierras del hemisferio occidental y trasladaron al oeste la Línea de Demarcación (pág. 26)

Townshend Acts [Actas de Townshend] *s.* actas aprobadas por el Parlamento en 1767 para intensificar el control británico de las colonias (pág. 160)

Trail of Tears [Marcha de las Lágrimas] *s.* el desplazamiento forzado de los cherokee desde su tierra natal hasta el Territorio Indígena (pág. 402)

transcontinental railroad [ferrocarril transcontinental] *s.* ferrocarril que recorría el continente norteamericano (pág. 596)

trench warfare [guerra de trincheras] *s.* guerra en la que los soldados cavan profundas trincheras en el campo de batalla (pág. 720)

triangular trade [comercio triangular] *s.* complejo sistema de intercambio transatlántico de esclavos, ron, azúcar y melaza (pág. 94)

tribute [tributo] *s.* pago a cambio de protección (pág. 352)

Truman Doctrine [doctrina Truman] *s.* política que prometía ayudas a los países que luchaban por mantener la democracia (pág. 844)

trust [*trust*] *s.* organismo legal creado para controlar acciones de muchas compañías, a menudo de la misma industria (pág. 630)

Tuskegee Airmen [aviadores de Tuskegee] *s.* famosa unidad segregada de pilotos afroamericanos (pág. 812)

Twentieth Amendment [Enmienda Vigésima] *s.* enmienda constitucional que trasladó la investidura presidencial de marzo a enero (pág. 784)

Twenty-sixth Amendment [Enmienda Vigésimo sexta] *s.* enmienda constitucional aprobada en 1971 que rebajó la edad para votar de 21 a 18 años (pág. 926)

U.S.S. *Maine* [*U.S.S.* Maine] *s.* acorazado estadounidense que explotó en La Habana, Cuba, el 15 de febrero de 1898 (pág. 698)

U-Boat [U-Boat] *s.* submarino alemán (pág. 720)

Uncle Tom's Cabin [La cabaña del Tío Tom] *s.* novela publicada por Harrriet Beecher Stowe en 1852 que mostraba la esclavitud como una práctica brutal e inmoral (pág. 480)

Underground Railroad [ferrocarril subterráneo] *s.* serie de rutas de huida utilizadas por los esclavos para escapar del Sur (pág. 464)

United Nations [Naciones Unidas] *s.* organismo internacional para mantener la paz fundado en abril de 1945 por 50 naciones (pág. 832)

uprising [levantamiento] *s.* rebelión (pág. 510)

urbanization [urbanización] *s.* crecimiento de las ciudades como resultado de la industrialización (pág. 640)

Valley Forge [Valley Forge] *s.* lugar al suroeste de Pensilvania donde Washington y su ejército acamparon el invierno de 1777-1778 (pág. 204)

vaquero [vaquero] *s.* término para una persona que trabaja con ganado (pág. 600)

vaudeville [vodevil] *s.* entretenimiento ligero que incluía canciones, bailes y comedia (pág. 662)

Versailles, Treaty of [Tratado de Versalles] *s.* tratado de 1919 que puso fin a la Primera Guerra Mundial (pág. 740)

veto [veto] *v.* impedir que se convierta en ley (pág. 570)

Viet Cong [Viet Cong] *s.* Survietnamitas que lucharon para derrocar al gobierno Diem y unir al país bajo el comunismo (pág. 908)

Vietnamization [vietnamización] *s.* estrategia de retirar las tropas estadounidenses y devolver el terreno de lucha a los survietnamitas (pág. 920)

vigilante [vigilante] *s.* persona que se toma la justicia por su mano (pág. 600)

Virginia Plan [Plan Virginia] *s.* propuesta de una legislatura con dos cámaras con representación en cada una según la población o riqueza de cada estado (pág. 242)

Virginia Statute for Religious Freedom [Estatuto de Virginia para la Libertad de Culto] *s.* declaración a favor de la libertad religiosa, escrito por Thomas Jefferson (pág. 222)

Voting Rights Act [Acta del Derecho al Voto] *s.* ley de 1965 que prohibía las pruebas de alfabetización y otras leyes que impedían a los negros registrarse para votar (pág. 884)

W

war bonds [bonos de guerra] *s.* préstamo a bajo interés de los civiles al gobierno que serían devuelto después de ciertos años (pág. 728)

war hawk [halcón de guerra] *s.* persona del Oeste que apoyó la Guerra de 1812 (pág. 352)

War Industries Board [Consejo de las Industrias de Guerra] *s.* dirigía la compra y distribución de materiales de guerra; establecía los objetivos de producción y también los precios (pág. 728)

War Powers Act [Acta de Poderes Bélicos] *s.* legislación aprobada en 1973 para limitar el poder del presidente para ir a la guerra (pág. 926)

War Production Board [Junta de Producción Bélica] *s.* agencia del gobierno creada durante la Segunda Guerra Mundial para coordinar la producción de equipamiento y suministros militares (pág. 812)

Watergate scandal [escándalo Watergate] *s.* acciones ilegales del presidente Nixon y sus ayudantes con el fin de tapar delitos relacionados con su campaña de reelección (pág. 936)

Whig Party [Partido *Whig*] *s.* partido político formado por Henry Clay, Daniel Webster, y otros opositores a Jackson (pág. 408)

Whiskey Rebellion [Rebelión del Whiskey] *s.* protesta contra los impuestos del gobierno sobre el whiskey que realizaron los granjeros campesinos (pág. 318)

Wilderness Road [*Wilderness Road*] *s.* sendero que terminaba en Kentucky (pág. 204)

Wilmot Proviso [Provisión de Wilmot] *s.* propuesta de 1846 que ilegalizaba la esclavitud en cualquier territorio ganado en la guerra con México (pág. 480)

Wounded Knee Massacre [Masacre de Wounded Knee] *s.* asesinato en masa de unos 300 sioux desarmados a manos de soldados estadounidenses en Wounded Knee, Dakota del Sur, en 1890 (pág. 608)

writ of habeas corpus [escrito de habeas corpus] *s.* ley que impide al gobierno retener a los ciudadanos sin cargo formal (pág. 542)

writs of assistance [escritos de allanamiento] *s.* orden judicial que se usa para entrar en domicilios o negocios en busca de mercancía de contrabando (pág. 160)

X

XYZ Affair [Asunto XYZ] *s.* incidente de 1797 en el que oficiales franceses demandaron de los diplomáticos norteamericanos un soborno (pág. 326)

Y

Yalta Conference [Conferencia de Yalta] *s.* conferencia en la que los Aliados planearon cómo sería el mundo después de la guerra (pág. 818)

yellow journalism [periodismo amarillo] *s.* estilo de periodismo que exagera las noticias, en busca del sensacionalismo (pág. 698)

Yorktown, Battle of [batalla de Yorktown] *s.* batalla final de la guerra, en la que fuerzas francesas y estadounidenses lideradas por George Washington derrotaron al general británico Cornwallis (pág. 212)

Z

Zimmerman telegram [telegrama Zimmerman] *s.* telegrama diciendo al embajador alemán que pidiera a México que declarase la guerra a EE.UU. (pág. 720)

Cambridge Lakes
Charter School

Index

Page references in **boldface** indicate Key Terms & Names and Background Vocabulary that are highlighted in the main text.

Page references in *italics* indicate illustrations, charts, and maps.

Hurston, Zora Neale, 763, *763, 765,* 766
Hussein, Saddam, 957
Hutchinson, Anne, **66, 70,** 71
hygiene, **516, 519**

I

"I Have a Dream" speech, 887, 901
I Love Lucy, 863
immigrant, **450, 451**
immigration, *452–453*
   in late 1800s, *628,* 643–645, *660*
   in mid-1800s, 450–455
   late 1900s–present, 958–959, *958*
   to Middle colonies, 111, 114–115, 119
   to New England colonies, 100, 119
   population of, *449*
   pre-Civil War, 482
   prejudice against, 445, 644–645
   to Southern colonies, 80, 119
   to West, 598, 603, 605, 607, 617, 618, 958–959
   See also individual immigrant groups.
immunities, **282**
impeach, *568, 570,* **575**
impeachment, **267,** *268*
   of Andrew Johnson, 575
   of Clinton, *268,* 952
imperialism, **694, 695,** *704–705*
   characteristics of, *696*
   See also global expansion.
impressment, *352,* **352, 354**
inaugurate, **312, 313**
Inca, *2,* **4,** *7, 8,* **8,** *32,* 33
income tax, 292, **542, 545,** 754
indentured servant, **60, 64,** 78, 104, 105
Independence Hall, *113, 232*
India, 441
Indian. *See* Native Americans.
Indiana, 209–210
Indian Removal Act, *402,* **402, 404**–407, *405*
Indian Territory, **402, 405**
indictment, **268**
indigo, *102,* **102, 106,** *127*
individual rights, *265,* **265**
   See also civil rights.
Indochinese Communist Party (ICP), 910
industrialization (1860–1914), *660*
   and corporations, 634–636
   during Gilded Age, *636,* 636–637
   growth of, 631–633
   and immigration, *628,* 643–646
   impact on cities of, 641–642
   impact on mass culture of, 663–665
   inventions for, 632–633
   and labor movement, 657–661
   and racial discrimination, 651–655
   and urban problems, 646–647
Industrial Revolution and growth (1800–1844), 362–389, *383*
   and nationalism, 379–381, 383–384
   and rise of factory system, 365–367, *366*
   and sectionalism, 381–382
   and slavery, 373–377, 381–382
   technology of, *368,* 368–371, *370–371,* 373, 381
industry
   in 1920s, 755–756
   before and after Civil War, 482, *561,* 562
infamy, **806**
inferior courts, **280**
inflation, **408, 411, 542,** *545,* **545,** 621, **936,** *938,* 939, 943
   during Civil War, 545, *545*
infringe, **872, 873**
inoperative, **294**
Inouye, Daniel, 817
installment buying, **752, 755**
insurgent, **954, 957**
insurrection, **290, 291**
integrate, **876, 878**
Intermediate-Range Nuclear Forces (INF) Treaty, 949
International Criminal Court, *835*
Internet, 959

Internet, using
   evaluating internet sources, R38
   recognizing bias, R39
   using search engines, R37
interstate highway system, 860
Intolerable Acts, **168,** 169–172, *170,* **170**
Inuit tribe, 8
inventions. *See* technology.
investment capital, *632*
investor, **60, 62**
Iran, 854, 947
Iran-Contra affair, **946, 949**
Iran hostage crisis, 947, 949
Iraq
   2003 invasion of, 957
   in Persian Gulf War, 951
Irish immigrants, *448,* 453–454, *470*
   in Civil War, 517
   in West, 598
Irish Potato Famine, 453
ironclad ships, *520,* 521
iron curtain, 847, *950*
Iroquois Great Law of Peace, 46–47
Iroquois nations, 46, 144
   earliest, 9
Iroquois tribe, 199–200
   See also Mohawk tribe.
Isabella I, 17, *17,* 28
Islam, **10, 12**
island hopping, **826, 829**
Israel, 943
   creation of, 837
   in Suez Canal conflict, 855
Italy, 28–29
   in World War II, 807–808, 811, 820
Iwo Jima, *805,* 830

J

Jackson, Andrew, *278,* **394, 395,** *396,* 396–398, *411*
   at Battle of New Orleans, 357–358
   election of, 395–396, 410
   in Florida, 384
   inauguration of, 392, 395, 398
   opposition to national bank by, 409–410
   removal of Native Americans by, 404–406
   and states' rights, 400–401
   wife of, 396–398
Jackson, Rachel, 396–398
Jackson, Thomas J., **510, 515**
Jacksonian democracy, **394, 397**
Jacksonian era, 392–415, *411*
   and democratic reform, 396–398
   economy of, 409, 411
   and Indian Removal, 403–407
   and Jacksonian democracy, 396–398
   and national bank, 409–411
   and sectionalism, 395, 398–401, *399*
   settlement during, *393*
   and spoils system, 398
   and states' rights, 399–401
   and Whig Party, 412
James, Jesse, 605
James I, 62–63, 65, 67
James II, 139, 140
Jamestown, **60, 63**–65, 104
Japan, 707–708
   in World War II, 807–808, 811, 827–831, 834
Japanese-American internment, **812,** *816,* **816**–817, *817*
Japanese immigrants, 643
Jaworski, Leon, 941
Jay, John, *250,* **312, 314,** 322–323
Jay's Treaty, **318, 323**
Jazz Age, *750, 751,* **758, 759**–761, *768*
Jefferson, Thomas, *176,* **176, 180,** 327, **338, 339**
   and Bill of Rights, 251, 253–254, 286
   and Constitutional Convention, 244–245
   and Declaration of Independence, **180**–184
   and democracy and government, 341–343, 356, *356*
   and election of 1800, *339,* 339–341
   and freedom of religion, 228
   and industrialization, 367

   inventions of, 340
   and Louisiana Purchase, 345–351
   and Native Americans, 348
   as president, 336–341
   as secretary of state, 314, 322, 328
   and slavery, 227
   and treasury policy, 316
   and War of 1812, 353–358
Jesuits, 143–144
Jews
   in American Revolution, 223, *223*
   and anti-Semitism, 644, 818
   in colonies, 80, 84
   in Holocaust, 824–825
   immigration of, 644–645
   in mid-1800s, 452
Jim Crow, **650, 652**–653, **872,** 873–875, **874,** *875*
   See also segregation.
John II (Portugal), 30
Johnny Tremain, 175
Johnson, Andrew, *568,* **570,** *572,* **572,** *589*
   impeachment of, 575
   and Reconstruction, 572–574, 581
Johnson, Elliot, 833
Johnson, James Weldon, 766
Johnson, Lyndon Baines, *916*
   and civil rights, 887–891
   and Great Society, 889
   and Vietnam, 913, 915–916, 923–924, 929
Johnston, Albert S., 524
joint-stock company, **60, 62**
Jones, Bobby, 760
Jones, John Paul, **204, 210,** *211*
Jones, Mary Harris "Mother," 657, *657*
Joseph, Chief, 610, *610,* 612
Journal (New York), 700
judicial branch, **242, 245,** 383
   in Constitution, 280
   under FDR, 789–790
   under John Adams, 342–343
   under Washington, 314
   See also Supreme Court.
judicial review, **338,** 342, **343**
Judiciary Act of 1789, **312, 314**
Judiciary Act of 1801, **338, 343**
Jungle, The, 676
jury trial, *288*

K

kamikaze, **826, 830,** *830*
Kansas, 487
Kansas-Nebraska Act, **480,** *486,* **486**–487, *503*
Kaskaskia, Fort, 209–210
Keegan, Elizabeth, *444*
Kelly, William, 632
Kennedy, John F., *300,* **906,** *912,* **912,** *950*
   and civil rights, 885–887
   election of, 863
   and Vietnam, 912–913
Kent State University, 921, *921*
Kentucky, 512
Kentucky and Virginia Resolutions, **326,** 331–**332**
Kerouac, Jack, 861
Key, Francis Scott, 357
Khomeini, Ruholla, 947
Khrushchev, Nikita, 855, 912
Kicking Bear, 611
King, B.B., 859
King, Martin Luther, Jr., *260,* **876, 880,** **880,** *890,* 891
   and antiwar movement, 322
   in Birmingham protest, 886–887
   "I Have a Dream" speech of, 887, 901
   in March on Washington, 887
   in Montgomery bus boycott, 880
   and nonviolence, 880, 889
King Philip's War, **94,** *99,* **99**–100
King's Mountain, Battle of, 213
Kingston, Maxine Hong, 597
Kissinger, Henry, 939
Knife River, 609
Knight, Margaret, 633

Acknowledgments

Text Acknowledgments

Chapter 6, page 175: Excerpt from *Johnny Tremain* by Esther Forbes. Copyright © 1943 by Esther Forbes Hoskins, copyright renewed © 1971 by Linwood M. Erskine, Jr., Executor of the Estate of Esther Forbes Hoskins. Reprinted by permission of Houghton Mifflin Company. All rights reserved.

Chapter 16, page 530: Excerpt from *Across Five Aprils* by Irene Hunt. Copyright © 1964 by Irene Hunt. All rights reserved. Reprinted by permission of Penguin Putnam.

Chapter 20, page 666: Excerpt from *Dragonwings* by Laurence Yep. Copyright © 1975 by Laurence Yep. Used by permission of HarperCollins Publishers.

Chapter 25, page 800: Excerpt from *Roll of Thunder, Hear My Cry* by Mildred Taylor. Copyright © 1976 by Mildred D. Taylor. Used by permission of Dial Books for Young Readers, a division of Penguin Young Readers Group, a member of Penguin Group (USA) Inc., 345 Hudson Street, New York, NY 10014. All rights reserved.

Chapter 26, page 838: Wartime Special: Victory Sandwiches recipe, from *Grandma's Wartime Kitchen: World War II and the Way We Cooked* by Joanne Lamb Hayes. Copyright © 2000 by Joanne Lamb Hayes. Reprinted by permission of St. Martin's Press, 175 Fifth Avenue, New York, NY 10010.

Chapter 27, page 859: Excerpt from *She's A Rebel: The History of Women in Rock & Roll, Expanded 2nd edition* by Gillian Gaar. Copyright © 2002 by Gillian Gaar. Reprinted by permission of Seal Press.

Chapter 28, page 880: Excerpt from "Stride Toward Freedom" by Martin Luther King Jr. Copyright © 1958 by Martin Luther King Jr., copyright renewed 1986 by Coretta Scott King. Reprinted by arrangement with the Heirs to the Estate of Martin Luther King Jr., c/o Writers House as agent for the proprietor New York, NY.

page 887: Excerpt from "Letter from Birmingham Jail" by Martin Luther King Jr. Copyright © 1963 by Martin Luther King Jr., copyright renewed 1991 by Coretta Scott King. Reprinted by arrangement with the Heirs to the Estate of Martin Luther King Jr., c/o Writers House as agent for the proprietor New York, NY.

pages 887, 901: Excerpts from "I Have a Dream" by Martin Luther King Jr. Copyright © 1963 by Martin Luther King Jr., copyright renewed 1991 by Coretta Scott King. Reprinted by arrangement with the Heirs to the Estate of Martin Luther King Jr., c/o Writers House as agent for the proprietor New York, NY.

page 890: Dec. 11, 1964 quote by Martin Luther King Jr. Copyright © 1964 by Martin Luther King Jr., copyright renewed 1992 by Coretta Scott King. Reprinted by arrangement with the Heirs to the Estate of Martin Luther King Jr., c/o Writers House as agent for the proprietor New York, NY.

page 890: Excerpt from telegram to Betty Shabazz from Martin Luther King, Jr. Copyright © 1965 by Martin Luther King Jr., copyright renewed 1993 by Coretta Scott King. Reprinted by arrangement with the Heirs to the Estate of Martin Luther King Jr., c/o Writers House as agent for the proprietor New York, NY.

page 890: Malcolm X quotes, TM 2007 Family of Malcolm X by CMG Worldwide, Inc., www.CMGWorldwide.com

The editors have made every effort to trace the ownership of all copyrighted material found in this book and to make full acknowledgment for its use. Omissions brought to our attention will be corrected in a subsequent edition.

Art Credits

All maps, with the exception of World Atlas maps, created by GeoNova LLC.

Cover and Title Page *Adams* The Granger Collection, New York; *Chavez* Najlah Feanny/Corbis; *eagle* iStockphoto.com; *flag* PhotoDisc/Getty Images; *Lincoln* Archivo Iconografico, S.A./Corbis; *MLK* Flip Schulke/Corbis; *Sacajawea* Connie Ricca/Corbis; *Washington* The Granger Collection, New York; *Yosemite* Jose Fuste Raga/Corbis; *clouds* PhotoDisc.

Section & American Spirit Banner *American flag* PhotoDisc Red/Getty Images; **Historic Decisions of the Supreme Court** *courthouse* Royalty-Free/Corbis; *justice* Royalty-Free/Corbis; **Geography &**

History Banner *compass* Harnett/Hanzon/Getty Images; **Interactive Primary Source Banner** *glasses, pen, document* Royalty-Free/Corbis; *quill pen, magnifying glass on letter* Royalty-Free/Corbis; *Constitution with quill pen* Comstock; **Table of Contents Banner** *American flag* Comstock; *Rocky Mountains* Digital Stock; *White House* Comstock; *Constitution* Comstock.

Table of Contents
iii McDougal Littell/Houghton Mifflin Co.; **vii** *bottom right* Detail, *Benjamin Franklin* (ca. 1785), Joseph Siffred Duplessis. Oil on canvas, 72.4 x 59.6 cm. National Portrait Gallery, Smithsonian Institution, Washington, DC. Gift of the Morris and Gwendolyn Cafritz Foundation/Art Resource, New York; **x** *bottom right* Courtesy of the State Preservation Board, Austin, Texas. CHA 1989.96, Photographer Perry Huston, 7/28/95, post conservation; **xii** *bottom right* The Granger Collection, New York; **xiv** *bottom right* Bettmann/Corbis.

Special Features & Reading for Understanding
xvii Bill Manns/The Art Archive; **xix** The Granger Collection, New York; **xx** Alexander Gardner (1863)/AP Images; **xxii** *center* Flip Schulke/Corbis; *inset* Hulton Archive/Getty Images; **xxx** *center left* Bizuayehu Tesfaye/AP Images; *bottom center* AP Images; *bottom right* Thinkstock Images/Jupiter Images; *frame* Shutterstock; *stamp* AP Images; **xxxi** *top right* National Museum of American History, Smithsonian Institution Negative # 74-2491; *center left* The Granger Collection, New York; *center inset* California Gold Rush Guide, 1849/The Granger Collection, New York; **xxxii** *top* Pixel Images, Inc./McDougal Littell/Houghton Mifflin Co.

Geography Handbook
S30 *top right* Peter Pearson/Getty Images; *bottom left* Bob Torrez/Getty Images; **A1** *top* Onne van der Wal/Corbis; *bottom* Andy Sacks/Getty Images; **A2** *top* Steve Dunwell/Index Stock Imagery; *bottom* Christopher Pfuhl/AP Images; **A3** Brian Snyder/Reuters/Corbis; **A4** *bottom left* Lockheed Martin; **A8** *top* Lester Lefkowitz/Corbis; *bottom* Tom Bean/Corbis; *center* George Steinmetz/Corbis; **A9** *top* Steve Satushek/Getty Images; *bottom* Keith Wood/Getty Images; **A10** *top* Jessica Rinaldi/Reuters/Corbis; **A11** Michael Melford/Getty Images; **A12** Illustration by Ken Goldammer/McDougal Littell/Houghton Mifflin Co.; **A14** *bottom* Atlantide Phototravel/Corbis; *center right* Bill Pogue/Getty Images; *center left* Walter Rawlings/Getty Images; **A15** *top* Najlah Feanny/Corbis SABA; *bottom* Jeff Greenberg/PhotoEdit; **A16** Brooks Kraft/Corbis; **A17** *left* Gregory Bull, Staff/AP Images; *right* James Leynse/Corbis; **A18** Medioimages/Getty Images.

World Atlas
A20 Image created by Reto Stockli with the help of Alan Nelson, under the leadership of Fritz Hasler/NASA. **A21–A39** All maps © Rand McNally.

Unit 1
1 Corbis; **2** *bottom right* Biblioteca Augusta Perugia/Dagli Orti/The Art Archive; *bottom center* Werner Forman/Corbis; *bottom left* Charles & Josette Lenars/Corbis; **3** *top right* The Granger Collection, New York; *center right* Werner Forman Archive; *center left* Macduff Everton/Corbis; *bottom* Sextant, English (brass), English School, (18th century)/Private Collection/The Bridgeman Art Library International; **5** *top right* Werner Forman/Art Resource, NY; *center right* Palazzo Pitti Florence/Dagli Orti (A)/The Art Archive; **6** *center right* SuperStock; **7** George H. H. Huey/Corbis; **8** *top* The Granger Collection, New York; *inset* Medioimages/Getty Images Royalty-Free; **8–9** Wide Group/Getty Images; **9** *top* George H. H. Huey/Corbis; **10** Illustration by Geoff Kornfeld; *bottom left* Gianna Dagli Orti/Corbis; *top left* Getty Images/Royalty-Free; *center left* Keith Dannemiller/Corbis; **12** *center right* Frans Lemmens/Getty Images; **13** *center right* Erich Lessing/Art Resource, NY; *top right* Sandro Vannini/Corbis; **14** Werner Forman Archive; **16** SSPL/The Image Works; **17** *center right* Stock Montage/Getty Images; *top right* Bibliothèque Universitaire de Mèdecine, Montpellier/Dagli Orti/The Art Archive; **18** The Granger Collection, New York; **19** *center* Sandro Vannini/Corbis; *right* Bibliothèque Universitaire de Mèdecine, Montpellier/Dagli Orti/The Art Archive; *left* Werner Forman/Art Resource, NY; **20** Four pocket compasses (wood & brass) by German School, (15th century) © British Museum, London, UK/© Boltin Picture Library/

The Bridgeman Art Library; **21** *top* Werner Forman/Art Resource, NY; *bottom left* Biblioteca Augusta Perugia/Dagli Orti/The Art Archive; **22** North Wind Pictures Archive/Alamy; **23** *The Venetian Ambassador's Interview in an Oriental City or, The Reception of Domenico Trevisani in Cairo in 1512* (oil on panel), Italian School, (16th century)/Louvre, Paris, France, Giraudon/The Bridgeman Art Library International; **24–25** Library of Congress, Washington, DC; **24** *bottom left* Museum of Modern Art Mexico/Dagli Orti/The Art Archive; *bottom right* Inca kero, or wooden beaker, Southern Highlands, Peru, 16th century © British Museum, London, UK/The Bridgeman Art Library; **25** *center* Jeffrey L. Rotman/Corbis; *bottom* The Granger Collection, New York; **26** New-York Historical Society, New York, USA/The Bridgeman Art Library; **27** *top right* Museo de la Torre del Oro Seville/Dagli Orti/The Art Archive; *center* Snark/Art Resource, NY; **28** Monastery of the Rabida, Palos, Spain/Dagli Orti/The Art Archive; **29** Archivo Iconografico, S.A./Corbis; **31** Bildarchiv Preusssischer Kulturbesitz/Art Resource, NY; **32** *right* American Museum of Natural History, New York, USA/The Bridgeman Art Library; *left* Gianni Dagli Orti/Corbis; **34** *The Launching of English Fireships on the Spanish Fleet off Calais with Queen Elizabeth I (1533-1603) on Horseback on Shore*, by Flemish School, (17th century) Private Collection/Rafael Valls Gallery, London, UK/The Bridgeman Art Library; **35** *center* Bettmann/Corbis; *top right* Museo de la Torre del Oro Seville/Dagli Orti/The Art Archive; **37** Elizabeth I, Armada portrait, c.1588 (oil on panel), English School, (16th century)/Private Collection/The Bridgeman Art Library; **40** Tom Bean/Corbis; **41** *center right* The Granger Collection, New York; *top right* Museo de la Torre del Oro Seville/Dagli Orti/The Art Archive; **42** Bettmann/Corbis; **43** Helmet and Shield: Collection of the Oakland Museum of California, Gifts of Herbert Hamlin and Dr. W. Michael Mathes. Body Armor: The DeYoung Museum of San Francisco; **48** *Slaves Below Deck of Albanez* (date unknown), Francis Meynell. Copyright © National Maritime Museum Picture Library, London.; **49** *center* Fotomas Index/Bridgeman Art Library; *top right* Museo de la Torre del Oro Seville/Dagli Orti/The Art Archive; **50** *Portrait of a Negro Man*, c.1780 (oil on canvas), Ramsay, Allan (1713-84) (attr. to)/Royal Albert Memorial Museum, Exeter, Devon, UK/The Bridgeman Art Library International; **51** Corbis; **53** *top* Museo de la Torre del Oro Seville/Dagli Orti/The Art Archive; *bottom right* Museum of Modern Art Mexico/Dagli Orti/The Art Archive; *bottom left* Archivo Iconografico, S.A./Corbis; **54** Museo de la Torre del Oro Seville/Dagli Orti/The Art Archive; **55** Museo de America Madrid Dagli Orti/The Art Archive.

Unit 2

56–57 *Old State House*, Boston, 1801 (oil on panel) by Marston, James Brown (1775-1817) Massachusetts Historical Society, Boston, MA, USA/The Bridgeman Art Library; **58** *bottom left* Getty Images; *bottom center* Tobacco plant (nicotiana tabacum) (1633), woodcut from Thomas Johnson's "Herball"/The Granger Collection, New York; **59** *bottom* British Library/HIP/Art Resource, New York; *center* Penn's Treaty With the Indians (1830 - 1840), Edward Hicks. Oil on canvas. The Bayou Bend Collection, gift of Alice C. Simkins in memory of Alice Nicholson Hanszen/Museum of Fine Arts, Houston (B.77.46) Photograph by Francis G. Mayer/Corbis; **61** *top right* Richard T. Nowitz/Corbis; *center* Carolina Algonquin Indians Fishing (ca. 1585), John White. Watercolor. The Granger Collection, New York; **63** *Detail*, *Pochahontas, Daughter of Powhatan Chief* (ca 1616), Anonymous, after 1616 engraving by Simon van de Passe. Oil on canvas, 76.8 cm x 64.1 cm. National Portrait Gallery, Smithsonian Institution, Washington, DC/Art Resource, New York; **64** Spencer Platt/Getty Images; **65** New Line/Merie W. Wallace/The Kobal Collection; **67** *center John Winthrop* (1834), Charles Osgood, after portrait by anonymous artist. Oil on canvas. The Granger Collection, New York; *top right* Richard T. Nowitz/Corbis; **68** Richard T. Nowitz/Corbis; **69** *inset* Tim Wright/Corbis; **70** Culver Pictures/The Art Archive; **71** *The Hanging of Mary Dyer* (1906), Basil King. Lithograph, after Howard Pyle/The Bridgeman Art Library; **73** Toby Talbot/AP Images; **74** Joseph Sohm/The Image Works; **76** Library of Congress Prints and Photographs Division (LC-USZ62-61452); **77** Illustration by Christian Hook; *top right* Richard T. Nowitz/Corbis; **79** The Colonial Williamsburg Foundation; **80** *inset* The Granger Collection, New York; **82** The Granger Collection, New York; **83** *center* Stock Montage/Getty Images; *top right* Richard T. Nowitz/Corbis; **85** Illustrations by Andrew Wheatcroft; *all* The Colonial Williamsburg Foundation; *cap* The Colonial Williamsburg Foundation. Gift of Mrs. Cora Ginsburg; **87** *top right* Richard T. Nowitz/Corbis; *bottom* Mary Evans Picture Library ; *top left* Snark/Art Resorce, New York; **88** Merie W. Wallace/New Line/The Kobal Collection; **89** *top left* Richard T. Nowitz/Corbis; *bottom left* John Winthrop (1834), Charles Osgood, after portrait by anonymous

artist. Oil on canvas. The Granger Collection, New York; **91** Public Domain; **92** *bottom left* The Granger Collection, New York; *center left* Howard Pyle/The Granger Collection, New York; **93** *bottom* The Granger Collection, New York; **95** *center Self-Portrait* (ca. 1680),Thomas Smith. Oil on canvas, 24.75 x 23.75 inches. Worcester Art Museum, Worcester, Massachusetts. Museum Purchase (1948.19); *top right* Detail, *Southeast Prospect of the City of Philadelphia* (1720), Peter Cooper. Oil on canvas, 20" x 87". The Library Company of Philadelphia; **97** *right* Mary Evans Picture Library; *left* © 2001, 2006 Stars and Stripes. Used with permission.; **98** *right inset Trade Castles and Forts of West Africa* (Stanford University Press, 1964), A.W. Lawrence. Plate 44; taken from "Tilforladelig Efterretning om Kysten Guinea" ("A reliable account of the coast of Guinea"), Ludwig Romer (Copenhagen, 1760)/Stanford University Press; *left inset* The Granger Collection, New York; **99** Hulton Archive/Getty Images; **100** *right John Freake* (ca.1671-1674), Anonymous. Oil on canvas, 42.5 x 36.8 inches. Worcester Art Museum, Worcester, Massachusetts. Sarah C. Garver Fund (1963.135) ; *left Portrait of Elizabeth Clarke Freake and Baby Mary* (ca. 1671-1674), Anonymous. Oil on canvas, 42.5 x 36.8 inches. Worcester Art Museum, Worcester, Massachusetts. Gift of Mr. and Mrs. Albert W. Rice (1963.134) ; **101** North Wind Picture Archives; **102** *yarn* Dorothy Miller; *indigo plant* The New York Botanical Garden; **103** *center right George Mason of Gunston Hall* (1858), Louis Mathieu Didier Guillaume, after John Hesselius. Oil on canvas, 76.20 x 63.50 cm (30 x 25 inches). (1858.2) Virginia Historical Society; *top right* Detail, *Southeast Prospect of the City of Philadelphia* (1720), Peter Cooper. Oil on canvas, 20" x 87". The Library Company of Philadelphia; **106** Angelo Hornak/Corbis; **108** David Lyons/Alamy; **108–109** Illustration by Sebastian Quigley/Linden Artists Ltd.; **110** The Granger Collection, New York; **111** *center right Penn's Treaty With the Indians* (1830 - 1840), Edward Hicks. Oil on canvas. The Bayou Bend Collection, gift of Alice C. Simkins in memory of Alice Nicholson Hanszen/Museum of Fine Arts, Houston (B.77.46) Photograph by Francis G. Mayer/Corbis; *top right* Detail, *Southeast Prospect of the City of Philadelphia* (1720), Peter Cooper. Oil on canvas, 20" x 87". The Library Company of Philadelphia; **112** Lithograph, 1875/The Granger Collection, New York; **113** Royalty-Free/Corbis; **114** Photograph by John Schilling, Courtesy of Peter Wentz Farmstead, Department of Parks and Heritage Services, Montgomery County PA; **116** Ric Ergenbright; **117** Illustration by Roger Stewart; *top right* Detail, *Southeast Prospect of the City of Philadelphia* (1720), Peter Cooper. Oil on canvas, 20" x 87". The Library Company of Philadelphia; **118** *inset* Michael P. Gadomski/Photo Researchers, Inc.; **121** *top left* Detail, *Southeast Prospect of the City of Philadelphia* (1720), Peter Cooper. Oil on canvas, 20" x 87". The Library Company of Philadelphia; *bottom left* New York Botanical Garden; **124** *both* The Granger Collection, New York; **125** *bottom right* Stuart Dee/Getty Images; *bottom left* The Granger Collection, New York; **126** Colonial Williamsburg Foundation; **127** *center* Illustration from Henry Mouzon, Jr., "Map of the Parish of St. Stephen's in Craven County" (1775), South Carolina Historical Society; *top right* Colonial Williamsburg Foundation; *bottom* Gown, silk textile 1740s, remodeled 1780-1795, silk damask with appliquéd silk. From the collection of Doris Langley Moore. The Colonial Williamsburg Foundation; **129** Colonial Williamsburg Foundation; **130** *top* The Granger Collection, New York; *center, bottom* Library of Congress Prints and Photographs Division; **131** Colonial Williamsburg Foundation; **132** *Benjamin Franklin* (ca. 1785), Joseph Siffred Duplessis. Oil on canvas, 72.4 x 59.6 cm. National Portrait Gallery, Smithsonian Institution, Washington, DC. Gift of the Morris and Gwendolyn Cafritz Foundation/Art Resource, New York; **133** *Franklin's Experiment, June, 1752* (1876), Currier & Ives. Museum of the City of New York/Corbis; **134–135** Illustrations by Luigi Galante; **135** The Colonial Williamsburg Foundation; **136** British Picture Library; **137** *center Increase Mather* (1688), Jan Van Spriett. Oil on canvas. Massachusetts Historical Society/The Granger Collection, New York; *top right* The Colonial Wiliamsburg Foundation; **138** David Frazier/Getty Images; **139** The Granger Collection, New York; **140** Illustrations by Rogue Element; **142** *Death of General Richard Montgomery* (1865), Alonzo Chappel. Oil on canvas. Chicago Historical Museum/The Bridgeman Art Library; **143** *center* The Granger Collection, New York; *top right* The Colonial Wiliamsburg Foundation; **145** *inset* Detail, *Braddock's Defeat* (1903), Edward Deming. State Historical Society of Wisconsin Museum Collection, SHSW #42.488.; **147** The Granger Collection, New York; **149** *top left* The Colonial Wiliamsburg Foundation; *bottom left* Detail, *Benjamin Franklin* (ca. 1785), Joseph Siffred Duplessis. Oil on canvas, 72.4 x 59.6 cm. National Portrait Gallery, Smithsonian Institution, Washington, DC. Gift of the Morris and Gwendolyn

Cafritz Foundation/Art Resource, New York; **151** *The Death of General Wolfe* (ca. 1771), Benjamin West. Oil on panel, 43.2 x 61 cm. Private collection/The Bridgeman Art Library.

Unit 3

152–153 Burstein Collection/Corbis; **154** Illustration by Thomas Bayley; *right* Military and Historical Image Bank; *left* George III (ca. 1762), Alfter Allan Ramsay. Oil on canvas. Scottish National Portrait Gallery, Edinburgh, Scotland/The Bridgeman Art Library; **155** *bottom left* Pennsylvania Society of the Sons of the Revolution; *bottom right* Don Troiani/Military and Historical Image Bank; **156** *George III* (1794), David Dodd. Oil on canvas. Private Collection/The Bridgeman Art Library; **157** *center Mrs. Richard Bache* (Sarah Franklin) (1793), John Hoppner. Oil on canvas, 30 1/8 x 24 7/8 inches. (76.5 x 63.2 cm). Catherine Lorillard Wolfe Collection, Wolfe Fund, 1901 (01.20),The Metropolitan Museum of Art, New York; *top right* Colored engraving (1770), Paul Revere. The Granger Collection, New York; **158** *bottom* Emmet Collection, Manuscripts and Archives Division, The New York Public Library; *top* The Granger Collection, New York; **159** The Granger Collection, New York; **161** Illustration by Patrick Faricy; *top right* Colored engraving (1770), Paul Revere. The Granger Collection, New York; **162** *window* Colonial Williamsburg Foundation; *dress* The Granger Collection, New York; *clock* Georgian longcase clock with marquetry case, 18th century/Private Collection/Bonhams, London/The Bridgeman Art Library; *fabric* Floral design with peonies, lilies and roses for Spitalfields silk (1744), Anna Maria Garthwaite/Victoria and Albert Museum/The Bridgeman Art Library; *book The Constitutions of the Freemasons* (1723), Dr James Anderson, London/Bibliotheque Nationale, Paris/Archives Charmet/The Bridgeman Art Library; *telescope* Reflecting Table Telescope (18th century), English. Brass and leather. Private Collection/The Bridgeman Art Library; *glasses* Wine glasses, (18th century), English. Private Collection/The Bridgeman Art Library; **164** Colored engraving (1770), Paul Revere. The Granger Collection, New York; **165** *right John Adams after 1783* (Detail) (ca. 1783), Anonymous, after John Singleton Copley. Oil on canvas, 20 1/4 x 13 5/8 inches (51.43 x 34.61 cm). Seth K. Sweetser Fund (23.180), Museum of Fine Arts, Boston; *left Samuel Adams* (Detail) (ca. 1772), John Singleton Copley. Oil on canvas, 49 1/2 x 39 1/2 inches (125.73 x 100.33 cm). Deposited by the City of Boston (L-R 30.76c), Museum of Fine Arts, Boston; **167** *right A Society of Patriotic Ladies* (1775), Philip Dawe. Mezzotint. British Cartoon Collection, (LC-USZC4-4617) Library of Congress; *left* Library of Congress, Prints and Photographs Division (LC-USZC4-1583); *bottom* The Granger Collection, New York; **168** *Paul Revere* (1768), John Singleton Copley. Oil on canvas, 35 1/8 x 28 1/2 inches (89.22 x 72.39 cm). Gift of Joseph W. Revere, William B. Revere and Edward H. R. Revere (30.781), Museum of Fine Arts, Boston; **169** *center* Art Resource, New York; *top right* Colored engraving (1770), Paul Revere. The Granger Collection, New York; **170** Bettmann/Corbis; **171** The Granger Collection, New York; **172** *Abigail Smith Adams* (ca. 1766), Benjamin Blyth. Pastel on paper, 57.3 x 44.8 cm. Massachusetts Historical Society, Boston MA/Corbis; **173** Illustration, Bibby's Annual (1909), Ernest Crofts. Mary Evans Picture Library; **175** McDougal Littell/Houghton Mifflin Co.; **176** Detail, *Thomas Jefferson* (1786), Mather Brown. Oil on canvas, 90.8 x 72.4 cm. Bequest of Charles Francis Adams, National Portrait Gallery, Smithsonian Institution/Art Resource, New York; **177** *center Mrs. Gage* (1771), John Singleton Copley. Oil on canvas. Private Collection/The Bridgeman Art Library ; *top right* Colored engraving (1770), Paul Revere. The Granger Collection, New York; **179** Lauren McFalls/McDougal Littell/Houghton Mifflin Co.; **180** *both* The Granger Collection, New York; **181** *all* Pennsylvania Society of the Sons of the Revolution; **182** *all* The Granger Collection, New York; **184** The Granger Collection, New York; **189** *top left* Colored engraving (1770), Paul Revere. The Granger Collection, New York; *bottom right* Don Troiani/Military and Historical Image Bank; *bottom left* The Granger Collection, New York; **191** Military and Historical Image Bank; **192** *bottom left* The Granger Collection, New York; **193** *bottom right* National Park Service, Harpers Ferry Center, artist Don Troiani http://www.cr.nps.gov/museum/exhibits/revwar/image_gal/vafoimg/csfront.html; *bottom left* Guilford Courthouse National Military Park; **195** *top right* Bob Krist/Corbis; *center right The Copley Family* (1776/1777), John Singleton Copley. Oil on canvas, 1.841 m x 2.292 m (72 1/2" x 90 1/4"). Andrew W. Mellon Fund, © 1999 Board of Trustees, National Gallery of Art, Washington DC; **196** *both* North Wind Picture Archives; **197** Réunion des Musées Nationaux/Art Resource, NY; **199** The Granger Collection, New York; **200** Photo courtesy of the Historical and Military Image Bank www. historicalimagebank.com; **202** *center left* Albert Konschak; *bottom left* Richard T. Nowitz/Corbis; *top left* Albert Konschak; **202–203**

Illustration by Sebastian Quigley/Linden Artists Ltd.; **203** *top right* Kelly Culpepper/Transparencies, Inc.; **204** Photograph courtesy Peabody Essex Museum, Joseph Howard, Watercolor 19 3/4 x 27 3/4 in. Built 1799, Salem, MA, 850 tons. ; **205** *center right* www. davidrwagner.com; *top right* Bob Krist/Corbis; **206** British Cartoon Collection, Library of Congress, (LC-USZ62-45442); **207** *Marquis de Lafayette* (1757-1834), c.1781-85 (oil on canvas) by Francesco Giuseppe Casanova (c.1732-1803), New-York Historical Society, New York, USA/Bridgeman Art Library; **208** *top left* Courtesy National Park Service, Museum Management Program and Guilford Courthouse, National Military Park, GUCO 1603 http://www.cr.nps.gov/museum/exhibits/revwar/image_gal/gucoimg/guco1603amputation.html; **208** *top right* Valley Forge National Historical Park ; *bottom left* National Park Service, Harpers Ferry Center, artist Don Troiani, http://www.cr.nps.gov/museum/exhibits/revwar/image_gal/gucoimg/medicalcare.html; *right* North Wind Picture Archives; **209** *George Rogers Clark* (1976), Rosemary Brown Beck. Oil on canvas. From the Collection of the Indiana State Museum and Historic Sites; **210** Historical Society of Pennsylvania (HSP), James Forten, n.d., Leon Gardiner Collection; **211** *top right* The Granger Collection, New York; **212** Robert K. Ander; **213** *center right* Andy Thomas; *top right* Bob Krist/Corbis; **214** *left* The Granger Collection, New York; *right* Heribert Proepper/AP Images; **217** The Granger Collection, New York; **218** Illustrations by Rogue Element; **220** *both* The Granger Collection, New York; **221** *center right* William L. Clements Library, University of Michigan; *center left* National Portrait Gallery, Smithsonian Institution/Art Resource, NY; *top right* The Granger Collection, New York; **222** The Granger Collection, New York; **223** *center right* United States Postal Service. All rights reserved. Used with permisssion/The Granger Collection, New York; *top right* Bob Krist/Corbis; **224** Illustrations by Rogue Element; **226** The Granger Collection, New York; **227** *inset* The Granger Collection, New York; *frame* PhotoDisc/Getty Images; **229** *top* Bob Krist/Corbis; *bottom* The Granger Collection, New York; **230** *Marquis de Lafayette* (1757-1834), c.1781-85 (oil on canvas) by Francesco Giuseppe Casanova (c.1732-1803), New-York Historical Society, New York, USA/Bridgeman Art Library; **231** The Granger Collection, New York; **232** *bottom left* The Granger Collection, New York; *bottom right* American flag, c.1781 (wool & cotton), American School, (18th century)/© Collection of the New-York Historical Society, USA,/The Bridgeman Art Library International; **233** *bottom right* Peggy & Ronald Barnett/Corbis; *bottom left* The Granger Collection, New York; **235** *center right* The Granger Collection, New York; *top right* Bettmann/Corbis; **238** *View of New Orleans from the Plantation of Marigny, 1803* (oil on canvas), Woiseri, J. L. Bouquet de (fl.1797-1815)/© Chicago Historical Museum, USA,/The Bridgeman Art Library International; **240** *center left* The Granger Collection, New York; *bottom right* Ohio Historical Society; **241** Illustration by Roger Stewart; *survey tool* Copyright © John E. Fletcher & Arlan R. Wiler/National Geographic Image Collection; **243** *center inset* The Granger Collection, New York; *center right* Dennis Degnan/Corbis; *top right* Bettmann/Corbis; **244** Corbis; **249** *center right* The Granger Collection, New York; *top* Bettmann/Corbis; **250** *right John Jay* (1745-1829) 1786 (oil on canvas), Wright of Derby, Joseph (1734-97)/© Collection of the New-York Historical Society, USA,/The Bridgeman Art Library International; *left* Bettmann/Corbis; **251** Bettmann/Corbis; **252** AP Images; **253** Bettmann/Corbis; **256** *bottom left* Corbis; **257** *top left* Bettmann/Corbis; **259** *The Constitutional Convention, 1787*, by Allen Cox, Negative # 70681. Architect of the Capitol; **260** *center left* The Granger Collection, New York; *bottom right* Bettman/Corbis; **261** *top left* Norm Dettlaff/AP Images; *center right* Karen Kasmauski/Corbis; *bottom left* Mike Lane; **262** J. L. Atlan/Corbis Sygma; **263** Steve Warmowski/Jacksonville Journal-Courier/The Image Works; **264** Illustrations by Rogue Element; **265** *top right* Terry Ashe/Time Life Pictures/Getty Images; *center right* David Bacon/The Image Works; **266** *top* National Archives; *bottom left* Richard T. Nowitz/Corbis; **267** The Granger Collection, New York; **268** Peter Lennihan/AP Images; **269** Bettmann/Corbis; **270–271** Illustrations by Rogue Element; **271** Jay Penni/McDougal Littell/Houghton Mifflin Co.; **272** *bottom left* Ahn Young-Joon/AP Images; *bottom center* U.S. Navy/Handout/CNP/Corbis; *bottom right* George Hall/Corbis; **273** *bottom left* Brownie Harris/Corbis; **273** *bottom right* Reuters/Corbis; **274** Royalty-Free/Corbis; **276** Illustrations by Rogue Element; **277** Bettmann/Corbis; **278** *top right* Library of Congress, Washington, DC (cwpb 01131); *center left* The Granger Collection, New York; *top left* Eric Draper/White House/Handout/CNP/Corbis; *center right* Wally McNamee/Corbis; *bottom* Bettmann/Corbis; **280** Mark Wilson, Staff/Getty Images; **283** Jack Kurtz/The Image Works; **284** Mike Theiler/Reuters/Corbis; **286** *top left* The Granger Collection,

New York; **286–287** Tom Dodge/AP Images; **287** *bottom right* Spencer Grant/PhotoEdit; **288** Alan Klehr/Getty Images; **289** The Granger Collection, New York; **290** Getty Images; **291** 1976 Matt Herron/Take Stock; **292** The Granger Collection, New York; **293** Bettmann/Corbis; **294** Bettmann/Corbis; **295** Francis Miller/Getty Images; **296** *bottom center* Wedgwood Slave Emancipation Society medallion, c.1787-90 (jasperware) by William Hackwood (c.1757-1829), © Private Collection/The Bridgeman Art Library; *bottom left* The Granger Collection, New York; *top right* Associated Press, AP Images; **297** *bottom center* The Art Archive/Museum of the City of New York/47.225.12; *bottom right* Franklin D. Roosevelt Library; **299** Bob Lang; **301** Bettmann/Corbis; Seth Wenig/Reuters/Corbis; **303** *bottom* Will & Deni McIntyre/Corbis; *center right* Royalty-Free/Corbis; **304** NewsCom/PR Newswire; **305** Mary Kate Denny/PhotoEdit; **306** Michael Newman/PhotoEdit.

Unit 4

308–309 Yale University New Haven/The Art Archive; **310** *bottom left* Library of Congress, Washington, DC (cph 3b52213); *bottom center* SSPL/The Image Works; **311** *bottom left* Birthplaces of John Adams and John Quincy Adams, G. Frankenstein (1849). Courtesy of the National Park Service, Adams National Historical Park; *bottom center* Chateau de Blerancourt/Dagli Orti/The Art Archive; **312** Larry Downing/Reuters/Corbis; **313** *top right* The Granger Collection, New York; *center right* New York Times; **314** The Granger Collection, New York; **315** North Wind Picture Archives; **316** Illustrations by Rogue Element; **319** *center right* North Wind Picture Archives; *top right* The Granger Collection, New York; **320** Ohio Historical Society; **322** *The Women of Les Halles Marching to Versailles, 5th October 1789* (watercolor on paper) Jean-Francois Janinet (1752-1814) © Bibliotheque Nationale, Paris, France/Archives Charmet/The Bridgeman Art Library; **324** *bottom right* The Philadelphia Museum of Art/Art Resource, NY; *top* Library of Congress, Washington, DC (LC-USZ62-88324); *bottom left* American Numismatic Society; **325** *center left* Joseph Sohm/Visions of America/Corbis; *bottom left* Andre Jenny/Alamy; *top right* British Museum/HIP/Art Resource, New York; *center, bottom center* Dagli Orti/The Art Archive; *center right* John Hicks/Corbis; **327** *both* The Granger Collection, New York; **328** Fenimore Art Museum, Cooperstown, NY; **329** Illustration by Andrew Wheatcroft; **330** The Granger Collection, New York; **331** Photos courtesy of the Military & Historical Image Bank www.historicalimagebank.com; **333** *top left* The Granger Collection, New York; **333** *bottom left* Chateau de Blerancourt/Dagli Orti/The Art Archive; **334** *bottom* A Thames Wharf, c1750 Samuel Scott, oil on canvas, Victoria & Albert Museum, London, UK/The Bridgeman Art Library ; **336** *bottom left* Smithsonian American Art Musuem, Washington, DC/Art Resource, NY; *bottom right* The Granger Collection, New York; **336–337** Library of Congress, Prints and Photographs Division (g3300-ct000584); **337** *center left* From the Archives of the Ernst Mayr Library of the Museum of Comparative Zoology, Harvard University; *bottom left* © 2006 Harvard University, Peabody Museum, 99-12-10/53110.2 T3042.1.1; *bottom right* Bettmann/Corbis; **339** *center right* Smithsonian Institution; *top right* Monticello/Thomas Jefferson Foundation, Inc.; **340** *top right* Thomas Jefferson Polygraph, Special Collections, University of Virginia Library (image provided by Monticello/Thomas Jefferson Foundation, Inc.); *all others* Monticello/Thomas Jefferson Foundation, Inc.; **342** *Chief Justice John Marshall* (date unknown). Rembrandt Peale. Oil on canvas. Collection of the Supreme Court of the United States; **344** *both* Independence National History Park; **345** *top right* Monticello/Thomas Jefferson Foundation, Inc.; *center right* The Granger Collection, New York; **347** *top* Sam Abell/National Geographic Image Collection; *center right* Historical Picture Archive/Corbis; *all others* Smithsonian American Art Museum, Washington, DC/(Detail) Art Resource, New York; **348** *right* Library of Congress, Washington, DC; *left* The Granger Collection, New York; **350** *bottom* Navaswan/Taxi/Getty Images; *top* David Muench Photography; **351** *top left* David Muench/Corbis; *top right* Connie Ricca/Corbis; *center left* Annie Griffiths Belt/Corbis; *bottom right* Olivier Cirendini/Lonely Planet Images; **352** The Granger Collection, New York; **353** *center right* The Granger Collection, New York; *top right* Monticello/Thomas Jefferson Foundation, Inc.; **354** *both* The Granger Collection, New York; **356** Bettmann/Corbis; **357** Brooklyn Museum/Corbis; **359** *top left* Monticello/Thomas Jefferson Foundation, Inc.; *bottom right* Smithsonian American Art Musuem, Washington, DC/Art Resource, NY; *bottom left* The Granger Collection, New York; **360** *both* The Granger Collection, New York; **361** The Granger Collection, New York; **362** *bottom right* Portrait of Euphemia Toussaint, c.1825 (miniature on ivory) by Meucci, Anthony (fl.1825) © Collection of the New-York Historical Society, USA/The Bridgeman Art Library;

bottom left Hulton Archive/Getty Images; **363** *bottom center* Collection of The New-York Historical Society, negative number X.48; *bottom right* National Museum of American History, Smithsonian Institution. Negative # 74-2491; **364** Hulton Archive/Getty Images; **365** *both* American Textile History Museum; **366** *background* The Granger Collection, New York; *inset* David H. Wells/Corbis; **367** The Granger Collection, New York; **368** *center* Thomas Kraft/TRANSTOCK INC.; *bottom* Michael Freeman/Corbis; *center left* Photo By Stock Montage/Getty Images; *top* The Granger Collection, New York; **370** *top left, center left* Bettmann/Corbis; *bottom left* Corbis; **370–371** Illustration by Michael Mundy; **372** National Museum of American History, Smithsonian Institution; **373** *center right* Library of Congress, Prints and Photographs Division; *top right* American Textile History Museum; **375** *right* Tim Rand/Getty Images; *left* The Granger Collection, New York; **376** *Nat Turner (1800-31) with fellow insurgent slaves during the Slave Rebellion of 1831* (coloured engraving) by American School, (19th century) © Private Collection/Peter Newark American Pictures/The Bridgeman Art Library; **377** *inset* The Granger Collection, New York; *top right* Art Media/Heritage-Images/The Image Works; **378** Joseph Sohm; ChromoSohm Inc./Corbis; **379** *center right* Portrait of Henry Clay (1777-1852) (oil on canvas) by Jarvis, John Wesley (1780-1840) Private Collection/© Christie's Images/The Bridgeman Art Library ; *top right* American Textile History Museum; **381** SSPL/The Image Works; **383** Hulton Archive/Getty Images; **385** Bettmann/Corbis; **387** *top* American Textile History Museum; *bottom left* National Museum of American History, Smithsonian Institution; *bottom right* Bettmann/Corbis; **388** *right* Bettmann/Corbis; *left* Stock Montage/Getty Images.

Unit 5

390–391 *Three American Indian Chiefs, c.1900* (photogravure) (b&w photo) by Curtis, Edward Sheriff (1868-1952) Private Collection/The Bridgeman Art Library; **392** *left* The Granger Collection, New York; **392** *right* Bettmann/Corbis; **393** *left* North Wind Picture Archives/Alamy; *right* The Granger Collection, New York; **394** Chateau de Blerancourt/Dagli Orti/The Art Archive; **395** *center right* Margaret Bayard Smith, Charles Bird King. Oil on canvas. Redwood Library and Athenaem, Newport, Rhode Island, www.redwoodlibrary.com; *top right* Sonda Dawes/The Image Works; **396** Topham/The Image Works; **397** Michael Dwyer/AP Images; **399** Illustration by Vilma Ortiz-Dillon; **400** *top* Corbis; *bottom* The Art Archive/Culver Pictures; **401** *Henry Clay (1777-1852)* (b/w photo) by American Photographer, (19th century) Private Collection/Peter Newark American Pictures/The Bridgeman Art Library ; *frame* PhotoDisc/Getty Images; **402** The Granger Collection, New York; **403** *center right* Library of Congress, Washington, DC (LC-USZC4-2566); *top right* Sonda Dawes/The Image Works; **404** Sash, c.1820s (wool and beads) American School (19th century), © Peabody Essex Museum, Salem, Massachusetts, USA/The Bridgeman Art Library ; **406** Billy E. Barnes/PhotoEdit; **407** *Portrait of Osceola (1804-38)* (oil on canvas), George Catlin (1794-1872)/Private Collection/The Bridgeman Art Library; **408** Bettmann/Corbis; **409** *center right* The Art Archive/National Archives Washington, DC; *top right* Sonda Dawes/The Image Works; **410** Panoramic Images/Getty Images; **411** The Granger Collection, New York; **412** The Granger Collection, New York; **413** *bottom left* Bettmann/Corbis; *top left* Sonda Dawes/The Image Works; **414** The Granger Collection, New York; **415** The Granger Collection, New York; **416** *bottom right* Courtesy of the Oakland Museum of California; *bottom left* Smithsonian American Art Museum, Washington, DC/(Detail)Art Resource, New York; **416–417** Ric Ergenbright; **417** *bottom left* Courtesy of the Oakland Museum of California; *bottom center* Photos courtesy of the Military & Historical Image Bank www.historicalimagebank.com; *center right* Gift of Ruth Koerner Oliver/Buffalo Bill Historical Center, Cody, Wyoming/The Art Archive; **419** *inset* The Granger Collection, New York; *center right* William Manning/Corbis; *top right* Robert Y. Ono/Corbis; **420** The Granger Collection, New York; **421** *inset* Museum of the American West/Autry National Center; **422** *bottom left* James L. Amos/Corbis; *top* Royalty-Free/Getty Images; *center right* Museum of the American West/Autry National Center; *bottom right* James L. Amos/Corbis; **424** *top left* North Wind/Nancy Carter/North Wind Picture Archives; *center left* David Muench/Corbis; *bottom left* The Granger Collection, New York; **424–425** Illustration by Steve Weston/Linden Artists Ltd.; **426** Richard Cummins/Corbis; **427** *center right* Prints and Photographs Collection, Mary Austin Holley File, The Center for American History, The University of Texas at Austin; CN00165; *top right* Robert Y. Ono/Corbis; **428** *both* The Granger Collection, New York; **429** The Granger Collection, New York; **430** Courtesy of the State Preservation Board, Austin, Texas (CHA 1989.96). Photograph by Perry Huston; **432** *right* Library of Congress Prints and Photographs

Division (LC-USZC2-3798); *left* Courtesy of the California History Room, California State Library, Sacramento, California; **433** *center right* The Granger Collection, New York; *top right* Robert Y. Ono/Corbis; **437** Christie's Images/Corbis; **438** *center right* Courtesy of the Oakland Museum of California; **439** *center right* Courtesy of the California History Room, California State Library, Sacramento, California ; *top right* Robert Y. Ono/Corbis; **440** *inset* Courtesy of The Bancroft Library University of California, Berkeley, General Vallejo. Houseworth & Co. Photographs. Houseworth's Souvenir Photographs: 5; *top left* Courtesy of The Bancroft Library University of California, Berkeley, Shaw, S. W., artist Kuchel & Dresel (active ca. 1853-ca. 1865), lithographer Britton & Rey (active 1851-1902), printer [18--] lithograph, color 53.9 x 68.8 cm. ; **441** Sherwin Crasto/Reuters/Corbis; **442** Courtesy of the Oakland Museum of California; **444** *bottom left* The Granger Collection, New York; *center right* Collection of the Oakland Museum of California, Gift of Anonymous Donor. Photography by Isaac W. Baker; *top right* The Granger Collection, New York; **445** *top left* Robert Y. Ono/Corbis; *bottom right* Courtesy of the State Preservation Board, Austin, Texas. CHA 1989.96, Photographer Perry Huston, 7/28/95, post conservation.; *bottom left* The Granger Collection, New York; **446** The Granger Collection, New York; **448** *bottom right* Stuart Ramson/AP Images; *bottom left* View of St. Paul's Chapel and the Broadway Stages, New York (color litho), American School, (19th century) /, © Collection of the New-York Historical Society, USA /The Bridgeman Art Library International; **449** Emigrant illustrations by Rogue Element; *others* The Granger Collection, New York; **450** Courtesy of the Milwaukee County Historical Society, Milwaukee, Wisconsin; **451** *both* Museum of the City of New York/Corbis; **454** Brown Brothers; **455** Library of Congress, Washington, DC; **457** *center right* The Granger Collection, New York; *top right* Museum of the City of New York/Corbis; **458** Archive Photos/Getty Images; **459** Brown Brothers; **460** Lauren McFalls/McDougal Littell/Houghton Mifflin Co.; **461** *top right* NBAE/Getty Images; *inset* Will & Deni McIntyre/Getty Images; **462** *left* Bettmann/Corbis; **464** *center right* The Granger Collection, New York; **465** *center right* General Research & Reference Division, Schomburg Center for Research and Black Culture, The New York Public Library, Astor, Lenox and Tilden Foundations; *top right* Museum of the City of New York/Corbis **466** Detail, *Frederick Douglass* (1844), Elisha Hammond. Oil on canvas, 69.9 cm x 71.1 cm. National Portrait Gallery, Smithsonian Institution/Art Resource, New York; **467** Hulton Archive/Getty Images; **468** *left* Mike Simons/Getty Images; *right* Library of Congress Prints and Photographs Division (LC-USZC4-4659); **469** *top right* Corbis; **470** *bottom right* Stuart Ramson/AP Images; **472** McDougal Littell/Houghton Mifflin Co.; **473** *top* Museum of the City of New York/Corbis; *bottom right* The Granger Collection, New York; *bottom left* Detail, *Frederick Douglass* (1844), Elisha Hammond. Oil on canvas, 69.9 cm x 71.1 cm. National Portrait Gallery, Smithsonian Institution/Art Resource, New York; **474** *bottom* Copyright © Collection of The New York Historical Society/The Bridgeman Art Library; *center* Bettmann/Corbis; **475** The Granger Collection, New York.

Unit 6

476–477 Carolyn Kaster/AP Images; Don Burk/AP Images; **478** *cards* (ca. 1850), American. Color lithograph. Dallas Historical Society, Texas/The Bridgeman Art Library; *bottom right* Schomburg Center/Art Resource, NY; **479** *both* The Granger Collection, New York; **481** *both* The Granger Collection, New York; **482** Illustrations by Rogue Element; **483** David J. and Janice Frent Collection; **484** *top right* Bettmann/Corbis; *center inset* Lithograph, Robertson, Seibert & Shearman, New York, ca.1859. Library of Congress Prints and Photographs Division (LC-USZC4-2356); **485** Stock Montage/Getty Images; **486** The Granger Collection, New York; **488** *bottom inset* *Bird's-Eye View of New Orleans and Suburbs* (1873), American School. Color lithograph. Collection of the New-York Historical Society/The Bridgeman Art Library; **488–489** Robert Holmes/Corbis; **489** *top left* *Loading the Steamboat with Cotton Bales from a Plantation* (ca1860), American School. Color engraving. Private Collection. Peter Newark American Pictures/The Bridgeman Art Library; **489** *center right* *Slave Quarters, Evan-Hall Plantation* (ca. 1860), George Francois Mugnier. Albumen photograph. Louisiana State Museum; **490** Getty Images; **491** *center right* *FugitiveSlave Law Convention, Cazenovia, New York, August 22, 1850,* Ezra Greenleaf Weld. (Accession Number 84.XT.1582.5). Daguerreotype, 1/6 Plate. Image: 6.7 x 5.4 cm (2 5/8 x 2 1/8 in.) ; Mat: 8.1 x 7 cm (3 3/16 x 2 3/4 in.). The J. Paul Getty Museum, Los Angeles; *top right* The Granger Collection, New York; **492** Illustration by Rogue Element; **493** *Frank Leslie's Illustrated Newpaper,* June 27, 1857. Wood engraving after photograph by Fitzgibbon. Library of Congress Prints and

Photographs Division (LC-USZ62-79305); **494** The Granger Collection, New York; **495** Rick Wilking/AP Images; **496** Richmond Times-Dispatch/AP Images; **497** *John Brown Going to His Hanging* (1942), Horace Pippin. Oil on canvas, 24 1/8" x 301/4" (61.3 x 76.8 cm). John Lambert Fund (1943.11), Pennsylvania Academy of the Fine Arts, Philadelphia; **498** Brady-Handy Photograph Collection, Library of Congress, Prints and Photographs Division (LC-BH82-2417); **499** *top right, center right* The Granger Collection, New York; *frame* PhotoDisc; **501** Courtesy of the Lloyd Ostendorf Collection; **502** South Carolina Historical Society; **503** The Granger Collection, New York; **505** *top left* The Granger Collection, New York; *bottom left* Bettmann/Corbis; **506** *bottom* The Granger Collection, New York; *top* Frank Leslie's Illustrated Newpaper, June 27, 1857. Wood engraving after photograph by Fitzgibbon. Library of Congress Prints and Photographs Division (LC-USZ62-79305); **508** *bottom left* Library of Congress, Prints and Photographs Division (LC-USZC2-2804); *center left, center right* The Chicago Historical Society; *bottom center* Museum of the City of New York/Corbis; **509** *center* Military and Historical Image Bank; *right* Military and Historical Image Bank ; **510** *Bombardment of Fort Sumter, Charleston Harbour, 12th & 13th April 1861* (ca. 1865), Currier & Ives. Color lithograph. Library of Congress/The Bridgeman Art Library; **511** *center right* Public Domain; *top right* Carolyn Kaster/AP Images; *frame* Jupiter Images; **512** Library of Congress Prints and Photographs Division (LC-USZ62-11897); **514** *left* Library of Congress Prints and Photographs Division (LC-DIG-ppmsca-08386); *right* Library of Congress Prints and Photographs Division (LC-DIG-cwpbh-03116); *left & right insets* Photograph by Hugh Talman/Smithsonian Images; **515** Museum of the City of New York/Corbis; **516** *The 'Monitor' and the 'Merrimac', the First Fight between Ironclads in 1862* (1886), after Julian Oliver Davidson. Lithograph. Published by Louis Prang & Co. Private Collection/The Bridgeman Art Library; **517** *center right* Bureau of Archives and History, New Jersey State Library; *top right* Carolyn Kaster/AP Images; *frame* Jupiter Images; **518** *top* Hulton Archive/Getty Images; *jacket & cap* Military and Historical Image Bank ; **519** *bottom* Bettmann/Corbis; *bottom inset* Hugh Talman/Smithsonian Institute; *top* Military and Historical Image Bank; **520** *top right* Corbis; *top left* Andrew J. Russell/Corbis; *rifle* Photograph by Dave King/Confederate Memorial Hall, New Orleans/Dorling Kindersley ; *bottom right* Time Life Pictures/Getty Images; *grenade* Armed Forces History, Division of History of Technology, National Museum of American History; **522** Bettmann/Corbis; *frame* Jupiter Images; **523** *top right* Carolyn Kaster/AP Images; **524** Library of Congress Prints and Photographs Division (LC-USZC4-1910); **525** *bottom right* Brad C. Bower/AP Images; **527** *Home, Sweet Home* (ca. 1863), Winslow Homer. Oil on canvas, 21 1/2" x 16 1/2", (54.6 x 41.9 cm). Patrons' Permanent Fund (1997.72.1), National Gallery of Art/Christie's Images/The Bridgeman Art Library ; **528** Military & Historical Image Bank ; **529** *top left* Library of Congress Prints and Photographs Division (LC-DIG-cwpb-00238); *top right* George Eastman House; *photograph in viewer* Confederate Soldiers as They Fell, Near the Burnside Bridge at the Battle of Antietam, September 1862, Alexander Gardner. Glass negative, wet collodion process. Library of Congress Prints and Photographs Division (LC-B811- 555); **530** McDougal Littell/Houghton Mifflin Co.; **531** *top left* Carolyn Kaster/AP Images; *bottom left* Library of Congress Prints and Photographs Division (LC-DIG-ppmsca-08386); **534** *bottom left* The Freedman (1863), John Quincy Adams Ward. Bronze, 19 1/2" x 14 3/4" x 9 3/4" (49.5 x 37.5 x 24.8 cm). Gift of Charles Anthony Lamb and Barea Lamb Seeley, in memory of their grandfather, Charles Rollinson Lamb, 1979 (1979.394), Metropolitan Museum of Art, New York; *bottom right* Siege of Vicksburg–13, 15, & 17 Corps, Commanded by Gen. U.S. Grant, Assisted by the Navy under Admiral Porter–Surrender, July 4, 1863 (1888), Kurz and Allison, Art Publishers, Chicago. Lithograph. Library of Congress Prints and Photographs Division (LC-USZC4-1754); **535** *bottom* Lee Surrendering at Appomattox, Thomas Lovell, National Geographic Image Collection; **536** Lee Snider Photo Images/Corbis; **537** *center right* Time Life Pictures/Getty Images; *top right* The Fall of Richmond, Virginia (1865), Currier and Ives. Lithograph. Private Collection/The Bridgeman Art Library; **538** *The Hour of Emancipation* (1863), William Tolman Carlton. Oil on canvas. Private Collection/© Christie's Images/The Bridgeman Art Library; **539** *Freedom to the Slave* (1863). Lithograph, Philadelphia. National Museum of American History, Smithsonian Institution; **540** Kean Collection/Getty Images; **541** Jonathan Wiggs/Boston Globe; **542** *both* Courtesy of the Federal Reserve Bank of Atlanta Monetary Museum; **543** *center* The Museum of the Confederacy; **543** *top right* The Fall of Richmond, Virginia (1865), Currier and Ives. Lithograph. Private Collection/The

Bridgeman Art Library; **544** The Granger Collection, New York; **546** Corbis; **547** Abraham Lincoln Presidential Library, Springfield, Illinois; **548** Eric Mencher/Getty Images; **549** *center right* Adams County Historical Society, Gettysburg, Pennsylvania; *top right The Fall of Richmond, Virginia* (1865), Currier and Ives. Lithograph. Private Collection/The Bridgeman Art Library; **550–551** Brad C. Bower/AP Images; **552** *right* Time Life Pictures/Getty Images; *left* Detail, *Ulysses S. Grant* (1864), Mathew Brady. Albumen silver print. National Portrait Gallery, Smithsonian Institution/Art Resource, New York; **554** *The Fall of Richmond*, Virginia (1865), Currier and Ives. Lithograph. Private Collection/The Bridgeman Art Library; **556–557** Illustration by Brian Berley; **558** Time Life Pictures/Getty Images; **559** *center right Portrait of Walt Whitman* (ca. 1853), Gabriel Harrison. Quarter plate daguerreotype, 4 1/4" x 3 1/4" (10.8 x 8.3 cm). Humanities and Social Sciences Library/Rare Books Division, New York Public Library; *top right The Fall of Richmond, Virginia* (1865), Currier and Ives. Lithograph. Private Collection/The Bridgeman Art Library; **560** *top right Incidents of the War: Harvest of Death* (Gettysburg,1863), Timothy H. O'Sullivan. Published by Alexander Gardner in "Gardner's Photographic Sketch Book of the War," Vol I, 1866. (LC-B8184-7964-A) Library of Congress Prints and Photographs Division; *top left* The Granger Collection, New York; *frame* PhotoDisc; **561** AP Images; **563** Alexander Gardner (1863)/AP Images; **565** *top left The Fall of Richmond, Virginia* (1865), Currier and Ives. Lithograph. Private Collection/The Bridgeman Art Library; *bottom left* Time Life Pictures/Getty Images; **567** *A Ride for Liberty, or The Fugitive Slaves* (ca. 1862), Johnson, J. Eastman. Oil on paper board, 21 15/16" x 26 1/8" (55.8 x 66.4 cm). Brooklyn Museum of Art, New York (40.59a-b), Gift of Gwendolyn O. L. Conkling/The Bridgeman Art Library ; **568** *bottom center* The Granger Collection, New York; *bottom left* Corbis; **569** Farmland illustrations by Rogue Element; *bottom left* Dorling Kindersley; *bottom right* Carolyn Kaster/AP Images; **571** *center right* The Granger Collection, New York; *top right* Hisham Ibrahim/Getty Images; **572** The Granger Collection, New York; **573** The Granger Collection, New York; **574** Michael Siluk/The Image Works; **575** The Granger Collection, New York; **576** The Granger Collection, New York; **577** *center right* Corbis; *center* Hisham Ibrahim/Getty Images; **578** *right* Medford Historical Society Collection/Corbis; *background* Richard T. Nowitz/Corbis; *background inset* Buddy Mays/Corbis; **579** The Granger Collection, New York; **580** Illustrations by Rogue Element; **581** *top inset* The Chicago Historical Society; *top* The Granger Collection, New York; **582** Bettmann/Corbis; **583** *bottom The Shackle Broken–by the Genius of Freedom.* Color lithograph. Published by E. Sachs & Co., Baltimore, 1874. The Chicago Historical Society; *center* Library of Congress, Washington, DC; *top right* Hisham Ibrahim/Getty Images; **584** *both* Bettmann/Corbis; **585** The Granger Collection, New York; **586** The Granger Collection, New York; **587** Illustration by Rogue Element; **588** Jeff Greenberg/Index Stock Imagery; **589** *top left* Hisham Ibrahim/Getty Images; *bottom right, bottom left* The Granger Collection, New York; **590** © 2006 The Children's Museum of Indianapolis, Inc. Photograph by Wendy Kaveney.

Unit 7
592–593 Library of Congress, Washington, DC (cph 3g04637); **594** *left* Library of Congress, Prints and Photographs Division Washington, DC (LC-USZC2-4891); *right* Craig J. Brown/Index Stock Imagery; **595** *bottom left* Werner Forman/Art Resource, NY; *center left* Bill Manns/The Art Archive; **596** Annie Griffiths Belt/Corbis; **597** *center right* Pajaro Valley Historical Association; *top right* The Granger Collection, New York; **598** *center left* Iris & B. Gerald Cantor Center for Visual Arts at Stanford University; **599** National Museum of American History/The Smithsonian Institution; **600** Smithsonian Institution; **601** *center right* Bill Manns/The Art Archive ; *top right* The Granger Collection, New York; **602** Courtesy of the Oakland Museum of California; **603** *cowboy* Bill Manns/The Art Archive; *cowgirl* Courtesy of Colorado Historical Society, (ID Number F40608, 10027838). All Rights Reserved; *boots* Dorling Kindersley; *hat* Kansas State Historical Society; *spurs* Museum of the American West/Autry National Center; **604** Royalty-Free/Corbis; **605** Bill Manns/The Art Archive ; *frame* PhotoDisc; **606** The Granger Collection, New York; **607** Courtesy of Colorado Historical Society, (William H. Jackson Collection, ID number 20101514. All Rights Reserved; **608** Smithsonian Institution; **609** *center right* State Historical Society of North Dakota; *top right* The Granger Collection, New York; **610** *all* National Archives Washington DC/The Art Archive ; **611** Southwest Museum Pasadena/Laurie Platt Winfrey/The Art Archive; **612** Burton Historical Collection, Detroit Public Library; **613** Buffalo Bill Historical Center, Cody, Wyoming; Chandler-Pohrt Collection, Gift of Mary J. and James R. Jundt; NA.204.4; **614** *bag,* Buffalo Bill Historical Center,

Cody, Wyoming; Gift of Mrs. Henry H.R. Coe; NA. 106.128A *calumet,* Buffalo Bill Historical Center, Cody, Wyoming; Gift of Mrs. Richard A. Pohrt; NA. 502.195.2 *basket* Buffalo Bill Historical Center, Cody, Wyoming; Simplot Collection, Gift of J.R. Simplot; NA. 506.69"; *moccasins* Southwest Museum of the American Indian/Autry National Center; *bottom* National Archives, Washington, D.C./The Art Archive; ; **615** *top* Bill Manns/The Art Archive; **617** *center right* Solomon D. Butcher Collection, Nebraska State Historical Society; *top right* The Granger Collection, New York; **618** Solomon D. Butcher Collection, Nebraska State Historical Society; **619** Bill Stormont/Corbis; **620** Illustrations by Rogue Element; **621** Bettmann/Corbis; **622** *right* National Archives and Records Administration; *left* Craig J. Brown/Index Stock Imagery; *center left* Royalty-Free/Corbis; *center right* National Archives, Washington, D.C./The Art Archive; **623** Library of Congress Prints and Photographs Division; **624** *top right* Corbis; *bottom right, center left* Bettmann/Corbis; *bottom center* Museum of the American West/Autry National Center; **625** *top* The Granger Collection/New York; *bottom left* Tom Bean/Corbis; **626** Library of Congress, Washington, DC; **627** *Indians Attacking a Pioneer Wagon Train* (oil on canvas), Remington, Frederic (1861-1909)/Private Collection, Peter Newark American Pictures/The Bridgeman Art Library; **628** *bottom left* Library of Congress, Washington, DC; *bottom right* Dinodia Images/Alamy; *bottom center* Bettmann/Corbis; **629** *bottom center* SSPL/The Image Works; *Rockefeller* The Granger Collection, New York; *Carnegie* Hulton Archive/Getty Images; *bottom right* Eric Risberg/AP Images; **631** *center right* The Queens Borough Public Library, Long Island Division, Latimer Family Papers Collection; *top right* Lake County Museum/Corbis; **632** Lake County Museum/Corbis; **633** *Edison & Bell* Stock Montage/Getty Images; *phone & lightbulb* SSPL/The Image Works; *background* Mansell/Time & Life Pictures/Getty Images; **634** Corbis; **635** *both* The Granger Collection, New York; **636** *left* Bettmann/Corbis; *right* Jacob A Riis/Museum of the City of New York/Getty Images; **637** Dagli Orti/The Art Archive; **638** *center left* Lake County Museum/Corbis; *bottom left* Dave King/Dorling Kindersley; *bottom right* Courtesy of Phil Baggley/Workington Iron and Steel; **639** *bottom* Bettmann/Corbis; *center right* Matther Warc/Dorling Kindersley; **641** *center right* The Granger Collection, New York; *top right* Lake County Museum/Corbis; **642** Bancroft Library/University of California at Berkeley; **643** The Granger Collection, New York; **644** Mario Tama/Getty Images; **645** *top* Jacob A. Riis/Getty Images; *center right* Bettmann/Corbis; **646** The Granger Collection, New York; **647** The Granger Collection, New York; **648** *both* The Granger Collection, New York; **648–649** Illustration by Nick Rotundo/Bizzy Productions, Inc.; **651** *center right* Marianne Barcellona/Time Life Pictures/Getty Images; *top right* Lake County Museum/Corbis; **652** *left* The Granger Collection, New York; *right* Library of Congress, Washington, DC; **653** *top right* The Granger Collection, New York; **654** *left* Time Life Pictures/Library of Congress/Getty Images; *right* C.M. Battey/Getty Images; **655** Mary Ann Chastain/AP Images; **656** Bettmann/Corbis; **657** *center right* Library of Congress, Washington, DC (LC- DIG-ggbain-18170); *top right* Lake County Museum/Corbis; **658** The Granger Collection, New York; **659** The Granger Collection, New York; **660** Bettmann/Corbis; **661** The Granger Collection, New York; **662** Bettmann/Corbis; **663** *center right* The Granger Collection, New York; **663** *top right* Lake County Museum/Corbis; **664** *bottom* Library of Congress, Washington, DC (LC-USZ62-21467A); *center right* The Granger Collection, New York; **665** Museum of the City of New York/The Art Archive; **666** McDougal Littell/Houghton Mifflin Co.; **667** *top left* Lake County Museum/Corbis; *bottom right, bottom left* The Granger Collection, New York; **668** Royalty-Free/Getty Images; **669** The Granger Collection, New York; **670** *left* Jeff Vanuga/Corbis; *center* Bettmann/Corbis; **671** *bottom left* Culver Pictures/The Art Archive; *bottom right* The Granger Collection, New York; **673** *center right* Corbis; *top right* Bettmann/Corbis; **674** Roswell Daily Record/AP Images; **675** Corbis; **676** Ric Ergenbright; **677** David J. & Janice L. Frent Collection/Corbis; **678** David J. & Janice L. Frent Collection/Corbis; **679** *center right* David J. & Janice L. Frent Collection/Corbis; *top right* Bettmann/Corbis; **682** The Granger Collection, New York; **683** *both* Bettmann/Corbis; **684** *bottom* Corbis; *left Abigail Smith Adams* (ca. 1766), Benjamin Blyth. Pastel on paper, 57.3 x 44.8 cm. Massachusetts Historical Society, Boston, MA/Corbis; **684** *center* The Granger Collection, New York; **685** *top left* Bettmann/Corbis; *bottom left* AP Images; *top right* David J. & Janice L. Frent Collection/Corbis; *bottom right* The Herald-Dispatch/AP Images; **686** Bettmann/Corbis; **687** *bottom* Culver Pictures/The Art Archive/Picture Desk; *top* Bettmann/Corbis; **689** *top left* Bettmann/Corbis; *bottom left, bottom right* Corbis; **690** The Granger Collection, New York; **691** Underwood & Underwood/Corbis; **692** bottom left Richard Cummins/SuperStock; bottom right Royalty-Free/Corbis; **692–693** Bettmann/Corbis; **693** bottom left Rout of Foreign Troops by Boxers at Beicang near Diantsin. Qing Dynasty (ca. 1900). Woodcut. Donated by E.B. Howell (1948,0710,0.6), The British Museum; bottom right Julie Plansencia/AP Images; **694** The Granger Collection, New York; **695** center MPI/Hulton Archive/Getty Images; right The Granger Collection, New York; **697** inset Frank and Frances Carpenter Collection/Library of Congress, Prints and Photographs Division (LC-USZ62-108293); top Charles O'Rear/Corbis; **698** The Chicago Historical Society; **699** center Richard Drew/AP Images; top right The Granger Collection, New York; **700** top The Yellow Kid (June 5, 1897), Richard Felton Outcoult. Magazine cover illustration. Library of Congress Prints and Photographs Division (AP2. Y5 1897); bottom Jeremy Horner/Corbis; **705** American insurance company advertisement, 1909/The Granger Collection, New York; **706** Corbis; **707** center Matthew Calbraith Perry (ca.1854). Color wood-block print. Published in Miki Kosai's Ikoku Ochiba Kage, Tokyo, ca. 1854. National Portrait Gallery, Smithsonian Institution/Art Resource, New York; top right The Granger Collection, New York; **709** Illustration by Nick Rotundo/Bizzy Productions, Inc.; **710** The Granger Collection, New York; **713** top left The Granger Collection, New York; bottom left Royalty-Free/Corbis; bottom right Detail, Matthew Calbraith Perry (ca.1854), Anonymous. Color wood-block print. Published in Miki Kosai's Ikoku Ochiba Kage, Tokyo, ca. 1854. National Portrait Gallery, Smithsonian Institution/Art Resource, New York; **715** Culver Pictures.

Unit 8

716–717 Over the Top, Neuville-Vitasse, 1918 (oil on canvas), Bastien, Alfred (1873-1955) Canadian War Museum, Ottawa, Canada/The Bridgeman Art Library; **718** top right Library of Congress, Prints & Photographs Division, [LC-USZ62-123456]; bottom left The Granger Collection, New York.; bottom right AP Images; **719** bottom right Bettmann/Corbis; bottom left Kevin Summers/Photographer's Choice/Getty Images; **720** MPI/Getty Images; **721** center right World War I Document Archive and BYU Library; top right The Granger Collection, New York; **722** Corbis; **723** bottom Lusitania Sinking (oil on canvas) by Crossley, Harley (Contemporary Artist) © Private Collection/The Bridgeman Art Library; top Armed Forces History, Division of History of Technology, National Museum of American History; **724** The Granger Collection, New York; **725** Bettmann/Corbis; top left The Granger Collection, New York; center left Hulton-Deutsch Collection/Corbis; bottom left Bettman/Corbis; **726–727** Illustration by Brian Berley; **728** Library of Congress, Prints & Photographs Division, WWI Posters, (LC-USZC4-8307); **729** center right Corbis; top right The Granger Collection, New York; **730** left The Granger Collection, New York; right Bettmann/Corbis; **731** Library of Congress, Prints & Photographs Division, WWI Posters, [LC-USZC2-1234] ; **733** The Granger Collection, New York; **735** both The Granger Collection, New York; **736** AP Images; **737** both The Granger Collection, New York; **738** The Granger Collection, New York; **741** center right Hulton Archive/Getty Images; top right The Granger Collection, New York; **742** Bettmann/Corbis; **743** Florida Division of Library and Information; **745** David J & Janice L. Frent Collection/Corbis; **747** both The Granger Collection, New York; **748** Library of Congress, Washington, DC; **750** Harding illustration by Patrick Faricy; left The Granger Collection, New York; right Library of Congress (cph 3b23344); **751** bottom Leonard de Selva/Corbis; center Bettmann/Corbis; **753** top right Frank Driggs Collection/Getty Images; center Ford Motor Co./AP Images; **754** H. Armstrong Roberts/Getty Images; **755** Hulton Archive/Getty Images; **756** Bettmann/Corbis; **757** AP Images; **758** Bettmann/Corbis; **759** top right Frank Driggs Collection/Getty Images; center Underwood & Underwood/Corbis; **760** Bettmann/Corbis; **761–762** Underwood & Underwood/Corbis; **762** Corbis; **763** center Mules and Men by Zora Neale Hurston. Dust jacket. Humanities and Social Sciences Library/General Research Division, New York Public Library; top right Frank Driggs Collection/Getty Images; **764** left Frank Driggs Collection/Getty Images; **764** bottom Church on Lenox Avenue (ca.1930), William H. Johnson. Smithsonian American Art Museum, Washington, DC/Art Resource, New York; **765** bottom Courtesy Harold Ober Associates, Inc. (Estate of Langston Hughes) Courtesy Victoria Sanders and Associates LLC (Estate of Zora Neale Hurston)/ Langston Hughes Papers, James Weldon Johnson Collection in the Yale Collection of American Literature, Beinecke Rare Book and Manuscript Library; **766** left SSPL/The Image Works; right Blank Archives/Getty Images; **767** Underwood & Underwood/Corbis; **768** top right, bottom right Bettmann/Corbis; top left CinemaPhoto/Corbis; bottom left New York Times/Getty Images; **769** bottom right Hulton Archive/Getty Images; top left Frank Driggs Collection/Getty

Images; bottom right National Photo Company Collection/Library of Congress Prints and Photographs Division (LC-USZ62-111369); **770** Illustration by Patrick Faricy; **771** David J. & Janice L. Frent Collection/Corbis.

Unit 9

772–773 Joe Rosenthal/Corbis; **774** center Corbis; left Minnesota Historical Society/Corbis; bottom Bettmann/Corbis; **775** right Library of Congress, Prints & Photograhs Division, FSA/OWI Collection, [LC-USF34-9058-C]; left Political Campaign Materials Collection, Franklin Delano Roosevelt campaign button with tri-ribbon. Duke University Libraries, Rare Book, Manuscript, and Special Collections Library; **776** Bettmann/Corbis; **777** center right Douglas Kirkland/Corbis; top right Bettmann/Corbis; **778** Franklin D. Roosevelt Library, Hyde Park, New York; **780** Bettmann/Corbis; **781** Library of Congress, Prints & Photographs Division, NYWT &S Collection, [LC-USZ62-111157]; **782** bottom left Royalty-Free/Corbis; center left AP Images; top left Bettmann/Corbis; **782–783** Illustration by Scott Cherba/3D Nature LLC; **784** Bettmann/Corbis; **785** both Bettmann/Corbis; **786** Oscar White/Corbis; **787** Philip Gould/Corbis; **788** top Franklin D. Roosevelt Library, Hyde Park, New York; bottom Blank Archives/Getty Images; **789** The Granger Collection, New York; **791** both Franklin D. Roosevelt Library, Hyde Park, New York; **792** Dorothea Lange/Corbis; **793** center right Library of Congress, Prints & Photographs Division, FSA/OWI Collection, [LC-USF34-9058-C]; top right Bettmann/Corbis; **794** inset Dorothea Lange, Photographer, Library of Congress, Prints and Photographs Division (LC-USF34-016109-E); **795** Tenement Flats (1934), Millard Sheets. Smithsonian American Art Museum, Washington, DC/Art Resource, New York; **796** Marvin Koner/Corbis; **798** both Bettmann/Corbis; **800** McDougal Littell/Houghton Mifflin Co; **801** top Bettmann/Corbis; bottom left Hulton-Deutsch Collection/Corbis; **803** Library of Congress, Prints & Photograhs Division, FSA/OWI Collection, [LC-USF34-9058-C]; **804** left Imperial War Museum/The Art Archive; right Corbis; center Shutterstock; **805** right Joe Rosenthal/AP Images; left Time Life Pictures/Getty Images; **806** National Archives/The Art Archive; **807** center right Mary Evans Picture Library; top right David James/Dreamworks LLC/The Kobal Collection; **809** inset AKG Images; **810** Hulton-Deutsch/Corbis; **811** both Time Life Pictures/Getty Images; **813** center right Alfred T. Palmer/Farm Security Administration, Office of War Information Collection, Library of Congress Prints and Photographs Division (LC-USW36-295) ; top right Photograph by David James/Dreamworks LLC/The Kobal Collection; **814** Bettmann/Corbis; **815** Time Life Pictures/Getty Images; **816** background Manzanar, California (July 3, 1942.), Dorothea Lange. WRA Photograph C-838/Corbis; left Mario G. Reyes/The Rafu Shimpo; **817** top Keystone/Getty Images; right inset Courtesy of Ruth Asawa; **818** AP Images; **819** center right Robert Capa/Magnum Photos; top right Photograph by David James/Dreamworks LLC/The Kobal Collection; **820** Bettmann/Corbis; **822–823** Illustration by Thomas Bayley; **824** Bettmann/Corbis; **825** top right CAF/AP Images; right inset United States Holocaust Memorial Museum (The views expressed in this book, and the context in which the image is used, do not necessarily reflect the views or policy of, nor imply approval or endorsement by, the United States Holocaust Memorial Museum.); **826** Bettmann/Corbis; **827** center right US Marine Corps/AP Images; top right Photograph by David James/Dreamworks LLC/The Kobal Collection; **828** NARA/Jeff Ethell Collection; **829** Getty Images; **830** Keystone/Getty Images; **831** Bettmann/Corbis; **832** Jon Riley/Getty Images; **833** center right AP Images; top right Photograph by David James/Dreamworks LLC/The Kobal Collection; **834** Yevgeny Khaldei/Corbis; **835** AP Images; **836** top Alfred T. Palmer/Farm Security Administration, Office of War Information Collection, Library of Congress Prints and Photographs Division (LC-USW36-295); bottom CAF/AP Images; **838** bottom Northwestern University; center Harold M. Lambert/Getty Images; top Illinois State Library; **839** top right Photograph by David James/Dreamworks LLC/The Kobal Collection; bottom Bettmann/Corbis; **840** The Granger Collection, New York; **841** Dorothea Lange (1942)/Corbis; **842** bottom U.S. Postal Service/AP Images; left Bettmann/Corbis; **843** bottom right Sovfoto; bottom Hulton Archive/Getty Images; **844** Illustration by Patrick Faricy; **845** center right Motion Picture and Television Photo Archive; top right John H. Clark/Corbis; **846** bottom Retrofile/Getty Images; top H. Armstrong Roberts/Corbis; **848** Romeo Ranoco/Reuters; **850** Time Life Pictures/Getty Images; **851** center right Robert W. Kelley/Time Life Pictures/Getty Images; top right John H. Clark/Corbis; **852** Corbis; **854** bottom Bettmann/Corbis; top Joe Raedle/Getty Images; **857** Bettmann/Corbis; **858** Time Life Pictures/Getty Images; **859** center right Getty Images; top right John H. Clark/Corbis; **860** AP Images; **861** right Bettmann/Corbis; left Takaharu Yoshizawa/Getty Images;

862 *left* Bettmann/Corbis; *right* GAB Archives/Redferns; 863 Everett Collection; 864 *inset* Historical Society of Western Pennsylvania; *bottom* Royalty-Free/Corbis; 865 *bottom left* Time Life Pictures/Getty Images; *top left* John H. Clark/Corbis; 866 Getty Images; 867 Corbis.

Unit 10

868–869 AP Images; 870 *both* Bettmann/Corbis; 871 *left* AP Images; *right* Wally McNamee/Corbis; 872 Bettmann/Corbis; 873 *top Civil Rights March, May, 1965*, Copyright James H. Karales; *center right* Hallinan Consulting; 875 David J. & Janice L. Frent Collection/Corbis; 877 *center right* Montgomery Sheriffs Department/AP Images; *top right Civil Rights March, May, 1965*, Copyright James H. Karales; 878 Bettmann/Corbis; 879 Bettmann/Corbis; Flip Schulke/Corbis; 881 Bob Daemmrich/Corbis; 882 Bettmann/Corbis; 883 Fred Blackwell; 884 Bettmann/Corbis; 885 *center right* Bettmann/Corbis; *top Civil Rights March, May, 1965*, Copyright James H. Karales; 886 *top* Guy Jarvis/McDougal Littell/Houghton Mifflin Co.; *bottom* Bill Hudson/AP Images; 888 Staff/AP Images; 890 AP Images; 891 Time Life Pictures/Getty Images; 892 *top* Courtesy of the NAACP/Library of Congress, Washington, DC; *center* Time Life Pictures/Getty Images; *bottom* Bettmann/Corbis; 893 *top right* Bettmann/Corbis; *bottom right* David J. & Janice L. Frent Collection/Corbis; *bottom left* Library of Congress, Washington, DC (cph 3g06525); *top left* Ivan Massar/Black Star; 895 *center right* Time Life Pictures/Getty Images; *top right Civil Rights March, May, 1965*, Copyright James H. Karales; 896 Time Life Pictures/Getty Images; 897 Bob Fitch/Black Star; 898 *left* Bettmann/Corbis; *right, center* Time Life Pictures/Getty Images; 899 *center* Bettmann/Corbis; *bottom* Wally McNamee/Corbis; 900 AFP/Getty Images; 903 *top left Civil Rights March, May, 1965*, Copyright James H. Karales; *bottom left* Flip Schulke/Corbis; 905 *A Man Was Lynched Yesterday. ca. 1938.* Copyprint. NAACP Collection, Prints and Photographs Division. Reproduction Number: LC-USZC4-4734/LC-USZ62-33793 (6-10b) Courtesy of the NAACP.; 906 *bottom* Paul Schutzer/Time Life Pictures/Getty Images; *left* Bettmann/Corbis; 907 *center left* Todd Gipstein/Corbis; *bottom* AP Images; *center right* Bettmann/Corbis; 909 *top right* Bettmann/Corbis; *center right* U.S. Air Force Photographs; 910 Time Life Pictures/Getty Images; 911 Bettmann/Corbis; 912 Bettmann/Corbis; 914 Staff/AP Images; 915 *both* Bettmann/Corbis; 916 Bettmann/Corbis; 917 *left* Bettmann/Corbis; *right* Francoise de Mulder/Corbis; 918 Tim Page/Corbis; 920 Smithsonian Institution, Washington, DC; 921 *center right* John Filo/Getty Images; *top right* Bettmann/Corbis; 922 Marc Riboud/Magnum Photos; 923 © 1995 Burt Glinn/Magnum Photos; 924 Larry Burrows Collection; 926 *both* Smithsonian Institution, Washington, DC; 927 *center right* Photo Courtesy of SFC David Bata; *top right* Bettmann/Corbis; 928 Bettmann/Corbis; 929 Peter Marlow/Magnum Photos; 930 McDougal Littell/Houghton Mifflin Co.; 931 *top, bottom right* Bettmann/Corbis; *bottom left* Todd Gipstein/Corbis; 932 Getty Images; 933 Reg Manning/Courtesy of Arizona State University; 934 *left* The Image Works ; *right* SSPL/The Image Works; *bottom* Corbis; *center* Terry Ashe//Time Life Pictures/Getty Images; 934–935 Image created by Reto Stockli with the help of Alan Nelson, under the leadership of Fritz Hasler/NAS; 935 *bottom left* Wally McNamee/Corbis; *bottom right* PhotoDisc Green/Getty Images; *bottom center* Vario Images GmbH & Co. KG/Alamy; 936 Bettmann/Corbis; 937 *top center, lower & upper* The Granger Collection, New York; *center right* Doug Menuez/Corbis; *top left, top right* Owen Franken/Corbis; 938 Royalty-Free/Corbis; 939 AP Images; 940 *background* Time Life Pictures/Getty Images; *top left, top right* AP Images; *bottom right* Jd, Staff/AP Images; *bottom left* Getty Images; 941 Bettmann/Corbis; 943 Corbis; 944 *top* NASA Glenn Research Center; *center* NASA Johnston Space Center; *bottom* NASA Headquarters - Greatest Images of NASA (NASA-HQ-GRIN); 944–945 Illustration by Brian Berley; 946 Royalty Free/Corbis; 947 *center right* Wally McNamee/Corbis; *top right* Purestock/SuperStock; 948 Time Life Pictures/Getty Images; 949 Martin Athenstaedt/dpa/Corbis; 950 *bottom* Wolfgang Rattay/Reuters; *top center* Corbis; *center, top right* Bettmann/Corbis; *center right* AP Images; 951 Wally McNamee/Corbis; 952 *bottom* Jeff Greenberg/The Image Works; *top* J. Scott Applewhite/AP Images; 954 PhotoDisc Green/Getty Images; 955 *center right* Tony Gutierrez/AP Images; *top right* Bill Ross/Corbis; *clouds* PhotoDisc; 956 Getty Images; 957 *bottom right* Ballard Karen/Corbis Sygma; *center right* Str Old/Reuters; *bottom left* Joel Page/AP Images; *top right* William Philpott/Reuters/Corbis; *bottom center* Gretchen Ertl, Staff/AP Images; *center* Ted S. Warren, Staff/AP Images; 958 *left* Ethel Wolvovitz/The Image Works; *center* Margot Granitsas/The Image Works; *right* Robert Brenner/PhotoEdit; 959 *top* David Arky/Corbis; *all others* Royalty-Free/Corbis; 960 ImageState/Alamy; 961 Royalty-Free/Corbis; 962 *top* Jeff Greenberg/PhotoEdit; *center right* Michael Newman/PhotoEdit; *center left* Erin Moroney LaBelle/The Image Works; *bottom center* Ariel Skelley/Corbis; 963 *top left* Bill Ross/Corbis; *bottom left* Doug Menuez/Corbis; *bottom right* Bettmann/Corbis; 964 Carter illustration by Patrick Faricy; *bottom* Corbis; 965 Getty Images.

Skillbuilder Handbook

R18 Library of Congress, Wahington, DC; R24 Courtesy of the Lloyd Ostendorf Collection; R25 McDougal Littell/Houghton Mifflin; R26 McDougal Littell/Houghton Mifflin; R34 The Granger Collection, New York; R36 Christopher Barth/AP Images.

Presidents of the United States
Illustrations by Patrick Faricy.

All other illustrations by
McDougal Littell/Houghton Mifflin Co.

Illinois Learning Standards for Social Science
Middle/Junior High School

MIDDLE/JUNIOR HIGH SCHOOL

STATE GOAL 14:
Understand political systems, with an emphasis on the United States.

A. *Understand and explain basic principles of the United States government.*

14.A.3
Describe how responsibilities are shared and limited by the United States and Illinois Constitutions and significant court decisions.

B. *Understand the structures and functions of the political systems of Illinois, the United States and other nations.*

14.B.3
Identify and compare the basic political systems of Illinois and the United States as prescribed in their constitutions.

C. *Understand election processes and responsibilities of citizens.*

14.C.3
Compare historical issues involving rights, roles and status of individuals in relation to municipalities, states and the nation.

D. *Understand the roles and influences of individuals and interest groups in the political systems of Illinois, the United States and other nations.*

14.D.3
Describe roles and influences of individuals, groups and media in shaping current Illinois and United States public policy (e.g., *general public opinion, special interest groups, formal parties, media*).

E. *Understand United States foreign policy as it relates to other nations and international issues.*

14.E.3
Compare the basic principles of the United States and its international interests (e.g., *territory, environment, trade, use of technology*).

F. *Understand the development of United States political ideas and traditions.*

14.F.3a
Analyze historical influences on the development of political ideas and practices as enumerated in the Declaration of Independence, the United States Constitution, the Bill of Rights and the Illinois Constitution.

14.F.3b
Describe how United States political ideas and traditions were instituted in the Constitution and the Bill of Rights.

MIDDLE/JUNIOR
HIGH SCHOOL

STATE GOAL 15:
Understand economic systems, with an emphasis on the United States.

A. *Understand how different economic systems operate in the exchange, production, distribution and consumption of goods and services.*

15.A.3a

Explain how market prices signal producers about what, how and how much to produce.

15.A.3b

Explain the relationship between productivity and wages.

15.A.3c

Describe the relationship between consumer purchases and businesses paying for productive resources.

15.A.3d

Describe the causes of unemployment (e.g., *seasonal fluctuation in demand, changing jobs, changing skill requirements, national spending*).

B. *Understand that scarcity necessitates choices by consumers.*

15.B.3a

Describe the "market clearing price" of a good or service.

15.B.3b

Explain the effects of choice and competition on individuals and the economy as a whole.

C. *Understand that scarcity necessitates choices by producers.*

15.C.3

Identify and explain the effects of various incentives to produce a good or service.

D. *Understand trade as an exchange of goods or services.*

15.D.3a

Explain the effects of increasing and declining imports and exports to an individual and to the nation's economy as a whole.

15.D.3b

Explain how comparative advantage forms the basis for specialization and trade among nations.

15.D.3c

Explain how workers can affect their productivity through training and by using tools, machinery and technology.

E. *Understand the impact of government policies and decisions on production and consumption in the economy.*

15.E.3a

Identify the types of taxes levied by differing levels of governments (e.g., *income tax, sales tax, property tax*).

15.E.3b

Explain how laws and government policies (e.g., *property rights, contract enforcement, standard weights/measurements*) establish rules that help a market economy function effectively.

MIDDLE/JUNIOR HIGH SCHOOL

STATE GOAL 16:
Understand events, trends, individuals and movements shaping the history of Illinois, the United States and other nations.

A. *Apply the skills of historical analysis and interpretation.*

16.A.3a

Describe how historians use models for organizing historical interpretation (e.g., *biographies, political events, issues and conflicts*).

16.A.3b

Make inferences about historical events and eras using historical maps and other historical sources

16.A.3c

Identify the differences between historical fact and interpretation.

B. *Understand the development of significant political events.*

16.B.3a

Describe how different groups competed for power within the colonies and how that competition led to the development of political institutions during the early national period.

16.B.3b

Explain how and why the colonies fought for their independence and how the colonists' ideas are reflected in the Declaration of Independence and the United States Constitution.

16.B.3c

Describe the way the Constitution has changed over time as a result of amendments and Supreme Court decisions.

16.B.3d

Describe ways in which the United States developed as a world political power.

C. *Understand the development of economic systems.*

16.C.3a

Describe economic motivations that attracted Europeans and others to the Americas, 1500–1750.

16.C.3b

Explain relationships among the American economy and slavery, immigration, industrialization, labor and urbanization, 1700–present.

16.C.3c

Describe how economic developments and government policies after 1865 affected the country's economic institutions including corporations, banks and organized labor.

D. *Understand Illinois, United States and world social history.*

16.D.3a

Describe characteristics of different kinds of communities in various sections of America during the colonial/frontier periods and the 19th century.

16.D.3b

Describe characteristics of different kinds of families in America during the colonial/frontier periods and the 19th century.

MIDDLE/JUNIOR
HIGH SCHOOL

E. *Understand Illinois, United States and world environmental history.*

16.E.3a

Describe how early settlers in Illinois and the United States adapted to, used and changed the environment prior to 1818.

16.E.3b

Describe how the largely rural population of the United States adapted, used and changed the environment after 1818.

16.E.3c

Describe the impact of urbanization and suburbanization, 1850-present, on the environment.

STATE GOAL 17:

Understand world geography and the effects of geography on society, with an emphasis on the United States.

A. *Locate, describe and explain places, regions and features on the Earth.*

17.A.3a

Explain how people use geographic markers and boundaries to analyze and navigate the Earth (e.g., *hemispheres, meridians, continents, bodies of water*).

17.A.3b

Explain how to make and use geographic representations to provide and enhance spatial information including maps, graphs, charts, models, aerial photographs, satellite images.

B. *Analyze and explain characteristics and interactions of the Earth's physical systems.*

17.B.3a

Explain how physical processes including climate, plate tectonics, erosion, soil formation, water cycle, and circulation patterns in the ocean shape patterns in the environment and influence availability and quality of natural resources.

17.B.3b

Explain how changes in components of an ecosystem affect the system overall.

C. *Understand relationships between geographic factors and society.*

17.C.3a

Explain how human activity is affected by geographic factors.

17.C.3b

Explain how patterns of resources are used throughout the world.

17.C.3c

Analyze how human process influence settlement patterns including migration and population growth.

D. *Understand the historical significance of geography.*

17.D.3a

Explain how and why spatial patterns of settlement change over time.

17.D.3b

Explain how interactions of geographic factors have shaped present conditions.

MIDDLE/JUNIOR HIGH SCHOOL

STATE GOAL 18:
Understand social systems, with an emphasis on the United States.

A. *Compare characteristics of culture as reflected in language, literature, the arts, traditions and institutions.*

18.A.3
Explain how language, literature, the arts, architecture and traditions contribute to the development and transmission of culture.

B. *Understand the roles and interactions of individuals and groups in society.*

18.B.3a
Analyze how individuals and groups interact with and within institutions (e.g., *educational, military*).

18.B.3b
Explain how social institutions contribute to the development and transmission of culture.

C. *Understand how social systems form and develop over time.*

18.C.3a
Describe ways in which a diverse U.S. population has developed and maintained common beliefs (e.g., *life, liberty and the pursuit of happiness; the Constitution and the Bill of Rights*).

18.C.3b
Explain how diverse groups have contributed to U.S. social systems over time.